WITHDRAWN

150 YEARS OF MUSIC FOR SAXOPHONE

Bibliographical index of music and educational
literature for the saxophone: 1844-1994

150 ANS DE MUSIQUE POUR SAXOPHONE

Répertoire général des oeuvres et des ouvrages
d'enseignement pour le saxophone: 1844-1994

by JEAN-MARIE LONDEIX

Conservatoire de Bordeaux

BRUCE RONKIN, Editor

Northeastern University

RONCORP
publications

Post Office Box 724

Cherry Hill, NJ 08003 USA

© Copyright 1994 Roncorp, Inc.
All rights reserved.

ISBN 0-939103-04-4
Library of Congress Catalog Card Number: 94-67611

Roncorp, Inc.
Post Office Box 724
Cherry Hill, NJ 08003 USA

Printed in the United States of America.   603

Table of Contents - Table des Matières

Introduction

150 YEARS OF MUSIC FOR SAXOPHONE includes more than 12,000 works of "classical music" for saxophone, 1844-1994. Not included are the 3,000 symphonic or operatic works in which one or several saxophones appear in the orchestration.

This book allows for the correction of the generally widespread idea that, "there are no pieces for the saxophone before 1937." In actuality, for the period more or less from Kastner to Vuataz, we can list no less than 700 titles! An impressive figure which shows at the very least that the saxophone was widely used outside of jazz and military music.

Descriptive paragraphs complete the basic data, allowing one to get an idea of the aesthetics and language used by the most well-known composers.

The quality of the ambitious pieces written in Germany during the 1930s by composers with solid technique shows that the "classical" saxophone was more highly regarded in Germany than anywhere else at that time, thanks no doubt to the enlightened initiative of Gustav Bümcke, Paul Hindemith, and their disciples. But perhaps this was also due to the spirit of liberty which the instrument embodied as it faced an inhuman regime that would unfortunately end up in getting the better of it.

This book underlines in particular the significance of certain composition instructors who favored the saxophone such as Paul Hindemith, Darius Milhaud, and above all, Nadia Boulanger. Indeed, from Yves de la Casiniere to Jean-Louis Dhaine, including Ross Lee Finney, Ingolf Dahl, Leslie Basset, Karel Husa, Jean Francaix, Marius Constant, Roger Boutry, Michel Legrand and Philip Glass, we mention no less than sixty composers who were students and disciples of the "Grande Mademoiselle." Nadia Boulanger generally shared with them her taste for neo-classicism and her concern with form.

Still to be noted is the impressive number of pieces to date with uncommon instrumentation:

- 150 pieces with organ;
- 350 pieces for saxophone ensembles of which approximately one hundred use a dozen saxophones from the bass to the sopranino;
- 400 pieces with magnetic tape, electronics, or synthesizer;
- 650 pieces for two or three saxophones;
- 600 pieces for solo saxophone, of which 400 are intended for the alto saxophone;
- 850 pieces with percussion.

The number of first-rate composers, of high caliber and of international fame, has markedly grown these last ten years… notably in countries where the saxophone is respected and officially taught alongside other orchestral instruments. Thus, their number shows the increasingly important place that the saxophone occupies as a concert instrument. The number of composers—particularly among the youngest—who reveal original qualities, particular and intrinsic to the saxophone multiplies from year to year. These "inventors" who are making the saxophone an instrument capable of answering to the highest musical demands of the time, have finally made the instrument indispensable to "classical" music and justify the involvement of our best musicians in the rendering of this concert music.

We wish to warmly thank all those who encouraged and helped us in our often long, tedious, and difficult research, as well as those who made the realization of this book possible.

Jean-Marie Londeix
Bordeaux, July 15, 1994

(Translated from the French by Karen J. Carlson)

For information contact:
Centre Européen de Saxophone
22, Quai Sainte-Croix
33800 Bordeaux, France
Fax: 56.92.22.30

Introduction

150 ANS DE MUSIQUE POUR SAXOPHONE compte plus de 12,000 oeuvres de "musique classique" destinées au saxophone, 1844-1994. Ne sont pas répertoriées les 3,000 oeuvres symphoniques ou lyriques dans l'instrumentation desquelles figure un ou plusieurs saxophones.

Cet ouvrage permet de corriger l'idée généralement répandue qu'"il n'y a pas d'oeuvres pour saxophone avant 1937." En effet, nous dénombrons pour cette période qui va grosso modo de Kastner à Vuataz, pas moins de 700 titres! Chiffre impressionnant qui montre pour le moins que le saxophone était largement utilisé en dehors du jazz et des musiques militaires.

Certains renseignements complètent les informations de base, permettant d'avoir une idée de l'esthétique et du langage utilisé par les compositeurs les mieux connus.

La qualité d'oeuvres ambitieuses écrites en Allemagne dans les années trente par des compositeurs nantis d'un solide métier, montre que le saxophone "classique" était mieux considérer en Allemagne que partout ailleurs à la même époque, sans doute grâce à l'action éclairée d'un Gustav Bümcke, de Paul Hindemith et de ses disciples, mais peut-être aussi grâce à l'esprit de Liberté que l'instrument incarnait alors, face à un régime inhumain, qui finira malheureusement par en avoir raison.

Cet ouvrage souligne en particulier l'importance qu'ont eu certains professeurs de composition favorables au saxophone, comme Paul Hindemith, Darius Milhaud et, surtout, Nadia Boulanger. En effet, d'Yves de la Casiniere à Jean-Louis Dhaine, en passant par Ross Lee Finney, Ingolf Dahl, Leslie Basset, Karel Husa, Jean Francaix, Marius Constant, Roger Boutry, Michel Legrand ou Philip Glass, nous ne mentionnons pas moins de soixante compositeurs, élèves et disciples de la "Grande Mademoiselle." Nadia Boulanger leur a généralement fait partager son goût pour le néo-classicisme et son souci de la forme.

A noter encore le nombre impressionnant d'oeuvres à l'instrumentation jusque-là rare:

- 150 pièces avec orgue;
- 350 pièces pour ensembles de saxophones dont une centaine utilisant une douzaine de saxophones du Basse au Sopranino;
- 400 pièces avec bande magnétique, appareillage électronique, ou synthétiseur;
- 650 pièces pour deux ou trois saxophones;
- 600 pièces pour saxophone solo, dont 400 destinées au saxophone-alto;
- 850 pièces avec percussion.

Le nombre de compositeurs de premier plan, de grande envergure et de notoriété internationale, s'est sensiblement accru ces dix dernières années… notamment dans les pays où le saxophone est considéré et enseigné officiellement comme les autres instruments de l'orchestre. Leur nombre montre ainsi la place de plus en plus conséquente qu'occupe le saxophone en tant qu'instrument concertant. Le nombre de compositeurs—surtout parmi les plus jeunes—qui dévoilent les qualités originales, particulières et intrinsèques du saxophone se multiplie d'année en année. Ces "inventeurs" faisant du saxophone un instrument capable de répondre aux plus hautes exigences musicales de l'époque, rendent l'instrument enfin nécessaire à la musique "classique" et justifient l'engagement de nos meilleurs interprètes dans la voie de cette musique de concert.

Nous tenons à remercier chaleureusement tous ceux qui nous ont encouragé et aidé dans nos recherches souvent longues, fastidieuses et difficiles, et ceux qui ont permis la réalisation de cet ouvrage.

Jean-Marie Londeix
Bordeaux, le 15 Juillet 1994

Pour toutes informations:
Centre Européen de Saxophone
22, Quai Sainte-Croix
33800 Bordeaux, France
Fax: 56.92.22.30

Abbreviations

Saxophones

Sx	Saxophone
Sno	Sopranino
SnoSx	Sopranino Saxophone
S	Soprano
Ssx	Soprano Saxophone
A	Alto
Asx	Alto Saxophone
T	Tenor
Tsx	Tenor Saxophone
B	Baritone
Bsx	Baritone Saxophone
Bs	Bass
BsSx	Bass Saxophone
CBs	Contrabass
CBsSx	Contrabass Saxophone

Orchestra

Orch	Orchestra; *Orchestre*; *Orchester*
Picc	Piccolo; *Petite flûte*; *Kleine Flöte*
Fl	Flute; *Flûte*; *Flöte*
Ob	Oboe; *Hautbois*
EH	English Horn; *Cor anglais*
Cl	Clarinet; *Clarinette*; *Klarinette*
BsCl	Bass Clarinet; *Clarinette basse*; *Baßklarinette*
Bsn	Bassoon; *Basson*; *Fagott*
CBsn	Contrabassoon; *Contre-basson*; *Kontrafagott*
Hn	Horn; *Cor*
Tpt	Trumpet; *Trompette*; *Trompete*
Trb	Trombone; *Posaune*
BsTrb	Bass Trombone
Tuba	Tuba; *Tuba basse*; *Baßtuba*
Perc	Percussion
Timp	Timpani; *Timbales*; *Pauken*
Str	Strings; *Cordes*
Vln	Violin; *Violon*; *Violine*
Vla	Viola; *Alto à cordes*; *Bratsche*
Vcl	Cello; *Violoncelle*; *Violoncell*
Bass	Double Bass; *Contrebasse*; *Kontrabaß*

Other

Guit	Guitar; *Guitare*
Harp	Harp; *Harpe*; *Harfe*
Harps	Harpsichord; *Cembalo*; *Clavecin*
Narr	Narrator; *Récitant*
Org	Organ; *Orgue*; *Orgel*
Pno	Piano; *Clavier*; *Klavier*
Synth	Synthesizer; *Synthétiseur*
Tape	Tape; *Bande Magnétique*
Vibr	Vibraphone
Voice	Voice; *Voix*; *Stimme*

composer of original work

year of composition — **ABBOTT, Alain** (1938) — duration

title — *Saxophonie* (1974) (8'45) (to Quatuor d'Anches de Paris) •Ob/Cl/Asx/Bsn •Bil — dedication

instrumentation — publisher

composer of arranged or transcribed work — ABEL, Carl-Friedrich (1725-1787)
Andante (from *3rd Symph.*) (BRINK) •SATB •Lis

arranger

General Index By Composer

Répertoire Général

AARON, Yvonne (1937)

Compositeur français né le 28 VI 1937 à Paris. Travailla avec N. Boulanger, P. Gaubert, M. Emmanuel, X. Leroux, et J. Gallon.

"La *Fantaisie sans poids ni mesure* exploite habilement les possibilités du saxophone pour établir une atmosphère mélancolique autour de thèmes bien attachants." (L. WERNSTEIN)

Fantaisie sans poids ni mesure... (1972) (13') •Asx/Pno •adr

AATZ, Michel

Engrenages (6') (to D. KIENTZY) •Sx/Mallet Perc [claviers]
Frühling (11') •Asx/Orch (2222/222/Pno/Perc/Str-30221)

ABBOTT, Alain (1938)

Compositeur français, né à Lille, le 15 IX 1938. Travailla avec Y. Desportes et O. Messiaen.

Métabole (1976) (8') (to J-M. LONDEIX) •Asx/Pno
Poème (1969) (12'30) •SATB •Bil
Saxophonie (1974) (8'45) (to Quatuor d'Anches de Paris) •Ob/Cl/Asx/Bsn •Bil
Le Tombeau de Bach (1984) •SATB/Tape

ABE, Komei (1911)

Compositeur japonais (voir également Komei, Abe), né à Hiroshima. Travailla avec K. Pringheim.

Divertimento (1951-53) 1) Andante sostenuto & Allegro 2) Adagietto 3) Allegro •Asx/Orch or Pno

ABECASSIS, Eryck

Dans 3 nuits (1984) •Asx/Fl/Cl/Vln/Vcl/Pno

ABEL, Carl-Friedrich (1725-1787)

Andante (from *3rd Symph.*) (BRINK) •SATB •Lis

ABELLAN, G.

Compositeur espagnol.

Fantasia Andaluza •SATB
Fantasia Exatona •SATB
Impresiones sobre el 23. F •SATB
Leoneras •SATB
Musica anacronica •SATB
Suite •SATB

ABLINGER, Peter (1959)

Compositeur autrichien, né à Schwanenstadt. Travailla avec Haubenstock-Ramati et G. Neuwirth.

Escapse (1989) •Tsx/Band •adr
7 X 7 (1993) •Ssx/Tape •INM
Verkündigung (1990) •Fl/Asx/Pno •adr

ABRAHAMSEN, Hans (1952)

Compositeur danois.

Flush (1974-79) (to Chr. A.) •Sx Solo •Gron

ABSIL, Jean (1893-1974)

Compositeur belge, né à Bonsecours (Hainault), le 23 X 1893, mort à Bruxelles, le 2 II 1974. Travailla avec P. Gilson.

"La forme de l'art important peu, je me range volontiers à l'avis de ceux qui considèrent comme condition essentielle l'expression de la sensibilité humaine." (J. ABSIL) "Jean Absil use avec mesure de toutes les nouvelles ressources de son époque." (P. PITTION) "Avant tout un

constructeur." (P. WOLFF) "Sa formation musicale semble avoir été dominée par une double influence: celle de la musique française et celle de l'école viennoise à laquelle le rattachait son amitié avec A. Berg." (B. GAVOTY) "Harmoniste raffiné et audacieux–il a écouté Ravel–Absil use d'un style polytonal original, vivant, concis, d'une parure instrumentale brillante: son art est d'un Latin authentique. (H. HALBREICH) "Il s'est éloigné de l'académisme de Gilson et de l'influence de Ravel pour se créer un langage polytonal s'exprimant en des formes libres dans la parenté de Milhaud et de Hindemith. Son style, dynamique, concis, coloré et rythmé, traduit un tempérament vif dans une production considérable, 150 oeuvres de tout genre." (Cl. ROSTAND)

"Jean Absil has evolved an individual style, characterized by rhythmic variety, free tonality and compact counterpoint." (BAKER) "Absil's work impresses by its spontaneity and sincerity and by the vigor and originality of his temperament. His later work shows a diminishing preoccupation with preconceived theoretical innovations and a consequent increase in creative spontaneity." (ANGLES) "This style is essentially polyphonic and polymodal, with different modes used in each work, although there is a predilection for intervals of an augmented 4th and diminished octave. Changes in meter and irrational divisions are frequent; sometimes there are superimpositions of triple and binary meters, or of differently divided gruppettos, so producing characteristically vigorous effects."

Ballade: Double Concerto, op. 156 (1971) •Asx/Chamber Orch or Pno
Berceuse (1932) (5') •1 Sx: A or T/Orch or Pno •An/Ger
5 Pièces faciles, op. 138 (1968) 1) Badinerie 2) Chant de marins 3) Pavane 4) Speen 5) Joyeux départ •Asx (or Cl)/Pno •Lem
Divertimento, op. 86 (1955) (20') (to Quatuor Belge de Sxph.) 1) Entrée 2) Romance 3) Scherzetto 4) Intermezzo 5) Finale •SATB/Chamber Orch (1100/3100/Perc/Str) •CBDM
Etude (3'30) •Sx Solo •Bil
Fantaisie-Caprice, op. 152 (1971) (5') (to Fr. Daneels) •Asx/Str or Band or Pno •Lem
Phantasmes, op. 22 & 72 (1936-50) (12') (textes de H. MICHAUX, L. HUGUER, M. BEERBOCK) 1) Télégramme de Dakar 2) Crachoirs de cuivre 3) Nostalgie d'Arabella •Contralt. Voice/Asx/Pno/Perc •CBDM
1er Quatuor, op. 31 (1937) (10') (to Quatuor Mule) 1) Andante 2) Allegro-vivo 3) Nocturne •SATB •Lem
Sicilienne (1950) (9') •1 Sx: A or T/Orch or Harp or Pno •An/Ger
Sonate, op. 115 (1963) (8'30) (to G. GOURDET) 1) Allegro 2) Andantino 3) Vivo •Asx/Pno •Lem
Suite d'après le Folklore Roumain, op. 90 (1956) (17') (to Quatuor Belge) 1) Allegro vivace 2) Andante con moto 3) Scherzo leggiero 4) Andantino cantabile 5) Rude et fortement rythmé •SATB •CBDM
Trois 3 Pièces en Quatuor, op. 35 (1938) (to Quatuor Mule) 1) Sérénade 2) Rêverie 3) Tarentelle •SATB •Lem

ACHENBERG, David

Compositeur belge.
4 Portraits •SATB

ACHRON, Joseph (1886-1943)

Impressions, op. 32, no. 1 (GUREWICH) •Asx/Pno •Uni

ACKERMANS, Johann Karl (1765-1792)

Ancient Scotch Melodies Fantasy •Asx/Pno •B&H
2 Poèmes •Asx/Pno •Led
Petite fantaisie italienne •Asx/Pno •Led

ACKERMANS, H.

Day Lilly •Asx/Pno •Kr
Fantaisie Tzigane (AUBEL) •Asx/Pno •Cra

Nordic Landscape •1 Sx: A or T/Pno •HE

ADAM, Adolphe (1803-1856)

Compositeur français, né à Paris le 24 VII 1803, où il est mort le 3 V 1856. Travailla avec Cherubini et Boieldieu. Membre de l'Institut de France. Ses opéras-comiques : *Le Chalet* (1834), *Si j'étais Roi* (1852) marquent la fin d'une époque.

"Chez Adolphe Adam le sentiments musical était totalement absent. Il faisait de la musique comme il eut fait autre chose." (V. d'INDY) "Abusant de ses dons d'improvisateur, Adolphe Adam se laisse aller à une déplorable facilité, voire même à une trivialité assez peu musicale." (N. DUFOURCQ)

"Studied with Boieldieu, whose influence was a determining factor in his career." (BAKER) "Adam was a prolific composer who wrote music with extreme facility, but a large amount of his huge output is of purely ephemeral interest." (GROVE)

Cantique de Noël (HOLMES) •Asx/Pno •Rub
Le Postillon de Longjumeau - Air •Sx Solo
Quintette (185x) •3 Cl (Eb, Bb, Bs)/2 Sx

ADAMIS, Michalis

Kalophonikon (1989) (12') (to Saxtuor) •4 Sx

ADAMS, Daniel

Compositeur américain.
Threshold (1987) (6') •SATB •Ron

ADAMS, Stephen David (1909)

The Holy City (BUCHTEL) •2 Sx: AT/Pno •Kjos
The Holy City (DELAMATER) •2 Sx: AA/Pno •Rub
The Holy City (GLENN) •Asx/Pno •B&H
The Holy City (A. LEMARC) •SATB or AATB •TM

ADAMSKI

Feelin fine •Asx/Pno •Sha

ADASKIN, Murray (1906)

Compositeur canadien, né à Toronto le 28 III 1906. Travailla avec J. Weinzweig, Ch. Jones, et D. Milhaud.

"The rhythms in Adaskin's music are energetic, extrovert and, in their irregular groupings and revolving or repeated chord patterns, reminiscent of Stravinsky. More recent orchestral works incorporate materials from Canadian folklore and evoke the country's vast space and vanising folk cultures." (W. AIDE)
Daydreams (1968-71) (2'40) •Asx/Pno •CMC

ADDERLEY, Mark (1960)

Compositeur norvégien.
Waver (1986) •Fl/Cl/Tsx/Vln •NMI
The Worm and the Toothache - A Cosmological Incantation from Ancient Mesopotamia: Concerto (1986) •Asx/Tsx/Vln/Fl/Trb/ Pno/Perc •NMI

ADLER, Samuel (1928)

Compositeur américain d'origine allemande, né le 4 III 1928 à Mannheim (Allemagne). Travailla avec W. Piston, P. Hindemith, A. Copland, et R. Thompson. Professeur à Eastman School of Music, Rochester, New York, U.S.A.
Canto IV (1970) (to D. SINTA) 1) Quite fast and steady 2) Slowly moving along 3) Fast and Furious •Asx Solo •DP
Concerto (1985) (20') •SATB/Orch •Gravis
Line Drawings (1978) (to S. Rascher Quartet) 1) Light drawing 2) Dark drawing •SATB •DP

ADRIET (18xx-18xx)

Chef de musique français.
Mélodie •8 or 10 Sx: SSAATTBBs •Marg

AGER, Klaus (1946)

Compositeur autrichien né à Salzburg. Travailla à Paris avec O. Messiaen et P. Schaeffer.
Shigöpotuu (1988) •SATB •ADE

AGNESENS, Udo (1961)

Compositeur allemand, né le 10 VII 1961, à Beckum. Travailla avec F.M. Beyer. I Yun, W. Szaloneck, et M. Bertoncini.
Aufbruch-Paradoxon (1989) (8') •SATB/String Quartet •adr
Petite sonate (1986) 1) Vivace lirico 2) Adagio molto - Poco presto •Asx/Vcl •adr
Quartet (1981) (12') •SATB •adr
Quartet II (1985) (12') •SATB •adr
Quartet III (1989) (12') •SATB
Suite populaire (1986) 1) Ruhing 2) Heiter 3) Adagio e vivace lyricossimo 4) Burlesque •Asx/Vla/Vcl •adr

AHLBERG, Gunnar (1942)

Compositeur suédois, né à Mora, le 29 III 1942. Travailla avec K. Birger, I. Lidholm et G. Ligeti.

"Gunnar Ahlberg already attracted attention as a composer in the mid-1960s, when he was regarded as a rational artist profoundly influenced by Darmstadt–but more Boulez than Stockhausen and preferring sound to intellectual theories."
Mosaïk (1964) (6') •SATB •STIM

AHO, Kalevi (1949)

Compositeur finlandais, né le 9 III 1949. Travailla avec E. Rautavaara puis avec B. Blacher à Berlin.

"His music is entirely in large-scale symphonic forms employing classical polyphony." (E. SALMENHAARA)
Quartet (1982) (22') •Fl/Asx/Guit/Perc •FMIC

AICHINGER, Gregor (1564/5-1628)

Jubilate Deo •SATB •WWS

AJOSA, A.

Technica Modern per Saxophone

AKI, Touru

Compositeur japonais.
Réla •Ssx/Perc

AKIMENKO, Fyodor Stefanovich (1876-1945)

Eglogue (EPHROSS) •Asx/Pno •South

AKKERMANN, Michel

Compositeur allemand.
"To be redreamed in colors pale but intense" (1991) (10') •4 Sx: SATB/Tpt/Pno

AKSES, Necil Kâzim (1908)

Compositeur turc, né à Istanbul le 6 V 1908. Travailla à Vienne avec J. Mark puis à Prague avec A. Haba. Directeur de l'Opéra d'Ankara.

"His music, derived from Turkish folk rhythms, is in the modern idiom." (BAKER) "Akses's works are few in number, but lengthy and important in reflecting the influence of modern musical movements of central Europe; at the same time he has skillfully incorporated into them melodies adapted from ancient Turkish art music and folk rhythms." (GROVE)
Allegro feroce (1931) •Asx/Pno •Uni

ALBAM, Manny (1922)

Compositeur américain.
Eubie Medley (1982) (to Amherst Saxophone Quartet) •SATB/Orch
Quartet no. 1 (1964) (to the New York Saxophone Quartet) •SATB

ALBEN, Denis
Concertino (1983) (to Paul COHEN) •Asx/Pno

ALBENIZ, Isaac (1860-1909)
Aragonaise (CORROYEZ) •Asx/Pno •Led
Berceuse (CORROYEZ) •Asx/Pno •Led
Chant d'amour (CORROYEZ) •Asx/Pno •Led
L'Automne (CORROYEZ) •Asx/Pno •Led
L'Eté (CORROYEZ) •Asx/Pno •Led
L'Hiver (CORROYEZ) •Asx/Pno •Led
Le Printemps (CORROYEZ) •Asx/Pno •Led
Mallorca, barcarola (AMAZ) •Tsx/Pno •UME
Mallorca, barcarolla (BAYER) •Asx/Pno •ME
Menuet (CORROYEZ) •Asx/Pno •Led
Puerta de Tierra, bolero (AMAZ) •Tsx/Pno •UME
Puerta de Tierra, bolero (Bayer) •Asx/Pno •UME
Scherzino (CORROYEZ) •Asx/Pno •Led
Sévilla (Mule) •SATB •Bil
Tango, op. 165/2 (CORROYEZ) •Asx/Pno •Led
Tango, op. 165/2 •Asx/Pno •Sch
Tango, op. 165/2 •Asx/Pno •CBet
Tango (STABER) •Asx/Pno •ME
Trois Pièces (MULE) (5') •SATB •Led

ALBERT, Eugen d' (1864-1932)
Pianiste virtuose et compositeur allemand, né à Glasgow, le 10 IV 1864, mort à Riga, le 3 III 1932. Travailla avec Richter et Fr. Liszt.

"D'esthétique wagnérienne avec influence italienne." (E. VUILLERMOZ)

"Style inspiré de Brahms."

"His musical idiom oscillates between the Italian melodic style and German contrapuntal writing, and fails to achieve originality." (BAKER)

Saxophon Musik (193x) •Asx/Orch

ALBERT, Karel (1901)
Compositeur belge né à Anvers, le 6 IV 1901. Etudia avec M. de Jong.

"At first this musical style ranked him with the expressionist school, but during World War II he turned to a more traditional, simple, and comprehensible style; in 1956 he became influenced by dodecaphony." (GROVE)

Quatuor (1960) (to Quatuor Belge de Sxph.) 1) Allegro 2) Moderato expressivo 3) Allegro •SATB •adr

ALBERT, Thomas (1948)
Compositeur américain, né à Lebanon (Pennsylvania) le 4 XII 1948. Travailla avec B. Johnston, P. Zonn, et M. Powell.

Devil's Rain (15') •SATB
Sound Frames (1968) (6') •Asx/Ob/Trb/Vibr •MP

ALBERTH, Rudolf (1918)
Chef d'orchestre et compositeur allemand, né à Frankfurt le 28 III 1918.

Divertimento (1941) •Asx/Str Trio •adr
Piece •Asx/Org •adr
Saxophonmusik (1950) (19') •Asx/Orch (3330-03300/Harps/Pno/Str) •adr

ALBINONI, Tomaso (1671-1750)
Adagio (Remo GIAZOTTO-LONDEIX) •Asx/Org •Lem
Adagio (Remo GIAZOTTO-PICARD) •Tsx/Pno •Phi
Concerto in D moll, op. 9, no. 2 (JOOSEN) •Tsx/Pno •Mol
Sonata, op. 2, no. 5 (SIBBING) 1) Adagio 2) Allegro •5 Sx: SAATB
Sonata, op. 2, no. 5 (SIBBING) 1) Adagio 2) Allegro •6 Sx: SAATTB

ALBRIGHT, William (1944)
Compositeur, pianiste, et organiste américain né le 20 X 1944 à Gary (Indiana). Travailla avec Finney, Rochberg et, à Paris, avec O. Messiaen.

"Albright's late works often combine a complex rhythmic and atonal style with elements of American popular music. Though his works are formally concise, he stresses the value of music as communication and supremacy in music of intuition, imagination and beauty of sound. Through his modern rag compositions and his performances of classical ragtime, stride piano, and boogie-woogie, he has been a principal figure in the revival of interest in Scott Joplin and other ragtime masters." (GROVE)

Doo-Dah (1975) (to D. SINTA) •3 Sx: AAA •DP
From Dawn to Dusk in the Valley of Fire (1989) (6'30) •4 Sx: SATB/Org •Hen/Pet
Heater (1977) •Asx/Band
Introduction, Passacaglia, and Rondo Capriccioso (14') •Pno/Fl/Cl/Asx/Hn/Tpt/Trb/Tuba/Perc •Pet
Pit Band (1993) •Asx/BsCl/Pno •INM
Sonata (1984) (20') (to D. SINTA, L. HUNTER, & J. WYTKO) 1) Two part invention 2) La Follia nuova: a lament for G. Cacioppo 3) Scherzo 4) Récitative e Dance •Asx/Pno •Pet

Album...
Album of Celebrated Folk Songs and Patriotic Airs •SATB or AATB •CF

ALCALAY, Luna (1928)
Trio (1964) •Asx/CBsn/Bass

ALDRICH, Henry (1648-1710)
Love and Flowers •2 Sx: AT/Pno

ALEN, Andrès
Tema con variaciones (1978) (to M. VILLAFRANCA) •Asx/Pno

ALESSANDINI, Raymond
Piazzolino •Asx/Pno •Bil

ALESSANDRINI, Pierluigi
Saxophoniste de jazz et compositeur italien.

Air - Dance •SATB •Piz
Blues for Sax •12 Sx: SnoSSAAATTTBBBs
Chassé-croisé •Asx/Pno •Bil
5 Etudes jazz (1988) •CoMu
Ellingtoniana (ELLINGTON) •12 Sx: SnoSSAAATTTBBBs
Improvisation & Sax in jazz •3 Sx: ATB
Melange •SATB •Ber
Notturno •3 Sx: ATB
Piazzolino •Asx/Pno •Bil
Sweetly (1987) (2'30) •3 Sx: AAT •CoMu
Traditione-Blues •SATB •Ber
Trilogie (1991) 1) Blues 2) Zazeau 3) Village •3 Sx: AAT •CoMu
Valse lente •Asx/Pno •Bil

ALESSANDRINI, R.
Travelling Suite •SATB •SL

ALESSANDRO, Raffaele d' (1911-1959)
Compositeur, pianiste, et organiste suisse, né à St-Gallen, le 17 III 1911, mort à Lausanne, le 17 III 1959. Travailla avec M. Dupré, P. Roes, et N. Boulanger.

"Son oeuvre, à l'écart des écoles témoigne d'un tempérament passionné s'exprimant par un lyrisme tourmenté et concentré, d'une inspiration très originale." (BORDAS)

"His eclectic style took elements from the varied musical currents of the time, but he retained a basis of sonata form and tonal harmony. He preferred driving rhythms and his writing is complex and compact." (L. MARRETA-SCHAR)

Serenade, op. 12 •Asx/Str Orch

ALEXANDER, Joseph
Masks and Mirrors (1986) •Ssx/Vcl/Perc/Pno

ALIPRANDI, Paul
Compositeur français.
Paysages •Asx/Harp •Chap

ALIS, Romàn (1931)
Compositeur espagnol, né à Palma de Majorca le 24 VIII 1931. Travailla avec Zamacois, Pich, et Toldra. Professeur au Conservatoire de Madrid.
"His early compositions employed 12-note serialism; later his technique became more open and flexible."
Ambitos, op. 135 (1982) (10'30) (to M. Mijan) 1) Allegro accentuado e con brio 2) Moderato muy calmado 3) Allegro vivo y marcial •Asx Solo •EMEC

ALIX, René (1907-1966)
Compositeur et chef de choeur français, né à Sotteville-les-Rouen, mort à Orly, le 30 XII 1966. Travailla avec L. Vierne, Caussade, et Bertelin.
"Alix revendique son appartenance à la tradition classique. Pour lui, la qualité des idées prime la recherche systématique de nouveaux moyens d'expression." (Bordas)
Prélude fantasque et Impromptu •Asx/Pno •Led

ALKEMA, Henk (1944)
Compositeur néerlandais.
Op avontuur (1988) (10') •Tsx/Pno •Don
Just music (1986) (12') •Sx/Marimba •Don
Quartet no. 1 (1983/84) (10') •SATB •Don
Rituelen II (1987) (11') •Bsx/Pno •Don
Sonatine (1980) (8') (to L. van Oostrom) •Asx/Pno •Don

ALLA, Thierry (1955)
Compositeur et professeur français, né à Libourne, le 24 III 1955. Travailla avec Michel Fusté-Lambezat, A. Bancquart, et Chr. Eloy, ainsi qu'à Darmstadt.
Aérienne (1994) (8') (Envol - Jet Stream - Khamsin Terres) •Fl/2 Sx/Pno/Perc/dispositif électroacoustique
La Terre et la Comète (1991) •Children's Choir (Choeur d'enfants)/Fl/Cl/Asx/Pno/Bass/Synth/Perc/Tape •adr
Météore (1986) •6 Sx: SAATBBs/Perc •adr
Offshore (1990) •SATB •Fuz
Polychrome (1994) (to J-M. Londeix) •12 Sx: SnoSSAAATTTBBBs

ALLARD, Joseph (1910-1991)
Saxophoniste et clarinettiste américain, né le 30 XII 1910 à Lowell (Massachusetts), mort à New York le 3 V 1991. Travailla la clarinette avec G. Hamelin et le saxophone avec Rudy Wiedoeft. Professeur à la Juilliard School de New York.
Advanced Rhythms •All Sx •DP
Jazz Progressive Studies
3 Octave scales & Chords (1947) •CC

ALLGEN, Claude Loyola (Klas-Thure) (1920-1990)
Compositeur suédois né le 16 IV 1920 à Calcutta, mort le 18 IX 1990. Travailla avec M. Melchers.
Karl-Birger Blomdahl referred to him as "a hyperintellectualist who denies all vertical relationships or observes only negative rules (for example, that different parts are not allowed to meet on the same note) and mostly enjoys writing nine-part fugues with 100 per cent utilization of his thematic material and practically unplayable tempi, and is a stickler for 'single absolute objectivity' (he just 'starts up' the music which then keeps going until it runs out')."

Adagio och Fuga (25') •Fl/Ob/EH/Cl/BsCl/2 Sx: AB/Bsn/Hn •STIM
Praeludium och Carmen Perlotense •Vln/Vla/Vcl/Asx/Pno/Harps/Org •SMIC/STIM/Ehr

ALLIK, Kristi
Compositeur canadien.
Integra (1986) •Ssx (or Asx)/Tape •CMC

ALSCHAUSKY
Walser-Arie no. 2 •Bsx/Pno •CBet

ALSINA
Rendez-vous •Cl/Asx/Trb/Perc •Led

ALTER, Louis
Manhattan Serenade (Wiedoeft) •Asx/Pno •Rob

ALTIERI, Roberto
Compositeur italien.
Untitled (1992) (10') •Asx/Pno

ALTISENT, J.
Compositeur espagnol.
Soliloquio •Asx/Pno •Boi

AMATO, Bruno
Sonatella (1977) (to K. Fischer) (3 movements) •Asx/Pno •Rub

AMBRIOSO, Alfred Joseph d' (1871-1914)
Canzonetta (Hummel) •Asx/Pno •Rub
Canzonetta, op. 6 (Teal) •Asx/Pno •GSch

AMBROSINI, Claudio (1948)
Compositeur italien, né à Venise.
Trobar clar (1982) •Fl/Ob/Cl/Tpt/1 Sx: S+A

AMDAHL, Magne (1942)
Cantilène (1973) (4') •Asx (or Ob)/Pno •NMI
Sintoley (1977) (4') •Asx/Pno •NMI
Tranquillo dolce (1973) (4') •Asx/Pno •NMI

AMEELE, D.
Sound poem •Sx/Perc

AMELLER, André (1912-1990)
Compositeur et contrebassiste français, né à Arnaville (M-&-M), le 2 I 1912. Mort à Courbevoie le 14 V 1990. Travailla avec S. Ple-Caussade, T. Aubin et Roger Ducasse. Directeur du Conservatoire de Dijon (1953-1987).
"Art essentiellement formulaire, André Ameller ne manque pas au demeurant de dextérité dans l'agencement des procédés stylistiques dûment consacrés." (R. Bernard).
Aria moderato (1960) (to J-M. Londeix) •Asx/Pno
Azuleros de Valencia (1965) (13') (to Sextuor à vent de Dijon) 1) Andante 2) Lento expressivo 3) Giocoso 4) Final •Fl/Ob/Cl/Asx/Hn/Bsn
Belle Province (1973) (3') 1) Baie Comeau 2) Pointe au Pic •1 Sx: A or T/Pno •Led
Capriccio (1974) (7'30) (to J-P. Caens) •Asx Solo •Com
Concertino, op. 125 (1959) (12'30) (to J-M. Londeix) 1) Lento-Allegro con fantasia 2) Come un'improvisazione 3) Vivace •Asx/Str Orch et Fl obligée (or Asx/Pno) •Phi
2 Pièces (1957/69) (2'30) 1) Haïz-Pian 2) Ené Bihotzian •Asx/Pno •Phi
Entrée, Deux petites pièces Estudio (1961) (to J-M. Londeix) •Asx Solo
Entrée et Danse (1977) (4'30) (to A. Bouhey) •Asx Solo •Com

Espressivo et Vivement (1959) (to J-M. LONDEIX) •SATB
Geneviève (1977) (7'30) •1 Sx: A or T/Pno •Mar
Gypsophile •Asx Solo •Mar
Jeux de table (1954) (8'30) (to J-M. LONDEIX) 1) Diamino 2) Mahh-
    jongg 3) Ping-pong •Asx/Pno •Lem
Kesa (1981) •1 Sx: A or T/Pno •Mar
Kryptos •BsSx/Pno •Pet
Lirico (1969) (2') •1 Sx: A or T/Pno •Phi
La Plata (1972) (1'30) •1 Sx: A or T/Pno •Com
15 Etudes expressives (1954-56) •Sx Solo •Pet
La Sauge (1976) (2'30) •1 Sx: A or T/Pno •Lem
Scherzo-Fugato (1959) •SATB
Suite d'après Rameau (1960) (9') (to J-M. LONDEIX) 1) Vivo
    2) Sarabande 3) Menuets 4) Rondeau gracieux 5) Final •Asx/Str
    or WW Quintet or Pno •ET
De Trois à Six (1960) (to J-M. LONDEIX) •Asx/Pno

AMIOT, Jean-Claude (1939)
Compositeur français.
1er Quatuor (1967) (to Quatuor de Lyon) •SATB
Sérénade (1969) •Asx/Pno •Mar

AMIROV, Fikret Mechadi Djamil Ogly (1922)
Compositeur d'Azerbaïdjan né à Gyandzha, le 22 XI 1922. Travailla
avec B. I. Zeïdman.
"In general his music combines the traditions of Azebaijani folk
music with those of Russian and European art music. His use of the
orchestra is notable above all for its clarity and at times, picturesque-
ness." (Y. GABAY)
Concerto (1974) •Mezzo Soprano Voice (or Asx)/Orch
Poême Symphonique (1977) •Asx/Orch

AMMAN, Benno (1904-1986)
Sonata •Asx/Pno

AMON, Klemens
Compositeur autrichien.
Sax with Mr. X (1993) •Asx/Perc •INM

AMORÉ, Daniel
Compositeur français. Travailla avec M. Fuste-Lambezat.
Aux Quatre vents (1988) •4 Sx: Sno+S ATB

AMOS
Compositae no. 11 •Asx/Pno
Compositae no. 12 •Tsx/Pno
Saxifrage •SATB

AMRAM, David Werner (1930)
Compositeur et chef d'orchestre américain, né à Philadelphie, le 7 XI
1930. Travailla avec V. Gianini. Fit du jazz avec le Dixieland band.
"In appearance, Amram has little of the maestro; like much of his
music he is casual, easygoing, genially unkempt, and no respecter of
categories." (A. RICH) "His music is romantic, dramatic, and colourful,
marked by rythmic and improvisatory characteristics of jazz." (O.
DANIEL)
Ode to Lord Buckley (Concerto) (1980) (30') (to K. RADNOFSKY)
    1) Overture 2) Ballad 3) Taxim; Ein Adir •Asx/Orch (221BsCl2/
    2221/Timp/3 Perc/Str) or Band or Pno •Pet
Trio (1965) 1) Allegro moderato 2) Andante quasi un poco adagio
    3) Allegro con brio 4) Epilogue •Tsx/Hn/Bsn •Pet

AMSDEN
Practice Duets •2 Sx: AA •WWS

AMY, Gilbert (1936)
Compositeur et chef d'orchestre français, né à Paris , devenu direc-

teur des concerts du Domaine Musical comme successeur de Pierre
Boulez (1967). Travailla avec D. Milhaud, O. Messiaen, puis P.
Boulez.
"Gilbert Amy s'est rapidement affranchi de l'influence de P. Boulez
pour développer, dans le style post-sériel, une des personnalités les
plus inventives, les plus raffinées et les plus rigoureuses de sa génération." (Cl. ROSTAND) "Se détournant d'un sérialisme très strict, au profit
d'un langage plus souple, Gilbert Amy conçoit toujours l'oeuvre
comme une totalité soumise à une forte cohérence logique, adoptant
cependant, pour chacune de ses compositions, une 'forme' différen-
ciée; chacune d'elles devient un organisme autonome, dont la rigueur
formelle n'empêche aucunement une certaine variabilité." (D. & J-Y.
BOSSEUR)
Trio (1993) •Vln/Sx/Trb

ANASTASI, Concetta
Compositeur italien.
Print (1992) (7') •Asx/Pno

ANCELIN, Pierre (1934)
Compositeur français né à Cannes, le 25 X 1934. Travailla avec O.
Messiaen.
"Est surtout un autodidacte. Sans se priver des apports de son temps,
Ancelin récuse tout procédé ou système d'écriture. Il a peu à peu
découvert son langage, que régit une très libre modalité, et son style,
fondé sur le primat de l'expression." (BORDAS) "Très modal, son
langage est fondé sur l'expression."
Saxophonie (1983) (8') (to D. DEFFAYET) •Asx/Str Orch or Pno •Bil

ANDERBERG, Carl Olof (1914-1972)
Compositeur, pianiste, et chef d'orchestre suédois, né à Stockholm,
le 13 III 1914 et mort à Malmö, le 4 I 1972.
"Anderberg's music of the 1930s and 1940s showed French influence, but later he went through a 12-note serial period, stimulated by
his profound analyses of Schoenberg's piano music. In this way he
integrated new techniques into an individual style, solidly craftsmanlike
in the orchestral works and instrumentally brilliant in the chamber
music." (H. ASTRAND) "As a creative artist, Anderberg was an explorer,
an experimental avant-gardist with a strong sense of social pathos. He
had begun in the footsteps of Hindemith, at an early stage he had taken
an interest in Schoenberg's 12-tone system and, finally, he had evolved
a personal form of serialism in which aleatory music and improvisation
became vital components."
Konsert (1969) •Asx/Orch (2222/2200/Str) or Pno •FS

ANDERSEN, Erling (1922)
Compositeur norvégien.
Movements (1976) •SATB

ANDERSEN, Joachim (1847-1909)
24 Etudes, op. 21 (LEGER) •Bil
24 Etudes instructives dans tous les tons, op. 30 (LEGER) •Bil
24 Petites études, op. 33 (LEGER) •Bil
18 Petites études, op. 41 (LEGER) •Bil

ANDERSEN, Michael
Sonata (1976) 1) Allegretto 2) Adagio 3) Vivace •Ssx/Pno

ANDERSON, Beth (1950)
Hallophone (1973) •Dancer/Voice/Sx/Guit/Tape

ANDERSON, Garland (1933)
Compositeur américain né le 10 IV 1933 à Union City (Ohio).
Travailla avec H. Gal et R. Harris.
Concerto •Asx/Band •DP
Quartet (1968) (to C. LEESON) •AATB •adr
Sarabande (1966) (to C. LEESON) •Tsx/Pno •adr

Sonata (1966) (to J. Anderson) 1) Adagio-Allegro-Adagio
2) Scherzo 3) Andante con moto 4) Allegro ma non troppo
•Asx/Pno •South
Sonata (1968) (to C. Leeson) •Tsx/Pno •South
Sonata (1976) (to N. Brightman) 1) Allegro con spirito 2) Andante
sostenuto 3) Adagio-Allegro •Bsx/Pno •South
Sonata no. 2 (1978) (to T. Baker) 1) Allegro 2) Andante molto
3) Allegro •Asx/Pno •South
Symphony for Saxophone Ensemble (1973) •12 Sx: ATB •adr

ANDERSON, Gerry
Compositeur irlandais.
Pastiche (1993) •Ssx/Pno •INM

ANDERSON, Jean
Compositeur canadien.
Introduction and Dance (1982) •Asx/Pno •CMC
Sonata (1983) •Asx/Pno •CMC

ANDERSON, Leroy (1908-1975)
Belle of the Ball •Asx/Pno •Mills

ANDERSON, Michael
Sonata (1977) (to D. Masek) •Asx/Pno

ANDERSON, Thomas Jefferson (1928)
Compositeur américain, né à Coatesville, Pennsylvania le 17 VIII
1928.
"His music reflects the influence of both jazz and post-Webern
styles. His predilection for rythmic complexities and his imaginative
use of instrumental color are particularly noteworthy." (E. Southern)
Intermezzi (1983) •Cl/Asx/Pno •B&B
Re-creation (1978) •Asx/Vla/Vcl/Pno/Tamtam
Variations on a Theme by M.B. Tolson (1969) •Ssx/Tpt/Trb/Vln/Vcl/
Pno

ANDERSON, Tommy Joe (1947)
Compositeur américain, né à Bristol. Travailla avec T. Canning.
Concerto, op. 23 (1976) (for J. Wytko) 1) Andantino 2) Larghetto
3) Presto •Asx/Wind Symphony •WWS
Impromptu, op. 29 (to K. Fischer) •Ssx Solo •DP
Liebeslied, op. 20 (1975) (to J. Wytko) •Ssx/Pno
Nemesis, op. 19 (1975) (to F. Hemke) 1) Quickly 2) Slow 3) Ener-
getically •Ssx/Woodwind Quintet •DP/WWS
24 Preludes, op. 28 •Asx Solo
Sonata, op. 10, no. 1 (1970) (4'30) (to J. Wytko) Very fast - Slow -
Fast •Asx/Pno •SMC
Sonata no. 2, op. 17 (1973) (To J.Wytko) •Asx/Pno •DP/WWS
Sonata no. 3, op. 30 (1988) (14'15) (for K. Fischer) 1) Andante-
Presto 2) Largo "Todeslied" 3) Presto •1 Sx: S+A/Pno •Ron

ANDERSSON, Magnus (1953)
Compositeur suédois.
Gömma (1989) (13') •Asx Solo •SMIC

ANDO, Jan
Futur (1976) (to Ryo Noda) •Asx/Pno
Max on the Man •Asx/Pno

ANDRAUD, Albert J. (1884-19xx)
Hautboïste et professeur français né à Bordeaux le 17 II 1884. Installé
aux U.S.A. en 1918.
1er cahier d'Etudes •Led
48 Etudes d'après Ferling •South
3 Duos concertants •2 Sx: AA or TT

ANDRÉ, Paul (18xx-1940)
Compositeur français.

Romance d'Automne •2 Sx: AA/Pno •Braun

ANDREIEV, E.
Saxophoniste russe.
Manuel d'Enregistrement initial du saxophone (1973)

ANDRES, Edouard
Compositeur français. Travailla avec J. Falk.
Méditation (5') (Pour M. Sieffert) •Asx/Org

ANDREWS
Threnos •Sx Solo •Sha

ANDRIESSEN, Jurriaan (1925)
Compositeur néerlandais, né à Harlem, le 15 XI 1925. Travailla avec
son père Hendrick, W. van Otterloo, et, aux U.S.A. avec A. Copland.
"His music exhibits sound professional skill in a style that draws on
diverse recently developed techniques without being bound to any
specific system." (J. Wouters)
Concertino (1966-67) •Asx/Orch •Don
Hommage à Milhaud (1945) (8') •Fl/Ob/Cl/Bsn/Hn/Tpt/Trb/Asx/
Vln/Vla/Vcl •Don

ANDRIESSEN, Louis (1939)
Compositeur néerlandais, frère du précédent, né à Utrecht, le 6 VI
1939. Travailla avec son père et L. Berio.
"Ses oeuvres instrumentales pour les formations les plus diverses en
font une des personnalités les plus originales de l'école hollandaise
moderne." (Cl. Rostand). "Pour certains compositeurs de musique
politique, comme Louis Andriessen, le désir d'un contact avec un
public vaste, porté par un message emphatique, a donné naissance à des
styles de composition et à des types de concerts relevant plutôt du
monde rock: puissante amplification, pièces répétitives, à pulsation
forte." (P. Griffiths)
"Since 1965 he has often made use of collage and other avant-garde
techniques."
Introspezione III (1959) •2 Pno/Tsx •Don
On Jimmy Yancey (1973) (10') Fl/2 Sx: AT/Hn/Tpt/3 Trb/Bass/Pno
•Don
Song lines (1989) •3 Sx: TTB or 6 Sx: TTTTBB/Perc •JG
De Volharping (Perseverance) (1972) (23') •3 Sx/3 Tpt/3 Trb •Don
Widow (1990) •3 Sx: TTB •JG

ANDRIEU, Fernand (1863-19xx)
Compositeur français.
L'Angélus du soir •1 Sx: A or T/Pno •Mar
Concertino n° 3 •Tsx/Pno •Mus
Divertissement (1923) •Asx/Pno •Bil
Impressions Napolitaines 1) Farniente 2) Tarentelle •2 Sx: SA or TB
•Mar
1er solo de concours •1 Sx: T or B/Pno •Alf
Rondo Caprice •Tsx/Pno •Mus
Rossignol d'amour •Asx/Pno •Braun
A une étoile •1 Sx: A or T/Pno •Mar

ANDRIX, Georges (1932)
Compositeur américain.
4 Pieces, Movements (to D. Sinta) •Asx/Pno

ANDROSCH, Peter
Compositeur autrichien.
Dr. Mabuse •12 Sx: SnoSSAAATTTBBBs

ANEST, Alex
Compositeur américain.
Last (1993) •Ssx/Guit •INM

ANGELINI, Louis (1935)

Sextet (to F. HEMKE) •Asx/Woodwind Quintet

ANGELO, Nicholas V. d' (see D'ANGELO)

ANGULO, Manuel

Bisonante (1983) (8'30) (to M. MIJAN) •Asx/Pno •Mun
Bucolica (1985) (13') (to M. VILLAFRUELA) •Ssx/Tape

ANONYMOUS

Chanson & Canon (EVERTSE) •SATB •TM
De montis lapis (BIRTWISTLE & MULDOWNEY) (3') •4 Sx: SSSS
15th Century German Trios (AXWORTHY) •3 Sx: ATB •TVA
Kyrie (from *Missa pro Defunctus*) (EVERTSE) •SATB •TM
O Virgo splendens (BIRTWISTLE & MULDOWNEY) (2'30) •4 Sx: SSSS
Pange melos lacrimosum (BIRTWISTLE & MULDOWNEY) (1') •4 Sx: SSSS
Regina Coeli (EVERTSE) •SATB or AATB •TM
Resurrexit (EVERTSE) •SATB or AATB •TM
Si domiero (DORN) •3 Sx: ATB •DP
16th Century Trios (BENTLEY) •Fl (or Ob or Cl)/Ob (or Cl)/Sx •Chap
Tart ara (DORN) •3 Sx: ATB •DP

ANSIND, Caroline

Compositeur néerlandais.
Het water zal de stenen breken (1986) (14'30) Choir/Ob/Cl/2 Sx: AB/2 Trb/Perc/Pno •Don

ANTOINE, R.

Gammes •Chou

ANTONINI, Félix (1906)

Pianiste, organiste, et compositeur français, né à Lyon le 18 IV 1906.
Adagio et Allegretto •Asx/Pno •adr
Arabesque •SATB •adr
Ave Maria •SATB •adr
Le Berger rêve •Asx/Pno •Bil
Concertino baroque •Ssx/Band •adr
Danse martienne •SATB •adr
Mixte concertino •Asx/Pno •adr
Saturno •SATB •adr
Saxo-Czardas •Asx/Pno •adr
Tzigane (1971) (2'45) •Asx/Pno •Bil

ANZALONE, Valentine

Breeze-Easy Method (1958) •Wit

APERGHIS, Georges (1945)

Compositeur français, né à Athènes. Autodidacte, impressionné par Mauricio Kagel. Installé à Paris depuis 1963.
"La musique de Georges Aperghis dépasse toujours le strict cadre du concert pour basculer dans l'histoire, à la manière d'un conteur extra-occidental dont la musique n'est qu'un véhicule, un moyen de communiquer." (C. LEBLÉ)
Signaux (1978) (9'30) •Quatuor d'instruments de même timbre et tessiture •Sal

APFELSTADT, Marc (1952)

Compositeur américain.
Duo for Wind Controllers (1990) 1) Introduction 2) Danse 3) Waltz 4) Duo Fantasies 5) Cantus •2 Yamaha WX7 MIDI Wind Controllers •adr
Industrial.Orient.90 (1990) •Yamaha WX7 MIDI Wind Controller •adr

APIVOR, Denis (1916)

Compositeur irlandais, né le 14 IV 1916 à Collinstown. Travailla avec P. Hadley, A. Rawsthorne, et E. Clark, disciple de Schoenberg.
"Presque toutes ses oeuvres sont composées selon les techniques sérielles." (BORDAS)
"After 1956, Apivor's style became more radical, the serialism atonal and athematic. Most of the works of this period exploit short forms, smaller instrumental groups, and more polyphonic textures. Apivor has shown no interest in either aleatory or electronic techniques, but from 1968 he favored a freer serialism." (A. WHITTALL)
Trio (The prostest) (1981) (to J. DAWSON) •Ssx/Vcl/Pno

APOTHELOZ, Jean (1900-1965)

Compositeur et peintre suisse, né à Lausanne, le 12 V 1900, mort à Nyon, le 10 VII 1965. Mena simultanément des études de peinture et de musique. Travailla avec Fornerod.
"Il a écrit une oeuvre très française de forme et d'inspiration dont le caractère plastique et mélodique révèle une délicate sensibilité." (BORDAS). "Jean Apotheloz est délibérément traditionnel; volontiers inspiré par la nature, il s'en tient au langage tonal le plus pacifique, langage qu'il manie en évitant les formules toutes faites, scolaires ou conventionnelles, témoignant d'une verve et d'une fraîcheur très personnelles." (Cl. ROSTAND)
Sérénade (1951) •Asx/Orch •adr

APPARAILLY, Yves (1936)

Accordéoniste et compositeur français, né à La Rochelle, le 24 XI 1936. Travailla avec A. Abott et J. Pernoo.
Danse sacrée (1980) (8') (to J-M. LONDEIX) •14 Sx: SnoSnoSSSAAAATTBBBs •adr
3 Danses (1975) (9'45) (to J-M. LONDEIX) •Asx/Pno •adr

APPERSON, Ronald

Concertino •Fl/Asx/Bsn
Quartet •SATB •TM
Suite antique •SATB •Mol

APPLEBAUM, Terry (1945)

Compositeur américain, né à Chicago, le 1 III 1945. Travailla avec G. Peters et T. Davis.
Fun with the Old Favorites •2 Sx •WWS
Progressive Duets •2 Sx •WWS
Quartet (1964) (4') (to F. HEMKE) •SATB •South

APPLEDORN, Mary Jeanne van

Compositeur américain.
4 Duos (1985) (4'30) Dialogue - Divertimento - Dirge - Dance •2 Sx: AA •DP
Liquid Gold (1981) (for D. UNDERWOOD) •Asx/Pno •DP
Matrices (1979) (7'10) •Asx/Pno

ARASHINO, Nidehiko (1940)

Compositeur japonais.
Sonatine (1964) (to A. SAKAGUCHI) •Asx/Pno

ARBAN, Joseph (1825-1889)

Cornettiste et chef d'orchestre français né à Lyon le 28 II 1825; mort à Paris le 9 IV 1889. Etudia la trompette avec Dauverné. Professeur au Conservatoire de Paris (1869-1889). Ami d'Adolphe Sax.
"On lui doit quantité de Fantaisies et morceaux de concerts, ainsi que d'importants ouvrages didactiques." (LAROUSSE)
"He acquired renown for conducting salon orchestras. Arban was the founder of the modern school of trumpet playing." (E. H. TARR)
Caprice et Variations (1861) (to A. SAX) •Asx/Pno •Ron/Sax
Oberto, Air varié •1 Sx: A or T/Pno •Mol
Perpetual Motion (1'30) (VANASEK) •Bb Sx/Pno •SC

ARCHER, Violet (1913)

Compositeur et pianiste canadien, né à Montréal, le 24 IV 1913.

Travailla avec D. Clarke, Cl. Champagne, et Béla Bartok à New York et Paul Hindemith à la Yale University (1949).

"There have been great executive artists among women but you could count the composers on the fingers of one hand. Indeed I can't think of one who has survived as a classic. But this slim, small, quiet Canadian doesn't write in what we have assumed to be feminine terms. When you listen to her strong austere music with its contrapuntal mastery you realize that such assumptions are arbitrary enough to be broken, like most arbitrary generalizations." (Th. ARCHER) "Her music is informed by some qualities which have become equated with the spacious Canadian country and its often rugged lanscape. She also uses Hindemith's system of progressive harmonic weights." (D. COOPER)

Divertimento (1979) (12') (to M. ECKROTH) 1) Preludio (Andante con moto) 2) Meditation (Largo molto, espressivo) 3) Festive (Allegretto energico) •SATB •DP

Moods (10') (for P. BRODIE) Theme and variations - Tranquil - Energetic - Sad - Restless - Whimsical - Rhapsodic •Cl/Asx •CMC

Sonata (1972) (15'30) (to P. BRODIE) 1) Préambule 2) Interlude 3) Valsette 4) Rondo •Asx/Pno •BML

Three Essays (1988) •Sx Solo: S+A •CMC

ARCURI, Serge
Compositeur canadien.
Prologue (1985) •Fl/Ssx/Cl/Hn/Perc/Tape •CMC

ARDITI, Luigi (1822-1903)
Il Bacio •2 Sx: AT/Pno or 3 Sx: AAA/Pno •Cen

AREND, A. den
Quartet •SATB •TM

AREND, Johann Krieger
Boismortier Suite •SATB •Mol

ARENSKY, Anton Stephanovitch (1861-1906)
The Cuckoo •AATB/(Pno ad lib.) •Bri

ARGERSINGER, Charles
Doxology Variations (1983) (to L. KLOCK) •Asx/Wind Ensemble
Drastic Measures (to Baylor Chamber Players) •Fl/Ob/Cl/Asx/Bsn/ Hn/Perc

ARIOSTI, Attilio (1666-1740)
Gigue (MULE) •Asx/Pno •Led

ARLT, Kurt
Liebeswalzer (H. KIRCHSTEIN) •Asx/Pno •Fro

ARMA, Paul (1905-1987)
Compositeur, pianiste et ethnomusicologue français, d'origine hongroise, né à Budapest, le 22 X 1905; mort à Paris le 28 XI 1987. Travailla avec B. Bartok. Etabli en France depuis 1933.

"Mes longues recherches m'ont conduit au "mobile" musical non-aléatoire, où la juxtaposition des plans et des espaces sonores est déterminée par le compositeur seul: alors la liberté naît, justement, comme toujours de la grande rigueur. J'ai écrit 62 "Transparences"... Je n'ai pas le moins du monde la prétention d'avoir en cela fondé un "genre". J'ai eu l'ambition, simplement, d'avoir créé des objets trans-parents, ce qui est une approche, tout de même de la pureté." (P. ARMA)

"As a composer he is known chiefly for his experimental work, though he has also published didactic pieces and folksong arrangements." (V. LAMPERT) "A composer of empiric music exploring the ultimate in complexity, he has developed a compromise method evocative of folksongs in an advanced rythmic style." (BAKER'S)

Comme une improvisation (1978) (7'30) (to J. DESLOGES) •Asx Solo •DP

3 Contrastes (1971) (6') (to J. DESLOGES) •Sx Solo •Chou
2 Convergences (1976) (7'30) (to A. BOUHEY) •Asx/Tape (African instruments)
7 Convergences (1974) (14'30) •SATB •DP
Divertimento no. 12 (1971) (15') •2 Sx: AA or TT •Chap
Divertimento no. 18 (1976) (13') •Asx/Fl
Divertissement 1600 (1960) (12'30) 1) Prélude 2) Branle simple 3) Branle gay 4) Branle de Montirandé 5) Pavane d'Angleterre 6) Volte 7) Postlude •SATB
6 Mobiles (1975) (12') •1, 2, 3, or 4 Sx
Musique (1980) (13') •4 Sx: SATB/Harp
Musique d'après des thèmes populaires roumains (1968) (12') 1) Danse lente 2) Pastourelle 3) Chant d'amour 4) Chant du berger 5) Ballade 6) Danse des jeunes 7) Chant du vagabond 8) Chant triste 9) Ronde •2 Sx
Petite Suite (1972) (10'30) (to Quatuor DESLOGES) •SATB •Lem
Phases contre Phases (1978) (13') (to G. WOLFE) •Ssx/Pno •Lem
Résonnance (1973) (16') •Ssx/Perc (1 player) •DP
Soliloque (1968) (10') (to J. DESLOGES) •Asx Solo •Bil
Transparences (to Quatuor d'Anches Français) •Ob/Cl/Asx/Bsn
7 Transparences (1968) (13'30) •SATB •Lem

ARMSTRONG, David (1927)
Compositeur anglais.
The Protest (1960) (9'30) •Cl/Trb/2 Asx/Tpt/Perc/Pno/Bass •BMic

ARNAUD-MARWYS & Frédéric ADAM
Saxolo •Asx/Pno •ME

ARNE, Thomas Auguste (1710-1778)
Finale (MERIOT) •Asx/Pno •Phi

ARNOLD, André (1910)
Compositeur français, né à Epone, le 18 IX 1910. Travailla avec A. Marchal, Ezat, et Thomas.
Mélopée (1971) (5') (to J. DESLOGES) •Asx/Pno •adr
Quatuor, op. 50 (1974) (to Quatuor Desloges) •SATB •MSC
Thème varié (1979) (to J. DESLOGES) •Asx/Org
Védéa (1971) (10') (to A-M. DESLOGES) 1) Prélude 2) Berceuse 3) Final-Rondo •Asx/Pno •Arp

ARNOLD, Hubert E. (1945)
Compositeur américain.
Anamesis (1977) (to R. RICKER) •Tsx/Pno
Dithyrambe (1969) •SATB •Art
La Fantaisie Eclectique (1984) (to the New York Saxophone Quartet) •SATB
Piano Trio (1992) •Ssx+EH/Vcl/Pno

ARNOLD, Jay
Easy Saxophone Solos or Duets (1960) •1 or 2 Sx •Ams
Everybody's Favorite Easy Saxophone Solos (1951) •Ams
Fingered Scales Including the Register Above High F (1951) •WMP
Homeless - Romance •Asx/Pno •CF
Introduction to the Saxophone: 50 Easy Lessons (1978) •ChH
Jazz Saxophone Basics for Improvisation (1982) •DP
Jazz Saxophone Studies in Improvisation (1982) •DP
Jazz Style for Saxophone (1963) •Ams/Mol
Modern Fingering System (1950) •WMP/SB
More Easy Saxophone Solos (with Herbert WISE) •Cons
Saxophone Quartets (1964) (with Charles LINDSAY) •AATB •Ams

ARSENEAULT, Raynald (1945)
Compositeur canadien.
Namo (1980) (7') (4 movements) •Sx Solo •CMC

ARTALLIO
4 Exercices pour la respiration circulaire

ARTIOMOV, Vyatcheslav (1940)

Compositeur russe né à Moscou, en 1940. Travailla avec N. Sidelnikov (+ études de physique).

"D'abord influencé par Prokofiev et Stravinsky, s'y ajoute la tendance néo-classique (Honegger, Hindemith) puis Jolivet et surtout Varèse. Il s'intéresse de façon croissante à la musique des peuples caucasiens; enfin, il revendique l'héritage romantique de Chopin à Scriabine. Son style se présente comme une large synthèse des ces différentes sources. Il privilégie le rythme et une écriture poly-tonale, puis se rapproche de la musique "minimale". La matière sonore se raréfie et devient scintillement, vibration, souffle, elle témoigne d'une quête intérieure fortement spirituelle, voire mystique, sans revendiquer une expression religieuse précise." (J. VANNI)

Automne Sonata (1977) •Asx/Pno
Caprice pour le Nouvel an 1975 (18-20') (In memoriam M. Ravel)
  •2 Sx: SB/Perc •ECS
Litania (1979) •SATB
Litania I (1982) •SATB •ECS
Little Concerto •Ssx/6 Perc
Recitative I (1978) (to L. MICHAILOV) •Ssx Solo
Sonate all pongo •Asx •ECS

ARTOT, J-B.
12 Quartets •AATB •CF
12 Trios •Fl/Cl/Asx •DG

ARZOUMANOV, Valery

Compositeur français, d'origine russe.
7 Chansons russes (1993) •Asx/Pno •INM

ASCHER, Joseph (1829-1869)
Alice, Where art Thou? (MOLLOY) •Asx/Pno •CF
Alice, Where art Thou? (BLAAUW) •Tsx/Pno •Mol
Love's Old Sweet Song (MOLLOY) •Asx/Pno •CF

ASCOUGH, R.
Quintet •Ssx/Fl/Ob/Cl/Bsn

ASHEIM, Nils Henrik (1960)

Compositeur norvégien.
Kvad (1975) (10') •4 Sx: SATB/Perc •NMI/DP
Midt iblant os...: a composition for pictures and music (1978) •Fl/Asx/Vla/Vcl/Bass/Perc •NMI

ASHFORD, Theodore
American Folksong Suite (to F. HEMKE) •SATB •South

ASHTON, John

Compositeur américain.
Dialogues, Discourses (1975) 1) Pucelete 2) Je languis 3) Domino
  •SATB •SeMC

ASPELMAYER, Franz (1728-1786)
Quatuor concertant (CORROYER) •2 Cl/2 Sx: TB •Buff

ASTON, David (1957)

Compositeur anglais.
Euphonium (1977) (5') •SATB

ATOR, James Donald (1938)

Clarinettiste, saxophoniste, et compositeur américain, né à Kansas City (Missouri), le 15 X 1938. Travailla avec J. Allard, V. Jennings, Adler, W. Latham, M. Ellis, et N. Jones.
Adagio (1981) •SATB •WWS
Duo (1981) •Asx/Tuba •DP/WWS

Duo for Saxophones (1983) •2 Sx
Enuffispluntee (1972) (9') •Asx/Perc •SeMC
Life Cycle (1973) (18') •Mz-Sopr Voice/Asx/Ob/Perc/Vcl •SeMC
Haikansona (1974) (10') •Mz-Sopr Voice/Ob/Asx/Vcl •SeMC
Three Pieces (1970) •Asx/Pno •SeMC
Woodwind Quartet (1969) (11') •Fl/Cl/Sx/Bsn •SeMC

ATWOOD, Charles

Compositeur américain.
Alienated Thing (1989) •Asx/Electr.Vln/Orch (2221CBsn/223/Timp/3 Perc/Str) •CMA

AUBART, Michael (1952)

Compositeur américain.
Deadly Sins (1982) (To R. DIRLAM) •Asx/Pno
Duo (1982) (to R. DIRLAM) •Asx/Tape
Hanblecheyapi: Crying for a Vision (1982) (to R. DIRLAM)
  1) Tenebrae 2) Hesperus •Asx/Pno

AUBERT, Esprit (1782-1871)
Angela Aria (from *Le Domino Noir*) (W. HEKKER) •1 Sx: S or A/Pno •TM
Prière (From *la Muette de Portici*) (W. HEKKER) •SATB or AATB

AUBERT, Jacques (1689-1753)
Gigue (MAGANINI) •1 Sx: A or T/Pno •Mus
Suite (LONDEIX) •2 Sx simil. •Led

AUBERT, Pierre (1763-1830)
1er solo de concours •Asx/Pno •Bil

AUBIGNY, L. d'
Prière (1890) •Ob (or Asx)/Pno (or Org)

AUBIN, Francine
Ainsi racontent les nuages (1987) (3'30) •Asx/Pno •Mar
Chanson dans la rue (1986) (2'45) •Asx/Pno •Mar
Frédéri (1990) (3') •1 Sx: A or T/Pno •Mar
Nocturne en forme de blues (1986) (3') •Asx/Pno •Mar

AUBIN, Tony (1907-1983)

Compositeur, professeur et chef d'orchestre français, né le 8 XII 1907, à Paris, où il est mort en 1983. Travailla avec S. Rousseau, N. Gallon, et P. Dukas.

"Son art dénote un constant souci de l'expression. On y rencontre, subtilement combinées, les influences de Franck et de Dukas, tandis que son écriture harmonique s'inscrit dans la tradition de Fauré et de Ravel." (BORDAS) "Il représente l'académisme. Il ne le nie pas. Il le proclame, au contraire, avec fierté comme un bienfait." (Cl. ROSTAND)

"His compositions pursue the more harmonically rich and colourful aspects of the music of Ravel and Dukas." (P. GRIFFITHS)

Petite rêverie (1980) •Asx/Pno •Mar

AUCLERT, Pierre (1905-1975)

Compositeur et pianiste français né à Djidjelli (Algérie) le 15 II 1905, mort à Boulogne-sur-Seine. Travailla avec Y. Nat, N. Gallon, et P. Dukas.
Comme un vieux Noël (1941/69) (1'30) •Asx/Pno •Bil

AUDOIN, Jean-Claude

Compositeur français.
Hommage à Fr. Valonne (1986) (2'30) (to M. JEZOIN) •4 like instruments (semblables)
Rue Descartes (1981) (3') (to M. JEZOIN) •3 like instruments (semblables)

AUDRAN, Edmond (1842-1901)
Fantaisie sur "La Mascotte" (SOHIER) •Asx/Pno •Marg

AURIOL, Hubert d'
Quatuor d'anches •Ob/Cl/Asx/Bsn •Bil

AUSEJO, Cesar
Compositeur espagnol.
Sax-Fantasy (1991) •Asx/Pno •Mun

AUSTIN, John
Farewell Music: Mixing with Wind and Light. Over the Waves (1985)
•Asx/Perc •DP
In Memoriam (1979) (to F. HEMKE) •Asx/Timp

AUSTIN, Larry (1930)
Compositeur américain, né à Duncan (Oklahoma), le 12 IX 1930.
Travailla avec D. Milhaud et S. Shifrin.

"Most of his works are cast for mixed media in which theatrical,
acoustical, and dynamic elements appear as manifestations of universal
vitality. He makes use of traditional instruments as well as electronic,
computerized, and aleatory resources. In order to secure a maximum
impact with a minimum of anarchy, he introduced the concept of
coordinated improvisation, which he terms *Open Style* ." (BAKER'S)
Improvisations for Orchestra and Jazz Soloist (15') •3sx: ATB/Tpt/
Cl/Bass/Perc/Orch •adr
J.B. Larry Plus •Improvisational Sx/Tape •DP

AVIGNON, Jean (1915)
Chef de musique français, né à Paris, le 31 VIII 1915. Travailla avec
Roger-Ducasse. Il étudia le saxophone avec G. Chauvet.
Spiritual et Danse exotique (1967) (4') •Asx/Pno •Bil

AVRIL
Bicentennial Quintet •5 Sx: SAATB •WWS
Introduction and Allegro •AATB •WWS

AXWORTHY (see ANONYMOUS)

AYOUB, Nick (19xx-1991)
Saxophoniste et professeur canadien, mort à Montréal en 1991.
Professeur au Conservatoire de Montréal.
Attaca (1977) •SATB •adr
Ballade et Improvisation •SATB •DP
Diversion No. 1 •SATB •DP
Diversion No. 2 •SATB •DP
Diversion No. 3 •SATB •DP
Diversion No. 4 •SATB •DP
Diversion No. 5 •SATB •DP
Diversion No. 6 •SATB •DP
Diversion No. 7 •SATB •DP
Diversion No. 8 •SATB •DP
Four of a Kind •4 Sx: AAAA •WWS
Jazz Suite (6'40) •SATB •WWS/DP
Joey's Place •AATB/Rhythm Section •DP
Saxtet •6 Sx: SAATTB/Bass/Drums •DP
Slightly Bluesy •SATB •DP
Three Movements •SATB •DP
12 Classical Etudes (1955) •DP

AYSCUE, Brian T. (1948)
Clarinettiste, saxophoniste et compositeur américain, né à Camden
(New Jersey), le 25 IV 1948. Travailla avec J. Thome, S. Rascher, et
A. Cicarelli.
Morning Piece (1970) (6') (to G. WEBBER) •Asx/Pno •adr
Permutations I (1972) (6'30) (to J. THOME) •Fl/Ob/Cl/Tpt/Tsx •adr
The Place of Peace (1972) (3'30) (to B. WEINBERGER) •Tsx/Pno •adr
Quartet (1982) •SATB •adr
Three Pieces (1969) (5'30) 1) Monodie 2) Aria 3) Reflections •Asx
Solo •Art

BABAYAN, Yahram (1948)

Compositeur arménien, né le 19 VIII 1948 à Erevan. Travailla avec E. Mirzoian et G. Eguiazarian.

Mantra - quasi sonata, op. 63 (1986) (7') •Ssx/Pno •Led

BABBITT, Milton (1916)

Compositeur américain, né à Philadelphia, le 10 V 1916.

"Je crois à la musique cérébrale et je ne choisis jamais une note sans savoir pourquoi je la veux à une place précise." (M. BABBITT) "Il représente l'abstraction sérielle la plus rigoureuse." (Cl. ROSTAND) "Milton Babbitt semble venu à la technique sérielle par amour pour la cérébralité et l'abstraction. Il affectionne les titres abstraits et la répartition mathématique des éléments, sans toutefois renoncer à une élégance d'expression qui favorise l'approche de sa musique." (A. GAUTHIER) "Milton Babbitt représente le type du compositeur chercheur et sera un des grands théoriciens américains des nouvelles musiques, le dodécaphonisme bien sûr, mais aussi tout ce qui joint les mathématiques à la musique. Il est donc très représentatif d'une certaine Amérique dans sa quête scientifique." (J. & B. MASSIN)

"His music is couched in an abstract style. In 1948 he adopted the 12-tone method of composition, expanding it into the domain of rhythm (12 basic rhythmic values in a theme) and into instrumentation (theme of 12 notes played successively by 12 different instruments)." (BAKER) "His early attraction to the music of Varese and Stravinsky soon gave way to an absorption in that of Schoenberg, Berg, and Webern—particularly significant at a time when 12-note music was unknown to many and viewed with scepticism by others." "Babbitt's interests in synthesis were not with the invention of new sounds per se, but with the control of all events, particularly in the timing and rate of changes of timbre, texture, and intensity." (E. BARKIN)

All Set (1957) •2 Sx: AT/Tpt/Trb/Vibr/Bass/Perc/Pno •adr
Images (1979) (10'30) (to H. PITTEL) •1 Sx: Sno+S+A/Synth Tape •adr
Whirled Series (1987) (13') (to J. FORGER, K. RADNOFSKY, & J. SAMPEN) •Asx/Pno •Pet

BABCOCK, David

Fenêtres prismatiques, op. 8 (1982) (to H. BOK) •Sx+BsCl/ Marimba+Vibr

BACH, Carl Philip Emanuel (1714-1788)

Sonate in A moll (from Fl) •Asx Solo •Ric
Spring's Awakening (GALLO) •1 Sx: A or T/Pno •CBet

BACH, Jan (1937)

Compositeur américain, né en 1937. Etudia avec R. Kelly, K. Gaburo, A. Copland, et R. Gerhard.

My Very First Solo (1974) (to M. SIGMON) •Asx/Elec. Pno

BACH, Johann Christian (1735-1782)

Allegro Siciliana (TRILLAT) •Asx/Pno •GD
Andante (JOHNSON) •Bsx/Pno •Bel
Sinfonia en Sib •SATB •Mol
Symphony no. 2 (AXWORTHY) •6 Sx: SAATBBs •TVA
Trio in Two Movements (CUNNINGHAM) •3 Sx: SAT •Eto

BACH, Johann Sebastian (1685-1750)

Adagio (MULE) •Asx/Pno •Led

Adagio (SCHMIDT) •Tsx/Pno •WIM
Adagio et Andante (MULE) •Asx/Pno •Led
Air (HEKKER) •SATB •Lis
Air (from *Suite in D*) (LEESON) •Asx/Pno •HilCol
Air (*Suite no. 3*) (HEKKER) •3 Sx: ATB/Cl or 3 Cl/Bsx •WaB
Air (from *Suite 3*) (HEKKER) •SATB •TM
Air (from *Suite no. 3, BWV 1068*) (T. SCHÖN) •SATB •ApE
Air de la fugue (DELGIUDICE) •SATB •Mar
Allegro (MULE) •Asx/Pno •Led
Andante (JOHNSON) •Bsx/Pno •Bel
Andante (MULE) •Asx/Pno •Led
Andante (SCHMIDT) •Tsx/Pno •WIM
Andante et Allegro (MULE) Asx/Pno •Led
Andante et Sinfonia (MEYNS) •Bb Sx/Pno •Mol
Aria (WATZ) •SATB •GB
Arioso (from *Cantata no. 156*) (KENT) •Tsx/Pno •CF
Arioso (KENT) •AATB •CF
Arioso (KENT) •Asx/Pno •CF
Ave Maria (GOUNOD) •2 Sx: AT/Pno •Cen
Bach for Saxophone (GEE) •Asx/Pno or Org •Ken
Badinerie (from *Orch. Suite No. 2*) (4') (POWELL) •SATB •TTF
Bist du bei mir •3 Sx: SAT or SAB or AAT or AAB •TM
Bourrée (OOSTROM) •SATB •Mol
Bourrées (Suite No. 3) (GEE) •Tsx/Pno •DP
Bourrées (TEAL Album) •Bb Sx/Pno •GSch
Brandenburg Concerto No. 2 (REX) •10 Sx: SAAAATTTBBs •WWS
Brandenburg Concerto No. 2 (REX) 6 Sx: SAATBBs •DP
Brandenburg Concerto No. 3 (GOINS) •9 Sx: SSAAATTBB
Brandenburg Concerto No. 3 (WAID) •7 Sx
Brandenburg Concerto No. 5 (3rd Mvt.) (REX) •5 Sx: SSATB/Pno •DP
Brandenburg Concerto No. 6 (WESTERN) •6 Sx: AATTBBs
Canon no. 4 (SMIM) •2 Sx: AT •Rub
4 Canons (from *The Art of the Fugue*) (MOROSCO) •2 Sx: ST & SB
Célèbre Aria (GILET) •SATB •Mar
Choralbearbeitung und Kantate 147 (EVERTSE) •4Sx: SATB or SSAB •TM
Chorale (from *Cantata No. 4*) (REX) •SATB or AATB •DP
Chorale "Ach Gott und Herr" (HARTLEY) •6 Sx: SAATBBs •adr
Chorale Variations (REX) •8 Sx: SAAATTBBs •DP
Chorale "Wachet Auf" (HARTLEY) •8 Sx: SnoSAATBBsCBs •DP
Chorales (LEWIS) •7 Sx: SAATTBB •WWS
2 Chorals (DYCK) •SATB •Braun
Concerto in G Major (POWELL) (6') •SATB •TTF
Contrapunctus 1 (OOSTROM) •SATB •Mol
Contrapunctus 5 (OOSTROM) •SATB •Mol
Contrapunctus 9 (OOSTROM) •SATB •Mol
Doppelfuge über ein neues Thema und das Hauptthema (Contrapunctus 9) (from *Art of the Fugue*) (T. SCHÖN) •SATB •ApE
Duet Cantata 78 (SIBBING) •2 Sx: AA/Pno •Eto
Duo Sonata •2 Sx: AA or TT •EM
Duo Sonata •2 Sx •Mus
Duos •2 Sx •Mil
Einfache Fuge über das Thema (Contrapunctus 1) (from *Art of the Fugue*) (T. SCHÖN) •SATB •ApE
Einfache Fuge über die Umkehrung des Themas (Contrapunctus 4) (from *Art of the Fugue*) (T. SCHÖN) •SATB •ApE
Etudes de Virtuosité (FAULX) •EMB
Fugue no. 4 (GRAINGER) •6 Sx: SATTBBs •PG
Fugue no. 7 (BRIEGEL) •AATB •Bri
Fugue no. 8 (SCHMIDT) •SATB •WIM
Fugue no. 9 (ROSENTHAL) •SATB •WIM
Fugue no. 16 (CHAPMAN) •SATB

Fugue XVI (A. Domizi) •Ob/Cl/Asx/Bsn
Fugue XVII (A. Domizi) •Ob/Cl/Asx/Bsn
Fugue no. 21 •3 Sx: SAB •WIM
Fugue no. 22 (Schmidt) •5 Sx: SAATB •WIM
Fugue Contrapunctus III (Rex) •SATB •DP
Fugue in E (Woodward) •SATB •SM
Fugue in E Minor (Kasprzyk) •SATB •Art
Fugue in G Minor "Little Fugue" (Schmidt) •5 Sx: SAATB
Fuguette (Mule) •Asx/Pno •Led
Gavotte and Bourrée (Rascher) •Bb Sx/Pno •Bel
Gavotte Favorite no. 2 (Vittmann) •3 Sx: SAB •ES
Gavottes (Mule) •Asx/Pno •Led
Gegenfuge über das variierte Thema und seine Umkehrung in drei verschiedenen Wertgrößen (Contrapunctus 7) (from *Art of the Fugue*) (T. Schön) •SATB •ApE
Goldberg Variations (Koulman) •SATB
If Thou Art Near (Gee) •Asx/Pno or Org •Lud
In Thou Be Near (Patrick) •Sx Ensemble
Invention no. 8 •3 Sx: SAB •Ken
3 Inventions (Avignon) •SATB •Mar
15 Inventions (Teal) •2 Sx: AA or AT •Pres
Jesu, Joy of Man's Desiring (Caravan) •Sx Ensemble: SATBBs
Jesus, Joy of Man's Desiring (Cluwen) •Tsx/Pno •Mol
Jesus, Joy of Man's Desiring (Evertse) •SATB •Elk
Jésus, que ma joie demeure (Jezouin) •14 Sx: SnoSSAAAATTTBBBsBs
Jésus, que ma joie demeure (Londeix) •Asx Solo/8 Sx: SSAATTBB
Kanon in der Oktave (from *Art of the Fugue*) (T. Schön) •2 Sx: AB •ApE
Koraalbewerking •4 Sx: SATB/Org •Lis
Largo and Allegro (Sibbing) •Asx/Pno •RS
Louré (Chauvet) •Asx/Pno •Com
March (Grainger) •6 Sx: SAATTB •PG
Minuet (Rascher) •Asx/Pno •Bel
Musette (Rascher) •Asx/Pno •Bel
O Mensch Bewein (Grainger) •5 Sx: SAABBs
Pièces d'orgue (Mule) •Asx/Pno •Led
22 Pièces en cinq suites (Corroyer) •Sx Solo •Buff
Prelude no. 4 •SATB or AATB •Mus
Prélude no. 12 (Maganini) •AATB •Mus
Préludes no. 12 & 156 (Rascher) •Asx/Pno •Chap
Preludium XVI (A. Domizi) •Ob/Cl/Asx/Bsn
Preludium XVII (A. Domizi) •Ob/Cl/Asx/Bsn
Preludium XX (A. Domizi) •Ob/Cl/Asx/Bsn
Preludium no. 26 (Oostrom) •SATB •Mol
Prélude et Fugue en Réb Maj. (Londeix) •SATB •Fuz
Prelude and Fugue in B minor (Sibbing) •5 Sx: SAATB
Prelude and Fugue in Bb minor (Gee) •5 Sx: SAATB •Sha
Prelude and Fugue in D, in E, in G (Eymann) •AATB •CF
Prélude et Fugue no. 5 (Grainger) •SATB •PG
Quartet, op. 17, no. 6 •SATB •WWS
Quartet, op. 17, no. 6 (Cunningham) •SATB or SAT/Bass •Eto
Ricercar a6 (from *Mus. Offr.*) (Patrick) •Sx Ensemble: SATBBs
Ricercar No. 4 (from *Mus. Offr.)* (Axworthy) •6 Sx: SAATBBs •TVA
Sarabande (from *French Suite I*) (Dawson) •SATB •Ron
Sarabande (Hemke) •SATB or AATB •South
Sarabande et Badinerie (Johnson) •AATB •Rub
Sarabande and Bourrée •AATB •Ru
Scherzetto (Londeix) •Bb Sx/Pno •Led
Siciliano (Maganini) •Bb Sx/Pno •Mus
Sicilienne (Mule) •Asx/Pno •Led
Sicilienne et Allegro (Teal) •Asx/Pno •GSch
Sicut Locutus Est (Garcia) •5 Sx: SAATB •DP
Sinfonia (from *Cantata no. 109*) (Sibbing) •Ssx/Brass Quint. •Eto

Sonata in A minor (Gallo) •Asx/Pno •CBet
Sonata in G minor (Scudder) •Asx/Pno
Sonate no. 2 (Gateau) •Asx/Pno •Bil
Sonate no. 2 (Gateau) •Tsx/Pno •Alf
Sonate no. 4 (Flute) (Mule) •Asx/Pno •Led
Sonate no. 4 (Gee) •Tsx/Pno •South
Sonate no. 6 (Flute) (Mule) •Asx/Pno •Led
6 Sonates en trio (Londeix) •3 Sx: SAB •KuD
Suite no. 2 en Si min. (Londeix) •Asx Solo/4Sx: SATB •Mol
Suite en Si min. Badinerie (Mule) •Asx/Pno •Led
Suite en Ut, Bourrée (Mule) •Asx/Pno •Led
Suite en Ré, Aria (Mule) •Asx/Pno •Led
Suites I, II, III, IV (Vcl) (Ricker) •Sx Solo •DP
Suite I (Vcl) (Londeix) •Asx Solo •Lem
Suite I (Vcl) (Kasprzyk) •Bsx Solo •South
Suite III (Vcl) (Kasprzyk) •Bsx Solo •South
Suite III (Vcl) (Londeix) •Asx Solo •Lem
Suite IV (Vcl) (Kasprzyk) •Bsx Solo •South
Suite no. 6, Gavotte, Musette (Mule) •Asx/Pno •Led
Suite of Bach (Buckland) (Bouree, Air, Badinerie) •SATB or AATB •PBP
Theme, Triple Fugue and Chorale (Axworthy) •SATB •TVA
3 Thèmes célèbres (Beun & Terranova) •5 Sx: AATTB •Mar
Toccata and Fugue in D Minor (Greenberg) •SATB •DP
Toccata and Fugue in D Minor, BWV 565 (Maeda) •19 Sx
Trio, op. 17, no. 3 (Cunningham) •3 Sx: ATB •DP
Vivace (Mule) •Asx/Pno •Led
Wie Schön leuchtet der Morgenstern, BWV 436 (Patrick) •Sx Ensemble: SATBBs

BACH, Wilhelm Friedmann (1710-1784)
6 Duets (2 Vol.) •2 Sx: AA or TT •EK

BACHMANN, Gottob (1763-1840)
Dance bretonne (Lefevre) •Asx/Pno •CF

BACHOREK, Milan (1939)
Compositeur tchécoslovaque.
Inspirace (1983) (12') •Ob/Asx/Cl+BsCl/Perc/Pno/Electr. Guit •CHF

BACHTISCHA, Michael
Compositeur français, d'origine russe.
Notation (1993) •2 Sx: SA •INM

BÄCK, Sven-Erik (1919)
Compositeur, violoniste et professeur suédois, né à Stockholm, le 16 IX 1919. Travailla avec H. Rosenberg et G. Petrassi.

"Son oeuvre peu abondante est d'une haute qualité. Un goût très développé de la tradition ne l'a pas empêché d'assimiler différentes tendances de la musique contemporaine." (Bordas) "Après ses premières oeuvres d'un néo-classicisme hindemithien, il a pris le virage sériel en 1953 et a bientôt évolué vers une forme de pointillisme quelque peu maniériste, puis vers une conception spatiale, enfin vers une écriture plus linéaire où se réaffirment ses qualités initiales de contrapuntiste, tandis que sa rythmique se raffine." (Cl. Rostand)

"He was born into a Protestant family and came into early contact with unpretentious chamber music, jazz, and Lutheran church music. Rosenberg's teaching had stressed melody as an essential element, even in polyphonic works, and Bäck introduced quite original melodic ornaments, easily recognized in his music of the 1950s." (H. Astrand)

"Contemplation, an introverted, ethereal atmosphere and an intensively extravert temperament are the hallmarks of Sven-Erik Bäck's music. He has employed numerous media and styles. His inspiration oscillates between historical examples and, on the other hand, the spirit of our own age and the successive advances of the new music."

Bagateller - Elegi (1961) •Asx/Pno •SMIC
Dithyramb (1949/89) (4') •Sx Solo •SMIC
Elegie (1952) •Asx/Pno •SMIC/WH

BACKE, Ruth (1947)
Fantasia Eg veit I Himmerik Ei Borg (1982) •Asx/Org

BACULEWSKI, Krzysztof (1950)
Compositeur polonais, né à Varsovie en 1950. Travailla avec W. Rudzinski, puis avec O. Messiaen, et au Groupe de Recherches Musicales.
Partita (1980) (12'-15') (to D. Pituch) •Asx/Harp or Prepared Pno
    •CPWN

BACULIS, Alphonse
Compositeur de jazz canadien.
Six Pieces for Five Saxophones •5 Sx: SAATB
Six Pieces for Saxophone Quartet (15') 1) Opening 2) Bebop
    3) Cadenza 4) Chorale 5) Bugaloo 6) Closing •SATB
Three Folk Songs •Soprano Voice/5 Sx: SAATB

BADAULT, Denis
Compositeur français.
En effet (1990) (8') (to Quatuor de Versailles) •SATB

BADINGS, Henk (1907-1987)
Compositeur néerlandais, né à Bandung, Java, le 17 I 1907; mort à Maarheeze, le 26 VI 1987. Travailla avec W. Pijper.
"Henk Badings est autodidacte si l'on excepte une courte période d'étude auprès de W. Pijper. Tout en demeurant fidèle aux formes classiques, il fait un usage original des modes et d'un système de huit sons." (Bordas) "Sa musique est de forme et de langage traditionnels en dépit d'incursions dans les domaines de la modalité, de la bitonalité et de la polytonalité, ainsi que de ses expériences électroniques." (Cl. Rostand) "Sa musique doit sa force d'expression, aussi bien à une puissance tragique, qui donne à ses adagios une tension et une profondeur qu'on n'avait guère retrouvées depuis Bruckner, qu'à une désinvolture pleine d'humour, qui allège très heureusement la complexité du style contrapuntique." (Fasquelle)
"His style may be described as romantic modernism; his harmonies approach polytonality; in his melodic material he often uses a scale of alternating whole tones and semitones." (Baker) "In some of his works the direct influence of Bach and other composers of his period is traceable, notably in the relations between the solo instrument and orchestra in his instrumental concerto. Practically everything he has written demands high executive skill and much of it large resources." (H. Antcliffe)
Cavatina (1952) (5') (to J. de Vries) •Asx/Pno •Don
Concerto (1951) (20') (to J. de Vries) 1) Allegro 2) Notturno
    3) Rondo •Asx/Orch (2222/3331/Perc/Str) or Pno •Don
Friere Trije •4 Sx: SATB or SATT •TM
Gelderse Peerdesprong •4 Sx: SATB or SATT •TM
Hollande Boerenplof •4 Sx: SATB or SATT •TM
Largo cantabile (1983) (6') (to Bilger Duo) •Asx/Pno •Don
La Malinconia (1949) (8') (to S. Rascher) •Asx/Pno •Don
Quadrupelconcert (1984) (20') •SATB/Orch or Band •Don

BAELTER, Karl
3 Affections (1983) (to B. Foley) •Asx/Pno

BAER, Walter
Compositeur américain.
Fragments of a Dream (1991) (to J. Sampen) •Asx/Pno

BAERMANN, Carl (1782-1842)
Foundation Studies, op. 63 (D. Hite) •Sx •South

BAEYENS, Henri (1897)
Compositeur belge-flamand, né à Leeuw-St-Pierre (Brabant), le 28 IV 1897. Travailla avec P. Gilson.
Adagio animato •Asx/Pno •EMB
Berceuse •Asx/Pno •Ver
Canzonetta •Bb Sx/Pno •EMB
Serenata •Asx/Pno •Ver

BAFILE, Giorgio
Compositeur italien.
Ricerca (1992) •Asx/Pno

BAGLEY
Thistledown (Harris) •2 Cl/Asx/Bsn •CF

BAGOT, Maurice (1896-198x)
Compositeur et chef d'orchestre français, né à Saint-Servan. Travailla avec Caussade.
Concerto (1951) •Asx/Orch or Pno
Quatuor (1965) (to D. Deffayet) 1) Lento-allegro 2) Lento 3) Finale
    (Rondo) •SATB
Saxophonie à Quatre (1975) (9') (to Quatuor de la Garde
    Républicaine) •SATB
Transmutation (1974) (to Quatuor d'Anches de Paris) •Ob/Cl/Asx/
    Bsn

BAGUERRE, Francis (1945-1982)
Compositeur français né à Cognac. Travailla avec L. Dallapiccola et N. Feldman.
Appolinaria (1982) (10') (to J-P. Caens) •SATB
Duo (1977) •Asx/Fl
Et la source des eaux devint amère..." (1980) •Ob/Asx/Cl/Bsn

BAILE, Paul
Saxophoniste de jazz.
10 Thèmes et improvisations •Sal

BAILEY, Judith (1941)
Compositeur anglais.
Quartet (1972) (15') 1) Allegro 2) Adagio 3) Allegro •SATB

BAILEY, Marshall
The Thaw •Asx/Actress

BAILLY, Jean-Guy (1925)
Compositeur français, né à Lyon, le 1er III 1925. Travailla avec O. Messiaen et N. Boulanger.
Capriccio •Asx/Pno •Sch
Contraires II (to Quatuor de Lyon) •SATB •adr

BAILY, Jean
Compositeur belge.
Ballade •Asx/Str or Pno •HM

BAINBRIDGE, Simon (1952)
Compositeur anglais.
People of the Dawn (1975) •Soprano Voice/Cl/Ssx/BsCl/Perc/Pno
    •UMPL

BAJUS, Louis
Prélude et Allegretto (1935) •Asx/Harmonie or Fanfare

BAKER, David N. (1931)
Compositeur américain.
Concerto (1987) (25') (to E. Krivda) 1) Jubilee 2) Spiritual 3) Ostinato Blues Waltz •Tsx/Chamber Orch •SOMI
Duet (1992) (10') •2 Sx: AA
Ellingtones (1987) (2'30) (D. Gordon) •Tsx/Orch •Dus

Faces of the Blues (1988) (8'49) (to F. Bongiorno) •Asx/SATB
•MMB
Fantasy (1977) (to J. Lansing) •Asx/Pno

BAKER, Ernest (1912)
Compositeur anglais.
Night Theme (1980) (4'45) •Asx/Pno •BMIC

BAKER, Michael C.
Compositeur canadien.
Capriccio (1986) •Asx/Orch or Pno •CMC

BALAKAUSKAS, Osvaldas
Polilogas (1991) (20') •Asx/Str •PWM

BALAY, Guillaume (1871-1943)
Piece de Concours (Meyer) •Asx/Pno •Led

BALBOA, Manuel (1958)
Compositeur espagnol.
Sombra Interrumpida (1980) (to M. Mijan) •Asx/Pno •EMEC

BALFE, Michael William (1808-1870)
Bohemian Girl •AATB •Bar
Cavatine •Asx/Pno •CF
Killarmey •Bb Sx/Pno •CBet
Then You'll Remember Me •Asx/Pno •CF

BALL, Derek
Compositeur irlandais.
Work (1973) (to S. Egan) •Asx/Pno

BALL, Leonard V.
Compositeur américain.
and they spoke of things transfigured... (10') (to K. Fischer)
•Yamaha WX11 MIDI Wind Controller and Korg Wavestation
Synth •adr

BALLIF, Claude (1924)
Compositeur français, né à Paris, le 22 V 1924. Travailla à Bordeaux avec J-F. Vaubourgoin, puis avec T. Aubin, O. Messiaen, et enfin B. Blacher et J. Ruffer.

"Musicien indépendant, Claude Ballif est un novateur audacieux. Il pratique la forme ouverte, utilise les moyens mathématiques, élargit la palette sonore, découvre de nouvelles structures musicales, mais surtout, il est l'inventeur d'un langage qui réconcilie tonalité et atonalité, diatonisme et chromatisme, la '*métatonalité*' dont sa musique atteste la souplesse expressive." (Bordas) "Son évolution et sa production sont les témoignages d'un solitaire." (Cl. Rostand) "La musique de Ballif ne craint pas les longueurs, l'aridité, et, pour avoir assimilé la plupart des conquêtes actuelles, elle n'est réellement inféodée à aucune des écoles régnantes. Ni musique de pointe ni musique de synthèse, elle se contente d'être une musique *nécessaire* autant pour ce qu'elle a à dire que pour la manière dont elle le dit. Le langage y est indissociable de l'expression." (M. Fleuret) "A la différence de maints compositeurs du siècle, loin de privilégier la quarte augmentée qui partage l'octave en deux parties égale, Ballif l'élimine comme seule note réellement atonale. Ses échelles, ou *référentiels*, se composent d'une sorte de gamme mobile majeure-mineure à 11 sons, à base de "variants" compris dans des "invariants" (qui délimitent les deux tétracordes, par exemple: *do-fa* et *sol-do*, seul manquant le *fa* dièse central). Un *référentiel* s'adosse à une note pôle qui détermine son *orient*." (B. F. Sappey) "Deux évidentes attitudes dans l'oeuvre du compositeur: l'une démonstrative et spectaculaire, ayant pour objectif la communication avec le monde qui l'entoure; l'autre est celle du dialogue intime avec Dieu, celle tout simplement de la prière." (J-M. Dieuaide)

"The chief characteristic of Ballif's work is his avoidance of conventional musical systems in favour of his own 'metatonality', which he sees as an enlargement of tonality in contrast with the evasion of tonality represented by atonal music. Ballif's metatonality is founded on a scale of 11 notes, and his musical discourse avoids the tonal disorientation of atonality, since the missing pitch suffices to give the music suggestions of tonality, while at the same time implying the presence of the total chromatic." (D. Charles)
Solfegietto, op. 36, no. 8 (1982) (12'30) (Commande de l'AsSaFra [Commissioned by French Saxo. Assoc.]) 1) Dolce e comodo (to D. Kientzy) 2) Allegro gioval 3) Quieto e con tenerezza (to Cl. Delangle) •Asx Solo •ET

BALTIN
Compositeur russe.
Concertino •ECS

BANASIK, Christian (1963)
Compositeur allemand, d'origine polonaise, né à Siemianowice, le 1 X 1963.
Melodien •Asx Solo
Begegbubg •Asx/Vla/Perc

BANK, Jacques
Finale (1984) (30') •Baritone Voice/Asx/BsCl/Perc •Don
Requiem voor een Levende (1985) (50') •Récit. Choeur/4 Sx/9 Accordion/3 Bass/3 Perc •Don

BANKS, Donald (1923)
Compositeur australien, né à South Melbourne, le 25 X 1923. Travailla avec Seiber, Babbitt, Dallapiccola, et Nono.

"Il était connu comme pianiste et arrangeur de jazz avant de commencer de sérieuses études de composition." (Bordas)

"Elements of jazz and 'soul' style continue to permeate his works."
Equation 1 (1964) (7') •Jazz Ensemble: Tpt/Asx/Pno/Harp/Guit/ Perc/Str Quartet •BMIC

BANTER, Harald (1930)
Compositeur allemand, né le 16 III 1930 à Berlin. Travailla avec B. A. Zimmermann et Hans Werner Henze.
Konzert (1979) (16') •Ssx/Jazz Orch •adr
Phönix (1989) •Ssx/Pno •B&B

BARAB, Seymour (1921)
Compositeur et violoncelliste américain, né à Chicago. Travailla avec G. Piatigorsky et Ed. Kurtz.
Quartet (1978) (13'45) 1) Allegro moderato with Mozartean elegance 2) Andante maestoso 3) Presto •SATB

BARAT, Jacques
Compositeur français.
Descente sur la neige (1972) (to Quatuor Desloges) •SATB •adr
Elégie dolente •Tsx/Pno •Map
Karanguez (1972) (1'30) (to Quatuor Desloges) •SATB •adr
Les porcelaines de Saxe •3 Sx: AAA •Chou

BARAT, Joseph-Edouard (1882-1963)
Compositeur français, né le 22 IX 1882. Travailla avec P. Vidal et E. Pessard.
Andante et Allegro •Asx/Pno •HS
Berceuse (Voxman) •Asx/Pno •Rub
Chant slave (album) •Bb Sx/Pno •GW
Danse espagnole •Asx/Pno •HS
Elégie (Voxman) •Asx/Pno •Rub
Nostalgie (4') •Asx/Pno •Led

BARBAUD, Pierre (1911)

Compositeur français, "né un 10 Octobre, au XXe siècle," promoteur de la "musique algoritmique." Travailla avec A. Jolivet.

"En France, Pierre Barbaud est le premier musicien à proposer 'd'introduire la pensée mathématique et les méthodes qui en découlent dans la composition musicale', et ceci dès 1950." (J. & B. Massin) "Pierre Barbaud élabore à la Bull General Electric, en 1960, la première oeuvre réalisée sur ordinateur, 7!. Pour lui, le recours aux lois aléatoires répond à une logique de la pensée musicale qui n'est nullement en rupture avec les systèmes du passé et les calculs qui leur sont sous-jacents. Toutefois, pour esquiver tout effet de séduction dramatique que pourraient produire des réminiscences tonales, il travaille fréquemment avec des échelles non tempérées, ou avec des divisions du champ sonore capable d'échapper à la suprématie de l'octave et des intervalles pivots de la musique traditionnelle." (D. J-Y. Bosseur)

"He has worked with a computer at Bull General Electric, producing music for conventional instruments that is defined by laws of probability; the computer-produced material is used without alteration: if Barbaud is dissatisfield with the result, changes are made to the programme rather than the score." (N. Lachartre)

Arthémise or la Rhétorique des Dieux (6'30) •Cl/Bsn/2 Sx •EFM
Pièces brèves pour Quatuor de cuivres (10') •Sx/Tpt/Trb/Tuba •EFM

BARBER, Clarence (1952)

Kiribilli (1988) (5') (to D. Schwartz) •Asx Solo •TTF
A Lincolnshire Whimsy (1991) (7') (to P. Cohen) •Sx Ensemble: SSAATTBBs •TTF
New York Concerto (1993) (12') (to D. Schwartz) 1) Manhattan 2) The Cathedral of St. John the Divine 3) Central Park 4) Madison Square Garden •Asx/Band or Pno •TTF
Vignettes (1993) (6') (to D. Schwartz) •4 Sx: A A+S TB •TTF

BARBER, Samuel

Adagio (Marr) •SATB

BARBIER, René (1890)

Compositeur belge, né à Namur, le 12 VII 1890. Travailla avec P. Gilson et S. Dupuy.

"His music is notable for the richness of its orchestration, recalling Dukas and Wagner." (H. Vanhulst)

Pièce concertante, op. 95 (1958) (10') (to F. Daneels) Allegro moderato - Andante - Allegro agitato •Asx/Orch or Pno •CBDM
Quatuor, op. 99 (1961) (14') (to Quat. Belge de Sxph.) 1) Allegro 2) Moderato espressivo 3) Allegro •SATB •CBDM

BARCE, Ramon (1928)

Compositeur et musicologue espagnol né à Madrid, le 16 III 1928. Travailla avec O. Messiaen et G. Ligeti. Fondateur du groupe 'Nueva Mùsica.'

"Nettement influencé par l'expressionnisme allemand, Ramon Barce écrit cependant une musique très personnelle. Ses recherches harmoniques basées sur le dodécaphonisme ont abouti à ce qu'il appelle l''harmonie des niveaux.' " (Bordas)

Anàbasis (1987) (10'15) (to M. Mijan) •SATB •RME
Concierto de Lizara V (1977) (10'45) •Cl/Tsx/Tpt/Trb/Harp/Pno/Vln/Vcl
Largo viaje (1988) (11') (to M. Mijan) •Asx/Pno
Obertura fonética (1968) (8'50) (to A.Tamayo) •Fl/Ob/Cl/Asx/Tpt/Trb •EMEC

BARCK, Ed.

Konzert, op. 6 •Asx/Orch

BARDEZ, Jean-Michel

Compositeur français.
Saxyphrage (1984) (1'45) (to M. Jezoin) •Asx/Xylophone

BARDI, Benno (1890)

Compositeur allemand, né à Königsberg, le 16 IV 1890.
Musik (1931) •Asx/Chamber Orch

BAREIS, Hermann

Compositeur anglais.
When the Cock Crows (1993) •Asx/Pno •INM

BARGIELSKI, Zbigniew (1937)

Compositeur polonais né à Lomiza, le 21 I 1937. Travailla avec Szeligowski et Szabelski, et N. Boulanger à Paris.

"His music follows the models of older Polish composers." (M. Hanuszewska)

Ikar (1981) (to H. Bok and E. Le Mair) •Sx+BsCl/Marimba+Vibr

BARGSTEM, Joey

Quintet for Winds •Ob/Cl/Asx/Trb/Bsn •DP

BARILLER, Robert (1918)

Professeur et compositeur français, né le 31 III 1918. Travailla avec H. Busser.
Fan'Jazz (3') •1 Sx: A or S/Pno •Led
Rapsodie bretonne (1953) (12') (to M. Mule) •Asx/Orch (2222/4331/Perc/Str) or Pno •Led

BARK, Jan (1934)

Compositeur suédois, né le 19 IV 1934 à Härnösand.

"Influenced by Varese and K. Dewey, and more pronouncedly by worldwide folk cultures, his compositions often feature music theater."

Ost-funk (1964) (10') •Tpt/Asx/3 Perc/Pno/2 Bass •SMIC

BARKER, Warren E.

Capriccio (1987) •SATB/Band •JP
CCI •BsCl/Bsx •WWS
Scherzo •SATB or SSTB •Ken
Voici le Quatuor… •SATB •Ken

BARKIN, Elaine (1932)

Media Speak (1981) •Fl/Asx/Bass/Tape

BARLETT, J.C.

A Dream (Hummel) •Asx/Pno •Rub

BARLOW, Wayne (1912)

Compositeur et professeur américain né à Elyria (Ohio), le 6 IX 1912. Travailla avec Royce, Rogers, Hanson, et A. Schoenberg.

"He is a prolific composer in an eclectic, tonal, free 12-note serial style." (T. Marrocco)

Concerto (1969) (14') (to J. Casagrande & D. Sinta) •Asx/Band or Pno •Tem

BARNARD, Allan F.

Panda Dance •Bsx/Pno •Bel

BARNARD, George D.

The Pals (Buchtel) •3 Sx: AAA/Pno •Kjos

BARNBY, Joseph (1838-1896)

Sweet and Low •AATB •Alf

BARNES, C.

Three Debonairs •3 Sx/Pno •Kjos

BARNES, Clifford P.
Saxophone Album (1956) 1) The young artist 2) The young genius
    3) The young maestro 4) The young virtuoso •Asx/Pno •B&H

BARNES, Milton
Compositeur canadien.
Concerto (1975) •Asx/Str Orch •CMC
Medley from Blood And Guts (1979) •1 Sx: A+S/Str Orch •CMC

BARNHOUSE, C.
Milennial •2 Sx: AT/Pno •Bar
Silver Lining •2 Sx: AT/Pno •Bar

BARON, Eugène (18xx-1964)
Solfège instrumental universel

BARON, Maurice (1889-1964)
Chef d'orchestre, arrangeur, et violoniste américain, d'origine française, né à Lille, le 1er I 1889, mort à New York, le 5 IX 1964.
Elegy •Fl/Asx/Harp (or Pno) •MBCo
The Last Tryst •Asx/Pno •MBCo
Chansonnette (GUREWICH) •Asx/Pno •GSch

BARONIJAN, Vartkes (1933)
Compositeur yougoslave, né le 23 IV 1933. Travailla avec Milojevic.
Sonatina (1957) •Asx/Pno •adr

BARRAINE, Elsa (1910)
Compositeur français, né à Paris le 13 II 1910. Travailla avec J. Gallon et P. Dukas. Grand Prix de Rome (1929).
"Son style a une âpreté, un tour hardiment personnel, des accents aussi peu conventionnels que possible." (R BERNARD)
She is one of the first romanticists of her generation, and after occasional essays in 'pure music', she soon reverted to the expression of tragic or at least highly strung lyricism." (GROVE)
Andante et Allegro •Asx/Pno •Sal
Improvisation (1947) •Asx/Pno •Bil

BARRAQUÉ, Jean (1928-1973)
Compositeur et professeur français, né à Puteaux, près de Paris, le 17 I 1928, mort à Paris le 17 VIII 1973. Travailla avec J. Langlais et O. Messiaen, ainsi qu'au Groupe de Musique Concrète au sein de l'ORTF.
"Dès le début il écrivit en musicien sériel, et restera inébranlablement fidèle à une technique de composition sur ce qu'il en viendra à appeler les 'séries proliférantes' (prolifération de séries différentes dérivées d'une série initiale, et lui restant apparentées). Les auteurs de référence de Barraqué resteront Beethoven, Debussy, et Webern." (A. POIRIER) "Bien qu'utilisant la technique sérielle, Jean Barraqué demeure un indépendant qui rejette certaines conceptions d'avant-garde, notamment le principe "aléatoire." Et c'est à travers une écriture rigoureuse que Barraqué —conjuguant les enseignements de Beethoven et de Debussy—parvient à un style d'improvisation essentiellement lyrique." (BORDAS) "Solitaire, échappant à tout académisme ancien ou récent, Jean Barraqué est un visionnaire apocalyptique et un démiurge dont le vocabulaire librement créé est à la mesure de ses ambitions colossales. C'est un des très grands inspirés de notre temps." (Cl. ROSTAND) "Sa musique est anguleuse, austère, agitée, avare de son expression. Elle est de son époque, mais en même temps elle traduit ou trahit une tension tragique exacerbée qui n'a rien à voir avec une rage, une violence révolutionnaire." (C. LEBLÉ) "En vérité, Barraqué est le romantique du mouvement sériel de l'après-guerre, ce qui ne lui enlève pas ses qualités de compositeur méticuleux, intensément conscient des problèmes de la création artistique." (P. GRIFFITHS)
"In adding the further commentaries of the music, Barraqué developed a technique of 'proliferating series': an original series gives place to a different but closely related series and so on, so that the basic material becomes increasingly distant from its first state. His music drew its power from the contradiction between the will to construct and the necessity of silence in a world tending to the destruction of values, whether musical or ethical. The outcome was a work of unprecedentedly enrmous proportions, but a work planned to remain incomplete." (D. JAMEUX)
... au delà du hasard (1968) •20 instr. (including [dont] 1 Asx) in 4 groups

BARRATT & JENKINS
Sounds for Sax 1 •1 Sx: T or A/Pno •Che

BARRAUD, Henry (1900)
Compositeur français, né à Bordeaux, le 12 IV 1900. Travailla avec J-F. Vaubourgoin, G. Caussade, P. Dukas, et L. Aubert.
"Barraud dont les lignes modales, dès qu'elles cessent d'être monodiques, tendent vers la dissonance sans mélange d'un contrepoint discordant, veut que son grégorianisme soit militant; ses connotations archaïques, médiévales, évoquent la cathédrale d'Albi, à la fois sanctuaire et forteresse: pierres hérissées de métaphysique et de détermination." (F. GOLDBECK) "L'oeuvre d'Henry Barraud est caractérisée par la maîtrise de son architecture." (BORDAS) "Son art est volontaire, tendu, mais cette réserve, qui est aussi celle de l'homme, cache de l'intensité. Il nous indique lui-même les principales caractéristiques de son langage, qui est celui d'un indépendant: emploi fréquent des gammes modales; rares emprunts au folklore; emploi de certains intervalles familiers comme le triton; peu de goût pour les thèmes mélodiques fondés sur des enchaînements d'accords et qui n'ont de sens que par l'harmonie sous-jacente; conception des thèmes en fonction de leur potentiel lyrique et non en vue de combinaisons contrapuntiques; attachement au principe tonal. Il est l'ennemi de la facilité, et la gravité lui sied plus que la gaieté." (Cl. ROSTAND)
"Barraud combines a reserved demeanour and a critical spirit with deep and imaginative religious conviction and a great sensitivity to people as also to the arts. This dualism is to be found in his music. In some works, felicities of scoring and elegant solutions of formal problems follow too smoothly, adding up to an effect that can seem academic." (J. GRIFFIN)
Quatuor (1973) (16') •SATB •B&H

BARREL, Bernard (1919)
Compositeur anglais.
A Shottisham Suite, op. 23 (1960) (4') •3 Treble Instruments
A Suffolk Suite, op. 24 (1960) (4') •3 Treble Instruments
Concerto, op. 29 •Ssx/Str Orch •BMIC

BARREL, Joyce (1917)
Compositeur anglais.
Quartet, op. 47 (1973) (15') •SATB

BARRET, Eric (1959)
Saxophoniste de jazz français, né au Havre, le 5 V 1959. Autodidacte.
"J'ai essayé d'écrire le *Quintet* (quatuor écrit, plus un soliste improvisateur), en favorisant l'échange entre musiciens classiques et musiciens jazz. Il ne s'agit pas simplement d'un 'chorus' de saxophone sur fond de quatuor. Improvisation et écriture sont étroitement liées. Le soliste participe lui-aussi aux parties écrites alors que le quatuor joue parfois des improvisations simulées. C'est une manière de fixer sur le papier la musique de jazz. C'est ce qu'évoque d'ailleurs le titre 'Kavisilak' qui, traduit du Lapon, exprime l'idée de la neige gelée, transformée en givre." (E. BARRET)
7 Thèmes et improvisations (1990) •Sal
Quintet Kavisilak (1990) (7'40) (to Quatuor de Versaille) •Tsx Solo/ SATB •Sal

BARRET, Reginald (1861-1940)
The Light Beyond, Ave Maria •Bb Sx/Pno •CF

BARRET, Richard (1958)
Compositeur anglais.
Quartet (1981) •SATB •BMIC

BARRIERE, Françoise
A Propos d'un chant de Noël (1979) •Asx/Perc/Vla/Vcl/Tape

BARRIGO, Don.
The Saxophone – A Modern Method (1952) •B&H

BARRINE
Andante et Allegro •Asx/Pno •WWS

BARROLL, Edward C.
Laf 'n Sax (1924) •7 Sx

BARROSO, Sergio Fernandez (1946)
Yantra IX (1979) •Sx/Tape

BARROW, Edgar L.
Compositeur américain.
Rustic Rondo (1954) •Asx/Pno
Semplice (1954) •Asx/Pno

BARTELS, Alfred
Compositeur américain.
Music for Symph. and Jazz Orch, op. 4 (20') •5 Sx: AATTB/4 Tpt/3 Trb/Tuba/Orch

BARTH, Marcel
Romance •2Sx: AA/Pno

BARTHALAY, Raoul (xxxx-1985)
Compositeur français, mort le 5 IV 1985.
Mini-variations sur une vieille ronde populaire (1978) (2'15) •3 Sx: AAA •Bil

BARTHOLOMEE, Pierre (1937)
Compositeur et chef d'orchestre belge né à Bruxelles le 5 VIII 1937. Travailla avec Schoenberg et Webern.
"Le souci d'élargissement de l'écriture, d'une confrontation à des mondes sonores diversifiés, qui ne se réduise pas à une simple juxtaposition anecdotique, est partagé par plusieurs compositeurs belges, qui souhaitent faire transparaître dans leur musique des horizons stylistiques avec lesquels ils se sentent de profondes affinités." (D. J-Y. BOSSEUR)
"One of his prime concerns as a composer is with the possibilities of harmony in new music; he has also taken a profound interest in the instruments, and intrumental practice, of the Baroque."
Ricercar (1974) (to Fr. DANEELS) •SATB

BARTLING, Stefan
Falsche Verse (1991) (6') •4 Sx: AABB

BARTOK, Béla (1881-1946)
6 Bagatelles (SCHMIDT) •SATB •DP
Bear Dance (Schmidt) •5 Sx: SAATB
Suite (L. LIVI) 1) Lentamente 2) Danza vorticosa 3) Pizzicato 4) Danza rutena 5) Cornamusa •Ob/Cl/Asx/Bsn
Three Folk Dances (GORDON) •AATB •South

BASEVI, Andrea
Compositeur italien.
6 Brecht-lieder (1993) •Voice/1 Sx: S+T •INM

BASSET, Leslie (1923)
Compositeur et professeur américain, né à Handford (California), le 22 I 1923. Travailla avec Finney, N. Boulanger, Gerhard, et Davidovsky.
"In his music, he pursues the ideal of structural logic within the judicial limits of the modern school of composition, with some serial elements discernible in his use of thematic rhythms and motivic periodicity." (BAKER'S) "His music is carefully structured, its formal process clear, conventional pitch materials are frequently deployed in an original manner. A strong religious feeling is evident in the serious and often serene tone of his work." (E. BORROFF)
Designs in Brass •2 Sx: BB/4 Hn/4 Tpt/3 Trb/Tuba/Timp/Perc •Pio
Duo Concertante (1984) (17') (to S. JORDHEIM) 1) Driving 2) Lyrical 3) Unhurried 4) Ascending 5) Dramatic •Asx/Pno •Pet
Music (1967/69) (10') (to D. SINTA) 1) Fast 2) Slow 3) Moderato 4) Fast •Asx/Pno •Pet
Wind Music •Fl/Ob/Cl/Asx/Hn/Bsn •THP

BASSI, Adriano
Movie •SATB

BASSI, Luigi (1766-1825)
27 Virtuoso Studies (IASILLI) •CF

BASSKIN, Ali (1962)
Compositeur allemand, né le 26 I 1962, à München. Travailla avec D. Acker et W. Killmayer.
Abushina (1983) (15') •Asx/2 Perc •adr

BASTEAU, Jean-François
Blue-Jean (1993) (1'30) •1 Sx: A or T/Pno •Mar

BATAILLE, Prudent (1888-1969)
Compositeur français, né à Roubaix, le 10 IV 1888, et mort à Paris le 11 II 1969.
Badine badine (1968) (2'30) •Asx/Pno •Bil

BATES, Norman C. (1927)
Contrebassiste et pianiste de jazz américain, né à Boise (Idaho), le 26 VII 1927.
Advanced Staccato Studies (1937) •RoMu

BATIAROV
Compositeur russe.
Rondo joyeux •SATB •ECS

BATTISTA, Tonino (1960)
Compositeur et chef d'orchestre italien, né à Gaeta. Travailla avec S. Sciarrino, K. Stockhausen, H. Ahronian, P. Eoetvos, et D. Gatti.
Narcisso (1989/91) (to E. FILIPPETTI) •1 Sx: S+B/Live Electron.

BAUCHWITZ, Peter (1953)
Guitariste et compositeur allemand, né le 14 IV 1953 à Berlin.
You came into my life (1986) (3'40) •Voice/Sx/Perc •adr

BAUCKHOLT, Carola
Schraubdichtung (12') •CBsSx/Vcl/Perc/Voice

BAUDRIER, Emile (1899)
Compositeur français, né à Neuille-Pont-Pierre (I&L), le 18 VII 1899.
Ballade •Bb Sx/Pno •Mol
Mes amis (1965) •SATB •Mol
Moderato •Bb Sx/Pno •Mol

BAUER, Robert P. (1950)
Compositeur canadien, né à Port Colborne (Ontario), le 24 I 1950. Travailla la guitare et le saxophone puis la composition avec J. Weinzweig et J. Beckwith.

NB 911 WR (1971) (2') •Asx Solo •CMC
Quatuor (1974) •SATB •CMC
Serenata Nerak (1972) (5') •Mezzo Soprano Voice/Ssx •CMC
A Sincere and Earnest Appeal (1974) (8') (To P. BRODIE) •SATB
   •CMC
Sokasodik (1974) (To P. BRODIE) •Any 4 Sx •BML
Three Pieces (1975) (9') (to P. BRODIE) •Ssx/Guit •CMC
Will Rag (1972) (1'10) (To . BRODIE) •SATB •BML/CMC

BAUMANN, (18xx-18xx)

2° Solo •Asx/Pno •Sax
Fantaisie •Asx/Pno •Sax

BAUMANN, Eric

Sonate •Asx/Pno •NoE

BAUMANN, Herbert (1925)

Compositeur et chef-d'orchestre allemand, né le 31 VII 1925 à Berlin. Travailla avec P. Höffer, B. Blacher, et S. Celibidache.
Monodie (1987) •Asx Solo •B&B
Variationen über ein englisches Volkslied (1968) (13'45) •Asx/Str
   Orch •MV

BAUMANN, P.

Concert in the Forest (RASCHER) •Asx/Pno •Bel

BAUMGART

Ein Hauch Lavendel •Tsx/Pno •Dux

BAUMGARTNER, Jean-Paul (1932)

Compositeur français, né à Strasbourg, le 26 IV 1932. Travailla avec O. Messiaen et T. Aubin.
"D'abord proche de Hindemith, de Honegger, puis de Messiaen, son art s'identifie désormais résolument aux recherches de l'avant-garde, par l'emploi des techniques sérielles et de celles de la musique concrète, sans esprit systématique toutefois." (BORDAS)
Cycle IV (1981) (15') (to Quatuor Elodia) 9 Sequences pour Quatuor
   d'anches, Trio d'anches, Duo et instrument Solo •Ob/Cl/Asx/
   Bsn
Séquence (1983) (to J-P. CAENS) •Asx Solo

BAUMGARTNER, Wilhelm (1820-1867)

Noch Sind die Tagen der Rosen (BLAAUW) •Bb Sx/Pno •Mol

BAUMONT, Chantal de (1954)

Angle de réflexion (to J. BATTEAU) •Asx

BAUR, John

Colors–O'Keefe 1) White 2) White Light 3) Black 4) Red •MIDI
   Wind Controller/MIDI Sequencer

BAUR, Jürg (1918)

Compositeur et professeur allemand né à Düsseldorf, le 11 XI 1918. Travailla avec Jarnach et M. Schneider.
"Jarnach's influence marks his first creative period, up to about 1954, when, as he stated, he was endeavouring 'to combine the contrapuntal principal and the musical styles of Hindemith and Bartok.' After 1952 he turned his attention to dodecaphonic techniques. He has described his attitude thus: 'I support those who wish to transform the compli-cated means of expression of the avant garde into a more accessible, more easily comprehensible language' (1968)." (R. LÜCK)
Ballata romana (1960-87) (11') 1) Elegia 2) Burletta 3) Aria
   4) Burletta 5) Elegia •Asx/Pno •Br&Ha
Cinqua Foglie (1986) (17'30) (to G. PRIESNER) 1) Allegro ruzzone
   2) Circulo ostinato 3) Ballo estatico 4) Sogno solitario 5) Finale:
   Fugato scherzando •SATB •B&H

BAUWENS, Alphonse

Compositeur belge.
London Concertino (8') (to Quat. Belge de Sxph.) 1) Piccadilly
   Circus 2) Mist Over Soho 3) Lyons Tea •SATB/Orch

BAUZIN, Pierre-Philippe (1933)

Compositeur et pianiste français, né à St-Emilion (Gironde), le 12 IV 1933. Travailla avec A. Honegger, M. Duruffle, et T. Aubin.
"La musique de Pierre-Philippe Bauzin ne manque ni de souffle ni d'inspiration, en somme celle d'un musicien qui a quelque chose à dire et qui le dit avec sincérité, parce que la musique est son moyen d'expression familier et qu'il connaît vraiment le langage tonal."
1er Concerto, op. 18 (1959) (16') (to J-M. LONDEIX) 1) Allegro
   2) Largo 3) Presto leggero •Asx/Orch (2222/221/Perc/Str or Pno
   •adr
Concerto, op. 32 (22') (to Quatuor D. Deffayet) 1) Tranquille
   2) Adage 3) Allègrement •SATB/Str Orch •adr
2me Concerto, op. 55 (1966) (18') (to D. DEFFAYET) Asx/Str Orch
   •adr
Divertimento, op. 63 (1968-69) (26') (to MM. LONDEIX, McGEE, &
   BOUHEY) 1) Moderatamente 2) Giocoso 3) Placabile 4) Allegria
   5) Rubando 6) Leggierissimo 7) Amarevole
   8) Vivacissimamente •3 Sx: AAT •Lem
Esquisses, op. 57 (1967-68) (to J-M. LONDEIX) Allegremente -
   Leggerissimo - Cantabile - Fughetta - Cadenzia - Finale-vivace
   •Asx Solo •adr
5 Mouvements en forme de musique, op. 19 (1960) (12') (to J-M.
   LONDEIX) En forme: 1) d'étude 2) de divertissement 3) de
   berceuse 4) de fugue 5) En pleine forme •Asx/Pno or Wood-
   wind Quintet •adr
Poême, op. 20 (1960) (14') (to J-M. LONDEIX) •Asx/Orch (2222/323/
   Perc/Harp/Str) or Pno •adr
Quatuor, op. 29 (1962) (20') 1) Allegretto 2) Scherzo 3) Larghetto
   4) Finale •SATB •adr
Sonate, op. 15 (1959) (15') (to J-M. LONDEIX) 1) Allegro moderato
   2) Vif et léger 3) Adage 4) Allegro vivo •Asx/Pno •adr

BAVICCHI, John

Compositeur américain.
Quartette no. 4 •SATB •DP

BAXTER, L.

Nocturne (5'30) •Sx/Vibr

BAY, Bill (1945)

Jazz Sax Studies (1979) •HD
Sax Improvisations •HD

BAYER, Marcelino Gaspa (1898)

Saxophoniste, clarinettiste, et compositeur espagnol, né à Montblanch (Tarragona).
Escalas y arpegios •UME

BAYLES, Philip

Compositeur américain.
Méditation •Sx/Dancer

BAZELAIRE, Paul (1886-1958)

Suite française (LONDEIX) (7') 1) Bourrée d'Auvergne 2) Chanson
   d'Alsace 3) Chanson de Bresse 4) Berceuse populaire
   5) Montagnarde d'Auvergne •Tsx/Pno •Sch

BAZELON, Irvin (1922)

Churchill Downs Concerto (1972) (to H. ESTRIN) •Asx/Pno

BAZZINI, Antonio (1818-1897)

Ronde des lutins, op. 25 (MUTO) •Asx/Pno •Lem

BEAL, Jeff

Compositeur américain.

Circular Logic (1986) (10') (for N. CORMAN) •Asx/Soprano Voice/
Vcl/Pno •PMCP

BEALL, John

Compositeur américain.

Concerto (1991) (to D. HASTINGS) •Asx/Orch (2222/221/Timp/Perc/
Str) or Wind Orch •adr

Shaker Tunes: Free Variations for Woodwind Sextet (1992) •Asx/Fl/
Ob/Cl/Hn/Bsn

Sonata (1976) •Asx/Pno •South

BEAUCAMP, Albert (1921-1967)

Chef d'orchestre et compositeur français, né à Rouen.

"Oeuvres solidement écrites, souvent pleines d'esprit." (P. PITTION)

Chant élégiaque (to H-R. POLLIN) •Asx/Pno •Led

Menuet d'Orphée •Asx/Pno •Led

Tarentelle (1946) (to M. MULE) •Asx/Pno •Led

BEAUME

Suite 1) Prélude 2) Molto moderato 3) Finale •Asx/Orch (1111/100/
Str)

Suite 1) Prélude 2) Nocturne 3) Interlude 4) Tambourin •SATB

BEAVERS, Kevin

Shadowplays (1994) 1) Drones of Mayhem and Repose 2) Higher,
Faster, Louder •Sx/Pno/3 Perc

BECERRA (SCHMIDT), Gustavo (1925)

Compositeur chilien, né le 26 VIII 1925, à Temuco. Travailla avec
Allende, Santa Cruz, Carvajal, et Salas-Viu.

"His extensive output includes works in almost all media and in a
great variety of styles, including neo-classical, serial, electronic, mixed-
media, aleatory, and graphic features." (J. ORREGO-SALAS)

Quartetto (1959) •SATB

BECHARD, René

Compositeur canadien.

L'Orgue de Barbarie •SATB

BECK, Conrad (1901-1989)

Compositeur suisse, né à Lohn (Schaffhouse), le 16 VI 1901, mort à
Bâle le 31 X 1989. Travailla avec J. Ibert, A. Honegger, A. Roussel, et
N. Boulanger.

"L'art de Beck est une synthèse fertile de la sensibilité alémanique et
des vertus latines. Son écriture utilise des moyens délibérément ré-
duits." (BORDAS) "Son écriture est résolument contrapuntique, incli-
nant vers le dépouillement acidulé et martelé de Hindemith, mais il
s'humanise et se tempère grâce à l'ascendant de Roussel et d'Ibert." (R.
BERNARD)

"His style shows a blend of Teutonic emotional depth and Latin sense
of form, and he has done more than any other Swiss composer to create
a new polyphonic-linear style." (K. von FISCHER)

Nocturne (1959) (3'30) (to J-M. LONDEIX) •Asx/Pno •Lem

BECKER, Charles (1944)

Compositeur belge, né à Verniers, en 1944. Travailla avec E. Quinet.

Triade (1974) (to Quat. Belge de Sxph.) 1) Trés lent 2) Vif 3) Trés
lent •SATB

BECKER, Günter Hugo (1924)

Compositeur et professeur allemand, né à Forbach-Baden, le 1 IV
1924. Travailla avec W. Fortner.

"It was his experience of Greek life and culture that caused Becker
to break away and develop his style, a style in which serial writing was
abandoned in favour of oscillating textures, comparable with those of

Ligeti, but lacking a similar structural function." (R. LÜCK)

Correspondances (1966/68) •Eb Cl/BsCl/Asx/Chamber Orch •HG/
IMD

BECKER, Holmer (1955)

Compositeur allemand.

Adagio (5') •Sx Solo

"Lacht das Licht..." (1988) (3') •3 Sx: SAB

Nocturne (1985) (4') •Asx Solo

Nocturno (6') •Asx/Pno

BECKERATH, Alfred von (1901)

Compositeur allemand, né à Hagenau/Elsass, le 4 X 1901. Travailla
avec A. Lipray, M. Bauer, J. Hass, et C. Rathauss.

6 Kleine Bilder (1970) (9') (to S. RASCHER) 1) Intrada-Allegro
moderato 2) Andante tranquillo 3) Moderato resoluto 4) Scherzo
aggresive-vivo 5) Interludio lirico-andante 6) Danza finale-vivo
•SATB •adr

BECKLER, Stanworth

Folksong Fantasy •Tsx/Pno •SeMC

Mixtures •Asx/Fl/Ob/Cl/Hn/Bsn •SeMC

BEDARD, Denis (1950)

Organiste et compositeur canadien.

Duetto (1988) (to Cl. BRISSON) •2 Sx: AA

Fantasie (1984) (6'30) •1 Sx: S or T/Pno •Bil

Sonate (1981) (11'30) (to Cl. BRISSON) 1) Allegro 2) Andante
3) Allegro •Asx/Pno •SEDIM/Do

Suite (1983) (to Quat. Bourque) 1) Burlesque 2) Aria 3) Final
•SATB •Do

BEDFORD, David (1937)

Compositeur anglais né à Londres, le 4 VIII 1937. Travailla avec
Lennox Berkeley avant d'aller travailler avec Luigi Nono.

"D'abord franchement atonal, laissant dans ses oeuvres une très large
liberté aux exécutants, David Bedford semble tenté par le minimalisme
et l'influence de la musique 'pop.' " (G. GEFEN)

"Bedford's music shows little dependence on traditional techniques.
It is freely experimental in the use of improvisatory processes, in choice
of instruments, in using unorthodox playing techniques and in ordering
events by dice throwing. From a traditional viewpoint, his music can
appear to be harmonically and rhythmically static, until the listener
adjusts to the very slow rate of textural change, and focuses attention
on the variations in timbre, types of articulation and attack." (H. COLE)

Five Easy Pieces (1987) •Asx/Pno •Uni

Fridiof Kennings (1980) (10') •SATB

BEECKMANN, Nazaire (18xx-19xx)

Compositeur français.

Concerto militaire, op. 23 (to C. BENDER) •Asx/Pno •Cos

Elégie, op. 14/3 (to L. MAYEUR) •Asx/Pno •Bil

Méthode complète élémentaire et progressive (revue et corrigée par
[revised and edited by] H. Rawson) (1874) •PB

*Méthode de Saxph. basse; de Saxph.-baryton; Saxph.-Alto; Saxph.-
Soprano* (1874) •Alf

2° Morceau de concert, op. 17 (1888) (to P. SEGOIN) •Asx/Pno •Bil

3° Morceau de concert, op. 27 •Asx/Pno •Cos

Souvenir du Château de Waterloo, op. 21 •Asx/Pno •Cos

BEEFTINCK, Herman (1953)

Compositeur hollandais.

Quartet (1977) (5') •SATB •Don

BEEKUM, Jan van

Animato — 107 short technical studies •Harm

Fair Play (1984) — 40 petites pièces •3 Instrum. Variables •Mol

BEERMAN, Burton (1943)

Compositeur américain.

Concerto I (1980) (to J. SAMPEN) •Asx/Taped Instruments
Fragments (1988) •1 Player: MIDI Wind Controller/Yamaha TX81Z
 Synth/Digital Delay •ACA
Moment (1978) (to J. SAMPEN) •Asx/Pno •ACA
Passager (1985) (to J. SAMPEN) •Ssx/Pno

BEERS, Jacobus Cornelis (1902-1947)

Compositeur et pianiste hollandais, né à Amersfoort, le 2 VI 1902,
mort à Amsterdam, le 15 VI 1947. Travailla avec J. Huré et N.
Boulanger.

Concerto •Voice/Asx/Orch

BEETHOVEN, Ludwig van (1770-1827)

Adagio et Finale (*Trio, op. 87*) (GEE) •3 Sx: AAT •MMB
Adelaïde (SEGOIN) •Asx/Pno
Adelaïde •Bb Sx/Pno •CBet
Allegro ("*Pathétique*") (BETTONY) •Bsx/Pno •CBet
Allegro (from *String Quartet no. 1*) (REX) •SATB •DP
Allegro and Minuet •2 Sx •Mus
Allegro con brio (SIBBING) •3 Sx: ATB •Eto
Allegro molto quasi presto (from *String Quartet, op. 18, no.
 2*) (FRASCOTTI) •SATB •Ron
Bagatelle in F minor (R. GUENTHER) •AATB •South
Duo •Ssx/Cnt •Mil
Duo (*Grand sextuor*) •2 Sx •Mil
Excepts from Rondo (*Sonata Pathétique*) •Cl/Asx/Bsn •CF
Fünf Mödlinger Tänze, WoO 17 (T. SCHÖN) •SATB •ApE
Fugue •3 Sx: AAT •Mus
Grand Trio, op. 87 •2 Cl/Asx or Fl/Ob/Asx •Braun
Heavens Resound (RASCHER) •Bsx/Pno •Bel
Larghetto (*2nd Symphony*) (TILLIARD) •SATB •Ma
Marche funèbre (ROMBY) •Asx/Pno •PB
Menuet (MAGANINI) •Bb Sx/Pno •Mus
Menuet (TRINKAUS) •Sx/Tpt (or Trb)/Pno •CF
Menuet de printemps (DYCK) •SATB •Braun
Minuet (THOMSON) •AATB •GSch
Minuet (TRINKAUS) •Bb Sx/Pno, or 2 Sx: AA or AT/Pno •CF
Minuet in G (ANDREANI) •Asx/Pno •Ric
Minuet in G (CAILLIET) •AATB •Bel
Minuet in G •Bb Sx/Pno, or 2 Sx: AA or AT/Pno •CBet/CF
Minuetto •Asx or Bb Sx/Pno •Mol
Moonlight Sonata (1st movement) •Asx/Pno •CF
Moonlight Sonata - Adagio •2 Sx: AA or AT/Pno •Cen
Petite valse (MULE) •Asx/Pno •Led
Romance, op. 50 (5'40) (ANZALONE) •Asx/Pno •Ken
Romance (LEFEVRE) •Asx/Pno •CF
Romance in F, op. 50 (FRASCOTTI) •Asx/Pno •Ron
Rondo, op. 17 (MAGANINI) •Asx/Pno •Mus
Scherzo (TEAL - Album) •Bb Sx/Pno •GSch
Scherzo (from *String Quartet no. 1*) (REX) •SATB •DP
Seven Variations on a theme from Mozart's 'Magic Flute'
 (SAKAGUCHI) •2 Sx •IM
Sonate, op. 5 •Bb Sx/Pno •Mil
Sonate Pathétique •Bb Sx/Pno •Mil
Symphony no. 5 (BERNARDO) •SATB •DP
Trio, op. 20 •Asx/Cnt/Pno •Mil
Trio, op. 20 •2 Cl/Asx •Mol
Trio, op. 87 •Fl/Ob/Asx •Bil
Trio, op. 87 •2 Cl/Asx •Mol
Trio, op. 87 (TEAL) •3 Sx: SAT or ATB •Eto

BEGLARIAN, Eve

Getting to Know the Weather •Bsx Solo •DP

Fresh Air •SATB/Tape •NP

BEHRENS, Jack

Compositeur américain.

Music from Wawerfree (1972) (8') (to P. BRODIE) •Ssx/Pno •CMC

BEINKE, Eckart

Compositeur allemand.

Quartett (1993) (14') (to l'Ensemble Bordeaux-Berlin) •SATB •adr

BEKKU, Sadao

Compositeur japonais.

Chant de ville •Asx/Pno

BELARDINELLI, Daniele

Tris (1992) •3 Sx: SAB

BELDA, J.

Compositeur espagnol.

Cuarteto •SATB

BELDON

Feather River •Asx/Pno •Bel

BELL, Derek (1923)

Compositeur américain.

Honest Pleasures (1981) (to J. SAMPEN) •Asx/Chamber Ensemble

BELLEMARE, Gilles

Compositeur canadien.

La chasse-galerie (1981) •Narr/Choir/2 Fl/2 Recorder/2 Cl/2 Tpt/1
 Sx

BELLINI, Luciano

Compositeur et chef d'orchestre italien, né à Roma.

Phos (1991) •Asx/Tape •adr

BELLINI, Vincenzo (1801-1835)

Air et variations (from "*La Somnambule*") •Bb Sx/Pno •CF
Concerto (JOOSEN) •Bb Sx/Pno •Mol
Duet from "Norma" •2 Sx/Pno •CF
Hear me Norma (LEWIS) •Asx/Tpt (or Trb)/Pno •CF
Norma - 20 mélodies (VERROUST) •Sx Solo •Bil
Les Puritains (MAYEUR) •Asx/Pno •Cos
La Somnambule •Ob or Cl/Asx/Pno •Bil

BELLISARIO, Angelo

Compositeur italien.

Improviso (1973) •Asx/Pno •Ber
Papillons 1) Allegro 2) Adagio 3) Adagio 4) Adagio misterioso
 5) Allegro •Tsx/Pno •adr

BELMANS, R.

Variations on an Old Christmas Song •Bb Sx/Pno •Scz
Romanza piccola •Bb Sx/Pno

BELON

Fantaisie Hongroise •Asx/Pno •Pre

BELSSEL

God, Ruler of All Nations (HARTLEY) •Sx Ensemble: SSAATTB •adr

BELTRAN

Metodo completo •UME

BENCRISCUTTO, Frank (1928)

Compositeur américain, né le 21 IX 1928, à Racine (Wisconsin).

Concerto Grosso (1962) (8') •4 Sx: AAAT/Band •Sha
Serenade •Asx/Band or Pno •adr

BENDA, Franz (1709-1786)

Introduction et Danse (FELIX) •Tsx/Pno •Mus
Sonata in F Major •Tsx/Pno •Mus

BENEJAM, Luis (1919)

Violoniste et compositeur espagnol, né à Barcelone.
Sonata 1) Allegro vivace 2) Andante 3) Allegro •Asx/Pno •adr

BEN-HAIM, Paul (FRANKENBURGER) (1897)

Compositeur israélien, né à Munich, le 5 VII 1897, fixé en Palestine depuis 1933.

"Aux influences de la musique de l'Europe centrale vinrent s'ajouter celles de la musique orientale et spécialement des juifs yéménites." (BORDAS) "Un des musiciens les plus importants d'Israël." (FASQUELLE) "Au contact de l'Orient, ses oeuvres postérieures à 1940 s'apparentent au chant populaire de son pays d'adoption." (Cl. ROSTAND)

"His works had been distinguished by their tender lyricism already in his pre-Palestinian period, and the pastoral pages are the most attractive in his later compositions." (GROVE) "Ben-Haim has stayed essentially within the Western tradition, he has absorbed influences from his adopted country. He became acquainted with Jewish and oriental folksong through Bracha Zefira, a folksinger of Yemeni descent, and much of his music is marked by the cantillation and pastoral mood of Middle Eastern peasant music, together with the rhythms of such dances as the *hora* ." (U. TOEPLITZ)

3 Songs Without Words (1952) (10') 1) Arioso 2) Ballad
 3) Sephardic Melody (traditional) •1 Sx: A or T/Pno •MCA

BENHAMOU, Lionel

Saxophoniste de jazz.
10 Thèmes et improvisations •Sal

BENHAMOU, Maurice

Mouvement (1979) •Fl/Sx/Vla/Vcl/Perc/Tape
Musique pour 13 instruments •Fl/2 Cl/Harmonica/Sx/2 Vln/3 Guit/
 Pno 6 hands (à 6 mains)

BENNET, Frank

Song (1975) (to D. SINTA) •Asx/Pno

BENNETT, David (1897)

Compositeur et arrangeur américain, né à Chicago, le 3 IX 1897.
Concerto in G Minor (1939) (7') •Tsx/Orch or Pno •CF
Latinata •Asx/Band or Pno •CF
Modern •Asx/Pno •CF
Sax Soliloquy •4 Sx: AATB or AATT/Band or Pno •B&H/South
Saxophone Symphonette •AATB •CF
Saxophone Royal •Asx/Band or Pno •South

BENNETT, Richard Rodney (1936)

Compositeur et pianiste anglais, né à Broadstairs (Kent), le 29 III 1936. Travailla avec L. Berkeley, H. Ferguson et P. Boulez.

"Il s'est constitué un style libre et personnel auquel l'influence de Britten n'est pas étrangère, style de synthèse qui s'apparente aussi à celui de Hans Werner Henze." (Cl. ROSTAND)

"His music is influenced mainly by Béla Bartok, but he has also pursued serial methods." (BAKER) "works show a sure sense of occasion and a brilliant instinct for that elusive blend of seriousness and approachability or, to put it in other terms, of the up to date and the not too challenging. Of the lighter pieces some are tonal, but most use basically modern harmonies in a clear, fresh, and effective, if not perhaps very memorable way. The more substantial and serious scores are usually 12-note, but Bennett always manages to avoid the more rebarbative associations of serialism." (S. WALSH)

Conversations (1983) •2 Sx: AA or TT •Uni
Comedia I (1972) •Fl/Asx/BsCl/Tpt/Vcl/Perc •Uni

A Jazz Calendar (1963-64) (31') 7 pieces for 12 players •Fl/3 Sx: ATB/2 Tpt/Hn/Trb/Tuba/Pno/2 Perc •Uni
Jazz Pastorale (1969) (25') •Voice/1 Sx: A+T/Bsx/2 Tpt/Trb/Tuba/ Pno/Bass/Perc •Uni
Soliloquy (1966) (14') •Voice/1 Sx: A+T/Tpt/Tuba/Pno/Bass/Perc •Uni
Sonata (18'30) 1) Poco allegro 2) Scherzando 3) Andante in Memory of Harold Arlen 4) Vivo •Ssx/Pno
Travel Notes (1979) (4') •SATB •Nov

BENNETT, Wilhelmine (1933)

Compositeur américain, né le 14 VI 1933, à Carmi (Illinois). Travailla avec A. Donata, W. Fortner et Chou Wen-Chung.
Five Quick Visions of the Apocalypse (1971) (25') Sx/Actress/Tape •DP

BENSON, Warren Frank (1924)

Compositeur et professeur américain, né à Detroit, le 26 I 1924.

"From his earliest works, Benson assimilated a neo-classical idiom, distinguished by compact contrapuntal writing and harmonic clarity without avoidance of justifiable dissonance." (BAKER) "His music is varied and selective in technique, giving prominence to lyricism and to colorful instrumentation." (J. Graue)

Aeolian Song (from *Concerto*) (5') Asx/Orch or Band or Pno •MCA
Cantelina (1954) (2'30) (to S. RASCHER & W. BRASK) •Asx/Pno •B&H
Concertino (1955) (13') (to S. RASCHER) 1) Very slowly 2) Slowly peacefully 3) Lively bouyantly •Asx/Orch (000/4431/Perc/Str) or Band or Pno •MCA
The Dream Net (1972) (to F. HEMKE) •Asx/Str Quartet •Bel
Farewell (1964) (2') (for D. SINTA) •Asx/Pno •MCA
Images •Asx/Band •adr
Invocation and Dance (1960) (5') (to S. RASCHER) •2 Sx: SA/Perc •MCA
Quartet •SATB •adr
Quintette •Ssx/Str Quartet •adr
Star Edge (1966-67) (18') (to D. SINTA) •Asx/Orch or Band •MCA
Wind Rose (1966) (7') (To F. HEMKE) 1) Legato 2) Free •SATB •MCA

BENT

Swiss Boy •2 Sx: AA/Pno

BENTLEY, Arnold (1913)

16th Century Trios •Fl (or Ob or Cl)/Ob (or Cl)/Sx •Chap

BENTZON, Jørgen (Liebenberg) (1897-1951)

Compositeur danois, né à Copenhague, le 4 II 1897, mort à Hoersholm, le 9 VII 1951. Travailla avec C. Nielsen et Karg-Elert.

"Bentzon se tourna plutôt vers Hindemith." "Son style fait remarquer une habileté réelle à combiner les timbres des instruments."

"As composer, he followed the romantic school, clearly related to Nielsen's ideals." (BAKER) "Bentzon's music ranges from a kind of witty, sometimes ironic entertainment, to works of highly crafted polyphony." (W. REYNOLDS)

Raconto n° 1, op. 25 (1935) (13') (for S. RASCHER) •Fl/Asx/Bsn/Bass •SOBM/BMCo
Introduction, Variations and Rondo (1938) (17') (to S. RASCHER) •Asx/Str Orch •SOBM

BENTZON, Niels Viggo (1919)

Compositeur danois, né à Copenhague en 1919. Travailla avec Jeppesen.

"Son oeuvre très vaste porte la marque de Brahms, Schoenberg, et Hindemith." (BORDAS) "Il se manifeste comme l'une des personnalités les plus en relief de son pays, d'abord dans un style influencé par

Hindemith, puis effectuant un léger virage vers l'atonal." (Cl. Ros-
TAND)

"Powerful and often bombastic, Bentzon's compositions are dissonant but tonal in concept, free-flowing with an almost improvisatory
character. His style was well developed early in his career and has
undergone relatively little evolution: his intellectual curiosity and
inventive approach have caused him to experiment frequently, with
many avant-garde procedures, but these essays have not significantly
altered his basic statement." (W. REYNOLDS)

Climatic Changes, op. 474 (1985) (20') •Bsx/Pno Soli/Orch (1111/
111/Perc/2 Vln/2 Vla/Vcl) •Hire/Sal

Emancipatio, op. 471 (1985) (9'30) •Asx/Pno •WH

Sonata, op. 320 (1973) (9') (to Ch. A. GRØN) 1) Allegro 2) Andante
3) Allegro moderato •Asx/Pno

Sonata, op. 478 (1985) (14') •Ssx/Pno •WH

Sonatina, op. 498 (1986) (6'30) (to P. EGHOLM) •Asx/Pno •WH

BENZIN, A.

Caprice russe •1 Sx: A or T/Pno •An

BERBIGUIER, Benoît Tranquille (1782-1838)

18 Etudes or Exercices (MULE) •Led

6 Easy Duets •2 Sx •Mus

BERENGUER, José-Manuel (1955)

Compositeur espagnol, né à Barcelone.

Fuego (1989) (8') (to D. KIENTZY) •BsSx/Tape

BERG, Gunnar Johnsen (1909-1989)

Compositeur et pianiste danois, né le 11 I 1909 à St Gall en Suisse.
Travailla à Paris avec A. Honegger.

"Berg's compositions were impressionistic and freely atonal, and,
with the exception of brief experiments with tonality, he has consistently employed atonal procedures. He has been influenced by many
composers, above all Messiaen and Webern." (W. REYNOLDS)

Prosthesis (1952) •Asx/Pno •adr

BERG, Olav (1949)

Compositeur et trompettiste norvégien, né à Oslo. Travailla avec A.
Bibalo puis, à Londres, avec L. Berkeley.

Fragments (1977) (8') •Fl/Cl/Asx/Vla/Vcl/Pno/2 Perc •NMJ

Quartet (1989) (12'45) (to H. Bergersen's Saxophone Quartet)
1) Allegro moderato - Adagio 2) Allegro 3) Lento - Allegro
•SATB

BERG, Paul

To Teach His Own (1984) (12') •Fl/Ob/Tsx/Trb/Vln/Vcl/Tape •Don

BERGEIJK, Gilius van

Life of Rosa Luxembourg •Pno/Vcl/4 Instr./Tape

BERGER, David

Contemporary Jazz Studies (2 vol.) •DP

BERGER, Jean (1909)

Chef de choeur et compositeur américain d'origine française, né à
Jamm, le 27 IX 1909. Travailla à Paris avec L. Aubert.

Divertimento •3 Instrument aigus •Bou

BERGERET, Emile

Romance sans paroles (1891) •Asx/Pno

BERGERON, Thomas

Saxophoniste et compositeur américain.

Designs on B Option 9 (1989) •Sx Solo •adr

Magical Dances •Cl/Sx/Pno

Saxophone Multiphonics: A Scalar Model •Sx •adr

Statement V •Asx Solo •adr

Untitled Work for Solo Saxophone (1975) •Asx Solo •adr

BERGH, Alja

Motivationen (1993) •Asx/Pno •INM

BERGHMANS, José (1921-1992)

Compositeur français d'origine belge, né à Moulins/Allier, le 15 VII
1921, mort en Mai 1992. Travailla avec T. Aubin, F. de Bourguignon,
et O. Messiaen.

Concerto Lyrique (1974) (14') •Asx/Orch (21EH22/423/Perc/Pno/
Str) or Pno •EFM

Telle qu'en elle-même (1977) Septuor chorégraphique •Tsx/Pno/5
Perc •Chou

BERGMAN, Erik (1911)

Compositeur finlandais, né le 24 XI 1911. Travailla avec Carlsson,
Tiessen, et Vogel.

"Erik Bergman is a composer of abundant youth, vitality and
creativity, in whose music lyricism and toughness, mysticism and
mischievous humour, sophistication and primitivism meet. He contin-
ues the work of the Finnish modernists of the twenties, above all Aarre
Merikanto, but when he took the decisive step towards dodecaphony
and serialism he went further than they had gone and, by freeing his
music of the last echoes of national romanticism, laid the foundations
of modern Finnish music." (P. HEININEN) "At the end of the 1960s
Bergman abandoned strict serial procedures for a freer technique
involving elements of improvisation and aleatory writing but retaining
a strict control over form." (LORAMO)

Etwas rascher, op. 108 (1985) (16') •SATB •Nov/FMIC

Mipejupa, op. 96 (1981) (17') (to P. SAVIJOKI) •Fl/Asx/Guit/Perc
•Nov/FMIC

Solfatara, op. 81 (1977) (15') (to P. SAVIJOKI) •Asx/Perc •Pa/FMIC

BERGSON, Michael (1820-1898)

Scène et air (from "*Luisa di Montfort*") •Asx or Bb Sx/Pno •Mol

BERGSTRÖM, Harry (1910)

Compositeur finlandais, né le 4 IV 1910.

"Harry Bergström must be counted among the most proliferous of
Finnish light music and film music composers. His list of works reads
like a history of Finnish light music."

Suite (1936) •Asx/Orch (2221/2210/Perc/Str) •FMIC

BERIO, Luciano (1925)

Compositeur italien, né à Oneglia, le 24 X 1925. Travailla avec
Ghedini et Dallapiccola.

"Tôt venu au mouvement sériel, Berio a rapidement pris sa liberté
pour écrire dans tous les styles avancés, pour exprimer une nature qui
est l'indépendance même; il est un baroque dont l'invention jaillissant
et la sensibilité mobile assimilent tout ce qui passe à sa portée, toutes
les impressions qu'il reçoit de la vie sous toutes ses formes, pour en tirer
de la musique également sous les formes les plus diverses. Quelles
qu'en soient les origines, matérielles ou intellectuelles, fussent-elles
les plus inattendues, ces musiques semblent couler de source. Il y a là
'cas' de verve fantaisiste toute italienne qui n'est d'ailleurs pas sans
laisser quelque déchet, le tout allant de la farce au sublime." (Cl.
ROSTAND) "Chez Berio la technique sérielle généralisée demeure souple et spontanée." (BORDAS) "Aussi distant à l'égard des structuralistes
rigoureux des années cinquante que sceptique devant l'esthétique
minimaliste américaine, Berio met en scène depuis quarante ans une
sorte de témoignage sonore de la vie: il fait sonner le monde." (C.
LEBLÉ) "Dans la série des *Sequenze*, la virtuosité est avant tout une
virtuosité mentale. Chaque *Sequenza* est un commentaire de l'histoire
de l'instrument lui-même; à la fois elle s'accorde à l'histoire de
l'instrument et elle innove pour l'instrument, sinon la virtuosité sans
contenu 'spirituel' ne m'intéresse absolument pas." (L. BERIO)

"His works, many of them written in a special optical notation..." (BAKER) "The predominantly static and elemantary nature of Berio's micro-structures recalls the craftsman's parsimony developed by him, for instance, in the repeated new elaborations of the two *Sequenze* for viola and harp. The use he made as a container of casual heterophony confirmed his overwhelming confidence in his own creative faculties, which the exploiting of virtuosity in the *Sequenze* for various soloists had meanwhile tested in entirely traditional terms." (C. ANNIBALDI)

Novissimum Testamentum (1991) •4 Sx: SATB/4 Voice/4 Cl
Prière (1970) (15') •Voice/Instruments (8 players minimum) •Uni
Sequenza IXb (1980) •Asx Solo •Uni

BERKELEY, Michael (1948)
Compositeur anglais.
Keening (1987) (10'30) (to J. HARLE) •Asx/Pno

BERLIN, David
Patterns (Marcato (fast) - Lento espressivo - Fast) •SATB

BERLIN, Irving
Cheek to Cheek (POLANSKY) •Ssx/Pno •Lem

BERLINSKI, Herman
Canons and Rounds (9 Pieces) •3 or 4 Sx •Pres

BERLIOZ, Gabriel-Pierre (1916)
Compositeur français, né à Paris. Travailla avec A. Roussel.
Air à danser (to R. LETELLIER) •Asx/Pno •Braun

BERLIOZ, Hector (1803-1869)
Compositeur français, né à La Côte-Saint-André (Isère), le 11 XII 1803, mort à Paris, le 8 III 1869.
Ami et vibrant défenseur d'Adolphe Sax, Hector Berlioz composa une oeuvre avec saxophone, qui fut jouée en première audition sous la direction du compositeur, à Paris, salle Herz, le 3 Février 1844, par MM.: Dufresne (nouveau cornet), Arban (bugle perfectionné), Dauvernay (trompette suraigüe), Leperd (clarinette), Duprez (clarinette-basse), et Adolphe Sax (saxophone baryton). Cette oeuvre est malheureusement perdue dans cette forme pour six instruments à vent.
Chant sacré (1843/44) •2 Tpt/Bugle/2 Cl/Bsx
Chant sacré (LONDEIX) •12 Sx: SnoSSAAATTTBBBs •Bil
Romance de Marguerite (MAYEUR) •Asx/Pno •Cos
3 Lieder (*Faust Verdammung*) •Asx/Pno •VAB
3 Songs (*Damnation of Faust*) (CLARK) •Bb Sx/Pno •Mus

BERNAOLA, Carmelo (Alonso) (1929)
Compositeur espagnol né à Ochandiano (Biscaye), le 16 VII 1929. Travailla avec Blanco, Masso, Calès Pina Gomez, Jolivet, Tansman, Petrassi, Celibidache, et Maderna.
"Influencé d'abord par Bartok, puis par la musique sérielle, Carmelo Bernaola est devenu rapidement l'un des représentants les plus avancés de sa génération." (BORDAS)
"He departed from his rigorous academic training to evolve a style assimilating some of the ideas of the avant-garde, though he has used these with flexibility and individuality. The strong influence on his music of his Basque-Castilian background should not be overlooked; though he has never used popular or traditional ideas, his work displays unmistakably Spanish traits." (E. FRANCO)
Superficie n°3 (1963) •Asx/Picc/Xylophone/Bongos •Alp

BERNARD, Jacques (1931)
Saxophoniste et compositeur français, né à Dôle (Juras), le 8 VIII 1931. Travailla avec M. Mule, J. Rivier, et D. Milhaud.
"Son langage est tout simplement atonal, mais pas forcément sériel, et tendant vers une architecture et une structure libres (développement sur place, improvisation, etc.)."

Andante et Scherzo (1965) (10'40) (to Quatuor Deffayet) •SATB •adr
Climats (1975) (to A. BEUN) •Asx/Perc •adr
Dialogues d'anches (1969) (13') (to Quatuor d'anches français)
1) Rencontre et présentation 2) Intermède 3) Reprise
4) Modération 5) Débat 6) Dénouement or conclusion •Ob/Cl/Asx/Bsn •EFM
L'Opéra de l'Espace (1970) (Poème de C. DOBZIJNSKY) •Narr/Ob/Cl/BsCl/1 Sx: S+A+B/Bsn/Perc •adr
6 Miniatures (1978) (8'30) (to A. BEUN) 1) Lyrique 2) Véloce
3) Contrastes 4) Ostinato 5) Ballet 6) Panorama •Ssx Solo •An

BERNARD, Jean-Emile Auguste (1843-1902)
Passacaglia •Asx/Pno

BERNARD, Robert (1900-1971)
Musicologue et compositeur français d'origine suisse, né à Genève le 10 X 1900. Travailla avec Templeton, Strong, Barblan, et Lauber.
"Dans sa musique, il utilise tous les modes y compris le chromatisme, mais sans s'opposer aux principes de la construction tonale. Les influences de Fauré, Debussy, Stravinsky, Roussel, et Bartok y sont assimilées avec l'indépendance la plus délibérée." (BORDAS) "Art sincère, volontaire, sérieux, se traduisant en des formes solidement architecturées et une polyphonie robuste." (Cl. ROSTAND)
Quatuor (1931-35) •SATB •adr

BERNARDINI, Giampiero
Compositeur italien.
Quartet (1992) •SATB

BERNARDS, B.
Compositeur allemand.
125 Übungen als tägliche Studies (1926) •Zim
Des Saxophonisten Repertoire •Zim
24 Virtuosenetüden mit Anang (1927) •Zim
10 Duos •2 Sx: AA or TT •Zim
10 Instruktive Duos •2 Sx: AA or TT •Zim

BERNAUD, Alain (1932)
Compositeur français, né à Neuilly/Seine, le 8 III 1932. Travailla avec J. Murgier et T. Aubin.
Final (Extrait de la *Sonate*) •Asx/Pno •Chou
Humoresque (1982) (to J. LEDIEU) 1) Pomposo 2) Molto ritmico
3) Andantino •Bsx/Pno •adr
Quatuor (24'30) 1) Moderato tranquillo 2) Dinamico 3) Adagio
4) Molto vivace •SATB •RR
Rhapsodie (1984) (to D. DEFFAYET) •Asx/Pno •Chou
Sonate en Duo •Ssx/Vcl •adr
Sonate pour deux saxophones (1974) (20'30) (for D. DEFFAYET & J. LEDIEU) 1) Allegro 2) Andante 3) Vivace 4) Lent, doux et rêveur - vivace •2 Sx: SB •adr

BERNIER, Anthony
Crépuscule - Fantaisie (1893) •Asx/Pno

BERNIER, René (1905)
Compositeur belge, né à St-Gilles-lez-Bruxelles, le 10 III 1905. Travailla avec P. Gilson. Appartint au group des 'Synthétistes.'
"Etrangères aux spéculations esthétiques, aux recherches alchimiques, mes aspirations visent avant tout à l'expression, à ce que je dénommerais volontiers 'l'au-delà des notes.' " (R. BERNIER)
"His harmony is essentially tonal, with modal suggestions, and his deeply lyrical and discreetly refined music creates an atmosphere of gentle melancholy." (H. VANHULST)
Capriccio (1957) (2'30) •Asx/Pno •Led
Hommage à Sax (1958) (10') •Asx/Orch (1121/211/Perc/Harp/Str) or Band or Pno •Led

Serinette en guise de bis (1974) (1') •SATB •Bil
Suite pour le plaisir de l'oreille (1973) (13') 1) Le joueur d'aulos: andantino 2) Ronde rituelle: graziosamente 3) Chant psalmodique 4) Caprice à danser: vivo capricioso •SATB •CBDM

BERNINGER, Hans
Musicien allemand.
Saxophon-Übungen (1933) •Hof

BERNSTEIN, Leonard (1918-1991)
America (WHITE) •8 Sx: SnoSAATTBCBs
West Side Story: America (DÖMÖTÖR) •SATB •KuD
West Side Story (Excerpts) (MAEDA) •19 Sx

BERRY, Hans
Tocsani Melody •SATB
Valse Lilibet •SATB

BERTAIN, Jules
Mazurka pastorale (1900) •Cl or Ssx/Military Orch or Pno

BERTAINA, Pier Michele (1951)
Compositeur italien.
5 Pezzi per quartetto d'ance (1988) (to Quart. d'Ance Italiano)
  1) Allegro ritmico 2) Movenze vibranti 3) Volante 4) Pulzar 5) Introduzione/Valzer •Ob/Cl/Asx/Bsn
Gnomus •SATB
Jongleurs (1990) (11') (to Quat. Aquilano) •SATB

BERTHELEMY, Norbert (1908)
Compositeur français, né à St-Omer, le 25 VIII 1908. Travailla avec Caussade et Pech.
Rondo pour rire (2') •2Cl/Tsx •Bil

BERTHELOT, René (1903)
Compositeur et directeur de conservatoire français, né à Orléans, le 11 I 1903. Travailla avec Mariotte.
Adage et Arabesque (1972) (4') (to G. BORDIER) •Asx/Pno •Led
Un Air triste, un air gai... (1982) (3') •Asx/Pno •Led
En Berçant l'ourson (1984) (1'45) •Asx/Pno •Lem
Le Roi Renaud (1974) (2'30) •Asx/Pno •Led
Siciliana malinconia (1984) (4'30) •Asx/Pno •Lem

BERTHOMIEU, Marc (1906-1991)
Compositeur français, né à Marseille. Travailla avec H. Busser.
Rondo (from *Suite brève*) (LETELLIER) •SATB •Elk
Suite brève (1958) 1) Bucolique 2) Gavotte 3) Forlane 4) Menuet 5) Rondo •Asx/Pno •Lem
Volubilis •Asx/Pno •Com

BERTOCCHI, Serge (1961)
Saxophoniste français, né le 24 IX 1961 à Albertville. Travailla avec J. Net et D. Deffayet.
Axolotl (1987) (4') •Ssx/Synth
Quatrième méridien (1986) (5') •SATB
Sphéroïde (1989) (6') •Sx Ensemble

BERTOMEU, Agustin
Compositeur espagnol.
Cuarteto romantico (1990) (to M. MIJAN) •SATB

BERTOUILLE, Gérard (1898)
Compositeur belge, né à Tournai, le 26 V 1898. Travailla avec Fr. de Bourguignon et J. Absil.
"Sa musique sans être classiquement tonale n'a rien de l'atonalité absolue. Gérard Bertouille reste avant tout un mélodiste." (E. MOUSSET)
"In his music he occupies a moderate position, writing in a contem-

porary idiom avoiding the extremes of modernism." (BAKER) "His melodically expressive music is cast in conventional forms." (H. VANHULST)
Prélude et Fugue (1955) (4') •SATB •CBDM
Trio (1955) (4') •3 Sx: SAB •CBDM

BERWALD, Franz (1796-1868)
Hymn (c. 1845) (HARTLEY) •Sx Ensemble: SAATBBs •Eth

BESOZZI, Jerome (1704-1778)
Sonata •Tsx/Pno

BESTOR, Charles (1924)
Compositeur américain.
Suite (1982) (to L. KLOCK) 1) Prelude 2) Chaconne 3) Moto perpetuo 4) Aubade 5) Scherzo 6) Postlude •Asx/Perc •DP

BESWICK, Aubrey
Six for Sax (1986) •Asx/Pno •Uni

BETTA, Marco
Compositeur italien, né en Sicile.
Mirrors •SATB

BETTARINI, Luciano (1914)
Compositeur italien.
Sonata (1959) •SATB

BETTS, Lorne (1918)
Compositeur canadien.
Concertino (1972) (to P. BRODIE) •Ssx/Orch (2020/2000/Perc/Harp/Str) •CMC

BEUGER, Antoine
Compositeur allemand.
Things taking place (1993) •Bsx/Bass •INM

BEUGNIOT, Jean-Pierre (1935)
Compositeur français, né à Bordeaux, le 27 IV 1935. Travailla avec R. Gayral, R. Gendreu, T. Aubin, et H. Sauguet.
Anamorphose (1976) (11') (to J-M. LONDEIX) •Ob/Hn/Bsx •adr
Omenage (to Fr. MISTRAL) (5'30) •Ssx/Org •adr
Pièces en Quatuor (1970) (11'30) (to Quat. J. Desloges)
  1) Dynamico 2) Martial 3) Andante 4) Final •SATB •EFM
Sonate (1975) (14') (to D. DEFFAYET) •Asx/Pno •Bil

BEURDEN, Bernard van (1933)
Compositeur hollandais.
Psychophony (1979) (to J. BOK) •SATB •Don
Triptyque (to H. BOK) •Asx/Pno

BEURLE, Jürgen (1943)
Variable Realisationen (1967) •Voice/Chamber Ensemble/Chamber Choir •EMod

BEVERIDGE, Thomas
Alborada (1980) (to G. WOLFE) •Asx/Pno

BEVELANDER, Brian
Compositeur américain.
Sonata •Asx/Pno •WWS
Synthecisms (1988) (to J. MURPHY) •1 Sx: S+A/Tape

BEVIN, Elway
Browning (RIPPE) •3 Sx: ATB •DP

BEYDTS, Louis (1895-1953)
Compositeur et chef d'orchestre français, né à Bordeaux, le 29 VI 1895, où il est mort, le 15 IX 1953. Travailla avec J-F. Vaubourgoin.

"Musicien délicat, héritier de Messager et de R. Hahn, utilise un langage à l'élégance harmonique toute fauréenne." (N. Dufourcq)

"His songs are delightful and gain enormously in atmosphere by the delicacy of their harmony, a trait which is equally characteristic of Beydt's orchestration of works by Duparc, Debussy, and Pierne." (G. Samazeuilh)

Romanesque (1935) (3') (to M. Mule) •Asx/Pno •Led

BEYER, Frank Michael (1928)

Compositeur, organiste, et pianiste allemand, né à Berlin, le 8 III 1928. Travailla en France.

Sanctus (1989) (12') •SATB •adr

BEYTELMAN, Gustavo

Compositeur sud-américain.

Jardin mélancolique (1990) (8') (to J-P. Baraglioli) •Asx Solo
Momentos (to Quatuor G. Pierné) •SATB

BEZOZZI, Alessandro (1702-1793)

Sonata II (1754) (Matzke) 1) Allegro 2) Andante 3) Allegro •Asx/Pno •adr

BIALAS, Günter (1907)

Compositeur allemand à Bielschowitz (Hte-Silésie), le 19 VII 1907. Travailla avec F. Lubrich et P. Hindemith.

"Il s'est intéressé aux techniques primitives, aux modes, enfin à la technique des douze sons, tout en recherchant une plus grande expression." (Bordas)

"Bialas' aesthetic view combines conservative tendencies with a discreet propensity for change, and his work of successive periods reveals a constant progress. After 1970, when any kind of predetermined structure became suspect in his view, he developed a manner based on organic combinations of timbres." (W. Brennecke)

6 Bagatellen (1985/86) (14') (for Rascher Quartet) •SATB •GrB

BIALOVSKY, Marshall (1923)

Compositeur américain, né à Clèveland, le 30 X 1923. Travailla avec R. Harris, E. Bacon, et L. Dallapiccola.

Fantasy Scherzo •Asx/Pno •WIM

BIANCHINI, Laura (1954)

Compositeur italien, né à Trevi nel Lazio. Travailla avec G. Bizzi et M. Lupone.

NO.DI - Note differenze (1987/88) (10') (to E. Filippetti) •1 Sx (S+A+T)/Computer "Fly" •adr
Tra le voci (1990) (15') (to Quat. Aquilano) •SATB/Tape •adr

BIANCHINI, Riccardo (1946)

Compositeur italien. Travailla avec B. Canino, A. Paccagnini ainsi qu'à l'Ingegneria al Politecnico de Milan.

Alberi (1990) (to Quat. Aquilano) •SATB

BIBER, Heinrich-Franz von (1644-1704)

Battalia (Londeix) •9 Sx: SSAAATTBB

BICHON, Serge (1935)

Saxophoniste français, professeur au Conservatoire Régional de Lyon.

Gammes pour tous (1977) •Chou
Jouons du saxophone (1969) •Chou

BIELAWA, Bruce

Compositeur américain.

Extended Dance Suite (1993) •4 Sx •INM

BIELER, Helmut (1940)

Professeur et compositeur allemand.

Fantasie (1987) (12') (to G. Priesner) •Asx/Org •adr

Reprisen (1982) (12') (to G. Priesner) •Asx/Perc/Pno •adr
Sounding Colours (1985) (to G. Priesner) •SATB •adr

BIENVENU, Lily (1920)

Compositeur français.

"Lily Bienvenu chez qui on discerne une certaine influence de Messiaen, qui s'exerce peut-être davantage sur le plan du climat spirituel que sur celui de la technique." (R. Bernard)

Symphonie concertante •Asx/Orch •adr

BIESEMANS, Janpieter (1939)

Compositeur belge.

Why not, Hans! (1990) (9') •Asx/Pno

BIGAGLIA, Diogeno (18th century)

Allegro (Londeix) •Bb Sx/Pno •Lem
Andante (Londeix) •Bb Sx/Pno •Lem

BIGOT, Eugène (1888-1965)

Chef d'orchestre et compositeur français, né à Rennes, le 2 II 1888, mort à Paris, le 17 VII 1965. Travailla avec Gedalge, Vidal, et X. Leroux.

"His work is chiefly remarkable for elegance of style and excellent workmanship." (F. Rizzelli)

Carillon et Bourdon •Tuba/Tsx/Pno
Prélude et Danses (1961) (10') (to M. Mule) •Asx/Orch or Pno •Led

BIGOT, Pierre

Sicilienne •Eb Sx or Bb Sx/Pno •Mar

BILIK, Jerry (1933)

Concertino (1973) (11') (to L. Teal) 1) Prelude 2) Ostinato 3) Song 4) Minuetto 5) Finale •Asx/Orch or Band or Pno •CL

BILLAULT

Grand solo de concert •Asx/Pno •Mar

BILOTTI, Anton (1906-1963)

Compositeur et pianiste américain, né à New York, le 17 I 1906, où il est mort, le 10 XI 1963. Travailla avec Busoni puis avec M. Ravel.

Sonata (1939) (to Winthrop & Palmer & C. Leeson) 1) Maestoso 2) Lento 3) Allegro non troppo 4) Allegro •Asx/Pno •Pres
Concerto •Asx/Orch

BINEGGER, Thomas

Compositeur allemand.

Phoenix (1993) •Tsx/Pno •INM

BINET, Jean (1893-1960)

Compositeur suisse, né à Genève, le 17 X 1893, mort à Trélex, le 24 II 1960. Travailla avec J. Dalcroze et E. Bloch.

"Répugnant aux contrastes violents, son harmonie, souvent subtile, est toujours guidée par des affinités tonales." (Bordas) "C'est un néo-classique qui écrit avec une élégance traditionnelle et qui a tout à la fois le sens du divertissement et de l'élégie." (Cl. Rostand)

"His works are inspired by the French spirit, full of fancy and delicate poetry. Without ever being superficial, he avoids what is heavily problematic and expresses himself with grace, often playfully; yet his music is by no means devoid of feeling and profundity." (P. Glanville-Hicks)

Pièce (1941) (3') •Asx/Pno

BINGE, Ronald (1910-1979)

Compositeur anglais, né à Derby, le 15 VII 1910, mort à Ringwood, le 6 IX 1979.

"Musicien et auteur de musique de théâtre, de café et de danse, il composa de nombreuses musiques de film."

Concerto (1956) (14') 1) Allegro spiritoso 2) Romance : Andante espressivo 3) Rondo: Allegro giocoso •Asx/Orch or Pno •IAC
Romance (from *Concerto*) •Asx/Band or Pno •MMC

BINNEY, Oliver Corcoran (1928)
Compositeur américain né le 12 V 1928, à New York. Travailla avec K.G. Roger.
Concert Suite (1964) (10') •Asx/Str Orch •adr

BIRD, Hubert
Compositeur américain.
Sonata (1987) (to M. BERNANDO) •Asx/Pno •HB

BIRKNER, Rudolf (1909)
Compositeur autrichien.
Pastorale und Fughetta (1992) •4 Sx: SATB/Org

BIRTWISTLE, Harrison (1934)
Compositeur anglais né à Accrington, le 15 VII 1934. Travailla aux U.S.A.
"La référence historique joue un rôle de tout premier plan chez les compositeurs anglais, tels Harrison Birtwistle mais leur appréhension du passé semble se rapprocher davantage d'une vision nostalgique d'un âge d'or à jamais éteint que résulter d'un souci d'entrer en tension, aujourd'hui, avec une forme musicale d'autrefois." (D. J-Y. BOSSEUR) "Harrison Birtwistle s'oriente vers un 'théâtre musical' où le son, le texte et le geste s'intègrent parfaitement. Pour lui, la salle de concerts est essentiellement un théâtre où solistes et choeurs font des déclarations, se défient mutuellement, se rejoignent, ce qui débouche parfois sur une action formalisée." (P. GRIFFITHS) "Initialement sensible à l'influence de Stravinsky, Varèse, et Webern, expert en musique médiévale, il occupe une position à part au sein de la musique anglaise. Attentif à l'aspect empirique des nouvelles expériences, il a été le premier dans son pays à se dégager réellement d'une tradition 'post-romantique'—issue d'Elgar—ou 'néo-classique.' " "Clarinettiste de formation, Birtwistle se consacre à son activité d'instrumentiste, conjointement à l'enseignement qu'il pratique régulièrement à partir de 1962. Birtwistle est d'abord marqué par l'influence de Stravinsky, Varèse et, indirectement, Messiaen. Comme ses condisciples au Royal Manchester College of Music, Birtwistle a très tôt manifesté son attirance pour les techniques d'écriture médiévales, qu'il utilisera à plusieurs reprises. Ce trait essentiel de sa personnalité musicale, qui n'a fait que se confirmer depuis, est à mettre en relation avec son goût pour élaborer une oeuvre à partir d'un élément mélodique qui fournira la base du travail compositionnel. Certains de ses biographes ont insisté sur la dimension 'allégorique' de sa musique dans la mesure où, de la majeure partie des ses oeuvres, découle une signification spirituelle ou psychologique." (A. POIRIER)
"At first influenced by Stravinsky, Varèse, Webern, and medieval music, he composed works of stark ritual form and expression. He has gradually developed a more organic technique in which ideas grow and evolve, often from work to work. Much of his music relates to myths of birth (physical or aesthetic), death, and regeneration." (S. WALSH)
Dinah & Nick's Love Song (1972) (5') •3 Sx: SSS/EH/Harp •Uni
Medusa (1969/70/78) •Fl/Cl/Ssx/Pno/Perc/Vln/Vla/Vcl/Tape

BIRUKOFF, Andrei
Compositeur russe.
Concerto (1975) •Asx/Orch

BISCHOF, Rainer
Compositeur autrichien.
Nightwoods •SATB •ECA/ApE

BISSELL, Keith (1912)
Compositeur canadien, né à Meaford (Ontario), en 1912. Travailla avec G. Keetman et C. Orff.

"A commentary on his philosophy of music composition may be indicated by his preferences in composers. High on his list of the legitimate giants of the twentieth century are the names Britten, Bartok, and Stravinsky."
3 Etudes (1972) (to P. BRODIE) 1) Allegro 2) Adagio 3) Moderato-Andante-Allegro •Asx/Pno •CMC

BISSELINK, Piet (1881-19xx)
Compositeur néerlandais.
Izegrim •1 Sx: T or B/Pno •Mol

BITSCH, Marcel (1921)
Compositeur français, né à Paris. Travailla avec N. et J. Gallon puis avec H. Busser. Grand Prix de Rome (1945).
Aubade (1978) (to D. DEFFAYET) •Asx/Pno •Led
Villageoise (1953) •Asx/Pno •Led

BIZET, Georges (1838-1875)
L'Arlésienne (LONDEIX) (25') 1) Prélude 2) Pastorale 3) La Cuisine du Castelet 4) Minuetto 5) Carillon 6) Farandole •12 Sx: SnoSSAAATTTBBBs •Kud
Adagietto (Album) •Bb Sx/Pno •Mus
Adagietto (CAILLIET) •AATB •Bel
Adagietto (MARTIN) •SATB •Mar
Adagio (from *Symphony in C*) •Bb Sx/Pno •Mus
Agnus dei •Asx or Bb Sx/Pno •Mol
Agnus dei •Tsx/Pno •Mus
Aragonaise (from *Carmen*) (Album) •Bb Sx/Pno •Mus
Carmen (Medley) (MULLER) •SATB •GB
Fantaisie sur Carmen (LEROUX) •Asx/Pno •Marg
Farandole de l'Arlésienne (DELAMARRE) •3 or 4 Sx: S (ad lib.) ATB •adr
Intermezzo (GEE) •Asx/Pno •CF
Menuet de l'Arlésienne •Asx or Bb Sx/Pno •Mol
Minuet (BUCHTEL) •Asx or Bb Sx/Pno •Kjos
Prélude (8 *Scènes bohémiennes*) •Asx/Cl •Mol
Quartet de l'Arlésienne (JOHNSON) •AATB •Rub
Romance of Nadir •Asx/Pno •CF
Les Soli de l'Arlésienne (CHARON) •Asx/Pno •Chou
Solo de l'Arlésienne (HUMMEL) •Asx/Pno •Rub
Spanish Serenade (HARVEY) •Asx or Bb Sx/Pno •Ron
Suite from Carmen (RONKIN) 1) Les Toréadors 2) Intermezzo 3) Habañera 4) Aragonaise-Finale •MIDI Wind Controller+Emu Proteus 2 Synth/Pno •adr
Toreador Song •Asx or Bb Sx/Pno •CF

BJORKLUND, Terje (1945)
Compositeur norvégien.
Herbarium : Suite in 5 Movements (1982) •Fl/Ssx/Vln/Hn/Bass/Pno/Perc •NMI

BLAAUW, L.
Ballade •Asx/Pno •Lis/TM
Ballet Scene •Bb Sx/Pno •TM
Concertino •SATB •TM
Humoreske •4 Sx: SATB or SAAT or SATT or SAAB •TM
Nocturne and Humoresque •Asx/Pno •Lis/TM
Quartet •SATB •TM
Romance •SATB •TM
3 Romances •Asx/Pno •Mol/TM
2 Eenvoudige Voordrachtstukken •Bb Sx/Pno •TM
2 Karalterstukken •Bb or Eb Sx/Pno •TM

BLACHER, Boris (1903-1975)
Compositeur allemand, né à Nou-tchouang en Chine, le 19 I 1903, d'origine Balte; mort à Berlin le 30 I 1975. Travailla avec F. E. Koch.

"Les compositions de Blacher se distinguent par leur écriture volontairement concise. On y sent des influences de la musique de jazz." (Bordas) "Brillant, spirituel, son art est strictement objectif, ennemi de la sentimentalité et du romantisme. Comme Stravinsky dont il a profondément subi l'influence, il a pour idéal suprême la clarté et la transparence de la matière musicale. Comme lui, il accorde la prépondérance à l'élément rythmique, l'organisant en un système mathématique très personnel, système dit 'des mètres variables' (des progressions arithmétiques préétablies définissent la structure métrique d'une oeuvre). Par contre, son langage harmonique demeure assez traditionnel et son contrepoint assez simpliste. C'est un linéaire, un dessinateur." (Cl. Rostand) "Il s'est illustré par ses recherches sur le rythme; dès 1950 il prônait le dodécaphonisme; comme déjà Ernst Krenek il s'est rapproché du jazz; il a cherché le renouvellement du langage dans le domaine lyrique." (J. & Br. Massin)

"His music is cast in a terse effective style; he has developed a system of 'variable meters' according to arithmetical progressions with permutations contributing to variety." (Baker's) "His ideal is a sparse, transparent instrumentation with delicately traced and coloured ornamental lines; and his best works are dominated by brightness of tone and an unobtrusive logic that reveals both agility of mind and a sure sense of formal proportioning." (Grove)

Jazz-Koloraturen, op. 1 (1929) 1) Slow fox 2) Allegro molto
    (Charleston tempo) •Soprano Voice/Asx/Bsn •B&B/AMP

BLACKMAN
Sax-Schule

BLAIR, Dean (1932)
Compositeur canadien.
Symphonette for Sotto Voce Saxophones (1990) (For Lyle) 1) Oblation and Priest's Dance 2) Meditations 3) Prayer Wheels
    4) Wind Pantomine and Vision •SATB •CMC

BLAKE, Eubie
Eubie Medley (1982) (M. Albam) (to Amherst Saxophone Quartet)
    •4 Sx: SATB/Orch

BLANC, Jean-Robert (1907)
Compositeur français, né à Bordeaux, le 11 IX 1907. Travailla avec E. Bigot et J. Lefebvre.
Aubade et Impromptu, op. 29 (1956) (4') (to M. Mule) •Asx/Pno
    •Bil

BLANCHARD, Harold
Pimiento (Lindemann) •1 Sx: A or T/Pno •Sal
Quicksilver (Lindemann) •1 Sx: A or T/Pno •Sal
Wistaria (Lindemann) •1 Sx: A or T/Pno •Sal

BLANCHETEAU
Fleur de rosée - air varié, op. 661 (1887) •Asx/Pno

BLANCO, Juan
Compositeur cubain.
Bucolica (H. Angulo) •Ssx/Tape

BLANES, Luis
Compositeur espagnol.
Tres impresiones (1990) •SATB

BLANK, Allan (1925)
Compositeur américain, né à New York, le 27 XII 1925.
"Prevalent in his music are flowing arabesque-like lines producing a sonorous polyphonic blend in which the quality of each instrument or voice remains nevertheless distinct." (E. Barkin)
Around The Turkish Lady (1991) (to R. Dowdy) •Asx Solo •Ron
Concert Duo •Asx/Pno •DP

Music for 3 Players •3 Instruments •ACA
Three Novelties (1971) (to K. Dorn) •Asx Solo •DP

BLANQUER, Amando
Sonatina Jovenivola (1986) (G. Castellano) 1) L'Ocell irisat
    2) Petita egloca 3) Rosa la sinia •Asx/Pno •Piles/AE

BLATNY, Pavel (1931)
Compositeur Tchèque né le 14 IX 1931. Travailla avec Schaefer et Borkovec.
"During the 1960s he began to experiment with serial techniques and then with jazz elements; he is a brilliant improviser, and improvisation plays an important part in certain pieces." (B. Large)
D-E-F-G-A-H-C •Fl/3 Sx: ATB/Pno/Bass/Tpt/Trb •CMIC
Dialogue (1959/64) •Ssx Solo/Jazz Orch •DP
Kreis •SATB
Kruh-Circolo (1982) (5') •SATB •CHF
Pour Ellis (1966) •Tpt/Ssx/Jazz Orch •IMD

BLATT, François-Thadée (1793-1856)
20 Exercises, op. 30 •Cos

BLAVET, Michel (1700-1768)
La Marc-Antoine (Meriot) •Asx/Pno •Phi
Siciliana (Londeix) •Asx/Pno •Lem
Sonata no. 5 (Wolfe) •Ssx/Pno •Ron
Sonatine en Sib (Joosen) •Bb Sx/Pno •Mol

BLEGER, Adolphe (1835-xxxx)
Les Echos de Barcelone •Asx/Pno •Mar
Souvenir de Valence - Air varié •Bb Sx/Pno •Mol
Souvenir de Valence - Duo •2 Bb Sx •Mol

BLEMANT, Louis (1864-1934)
Chef de musique français.
Nouvelle Méthode Pratique (1920) •Led
Sous les sapins •Bsx/Pno •Led
20 Etudes mélodiques (1918) (2 Volumes) •Led

BLEUSE, Marc (1927)
Compositeur français, né à Niort, le 23 II 1927.
Proper (1980) (to J-P. Baraglioli) •Asx/Perc

BLICKHAN, Tim
State of the Art (1977) (to G. Kirck) •Asx Solo •DP
Music for 7 Saxophones (1979) •7 like saxophones •DP

BLIN, Lucien (1906)
Violoncelliste et compositeur français, né au Mans.
Gentiment (to M. Gabillet) •Asx/Pno •Phi
Grupettino •Cl/2 Sx: AT •GD

BLINKO, Timothy
Compositeur anglais.
Sculptures •SATB

BLOCH, André (1873-1960)
Compositeur français, né à Wisembourg, le 18 I 1873; mort à Paris, le 7 VII 1960. Travailla avec E. Guiraud et J. Massenet.
"Certaines de ses pages contiennent une fervente émotion, écrites dans une forme très pure." (P. Pittion) "André Bloch possède un talent souple et fin qui trouve dans le langage le plus classique toutes les ressources nécessaires pour traiter les sujets les plus différents." (E. Vuillermoz)
Goguenardises (1953) (2'30) •Asx/Pno •PN
Les Maisons de l'éternité (1930) (8') •Asx/Pno •Gras

BLOCH, Augustin (1929)

Compositeur polonais, né le 3 VIII 1929, à Grandziadz. Travailla avec F. Raczkowski et T. Szeligowski.
A Due (1984) (7'30) 1) Corale 2) Canto 3) Scherzino 4) Furioso •Asx+BsCl/Vibr+Marimba •PNS
Notes for Saxophone (1980) (6') (to D. Pituch) •Asx Solo

BLOMBERG, Erik (1922)

Compositeur suédois.
Melos (1992) •SATB •SMIC

BLOMENKAMP, Thomas

Compositeur allemand.
Background Music (12') •2 Sx: AT/Perc •Asto
Vier Stücke (13'30) •Asx/Marimba/Tam-tam •Asto

BLOOM, Shirley (1931)

Compositeur américain, né à New York, le 7 III 1931. Travailla avec D. Milhaud, N. Flagello, et E. Tanenbaum.
Suryanamaskar (1971) (10') •Asx/Vcl/Dancer/Chanter •DP

BLUMENTHALER, Volker (1951)

Compositeur allemand, né le 2 I 1951.
Elégie (1981) •Tsx/Bass/Vibr •B&B
Tez Thelon langlo (1993) •Asx/Vibr •INM

BLUMER, Theodor (1881-1964)

Compositeur allemand, né à Dresden, le 24 III 1881, mort à Berlin, le 21 IX 1964.
Zwei Lieder ohne Worte, op. 67 1) Serenade 2) Walzer •Asx/Pno •Zim

BLYTON, Carey (1932)

Compositeur anglais, né à Beckenham (Kent), le 14 III 1932. Travailla avec W. Lovelock.
"Carey Blyton is primarily a miniaturist, composing mostly songs and chamber music. His recent works include several groups of folk song arrangements commissioned for commercial recording educational music."
Dance Variations, op. 73 (1975) (12'30) •SATB •Mau
Flying Birds (Theme and 9 Variations), op. 67 (1972) (8') •SATB •adr
Fugue in G minor (Frescobaldi), op. 62 (4') •SATB •adr
In Memoriam Django Reinhardt, op. 64b (1972) (6'30) (to London Saxophone Quartet) 1) Prelude 2) Blues 3) Dj. Reinhardt's Stomp •SATB •adr
In Memoriam Scott Fitzgerald, op. 60a (1971) (2'30) (to London Saxophone Quartet) •SATB •adr
Market (1964) (30') •Ob/Asx/Harp/Vcl •adr
Mock Joplin, op. 69 (1974) (2') (to J. Houlik) •SATB •Ken
Pantomine, op. 43 (1972) (3'30) 1) Harlequin 2) Columbine 3) Pantaloon •SATB •adr
Patterns, op. 31: Designs (1973) (5'30) 1) Waltz 2) Pastoral 3) The Organ Grinder •SATB •adr
Rainbow Snake - Cantata (1974) •Voices/4 Sx: SATB •BBC
Saxe Blue, op. 65 (1972) (2'30) (to London Saxophone Quartet) •SATB •adr
3 Musical Mishaps, op. 32 (1975) (5') (to London Saxophone Quartet) 1) The 3-stringed diddle 2) The damaged bagpipes 3) The broken pianola •SATB •adr
What then is love?, op. 26c (1972) (6') 1) Western wind, when will thou blow? 2) Telle me where is fancy bred? 3) Stay, o sweet, and do not rise! 4) Love is a sickness full of woes •SATB •adr

BOBILIOV, Leonid

Compositeur russe.

Sons de Forêt (1980) •SATB •ECP

BOCCHERINI, Luigi (1743-1805)

Adagio (Mule) •Asx or Bb Sx/Pno •Led
Menuet •Bb Sx/Pno •CBet
Menuet •Bb Sx/Pno •Mol
Menuet •SATB •Mol
Menuet (Cailliet) •SATB •South
Menuet (Mule) (3') •SATB •Bil
Menuet (Signard) •SATB •Mil

BOCKMAN, R.

Serenade •Asx/Pno

BODA, John (1922)

Opus (1984) (to Rascher Quartet) •SATB
Perambulations •2 Sx: AT/Pno

BODART, Eugen (1905)

Compositeur allemand, né le 8 X 1905 à Kassel.
Concertino (14') •Asx/Orch •Hen
Sonatine (10'30) •Asx/Pno or Orch (2222/2220/Harp/Perc/Str) •Hen

BODEGRAVEN, Paul van

Adventures in Saxophone Playing (1960) •SMP

BODSON, Dominique

Compositeur belge.
Atikte (1992) •Asx/Pno

BOEDJIN, Gérard (1895)

Compositeur hollandais.
Badinage in Een Knollenland, op. 163 (1961) •SATB •Mol

BOEGEN, Bruno

40 Duos (1992) •2 Instruments de même famille •Com

BOELL, Eric

Technique d'improvisation (1984) (2 Volumes) •OM

BOELTER, Karl (1952)

Compositeur américain.
3 Affections (1982) (to B. Foley) 1) Grandeur 2) Réflection 3) Héroïsme •Asx/Pno

BOERLIN, Richard

Elegy (to T. Hegvik) •Asx/Pno •Sha

BOESWILLWALD, Pierre

Compositeur français, professeur d'électro-acoustique.
La vie des Saints aux bars des hôtels - Théâtre musical (1989) (45') •2 Sx: AT/Cl/Tape/Comédienne

BOEUF, Georges (1937)

Compositeur, saxophoniste et professeur français, né à Marseille, le 21 XI 1937. Travailla avec M. Prevot, J. Gabriel-Marie et, le saxophone, avec D. Deffayet. Anime à Marseille, le Groupe de Musique Expérimentale (GMEM).
Em Misma Puerto del Suêno (1971) (10') (to D. Feilane) •Vln/Fl/Cl/Asx •adr
Espace (1979) •Asx/Pno •adr
L'Image poursuivie (1973) (12') (to Quatuor Desloges) •SATB •adr
Parallèles (1967) (12') (to Quatuor Deffayet) 1) Lent 2) Vif •SATB •CANF
Phrases (1975) (15') •Ssx/Tape •adr
Rythmes et Déchiffrage •Mar
Sonate au berceau (1991) (4'30) 1) Allegro à quatre pattes 2) Adagio pour s'endormir 3) Espoir de fugue •3 Identical Sx •Led

Tryptique pour une évasion (1985) (15') (to Saxtuor) •2 Sx/Group of 8 to 14 Sx •adr

BOEUF, Sylvain
8 Thèmes et improvisation •Sal

BOGULAWSKI, Edward (1940)
Compositeur polonais né à Chorzow, le 22 IX 1940. Travailla avec B. Szabelski et R. Haubenstock-Ramati à Vienne.
"He has adopted post-serial methods, and later pieces lean towards a free play of short repeated motifs and quasi-aleatory music." (M. HANUSZEWSKA)
Musica concertante (1988) (to Fr. DANEELS & D. PITUCH) •Asx/Orch •PWM

BOHM, Charles (1844-1920)
Laender •Eb Sx/Pno •CF

BOIËLDIEU, François Adrien (1775-1834)
Le Calife de Bagdad (ROMBY) •Asx/Pno •PB
Souvenir de l'opéra "La Dame Blanche" (W. HEKKER) •SATB or AATB •TM

BOINOT, Rémi
Compositeur français.
Apparcir (1982) •Asx/Pno

BOIS, Rob du (1934)
Compositeur et pianiste néerlandais né le 28 V 1934. Autodidacte.
"His principal influences are Schoenberg and Berg; he also follows the ultra-modern techniques of the cosmopolitan avant-garde." (BAKER's) "His work shows remarkable facility in an adventurous style." (M. STARREVELD-BARTELS)
Brueker Concerto (1968) •4 Sx: SATB/2 Cl/21 Str •Don
The 18th of June •(1978) (12') •SATB •Don
Herman's Hide-Away (1976) •Ssx/Pno •Don
Springtime (1978) •Picc/3 Sx/Hn/2 Tpt/2 Trb/Tuba/Pno •Don
Stuleken (1960) •Fl/Tsx/Vla/Perc •Don
Summer Music (1967) (7'15) (to F. FUKUSHIMA) •Asx/Vln/Vcl •Don

BOISDEFFRE, Charles-Henri René de (1838-1906)
3 Pièces, op. 20 (DAILEY) 1) Mélodie 2) Pièce dans le style ancien 3) Barcarolle •Bb Sx/Pno •GW

BOISMORTIER, Bodin de (1691-1755)
Suite (AREND) •SATB •Mol
2 Sonatas, op. 6 •2 Sx: AA or TT •EK

BOISSELET, Paul (1917)
Compositeur français, né à Bar-St-Martin (Moselle), le 5 VII 1917. Travailla avec H. Forterre et Fl. Schmitt. Auteur d'ouvrages révolutionnaires sur "l'Ars novissima."
"Promoteur d'un nouveau système esthétique musical, Paul Boisselet travaille la masse sonore en utilisant la musique traditionnelle, la musique concrète, le matériau sonore naturel, le matériau électroacoustique dans son Atelier de Composition Musicale." "Le *Quatuor de saxophones* est une oeuvre courte, simple, dynamique. Quelques éléments mélodiques et rythmiques bien dessinés que la mémoire enregistre rapidement sont à la base de ces pages qui n'aspirent qu'à distraire. Paul Boisselet cherche à mettre la musique de chambre à la portée du plus grand nombre, il reste ainsi fidèle aux principes énoncés dans son système esthétique musical." (Le Romantisme Révolutionnaire) "Il y a un curieux mélange d'ironie et de lyrisme, de scepticisme et de passion dans le style de Paul Boisselet qui met une évidente coquetterie à se dérober à toute classification simplificatrice, dût-il déconcerter ses auditeurs jusqu'à se les aliéner." (R. BERNARD)

Quatuor (1946) (12') (to Quatuor de la Garde Républicaine) 1) Allègre 2) Lent 3) Rythmique •SATB •adr

BOITOS, James (1946)
Saxophoniste de jazz américain, né le 1 VII 1946.
Conversations: Lament-Goin' to Charm-Jive Talkin' •Asx/Pno
Song for Nicole •Asx/Pno
Sweet Candy (to Floyd 'Candy' JOHNSON) •Asx/Pno

BOIZARD, Gilles (1933)
Concert (1981) (14') (to A. BOUHEY) •Asx/Vcl/Harp

BOKHOVE, H.
Pro Musica •4 Sx: SATB or SAAT or SATT or SAAB •TM

BOLCOM, William (1938)
Professeur, pianiste, et compositeur américain, né le 26 V 1938 à Seattle. Travailla avec J. Verrall, D. Milhaud, et O. Messiaen.
"Bolcom has also been deeply involved in the ragtime revival: he has recorded piano rags and composed original ones, he has included ragtime moments in larger works." (A. CLARKSON)
A Short Lecture on the Saxophone (1979) (to J. SAMPEN) •Asx+Narr
Lilith (1984) (14'15) (to D. SINTA, J. WYTKO, L. HUNTER & CONNELLY) 1) The Female Demon 2) Succuba 3) Will o'the Wisp 4) Child-Stealer 5) The Night Dance •Asx/Pno •EBMM

BOLDUC, David J.
Saxophoniste et professeur américain.
Complete Course of 12 Lessons in the Art of Playing High Notes (1922)

BOLIART I PONSA, Xavier
Compositeur espagnol, né à Barcelone.
5 X 12 (1993) (12') 1) Amabile 2) Spiritoso 3) Sensible 4) Grazioso 5) Deciso •12 Sx: SnoSSAAATTTBBBs •adr

BOLLING, Claude (1930)
Pianiste et chef d'orchestre de jazz français né le 10 IV 1930.
Un papillon sur l'épaule •Sx/Pno

BOLZONI, Giovanni (1841-1919)
Minuetto (MULE) •SATB •Bil

BOMBARDELLI, Umberto (1954)
Compositeur italien né à Milan, le 21 III 1954. Travailla avec L. Benedetti et P. Molino.
12 Sounds (1988) •12 Sx: SnoSSAAATTTBBBs

BOMBERG, David (1959)
Compositeur américain.
Interactions (1980) •Ssx/Pno •WWS
Music for Nürnberg (1982) •Tsx Solo

BON, André
Fragments (1984) (25') (to D. KIENTZY) •Tsx/2 Harp/Processeur de son numérique

BON, Maarten (1933)
Pianiste et compositeur néerlandais, né à Amsterdam, le 20 VIII 1933. Travailla avec J. Spaanderman, T. Bruins, et K. van Baaren.
Canzon Francese del principe display •SATB •Don

BONA
Rhythmical Articulation Studies •Sch

BOND, C.
I Love You Truly •3 Sx/Pno •Kjos

BOND, Victoria (1949)

Compositeur américain.

Concerto (1993) (to C. Sikes) •Asx/Orch
Ménage à trois •Fl/Asx/Cl •SeMC
Notes from Underground (1985) (to N. Ramsay) •Asx/Pno
Scat (1985) (to N. Ramsay) •Sx/Pno or Guit •SeMC

BONDON, Jacques (1927)

Compositeur français, né à Boulbon, le 6 XII 1927. Travailla avec Ch. Koechlin, J. Rivier, et D. Milhaud.

"L'insolite, le fantastique et le merveilleux sont pour lui des thèmes constants d'inspiration. Novateur dans le domaine des timbres et du coloris orchestral, Bondon a renouvelé le langage et l'écriture impressionnistes." (Bordas) "Son esthétique demeure traditionnelle et sa sensibilité le situe dans la descendance post-romantique." (Cl. Rostand)

"A prolific composer, he has drawn on a wide range of tonal precedents, and also on ideas from science fiction. He was able, without fearing triviality, to write music for the 1968 Winter Olympic Games in Grenoble, matching the setting in the brittle iciness of his orchestration." (P. Griffiths)

Movimenti (1980) (to Quatuor Desloges) 1) Allegro poco vivace 2) Adagio cantabile 3) Allegro deciso •SATB •ME
Sonate à Six (1980) •2 Fl/2 Cl/2 Asx •ME

BONI, Pietro (18th Century)

Largo and Allegro (Voxman) •Asx/Pno •Rub

BONNARD, Alain (1939)

Compositeur français, né à l'Horme (Loire), en 1939. Travailla avec J. Chailley, Challand, Y. Desportes, J. Rueff, et J. Giraudeau.

Bis, op. 42 •Fl/Ob/Cl/Asx •Bil
Da Pacem Domine, op. 67 •Ob/Asx/Vcl •adr
Danse initiatique, op. 84b •Ob/Ssx/Vcl •adr
Double invention et Fugue, op. 18 •SATB •adr
Menuet (1985) (2'45) •4 Sx: AAAA •adr
Quintette (1976) •SATB/Pno •adr
Sonate, op. 1, no. 1 (1954/71) (15') (to S. Bichon) 1) Andante moderato 2) Allegro 3) Recitativo 4) Scherzo •Ssx/Pno •EFM
Sonate, op. 10 •Tsx/Pno •adr
Stochateïs •SATB •adr
Treble, op. 79 (1979) (to S. Bichon) •Ob/Asx/Vcl
Variations sur un chant populaire basque, op. 97 •Ob/Asx/Vcl •adr
Villancico, op. 47 •Ssx/Pno •adr
Virelai en Trio, op. 74 •Ob/Asx/Vcl •Chou

BONNEAU, Paul (1918)

Chef d'orchestre et compositeur français, né à Moret-sur-le-Loing, le 4 IX 1918. Travailla avec H. Busser.

"Paul Bonneau a écrit avec aisance des oeuvres faciles et accessibles à tous." (R. Bernard)

Caprice en forme de valse (1950) (4') (to M. Mule) •Asx Solo •Led
2 Caprices en forme de valse (1950-80) •Asx/Str Orch or Pno (ad lib.) •Led
Concerto (1944) (15'30) (to M. Mule) 1) Allegro 2) Andante 3) Allegro •Asx/Orch (3323/422/Perc/Harp/Str) or Pno •Led
Pièce concertante dans l'esprit jazz (1944) (10') (to M. Mule) •Asx/Orch (2222/333/Perc/Guit/Pno/Str) or Pno •Led
Suite (1944) (7') (to M. Mule) 1) Improvisation 2) Danse des démons 3) Plainte 4) Espièglerie •Asx/Orch (2222/200/Perc/Harp/Str) or Pno •Led

BONTEMPELI, Bruno (1948)

Compositeur et romancier italien.

Jeu d'anches (1979) (to Quatuor Contemporain) •SATB
Quatuor (1979) •SATB

BOOGARD, Bernard van den (1952)

Compositeur et pianiste néerlandais, né à Castricum, le 17 I 1925. Travailla avec P. Schat, H. Dercksen, et T. Leeuw.

Syntetisch Gedicht (1971) (20') •Mezzo Soprano Voice/Asx/BsCl/ Pno •Don
Kwartet (1985) (12') (to Rijnmond Saxo. Kwartet) •SATB •Don

BOONE, Ben

Compositeur américain.

Election Year (1994) (to K. Radnofsky) •Sx Solo: S or A or T or B •INM/adr

BOOREN Jo van den

2 Pièces caractéristiques, op. 84 (1992) (9') •Sx/Tpt/Trb/Perc •Don

BORÄNG, Gunnar (1947)

Compositeur suédois.

Estimerat val (1984) (8') •Ssx/Orch •Tons/Smic

BORBOUSSE, P.

Simple mélodie •1 Sx: A or T/Pno •An

BORCHARD, Adolphe (1882-1967)

Pianiste et compositeur français, né au Havre, le 30 VI 1882, mort à Paris le 13 XII 1967. Travailla avec Diemer et Lenepveu.

Fileuse (to M. Mule) •SATB •adr

BORCK, Edmund von (1906-1944)

Compositeur et chef d'orchestre allemand, né à Breslau, le 22 II 1906, tué en Italie, le 16 II 1944.

"Subit à Berlin, l'influence de P. Hindemith." "Son écriture contrapuntique vise à l'élargissement de la tonalité et recourt souvent à la dissonance, parfois rude, dans un lyrisme expressionniste concentré et puissant." (Larousse)

"His style of composition is neo-classical, with strong contrapuntal structure; the rather austere and reticent mode of expression assume in Borck's music a colorful aspect through a variety of melodic and rhythmic devices, often in a rhapsodically romantic vein." (Baker) "His music has more hardness and less humour than that of Hindemith and is often as massive in harmony as that of Richard Strauss, though more angular; towards the end of his short career it struck out on a line of its own." (H. Strobel)

Concerto, op. 6 (1932) (16') (to S. Rascher) 1) Lento-Allegro vivo 2) Adagio 3) Presto •Asx/Orch or Pno •Kal
Introduktion und Capriccio, op. 11 (1934) •Asx/Vln/Pno •IMD

BOREL, René

Compositeur suisse.

Fugato in F (1976) (to Rascher Quartet) •SATB •Bou

BORENSTEIN, Daniel (1956)

Compositeur français.

Eshet-Haïl (1983) (8') (to D. Kientzy) •Tsx Solo •Sal
M-Tango (1982) (6') (to D. Kientzy) •1 Melody Instr/Electr. •Sal

BORESEL, Fedoroff

Method •Pet

BORGHINI, Louis (1874-1933)

Compositeur français.

Romance •Asx/Pno •ES

BORGO, Del (see Del Borgo)

BORGULYA, Andràs (1931)

Burlesque (1966) •Asx/Fanfare

BORIK, Reginald (1960)

Saxophoniste et compositeur américain, né le 7 VI 1960. Travailla avec J-M. Londeix.
Last Dance (1988) •SATB

BORISOV, Lilcho (1925)

Compositeur bulgare.
Concertino (1983) (to O. VRHOVNIK) •Asx/Orch

BÖRJESSON, Lars-Ove (1953)

Compositeur suédois, né à Borlänge, le 18 VII 1953. Autodidacte, il a toutefois travaillé avec M. Makros.
Divertimento, op. 38 (1983) •Asx/BsCl/Bsn/Guit/Harp/Marimba/ Vln/Vcl •STIM
Interparolo III, op. 45 (1986) •Asx/BsCl/Org •SMIC
Sipapu, op. 36 (1983) (16') •Ssx/Orch •STIM

BORMANN, Emile von (1864-1911)

Compositeur allemand.
Frühlingsmärchen •Asx/Pno
Suite im alten Stil •SATB •Fro
Valse Impromptu •Asx/Pno •Fro

BORODIN, Alexandre (1833-1887)

Intermezzo (LONDEIX) •Asx/Pno •Lem
Introduction - Allegro vivo (AREND) •Cl/Asx/Pno •Mol
Peasant's Chorus (4') (MIDDLETON) •Sx Ensemble: SAATTBBs •TTF
Polovetsian Dance (WALTERS) •Asx or Bb Sx/Pno •Rub
Solicitude (MAGANINI) •2 Sx: AT/Pno •Mus

BOROS, Jim

Compositeur américain.
Shreds (1986) •Asx Solo

BORREL, H. (18xx-xxxx)

Chef de musique français, du 66° de ligne.
Au bord de l'eau - Fantaisie variée (1893) •Asx/Pno
Sous les tonnelles - Fantaisie (1893) •Asx/Pno

BORRIS, Siegfried (1906)

Compositeur, musicologue, et professeur allemand, né à Berlin, le 4 XI 1906. Travailla avec P. Hindemith.
"His compositions sometimes bear the influence of Hindemith, but Borris often deliberately cultivates a clearer and simpler style in which folk music plays a role." (G. LOOMIS)
Konzert (1966) (to C. PETERS) •Ssx/Orch or Pno
Sonatina per tre, op. 45/1 •3 Sx: AAA •SV

BORROFF, Edith (1925)

Musicologue américain né à New York, le 2 VIII 1925.
Mottos (1989) •Sx Ensemble
Trio (1982) •Tsx/Pno/Perc
Two Rags From the Old Bag (1989) (to the Empire saxophone Quartet) •SATB

BORSARI, Amédée (1905)

Compositeur français, né à Paris, le 23 XII 1905. Travailla avec V. d'Indy.
"De tendances éclectiques, Amédée Borsari ne refuse pas au besoin, d'écrire des oeuvres directes et qui n'exigent du public aucune compétence spéciale, mais sans se permettre cependant de concessions à la facilité." "Par son style clair et concis, son langage direct, son sobre lyrisme, Borsari s'inscrit dans la tradition française." (Bordas)
Blues (d'après le *1er Concerto pour piano*) (1941) (4') •Asx/Pno •Bil

Concerto (1947) (18') (to G. GOURDET) 1) Allegro 2) Lent 3) Allegro giocoso •Asx/Str Orch or Pno •Bil
Prélude et Choral varié (1943) (to Quatuor Mule) •SATB •Bil

BORSCHEL, E.

Kubanisches Liebeslied •1 Sx: A or T/Orch or Pno •Fro
Pastell •Asx/Pno •Fro
Silberner Mond •Tsx/Pno •Fro

BORSTLAP, Dick (1943)

Compositeur néerlandais, né à Bilthoven, le 3 V 1943. Travailla avec K. van Baaren, D. Raymakers, et H. Kien.
Fanfare II (1975) (6') Fl/Picc/2 Sx: AT/Hn/Tpt/2 Trb/BsTrb/Pno/ Bass •Don
From here to eternity (1966) (6') (to L. OOSTROM & E. BOGAARD) •Sx Solo •Don
Over de verandering en de gelÿkheid (1974) (5') •Fl/Picc/2 Sx: AT/ Hn/Tpt/2 Trb/BsTrb/Pno/Bass •Don
Vrijheidslied (1978) (2') •Picc/3 Sx: SAT/Hn/2 Tpt/2 Trb/Tuba/Pno •Don

BORSODY, Làszlo

Duo (1983) (to BOK & LE MAIR) •Asx/Vibr

BORTOLOTTI, Mauro (1926)

Compositeur italien, né à Narni (Terni), le 26 XI 1926. Travailla avec Caporali, Germani, P. Grossi, et Petrassi.
"In his subsequent concern with total serialism, aleatory processes and electronic music, he has avoided any extreme or dogmatic approach. And the progressively increasing antidiscursiveness of *Studi per trio*, *Studio per E.E. Cummings n° 2*… has not inhibited the urge to communicate which he inherited from the realistic tendencies in postwar Italian culture." (C. ANNIBALDI)
Luogo dell'Incontro 1 (1985/90) •Sx Solo: S+A •adr
Os deuses são felizes (1991) •Asx/Pno •adr
Studio per E.E. Cummings n° 2 (1964) •Vla/Vcl/Bass/Ob/Cl/BsCl/ Sx/Hn/Perc •adr

BÖRTZ, Daniel (1943)

Compositeur suédois, né à Osby (Hässleholm), le 8 VIII 1943. Travailla avec J. Fernström et H. Rosenberg puis avec K-B. Blomdahl et I. Lidholm.
"The wide span of his largest works recalls the music of the high and late Romantic period, and Börtz himself has described the music of Anton Brückner as a source of understanding to him where the essential art of composition is concerned."
Monologhi 7 (1979) (8') (to P. SAVIJOKI) •Asx Solo •SMIC/CG

BOSCH, A. Jr.

Concert Studies •HE
Etude voor Saxofon •Mol

BOSSE, Denis (1956)

Compositeur français, né à Bordeaux. Travailla avec M. Fusté-Lambezat.
…d'un léger souffle cosmique (1987) (10') (to J-M. LONDEIX) •Sx Solo: B+A+S/2 Vln/Vla/Vcl/Bass

BOSSERT, Margo

Mystic •Asx/Pno

BOSSEUR Jean-Yves

Ecrivain, musicologue et compositeur français.
43 Miniatures (1992) •Vln/Cl/2 Sx: AB/Harp/Pno/Perc

BOTTENBERG, Wolfgang (1930)

Compositeur canadien d'origine allemande, né à Frankfürt en 1930. Vit au Canada depuis 1958. Travailla avec R. A. Stangeland et T. S.

Huston.
Concertino (1989) •Tsx/Str Orch •CMC
Fa-Sol-La-Si-Do-Ré (1972) (21') (to P. Brodie) 1) Ricercare
2) Textures 3) Rondo concertato •Ssx/Str Orch •CMC

BOTTJE, Will Gay (1925)

Compositeur américain, né à Grand Rapids, Michigan, le 30 VI 1925.
Travailla avec N. Boulanger, Giavini, et Badings.
Concertino (1958) (13') •Asx/Str Quartet •Pio
Modalities •AATB/Tape •AMA
Quartet no. 1 (1963) (13') 1) Delicato un poco rubato 2) Leggiero
3) Quietly thoughout 4) Rondo •SATB •Pio/ACF

BOTYAROV, Yergeni

A Merry Rondo •SATB

BOUCHARD, Marcel Alexandre (1892-19xx)

Compositeur français, né à Tarbes, le 24 XII 1892. Travailla avec son
père puis avec D. Fouchet et Pierson.
"Mélodiste, aux tendances bien françaises." (J. P.)
Chant nostalgique (1972) (4') •Asx/Pno •adr
Complainte d'amour (1969) (4') •Asx/Pno •Bil
Miniature (1966) (6'30) 1) Allegro 2) Moderato 3) Minuetto
4) Scherzo •SATB •adr
1er Solo (1941) (5') •Asx/Pno •adr
1ère Sonatine (1964) (8') •Asx/Pno •Mar
Quartet sinfonia (1965) (11'30) (to Chesnel) 1) Allegro non troppo
2) Andante 3) Minuetto 4) Scherzo •SATB •Bil
Rêverie (1974) (4') •Asx/Pno •Bil
Triade (1970) (7'30) 1) Allegro 2) Moderato 3) Andante •Asx/Ob/Cl
•Bil
Vistas de Spana (1971) (8'30) 1) Jota 2) Habanera 3) Danza •SATB
•adr

BOUDREAU, Walter (1943)

Compositeur et saxophoniste canadien.
"Artiste bien engagé dans la musique d'avant-garde de son pays." (R.
Whith)
Le Cercle gnostique IV (1979) (to A. Pelchat) •SATB •CMC
Chaleurs (1985-89) (40') •SATB •CMC
Cocktail music (1984) (to R. Masimo) •Asx/Pno •CMC
Demain les Etoiles (1980) (14') (to J-M. Londeix) •12 Sx:
SnoSSAAATTTBBBs •CMC
Incantations I (1979) (23') •SATB •CMC
L'Odyssée du Soleil II (1979) •SATB •CMC
Variations (1975) •Ssx/Asx+Fl/Tsx+Picc/Tuba/Pno+Celesta/Guit
•CMC

BOUHEY, Alain (1949)

Saxophoniste-interprète, professeur et écrivain français, né à Dijon,
le 16 II 1949. Travailla avec J-M. Londeix, M. Nouaux. Maîtrise
Lettres Modernes.
"Consacre son activité créatrice à la recherche "scriptorale" dont il
est le fondateur: recherche des conditions d'une relation évolutive
entre l'"oral" et le 'script', qu'il redéfinit à sa manière: le premier
représente le 'flash' d'inspiration, et le second en est la réalisation, ou
fixation. Il s'attache en somme à comprendre comment apprendre à
sentir et exprimer toujours mieux et plus, à partir de ce que lui enseigne
la technique saxophonistique."
Improvisations et modes (avec Y. Seffer) (1992) •Sx •Lem

BOUILLAGUET, Gérard

Compositeur français. Travailla avec R. Boutry, A. Challan, et O.
Messiaen.
Quatuor (1973) 1) Allegretto 2) Andantino 3) Prestissimo •SATB

BOUILLON, Pierre (18xx-1883)

L'auriole - Fantaise (1884) •Asx/Pno
Diavolino - Air varié •Asx/Pno •Marg
Dolcissimo - Air varié (1884) •Asx/Pno
L'Oiseau-mouche - Fantaisie variée (1883) Asx/Pno •Marg
Papillons - Fantaisie variée (1885) •Asx/Pno •Mol
La Pluie d'Or - Air varié •Bb Sx/Pno •Mol

BOURDIN, François

Compositeur français.
Choral en canon (2') (to M. Jézouin) •Ob/Asx (or Tsx)/Vcl/Bass
Fugue (1983) (2') (to M. Jézouin) •Asx/Ob
Quatuor (1985) (to M. Jézouin) •SATB
Rêverie (1984) (to M. Jézouin) •Fl/Asx/Pno

BOURGEOIS, César (1870-1950)

Chef de musique français.
Rêverie, Introduction, et Andante •Asx/Pno •Bes

BOURGUIGNON, Francis de (1890-1961)

Pianiste et compositeur belge, né à Bruxelles, le 28 V 1890, où il est
mort, le 11 IV 1961. Travailla avec E. Tinet et P. Gilson. Membre du
groupe des 'Synthétistes.'
"De Bourguignon ne recherche jamais l'effet, et exprime avec
simplicité et pondération, mais non sans accent, des idées musicales
clairement délimitées." (R. Bernard) "Son style est clair, vivant et
raffiné à la fois, auquel l'exemple de Ravel n'est pas étranger." (H.
Halbreich) "Il se manifesta dans un style éclectique et néo-classique
agréable et pittoresque." (Cl. Rostand)
"After 1937 he composed in a neo-classical style, often writing
fugally though retaining the lyrical quality of his music." (H. Vanhulst)
Prélude et Ronde, op. 72 (1941) (5') •Asx/Pno •Ger/An

BOURLAND, Roger

Double Concerto ("Far in the Night") (1983) (11') (to K.
Radnofsky) •Ssx/Bsn/Str/Harp •ECS
Fire From Fire •Ssx Solo •ECS
Minstrel (1982) •Asx/Orch
Quintet (1985) (15') (to K. Radnofsky) •Ssx/Str Quartet •ECS
Stone Quartet (to R. Stone) •Ssx/Vla/Vcl/Pno •ECS
Three Dark Paintings (to K. Radnofsky) •Ssx/Vla/Vcl •ECS

BOURNE - LEIDZEN

Bourne Trio Album •3 Sx: AAT •Bou

BOURNONVILLE, Armand

Danse pour Katia (Gee) •Asx/Pno •South

BOURQUE, Pierre

Saxophoniste et compositeur canadien.
Quatuor (1970) (41') •SATB •CMC

BOURREL, Yvon (1932)

Compositeur français, né à Vendegies-sur-Ecaillon (Nord), le 3 XII
1932. Travailla avec S. Ple-Caussade, J. Rivier, et D. Milhaud.
Sonate, op. 18 (1964) (14') (to Gourdet-Mellinger) 1) Modéré
2) Trés vif 3) "In memoriam" 4) Animé •Asx/Pno •Bil

BOUSSAGOL, Emile (1854-1917)

Harpiste et chef d'orchestre français, né le 30 XII 1854, mort le 2 XI
1917.
Duo •Asx/Cl

BOUTIN, Pierre

Berceuse (1985) •Asx/Pno •Com

BOUTRY, Roger (1932)

Compositeur, pianiste et chef d'orchestre français, né à Paris, le 27

II 1932. Travailla avec N. Boulanger, T. Aubin, et H. Challan.

"Il compose des oeuvres d'une facture traditionnelle teintée de debussysme et de ravélisme, et indiquant ainsi l'admiration que l'auteur porte à Prokofiev et à Bartok." (Cl. ROSTAND) *"Sérénade pour Saxophone et Orchestre* partition vivante et gaie, saine où aucune concession n'est faite au mauvais goût et à la facilité. Cet ouvrage est en réalité un véritable concerto dont l'expression est très directe et qui n'a d'autre but—hormis celui de réserver au virtuose les possibilités d'exploits instrumentaux peu courants—que de créer un climat de bonne humeur tout à fait tonifiant."

His music is deeply influenced by Debussy and Ravel, and is notable for its uncommonly expressive melody." (A. GIRARDOT)

Alternances (1974) •SATB/Orch or Band •adr
Cadence et mouvement (to D. DEFFAYET) •Asx/Pno
Divertimento (1964) (9') (to M. MULE) 1) Allegro non troppo
    2) Andante 3) Presto •Asx/Str Orch or Pno •Led
Improvisations (1978) •SATB •adr
Prélude Danse (2') ("Panorama" Recueil 2) •Asx/Pno •Bil
Rapsodie pour piano et ensemble à vent (14') •2 Fl/2 Cl/3 Sx: SAT/
    2 Hn/3 Tpt/3 Trb/Tuba •adr
Sérénade (1961) (14') (to M. MULE) 1) Introduction et cadence
    2) Divertissement 3) Sérénade 4) Final •Asx/Orch (111/110/
    Pno/Str) or Pno •Sal

BOUVARD, Jean (1905)

Organiste et compositeur français, né à Lyon, le 29 IX 1905. Travailla avec Fl. Schmitt, P. Dukas, V. d'Indy, et M. Dupre.

Adagio et ronde populaire (1970) •Asx/Pno •Bil
Andantino (1976) (to S. BICHON) •Asx/Org •adr
Bagatelle (1973) (2'15) •Asx/Pno •Mar
Chanson à danser du Vivarois •3 Sx: AAA or TTT •adr
13 Chansons et danses populaires étrangères (Allemagne - Bohème -
    Corinthie - Espagne - Haute - Autriche - Irlande - Italie - Souale
    -Thuringe) •2 Sx: AA or TT •adr
Chant élégiaque et final (1976) (2'45) •Asx/Pno •Bil
Choral dialogue •3 Fl/3 Cl/3 Asx •adr
Choral varié •Ob/Cl/Asx/Bsn •adr
3 Danceries (1970) (5'30) (to D. DEFFAYET) •3 Sx: AAA or TTT
    •adr
4 Danses (1969) 1) Menuet 2) Sarabande 3) Bourrée 4) Gigue •3 Sx:
    AAA or TTT •Bil
7 Duos faciles •2 Sx: AA or TT •adr
13 Etudes progressives •adr
4 Fabliaux •Ob/Asx/Bsn •adr
3 Images •Fl/Vln/Asx/Pno •Bil
5 Images (1970) (7'30) (to J-M. LONDEIX) 1) Aubade 2) Légende
    3) Marine 4) Eglogue 5) Danse •3 Sx: AAA or TTT •Bil
21 mini duetti sur les chansons populaires françaises (1979) •2 Sx:
    AA or TT •Bil
Noëls (1983) •SATB •Mar
Ouverture dans le style ancien (1971) •3 Sx: AAA or TTT •adr
6 Pages enfantines (1973) •4 Sx: AAAA •adr
3 Paraphrases •Asx/Org •adr
Pastourelle (1984) (2') •Asx/Pno •Bil
Petit concerto (1984) •Asx/Str Quartet •Mar
Petite chanson (1982) •Asx/Pno •Bil
3 Pièces brèves (1972) (to Quatuor d'Anches Français) •Ob/Cl/Asx/
    Bsn •adr
12 Pièces faciles (1970) 1) Joyeuse marche 2) Paysage 3) Le petit
    mousse 4) Feuilles d'automne 5) Carillon 6) Pavane 7) Le jeune
    cavalier 8) La chanson du ruisseau 9) Ronde des enfants
    10) Dans la forêt ensoleillée 11) Vers les cimes du matin 12) La
    fête au hameau •3 Sx: AAA or TTT •Bil
3 Pièces rustiques (1971) (6') (to J-M. LONDEIX) 1) Largo 2) Andante
    3) Vif •Asx/Org •adr

Portraits d'enfants (1973) •4 Sx: AAAA •adr
6 Préludes pour débutants (1973) •4 Sx: AAAA •adr
Rencontre à quatre (1971) •4 Sx: AAAA •Mar
Sonatine en 3 mouvements •Asx/Pno •adr
Suite française (1973) (to Quatuor de Lyon) •SATB •Chou
Suite montagnarde •Ob/Cl/Asx/Bsn •adr
Trio •2 Sx: SB/Pno •adr
Variations sur 4 chansons populaires (1979) •3 Sx: AAA or TTT
    •Mar
Variations sur un thème de Haydn (1978) •3 Sx Soloists/Sx
    Ensemble •adr
Variations sur un thème populaire tchèque •SATB •adr
Variations sur une chanson populaire grecque (1970) (to S. BICHON)
    •3 Sx: AAA or TTT •Bil
Vive Henri IV (4') •6 Sx: AAAATB •adr

BOWLES, Anthony (1931)

Compositeur anglais.
Quartet (1974) (15') (to London Saxophone Quartet) •SATB

BOYCE, William (1710-1779)

Moderato & Larghetto (from *Ode for his Majesty's Birthday*) •Bb
    Sx/Pno •TM

BOYLE, Rory (1951)

Compositeur anglais.
Passacaglia (1975) (3'30) (to London Saxophone Quartet) •SATB

BOZZA, Eugène (1905-1991)

Directeur de conservatoire et compositeur français, né à Nice le 4 IV 1905; mort à Nice, le 28 IX 1991. Travailla avec H. Busser.

Andante et Scherzo (1943) (7') (to Quatuor Mule) •SATB •Led
Aria (d'après le Manuel de la Fantaisie en Fa de J-S. BACH) (1936)
    •Asx/Pno •Led
Le Campanille (1964) (1'15) •Asx/Pno •Led
Chanson à bercer (1964) (2') •Asx/Pno •Led
Concertino (1938) (15') (to M. MULE) 1) Fantasque et léger
    2) Andantino sostenuto 3) Allegro vivo •Asx/Orch (2222/211/
    Perc/Str) or Pno •Led
Diptyque (1970) •Asx/Pno •Led
Divertissement (HITE) •Asx/Pno •South
Etudes caprices (1944) (to M. MULE) •Led
Fantaisie italienne (MULE) •Asx/Pno •Led
Gavotte des Damoiselles (1964) (2') •Asx/Pno •Led
Impromptu et Danse (1954) (4'30) (to M. KOZA) •Asx/Pno •Led
Improvisation et Caprice (d'après BLANCOU) (to M. MULE) •Asx Solo
    •Led
Introduction et Scherzo •SATB
Menuet des Pages (1964) (2'30) •Asx/Pno •Led
Nocturne et danse (1968) (6'30) (to R. DESMONS) •Asx/Pno •Led
Nuages (1946) (to Quatuor Mule) •SATB •Led
Ouverture pour une cérémonie •3 Tpt/4 Sx/3 Trb/BsTrb/Tuba/Perc
    •Led
Parades des Petits soldats (1964) (1') •Asx/Pno •Led
Petite Gavotte (1964) (1'30) •Asx/Pno •Led
Pièce brève (1955) (to M. MULE) •Asx Solo •Led
Prélude et divertissement (1960) (6') •Asx/Pno •Led
Pulcinella et Scaramouche, op. 53 (1944) (to M. MULE) •Asx/Pno
    •Led
Rêve d'enfants (1964) (2') •Asx/Pno •Led
Tarentelle (Final du *Concertino*) (5'30) •Asx/Pno •Led

BRABANT, Eric (1941)

Saxodrome (1982) (22') (to D. KIENTZY) •1 Sx: Sno+S+A+T+B/Tape

BRACHT, Thomas (1957)

Concertino (1982) (15') (to Cl. DELANGLE) •Asx/Str Orch or Pno

BRADY, Timothy (1955)

Compositeur canadien né au Québec.

Sonata (1979) •Asx/Pno •CMC

Unison Rituals (1991) (12') •SATB •CMC

BRAGA, Francisco (1868-1945)

Compositeur brésilien, né le 5 IV 1868 à Rio-de-Janeiro, où il est mort le 14 III 1945. Travailla à Paris avec J. Massenet.

"As a composer he followed late Romantic European models, sometimes taking thematic material from national sources."

Dialogue sonore ao lunar ("Seresta") •Asx/Pno •IMD

BRAGA, Gaetano (1829-1907)

Angel's Serenade •Fl/1 Sx: A or T/Pno •CF

Angel's Serenade •2 Sx: AT/Pno •CF/Cen

Serenata (BRANGA) •Asx/Pno •Dur

BRAHE, May H.

Bless This House (GLENN) •Asx/Pno •B&H

BRAHMS, Johannes (1833-1897)

Célèbre valse (MARTIN) •SATB •Mar

Chant populaire (BAUDRIER) •Bb Sx/Pno •HE/Mol

Chorale Preludes Nos. 3, 6, 8 (CARAVAN) •SAATBBs •Eth

Danse hongroise n° 5 (ROMBY) •Asx/Pno •PB

Famous Waltz, op. 39/15 •2 Sx/Pno •CF

Hungarian Dance No. 1 (TEAL) (Album) •Bb Sx/Pno •GSch

Hungarian Dance No. 5 (DAVIS) •Asx/Pno •Rub

Hungarian Dance No. 5 •Asx/Pno •Rub

Intermezzo in A, op. 118, no. 2 (YOUNG) •Ssx/Pno •Ron

Quintet, op. 88, no. 1 (SIBBING) •5 Sx: SAATB

Sapphic Ode (RASCHER) •Bb Sx/Pno •Bel

Sonata in F minor, op. 120, no. 1 (ROUSSEAU) 1) Allegro appasionato 2) Andante un poco adagio 3) Allegretto grazioso 4) Vivace •Asx/Pno •Eto

Sonata no. 2 in Eb Major, op. 120 (ROUSSEAU) 1) Allegro amabile 2) Andante con moto 3) Allegro non troppo •Asx/Pno •Eto

Sonate en Mib, op. 120, no. 2 (GOURDET) 1) Allegro amabile 2) Andante con moto 3) Allegro non troppo •Asx/Pno •Bil

Valse, op. 39, no. 15 •Asx/Pno •Fro

Variation & Fugue, op. 24 (SCHAEFFER) •9 Sx: SnoSAAATTBBs •DP

Wiegenlied •Asx/Pno •Fro

BRAMUCCI, Rodolfo

Compositeur italien.

Spiel (1992) •SATB

BRANCOUR, René (1862-1948)

Critique musical et compositeur français, né à Paris, le 17 V 1862, où il est mort le 16 XI 1948.

Suite, op. 99 (1923) (to R. BRIARD) 1) Improvisation 2) Pastorale 3) Humoresque •Tsx (in C [en Ut])/Pno •ES

BRÄNDLE

Ganz eintach •Asx/Pno •Fro

March's gut •Asx/Pno •Fro

BRANDMÜLLER, Theo (1948)

Compositeur allemand.

Quatuor - Silhouetten (1987) (13') (to Rascher Quartet) 1) Quasi una melodia 2) Quasi una danza •SATB

BRANDOLICA, Ljubomir (1932)

Compositeur yougoslave, né à Herceg-Hovom, le 19 VIII 1932.

Improvizacija (1959) •Asx Solo •adr

BRANDON, Seymour (1945)

Compositeur américain.

Bachburg Concerto No. 2 (1978) (to Bilger Duo) •Asx/Pno/Orch (2222/4331/Timp/Perc/Str) or Pno •adr

Chaconne and & Variations •Ob/Asx/2 Hn/Trb/Pno •MaPu

Concert Overture •AATB •PA/MaPu

Concerto (to J. HOULIK) •Tsx/Orch or Pno

Conversations (1977) (6'30) (to D. BILGER) •Asx/Pno •MaPu

Introduction and Dance (1969) (to D. & D. BILGER) •Asx/Pno •MaPu

Micro Pieces (1973) (to J. HOULIK) •Tsx Solo •MaPu

BRANT, Henry Dreyfus (1913)

Compositeur américain d'origine canadienne, né à Montréal, le 15 IX 1913. Travailla avec Goldmark, Copland, et Riegger.

"Son étonnante précocité et sa rare fécondité semblent avoir été plutôt préjudiciables à son évolution, comme il advient, hélas! si souvent aux artistes très doués et qui sont victimes de la dangereuse illusion que la création artistique est aisée, et qui ne résolvent pas les problèmes dont ils ne sont pas contraints de prendre conscience." (R. BERNARD) "C'est comme expérimentaliste qu'il convient de le situer dans la musique de notre temps. Il mettait un point d'honneur à n'avoir jamais réalisé deux oeuvres semblables par la technique ou par le style; brassait d'une humeur joyeuse les influences les plus diverses, celle du jazz notamment, dans des pages à la forme volontairement insolite. Intéressé par tous les aspects de la polyphonie, il n'hésite pas à les présenter à travers les combinaisons instrumentales les plus singuliè-res." (A. GAUTHIER) "Henry Brant explore très tôt l'éventualité d'un éclatement de l'espace de jeu réservé aux musiciens, cherchant à abolir la coupure entre espaces de la scène et de la salle, ou bien, en ce qui concerne l'écriture musicale proprement dite, pratique des superposi-tions de tempos d'une complexité inégalée, qui fait surgir l'idée de 'collage' si chère à Charles Ives." (J. & Br. MASSIN)

"In his music, he explores unusual sonorities; has experimented with directional sound, in which the location of the instruments is widely varied in performance; has also written scores for unspecified instru-ments." (BAKER) "Material for large groups is conventionally notated except where rhythmic noncoordination or indefinite vocal pitches require special indications; solo parts are treated similarly, though several have opportunities for virtuoso improvisation." (K. STONE)

Barricades (1961) •Tenor Voice/Ob/Ssx/Cl/Bsn/Trb/Pno/Xylo-phone/Str •adr

Concerto (1941) (20') (to S. RASCHER) •Asx/Orch (2222/0320/Perc/Pno/Harp/Str) or Fl/6 Cl/Tuba/Perc •CFE

Dialogue in the Jungle (1964) (15') •Tenor Voice/Fl/Ob/Cl/Bsx/2 Tpt/Trb/Hn/Tuba •adr

From Bach's Menagerie (1974) •SATB •adr

Millennium •Soprano Voice/10 Tpt/10 Trb/8 Hn/2 Tuba/6 Sx/5 Perc •MCA

Nomads (1974) •3 soloists: Vln/Perc/Sx/Brass Orch •adr

Strength through Joy in Dresden •Ob/Asx/Pno •adr

Underworld (1963) •2 Sx: AB/Orgue à bouche •adr

BRÄU, Albert

Eitelkeit •Asx/Pno •Fro

Episode in Blue •Asx/Pno •Fro

Errinnerung (KLETSCH) •Asx/Pno •Fro

Irrlucht •Asx/Pno •Fro

Karussel (Bravour Polka) •Asx/Pno •Fro

Kleiner Ballett •Asx/Pno •Fro

Kleiner Much •Asx/Pno •Fro

Leibelei •Asx/Pno •Fro
Leichte Kost •Asx/Orch or Pno •Fro
Margit •Asx/Pno •Fro
Mully •Asx/Pno •Fro
Parfum •Asx/Pno •Fro
Regenbogen •Asx/Pno
Saxo Step •Asx/Pno •Fro
Saxophon Akrobatik •Asx/Pno •Fro
Saxophone Groteske •Asx/Pno •Fro
Saxophone Kapriolen •Asx/Pno •Fro
Der Saxophonist im Modernen Tanz-Orchester (1936) •Zim
Schattenspiele •Asx/Pno •Fro
Süsse Träume •Asx/Pno •Fro
Uebermut •Asx/Pno •Fro

BRAUN
2 Grand duos, op. 3 •2 Sx •Cos

BRAUN, R.
An Air from Erin •Fl/3 Cl/2 Sx: AT •Yb
Angevin Carol •Fl/3 Cl/2 Sx: AT •Yb

BRAUNEISS, Leopold
Compositeur autrichien.
2 Inventionen über Dreiklänge (1992) (7') •12 Sx:
　SnoSSAAATTTBBBs •CA

BRAUNFELS, Michael (1917)
Pianiste et compositeur allemand, né à München, le 3 IV 1917. Travailla avec P. Baumgartner.
Encore (1986) (3') •SATB
4 X 4 (1985-86) (19') •SATB

BRAXTON, Anthony (1945)
Compositeur et saxophoniste de jazz américain, né à Chicago, le 4 VI 1945. Travailla avec J. Gell.
"Anthony Braxton tantôt se frotte au ragtime, tantôt écrit de somptueux arrangements pour grand orchestre qui débordent de swing, au sens classique du mot, et tantôt encore se livre à des recherches qui n'ont rien à voir avec le jazz et seraient mieux à leur place dans les ateliers de 'musique contemporaine.' " (J. & B. MASSIN)
"In 1968 Anthony Braxton revealed new structured approaches to what was then called 'New jazz.' In this period he also began to explore new possibilities for solo saxophone, new methods of using mathematics which have come to be called *conceptual math*."
G 10 4 ZI (to F. RWEZKI) •2 Sx: ABs/Perc
RKM (to J. BARR) •Ssx/Vcl
S-37 C-67B (to J. COOPER) •2 Sx: ABs/Perc
W12-B46 (to J. LEE) •Voice/Reeds/BsTrb/Perc

BRAYTON, Dana
Compositeur américain.
Quartet (1992) (for J. SAMPEN) •Sx/Str Trio

BREARD, Robert (1894-19xx)
Compositeur français, né à Rouen. Travailla avec Ch-M. Widor.
10 Etudes de style (1925) •Led
1ère suite (1928) (to V. GUCHTE) 1) Prélude et Cadence 2) Les Rameurs nubiens 3) Allegro finale •Asx/Pno •Led

BREDEMEYER, Reiner (1929)
Compositeur allemand, né à Velez (Columbie) le 2 II 1929. Travailla à Munich avec K. Höller et à Berlin avec Wagner-Regeny.
"Consciously turning against any convention, he writes music that is firmly constructed and well defined in sound, although there is also a certain improvisatory treatment, and a poetic feeling is apparent alongside the aggressiveness." (GROVE)

Sonate •Asx/Pno

BREEDAM, J. van
Ecoutez-moi •1 Sx: A or T/Band •An

BREGENT, Michel-Georges (1948)
Compositeur canadien.
Melorytharmundi (1984) •Fl/Cl/Sx/2 Perc/Pno/Vcl/Guit •CMC
Mitzvot, en vue de l'omniprésence divine (1982) •SATB/Tape

BREHME, Hans Ludwig (1904-1957)
Pianiste et compositeur allemand né à Postdam, le 10 III 1904; mort à Stuttgart, le 10 IX 1957.
"Brehme's compositions stand squarely in the German Romantic mainstream: while his harmony and rhythm show the influence of modern currents, his pieces depend essentially on older models." (W. GUDGER)
Sonata, op. 25 & 60 (1932-57) (to S. RASCHER) •Asx/Pno

BREHU, Jean-Pierre
Compositeur français.
Sonate (1978) (to J-P. MAGNAC) •Asx/Pno

BREILH & DECRUCK (see DECRUCK & BREILH)

BRENET, Thérèse (1935)
Compositeur français.
Calligramme (1982) (16') (to J. CHARLES) •1 Sx: S+A •Bil
Flânerie - Autour d'un Ré (to Mlle. HUGUENIOT) •3 Sx: AAA or AAB •Phi
Gemeaux I & II •SATB or 8 Sx: SSAATTBB •Lem
Incandescence (1984) (8') (to J. LEDIEU) •Bsx/Pno •Lem
Phoenix (1984) (3') (to M. JEZOUIN) •Asx Solo •Lem
Tetrapyle (1978) (19') (to Quatuor Deffayet) 1) Prelude & 1er mouvement - 2° mouvement - Interlude - 3° mouvement - 4° mouvement •SATB/Pno

BRENTA, Gaston (1902-1969)
Compositeur belge, né le 10 VI 1902 à Shaarbeck, près de Bruxelles, où il est mort, le 30 V 1969. Travailla avec P. Gilson. Membre du groupe des 'Synthétistes.'
"D'une facture moderne, ses oeuvres se caractérisent par un grand souci de la ligne mélodique." (N. DUFOURCQ) "Gaston Brenta use volontiers d'harmonie âpres, mais son inspiration ne s'en épanouit pas moins en de grandes mélodies d'un généreux lyrisme." (H. HALBREICH)
"Brenta was a romantic composer, giving pride of place to amply developed and expressive melodic line. He usually employed conventional forms, and his tonal harmony included unexpected use of dissonance." (H. VANHULST)
Adolphe Sax et la facture instrumentale •EPA
Saxiana (1962) (7'30) •Asx/Str Orch/Timb/Pno or Asx/Pno •Led

BRESNICK, Martin
Tent of Miracles •Bsx Solo/3 Bsx

BREVER, Karl Günther
Atonalyse II (1957) •5 Soloists: Tpt/Cl/Vln/Vla/Sx/Str Orch •Led

BREVILLE, Pierre Onfroy de (1861-1949)
Compositeur français, né à Bar-le-Duc, le 21 II 1861, mort à Paris le 23 IX 1949. Travailla avec Th. Dubois et C. Franck.
"Oeuvres nombreuses d'une aimable inspiration, d'une élégante adresse, d'un style parfois un peu efféminé." (N. DUFOURCQ)
"They are all skillfully written, with rhythmic inventiveness, meticulous prosody and sensitivity to the poetry." (M. DEGAL DAITZ)
Prélude, trois interludes et postlude (1946) (To Quatuor de la Garde Républicaine) •SATB

BRIARD, Raymond (18xx-19xx)

Clarinettiste et saxophoniste français soliste à la Garde Républicaine, à l'Opéra et à l'Opéra-comique de Paris.

Méthode pour l'étude de tous les saxophones (1919) •Bil
Pastorale et Tarentelle (193x) •Asx/Pno •Marg

BRIE, Jérôme

"Comme la main gauche de Thelonious Monk" (1994) (10') •12 Sx: SnoSx Solo/SSAAATTTBBBs

BRIEGEL, George F.

Cathedrale echoes •4 Sx: AATB or 2 Sx: AA/Pno •Bri
Soloette •2 Sx: AT/Pno or 3 Sx: AAT/Pno •Bri
3 Stars •3 Sx: AAT/Pno •Bri
Triplets (TUCKER) •3 Sx: AAT or 2 Sx: AT/Pno •Bri

BRIGHT, Greg

Compositeur anglais.

Music of the Maze (10') •6 woodwind instruments •EMIC

BRIGHT, W. W.

Regrets d'amour •Bb Sx/Pno •CF

BRIGGS, Thomas

Compositeur américain.

Festival •Ssx/Marimba •DP
Montage •Asx/Vibr •DP

BRINDEL, Bernard (1912)

Compositeur américain né à Chicago, le 23 IV 1912. Travailla avec P. Held, M. Wald, et I. Levin.

Autumnal Meditation (1938) (to C. LEESON) •Asx/Pno •MCA/Pro
Suite (1938) (17') (to C. LEESON) 1) Andante espressivo 2) Allegro molto 3) Adagio ma non troppo 4) Presto •Asx/Pno •Pres

BRINDUS, Nicolae

Compositeur roumain.

Kitsh II-N (20') (to D. KIENTZY) •1Sx: Sno+S+A+T+B/Tape
Ouvennérode (1991) (12') (to D. KIENTZY) - Théâtre musical •(avec apparition/présence féminine)
Saxonatina (1985) (to Saxtuor) •8 Sx

BRINGS, Allen

Compositeur américain.

Ricercar •Asx Solo •SeMC
Three Fantasies •SATB •SeMC

BRITTEN, Benjamin (1913-1976)

6 Metamorphoses after Ovid, op. 49 (12') •Ob or Sx •B&H

BRIXEL, Eugen (1939)

Compositeur autrichien.

Saxophonissimo (1983) (6'30) (to O. VRHOVNIK) 1) Méditation 2) Exercice •Asx Solo
3 Bagatellen (to O. VRHOVNIK) (1983) •Asx/Pno

BRIZZI, Aldo

D'après une esquisse (1987) (8') (Commande de l'AsSaFra [Commissioned by French Sx Assoc.]) •1 Sx: A+S/Vln/Cl/Pno
De la Transmutazione del Metalli (1983-86) (9') (to D. KIENTZY) •Sx Solo: S+T
Mi ha sefer (12') (to D. KIENTZY) •Tsx/SnoTBs en magnétoph. multipistes or Saxophones/Perc •Sal

BRNCIC, Isaza Gabriel (1942)

Compositeur chilien né à Santiago du Chili, le 16 II 1942. Travailla avec Becerra-Schmidt, Ginastera, Grandini, et Kröpfl.

"He has written works in an aleatory style and has combined electronic sounds with voices and various ensembles." (J. SCHECHTER)

Kientzy - Concert (1989) (12') •Tsx/Tape
Melodies (1987) •Asx
Quodlibet I (1966) •Sx/Vla/Tpt/Electr. Guit/Electr. Org or 2 Asx/Vla/Vibr

BROCKMAN, Jane (1949)

Divergencies (1975) (to S. MAUK) •Fl/Ssx/Pno

BROEGE, Timothy (1947)

Compositeur américain.

Characteristic Suite (Fantasia - Recitative - Aria - Canzona - Trio - German dance - Round - O jigg) •Sx/Pno
9 Arias (1978) (to P. DeLIBERO & M. SMELLIE) •Asx/Pno •DP
Partita IV (1975) (7') 1) Motet 2) Minuet 3) March 4) Tartantella 5) Gymnopédie •5 Sx: SATTB •adr

BROEKHUIJSEN, H.

Glorification •4 Sx: SATB or SAAB •TM
Op de Heide •SATB •TM
'S Morgens Vroeg/Paraphrase •SATB •TM

BROGUE, Roslyn Clara (HENNING) (1919)

Compositeur américaine, née à Chicago, le 16 II 1919. Travailla avec W. Piston.

"Her music follows dodecaphonic precepts." (BAKER)

Equipoise (1971) (10') •Asx/Harp

BRONS, Carel (1931-1981)

Pianiste et compositeur néerlandais né à Groningen, le 1er I 1931.

"Characteristic of his work are rich contrasts and a particular attention to formal structures." (R. STARREVELD)

Ballade '81 (1981) (12') •SATB •Don

BROOKS, E.

The Message (BUCHTEL) •Asx/Pno •Kjos

BROR, Lille

Idea I •4 Sx

BROSH, Thomas (1946)

Saxophoniste et compositeur américain.

Aeolian Suite (1985) (to H. GEE) •Tsx/Tape
Dialogue for Treble Clef Instruments •Several Asx
Misterioso •3 Sx
3 Movements (1985) •Asx Solo
Trio (1967) •3 Sx: AAT

BROTONS, Soler Salvador (1959)

Compositeur espagnol, né à Barcelonne, le 17 VII 1959.

Quinteto de viento (1978) •Fl/Ob/Asx/Hn/Bsn •EMEC
Planyiment, op. 24 (1980) (12'10) 1) Mecanitzacio 2) Clam apressiu 3) Massificacio •SATB

BROTT, Alexander (1915)

Violoniste, chef d'orchestre et compositeur canadien, né à Montréal, le 14 III 1915. Travailla avec McGill.

"Brott's style derives largely from neo-classical contrapuntal procedures, from simple fragmentation to dense mass structures. Generally he uses familiar material in new ways... He has sometimes used a familiar tune in a satirical way (but unlike Ives), or uses folksong material from each main region of Canada." (D. COOPER)

Berceuse (1962) •SATB •CMC

Saxi-Foni-Saties (1972) (16') (to Cl. KIRKLAND-CASGRAIN) 1) Me
  Luhan's Extension (IBM-12-BMI) 2) In nomine (Vestal virgin,
  where is thing sing?) 3) Cortège ivre 4) Aus Gewehr 5) Mein hut
  - "hot-foot" 6) Chez ma tante 7) Pushkin's last Chekov
  8) Marconi's Itch 9) Woman's Lib (la dolce vita) 10) Sum-Mary
  (BMI-12-IBM) •SATB •CMC
7 for seven (1954) (14'30) •Narr/Cl/Asx/Vln/Vla/Vcl/Pno •CMC
Three Acts for Four Sinners (1961) (11') 1) Allegro giocoso
  2) Andante 3) Finale •SATB •CMC

BROUQIERES, Jean
Compositeur français.
Côtes-d'Armor (1992) (3') •1 Sx: A or T/Pno •Mar
Lamentation et Danse (1982) (3'45) •Asx/Pno •Bil
Phonetic (1993) (2') •Asx/Pno •Mar
Songes (1982) •Asx/Pno •Mar

BROUWER, Leo (1939)
Compositeur et guitariste cubain, né à La Havane, le 1er III 1939.
Travailla aux U.S.A. avec Persichetti et Wolpe.
"Brouwer's early works show him as a typical nationalist, drawing
on indigenous materials and dance patterns. Since 1962, however, he
has rapidly adopted the newest avant-garde techniques and has been
open to influence from those Western composers who have visited
Cuba, Nono in 1967 and Henze in 1969-70." (GROVE)
Ludus metallicus (1972) •SATB

BROWN, Anthony
Compositeur américain.
Beyond Oblivion •Asx/Chamber Orch or Tape •SeMC
Interpolations •Asx/Film/Lights •SeMC
Quartet •SATB •SeMC
Quartet No. 2 •SATB/Tape •SeMC
Soundscapes 1 •Asx/Bsn/Tpt/Vln/Voice/Pno/Perc/Tape •SeMC
Soundscapes 3 •Ssx/Tape •SeMC
Surface Textures (1977) •3 Sx: AAT •SeMC

BROWN, Charles (1898-1988)
Violoniste, compositeur et chef d'orchestre français, né à Boulogne-
sur-mer, le 9 IV 1898. Travailla avec G. de Lioncourt et A. Steck.
"Charles Brown s'efforce d'obtenir une variété de moyens aussi
étendue que possible, ayant pour but essentiel la sincérité de l'expression
et la solidité de la forme." "Le Quatuor de saxophone de Charles Brown
est une oeuvre bien construite, agréable à entendre, dont l'écriture est
assez habile pour triompher du danger constitué par la similitude des
timbres." (R. DUMESNIL)
Arlequinade (1969) (7'30) (to M. MULE) •Asx/Pno •Led
Au fil du vent (1963) (3') (to J. et G. BARDIN) •Asx/Pno •Phi
En promenade (3') •Asx/Pno •Lem
Quatuor (1959) (20') (Au Quatuor Mule) 1) Modéré 2) Scherzo
  3) Lent 4) Final •SATB

BROWN, Tom (1882-1950)
Bull Frog Blues (GEE) •SATB or AATB •Ron
Chicken Walk (c. 1913) (2'30) (GEE) •5 Sx: SAATB •Eto

BROWN & SHRIGLEY
Bull Frog Blues (GEE) •SATB or AATB •Ron

BROWN, Earle (1926)
Compositeur américain, né à Lunenberg (Massachusetts), le 26 XII
1926. Etudia les mathématiques. Travailla avec R. Drogue Henning, J.
Cage, et D. Tudor.
"Impliqué dans la génération même de l'oeuvre, l'exécutant doit
mettre tout en mouvement." (E. BROWN) "La notation graphique
représente pour Earle Brown un moyen d'obtenir une non-fixité des
évènements musicaux, et, par suite, des 'improvisations solistes ou

collectives.' " (D. J-Y. BOSSEUR) "Plutôt que s'efforcer de 'conserver'
les caractéristiques d'une oeuvre la notation devrait constituer un
catalyseur pour le jeu musical. C'est pourquoi des compositeurs
comme Earle Brown, ont pu se sentir plus proches, dans leur travail de
notation et de communication avec les interprètes, des pratiques de la
Renaissance ou de l'ère baroque que de celle du Romantisme, qui tend
à sacraliser la création du compositeur." (J. & B. MASSIN) "Earle Brown
qui prend note de ce qu'il appelle 'la fonction créatrice du 'non-
contrôle' dans l'art de Pollock et de Calder, introduit l'indétermination
au niveau de la forme." (P. GRIFFITHS)
"Composer of the avant-garde ... He studied the Schillinger System
and expanded it to include aleatory processes; also devised an optical
system of notation in which pitch, duration and dynamics are indicated
by symbolic ideograms. In his pioneer work *In 25 pages* (1953) he
introduced the concept of 'open end' composition in which the
performer is free to select the order of notated fragments of the piece."
(BAKER'S)
4 Systems unspecified instrumentation (1954) •AMP
Sonata •Asx/Pno •CAP

BROWN, John R. (1947)
Compositeur anglais, né à Bolton, le 7 V 1947.
The Millet of Dee (traditional) •SATB •SM
The Squirrel •SATB •SM

BROWN, Newel Kay (1932)
Compositeur américain né à Salt Lake City. Travailla avec L.
Robertson, B. Rogers, H. Hanson, et W. Barlow.
Déjeuner sur l'herbe (14') •Mezzo Voice/Fl/Sx/Pno •SeMC
Figments •Sx/Tpt/Bsn/Vcl •SeMC
Four Meditations (1982) •Voice/Asx/Perc •DP
Pastorale and Dance •Fl/Cl/Asx/Tpt/Trb •SeMC
Sonata •Asx/Pno •SeMC

BROWN, Rayner
Fugues •SATB •WWS
Sonata (1981) 1) Cadenza 2) March 3) Andante 4) Fugue 5) Dia-
  logue •Asx/Org •WIM
Sonata (1987) 1) Prelude 2) Scherzo 3) Pacato 4) Fugue •Ssx/Org
Suite 1) Prelude 2) Fugue 3) Vexilla Regis 4) Pastorale 5) Scherzo
  6) Postlude •2 Sx: Eb or Bb •WIM

BROWN, Robert
Ken's Patience •Ssx Solo

BROWN, Tony (1950)
Compositeur américain.
Concerto, op. 18 (1968) 1) Moderato - Faster 2) Andante 3) Finale
  •Asx/Orch
Sonata, op. 35 (1968) 1) Fast 2) Slowly 3) Fast •Asx/Pno
Suite, op. 22 (1968) (5'30) 1) Moderately 2) Slowly 3) Moderately
  4) Slow - Quickly •Asx/Pno

BROWNING, Zack
Compositeur américain.
Black Notes (to J. LULLOFF) •Asx/Pno

BRUBECK, Dave (1920)
Pianiste et compositeur de jazz américain, né à Concord (California),
le 6 XII 1920. Travailla avec D. Milhaud et A. Schoenberg.
"He was largely responsible for introducing pieces in non-binary
meters into the jazz repertory, and until the late 1960s his group
featured excellent playing by the alto saxophonist Paul Desmond, who
greatly contributed to the quartet's personality." (J. HOSIASSON)
Blue Rondo A La Turk •Asx

BRUCE, Neely
Analogues (1993) •Sx/Vln

BRUCH, Max
Three Pieces, op. 8 (GEE) •Cl/Sx/Pno •DP

BRUGK, Haus Melchior (1909)
Zum Vortrag •3 Eb or Bb Instruments •PGM

BRÜLL, Ignaz (1846-1907)
Bauerntanz (to KLEMARC) •SATB •TM

BRUN, François-Julien
Chef d'orchestre français.
Fantaisie (Au Quatuor de la Garde Républicaine) •SATB

BRUNARD, Gaston (18xx)
2° Pastorale - Thème varié (1891) •Bb Sx/Pno •Mil
Offertoire •1 Sx: A or T/Org or Pno •Mil

BRUNIAU, Augustin (18xx-19xx)
Fantaisie Tyrolienne •Asx/Pno •Bil
Fantaisie variée •Asx/Pno •Bil
Grande introduction et Polonaise •Asx/Pno •Bil
Sur la montagne - Pastorale •Asx/Pno •Bil
Toi et moi - Fantaisie duo •2 Sx: SA •Bil

BRÜNINGHAUS, Rainer (1949)
Compositeur allemand, né le 21 XI 1949 à Bad Pyrmont.
Minimal-paraphrasen (1990) •2 Sx •B&B

BRUNNER, Hans (1898-1958)
Altiste et compositeur suisse, né à Bâle, le 18 VI 1898.
"A distinguishing characteristic of his work is easy flow and spontaneous musicianship." (von FISCHER)
2 Oeuvres, op. 19 1) Allegro molto vivace - Impetuoso - Adagio 2) Allegro •Asx/Pno
Fantaisie •Asx/Str Orch or Pno •Kneu

BRUNO, Mauro
Trompettiste et compositeur américain, né à Boston (Massachusetts). Travailla avec G. Tremblay.
California Concerto Grosso 1) Allegro 2) Adagio 3) Finale •SATB/ Wind Ensemble
Circus Saxophonius (1990) •15 Sx: SSAAAAAATTTTBBBs
Fancy Flight •SATB
Happy Birthday Adolphe Sax •15 Sx: SSAAAAAATTTTBBBs
The Hitch-Hiker •SATB
Little, op. 1 •SATB
Salutations, Fugue and Finale (5') •SATB
Saxes Strike Up (1990) •15 Sx: SSAAAAAATTTTBBBs
A Short Encore •SATB
Texture & Colors (7'30) •SATB

BUBALO, Rudolph (1927)
Compositeur américain.
Conicality (1977) •SATB
Electrum (1977) (5'45) •Asx/Tape
Organic Concretion (to F. HEMKE) •Asx/Org/Perc/Tape

BUCKINX, Boudewin
Compositeur américain.
Clink of Sounds on Chair •Ssx/Actress •AMP

BUCKLAND, Rob
Irish Air •SATB or AATB •PBP

BUCQUET, P.
1st Suite •2 Sx •Mus
2nd Suite •2 Sx •Mus

BUCZKOWNA, Anna
Hipostaza (1984/85) (15') (to D. KIENTZY) •1 Sx: S+A+T/Fl/Vcl/ Vibr/Soprano Voice

BUDD, Harold (1936)
Compositeur américain, né à Los Angeles, le 24 V 1936. Travailla avec G. Strang, A. de la Vega, et I. Dahl.
"His compositions are mostly for mixed media, some of them modular, capable of being choreographed one into another; some are more verbalizations of the mode of performance in a frequently benumbing stultifying, mesmerizing, or fantastic manner."
Black Flowers (1968) •4 Performers
The Candy Apple Revision (1970) •Sx Solo
Intermission Piece (1968) •Any number of players
September Music (1967) •Any number of players

BUEL, Charles Samuel (Charlie) (1943)
Compositeur américain, né le 3 II 1943, à San Francisco. Travailla avec R. Nixon, H. Onderdonk, R. Erickson, K. Gaburo, et P. Oliveros.
Chimera, Avatars and Beyond (1972) (15-20') •Fl/Ob/2 Sx: AT/Perc •adr
Reflections on Raga Todi (1972) (6') •Asx Solo •adr
37 Dream Flowers (1971-72) (9') •Asx/Bsn/Pno/Electr. Pno/Perc •adr

BUESS, Alex (1954)
Compositeur, saxophoniste italien, né à Cunéo.
Audio konstrukt Arch II (1990) •Asx/Band/Syst. électron.
Hyperbaton (1991) (7') (to S. BERTOCCHI) •4 Sx: TTBB •adr

BUHR, Glenn
Compositeur canadien.
The Ebony Tower (1986) •Asx/Orch (1221/2110/Perc/Pno/Bass) •CMC

BULL, Edward Hagerup (1922)
Compositeur norvégien, né à Bergen, près d'Oslo, le 10 VI 1922. Travailla avec B. Blacher à Berlin, puis à Paris, avec Ch. Koechlin, J. Rivier, et D. Milhaud. Vécu longtemps à Paris.
"Musicien d'une technique solide et d'une personnalité vraiment très attachante, vigoureuse et pleine de fantaisie." (D. MILHAUD) "Un indépendant (et c'est peut-être un trait de sa race). Il laisse parler son coeur au gré de son inspiration, sans s'imposer de directives préétablies, sans se laisser influencer par un mode d'expression particulier ni une tradition quelconque. Le résultat est une musique singulièrement pittoresque et vivante." (HEU)
"He is an independent composer completely uninfluenced by specific traditions and modes of expression, but he has a keen appreciation of all currents and trends of the twentieth century. Complex nuances, rhythms and dynamics characterize his music. He says 'I take care not to obtain my inspiration from today's 'recipe' for musical writing and expression. The dictates of fashion, with all their speculation in 'structure and context' are calculated only to pull the wool over people's eyes.'" (The American Biograph. Instit.)
Concerto, op. 52a (1980) (17') 1) Risoluto 2) Energico 3) Marcato •Asx/Orch (222/220/Harp/Str/Perc) •NMI
Duo concertant, op. 52b (1980) (13') (to H. JEFTA & H. G. ELVING) 1) Risoluto 2) Ernergico 3) Marcato •Asx/Pno •NMI
3 Morceaux brefs, op. 17 (1955) (11'30) 1) Allegretto 2) Andante 3) Allegro molto •Asx/Orch (2222/220/Perc/Harp/Str) or Pno •ET
Perpetuum mobile (1992) (2') •Asx/Pno •adr

Sextuor, op. 31 (1965) (11') (to Sextuor à vent de Dijon) 1) Molto marcato 2) Andante 3) Poco leggiero •Fl/Ob/Cl/Asx/Hn/Bsn •NMI

Sonatine, op. 59-2 (1986) (7'15) •Asx/Pno •adr

BULLARD, Alan
Compositeur anglais.
Circular Melody (1990) •14 Sx
Three Picasso Portraits •SATB

BULOW, Harry T.
Compositeur américain.
Concerto (1985) •Asx/Orch •adr
Crystal Cove •Tpt/3 Sx: AAT/Pno/Bass/Guit/Drums •adr
Elegy •Sx Solo •Sil
Introduction and Allegro •Sx Solo •Sil
Syntax II •Sx Solo •Sil

BUMCKE, Gustav (1876-1963)
Pédagogue, saxophoniste et compositeur allemand, né à Berlin, le 18 VII 1876, mort à Klein Machnow, près Berlin, le 4 VII 1963. Travailla avec Max Bruch. Enseigna au Conservatoire Stern de Berlin.
Burleske, op. 87 (1957) •Asx/Pno
Concertino, op. 95 (1961) •Asx/Chamber Orch (2 Hn/2 Tpt/1 Trb/ Timb/Str) or Wind Ensemble or Pno •R&E
"Der Spaziergang" in 5 Sätzen, op. 22 •Fl/Ob/EH/Cl/Bsn/Hn/ BsTrb/Bsx/Harp
38 Duette, op. 43 •2 Sx •VAB
Elegie •Asx Solo/Orch or Pno
36 Einfache Etüden, op. 43 •VAB
36 Leichte original Etüden, op. 43 •VAB
3 Fantasien, op. 50 (1930/31) 1) Fantasie über das "Wolgalied" 2) Fantasie über "Näher mein Gott zu Dir" 3) Fantasie über das "Polnische Lied" •10 Sx: SnoSAAAATTBBs
4 Fantasien, op. 51 (1931) 1) "Weisst Du wieviel Sternlein" 2) "Ich hatte einst ein schönes Vaterland" 3) "Fahr wohl" 4) "Nun ade" •4 Sx
Grifftabelle für Saxophon •VAB
2 und 3 Humoreske, op. 74 (1944) •4 Sx
Inka - Fantasie, op. 62 •Asx/Orch or Wind Ensemble or Pno
3 Intermezzi, op. 55 1) As-Dur 2) G-Dur 3) H-Dur •Asx/Pno
24 Jazz Etüden, op. 43 (1927) •VAB
"Kaffekränzchen" kleine U-Musik über Töne CAFFEE, op. 78 (1951) •3 Sx
Kleines Trio, op. 96 (1961) •3 Sx
Konzert in F min., op. 57 (22') (1935) 1) Allegro 2) Larghetto 3) Vivace •Asx/Orch (2122/4331/Perc/Perc/Str) •R&E
2 Konzertwalzer, op. 48 (1929) •Asx/Pno or Orch or Wind Ensemble •VAB/Benj
Liedbearbeitung, op. 64 (1937) 1) Die Blümelein sie schlafen 2) Frühmorgens wenn die Hähne 3) Es fiel ein Reif •Voice/Sx/ Pno
3 Lieder für tiefe Stimme, op. 63 1) Inkalied 2) Der Engel 3) Das Alphorn (R. ZIEGLER) •Low Voice (Voix grave)/Asx/Pno
Morceaux instructifs choisis •Asx/Pno •VAB
Notturno, op. 45 •Asx/Harp •R&E
Präludium und Fuge, op. 20 (1903) •Fl/Ob/EH/Sx/Cl/BsCl/2 Bsn/2 Hn
Präludium und Rondo, op. 61 •4 Sx
3 Kleine Präludien, op. 54 (1932) •4 Sx
3 Präludien, op. 7 (1897) •4 Sx
Quartett As-Dur (1902) •4 Sx
Quartett, op. 46 •4 Sx
Quartett, op. 49 (1930) 1) Humoreske 2) Präludium 3) Scherzo •4 Sx •Fro

2 Quartette, op. 23 (1908) 1) Abendgang 2) Elegie ("Klage") •SATB •E&R
2 Quartette über amerikanische Lieder, op. 52 (1931/32) 1) Fantasie über "My old Kentucky Home" 2) Fantasie über "Swannee River" •4 Sx
Quintett "Abendgang und Elegie", op. 23b •Cl/EH/Wald Horn/Bsn/ Bsx
2 Romanzen, op. 44 1) Ges-Dur 2) G-dur •Sx/Pno
Saxophon Schule (1926) •VAB/AMP
2 Saxophon Trios, op. 53 (1931/32) 1) Fantasie über Santa Lucia 2) Fantasie über Schöne Rotraut •3 Sx
Scherzo, op. 67 (1937/38) •Asx Solo/Pno or Harp or Orch or Wind Ensemble
Sextet, op. 19 (1903) •Cl/EH/Wald Horn/BsCl/Sx/Bsn •Diem
Sextuor, op. 20 en Lab •2 Sx: AA/EH/Hn/BsCl/Bsn •VAB
Sonate in B-Moll, op. 68 (1938) 1) Allegro appasionato 2) Sostenuto 3) Allegro molto •Asx/Pno •R&E
45 Studien und Etüden
Suite G Dur "Von Liebe und Tod" Tondichtung, op. 24 1) Begegnung 2) Sehnsucht 3) Erfüllung 4) Eifersucht 5) Herbestentschluss •Tenor voice (in 5)/Fl/Ob/Cl/Bsn/Hn/Bsx/ Harp •VAB
Tägliche, Technische Übungen, op. 43 •VAB
Tonleiter Studien, op. 70 (1943) •VAB
Variations sur "Le beau Danube bleu", op. 56 (1932) •Asx/Orch or Pno
2 Volksliedbearbeitungen für 2 Männerstimmen, op. 58 1) Treue Liebe 2) Das Wandern •Tenor Voice/Baritone Voice/4 Sx
4 Volksliederbearbeitungen, op. 59 1) Das Heideröslein 2) Das Wandern 3) Treue Liebe 4) Schätzle, ruck, ruck, ruck •Soprano Voice/Tenor Voice/Sx/Pno

BUNTON, Eldridge
Alto Mood (1966) (4') •Asx/Band •Ken
Theme from Lushabye •Asx/Band •DP

BUONO, Michel (1899-1951)
Concertino (1942) (11') (to M. PERRIN) •Asx/Orch or Pno

BUOT, Victor (18xx-xxxx)
Chef de musique et compositeur français.
Air varié sur "Le Carnaval de Venise" (1879) •Asx/Pno •ES
Morceau d'élévation (1880) •Asx/Org (or Pno or Harmonie) •ES
Tyrolienne variée (1876) (to L. MAYEUR) •Asx/Pno •ES

BURCH, John Robert
Capriccio (1966) •SATB

BURGERS, Simon (1958)
Compositeur néerlandais.
Trio (1983) (10') •Asx/Vla/Pno •Don

BURGHARDT, Victor
Abendstimmung (1986) •3 Sx •B&B
Divertimento (1986) •3 Sx •B&B
Rigaudon (1986) •3 Sx •B&B

BURGSTALHER
Quartet •4 Sx: AAAA or TTTT

BURKE, John (1951)
Compositeur canadien.
Near Rhymes (1984) (14') •SATB •CMC

BURKHARDT, Joel G.
Chanson (1987) (1'30) •Asx/Pno •South

BURKHOLDER, Reed
Compositeur américain.
Sonata in One Movement (1975) (to B. STANLEY) •Tsx/Pno •DP

BURNETTE, Sonny
Compositeur, saxophoniste, jazzman américain.
Collegiate Edition–Scales and Arpeggios for Saxophone (1994) •adr
Jazz Base Music (1978) •Asx/Pno
Nuage Musique •Asx/Pno •Ron
Stained Glass Window •Asx Solo/Optional Echo Delay •Ron
Winter Wind (1993) •Ssx/Pno •Ron

BURRITT, Lloyd Edmund (1940)
Compositeur canadien, né à Vancouver (British Columbia), le 6 VII 1940.
Crystal Earth (1990) •Soprano Voice/1 Sx: S+A/Pno •CMC
The Electric Chair (1971) (5') •Asx/Actress/Tape •Ken

BURSA, Lech (1904-1961)
Compositeur polonais, né le 26 IV à Krakow où il mort le 18 XI 1961.
Suite, op. 3 (1928) •Vln/Sx/Pno

BURTON, Stephen
Compositeur américain.
Rhapsody (1976) (to M. SIGMON) •Asx/Pno

BUSCH, Adolph (1891-1952)
Violoniste et compositeur américain d'origine allemande, né à Siegen (Westphalie), le 8 VIII 1891, mort à Guilford (Vermont), le 9 VI 1952. Vivait aux U.S.A. depuis 1939.
"As a composer Busch was at first closely allied to M. Reger, but later he achieved a free and more personal style." (H. COLLER) "His compositions, rarely performed, show the influence of Reger." (R. PHILIP)
Nocturne, op. 58a (1932) •Asx/Orch (1011/200/Harp/Org/Str) or Pno •Pet
Quintett, op. 24 (1927-28) 1) Vivace, ma non troppo 2) Scherzo 3) Andante sostenuto 4) Vivacissimo •Asx/Str Quartet •HD/Tong
Quintette Es-Dur, op.34 (1925) (20'15) 1) Vivace ma non troppo 2) Scherzo: Allegro vivo 3) Andante sostenuto •Asx/Str Quartet •PJT
Suite (1926) 1) Praeludium 2) Sarabande 3) Gavotte 4) Gigue •Vln/Asx •AmV

BUSCH, Carl (1862-1943)
Compositeur danois, né à Bjerre, le 29 III 1862, mort à Kansas City (U.S.A.), le 19 XII 1943. Travailla avec Hartmann et Gade.
Valse élégiaque (1933) (to B. HENTON) •Asx/Pno •Wit

BUSCHMANN, Rainer Glen (1928)
Compositeur allemand.
Tenor Talen (1965) (15') •Tsx/Orch (2222/1311/4 Perc) •Br&Ha
Quartett n°1 1) Obstler 2) Ruländer 3) Kuckuck 4) Pils time •SATB

BUSSER, Henri (1872-1973)
Compositeur chef d'orchestre et pédagogue français, né à Toulouse, le 16 I 1872, mort à Paris le 30 XII 1973. Travailla avec C. Franck, Ch-M. Widor, E. Guiraud, et Ch. Gounod.
"Disciple préféré de Gounod, Busser doit à son maître l'orientation de son lyrisme essentiellement élégiaque et mélodique." (R. BERNARD) ' "Style académique' et assez peu personnel." (Cl. ROSTAND)
"His musical activity displayed itself in works of varying styles, in which he appears wholly at ease." (M. PEREYRA) "His pieces are sophisticated in orchestration and accomplished in craftsmanship; although there is sometimes an indebtedness to Debussy, Busser remained faithful to the French 19th-century tradition." (A. HOEREE)
Aragon, op. 91(MULE) •Asx/Pno •Led

Asturias, op. 84 (MULE) •Asx/Pno •Led
Au pays de Léon et de Salamanque, op. 116 (1943) (4'30) (to M. MULE) •Asx/Orch (2222/220/Perc/Harp/Str) or Pno •Led
12 Etudes mélodique (PAQUOT) •Asx/Pno •Led

BUSSEUIL, Patrick (1956)
Compositeur français, né à Lyon. 1er Prix du Concours de composition Marcel Josse (1981).
Arêne (1985) (to Cl. DELANGLE) •Asx/Pno
Light Shade (1985) •Asx/3 Cymb.
Musiques pour illustrer la chute d'Icare •Asx/Pno
Trans (1982) •8 Sx: SSAATTBB
Trio - Inertie (1981) •Ob/Asx/Vcl

BUSSOTTI, Sylvano (1931)
Compositeur, peintre, cinéaste, directeur d'Opéra, metteur en scène et décorateur italien, né le 1er X 1931, à Florence. Travailla avec Dallapiccola, M. Deutsch et subit l'influence de P. Boulez et J. Cage.
"La seule façon de sauver l'art est de le pousser au paroxysme. En face d'un mécanisme qui annule tout et sous lequel suffoque la grande majorité des hommes, le devoir de l'artiste est de tendre vers la complexité." (S. BUSSOTTI) "Son style se cherche depuis le début, mais témoigne de dons incontestables, fréquemment sur la pente du néo-dadaïsme, qui le conduira à ses expériences de 'théâtre total' et de 'théâtre musical', à mi-chemin entre le concert et le spectacle." (Cl. ROSTAND) "Bussotti est de ces trublions qui ont subverti le dogme post-sériel en y introduisant une dimension fortement théâtrale, sinon totalement baroque. Sa musique brasse toutes les formes d'expression, convoque les compositeurs du passé, multiplie les références littéraires, fait place à l'expérimentation, et n'hésite pas à parler à la première personne, non sans narcissisme." (J-E. FOUSNAQUER)
"A man of, at once, glaring decadence and discerning modernism, he is the most many-sided and controversial Italian composer of his generation." (Cl. ANNIBALDI)
1) Concerto a L'Aquila 2)Ballerina Gialla e Pettirosso (1986) •(variabl.) 1) Ensemble 2) Sx Solo •Ric
Trio "Voliera" (1992) (12') (to G. ANTONGIROLAMI) •Fl+Picc/Asx/Pno

BUTTERFIELD, N.
When you and I were young •2 Sx: AT/Pno •Cen

BUTTERWORTH, Arthur (1923)
Chef d'orchestre, compositeur et professeur anglais, né le 4 VIII 1923 à Manchester. Travailla avec R. Hall.
"The major inspirational source of his music is the north country in which he lives, its poetry, its painting, and its landscapes." (G. LARNER)
Old English Songs - Duo (1962)
3 Dialogues (1962) 1) Andante con moto e molto legato 2) Allegro 3) Presto •2 Sx: SS •Pet/Hin

BUTTS, Carrol
Chameleon •3 Sx •SH&MC
Moderato and Allegro •3 Sx: AAA •Ken
Trio •3 Sx •Pro

BUTTSTEDT
Aria •Asx/Pno •WWS

BUWEN, Dieter (1955)
Organiste, compositeur, et professeur allemand, né à Losheim/Saar. Travailla avec T. Brandmüller et H. Lohse, puis, à Paris, avec G. Litaize.
Nachtgedanken (1990) (8') (to G. PRIESNER) 1) Berceuse-Elegie 2) Vision 3) Notturno-Lamento •SATB •CA

Die Sephiroth (1991) (18') - 10 Inventionen - 1) Kether
  2) Chockmah 3) Binah 4) Chesed 5) Geburah 6) Tipheret
  7) Netzach 8) Hod 9) Jesod 10) Malkuth •Asx/Org •adr

BYRD, William (1543-1623)

Fantasie (AXWORTHY) •6 Sx: SSAATB/Optional Perc
Pavane for the Earl of Salisbury (HARVEY) •SATB •Che
This Sweet and Merry Month (HARVEY) •SATB •Che

BYRNE, Andrew (1925)

Compositeur anglais.

Introduction, Blues & Finale (1966) (6') •3 or more instruments of
  equal pitch •Hin
3 Pieces, op. 14 (1964) (4'30) •3 or more instruments of equal pitch
  •Hin

BYTZEK, Peter (1954)

Compositeur allemand, né à Reichenau, le 27 VIII 1954. Autodidacte.

Gefühle auf dem Eis (1985) (3'45) •2 Voice/Guit/Pno/Sx/Perc/Bass
  •adr

CABEZON, Antonio (c. 1510-1566)
Prelude in the Dorian Mode (GRAINGER) •3 Sx: SAT or 6 Sx: SnoSATBBs •PG

CABUS, Peter
Compositeur belge flamand.
Facetten (1974) (to E. APPER) Canto I - Allegro - Canto II - Danza I - Cadenza - Danza II •Asx/12 Str •Mau
Preludium & Rondo (1979) •6 Sx: SAATTB •Mau
Rapsodie (1974) (to E. APPER) Lento - Allegretto •1 Sx: A+T/Perc/ Pno •Mau

CACAVAS
Montage •Asx/Band •DP

CADEE, J. L.
Compositeur français.
Nocturnes (1986) (14'30) •Bsx/Pno •adr
Suite (1986) (6'30) •Ssx/Perc •SL

CADWALLADER, Rex
Compositeur américain.
Rhapsody (1987) (to R. GREENBERG) •Asx/Wind Ensemble •adr
Quartet (1987) (to R. GREENBERG) •SATB •adr

CAENS, Jean-Pierre (1948)
Saxophoniste, musicologue, et professeur français, né à Dijon. Travailla avec J-M. Londeix, D. Deffayet, et J. Chailley.
"L'A.B.C. du saxophoniste. Apprendre en duo" Method (2 Volumes) (1992) •Bil

CAFARO, Sergio
Compositeur italien.
Sax (1985) (to Quart. di Sassofoni Aquilano) •SATB

CAGE, John (1912-1992)
Compositeur, philosophe, et penseur américain, né à Los Angeles le 5 IX 1912, mort le 18 VIII 1992. Travailla à Paris, puis avec R. Buhling, A. Weiss, H. Cowell, et A. Schoenberg.

"L'élément le plus important de la musique est le temps... Le son a quatre qualités: hauteur, timbre, intensité et durée, et un complément: le silence, la durée étant la seule commune mesure entre le son et le silence. C'est pourquoi le principe de construction fondé sur des durées rythmiques est valable (adéquat à la nature du matériau), alors que la construction fondée sur l'harmonie ne l'est pas, parce que dérivée de la hauteur du son, laquelle n'a pas d'équivalent dans le matériau complémentaire qu'est le silence." (J. CAGE) Il se plut à dire "Laissons les sons être ce qu'ils sont." "Une des personnalités les plus originales et les plus inventives de la jeune école, en dépit des extravagances quelque peu néo-dadaïstes susceptibles de donner des apparences peu sérieuses à des travaux qui sont cependant extrêmement sérieux et significatifs des recherches, des tendances et des vérités de notre époque. Avec Charles Ives, c'est probablement le plus profondément américain des compositeurs américains... Il est l'un des premiers et principaux explorateurs de la tendance qui incorpore à la musique traditionnelle des sons qui étaient jusqu'alors considérés comme des bruits... Il est également parti à la découverte du hasard, et il est l'un des initiateurs de la musique aléatoire." (Cl. ROSTAND) "Les concepts compositionnels de Cage, même sous leur forme la plus aléatoire, comportent une discipline mentale particulière, discipline d'intention

qui n'a rien à voir avec le négativisme qu'on trouve dans un torrent apparemment sans fin de compositions 'libres.'" (S. BRADSHAW) "John Cage est de ceux à qui l'on doit une nouvelle façon non plus de *penser en musique*, mais de *penser la musique*." (Marc VIGNAL)

"In his desire to eliminate the subjective element in composition, Cage has adopted a method of composing with a set of Chinese dice, each throw indicating the pitch, note value, dynamics, instrumentation, etc., according to a predetermined range system of indices." (BAKER's) "His earliest compositions are based on a schematic organization of the 12 pitches of the chromatic scale. Such works as the *Six Short Inventions* (1933) and the *Composition for 3 Voices* (1934) deal with the problem of keeping repetitions of notes among the different voices as far apart as possible, even though each voice uses the same 25-note range and must itself state all 25 notes before repeating any one of them. *Music for Wind Instruments* (1938) and *Metamorphosis* (1938) use fragments of 12-note series transposed to various pitches determined by the intervallic structure of the series itself. These works are all for small combinations of instruments and show the influence of the theories and compositions of his teachers.

Composition for 3 Voices (1934) (to P. SCHLINDER) •3 or more instruments
Four 5 (1992) (8') (to J. SAMPEN) •Sx Ensemble: SATB
4'33" (1952) •Tacet for any instrument(s)
4'33" (no. 2) (0'0") (1962) •Solo for any player
Score (40 Drawings by Thoreau) and 23 Parts (1974) •Any Instruments/Winds
Solo with Obbligato Accompaniment of Two Voices in Canon, and Six Short Inventions on the Subjects of the Solo (1933) •3 or more instruments •Pet
Sonata for 2 Voices (1933) •2 or more instruments •Pet
Theatre Piece (1960) 1-8 Performers
Variations I and II (1958) (1961) •Any number of players, any means •Pet
Variations III (1963) •Any number of people performing any actions
Variations IV (1963) •Any number of players, any means

CAHARD, André-Armand-Alfred (1918)
Broderie sur l'Echappée •Asx/Pno

CAIAZZA, Nick
Portraits •Asx/Band •DP

CAILLIERET, A.
15 Etudes (d'après les Sonates pour Vl. seul de Bach) •Led

CAILLIET, Lucien (1897-1985)
Clarinettiste, chef d'orchestre, professeur, et compositeur américain d'origine française, né à Dampierre près de Dijon, le 22 V 1897; mort à Redondo Beach (California), le 3 I 1985. Travailla avec Caussade, A. Gedalge, G. Pares, et V. d'Indy. Aux U.S.A. depuis 1916.
Andante and Allegro (LEFEBVRE) •Asx/Pno •South
Canzonetta (TSCHAIKOVSKY) •Asx/Cl Choir •LCP/South
Carnaval (1962) •SATB •SMC/South
Divertimento (FARHART) •SATB •LCP/South
Elementary Method •Bel
Fantasy and Fugue on "Oh Suzanna" •AATB •LCP/South
Menuet (BOCCHERINI) •SATB •LCP/South
Method for Alto and Tenor Saxophones (1941) (2 Volumes) •Bel
Quartet Album (10 Pieces) (1942) •AATB •Bel
Theme and Variations •Asx/Pno •adr

CAIOLA, A. (1920)
You are the Soloist •1 Sx: A or T/Pno •MCA

CAIX D'HERVELOIX, Louis (1680-1760)
La Marche du Csar (CLASSENS-MERIOT) •SATB •Com

CALENS, P.
Compositeur belge.
Prélude et Rondo •6 Sx: SAATTB

CALHOUN, William
Sonata (1982) (to M. JACOBSON) •Ssx/Pno •DP

CALI, Giuseppe
Compositeur italien.
Bagatelle I, II, III, IV •SATB
Musical & Masque •SATB

CALLHOFF, Herbert (1933)
Compositeur et organiste allemand, né le 13 VIII 1933 à Viersen. Travailla avec Reda.
Facetten (1986) •Asx/BsCl/Cl/Perc •adr

CALMEL, Roger (1921)
Compositeur français, né à Creissan, près de Béziers (Hérault), le 13 V 1921. Travailla avec D. Milhaud et J. Rivier.
"Après avoir expérimenté la technique sérielle, il l'a abandonnée sous sa forme stricte. Cependant, depuis 1959 il utilise les éléments dodécaphoniques, mais dans un esprit de liberté, car l'essentiel pour lui, réside dans le choix des lignes mélodiques, qui déterminent les rapports harmoniques et rythmiques. Ses travaux récents sont orientés vers la musique occitane et la recherche de la pureté linéaire." (BORDAS)
"Il est normal que, pour ce méditerranéen, l'émotion et la sensibilité priment tout. Peu lui importe d'employer tel ou tel procédé. Il estime que l'oeuvre naissante trouve d'elle-même son climat et sa technique, et que la mélodie doit rester la préoccupation essentielle du compositeur." (HEU)
Aria (1950) •Asx/Pno •adr
Cantate "Liberté" •Ob/Cl/Asx/Bsn/Chorus/Soloists •adr
Les Caractères (15') (to M. PERRIN) •Vln/Asx/Vcl/Pno •adr
Concertino (1952) (11') (to G. GOURDET) 1) Vif et léger 2) Andante 3) Allegro •Asx/Orch (1100/Pno/Perc/Str) or Pno •Heu/Led
Concertino (1958) (14') (to Fr. DANEELS) 1) Allegro vivo 2) Andante 3) Finale, joyeux et animé •Asx/Chamber Orch •Heu/Led
Concertino (1974) (to D. DEFFAYET) •Asx/Wind Ensemble •Chou
Concerto (1972) (to F. DANEELS) •Asx/Orch or Pno •Chou
Concerto Grosso (1956) (17') (to Quatuor Mule) 1) Introduction, Allegro vivo 2) Scherzando 3) Grave et soustenu 4) Allegro con fuoco •SATB/Str Orch/Perc •Heu/Led
Incantations thibétaines (1974) 1) Trés allant 2) Vif et scherzando 3) Final •Ob/Cl/Asx/Bsn •adr
Messe du Pays d'Oc •Ob/Cl/Asx/Bsn/Chorus/Soloists •adr
Nocturne (1961) (1'30) •Asx/Pno •Phi
Quatuor d'anches (to P. PAREILLE) •Ob/Cl/Asx/Bsn •adr
Quatuor de saxophones (1957) (to Quatuor Mule) 1) Gaiment 2) Lent et Mystérieux 3) Joyeusement •SATB •adr
Quatuor méditerranéen (1982) (to Quatuor Deffayet) •SATB •adr
7 Séquences (12'15) 1) Andante 2) Allegro con brio 3) Andante espressivo 4) Lent et soutenu 5) Scherzando 6) Vif et gaiement 7) Lento •SATB or Ob/Cl/Asx/Bsn •EFM/adr
Sonate d'Automne (1991) (10'30) •Asx/Pno •Com
Suite (1961) (8') (to Fr. DANEELS) 1) Prélude 2) Sarabande 3) Tambourin •Asx/Pno •adr

CALTABIANO, Ronald
Compositeur américain.
Concerto (1983) (22') (to P. COHEN) •Asx/Orch (2222/4221/4 Perc/Str) •MeM

CAMARATA, Salvador (1913)
Compositeur américain, né à Glen Ridge (New Jersey), le 11 V 1913. Travailla avec B. Wagenaar, C. Sodero, et S. Meyerwitz.

Rhapsody (1949) Maestoso - Slowly - Presto •Asx/Pno •Mills

CAMBRELING, Sylvain (1948)
Chef d'orchestre et compositeur français.
Facette I •SATB

CAMIDGE, Mattew (1758-1844)
Sonatine in B (JOOSEN) •Bb Sx/Pno •Mol

CAMILLERI, Charles Mario (1931)
Compositeur canadien d'origine maltaise, né le 7 IX à Hamrus.
"Many works belonging to his early period are influenced by the Ghana type of Maltese folk music, but after his 'conversion' at the 'serious' music, he became immersed in a study of African and Asiatic folk musics and Indian mysticism in an attempt to encompass the essence of Eastern and Western musical thought in closer unity." (Ch. PALMER)
Fantasia concertante no. 6 (1974) (11') (to P. BRODIE) 1) Moderato e lirico - Vivo 2) Lento recitativo 3) Agitato •Asx Solo •Ram
Suite (1960) (to P. BRODIE) 1) Soliloquy 2) Fileuse 3) In Memoriam Garcia Lorca •Asx/Str/Harp or Pno •Wa/Che

CAMPANA, José Luis (1949)
Compositeur franco-argentin, né à Buenos Aires. Travailla avec B. Jolas, G. Reibel, et I. Malek. Vit en France depuis 1979.
"Campana dispose d'une grande gamme de moyens d'expressions et d'une évidente capacité concertante. Sa musique prend de l'élan et connaît aussi des espaces de repos. Elle témoigne d'un grand amour pour les couleurs sonores, exploitées au maximum." (Badische Zeitung)
"Face à des constructions sonores parfois trop calculées, José Luis Campana oppose une musique sensible, physique, psychodramatique... Peut-être sommes-nous devant une néo-sensibilité libérée?" (SUEDKURIER)
Acting-In (1983) (16'15) •1 Sx: A+T •Sal
Acting out (1982) (to Cl. DELANGLE) •Ssx Solo •Sal
Du sonore (1986) (7') (to Cl. DELANGLE) (3 Movements) •Asx/Perc •Lem
Insight (1987) (18') •Fl/Voice/Sx/Bass/Perc/Tape/Video •Bil
Pezzo per Claudio (Commande d'Etat) (1985) (6') •Asx Solo •Lem

CAMPBELL, John
Voices of America (1984) 1) America and Liberty 2) I Gave Them Fruits 3) America and Liberty 4) America 5) America and Liberty 6) Alabama Centennial 7) America and Liberty •Voice/Ssx/Vibr/Bass •adr

CAMPRA, André (1660-1744)
Achile et Deidanie - Gavotte (MULE) •Asx/Pno •Led
Fêtes vénitiennes (MULE) •Asx/Pno •Led
Musette (LONDEIX) •Asx or Bb Sx/Pno •Lem

CAMPS, Pompeyo
Compositeur, critique musical, auteur, et pédagogue argentin. Travailla à Barcelone avec J. Pahissa.
Fantasia, op. 93 (1989) (7') •Asx/Pno •CIDEM

CANAT de CHIZY, Edith (1950)
Compositeur française, née à Lyon en 1950. Travailla avec I. Malec, M. Ohana, G. Reibel puis Donatoni.
Saxy (1985) (3'30) - Collection Panorama III •Asx/Pno •Bil

CANET, Jacques
Suite brève •SATB

CANGINI, Giuseppe
Compositeur italien.
Ecate •Asx/Pno/Dancer
Spiandoti e ciecamente...!! (1992) •Asx/Str Quartet

CANIVEZ, L.
Fantaisie de concert, op. 127 •Asx/Pno •TM

CANNING, Thomas (1938)
Concert Piece (1974) (to J. WYTKO) •Asx/Pno
Two Chorales after Bach •SATB

CANTON, Edgardo (1934)
Compositeur argentin. Travailla à Paris au GRM.
Phares et Balises •Fl/Ob/Sx/BsCl/Hn/Tpt/Trb

CAPDEVIELLE, Pierre (1906-1969)
Compositeur et chef d'orchestre français, né à Paris le 1er II 1906, mort à Bordeaux, le 9 VII 1969. Travailla avec Gedalge, P. Vidal, et V. d'Indy. Fondateur du "Dixtuor de Paris."

"C'est un néo-romantique qui pense que l'art est rituel et non jeu d'esthète, et qu'il a mission de traduire aussi bien le divin que l'humain en nous conduisant tout à la fois au-delà et en deçà des choses et des êtres." (ROSTAND)

"On the whole he is a romanticist who takes to classic subjects and treats them in a picturesque manner (F. GOLDBECK) "His music is the expression of a stormy, romantic temperament, moderated somewhat in the manner of Roussel." (P. GRIFFITHS)

Danse des 7 Voiles de Salomé (1956) (4') (to G. GOURDET)
　1) Mimodrame 2) Danse •Asx/3 Timp •Bil
Exorcisme (1936) (9'30) (to M. MULE) •Asx Solo •Aug
Schandh'Ebhen (to J. J. MACPHERSON) •Asx/Pno •HS

CAPELLE, Achille-Joseph (1848-xxxx)
20 Grande études (2 Volumes) •Led

CAPLET, André (1878-1925)
Compositeur et chef d'orchestre français, né au Havre, le 23 XI 1878. Mort à Neuilly près de Paris, le 22 IV 1925. Travailla avec H. Woolet, X. Leroux, P. Vidal, et Lenepveu. Grand Prix de Rome (1901).

"Adopte en partie le style de ses amis Cl. Debussy et G. Fauré." (LAROUSSE) "A été le plus fidèle debussyste, le seul qui ait tiré la leçon profonde du musicien, sans pour cela abdiquer sa personnalité." (P.WOLFF) "Ami et collaborateur de Debussy, André Caplet n'en poursuit pas moins ses recherches vers une musique plus libérée, plus personnelle, parfois ésotérique, toujours exempte de formules stéréotypées." (BORDAS) "Ce fut sous l'influence de Cl. Debussy, dont il était le familier que Caplet commença à composer, mais son profond sentiment chrétien, avivé encore par les années de guerre, le conduisit bientôt vers une musique originale, complètement dégagée de Debussy et du flou impressionniste, au dessin net et même un peu rude, à la fois très moderne d'inspiration et retrouvant l'inspiration joyeuse, exaltante, du catholicisme grégorien." (R. DUMESNIL) "L'art objectif, ornemental de Caplet, prend son archaïsme moderne à celui de Debussy, mais l'applique à une sphère musicale qui n'entra jamais dans le champ de Debussy, et où le recours aux modes médiévaux est entièrement justifié." (F. GOLDBECK)

"Caplet's music is unequivocally impressionistic, with a lavish use of whole-tone scales and parallel chord formations; he combined this impressionism with neo-archaic usages and mystic programmatic ideas." (BAKER) "Among his contemporaries Caplet ranked as a composer who employed modern harmony and instrumental colour with authority and taste. He was a sensitive poet before all else. He understood how to create a dreamlike or magic atmosphere in the most spontaneous way, from the first notes of any of his works. A refined artist, he always succeeded in expressing the most delicate fugitive shades of thought and feeling with an exquisite choice of expression." (F. RAUGEL)

Impression d'Automne - Elégie (1905) (3') •Asx/Ob/2 Cl/Bsn/Harp/ Org/2 Vcl

Légende (1903) (13') (to E. HALL) •Asx/Ob/Cl/Bsn/2 Vln/Vla/Vcl/ Bass •Fuz

CAPOËN, Denis
Compositeur français.
Euphonie (1987) (8-10') •1 Sx: T+B or A+T

CAPPETO, Michael
Quartet in 3 Movements •SATB

CAPURSO, Elisabetta
Compositeur italien.
Due per tre (1992) (9') •Asx/Pno

CARAGO
Dance of the Silhouettes •Asx/Pno •Mills

CARAMAZZA, Filippo Maria
Compositeur italien.
Saxenty 115 (1992) •Asx Solo

CARAVAN, Ronald L. (1946)
Clarinettiste, saxophoniste, et compositeur américain, né à Pottsville (Pennsylvania), le 20 XI 1946. Travailla avec W. Willet et S. Rascher.
Call to Worship (to C. L. BENCE) •Asx Solo •adr
Canzona (1978) •AATB •Eth
Declamation: A Rhetorical Fanfare (1984) •6 Sx: SAATBBs •Eth
Extensions of Technique for Clarinet and Saxophone (1974) •adr
Four Miniatures (1971) •SATB •adr
Four Movements (1968) •SATB •adr
Improvisation (Romani) (to M. CRUMB) (1980) •Tsx Solo •Eth
Jubilate! (1982) (4') (to S. RASCHER) •8 Sx: SSAATTBBs •Eth
Lament for Unknown Infant Victims of War (1979) •SATB/Pno •Eth
Little Showpiece (1985) •2 Sx: SnoBs •adr
Love (I Corinthians 13) (1973) (4') •2 Sx: AT/Org •adr
Monologue (1975) •Asx Solo •Eth
Paradigms I -10: graded compositions using contemporary techniques (1976) (30') (to E. GATES) •Sx Solo •DP
Paradigms II: "Images of the infinite" (1990) 1) Creation 2) Temptation •Asx Solo •adr
Pastorale •6 Sx: SAATBBs •Eth
Preliminary Exercices and Etudes in Contemporary Techniques (1980) •DP
Quiet Time (1980) •1 Sx: S+T/Pno •Eth
Sketch (1973) (3') (to J. RADWAY) •Asx Solo •SeMC
Three Modal Dances (1978) •2 Sx: SB •Eth
Three Pieces (1973) •Asx Solo •adr

CARDEW, Cornelius (1936-1981)
Compositeur anglais, né à Winchcombe, Gloucester, le 7 V 1936. Travailla avec H. Stockhausen.

"Ses oeuvres musicales, en général accompagnées de longues notices explicatives, portent souvent des titres très classiques (sonate, octuor, etc.), mais leur écriture et leur caractère aléatoire les placent à la pointe de l'extrême avant-garde. Dans le climat "post-soixante-huitard", Cornelius Cardew fut salué comme le nouveau génie de la musique britannique. Cet enthousiasme est fort retombé depuis et l'on ne saurait guère prendre l'oeuvre de C. pour autre chose que ce qu'elle est: une musique expérimentale, au sens strict de ce terme." (G. GEFEN).

"Composer of the avant-garde. His compositions are preponderantly latitudissarian and disestablishmentarian, replete with unpremeditated verbalization. But he also wrote explicitly performance music." "Cardew's earlier compositions reflect the influence of Webern and the European post-Webern avant-garde. While working in Germany with Stockhausen, he met Cage and Tudor, and was attracted by Cage's ideas concerning indeterminacy and the involvement of performers directly in the creation of a work. *Autumn '60* reflects this influence."

(M. Parsons)
Autumn '60 (1960) (10') •Any ensemble •Uni
Material (1960) (10') •Any ensemble of harmony instruments •Uni
Solo with Accompaniment (1964) (10') •2 Performers •Uni

CARDEW, P.
Compositeur américain.
Alto Reverie •Asx/Pno •Ka

CARDONI, Alessandro
Musicien italien.
Introdizione allo Studio del Saxofono (1947) •Ric

CARDY, Patrick
Compositeur canadien.
Mirages (1984) •Sx (or Fl)/Pno •CMC

CARION, F.
Elegy •Asx/Pno •HE

CARISCH
Concertino (1940) •Asx/Orch or Pno •Car

CARISI, John
Quartet No. 1 (to the New York Saxophone Quartet) •SATB •NYSQ

CARL, Gene
Gray Matter (1983) (23') (Text: Luria) •2 Sx: AA/2 Pno/2 Bass Guit/2 Trb •Don

CARL, Robert
Compositeur américain.
Duke Meets Mort (1992) (9') (to the Nice Guy Saxophone Quartet) •SATB

CARLE
Enchantment (Wheeler) •Asx/Pno •Volk

CARLES, Marc (1933)
Compositeur français, né à Castres, le 9 VIII 1933. Travailla avec M. Bitsch et Tony Aubin.
"Marc Carles témoigne d'une solidité d'écriture qui anime. Rien de banal chez lui, s'il pousse loin la recherche, jamais il ne s'égare." (Le Figaro) "Exemple merveilleux de ce que le langage musical de notre temps peut créer." (C. A.) "Son oeuvre pénétrée d'un lyrisme de qualité nous permet de constater les possibilités naturelles de l'auteur." (I.)
Cantilène (1963) (2'30) •Asx/Pno •Led
3 Chants Incantatoires (1965) (14'30) (to D. Deffayet) 1) Sortilège 2) Magie 3) Enchantement •Asx/Str Orch •ET
Cycliques (1976) (to D. Deffayet) •Asx/Pno
Fragmentaires (1971) (12') (to Quatuor d'anches Français) Prélude - Choral - Incantation - Scherzo - Chant - Improvisation - Postlude •Ob/Cl/Asx/Bsn •adr
Quatuor (1973) •SATB •adr

CARLID, Göte (1920-1953)
Compositeur suédois né à Gävleborg, le 26 XII 1920; Mort à Stockholm, le 30 VI 1953. Autodidacte.
"In his compositions he tried to free himself from traditional structures, taking models from Debussy, Berg, and Ture Rangström, and in part from Varèse and Schoenberg, whose importance he was one of the first in Sweden to recognize. The best of his works might be characterized as expressionist 'interior monologues.'" (H. Astrand) "His compositions have to a great extent peaceful tonal language."
Triad (1950) (5'30) (to J. de Vriès) •Asx/Pno •STIM/Ehr

CARLOSEMA, Bernard (1949)
Compositeur français, né à Pont-de-Ruau (Indre & Loire), le 1er VI 1949. Travailla avec A. Herzog, G. Carriere, et A. Louvier.
Azulejos (1987) (6') •12 Sx: SnoSSAAATTTBBBs •Fuz
L'eau (1985) (5'30) •SATB •Fuz
Radiance (1988) (5'30) •Fl/Asx/Hn/Tpt/Trb/Tuba •Fuz
Vésanie II (1985) (5') •Asx/Pno/Tape
Zeugma (1986) (3'10) •Asx (or Tsx)/Perc •Fuz

CARMICHAEL, John
Compositeur australien.
Introduction and Allegro •Asx/Pno

CARNAUD
30 Progressive duets

CARNES, Micahel
Before We Were so Rudely Interrupted (for R. Stone) 1) Cat Dance 2) Slow 3) Gig Music Asx/Vln/Pno •DP

CARNEY, Harry Howell (1910-1974)
Saxophoniste de jazz américain, né à Boston, le 1er IV 1910; mort à New York, le 8 X 1974.
"Est reconnu comme l'un des meilleurs saxophonistes-baryton jazz."
Harry Carney's Warm-Up Method •Bsx •NYPL
Warm-Up •Bsx/Pno •MCA

CARPENTER, Gary (1951)
Compositeur anglais.
Dances for Mutilated Toys (1970) (15') •Fl/Ob/Cl/Asx/Bsn •BMIC

CARPENTER, Kurt (1948)
Compositeur américain, né à Détroit, le 15 XI 1948. Travailla avec E. Kurtz, G. Crumb, R. Lee Finney, L. Bassett, et L. Barzin.
The Marlboro Concerto "alla Stravinsky" (1971-72) (12'30) (to E. Zajac) •Asx/Str Orch or Pno •adr

CARRE-CHESNEAU, Thierry (1950-1992)
Compositeur français, né à Blois, le 12 X 1950, mort le 7 IV 1992.
Conduit (1990) (to B. Knops) •8 Sx
2 Etudes en ¼ de ton (1975) (to J. Charles) •Asx Solo
2 Pièces (1979) 1) Bouffée d'air chaud 2) Lumière sous bois •1 Sx: S+A/Pno
Rencontres (1977) (to G. Mathiot) •Asx/Pno

CARRIERE
Air médévial •Bb Sx/Pno •Mar

CARRON, Willy
Compositeur belge.
Quartet (1978) 1) Prélude 2) Scherzo 3) Blues 4) Postlude •SATB •CBDM

CARSTE, Hans Friedrich (1909-1971)
Compositeur, chef d'orchestre allemand né le 5 IX 1909 à Frankenthal et mort à Bad Wiessee le 11 V 1971.
Ballettreigen •Asx/Pno •Fro
Kleine Kavallerie •Asx/Pno •Fro

CARTER, Elliott (1908)
Compositeur américain, né à New York, le 11 XII 1908. Travailla avec N. Boulanger. Prix de Rome (1953).
"Carter est aux U.S.A. le chef de file respecté de la génération correspondant en France à celle de Jolivet et Messiaen." (de Nussac) "Tout américain qu'il soit, Elliot Carter se définit comme un musicien d'esprit européen, c'est-à-dire solidaire des choix esthétiques développés là depuis l'immédiat après-guerre." (C. Leblé) "D'abord attiré par le néo-classicisme d'un Stravinsky ou d'un Hindemith, il évolue vers

une plus grande complexité d'écriture, en particulier rythmique, tout en se libérant progressivement de la tonalité." (A. POIRIER) "Très influencée par Copland, Piston, Hindemith, et Stravinski, son oeuvre est caractérisée par l'emploi de la modalité et de la polytonalité, ainsi que par un caractère expressif soutenu. Ses rythmes sont vigoureux et asymétriques." (BORDAS) "Carter est un chercheur de tempérament, et il a expérimenté tous les moyens de composition, depuis ceux de la Grèce ancienne jusqu'au dodécaphonisme, mais son esprit hautement intellectuel et sa conscience musicale transforment toujours son idiome avancé en un accent personnel, d'où ressort une musique émouvante, américaine sans doute, mais dont l'expression est universelle." (N. DUFOURCQ) "Compositeur d'une classe internationale. Curieux de tous les problèmes de la technique musicale, de toutes les formes d'expression; en possession d'une large et solide culture, il s'est édifié un langage en marge de tous les systèmes accrédités, mais qui retient de chacun d'eux ce qui lui semble opportun. Un musicien qui ne recule devant aucune audace, compris le système dodécaphonisme. Si accueillant que soient son esprit, sa sensibilité et son oreille aux agrégations sonores les plus hardies, il y a chez lui un constant souci d'humanisme qui l'a incité à considérer avec non moins de vigilante attention les lois de la musique grecque antique. L'étendue de ses vues et cette volonté d'atteindre au permanent, à ce qu'il y a de fondamental et d'immanent derrière les apparences contradictoires donnent un intérêt et un sérieux peu communs à ses chroniques de *Modern Music* et à son enseignement au Peabody Conservatory de Baltimore." (R. BERNARD) "Je considère mes partitions comme des scénarios auditifs dans lesquels les exécutants interviennent comme des personnages avec leurs instruments, soit à titre individuel, soit comme participants à l'ensemble" (E. CARTER) "L'oeuvre de Carter est quantivement limitée, mais elle prouve une extrême concentration de pensée, un sérieux et une originalité, un sens de la perfection formelle et du contraste tels que la convergence de ces qualités peut produire des chefs-d'oeuvre." (Cl. SAMUEL) "A l'heure de la maturité, Carter apparaît -et on ne l'a pas suffisamment fait ressortir- comme un héritier d'Alban Berg, non pas, sans doute, sur le plan de la sensibilité, mais sur celui de la plastique et de la dialectique musicales." (Cl. ROSTAND)

"His reputation rests squarely on a comparatively small number of large-scale works; at best his music sustains an energy of invention that is unrivalled in contemporary composition." (GROVE) "Elliot Carter's work is essentially neo-classic in style and is a good example of how the American idiom can evolve within this structural type. The music is economical, linear, rhythmically intricate and syncopated, and he has a notable gift for achieving dramatic effects by unusual and yet simple technical devices. This is apparent both in his orchestral and in his choral scores. His music is remarkably free of mannerisms, either idiomatic or technical, but it has a distinct individuality in spite of its abstract nature." (P. GLANVILLE-HICKS) "In his music, Elliot Carter adopts a modern contrapuntal style, with a pronounced feeling for modal writing; his rhythms are vigorous and often asymmetrical; his treatment of the instruments and the voice is invariably idiomatic… About 1955 he changed his style radically, adopting the method of serialization of intervals and dynamics." (BAKER)

Canonic Suite (1939) (6'30) 1) Deciso 2) Allgretto con moto 3) Allegro •4 Sx: AAAA •Bro/ME

Prelude, Fanfare, and Polka (1938) (6') •Fl/Ob/2 Sx: AT/3 Tpt/2 Trb/Perc/Str •ACA

CARVALHO, F. Urban

Compositeur américain.

Song and Dance (1970) (for D. UNDERWOOD) •Asx/Orch (2222/4221/ Perc/Str) or Band or Pno •Pres

CASABLANCAS, Benet Domingo (1956)

Concerto (1977) •Asx/Ensemble

CASADESUS, Francis (1870-1954)

Romance et Danse pastorale (MULE) •Asx/Pno •Lem

CASANOVA, André (1919)

Compositeur français, né à Paris, le 10 X 1919. Travailla avec R. Leibowitz.

"André Casanova est, chronologiquement, le premier des jeunes compositeurs français à avoir abordé la technique sérielle. Mais il n'a jamais envisagé cette dernière comme une discipline systématique et stricte, et il l'utilise en une évolution qui va avec souplesse vers une sorte de néo-romantisme dans la descendance d'Alban Berg. Il est, par contre, demeuré étranger à l'héritage Webernien. Ses compositions témoignent d'un tempérament intense et chaleureux, et elles ont vite pris place dans le circuit des manifestations internationales." (Cl. ROSTAND) "Ecriture élégante et raffinée. Et quelle maîtrise dans l'instrumentation!" (M. SCHNEIDER) "Technique solide mise au service d'une richesse expressive peu commune." (A. GOLEA)

"His music is cast in a neo-classical framework, with some atonal deviations." (BAKER'S)

Duo Canzoni (1973) (10'30) •Asx/Cl/Tpt/Perc/Small Org/Electr. Bass Guit •adr

CASINIERE, Yves de la (see LA CASINIERE)

CASKEN, John Arthur (1949)

Compositeur anglais né à Barnsley, le 15 VII 1949. Travailla avec J. Joubert et P. Dickenson.

"John Casken se situe dans la ligne de Lutoslawski." (G. GEFEN)

"He was at first influenced by contemporary Polish composers, particularly Lutoslawski, he began to develop a more personal style. The starting point for his compositions is serial, but the method may be applied with various degrees of strictness and freedom, and his flexible approach to timbre and texture is equally important." (GROVE)

Kagura (1972-73) (15') •Asx/Wind Ensemble •Sch

Visu for Three (1974) 1) Any melodic instr 2) Any keyboard instr 3) Any bass instr •3 Instruments •BMIC

Music for a Tawny-Gold Day (1975-76) (10') (for the Aulos Ensemble) •Asx/BsCl/Vla/Pno •Sch

CASSEDAY, A.

Quartet in G minor •AATB •Bou/WWS

CASTELLANO, Mauro

Compositeur italien.

Vento di mare (1992) •Asx Solo

CASTEREDE, Jacques (1926)

Compositeur français, né à Paris le 10 IV 1926. Travailla avec Tony Aubin, Olivier Messiaen, et Samuel Rousseau. Grand Prix de Rome (1953).

"Je suis parti d'une musique à tonalité élargie de forme assez traditionnelle pour m'orienter vers plus de liberté dans les structures et une cohérence plus consciente du langage par l'emploi de plus en plus fréquent d'une écriture modale, chromatique et diatonique." (J. CASTEREDE) "Langage traditionnel." (LAROUSSE) "Production de caractère néo-classique." (Cl. ROSTAND) "Résolument opposé à tous les systèmes d'écriture, il demeure attaché à la tradition en se refusant d'abroger le principe d'opposition entre la consonance et la dissonance, ces termes n'ayant nullement une signification scolaire dans son esprit; par ailleurs, il accepte l'apport rythmique du jazz, mais c'est là un élément qu'il a suffisamment assimilé pour qu'il se fonde harmonieusement avec de tout autres données stylistiques." (R. BERNARD)

Libre parcours (1984) (to J-P. BARAGLIOLI & A. BEGHIN) 1) Ouverture 2) Molto perpetuo 3) Aria 4) Contrapunti •Sx/Perc •Led

Pastorale (1981) •Asx/Pno •Led

Scherzo (1954) (4') •Asx/Pno •Led

Trois Nocturnes (1981) (5') •SATB •Led

CASTO
Heart Strings Intermezzo (HOLMES) •AATB •Bar

CASTRO, Dino (1920)
Concerto (1978) (to A. BEUN) •1 Sx: S+A+B/Chamber Orch

CATEL, Charles-Simon (1773-1830)
Symphonie militaire (FERSTL) •SATB •GB
Thermidor de l'An II (LONDEIX) •12 Sx: SnoSSAAATTTBBBs

CATURANO, Francesco
Out of the time (1987) (10') •SATB •Ber

CAVALLINI, Ernesto (1807-1874)
30 Caprices (IASILLI) •Asx/Pno •CF

CAVANA, Bernard (1951)
Compositeur français. Travailla avec H. Dutilleux et A. Stroé.
Cache-sax - Théâtre musical (1984) (10') (to D. KIENTZY) •BsSx
Solo •Sal
Goutte d'or blues (1985) (7') (for E. D'OSENAY) •1 Sx: Sno+S/Tape
or 12 Sx: SnoSnoSnoSSSAAABBB •Sal
Mariage (1984) (to D. KIENTZY) •1 Sx: Sno+S+T+Bs+CBs/Cl/Pno/
Singers
Quatuor (1982) (to Quatuor Contemporain) •SATB
Sax déminé - Théâtre musical (Text by C. VESCHAMBRE) (to D.
KIENTZY) •2 Soprano Voices (high & low)/1Sx: Sno+S+T+Bs/
Echo Chamber
La Villette (1984-85) (to D. KIENTZY) •1 Sx: S+T+CBs/Tape

CAZDEN, Norman (1914)
Pianiste, musicologue, et compositeur américain, né à New York, le
23 IX 1914. Travailla avec Piston et A. Copland.
"A versatile composer, he writes music broad in expressive range,
with marked rhythmic impulse, frequent polyphony (from sparse to
massive in density) and widely expanded tonality, and melodies that
sometimes reflect his deep interest in folk music." (R. HILTON)
Six Discussions for Wind Ensemble No. 4 •5 Sx •EK

CECCARELLI, Luigi (1953)
Compositeur italien, né à Rimini. Travailla avec G. Baggiani, W.
Branchi, et G. Zosi.
Compose de nombreuses partitions pour instruments et électronique.
Koan II fait parti d'une série d'oeuvres pour piano préparé et un
instrument soliste, toutes dénommées *Koan*.
Koan II (1989) (9') •Ssx/Prepared Pno •adr
Neuromante (1993) •Asx/Tape •INM

CECCONI, Monique-Gabrielle (1936)
Compositeur français, né à Courbevoie (près Paris), le 30 IX 1936.
Travailla avec J. Rivier et H. Dutilleux.
"Expression du langage musical très actuel, avec un lyrisme parfois
prenant, éveillant toujours l'intérêt."
Ariette (1962) (5') (to P. PAREILLE) •Asx/Pno •Com/Phi
Aubade et Danse (1964) (3') •3 Sx: AAA •Phi
Hommage à... •2 Str Quartets/Ob/Cl/Asx/Bsn •Phi
Silences (1971) (10') (to Quatuor d'Anches Française) •Ob/Cl/Asx/
Bsn •EFM/Bil

CEKOW, André
Etude en forme de fugue (1971) (4'30) •SATB

CELERIANU, Michel
Aus (1985) (to D. KIENTZY) •1 Sx: S+Bs/Ensemble/Choir
Janvier (1983) (to D. KIENTZY) •Ssx/Fl/2 Bass/Perc •Sal
Ouverture trio (to D. KIENTZY) •Sx/BsCl/Perc

CENSHU, Jiro
Compositeur japonais.
Spring in the wind (1992) •15 Sx: SSAAAAAAAAATTBBB

CENTEMERI, Gian Luigi (1903)
Compositeur italien.
Sonate (1953) •Asx/Pno
Concerto (1964) •Asx/Str

CERHA, Friedrich (1926)
Chef d'orchestre, violoniste, et compositeur autrichien, né à Vienne
en 1926. Travailla avec A. Uhl. On lui doit l'orchestration des parties
manquantes du 3° acte de l'opéra *Lulu* d'A. Berg.
"Un Boulez autrichien avec une personnalité plus accessible." "Pour
lui, les innovations sont décelables aujourd'hui, peut-être moins au
niveau du matériau proprement dit qu'en ce qui concerne la visée,
intellectuelle et spirituelle, et les instruments conceptuels accordés par
le compositeur à chaque oeuvre." (D. J-Y. BOSSEUR)
Concertino •Ssx/Orch
Exercices for Nine, No. 1 •BsCl/Bsx/Bsn/Tpt/Trb/Tuba/Vcl/Bass/
Harp •Uni
Fantasies nach Cardw's Herbst 60 •Cl/BsCl/Tsx/Vln/Vla/Vcl/Pno
•EMod

CERINO, Sandro
Compositeur italien.
L'Estasi del Karma •7 Sx
Into the Karma •7 Sx

CERRO, Emiliano del (see DEL CERRO)

CERVELLO, Garriga Jordi (1935)
Compositeur espagnol.
Shoshanna (1979) (to Quatuor de Bordeaux) •SATB •adr

CEUGNART, Robert (1913)
Compositeur français, né à Merville (Nord), le 27 IV 1913.
Berceuse •SATB •adr

CHADABE, Joel
Sean •Any instrument, any number

CHAGNON, Roland
Compositeur français.
Image pour un enfant (1974) (to Quatuor d'Anches de Paris) •Ob/Cl/
Asx/Bsn

CHAGRIN, Francis (1905-1972)
6 Duets •2 Sx •Nov
4 Lyric Interludes (1963) (5') •Any solo instrument/Str Quartet or
Pno •Nov
Sarabande (1951) (6') •Ob/Hn/Vln/Asx/Str Quartet •ALC
2 Studies for Jazz Quartet (1959) •Tpt/Sx/Bass/Drums •BMIC

CHAIKIN, Linda
Saxophoniste américaine.
Mood Escapades 1) Temperamental Burgundy 2) Lament in Blue
3) Rose Colored Rhyyls •Sx Solo

CHAILLEUX, André (1904)
Compositeur français.
Andante et Allegro (1958) (3') •Asx/Pno •Led

CHAILLY, Luciano (1920)
Compositeur italien, né à Ferrara, le 19 I 1920. Travailla avec
Righini, Bossi, et P. Hindemith.
"His abundant compositional output, initially rather traditional, was
later influenced by Hindemith and then by avant-garde tendencies,

though Chailly's use of these has been cautious." (A. Pironti)
Improvisation n° 10 (1978) •Sx Solo

CHALFONTE, Richard (1924)
Compositeur américain, né le 4 III 1924, à Muncie (Indiana). Travailla avec M. O'Toole et R. Schramm.
"Intricate, well-constructed, creating quiet, nostalgic wonderment." (PTM Magazine) "Composer gets praise from New York debut of saxophone piece." (OCO)
Sorrows of Werther (1961) •Asx/Pno/Soprano Voice •adr
Suite (Children Pieces) (1962) •3 Sx •adr

CHALLAN, René (1910)
Compositeur français, né à Asnières, le 12 XII 1910. Travailla avec J. et N. Gallon, et H. Busser. Grand Prix de Rome (1935).
"Musique délicate, mélodique à souhait." (D. Blaize)
Concerto (1946) (20') (to M. Mule) 1) Allegro con brio 2) Largo 3) Vivace •Asx/Orch (2222/221/Perc/Harp/Str) or Pno •Led
Jacasserie •SATB

CHALLULAU, Tristan-Patrice
Compositeur français.
Brisures (1993) •Sx/Pno •INM
Chaud! Chaud! (1993) •Sx/Pno •B&N
Sur quelque étoile morte: l'homme •Asx/Fl/Cl

CHAMBERS, Evan K.
Compositeur américain.
The Trouble With the Wind (1991) (4') •SATB
Untitled (1992) (10') •Asx/Pno

CHAMINADE, Cécile (1857-1944)
The Flatterer (Thomson) •AATB •Alf
Pastorale enfantine •Bb Sx/Pno •CBet

CHAMPAGNAC, René
Eglogue •Bb Sx/Pno •Bil

CHAN, Francis Ka-Nin (1949)
Compositeur canadien, d'origine chinoise.
Wild nights wild nights (1978) •Soprano Voice/Sx/Vcl •CMC
Quartet (1989) (14') Allegro con spirito •SATB •CMC

CHANCE, Nancy Laird (1931)
Compositeur américain, né le 19 III 1931. Travailla avec Vl. Ussachevsky et O. Luening.
Bathseba's Song (1972) (7') (to K. Dorn) •Asx (live)/Tape (6 tracks prerecorded Asx)/Speaker/Dancer •SeMC

CHANDLER, Erwin (1944)
Concert Music •Asx/Ob/2 Hn/Pno
Sinfonia (1982) (to D. Bilger) •8 Sx :SSAATTBBs
Sonata, op. 25 (1969) (to D. Bilger) 1) Allegro vivace 2) Andantino 3) Allegro molto •Asx/Pno
Suite (1985) (to Bilger Duo) •Asx/Pno
3 Pieces (1982) (to Bilger Duo) •Asx/Pno

CHANG, Li-ly (1952)
Impromptu (1979) (5') (to J. Cunningham) •Asx/Pno

CHARBONNIER, Janine
Compositeur français.
Exercice (4') •2 Sx: SA/BsCl/Bsn •EFM
Prélude, Canon et Choral (5') •Asx/Tpt/Trb/Tuba •EFM

CHARCHOVSKY, Willis
Fantasy Sonata (1958) (to J. Bestman) •Asx/Pno

CHARLTON, Andrew
Diversions (1980) (to R. Greenberg) •Fl/Asx
Fantaisie on the Chaconne (from *Partita no. 2* for unaccompanied violin by J. S. Bach) •SATB

CHARPENTIER, Jacques (1933)
Compositeur français, né à Paris, le 18 X 1933. Travailla avec O. Messiaen et Tony Aubin. Il étudia la musique traditionnelle de l'Inde.
"La grande aventure de sa jeunesse est un séjour en Inde (1952-54) où il s'initie à la musique classique traditionnelle du pays." (Cl. Rostand) "Il affirme une vocation d'intemporalité." (G. Brelet) "Un pouvoir étrange et mystérieux se dégage de sa musique. Et aussi une poésie envoûtante, d'une gravité mystique." (Cl. Chamfray) "Maître verrier, vitrail des sonorités suspendues ou des mouvements en rosace; lent étirement de la monodie qui suspend le temps et remplit l'espace de sa seule présence. Voilà qui enrichit le répertoire et témoigne en faveur du talent, déjà affirmé, d'un jeune maître." (J. Roy) "Plusieurs modes de pensée, éloignés dans le temps et dans l'espace, interviennent dans l'écriture de Jacques Charpentier références aux *sinfonie* allemandes du XVIIIe siècle; de manière plus systématiquement généralisée, l'organisation modale hindoue. La dimension temporelle qui dérive de cette conception modale de l'univers musical a laissé une forte empreinte sur une grande partie de son oeuvre à vocation spirituelle." (D. J-Y Bosseur) "Charpentier adosse son langage aux 72 modes karnâtiques, c'est-à-dire à des échelles de 7 notes dans un système hémitonique à 12 sons (échelles réparties en deux classes de 36, l'une avec quarte pure, l'autre avec quarte augmentée)." (G. Cantagrel)
"He traveled to India where he made a thorough study of Indian music; several of his works contain thematic allusions to Indian ragas." (Baker's)
Concert n° 5 (1974) (23') (to J-M. Londeix) Asx/Str Orch or Pno •Led
Gavambodi 2 (1966) (8') (to G. Gourdet) •Asx/Pno •Led

CHARPILLE, Jean-Louis
Compositeur français né à Nancy.
Jardins provisoires (1991) •Bsx/Vcl/Perc
Lettrine (1990) •Tsx Solo

CHARRON, Damien (1957)
Compositeur français, né à Epinal. Docteur es lettres. Autodidacte. A toutefois travaillé avec C. Lefebure (électro-acoustique), B. Ferneyhough et Y. Taira (composition).
Carrière d'étincelles (1991) (10') •12 Sx: SnoSSAAATTTBBBs
Extraits du corps (poèmes de B. Noël) (1985) •Mezzo Soprano Voice/Tsx/BsCl/Bass/Perc
Vers tous les chemins (1987-88) (5') •Tsx Solo •Dur
Vers tous les chemins (1988) (3') •2 Sx: AA •Dur

CHATILLON, Jean
Compositeur canadien.
Sonate (1966) (to J. Larocque) 1) Agitato 2) Andante 3) Allegro agitato molto •Asx/Pno •Reb
Suite renaissance (1966) 1) Joyeuseté 2) Esprit de contradiction 3) Sagesse 4) Invention •Asx/Vcl •Reb

CHATMAN, Stephen (1950)
Compositeur américain.
Music for Two Saxophones •2 Sx: AA
O lo velo! (1973) (9') (to T. Hulick) 1) Con ansieta 2) Con delicatezza 3) Con forza •Asx/Perc •Eto
Outer Voices (1978) •Fl/Cl/Asx/2 Perc/Celesta/Guit/Harp/Tape •CMC
Quiet Exchange (1976) (to D. Sinta) •Asx/Cymbals •DP
Whisper Rachel (1976) (8') (to D. Sinta) •Asx/Harps •DP

CHATTAWAY, Jay
Compositeur américain.
Double Star (1985) (for D. Underwood) •2 Sx: AT/Band
Nocturne and Ritual Dance (1976) (for D. Underwood) •Asx/Band
The Prize (1988) •Sx/Jazz Ensemble

CHAUDOIR, James
Compositeur américain.
Textures (1980) (to Mitchell) •AATB •DP
Dialectics (1985) •Asx
Sonatine (1988) (to A. Reilly) 1) Allegretto 2) Adagio con espress.
   3) Tarantella •Asx/Pno

CHAUVET, Georges (1906)
Saxophoniste français, de la Garde Républicaine. Membre avec Marcel Mule du Quatuor de Saxophones de la Garde Républicaine.
Chant du soir (Schlimann) •Asx or Bb Sx/Pno •Com
Etudes de perfectionnement •G&F/Com
Quatuor concertant •SATB •Bes
15 Grande études (Barret) •2 Sx: AB or ST •Com
Le saxophone classique (2 Volumes) •Com

CHAVIANO, Flores
Compositeur espagnol.
Soledad (1991) (to M. Mijan) •Asx/Pno

CHEBROU, Michel
Au revoir mon pays (1989) (5'30) (Dédié à Albert Ier, roi des Belges, ayant vécu à Ste-Adresse pendant la guerre 1914-18) •Asx/Pno

CHEDEVILLE, Esprit (1696-1782)
Scherzo - Trio (Clark) •2 Sx: AT/Pno •Mus
La Chicane (Londeix) •Bb Sx/Pno •Lem

CHEDRINE, Rodion, Konstantinovitch (1932)
Compositeur et pianiste russe, né à Moscou. Travailla avec J. V. Flier, et Y. Chaporine.
"D'abord à l'écart des tendances 'modernistes' au début des années 60, il évolue progressivement vers un langage plus original, où certains éléments (aléatoire, jazz) de cette modernité sont pris en compte. L'humour, l'inspiration liturgique appartiennent à ses préoccupations récentes." (J. Vanni)
Hommage à Albeniz •Asx/Pno

CHEN, Qigang (1955)
Compositeur chinois, né a Shanghai. Travailla d'abord avec Zhong-rong Luo, puis à Paris, avec Olivier Messiaen, Ivo Malec, Claude Ballif, Betsy Jolas, et Jacques Casterede, enfin à Sienne, avec Franco Donatoni.
"Doué d'une intelligence exceptionnelle et d'une excellente audition intérieure, Qigang Chen a assimilé très vite la musique européenne et toutes les musiques actuelles. Ses compositions témoignent d'une réelle invention, d'un très grand talent, et d'une parfaite assimilation de la pensée chinoise aux conceptions musicales européennes. Toutes ses oeuvres écrites depuis 1985 sont très remarquables par leur pensée, leur poésie, leur instrumentation." (O. Messiaen)
"Endowed with exceptional intelligence, and an excellent internal 'ear,' Qigang Chen has very quickly assimilated European music and all contemporary music. I can state that his compositions display real inventiveness, very great talent and a total assimilation of Chinese thinking to European musical concepts. All his works written since 1985 are remarkable by their thought, their poetry and their instrumentation." (O. Messiaen)
Feu d'ombres (1990) (16'30) •Ssx/Orch (1111/2220/Perc/Harp/ Bass) •Bil

CHENETTE, Edward Stephen (1895-1963)
Pep and Peppy •Asx or Bb Sx/Pno •Bel
Sax Simplicity •Asx or Bb Sx/Pno •CF
Sax Sweetness •Asx or Bb Sx/Pno •CF
Valse Joliet •Asx or Bb Sx/Pno •CF

CHERNEY, Brian
Compositeur canadien.
Quintet (1962) (20') •2 Vln/Asx/Vla/Vcl •CMC

CHERUBINI, Luigi (1760-1842)
Canon •3 Sx: SAT/Pno •Mol
2° Sonate (Pala) •Tsx/Pno •Mol

CHESKY
Contemporary Duets •2 Sx

CHEVALIER, Christina
Iris •Ssx/Synth

CHEVREUILLE, Raymond (1901)
Compositeur belge, né à Watermael, le 17 XI 1901. Travailla à Bruxelles, avec G. Minet et Fr. Massé.
"Je suis un ennemi du système et de la musique fabriquée. La musique est un langage simple, qui doit exprimer quelque chose. La musique est question d'entrailles, de coeur, etc., de cerveau ensuite. Il faut parler au coeur des hommes et ils écouteront. Au créateur à trouver les mots qu'il faut dire." (R. Chevreuille) "Les éléments constitutifs de son oeuvre sont harmoniquement articulés et sont soumis avant tout à l'expression, ce à quoi le compositeur accorde une importance essentielle." (P. Chevreuille) "Ce musicien, à partir de Roussel, de Debussy et de P. Hindemith, multiplie les expériences les plus intéressantes et se taille un langage solidement charpenté." (E. Meynaerts-Wathelet) "Il s'est surtout efforcé d'atteindre à un art clair, simple et directement expressif dans un langage des plus traditionnels." (Cl. Rostand)
"He has written works in every genre; his style is greatly advanced in the direction of modern harmony; his liberal eclecticism allows him to use means of expression ranging from neo-classicism to individual expressionism, applying the devices of atonality and polytonality." (Baker)
Double Concerto, op. 34 (1946) (21') (to Fr. Daneels) 1) Moderato - Allegro scherzando 2) Andante grazioso 3) Giocoso •Pno/Asx/ Orch (4222/4220/Perc/Str [Vcl & Bass]) •CBDM

CHEYETTE, Irving (1904)
Viennese Lullaby •AATB •Sha

CHIARPARIN, Antonio
Compositeur italien.
Omaggio à Zoltan Kodaly - Divertimento •2 Fl/6 Sx: AAATTB/ Bugle (Flicorno)/BsTrb •Piz

CHIC, Léon (1819-1916)
Tyrolienne variée (1861) (to A. Sax) •Asx/Pno •Sax

CHIEKO - MIYAMAE
Poélégie (1978) •Sx Solo •Chou

CHIHARA, Hideki
Compositeur japonais.
Lied •Asx Solo

CHIHARA, Paul (1938)
Compositeur américain, né à Seattle (Washington), de parents japonais. Travailla avec N. Boulanger et E. Peppine.
Concerto (1980) (13'30) (to H. Pittel) •1 Sx: Sno+S+A/Orch

CHILDS, Barney (1926)

Compositeur américain, né à Spokane (Washington), le 13 II 1926. Travailla avec L. Ratner, G. Chavez, A. Copland, et E. Carter.

"Not overly concerned with public tastes and current fashions of cosmopolitan styles in music he cultivates indeterminate structures." (BAKER'S)

Bayonne Gum and Barrel Cie •Asx/Band •ACA
Four Pieces for Six Winds (1977) •1 Sx: S+A/Fl/Ob/Cl/Hn/Bsn •WWS
Interbalances V •Fl/Ob/Cl/Asx/Hn/Bsn •CFE
Music for One Player •Sx •ACA
Music for... Saxophone •Sx •BMI
Operation Flabby Sleep •3 or more instruments •ACA
Sonatina (1958) (6'30) (to J. HELDER) •Asx Solo •TP
The World from Department R (1979) (to J. ROTTER) •Asx/Cl/Pno •CFE

CHINI, André (1945)

Chef d'orchestre, hautboïste, et compositeur suédois d'origine française, né à Roumengoux, le 18 V 1945. Travailla avec A. Jolivet. En Suède depuis 1975.

"He uses a dynamic, vivid tonal language and his expressive range extends from brittle, very subdued effects to tempestuous brutality."

3 Cris pour 4 (1974) (7') (to Quatuor d'Anches de Paris) •Ob/Cl/Asx/Bsn •STIM
Skateboard (1992) •Fl/Sx/2 Perc/Pno/Bass
Trafic (1992) •Fl/Ssx/Pno/2 Perc/Bass

CHLEIDE, Thierry

Compositeur belge.

Suite brève (1991) (10') (to D. DUHEN & M. MERGNY) 1) Pavane 2) Gaillarde 3) Sarabande 4) Gigue •Asx/Pno •An

CHO, Gene J. (1933)

Compositeur américain, né à Taiwan (Formosa), le 27 IX 1933. Travailla avec A. Donato.

Sonata (1971) (7'30) 1) Largo-Allegretto 2) Andantino 3) Adagio-Allegro •Asx/Pno •South

CHOPARD, Patrice (1953)

Guitariste et compositeur allemand, né le 28 III 1953 à Zurich. Travailla avec S. Thomatos.

3 Stücke (1980) (7') •Sx Solo •VDMK

CHOPIN, Frédéric (1810-1849)

Chopin Favorite (DEDRICK) •AATB or SATB
Dis lui que je l'aime (VIARD) •Asx/Pno •Sal
Largo (HOULIK) (2 Lyric pieces) •Tsx/Pno •South
Largo (from cello sonata) (ROUSSEAU) •Asx/Pno •Eto
Minute Valse (CHAUVET) •Asx/Pno •Led
Minute Waltz, op. 64, no. 1 (BRIEGEL) •2 Sx: AT/Pno •Bri
Nocturne (COLMIER) •Bb Sx/Pno •Mil
2° Nocturne (MULE) •Asx/Pno •Led
2° Nocturne (CHAUVET) •Asx/Pno •Com
5° Nocturne (CHAUVET) •Asx/Pno •Com
15° Nocturne (MULE) •Bb Sx/Pno •Led
Nocturne, op. 9, no. 2 (DELCHAMPE) •Asx/Pno •EMB/HE
Nocturne, op. posthumous (TEAL) (Album) •Asx/Pno •GSch
Noturno •Asx/Pno •GSch
Noturno, op. 32, no. 1 •Eb Sx/Pno •CF
Polonaise (EDWARDS) •Asx/Pno •Mills
15° Prélude (MULE) •Asx/Pno •Led
Prelude, op. 29, no. 20 (ROSSI) •8 Sx: SAATTTBBs •DP
La Tristezza (CHAUVET) •Asx/Pno •Com
Tristesse (MARTIN) •Asx/Pno •Mar
Tristesse, op. 10, no. 3 (MULE) •Asx/Pno •Led

6° Valse (MULE) •Asx/Pno •Led
7° Valse (MULE) •Asx/Pno •Led
Valse du Petit chien (CHAUVET) •Asx/Pno •Com
Valse, op. 64, no. 1 (DELCHAMPE) •Asx/Pno •EMB/HE

CHOQUET, Patrick (1947)

Quatuor (1974) (to Quatuor de Saxophones de Paris) •SATB
Aires (1992) (4') •Sx Solo •Lem

CHOSTAKOVITCH, Dmitri (see SHOSTAKOVICH)

CHOUT, Wadislav (see SHOUT)

CHRETIEN, Hedwige (1859-1944)

Allegro appassionato •1 Sx: A or T/Pno •Mil
Duo •Asx/Fl

CHRISTENSEN, James

Comedy for Saxophones •AATB •Kjos
Hey Ride! •SATB or AATB •Ken

CHRISTOPHE

Les Petits oiseaux •Eb Sx/Pno •TM

CHRISTOL (18xx-1956)

Le coeur de Mamie - Air varié •Asx/Pno •Mol
Grand solo, Andante et Allegro •1 Sx: A or T/Pno •Mil

CIAPOLINO, R.

Andante et Scherzo •SATB
Quatuor •SATB

CIBULKA, Franz Peter (1946)

Compositeur et clarinettiste autrichien. Travailla avec A. Dobrowolski.

Capriccio (1980) (to O. VRHOVNIK) •Asx/Pno
Garuda, Phantasia, Indonesia (1991) (6') •Asx/Org+Marimba
Kaleidoscop (1981) (4'30) (to O. VRHOVNIK) •Asx/Orch or 7 Sx: AAATTBBs
Konzert (1990) (23') •SATB/Str Orch •CA
Quartet n° 1 (1984) (12') (to O. VRHOVNIK) •SATB •CA
Saxophonic (1981) (to O. VRHOVNIK) •Asx/Orch or 12 Sx: SnoSSAAATTBBBs
Saxophonquartett n° 3 (15') 1) Allegro 2) Adagio 3) Rondo •SATB
Solo (1982) (to O. VRHOVNIK) •Sx/Tape
Studie (6') •Asx/Pno
Studie für Altsaxophon & Echo (1982) •Asx/Tape

CICONIA, Johannes (1355-1411)

O Padua (AXWORTHY) •3 Sx: ATB •DP/TVA

CIMAROSA, Domenico (1749-1801)

Sonate en Sib (JOOSEN) •Bb Sx/Pno •Mol

CIRRI, Giovanni Battista (1724-1808)

Arioso (MAGANINI) •1 Sx: A or T/Pno •Mus

CIRY, Michel (1919)

Compositeur, peintre, et graveur français, né à La Baule, le 31 VIII 1919. Travailla avec N. Boulanger et A. Dieudonné.

"Musicien d'inspiration mystique." (LAROUSSE) "C'est dans la rigueur du style que Michel Ciry cherche et trouve l'expression. Il s'attache en tout premier lieu à des sujets religieux et de haute spiritualité." (R. BERNARD) "Il marque une prédilection (qui situe d'ailleurs sa personnalité) pour Dallapiccola, Fr. Martin, Hindemith, et tend vers un lyrisme qui évite "les débordements indécents d'une fausse sensibilité." (Cl. SAMUEL)

Capriccio, op. 52 (to M. & M-A. ALTOFER) •Asx/Pno •Sch

CITRON, Ronald (1944)
Suite Harlequin (1976) (to E. GREGORY) •Asx/Pno

CIVITARIALE, Walter
   Compositeur luxembourgeois.
Aubade •Asx/Pno
Un soir à Moscou (in 6 parts [en 6 parties])
Sonatine •Ssx

CLAIRVAL, Jean
Saxophone par l'image (1984) (Method) •PB

CLARK, Keith
Different Callings (1977) (to R. GREENBERG) •Asx/Pno/Perc

CLARK, Scotson Frederick (1840-1883)
Belgian March (WILLIAMS) •4 Sx: AATB or 5 Sx •South
Seicento - Trio •3 Sx: AAT •Mus
Supplementary Studies

CLARK, Thomas
   Compositeur américain.
Dreamscape •Fl/Ob/Cl/Sx/Tpt/Trb/Pno/Perc/Bass •SeMC

CLARKE, Herbert Lincoln (1867-1945)
Artemis Polka •Eb Sx/Pno •CF
An Autumn Day - Scherzo •Eb Sx/Pno •CF
Beryl - Valse Lente •Eb Sx/Pno •CF
Fontana - Valse Caprice (To H. STEPHENS) •Eb Sx/Pno •CF
Lavinia - Mazurka Gracieuse •Eb Sx/Pno •CF
May Day, Country Dance •Eb Sx/Pno •CF
Memory Sweet Midst Battle's Roar •Eb Sx/Pno •CF
My Lady Dreams •Eb Sx/Pno •CF
Norine •Eb Sx/Pno •CF
Supremacy of Right •Eb Sx/Pno •CF
Trixie Valse, Venus Valse •Bb Sx or Eb Sx/Pno •CF
Victory - Original Fantasia •Eb Sx/Pno •CF

CLASSENS, Henri (1896)
   Compositeur français.
Caprice •Asx/Pno •Com
1er Concertino, op. 85, no. 1 (1961) (3') (to J-M. DEPELSENAIRE)
   •Asx/Pno •Phi
2° Concertino •Asx/Pno •Phi
Introduction et Scherzo (2'45) •Asx/Pno •Com
Jérusalem •Asx/Pno •Com
Le Nouveau Saxophone Classique (MERIOT) •Com
Venise (1'30) •Asx/Pno •Com

CLAY, Carleton
Lullaby for J.Y.C. (1993) (to the Empire Saxophone Quartet) •SATB

CLAYTON, Laura (1943)
Simichai-ya (1976) (to D. SINTA & L. HUNTER) •Asx/Tape

CLEAR, Th.
Romance •Asx/Pno •ES

CLELLAND, Kenneth P.
   Compositeur américain.
Dream So Real (1991) •Sx Solo •adr

CLEMENT
Evening Zephyr •Bb Sx/Pno •Bar

CLEMENT, Nicole
   Compositeur français
Saxophonie (1962) •Sx

Sonata (1983) (to M. MIJAN) •Asx Solo

CLEMENTI, Muzio (1752-1832)
Canon (from *Gradus & Parnassum*) (EVERTSE) •4 Sx: SATB or 2 Cl/
   2 Sx: AB •Lis/TM

CLERGUE, Jean (1896-1966)
   Chef d'orchestre et compositeur français, né à Luchon. Travailla
   avec P. Vidal, Gedalge, et V. d'Indy.
Volutes et Primavera (1965) (3') •2 Sx: AA or TT •Phi

CLERISSE, Robert (1899)
   Chef de musique et compositeur français.
A l'ombre du clocher •Bb Sx/Pno •Led
Bergerette (1937) (3') •Asx/Pno •Braun
Cache-cache (to M. MULE) •SATB •Led
Caprice (1') •Asx/Pno •Phi
Caravane •SATB •Led
Chanson à bercer (4') •Asx/Orch (2222/010/Harp/Str) or Pno •adr
Chanson du rouet •SATB •Led
Feuillet d'album •Bb Sx/Pno •Braun
Improvisation •SATB •Led
Introduction et Scherzo •SATB •Led
Le P'tit prince a dit... •4 Sx: SATB or Fl/Ob/Cl/Asx/Hn/Bsn •adr
Polka valaisanne (3'40) •SATB •Mar
Polka valaisanne (3'40) •Fl/Ob/Cl/Asx/Hn/Bsn •adr
Prélude et Divertissement •1 Sx: T or B/Pno •Bil
Promenade (DAILEY) Album •Bb Sx/Pno •WA
Recueil de Quatuor classiques (HAYDN, MOZART) •SATB •Mar
Rêverie (1958) (2'30) •Asx/Pno •Led
Sérénade mélancolique (to G. CHAUVET) •SATB •adr
Sérénade tessinoise •Asx/Pno •Phi
Sérénade variée •Bb Sx or Asx/Pno •Led
Vieille chanson (DAILEY) Album •Bb Sx/Pno •WA

CLINCH, Peter (1930)
   Clarinettiste et saxophoniste australien, professeur au Conservatoire
   de Melbourne.
Inventions •Asx/Pno

CLIPPARD, Michael
   Compositeur américain.
Metamorphical Suite •Asx/Pno
Mitosis-Kinetics (1968) •Asx/Pno

CLODOMIR, Pierre (18xx-1900)
12 Duos in B •2 Sx: TT •Elk/Mol
1er Trio •3 Sx: SSA •Mol

CLOEDT, Emile de (1931)
   Compositeur belge, né le 13 II 1931, à Bruge. Travailla avec J.
   Demiddeleir et M. Dezoo.
Dorpsdans (1958) •5 Sx: SATBBs •An
Entrée - Danse villageoise •5 Sx: SATBBs •An

CLOSTRE, Adrienne (1921)
   Compositeur français, né le 9 X 1921, à Thomery (Seine-et Oise).
   Travailla avec O. Messiaen, H. Busser, J. Rivier, et D. Milhaud. Prix
   de Rome (1949).
   "Adrienne Clostre est sensible aux recherches contemporaines les
   plus avancées, passionnées même par elles, mais considère qu'elles
   n'aboutissent généralement pas à des systèmes de langage cohérents."
   (Cl. ROSTAND) "Son style est atonal. La musique sérielle l'attire aussi,
   mais elle prend avec elle certaines libertés. Enfin, le style harmonique
   l'intéresse moins que la superposition de lignes sinueuses et complexes." (HEU)
Kalamar (1954) (3') (Album) •Asx/Pno •PN

COATES, Eric (1886-1957)

Compositeur et altiste anglais, né à Hucknall (Nottinghamshire), le 27 VIII 1886, mort à Chichester, le 21 XII 1957. Travailla avec Corder. "Melodically conventional, unadventurous but sometimes piquant in harmony and always safe and effective in orchestration." (H. COLLES) "The popularity of his music received its greatest boost when the march *Knightsbridge* (from the *London* suite) was adopted as a radio signature tune."

Saxo-Rhapsody (1936) (11') (to S. RASCHER) •Asx/Orch or Band or Pno •B&H/Chap

COCCO, Enrico (1953)

Compositeur italien, né à Rome. Travailla avec D. Guaccero, M. Bortolotti, et G. Nottoli. Depuis 1988, Enrico Cocco est membre du Laboratoire de Recherche Musicale Spaziomusica. (CAGLIARI)

Actings (1990) (10') (to E. FILIPETTI) •1 Sx: A+B/Electronics •adr

Il Sogno di Chuang Tzu - Balletto (1989/91) (40') (to E. FILIPETTI & G. ROGGERI) •Dancer/Perc/1 Sx: S+A+T+B/Electronics •adr

COCO, Remigio (1965)

Compositeur italien.

Rag-time (1987) (to Quart. d'Ance Italiano) •Ob/Cl/Asx/Bsn

CODINA, M. A.

Compositeur espagnol.

Sélène (12') •SATB •adr

COE, Tony

Compositeur anglais.

The Buds of Time (1979) (20') •10 Performers: Cl+Sx/Cl+BsCl/Str Quartet/BsTrb/Pno/Bass/Perc •adr

COENEN, Paul (1908)

Compositeur allemand né le 8 XII 1908 à Saarlouis.

Trio (22'30) •Tpt/Asx/BsTrb •Asto

COFIELD, Frank D.

Chartreuse •Asx/Pno •Rub

Estilian Caprice •Asx/Pno •Rub

COGGINS, Willis Robert (1926)

Professeur de saxophone et de clarinette américain, né le 20 VIII 1926 à Winston-Salem (North Carolina).

Aria •Asx •Bel

Duets •2 Sx •Bel

Studies and Melodious Etudes •Asx •Bel

Studies and Melodious Etudes •Tsx •Bel

Tenor Saxophone Student •Tsx •Bel

Tunes for Alto Saxophone Technique •Asx •Bel

COHANIER, Edmond

Saxophoniste suisse.

Silhouette •Asx/Pno •Bil

COHEN, Paul

Dance Whirlwinds •Ssx •adr

The Renaissance Book II (8') (COHEN) 1) La Bouree 2) Un Sonar de Piva 3) El Grillo 4) La tura tu 5) Et la la la •SATB •TTF

COHEN, Sol B.

Compositeur américain.

Introduction et Czardas •Tsx/Pno •Wit

Novelette •AATB •Bel

COHEN, Steven

Compositeur américain.

Quartet (1980) (to P. COHEN) •SATB •DP

COHEN, Veronika Wolf

I Remember •Sx/Dancer/Tape

COHN, Arthur (1910)

Violoniste, compositeur, et chef-d'orchestre américain, né à Philadelphia, le 6 XI 1910. Travailla avec Happich et R. Goldmark.

Variations (1945) •Cl/Asx/Str Orch •EV

COHN, James (1928)

Baroque Suite (from Flute) •Sx Solo •Mus

COITEUX, Francis

Aria (1989) (1'45) (to J. N. PAPUT) •Asx/Pno •Mar

Delta plane (1'30) (to E. DEVALLON) •Asx/Pno •Mar

COKKEN

Méthode complète de saxophone (1846) •Ed. Meissonnier

COLARDO, Giuseppe

Divertimento (1983) (to BOK & LE MAIR) •Sx+Cl/Marimba+Vibr

COLBORNE-VEEL, John

Compositeur australien.

Quartet (1988) (to P. CLINCH) 1) Andante - Allegro 2) Adagio 3) Rondo 4) Allegro •SATB

COLE, Bruce (1947)

Compositeur anglais.

Pantomimes (25') •Soprano Voice/Fl/Cl/BsCl/Ssx/Perc/Pno/Guit/ Vln/Vla/Vcl •B&H

COLE, Helen Wert (1911)

Pianiste et compositeur américaine, née à Portland (Oregon), le 2 V 1911.

Serenade •Fl/Ob/2 Cl/BsCl/Hn/Asx/2 Bsn •Nov

COLE, Hugo (1917)

Compositeur et critique musical anglais né à Londres, le 6 VII 1917. Travailla avec Morris, Howells et, à Paris, avec Nadia Boulanger.

"Cole's music has something of the same quality as his criticism. It is fresh, never short of good ideas and, if limited in expressive and structural scope, never pretentious. The clarity of his writing, its uncomplicated rhythms, and the general familiarity of his idiom— basically neo-classical and recognizably English in spite of the echoes of Copland—have made him a particularly successful composer of operas and other pieces for young and amateur performers." (G. LARNER)

Serenade for Winds (1965) (15') •2 Fl/Ob/2 Cl/Asx/2 Bsn/2 Hn

COLEMAN, Randolph (1937)

Divertimento (to F. HEMKE) •SATB

COLERIDGE-TAYLOR, Samuel (1875-1912)

Demande et Réponse (BISHOP) •Asx/Pno •B&H

COLGAN, J. R.

Concert Duet •Eb or Bb Sx

COLIN, Charles Joseph (1832-1891)

Hautboïste et professeur français, né à Cherbourg, le 2 Juin 1832. Elève de A. Thomas et A. Adam. 2me Grand Prix de Rome (1857).

Airs Italiens - Fantaisie •Bb Sx/Pno •Mil

Etudes Modernes •Bb Sx/Pno •CC

Mélodie •Bb Sx/Pno •Mil

1er Solo •Asx/Pno •Mil

2° Solo •Asx/Pno •Mil

3° Solo, op. 40 (1884) •Asx/Pno •Mil

4° Solo, op. 44 (1884) •Asx/Pno •Mil

5° Solo (J. BERTAIN) (1886) •Asx/Pno •Mil
8 Solos •Asx/Pno •South

COLIN, Jean-Marie (1951)
Compositeur français, né à Paris, le 17 II 1951. Travailla avec L. Thiry, J. Feuillie, M. Battier, et I. Xenakis.
L'Homme cage (1976) (sur des textes d'Y. PINGUILLY) •Soprano Voice/2 Cl/Sx
Médecines douces (1984) (Y. SEFFER) •Sx/Org
SaXaf (1991) •1 Sx: S+T/African Instruments/Tape or Synth
Saxanzesse (1990) (10') (to S. BERTOCCHI) •Bsx/Tape

COLIN, Jeanne (1924)
Compositeur belge née le 9 I 1924 à Bruxelles.
Fantaisie, op. 27 (1978) (9') (to Fr. DANEELS) •Sx Solo •Bil
Quatuor (to Quatuor Belge de Saxophones) •SATB

COLLECTIONS
Collection of 25 Gospel Hymns (LAURENDAU) •SATB •CF
Collections 5 and 6 for Pleasure •2 Sx: AT •SeMC
Harmony Trio Album (14 Pieces) (ROBERTS) •3 Sx (diverse combinations) •CF

COLLER, Father Jerome (1929)
Sonatina (1966) (to R. KNUESEL) 1) Dry and lively 2) Scherzo 3) Very slow 4) Theme with variations •Asx/Pno
Trio (1984) (to D. DEFFAYET & R. KNUESEL) •2 Sx/Pno

COLUMBRO, Carmelo
Compositeur italien.
Acedia •SATB

COMBELLE, François (1880-1953)
Saxophoniste et compositeur, né à Marcigny (Saône & Loire), le 26 VII 1880, mort à Paris, le 3 III 1953. Appartint à l'orchestre de la Garde Républicaine.
Ballade et Divertissement •Sx Solo •HS
Le Barbier de Séville n° 1 (1920) •Asx/Pno •HS
Le Barbier de Séville n° 2 (1920) •Asx/Pno •HS
Esquisse •Asx/Pno •HS
Fantaisie mauresque (1920) (to Mme HALL) •Asx/Pno •HS
Grande Méthode moderne (1910) (to G. PARÈS) •HS
Invocation •Asx/Pno •HS
Marlbrough, Variations (1938) •Asx/Pno •Bil
1er Solo de concert (to M. PILOT) •1 Sx: B or T/Pno •Alf
1er Solo de concert (1911) •Asx/Pno •Bil
Rapsodie Cypriote (1932) (to H. SELMER) •Asx/Pno •HS
Sérénade italienne (1920) (to MM. CHAUVET et LÉGÉ) •Asx/Pno •HS
Sur l'Essonne - Barcarole (1920) (to MM. BRIARD et RAFFY) Asx/Pno •HS
Triolette mazurka (1920) •Asx/Pno •HS

COMBES-DAMIENS, Jean-René
Fable du Souffle (1990) (3') (to Ph. CAPERAN) •Asx/Pno •Led

COME, Tilmant
Compositeur belge.
Capriccio (to E. APPER) •Asx/Pno •Mau

CONCERT
Concert Album of French Classics (DAHM) •1 Sx: A or T/Pno •Mus
Concert Pieces (DAILLET) •Tsx/Pno •Mus
Concert Album (MAGANINI) 12 pieces •Tsx/Pno •Mus

CONCONE, Giuseppe (1801-1861)
Racconto (SANSONE) •Asx/Pno •South
A Little Story (SANSONE) •Asx/Pno •South

CONDÉ, Gérard (1947)
Critique musical et compositeur français.
Invocations (1983) (12'30) (Commande de l'Etat) Le Miroir - Le Chien et le flacon - Ritournelle - Interlude - Un hémisphère dans une chevelure •Baritone Voice/4 Sx: SATB •Sal
Monarch of Gods and Deamons - Théâtre musical (1983) (22') (to D. KIENTZY) •1 Sx: Sno+S+A+T+B+Bs

CONFREY, Zez
Dizzy Fingers (POTTER) •Asx/Pno •Mills

CONKLIN
Handy Andy •2 Sx/Pno •CF

CONLEY, Lloyd
Christmas for Two (1981) •2 Sx: AA or TT •Ken
Song and Caprice •AATB •Ken

CONNOLLY, Justin (1933)
Compositeur anglais né à Londres, le 11 VIII 1933.
"In 1963 Justin Connolly went to Yale University on a Harkness Fellowship and during a three-year stay there, first as a student, later as a teacher, he found a path forward. The newly perfected technique depended largely on continuous discourse between individuals, perhaps the most obvious stylistic outcome of his stay in the U.S.A. There are precedents for Connolly's characterization of instruments, for example, in the music of Carter." (A. PAYNE)
Abraxas (1966) (14') •Ensemble with Saxophone •BMIC

CONRAD, Tony
3 Loops for Performers and Tape •Performer/Tape

CONSOLI, Marc-Antonio
Saxoldie (to L. KLOCK) •Asx/Pno

CONSTANT, Franz
Pianiste et compositeur belge né à Montigny-le-Tilleul, le 17 XI 1910. Travailla avec Fr. de Bourguignon et J. Absil. Il obtint le Prix de composition de l'Académie Royale de Belgique avec sa *Fantasia*, op. 41 pour Saxophone et Orchestre.
Concerto, op. 13 (1963) (13') (to Fr. DANEELS) 1) Allegro 2) Lento molto espressivo 3) Vivace •Asx/Orch or Pno •Met
2 Episodes, op. 119 (1986) (5'30) (Coll. Panorama III) •Asx/Pno •Bil
Fantaisie, op. 41 (12') •Asx/Orch or Pno •Bil
4 Séquences, op. 16 (1966) (12') (to Quatuor Belge de Saxophones) 1) Rythme 2) Nostalgie 3) Contraste 4) Exultation •SATB •CBDM
Rythme et Expression, op. 49 (1972) (13') 1) Vivace 2) Andante 3) Vivace •Vln/Pno/Asx/Perc •CBDM
Sax ambiance (1974) (to Quatuor Belge de Saxophones) •SATB •adr
Sonatine à deux, op. 136 (1992) •Pno/Asx •HM
Tension (1976) •Asx/Pno •adr
Triade, op. 30 (1967) (10') (to Quatuor Belge de Saxophones) 1) Poème des bruits 2) Rythmes 3) La Grande Brosse •SATB •CBDM

CONSTANT, Marius (1925)
Compositeur et chef d'orchestre français, d'origine roumaine, né à Bucarest, le 7 II 1925. Travailla avec G. Enesco, O. Messiaen, et Nadia Boulanger.
"Toutes ses recherches tendent à l'élargissement des limites de la matière sonore." (BORDAS) "Il ne ressentira jamais pour lui-même le besoin d'une référence à l'univers du sérialisme, en revanche son oeuvre sera en grande partie guidée par un souci 'd'ouverture.' " (J. & Br. MASSIN) "Marius Constant a le sens du mouvement, des contrastes,

des gradations, de la couleur." (R. Bernard) "Compositeur d'un métier raffiné, Constant est ouvert à toutes les curiosités, apte à toutes les orientations." (N. Dufourcq) "Empruntant des itinéraires ne passant pas par le post-wébernisme il rejoint certaines recherches actuelles jusqu'à l'aléatoire et jusqu'à certaines trouvailles sonores avancées, cela progressivement et par un développement incessant de sa personnalité et de son art." (Cl. Rostand) "Compositeur touche-à-tout, figure remuante des années soixante et soixante-dix, Constant refuse tout système (et plus précisément celui par lequel dominaient quelques compositeurs à l'époque, le sérialisme). Il est de ceux qui examinent la musique, drôle de chose, sous toutes les coutures. Ce n'est pas un théoricien, sa musique est un laboratoire. Ce n'est pas un musicien institutionnel, ses oeuvres sont autant de rencontres." (C. Leblé) "Estimant que le problème de la composition musicale consiste avant tout à s'affronter à la question de la forme et de son déroulement dans le temps, Marius Constant accuse l'aspect 'lyrique' de sa musique en jetant des ponts entre différentes disciplines artistiques, comme s'il s'agissait de retrouver, sous la spécificité de chacune, la poétique commune à toutes." (D. J-Y. Bosseur)

Concertante (1978-79) (20') 1) Raga 2) Cake-Walk 3) Passacaglia •Asx/Orch (2221/221/Harp/Perc/Str) or Pno •Ric

Musique de concert (1954) (10') (to M. Mule) •Asx/Orch (1101/111/Perc/1 Vln/1 Vcl/1 Bass) or Pno •Led

Traits (1991) (11') (to J-M. Goury & S. Bertocchi) •2 Sx: Sno+S+A+B/S+A+T+Bs

CONSTANTINIDES, Dinos

Legend (1988) (11') (to G. M. Campbell & J. Raush) •Asx/Perc

CONTE, David

Sonata (1979) (to M. Taggart) •Ssx/Pno

CONTI, Francis

Quintet (1972) •Fl/Picc/1 Sx: A+S/Cl/Bsn •adr

CONYNGHAM, Barry (1944)

Compositeur et pianiste de jazz australien, né le 27 VIII 1944 à Sydney. Travailla avec Takemitsu.

Jazz Ballet (1964) •Fl/Asx/Bass/Perc/Pno •Uni

Mirror Images (1975) •4 Actors/Asx/Vcl/Bass/Perc •Uni

COOKE, Anthony

Pictures at Hemke's Exhibition (to F. Hemke) •Asx/Band

COOKE, Charles L. (1891-19xx)

Lazy Lute •Tsx/Pno •MBCo

COOLIDGE, Richard (1929)

Ballade (1993) (to R. Navarre) •Tsx/Pno •adr

Weeping Dancer •Asx/Pno •WWS

COOLS, Eugène (1877-1936)

Compositeur français, né à Paris, le 27 III 1877, où il est mort le 5 VIII 1936. Travailla avec Gedalge, G. Fauré, et Widor.

Allegro de concert •Bsx/Pno •Bil

COOPER, David (1956)

Compositeur anglais. Travailla avec Alex Goehr et D. Blake.

Quartet (1985) 1) Lento lontano 2) Presto scherzando 3) Lento •SATB

COOPER, Kenneth

Rondo •SATB

COOPER, Paul (1926)

Compositeur et professeur américain, né à Victoria (Illinois) le 19 V 1926. Travailla la composition au Conservatoire de Paris.

"His formally economical and varied music ranges in style from the

highly dissonant to the softly contemplative." (E. Borroff)

Concertino (1982) (18') (to D. Sinta) •Asx/Orch (2282/4442/Pno/Vcl/Bass/Timp/Perc) •Sal

Four Impromptus (1983) (12') (to L. Hunter) 1) Presto e misterioso 2) Andante e espressivo 3) Animato e giocoso 4) Largo cantabile •Asx/Pno •WH

Variants IV (1986) (to L. Hunter) Thema: molto adagio - Tempestoso - Tranquillo - Semplice - Dramatico - Tempestoso - Thema: molto adagio •Asx/Pno •Che

COPE, David (1941)

Compositeur américain, né à San Francisco, le 17 V 1941. Travailla avec I. A. MacKenzie, G. Perle, et I. Dahl.

"Rich creative forces of vitality and imagination." (Music Magazine 71)

Clone (1976) (7'30) (to J. Houlik) •Tsx/Pno •SeMC

Concerto (1975) (for J. Houlik) 3 Movements •Tsx/Orch (2222/4330/4 Perc/Str) •adr

Probe No. 3 (1970) (10') (to K. and S. Dorn) •Sx/Actress+Dancer •DP

Towers (1968) •Unspecified Ensemble •MP

COPELAND, Eugene

Compositeur américain.

Petite suite •Asx/Pno •DP

Sonatine •Asx/Pno •DP

Three Chorale Preludes (6') •SATB •DP

COPLEY, Evan (1930)

Trio (1981) (to R. Greenberg) •Asx/Hn/Pno

COPPENS, Claude A. (1936)

Pianiste, compositeur belge, né le 23 XII 1936, à Schaarbeek.

"His early music was dodecaphonic; since 1961 he has increasingly used serial techniques and electronic means, including, since 1967, the composer at the IPEM studios in Ghent." (C. Mertens)

Quartet •SATB

Wheels within wheels (1972) (to N. Nozy) •Asx/Variable Ensemble •CBDM

COPPOOLSE, David (1960)

Compositeur néerlandais.

Canto XVII (Divina comedia) (1984) (12') •Asx/2 Hn/2 Trb/Vln/Vla/Vcl/Bass/Pno •Don

CORBIN, A.

L'Aurore - Fantaisie mélodique (1887) •Asx/Pno •Marg

Beau soleil d'Espagne - Fantaisie Boléro (1887) •Asx/Pno •Marg

Canzonetta - Petite fantaisie (1887) •Asx/Pno •Marg

Elégie - Adagio (1887) •Asx/Pno •Marg

Fantaisie variée sur un thème original (1890) •Asx/Pno •Marg

Le Labrador - Fantaisie variée (1887) •Asx/Pno •Marg

Rayon d'or - Fantaisie variée (1884) •Asx/Pno •Marg

Tout le long du Rhin - Valse caprice (1890) •Ssx/Pno •Marg

CORDELL, Frank (1918)

Compositeur anglais.

Patterns (1972) (8') (to London Saxophone Quartet) 1) Preamble 2) Polygrams 3) Prolation 4) Postlude •SATB •NOV

Gestures (1972) (8') •SATB •NOV

The King Charles Galliard (1979) (2') •SATB

CORDERO, Roque (1917)

Compositeur, chef d'orchestre, et professeur Panaméen, né à Panama City, le 16 VIII 1917. Travailla avec E. Krenek, S. Chapple, et L. Barzin.

"C'est l'une des figures les plus représentatives de la musique contemporaine américaine." (Bordas)

"Up to 1954, Cordero's music was generally tonal. In that year he wrote his first 12-note composition." (G. Chase)

Soliloquios No. 2 (1976) (to J. Boitos) •Sx Solo •Peer/SMPC

CORDEIRO, George

Christmas Folio •4 Sx: AATB or SATB •DP
Saxophone Quartet No. 3 •SATB •DP

COREA, Chick

Crystal Silence •Asx/Perc

CORELLI, Arcangelo (1653-1713)

Adagio (Mule) •Asx/Pno •Led
Air et Dance (Maganini) •1 Sx: T or A/Pno •Mus
Baroque Etude •Tsx/Pno •PA
Chamber Sonata, op. 2, no. 2 (Schmidt) •3 Sx: SAB •DP
Gavotte et Courante (Chauvet) •Asx/Pno •Com
Gigue (Coggins) •Asx/Pno •Bel
Gigue (Harris) •2 Cl/Asx/Bsn (or BsCl) •CF
Gigue (Maganini) •Bb Sx or Asx/Pno •Mus
Prélude et Gigue (Chauvet) •Asx/Pno •Com
Sarabande and Courante (Johnson) •AATB •Rub
Sarabande and Gigue (Voxman) •Bb Sx/Pno •Rub
Sarabande et Gavotte (Chauvet) •Asx/Pno •Com
Sarabande et Gigue (Chauvet) •Asx/Pno •Com
6 Sonatas (Teal) •Asx/Pno
Sonate in F (Felix) •Bb Sx/Pno •Mus
Suite in Bb (Maganini) •Asx or Bb Sx/Pno •Mus
Variations on a Gavotte (Glaser-Rascher) •Asx/Pno •Chap

COREY, Kirk

Three Vignettes (1993) •Sx Solo

CORIGLIANO, James

Serenade and Rondo (1977) (5'15) (to Violet & Anthony Corigliano) •Asx/Pno •Sha

CORINA, John Hubert (1928)

Compositeur américain, né le 21 IV 1928, à Cleveland (Ohio).

Partita (1974) (to K. Deans) •Asx/Pno •adr
Partita 1) Moderato 2) Slowly 3) Quicker 4) Lively 5) Liltingly 6) Moderately 7) Slowly •2 Sx: AA

CORIOLIS, Emmanuel de (1907)

Compositeur français, né à Marseille, le 23 V 1907. Travailla avec P. Jeanjean.

Barcarolle (1973) •1 Sx: A or T/Pno •Bil
Pavane (1970) (2'10) •Asx/Pno •Led

CORNER, Philip (1933)

Compositeur américain, né le 10 IV 1933, à New York. Travailla à Paris avec O. Messiaen.

"After he spent a year in Korea studying Oriental calligraphy in order to apply it to the needs of graphic music notation, he turned to serial music, but mitigated its doctrines by aleatory indeterminacy; he often composes works after their first performances so as to avoid the stigma of premeditation." (Baker's)

Composition With or Without Beverly •Sx/Tape

CORNETTE, Victor (1795-1886)

Petite méthode •Cos
Tablature •Cos

CORNIOT, René (1901)

Chef d'orchestre et compositeur français, né à Lyon. Travailla avec P. Dukas et Noël Gallon.

Eglogue et Danse pastorale (1946) (14') (to M. Mule) •Asx/Orch (2222/221/Perc/Harp/Str) or Pno •Led

CORNU, Françoise (1960)

Compositeur français, né à Poitiers, le 1er IV 1960. Membre de l'Ensemble Instrumental Electro-Acoustique TM+.

Sentiers (1988) (2'15) •Asx/Perc •Lem
Filigranes I & II (1988) (4') (to S. Bertocchi) •2 Sx: AA

CORREGIA, Enrico

Augenblick der Stille (1985) (to Quart. Italiano Sassof.) •SATB

CORROYEZ, Georges (1871-1950)

Recueil de Quatuors classiques •Diverse combinations •Mar
20 Petites pièces en Quatuor •Diverse combinations •Mar
22 Pièces de J-S. Bach en 5 Suites •Mar
26 Pièces concertantes en Trio •Diverse combinations •Mar

CORTES, Ramiro (1933)

Compositeur américain, d'origine mexicaine, né à Dallas, le 25 XI 1933. Travailla avec Cowell, Donovan, Stevens, Dahl, Petrassi à Rome et Giannini à New York.

"Until the late 1960s his music was serially organized, under the influence of late Stravinsky and Dallapiccola; thereafter it became more freely structured, while remaining fully chromatic." (H.W. Hitchcock)

Five Studies (1968) (for R. Wojciak) •Sx Solo •USC

CORVALHA, Urban F.

Song and Dance (1971) •Asx/Band

CORY, Eleanor (1943)

Waking (1974) •Tsx/Bsn/Vln/Vcl/Bass/Perc

COSMA, Edgar (1925)

Compositeur français.

Graphiques (1981) (14') (to Saxtuor) •4 Sx
Invocation •Asx/Orch or Pno
Quatuor •SATB
7 Séquences (1963) (12'30) (to Quatuor Deffayet) 1) Pas trop vite 2) Rythmé 3) Assez libre 4) Vite 5) Capricieuse 6) Allant 7) Avec soins •SATB
Soliloque (1984) (10') •Ssx Solo

COSMEY

Louise •Bb Sx/Pno •Rub

COSSABOOM, Sterling

Fragments (to B. Rose) •Ssx/Pno

COSTANTINI, Andreina

Compositeur italien.

Nicht nur, noch nicht (1988) (6') •Tsx/Pno •adr

COSTE, Napoléon (1806-1883)

Guitariste et compositeur français né dans le Doubs, le 28 VI 1806, et mort à Paris le 17 II 1883.

"His compositions are often in the form of a fantasia and are frequently contrapuntal." (J. Cooper)

Fantaisie de concert •2 Sx •Mil
Regrets - Cantilène, op. 36 (1880) •Bb Sx/Pno •Mil

COSTEN, Roel van

Prisma (1984) (8') •Vla/Fl/Cl/Asx/BsCl/Trb/Vcl/Bass/Perc/Pno •Don

COTTET, Jean-Marie (1959)

Compositeur français.

Variations (1976) •Asx/Pno •Chou

COUF, Herbert

Saxophoniste, professeur, et compositeur américain.
Introduction, Dance et Furioso (1959) •Asx Solo •Band

COUINEAU, Patrice (1958)

Compositeur français, né à Toulouse, le 17 II 1958.
Mouvements volcaniques (1992) (9') •Bsx/Orch (1111/121/Str/Perc)
   or Pno •adr

COULEUVRIER, Alphonse-Louis (1848-1917)

Andante reliogioso n° 1 (1897) •Ssx/Fanfare or Pno •Cos
Andante relligioso n° 2 •Asx/Pno •Mar

COUPERIN, François (1668-1733)

Air du Diable (CLARK) •Bb Sx/Pno •Mus
Berceuse en rondeau (MULE) •Asx or Bb Sx/Pno •Led
Les Jeunes seigneurs (MULE) •Asx/Pno •Led
Les Moissonneurs - Rondeau •Asx/Pno •Led
Musette de Taverny (MULE) •Asx/Pno •Led
Le Petit Rien (MERIOT) •Asx/Pno •Phi

COURNET, Francis

Jazzman français.
10 Thèmes et Improvisations •Sx •Sal
Le "Thesaurus" du saxophoniste - Tablature générale de doigtés
   (1992) •Bil

COURROYER, Bernard (1921)

Saxophoniste et compositeur belge, né à Leval Trahegnies, le 18 VIII
1921. Travailla avec Fr. Daneels.
Improvisation •Asx/Pno •HM
Ventose (1969) (10') (to Fr. DANEELS) •7 Sx: SnoSATBBsCBs •adr

COURTIOUX, Jean (1931)

Percussionniste, arrangeur de jazz, et compositeur français, né le 26
XI 1931 à Paris.
Manu reva (1983) •2 Sx: TB/Fluegelhorn/Trb/Bass/Drums •DP
Opus market (1983) (to J. MELZER) •SATB •DP
Les Quatre éléments - Ballet •12 Sx: SnoSSAAATTTBBBs/Electric
   Pno/Perc/Bass

COUTU, Jacques

Compositeur canadien.
Etude de comportement et d'expression mélodique (1983) (12'30) (to
   G. TREMBLAY) •Ssx Solo •CMC

COWAN, Don

Compositeur canadien.
Impressions (1968) (3') (to P. BRODIE) •Asx/Pno •B&H
Morceau de genre (1968) (4') (to P. BRODIE) •Asx/Pno •B&H
Réflections (1969) (4') (to P. BRODIE) •Asx/Pno •B&H
Shadows (1975) •Tsx/Pno •B&H

COWELL, Henry Dixon (1897-1965)

Compositeur, pianiste, et musicologue américain, né à Palo Alto
(California), le 11 III 1897, mort à Shady (New York), le 10 XII 1965.
Travailla à Berlin avec E. von Hornbostel et R. H. Woodman.
   "Un des inventeurs de la musique américaine contemporaine." (C.
LEBLÉ) "La musique d'Henry Dixon Cowell a suscité de violentes
réactions : le fait est qu'elle est hardiment subversive. On relève une
volonté constante de chercher quelque chose d'inexploré, tentative
souvent couronnée de succès. Chercheur inlassable, Cowell—qu'on a
surnommé 'l'homme qui joue avec les coudes'—s'est particulièrement
attaché à renouveler le matériau sonore dans le sens d'un accroissement
et d'une identification du dynamisme." (R. BERNARD) "Henry Dixon
Cowell semble, par l'abondance des étiquettes que son attitude a pu
suggérer, depuis un demi-siècle, reculer les limites de l'éclectisme

généralement admis pour la plupart de ses compatriotes." (A. GAUTHIER)
"Cowell se tourna aussi vers les musiques asiatiques—Inde, Japon
entre autres—dont il explora avec réussite les échelles (tiers et quarts
de ton japonais, les rythmes et les tournures mélodiques; il ne négligea
pas davantage la culture musicale américaine, les ballades de son
folklore, ses anciens hymnes et airs fugués." (F-R. TRANCHEFORT)
"Dans ses oeuvres récentes, il s'est assagi: sa musique, d'inspiration
romantique, revêt fréquemment un caractère folklorique." (BORDAS)
"Une des personnalités les plus originales et les plus audacieuses de
l'école américaine." (Cl. ROSTAND) "Cowell est un personnage central
dans ce qu'il est convenu d'appeler musique 'moderne' ou même 'ultra
moderne'. Pour lui la musique est un terrain ouvert à toutes les
ressources, toutes les expériences, toutes les traditions (y compris les
traditions exotiques et ethniques) qui peuvent se révéler précieuses."
(GRIFFITHS)
   "Cowell is one of the most activve of American modern composers;
he has written more than one thousand works of various descriptions;
has championed serious new music in the U. S. and abroad." (BAKER)
"There is a persistent undercurrent of folk material audible in most of
Henry Cowell's works though they vary much according to their
particular function and particular instrumentation. His musical style is
melodic, whimsical, and very free." (GROVE) "It will take many years
before an adequate appraisal of Cowell as a composer can be made,
because of the abundance of his work and its nonlinear evolution. His
place in the history of contemporary music is assured, however, by his
seminal influence as a composer and as a person." (B. SAYLOR)
Air and Scherzo (1961) (for S. RASCHER) •Asx/Chamber Orch or Pno
   •AMP/ACA
Chrysanthemus (1937) •Soprano Voice/2 Sx/2 Vln/Vla/Vcl
Hymn and Fuguing Tune No. 4 (1945) •Any 3 instruments (SAT)
   •ACA
Hymn and Fuguing Tune No. 18 (1964) •2 Sx: SA
Hymn and Fuguing Tune No. 18 (1964) (4') (to S. RASCHER) •2 Sx: S
   CBs •TTF
Quartet (1946) (6') •AATB •PIC
Sailor's Hornpipe (4') •AATB •PIC
Sax-happy (1949) (4') •AATB •PIC
"60" (1942) (2') (for Percy Grainger's 60th Birthday) •3 Sx: SAB
   •TTF

COWLES, Colin E. (1940)

Compositeur anglais.
Concertante (1973) (to P. HARVEY) •4 Sx: SATB/Str Quartet •adr
Elegy (1973) (12') •Ssx/String Orch •adr
Five Little Pieces 1) Soliloquy 2) Promenade 3) Slightly blue
   4) Pirate Tella •SATB
Five Pieces (10') 1) Tolmers village 2) Octagon 3) Blacker & Blues
   4) Poem 5) Scherzo •Asx/Pno •Stu
Four Features (1979) (12') (To English Saxophone Quartet) •SATB
   •adr
Four in Popular Style (1979) (12') •SATB •Stu
From Barrak Hill No. 2 (1979) (8') (to London Saxophone Quartet)
   •4 Sx Quartets: SATB/SATB/SATB/SATB •adr
From the King's Chamber •Tsx/Narr/Chamber Orch •adr
Fun Piece (2') •Bsx/Pno •adr
Fweekout •Sx Choir: SnoSATBBs •adr
"I will give my love an appel" (1975) (3') (to P. HARVEY) •Sx Solo
   •adr
In Memoriam (to a little white Rabbit) (1976) (13') •Tsx/Str Orch
   •adr
Intermezzo (1979) (1'30) •2Sx: BB •BMIC
Miniature Suite •1 Sx: B or A/Pno •Stu
Of Spain •Tsx/Pno •DP
On the Other Hand (1985) •Jazz Sx Quartet: SATB •DP
Pastoral •Tsx/Pno •DP

Quartet no. 1 (1977) 1) Preamble 2) Intermezzo 3) Toccata •SATB
•adr

Recitative and Air (3') •Ssx/Harp or Pno •adr

Rhapsody (1977) (10') •Asx/Str Orch •adr

Sarabande (2') •Ssx/Pno •adr

Sarabande, Ben ritmico, Air, Em-Bari-Swing (1975) (8') •1 Sx:
S+A+T+B/Str quartet •adr

Scherzino •Asx/Pno •Stu

Six Easy Quartets in Recognizable Forms (1975) (15') (to the
London Saxophone Quartet) 1) Promenade 2) Pinata-tella
Litanies 3) Slightly Blue 4) Presco •SATB •adr

Sonata (1978) (18') 1) Moderato 2) Fuoco feroce 3) Pastoral •Tsx/
Pno •adr

Sopsonare (1973) (12') 1) Moderato 2) Intermezzo blues 3) Rondo
•Ssx/Pno •adr

Suite (1978) (20') •4 Sx: SATB/Harp or Pno •adr

Swinging the Cat (4') •2 Eb Sx or 2 Bb Sx •adr

Tears (2') •Bsx/Pno •adr

Three Sketches from Bala (8') •Tsx/Pno •adr

COX, J. S.

Call Me Time Own •Eb Sx/Pno •CF

COX, Rona (1942)

Compositeur américain, né le 9 VI 1942, à Fort Smith (Arkansas).
Travailla avec M. Ellis.

A Saxophone (1968) (6') •2 Sx: AT/Tape •adr

Two Expressions (1968) •Fl/Ob/Cl/2 Sx: SB/Hn/Bsn/Bass/Perc •adr

COYNER, Lou

Compositeur américain.

Music-Piva •Asx/Perc/Tape

Saxifrage II •SATB •WWS

Solo Saxophone with Ensemble (1985) (to J. SAMPEN) •Asx/
Ensemble: EH+Ob/BsCl/Bsn/Harp/Pno/Perc/Str

CRAEN, Nikolauss (xxxx-1507)

Si ascendero in Caelum (RIPPE) •3 Sx: ATB •DP

CRAGUN, J. Beach (18xx-19xx)

Saxophoniste, professeur, et compositeur américain d'origine allemande, né à Berlin. Travailla avec G. Bumcke.

The Business Saxophonist (1923) •F&U/Rub

Concerto No. 1, op. 21 (1925) 1) Allegro brillante 2) Romanza
3) Allegro giocoso •Asx/Orch or Pno •Rub

Cragun Conservatory Method (3 Volumes) •F&U/Rub

8 Concert Duets (1926) •2 Sx •Rub

11 Cadenzas •Rub

52 Progressive Etudes •Rub

Finishing Routine Studies for Daily Practice (1926) •Rub

95 Duets and Trios •Rub

30 Melodic Caprices in all Major and Minor Keys •Rub

36 Etudes •Rub

20 Etudes for the Development of Technic Difficulty •Rub

CRAIG, Jack

Slap 'n Sax (1924) •Sx Ensemble

CRAS, Jean (1879-1932)

Compositeur français, né à Brest, le 22 V 1879, où il est mort le 14
IX 1932. Travailla avec H. Duparc.

"Duparc qui le forme, a exercé une profonde influence sur l'orientation de la pensée de ce musicien délicat, farouchement indépendant, et
qui n'a jamais obéi à d'autres impératifs qu'à ceux d'une conscience
exigeante et superbement indifférente aux sollicitations du succès et de
la mode." (R. BERNARD) "Le message franckiste se teinte chez lui
d'orientalisme inspiré par ses voyages." (R. STRICKER) "Personnalité

passionnée et attachante dont l'oeuvre nous réserve encore des surpri-
ses." (J. & B. MASSIN)

Danse (1924) •SATB •Sen

Demain (1929) •Asx/Tpt/Trb/Perc/Vln/Vcl/Bass •Sen

CRAWFORD, Jerry (1947)

Sonata •Asx/Pno •adr

Music (1969) (7') (To J. CUNNINGHAM) •Asx/Pno

CRAWLEY, Clifford (1929)

Compositeur canadien.

Boutade (1977) (4') (to P. BRODIE) •SATB •CMC

CREPIN, Alain

Compositeur belge.

Céline Mandarine (1991) (3'15) (Pour ma fille Céline) •Asx/Pno
•Lem

Green Apple •Asx/Pno

Saxoflight •Asx/Orch d'harmonie or Pno •Scz

Sicilienne •1 Sx: A or S/Pno •HM

CREQUILLON, Thomas (1480-c. 1500)

Canzona (REX) •AATB •DP

CRESSONNOIS, Jules (1823-xxxx)

Chef de musique et compositeur français, né à Mortagne (Orne), le
17 IV 1823. Travailla avec G. Kastner.

Fantaisie d'après Mayeur •Asx/Pno •Cos

Pifférari •SATB •Sax

Romance de Proserpine - Trio •3 Sx •Sax

Tambourin d'après Rameau •SATB •Sax

CRESTON, Paul (Joseph GUTEVECCHIO) (1906-1985)

Compositeur et organiste américain d'origine italienne, né à New
York, le 10 X 1906; mort le 24 VIII 1985.

"Autodidacte et éclectique, Paul Creston s'est imposé par un langage
simple et naturel, qui a résolu la plupart des problèmes posés aux
compositeurs de sa génération." (A. GAUTHIER) "C'est de façon éclectique et également empirique qu'il a résolu la plupart de ses problèmes
se posant aujourd'hui à un symphoniste. Les influences les plus
diverses se retrouvent dans ses oeuvres, de Brahms à Stravinski." (Cl.
ROSTAND)

"His music is characterized by spontaneity, with strong melodic lines
and full-bodied harmony; his instrumental writing is highly advanta-
geous for virtuoso performance." (BAKER) "Creston has made rhythm
the keystone of his style, his technique depending primarily on
constantly shifting subdivisions of a regular metre. The other main
features of his music are long, florid, but motivically generated
melody, lush impressionistic harmony and very full orchestration. The
texture is generally homophonic, the tonality free and the form classical in its clarity and concision despite the flamboyantly romantic
gestures." (W. G. SIMMONS)

Concerto, op. 26 (1941) (17') (To C. LEESON) 1) Energetic 2) Medita-
tive 3) Rhythmic •Asx/Orch (3222/4231/Timp/Str) or Band
(3252/4232/3 Cnt/4 Sx/Perc) or Pno •GSch

Rapsodie, op. 108 (1976) (10') (to J-M. LONDEIX) •Asx/Org •Sha

Rapsodie, op. 108b •Asx/Pno •Sha

Sonata, op. 19 (1939) (13') (to C. LEESON) 1) With vigor 2) With
tranquility 3) With gaiety •Asx/Pno •Sha

Suite, op. 6 (1935) (10') (to C. LEESON) 1) Scherzo 2) Pastorale
3) Toccata •Asx/Pno •Sha

Suite (1978) (15') (to the Swiss Saxophone Quartet) 1) Prelude
2) Scherzino 3) Pastorale 4) Rondo •SATB •Sha

CRIVELLI, Carlo

Compositeur italien. Travailla avec D. Guaccero.

Nel buio del Mare (1988) (12') (to Quatuor di Sassof. Aquilano)
•SATB

CROLEY, Randall

Compositeur américain.
Gli Occhi (1984) (8'30) •Asx Solo
Sette Momenti (1967-72) •SATB •AEN
Trè Expressioni (1969) (to M. TAYLOR) •SATB •AEN

CROUSIER, Claude

Clarinettiste, professeur, et compositeur français, né à Nîmes. Travailla avec J-P. Guezec, O. Messiaen, et Cl. Ballif.
Mon 1er cycle - ça démarre! (1991) (5') •Asx/Pno •Fuz
Mon 2e cycle - ça roule! (1991) (5') •Asx/Pno •Fuz

CRUFT, Adrian (Francis) (1921)

Compositeur anglais né à Mitcham, le 10 II 1921. Travailla avec G. Jacob et E. Rubbra.
"His music is diatonic, firmly based in tradition and generally straightforward in idiom." (H. COLE)
Chalumeau Suite, op. 81 (1975) (6') •Tsx/Pno •JP

CRUMB, George (Henry) (1929)

Compositeur américain né à Charleston (West Virginia), le 24 X 1929. Travailla avec Finney.
"Il est sans doute avec Carter le compositeur le mieux intégré à l'*establishment* musical américain. Son oeuvre est doctement étudiée sur les campus et connaît les faveurs d'un nombre grandissant d'interprètes prestigieux. Sous des dehors de stricte et sévère modernité, sa musique cache des réserves de fantaisie et de liberté créatrice. Si elle obéit à une logique, c'est apparemment à celle du rêve ou, au mieux, du rituel. Crumb semble avoir toujours manifesté une indépendance d'esprit ombrageuse: il n'a notamment jamais adhéré au système sériel. Les recherches de timbre, l'exploration poétique, la spiritualité l'emportent chez lui apparemment sur toute considération d'organisation formelle." (J-E. FOUSNAQUER) "Redevable à Cage—même s'il se réclame d'autres sources, comme le Berio de *Cries of London* et de *Coro*—il puise à différents courants ethniques. Celui de l'Inde ou de l'Extrême-Orient et propose des effets vocaux et instrumentaux spéciaux." (J-N. von der WEID)
"Crumb has stated that Debussy, Mahler and Bartok were the principal influences on his music." (L. A. PEARLMAN)
Quest (25') •Guit/ 1 Sx: S+A+T+Harmonica/2 Perc/Harp •BR

CRUZ, Zulema de la (1958)

Compositeur espagnole, née à Madrid en 1958. Travailla avec C. Bernaola, L. de Pable, A. Garcia, Abril, L. Hiller, R. Bauer, et L. Smith.
Chio (1989) (to D. KIENTZY) •BsSx/Tape

CUI, César (1835-1918)

Cantabile, op. 36 •Bb Sx/Pno •CBet
En partant (MULE) •Asx/Pno •Led
Orientale (from *Kaleidoscope*) (GUREWICH) •Asx or Bb Sx/Pno •CF
Orientale (HARRIS) •2 Cl/Asx/Bsn (or BsCl) •CF
Orientale (WHEELER) •Asx or Bb Sx/Pno •Mills

CULBERTSON, D. C.

Dream Music I (1979) •Sx/Vibr

CULPO, Christopher (1960)

Compositeur américain, né à Pittsfield (Massachussetts). Travailla avec M. Babbitt, B. Rands, J. McKeel, et R. Sirota.
Metaphor (1988) •Asx/Pno

CUNCHE, Jean Alexandre Octave (1930)

Compositeur belge, né le 8 V 1930 à Chatelet. Travailla avec H. Barbier, F. de Bourguignon, et P. de Leye.

Introduction et Tarentelle (1958) (6') (to Quatuor Belge de Saxophones) •SATB •adr

CUNEO, Angelo Francesco (1870)

Contrebassiste et compositeur italien, né à Turin, le 13 XII 1870.
Capriccio •Asx/Pno •Ric
Metodo completo (1946) •Ric

CUNLIFFE

Farewell to Peace •Ssx/Pno •WWS

CUNNINGHAM, H.

Concerto (1960) •Asx/Orch

CUNNINGHAM, Michael G. (1937)

Compositeur américain, né le 5 VIII 1937, à Warren (Michigan). Travailla avec R. L. Finney, L. Bassett, et B. Heiden.
Cat Feet - Jazz Piece •5 Sx/4 Tpt/4 Trb/Guit/Pno/Bass/Drum •SeMC
French Fantasy (1985) (to J. HOULIK) •Tsx/Pno
Linear Ceremony •2 Quintets: Fl/Ob/Cl/Hn/Bsn & Fl/Ob/Sx/Cl/Bsn •SeMC
Mazurka (DEBUSSY) •SATB •Eto
Miro Gallery - Jazz Piece •Fl/Ob/Cl/Asx/Bsn •SeMC
The Nightingale (1964) (4') •Asx/Pno •DP
Pleasantries (1991) (to S. GETZ) 1) Moderato 2) Andante 3) Con spirito •Tsx/Pno
Quartet, op. 103 (1986) •SATB •SeMC
Rara Avis, op. 19b (1966) (4') •Sx Solo •Eto
Rondo (C. P. E. BACH) •SATB •Eto
Serenade, op. 13a (1961) (7') •Cl/Asx/Bsn •SeMC
Shorty - Jazz Piece •5 Sx/4 Tpt/4 Trb/Guit/Pno/Bass/Drum •SeMC
Sonata, op. 50 (1972) (10') 1) Vivo 2) Subdued 3) Theme and variations •Asx/Pno •SeMC
Sonata •Ssx/Pno •SeMC
Spring Sonnet •Fl/2 Cl/BsCl/2 Sx/3 Hn/Bass •SeMC
Three Quaint Cameos •3 Sx: ATB •SeMC
Trigon, op. 31 (1969) (10') (to J. HOULIK) 1) Constant driving rhythm 2) Quiet and calm 3) Quite fast •Tsx/Pno •Eto
Trio in Two Movements (J. C. BACH) •3 Sx: SAT •Eto
Trio no. 3, op. 59 (1974) (to K. DEANS) 1) Mystical 2) Pensive 3) May song •2 Sx: SA/Pno •Eto

CURTI, Guido

Ambition - Valse caprice •Asx/Pno •Col
Dancing saxophone •Asx/Pno •Col
Gouttes perlées - Valse •Asx/Pno •Col
Le Jongleur de notes •Asx/Pno •Col
Passion •Asx/Pno •Col
Plaisanterie •Asx/Pno •Col
Ris donc, saxophone •Asx/Pno •Col
Saxo aviateur •Asx/Pno •Col
Saxo mitrailleuse •Asx/Pno •Col
Saxopanie - Novelty fox •Asx/Pno •Col
Le secret du saxophone •Asx/Pno •Col
Swinging saxophone •Asx/Pno •Col
Triumphal saxophone •Asx/Pno •Col
Va et vient - Novelty fox •Asx/Pno •Col
Virage dangereux •Asx/Pno •Col

CURTIS-SMITH, Curtis (1941)

Compositeur américain, né à Walla Walla (Washington), le 9 IX 1941.
Unisonics (1976) (14') (to T. KYNASTON) 1) Prelude 2) 66-69 3) 126 4) ca. 60 5) Postlude •Asx/Pno •Pres

Sundry Dances (1981) 1) Death Jig (Totentanz) 2) In dulci jubilo
(like a calliope) 3) Dream blues 4) Wie lieblich ist doch Herr, die
Statte (Jig for an elephant) 5) Pipes and Drones (Bagpipes) •Fl/
Ob/Cl/3 Sx: SAB/Bsn/CBsn/Tpt/Trb/Tuba/Bass •adr

CUSHING, Charles (1905)

Compositeur américain, né à Oakland (California), le 18 XII 1905.
Travailla en France avec N. Boulanger.

"His compositions are best known on the west coast of the U.S.A.
where many of them have been performed." (GROVE) "His music is
lyrical and makes use of impressionist harmonies." (V. B. SAMSON)

Hommage à A. Roussel (1954) (3') Collection •Asx/Pno •PN/Bil

CUSTER, Arthur (1923)

Compositeur américain, né le 24 IV 1923, à Manchester (Connecticut).

Cycle for Nine Instruments •Asx/BsCl/Tpt/Hn/Vln/Vla/Vcl/Bass/
Perc •JM

DABNEY, Denise & Donald SINTA
Voicing: An approach to the saxophone's third register •SiMC

DACHEZ, Christian
Melodi-lène (1986) (2'10) •1 Sx: A or T/Pno •Led
Saxorama (1986) (2') •1 Sx: A or T/Pno •Led

DADELSEN, Hans-Christian von (1948)
Compositeur, pianiste, et professeur allemand, né le 4 XII 1948 à Berlin. Travailla avec D. de la Motte et Ligeti.
Cries of Butterflies (1979) (16') 1) Adagio assai, espressivo e cantabile - Allegro apassionato 2) Adagio assai, espressivo e cantabile - Adagio 3) Lento - Allegro tenchroso - Rock 'n roll 4) lento - Adagio assai •Asx/Hn/Vla/Synth •Kodasi
Kra / Dark (1993) •Asx/Vla •INM

DAETVYLER, Jean (1907)
Concerto (1980) •4 Sx: SATB/Perc

DAHL, Ingolf (1912-1970)
Compositeur, professeur, et chef d'orchestre américain, d'origine suédoise, né à Hambourg, le 9 VI 1912, mort à Frutigen (Suisse), le 7 VIII 1970. Travailla à Cologne avec Ph. Jarnach et H. Abrendroth, à Zurich avec Andrea et W. Frey, puis en Californie avec Nadia Boulanger.
"A un style nettement américain, diatonique, avec une rythmique de grande énergie."
"As composer, he adheres to an advanced polyphonic style in free dissonant counterpoint." (BAKER) "He began in an expressionistically oriented dissonant and polyphonic style which later developed into an idiom based on clear-cut diatonic elements, with strong emphasis on the sonorous and virtuosic potentialities of his instrumental materials."…"His collaboration with Stravinsky resulted in increasing clarification of texture, a trend towards diatonicism and pronounced interest in timbre and instrumental virtuosity." (K. STONE)
Concerto (1949/53) (19') (to S. RASCHER) •Asx/Wind Orch •(3353/ 4432/4 Bass/Perc) or Pno •EAM

DAHM
Concert Album of French Classics •1 Sx: A or T/Pno •Mus
Paris soir •1 Sx: A or T/Pno •Mus

DAIGNEUX, A.
Sinuosity •Asx/Pno •Sez

DAILEY, Dwight Morris (1923)
Clarinettiste et saxophoniste américain, né à Coldwater (Michigan) le 22 VI 1923. Travailla avec A. Luconi, W. Stubbins, R. Howland, W. Revelli, et S. Rascher.
Reflections in Gold, Silver and Ebony (1982) •Sx/Fl/Cl/Pno
12 Concert Pieces (1950) •Tsx/Pno •GW

DAILLET
Concert Pieces •Tsx/Pno •Mus

DAKEN, K.
Compositeur russe.
Cuckoo •5 Sx: SAATB/Pno/Bass/Drums

DAKIN, Charles (1930)
Compositeur anglais
Epona (1981) (11') (to J. DAWSON) •Ssx/Vcl/Pno •DP
Kinnari (1982) (5'35) •Ssx/Tpt
Leda and the Swan (1977) (7') •Ssx/Tpt/Trb •DP
Mobiles (1982) (11'15) (for J. DAWSON) 1) Brazen 2) Calm 3) Solemn 4) Fragile 5) Firm 6) Thrusting •2 Sx: ST •DP
Prélude and Dance (1956) (5'30) •SATB •Pet
Quartet (1981) •SATB
Ragamala (1980) (2'30) (for J. DAWSON) •Ssx/Vcl
Sonata da camera •Asx/Pno •DP
Straight Jazz •SATB •WWS
Suite Concertante (1974) (25') •4 Sx: SATB/Str Orch •DP
Syra (1979) (8'30) •2 Cl/2 Tsx/2 Tpt/2 Trb/4 Vla/4 Vcl/2 Bass
The Tarots of Marseille (1981) (17') (for J. DAWSON) •Sx Solo

D'ALBERT, Eugen (See ALBERT)

D'ALESSANDRO, Raffaele (See ALESSANDRO)

DALLIN
Aubade in Blue (WESTPHAL) •AATB •Bel
Aubade in Blue •6 Sx: AATTBBs •WWS

DALLINGER, Fridolin
Compositeur autrichien.
Piece (1974) (10') (to S. FASANG) •Asx/Pno
Suite (7') •SATB •CA

DAM, Hermann van (1956)
Compositeur néerlandais, né à Harderwijk, le 25 IV 1956. Travailla à Utrecht avec J. Straesser.
Rage, rage against the dying of the light (1984) (8') (In memoriam Gustav Martin BLOK) •SATB •Don
Rituals in transfigured time (1988) (8') •Sx Solo: A or T •Don
Who's afraid of black, white and time, contrast II (1988) (35') •Asx/ Pno •Don

DAMAIS, Emile (1906-198x)
Compositeur et professeur français, né à Paris.
"Parisien de Paris, Emile Damais fait figure d'indépendant parmi ses pairs. L'écriture, d'où tout système est banni, participe de l'atonalité, de la polytonalité sans exclure d'autant une base tonale." (M. IMBERT)
Esquisse symphonique (1944) (10') (to LEMAGNENT) Asx/Orch or Pno •Bil
5 Divertissements (1946) (17') 1) Rapidité 2) Lent mélancolique 3) Rythmico 4) Spiritual 5) Staccato •Asx Solo •Bil
Quatuor •4 Sx

DAMASE, Jean-Michel (1928)
Compositeur et pianiste français, né à Bordeaux, le 27 I 1928. Travailla avec Cl. Delvincourt. Grand Prix de Rome (1947).
"Je préfère la sincérité à la nouveauté." (J-M. DAMASE) "Il réussit à concilier l'inconciliable, en infusant un peu d'esprit d'austérité et de scrupuleuse ascèse syntaxique à une esthétique non seulement hédonique mais que conditionne une recherche délibérée de l'efficacité ou, si l'on préfère, du succès." (R. BERNARD)
"Damase's youthful compositional maturity helped to foster a considerable technical facility, and he has produced a great deal of music in a style that is attractive and elegant, remaining close to the traditions of the Conservatoire. All his works demonstrate a deep knowledge of the possibilities of instruments." (A. GIRARDOT)
Aria, op. 7 (1947) (4') •Asx/Pno •Sal
Azur (1990) •Asx/Pno •Bil
Concertstück, op. 16 (1950) (9'30) (to M. MULE) •Asx/Orch (1111/ 100/Harp/Str) or Pno •Led

Mélancolie - Recueil (Album) (1974) (2'30) •Asx/Pno •Zu
Note à note (1990) (2'30) (to J-Y. FOURMEAU) •Asx/Pno •Bil
Quatuor (1976) (11') 1) Allegro 2) Andante 3) Allegro vivo •SATB
    •Lem
Thème varié (1987) (4') (to M. MÉRIOT) •Asx/Pno •Comb
Vacances (1990) (2'30) (to J-Y. FOURMEAU) •Asx/Pno •Bil

D'AMBRIOSO, Alfred Joseph (see AMBRIOSO)

DAMICO, John
Compositeur américain.
Avilion (1960) •Asx/Str (2 Vln/Vla/Vcl/Bass) •DP

DANCEANU, Liviu
Florilège (15') (to D. KIENTZY) •Sx/Fl/Fl-à-bec/Pno
Quasi concerto (1983) (15') (to D. KIENTZY) •1 Sx: S+T/Bsn/Trb/
    Vcl/Bass/Pno/Perc

DANCLA, Jean-Baptiste (1817-1907)
Air varié - sur un air de Donizetti •Bb Sx/Pno
Andante et Mazurka •Bb Sx/Pno •Mol
Ballade et Air de ballet •Bb Sx/Pno •Mol
Petite étude et Polonaise •Bb Sx/Pno •Mol
Rêverie et Polka •Asx/Pno •Mol
Romance et Valse •Bb Sx/Pno •Mol

DANDELOT, Georges (1895-1975)
Professeur et compositeur français, né à Paris, le 2 XII 1895.
Travailla avec A. Roussel, V. d'Indy, et P. Dukas.
"Ses oeuvres sont dans le style néo-classique." (Cl. ROSTAND) "Georges Dandelot tente d'exprimer un romantisme naturel, que le langage contemporain refuse généralement." (R. STRICKER)
Sonatine (1967) (7') (to M. MULE) 1) Allegro 2) Lent 3) Final •Asx/
    Pno •ME

D'ANDREA, O.
Altair •Asx/Pno

DANEAU, N.
Piasaxo •Asx/Pno •TM

DANEELS, François (1921)
Saxophoniste virtuose et professeur belge, né à Tubize (Brabant) le 4 XI 1921. Professeur au Conservatoire Royal de Bruxelles de 1954 à 1988. Fondateur du Quatuor Belge de Saxophones (1953).
S'est fait entendre en soliste ou avec son quatuor principalement en Europe et aux U.S.A., et a enregistré de nombreux disques. Peut être considéré comme un des principaux promoteurs du saxophone 'classique' en Belgique.
Le saxophoniste en herbe - Exercices pour la 1ère année (1969)
    •Sch
4 Miniatures (to N. NOZY & W. DEMEY) 1) Lento 2) Vif 3) Calme
    4) Energique •Asx Solo •Sch
Suite (1973) (7') •Asx Solo •Sch

D'ANGELO, Nicholas V. (1929)
Compositeur américain, né à Erie (Pennsylvania), le 2 XII 1929.
Travailla avec V. Giannini, B. Rogers, et P. Hindemith.
"Few composers have an output, sufficiently varied in style and scope to make such a *one-man show* work. You are certainly one of the exceptions." (F. PREAUSNITZ)
Capriccio and Improvisations (1967) (8') •Asx/Orch •adr
A Child's Prayer (1966) (6') •SATB •adr
Dimensions Three (1965) (7') •3 Sx: ATB •adr
Five Mobiles (1972) (15') •Asx/Pno •adr
Introduction and Fantasy (1967) (10') (to J. KRIPL) •Asx/Chamber
    Orch or Pno •adr

Mosaics (1970) (8') •SATB •adr
The Seventh Star of Paracelsus (1968) (16') •Fl/Vln/Asx/Vcl/Pno
    •adr

DANIELS, Edward Kenneth (1941)
Musicien de jazz américain, né le 9 X 1941, à Brooklyn (New York).
The Budding Saxophonist •Pet

DANKS, Hart Pease (1834-1903)
Silver Threads Among the Gold •2 Sx: AT/Pno or AATB/Pno

DANKWORTH, John (1927)
Compositeur et musicien de jazz anglais né le 20 IX 1927, à Londres.
Joue de la clarinette et du saxophone.
Fairoak Fusion (1979) (45') •4 Sx: SATB/Vln/Jazz Quartet

DANNENBERG, Torsten
Compositeur suédois.
Skizze no. 1 (3'30) •Tsx/Big Band •SMIC

DAPPER, Klaus (1948)
Saxophoniste de jazz.
Das Saxophonbuch (1989) •Vog

DARBELLAY, Jean-Luc (1946)
Compositeur suisse, né 2 VII 1946. Travailla avec Th. Hirsbrussner et Chr. Halffter.
Plages (5') (to M. SIEFFERT) •Asx Solo
Quatuor (to M. SIEFFERT) •SATB

DARCY, Robert
Four Movements •SATB

DARIJAN, Bozii
Concert •Asx/Orch •YUC

DARLING, John
Quatre de la famille (1982) 1) Entrée 2) En forme de slow 3) En
    forme de disco 4) Finale dixieland •SATB •Mar

DARROW, Melissa (1959)
Rites of Passage (1992) 1) Monday Night Wake 2) Contredanse •Sx
    Ensemble: SATBBs

DASKE, Martin (1962)
Compositeur allemand, né à Berlin. Travailla aux U.S.A. avec C.
Wolff, à Cracovie avec B. Schaeffer, puis à Salzbourg.
Sisaxason (1991) (13') •4 Sx: SATB/Tape

DASSONVILLE
Elsida la Créole - Fantaisie berceuse concertante (1895) •Asx/Pno

D'AURIOL, Hubert (See AURIOL)

DAUTREMER, Marcel (1906-1978)
Compositeur et chef d'orchestre, né à Paris, le 11 VI 1906; mort à Paris, le 25 XI 1978. Travailla avec P. Dukas.
"La musique de Marcel Dautremer use d'un langage néo-classique où prime la mélodie, non dénué d'élégance."
Concerto, op. 61 (1962) (12'30) (to G. GOURDET) 1) Allegro 2) Largo
    cantabile 3) Finale •Asx/Str Orch or Pno •Lem
Incertitude - Recueil (Album) (1974) •Asx/Pno •Zu
Quatuor •SATB
Rêverie interrompue (1954) (4') •Asx/Pno •Led
Tango et Tarentelle (1946) (6') (to M. MULE) •Asx/Pno •Led
Tetraventi (1975) (to Quatuor Deffayet) •SATB

DAVENPORT, La Noue (1922)
3 Duets •HE

DAVIA, Moises

Compositeur espagnol.
Dialogo (1982) (to M. Mijan) •SATB
Quatuor (1981) (to Quatuor Mijan) •SATB

DAVID, Karl Heinrich (1884-1951)

Compositeur, chef d'orchestre et critique musical suisse, né à Saint-Gall, le 30 XII 1884, mort à Nervi (Italie), le 17 V 1951. Travailla en Thuille. Appartint au groupe dit "de Munich."

"Although he is not of the younger generation David's compositions are thoroughly modern in style and characterized by vigour and virility. He is among the few Swiss composers who have really grasped the essentials of music for the stage." (H. Ehinger)
Concerto (1947) •Asx/Str Orch
1° Quartet (1934) •Vln/Asx/Vcl/Pno
2° Quartet (1936) •Vln/Asx/Vcl/Pno

DAVIDSON, Tina

Berceuse (1991) •Asx/8 Vcl

DAVIES, Terry

Compositeur anglais.
Whale (1990) •Sx+WX7 MIDI Wind Controller/Tape

DAVIS, Michael

Compositeur américain.
Night Poem (to the US Air Force Saxophone Quartet) •SATB

DAVIS, Rick

Concerto (1966) •Electronic Asx/Jazz Band

DAVIS, William (1949)

Recitative and Scherzo (1984) (to T. Liley) •Asx/Pno
Variations on a Theme of Richard Schumann (1982) •Bsx/Pno
  •South

DAWES, Charles G.

Melody (Sears) •Asx/Pno •Rem

DAWSON, Carl

Compositeur américain
Quartet (1968) (to C. Leeson) •AATB

DEAK, Csaba (1932)

Compositeur suédois né le 16 IV 1932 à Budapest (Hongrie). Travailla avec F. Farkas puis, à Stockholm avec H. Rosenberg. En Suède depuis 1957.

"From the 1960s his works are based on a 12-tone melody. Since then Deak has evolved personal systems which are by no means entirely free but are flexibly varied from one composition to another." (H-G. P.) "Deak has composed a great deal more besides the works for wind instruments which perhaps have earned him most attention."
Kvartett (1988) (15') (to Stockholm Saxophone Quartet) •SATB
  •SUE/SMIC
Quintet (1989) (15') (to J. Pettersson) •Asx/Str Quartet: 2 Vln/Vla/
  Vcl •SUE

DEASON, David (1945)

Compositeur américain.
Double-take (1979) (4'45) (to D. Demsey) 1) Allegro moderato
  2) Lento 3) Allegro •Asx/Tpt •Pres
Blues-Walk (1984) (to J. Stoltie) •1 Sx: S+A+T/Pno
Epigrams •Ssx/Pno •DP
Five Diversions (1980) (to D. Demsey) 1) Allegro 2) Lento
  3) Moderato 4) Andante 5) Allegro molto •Ssx/Fl •DP
Glow (1980) •2 Sx: AT •DP
Gossamer Rings (1982) (to S. Mauk) •Ssx/Wind ensemble

Jazz Partita (1983) (to D. Demsey) •Sx Solo
Quartet (1983) (to Adirondack Saxophone Quartet) •SATB
Quartet (1985) (For the Amherst Saxophone Quartet) Allegro -
  Mesto - Allegro •SATB
Sonata (1980) •Asx/Tuba/Pno •DP
Tenor-ventions (1980) (to H. Gee) •Tsx/Pno •DP
Two Studies (1980) •Ssx/Fl •DP

DEBAAR, Mathieu

Prélude et Humoresque •Asx/Pno •EMB

DeBLASIO, Chris (1958-1993)

Music for a Short Subject (1990) (8') (to H. Huff) •Ssx/Org •TTF
Prelude and Fugue (1991) (9') (to A. Paulsson) •Ssx/Str Quintet
  •TTF

DEBONDUE, Albert

25 Etudes déchiffrages •Led
48 Etudes déchiffrages •Led
50 Etudes déchiffrages •Led
Etudes progressives •DP
Méthode pour hautbois ou saxophone •Bil

DE BUERIS, John

Miami Moon - Valse brillante •Asx/Pno •CF

DEBUSSY, Claude-Achille (1862-1918)

Compositeur français, né à Saint-Germain-en-Laye, le 22 VIII 1862, mort à Paris, le 25 III 1918.

"L'essence même du génie français." (Ch. Du Bos) "Après les grandioses architectures de l'époque classique, après le flamboiement du romantisme, la musique française par Claude Debussy s'est vu couronnée de toute une floraison inattendue de fraîcheur nouvelle, dont l'éclosion fut la surprise enchantée de notre jeunesse, et dont l'épanouissement, en une gloire désormais universelle, ne peut être salué avec plus de joie que par l'un de ceux qui en respirèrent dès l'aurore, le premier parfum." (P. Dukas) "Cette personnalité dans la façon non seulement de s'exprimer, mais surtout de *sentir*, qui est le privilège des natures exceptionnelles, Claude Debussy a eu la rare fortune de la posséder très tôt, et de la développer dans le meilleur sens, suivant les aspects les plus variés." (G. Samazeuilh) "Dans la *Rapsodie avec saxophone*, Claude Debussy s'affirme comme un musicien de plein air, aimant respirer longuement, sachant ouvrir des horizons, comme un peintre étincelant qui sait faire vibrer une palette somptueuse, faire chanter les jeux d'ombre et de lumière." "Loin d'être une oeuvre mineure, la *Rapsodie avec saxophone* est un chaînon indispensable entre *La Mer* et *Le Martyre de St. Sébastien.*" (J-M. Londeix)

In April 1902, Debussy wrote: "I wanted from music a freedom which it possesses perhaps to a greater degree than any other art, not being tied to a more or less exact reproduction of Nature but to the mysterious correspondences between Nature and Imagination." "Debussy is regarded as the creator and chief protagonist of musical Impressionism, despite the fact he deprecated the term and denied his role in the movement... He created a style peculiarly sensitive to musical mezzotint from a palette of halflit delicate colors. To accomplish the desired effect, Debussy introduced many novel technical devices. He made use of the Oriental pentatonic scale; and of the whole-tone scale; he emancipated dissonance, so that unresolved discords freely followed one another; he also revived the archaic practice of consecutive perfect intervals. In Debussy's formal constructions, traditional development is abandoned, and the themes themselves are shortened and rhythmically sharpened; in instrumentation, the role of individual instruments is greatly enhanced and the dynamic range subtilized." (Baker)
Air de Lia (Maganini) •1 Sx: A or T/Pno •Mus
Andantino and Vif (Teal) •SATB •Eto

Arabesque no. 2 •SATB •WWS
Ballet (from *Petite suite*) (WORLEY) •9 Sx: SnoSAAATTBBs •DP
Beau soir •SATB •WWS
Beau soir (*2 Lyric Pieces*) (HOULIK) •Tsx/Pno •South
Bruyères (SIBBING) •5 Sx: SAATB
Clair de lune (MULE) •Asx/Pno •JJ
Clair de lune •SATB •DP
Children's Corner Suite (SCHMIDT) •6 Sx: SAATBBs
Cortege (from *Petite suite*) (WORLEY) •9 Sx: SnoSAAATTBBs •DP
Debussy Album •Sx/Pno •Uni
En Bateau (from *Petite suite*) •Asx/Pno •Dur
En Bateau (from *Petite suite*) (WORLEY) •9 Sx: SnoSAAATTBBs
      •DP
Estampes (LONDEIX) •10 Sx: SnoSSAATTBBBs
La Fille aux cheveux de lin (OOSTROM) •SATB/Pno •Mol
La Fille aux cheveux de lin (REX) •9 Sx: SAAATTTBBBs •DP
La Fille aux cheveux de lin (SAKAGUCHI) •SATB •EFJM
La Fille aux cheveux de lin (VIARD) •Asx/Pno •Dur
Golliwogg's Cake-walk (TESEI) •Ob/Cl/Asx/Bsn
Golliwogg's Cake-walk (VIARD) •Asx/Pno •Dur
Golliwogg's Cake-walk (ZAJAC) •SATB •Eto
Jimbo's lullaby (VIARD) •Asx/Pno •Dur
The Little Shepherd (ZAJAC) •SATB •Eto
The Little Shepherd & Golliwogg's Cake-walk •SATB •WWS
Mandoline •Tsx/Pno •Mus
Mandoline (FORST) •Bb Sx or Eb Sx/Pno •Mu
Mazurka •SATB •WWS
Mazurka (3') (CUNNINGHAM) •SATB •Eto
Menuet (from *Petite suite*) (WORLEY) •9 Sx: SnoSAAATTBBs •DP
Miniatures - 7 Pièces (LONDEIX) •10 Sx: SnoSSAATTBBBs
Minstrels (from *Préludes*) •Asx/Pno •Dur
La Plus que lente (VIARD) •Asx/Pno •Dur
Le Petit nègre (LOERCH) •SATB •GB
Le Petit nègre (MULE) •Asx/Pno •Led
Le Petit nègre (MULE) •SATB •Led
Le Petit nègre (TESEI) •Ob/Cl/Asx/Bsn
Rapsodie (1904) (10') (to Mme E. HALL) •Asx/Orch (3322/424/
      Harp/Perc/Str) or Pno •Dur
Rapsodie (ROUSSEAU) •Asx/Pno •Eto
Rêverie (MULE) •Asx/Pno •JJ
Sarabande (CARAVAN) •6 Sx: SAATBBs •Eth
Sarabande (TEAL) (Album) •Bb Sx/Pno •GSch
Syrinx (LONDEIX) (2'45) •Sx Solo: A or S •JJ
Syrinx (REID) •Ssx Solo •Ken

DECADT, Jean (1914)

Compositeur belge, né à Ypres, en 1914. Travailla avec J. Absil.
Canto espressivo e molto giocondo (1974) (to Quatuor Belge de
      Saxophones) 1) Canto espressivo 2) Molto giocando •SATB
      •CBDM
Concerto 1 (1973) (to Fr. DANEELS) 1) Intrada - Allegro non troppo
      2) Andante molto espressivo 3) Finale giocoso con spirito •Asx/
      Orch •CBDM
Notturno (1975) •SATB •CBDM
Quartet (1979) 1) Molto vivo, Spirit 2) Lento molto espressivo,
      Spleen 3) Allegro giocoso, Joyfully •SATB •CBDM

DECLOEDT, E.

Entrée - Danse villageoise •SATB •An

DE CORDOBA, Hafid

Compositeur espagnol.
Mijanianas (1989) (to M. MIJAN) •Asx/Pno

DECOUAIS, René (1930)

Saxophoniste et professeur français, né le 25 XI 1930 à La Riche
(Indre & Loire). Travailla avec Marcel Mule. 1er Prix de Saxophone du
Conservatoire de Paris. Professeur au Conservatoire de Limoges.
35 Etudes techniques (1972) (to D. DEFFAYET) •Bil
3 Pièces de concert (1983) (8') •Asx/Pno •Bil

DECOUST, Michel (1936)

Compositeur français, né à Paris, le 19 XI 1936. Travailla avec D.
Milhaud, O. Messiaen, K. Stockhausen, H. Pousseur, et P. Boulez.
      "Apartir d'une réflexion à distance sur les conséquences prospecti-
ves du sérialisme, Michel Decoust assume la volonté d'une prise en
charge active et de maîtrise du matériau. L'intérêt qu'il porte depuis
1977 au travail sur ordinateur apparaît alors, dans une parfaite logique
de pensée, en continuité avec l'héritage viennois. A la conjonction des
domaines de la composition musicale, de la recherche et de la technique, en particulier depuis son entrée à l'I.R.C.A.M. en 1977, Michel
Decoust s'efforce de découvrir les structures mentales de la recherche,
ses processus moteurs, ce qui n'est possible qu'en renonçant au statut
isolationniste du compositeur et en multipliant les chances d'un travail
en équipe où l'activité musicale entre en interaction avec les horizons
de la science, de la sociologie et de la technologie." (D. J-Y. BOSSEUR)
      "He has been influenced by Cage's work as much as by
Stockhausen's." (A. GIRARDOT)
Olos (1983-84) (11') (to D. KIENTZY) •Tsx/Dispositif électro-acoust.
      •Sal
Ombres portées (1986) (9') •2 Ob/Cl/2 Asx/Harp/Pno/Perc •Sal
Quatuor (1980) •SATB

DECRUCK, Maurice (1896-1954) & Fernande BREILH (xxxx-1954)

Maurice Decruck, saxophoniste solo à l'orchestre philharmonique
de New York, publia de nombreux ouvrages en collaboration avec sa
femme Fernande Breuilh, morte le 6 VIII 1954.
      "Musique aimable et facile." (R. BERNARD)
Chant lyrique, op. 69 (1932) (to Fr. COMBELLE) •Asx/Pno •HS
3me Chant lyrique •Asx/Pno •Led
5me Chant lyrique •Asx/Pno •Led
Complainte de Dinah •Asx/Pno •EP
12 Duos (1934) (2 Volumes) A): 1) Prélude à deux 2) Fugue en duo
      3) Pastorale rustique 4) Intermission 5) The Spinning Wheel
      6) Brothers B): 1) Ostinato 2) Jazz et fugue 3) Romance et
      double 4) Ecossaise 5) Prélude et valse 6) Introduction et tierce
      •2 Sx: AA •EP
Ecole moderne du saxophone (1932) •Led
The Golden Sax (1934) (to R. WIEDOEFT) •Asx/Pno •EP
8 Pièces françaises (1943) (17') (to M. MULE) 1) Tambourin
      2) Vieux calvaire 3) Villageoise 4) Forlane 5) L'horloge
      6) Rondel 7) Rigaudon 8) Toccata •Asx/Pno •Bil
Pavane •SATB •EP
Printemps •SATB •EP
Rex Sax (to C. SAUVAGE) •Asx/Pno •EP
Saxophonie •SATB •EP
Selméra-sax (1934) •Asx/Pno •HS
Sicilienne •SATB •EP
Sonate en Do dièse (1944) (16') (to M. MULE) 1) Trés modéré -
      Expressif 2) Andante 3) Fileuse 4) Nocturne et final •Asx/Pno
      •Bil
Totem •SATB
Variations symphoniques •SATB •EP

DE DECKER, George

Quatuor •SATB

DEDIU, Dan

Compositeur roumain.
Parerga agonica (1993) •Mezzo Soprano Voice/1 Sx: S+A+B
      •INM

DEDRICK, Art

Waltz for Four •AATB •Ken

DEDRICK, Chris

Sensitivity (6'15) •SATB or AATB •AMI/Ken

DEDRICK, Rusty (1918)

A Tune for Christopher •Asx/Pno •Ken
The Modern Art Suite (13') (to the New York Saxophone Quartet)
    1) Impressionism 2) Purism 3) Mysticism 4) Surrealism
    5) Realism •SATB •Ken
Saxafari •SATB/Optional Perc •Ken

DEFAYE, Jean-Michel (1932)

Compositeur français.
Ampélopsis (1976) (to D. Deffayet) •Asx/Pno •Led
Concerto (1983) (15') (to W. Street) •Asx/Orch (2222/0000/Harp/
    Perc/Str) or Pno •SL
Dialogues •5 Sx: SAATB
Six études (1993) •Led

DE FESCH, Willem (1687-c. 1757)

Sonata •Asx/Pno •WWS
Sonata (Stanton) •SATB •Eto

DEFONTAINE, M.

Prélude, Menuet et Gigue •SATB

DEFOSSE, Henry (1883-1956)

Compositeur français.
Bucolique nocturne (1931) (7') (to M. Perrin) •SATB
Elégie (1952) (6') (to M. Perrin) •Asx/Orch or Pno
Sicilienne et Gavotte (1940/42) (3'30) (to M. Perrin) •Asx/Orch or
    Pno

DEFOSSEZ, René (1905)

Chef d'orchestre et Compositeur belge, né à Spa, le 4 X 1905. Prix
de Rome (1935).
    "Later he moved towards an eclectic neo-classical style, including
novel touches within strictly conventional molds." (H. Vandhulst)
Mélopée et Danse •Asx/Pno or Fl/Ob/Cl/Asx/Bsn •An
Mouvemento perpetuo (1973) (to Quatuor Belge de Saxophones)
    •SATB
Suite "Souvenirs" 1) Trés lent 2) Vif et Joyeux 3) Trés modéré
    4) Berceuse 5) Galop •Vln/Asx/Pno/Perc

DEGASTYNE, Serge (1930)

Compositeur américain.
Quartet (1968) (to C. Leeson) •AATB
Quartet, op. 53 •SATB •FP
Suite Rhetaise, op. 26 (1961) (to C. Leeson) •Asx/2 Vln/Vla/Vcl
    •FP/SMC

DEGEN, Helmut (1911)

Compositeur et chef d'orchestre allemand, né à Aglasterhausen,
Baden, le 14 I 1911. Travailla avec Wuilliam Maler, Jarnach, et
Klussmann.
    "Under his teacher Wuilliam Maler, Degen fashioned a polyphonic
idiom sometimes reminiscent of Hindemith. Without embracing 12-
note technique he has employed similar methods of organizing pitch
content, particularly in the later works." (G. W. Loomis)
Sonate (1950) •Asx/Pno •Sch

DEGEN, Johannes Dietz (1910-1989)

Compositeur suédois d'origine allemande, né à Leipzig, le 11 I 1910.
Mort le 6 XII 1989. Travailla avec S. Karg-Elert et H. Grabner. En
Suède depuis 1947.

"In the course of a long and rewarding life it has been my privilege
to travel between two worlds. One of them is governed by the chilly
intellectualism of the natural sciences, research and philosophy. The
other stands for creative intuition: composition, publishing of fiction
and poetry, painting and sculpture. If there is any common denomina-
tor, it is my romantic belief in the life force of intuitive invention, solid
craftsmanship and an unfailing artistic integrity." (H-G. P.)
Canzone devota (1981) (4') •SATB •STIM

DEJONCKER, Théodore (1894)

Compositeur belge, né à Bruxelles, le 11 IV 1894. Travailla avec P.
Gilson. Fit partie du 'Groupe des Synthétistes.'
    "Musique où un humour discret n'est pas exclu."
Quatuor •SATB

DE JONG, Conrad (1934)

Compositeur américain, né le 13 I 1934 à Hull (Iowa). Travailla avec
B. Heiden et T. de Leeuw.
Fun and Games (1967/70) (duration open) (to R. Sammaroto) •Any
    instrument/Pno •MP

DE JONGHE, Marcel

3 Bagatelles (1982) (to Saxofonio Ensemble) •SATB

DEKKER, Dirk

Compositeur néerlandais.
Obsessie (1986) (10') •SATB •Don

DE KOVEN, Henry-Louis-Reginald (1859-1920)

Oh Promise Me (Leidzen) •Tsx/Pno •ECS

DELA, Maurice (1919-1978)

Compositeur, professeur, et organiste canadien, né à Montréal, le 9
IX 1919; mort le 28 IV 1978. Travailla avec L. Bailly, S. Moisse, et Cl.
Champagne.
    "Maurice Dela has been attracted by the avant-garde in music and has
always been indifferent to the opinions of music critics. He is content—
in his words: "to let my music go its own little way." Although he leads
a busy life as a teacher, arranger and church organist, he still manages
to find time for composition and revision, for he is a meticulous worker
who frequently goes back to a composition, refining and reshaping it
until he is satisfied." (C.M.C.) "His work is couched in an ingratiating
romantic idiom." (Baker)
Divertimento (1972) (12') 1) Festival 2) Incantation 3) Danse
    •SATB •CMC

DELACRUZ, Zulema

Compositeur espagnol.
Chio (1989) (7'30) (to D. Kientzy) •1 Sx: S+A+B/Tape

DELAGE, Jean-Louis (1960)

Saxophoniste et compositeur. Travailla avec J-P. Vermeeren et B.
Totaro.
Chromadence - Cadence pour tous les saxophones (1987) •Sx Solo
Climat (1989) (to A. Ghidoni) •Sx Solo: A or T
Illusions, Rêves et Caprices (1990) (12') (to J-P. Vermeeren) •Asx/
    Pno/Synth/Perc or Asx/Pno •Bil

DELAMARRE, Pierre (1947)

Saxophoniste, professeur, et compositeur français, né à La Baule, le
6 V 1947. Travailla avec J. Terry et D. Deffayet.
Ballade (1983) (7') •Bsx Solo •adr
Détente •5 Sx: AAAAA •adr
Farandole de l'Arlésienne (Bizet) 3 or 4 Sx: S (ad lib.) ATB •adr
La 8 (1981) (3') (to B. Rehak) •Fl/Ob/Cl/Asx/Pno 4 hands [à 4
    mains]/Bass/Perc •adr
Inéquation (1981) (2') •Tpt/Asx •adr

Nazaireïdes - 4° Episode •Asx Solo/5 Sx: AAATB •adr
Quatuor pour rire (1977) (3') •SATB •Bil
Rhapsodie (1979) (5') •Asx/Band •adr
Trio n° 1 •3 Sx: SAT •adr

DELAMATER, Eric (1880-1953)
Adeste Fidelis •2 Sx: AA/Pno •Rub

DELAMONT, Gordon
Divertimento •4 Sx: AATT •WWS
Three Entertainments (8'35) •SATB or AATB •Ken

DELANNOY, J.
The Last Thought of Weber •Asx/Pno •HE

DELANNOY, Marcel (1898-1962)
Compositeur français, né à La Ferté-Alais, le 9 VII 1898; mort à Nantes, le 14 IX 1962. Encouragé par A. Honegger, il abandonna des études aux beaux-arts pour se consacrer à la musique.

"Autodidacte, Delannoy fut aidé dans sa formation musicale par A. Honegger et R. Manuel. Sa musique se caractérise par une constante franchise." (N. Dufourcq) "C'est un traditionaliste et un néo-classique doué d'une certaine facilité d'invention et chez qui l'on retrouve fréquemment les influences de la chanson populaire française et du jazz." (Cl. Rostand)

"A composer of great talent with an original style of his own. A countryman by origin, Delannoy writes music in which 'folk' and even 'popular' elements are blended, but without affectation." (R. Myers) "While slightly influenced by Honegger, he pursued an individual path and remained on the edge of contemporary currents." (A. Hoeree)

Ballade concertante, op. 59 (1955) •Pno/Sx/11 Instruments
Le Marchand de notes 3 Vln/Bass/4 Sx/2 Tpt/Trb/Perc/Pno
Rapsodie (1934) (to R. Delange) •Asx/Tpt/Vcl/Pno •Heu

DELAUNAY, René (1880-19xx)
Compositeur français. Directeur du Conservatoire de Metz.

Au fil de l'eau (to M. Hermann) 1) Murmure du ruisseau 2) A travers la prairie ensoleillée 3) Cascadelle •Asx or Bb Sx/Pno •Bil/ Braun
Sérénade matutinale (to F. Lamy) •Asx/Pno •Bil

DELBECQ, Laurent (1905)
Compositeur de musique légère français, né à Leers (Nord), le 26 X 1905.

A batons rompus •SATB •Mar
A saute mouton •SATB •Mar
Accord tripartite (1983) (10') 1) Triade 2) Trianon 3) Triplette 4) Troïka •3 Sx: AAA or TTT •Mar
Chanson de Bourgogne •SATB
Chanson de Bresse •SATB
Dans la montagne •2 Bb Sx or Cl/Bb Sx •Mol
Enfantillage (1970) (2') •Bb Sx/Pno •Mol
Fantaisie duo •2 Bb Sx •Mol
Flanerie (1970) (1'30) •Bb Sx/Pno •Mol
Gemini I (1970) (2'00) •Bb Sx/Pno •Mol
Impromptu •SATB •Mar
Juliana •Bb Sx/Pno •Mol
Mélodia •Bb Sx/Pno •Mar
Menuet (Bolzoni) •SATB
Mona Lisa •2 Sx •Mol
4 Saxophones en récréation •SATB •Mar
Sévilla (Albeniz) •SATB

DEL BORGO, Elliot (1938)
Compositeur américain né à Port Chester (New York). Travailla avec V. Persichetti.

Canto (1973) (to J. Stoltie) •Asx Solo •DP

Concertino (1972) (to J. Stoltie) •Asx/Str Orch
Elegy II (1989) (for D. Underwood) •Asx/Pno
Quartet (1987) (For the Texas Saxophone Quartet) •SATB
Soliloquy and Dance (1978) (for D. Underwood) •Asx/Band •DP
Sonata No. 1 (1973) (to J. Stoltie) 1) Pensively 2) With vigor 3) Quietly 4) With spirit •Asx/Pno •Sha
Sonata No. 2 (1983) (for J. Stoltie & D. Underwood) •Asx/Pno •Sha

DEL CERRO, Emiliano
Compositeur espagnol.
Quejumbroso metal (1992) (8') (to M. Mijan) •Asx/Tape

DELDEN, Lex van (1919)
Compositeur néerlandais, né le 10 IX 1919. Entreprit des études de médecine avant de se consacrer à la musique.

"Autodidacte, Delden écrit dans un style aisé, mais solide, loin de toute préoccupation sérielle." (H. Halbreich)

"He often builds a work from one fairly concise idea, and the tenacity to this starting-point generates a conflict which provides the impetus for the music. The resolution takes the initial idea through a mosaic of shifting variations." (J. Wouters)

Concerto, op. 91 (1967) •2 Sx: SS/Orch •Don
Sonatina, op. 36 (1952) (6'45) (to J. de Vries) 1) Allegro 2) Aria 3) Rondo alla polka •Asx/Pno •Don
Tomba, op. 112 (in memoriam Uxoris) (1985) (10') 1) Agonia - Allegro 2) Rassegnazione - Lento •SATB •Don

DELERUE, Georges (1925-1992)
Compositeur français, né à Roubaix, le 12 III 1925, mort à Los Angeles, le 22 III 1992. Travailla avec H. Busser et D. Milhaud. A composé en quelques 40 ans de carrière, pas moins de 400 partitions pour l'image dont 150 musiques de musiques de films!

"Son style direct orienté vers la simplicité et l'efficacité, le prédestinait à la musique illustrative, où il a trouvé son domaine d'élection." (Bordas) "Si j'écris de la musique hors d'un film, c'est alors de la musique 'complètement à moi', une musique pure, un concerto, un quatuor ce n'est pas la même démarche; moi, ce sont les images, l'histoire, les personnages qui me parlent, qui m'inspirent..." (G. Delerue)

"Delerue is one of the most respected writers of film music." (D. Amy)

Prisme (1977) (to D. Deffayet) •Asx/Pno •ET

DELGIUDICE, Michel (1924)
Chef de musique et Compositeur français, né à Nice, le 18 II 1924.

Badinage (1988) (2'30) •1 Sx: A or T/Pno •Led
Complainte et Divertissement •Asx or Bb Sx/Pno •Bil
Jouer à deux - 12 Duos progressifs (1990) •2 Identical Sx •Com
Phrygienne (1983) (2') 1) Andante 2) Allegro con spirito •Asx/Pno •Led
Quatuor •SATB •adr
Saxboy (2'30) •1 Sx: S or A or T/Pno •Mar

DELHAYE, Alyre (1875-1952)
5 Bagatellen •Asx/Pno •Sez
Silver Threads - Air varié •Bb Sx/Pno •Mol

DELIBERO, Phillip
Contemporary Saxophone Studies (1975) •DP

DELIBES, Léo (1836-1891)
Coppélia (Davis) •Asx/Pno •Rub

DELIO, Thomas
Compositeur américain.
Congruent Formalizations •Fl/3 Cl/4 Sx •DP

Gestures •Ssx/Pno •DP
Partial Coordinates •Asx Solo •DP

DELISSE
Duo •2 Sx •Mil
Menuet (RAMEAU) •2 Sx: SA/Pno •Mil

DELLE-HAENSCH
Modern Saxophonschule Mein Steckenpferd •Tsx/Pno •Dux

DELLI PIZZI, Fulvio
Elegia per F. (1982) •SATB
Quinta bagatella (1985) •Asx Solo

DELMAS, Marc-Jean-Baptiste (1885-1931)
Clair de lune (LAURENT) •Asx/Pno •Bil
Conte rose (COMBELLE) •Asx/Pno •Bil
Soir d'été (COMBELLE) •Asx/Pno •Bil
Variations tendres •Asx/Pno •Bil

DE LONG
Sonata francese •Tsx/Pno •Ken

DEL PRINCIPE, Joseph
Compositeur américain.
Lyric Pieces for Octet •Fl/Ob/Sx+Cl/BsCl/Tpt/Hn/Trb/Tuba •SeMC

DE LUCA, Joseph
Beautiful Colorado - Valse caprice •Asx or Bb Sx/Pno •CF
Thoughts of Gold - Valse caprice (to E. HENEY) •1 Sx: A or T/Pno
    •CF

DELVINCOURT, Claude (1888-1954)
Compositeur français, né à Paris, le 12 I 1888, mort accidentellement
à Orbetello (Italie), le 5 IV 1954. Grand Prix de Rome (1913). Directeur
du Conservatoire de Paris (1941-1954). Confia en 1942 la réouverture
de la classe de saxophone à Marcel Mule.

"Disciple indirect de Saint-Saëns et de G. Fauré, Claude Delvincourt
a continué la tradition de Ravel, retenu l'esprit bouffe de Janequin et
de Chabrier, sans oublier Debussy et Stravinsky." (N. DUFOURCQ) "De
caractère néo-classique et d'esprit plutôt antiromantique, son oeuvre
échappe aux formules toutes faites et s'exprime avec une verve, sinon
un langage très personnels." (Cl. ROSTAND)

"Delvincourt was one of the most enlightened composers of the
modern French school, with a particular feeling for comedy in music."
(R. MYERS) "Delvincourt's music is marked by a Cartesian control
which does not preclude the depth of feeling, the humour (of his
Croquembouches). After Debussy and Ravel, he was one of the most
ardent of French composers in trying to recapture the spirit of the
Middle Ages and the Renaissance." (A. LOUVIER)
6 Croquembouches (1946) (14') 1) Plum pudding 2) Linzer tart
    3) Puits d'amour 4) Rahat loukhoum 5) Nègre en chemise
    6) Grenadine •Asx/Pno •Led
Scapin joué (3'30) •1 Sx: S or T/Pno •Lem

DE MAN, Roderik
Compositeur hollandais.
Discrepancies (1993) •4 Sx •INM

DEMARET, R
Habanera •Asx/Pno •Che

DE MARS, James (1952)
Pianiste et compositeur américain né à Minneapolis. Travailla avec
D. Argento et E. Stokes.
Desert Songs (1983) 1) There is One 2) The woman Who
    3) Dedicace 4) Night speech 5) Crossing atomland 6) Mis-one-
    ism •Soprano Voice/Asx/Vcl/2 Perc/Pno •adr

Premonitions of Christopher Columbus (16'30) •Native American
    Fl/African Perc/Asx/Vcl/Pno/Perc •adr
Seven Healing Songs of John Joseph (Blue) (1982) (9'20) (to J.
    WYTKO) •Asx/Tape •adr

DEMERSSEMAN, Jules (1833-1866)
Flûtiste et Compositeur belge, né à Hondschoote, le 9 I 1833, mort
à Paris, le 1er XII 1866.
Allegretto brillante, op. 46 •Asx/Pno •Rub
Ave Maria (1865) •Voice/Asx
Chant religieux, op. 45 •Asx/Pno •Cos/CF
12 Etudes mélodiques et brillantes (1866) •Marg
Fantaisie, op. 32 (1862) •Asx/Pno •Cos
Fantaisie pastorale •Bb Sx/Pno •Bil
Fantaisie pastorale - In Arcadie •Bb Sx/Pno •Mol
Fantaisie sur un thème original (1860) (to M. VUILLE) •Asx/Pno
    •Bil/HM
Introduction et variations sur "Le Carnaval de Venise" •Bb Sx/Pno
    •Marg
Sérénade, op. 33 (1862) •Asx/Pno •Cos/HM
Solo, op. 47 •Asx/Pno •Bil
1er solo (1865) •Ssx/Pno
1er solo (1865) •Bsx/Pno
1er solo - Allegro et Allegretto (1866) (to M. STAPS) •Asx/Pno •Sax
1er solo - Andante et Boléro (1866) (to C. PANNE) •Tsx/Pno •Sax/
    Ron
2me solo (1866) •Ssx/Pno
2me solo - Cavatine (1866) •Bsx/Pno

DEMETRY, Zebre
Intermezzo saxofonico •YUC

DEMIDDELER, Jean
Compositeur belge.
Recitativo •Asx/Pno

DEMILLAC, Francis Paul
Compositeur français.
Concerto pour Suite de 4 Saxophones (1974) (20') (to J. MAFFEI)
    •SATB/Orch •Bil
Jeux de vagues •Asx/Pno •Com
Sicilienne et Tarentelle •Asx/Pno •Com

DEMOULIN (See VINCENT-DEMOULIN)

DEMUTH, Norman (1898-1968)
Compositeur anglais, né à South Croydon (Londres), le 15 VII 1898;
mort à Bognor Regis (Sussex), le 21 IV 1968.

"Autodidacte, Norman Demuth subit l'influence de C. Franck, V.
d'Indy et d'A. Roussel." "Il a une conception essentiellement contrapuntique de la musique, non pas dans le sens d'un retour à l'écriture de
la Renaissance, mais bien celui de l'opposition simultanée de 2, 3 ou
4 éléments, qui peuvent être homophones ou harmoniques, mais qui
conservent leur autonomie, se combinent en se superposant, se répon-
dant, se complétant, s'opposant." (R. BERNARD)

"Demuth has devoted a good deal of study to modern French
composers, his music avoids the more fashionable 'Gallic' characteristics. In his most recent works his harmonics are rather hard and
severe, with more bare fourths and fifths than thirds, and more major
than minor seconds... Its somewhat austere melody, in which defin-
able tunes have little part, and its complex but subtle harmony displays
a more general affinity with d'Indy or Roussel. His harmonic awareness was keen, and the corresponding range broad." (C. MASON)
Concerto (1938) (12') •Asx/Band or Pno •adr
Sonata (1955) (to M. MULE) 1) Andante con moto 2) Allegretto
    scherzando •Asx/Pno •adr

DENBURG, Moche

Compositeur canadien.

Jericho (1992) •Asx/Pno

DENHOF, Robert

Compositeur allemand.

Orion (1993) •Bsx/Pno •B&N

DENHOFF, Michael (1955)

Compositeur allemand né le 25 IV 1955 à Ahaus. Travailla avec J. Baur et H. W. Henze.

Gegen-Sätze (1984) (14') (to the Rascher Saxophone Quartet) •SATB •GrB

Svolgimenti (1986) (26') (to the Rascher Saxophone Quartet) 1) Rappresentazione 2) Svolgimento I 3) Svelgimento II 4) Svolgimento III 5) Svolgimento IV 6) Svolgimento V 7) Conclusione •SATB •GrB

DENISOV, Edison Vasilievitch (1929)

Compositeur russe, né le 6 IV 1929 à Tomsk (Sibérie). Après des études de mathématiques travailla avec W. Chebaline et N. Peiko. Actuellement professeur au Conservatoire de Moscou.

"Quoique marqué par le folklore sibérien et ses échelles non tempérées, Edison Denisov a commencé à composer dans le style officiel de Shostakovich et de Prokofiev, puis a évolué vers un langage et une esthétique plus moderne, sous l'influence de Boulez et de Nono, adaptant certains procédés sériels et même aléatoires." (Cl. ROSTAND) "Il apparaît aujourd'hui comme l'un des compositeurs soviétiques de premier plan, mais insuffisamment reconnu sur le plan international." (J. DI VANNI) "Oeuvre personnelle à l'inspiration ferme, où la rigueur veille comme chez Boulez, en évitant tout didactisme" (Cl. GLAYMAN) "Continuant à être extrêmement attentif aux musiques de l'Ouest et de l'Europe, Edison Denisov pratique l'aléatoire, voire le collage ou les micro-intervalles." (J. & Br. MASSIN) "J'aime beaucoup le saxophone et c'est dommage que les meilleurs compositeurs n'écrivent pas plus pour cet instrument magnifique et tellement riche par ses possibilités." (E. DENISOV) "La plupart de mes oeuvres, même instrumentales, sont spirituelles." (E. DENISOV)

"An experimenter by nature, he wrote instrumental works of an empirical genre." (BAKER) "In his mature compositions he has exploited serial procedures, aleatory writing, unconventional instrumental techniques, electronic means and microtones." (V. KHOPOPOVA)

Concerto (1986-92) (25') (4 movements) •Vla (or Asx)/Orch •Led

Concerto piccolo (1977) (22') (to J-M. LONDEIX) •1 Sx: S+A+T+B/6 Perc •Led

Deux Pièces brèves (1974) (5'10) (to L. MICHAILOV) •Asx/Pno •Led

Quintette (1991) (20'15) (to C. & O. DELANGLE) 1) Agitato 2) Moderato 3) Tranquillo •4 Sx: SATB/Pno •Led

Sonate (1970) (12') (to J-M. LONDEIX) 1) Allegro 2) Lento 3) Allegro moderato •Asx/Pno •Led

DENIZOT, Anne-Marie

Compositeur français.

Trois petits sons et puis s'en vont (1993) •1 Sx: S+A/Harp or Pno •INM

DENNEHY, Donnacha

Compositeur américain.

Contingency, Irony and Temporal Brutality (1993) •Asx/Pno •INM

DENZA, Luigi (1846-1922)

Funiculi-Funicula (HARRIS) •2 Cl/Asx/Bsn (or BsCl) •CF

DEOM, Michel

Compositeur belge.

Les pêcheurs d'ombres, op. 7 (1980) (16'30) (to Quatuor Belge de Saxophones) •SATB •Bil

DEPABLO, Luis (see PABLO, Luis de)

DEPELSENAIRE, Jean-Marie (1914-1986)

Compositeur français, né à Maubeuge, le 6 V 19124; où il est mort le 22 VII 1986.. Travailla avec E. Gaujac et N. Gallon.

Baroque (1960) (2'30) •Asx/Pno •GD

Concertino (1969) (9') (to R. FERREAUX) •Ob/Asx/Orch or Pno •Chou

Concertino (1972) (9') (to F. DANEELS) •3 Sx: AAA/Orch or Pno •ET

Concertino da camera (1959) (5') (to Ch. BROWN) •Asx/Pno •ET

Concertino mélodicorythmique (1964) (3') (to M. EHRMANN) •Asx/Pno •Gras

Concertino n° 6 "Confidences" (1961) (3'30) (to A. DEFER) •Asx/Pno •Lem

Dialogue (1966) (6'30) (to MM. JOUX et DUDICOURT) •Tpt/Asx/Orch (1121/Str) or Pno •ET

Divertissement (1964) (2'30) (to R. DUDICOURT) •Asx/Pno •Com

Dixtour (1971) •2 Fl/2 Tpt/2 Sx/4 Cl •adr

Entre la vie et le rêve (to M. JÉZOUIN) •6 Sx: SnoSATBBs •adr

Evocations d'Ardennes (1974) (3') •Asx/Pno •ET

Funambules (1961) (5') (to F. AMADIO) •Asx/Pno •ET

Le donjon dans la brume (1964) (2'30) (to R. DUDICOURT) •Asx/Pno •Com

Le Dragon de jade (to M. JÉZOUIN) •2 Sx: SA/Pno •adr

Le fil d'Ariane (1971) (3') (to Fr. DANEELS) •SATB

Les approches de l'invisible (1973) (4') •Vln/Asx/Pno/Perc •adr

Les Métamorphoses d'Arlequin •Ob/Cl/Asx/Bsn •adr

Les sentiers de la nuit (1972) (2') (to F. BERTRAND) •Asx/Pno •Chou

L'heure paisible (to M. JÉZOUIN) •SATB •adr

Mosaïque (1979) (2'30) •Fl/1 Sx: A+T+B/Harp •adr

Octuor moderne (1978) •2 Tpt/2 Asx/4 Perc •Chou

Petit concert à quatre (1973) (2') (to R. DRUET) •Fl/Tpt/Asx/Cl •Phi/Com

Petit rituel occidental (1974) (2'30) •Asx/Perc

Pour une nuit de Printemps (1971) (1'30) (to ROLAND) •Asx/Pno •Com

Prélude et Danse (1972) (3'30) •Asx/Pno •Ham

Prélude et Divertissement (1958) (5') •Asx/Pno •Chou

Prélude et Scherzetto (1963) (4') •Asx/Pno •Chou

Récitatif et Air (1962) (2'30) (to A. MASURE) •Asx/Pno •GD

Recréation (to M. JÉZOUIN) •Orch including [dont] 3 Sx: AAT •adr

Sonatine en Fa mineur (1958) (10') (to E. BROUDEHOUX) •Asx/Pno •Com

Suite concertante (1971) (10') (to R. DUDICOURT) •Asx/Orch or Pno •ET

Trio de saxophones (1979) (3') •3 Sx: AAA or TTT •adr

Trio surprise (1975) (4') •Asx/Tpt/Cl •Phi/Com

Vers la lumière (1979) (5') (to D. KIENTZY) •1 Sx: S+A+T+B/Perc

Volutes (1963) (4') (to NICOLAS) •Asx/Pno •GD

DEPRAZ, Raymond (1915)

Compositeur français, né en Savoie, en 1915. Travailla avec D. Lesur, T. Aubin, et O. Messiaen.

"Depraz revendique les influences de Messiaen, Webern, Bartok, Moussorgsky, Varèse, du grégorien, des folklores jaunes et noirs. Ses oeuvres sont fréquemment d'inspiration religieuse (la pensée de Teilhard de Chardin ayant joué chez lui un rôle capital)." (Cl. ROSTAND)

2e Symphonie (1973) (32'30) (to Quatuor Deffayet) •SATB/Orch (2111/433/EH/BsCl/CBsn/Str/3 Perc/Pno) •EFM

Quatuor n° 2 (1974) (17'15) (to Quatuor Deffayet) 4 movements •SATB •EFM

DERKSEN, Bernard (1896-1965)
Kapriolen - Waltz, op. 28 •Asx/Pno •EB/AMP/B1B

DE ROSE, Peter
Deep Purple (WIEDOEFT) •Asx/Pno •Rob

DE ROSSI RE, Fabrizio (1960)
Compositeur italien, né à Rome. Travailla avec M. Bortolotti, S. Sciarrino, et S. Bussotti.
Allegro nero (1986) (5') •SATB •EDP
Aria di Strepido (1992) (6') •Tsx/Orch

DERR, Ellwood (1932)
Compositeur américain.
Elegy (1963) •Asx/Orch or Pno •adr
I Never Saw Another Butterfly, op. 11 (1966) (for Michele, Nelita, and Don) 1) Prologue: Terezín 2) The Butterfly 3) The Old Man 4) Fear 5) The Garden •Soprano Voice/Asx/Pno •UMM/DP
One in Five in One, op. 10 (1955-65) (to D. SINTA) 1) Improvisation 2) Canzona 3) Recitativo 4) Scherzo 5) Elaboration •Asx/Pno •UMM/DP

DERVAUX, André-Jean (1918)
Kopak et Ciolina (4') •SATB •Phi
Nocturne en Saxe (1955) (MOUTET) •Asx/Orch or Pno •Com
Petite suite en Saxe (1970) (2'30) •Asx/Pno •Bil
Saxophonissimo •Asx/Pno •Bil
Saxorama •Asx/Pno •Marg

DESCARPENTRIES, Hugues (1961)
Compositeur français, né à Bordeaux. Travailla avec M. Fusté-Lambezat.
Braer (1992) •Pno/3 Sx: SSS
ô (1993) (3'30) •Voice/5 Sx: SATBBs/Pno/Perc

DESCHAMPS, Jean-Henri (dit Jean RIDESS) (1894)
Compositeur français, né à Bordeaux, le 10 VII 1894.
Danses anciennes •SATB •Bil
Danse arabe (1970) (4') (to J. GRANT) •Asx/Pno •Bil
Elégie (1971) (3'30) •SATB •adr
Menuet •SATB •adr
Sonatine 1) Andante 2) Allegro 3) Menuet •2 Sx: AA/Pno •Bil

DE SCHRISVER, K. (see SCHRIJVER, K. de)

DESENCLOS, Alfred (1912-1971)
Compositeur français, né à Portel (Pas-de-Calais), le 7 II 1912; mort à Paris, le 3 III 1971. Grand prix de Rome (1942). Travailla avec F. Bousquet.
"Ses oeuvres se situent dans la plus élégante tradition française." (LAROUSSE) "Les inflexions de son discours ont beaucoup de souplesse et de variété expressive; sans s'écarter du strict domaine musical, il a le pouvoir de suggérer des états émotifs logiquement coordonnés. Sans nul souci d'attitude, sans prétention et sans ambition, il accomplit son oeuvre en suivant des disciplines qui, sans s'insurger contre la science musicale qu'il a acquise et qui lui a valu le Prix de Rome et d'autres distinctions officielles, ne sont ni timorées ni orientées vers une servile exploitation de procédés rentables." (R. BERNARD) "*Prélude, Cadence et Final* a confirmé mon opinion sur ce musicien sincère et vrai. Il met ici magnifiquement en valeur les ressources du saxophone. La partie de piano dialogue et soutient le saxophone sans jamais toutefois prendre le pas sur lui." (F. VELLARD) "Le *Quatuor de saxophones* d'Alfred Desenclos, dans un contrepoint riche que détendent parfois de larges élans, séduit par la poésie autant que la maîtrise du style. Son souffle et sa retenue en font une oeuvre qui à elle seule, mériterait l'attention et l'adhésion." (P. GERMAIN)

Prélude, Cadence et Finale (1956) (11') (to M. MULE) •Asx/Pno •Led
Quatuor (1964) (15'30) (to Quatuor Mule) 1) Allegro non troppo 2) Calmo 3) Poco largo, ma risoluto Allegro •SATB •Led

DESJARDINS, Luc
Compositeur canadien.
Autodafé (to Cl. BRISSON) •Ssx/Tape

DESLOGES, Jacques (1933)
Saxophoniste, quartettiste, professeur, et compositeur français, né à Paris, le 2 IX 1933. Travailla avec M. Mule.
Chanteries (1983) (3') •Asx/Pno •Com
Fabliau (1984) •1 Sx: A or T/Pno •Mar
Prélude et Danse - Rondo valse (1983) •SATB or Ob/Asx/Cl/Bsn (or Vcl or Trb) •IMD/Arp
Rondo (1972) •SATB •CANF
6 Pièces faciles (1978) (to ARNOLD) •4 Sx: AAAA or TTTT/Pno •Bil

DE SMET, Raoul (1936)
Compositeur belge.
Soledad Sonora (1988) (5'45) •Asx/Pno

DESMONS, René (19xx-1990)
Professeur de saxophone français.
Méthode nouvelle (1983) •LF

DESPALJ, Pavle (1934)
Chef d'orchestre et compositeur yougoslave né à Blato (Korcula), le 18 III 1934. Travailla avec Sulek.
"His miusic bears witness to the breadth of his interests and to his particular affinity with the Baroque. His finest piece is the *Saxophone Concerto*, but the development of his conducting career left him less time for composition in the later 1960s." (K. KOVACEVIC)
Concerto (1966) (11') (to C. LEESON) 1) Allegro 2) Andante 3) Presto •Asx/Orch or Pno •South

DESPARD, Marcel (1920)
Quatuor (to Quatuor Deffayet) •SATB

DESPORTES, Yvonne (1907)
Professeur et compositeur français, né à Cobourg (Saxonie), le 18 VII 1907. Travailla avec P. Dukas. Prix de Rome (1932).
"Compositeur se tenant à l'écart de l'avant-garde, traditionaliste, mais résolument non conformiste." (Cl. ROSTAND) "Yvonne Desportes se consacre, souvent, à l'illustration d'un argument où elle trouve le ferment d'une inspiration pittoresque." (R. STRICKER) "Le fond de l'écriture de ma musique reste toujours thématique et contrapuntique, et l'inspiration avant tout humaine." (Y. DESPORTES)
Blablabla (1971) (15') (to D. DEFFAYET) •2 Sx: AT/Pno •Dom
Cantilène (2'15) (Album) •Asx/Pno •Bil
Danses saxsonnantes (6'30) •8 Sx •DP
Dédicace (1979) (to J. BOK) •SATB •adr
Discordances •2 Voices/1 Sx: S+A+B •EFM/Bil
Divertissement (9') 1) Jean qui pleure 2) Jean qui rit •SATB •DP
Fugue en La mineur (BACH) (3') •SATB •DP
4 Fuguettes (1977) (13'30) (to J. DESLOGES) 1) A la manière de… 2) La fugue enchantée 3) Schumanneske 4) Le Tombeau de Ravel •SATB •adr
Gigue saxonne (1984) (5'30) •Asx/Pno ad lib. •Bil
9 Images •4 Sx: AAAB •Bil
La maison abandonnée (1961) (20') (to M.E. von AZOV) 1) Allegro 2) Andante 3) Vif •Vln/Vla/Vcl/Asx/Perc/Pno •adr
Le noir et la rose (5'30) •Tsx/Harp or Pno •DP
Les trois demeures (15'15) •Asx/Pno •DP
L'Homme des cavernes (6') •Tsx/Accordion or Pno •DP

L'Horloge jazzante (1984) (8') •Asx/Guit •Bil
Mélopée dorienne •Asx/Pno •Com
3 petits contes (Album) (DAILEY) 1) Sérieux 2) Sentimental 3) Gai
    •Bb Sx/Pno •WA
16 petites pièces •4 Sx: AAAB •VB
Per sa pia (1978) (to Cl. Delangle) 1) Dédicace 2) Andante 3) Trés
    vif et rythmé •Sx/Perc •adr
Pièces faciles pour quatuor de saxophones •4 Sx: AAAB
Plein air (1975) (16'30) (to Quatuor Desloges) •SATB •Dom
Pour copie conforme (4') •2 Sx: AT •DP
Saxo danses (1989) (4'30) Danse sentimentale - Danse joyeuse
    •Asx/Pno •Com
Saxophonades (9') •8 Sx •DP
Sonate pour un baptême (1959) (18') (to LILIANE) •Fl/Asx/Soprano
    Voice (or EH)/Perc/Pno •Bil
Souvenir de Chambéry (20'15) •Ssx/Org •DP
Un choix difficile (1980) (17') •Asx/Marimba+Vibr •DP
Une fleur sur l'étang (1977) (12') (to D. KIENTZY) •Asx/Harp •Dom

DES PRES, Josquin (c. 1449-1521)
La Bernardina (GRAINGER) •3 Sx: AAA •PG

DESROCHERS, Pierre
Compositeur canadien, né au Québec.
5 Miniatures •Fl/Tsx/Pno

DESSAU, Paul (1894-1979)
Compositeur et chef d'orchestre allemand, né à Hamburg, le 10 XII 1894, mort à Berlin, le 28 VI 1979. Travailla avec M. Loewengard.

"Le plus exclusivement 'brechtien' des compositeurs de Brecht. Paul Dessau se plaisait à reconnaître comment, grâce au dramaturge, il avait pu définir enfin clairement son art et sa conscience politique." (J. & Br. MASSIN)

"He had been striving in his music for a genuine expressiveness and clear, coherent construction; the expressionist influences of his early works had given place to exploration of 12-note technique and to a preoccupation with Jewish folk music." (GROVE)
Suite (1935) (8') (to S. RASCHER) 1) Petite ouverture 2) Air
    3) Sérénade •Asx/Pno •B&B

DESTOUCHES, André-Cardinal (1672-1749)
Issé - Pastorale et passepied (MULE) •Asx/Pno •Led

DE SWERT, Jules (1843-1891)
Ballade •Eb Sx/Pno •CF

DETTLEFSEN, H. C.
Compositeur néerlandais.
Mirage (1982) (13') •Asx/Pno/Perc •Don

DEUTSCHMANN, Gerhard
Compositeur allemand.
Lyrische Impressionen (198x) (8') 1) Etwas bewegt 2 Fliessend
    3) Rasch •Asx/Pno

DEVENIJNS, Gaston
3 Mouvements •SATB

DEVEVEY, Pierre (1919)
Chef d'orchestre et compositeur français, né à Paris, le 17 VIII 1919.
A la claire fontaine •SATB •adr
L'Alouette •SATB •adr
Arabesque •Asx/Pno •ELC
Caprice •SATB •ELC
Pièce en forme de valse •SATB •ELC
4 saxophones s'amusent •SATB •adr

DEVIENNE, François (1760-1803)
Largo and Allegretto (JAECKEL) •Tsx/Pno •South
6 Sonatas (ANDRAUD) •2 Sx: AA •South
Trio •2 Cl/Tsx or 3 Sx: TTB •Mol

DE VILLE, Paul
Blue Bells of Scotland •Eb Sx/Pno •CF
Happy be Thy Dreams •Eb or Bb Sx/Pno •CF
Major and Minor Scales •CF
60 Exercices of Mechanism •CF
The Swiss Boy •Ssx/Tpt/Pno •CF
27 Exercices and 15 Cadenzas (KAPPEY) •CF
Universal Method •CF
Ye Banks and Braes of Bonnie Doon •Eb Sx/Pno •CF

DEVOGEL, Jacques
Chef de musique français.
Graciella (1993) (2'15) •Asx/Pno •Com
Sans Lassie (1982) (1'15) •Asx/Pno •Com
Suite enfantine •6 Sx: SAATTB/Pno •Bil
Tiffany (1991) (2'30) •Asx/Pno •Com
Volupté (1989) (2'30) •1 Sx: A or T/Pno •Mar

DEWIT, A.
Hungarian Fantasy (HARRIS) •2 Cl/Asx/Bsn (or BsCl) •CF
On the Lake (HARRIS) •2 Cl/Asx/Bsn (or BsCl) •CF
Polonaise no. 1 (HARRIS) •2 Cl/Asx/Bsn (or BsCl) •CF
Spanish Waltz •2 Cl/Asx/Bsn (or BsCl) •CF
Summertime •2 Cl/Asx/Bsn (or BsCl) •CF

DE WOLF, Karel
4 Easy Pieces (2') 1) Choral 2) Cancion de la mulinera 3) A jazzy
    funeral 4) Rondo alla ragtime •SATB •Scz

DE YOUNG, Lynden (see YOUNG, Lynden de)

D'HAEYER, Frans C.
Introduction et Allegro (1953) •Asx/Pno •Met/An

DHAINE, Jean-Louis (1949)
Compositeur français, né le 29 XI 1949, à Armentières (Nord). Travailla avec N. Boulanger et D. Milhaud.
Cantabile •Asx/Accordion (or Pno)
3 Chants lyriques •3 Voice/2 Tpt/Asx/Pno
1er Concertino (1978) (to M. MÉRIOT) 1) Prélude 2) Nocturne
    3) Caprice •SATB
2me Concertino (1979) (13') (to D. MARTIN) 1) Prélude 2) Cantabile
    3) Finale •SATB
4me Concertino •2 Tpt/2 Sx: AT/Trb
9me Concertino (1983-84) (17') (to Quintet de Saxophones de Paris)
    1) Toccata 2) Gavotte 3) Adagio 4) Final •5 Sx: SnoSATB •Fuz
Entrechants (1978) (3') (to B. BEAUFRETON) •2 Sx: AT •Fuz
Fantaisies à 16 voix instrumentales •4 Fl/4 Cl/4 Sx: AATT/2 Tpt/2
    Trb
Grave (3') •Bb Sx/Org (or Pno)
3 Hymnes (14') •Asx/Org
Sonate (1983) (to B. COLLINET) 1) Prière aux Lémures 2) Scherzo
    3) A l'âme qui s'endort à midi 4) Final ou 'Ronde des esprits et
    des zéphiles' •Asx Solo
Sonatine (1983) (11') 1) Sinfonietta 2) Ostinato •Asx/Pno

DHOSSCHE
Invocation •Bb Sx/Pno •South

DIAMOND, David (Leo) (1915)
Compositeur américain, né à Rochester (New York) le 9 VII 1915. Travailla avec Rogers, Boepple, et Sessions, puis à Paris, avec N.

Boulanger.

"Clear structures, often evolved from contrapuntal or sonata-allegro procedures, are frequently fashioned into unusual one- or two- movement forms; among the later works are many masterful fugues and sets of variations. His harmony has developed gradually from a diatonic-modal to a more chromatic style without losing a strong personal character. Diamond's meticulous craftsmanship and his sensibility assured his position as a 20th-century classicist." (F. THORNE)

Duo concertante (1984) (to L. HUNTER) •Asx/Pno
Sonata (1984) (to D. SINTA & J. WYTKO) 1) Allegro vivo 2) Andante molto, quasi adagio 3) Allegro vivo •Asx/Pno

DIAZ, F.
Meu Bem •Sx/Tpt/Trb/Perc •PMP

DIAZ, Rafael (1943)
Compositeur espagnol.
Nudos (1981) (5') (to M. MIJAN) •SATB
Perfil reflejado (1986) •Asx Solo
Quatuor (1980) (to M. MIJAN) •SATB
3 Preludios del CEI (1984) (to M. MIJAN) •Asx Solo

DI BARI, Marco (1958)
Compositeur italien. Travailla avec G. Pernaiachi, L. Lombardi, A. Gentilucci, et R. Bianchini.

"Young Marco di Bari's work leads us to a homogeneous world of dreams and significance, their communicative force being born out of their ductility, their adaption to the tenets of listening considered as a natural dimension." (L. BRAMANI)

1° studio sugli oggetti in movimento (1989) (7') (to M. MAZZONI) •Bsx/Pno •Ric

DI BETTA, Philippe (1962)
Compositeur et saxophoniste français, né à Taverny, le 3 I 1962. Travailla avec D. Kientzy.
Croquis (1991) (6') •Fl/Asx •adr
Echantillons couleurs de bois (1993) (9'30) •Cl/Asx •adr
Fissures (1991) (3') •BsSx/Harp •adr
Passages (1990) (12') 1) Lento 2) Très lent, méditatif 3) = 40 4) = 104 5) 6) = 92 7) **Très calme, mystérieux** •2 Sx: AA •Fuz
Répertoire de toutes les possibilités similaires des doigtés mécaniques pour les saxophones (1990) •adr
Tempête de souffleurs (1993) •Ensemble ad lib of wind instruments [Ensemble ad libit. d'instruments à vent] •adr
Vents pluvieux (1992) (6') •Fl/Cl/Asx •Fuz

DI BIASE, Paolo (1942)
Professeur, pianiste, et compositeur italien, né le 16 I 1942.
Habanera (1993) (2'30) (to G. DI BACCO) •Asx/Pno •PT
Sirio (1993) (2') (to Quart. Accademia) •SATB •PT
Solarium (1992) (2') (to R. MICARELLI) •Asx/Pno •PT

DI CAPUA, Eduardo (1864-1917)
O sole mio •2 Sx: AT/Pno or 3 Sx: AAT or AAA or ATT/Pno •Cen

DI DOMENICA, Robert (1927)
Compositeur américain, né à New York, le 4 III 1927. Travailla avec J. Schmid.
Sonata (1967) (5'30) (to V. MOROSCO) 1) Fast 2) Very slow 3) Very fast 4) Slow •Asx/Pno •MJQ

DI DONATO, Vincenzo (1887-1971)
Compositeur italien, né le 15 VIII 1887, à Rome; mort en 1971.
Pastorale •Asx/Pno •DS

DIEDERICHS, Yann (1952)
Compositeur français, né à Lyon. Etudes de linguistiques générales.

Autodidacte en musique, se forme en assistant A. Boucourechliev et B. Jolas dans les studios du G.R.M., puis Bruno Maderna, chef d'orchestre. Vit depuis 1980 en Allemagne.
Dogme (1985/88) (8'10) •Sx
Inkrustowana (1982) (14'30) (to D. KIENTZY) •Asx/Lyricon
M.L.K. (1981) (10'30) (to D. KIENTZY) •1 Sx: S+A+T+B/Dispositif électro-acoust. ad lib.
Neumae (1982) (4'30) •Sx
Pentes (1985/88) (12'30) •Ssx/Perc
Prismes (1983/88) (12'30) •Fl/Asx/Pno
Shrills (1982) (6'30) •Asx/Dispositif électro-acoust.
SPC 834 (1984) (5') •Bsx/Perc
Subférence (1983) (5') •Asx/Dispositif électro-acoust. ad lib.
Shreds (1983) (5') (to D. KIENTZY) •Ssx/Dispositif électro-acoust.
Valence (1984) (10'30) •Sx/Tape
Versants (1985/88) (10'30) •3 Sx

DIEMENTE, Edward (1923)
Compositeur américain né à Cranston (Rhode Island), en 1923.
Diary Part II (1972) (to D. SINTA) •2 Sx: AA/Tape •DP
Dimensions I •Any 3 Instruments •SeMC
Dimensions II •Any 1 to 6 Instruments/Tape •SeMC
Dimensions III (1971) (to K. DORN) •Any Sx/Tape •SeMC
For Lady Day •Fl/Ob/Cl/Tpt/Trb/Vln/Vla/Sx/Bsn/Tape •SeMC
Mirrors IV - Etudes (1974) •Asx Solo •DP
Mirrors VI (1974) (to D. SINTA) •Asx/Pno •DP
Quartet in Memory Fl. O'Connor (1967) 1) Fast 2) Slow blues 3) Fast jazz beat •Asx/Trb/Bass/Perc •OKM/SeMC
Response (1969) (4'30) •Asx/Pno •OKM/SeMC
3-31'70 •Voice/Tpt/Trb/Sx/Guit/Bass/5 Perc •SeMC
Trio (1969) •Asx/Tpt/Perc •SeMC

DIERCKS, John (1927)
Compositeur américain, né à Montelain (New Jersey), le 19 IV 1927. Travailla avec H. Elwell, A. Hovhaness, B. Rogers, et H. Hanson.

"… a richly endowed musical personality, who possesses humor and depth; 'a simple, direct style'; 'charming.' "
Suite (1972) (6'30) (to F. WILLIAMS) 1) Chase 2) Barcarolle 3) Plaint 4) Gig •Asx/Pno •Pres/TP/Ten

DIERGUNOV, Fevgen
Dream in Blue of All Life •SATB

DIESSEL, Karl (1919)
Compositeur français, né en Allemagne, à Osnabruck, le 6 XI 1919.
Danse des spectres •SATB •adr

DIJK, Gijs van (1954)
Compositeur hollandais, né à Delft. Travailla avec Tr. Keuris.
Quintette for Saxophones and Piano (1986) (11'30) 1) Allegro assai 2) Lento, molto tranquillo 3) Coda •4 Sx: SATB/Pno •Don

DIJK, Jan van (1918)
Compositeur néerlandais. Travailla avec Püpper
7 Bagatellen (1982) •SATB
Concertino •Vln/Fl/Cl/Asx •Don
Concertino (1953) (9') 1) Prélude 2) Berceuse 3) Aubade 4) Finale •Asx/Orch (2222/2200/Timp/Str) or Pno •Don
Sonate (1953) (9') 1) Prélude 2) Berceuse 3) Aubade 4) Finale •Asx/Pno •Don

DIJK, Rudi Martinus van (1932)
Compositeur canadien d'origine néerlandaise, né à La Haye en 1932. Vit au Canada depuis 1953. Travailla avec H. Andriessen, R. Harris, et M. Deutjel.
Sonata movement (1960) (to Ph. LAIRD & P. BRODIE) •Asx/Pno •CMC

DIJOUX, Marc

Le déchiffrage pour tous (1992) •Mar
60 Duos sur des airs populaires •2 Sx: AA •Mar
Initiation progressive au déchiffrage instrumental •Mar
La technique du déchiffrage (2 Volumes) •Mar

DIKKER, Loek (1944)

Pianiste, compositeur, et arrangeur hollandais, né à Amsterdam.
Kwartet (1989) (8'15) (to Amsterdam Saxophone Quartet) •SATB

DI LASSO, O.

Matona lovely maiden (CHEYETTE) •2 Cl/Asx/Bsn (or Bsx) •Ken

DILLENKOFER, Josef Toni

Junior - Music - Camp (Book 4) •4 Sx: AATT •Zim

DILLON, Henry (1912-1954)

Musicien français, né à Angers, le 9 X 1912; mort en Indochine durant la guerre, le 9 VII 1954.
"He was largely self taught in music, and adopted a classical style of composition." (BAKER)
Sonate (1949) (7') (to S. M. S. SIHANOUKK 1er) 1) Allegro con brio 2) Andante 3) Vivace •Asx/Pno •Sal

DILLON, Robert

Compositeur américain.
Night Shade (1956) •SATB •B&H

DI LOTTI, Silvana (1942)

Intonazione (1985) •Asx/Pno

DINDALE, E.

Bucolique •1 Sx: A or T/Pno •HE
Canzonetta •1 Sx: A or T/Pno •HE
Eglogue •Asx/Pno •Sch
Lied •Asx/Pno •HE
Peasant Dance •1 Sx: A or T/Pno •HE

DINESCU-LUCACI, Violeta (1953)

Compositeur et professeur allemand, d'origine Roumaine, né le 13 VII 1953 à Bucarest. Travailla avec G. Enesco, K. Klinger, et P. Hindemith.
"Auf der Suche nach Mozart" (1983) (19') •Fl/Sx/Bsn/Hn/Vln/ Pno+Celesta •adr
Méandre (1993) •Asx/Pno •INM
Mondnacht (12') •Sx/Mezzo Soprano Voice •adr
Nakris •SATB •adr
3 Miniatures (1982) (5') (to Rascher Saxophone Quartet) •SATB •adr

DINICU, Grigoras (1889-1949)

Hora Staccato (HEIFETZ) •1 Sx: A or T/Orch or Pno •CF
Hora Staccato (ZAJAC) •Asx/Wind Ensemble

DININNY, John Ernest (1945)

Compositeur américain, né le 18 XII 1945.
Crab (1972) (12'30) (to K. & S. DORN) •Sx/Dancer •DP
Rhinoceros •Any numbers of players/Electronic Equipment •adr

DI NOVI, Eugene

Blues (1964) (to the New York Saxophone Quartet) •SATB

DI PASQUALE, James (1941)

Saxophoniste et compositeur américain, né à Chicago, le 7 IV 1941. Travailla avec F. Hemke, S. Rascher, D. Diamond, A. Donato, et L. Uhlehla.
"His music is rhythmically and melodically fresh with lots of good thematic ideas and effective use of the coloristic possibilities." (C. S-

T.) "Most of all, it was music filled with delight in being alive." (C. T.)
Quartet (1964) (10') •Tsx/Tpt/Vla/Vcl •adr
Radical Departures •14 Sx: SSAAAAATTTBBBBs
Sonata (1967) (10') (to J. HOULIK) 1) Andante - Allegro moderato 2) Adagio ma non troppo 3) Allegro con brio •Tsx/Pno •South

DI PIETRO, Rocco

Phantom Melos (1981) (to Amherst Saxophone Quartet) •SATB

DI SALVO

Rhapsody (1973) (to N. KOVAL) •Ssx/Pno

DIXON, Mary Morrison (1948)

Southern Soliloquies (1992) 1) The Old Farm 2) Debutantes 3) Spring Snow 4) The Bridge Club 5) South Main 6) Rope Swinging Out Over The Hill •Asx/Pno

DJEMIL, Enyss (1917)

Chef d'orchestre directeur de conservatoire et compositeur français, né à Paris, en 1917. Travailla avec L. Aubert et G. Ropartz.
Concerto (1974) (16') (to J. MAFFEI) 1) Pour l'alto 2) Pour le ténor 3) Pour le soprano •1 Sx: S+A+T/Orch or Pno •adr

DJORDJEVIC, Aleksandra

Compositeur ex-yougoslave.
Menace, Incantation (1993) •Asx/Org •INM

DMITRIEV, Gueorgui Petrovitch (1942)

Compositeur russe né à Krasnodar (Kouban caucasien). Travailla avec D. Kabalevsky.
"Son oeuvre est abondante et variée, il utilise différents éléments : chants populaires archaïques, liturgies byzantines, recherches de timbres et de langage influencées par les courants occidentaux. Il se rattache en partie à la tendance 'Vieille Russie.' " (J. di VANNI)
In the Character of Herman Hesse •SATB
Labyrinth (20') (to K. RADNOFSKY) •Asx/Orch •adr
Quartet (1986) (22') •SATB
Quartet (1990) (19'30) Allegro energico - Andante flessibile - Agitato molto - Con fuoco - Moderato •SATB

DMITRIEV, Sergej (1964)

Compositeur suèdois.
Fanfar (1992) •SATB •SMIC
Hâgrigar (Mirages) (1992) •SATB •SvM

DOBBINS, Bill

Pianiste et compositeur de jazz américain.
Echoes Distant Land •Asx Solo •WWS
Sonata (1991) (13') 1) Somewhat freely-Jazz waltz 2) Somewhat freely 3) With drive •1 Sx: S or T/Pno •AdMu

DOBROWOLSKI, Andrzej (1921)

Compositeur polonais né le 9 IX 1921. Travailla avec Rutkowski et Malawski.
"His contacts with Lutoslawski, Serocki and others over the years 1958-64 caused him to work intensively to develop a more individual style." (B. SCHÄFFER)
Passcaglia (1988) (16') •Tsx/Perc

DOBRZYNSKI, Ignacy Feliks (1807-1867)

Duo •Asx/Cl •WWS

DOERR, Clyde

Saxophone Moods •Asx/Pno or SATB •Sal
Valse Impromptu •Asx/Orch

DOLDEN, Paul

Revenge of repressed, Resonance #2 (1993) •Ssx/Tape •INM

DOMAGALA, Jacek (1947)

Compositeur allemand, d'origine polonaise, né le 19 VIII 1947 à Szczenicek. Travailla à Poznan puis à Berlin.
Ballade (1986) (15') •Asx/Pno •adr
Impression (5'30) •Asx Solo •Asto

DOMAZLICKY, Frantisek (1913)

Compositeur tchécoslovaque.
Musica, op. 54 (12') •SATB •DHF
Suite danza, op. 52 (17') •4 Sx/Hn/2 Tpt/Trb/Tuba

D'OMBRAIN, Geoffrey

Compositeur australien.
Continuo (1982) •Asx/Tape
Introspections (1975) (to P. CLINCH) •Asx/Tape

DONAHUE, Robert (1931)

Compositeur américain.
Sonata (1972) (to K. DEANS) •Asx/Pno
Sonata (1988) •Asx/Pno

DONAL, Michalsky

3 Time Four (1928/1974) 1) Fanfare 2) Lince 3) Canto firmo: fantasia a quatro •SATB •Sha

DONATO, Anthony (1909)

Compositeur américain, né le 8 III 1909 à Prague (Nebraska). Travailla avec Hanson, Rogers, et Royce.
Discourse II (1975) (to F. HEMKE) •Asx/Pno

DONATO, Vincenzo (See DI DONATO)

DONATONI, Franco (1927)

Compositeur et professeur italien, né à Vérone le 9 VI 1927. Travailla avec Bottagisio, Desderi Zecchi, Liviabella, et Pizzetti.

"Il est aujourd'hui admis comme l'un des compositeurs italiens qui comptent, avec Berio, Nono, Maderna ou Bussotti. Volubile, extravertie, la 'patte' de Donatoni est aisément reconnaissable: elle est celle d'un musicien réconcilié avec l'expressivité, le lyrisme, les caprices de l'invention." (J-E. FOUSNAQUER) "Après une première période néo-classique, il compose dans un style post-webernien librement et personnellement adapté. Sans maniérisme excessif, il a trouvé des solutions personnelles et originales à l'utilisation des techniques actuelles." (Cl. ROSTAND) "Il faudra longtemps pour comprendre comment à force de doute, de refus, de négation, de perte de soi-même, Donatoni a pu arriver à un art aussi convaincant dans son évidence, aussi positif pour tout dire. C'est peut-être que, ici comme chez Xenakis, la pensée est si forte, si cohérente, si globale qu'elle fait langage de toutes les situations." (M. FLEURET) "On a parlé à son propos d''émiettement du matériau', de 'revanche du matériau', c'est pour lui cet émiettement même qui doit forcer à chaque instant l'attention au matériau lui-même: "Les matériaux libérés se composent d'eux-mêmes en images, dit le compositeur." (J. & B. MASSIN) "Hot: Il s'agit d'un jazz 'imaginaire.' Rien qui soit d'une évidence immédiate, selon une pratique qui m'est chère et qui transpose, dans mon expérience artisanale de l'écriture, des gestes appartenant à la mémoire d'une pratique instrumentale 'improvisée', modulée par l'imagination." (F. DONATONI) "Pour chaque oeuvre, Franco Donatoni forge un processus en tant que 'phénomène dynamique qui précède la forme. Son invention ne peut donc être rien d'autre qu'une conséquence de l'attention dirigée vers la matière qui doit être transformée et fait partie intégrante non de la forme mais de l'oeuvre'. Composer implique moins de produire une oeuvre que de se soumettre aux conditions de l'oeuvre produite." (D. J-Y BOSSEUR)

"At best the listener's response to such works may end in a sort of philosophical meditation, like Bortolotto's or Baroni's, whose criti-cism, however, should be counterbalanced by the appreciation of Donatoni's ability in accommodating his cultural roots to the crisis of the European avant garde in the late 1950s, a crisis which he thus succeeded in turning into a personal possibility for continuing to compose: in his case, for continuing to give artistic evidence of a far-reaching crisis in values." (Cl. ANNIBALDI)
Hot (1989) (14') (Commande de l'AsSaFra [Commissioned by French Saxo. Assoc.]) •1 Sx: T+Sno/Cl+Eb Cl/Tpt/Trb/Perc/ Bass/Pno •Ric
Rasch (1990) (5'30) •SATB •Ric

DONDEYNE, Désiré (1921)

Chef d'orchestre et compositeur français, né à Laon (Aisne), le 20 VII 1921. Travailla avec N. Gallon et T. Aubin.
"Langage conventionnel essentiellement lyrique."
Berceuse et gavotte (from *Suite*) •SATB •SF
9 Déchiffrages (1986) •Sx Solo •Bil
13 Déchiffrages (1985) (5 Volumes) •Sx Solo •Bil
Mercure (1993) (1'30) •Asx/Pno •Mar
Pluton (1993) (1'30) •Asx/Pno •Mar
Quatuor •SATB •adr
Saturne (1993) (1'30) •1 Sx: A or T/Pno •Mar
Suite (19') 1) Ouverture 2) Berceuse-chanson 3) Gavotte 4) Valse lente 5) Rondo final •SATB •adr
Symphonie concertante (1970-71) (16'30) •Asx/Orch (2222/2200/ Harp/Str) or Pno •Chou
Variations sur un air tyrolien (1971) (10') •8 Sx: SAATTBBBs •EMRF
Voyages imaginaires (1989) (12') (to B. DUPAQUIER) 1) La lumière 2) La ville blanche 3) La lune blafarde 4) Animation sur la place 5) volubilis 6) Tanagras 7) Beautés intérieures 8) Marchands orientaux 9) Ciel bleu 10) Le chant de l'eau •Asx/Pno or Asx/2 Vln/Harp/Vcl •Com

DONIZETTI, Gaetano (1797-1848)

Belisaire (MAYEUR) •Asx/Pno •Led
Elisir d'amore (VERROUST) - 20 mélodies •Sx Solo •Bil
Fausta (VERROUST) - 15 mélodies •Sx Solo •Bil
Gemma di Vergy (MAYEUR) •Asx/Pno •Cos
Lucia de Lammermoor •2 Sx: AT/Pno •Cen
Lucia de Lammermoor •AATB •Rub
Lucia di Lammermoor (DIETZE) •AATB •Rub
Lucia di Lammermoor (MAYEUR) •Asx/Pno •Led
Pia di Tolomei (VERROUST) - 8 mélodies •Sx Solo •CF

DONJON, Johannes

Invocation •Bsx/Pno •CBet
Madrigal (1897) •Asx/Pno

DONORA, Luigi

Compositeur italien.
5 X 5 - Canoni •Asx/Pno •Piz

DORADO

Two Friends (WHEELER) •2 Sx: AA or AT/Pno •Volk

DORAN, Matt H. (1921)

Compositeur américain, né le 1er IX 1921, à Cavington (Kentucky).
Lento and Allegro (1962) •Asx/Pno •AvMu/WIM

DORFF, Daniel

Fantasy, Scherzo, Nocturne (1978) •SATB •Sha

DÖRFLINGER, Kurt (1910-1986)

Saxophoniste, chef d'orchestre, et Compositeur allemand, né le 5 VIII 1910 à Karslsruhe où il est mort le 6 I 1986. Auteur de musique de salon.

Illusion •Asx/Pno •Fro

DORHAM, Kenny
Blue Bossa (Moscatelli) •12 Sx: SnoSSAAATTTBBBs

DORN, Kenneth
Saxophoniste et éditeur américain.
Multiphonics •DP
Saxophone Technique •DP
Benedictus (Isaac) •3 Sx: ATB •DP
Si domiero (Anonymous) •3 Sx: ATB •DP
Tart ara (Anonymous) •3 Sx: ATB •DP

DORNBY, Finn
Compositeur danois.
Musickus dornby (to Ch. A. Gron) •2 Sx: AB/Org/Electric Guit/
Electric BsGuit/Perc

DORSAM, Paul
Sax Section - a catch and contemplation for saxophone quartet
•SATB

DORSEY, Jimmy (1904-1957)
Clarinettiste et saxophoniste de jazz américain, né le 29 II 1904 à
Shenandoah (Pennsylvania); mort à New York, le 12 VI 1957.
Oodles of Noodles •Asx/Pno •RoMu
Metodo per sassofono •Cur
Finger Bustin •Asx/Pno •WWS

DORSSELAER, Willy van (1918)
Compositeur français, né le 5 VIII 1918. Travailla avec Alpaerts,
Motelmans, et van Hoof.
Andantino, op. 68 (1966) (2'30) •Asx/Pno •Bil
Andantino (d'après A. Lavignac) (2') •Eb Sx or Bb Sx/Pno •Lem
Arabesque en Sib, op. 57 (1960) (4'30) •1 Sx: A or T/Pno •Met
A coeur joie (1971) (4') •Asx/Pno •Bil
Conte de Versaille - Menuet (1971) (2') •Asx/Pno •Bil
Dixieland (1969) (2'30) •Asx/Pno •adr
En regardant la mer (1971) (2'30) •Asx/Pno •Lem
Féérie sur glace, op. 82 (1970) (2'30) •Asx/Pno •adr
Feux follets, op. 67 (1966) (4') •Asx/Pno •Bil
Musicolor, op. 88 (1970) (1'30) •Asx/Pno •Bil
Solo de concours, op. 60 (1963) (4') (to G. Billaudot) •Tsx/Pno
•Braun

DORWARD, David
Quartet (1979) •SATB

DOTT, Hans-Peter (1952)
Compositeur allemand né le 21 XII 1952 à Koblenz.
Sonanzen (1984) (6') (to the Rascher Quartet) •SATB •adr

DOUANE, Jules-Albert (1891-19xx)
Capriccio (1960) (4') (to M. Mule) •Asx/Pno •Lem

DOUGHERTY, William (1956)
Compositeur américain.
Seven Bagatelles (1990) (12'-14') (to M. Cox) •Asx Solo •Heil

DOUGLAS, William (1944)
Compositeur américain.
Flower (1973) •Asx/Pno
Jig (1975) •Asx/Pno
Vajra (1972) •Asx/Pno

DOULIEZ, Victor
Compositeur belge.
Prélude et Scherzo (to Quatuor Belge de Saxophones) •SATB

DOULLON
Auréole - Fantaisie •Asx/Pno •Mil
Dolcissimo - air varié facile •Asx/Pno •Mil

DOURSON, Paul
Allegretto grazioso (1993) •Eb or Bb Sx/Pno •Led

DOURY, Pierre (1925)
Compositeur français. Travailla avec Alex. Cellier, A. Steck, M.
Samuel Rousseau, A. Hoeree, et J. Fournet.
Spécialiste de chant grégorien.
Caprice en Rondeau (2'10) (Recueil 1) •Asx/Pno •Bil
Quatuor •SATB

DOUSA, E.
Compositeur tchèque.
Jazz tones 1) Pozor jedeme 2) Baroque-jazz fuga •SATB

DOUSE, Kenneth (1906)
Violoniste, saxophoniste, et compositeur américain, d'origines an-
glaises, né à Tunbridge Wells (Kent), le 30 IV 1906.
Cynthia (1939) •Asx/Pno •CF
How to Double and Triple Staccato (1947) •BMCo

DOYEN, Henri (1905)
Organiste, compositeur français, chanoine, né à Soissons en 1905.
Travailla avec L. Vierne, Bonnet, et J. Dere. Maître de chapelle à la
Cathédrale de Soissons.
Canzona •Asx/Org •adr

DRDLA, Franz (1868-1944)
Souvenir (Harger) •5 Sx: AATTB •Band

DRESSEL, Erwin (1909-1972)
Compositeur et pianiste allemand, né à Berlin, le 10 VI 1909, où il
est mort le 17 XII 1972. Travailla avec Klatte et Juon. Fut très tôt
acclamé comme "enfant prodige."
Bagatellen (1938) (14') (to J. de Vries & S. Rascher) 1) Elegie
2) Aria 3) Scherzo 4) Gigue •Asx/Pno •RE
Capriccio, op. 45 (9') •Asx/Str Orch or Pno
Concerto, op. 27 (1932) (24') (to S. Rascher) •Asx/Orch or Pno
•RE
Concerto (1965) (to S. & C. Rascher) •2 Sx: SA/Orch
Partita (1965) (18') (for S. Rascher) 1) Prelude - Allemande
2) Canzone 3) Courante 4) Pavane 5) Gigue •Asx/Pno •RE
Sonate (1932) (to S. Rascher) •Asx/Pno

DRIGO, Riccardo (1846-1930)
Canzone Barcarolle •Asx or Bb Sx/Pno •Bel
Demande d'amour •Asx or Bb Sx/Pno •Bel
Serenade •Eb Sx or Bb Sx/Pno •CF/Cen
Serenade "Les Millions d'Arlequin" •1 Sx: A or T/Pno •Bel/Cen/
Zim
Smile of Colombine •Tsx/Pno •Bel
Valse bluette •2 Sx: AA/Pno •CF
Valse mélodie •Asx or Bb Sx/Pno •Bel

D'RIVERA, Paquito
Compositeur américain.
Suite 1) Elegy to Eric Dolphy 2) Wapango •SATB

DROGOZ
Triptyque pour 3 fois 3 instruments •Led

DROUET, Raymond (1919)
Compositeur français, né à Parthenay, le 13 VI 1919.
Quatuor •SATB •adr

DROZIN, Garth

Parabolics (1981) (to M. Taggart) •Ssx/Tape •ACA

DRUET, Robert (1920)

Saxophoniste français. Travailla avec Marcel Mule.

Air et danse (1976) •Asx/Pno •Bil
L'Ecole française du saxophone (Gourdet) (1963) (to M. Mule) (3 Volumes) •Braun
Mélodie •Asx/Pno •Bil
Sérénade - impromptu (1990) •Asx/Pno •Bil

DRUICK, Don

Sonatine •Asx/Pno

DRUMHALLER, Jonathan

Compositeur américain.

Wednesday: I will not be afraid (1992) (6') •SATB

DUBEDOUT, Bertrand (1958)

Compositeur français, né à Bayonne, le 8 V 1958. Travailla avec G. Maneveau et M-Françoise Lacaze, puis avec P. Schaeffer et G. Rebel.

Cycles de transparence (1984-85) (8') (to D. Kientzy) •Asx/Tape

DUBOIS, A.

Trio •Fl/Tsx/Pno •CDM

DUBOIS, Pierre-Max (1930)

Compositeur français, né à Graulhet (Tarn), le 1er III 1930. Travailla avec D. Milhaud et J. Rivier. Grand Prix de Rome (1955).

"C'est un traditionaliste qui se meut avec une extrême ingéniosité parmi les possibilités les plus diverses de l'écriture tonale, à laquelle il est sincèrement attaché. Doué d'une grande facilité de travail, il est à la tête d'un catalogue important qui sollicite tous les genres avec la même adresse et où passe fréquemment le souvenir de Darius Milhaud, qui fut son maître." (Cl. Rostand)

"The main influences on his music have been those of Milhaud, Françaix and Prokofiev." (P. Griffiths)

A Pas de loup •Asx/Pno •RR
2 Caprices en forme d'études (1964) •2 Sx: AA •adr
6 Caprices (1967) •2 Sx: AA •Led
Circus parade (1965) (15') (to Fr. Daneels) 1) Allegro moderato 2) Adagio 3) Marche •Asx/Perc •Led
Come back (1992) (16') (to D. Gremelle) •Asx/Pno •Bil
Concertino (d'après le *Quatuor de Saxophones*) (1967) (12') •SATB/Chamber Orch •Led
Concerto (1959) (17') (to J-M. Londeix) 1) Lento e Allegro (Cadence de [Cadenza by] J-M. Londeix) 2) Sarabande 3) Rondo •Asx/Str Orch or Pno •Led
Concertstück (1955) (10') 1) Aria 2) Allegro vigoroso e marcato •Asx/Orch or Pno •Led
Conclusions (1978) (12') (to J-Y Fourmeau) 1) Variations 2) Lamento 3) Scherzo •Asx Solo •Led
Danses provençales •2 Sx: AA/Perc •adr
Dessins animés (1978) (16') (to E. Tangvold) •2 Sx: SA/Cl/BsCl •FroMu
Divertissement (1953) (10') (to M. Mule) 1) Allegro vivo 2) Lent et doux 3) Scherzando •Asx/Orch (2222/221/Perc/Harp/Str) or Pno •Led
Dix Figures à danser - Petit ballet (1962) •Asx/Pno •Led
Les écureuils (1971) (1') •Asx/Pno •RR
Fantaisie •Bsx/Pno •Led
Feu de paille (1986) (8') (to Cl. Brunel et C. Arnoux) 1) Prélude et Gavotte 2) Fanfare et Final •Vln/Asx •Bil
Grave et Scherzo mécanique (1973) (to Fr. Daneels) •Asx/Pno •RR
Hommage à Hoffnung (with J-M. Londeix) (1980) (25') •11 Sx: SnoSSAAATTBBBs/Perc •adr

L'Imprévu (1987) •SATB •Bil
Le Lièvre et la Tortue - Impromptu (1957) (4'30) (to J-M. Londeix) •Asx/Orch or Pno •Led
Le récit du chamelier (1964) (5') •Asx Solo •Bil
Les Métamorphoses (1982) (24') (to Quatuor Deffayet) Allegro inquieto - Allegro molto - Andante (quasi recitativo) subito molto vivo - Andante - Intermezzo - Le miroir (Allegro vivo) •SATB •Bil
Les Tréteaux (1966) (7'30) 1) Prologue en fanfare 2) Romantica 3) Valse vulgaire •Fl/Asx/Pno •Chou
Les trois mousquetaires (1966) (10') (to P. Pareille) 1) Lentement 2) Allègrement 3) Allegro 4) Andante 5) Presto •Ob/Cl/Asx/Bsn •Led
Mazurka, Hommage à Chopin (1961) (4') (to G. Gourdet) •Asx/Pno •Led
Menuet de Beaugency •Asx/Pno •Led
2 Mini romances (1979) (5') (to G. Gourdet) •1 Sx: A or T/Pno •Bil
3 Miniatures (1981) •3 Sx: AAT •Ly
Moments musicaux (1985) (17'30) (to S. Bichon) 1) Andante 2) Agitato 3) Tempo di marcia 4) Coda - Prestissimo •Asx/Orch or Pno •Bil
Mominettes (1992) (13') (5 short movements) •Asx/Pno •Bil
Olga valse (1982) (1'30) •Asx/Pno •Bil
Petit Quatuor (1980) (8'30) •AATB •Ly
3 Petites sonates à Scarlatti (1990) •SATB •Bil
Pièces caractéristiques (1962) (16'30) (to J-M. Londeix) 1) A L'espagnole 2) A la russe 3) A la française 4) A la hongroise 5) A la parisienne Asx/Pno •Led
Prélude et Rengaine (1979) (to G. Gourdet) •1 Sx: A or T/Pno •Bil
10 Préludes imaginaires (1993) •4 Sx: SATB/Orch
Quatuor (1956) (17') 1) Ouverture 2) Doloroso 3) Spirituoso 4) Andante •SATB •Led
Respirations (1982) (8') (to D. Deffayet) •Asx/Pno •Bil
Sinfonia da camera (1964) (10') (to Sextuor à vent de Dijon) 1) Entrée 2) Gigue en rondeau 3) Variations •Fl/Ob/Cl/Asx/Hn/ Bsn •Led
Sonate (1956) (20') (to D. Deffayet) 1) Allegro vivo 2) Andante 3) Tempo di gavotte 4) Rondo •Asx/Pno •Led
Sonate d'étude (1970) (to D. Deffayet) 1) Comme une fileuse 2) Comme une cornemuse 3) Hommage à Paganini 4) Comme une guitare •Sx Solo •Led
Sonate fantaisie (1979) (13'30) (to G. Gourdet) 1) Avec souplesse et lyrisme 2) Incantatoire 3) Sérénade •Asx/Pno •Bil
Sonatine (1966) (8') (to Fr. Daneels) Lento - Allegro vivo - Andante - Allegretto prestissimo •Asx/Orch (1011/000/Perc/Str) or Pno •Led
2me Sonatine (1968) (9') 1) Allegro 2) Andante 3) Presto •Asx/Pno •Led
Sonatine (1974) (7') •Fl/Cl/Asx/Tpt/Trb •adr
Suite •Vln/Asx/Pno/Perc •Mau
Suite française (1962) (16') (to G. Gourdet) 1) Prélude 2) Courante 3) Sarabande 4) Gavottes 5) Bourrées 6) Menuet 7) Gigue •Asx Solo •Led
Triangle (1974) (19') (to J-P. Vermeeren) •1 Sx: S+A+T/Pno •RR
Trio •Fl/Tsx/Harp •adr
Trio •Ob/Asx/Vcl •adr
Variations (1968) (16') (to Quatuor Belge de Saxophones) 1) Thème andantino 2) Allegretto 3) Lento misterioso 4) Vivo 5) Religioso 6) Vif 7) Andante dramatico 8) Pastourelle 9) Final-presto •SATB •adr
Vieille chanson et Rondinade (1982) (3'30) •Tsx/Pno •Bil

DU BOIS, Rob (See BOIS, Rob du)

DUBUS, Georges (1909)
> Compositeur français, né à Roubaix (Nord), le 23 I 1921.
Adagio, Larghetto et Largo •SATB •adr

DUCHEMIN, Lucien (1909)
> Compositeur français, né à Paris. Travailla avec E. Bloch et Caussade.
Suite •SATB

DUCKWORTH, William (1943)
> Compositeur américain, né à Morganton (North Carolina), le 13 I 1943. Travailla avec B. Johnson, T. Fredukson, et M. Mailman.
> "Duckworth's music had some perky sonorities that gave it more character then anything else on the evening." (A. HUGHES)
A Ballad in Time and Space (1968) (3') (to J. HOULIK) •Tsx/Pno •SeMC
Fragments (1967) (12') (to J. HOULIK) •Tsx/Wind Orch/Perc •SeMC
Memory of You •Any 4 instruments •adr
Midnight Blue (1976) (4'30) (to BOK & LE MAIR) •Asx/2 Channels of self-preprared tape •adr
Pitch City •Any 4 instruments •MP
Pitt County Excusrsions (1972) (to J. HOULIK) 1) March 2) Serenade 3) Air 4) Ragtime •Tsx/Pno •SeMC
Real Music (1970) •SATB •MP

DUCLOS, René (1899-1964)
> Compositeur né à Bordeaux, le 12 X 1899. Travailla avec P. Dukas et J. Gallon.
Pièce brève (1950) (2'30) (to A. BEAUCAMP) •Asx/Pno •Led

DUFFAU, Lionel (1951)
> Compositeur et trompettiste français, né à Bordeaux le 29 V 1951. Travailla avec M. Fusté-Lambezat, H. Challan, et M. Constant. Directeur du Conservatoire de Pau.
Diffluence (1983) (9') (to Fr. VALONNE) •SATB
Questions (1985) (8') (to J-M. LONDEIX) 12 Sx: SnoSSAAATTTBBBs
3 Images (1982) 1) Modéré 2) Lent 3) Vif •SATB

DUFLOT, Raoul
Lido (1991) (1') •Asx/Pno •Com

DUFOUR, Denis (1953)
> Compositeur français, né à Lyon. Travailla avec Michel Fusté-Lambezat et J. Fontyn. Appartient avec Laurent Cuniot, Yann Geslin, et Philippe Mion au groupe TM+ issu du GRM.
> "Participe à l'amorce d'une nouvelle organologie, en alliant des lutheries acoustique et électronique."
Cueillir à l'arbre un petit garçon (1978) (8') •Asx/Synth

DUFRESNE, Gaston
Develop Sight Reading for Radio, TV, Symph. (1954) •CC

DUHA, Isabelle (1951)
Scherzo (1981) (2'30) (to G. GOURDET) •Asx/Pno •Bil

DUHAMEL, Antoine (1925)
> Compositeur français, né à Paris, le 30 VII 1925. Travailla avec De La Presle, O. Messiaen, et R. Leibowitz.
> "Travaille dans des directions proches du théâtre musical."
Hommage à Mingus (12'30) •5 Sx: AATTB •EFM
Le Transibérien (1983) •Asx/Tpt/Pno/Perc/Harmonica/3 Armenian Instruments

DUIJK, Guy Christian Désiré (1927)
> Chef d'orchestre et compositeur belge, né le 28 IV 1927, à Gand. Travailla avec J. Leroy et Fr. Bourguignon. Chef de musique de la Force Nationale Belge.
Contest + 5 •Asx/Pno •An
Introduction et Danse (10') •Asx/Orch or Pno •Mau

DUKAS, Antonia (1960)
Fantasia (1981) (to F. BONGIORNO) •Asx/Pno

DUKAS, Paul (1865-1935)
Alla gitana (MULE) •Asx/Pno •Led

DUKE, Lewis Byron (1924)
> Compositeur américain, né à Upland (California), en 1924. Travailla avec M. Castelnuovo-Tedesco et R. Gross.
Eingang (1969/71) •2 Sx: AB/Narr •BPb
Variations on a Tone Row (1952/70) (13'30) •Asx/Pno •BPb

DULAT, Philippe
> Compositeur français.
Quatuor à l'enfant malade - Le Phénix (1980) (to J. CHARLES) •SATB

DÜMKE, Ulrich (1964)
> Compositeur allemand.
Oktett (1989) •8 Sx: SSAATTBB
1058 (1990) (6') •Bsx Solo •Wu

DUNKEL, Elmar
> Compositeur allemand.
B / S new (1993) •Asx/Pno •INM

DÜNKI, Jean-Jacques (1948)
Lutezia, 1842 (1978) •Ssx/Tpt/Vcl/Pno/Perc

DU PARC
4 Love songs (DAVIS) •Ssx/Pno •WWS

DUPERIER, Jean (1886-19xx)
> Compositeur, écrivain suisse, né à Genève, le 17 VI 1886.
> "La caractéristique la plus saillante du talent de Jean Duperier est incontestablement l'esprit… Musicien authentique, qui parle une langue personnelle vigoureuse et châtiée." (R. BERNARD)
3 Airs pour un soir de Mai (1936) (to Quatuor Mule) •SATB •Lem

DUPIN, Paul (1865-1949)
> Compositeur français, né à Roubaix, le 14 VIII 1865; mort à Paris, le 5 III 1949. Travailla avec P. Durand.
Chant (1910) (to E. HALL) •Asx/Harps/Vla/Chorus

DUPONT, Jacques
Bercement (Recueil [Album]) (1974) (3'30) •Asx/Pno •Zu
Saxophonie •SATB

DUPONT, Pierre (1898-19xx)
> Chef d'orchestre français, né à St-Omer. Travailla avec Lavignac et P. Fauchet. Chef de musique de la Garde Républicaine (1927-1945).
Romance en Sib •Asx (or Vln)/Pno •Led

DUPORT, Jean-Louis (1749-1819)
Romance •Bb Sx/Pno •JS

DUPRÉ, René (1933)
> Chef de musique et compositeur français, né au Creusot, le 27 II 1933. Travailla avec C. Guidani, F. Foret, et G. Hugon.
> "Musicien sincère qui pense que la musique atonale, plate-forme entre la musique d'hier et celle scientifique de demain, est celle de notre temps."
Ballade chromatique •4 Sx: AAAA/Tpt •adr
Canon chromatique à 8 voix •4 Sx: SATB/2 Tpt/2 Trb •adr
Canon chromatique à 12 voix •12 Sx: 6 Asx/6 Tsx •adr

Canon perpétuel •4 Sx: AAAA/4 Tpt •adr
Canon perpétuel à 4 voix •4 Sx: AAAA •adr
Canon perpétuel pour 4 Saxophones alto •4 Sx: AAAA •adr
Canon perpétuel pour 5 Saxophones •5 Sx: SATBBs •adr
Canon perpétuel sur basse obstinée •5 Sx: AAAABs •adr
Les carrés magiques •5 Sx: AAAAA •adr
L'élastique •4 Sx: AAAA •adr
Intermède •3 Sx: ATB/Tpt/Trb •adr
Mouvement atonal (1967) (10') •5 Sx: SATBBs •adr
14 mouvements lents •5 Sx: SATBBs •adr
Quatre Saxophones alto en canon perpétuel •4 Sx: AAAA •adr
Rêve - Pièce canonique •4 Sx: AAAA •adr
Trio en canon •Cl/Tpt/Asx •adr

DURAND, André (1917)

Compositeur français, né à Marseille, le 20 V 1917.
Divertissement •SATB •adr

DURAND, Emile (1830-1903)

Compositeur et pédagogue français, né à St-Brieuc, le 16 II 1830;
mort à Neuilly (Paris), le 6 V 1903.
Le biniou •Sx Solo •Sal
1ère valse, op. 83 •Bb Sx/Pno •CBet

DURAND, Pierre-Hubert

A Piacere (1984) (9') (to J-P. CAENS) •SATB
Saxovéloce (1989) (4'30) •1 Sx: A or T/Pno •Com

DURANT, Douglas

Compositeur américain.
Skelter Memory (1994) (to B. RONKIN) •MIDI Wind Controller Solo
•adr

DURBIN, Jean (1919)

Compositeur français et critique musical, né au Croisic, en 1919.
Mena de front des études médicales et musicales avant de se consacrer
vers 1940 uniquement à ces dernières.
"Sa musique est celle de la sensibilité humaine, même dans le jeu
abstrait des lignes, des volumes, des couleurs. Jean Durbin est constamment tendu dans une volonté de système entre les exemples qu'il
admire (Debussy, Fauré, Ravel) et les objectifs qu'il poursuit." (Cl.
ROSTAND)
1ere suite d'Alain Fournier •Pno/Org/Vln/Vla/Sx

DUREY, Louis (1888-1979)

Compositeur et animateur français né à Paris le 27 V 1888; mort à St.
Tropez, le 3 VII 1979. Se trouva en 1919 parmi ceux que l'on désigna
alors sous le nom de 'Groupe des Six.'
"Satie's simplicity and Stravinsky's polytonality formed the foundation for his work, but Durey's music always has a sober gravity distinct
from these composers." (A. HOEREE)
Feu la mère de Madame, op. 49 (1945) (5') (d'après FEYDEAU)
1) Ouverture 2) Entrée de lucien - Menuet 3) Cortège
d'Amphritite 4) Entrée d'Annette 5) Entrée de Joseph
6) Evanouissement d'Yvonne 7) Final •Fl/Ob/Asx/Bsn/Tpt/
Tuba/Perc/2 Vln/Vla/Vcl/Bass •BRF

DURRANT, Frederick (1895)

Compositeur anglais.
Sonata for Saxophone Quartet (1972) (20') (to London Saxophone
Quartet) 1) Allegro 2) Adagio 3) Scherzo 4) Fuga •SATB

DURY, Martial

Divertissement, op. 5 •SATB •EMB

DUSCHINGER, Jean (1932)

Chef de musique luxembourgeois.

Escapade (1982) •Asx/Orch d'Harmonie

DUSSEKK, Johann Ludwig (1760-1812)

Andante (MERIOT) •Asx/Pno •Phi

DU TERTRE, Etienne (16th Century)

Pavane and Gailliarde (HARVEY) •SATB •Che

DUTJER, Heiner (1950)

Compositeur allemand.
Präludium, Adagio, Fugue (1985) (8') (to H. CORDES) •Asx/Pno

DUTKIEWICZ, Andrzzei (1942)

Compositeur et pianiste polonais. Travailla à Varsovie puis aux
U.S.A.
Capriccio (1984) (9') (to L. KLOCK) •Asx/Hn
Danse triste (1977) (13') (to L. KLOCK & M. PITUCH) 1) Introduction
2) Danse triste 3) Finale •Bb Sx/Pno •DP

DUTTON, Brent

Sonata (1981) 1) Allegro vivo 2) Fantasia - Allegro con brio •Asx/
Pno

DUVAL, François (1673-1728)

Rondeau (LONDEIX) •Asx/Pno •Lem

DUYCK, Guy

Introduction et Danse (to Fr. DANEELS) •Asx/Pno •Mau

DUYSBUTG, F.

Prélude et Danse •Asx/Pno •EMB

DVORAK, Anton (1841-1904)

Danse slave n° 8 (CAENS) •SATB •Mar
Humoreske, op. 101, no. 7 (BUMCKE) •Asx/Pno •VAB
Humoreske •Eb Sx/Pno •CF
Humoresque •Bb Sx/Pno •Mol
Humoresque •2 Sx: AA or AT/Pno or 3 Sx: AAA or ATT or AAT
•Cen
Humoresque (DELBECQ) •SATB •Mar
Humoresque (VERRECKEN) •AATB •CF
Lament (TEAL) (Album) •Bb Sx/Pno •GSch
Larghetto (TEAL) (Album) •Asx/Pno •GSch
Largo •Bb Sx/Pno •Pres
Largo (from *New World Symphony*) (P. GORDON) •AATB •South
Largo (GORDON) •AATB •South
Largo and Deep River (TOMPSON) •AATB •Alf
Prelude and Polka (from op. 39) (RONKIN) •SATB •Ron
1er mouvement (JOHNSON) •6 Sx: AAATTB •Rub
Quatuor, op. 96 (VOIRPY) •SATB •Lem
Romantic Piece, op. 75, no. 1 (TEAL) (Album) •Asx/Pno •GSch
Slavonic Dance, op. 72 (SAKAGUCHI) •SATB •EFJM
Song My Mother Taught Me (BRIEGEL) •2 Sx: AA/Pno or 4 Sx:
AATB •Bri

DWYER, Benjamin

Compositeur irlandais.
Tiento (1993) •Ssx/Pno •INM

DYCK, Vladimir (1882-1943)

Compositeur israélite français, né à Odessa, mort en déportation.
Elève de Gédalge et de Widor. Fondateur avec Léon Algazi de la
collection de musique juive 'Mizmor.'
5 Quatuors classiques (BACH, HANDEL, BEETHOVEN, MOZART,
MENDELSSOHN) •SATB •Bil
Easy Saxophone Solos (ARNOLD) •1 or 3 Asx/Pno •Cons
Invocation to Euterpe (DAILET) •Bb Sx/Pno •WA
1ère Légende hébraïque (1936) (to M. MULE) •Asx/Pno •Bil

2me Légende hébraïque (1936) (to M. MULE) •Ssx/Pno •Bil
Quatuor moderne Leblanc •SATB •Bil

DYFFORT, Jens-Uwe
Compositeur allemand.
Bewegtes Stück (1993) •Asx/Tape •INM

EARLY, Judith
Compositeur anglais.
Variations on a Theme for Saxophone Quartet (1972) (4') (to London Saxophone Quartet) •SATB

EBEN, Petr (1929)
Dré Invokace (to G. PRIESNER) •Ssx (or Tsx)/Org

EBENHÖH, Horst (1930)
Compositeur autrichien, né le 16 V 1930 à Wien.
Konzert für Saxophone Quartett und Orchester, op. 73 (25') •SATB/Orch (1101/1110/Perc/Str) •CA
Konzert, op.76 (25') •BsSx/Orch (1111/1110/Perc/Str) •CA
Saxzyklus, op. 70/2 (20') Vivace - Tempo libero - Allegro vivace - IV - Vivo •SATB •CA
Short Tale, op. 70, no. 3 •SATB •CA/ApE

EBERT, Hans (1889-1952)
Concerto •2 Sx/Orch

EBY, Walter M.
Professeur américain.
Scientific Method for Saxophone (1922) •WJ

ECCLES, Henry (1652-1742)
Sonata (RASCHER) •Asx/Pno •ElVo/Pres

ECHPAÏ, Andreï Iakovlévitch (see ESHPAY)

ECKARD, Walter
Highlights of Familiar Music (46 pieces) •Asx/Pno •Pres

EDELSON
Night Song •Asx/Pno •Mus

EDER de LASTRA, Erich
Compositeur autrichien.
Suite für vier Saxophone (14') •SATB •ECA

EDLUND, Mikael (1950)
Compositeur suédois, né à Tranâs, le 19 I 1950. Travailla avec I. Lidholm et A. Mellnas avant de se rendre aux U.SA. (1977-78).
"Mikael Edlund works in exceedingly minute detail, composing in the field of tension between penetrating reflection and unpredictable but rewarding intuition. His harmony is on the one hand bright and buoyantly impetuous and, on the other hand, vigorously austere and full of tension. Similarly, his compositions vary in character between the freely improvisational and the insistently, subtle expressive." H-G. P.)
Trio sol (1980) (9') •2 Sx: SS/Pno •TIM

EDMONDSON, John
Essay in Blue (1981) •Asx/Band or Pno •Ken

EECHAUTE, Prosper van
Compositeur belge.
Quatuor, op. 42 (1963) (to Quatuor Belge de Saxophones)
1) Champs de blé 2) Vieille chapelle 3) Matin printanier
4) Batifollage •SATB

EETVELDE, Van J.
Compositeur belge.
Quatuor (1980) •SATB

EFFINGER, Cecil (1914)
Compositeur et hautboïste américain, né le 22 VII 1914, à Colorado Springs (Colorado). Travailla avec F. Boothroyd, B. Wagenaar, et Nadia Boulanger.
"He is the inventor of a practical music typewriter patented in 1954, and marketed, under the name Musicwriter, in 1955." (BAKER) "His large output includes many original works and arrangements for orchestra, miliraty band and dance band, as well as choral compositions, chamber music and piano pieces." (P. GLANVILLE-HICKS)
Solitude (1960) (3'30) •Asx/Pno •Pres

EGEA, Jose Vincente
Compositeur espagnol.
Affa •SATB

EGGLESTON, Anne
Compositeur canadien.
Quartet (1972) (to P. BRODIE) •SATB •CMC
6 Pieces in Popular Style (1972) •Sx Solo •CMC

EHLE, Robert C.
Compositeur américain.
Hypothetical Orbits •Asx/Tape •DP
Prelude and Fugue for French Saxophone Quartet •SATB •WWS
Quartet, op. 90 (1987) (to R. GREENBERG) •SATB
Sonata •Ssx/Pno

EHRLICH, Abel (1915)
Compositeur israélien, d'origine allemande, né à Cranz, le 3 IX 1915. Travailla avec V. Huml puis à Jerusalem avec S. Rososky, à Darmstadt enfin, avec Stockhausen et H. Pousseur.
The Answer (1970) •Tenor Voice/Fl/Sx

EICHENWALD, Philipp
Compositeur suisse.
D.V.6 •6 Instruments including [dont] 1 Sx: (S+A+T+B)

EICHLER, Matthew
Saxophoniste et compositeur américain. Travailla avec R. Linn.
Beach Dance (1982) (to G & L KENT) •Vln/Asx
"(Colloquy) (Charter) 1980" (from Gregory) •Asx/Tape

EICHMANN, Dietrich (1966)
Musicien de jazz, arrangeur et compositeur allemand, né le 21 I 1966 à Erlangen.
Damnation du Pouls (1991) (19') •Tpt/Pno/4 Sx: SATB •adr
3 Dialoge (1984-85) •Tpt/Tsx •adr
George in the Forest (1984) (35') •3 Fl/Cl/2 Sx: AT/2 Tpt/Trb/2 Perc/Pno/Bs Guit •adr
Situations of a Saxophone Player (1985) (30-40') •Variables Sx Solo •adr

EIMERT, Herbert (1897-1972)
Compositeur, théoricien, et critique musical allemand, né à Bad Kreuznach, le 8 IV 1897; mort à Cologne, le 15 XII 1972. Travailla avec Bölsche, von Othegraven, et Abendroth.
"Pionnier de la *musique électronique* au studio de la Westdeutsche Rundfunk de Cologne."
"Eimert's importance rests chiefly in his foundation-laying research. In 1923, while still a student, he wrote an *Atonale Musiklehre* in which—independently of Schoenberg, Hauer and their colleagues—he gave the first systematic description of 12-note technique, together with an aesthetic basis and many music examples." (R. LÜCK)

Tanzmusik (1926) Fl/Sx/Mechanical Instrum. •Br&Ha
Der weisse Schwan - ballet (1926) •Fl/Sx/Mechanical Instrum.
  •Br&Ha/Uni

EINFELD, Dieter (1935)
Compositeur allemand.
Imaginationen II (1980-81) (19') (to J-P. Caens) Fantasia -
  Recitativo - Rondo •Asx/Orch (12222/4231/2 Perc/Str) or Pno

EISENMANN, Will (1906)
Compositeur allemand, né à Stuttgart, le 3 III 1906. Travailla à Paris,
avec P. Dukas et Ch. Koechlin.
Capriccio, op. 92 (1977) •Asx/Pno •adr
Concertino, op. 69 (1962) (11') (to S. Rascher) •Asx/Chamber Orch
  •adr
Concerto, op. 38 (1937) (14') (to S. Rascher) •Asx/Str Orch or Pno
  •Uni
Concerto da camera (1945-48) (15') (to H. Ackermann) 1) Andante
  amoroso 2) Molto vivace e energico 3) Allegro scherzando
  •Asx/Str Orch or Pno •Uni
Divertimento - Trio (1954) •2 Sx: SA/Bsn •Uni
Duo concertante, op. 33 (1951) (10') (to S. Rascher) 1) Deciso
  2) Energico •Asx/Pno •CF
Konzert (1962) (12') •2 Sx: SA/Orch
Movements, op. 68 (1961) (to S. Rascher) •Asx/Pno •adr
Nevermore - Ballade, op. 28 (to S. Rascher) •Asx/Pno •Ken

EISMA, Will (1929)
Compositeur et violoniste néerlandais, né à Soengaillat en Indonésie
le 13 V 1929. Travailla avec G. Stam, K. van Baaren, et Goffredo
Petrassi.
  "His music is based on trips in the frameworks of the 12-tone
technique." (Baker) "His pieces are notably successful in creating
distinctive atmospheres." (M. Starreveld-Bartels)
Affairs no. 1 •Fl/Asx/Vibr/Pno/Bass/Perc •Don
Non-lecture II (1971) (7'15) (to J. Houlik) •Sx Solo •Don

EITHLER, Estaban (1913-1960)
Compositeur Austro-Chilien, né à Bolzano (Tyrol), le 25 VI 1913;
mort le 12 II 1960.
Concertino (1953) (to J. de Vries) •Asx/Str Orch or Pno
Congaja •Bsx Solo •Lee/EMBA
Dicha •Asx/Pno •EMBA
Quartet (1945) •Picc/Fl/Tpt/Sx
Sonatina (1953) (to J. de Vries) •Asx/Pno •BBC
3 Canciones •Asx/Orch
Trio (1944) •Fl/Asx/Bass •BBC
Trio (1945) •Fl/Ob/Asx •BBC

EK, Hans (1964)
Compositeur suédois.
And down goes the bandit (1989) •Asx/2 Perc. •SvM

EKIMOVSKY, Victor (1947)
Compositeur russe.
Cantus figuralis, op. 32 (1980) (to J-M. Londeix) 1) Organum 2) Air
  3) Fugue 4) Choral 5) Recitatif •12 Sx: SnoSSAAATTTBBBs

EKLUND, Hans (1927)
Compositeur et professeur suédois né le 1er VII 1927 à Sandviken.
Travailla avec Ernst Pepping et Lars-Erik Larsson.
  "Most of his compositions are instrumental and are marked by a
solid technique developed principally from Hindemith and Reger." (R.
Haglund) "His artistic temperament is made up of aggressive power
and a plaintive introversion. His humour is equally obvious, but also
equally ambivalent, oscillating between the exuberantly burlesque and
more complicated, grotesque eruptions." (H-G. P.)

Omaggio a San Michele (1980) (12') •SATB •STIM/SMIC

EKSTRÖM, Lars
Compositeur suédois.
Vargtimen (1990) •Cl/Asx/Vln/Pno •SR/STIM

ELBE, Carl
Compositeur allemand.
Giocondita •Asx/Pno •Fro
Konzert (1936) (15') •Asx/Orch or Pno •HR/Fro

ELBE, Julian
Valdemosa •Asx/Pno

ELGAR, Sir Edward (1857-1934)
Land of Hope and Glory •4 Sx: SATB or SAAT or SATT or SAAB
Love's Greeting (Trinkaus) •Bb Sx/Pno •FMH
Love's Greeting (Trinkaus) •Sx/Tpt (or Trb)/Pno •CF
Nimrod (from *Enigma Variations*, op. 36) (1899) (Worley) •Sx
  Ensemble
Pomp and Circumstance (Akers) •Bb Sx/Pno •CF
Salut d'amour •2 Sx: AT/Pno
Salut d'amour •AATB •Rub
Salut d'amour (Staber) •Asx/Pno •Sch

ELIASSON, Anders (1947)
Compositeur suédois, né le 3 IV 1947, à Borlänge. Travailla avec I.
Lidholm et V. Söderholm, puis à l'Electronic Music Studio Foundation.
  "His tonal language has possessed an inexplicable but unmistakable
poetic impression which conveys an intensive spirtituality." (H-G. P.)
The Green Rose - Cantata (1976) (11'15) •Soprano Voice/4 Sx:
  SATB/Perc •STIM
Poem (1986-88) (10') •Asx/Pno •SMIC/STIM
Sinfonia concertante (1989) (27') •Asx/Orch (3333/4230/Perc/Str)
  •SMIC

ELLINGTON, Edward Kennedy (Duke) (1899-1974)
Ellingtoniana (Alessandrini) •12 Sx: SnoSSAAATTTBBBs

ELLIS, Donald (1934)
Trompettiste et compositeur américain, né à Los Angeles, le 25 VII
1934. Travailla avec G. Read et J. Vincent.
  "In his compositions and arrangements he boldly introduces non-
binary meters and asymetrical rhythms." (Baker)
Improvisational Suite No. 1 •Tpt/Asx/Bass/Perc •MJQ

ELLIS, James
Compositeur anglais.
Dixieland Duet •2 Sx •WWS
Napoli •Asx/Pno •WWS
Poems and Transitions (1972) (30') (to London Saxophone Quartet)
  •SATB

ELLIS, John Tilstone (1929)
Compositeur anglais.
Ollersett Suite (1978) (8') 1) Frolic 2) Aubade 3) Hurla burla
  4) Square dance •SATB •BMIC

ELLIS, Merrill (1916)
Compositeur américain, né le 9 XII 1916, à Cleburne (Texas).
Electro-acousticien.
Dream Fantasy (1974) (to M. Moore) •Asx+Cl/Prepared Tape/Perc/
  Visuals •CF

ELLIS, Norman A.
Compositeur américain.
Before a D'BL Scherzo (1971-72) •Asx Solo •DP

ELLO, William J.
The Eyes of the Dragon (1977) 1) Prelude 2) Movement 3) Epilogue
•Asx/Perc/Pno

ELOY, Christian (1945)
Compositeur et professeur d'électroacoustique français, enseignant au Conservatoire de Bordeaux. Travailla avec I. Malec.
Archipel - Trio (1990) •Fl/Asx/Guit •adr
Deux Pièces •Asx/Perc •Lem
Moai (1986) (5') •Asx/Electronics
Quattrocento (1991) (7') (to J-M. LONDEIX) •10 Sx: SnoSATB & SATBBs •adr
Saxotaure (to S. BERTOCCHI) (1985) (8') •Asx Solo •Com

ELSENAAR, Evert (1892-1965)
De saxofoon •Mol

EMMER, Huib (1951)
Compositeur néerlandais.
Camera eye (1978-79) (15') •2 Sx/2 Guit/2 Pno/2 Perc •Don
Koud zoud (1984) (5') •Ob/Asx/Trb/Bass •Don

EMMERECHTS, Raymond (1908)
Compositeur français, né à Lille (Nord), le 22 I 1908.
Ferroluro •SATB •adr

EMMETT, Daniel Decatur (1815-1904)
Dixie's Land •2 Sx/Pno •McK

END, Jack
Compositeur américain.
Two Modern Saxophone Quartets •SATB •Ken

ENDRESEN, R. M.
Compositeur américain.
Indispensable Folio (11 pieces) •Asx/Pno •Rub
Supplementary Studies (1936) •Rub

ENDRICH, Tom
Compositeur américain d'origine anglaise. Installé aux U.S.A. depuis 1971. Travailla avec B. Rands.
Lifelines (1983) •SATB

ENESCO
Concertstück •Asx/Pno •Eno

ENGEBRETSON, Mark (1964)
Compositeur et saxophoniste américain, né le 26 IX 1964. Travailla avec J-M. Londeix et M. Fusté-Lambezat. Membre du Vienna Saxophone Quartet.
An Arc in Solitude (1991) (8') (to S. FANCHER) •2 Sx: AA •ApE
For Anders (1991) (9') •Asx/Perc •adr
Four Short Songs •SATB •ApE
L'idéal (1987) (6') (to L'Ensemble International de Saxophones) •12 Sx: SnoSSAAATTTBBBs •adr
I Want (1992) •SATB •ApE
Not Loud (1990) (10'30) •SATB •adr
Tell No More of Enchanted Days (1993) (14') (to Vienna Saxophone Quartet) •SATB •adr

ENGELMANN, Hans Ulrich (1921)
Professeur et compositeur allemand, né le 9 IX 1921 à Darmstadt. Travailla avec Fortner, Krenek, Leibowitz, et Adorno.
"C'est une nature: après des débuts passablement laborieux et non dénués d'un certain académisme post-webernien, il s'exprime avec invention, puissance, diversité et fantaisie." (Cl. ROSTAND)
"His early works are impregnated by chromaticism with an impressionistic tinge; rhythmically his music is affected by jazz techniques.

Under the influenece of Leibowitz and Krenek he adopted the 12-tone method of composition, expanding it into a *sui generis field technique* of total serialism, in which rhythms and instrumental timbres are organized systematically. In his theater music he utilizes aleatory devices, musique concrete and electronic sonorities." (BAKER) "Initially his work was freely atonal, but after about 1949 he employed dodecaphonic, then serial procedures. Since 1968 he has incorporated new compositional techniques into his music (controlled chance, graphic notation, live electronic music)." (R. LÜCK)
Incanto, op. 19 (1959) •Soprano Voice/Asx/Perc •A&S
Intégrale, op. 14a (1959) (6') (to M. SEIBER) •Asx/Pno •A&S
Interlineas, op. 50b (1985) (16') •Sx/Perc •Br&Ha
Permutagioni •Fl/Ob/Sx/Bsn •A&S

ENSTRÖM, Rolf
Compositeur suédois.
Vigil (1993) •4 Sx •B&N

ERB, Donald (1927)
Compositeur américain, né à Youngstown (Ohio), le 17 I 1927. Travailla avec M. Dick et B. Heiden.
"His composing began in traditional style but Erb's own inclination lay in a more experimental direction. He has successfully combined his full technical knowledge of music, gained from formal study, with the jazz influences acquired during his own performing years. His imagination and sense of innovation have also led him into the field of electronic music, in which he has at times mixed recorded sounds with live instrumental music." "His music combines classical structural elements with ultramodern serial and aleatory techniques." (BAKER) "His works of the 1950s reveal his jazz background and the influence of neo-classicism and serialism. In the 1960s he developed a more individual style, based on experiments with unusual sounds, but his music is always structurally straightforward and formally clear." (J. SUESS)
Concert Piece no. 1 (1966) •Asx/Band
Hexagon (1962) (6') •Fl/Asx/Tpt/Trb/Vcl/Pno •CMC
Quartet (1962) (7') (to TUVETZKY) 1) Moderato 2) Andante 3) Allegro 4) Adagio •Fl/Ob/Asx/Bass •CMC
I "Mixed-Media": Fission (1968) (13') •Ssx/Pno/Tape •adr

ERB, Marie-Joseph (1858-1944)
Quartet •4 Sx

ERDMANN, Dietrich (1917)
Pédagogue, organiste, et compositeur allemand, né à Bonn, le 20 VII 1917. Travailla avec P. Hindemith, L. von Knorr, H. Genzmer, P. Höffer, et K. Thomas.
"Les expériences de la guerre ont tellement marqué Erdmann—dont le père est mort dans un camp de concentration—que jusqu'à aujourd'hui nombre de ses oeuvres font penser à l'atmosphère de la guerre. Du point de vue stylistique, il est toujours resté un expressionniste." (D. BENSMANN)
Akzente (1989) (8'30) 1) Allegro con fuoco 2) Adagio espressivo 3) Presto •Tsx/Pno
Fantasia colorata (1987) (6'50) Adagio - Allegro con fuoco •Tsx Solo •R&E
Konzert 1) Sostenuto-Allegretto scherzando 2) Adagio molto espressivo 3) Allegro assai •1 Sx: A+S/Orch (Picc 11 EH 1 BsCl 1/2220/Perc/Str) •R&E
Konzertstück •Asx/Chamber Orch or Pno •R&E
Resonanzen (1984) (12'30) 1) Sostenuto 2) Theme mit variaten 3) Allegro con fuoco •SATB •Br&Ha
Saxophonata (1986) (12') 1) Andante espressivo 2) Vivo 3) Largo con espressione •Sx Solo: S+A+T •R&E

ERDNA
6 Pieces Swing •1 Sx: A or T/Pno •Sal

ERICKSON, Frank (1923)
Compositeur et chef d'orchestre américain, né le 1er IX 1923, à Spokane (Washington).
Concerto (1960) (14') (to S. Rascher) •Asx/Band or Pno •Bou
Rondino •AATB •Bel

ERICKSON, Nils (1902-1978)
Compositeur suédois, né à Norrköping, le 3 IX 1902, mort le 12 III 1978.
Concerto (1952) (23') •Asx/Orch (2222/2220/Perc/Str) •STIM
Konsert (1980) (17') •Ssx/Str Orch •STIM
Konsert (1981) (16') •Tsx/Orch •STIM

ERIKSON
Nocturne •SATB
Scherzo •SATB
Serenade •SATB

ERIKSON, Ake (1937)
Compositeur suédois, né à Uppsala, le 3 II 1937.
The rest is silence (1971/73) •Fl/Asx/Cl/Pno/Bass/Perc •SMIC

ERIKSSON, Joseph (1872-1957)
Organiste et compositeur suédois, né à Söderfors, le 8 XII 1872, mort le 4 VII 1957 à Uppsala. Travailla avec R. Liljefors.
"Joseph Eriksson est sans doute le premier Suédois qui ait subi l'ascendant des théories de Busoni et d'A. Schoenberg, mais il s'en est imprégné avec une indépendance caractéristique de l'attitude scandinave... Dans le cas d'Eriksson cette attirance pour un art de cérébralité spéculative est contrebalancée par une adhésion à certains principes fondamentaux de la technique debussyste, sans que sa sensibilité nordique, toute de repliement méditatif et grave, où il entre autant de bonhomie sereine que de rêverie ingénue, ne perdent rien de ses droits."
(R. Bernard)
Konsert (1959) (14') (to S. Rascher) •Asx/Orch or Band •Ton

ERNRYD, Bengt (1943)
Compositeur suédois.
Rödingsjön II (1967) •Fl+Picc/Trb/Tsx+Perc/Bsx+Perc/Vcl/Bass/2 Perc •SMIC

ERNST
Elegie •Bb Sx/Pno •CBet
The Ernst Modern Graded Studies for Saxophone (1929)

ERNST-MEISTER, Sigrid
Compositeur allemand.
"*E... Staremo Freschi!*" (1992) (8') (to Chr. Hansen) •Sx Solo: S+T

ESCAICH, Thierry
Compositeur français.
Antiennes oubliées (1994) •Vln/Fl/Asx/Tpt/Trb/Vcl/Vibr •Bil
Le chant des ténèbres (1992) (18') •Ssx Solo/12 Sx: SnoSSAAATTTBBBs •Bil
3 Intermezzi (1994) •Fl/Cl/Sx •Bil
8 Pièces (1992) (to J-P. Baraglioli) 1) Valse 2) Romance 3) Air de cour 4) Nocturne 5) Pavane 6) Marche 7) Choral en trio 8) Antienne grégorienne •Asx (or Cl)/Pno •Mis

ESCOT, Pozzi (1931)
Pluies •Asx Solo •WWS
Sands II (1966) •5 Sx/Guit/4 Perc/17 Vln/9 Bass
Visione (1964-87) •Fl/Asx/Vibr/Soprano Voice/Bass/Perc/Narr

ESCUDIER, H. (1816-1881)
Ecrivain et musicien français, né à Castelnaudary, le 17 IX 1816, mort à Paris, le 22 VI 1881. Auteur de nombreuses pièces instrumentales.
6 Andantes religioso (1875) •Asx/Org (or Pno) •Mar
Fantaisie "Carnaval de Venise," op. 7 (1875) •Asx/Pno •Mar
1ère fantaisie originale avec variations, op. 3 (1875) •Asx/Pno •Mar
3me fantaisie avec thème et variations, op. 46 (1878) •Asx/ Harmonie or Fanfare or Pno •Mol
4me fantaisie avec variations, op. 55 (1880) Ssx/Harmonie or Fanfare or Pno •Mol
Le chant des vaux, op. 48 (1878) •Asx/Org (or Pno) •Cos/Bil
Les premiers pas des jeunes saxophonistes, op. 45 (25 Etudes mélodiques faciles et graduées) (1877)
Nouvelle tablature du saxophone (1878)
Quatuor - Andante •SATB/Pno •Mar

ESHPAY, Andrei Yakovlevich (1925)
Compositeur russe, né à Koz'modem'yansk, le 15 V 1925. Travailla avec Myaskovsky, Golubev, V. Sofronitsky, et Khachaturian.
"Son oeuvre est d'un langage académique qui fait parfois référence au folklore de Marii (petit peuple de Haute Volta proche des Finnois) (son père était lui-même compositeur et folkloriste de cette république des Marii)." (J. di Vanni)
"The folk music plays an important part in shaping his compositions, which show harmonic and orchestral variety. Eshpay has written concert works in all genres, variety songs and film scores, all with equal success." (G. Grigor'yeva)
Concerto (1988) •Ssx/Orch or Pno •ECP
Danse russe (3') (Album) •Asx/Pno •Bil
Miniature •Asx/Pno •ECP

ESPEJO, César (1892-19xx)
Complainte andalouse (Mule) •Asx/Pno •Lem

ESPOSITO, Patrizio
Compositeur italien.
Agressivo II •SATB
Attraverso (1991) (6') •8 Sx: SnoSAATTBBs

ESSL, Karlheinz (1961)
Compositeur autrichien né à Vienne.
"*Close the gap*" (1990) (13') •3 Sx: TTT •adr

ESSLINGER, Paul
Compositeur allemand.
Yak (1993) •1 Sx: A+S/Bass •INM

ESTEBAN, C.
Compositeur espagnol.
3 Canciones alicantinas •SATB

ETTORE, Eugene
L. T. the kid •Asx/Pno •CAP

EVANGELISTA, José
Saxfolly (1985) (12') (to Saxtuor) •8 Sx

EVANS, Edwin Jr. (1874-1945)
Spanish Eyes - Danza espanola •Bb Sx/Pno •CF
Sweet and Dainty •Bb Sx/Pno •CF

EVANS, O. A.
Jazz-Intermezzo •Asx/Pno •Zim
99 Breaks •Asx Solo •Zim

EVANS, Stanford (1938)

Compositeur américain, né à Palo Alto (California), le 14 I 1938.
Chor •Sx/Tape •adr
Each Tolling Sun (1972) (17') (Theatre Piece) •Sx/Tape/Actress
•adr

EVANS, Tolchard

Lady of Spain (KLICKMANN) •Asx/Pno •SF

EVARTT, R.

Eleonora •Asx/Pno •Me/An

EVENSEN, Kristian (1953)

Compositeur norvégien.
Quartet (1982-83) (10') (to the Bergersen Saxophone Quartet)
•SATB •NMI

EVERAARTS, Mathieu

Solo •Asx/Harmonie •TM

EVERETT, Thomas G. (1944)

Compositeur américain, né en 1944, à Philadelphia.
Three Comments: Vietnam 70 (1970) (4-10') (to P. STROMPER) •Tsx/
Bass/BsTrb •SeMC

EVERTT, Steven

Interactive Electronics •Asx+MIDI Wind Controller+Narr/Computer

EWAZEN, Eric

Compositeur américain.
Concerto (1993) (22') (to J. HOULIK) (three movements) •Tsx/Orch

EXAUDET, André Joseph (1710-1762)

Tambourin (LONDEIX) •Asx/Pno •Lem

EYCHENNE, Marc (1933)

Compositeur français, né le 17 XII 1933, à Alger (Algérie). Autodi-
dacte.
Cantilène et danse - Trio (1961) (13') (to M. PERRIN) •Vln/Asx/Pno
•Bil
Concerto (1966) •Asx/Str Orch/Perc •adr
Nuances et rythmes (1968) (10') (to P. PAREILLE) •Ob/Cl/Asx/Bsn
•adr
Petite suite •Ob/Ssx/5 Hn •adr
Sextuor (1964) (12'15) (to J-M. LONDEIX) 1) Allegro 2) Andante
3) Final •Fl/Ob/Cl/Asx/Hn/Bsn •Fuz
Sonate (1963) (11') (to MM. GOURDET-MELLINGER) 1) Allegro
2) Andante 3) Rondo •Asx/Pno •Bil

EYMANN

Prelude and Fugue •4 Sx: AAAA •CF

EYSER, Eberhard (1932)

Violoniste et compositeur suédois, d'origine allemande, né à
Marienwerder, le 1 VIII 1932.
Aubade (Salut de Drottningholm I) (1981) (4'30) •Asx/Vibr •STIM
Baroque (Le saxophone bien tempéré) (1976) (8') •5 Sx: SAATB
•STIM
Baroque (1987) •Fl/4 Sx: SATB
Canciones Nuevas (1988) (10') •Mezzo Soprano Voice/4 Sx: SATB
•EMa
Colloquium (1987) (4') •Sx/Pno •SMIC
Cuarteto antiguo español (after anonymous circa 1675) (1986) (6')
•SATB •EMa
Dosonat (1986) •Tsx/Marimba •EMa
Duo 2D (1989) (10') •2 Sx: S+T/A+B •EMa
Edictus to the honour of J-S. Bach (1985) •Fl/Ssx/Cl/BsCl •STIM
Ghiribizzi (1980) (12') •Sx Solo •EMa

Liebeslied im Regen (1993) •Ssx/Harp •INM
Livre des jeux faciles et progressifs (1959-86) (23'30) 1) Mélodie
basque (2 Sx) 2) Pastorelles (Asx/Harp or Pno) 3) Nocturne
4) Aubade (Asx/Vibr/Pno/Guit/Vln) •Asx/Harp/Pno/Vibr/Guit/
Vln •EMa
Nocturne (Salut de Drottningholm II) (1981) (6') •Asx/Vibr •STIM
Notados (1993) •Tsx/Marimba •INM
3 Paraphrases (1979) (8') 3 Sx: ATB/3 Cl/BsCl/CBsCl •EMa
Petit caprice & Cavatina (1977-79) (9') •Asx/Harp or Pno •EMa
Petite suite [Liten suite für 8 blasure] (1978) (10') •3 Sx: SAB/2 Cl/
Basset Horn/BsCl/CBsCl •STIM
Por los senderos del aire (1980) (13') •Sx Solo •STIM
Quartet I "Tris" (1976) (12') •SATB •EMa
Quartet II (1986) (15') •SATB •EMa
Quartet III - "Bagatelles" (1987) (11'30) •SATB •EMa
Quartet IV - "Deliciae scanienses" (1987) (14') •SATB •EMa
Quartet V (1989) (15') - *Divertimento* •SATB •EMa
Quartet VI (1992) •SATB •SvM
Quartetto italiano antico (after anonymous circa 1675) (1986) (14')
•SATB •EMa
Quintette à la mode dodécaphonique (1988) (8') •5 Sx: SAATB
•EMa
Salinas nocturnas (1979) (11') •Ssx/Cl/Vcl (or Bsn) •STIM
The Seasons - Die Jahreszeiten (after songs by C. A. Strindberg circa
1900) (1988) (8') •Voice/2 Sx •EMa
Suite classique I (after anonymous circa 1790) (1986) (14') •SATB
•EMa
Suite classique II (after anonymous circa 1790) (1986) (14') •SATB
•EMa
Symphonie Orientale (1978) (18') •3 Sx: SAT/3 Cl/BsCl/CBsCl
•EMa
Tremelin (1974) (3'30) •Any 3 melodic instruments •STIM
Tris - Suite (1987) •SATB
Watermusic - Submarine (1979-84) •1 Sx: A+T/Cl+BsCl/Tape
•STIM

FABRE, C.
Rêverie (HARRIS) •Cl/Sx/Pno or 2 Sx: AA/Pno •CF
2nd Rêverie (HARRIS) •Cl/Sx/Pno or 2 Sx: AA/Pno •CF

FAILLENOT
Air rustique •Tsx/Pno •WWS

FAILLENOT, Maurice
Rapsodie occitane (1992) (9'30) •Asx/Orch d'Harmonie or Pno
•Mar

FAITH, Walter (1921)
Compositeur allemand, né à Francfort-sur-le-Main. Autodidacte qui subit l'influence de G. Mahler et de Schoenberg.
Aria (to J. DE VRIES) •Asx/Pno •adr
Divertimento (1951) (to J. DE VRIES) •Asx/Pno/Tpt/Str •adr
Phantasies (1966) (to E. ERVIN) •Asx/Perc

FALK, Julien (1902)
Compositeur français, né à Menton. Travailla avec A. Gedalge et P. Vidal.
Prélude et fugue (1949) (to Quatuor Mule) •SATB •adr
Quatuor (1960) 1) Allegro giusto 2) Andante non troppo 3) Allegro agitato •SATB •adr
Quatuor d'anches (to Quatuor d'Anches Français) •Ob/Cl/Asx/Bsn •adr

FANTICINI, Fabrizio (1955)
Compositeur italien, né à Reggio Emilia.
Canto notturno (1987) (8') •SATB •Ric

FANTI-PAWLICKI
Etudes de style

FANTONI, Corrado
Compositeur italien.
4 Della vergino (1993) (13'45) (to MM. DONNINELLI & MARTELLI)
•Bsx/Org

FARBERMAN, Harold (1929)
Compositeur, chef d'orchestre, et percussionniste américain, né à New York, le 2 XI 1929.
"His music ranges from percussion pieces to expressionist opera, from jazz-influenced works to mixed media." (J. LEVINE)
For Erik and Nick (1964) •Tenor Voice/Asx/Vcl/Bass/Tpt/Trb/Vibr/ Perc
Concerto (1965) (10'30) (to H. ESTRIN) 1) Moderato 2) Allegro 3) Largo 4) Allegro •Asx/Str Orch or Pno

FARHART, H.
Divertimento •SATB •Lebl

FARIGOUL, Joseph-Marie (1860-1933)
Arioso •Asx/Pno •And

FARINA, Carlo (1600-1640)
Fragmento verdo musimo •Sx/Pno •SeMC

FARMER, John (16th century)
A Little Pretty Bonny Lass (CAWKWELL) •SATB •SM
Fair Phyllis I Saw (HARVEY) •SATB •Che

FARNABY, Giles (1565-1660)
Fayne would I wedd •Asx/Pno •WWS
Nobodyes gigge •Asx/Pno •WWS
Sometime she would and sometime not (HARVEY) •SATB •Che

FARNON, Dennis
Compositeur anglais.
Bouquet of Barbed Wire (1978-79) (3'30) •SATB •WOC

FASCH, Johann Friedrich (1688-1758)
Sonata (RASCHER) •Bsx/Pno •GiMa

FASOLO, Giovanni Battista (1600-1659)
Ballade •Tsx/Pno •WWS

FAULCONER, Bruce L.
Compositeur américain.
Music (1972) •Tsx/2 Perc •DP

FAULKNER, Elizabeth (1941)
Compositeur anglais.
Quartet (1978) (12') (to Myrha Saxophone Quartet) 1) Prelude 2) Promenade 3) Nuances 4) Finale •SATB

FAULX, J. B.
Bagatelle •1 Sx: A or T/Pno •HE/EMB
Concert Piece •Asx/Pno •HE
Little Piece •Tsx/Pno •HE
Romance •Asx/Pno •HE/EMB
20 Virtuoso Studies After Bach •HE

FAURÉ, Gabriel (1845-1924)
Pièce (DONEY) •Asx/Pno •Led
Après un rêve (Album) (DAILEY) •Bb Sx/Pno •WA

FAURÉ, Jean-Baptiste (1830-1914)
The palms (BROOKE) •AATB •CF
The palms, Let me dream (SULLIVAN) •Asx/Pno •CF
Les Rameaux •2 Sx: AT/Pno •Cen

FAUSTIN-JEANJEAN
Compositeur français.
Danse des violons (3') •SATB
Polka des Elfes (to J. ANQUETIL) •SATB
4 Pièces •SATB •HS
Quatuor (1949) (11'30) 1) Gaieté villageoise 2) Doux paysage 3) Papillons 4) Concert sur la place •4 Sx •Sal/Ric

FEDELE, Ivan (1953)
Magic (1985) •SATB

FEDIE, Jessie
Compositeur américain
Room 120 (1975) •Asx Solo

FEDOROW, N.
Compositeur allemand.
Saxophon Neubearbeitung (for Soprano, Alto, Tenor, Baritone, Bass) •HD
Schule für Saxophon (2 Volumes) •Zim

FEIFMAN, Alexander
Compositeur russe.
Romance (to L. MICHAÏLOV) •Asx/Pno

FEILER, Dror (1951)
Instrumentiste et compositeur suédois, né à Tel Aviv, le 31 VIII 1951. Travailla avec G. Bucht et B. Ferneyhough. Depuis 1976, il joue des saxophone, des clarinettes, de la percussion et des instruments

électroniques dans le 'Lokomotiv Konkrest music group.'
Antafada (1988) •Asx/Electronics •Tons
Don't walk out on me (1984) •Ssx Solo •SMIC/Tons
Gavona (1984) •Ssx/Tape •STIM
Hallel (1984) •Ssx Solo •SMIC/Tons
The Heart (1991) •Sx/Tape •Tons
Hive (1985) •2 Ssx/2 Electr. Guit/2 Perc •Tons/SMIC
Om (1985) •Ssx/Electr. Guit/3 Perc •Tons/SMIC
Schlafbeand (1985) •Ssx/Electr. Guit/3 Perc •Tons/SMIC
Sendero Luminoso II (1991) •Sx/Live Electronics/Tape •Tons
Slichot (1986) (4') •Sx/Guit •SMIC
Tändstickorna - The Matches (1979-80) •Ssx/2 Electr. Guit/2 Perc
  •SMIC
Too much too soon •Asx/Perc/Tape •Tons
Yad (1984) •2 Ssx/Electr. Guit/2 Perc •Tons/SMIC

FEIMAN, Alexander
Romance (1978) (to L. Michailov) •Sx Solo •SC

FELD, Jindrich (1925)
Compositeur tchécoslovaque, né à Prague, le 9 II 1925. Travailla avec Hlobil et Ridky.
Concerto (1980) (to E. Rousseau) 1) Con moto 2) Lento 3) Allegro
  con brio •1 Sx: S+A+T/Orch or Band •Kjos
Elegie (1981) (6') (to Kupferman) •Ssx/Pno •Led
Quatuor (1981) (26') (to Quatuor Deffayet) 1) Moderato assai
  allegro 2) Elegia 3) Scherzo 4) Intermezzo 5) Final •SATB
  •Led
Sonate (1982) (14') 1) Molto moderato 2) Scherzo (allegro assai)
  3) Finale (allegro con brio) •Ssx/Pno •Led
Sonate (1989-90) (21') (to E. Rousseau) 1) Allegro ritmico 2) Clo-
  ches de la liberté (1989) 3) Scherzo 4) Allegro con fuoco •Asx/
  Pno •Led

FELDMAN, Morton (1926-1987)
Compositeur américain. Travailla la peinture avant de se consacrer à la musique après sa rencontre (1949) avec J. Cage. Travailla avec W. Riegger et S. Wolpe.
"Cet américain fit partie de la mouvance expérimentale new-yorkaise dans les années cinquante et fut, à ce titre, l'un des compagnons d'armes de John Cage. Mais il n'a cessé, depuis lors, de tempérer ses ardeurs provocatrices, pour s'engager sur une voie plus solitaire. C'est ainsi que jusqu'à sa mort, il a produit une oeuvre singulière (largement tournée vers le piano), à l'expression épurée et contemplative, dans l'ensemble, d'un abord assez hermétique, rétive au contact familier." (J-E. Fousnaquer) "Les sons qui surviennent dans ses oeuvres ne sont subordonnés à aucune logique compositionnelle connue. Morton Feldman compose 'd'oreille'; le phénomène de construction étant mis entre parenthèses, c'est sur chaque évènement—qui naît du silence et retourne au silence—que l'auditeur peut se concentrer." (D. J-Y. Bosseur) "Morton Feldman reste très proche de l'expression plastique et des jeunes peintres de New York. Sa musique s'orientera vers une conception minimaliste, mais reste toujours orientée par une recherche sur le son." (J. & B. Massin) "Avec cette même confiance et avec ce qu'il nomme la 'permission' implicitement contenue dans l'oeuvre de John Cage, Feldman entreprend de composer des pièces sans prétention, faites de sons simples, délicats, fragiles. Sa musique semble prolonger les premières oeuvres de Webern par sa sérénité. Dans les années 70 et 80, il tendait vers des paysages musicaux plats parfois de vaste dimensions où les sonorités tranquilles et isolées qu'il chérissait pouvaient se développer avec certaines formules de la nouvelle musique, mais rien de son dynamisme." (P. Griffiths) "L'oeuvre de Feldman tout entier consiste en 'séries de réverbérations à partir d'une source sonore identique', se situe entre deux catégories, 'entre temps et espace', entre peinture et musique, entre construction de la musique et

sa surface." (J-N. von der Weid)
Round I •2 Sx: AA •Cen

FELICE, John
An American Ceremony •2 Sx: AA

FELIX
Burlesken •Asx/Pno •Mus
3 Canzonettas of the 17th Century •1 Sx: A or T/Pno

FENIGSTEIN, Victor (1924)
Pianiste et compositeur suisse, né à Zurich. Travailla avec E. Frey et E. Fischer.
Memento et épitaphe (1980) (8') (to O. Vrhovnik) •Asx/Pno •Ku

FENNELLY, Brian (1937)
Compositeur et professeur américain, né à Kingston (New York), le 14 VIII 1937. Travailla avec A. Powell, G. Schuller, et A. Forte.
"He has written both 12-note serial and free atonal compositions, and has shown an increasing concern with instrumental virtuosity. His music often unites a rhythmically complex surface with dramatic, expressive gestures." (E. Murray)
Concerto (1982-84) (32') (to D. Pituch) 1) Prelude 2) Dialogue
  3) Scherzando •Asx/Str Orch or Pno •EPN
Corollary II (1988) (8') (to D. Pituch) •Asx/Pno •NP/ACE
Tesserae VIII (1980) (6') (to D. Pituch) 1) Rhapsodie 2) Polyphonie
  •Asx Solo •PRO/PNS

FENZL, Helmut F.
Compositeur allemand.
3 Bagatellen (1985) (8') •SATB

FERLING, Wilhelm-Franz (1796-1874)
Duo Concertante No. 1 (Gee) •2 Sx: AT •MMB
3 Duos Concertante (Gee) •2 Sx: AA or AT •PA/South
4 Etudes (Gee) •Asx/Pno •DP
48 Etudes (Bleuzet) •Bil
48 Etudes augmentée de 12 nouvelles par M. Mule •Led
48 Famous Studies (Andraud) •South

FERM, Thomas
Compositeur suédois.
Elegie •SATB

FERNADINO, Steve
Klockwork Rag (1980) (to L. Klock) •Asx/Pno

FERNANDEZ, C.
Suite •Asx/Pno

FERNANDEZ, Oscar Lorenzo (1897-1948)
Compositeur brésilien, né à Rio-de-Janeiro, le 4 XI 1897, où il est mort le 26 VIII 1948. Travailla avec Braga et Nascimento. Abandonna des études de médecine pour s'adonner à la musique.
"S'inspira fréquemment du folklore brésilien." (Larousse) "Se place aux côtés de Villa-Lobos dans la génération qui porte à son point culminant la tendance musicale nationaliste." (Fasquelle)
"In his music he adopted a strongly national style, derived from Brazilian folksong, without, however, actual quotation; his mastery of the technique of composition was indisputable." (Baker) "While the source of inspiration is purely native, the technique is modern." (N. Slonimsky)
Noturno •Asx/Orch (1020/200/Str) or Pno
Sombra suave •Asx/Str Orch or Pno

FERNANDEZ ALVEZ, Gabriel
Compositeur espagnol.
Sonata Lirica (1990) (to M. Mijan) •Asx/Pno

FERRABOSCO, Alfonso (1575-1628)
Four notes pavan (GRAINGER) •5 Sx: SATTB •PG

FERRAND-TEULET, Denise
Compositeur français.
Dialogue II •Asx/Pno
Octuor (1975) •4 Sx: SATB/3 Cl/Bsn
Trio (to P. PAREILLE) •Vln/Asx/Pno

FERRANTE, Mauro (1956)
Compositeur italien.
Do-Mi-Si (1985) (to A. DOMIZI) •Asx Solo
"In prossimità dell'evento" (1992) (8') (to A. DOMIZI) •12 Sx: SnoSSAAATTTBBBs

FERRARI, Luc (1929)
Compositeur et professeur français, né à Paris le 5 II 1929. Travailla avec A. Honegger, O. Messiaen, puis au Groupe de Recherche de l'ORTF.

"Dans le cadre des techniques électro-acoustiques, il a fait une synthèse des suggestions de Webern et de Varèse, et aboutit à un style incisif très personnel." (Cl. ROSTAND) "Luc Ferrari fait partie de ces quelques imprudents qui s'insinuent par effraction dans le tissu social par espoir de s'y fondre pour mieux l'exprimer. Peuvent-ils alors s'attendre à payer cher le prix de leur audace: notre société n'est pas faite pour accueillir les éveilleurs de conscience collective, ces fauteurs de troubles!" (M. FLEURET) "Luc Ferrari se pose en observateur, effaçant autant qu'il est possible, toute considération esthétique ou formelle, afin de se tenir au plus près d'une situation donnée et d'en reconstituer les contours sonores, sans volonté d'appropriation artistique, à partir de son expérience 'artisanale' de musicien." (D. J-Y BOSSEUR) "Son oeuvre provocatrice, dynamique, exaltante, se dote des 'armes' musicales les plus efficaces: rythmes obsédants, itérations, éléments de jazz." (J-N. von der WEID)

"His music is characterized by virtuosity and violent contrasts and by an individual humour which is obvious even from the titles of his works, and which has its roots in a sophisticated irony and a gentle cynicism. His aim throughout has been to call into question the nature of art; in this he shows a sympathy with Cage's ideas, while not completely subscribing to them." (F-B. MÂCHE)
Tautologos III (1969) •Choice and number of various instruments [Choix et nombre d'instruments variable]
Apparitions et disparitions mystérieuses d'un accord (1979) •4 Sx: AAAA •ET

FERRE, Stephen
Compositeur américain.
From Her Husband's Hand... (1990) •Asx/Orch (2222/22/2 Perc/Str)

FERRERO, A.
3 Piezas breves •SATB

FERRITO
Concertino •Asx/Ob/2 Perc/Bass •DP

FERRO, Pictro
Amphitrion divertimento •2 Fl/2 Sx/CBsn/Perc •Ric

FERSTL, Emil
Ballade •AATB •Fro
Bauern-polka •AATB •Fro
Parade der saxophone •AATB •Fro
Rheinländer •AATB •Fro
Scherzo •AATB •Fro
Thema und variationen •AATB •Fro

FERSTL, Herbert
15 Duette (UHDE, DI LASSO, CASTOLDI, etc.) •2 Sx: AT

FESCA, Alexander Ernst (1820-1849)
The Wanderer •Eb Sx/Pno •CF

FESCH, Willem de (1687-1757)
Canzonetto •Bsx/Pno •Spr
Sonata in F (R. JONES) •Asx/Pno •Eto

FIALA, George (1922)
Compositeur, pianiste, organiste, et professeur canadien d'origine Ukrainienne, né à Kiev, le 31 III 1922. Vit au Canada depuis 1949. Travailla avec Revutsky, Liatoshinsky, et L. Jongen.

"He likes clarity: clear structure, and nowhere is this more evident than in the chamber music. 'Chamber music,' Fiala says, 'is different from any other kind of music. I try to make the players enjoy what they are doing. Music should exist outside philosophy or aesthetic issues, as a self-sufficient art with no literary explanation. I would like to see a return to the practices of Haydn and Mozart: optimistic music, not necessarily easy, not simply recreational, but pleasing, full of light and fun, though of course, I would not write like this for large orchestra.' Beginning with a romantically colored Russian type of composition, Fiala went through a neo-classical phase, and after 1961 adopted the dodecaphonic method and other serial procedures." (BAKER)
Quartet no. 1 (1955-62) (12') 1) Allegretto 2) Adagio 3) Finale: Allegro non troppo •SATB •BML
Quartet no. 2 (1961) (12') (to P. BRODIE) 1) Moderato 2) Andante 3) Presto •SATB •BML
Quartet no. 3 (1983) •SATB •CMC
Sonata (1970) (14') (to P. BRODIE) 1) Moderato sostenuto - Allegretto giusto 2) Cavatina 3) Finale •Asx/Pno •CMC/DP
Sonata for Two (1971) (14'30) (to P. BRODIE and J. MACEROLLO) 1) Allegro giusto 2) Lamento 3) Finale-badinage •Ssx/Accordion •CMC

FIBICH, Zdenko (1850-1900)
Poème (BUCHTEL) •Asx/Band or Pno •Kjos/Eto

FICHE, Michel
Musicien français.
Menuet pour la lune (1977) (2'15) •Asx/Pno •Comb
Mirage IV (1975) (2'30) •Asx/Pno •Comb
Retour d'un cosmonaute (1'30) •Asx/Pno •Bil

FICHER, Jacobo (1896-1978)
Compositeur, violoniste et chef d'orchestre argentin, d'origine russe, né à Odessa, le 15 I 1896. Travailla avec Stolyarsky, Hait, Korguyev, et Auer. Se fixa en Argentine en 1923.

"Mêle à son chromatisme oriental la volonté formelle des derniers romantiques." (DUFOURCQ)

"Much of his early music was inspired by Jewish melodies; the influence of the Russian school was also noticeable. His mature style is characterized by a rhapsodic fluency of development, harmonic fullness, and orchestral brilliance." (BAKER) "Ficher's music is imbued with the spirit of Hebrew melody but in his later works he reveals interest in the folk music of his adopted country." (N. FRASER)
Los invitados, op. 26 •Fl/Cl/2 Sx: AT/2 Tpt/Tuba/Pno/Perc
Quartet, op. 89 (1957) •SATB
Rhapsodie, op. 88 (1956) •Sx Ensemble: SATB
Sonatina, op. 21 (1932) (8') (to I. NUGUES) •Asx/Tpt/Pno •NMSC

FIEBIG, Kurt (1908)
Organiste et compositeur allemand, né à Berlin, le 28 II 1908. Travailla avec F. Schreker.
Clementi variations (1953) (to J. DE VRIES) •Asx/Pno •adr

FIELD, John (1782-1837)

Notturno •Bb Sx/Pno •Mol

FIEVET, Paul (1892-19xx)

Compositeur français, né à Valenciennes (Nord). Travailla avec C-M. Widor.

"Paul Fievet possède la netteté d'accent, la maîtrise d'écriture qui lui ont facilité la mise au point de pages qui ont sincérité et vigueur." (P. LE FLEM)

Méditation, op. 69 (1904) •Asx/Pno •Com
Chant lyrique (1962) •Asx/Pno •GD
Fantoche (1962) •Tpt/Bugle/Asx or Asx/Pno •Com

FILAS, Thomas J. (1908)

Concerto for Reed Doubles (13'30) •CF

FILIPOVITCH, Remy (1946)

Saxophoniste et compositeur allemand d'origine lituanienne, né à Wilna, le 21 IV 1946.

Stück (10') •Asx/Band •adr

FILLMORE, Henry (1881-1956)

Ann Earl •Bb Sx/Pno •FMH

FINGER, Peter (1954)

Compositeur allemand, né le 11 X 1954 à Weimar.

Neue Wege (1983) (11') •Guit/Ssx/Perc •adr

FINNEY, Ross Lee (1906)

Compositeur et professeur américain, né à Wells (Minnesota), le 23 XII 1906. Travailla avec Ferguson, R. Sessions, N. Boulanger, et A. Berg.

"Most characteristic of Finney's technique is the use of a structured series, particulary with balancing or mirror-image hexachords. These hexachords are generative and are fulfilled both in interaction and compression." (E. BORROFF)

Concerto (1974) (to L. TEAL) 1) Moderato 2) Allegro enertgico •Asx/Orch or Band or Pno •Pet
Sonata (1971) (13'30) (transcription of viola sonata by L. HUNTER) 1) Allegro moderato con moto 2) Largo sostenuto 3) Allegretto con spirito •Asx/Pno •Pet
Two Studies (1980) (10') (to L. HUNTER) •1 Sx: A+S/Pno •Pet

FINNISSY, Michael (Peter) (1946)

Compositeur anglais, né le 17 III 1946 à Londres. Travailla avec Stevens, Searle et, en Italie, avec Vlad.

Défendant le mouvement dit 'The New Complexity' auquel il est assimilé, Michael Finnissy répond: "La musique ne l'est pas, si ce n'est dans le domaine très superficiel du détail. Elle est complexe, si vous admettez que les êtres humains sont complexes et que tout art est complexe." "Il a parfois utilisé les techniques aléatoires, mais son oeuvre n'en porte pas moins la marque d'un lyrisme naturel, et s'intéresse beaucoup à la musique pour la scène et pour le film." (G. GEFEN)

"Finnissy's music has a severe, uncompromising quality, and the mood is often one of explicit violence. Tough, angular textures of elaborate counterpoint are contrasted with sustained chordal passages or with long 'structural silences.' Many new instrumental techniques are used, together with a variety of semi-aleatory procedures, including space-time notation." (R. COOKE)

Babylon (1971) (19') •Mezzo Soprano Voice/Ob/Cl/Asx/Bsn/Guit/ Harp/Pno/2 Perc/2 Vcl/Bass •Uni
Evening (Abend) (1974) •Asx/Hn/Tpt/Perc/Harp/Vcl/Bass
First sign a sharp white mons (1964-67) (45') •2 Fl/2 Cl/Asx/CBsn/ Hn/Accordion/Guit/Vln/2 Vcl/Pno •BMIC
Moon's goin' down' (1980) (8') •Voice or Ssx Solo •Uni

N (1969) (8-10') •1 or 4 instruments •Uni
Runnin' wild (1978) (7'30) •Cl or BsCl or Bb Sx or Eb Sx

FINZI, Graciane (1945)

Compositeur français.

5 Séquences (1982) (10'30) (to Quatuor Deffayet) •SATB •Bil
De l'un à l'autre (1977) (2'30) •Asx/Pno •Led

FIOCCO, Joseph-Hector (1703-1741)

Allegro (BALBO) •Tsx/Pno •OMC
Allegro (CORDEIRO) •1 Sx: A or T/Pno •DP
Allegro (RASCHER) •Asx/Pno •Bou
Aria and Rondo (FRACKENPOHL) •Tsx/Pno •Ken
Concerto (LONDEIX) (15') 1) Allegro 2) Modéré et gracieux 3) Lent et trés expressif 4) Trés animé •Tsx/Orch or Pno •Sch

FIORENZA, Eduard

Soundscape Suite for Jazz Quartet •Tsx/Pno/Bass/Perc •DP

FIRSOVA, Elena (1950)

Compositeur russe, né à Moscou en 1950. Travailla avec A. N. Piroumov, bénéficiant des conseils d'E. Denisov. Elle est l'épouse du compositeur Dmitri Smirnov.

"Son style, à la fois lyrique et dramatique, se place dans le cadre d'un sérialisme libre, traversé de violence ou d'un souffle romantique, un peu dans la descendance d'Alban Berg." (J. di VANNI)

Capriccio: Quintette avec flûte (1976) (8') •4 Sx: SATB/Fl
La Nuit (d'après B. PASTERNACK) (1978) •Soprano Voice/4 Sx: SATB

FISCHER

Here I Sit in the Deep Cellar •Tsx/Pno •Ken

FISCHER, Clare

Compositeur américain.

Rhapsody •Asx/Chamber Orch •adr
Rhapsody Nova (1988) (to G. FOSTER) •1 Soloist: Fl+Cl+Asx/Band •adr

FISCHER, Eric (1961)

Saxophoniste et compositeur français, né le 29 VII 1961.

Blues (1980) •Ssx/Vibr/Org •adr
Concerto (1982) (to A. BEUN) •Asx/Orch
La force 50 - Musique de scène •5 Sx: SAATB •adr
Kephas a Antioche (1984) (10') 1) 69 2) Trés lent 3) 108 •Tsx/Pno •Bil
Prière (1979) •Ssx/Org •adr
Prière au Christ (1980) •Asx/Org •adr
Quatuor n° 2 - Le martyre des quatorze de Meaux (1984) •SATB •adr
Sonate •Tsx/Pno •adr
Spleen - Cité d'hiver - Vers la vraie vie - La Reine morte •(1984) Jazz Group including [dont] 4 Sx: SATB/Electr. Bass/Perc •adr
Tango (1982) •2 Cl/4 Sx: SATB/Mallet Perc [Perc à clavier]/Synth/ Pno •adr
Variations •SATB •adr
Visions du Christ - en 8 mouvements •4 Sx: SATB/Mallet Perc [Perc à clavier] •adr

FISCHER, M.

Saxonetta •Asx/Pno •Fro

FISCHER, Michael Gotthard (1773-1829)

Kaprizioser •Asx/Pno

FISCHER-MÜNSTER, Gerhard (1952)

Compositeur allemand, né le 17 XI 1952 à Münster-Sarmsheim.

Fantasiestücke (1977) (8') •Tarogato Solo or Ssx Solo/Orch (1111/ 20000/Perc/Harp/Str) •adr
Fossilien (1981) (9') •BsCl/Ssx/Perc •VDMK

FISH, Greg
Compositeur américain.
The Hammer and the Arrow (to J. SAMPEN) (1990) •Yamaha WX7 MIDI Wind Controller/Computer •adr

FISHER, Alfred Joel (1942)
Compositeur américain.
5 Time Prisme •3 Sx: STBs/Vibr/Pno •SeMC
Tour de France (1990) (12'30) 1) Jour de marché: MM. RAVEL & DREYFUSS 2) M. le Postmoderne 3) Carpentras 4) Le mignon minime •Asx/Pno

FITCHORN, E. J.
Practical Procedures for Sight Reading (1968) •HE

FLADT, Hartmut (1945)
Compositeur allemand, né le 7 XI 1945. Travailla avec R. Kelterborn.
Die Abnehmer (1980) •2 Voice/Sx/Perc •adr
Im Fabelreich (1982) •Voice/Sx/Perc •adr

FLAMENT, Edouard (1880-1958)
Compositeur français, né à Douai, le 27 VIII 1880, mort à Bois-Colombes, prés Paris, le 27 XII 1958.
Romance (MULE) •Asx/Pno •Led
Sonate, op. 151 •Asx/Pno

FLEGIER, André-Ange (1846-1927)
Love Song (STANCES) •Eb Sx/Pno •CF
Vilanelle (SMIM) •Asx or Bb Sx/Pno •VAB

FLEISHER, Robert
Oblique Motions •2 Sx

FLEMING, Robert James (1921-1976)
Compositeur canadien né à Prince-Albert (Saskatchewan), le 12 XI 1921; mort à Ottawa, le 28 XI 1976. Travailla avec H. Howells et H. Willan.
"The Canadian nature of most of the film subjects for which he provided music caused him to seek a matching flavour in his scores by drawing on Canadian folksong. The wit and delicacy of touch shown in his early works are futher enhanced by jazz elements." (G. RIDOUT)
Threo (1972) (to P. BRODIE) •Ssx/Pno •CMC

FLEMMING, Hansen Chr. (see HANSEN)

FLETA POLO, Francisco (1931)
Compositeur espagnol, né le 18 VII 1931.
Divertimento 26 (1985) •Sx/Cl/Accordion/Bass/Timp
Impromptu n° 7a, op. 69 (1979) •Ssx/Pno
Impromptu n° 8, op. 79 (1979) •Asx/Pno •Cil
Quartetto n° 13, op. 79 "*El Manco de Lepanto*" (1980) 1) Tambores y clarines 2) Don Quijotte 3) Finale •SATB
Sonata - Cantarer le Rio Cid, op. 62 (1978) •Asx/Pno •Cil

FLETCHER, Grant (1913)
Compositeur et chef-d'orchestre américain, né le 25 X 1913 à Hartsburg (Illinois). Travailla avec H. Willan, B. Rogers, H. Hanson, et H. Elwell.
Sonata III •Asx/Pno •adr
Sax-son I (1977) (to J. WYTKO) •Asx/Pno •adr

FLIARKOVSKI
Compositeur russe.
Concerto •Asx/Orch or Pno •ECP

FLODI, John (1944)
Compositeur canadien, d'origine hongroise, né le 22 III 1944 à Nagyteval. Travailla avec J. Weinzweig, J. Beckwith, I. Anhalt, G. Ciamaga, et M. Davidovsky.
Signals, op. 22 (1968-69) (5'30) (to P. G. SMITH) •2 Sx: ST/Trb/ Perc/Pno •CMC

FLORENDAS, Paul
Tendre sérénade (1946) •Vln Solo or Asx/Small Orch/ Pno+Conductor •Chap

FLORENZO, Lino (1920)
Süd America Suite (1978) (10'30) 1) Tempo di cha-cha 2) Tempo di valse 3) Lento mysterioso 4) Tempo di samba •SATB •ME

FLORIAN
Pacific Poem no. 2-5 (1983) •1 Sx: S+B/Perc/Tape

FLORIO, Caryl (1843-1920) (see ROBJOHN, W. J.)

FLOTHUIS, Marius (1914)
Compositeur, pianiste, et musicologue néerlandais, né à Amsterdam, le 30 X 1914. Travailla avec Kempers.
"Peut être considéré comme un autodidacte." (LAROUSSE) "L'un des musiciens hollandais les plus fins et les plus châtiés." (H. HALBREICH) "Le style de sa musique est direct, simple, sans être réactionnaire pour autant." (R. BERNARD) "Marius Flothuis s'est surtout consacré à la musique instrumentale dans un langage traditionnel." (Cl. ROSTAND)
"He developed an individual style, redolent of neo-romanticism, but marked by a severely disciplined contrapuntal technique." (BAKER) "Flothuis' music is in general lyrical and intimate, tonal and extensively contrapuntal." (J. WOUTERS)
Capriccio, op. 86 (1985-86) (8') (to the Rascher Saxophone Quartet) •SATB •Don
Impromptu, op. 76, no. 3 (1976) •Asx Solo •Don
Kleine Suite (1952) •Ob/Cl/Ssx/Tpt/Pno •Don
Negro Lament (Poem by Langston HUGHES) (1953) 1) Andante: Poem 2) Sostenuto: "Harlem Night Song" 3) Adagio: "Troubled Woman" 4) Sostenuto: "The White Ones" 5) Allegro agitato: "Roland Hayes beaten" 6) Maestro e tranquillo: Epilogue •Contralto Voice/Asx/Pno •Don
Sinfonietta concertante, op. 55 (1954-55) (15') •Cl/Asx/Orch (2000/ 200/Timp/Str/Pno) or Pno •Don
3 Moments musicaux, op. 82 (1982) (12') •Asx/Pno •Don

FLOTOW, Friedrich von (1812-1883)
Aria - Martha (BLAAUW) •Asx/Pno •Mol
Martha (ROMBY) •Asx/Pno •PB

FLYNN, George (1937)
Compositeur américain, né à Miles City (Montana), le 21 I 1937.
Quartet (1982) •SATB •adr

FOARE, Charles
Chef de musique français, au 77e de ligne.
Doux espoir - Romance (1893) •Vcl (or Asx)/Pno

FOISON, Michèle (1942)
Compositeur français, né à Paris, le 6 VI 1942. Travailla avec O. Messiaen, A. Weber, Y. Desportes, et I. Markevitch.
"Je cherche d'une façon générale à ce que la musique que j'écris soit un véritable 'prolongement' de mon système nerveux, de mon émotion." (M. FOISON)
10 Variations sur un thème de berceuse (1966) (8') (to Quatuor Desloges) (Album) •Asx/Pno •Bil

FOLLAS, Ronald
Compositeur américain.
Ballade and Allegro (1985) (to J. HOULIK) •Tsx/Band

FOLLMAN, G.
3 Improvisations •Bb Sx/Pno •Sez

FONGAARD, Bjorn (1919-1990)
Compositeur norvégien, né à Oslo le 2 III 1919. Travailla avec P. Stenberg, S. Islandsmoen, B. Brustad, et K. Andersen.
Concerto, op. 120, no. 11 (1976) (17') •Asx/Orch •NMI
Quartet, op. 129, no. 5 (1975) (12') •SATB •NMI
Solosonata, op. 117, no. 2 (1973) (9') •Asx Solo •NMI
Sonata, op. 95 (1971) (8') (to K. DORN) •Asx/Tape •HL/Pet
Sonata, op. 125, no. 13 (1973) (7') •Asx Solo •NMI

FONTAINE, E.
Interlude Melody •Bsx/Pno •PA

FONTAINE, Fernand Marcel
Compositeur belge.
Concertino de Dinant (1975) (to Quatuor Belge de Saxophones) 1) Presto 2) Larghetto 3) Molto vivace 4) Presto •SATB •CBDM
Résonance •Asx Solo/3 Sx: STB or Pno or Chamber Orch

FONTAINE, Louis-Noël (1956)
Saxophoniste et compositeur canadien, spécialiste du saxophone baryton, né le 24 XII 1956 à Montréal. Travailla avec P. Gosteau, R. Masino, J. Ledieu, D. Deffayet, J-M. Londeix, puis J. Hétu et André Prevost.
Berceuse (1979) (2') •Asx/Pno
Concertante (1991) (13') •Asx Solo/11 Sx: SnoSSAATTTBBBs •Capri
Divertimento (1992) (10') •Asx/Pno •Capri
Duo pour les jours de pluie (1979) (6') •2 Sx: AB •Capri
Estudiantine (1993) (10') •SATB •Capri
Folia (1992) (12') (to J-F. GUAY & J. BÉCHARD) •Asx/Perc •Capri
Fugue en Lab dans un style baroque (1979) (4') •SATB
Mauresque (1992) (8') •Fl/Ssx/Cl/Vcl/Perc •Capri
Musique (1978) (8') •Cl/2 Hn/2 Sx: AB •Capri
Musique pour la fin des camps (1981) (9') •4 Sx: BBBB •Capri
Polymorphie (1992) (13') •12 Sx: SnoSSAAATTTBBBs •Capri
Prélude et fugue sur B.A.C.H. (1977) (5') •SATB
Quatuor (1982) 1) Andante 2) Allegro 3) Adagio 4) Allegro final •SATB •adr
Quatuor n° 1 "Requiem" (1982-93) (15') 1) Adagio-Allegro-Adagio-Allegro vivace 2) Lento-Moderato-Vivace •SATB •Capri
Scherzo (1992) (8') •Ssx/Pno •Capri
Sonatine (1992) (8') •Tsx/Pno •Capri
Sonate (1993) (15') •Bsx/Pno •Capri

FONTBONNE, Léon-Pierre (1858-1940)
Musicien français.
Méthode complète élémentaire, théorique et pratique, précédée des principes de musique et d'un historique de l'instrument •Cos

FONTYN, Jacqueline (1930)
Compositeur belge, née à Anvers, le 27 XII 1930. Travailla avec I. Bolotine, M. Quinet, et M. Deutsch.
"A la virtuosité d'écriture (des *Dialogues* pour saxophone et piano)—virtuosité ne serait-ce que par les controverses prestes et serrées d'un agile contrepoint—s'ajoute la pression d'un débordement d'invention, de trouvailles qui marquent un des aspects de la personnalité du compositeur." (M. & I.)

Cheminement (1986) (15') •Soprano Voice/Fl/Cl/Hn (or Asx)/Vcl/Bass/Perc/Pno
Controverse (1983) (7') •Tsx/Perc •B&B
Dialogues (1969) (13') (to Fr. DANEELS) 1) Introduction - Grazioso - Maestoso 2) Prestissimo 3) Cantabile - Sereno - Memi mosso •Asx/Pno •Chou
Fougères (1981) (5') (to J. CHARLES) •1 Sx: S+A/Pno or Harp •Sal
Mime III (1980) (5') (to J. CHARLES) •1 Sx: S+A/Pno •Sal

FORAY, Claude (1933)
Compositeur français.
Quatuor (to Quatuor Contemporain) •SATB

FORD, Andrew (1957)
Compositeur néerlandais.
Boatsong (1982) (to BOK and LE MAIR) •Sx+BsCl/Marimba •Don
Four Winds (1984) •SATB •Don

FORD, Clifford (1947)
Compositeur canadien, né à Toronto, en 1947. Travailla avec J. Beckwith et J. Weinzweig.
5 Short Pieces in Circular Motion (1971) (6') (to P. BRODIE) •Ssx/Pno •CMC

FORD, Trevor
Suite (1978) (to R. NODDELUND) 1) Allegretto 2) Andante 3) Allegro •SATB •Mol

FORENBACH, Jean-Claude (1925)
Dialogues (1982) (to Quatuor G. Pierné) •SATB
Week Chronicle (to J-P. BARAGLIOLI) •Asx/Perc

FORESTIER, J.
Solo (to C. van LEEUVEN) •Asx/Pno •Mol

FORET, Félicien (1890-19xx)
Sous-chef de la Musique de la Garde Républicaine.
Célèbre berceuse de Reber •SATB •Cos
2 Pièces •Asx/Pno •Dur
Pâtres et Rythmes champêtres (MULE) •Asx/Pno •Bil

FORSSELL, Jonas (1957)
Compositeur suédois.
Den Kortaste natten "En naturbild" (1979) •Bsx Solo •STIM
Epitaphinum (1978) •Asx/Org •STIM
Mia (1981) (10') •Asx/Pno •STIM
Tyst vâr (Printemps silent) (1986) (20') 1) Prolog 2) I 3) II 4) Epilog •SATB •STIM

FORSYTH, Malcolm (1936)
Breaking Through (1991) (5'15) (to W. STREET) •Asx/Pno •Ric
Tre vie (1992) (20') (to W. STREET) 1) Presto, ritmico: Like a meteor 2) 48 3) Relaxed and Singing 4) Final •Asx/Orch •Ric

FORTERRE
Quatuor •SATB

FORTIER, Marc
Tempo I (1968) (to Quatuor Bourque) •SATB

FORTINO, Mario
Prelude and Rondo •Asx/Pno •TP

FORTNER, Jack (1935)
Compositeur et saxophoniste américain, né à Grand-Rapids (Michigan), en 1935. Travailla avec G. Wilson et R. Lee Finney.
"Quoique à l'occasion, une série ait été utilisée, *S pr ING* est essentiellement d'un chromatisme libre."

S pr ING sur des poèmes de E. E. Cummings (1966) (11') •Mezzo Soprano Voice/Fl/Asx/Bsn/Vla/Vcl/Bass/Vibr/Harp/Pno •JJ

FORTNER, Wolfgang (1907-1987)

Compositeur, chef d'orchestre, et pédagogue allemand, né à Leipzig, le 12 X 1907; mort à Heidelberg, le 5 IX 1987. Travailla avec H. Grabner.

"Wolfgang Fortner allie le langage polyphonique traditionnel au chromatisme de Reger, à l'esprit de Schoenberg." (N. DUFOURCQ) "Il a fait des études fortement traditionnelles et a été conduit par les circonstances et l'esthétique officielle du régime nazi à s'exprimer d'abord dans un style néo-classique affirmé, ce qui n'était peut-être pas absolument contraire à son tempérament, où se trouve un fond d'académisme." (Cl. ROSTAND) "Néo-baroque, sa musique de 1928 fait découvrir son goût pour le contrepoint linéaire, les imitations, le tout empreint des vues et concepts d'alors: antiromantisme, antisubjectivité, clarté formelle. Sa musique d'Eglise est à base d'une renaissance de la liturgie musicale luthérienne." (J-N. von der WEID)

"The style of Fortner's middle period (1930-1945) may be termed 'neo-baroque' for its combination of baroque polyphony with a strangely abstract and novel mode of expression which is sometimes harsh and uncompromising." (K. BARTLETT) "He thus grew up in the Protestant church music tradition of Leipzig, and several of his earliest works were settings of sacred texts." (H. KRELLMANN)

Sweelinck Suite (1930) •AATB •adr

FOSS (FUCHS), Lukas (1922)

Compositeur, chef d'orchestre, et pianiste américain d'origines allemandes, né à Berlin, le 15 VIII 1922. Travailla à Paris avec N. Gallon et F. Wolfes. Installé aux U.S.A. en 1937 il étudia avec Thompson, Reiner, Koussevitzky, et P. Hindemith.

"In his first decade as an 'experimental' composer, Foss assimilated most of the devices identified with the avant garde of the 1960s and added some variants of his own devising." (G. CHASE)

Map •Any 4 Instruments •CF
Music for Six •Any 6 Instruments •CF
Quartet (1985) (for the Amherst Saxophone Quartet) •Anime - Choral - Mouvement de valse - Vif •SATB •Ron

FOSTER, Stephen Collins (1826-1864)

Beautiful Dreamer •Bb Sx/Pno •Mol
Come Where my Love Lies Dreaming •2 Sx: TT/Pno •CF
Old Dog, Beautiful Isle (THOMAS) •Asx/Pno •CF
Old Folks, Sweet By and By •Asx/Pno •CF
Jeannie with the light brown hair •Bb Sx/Pno •Mol
Massa's in the Cold Ground •Asx/Pno •CF
Sweetly She Sleeps •Tsx/Pno •HE
12 American Songs •Eb Sx/Pno •CF
Two Melodies •AATB •Bri

FOTE, R.

Amigos •2 Sx: AA/Pno •Ken
Waltz for Juliet •1 Sx: A or T/Pno •WWS

FOTEK, Jan (1928)

Compositeur polonais né à Czerwinsk, le 28 XI 1928. Travailla avec Wiechowicz et Szelogowski.

"His music uses techniques common to Polish composers of his generation." (M. HANUSZEWSKA)

Musiquette (1983) (3') (to D. PITUCH) •3 Sx: AAA
Wariacje (1985) •Asx/Pno

FOUILHAUD, Patrice

Volumen III (1986) (7') (to D. KIENTZY) •Bsx/ Solo •Dur

FOUQUE (Pierre) Octave (1844-1883)

Musicologue et compositeur français, né le 12 XI 1844 à Pau, où il est mort le 22 IV 1883. Travailla avec Ch. Chauvet et A. Thomas.

Adagio et variations •Asx/Pno •Mil
Mélodie •Asx/Pno •Mil

FOURCHOTTE, Alain (1943)

Compositeur français né à Nice.

Disgression I (1981) (5') (to D. KIENTZY) •SnoSx Solo •Sal
Disgressions II (1981-82) (5') (to D. KIENTZY) •Ssx Solo •Sal
Disgressions III (1982) (5') (to D. KIENTZY) •Asx Solo •Sal
Disgressions IV - Multiples (1984) (6') (to D. KIENTZY) •Tsx Solo or 6 Sx: SnoSABBsCBs
Disgressions V (1983) (5') (to D. KIENTZY) •Bsx Solo
Disgressions VI (1983-84) (5') (to D. KIENTZY) •BsSx Solo
Disgressions VII (1984) (5') (to D. KIENTZY) •CBsSx Solo
Echanges (1975) (15') •4 Sx
Pour K. (1985) (6') (to D. KIENTZY) •5 Sx

FOURNES, Siegfried

Stück (1932)

FOURNIER, Marie-Hélène (1963)

Compositeur français. Travailla avec G. Reibel, J-P. Drouet, M. Viard, et M. Lonsdale.

Aliénage (1987) (20') (Ballet - Instr. improv.) •Ad lib./Tape
Cinq Muses (1990) (20') (to S. BERTOCCHI) •Saxophones/Tape
Deux Pièces : Sentiers et Regards sur l'île d'Alcine (CORNU) (1987) •Asx/Perc •Lem
Hippogriffe III (1988) (11') (to S. BERTOCCHI) •1 Sx comédien: S+B/ Tape
Hippogriffe IV (1991) (11') •2 Musiciens-comédiens: Sx/Perc/Tape
Horoscope (1986) (3'30) •Asx Solo •Com
Les muses inconnues •1 Sx: A+S+T/Tape
Oxydes (1986) (3'40) (to J-M. GOURY & S. BERTOCCHI) •2 Sx: AA •Lem
Quatre Duos (1988) (10') •2 Sx: AA •Com
Sétiocétine (1987) (3'30) •Asx Solo •Com
Supplément nécessaire (1990) (50') (Théâtre musical) •5 Instrum. comédiens: 2 Perc/Bsx/Harp/Soprano Voice
What's what (1989) (Caractère théâtral) •SATB

FOX, Christopher

Stone-Wind-Rain-Sun (1990) (10') •SATB

FOX, Frederick (1931)

Compositeur et professeur anglais.

Annexus (1981) (10') (to T. LILEY) •Asx/Pno
S.A.X. (1979) (10') (to L. TEAL) •Asx/4 Sx: SATB
Shaking the Pumpkin (1987) (to K. FISCHER) •Asx/Pno/2 Perc
Three Diversions •SATB
Visitations (1982) (10') (to E. ROUSSEAU) •2 Sx: AA

FOX, Oscard J.

Aria and Scherzo •Asx/Pno •WWS
The Hills of Home (IASILLI) •Asx/Pno •CF
Minuet (RASCHER) •Asx/Pno •Bel
Waltz and Air •Asx/Pno •WWS

FOX, Tony

Symmetry (1979) (to D. MASEK) •Asx/Pno

FRACKENPOHL, Arthur (1924)

Compositeur américain, né à Irvington (New Jersey), le 23 IV 1924. Travailla avec B. Rogers, D. Milhaud, et N. Boulanger.

Air for Alto (1979) (to J. STOLTIE) •Asx/Pno •Ken
Chorale and Canon (1968) •SATB •Pres
Christmas Jazz Suite •SATB •Ken
Dorian Elegy (on a melody by STOLTIE) (1981) •Asx/Pno •Ken

Expressive Excursion in the Contemporary Idiom •Sx Solo •Ken
Fanfare, Air and Finale •SATB •JB
Intrada (1984) (to J. Stoltie) •SATB •Sha
Quartet (1967) 1) Fanfare 2) Song 3) Canon 4) Choral 5) Finale
     •SATB •RPS
Quartet (1969) (12') 1) March 2) Waltz 3) Interlude 4) Scherzo •Ob/
     Cl/Asx/Bsn •RPS/DP
Ragtime Suite (9'15) 1) Pan Am Rag (Turpin) 2) Something Doing
     (Joplin & Hayden) 3) The Cascades (Joplin) •SATB •Sha
Rhapsody (1984) (3'30) (to J. Stoltie) •Sx Solo •Ken
Sonata (1982) 1) Fast 2) Slowsly 3) Fast •Tsx/Pno
Tango and Two-Step (1993) (8') (to the Crane Saxophone Quartet)
     •4 Sx: SATB or 5 Sx: SSATB •Ken/adr
Three Waltzes (1994) (8') (to R. Faub) 1) Medium Rag 2) Slow Ballad
     3) Fast Jazz •Asx/Pno •adr/Ken
Trio •Ssx/Hn/Bsn •DP
Two Rags 1) Sad Rag 2) Glad Rag •6 Sx: SAATBBs •Sha
Variations (1969) (7') (to J. Stoltie) •Asx/Pno •Sha/RPS
Waltz Ballad (1979) •Asx Solo

FRANCAIX, Jean (1912)

Compositeur et pianiste français, né au Mans, le 23 V 1912. Travailla
avec Nadia Boulanger.

A propos de son *Concerto pour 15 instruments* 'soli': "Je n'y ai pas
inclus le saxophone, car il me semble plus proche des Maisons Closes
de Toulouse-Lautrec que des Palais de Haydn." (Jean Francaix) "Fut
un enfant prodige, et en garde un excès de facilité." (P. Wolff)
"Manque de vie intérieure." (P. Collaert) "Le style de Francaix paraît
parfois d'une gracilité un peu excessive et on souhaiterait que cette
grâce spirituelle et papillotante demeurât une modalité, une forme
d'expression de la pensée, alors que trop souvent chez lui, elle en
usurpe la place ou, du moins, elle joue un rôle prépondérant." (R.
Bernard) "Jean Francaix semble prédestiné par son nom à porter au-
delà de nos frontières un art qui répond exactement à l'image un peu
sommaire que s'en fait déjà l'étranger." (R. Stricker) "Miraculeuse-
ment doué, il continue imperturbablement de produire une musique
aimable, divertissante en des oeuvres qui ne se renouvellent nullement." (Cl. Rostand) "Molière dixit, (la *Suite* pour Quatuor de
saxophones) est une "suite" à la suite et à la fuite de ma jeunesse." J.
Francaix)

"In his music, Francaix associates himself with the neo-French
school of composers, pursuing the twofold aim of practical application
and national tradition." (Baker) "His music is characterized by an
engaging spontaneity and great technical proficiency. It is often witty,
but rarely profound; not selfconsciously 'neo-classic,' but marked on
the whole by a classical restraint and sobriety—in a word, by those
qualities of clarity, proportion and elegance which have always been
the hallmark of Gallic spirit in the arts." (R. Myers)

5 Danses exotiques (1962) (6') (to M. Mule) 1) Pambiche 2) Baïao
     3) Mambo 4) Samba lenta 5) Merengue •Asx/Pno •Sch
Concerto (1959-92) ("L'Horloge de Flore") •EH or Ssx/Orch (2022/
     200/Str) •ET
Paris à nous deux (1954) (30') (Opéra bouffe) •Soli de chant/4 Sx:
     SATB •ET
Petit quatuor (1939) (7') 1) Goguenardise 2) Cantilène 3) Sérénade
     comique •SATB •Sch
Suite (1990) (16'30) (to Quatuor de Versailles) 1) Prélude 2) Subito
     presto 3) Scherzo 4) Larghetto - Subito moderato 5) Finale
     •SATB •Sch

FRANCESCHINI, Romulus

Celebrations •Sx/Tape

FRANCESCONI, Luca (1956)

Compositeur italien, né à Milano. Travailla avec A. Corzhi et
Stockhausen, puis fut pendant quatre ans l'assistant de L. Berio à
Tanglewood (U.S.A.).

"… Music is Seduction. But this occurs, or should occur, at a level of
true profundity and not only skin-deep as happens for the most part with
consumer music. In other words, it becomes an enriching experience
involving our minds as well, beyond the first level of sensorial fascination; it is truly a profound dance between instinct and reason, in
continuous search of an equilibrium, consumed in our truest perceptual
experience." (L. Francesconi)

Piccola trama (1989) (14') •1 Sx: S+A/Fl/Cl/Guit/Perc/Vln/Vla/Vcl
     •Ric
Trama (1987) (20') (to J. Sampen) •Asx/Orch (2242/221/Perc/Str)
     •Ric

FRANCHETTI, Arnold (1909)

Compositeur américain d'origine italienne, né le 18 VIII 1909, à
Lucca (Italie). Travailla au Mozarteum de Salzburg avant de s'installer
aux U.S.A.

Canti (1969) (12') (to D. Sinta) •Asx/Wind Ensemble •SeMC
Concertino (1960) •Asx/Wind Ensemble •adr
Do - Ré - Mi •Asx/Pno •adr
Quartetto (1971) (10') (to D. Sinta) •AATB •DP
Seven Little Steps on the Moon (1976) •Asx/Chamber Ensemble
     •adr
Sonata (1970) (14') (to D. Sinta) "Love be in the midst of this
     dance;/ and who is his servant: but if Someone has suspicion and
     jealously,/ Then he should not dwell her." (Lorenzi De Medici -
     1489) •Asx/Pno •Led

FRANCIS, Mark

Divertimento •Cl/Asx/Perc

FRANCK, César (1822-1890)

Aux petits enfants (Cluwen) •2 Sx: AA/Pno •TM
Panis angelicus •AATB/Pno ad lib. •Bri
Panis angelicus (Lemarc) •SATB or AATB •TM
Pièce (Mule) •Asx/Pno •Led

FRANCK, Marcel G. (1894)

Légende (3') •Asx/Pno •EMa

FRANCO, Clare

Dance Piece •Asx/Pno
Four Winds in Search •Asx/Harp/Vibr/Fl/Ob/Cl/Hn/Bsn

FRANCO, Johan Henri (1908)

Compositeur américain d'origine hollandaise, né à Zaandam, le 12
VII 1908. Travailla à Amsterdam avec W. Pijper. Vit aux U.S.A.
depuis 1934.

"He is a prolific composer; his works, are tonal in style (many are
didactic)."

Sonata (1964) (to G. Etheridge) •Asx Solo •CFE

FRANGKISER, Carl (1894-19xx)

Compositeur et chef d'orchestre américain, né à Londonville (Ohio),
le 18 IX 1894.

Canzona •Bsx/Pno •Bel
Chant de l'orchidée •4 Sx •B&H
Jennadean •4 Sx •B&H
Luxury Lane •AATB •Bel
Melody variante •BsSx/Pno •Bel
Moraine •Asx/Pno •Bel
Song of the Orchid •AATB •B&H
Theme from Alaskan Night •Tsx/Pno •Bel

FRANK, Andrew

Compositeur américain.

Alto Rhapsody (1973) •Asx Solo •SMT

FRANK, Fred L.
Minka, Minka •3 Sx: AAT/Band or Pno •Rub

FRANK, M.
Centurion •Tsx/Pno •WWS
Conversation Piece •AATB •Ken

FRANZEN, Bengt
Compositeur suédois.
Suite •4 Sx •ACS

FRANZEN, Olov (1946)
Violoncelliste et compositeur suédois, né à Umeâ, le 22 I 1946. Travailla avec I. Lidholm.
Heptyk : sju satser (1987) (14'30) •AATB •SMIC/Faimo

FRASCOTTI, Robert & Bruce RONKIN
The Orchestral Saxophonist (2 Volumes) (1978/1984) •Ron

FRAZEUR, Theodore (1929)
Percussionniste américain, né le 20 IV 1929, à Omaha (Nebraska).
Frieze (1972) •Tsx/Perc •adr

FREE, John
Compositeur canadien.
A Wind of Changes I - XII (1990) •Cl/Bsn/Sx/Perc/Pno •CMC

FREEDMAN, Harry (1922)
Compositeur canadien d'origine polonaise, né à Lodz, le 5 IV 1922. Vit au Canada depuis 1925. Travailla avec J. Weinzweig, O. Messiaen, A. Copland, et E. Krenek.
"Several of Freedman's early compositions are 12-note serial pieces. By 1953 his dissatisfaction with the idiom was leading him to search for an alternative to serialism. His penchant for jazz was rekindled when he came across Bartok's music, which he found to have great affinities with jazz. Syncopation and melodic inflections similar to 'blue notes' are frequent. In certain 'third stream' works, jazz percussion instruments and Latin American rhythms are used." "Freedman's reliance on Canadian poets, painters and performers is noteworthy. To a large degree his musical imagination has been shaped by the North American jazz experience and furthermore by his more immediate intellectual landscape, or 'goût de terroir.' " (D. R. Cooper)
Celebration (1977) •Sx Solo: S+B/Orch (3030/4330/3 Perc/Harp/ Str) •CMC
Scenario (1970) •Asx/Electr. BsGuit/Orch •CMC
3 for 2 (1980) (to P. Brodie) 1) Not too fast 2) Slow 3) Lively •1 Sx: S+A/Cl •CMC

FRESCOBALDI, Girolamo (1583-1643)
Canzona (Hemke) •SATB
Fugue (Caravan) •5 Sx: SATBBs •Eth
Fugue in G Minor (Blyton) •SATB •DP
Gagliarda (Aron) •4 Sx: ATTB/Hn •GSch

FREUDENTHAL, Otto (1934)
Chef d'orchestre, pianiste, et compositeur suédois, né à Gothenburg, le 29 VII 1934.
"Stylistically he shows the influences of Schoenberg, Malher and the masters of the Baroque, but he has made them very much his own."
Duo (1978) •Ssx/Vla •SMIC
Intermezzo & Scherzoso (1992) •Asx/Perc •SMIC

FREUDENTHALER, Erland Maria
Compositeur autrichien.
Capriccios (8'36) •SATB
Fata Morgana (5'45) •12 Sx: SnoSSAAATTTBBBs

Saxophon-Fanfare (1990) (1'30) •12 Sx: SnoSSAAATTTBBBs

FREUND, Donald
Compositeur américain.
Killing Time (1980) (to A. Rippe) •Amplified Asx/Amplified Pno/Tape •adr
Not Gentle (to A. Rippe) •MIDI Wind Controller/Computer

FREUND, J.
Concertino •Asx/Orch

FRIBERG, Tomas (1962)
Compositeur suèdois.
Längs ett oavslutat ögonblick (1989) (8') •SATB •SMIC

FRICKER, Peter Racine (1920)
Compositeur anglais, né à Londres, le 5 IX 1920. Travailla avec M. Seiber. Installé aux U.S.A. depuis 1964.
"Peter Racine Fricker s'est créé un style clair et solide, sériel sans rigueur. Sa polyphonie est d'une richesse exceptionnelle. Sans rien sacrifier de sa richesse, il s'est orienté vers une expression plus humaine vers un souffle mélodique plus lyrique." (H. Halbreich) "Avec H. Searle, il est le musicien le plus remarquable de sa génération. Polyphoniste savant et austère, il pratique un style sériel cependant sans rigueur, clair et solidement architecturé." (Cl. Rostand) "Tenta de marier le sérialisme avec une expression plus personnelle et plus lyrique dans ses symphonies, ses quatuors et, surtout sa pièce chorale *The Vision of Judgement.*" (G. Gefen)
"His music is more harmonic in interest than contrapuntal, and the foundation of his harmony is the interval of the thirds, as used by Bartok—rather than Britten, for instance." (Ch. Mackeson) "The most prominent British composer to emerge immediately after World War II, he developed a free atonal style which exerted a strong influence at a time when British composers were turning from the insularity of the war years."
Aubade (1951) (4') (to W. Lear) •Asx/Pno •Sch
Serenade no. 3, op. 57 (1969) (8') •SATB

FRID, Geza (1904)
Compositeur et pianiste néerlandais né à Màaramarossziget, le 25 I 1904. Travailla avec B. Bartok et Z. Kodaly.
"A prolific composer, he has employed novel techniques within a conventional style that shows the influence of Hungarian folk music." (R. Starreveld)
Kleine Suite, op. 88 (1975) (10') •Asx/Pno •Don
3 Poems (1976) •Narr/Asx/Guit •Don
Vice versa, op. 96 (1982) •Sx/Marimba •Don

FRIED, Alexej (1922),
Compositeur tchécoslovaque.
Guernica (1978) (15') •Ssx/Str Quartet •CHF
Sonate fÿur saxophonquartett •SATB •Peer
Tympanon (1982) (21') •Vln/Soprano Voice/Sx/Pno

FRIEDMAN, Jeffrey
Compositeur américain.
Music for Solo Baritone •Bsx Solo •DP

FRIEDRICH, Burkhard
Compositeur allemand.
Liezwicht (1993) •Tsx/Vla •B&N

FRIEDRICHS, Günter (1935)
Compositeur allemand, né à Tiegenhof près Danzig, le 25 XII 1935. Travailla avec Klussmann et O. Messiaen.
"His music has developed through 12-note serial and newer methods to a style he has described as 'free tonality.' " (C. Erwin)

Pas de deux - Duettino (1981-82) (6') •2 Sx: AT •B&B

FRIIS, Flemming
Compositeur danois.
Angelus (1988) (6') (to P.EGHOLM) •Asx/Org
Kwartet 1 (1989) (25') •SATB
Vox humana (1990) (7') •SATB

FRISK, Henrik
Compositeur suédois.
Variations in three parts (1993) •Ssx/Vla •INM

FROBERGER
Capriccio •SATB •WWS

FROIO, Giovanni
Compositeur italien.
Vita (1988) (to Fr. SALIME) •Asx Solo

FROMIN, Paul
Compositeur français.
Ballade pour Angèle •Asx/Orch d'harmonie •Mar
Danceries •SATB •Mar
Le Grand Canyon - Air de chasse •Asx/Pno •Cham
Mexicana •Cham
Le petit orchestre - Western Hastings (1985) •Asx/Orch d'Harmonie
 •Mar

FROSCHAUER, H.
Rhapsody •Asx/Orch

FUCIK, Julius (1872-1916)
Entrée des Gladiateurs •Asx/Pno •Sal

FUCHS, Christina
Compositeur allemand.
Suite I (1993) •Ssx/Bass •INM

FUENTES, Tristan
Compositeur allemand.
Auerbachs Keller (Quartet - Part I Faust) •Ssx/Pno/Vibr/Marimba
 •HMC
Gretchen (Quartet - Part IV Faust) •Cl+Ssx/Synth/Vibr+Sgl-lead/
 Marimba+Steel Drum
Pan Am (Quintet with tape introduction and coda) •BsCl+Ssx/Synth/
 Vibr+Steel Drum/Marimba+Accordion/Tape •HMC
Quartet (Walpurgisnacht - Part V Faust) •Bscl+Asx/Synth/
 Vibr+Tabla/Marimba+Drums •HMC
Risas de los Incas (Quartet) •BsCl+Ssx/Pno/Vibr/Marimba+Bass
 Drum •HMC

FUERSTNER, Carl
Pianiste et compositeur américain.
Incantations, op. 45 •Ssx/Pno •Eto

FUJI, K.
Aya VIII •Asx/Pno

FUKUDA, Wakako (194x)
Divertissement •4 Sx/Bass/Perc

FURMANOV, V.
Compositeur russe.
Inspiration (1991) (5') •5 Sx: SAATB/Pno/Bass

FURRER, Beat (1954)
Compositeur suisse, né à Schaffhausen. Travailla à Vienne avec R.
Haubenstock-Ramati.
Trio (1985) •Fl/Cl/Asx (or Ob) •Uni

FURRER-MÜNCH, Franz (1924)
Compositeur suisse né à Winterthur. Abandonna des études de
physique avant de se consacrer à la musique. Travailla à Berne, Bale et
Zürich, puis la musique électronique aux U.S.A. et à Freiburg.
Aufgebrochene Momente (1991) •Tsx/Harps •adr
Momenti unici (1989) •Tsx/Harps/Perc •adr

FUSTÉ-LAMBEZAT, Arnaud (1963)
Pianiste jazz, compositeur, et percussionniste français. Travailla
avec son père, puis avec I. Malek et Cl. Ballif.
Blanc et noir (1982) (12') (to J-M. LONDEIX) •12 Sx:
 SnoSSAAATTTBBBs •adr
Catalogue d'étoiles (1983) •Asx/Fl/Cl/Vln/Vcl/Pno •adr

FUSTÉ-LAMBEZAT, Michel (1934)
Compositeur, chef d'orchestre, et professeur français, né à Bor-
deaux. Travailla avec D. Milhaud. Directeur du Conservatoire de
Bordeaux.
Forme-couleurs (1988) (18'30) (Commande de l'Etat) (to J-M.
 LONDEIX) (5 strophes) •12 Sx: SnoSSAAATTTBBBs •adr
Fragments imaginaires (1987) Chamber Orch including [dont] 1 Asx
 •adr
Mouvements (1978-84) (13') (to J-M. LONDEIX) •12 Sx:
 SnoSSAAATTTBBBs •adr
Polyphonies (1975) (15') •Cl/Asx/Vla/Vcl •SeMC

GABAYE, Pierre (1930)

Compositeur et pianiste français, né à Paris, le 20 II 1930. Travailla avec Y. Desportes, S. Ple-Caussade, et T. Aubin. Grand Prix de Rome (1956).

Printemps (1959) (2'30) •Asx/Pno •Led

GABBRIELLI, Michelangelo

Compositeur italien.
Sigla, Epigramma in 4 Aforismi •SATB

GABELLES, Gustave (1883-1959)

Chef de musique et compositeur français.
Andante appasisionato (1954) (3'30) •Asx/Pno •Bil
Au bord du torrent (1934) (to MM. LICKERT & d'IVERNOIS) •Asx/Pno •Cham
2 Pièces (to Quatuor Mule) 1) La roche lumineuse 2) Shipping tones •SATB •Mar
Fantaisie (to M. BACHELET) •Asx/Pno •Bil
Fantaisie caprice (to P. SANTANDREA) •Asx/Pno •Gras
3 Pièces (to M. MATHIEU) 1) Paysage 2) Rêverie 3) Negro •SATB •Mar

GABRIEL

Canzona crequillon •SATB •WWS

GABRIELI, Giovanni (1557-1612)

Canzona a 4 (BULOW) •SATB •Ron
Canzona nono toni a 12 •3 x 4 Sx: SATB SATB SATB •DP
Canzona per sonare no. 2 (AXWORTHY) •SATB •DP
Canzona XIV (LONDEIX) •2 x 5 Sx: SAATB SAATB •Fuz
Canzona XV (LONDEIX) •12 Sx: SnoSSAAATTTBBBs •Ron

GABRIELI, Maurizio (1957)

Compositeur italien.
Do.Dicis.Acs (1991) (8') (to A. DOMIZI) •12 Sx: SnoSSAAATTTBBBs

GABRIEL-MARIE (1852-1928)

Cassandre - Bouffonnerie •Asx/Pno •Cos
La Cinquantaine (CHAUVET) •Asx/Pno •Bil
La Cinquantaine (DIAS) •Asx/Pno •Bil
La Cinquantaine (WIEDOEFT) •Asx/Pno •Bil
Golden Wedding •AATB •Alf
Intermezzo (CHAUVET) •Asx/Pno •Bil
Pasquinade (DIAS) •Asx/Pno •Bil
Près du gourbi •Asx/Pno •Bil
Sérénade badine (CHAUVET) •Asx/Pno •Bil
Sérénade badine (WIEDOEFT) •Asx/Pno •Bil/Rub
Sur la route •Asx/Pno •Cos
Tyrolienne - variations •Asx/Pno •Mar
Vieille histoire (CHAUVET) •Asx/Pno •Bil

GABUCCI, A.

60 Varied Etudes (ALLARD) (1937) •Ric

GABURO, Kenneth (1926)

Compositeur américain, né à Somerville (New Jersey) le 5 VII 1926. Travailla avec B. Rogers, puis, à Rome, avec G. Petrassi.

"Although his earlier compositions were orientated towards tonality, since 1954 Gaburo has based his works on serial principles and complex structural systems. In 1959 he began to investigate the physiological, acoustical and structural domains of language as compositional elements, leading to a conception of 'compositional linguistics.' " (J. ROSEN)

The Flight of Sparrow •Asx/Tape

GABUS, Monique

Compositeur français.
Etude (to G. GOURDET) •Asx Solo

GADE, Niels Wilhelm (1817-1890)

Novelette, op. 19 (GEE) •4 Sx: AATB or AATT •DP

GADENNE, G.

Marjolaine - Mazurka (1946) •Asx/Fanfare •BC

GAGNÉ, Marc (1939)

Compositeur canadien.
Quatuor du petit Chaperon Rouge (1981) (16') (to Quatuor Bourque) •SATB •CMC

GAGNEUX, Renaud (1947)

Animateur et compositeur français né à Paris. Travailla avec H. Dutilleux.

"Renaud Gagneux rattache certaines de ses préoccupations à une réflexion sur l'environnement sonore, naturel ou artificiel. Il envisage à cet égard trois principaux types d'éléments: 'le *hasard*, la *répétition*' que l'on retrouve dans les musiques à processus modulaire, dites répétitives, dont la fonction est avant tout de créer un paysage sonore à vocation incantatoire et enfin, la *synthèse* (et le domaine électro-acoustique en général) particulièrement adaptés à la reproduction et à la production sonores en plein air dont l'utilisation 'live' peut convenir avec plus d'efficacité au contexte ambiant." (D .J-Y. BOSSEUR)

"Compositeur de grande imagination." (J. & B. MASSIN)

Babel (1978) (7') •1 Sx:A+S/Dispositif électro-acoustique simple
Etude pour les sons multiples (1982) (3') (to D. KIENTZY) •1 Sx: S+A+T
Première •Asx/Tape

GAGNON, Alain (1938)

Compositeur canadien. Travailla avec H. Dutilleux.
"Langage évoluant vers une poésie de type cosmique."
Fantaisie lyrique, op. 28 (1982) (9'30) (to R. MÉNARD) •Asx/Pno •Led
Suite (1976) •Asx/Pno

GAGO, José Garcia

Compositeur espagnol.
Elegiaca (6') •SATB •adr
Escena (4'30) •SATB •adr
Poema del sur (7') •SATB •adr

GAILLARD, Marius François (1900-1978)

Pianiste, chef d'orchestre, et compositeur français, né à Paris le 13 X 1900.

"Gaillard a une palette très personnelle qui se caractérise par des débordements de sensualité très attachants." (P. WOLFF)

"His compositions follow a neo-Impressionist trend." (BAKER) "In his own works he made perspicacious use of a variety of styles and ideas." (A. GIRARDOT)

Note sobre o Tejo (1934) (3') (to M. MULE) •Asx/Pno •Bil

GAL, Hans (1890-1987)

Musicologue et compositeur autrichien, né à Vienne, le 5 VIII 1890. Travailla avec Mandyczewski.

"His style has remained resolutely uninfluenced by the output of Schoenberg and his school, however attractive that must have been to a composer serving his apprentice years in Vienna before World War I. His musical roots lay in Brahms and Strauss, and it was in the tonal tradition of those composers that he continued to work, pouring out a tireless flow of classically constructed, glowing-toned pieces, finely crafted, courteous, orderly, and unhurried in their musical discourse." (C. WILSON)

Suite, op. 102b (1949) (18') (to J. de VRIES) •Asx/Chamber Orch or Pno •WWS

GALANTE, Steven (1953)

Compositeur et saxophoniste américain. Travailla avec J. Bach, R. Peck, W. Bolcom, et W. Albright.

Saxsounds I "Sealed with a Kiss" (1972) •for multiple or amplified Sx Quartet: SATB •DP

Saxsounds II "Cry Baby" (1975) (10') •2 x 4 Sx: SATB SATB •adr

Saxsounds III (Diminishing Returns) (1978) (10') (to L. TEAL) •2 Asx/Digital delay effect •EMP

Shu Gath Manna (1987) (12') (to D. SINTA) Prologue - Silicon Dance - Threnody and Regeneration •Asx/Yamaha DX7 Synth •adr

GALARINI, Marco

Compositeur italien.

Speculazioni (1992) (10') •SATB

GALAY, Daniel

Exotique à l'envers (1984) (5') (to D. KIENTZY) •Asx Solo
Le nom dernier (1984) (4') (to D. KIENTZY) •Tsx Solo

GALLAHER, Christopher (1940)

Compositeur américain né le 10 IV 1940 à Ashland (Kentucky). Travailla avec B. Heiden, J. Orrego-Salas et J. E. Duncan.

Impressions of Summer (1960) (5') (to J. E. DUNCAN) •Asx/Pno •South

Quartet No. 2, op. 31 (1969) (9'30) (to my son Brent) •SATB or AATB •adr

Sonatina (1968) (7') (to E. ROUSSEAU & J. REZITS) •Asx/Pno •SP

Three Thoughts (1961) (8') •SATB •adr

GALLET, Jean

Compositeur français.

Berceuse et promenade (1968) •Asx/Pno •Bil
Andante et Jeu (1969) •Asx or Bb Sx/Pno •Bil

GALLIARD, Johann Ernst (1680-1749)

Allegro (LONDEIX) •Asx or Bb Sx/Pno •Lem
Hornpipe (LONDEIX) •Asx or Bb Sx/Pno •Lem
Sarabande and Minuet •Tsx/Pno •CPP
Sonata No. 4 (RASCHER) •Tsx/Pno •Gi&Ma/Pet

GALLOIS-MONTBRUN, Raymond (1918-1994)

Violoniste et compositeur français, né à Saigon, le 15 VIII 1918, où il est mort le 14 VIII 1994. Travailla avec H. Busser, J. et N. Gallon. Grand Prix de Rome (1944).

"Il écrit une musique d'une très fine sensibilité poétique." (R. BERNARD) "Il se situe dans la tendance néo-classique et tonale." (Cl. ROSTAND)

Complainte •Asx/Pno •Com
Intermezzo (1952) (1'30) •Asx/Pno •Led
6 Pièces musicales d'étude (1954) (16'30) 1) Ballade 2) Intermezzo 3) Ronde 4) Lied 5) Valse 6) Finale •Asx/Pno •Led

GALUPPI, Baldassaro (1703-1785)

Toccata •3 Sx: AAA or TTT •Mus
Toccata (MAGANINI) •AATB •Mus

GAMSTORP, Göran (1957)

Compositeur suédois.

Barnet i skogen / Barn i stjärnljus (1987) (9'30) •Mezzo Soprano Voice/4 Sx: SATB •SMIC

GANDOLFO

Pièce •SATB

GANNE, Louis (1862-1923)

Compositeur et chef d'orchestre français, né à Buxières-les-Mines, le 5 IV 1862; mort à Paris, le 14 VII 1923. Travailla avec Th. Dubois et C. Franck. Auteur de deux marches devenues populaires: *Marche lorraine* (1887) et *Le père la victoire* (1888).

"His works, though intended for popular consumption, never became banal." (A. LAMB)

Le val fleuri - Mélodie (1888) •Asx/Pno

GARCIA, José (see GAGO, José Garcia)

GARCIA, Manuel D.

Concert Duet •Asx/Tuba •DP
Crucibus (1984) •Asx/Perc

GARCIA, Russell (1916)

Compositeur, chef d'orchestre, et arrangeur américain, né à Oakland (California), le 12 IV 1916. Travailla avec E. Ross, Castelnuovo-Tedesco, et A. Coates.

Miniature Symphony 1) Moderato 2) Fugue 3) Scherzo 4) Finale •SATB •EMod

GARCIA LABORDA, José Maria (1946)

Compositeur espagnol.

Amalgama (1989) (6'30) (to M. MIJAN) •Asx/Pno
Paisaje biografico (1991) (to M. MIJAN) •SATB

GARCIA ROMAN, José

Compositeur espagnol.

Musica para el otono (1990) (to M. MIJAN) •SATB

GARCIN, Gérard (1947)

Compositeur français né dans le Vaucluse. Etudes de flûte, de saxophone, d'harmonie, de contrepoint et d'électro-acoustique. Bien qu'ayant travaillé avec Fr. Donatoni, se considère comme autodidacte.

A la recherche du chant sacré (1991) •58 Sx including [dont] 12 soloists

A Sax (1991) •12 Sx: SnoSSAAATTTBBBs/Perc
Après... (1981) (14') •Asx/Tape •Sal
Après, bien après, enfin, elle arriva (1981) •4 reeds (SATB or other combinations)/Tape •Sal
Dialogosax (1971) •2 Sx
Duel à la recherche du chant sacré (1988) (15') (to J-M. LONDEIX) •12 Sx: SnoSSAAATTTBBBs
Elle arriva... (1981) •Bsx/Tape •Sal
Encore plus tard (1984) (12') (to D. KIENTZY) •1 Sx: Sno+A+Bs/Fl/Cl/Bsn/Vla/Vcl/Bass/Perc/Tape •Sal
Enfin... (1981) (13') (to Fr. JEANNEAU) •SnoSx/Tape •Sal
Enfin, après, elle arriva (1981) (14') •3 Sx: SnoSB •Sal
Le retour d'Uswann (1987) •Sx+BsCl/Perc/Bass
Méditations (1971) •2 Sx/Pno/Bass/Perc
6me Musique pour un 13 Juillet (1984) (6') •1 to 7 Asx/Tape •Sal
SA - Cadence (1986) (AsSaFra [French Saxo Association]) •Asx/Fl/Cl/Vln/Vcl/Pno

GARDNER, Samuel (1891-19xx)

Violoniste, compositeur, et chef d'orchestre américain, d'origine ukrainienne, né à Elizabethgrad, le 25 VIII 1891. Travailla avec Kneisel et Goetschius.

From the Canebrake •Asx/Pno •GSch

GARIN, Didier-Marc
Compositeur français. Travailla avec M. Fusté-Lambezat.
Aï fec (1985) •1 Sx: Sno+S+B+Bs/Perc/Tape
Da caccia IV - Flux d'estive (1992) (to l'Ensemble Proxima
    Centauri) •Fl/2 Sx: AT/Perc

GARIQUE
Mélodie •Asx/Pno •Mil

GARLICK, Antony (1928)
Compositeur anglais, né à Londres en 1928. Travailla avec W.
Harris, H. Darke, F. Germani, H. Olnick, et J. Weinzweig.
Bagatelle •Asx/Pno •SeMC
5 Study Patterns (1969) (11') •Asx/Pno •SeMC
Pièces •Ssx/Pno •SeMC
Rhapsodie (1969) (7') •Asx/Pno •SeMC

GARNOT, Claude
Quatuor (1989) (14') - Moderato - Vivace - Lent - Vif - Moderato
    •SATB

GARRIDO, Pablo (1905-1982)
Compositeur et ethnomusicologue chilien, né le 26 III 1905 à
Valparaiso où il est mort en 1982. Travailla avec G. Quintano et E. Van
Dooren.
"His compositions reflect a nationalist orientation, frequently em-
ploying folk material." (J. SCHECHTER)
Ventana de jazz •Sx/Pno

GARRIGUENC, Pierre
N. O. Rhapsody •Asx/Pno •EP

GARTENLAUB, Odette (1922)
Professeur et compositeur français.
Dialogue (1981) (to J-Y. FOURMEAU) •Asx/Pno

GASLINI, Giorgio (1929)
Compositeur, pianiste, et chef d'orchestre italien, né à Milan, le 22
X 1929.
"His compositional language is based substantially on a fusion of
jazz with 12-note serialism, also drawing on a wide range of other
contemporary musical currents from aleatoricism to electronic music
to pop; the aim is a stylistic synthesis which Gaslini describes as 'total
music.' " (P. SANTI)
Magnificat (1963) (4') •Soprano Voice/Asx/Pno/Bass •Uni
Silver concert (1992) (12') (to M. MAZZONI) •Bsx/Orch

GASSMAN, Florian (1729-1774)
Rococo Quartet No. 2 in Bb (AXWORTHY) •SATB •TVA

GASTINEL, Gérard (1949)
Compositeur français, né à Lyon, le 23 VI 1949. Travailla avec R.
Boutry, A. Weber, M. Bitsch, J. Casterede, et O. Messiaen.
Assonance •Asx/Str (33221)
5 Poèmes anciens (1974) (to Quatuor de Paris) •Mezzo Soprano
    Voice/4 Sx: SATB/Pno •Chou
Concerto (1984) (to J. NET) •Asx/Str Orch
Dilemne (1984) •Asx/Pno
Gamma 415 (1976) (to Quatuor J. Desloges) •SATB •Chou
8 Pièces en trio (1981) (8') •Asx/Ob/Vcl
Improvisation II (1976) (12'30) (to J. NET) 1) Modéré 2) Vif
    3) Calme 4) Trés vif •Asx/Pno •Chou
Pièce (1992) (6') •Asx/Pno
Quintette (1977) •Ssx/Ob/Cl/Hn/Bsn
Sax appeal (1988) (12'30) •14 Sx: SnoSSSAAAATTTBBBs

Suite en 4 mouvements (1982) (10') (to J. NET) - Moderato - Vivo -
    Lento - Animento •Asx Solo

GASTYNE, Serge de (see DEGASTYNE)

GATES, Everett (1921)
Compositeur et professeur américain.
Debu Yesque •Asx/Pno
Declamation and Dance •SATB
Foursome Quartet (1957) (7') (to S. RASCHER) 1) Four-Square
    Ostinato 2) Four-In-Three 3) Two-by-Two Canon 4) Four-Ward
    March •AATB •TTF
Incantation and Ritual (1963) (4') (to C. PETERS) •Asx Solo •EG
Odd Meter Duets •2 Sx •SF
Odd Meter Etudes (1962) •DG

GATTERMANN, Philippe
Fantaisie concertante •Fl (or Ob or Cl)/Asx/Pno •Bil

GATTI, Domenico
Concertino in Bb Major •Tsx/Pno •CF
Studies on Major and Minor Scales •CF
30 Progressive Duets (IASILLI) •2 Sx •CF
35 Melodious Technical Exercices (IASILLI) (1924) •CF

GAUBERT, Philippe (1879-1941)
Flûtiste, chef d'orchestre, et compositeur français.
Deux Pièces (PAQUOT) •Asx or Bb Sx/Pno •Led
Intermède champêtre (MULE) •Asx/Pno •Led
Poème élégiaque (1911) (8') (to E. HALL) •Asx/Orch (3222/EH/403/
    Timp/Harp/Str) or Pno •South

GAUDRIOT-SCHNEIDER
20 Etudes I & II •Dob

GAUDRON, René
Andante et allegretto •Tsx/Pno •Bil

GAUJAC, Edmond
Compositeur et chef d'orchestre français.
Funambule •Asx/Pno •Bil
Rêves d'enfant (1957) (10') (to D. DEFFAYET) 1) Le petit conquérant
    2) La grande soeur 3) Jeux •SATB •Bil

GAUTHIER, Brigitte
Like the Sweet Blonde (1983) •Fl/Asx/Cl/Vln/Vcl/Pno

GAUTIER, Leonard
Le secret (DAVIS) •Asx/Pno •Rub

GAY, Harry Wilbur (1925)
Compositeur et organiste américain, né à Montgomery (West
Virginia), le 1 XII 1925. Travailla avec A. Fuleihan et A. Marchal.
Ishtar (1971) (12') •Sx/Tape/Narr •Eri
Quartet with Percussion (1972) (8') •4 Sx: SATB/Perc •Eri
Soliloquy (1968) (3'30) •Sx Solo •Eri

GAYFER, James McDonald (1916)
Compositeur canadien, né à Toronto, le 26 III 1916.
Quintet concertante (1972) (4') (to P. BRODIE) •5 Sx: SAATB
    •CMC

GEARHART
Duet Sessions Serious and Amusing •2 Sx: AA or TT •Shaw

GEBHARDT-MANZ
Jazz-schule für Saxophon (1937) •Zim

GEBHARDT, Rochus (1922)

Compositeur allemand, né le 4 XI 1922 à Würzburg. Travailla avec K. Höller et C. Orff.
Sonate •Asx/Pno •adr

GECKELER

Belwin Saxophone Method (3 Volumes) •Bel

GEDDA, Giulio Cesare (1899-1970)

Concerto (1952) •4 Sx: SATB/Pno/Str/Perc

GEDDES, Murray (1950)

Inner time/in her time (1980) (10') •Sx/Reverberant room •CMC

GEE, Harry (1924)

Clarinettiste, saxophoniste, professeur, compositeur, et arrangeur américain, né à Minneapolis (Minnesota), le 20 II 1924. Travailla avec E. Handlon, B. Portnoy, R. McLane, P. Fetler à Paris, avec G. Hamelin, puis avec D. Deffayet et E. Rousseau.
1st Ballade (1962) (to N. Hovey) •Asx (or Fl)/Pno •Ken
2nd Ballade (1981) •Asx (or Fl)/Pno •Ken
25 Daily Exercises (Klosé) •DP
Essay for Saxophone and Piano •Asx/Pno •adr
Festival Solo •1 Sx: S or T/Pno •DP
Four Ferling Etudes •Asx/Pno •DP
Fugue in Baroque Style (1976) •3 Sx: AAT •CPP
Hommage to Vaughan Williams •Asx/Pno •DP
16 Intermediate Duets (various composers, arr. Gee) •2 Sx: AT •CPP
Intrada (1978) (to D. Bilger) •Asx/Pno •adr
Prelude and Passacaglia •5 Sx: SAATB •DP
Progressive and Varied Etudes (1981) •SMC/South
12 Rose Studies for Saxophone •DP
Saxophone Soloists and their Music, 1844-1985 •IUP
Sextet (1978) •6 Sx: SAATTB •adr
12 Saxophone Trios (various composers, arr. Gee) •3 Sx: AAA or AAT •CPP

GEELEN, Mathieu

Compositeur néerlandais.
Invention (1983) (6') •Asx/Electr. Org/Perc •Don

GEHLHAARD, Rolf (1943)

Compositeur américain, d'origines allemandes, né à Breslau, le 30 XII 1943. Aux U.S.A. depuis 1953. Travailla avec Stockhausen et J-Cl. Eloy.
"Rolf Gehlhaard poursuit des recherches acoustiques à partir de la musique électronique." (J. & B. Massin) "Rolf Gehlhaard définit dans son oeuvre deux types d'approches compositionnelles; dans les compositions de type 'analytique,' les sources sonores qui doivent être utilisées sont étudiées, enregistrées, transposées, filtrées, analysées… et le résultat employé pour générer des structures temporelles et spatiales qui manifestent à leur tour les caractéristiques microstructurelles découvertes. Ces structures sont ensuite reliées les unes aux autres afin de construire un processus musical qui récapitule et souligne le procédé analytique. Dans les compositions de type 'synthétique,' les structures fondamentales, temporelles et spatiales, proviennent d'un ensemble de proportions ou de relations numériques; celles-ci, en retour, sont utilisées pour engendrer des structures sonores qui transforment l'ensemble de relations abstraites en un ensemble ordonné de relations spatio-temporelles." (D. J-Y. Bosseur)
Hélix (1967) •Soprano Voice/Sx/Trb/Bass/Pno/Perc •FM

GEISER, Walther (1897)

Compositeur, chef d'orchestre, violoniste, et altiste suisse, né le 16 V 1897 à Zofingen. Travailla avec H. Suter, B. Eldering, et Busoni.
"Geiser's music is small in quantity but of considerable weight, showing a self-critical and carefully calculating attitude. A clear line of development may be traced from a late Romantic style of subjective lyricism, with an evident influence of impressionism, to a manner characterized by clear and unified formal ideas. Baroque elements, particularly fugue, are prevalent in his later music, and the melodic and rhythmic expression is tightened through the reduction of themes to short motifs." (F. Muggler)
Danza notturna, op. 36a (1947) •Asx/Pno •B&N

GEISSLER, Fred

Timelife I (to N. Ramsay) •Asx/Pno

GEKELER, Kenneth

Saxophone Method (1949) (3 Volumes) •Bel

GELALIAN, Boghos

Compositeur libanais.
2 Monodies orientales (1990) (8'30) (to L. Chaikin) •Asx Solo

GELLER, Gabriel

Compositeur allemand.
Osculum infame (1993) •Ssx/Pno+Synth •INM

GENEST, Pierre (1945)

Compositeur canadien.
Phonie-M.A. (1976) (to Quatuor Bourque) •SATB •adr
Saxologie (1971) (to Quatuor Bourque) •SATB •adr
Saxolo (1972) (4'30-5') •Asx Solo •adr

GENIN, Paul Agricol (1832-1904)

Compositeur français ami d'Adolphe Sax.
Air florentin avec variations, op. 65 (1892) •Asx/Pno •Bil
Cantilène, op. 64 (1892) •Asx/Pno •Bil
Fantaisie sur un air florentin •Asx/Pno •Bil
Fantaisie variée sur "Le Carnaval de Venise," op. 14 (Mule) •Asx/Pno •Bil
Mélodie avec variations, op. 63 (1892) •Asx/Pno •Bil
Moderato, op. 57 •Asx/Pno •Bil
Polacca, op. 55 (1887) •Asx/Pno •Bil
6 Morceaux, op. 15 (1875) 1) Pastorale 2) Introduction et polacca 3) Variations sur "Malborough" 4) Fantaisie sur "Il pleut bergère" 5) Fantaisie sur un thème napolitain 6) Fantaisie sur un thème espagnol •Asx/Pno •Bil
Solo de concours du Conservatoire, op. 13 (to A. Sax) •Asx/Pno •Cos/Bil
Tempo di redowa, op. 56 •Asx/Pno •Bil

GENIN, Raphael E. (1896-1975)

Sonate, op. 36 (1969) (to M. Perrin) •Asx/Pno

GENTILUCCI, Armando (1939)

Compositeur italien né à Lecce, le 8 X 1939. Travailla avec Bettinelli et Donatoni.
"Gentilucci has, for a long time, expressed only the negative aspect of his convictions as a left-wing critic, convictions which are decidedly hostile to the decadent and experimantal tendencies in the new music. This may be a result of his twofold activity, which made him doubly aware of the difficulties in accepting Nono's alternatives, or it may be because of his delay in throwing off the pre-war modernism of early works." (C. Annibaldi)
La trame di un labirinto (1986) (8') (to F. Mondelci) •Asx Solo •Ric

GENZMER, Harald (1909)

Compositeur allemand, né à Bremen, le 9 II 1909. Travailla avec P. Hindemith à la Hochschule für Musik de Berlin.
"Genzmer is the leading figure among those German composers who

have continued in the direction of Hindemith. His later work is more propulsive in rhythm and more ambitious in scope." (K. Wörner)

Konzert •Asx/Orch •R&E
Konzertantes Duo •Bsx/Org •R&E
Konzertantes Duo •Asx/Perc •R&E
Paergon (14') 1) Tranquillo 2) Allegro 3) Elégie 4) Finale •Sx Orch: SAATBBs/1 Perc •Pet
Quartett I (1982) (8') (to Rascher Quartet) 1) Tranquillo - allegro 2) Molto tranquillo 3) Allegro giocoso •SATB •WWS/R&E
Quartett II (1989) (16'30) 1) Allegro 2) Amabile tranquillo 3) Intermezzo 4) Final •SATB •R&E
Quartett III (1989) 1) Allegro moderato 2) Fuge 3) Scherzo 4) Intermezzo 5) Finale •SATB •RE
Rhapsodie (1987) (10') •Bsx/Pno •R&E
Sonate (1982) (14') (to C. Peters) 1) Tranquillo - Allegro 2) Lento 3) Burleske 4) Finale •Ssx/Pno •R&E
Sonate (1985) (12') 1) Allegro 2) Largo 3) Finale •Asx/Pno •R&E
Sonatine •Asx/Pno •R&E
Sonatine 1) Ritenuto - Allegro 2) Tranquillo 3) Presto 4) Finale •2 Sx: SA •R&E
10 Stücke •2 Sx: SA •RE

GEORGE, Graham (1912)
Compositeur et chef d'orchestre canadien d'origine anglaise, né à Norwich (Angleterre), en 1922. Vit au Canada depuis 1928. Travailla avec P. Hindemith.
Quartet (1972) 1) Serenely 2) Lively 3) Tranquil 4) Rhythmic and gay •SATB •CMC

GEORGE, Thom Ritter (1942)
Compositeur américain né à Detroit (Michigan), le 23 VI 1942. Travailla avec L. Mennini, W. Barlow, J. La Montaine, et B. Rogers.
Introduction and Dance, op. 150 (1963) (5') (to G. Welker) •Asx/Pno
Suite in Homage to J. S. Bach (1963-76) (19') 1) Prelude: Andante 2) Moderato 3) Canon: vivace 4) Passacaglia: Andante 5) Allegro moderato 6) Allegro (Scherzo) 7) Adagio 8) Epilogo: Più andante •Asx/Pno •South

GERAEDTS, Jaap (1924)
Compositeur, critique musical, et flûtiste néerlandais né le 12 VII 1924 à La Haye. Travailla avec Badings et Andriessen, puis J. Absil.
"For the most part his compositions indicate a link with tradition, finding a starting-point in a basis in tonality." (J. Wouters)
Moto perpetuo (1968) (4') •SATB •Don

GERARD, Marc
Compositeur belge.
Ouverture pour Clevremont •SATB

GERBER, René (1908)
Compositeur suisse, né à Travers (Neuchâtel), le 29 VI 1908. Travailla à Paris avec N. Boulanger et P. Dukas.
"Un des musiciens les plus représentatifs de sa génération." (N. Dufourcq)
"His style at first showed the influence of the recent French music, but later he went his own way and attained a very picturesque and powerful personal manner." (K. von Fischer)
Concertino (1937) •Sx/Tpt/Pno
Concertino (1944) •Sx/Vla/Vcl/Pno
Sonate (15') •Asx/Pno

GERHARD, Fritz Chr. (1911)
Compositeur allemand.
Concerto breve (14') •Asx/Str Orch •Sal

Fantaisie "Ben venga amre" (1970) (7') (to S. Rascher) •SATB •AMP
Rhapsodie (1980) (to C. Peters) •Ssx/Pno

GERHARD, Roberto (1896-1970)
Compositeur anglais, d'origine espagnole, né à Valls (Catalogne), le 25 IX 1896; mort à Cambridge, le 5 I 1970. Travailla avec Granados et Pedrell à Barcelona, puis avec A. Schoenberg à Vienne. S'installa en Angleterre lors de la guerre d'Espagne, en 1938.
"Dodécaphoniste convaincu." (G. Gefen)
"The one vital characteristic of Gerhard's work which was fundamental to every piece of music he wrote was the basic fact of rhythmic pulsation. It was this apparently alien force which, once harnessed to the cause of his serial ideas, enabled him to give such rare and powerful expression to his vision of music as a buoyant art: as the techniqqe of setting sounds in motion and of propelling them through the space of their collective time span." (S. Bradshaw)
Quartet (to Rascher Quartet) •SATB

GERHARDT, Frank
Compositeur allemand.
Geschichten vom Erwachen (1993) •Ssx/Pno •INM

GERIN, Roland
Suite en concert (1978) •SATB

GERMAN, Edward Sir (1862-1936)
Morris Dance (Thompson) •AATB •Alf
Pastorale et Bourrée (Voxman) •Tsx/Pno •Rub
Torch Dance (Thompson) •AATB •Alf

GERMETEN, Gunnar (1947)
Applaus (1985) •Cl/Sx/Trb/Accordion

GERSCHEFSKI, Edwin (1909)
Compositeur, pianiste, et professeur américain, né à Meriden (Connecticut), le 19 VI 1909. Travailla avec Schnabel et Schillinger.
"In general, his music is marked by strong rhythmic propulsion, a clear lyrical strain and frequent ostinato passages." (D. Campbell)
America, op. 44, no. 6 (1962) •Fl/Cl/Asx/Bsn •CFE
America, op. 44, nos. 8 & 9 •Ensemble of 4 Winds/Pno
America, op. 44, no. 13 •Fl/Cl/Asx/Bsn •CFE
America, op. 44, no. 14a •Fl/Cl/Asx/Tpt/Bsn/Pno •CFE
Workout, op. 10 (1933) •Asx/Pno •ACA

GERSHWIN, George (1898-1937)
Andante and Final (from *Rhapsody in Blue*) (Stone) •1 Sx: A or T/ Pno •MPHC
Blues (Sears) •Bb Sx/Pno •WaB
A Gershwin Fantasy (R. Martino) •Asx/Pno
Liza (Holcombe) •SATB •SMC
The Man I love (Marshall) •SATB •APA
Music Spelles (23'30) (Londeix) •SATB
Oh! Lady Be Good •Bb Sx/Pno •WaB
Oh! Lady Be Good (A. Marshall) •SATB •APA
2nd Prelude (Rascher) •Asx/Pno •MPHC
3 Preludes (Perconti) (published separately) •SATB •Ron
3 Preludes (Radnofsky) •Asx/Pno •Lem
3 Preludes (W. Schlei) •SATB •Uni
Rhapsody in Blue •3 Sx: AAT •Sal
Rhapsody in Blue (Worley) •Pno/Sx Ensemble
Rialto Ripples (Perconti) •SATB •Ron
Strike up the Band (Albam) •SATB/Orch
Suite American stories (16') (Londeix) •12 Sx: SnoSSAAATTTBBBs
Summertime (Beun) •5 Sx: SAATB •Mar
Summertime (Teal) •6 Sx: AATTBB

GERVAISE, Claude (16th century)
Bransle Gay (Harvey) •SATB •Che

GEUSEN, F.
Compositeur belge.
Saxo trio (to N. Nozy) •1 Sx: A+T/Pno/Perc

GHEZZO, Dinu
Pontica II •Fl/Sx/2 Tpt/2 Hn/Pno/Narr •SeMC
Sound shapes - solo wind •Fl/Ob/Cl/Sx/Bsn •SeMC

GHIDONI, Armando
Compositeur italien.
Blues & Boogie (1991) •SATB •CoMu
Douce chansonnette (1989) (5') (to B. Totaro) •Asx/Pno •Led
E. S. (1986) (2'30) •Asx/Pno •Ma
Mélodie (1991) (3'15) •1 Sx: A or T/Pno •Led
Pièce brève (1994) •Bb or Eb Sx/Pno •Led
Prelude et Fugue (in stile jazz) •SATB •adr
Quadricromatik •SATB •adr

GIAMPIERI, Alamiro
Metodo progressivo (1954) •Ric
16 Studi giornalieri di perfezionamento (1954) •Ric

GIARO, Paolo
Compositeur italien.
Su in aire (1992) •Asx/Live electronics

GIAZOTTO
Adagio in G minor on a theme of Albinoni •Asx/Pno •Ric

GIBBONS, Orlando (1583-1625)
Fantasia à 3 (Athmann) •3 Sx: SAB •K&D
Fantasia for Three •3 Sx: AAT •Mus
Fantazia (Hemke) •SATB •South

GIBBS, Cecil Armstrong (1889-1960)
Compositeur anglais, né à Gret Baddow (Essex), le 10 VIII 1889; mort à Chelmsford, le 12 V 1960. Travailla avec Vaughan Williams.
"Gibbs published an enormous quantity of utility music for choirs and amateur orchestras, and achieved an immense commercial success with his slow waltz *Dusk* in the late 1940s." (S. Banfield)
Harlequinade •3 Sx •Pet

GIBSON, Kenneth
Compositeur anglais.
Prologue and Epilogue (1968) (5') •5 Sx: SAATB
Quartet (1972) (17') (to London Saxophone Quartet) 1) Andantino 2) Andante 3) Prestissimo 4) Allegro 5) Andantino •SATB
Symphony for 18th Century (1973) (3'30) •SATB •SM

GIEFER, Willy
Compositeur allemand.
Saxopercumovi (1993) •1 Sx: S+A+T/Perc •INM

GILARDIN, Jean-Paul
Compositeur français.
Allegro (1984) •Asx/Pno •adr
Concertino (1986) •Asx/Pno •adr
2 Danses yougoslaves •2 Sx: ST/Pno •adr

GILLET, Bruno
Hornpipes (to J-P. Caens) •Ob/Cl/Asx/Bsn

GILLET, Ernest (1856-1940)
Caprice, Gavotte (Lefebre) •Asx/Pno •CF

GILLET, Roger
Compositeur français.
Promenade •SATB •Mar
Quartet-valse (to Quatuor de Paris) •SATB •Mar

GILLETTE, Mickey
Saxophone Method (1944)

GILLINGHAM, David
Compositeur américain.
Sonata (1988) (15') •Asx/Pno

GILMORE, Cortland P.
Martinello •Tsx/Pno •Rub

GILSON, Paul (1865-1942)
Compositeur et pédagogue belge, né à Bruxelles, le 15 VI 1865, où il est mort, le 3 IV 1942. Travailla avec Gevaert. Prix de Rome (1889).
"Sa culture extraordinaire, sa curiosité pour les nouvelles recherches de style et sa conscience pédagogique, attirèrent à lui un grand nombre de jeunes compositeurs qui le choisirent comme maître, particulièrement pour l'étude de l'orchestration. Ses plus fervents disciples se groupèrent sous le titre de 'Synthétistes' (Poot, de Bourguignon, Brenta, Bernier, Schoemaker, Dejoncker, Strens, et Otlet)." (R. Vannes) "Sa musique est d'une grande richesse orchestrale, qui évoque les rutilances de Rimsky-Korsakov. Les lignes mélodiques et la construction harmonique portent la trace de l'influence debussyste sur un goût très sûr." (P. Wolff)
"Though of Flemish race, Gilson is the spiritual descendant of the Russian school, whose works he studied with marked attention. It revealed a most remarkable mastery of orchestral technique, a strong sense of picturesque instrumentation, an uncommon knowledge of harmony joined to an interesting originality of invention, together with a clever employment of rhythms taken from Oriental folk-music." (M. Kufferath) "Gilson's importance lies above all in his activities as a teacher." (H. Vanhulst)
1er Concerto (1902) (11'30) (to E. Hall) 1) Deciso 2) Andante ritenuto 3) Presto scherzando •Asx/Orch •Ger/An
2me Concerto (1902) (10'30) •Asx/Orch (2222/4231/Perc/Str) or (1121/2210/Perc/Str) •RTB
Fackelzug (Strauwen) •5 Sx
Pièces romantiques (1933-36) (32') 1) Scherzetto 2) Romance 3) Arioso 4) Impromptu 5) Cantabile 6) Alla Polacca 7) Barcarolle 8) Improvisata •Asx/Pno •An
Quatuor (unfinished [inachevé]) •SATB

GIMENO, J.
Compositeur espagnol.
Caprici •Asx/Orch or Pno

GINER, Bruno (1960)
Compositeur français, né à Perpignan, le 13 XI 1960. Travailla notamment avec D. Tosi, J-L. Campana, S. Srawley, et Ivo Malec.
Con brio (1991) (13-17') •Vcl/Bsx/Perc/Tape
Entrechocs I (1985) (14') (to D. Kientzy) •1 Sx: Sno+S+B/Tape/ Synth
Io (1992) (8') (to S. *Bertocchi*) •Bsx Solo

GINER, C.
Compositeur espagnol.
Conversaciones •Asx/Cl •Piles

GINGRAS, Guy (1961)
Compositeur québécois, né le 22 IX 1961 à St-Raymond-de-Portneuf. Travailla avec P. Bourque, P. Houdy, Cl. Pepin, J. Faubert, et G. Tremblay.
"Guy Gingras se produit régulièrement dans des orchestres de jazz.

Souhaitant que sa musique accessible, son langage, bien que conservateur dans la notation, présente des combinaisons harmoniques recherchées. L'innovation n'est pas pour lui un but. Vivant en terre francophone, entouré d'anglophones, Guy Gingras attache une grande importance à ses origines latines, mais sait tirer profit de l'influence américaine toute proche."

Anagramme (1984) (12') (to J. Royer) •SATB •Med
Choral et Fugue (1982) (12') •SATB •Med
Choral et variations (1984) •Asx/Org •Med
3 Duos scabreux (1987) 1) L'embarrassant 2) L'indécent 3) Le grivois •2 Sx: AA •Med
Equistares, au seuil des saisons (1989) (17') 1) Equinoxe d'automne 2) Solstice d'hiver 3) Equinoxe de printemps 4) Solstice d'été •Asx Solo •Med
Fugue (1984) •SATB •Med
Girandoles (1992) (9') (to Quatuor Réunion) (2 movements) •SATB •Med
Perseides (1993) (to S. Bertrand) •Tsx Solo •Med
Trois duos scabreux (1987) (7') •3 Sx: AAA •Med

GIORDANI, Giuseppe (1753-1798)
An 18th Century Air •Eb Sx or Bb Sx/Pno •Mus

GIORDANO, John (1937)
Compositeur américain, né à Ijjunkirk, le 11 XII 1937.
Fantasy (1968) (5') (to Fr. Daneels) •Asx/Pno •South
Quatuor (1966) (to Quatuor Belge de Saxophones) •SATB

GIORGIO, Babbini
Compositeur italien.
Suite Medioevale •Sx/Bass

GIOVANNINI, Caesar (1925)
Pianiste et compositeur américain, né à Chicago.
Rhapsody (1977) •Tsx/Pno •APC
Romance (1988) (4') •1 Sx: B or A/Pno •South

GIPPS, Ruth (1921)
Compositeur et chef d'orchestre anglais né à Bexhill-on-Sea le 20 II 1921. Travailla avec Morris, Jacob, et Vaughan Williams.
"Her works showed some influence of Vaughan Williams, though with a degree of originality that has been developed in a brilliant and vigorous manner in her later music." (L. Beckett)
Seascape, op. 53 (1958) (6') •10 woodwind instruments •KP

GIRARD, Anthony (1959)
Compositeur français, né le 14 V 1959 dans l'état de New York. Etudes à Paris. Premier Prix au Concours Marcel Josse (1981).
Trio (1981) •Ob/Asx/Cl •adr

GIRARD, L.
Le sommeil de Polyphème •CBsSx Solo

GIRARDIN, Jean-Paul (1955)
Compositeur français.
L'Insolitude (1983) •Asx/Vibr/Str Orch

GIRNATIS, Walter (1894)
Compositeur autodidacte allemand, né à Hambourg.
Sonate (1962) •Asx/Pno •Sik

GISSELMAN, Philippe (1953)
Compositeur français, né à Chaumont. Travailla avec S. Ortega et P. Boulez.
Rebonds (Pièce interactive) (1989) (15') •Bsx/Ordinateur •adr
Série L. (4'30) (to S. Bertocchi) •Ssx Solo •adr

GITTLEMAN, Arthur
Israeli Folk Song •Asx

GIUFFRE, James Peter (Jimmy) (1921)
Clarinettiste, saxophoniste, et compositeur de jazz américain, né le 26 IV 1921 à Dallas. Travailla avec B. Raeburn, Jimmy Dorsey, B. Rich, et W. Herman.
Fine •Tsx/Guit/Vibr/Pno/2 Bass/Perc •MJQ
Four Brothers •3 Sx: ATB
Jazz Phrasing and Interpretation •Eb Sx •B&B
Suspensions •MJQ

GIULIANO, Giuseppe
Tempi della mente (1986) (11') •1 Sx: Sno+S/Tape

GLASER, Werner Wolf (1910)
Compositeur et chef d'orchestre suédois, d'origine allemande, né le 14 IV 1910 à Cologne. Travailla avec P. Hindemith.
"In his extensive output, Glaser develops a modernist tonal language." (H-G. P.) "His music is of enormous variety of genre and style. In the later work he has developed a formal freedom by avoiding conventional thematic working; he has written for unusual instrumental combinations, and his polyphonic writing is often harsh, though not without warmth." (R. Utterström) "In his extensive output, Glaser develops a modernist tonal language, based on his studies under Paul Hindemith. His confident handling of melody and his inspired treatment of form bear witness to the fluency of his inspiration and to his attainment of a personal style of craftsmanship." (H-G. P.)
Allegro, Cadenza e Adagio (1950) (9') (to S. Rascher) •Asx/Pno •STIM
Canto (1970) (6') (to S. Rascher) •Ssx/Str Orch •STIM
Concertino (1935) (to S. Rascher) •Asx/Orch •STIM
Concerto (1981) (16') •Tsx/Str Orch •STIM
Duo (1981) (9') •Asx/Vcl •STIM
Duo (1985) (12') •Asx/Pno •STIM
3 Fancies (1982) (12') •8 Sx: SnoSSAATTB •STIM
4 Kleine Stücke, op. 8a (1934) (6') (to S. Rascher) •4 Sx: SAAT •Pres
Konsert (1980) (17') (to C. Rascher) 1) Andante 2) Grave 3) Allegro palpando •Ssx/Orch •Ton
Konzertstück (1992) •Bsx/Str Orch •SMIC
Kvartett (1950) (to Rascher Quartet) •Asx/Vln/Vla/Vcl •STIM
Linda - Quartett (1970-85) (17') •Bsx/Vln/Vla/Vcl •STIM
Little Quartet (1970) (to S. Rascher) •Asx/Vln/Vcl/Pno •STIM
4 Phantasies (1982) (12') (to Rascher Saxophone Quartet) •SATB •STIM
3 Pieces (1981) (12') (to S. Rascher) •11 Sx: SSAAAATTBBBs •STIM
Quartet (1984) (17'30) 1) Sostenuto - Presto 2) Interludio 3) Vigoroso •SATB •SMIC/STIM
Quintet (1964-77) (15') (to S. Rascher) •5 Sx: SAATB •STIM
Ritornello (1989) (7') •2 Sx •SMIC
Solosonat (1936) (10') •Asx Solo •STIM
Sonata (1986) (15') •Bsx/Pno •STIM
3 Sonaten im alten Stil (1934) (12') (to S. Rascher) •Asx Solo •STIM
5 Strukturer •Soprano Voice/Fl/Sx/Vcl •STIM
Suite No. 3, op. 16 (1935) (8') (to S. Rascher) •Asx/Str Orch or Pno •STIM
Tale (1977) (12') (to L. Bangs) •Bsx/5 Perc •STIM
Triade (1992) •Fl/Marimba/Bsx
Trio (1981) (10') •3 Sx: ATB •ECA
Trio (1981) (14') •Ob/Asx/Vcl •STIM
Trio (1989) (14') (to L. Patrick) •3 Sx: ATB/Pno •SMIC
Variations on a Gavotte by Corelli •Asx/Pno •Chap/Pres

Variations on a Theme by Paganini (Carnaval of Venize) •Asx/Pno •Pres

GLASS, Philip (1937)

Compositeur américain né le 31 I 1937 à Baltimore (Maryland). Travailla avec Nadia Boulanger et Ravi Shankar à Paris.

"Partant d'une musique fondée sur une simple monophonie (une ligne de musique sans harmonie ni contrepoint jouée à l'unisson par exemple), j'ai introduit l'idée que la musique, quoique jouée rythmiquement à l'unisson, peut être jouée avec des parties différentes sur des 'plates-formes' différentes qui bougeraient en mouvement parallèles, contraires ou semblables, les uns par rapport aux autres." (Ph. GLASS) "Toutes les limites de Philip Glass sont inscrites dans sa musique, au premier degré: répétition à outrance, simplicité rythmique et harmonique, système élaboré une fois pour toutes il y a vingt-cinq ans, et quasiment immuable depuis… Il suffit de sélectionner cinq minutes au hasard dans cette musique pour être à même d'en stigmatiser les tics, les redites, les facilités. Sa production s'inscrit au moins autant dans l'univers du show-biz que dans celui de la 'musique contemporaine.'" (J-E. FOUSNAQUER) "Toute une frange de compositeurs américains, non directement concernés par les discussions et palabres sur les problèmes d'écriture et de langage de leurs confrères européens, vont s'engager sur les voies précédemment ouvertes par Morton Feldman ou Earle Brown et, simplifiant à l'extrême les données de départ de la composition, créer ce courant de musique dit 'répétitive,' qui ne désavoue pas la tonalité, se construit sur un principe rythmique, se déroule par variations imperceptibles, et où l'électronique prend souvent sa place, mêlée à l'instrumental. Les trois représentants les plus éminents de cette nouvelle école sont Terry Riley, Steve Reich et Philip Glass." (J. & B. MASSIN) "Indian rhythm influenced Glass in composing a series of ensemble pieces which, though they vary considerably in density, all share the technique of extending and contracting rhythmic figures in a stable diatonic framework. This may suggest some similarity with the work of Steve Reich, but Glass' music differs essentially in points of rythmic procedure; it is also, as performed by his own ensemble, much louder and stronger in sound, drawing close in this respect to rock music." (GROVE)

8 for John Gibson (1968) •Ssx Solo
Play (1966) •2 Sx

GLASSMAN, Ben

The Famous Style Series of Saxophone Studies

GLAZOUNOV, Alexander Konstantinovich (1865-1936)

Compositeur russe, né à Saint-Pétersbourg, le 10 VIII 1865, mort à Paris, le 21 III 1936. Travailla avec Rimsky-Korsakov.

"Glazounov est considéré comme le dernier représentant de la grande école russe du XIXe siècle." (LAROUSSE) "Foncièrement *symphonique*." (N. DUFOURCQ) "Point de nationalisme spectaculaire, mais un caractère russe en profondeur (une âme, un sentiment russe et non pas de constantes références au folklore)." (R. HOFMANN) "Sa gloire fut éphémère, sans doute parce que le caractère russe de son oeuvre s'attache—assez superficiellement—davantage aux idées littéraires de départ qu'à la matière musicale proprement dite: l'influence allemande est évidente." (J. & B. MASSIN) "Quelques compositions non dépourvues de mérites attestent d'une part l'influence romantique de Schumann, d'autre part celle du style national hérité du Groupe des Cinq." (A. LISCHKÉ)

"His music is often regarded as academic; yet there is a flow of rhapsodic eloquence that places Glazounov in the Romantic school." (BAKER) "With Russian music, Glazounov has a significant place because he succeeded in reconciling Russianism and Europeanism. There was a streak of academicism in Glazounov which at times overpowered his inspiration, an eclecticism which lacks the ultimate stamp of originality." (B. SCHWARZ)

Canzona, 2 Variations and Scherzo (GEE) •AATB •adr
Concerto en Mib (1934) (14') (to S. RASCHER) •Asx/Str Orch •Led
In modo religioso (BETTONEY) •2 Cl/Asx/Bsn (or BsCl) •CF
In modo religioso (EYMANN) •AATB •Bel
Quatuor en Sib, op. 109 (1932) (24') (to Quatuor Mule) 1) Allegro piu mosso 2) Canzona varie 3) Finale: Allegro moderato, piu mosso •SATB •B&H
Sérénade espagnole (LEESON) •Asx/Pno •Hil/Col

GLEMINOV, Michail

Compositeur autrichien.
Coyote (1993) •Bsx/Tape •INM

GLEN, Rainer

Einfach für Drei (198x) (5 movements) •3 Sx: AAT •Schu

GLICK, Srul Irving (1934)

Compositeur canadien, né à Toronto. Travailla avec J. Weinzweig, O. Morawetz, et J. Beckwith, puis avec D. Milhaud, M. Saguer, et M. Deutch.

Lament and Cantorial Chant (1985) •Sx/Str Orch •CMC
Sonata (1992) (10') 1) Andante 2) Calm 3) Fast •Asx/Pno
Suite Hebraique (1968) (14'45) (to P. BRODIE) 1) Cantorial Chant 2) Chasidic Dance 3) Hora 4) Lullaby 5) Dialogue 6) Circle Dance •Ssx/Pno

GLIERE, Reinhold (1875-1956)

Russian Sailor's Dance (HURRELL) •Bsx/Pno •Rub

GLINKA, Mikhail (1804-1857)

The Lark - Romance (BELLINI) •Asx/Pno •CF
Romance Melody (SCHUMANN) •Bb Sx/Pno •JS

GLINKOWSKI, Aleksander (1941)

Compositeur polonais, né à Stiring-Wendel, le 4 IV 1941. Travailla avec B. Szabelski, W. Szalonek et, à Paris, avec I. Xenakis.

Capriccio (to P. PRONKO) •Contralto Voice/Bsx/Pno •adr
Sequentia (1971) (11') (to J-M. LONDEIX) •Asx/Pno •adr

GLOBOKAR, Vinko (1934)

Compositeur et tromboniste français d'origine yougoslave né le 7 "Srpnja" 1934 à Andernyu. A Paris depuis 1955. Travailla avec R. Leibowitz et L. Berio.

"Dans les années soixante-dix, il se livrait au sein du New Phonic Art Ensemble à d'exubérantes improvisations qui fleuraient bon l'expérimentation sauvage. L'homme collait à son instrument. Aujourd'hui, il semble avoir rangé son trombone et s'être assagi. Assombri, peut-être. Ce musicien toujours à l'affût du monde et de la société ne manque pas de raisons de broyer du noir, à l'heure où survient la tragédie yougoslave." (J-E. FOUSNAQUER) "Il fait partie de cette nouvelle génération de musiciens pour qui la pratique musicale correspond à une activité globale, le travail de composition étant indissociable de celui de l'interprète; sa formation de virtuose lui permet d'aborder la composition d'une manière spécifique, d'introduire dans son projet compositionnel une attention particulière à l'instrument, mais aussi à l'instrumentiste, aux rapports intimes qui naissent entre eux." (D. J-Y. BOSSEUR) "Globokar's cosmopolitan approach, his prodigious technique and his riotous imagination, his early interest in jazz and his theatrical sense of humour have all combined to produce a series of original works." (N. O'LOUGHLIN)

Discours V (Ouverture et final) (1982) (22') •SATB •Pet
Plan (1965) Tsx/BsCl/Cnt/Trb •Pet
Vostellung (1976) •1 Soloist/2 Instruments •Pet

GLOVER, Sarah Ann (1786-1867)

Rose of Tralee •Asx/Pno •Mol

GLUCK, Christoph Willibald (1714-1787)

Ach, Ich habe sie verloren •Bb Sx/Pno •Mol
Air (from Orfeo) (MAGANINI) •Bb Sx/Pno •Mus
Air de ballet (JOHNSON) •AATB •Rub
Armide - Andante et Musette (MULE) •Asx or Bb Sx/Pno •Led
Divinities de Styx (MAGANINI) •Bb Sx/Pno •Mus
Gavotte (MULE) •Asx or Bb Sx/Pno •Led
Grazioso (BAUDRIER) •Bb Sx/Pno •Mol
Iphigénie en Tauride (CLASSENS-MERIOT) •SATB •Com
Orphée - Scène des Champs-Elysées (MULE) •Asx/Pno •Led
Pièce récréative (LETELLIER) •3 Sx: AAA or TTT •Mar
Two Classic Airs (MAGANINI-CLARK) •1 Sx: A or T/Pno •Mus

GNATTALI, Radamès (1906)

Compositeur, chef d'orchestre, et pianiste brésilien, né à Pôrto Alegre, le 27 I 1906.

"He achieved wide popularity through his music for radio serials, and through his skillful arrangements and orchestrations of fashionable popular tunes and dance rhythms. During the 1950s Gnattali deliberately attempted to remove himself from music nationalism. He then turned to neo-romantic and neo-classical molds while maintaining the light style often associated with symphonic jazz." (G. BEHAGUE)

Brasiliana No. 8 (1957) •Tsx/Pno •Ric

GNIOT, Walerian Jozef (1902)

Compositeur et professeur polonais, né à Proszyska, le 8 XI 1902. Travailla avec Wiechowicz.

"His compositions are frequently based on folk themes from Wielkopolska." (M. HANUSZEWSKA)

Allegro de concert (1951) •Asx/Pno

GOCA, Vladimir

Compositeur tchécoslovaque.

Etude •3 Sx: SAT
Musica camera •SATB
Na dostizich •SATB
Suite No. 1 •SATB
Suite No. 2 •SATB

GOCHT, J.

Impressions 65 •Asx/Pno •AMP

GODAR, Vladimir (1956)

2 Frammenti (1977) •Narr/Sx/Bass/Pno

GODARD, Benjamin (1849-1895)

Berceuse (BROOKE) •AATB •CF
Berceuse (ROBERTS) •Bb Sx/Pno •CF
Berceuse de Jocelyn (FERNAND) •Eb Sx or Bb Sx/Pno •Mol
Jocelyn - Berceuse (BUCHTEL) •Asx/Pno •Kjos

GODEL, Didier

Compositeur français.

Quintette (1975) •5 Sx: SAATB •adr

GODFREY, Paul Corfield (1950)

Compositeur anglais.

Sonata (1979) (9') 1) Andante - larghetto 2) Allegro vivace 3) Andante cantabile •Tsx/Pno •BMIC

GODFREY-HARRIS (1905)

Lucy Song •Bsx/Pno •CBet

GODFROID

Valsette •Bb Sx/Pno •TM

GODZINSKY, George de (1914)

Compositeur finlandais, né le 5 VII 1914.

Pièce romantique (1966) (4'15) •Asx/Orch (2121/2220/Perc/Harp/Str) •FMIC
Sxysrunoelma ("*Autumn elegy*") (1969) (4'30) •Asx/Orch (2121/2200/Timp/Str) •FMIC

GOEHR, Alexander (Peter) (1932)

Compositeur anglais d'origine allemande, né le 10 VIII 1932 à Berlin. Travailla avec Hall et Schoenberg, puis à Paris, avec O. Messiaen. Fixé en Angleterre dès 1933.

"Fait d'abord partie de la célèbre "Manchester School," avec Davies et Birtwistle, puis change de voie pour le sérialisme polyphonique, où fusionnent Messiaen et Schoenberg (1974-76). Retour à une écriture plus traditionnelle et à des formes polyphoniques du passé (1980-85), puis recherche de synthèse entre les formes de la sonate et de la variation (1987-92)." (J-N. von der WEID) "S'il manifesta immédiatement ses affinités avec la seconde Ecole de Vienne, il semble cependant que les traits post-romantiques de Schoenberg l'attiraient davantage que le rigoureux sérialisme de Webern. En 1968, ses saynètes musicales pour le Music Theatre Ensemble, qu'il dirigeait, avaient un contenu volontiers iconoclaste ou politique. Après 1970, Goehr se détachait progressivement des recherches 'technologiques et matérialiste' de l'avant-garde pour se tourner vers un style de composition 'plus humain et traditionnel.' " (G. GEFEN)

"Goehr's own attitude to music-making has been humanistic rather than therapeutic, political or mystical, and he has judged the many contradictory fashions since World War II neither from an 'avant-garde' nor 'conservative' standpoint, but according to whether they have tended to enrich the language or to distort or suppress some of its possibilities." (B. NORTHCOTT)

Shadowplay, op. 30 (1976) (20') •Actor+Tenor Voice/Narr+Fl/Asx/Hn/Vcl/Pno •Sch

GOEYENS, Alphonse

Compositeur belge.

Berceuse •Asx/Pno •HE
English Melody •1 Sx: A or T/Pno •HE
Introduction et Polonaise •Asx/Harmonie •An
Prélude, Sarabande et Final •Asx/Pno •EMB

GOEYENS, F.

Solitude •Asx/Pno •Scz

GOJKOVIC, Dusan (1931)

Trompettiste de jazz et compositeur allemand d'origine yougoslave, né à Jajce, le 14 X 1931.

Swinging macedonia (1966) (35') •Tpt/2 Sx: AT/Pno/Bass/Perc •adr

GOLBERG, Johann Gottlieb (1727-1756)

Le Chardonneret (ROMBY) •Asx/Pno •PB

GOLDBERG, Theo

Compositeur canadien.

Anti thesis (1974) (to D. PULLEN) •Asx/Pno or Tape

GOLDBERG, William B. (1917)

Compositeur américain, né à New York, le 24 I 1917. Travailla avec J. Weinberg.

Pelagos (1971) (to K. DORN) •Narr/Asx/Tape •adr
Sonatina (1987) •Asx/Pno •adr

GOLDMAN, Edwin Franco (1878-1956)

Air and Variations (BELLINI) •Eb Sx/Pno •CF
American Caprice •Tsx/Pno •CF
Reponse - Waltz •Tsx/Pno •ECS

GOLDMANN, Marcel (1936)

Compositeur français, né à Paris, le 28 IV 1936. Travailla avec M. Deutch.

"Avec ses *Hével*, Marcel Goldmann montre qu'on peut faire du cohérent avec des éléments qui ne le sont point, sous réserve d'avoir un sens musical." (N. M.)

Hével II (1970) (10') (to P. PAREILLE) •Ob/Cl/Asx/Bsn •EFM
Trio (1985) (20') •3 Sx

GOLDSTAUB, Paul R. (1947)

Compositeur américain né le 8 VII 1947. Travailla avec W. Benson et K. Husa.

Graphic IV (1973) (to R. CARAVAN) •Asx/Celesta or Pno •DP
Sonata (1972) (8'30) •Asx/Pno or Celesta •adr
3 Pieces (1966-67) (3'30) 1) Eolian dance 2) Pastorale 3) Duet •Asx/Pno •adr

GOLDSTEIN, Malcolm (1936)

Compositeur américain, né à New York, le 27 III 1936.

Frog Pond at Dusk (1970) (duration indeterminée) •Wind & String Instruments •adr
Ludlow Blues (1963) (12') •Asx/Fl/Trb/Tape •adr

GOLESTAN, Stan (1875-1956)

Compositeur roumain, né à Bucarest, le 26 V 1875; mort à Paris, le 22 IV 1956, où il a fait une brillante carrière de critique musical. Travailla avec V. d'Indy, A. Roussel, et P. Dukas.

"Se retrouvent dans ses oeuvres, les rythmes, les intervalles, les dessins mélodiques typiques du folklore roumain auquel, à la suite d'Enesco, il a donné droit de cité dans la musique savante." (N. DUFOURCQ) "Il nous apparaît sous deux aspects contradictoires, qui ne parviennent pas à se concilier harmonieusement: il y avait en lui une veine populaire, un instinct de l'improvisation à la fois brillante et pittoresque, caractéristique de l'art du rhapsode, qui s'accommodaient assez mal des rigueurs des grandes formes." (R. BERNARD)

"His works are impregnated with the poetry and colour of Rumanian folklore, wich gives them a tender and candid beauty, and he makes skillful use of melodies. He has been particulary successful in the composition of chamber music, though he has also written orchestral works." (GROVE) "Essentially a lyrical composer, Golestan summarized his standpoint in his preface to the *Doines et chansons* of 1922, 'I wanted to achieve a musical recollection of the raw, melancholy, pastoral atmosphere that vibrates in our open skies.' " (V. COSMA)

Divertissement champêtre (to Quatuor de la Garde Républicaine) •SATB

GOLTERMAN, George (1824-1898)

Cantilena (TEAL) •Bsx/Pno •GSch
Cantilena (WEBB) •Asx/Pno •CF/Bel
Concerto No. 4, op. 65 (TEAL) •1 Sx: A or T/Pno

GONZALES, Jean-François

Page d'album •Sx/Harp/Bass

GONZALEZ, Luis Jorge

Compositeur américain d'origine argentine, né à San Juan. Travailla avec E. Leuchter à Buenos Aires, puis, à Baltimore dans le Maryland, avec E. Brown et R. Hall Lewis.

Israel Concertino (1992) (to D. GORDON) •8 Sx: SSAATTBBs
Partita para un Virrey Mestizo (1992) (12'30) (to T. MYER & D.GORDON) 1) Galliarda 2) Zarabanda 3) Folia •8 Sx: SSAATTBBs

GOODE, Jack C. (1921)

Organiste et compositeur américain, né à Marlin (Texas), le 20 I 1921. Travailla avec B. Rozsa et L. Sowerby.

Dance of Joy (to F. HEMKE) •Sx/Org
Petite Suite (1964) (to M. TAYLOR) 1) Ouverture 2) Elegie 3) Impromptu •AATB •adr
Rondino (1962) (5'30) •Asx/Band or Pno •Kjos

GOODMAN, Alfred Grant (1920)

Compositeur allemand, né à Berlin, le 1 III 1920. Travailla aux U.S.A. avec H. Cowell et O. Luening.

"A skilled arranger, Goodman has proved adept at producing music with a direct appeal." (A. OTT)

Divertimento (1950) (12') •3 Sx: AAT •RG
3 Chants •Voice/Sx/Harp (or Pno) •adr
3 Gesänge für Gresang •Soprano Voice/Fl/Ob/Asx/Cl/Vla/Vcl/ Prepared Pno/Guit/Perc •adr
Duo (1968) (11'30) 1) Allegro giusto 2) Recitativo 3) Scherzoso •Asx/Harp •adr
Suite (1990) (13') (to S. RASCHER) •Ssx/Asx/Harp/Bass •adr
Universum (1993) •Asx/Harps •INM
We Two (1981) (7') •1 Sx: S+T/Vcl

GOODWIN, Gordon

Compositeur et professeur américain.

Anonymous V (1971) (6') (to H. JOHNSON) •Asx Solo •SeMC
The Gold Commode (1968) •5 Sx/5 Tpt/4 Hn (ad lib)/4 Trb/Tuba/ Pno/Guit/Bass/Perc •adr
Heterophonie Conuberations •5 Sx: SATTB/Electr. Bass •adr
Levittation •Sx/Tpt/Pno/Bass/Perc •adr
Quiet Canzona (1978) •SATB •adr

GORBUISKIA, Vladimir

Compositeur russe.

Concerto •Asx/Jazz Orch

GORBULSKIS, Benjaminas (1925)

Concerto (1969) •Asx/Orch

GORDON, Jacob

Three Movements •SATB •Sha

GÖRNER, Hans Georg (1908)

Compositeur et organiste allemand né à Berlin, le 23 IV 1908. Travailla avec L. Schrattenholz.

"In his preference for Baroque forms he stands close to Reger; his brilliant orchestration is used to dramatic, and sometimes humorous effect." (GROVE)

Concertino, op. 31 (1957) 1) Allegro moderato 2) Moderato, all' antico 3) Recitativo cantando 4) Rondo con allegrezza •2 Sx: AT/Orch or Pno •Hof

GORNSTON, David (18xx-19xx)

Musicien, saxophoniste, et professeur américain.

All Chords (1948) •GM
Brahms Studies (1962) •DG
Chopin Studies (1944) •DG
Dailies (1965) •Kjos
40 Rhythm Etudes (1949) •DG
Fun with Scales (Ben PAISNER) •DG
Fun with Swing (1964) •DG
Peer International Method •Shu/Peer
Progressive Swing Readings (1944)
Saxophone Mechanisms (1945) •DG
Saxophone Velocite (HUFFNAGLE) (1947) •Mor
Streamlined Etudes (1968) •DG
Valse Moment (HANSON) •Eb Sx/Pno •CF
Valse Syncopate (HANSON) •Eb Sx/Pno •CF
Weird Etudes (1936)

GORTHEIL, Bernhard
Compositeur allemand.
Die Kirmes (1993) •3 Sx/Cl •INM

GOSSEC, François Joseph (1734-1829)
La fête au village (MULE) •Asx/Pno •Led
Gavotte (DAWSON) •Asx/Pno •South
Ouverture •2 Sx: AA •Mol
Sonata •Bb Sx/Pno •Mol

GOTKOVSKY, Ida (1933)
Compositeur français, né à Paris, le 8 VIII 1933. Travailla avec N. Gallon et Tony Aubin.
"Langage conventionnel." (H. SOULE) "L'esthétique d'Ida Gotkovsky révèle une structure rigoureuse ainsi qu'une thématique se basant sur l'impressionnisme." (H. KNEIFER)
Brillance (1974) (12') 1) Déclamé 2) Désinvolte 3) Dolcissimo 4) Final •Asx/Pno •EFM
Concerto (1966) (16'30) (to M. MULE) 1) Allegro con fuoco 2) Andante cantabile 3) Presto •Asx/Orch (2222/4221/Perc/Harp/Str) or Orch d'Harmonie or Pno •ET
Eolienne (1979) (15') (to A. BOUHEY) 1) Lyrique 2) Intermezzo 3) Intense 4) Perpetuum mobile 5) Declamative •Asx/Harp •Bil
Golden symphonie (1991) (26'30) 1) Andante 2) Scherzo 3) Final •12 Sx: SSSAAATTTBBB •Bil
Poème lyrique (1987) •Soprano Voice/Baritone Voice/Pno/Fl (or Vln)/Asx (or Vla)/Bsn (or Vcl)
Quatuor (1983) (26'30) 1) Misterioso 2) Lent 3) Linéaire 4) Cantilène 5) Finale •SATB •Bil
Sonate •Asx/Pno •Bil
Variations pathétiques (1983) (28') 1) Declamando 2) Prestissimo 3) Lento 4) Rapido 5) con simplicite - anima 6) Prestissimo con fuoco •Asx/Pno •Bil

GOTLIB, A.
Compositeur russe.
Concerto •Asx/Orch

GOTSKOSIK, Oleg (1951)
Chef d'orchestre et compositeur suédois d'origine sibérienne. Travailla avec T. McKinley.
"In his representative works of today he uses a tonal language whose technical structure and expressive properties belong entirely to our own time." (H-G. P.)
Svit för unga musiker (1986) 1) Fanfar 2) Cirkus marschen 3) När skymningen faller 4) Tango 5) Gelsomina •Ob/Asx/Bsn/2 Vln/Pno •SMIC

GOTTSCHALK, Arthur William (1952)
Compositeur américain, né à San Diego (California), le 14 III 1952. Travailla avec R. L. Finney, L. Bassett, et W. Bolcom puis en electronic music avec M. Davidovsky et G. Wilson.
Cycloid •Cl/Asx/Hn/Tpt/Harp/Vibr/2 Vln/Vla/Vcl •SeMC
Jeu de chat (1981) (10') (to L. HUNTER & B. CONNELLY) •Asx/Pno
The Sessions - jazz piece •Fl/Asx/Vibr/Bass •SeMC

GOTTWALD
Friendship (SANSONE) •Asx/Pno •South

GOUGEON, Denis (1951)
Compositeur canadien né au Québec.
Heureux qui comme… (1987) •Soprano Voice/Picc/EH/Bsx/2 Vln/Vla/Vcl/Bass/Perc •CMC
Mercure (1992) •Asx Solo
6 thèmes solaires •Asx Solo •CMC

GOULD, Alec
Compositeur anglais.
Swing Suite •SATB •SM
Three Piece Suite •SATB •SM

GOULD, Elizabeth
Compositeur américain.
Tunes for a Madrigal (1987) (to J. SAMPEN) •Asx/Pno

GOULD, Morton (1913)
Compositeur et chef d'orchestre américain né à New York, le 10 XII 1913. Travailla avec V. Jones.
"His lighter works generally draw on American subject matter and music, whether jazz, folk or composed." (R. BYRNSIDE)
Diversions (1990) (25') (to J. HOULIK) 1) Recitatives and Preludes 2) Serenades and Airs 3) Rags and Waltzes 4) Ballades and Lovenotes 5) Quicksteps and Trios (Finale) •Tsx/Orch (2222/3321/Perc/Str) •GSch

GOULD, Tony
Compositeur australien.
Introduction for Two Players (1988) (to B. BROWN) •Ssx/Pno

GOUNAROPOULOS, Yrjö (see GUNAROPULOS)

GOUNOD, Charles (1818-1893)
Ave Maria (BACH) •Eb Sx or Bb Sx/Pno •Mol/Cen
Ave Maria & Only a Dream (WALLACE) •Eb Sx/Pno •CF
Ballet Music (from *Faust*) •Eb Sx/Pno •CF
The Calf of Gold (from *Faust*) •Asx/Pno •Mus
Cavatina (from *Faust*) (MULLALY) •Bb Sx/Pno •CBet
Fantaisie sur Faust (MOUSSARD) •Asx/Pno •Marg
Fantaisie sur Mireille (LEROUX) •Asx/Pno •Marg
Le soir (F. LEROUX) •Asx/Pno
March of a Marionette (WALTERS) •Tsx/Pno •Rub
Marche pontificale •AATB/Pno (ad lib.) •Bri
Recitatif, cavatine & Allegretto (from *La Reine de Saba*) (LUREMAN) •Bb Sx/Pno •TM
Sérénade (MULE) •Asx/Pno •Led

GOWER
Elegy and Presto •Ssx/Pno •WWS

GRABNER, Hermann (1886-1969)
Théoricien, pédagogue, et compositeur autrichien, né à Graz, le 12 V 1886; mort à Bolzano, le 3 VII 1969. Travailla avec M. Reger.
"Développe d'une manière personnelle, le style de son maître." (LAROUSSE)
"His compositional style evolved directly from that of Reger, though in some works, particulary those for organ, he introduced more modern features." (H. KRELLMANN)
Sextet, op. 33 •Fl/Ob/Cl/Tsx/Hn/Bsn •K&S

GRAEF, Friedemann (1949)
Compositeur allemand, né à Berlin le 9 I 1949.
Bearbeitungen •SATB •adr
Brandenburgische Messe (1989) (15') •SATB •adr
Canzona rhythmica (1990) (6') •Ssx/Org •R&E
Duos •Asx/Perc •adr
Facettes (1992) •Bsx Solo •R&E
Kammersinfonie (1992) (20') 3 Voices/Str Quartet/4 Sx: SATB/2 Perc
Karorak 7Z (14') •Ssx Solo •adr
Lieder zwischen Himmel und Erde (1989) (18') •Chorus/4 Sx: SATB •adr
Nocturne (1988) (11'30) •Bsx/Org •B&B
Rondo (1985) (10'30) •SATB •R&E

Sonata urbanisata (1993) •1 Sx: T+S/Perc •INM
Werke •Asx Solo •adr

GRAETZER, Guillermo (1914)
Divertimento •Bsx/Pno •Mus

GRAHN, Ulf (1942)
Compositeur suédois, né à Solna, le 17 I 1942.

"He is a traditionalist in the thoroughness of his musical craftsman-ship, but his musical vocabulary has constantly been absorbing new techniques which he uses in a manner both free and personal." (Sj)

Ballad (1985) (8') (to J. Sampen) •Asx Solo •NGlani
Soundscape II (1974) (7') •Fl/Cl/EH/Asx/2 Trb/2 Vln/Vcl/Bass •SMIC

GRAINGER, Christian
Compositeur américain.
Introduction and Allegro •Asx/Marimba
Sonata •Tsx/Pno

GRAINGER, Ella (1889-1979)
Mélodiste anglaise.
Honey Pot Bee (1948) (P. Grainger) •Voice or Ssx/Chamber Orch •GS
There's a Thing You Never Knew (1946) •Voice or Asx •GS
To Echo (1945) (P. Grainger) •Soprano Voice/Picc/Fl/Cl+Asx/Tsx/ Vla/BsCl/Bass/Marimba •GS

GRAINGER, Percy Aldrige (1882-1961)
Pianiste et compositeur australien naturalisé américain, né à Brigh-ton (Australie), le 8 VII 1882; mort à White Plains (New York), le 20 II 1961. Travailla à Berlin avec Busoni et à Londres avec Grieg. Naturalisé américain en 1914.

"Haïssant tous les genres traditionnels, il se fit l'apôtre d'une 'free music' pour la composition et la reproduction de laquelle il construisit d'étranges machines, dignes de la science fiction—on peut rêver à ce qu'il aurait tiré des ordinateurs d'aujourd'hui! Si ses capacités d'arrangeur et, parfois, son humour sont indéniables, il se peut, comme on l'a dit 'qu'un psychanalyste serait meilleur juge de sa personnalité qu'un historien de la musique.' Pervers sexuel, masochiste, complètement mégalomane, il se montrait à la fois anti-latin, antisémite et anti-allemand, prônant la domination d'une race anglo-scandinave de grands hommes blonds aux yeux bleus..." (G. Gefen)

"Grainger's philosophy of life and art calls for the widest commun-ion of peoples and opinions; his profound study of folk music underlies the melodic and rhythmic structure of his own music; he made a determined effort to recreate in art music the free flow of instinctive songs of the people; he experimented with 'gliding' intervals within the traditional scales and polyrhythmic combinations with independent strong beats in the component parts. He has introduced individual forms of notation and orchestral scoring, rejecting the common Italian designations of tempi and dynamics in favour of colloquial English expressions." (Baker) "The music by which Grainger is best known, consisting largely of arrangements of folk or folk-like tunes from England and Ireland, does not seem to encourage nationalistic Austra-lian claims on his identity in music." "His exquisite folksong settings alone assure him a place among the minor masters of his age, but his large-scale original works have been slow to gain acceptance. Like the best of his music, they bear the stamp of an original musical spirit whose measure has yet to be taken." (D. Josephson)

The Annunciation Carol •Sx/Band •PG
The Annunciation Carol (c. 1943) (4') •Sx Ensemble: SAATTBBs •TTF
The Duke of Marlborough (1905-39-49) •4 Tpt/4 Hn (or 2 Sx: AT/2 Bsn)/3 Trb/Tuba/Bass/Cymb. •Sch

The Immovable Do or Cyphering "C" (1933-39) •Sx Choir: SAATTBBs •GSch
Irish Tune from County Derry (4') (Cohen) •5 Sx: SAATB or SATBBs •TTF
Lisbon - Dublin Bay (1943) (3') •Sx Choir: SAATB •PG/TTF
The Lonely Desert Man Sees the Tents of the Happy Tribes (1949-54) •Ssx/Chamber Group or Pno •GSch
The Merry King (1939) •Fl/3 Cl/BsCl/Bsx/CBsn/Hn/Tpt/10 Str/Pno •GSch
Molly on the Shore (1914) •Asx/Pno •PG
Molly on the Shore (reconstructed by P. Cohen) (4') (to C. Leeson) •Asx/Pno •TTF
The Power of Love (1922-41-50) •Ssx/Pno •PG
Shepard's Hey (4') (Cohen) •5 Sx: SAATB or SATBBs •TTF
Sonata 1) Moderato 2) Allegro molto •Tsx/Pno •PG
A Song of Vermeland (4') (Cohen) •5 Sx: SATBBs •TTF
Spoon River (4') (Cohen) •5 Sx: SAATB or SATBBs •TTF
Stalt Vesselil (1951) •Voice/Bsn/Sx/Str •GSch
Ye Banks and Braes o' Bonnie Doon (1932-37) •7 Sx: SAATTBBs •GSch

GRANADOS, Enrique (1867-1916)
Danza espanola no. 2 "Oriental" (Amaz) •Tsx/Pno •UME
Danza espanola no. 2 "Oriental" (Bayer) •Asx/Pno •UME
Danza espanola no. 2 (Sakaguchi) •SATB •EFSM
Danza espanola no. 5 "Andaluza" (Amaz) •Tsx/Pno •UME
Danza espanola no. 5 "Andaluza" (Bayer) •Asx/Pno •UME
Danza espanola no. 5 "Andaluza" (Rooij) •Asx/Pno •Mol
Danza espanola no. 6 "Rondalla aragonesa" (Amaz) •Tsx/Pno •UME
Danza espanola no. 6 "Rondalla aragonesa" (Bayer) •Asx/Pno •UME
Intermezzo des Goyescas (Lacour) •Ob/Cl/Asx/Bsn
Intermezzo (from *Goyescas*) (Teal) •Asx/Pno •GSch
Pleyera (Album) (Teal) •Bb Sx/Pno •GSch

GRANDE, Miguel
Compositeur espagnol.
Reflection in the Mirror II (1990) (to M. Mijan) •Asx/Pno

GRANDERT, Johnny (1939)
Compositeur suédois, né à Stockholm, le 11 VII 1939.

"His music gave vent to his private anguish, in a protest against an evil world order. But it also included a healthy sarcasm and a telling humour. His pieces were liable to be unconventional, full of surprising effects." (Sj)

Etyd (1990) (5'30) •Asx/Pno •SMIC
Kvartett no. 2 (1989-91) (16') •SATB •SMIC
Kvintett (1975) (6'30) •5 Sx: SAATB •STIM
Quattro pareri (1983) (13'30) •SATB •SMIC/Tons
86 T •Fl/EH/BsCl/Bsx/CBsn/2 Tpt/Perc/Pno •STIM

GRANDIS, Renato de (1927)
Compositeur italien. Travailla avec Malipiero et B. Maderna.

"His dramatic writing, his subtlely of expression and the ever-present cantabile elements (which stem from bel canto and are found even in his instrumental music) all indicate a direct relation to tradition, although Grandis also employs serial technique and aleatory forms." (M. Lichtenfeld)

Canti sulle pause •Vln/Vcl/Tsx/Vibr/Trb/Perc •SeMC
Scotter Sud-est •Vln/Vla/Vcl/Bass/Sx/Hn/Tpt/Trb/Pno/Perc •SeMC

GRANITZE, M.
Suite •Asx/Pno

GRANOM, Lewis (18th century)
Sicilienne (MERIOT) •Asx/Pno •Phi

GRANT, Bruce
Compositeur canadien.
Everything Comes from the Blues (1978) (12') (to B. WEINBERGER)
  •Tsx/Pno

GRANT, Jerome (1936)
Compositeur américain, né à Détroit (Michigan) le 31 XII 1936.
Classical Woodwind Quartet (1966) (20') •Asx/Cl/Fl/Bsn •adr
Dance Frames (1980) (to D. MASEK) •Asx/Pno •adr
Dialogue (1966) (6') •Asx/Pno •adr
Duo 1 (to D. SINTA) •Eb Sx or Bb Sx/Tape •DP
Prelude, Aria and Fugue (1971) (9') •Asx/Pno •adr

GRANT, Parks (1910)
Compositeur américain, né le 4 I 1910, à Cleveland. Travailla avec
  H. Elwell et B. Rogers.
Varied Obstinacy, op. 61 (1972) (3'30) •Asx/Tape (Sx) •ACA

GRANT, Stewart (1948)
Compositeur canadien.
Fantasia No. 2 (1982) •Ob d'amore or EH/Ssx •CMC

GRÄSBECK, Mannfred
Compositeur finlandais.
Rapsodia del diabolo •2 Vln/Vla/Vcl/Sx/Pno/Perc

GRATZER, Carlo
Failles fluorescentes (1990) (16') (to D. KIENTZY) •Asx/Tape

GRAUN, Carl Heinrich (1703/4-1759)
Trio •Any 3 Instruments •HE

GRAUPNER (Johann) Christoph (1683-1760)
Intrada •Tsx/Pno •WWS

GREAVES, Terence (1933)
Compositeur anglais.
Three Folk Songs (1978) (7') (to English Saxophone Quartet)
  1) Gossip Joan variations 2) Flow gently sweet Afton, Oh dear?
  3) What can the matter be? •SATB •SM

GREEN, George
Compositeur américain.
Demonic Rites 1) Convocation 2) Incantation 3) Prayer 4) The Spell
  Dispelled •4 Sx

GREEN, John
Compositeur américain.
Mine Eyes Have Seen (1978) (37') •Tsx/Tpt+Flugelhorn/Electr.
  Guit/Orch (3333/4331/Timp/Perc/Pno+Celesta/Org/Synth/Str)
  •B&H

GREEN, Scott
Vindellia stonkie Tu-bong •Asx/Pno

GREEN, Stuart
Compositeur anglais.
Consortium (1976) (8') (to Myrha Saxophone Quartet) •SATB
Pipedreams (1978) (7') •Fl/Asx/Ob/BsCl

GREENWOOD, Allan
Compositeur anglais.
Junctions (1992) (8') •Sx/Yamaha WX7 MIDI Wind Controller/
  Tape

GREENE
From Out of Bartok •Asx/2 Bass/Perc/Pno

GREER
Flapperette •Bb Sx/Pno •Mills

GREIF, Olivier
Bomber auf Engelland •Soprano Voice/Asx/Pno

GRETCHANINOFF, Alexandre Tikhonovitch (1864-1956)
Compositeur russe, né à Moscou, le 13 X 1864; mort à New York, le
3 I 1956. Travailla avec Rimsky-Korsakov. Aux U.S.A. depuis 1939.
  "La musique de Gretchaninoff s'inscrit dans la tradition du 'Groupe
des Cinq,' cependant il est peu attiré par le contrepoint ou les recherches
harmoniques; c'est un romantique, mais ce ne sont pas les grandes
fresques bruyantes qui l'attirante: il est plus l'interprète des sentiments
intimes, du mystère, et souvent sa musique plaît plus par son côté
aimable qu'elle n'attire l'attention par quelque choc nouveau."
(FASQUELLE)
At the Hearth (VOXMAN) •Asx/Pno •Rub
2 Miniatures, op. 145 (4') 1) Souvenir de l'ami lointain 2) Phantasme
  •Asx/Pno •Led
Evening Waltz (VOXMAN) •Asx/Pno •Rub

GRETRY, André-Modeste (1741-1813)
Panurge - Ariette (LONDEIX) •Bb Sx/Pno •Led
Sarabande et menuet •SATB •Mol
Suite rococo (8') (LONDEIX) 1) Chasse 2) Ariette 3) Gavotte
  4) Tambourin •Tsx/Str Orch or Pno •Sch
3 Danses villageoises •SATB •Mol

GREUSSAY, Patrick
L'Intinéraire •Sx/Tape

GREY, Geoffrey (1934)
Compositeur anglais.
Quartet (1973) (14') (to London Saxophone Quartet) •SATB

GRIBOJEDOV, A.
Compositeur russe.
Waltz (3') •5 Sx: SAATB/Pno/Bass

GRIEBLING, Karen
English Post Cards •Asx/Pno

GRIEG, Edvard (1843-1907)
Album Leaf (from *Lyric Pieces*, op. 12) (TEAL) (Album) •Asx/Pno
  •GSch
An der Wiege •SATB •DP
Ase's Death (from *Peer Gynt*) •AATB/Pno ad lib. •Bri
Berceuse •Bb Sx/Pno •CBet
Elegie (TAYLOR) •AATB •Mills
Hochzeitslag auf Troldhaugen (HOLTZ) •SATB •Sim
Huldigung's March (THOMSON) •AATB •Alf
Ich liebe Dich •Bb Sx/Pno •Mol
I Love You •2 Sx: AT/Pno •Cen
The Last Spring, op. 34, no. 2 (1880) (WORLEY) •10 Sx:
  SSAAAATTBBs
Letzter Frühling •Bb Sx/Pno •Mol
March of the Dwarfs (JOHNSON) •AATB •Rub
Norvegian Dance (BROOKE) •AATB •CF
Poème érotique •Bb Sx/Pno •Mol
Soir dans les montagnes (STRAUWEN) •Asx/Pno •Sch
Solvejg's Lied •Bb Sx/Pno •Mol
Sonata No. 1 for Violin (Selection) (TEAL) •Bb Sx/Pno •GSch
Spring (Rousseau) •Asx/Pno •BM

Suite in Olden Style (from *Holberg*, op. 40) (WORLEY) •10 Sx: SSAAAATTBBs
To Spring •2 Sx: AT/Pno or 3 Sx: AAA •Cen
Watchman's Song (URBAN) •AATB •Mills
Wedding Day at Troldhaugen, op. 65, no. 6 (1897) (HEYBURN) •Sx Ensemble: SATBBs

GRIFFITHS, James (1948)
Dialogue on a Tone Row (1969) (4') •Asx/Perc

GRIFFITH, Oliver
Prelude and Fugue for Jazz Saxophone Quartet •SATB •WWS/DP

GRIGORIOU, Lefteris
Musique "Tu, toi, moi" (1991) (to S. BERTOCCHI) •Asx Solo

GRILLAERT, Octave (19xx-1979)
Compositeur belge.
Fantaisie variée, op. 1531 •Asx/Pno •Met/HE
Saxo voice (1976) (1'30) •Asx/Pno
Sopran song, op. 9393 (1978) (2'30) (to L. SCHOLLAERT) •Ssx/Pno
Spirito, op. 9331 (1') (with F. DANEELS) •Bsx/Pno
Suite baroque (F. DANEELS) •SATB

GRIMAL, A.
Chef de musique du 28e Régiment d'Infanterie.
Bravura - solo brillant (1879) •SnoSx/Pno •Mil

GRIMS-LAND, Ebbe (1915)
Compositeur suèdois, né à Malmö, le 11 VI 1915.
Thema des Tages II (1977) (6-7') •Asx Solo •STIM

GRISEY, Gérard (1946)
Compositeur français né à Belfort. Travailla avec O. Messiaen, H. Dutilleux, Stockhausen, Ligeti, Xenakis, ainsi qu'avec J-Etienne Marie l'électro-acoustique.
"Nous sommes des musiciens et notre modèle, c'est le son, non la littérature, le son, non les mathématiques, le son, non le théâtre, les arts plastiques, la théorie des quanta, la géologie, l'astrologie ou l'acupuncture." (G. GRISEY) "Fondée sur une approche exclusive du son, l'esthétique de Gérard Grisey refuse tout matériau de base et privilégie la mutation du son à l'intérieur de ce que le compositeur nomme un 'faisceau de forces.' C'est la mutation du son qui est au centre de sa préoccupation, le devenir sonore en tant qu'il atteint également l'auditeur, le corps de l'auditeur. La réception de ce dernier, son temps d'écoute soulèvent aussi un intérêt majeur. Gérard Grisey appartient à un groupe de musiciens dits 'spectraux' comme Tristan Murail, Eric Tanguy et d'autres..." (C. GLAYMAN) "Gérard Grisey déclare lui-même s'être rapidement éloigné du sérialisme qu'il juge trop abstrait, pour découvrir 'à travers l'acoustique et la psychologie de la perception une écriture en évolution continue dans laquelle la place de l'objet sonore importe autant, sinon plus, que sa structure même." (D. J-Y. BOSSEUR) "Imaginant une nouvelle spatialisation de la musique, Gérard Grisey entend découvrir à travers l'acoustique et la psychologie de la perception une écriture en évolution continue dans laquelle la place de l'objet sonore importe autant sinon plus, que sa structure même." (J. & B. MASSIN)
Anubis et Nout (1992) •1 Sx: Bs or B •Ric
2 Incantations •2 Sx: AA •Ric

GRISONI, Renato
Compositeur suisse.
Albumblat, op. 60 (to S. RASCHER) •Asx/Pno •Pet
Für Sigurd, op. 60 (5'30) •SATB •Kneu
Kabbalah, op. 58 (19'30) •4 Sx: SATB/Str Orch •CA
Sonatina, op. 64 (to S. RASCHER) (3 Movements) •Asx/Pno •Cur

Suite italienne, op. 26 (to S. RASCHER) 1) Preludium 2) Bullu tundu 3) Pavana 4) Courante 5) Siciliana 6) Ossolana 7) Aria 8) Sastarello •Asx/Pno •Pet

GROBA, Rogelio
Compositeur espagnol.
Tensiones - Quatuor n° 4 (1979) (to A. VENTAS) 1) Allegretto tenso - ritmique 2) Andante tenso - lyrique 3) Vivace tenso - calido •SATB •adr

GROFÉ, Ferde (1892-1972)
Diana •Asx/Pno •Rob
Gallodoro's Serenade (1959) (to A. GALLODORO) •Asx/Pno •Rob

GROHNER, Franz
Compositeur allemand.
Koboldsprünge - Foxtrott •Asx/Pno •CH

GROOME, Richard
Compositeur américain.
4 Quartzoids (to J. STOLTIE) •Asx/Pno
Variations •SATB

GROOT, Hugo de
Hasta la vista - Little Spanish Fantasy (1987) •SATB •Mol

GROOT, Rokus de (1947)
Kontur (1982) (25') (to L. OOSTROM) •Sx Solo: S or A •Don

GRÖSCHKE, Heinz
Compositeur allemand. Travailla avec G. Bumcke.
Quintett (1935) (21') •AATB/Pno •RE

GROSS, Eric (1926)
Compositeur australien d'origines autrichiennes, né à Vienne. Vit à Sydney, depuis 1958.
Quartet No. 1 (1987) (to Adolphe Sax Quartet) 1) Prologue 2) Scherzo 3) Fantasia 4) Epilogue •SATB
Quintet, op. 102 (1977) 1) Allegro 2) Romance 3) Allegro •Asx/Str Quartet •Lee
Three Bagatelles, op. 96 (to P. Clinch) •Asx Solo •Lee

GROSSE, Erwin (1904-1982)
Pianiste et compositeur allemand, né à Hannover, le 4 XII 1904, mort à Ettlingen le 4 III 1982.
Capriccio, op. 43 (1954) (5') •Asx/Orch (2212/2230/Perc/Harp/Str)
Concerto •Asx/Orch •adr
Konzerte •Tpt/Vln/Asx/Bass •adr

GROSSE-SCHWARE, Bernhard
Compositeur allemand.
Drei Kleine Stücke (1993) •Asx/Pno •INM

GROSSE-SCHWARE, Hermann (1931)
Compositeur allemand né le 1 IV 1931 à Castrop-Rauxel. Travailla avec H. Schroeder.
Fantasiestück •Asx/Harps •PJT

GROSSI, Daniel
Compositeur français.
"Sur le tombeau de Florence" (1986) (14') •13 Sx: SnoSSAAAATTTBBBs •adr

GROUVEL, Pierre (1939)
Compositeur français.
Les humeurs du jour (1982) •SATB
Volcan - Concerto poème (1993) (16'15) (to J-M. GOURY) •Sx Solo: A+T+B/12 Sx: SnoSSAAATTTBBBs/3 Perc

GROVLEZ, Gabriel (1879-1944)

Compositeur chef d'orchestre et pianiste français, né à Lille, le 4 IV 1879; mort à Paris, le 20 X 1944. Travailla avec Gedalge et G. Fauré.

"Musique où trouve à s'exprimer une délicate sensibilité." (LAROUSSE) "Le 'bon goût' caractérise sa personnalité. Il sait fixer la sensation fugitive et l'exprimer de façon directe sans rien lui laisser perdre de sa fraîcheur. Musique imagée. Les influences qu'il a subies, les affinités à son tempérament se rencontrent bien plutôt chez G. Fauré dont il fut l'élève, chez Debussy et chez Ravel, claire, intelligente, sensible, élégante, modérée, éloignée de toute outrance et n'exerçant jamais son audace que dans le sens de la finesse." (Y. DAUVRIL)

"Grovlez was perhaps too versatile an allround musician to make his mark very decively as a composer, though here, as in other departments of his art, he lacked nothing in technique and general accomplishment." (M. PEREYRA) "Grovlez's compositions are cultivated and finely coloured, achieving individuality despite a melodic and harmonic indebtedness to Fauré." (A. LOUVIER)

Lamento et Tarentelle (DAILEY) (Album) •Bb Sx/Pno •WA
Sarabande et allegro •Asx/Pno •Led
Suite (1915) (16') (to E. HALL) •Asx/Str/Fl/Hn/Harp •Fuz/South

GRUBER, Heinz Karl (1943)

Compositeur et contrebassiste autrichien, né à Vienne, le 3 I 1943. Travailla avec E. Ratz, H. Jelinek, et G. von Einem.

"During the mid-1960s he worked with relatively traditional serial techniques and with electronic resources; but even in the works of this period he maintained certain links with tonality. In the late 1960s he reverted to a fundamentally tonal idiom, which was influenced, however, by his experience of serialism and of electronics." (A. SCHARNAGL)

Concerto No. 2 (1961) •Tsx/Bass/Perc •B&H

GRUND, Bert (1920)

Compositeur allemand, né le 24 I 1920 à Dresden. Travailla avec H. Schneider, K. Striegler, C-M. Pembaur.

Triple-Konzert •Asx/Orch

GRUNDMAN, Claire (1913)

Concertante (1972) (for D. UNDERWOOD) 1) Slowly 2) Rather Bright •Asx/Orch or Band or Pno •B&H

GUACCERO, Domenico (1927-1984)

Compositeur et pianiste italien, né à Pablo del Colle (Bari), le 11 IV 1927, mort à Roma. Travailla avec G. Petrassi.

"The versatility displayed in his activities also marks Guaccero's music. He has accepted a wide range of new techniques, particulary those bearing on the theatre, which has always been the medium of his choice." (C; ANNIBALDI)

Esercizi (per clarinet version per saxophone) (1965) (9') •1 Sx: A+S/Pno •CRM
Luz (da 'Descrizioni del corpo') (1973) (7-10') 1 Low Instrument/Tape •CRM
Quartetto •Tsx/Cl/Soprano Voice/Tenor Voice •DP

GUAGNIDZÉ

Compositeur russe.
Solo •Asx Solo •ECS

GUALDA JIMENEZ, Antonio

Compositeur espagnol.
Noneto Zarco (1988) (16') •Vln/Vcl/Cl/2 Sx: SA/Vibr/Marimba/Guit/Pno
Soledades rojas (1988) (to M. MIJAN) •SATB

GUEÏFMAN, A.

Compositeur russe.
Romance (1977) •Asx/Pno

GUENTZEL

Indian Dance •6 Sx: AATTBBs •Rub
Mastodon •Bb Sx/Pno •Mills

GUERIN, Roland

Compositeur français.
Divertissement (1976) (to J. DESLOGES) •2 Sx: SB
Suite (1978) (to Quatuor Desloges) •SATB

GUERRERO, Francisco (1951)

Compositeur espagnol, né à Linares (Jaen).
Rhéa (1988) (6') (to J-M. Londeix) •12 Sx: SnoSSAAATTTBBBs

GUERRINI, Guido (1890-1965)

Compositeur italien, né à Faenza, le 12 IX 1890. Travailla avec Busoni.
"Guerrini's work is copious and greatly caried." (GROVE)
Canzonetta e ballo Forlinese (1938) •SATB
Chant et danse dans un style rustique (1946) (to Quatuor M. Perrin) •4 Sx SATB or AATB
Dialogo sui Fiori (1956) •Fl/Tsx/Pno

GUIBERT, Alvaro

Compositeur espagnol.
Del aire (1992) (10') (to Cuarteto orpheus) •SATB

GUICHARD, Christophe

Compositeur et percussionniste français né à Bordeaux. Travailla avec J. Courtioux, M. Fusté-Lambezat, et Chr. Eloy.
Glu et gli (d'après H. MICHAUX) (1991) (10') •Soprano Voice/Baritone Voice/Bsx/Perc

GUICHERD, Yves

Saxophoniste et compositeur français. Travailla avec D. Deffayet.
Ballade (1992) (3'40) •Asx/Pno •Bil
Chanson pour maman (1992) (2'15) •Asx/Pno •Bil

GUILHAUD, Georges (1851-19xx)

1er Concertino (MULE) •Asx/Pno •Bil
1er Concertino (VOXMAN) •1 Sx: A or T/Pno •Rub

GUILLAUME, Eugène (1882-1953)

Poète et compositeur belge, né à Namur, le 29 VI 1882; mort à Scheerbeek.
"La langue de Guillaume très marquée par le chromatisme, dénote une nette évolution de l'école musicale belge du style franckiste vers la tendance atonale des jeunes générations." (FASQUELLE)
Andante et scherzo •Asx/Pno •EMB

GUILLAUME, Georges

Humeurs (1986) (5'15) (to Fr. VALONNE) •Asx/Pno •Bil

GUILLAUME, Marie-Louise

Turquie •Ob/Cl/Asx

GUILLONNEAU, Christian

Compositeur français.
Eolithes (1988) (7') (to B. RUIZ) •4 Sx: AAAA/Perc/Tape
Evocation et Danse (1993) (4') •1 Sx: A or T/Pno •Mar
Rapsodie occitane (1992) (9'30) •Asx/Harmonie or Pno •Mar
Sax promenade (1989) (4') (to l'Ensemble de Saxophones des Pays de Loire) •12 Sx: SnoSSAAATTTBBBs

GUILLOU, René (1903-196x)

Organiste et compositeur français, né à Rennes, le 8 X 1903. Travailla avec Ch-M. Widor. Grand prix de Rome (1926).
Pièce concertante •SATB
Sonatine (1946) (5') (to P. BRUN) 1) Andantino grazioso 2) Andante 3) Vif •Asx/Pno •Led

GUILMAIN, Paul
Espoir, Impatience (to E. COHANNIER) •SATB

GUILMANT, Alesandre (1837-1911)
Cantilène pastorale (TAYLOR) •6 Sx: AAATTB •Mills
Finale in E Major (REX) •9 Sx: SAAAATTTB •DP

GUIMAUD, Olivier
Compositeur belge.
Sérénade alla Lupesca (16'15) •Tpt/Sx/Vcl/Perc •adr

GUINJOAN, Juan (1931)
Compositeur et chef d'orchestre espagnol né à Riudoms (Tarragona), le 27 XI 1931. Travailla avec C. Taltabull et, à Paris, avec Pendleton, Wissmer, et la 'musique concrète' avec J-Etienne Marie.
Musique intuitive - Diari (1969) •Cl/Tsx/Tpt/Vln/Vcl/Pno

GUINOVART, Carles
Compositeur espagnol.
Pièce (1992) •Asx/Instrumental Group

GUIOT, Raymond (1930)
Compositeur français.
Opium (1976) (6'30) (to J-Y. FOURMEAU) •Asx Solo •Bil

GULDA, Friedrich (1930)
Pianiste et compositeur autrichien né à, Vienna, le 16 V 1930. Travailla avec Pazofsky, Bruno Seidlhofer, et J. Marx.
"By mixing sharply contrasted programmes he intended to confront classical audiences with jazz, and vice versa. He initiated a modern jazz competition at Vienna in 1966 and, deeply interested in all aspects of improvisation, he founded the International Musikforum at Ossiach, Carinthia, in 1968. Occasionally he plays the flute and baritone saxophone." (G. BRUNNER)
Music for 4 soloists n° 2 •Trb/Bugle/Sx/Orch

GULLIN, Peter (1959)
Adventures •2 Sx: AT/Pno/Bass/Perc •SMIC/WIM
Tre suna julsagor (1988) •Bsx/Str Quartet/Bass

GULLY, Michel
Conte (1983) (1'30) •Asx/Pno •Com

GUNAROPULOS, George (Yrjö) (1904-1968)
Compositeur et chef d'orchestre finlandais, né à St-Petersbourg, le 28 V 1904; mort à Helsinki, le 28 V 1968.
Concerto No. 1 in C Minor (1935) (22') •Asx/Orch •FBC/FMIC
Concerto No. 2 in B Major (1946) (22') •Asx/Orch (2222/4220/Perc/ Str) •FBC/FMIC

GUNDLACH, Eric
Elfentraum (LÖBEL) •Asx/Pno •Rot

GUNJI, Takashi
Compositeur japonais.
Quatuor 1) Andante 2) 96 3) Final •4 Sx: S+A ATB

GUNSENHEIMER, Gustav (1934)
Compositeur allemand.
Concertino n° 3 (1982) (10') 1) Bagatelle 2) Blues 3) Capriccio •Ssx/Str Orch •VF
Concertino n° 4 (1986) (10') 1) Whistling 2) Strolling 3) King Rag 4) Dreaming •1 Sx: Sno+S+A/Str Orch •VF

GURBINDO, Jose Fermin
Compositeur espagnol.
Sonatina (to M. MIJAN) •Asx/Pno •RCSMM

GUREWICH, Jascha (1896-1938)
Saxophoniste et compositeur américain d'origines russes.
Ballet fantastique •Asx/Pno •GSch
Capriccio, op. 120 (to E. STOCK) •Asx/Pno •GSch
Concerto in E Minor, op. 102 (1926) (to J. P. SOUSA) 1) Maestoso 2) Andante sostenuto 3) Presto •Asx/Orch or Pno •Rub
The Coo-Coo Clock (1923) •Asx/Pno
Fantasia in F Minor (1924) •Asx/Pno •Ric
Italian Serenade •Bb Sx/Pno •SF
Jota •Asx/Pno •GSch
Kathryne -Valse Caprice •Asx/Pno
Melodie d'amour (1926) •Asx/Pno •GSch
One Minute •Bb Sx/Pno •SF
Passing Thought •Eb Sx/Pno •CF
Saxophonist's Daily Dozen •CF
Seguidilla (1924) •Asx/Pno
17 Classic Duets •2 Sx •CF
16 Artistic Etudes •Mills
Sonata, op. 130 (1928) •Asx/Pno •CF
Souvenir de Chamonix •Eb Sx/Pno •CF
Spinning Valse •Asx/Pno •SF
Staccatos and Legatos (1927) •SF
Suite orientale •Asx/Pno •GHS

GURILIOV, A.
Compositeur russe.
Nocturne (5') •5 Sx: SAATB/Pno/Bass

GÜRSCH, Günther (1919)
Pianiste, arrangeur, et compositeur allemand, né le 7 XII 1919, à Halbstadt.
Madison - Party (1963) (3') •3 Sx/Tpt/Trb/Perc •adr

GUTAMA SOEGIJO, Paul
Quartet (1992) •SATB
3 Motions (1992) (20') •SATB

GUTWEIN, Daniel
Reliquary for Rahshaan •Tsx/Tape •DP

GUY, Georges
Concerto en forme de jazz •Asx Solo/Pno Solo/Fl/Ob/Cl/Hn/Bsn/ Bass

GUYENNON, Bernard
Compositeur français.
100 chansons à jouer •Asx/Pno •Mar
Jouons en trio (NICOLLET) •3 Bb Sx or 3 Eb Sx •Mar

GYSELYNCK, Jean F.
Compositeur belge.
Adagio et Allegro •Asx/Perc/Pno
Sorrow (to N. NOZY) •Asx/Vibr

HAAN, Jan de
Fryske variaties (1981) (6') •Variable Orch Instrumentation •Mol

HAAS, Hans (1897-1955)
Compositeur et musicologue allemand.
Mixtura 1) Preludio 2) Scherzino 3) Sarabande 4) Rondo •Asx/Pno
•IMD

HAAS, Konrad (1954)
Compositeur allemand né à Riedlingen, le 19 X 1954. Travailla au
Conservatoire de Paris.
Steinwolke I (1980) (45') •Voice/Fl/Sx/Pno/Perc/Guit/Bass •Holz
Steinwolke II (1981) (45') •Voice/Fl/Sx/Pno/Perc/Guit/Bass •Holz
Steinwolke live (1982) (45') •Voice/Fl/Sx/Pno/Perc/Guit/Bass •Holz
Steinwolke (1983) (45') •Voice/Sx/Perc/Pno/Guit/Bass •Holz
Steinwolke - In wilder Zeit (1984) (45') •Voice/Fl/Sx/Pno/Perc/Guit/
Bass •Holz

HAASE, Milos
Echoes (1982) (to Bok & Le Mair) •Sx/Vibr

HÂBA, Alois (1893-1973)
Compositeur tchécoslovaque, né à Vizovice (Moravie), le 21 VI
1893, mort à Prague. Travailla avec V. Novak et Fr. Schreker.
"Dès le lendemain de la Première Guerre mondiale, Alois Hâba
s'affirma comme le pionnier résolu du fractionnement de l'échelle
chromatique tempérée, ainsi que de l'athématisme (abandon de la
notion de thème et de tout développement thématique). Il a trouvé des
micro-intervalles dans certaines inflexions de la musique folklorique
tchèque et morave, dont il s'est inspiré. Alois Hâba est, certes un
pionnier dont il ne faut pas mésestimer les travaux, mais il est comme
beaucoup de précurseurs, qui, découvrant un langage nouveau, n'en
saisissent pas du même coup la syntaxe et l'esprit, car ce n'est guère
qu'à la tradition de Brahms qu'il a appliqué son vocabulaire de ton
fractionné." (Cl. Rostand) "Parmi les compositeurs de la 'troisième
génération' tchèque, Alois Hâba tient une place bien particulière, en
tant que l'un des principaux promoteurs de la musique micro-tonale."
(J. & B. Massin) "Le catalogue de Hâba comporte plus de cent numéros
d'opus, parmi lesquels des oeuvres écrites traditionnellement." (J-N.
von der Weid)
"He became interested in the folk music of the Orient, which led him
to consider writing in smaller intervals than the semi-tone; he was also
influenced in this direction by Busoni's ideas. As a composer he has
developed a *non-thematic* method of writing (i.e. without repetition of
patterns, or development). He has also written a considerable amount
of music for ordinary instruments, in a diatonic style, and in the tweve-
tone system." (Baker) "Hâba may justly be regarded as the originator
of the use of quarter- and sixth-tones in Western art music. Hâba's
microtonal music employs the same compositional techniques as his
work in the semitone system, and he has avoided opposing the two. All
Hâba's music reveals a composer of fresh invention whose primary
sources are to be found in the music of his native region." (J. Vyslouzil)
Partita, op. 99 (1968) (9') (to S. Rascher) Allegro leggiero -
Andante cantabile - Allegro scherzando - Moderato •Asx Solo
•FM/CMIC

HÄBERLING, Albert
Music für Saxophon (1983) (to Quatuor Desloges) •SATB

HACHIMURA, Yoshiro
Concerto per 8 soli •Fl/Cl/Sx/Vibr/Vcl/Vla/2 Perc •OE

HACKBARTH, Glen
Metropolis (1979) (18') (for J. Wytko) •Asx/Wind Ensemble •DP

HADDAD
Andante and allegro •Asx/Pno •Sha

HADER, Widmar (1941)
Compositeur allemand né à Elbogen a.d. Eger, le 22 VI 1941.
Antizipation (6') •Asx Solo •Asto

HAENDEL, Georg-Friedrich (see HANDEL)

HAENSCH, Gerhard Delle (1926)
Compositeur, saxophoniste, et professeur allemand, né le 10 V 1926
à München. Auteur de plusieurs musiques de films.
Andantino •4 or 5 Sx •adr
Modern Etuden für Saxophon •adr

HAERL, Dan
Compositeur américain.
Quintet •Fl/Asx/Tpt/Trb/Bass •adr

HAESSIG, Bernhard
Compositeur suisse.
Sonate •Asx/Pno

HAGEN, Earl
Harlem Nocturne (Haring) •Asx/Band •SB

HAGI, Kyôko
Compositeur japonais.
Par avion •Bsx/Pno

HAGSTRÖM, Nils (1933)
Compositeur suédois.
Suono per fiati (1979) (11') •Fl+Picc/Ob+EH/Asx/Cl/Hn/Bsn
•STIM

HAHN, Reynaldo (1875-1947)
Compositeur et chef d'orchestre français, né à Caracas (Venezuela),
le 9 VIII 1875; mort à Paris, le 28 I 1947. Travailla avec Massenet.
Membre de l'Institut de France (1946).
"Son style mélodique, aimable et sensible témoigne d'une solide
technique mise au service d'un talent élégant et distingué." (N.
Dufourcq) "Lyrisme parfois affadi." (P. Wolff) "Obstinément et
radicalement hostile à toute évolution du langage, il en était resté
jusqu'à sa mort aux ressources expressives et stylistiques d'un Massenet." (Cl. Rostand)
"His music is distinguished by its facile melodic flow; some of his
songs have become very popular in recitals." (Baker) "He was the
equal of Messager in his freshness of melodic invention, his harmonic
zest and the aptness of his word-setting and form." (A. Hoeree)
Divertissement pour une fête de nuit (1933) (25') 1) La nuit, le parc
2) 3 Tableaux mimés: a) Haydn chez le Prince Esterhazy;
b) Adieu pour toujours - dessus de pendule; c) Le jugement de
Partis - danse lente; 3) Canzone - sur le lac 4) Lumières, valse
dans les jardins •2 Vln/Vla/Vcl/Bass/Asx/Bsn/Timp/Perc •Sal

HAIDMAYER, Karl (1927)
Professeur et compositeur autrichien.
Altorgano (1991) (3'15) •Asx/Org
Antispasmodium (1990) •SATB
Concerto n° 1 (1980) (to O. Vrhovnik) •Asx/Wind Orch
Concerto n° 2 (1981) (to O. Vrhovnik) •Asx/Orch
Duet (to O. Vrhovnik) •2 Sx: SB

Das Gebet (1991) •Asx/Org
Impromptu n° 1 (1980) (to O. VRHOVNIK) •Asx Solo
Pätzoludium and Toccata (1992) •Asx/Org •INM
Popludium III (1991) (11') •4 Sx: SATB/Org
Popludium IV (1988/91) •Asx/Str Orch
Quartet (to O. VRHOVNIK) •SATB
Romanesca 8 (1982) (to O. VRHOVNIK) •Asx/Pno
Romanesca 10 (4'20) •Ssx/Pno
Romanze (1989) •Asx/Synth
Saxophone 10 (3'45) •5 Sx: SAATB
Saxophonie X (1982) (to O. Vrohvnik) •7 Sx: SnoSATBBsCBs
Sonate n° 1 (to O. VRHOVNIK) •Ssx/Pno

HAÏK-VANTOURA, Suzanne (1912)

Compositeur français, né à Paris, le 12 VII 1912. Travailla avec G. Caussade, M. Dupré, et Roger Ducasse.
Adagio (1962) (4'30) (to J-M. LONDEIX) •Asx/Org •Bil
Visages d'Adam (1966) (20') (to J-M. LONDEIX) 1) Moderato maestoso 2) Molto tranquillo 3) Allegro •Asx/Orch •adr

HAJDU, Georg

Die Stimmen der Sirenen (1990) (12') •4 Sx/Tape •Peer

HALETZKI, P.

Father and Son - Intermezzo scherzoso (1938) •Picc/Asx/Bsn/Pno •Sch
Vater und Sohn •Asx/Pno •WWS

HALÉVY, Jacques François Elie (1799-1862)

Bright Star of Hope (*L'Eclair*) •Bb Sx/Pno •CF
The Cardinal's Air •Asx/Pno •Mus
Rachel (*La Juive*) •Eb Sx/Pno •CF

HALFFTER, Ernesto (Escriche) (1905-1989)

Compositeur et chef d'orchestre espagnol né à Madrid, le 16 I 1905. Dit parfois pour le différencier de son frère Rodolfo "le Halffter portugais" à cause de ses fréquents séjours dans ce pays. Travailla avec M. de Falla et O. Espla.
"Son style très éclectique est peu personnel." (Cl. ROSTAND)
"Halffter has always held an immutable belief in tonality, but in the 1960s he listened to some post-Webernian scores, and this stimulated him to undertake a thorough cleansing of his style in these later works. At the same time they display a return to his past manner, with its imitation of the Spanish Renaissance." (E. FRANCO)
Cavatina sobre el nombre de Arbos •Asx/Orch •ME

HALE, Jack

Sintage (1964) (to D. SINTA) •Asx/Pno

HALL, Helene

Compositeur canadien né au Québec.
Music for the consolation of philosophy (1990) •5 Soprano Voices/3 Sx: SAB/Vcl/2 Perc •CMC
Ruisselle/Fluvial (1988) •12 Sx: SnoSSAAATTTBBBs
Zones (1983/84) •5 Soprano Voices/3 Sx: SAB/Vcl/2 Perc •CMC

HALL, Morris Eugene (1913)

Bandmaster et arrangeur américain, né à Whiterright (Texas), le 12 VI 1913.
Stage Band Techniques •South

HALL, Neville (1962)

Saxophoniste et compositeur zélandais, né à Wellington, le 12 VII 1962. A été membre du groupe Pop 'Peking man.' Travailla la composition avec J. Rimmer et J. Elmsley.
Encounters (1992) (12'30) •Asx/Pno •adr
For a Single Point (1990) (11') •Cl/Tsx/Pno/Vla/Vcl •adr

For Two (1990) •Tsx/Perc •adr

HALLBERG, Bengt (1932)

Pianiste de jazz et compositeur suédois, né à Gothenburg, le 13 IX 1932.
"Since the 1960s he has written music for a host of different contexts and combinations, often attempting to combine the language of jazz with western art music tradition, folk, music etc." (SJ)
Quatuor (1992) •SATB
Sax vobiscum: Konsertstycke (1992) 5 Sx: SAATB (or 4 Sx: SATB)/ Orch (2222/2210/11/0/Str) •Tons/STIM

HALMRAST, Tor (1951)

Compositeur norvégien.
Fire Fall (1984) •SATB •NMI

HALPRIN, Ann

Compositeur américain.
Male-Female Ritual •Sx/Actress

HALSTENSON, Michael (1956)

Ballade (1984) (13') (to S. JORDHEIM) •Asx/Orch
Essay (1982) (to S. JORDHEIM) •Asx/Pno
Trio (1984) (8') (to S. JORDHEIM) •Sx/Fl/Pno

HAMBRAEUS, Bengt (1928)

Organiste et compositeur suédois, né à Stockholm, le 19 I 1928. Travailla avec Moberg.
"Presque entièrement autodidacte, mais ayant fait des études très poussées sur l'harmonie traditionnelle, sur la musique de la Renaissance et sur les systèmes extrême-orientaux, il se situe dans le groupe de tête de la jeune musique scandinave. Il a fréquenté les cours d'été de Darmstadt, ainsi que le studio électronique de Cologne: les recherches dans le domaine du timbre ont pour lui comme un caractère mystique, ce qui correspond à la synthèse qu'il effectue tout naturellement entre musique ancienne, musique extrême-orientale et musique d'avant-garde." (Cl. ROSTAND)
"He took courses in modern techniques in Darmstadt; became one of the pioneers of electronic music in Scandinavia. In his works he combines the constructivism of the cosmopolitan avant-garde with the linear polyphony of medieval modality." (BAKER) "As a composer Hambraeus has been stimulated by medieval music, extra-European musics (especially Japanese) and the avant-garde of the 1950s (above all the 'Darmstadt school'). He was one of the first to work in the electronic studios at Cologne (1955) and Milan (1959), and has engaged in many experimental activities.
Kammarmusik for 6, op. 28 (1950) (8') •Fl/Ob/Cl/Asx/Vla/Harp •STIM/Ehr

HAMBURG, Jeff

Elegie (1985-86) (9') •Fl/BsCl/Bsx/Perc •Don

HÄMEENIEMI, Aero (1951)

Compositeur finlandais, né le 29 IV 1951.
Chamber Music Book (1980) (to P. SAVIJOKI) •Fl/Guit/Asx/Perc •FMIC

HAMILTON, Tom

Dialogue •Asx/Fl

HAMMAN, Michael

Compositeur américain.
Variant Forms-Derivatives I (1985) •Any instrument

HAMMERTH, Johan (1953)

Compositeur suédois.
Under tiden (1993) •SATB •SvM

HAMPTON, Calvin (1938-1984)

Compositeur américain.

Bach's Fireworks Music (1984) (4') (to New York Saxophone Quartet) •SATB •TTF

Concerto (1974) (To New York Saxophone Quartet) •4 Sx: SATB/ Str Orch/Perc

Fugue (1978) (6') (To New York Saxophone Quartet) •SATB •TTF

Labyrinth (1986) (6') (text by Mic. ABREU Part I & II) •Soprano Voice/4 Sx: SATB •NYSQ

HANDEL, Georg-Friedrich (1685-1759)

Adagio and Allegro (GEE) •Bb Sx or Asx/Pno •South

Adagio and Allegro (HERVIG) •AATB •Rub

Adagio and Allegro (ROUSSEAU) •Asx/Pno •Wi&Jo

Adagio, Larghetto et Final (MULE) •Asx/Pno •Led

Andante and Allegro (GEE) •Tsx/Pno •South

Angels Ever Bright and Fair •Bb Sx/Pno •CBet

Air (SKOLNIK) •AATB •South

Air and Variations (RASCHER) •Asx/Pno •Bou

Allegro (MULE) •Asx/Pno •Led

Arrival of the Queen of Sheba (J. BROWN) •SATB •SM

Arrivée de la reine de Sabhat (FOURMEAU) •SATB •SL/Bil

Bourrée (MULE) •Asx/Pno •Led

Bourrée (CHAUVET) •Asx/Pno •Com

Bourrée, Air et Gavotte •SATB •Mol

Cantelina (BUCHTEL) •Asx/Pno •Kjos

Célèbre largo (MULE) •Asx/Pno •Led

Célèbre largo (NOSLIN) •Asx/Pno •Mar

Choralbearbeitung ans den Johannes Passion •SATB or AATB •TM

Concerto in G Minor (VOXMAN) •Bb Sx/Pno •Rub

3 Concertos (CORROYEZ) •2 Cl/2 Sx: TB •Buff

Concerto Grosso in C Major (1st movement) •9 Sx: SAT + AATTBBs •WWS

3 Dances and an Air (MAGANINI) •Bb Sx/Pno •Mus

Gavottes (MULE) •Asx/Pno •Led

L'Harmonieux forgeron (MULE) •Asx/Pno •Led

Hornpipe (Water Music) (1717) (PANHORST) •Sx Ensemble: SATBBs

How Beautiful are the Feet ("Messie") (STANG) •2 Cl/Asx/Bsn (or BsCl) •CF

Koraalbewerking (St. John's Passion) (EVERTSE) •4 Sx •TM

Largo •Bb Sx or Eb Sx/Pno •Mol

Largo (BROOKE) •AATB •CF

Largo (DYCK) •SATB •Braun

Largo (MULE) •Asx/Pno •Led

Largo (RASCHER) •Tsx/Pno •Bel

Largo (Xerxes) (STANG) •2 Cl/Asx/Bsn (or Bscl) •CF

Largo (VIARD) •Asx/Pno •Sal

Largo and Allegro (Sonata VI) (VOXMAN) •Asx/Pno •Rub

Menuet (LEMARC) •SATB •Lis

Pastorale (MULE) •Asx/Pno •Led

Sarabande •Eb Sx/Pno •Mol

Sarabande (GORDON) •AATB •South

Sarabande (WILLIAMS) •AATB/Pno •South

Sarabande and Air (JOHNSON) •AATB •Rub

Sarabande and Menuet (CLUWEN) •SATB •Mol

Sicilienne et Gigue (MULE) •Asx/Pno •Led

Sinfonia ("Entrance of the Queen of Sheba") (MARR) •SATB

Sinfonia ("Messie") (STANG) •2 Cl/Asx/Bsn (or Bscl) •CF

Sonata (KAPLAN) •Bb Sx/Pno •JS

Sonata in F •Tsx/Pno •Mus

Sonate en Sol mineur (LONDEIX) •Bb Sx/Pno •Led

Sonate n° 1 (LONDEIX) •Bb Sx/Pno •Led

1° Sonate (Fl) (MULE) •Asx/Pno •Led

2° Sonate (Vln) (MULE) •Asx/Pno •Led

3° Sonate •Bb Sx/Pno •Mol

3° Sonate (Vln) (MULE) •Asx/Pno •Led

Sonate No. 3 (RASCHER) •Asx/Pno •Chap

4° Sonate (Fl) (MULE) •Asx/Pno •Led

Sonate No. 5 (EPHROSS) •Tsx/Pno •South

Sonata No. 6 (GEE) •Asx/Pno •Lud

6° Sonate (Vln) (MULE) •Asx/Pno •Led

Sonata XIII (RASCHER) •Asx/Pno •Elvo/Pres

Sound an Alarm •Bsx/Pno •Spr

Trio C-Dur (V. WÜRTH) •3 Sx: ATB •VW

Trio Sonata No. 1 (VOXMAN-HERVIG) •2 Sx: AA/Pno •South

HANDY, George (1920)

Quartets Nos. 1 - 2 - 3 (1964) (to New York Saxophone Quartet) •SATB

HANKS, Sybil

Concertino, op. 16 •4 Sx: AATT/Orch or Pno •WB

HANLON, Kevin

Variations for Saxophone and Tape Delays •Asx/Tape Delay

HANNAY, Roger (Durham) (1930)

Compositeur et professeur américain, né à Plattsburgh (New York), le 22 IX 1930. Travailla avec Hanson et Foss.

"His music from 1955 to 1964 exhibits an individual alternation and mixture of serial techniques with free atonality and tonal elements. From 1966 to 1969 he was deeply involved with experimental electronic and percussion music and with mixed-media theatre works containing social and political comment. Since 1970 his music has reflected a new lyricism, often involving reinterpretations of music of the past." (D. GILLESPIE)

Cabaret Voltaire •Female Voice/Ssx/Perc •SeMC

HANNIKEN, Jos

Blues & Scherzo, op. 5a •SATB •An

Variations •SATB •An

HÄNSEL, Arthur (1877-19xx)

Concertino, op. 80 (SANSONE) •2 Sx: AT •South

HANSEN, Flemming Christian (1968)

Clarinettiste, saxophoniste, pianiste, organiste, et compositeur danois. Travailla avec A. Pape et I. Norholm.

A la mémoire de Dali (1989) (10'30) 1) Apparition 2) Existence fugitive 3) Dali parmi nous •SATB

HANSEN, Ted

Compositeur danois.

Contrasts (1983) •Asx or EH/Str •SeMC

Elegy (1978) (to D. DAILEY) •Asx/Pno •SeMC

HARBISON, John Harris (1938)

Bermuda Triangle (1970) •Vcl/Tsx/Electr. Org

Confinement (1965) (15'15) •Fl/Ob/EH/Cl/BsCl/Asx/Tpt/Trb/Vln/ Vla/Vcl/Bass/Pno/Perc

The Flower-fed Buffaloes (1976) •Voice/Cl/Tsx/Fl/Vcl/Bass/Pno/ Perc

Sonata (1995) (15') (commissioned by World-Wide Concurrent Premieres and Commissioning Fund) •Asx/Pno •AMP

HARDING, Taylde

Compositeur américain

Quartet •SATB

HARGER, Earle K.

Beguine •5 Sx: AATTB •Band

The E. Harger Saxophone Ensemble •5 Sx: AATTB •Band

HARLE, John (1956)

Saxophoniste concertiste et professeur anglais, né le 20 IX 1956 à Newcastle. Travailla avec Stephen Trier et D. Deffayet.

Bonjour... triste dame •6 Sx: SSSSSS
Classical Album •Uni
Easy Classical Studies •Uni
Foursquare for Saxophones (1980) (13') •SATB
Sax Album - to Baker Street and Bach (1985) •Asx/Pno •B&H
Saxophone Studies (1981-83) •Uni
Scales and Arpeggios (2 Volumes) (1984) •Uni

HARREX, Patrick (1946)

Compositeur anglais, né à Londres, le 26 IX 1946. Travailla avec G. Amy.

Mobile •adr
Passages III (1972) (9-12') (to K. Dorn) •Sx Solo •DP

HARRIS, Arthur

Farewell to Cucullain •AATB •CF
4 Heart Songs •AATB •CF
Quintette •Asx/Str Quartet

HARRIS, David

Moments •Tsx/Pno

HARRIS, Eddie (1938)

Musicien de jazz, saxophoniste américain, né le 20 X 1938, à Chicago.

The Intervallistic Concept •CC
Jazz Cliche Capers •HD

HARRIS, Floyd O.

Ballroom Echoes •1 Sx: A or T/Pno •Lud
2 Buckaroos •2 Sx: AA or TT/Pno •Lud
3 Cadets •3 Sx: AAT/Pno •Lud
3 Cubs •3 Sx: AAT/Pno •Lud
Fairy Princess •Asx/Pno •Lud
Gallant Brigadiers •3 Sx: AAT/Pno •Bar
2 Marionnettes •2 Sx: AA or TT/Pno •Lud
Ocean Beach •1 Sx: A or T/Pno •Lud
Old Refrain and Dark Eyes •2 Sx: AA/Pno •Lud
Sacred Melodies •2 Cl/Asx/Bsn (or BsCl) •CF
Sax Caprice •1 Sx: A or T/Pno •Lud
Scottish Airs •2 Cl/Asx/Bsn (or BsCl) •CF
Songs of America •2 Cl/Asx/Bsn (or BsCl) •CF
Syncopators •3 Sx: AAT/Pno •Lud
Three For the Show •3 Sx: AAA or AAT/Pno •Lud
Vesper Moods •AATB •Lud

HARRIS, Roger W.

Caliban in Apartment 112 •Tenor Voice/Asx/Pno/2 Perc •SeMC
Concert Etudes •Asx/Cl/EH •SeMC
4 Pieces for 3 •Any 3 instruments •Bou
Sopwith Hemke (1972) (to F. Hemke) •4 Sx: SSSS/Tape •Bou

HARRISON, Jonty (1952)

CQ (1989) (16') (to D. Kientzy) •1 Sx: S+B/Instrumental Ensemble •adr
EQ (1980) (13'30) (to J. Harle) •Ssx/Tape dispositif acoustique or Asx/Pno •adr
SQ (1979) (17') •SATB •adr

HARTL, Heinrich J. (1953)

Organiste et compositeur allemand.

Meditation, op. 42 (1989) •Bsx/Org
Quartett, op. 16 (1984) (8') (to Akademie Quatuor Nürnberg)
    1) Allegro 2) Largo 3) Spanischer Tanz •SATB •Tong

Sonate im Jazz Stil, op. 32 (1991) (7') 1) Dialog 2) Abschied 3) Chromatisches Thema •Asx/Pno •Hag
Trio concertante, op. 41 (1989) (8') 1) Lento 2) Vivace •3 Sx: SAB •VW

HARTLEY, Walter S. (1927)

Compositeur américain, né à Washington, le 21 II 1927. Travailla avec B. Phillips, B. Rogers, et D. Fiorillo.

Adagio (1994) (2'40) •8 Sx: SAAATTBBs •adr
Antiphonal Prelude (1984) (5') (to Rascher Saxophone Quartet) •4 Sx: SATB/Org •Eth
Aubade (1985) (1'20) (for S. Rascher - May 15, 1985) •6 Sx: SAATBBs •Eth
Cantilena (1984) (2'40) •Asx/Marimba •Eth
Chamber Concerto (1988) (9'30) •Bsx/Wind octet •DP
Chamber Music (1960) (8'30) (to S. Rascher & R. Resnick)
    1) Andante 2) Adagio 3) Allegretto •Asx/Fl/Ob/Cl/Hn/Bsn •Wi&Jo
Chorale Fantasia (1969) •SATB •adr
Concertino (1977-78) (9') (to J. Houlik) 1) Humoresque 2) Rêverie 3) Toccata •Tsx/Band or Pno •DP
Concertino da Camera (1994) (to M. Jacobson) 1) Allegro 2) Presto 3) Andante 4) Molto Vivace •Ssx Solo/2 Tpt/Hn/Trb/Tuba •adr
Concerto (1966) (12') (to D. Sinta) 1) Adagio - Allegro molto feroce - Adagio 2) Andante 3) Allegro scherzando •Asx/Band or Pno •Pres
Concerto No. 2 (1989) (10'30) (to D. Underwood) •Asx/Orch (2121/2210/Timp/Perc/Str) •DP
Dance (1990) (2') •2 like Sx •Eth
Dance Suite (1985) (6'30) •Asx/Vln/Pno •Eth
Diversions (1979) (7'30) (to R. Caravan) 1) Balkan Dance 2) Lines and Bells 3) Rigodon •Ssx/Pno •Eth
Double Concerto (1969) (7'30) •Asx/Tuba/Wind Octet (Fl/Ob/Cl/Bsn/Hn/2 Tpt/Trb) •PhC
Double Quartet (1994) (7'30) •4 Sx: SATB/Hn/Tpt/Trb/Tuba •adr
Duet - Sonatina (1986) (4'40) •2 Sx: AT •Eth
Duo (1964) (5'30) (to D. Sinta) •Asx/Pno •TP/Ten
Intermezzo (1970) (from *Suite* for Saxophone Quartet) •SATB •Cres
Little Suite (1974) (5'30) (to L. Bangs) •Bsx/Pno •DP
Lyric Suite (1993) (8'15) •Tsx/Vla/Pno •adr
Octet for Saxophones (1975) (8'30) (to S. Rascher) 1) Allegro agitato 2) Adagio molto 3) Presto 4) Andante con moto •8 Sx: SAAATTBBs •DP
Overture, Interlude and Scherzo (1988) (8'30) Sx Orch: SSAAATTBBs •DP
Petite Suite (1961) (5'30) (to D. Sinta & F. Hemke) 1) Intrada 2) Tango 3) Scherzo 4) Noturno 5) Capriccio •Asx Solo •Wi&Jo
Poem (1967) (3'30) (to J. Houlik) •Tsx/Pno •Ten/Pres
Prelude and Finale (1966) (5') •Ssx Solo (or Ob Solo) •RMP
Quartet Concerto (1992) (12') •4 Sx: SATB/Orch or Wind ensemble •EK
Quartet for Reeds (1977) (9'30) (to M. Sigmon) •Ob/Cl/Asx/Bsn •DP
Quartet 1993 (1993) (8'15) •Asx/Ob/Hn/Bsn •DP
Quintet for Saxophones (1981) (10') •5 Sx: SAATB •DP
Rhapsody (1979) (6'15) (to J. Houlik) •Tsx/Str Quartet or Str Orch •DP
The Saxophone Album (1974) (5'30) (to S. Rascher) (one solo each) •1 Sx: S+A+T+B/Pno •DP
Saxophrenia (1976) (2'30) (to T. Hegvik) •Asx/Band or Pno •DP
Scherzino (1986) (1'15) •Tsx/Pno •Eth
Serenade (1991) (10') 1) Pastorale 2) Tango 3) Canzona 4) Manchega •Sx Ensemble: SAATBBs •Eth
Seven "Sacred Harp" Songs (1992) •Asx/Keyboard •EK

Sinfonia VI (1984-85) (8'30) (to L. Patrick) Adagio - Allegro
  Marcato - Grave -Allegro con brio •11 Sx: SSAAAATTBBBs
  •Eth
Solemn Postlude (1985) (4'30) (to Rascher Saxophone Quartet) •4
  Sx: SATB/Org •Eth
Sonata (1973-74) (10'30) (to J. Houlik) •Tsx/Pno •DP
Sonata (1976) (10'30) (to L. Klock) 1) Allegro - Andante 2) Adagio
  3) Lento 4) Molto allegro •Bsx/Pno •DP
Sonata Elegiaca (1987) (13'45) (For L. Gwozdz) 1) Andante sonore
  2) Presto misterioso 3) Adagio •Asx/Pno •TP
Sonatine Giocosa (1987) (5') 1) Allegro molto 2) Allegretto grazioso
  3) Quolibet: poco vivace scherzando •BsSx/Pno •TP
Song (1972) (3') (from *Southern Tier Suite*) •Asx/Pno •Ten/Pres
Sonorities IV (1976) (3') (to D. Sinta) •Asx/Pno •DP
Sonorities VII (1985) (2') (to J. Moore) •Tsx/Pno •Eth
Suite (1972) (11') (to Rascher Quartet) 1) Prelude 2) Scherzo
  3) Nocturne 4) Intermezzo 5) Finale •SATB •PhiCo
Suite for 5 Winds (1951) (7') 1) Prelude 2) Scherzo 3) Pastorale
  4) Finale •Fl/Ob/Cl/Asx/Trb •Wi&Jo
Three American Folk Hymns (1987) •2 like Sx •DP
Three "Sacred Harp" Songs (1987) •Sx Ensemble: SSATTBBs
  •DP
Toccata Concertante (1984-85) (3'40) (to Rascher Saxophone
  Quartet) •4 Sx: SATB/Org •Eth
Trio (1984) (11') (to L. Patrick) •3 Sx: ATB •Pres
Trio Estatico (1991) (8'45) •2 Sx: AT/Pno •Eth
Trio for Reeds & Piano (1987) (10'30) •Ssx (or Ob)/Tsx (or
  Heckelphone)/Pno •DP
Valse Vertigo (1978) (3'40) •Asx/Pno •DP
A William Billings Suite (1987) •Sx Ensemble: SAATBBs •DP

HARTMAN

Methode élémentaire (1846) •Sbg

HARTMANN, John (1805-1900)

Auld Lang Syne •Eb Sx/Pno •CF
De Beriot's (De Ville) •Asx/Pno •CF
Fatherland (Blauw) •1 Sx: A or B/Pno •Mol
Longing for Home •Eb Sx/Pno •CF
Mia (Francis) •1 Sx: A or B/Pno •Mol
The Return - Air varié •Bb Sx or Eb Sx/Pno •Mol

HARTMANN, Otto B. (1939)

Saxophoniste, arrangeur, et compositeur allemand né le 8 VII 1939
  à Berlin-Charltenburg. Travailla avec Reimann et B. Blacher.
E-Musik ("L'Arlecchino") •SATB •adr

HARTWELL, Hugh

Soul Piece (1967) •2 Sx: AT/Tpt/2 Pno/Bass/Perc •CMC/BMI

HARTZELL, Doug

Compositeur américain, né à Dayton (Ohio).
Ballade •Asx/Pno •WWS
Ballade for Young Cats •Tsx/Pno •WWS
The Egotistical Elephant (1957) (3'30) •Bsx/Pno •Sha
Potato Sax (1965) •AATB •RM
Sax Symbol •Asx/Pno •Sha
Two Rogues (1968) (2'30) •2 Sx: AA or 1 Sx Solo/Pno •Tmp

HARTZELL, Eugene (1932)

Compositeur américain, né le 21 V 1932, à Cincinnati (Ohio).
  Travailla à Vienne avec H-E. Apostel. Vit en Autriche depuis 1956.
Divertimento (1992) (7') •SATB •CA
Monologue V (1965) Adagio - Andante - Molto lento •1 Sx: A or T/
  Perc •AMP/VD
Variants (1965) (7') •1 Sx: A or T/Perc •ECA

HARTZELL, L.

Jefferson Variations •Sx/Perc

HARVEY, Jonathan (1939)

Compositeur anglais, né à Sutton Coldfield (Warwickshire), le 3 V
1939. Travailla avec E. Stein et H. Keller, puis avec Babbitt. Tra-
vaillera ensuite à Paris à l'IRCAM, subissant alors l'influence de P.
Boulez.
  "L'art du peintre Turner influa sur Jonathon Harvey, tout proche
qu'il soit de la spectralité française et de la religiosité de Messiaen.
Ainsi dans *Valley of Aosta*. C'est à juste titre que nous connaissons
Harvey surtout pour ses oeuvres évoluant dans l'orbite de l'électronique, sans doute parce qu'il élève celle-ci à un niveau de subtilité, de
couleur rares en ce domaine." (J-N. von der Weid) "Harvey utilise aussi
bien les instruments que la bande magnétique, et son oeuvre sacrée
témoigne de ses efforts pour assortir, à la manière d'Olivier Messiaen,
le langage le plus avancé à la tradition liturgique." (G. Gefen)
The Valley of Aosta (1985) (13'30) •Fl/Ob/Ssx/Tpt/2 Yamaha DX7
  Synth/2 Harp/Pno/2 Vln/Vla/Vcl/Perc •FM

HARVEY, Paul Milton (1935)

Clarinettiste, saxophoniste, professeur, compositeur, chroniqueur,
et arrangeur anglais, né à Sheffield (Yorkshire), le 14 VI 1935.
Travailla avec T. Addison. Professeur à Londres. Fondateur du Lon-
don Saxophone Quartet.
Agincourt Song (1976) (2') •SATB •Nov
Bubble and Squeak - Duet •2 Sx: SnoB •adr
Le Cauchemar d'un saxophoniste (1974) (10') •SATB •adr
Celtic Collage •SATB
Choreographic Suite (1970) 1) Dance of Welcome 2) Virgin's Dance
  3) Mating Dance 4) Funeral Dance 5) Dance of the New Reeds
  •SATB •adr
Christmas Fantasy •SATB •adr
Common Market Suite (to E. Apper) •2 Sx: AT/Perc/Pno •Mau
Concert Duets (1981) •2 Sx: AT •Ron
Concertino (1973) (15') (to P. Brodie) Ssx/Orch (1111/110/Str
  Quartet) or Cl Choir (3 Bb/Alto/Bs/CBs) or Pno •Mau
Concertino (1974) (15') (to J. Houlik) •Tsx/Chamber Orch or Band
  or Pno •Mau
Concertino (1976) (15') (to D. Lawrence) Bsx/Orch or Band or Pno
  •Mau
Concertino Grosso (1974) (13') •4 Sx: SATB/Orch (1111/100/Str)
  •Mau
Contest Solos •Various Instruments/Pno •SMC
Damenesque (1973) (to J. Deman) •Asx Solo •Mau
7 Deadly Virtues (1975) •Ssx/4 Sx: SATB •adr
Equal Partners (1988) •2 Sx: AT •CasM
6 Elizabethan Madrigals (to London Saxophone Quartet) 1) "April is
  in my mistress fair" (Morley) 2) "Adieu sweet amarillis"
  (Wilbye) 3) "This sweet and merry month" (Byrd) 4) "Fair
  Phyllis I saw" (Farmer) 5) "Sometime she would and sometime
  not" (Farnaby) 6) "Amynstas with his Phyllis fair" (Pilkington)
  •SATB •adr
58 for 4 (1972) (3') •SATB •adr
The Hartfleur Song (1978) (2') •SATB •Nov/DP
3 Mouvements (1975) (15') (to Quatuor Belge de Saxophones)
  •SATB •adr
12 Pièces de la Renaissance •SATB •adr
Pieces for Nine (1979) (5') •4 Sx: SATB/2 Tpt/Hn/Trb/Tuba •adr
Quartet (to Fr. Daneels) •SATB •adr
Robert Burns Suite (1971) (10') (to London Saxophone Quartet)
  1) "My wife's a winsome wee thing" 2) My love is like a red,
  red rose 3) Nabbocks O' Bearmeal •SATB •Nov/ML
Saxequality (1971) (4') (to London Saxophone Quartet) •SATB •adr
Saxophone Quartets (2 Volumes) •SATB •Che

Saxophone Solos (2 Volumes) •Asx/Pno •Che
Saxophone Spectrum (1989) •Sx Ensembles •RSC
7 Saxophonian Folk Dances (1970) (10') (to London Saxophone
    Quartet) •SATB •Kjos
The Singing Saxophone (1989) •1 Sx: A or T/Pno •SMC
The Tale of Billy Goats and the Troll (1973) (15') •4 Sx: SATB/Narr
    •adr
Trio (to J. HOULIK) 1) Overture 2) March 3) Pavane 4) Fugue
    5) Incantation 6) Ritual 7) Finale •Fl (or Ob)/Cl/Tsx •DP

HASENPFLUG, Curt
Puck •AATB •Fro
Tarantella •AATB •Fro
Vater un Sohn •2 Sx/Pno •Fro

HASQUENOPH, Pierre (1922-1982)
Compositeur français, né le 20 X 1922. Travailla avec J. Rivier et D.
Milhaud.

"Les grandes préoccupations de Pierre Hasquenoph sont l'invention
thématique, la recherche rythmique et la clarté de l'orchestration. Ses
développements sont en général courts et traités plutôt comme des
variations. Quant à son écriture elle est atonale, mais basée sur le
contrepoint plus que sur l'harmonie." (HEUGEL) "Son style, en constante évolution, qui revendique la plus complète indépendance, est
cependant en partie conditionné dans son ensemble par les recherches
de structures et les jeux de timbres caractérisant notre époque." (Cl.
ROSTAND)

Concertino, op. 20 (1960) (10'30) 1) Allegro vivo 2) Adagio
    3) Presto •Asx/Str Orch or Pno •Heu
Concertino, op. 34b (1976) (10'30) •Tsx/Str Orch or Pno •ME
Concerto, op. 43a (1982) (14') (Work finished by [Oeuvre achevée
    par] J-J. WERNER) •Asx/12 Str •ME
Inventions •2 Vln/Vla/Vcl/Bass/Fl/Ob/Cl/Asx/Bsn/Hn/Tpt •Heu
Petite sérénade (1952) •3 Sx
Sonate à quatre, op. 7 (1954) (18') •SATB •ME
3me Symphonie concertante, op. 12 (1954) (24') 1) Vif 2) Lent et
    Scherzo 3) Vif •4 Sx: SATB/Orch (2222/3221/Perc/Pno/Str)
    •Chou
4° Symphonie, op. 17 (1954-58) (30') •4 sx: SATB/Orch (Str/Pno/
    Perc) •ET

HASSE, Johann Adolf (1699-1783)
Concert in G moll (JOOSEN) •Bb Sx/Pno •Mol

HATCHARD, Michael
Compositeur anglais.
Quartet (1977) (10') (to Myrha Saxophone Quartet) •SATB
Quartet for the Bean •SATB •SM

HATORI, Ryoichi (1907)
Compositeur japonais.
Concerto (1948) •Asx/Orch

HATTON, John Liptrot (1808-1886)
Goodbye, Sweetheart, Goodbye •Eb Sx/Pno •CF

HAUBENSTOCK-RAMATI, Roman (1919)
Compositeur et professeur israélien d'origine polonaise, né à Cracovie, le 27 II 1919. Travailla avec Malawski et Koffler. Vit à Vienne
depuis 1957.

"C'est une des personnalités les plus fines et les plus séduisantes de
l'avant-garde actuelle, et ses oeuvres, réalisées dans un langage et un
style des plus avancés, témoignent de la sensibilité poétique et sonore
des plus rares." (Cl. ROSTAND) "L'aspect symbolique de l'écriture
musicale; la recherche d'une notation où le signe ne renvoie plus
immédiatement à une syntaxe préétablie mais engendre sa propre
grammaire, favorise, sans doute, une certaine mouvance dans les

rapports entre l'interprète et la partition, autorise le compositeur à
appréhender la page comme prétexte de jeu; en revanche, la complexité
de la symbolique, exigeant un décryptage en fonction d'un mode
d'emploi établi plutôt par analogie avec l'écriture traditionnelle que
par souci de susciter de nouveaux modes de jeu, risque peut-être de
faire écran à une libre interprétation, en se substituant finalement au
codage solfègique." (D. J-Y. BOSSEUR)

Enchaîné (1987) (19') •SATB
Multiple II (1969) (12') •7 players: 3 Str/2 Woodwind/2 Brass ad lib
    •Uni
Multiple III (1969) (10') •7 Players ad lib •Uni
Multiple IV (1969) (10') •2 players: 1 Woodwind/1 Brass ad lib
    •Uni
Multiple V (1969) (10') •2 players ad lib •Uni
Self II (1978) •Sx •Uni
Versione 9 (1981) •Sx/Tuba •Uni

HAUBIEL, Charles Trowbridge (1892)
Compositeur et pianiste américain, né à Delta (Ohio), le 30 I 1892.
Travailla avec R. Scalero.
For Louis XVI (1940) (6') •AATB •BM/B&H
Jungle Tale •Asx/Pno/Male Choir (TTBB) •SeMC
Suite Concertante (1975) (22') Calmly - Severely - Anxiously -
    Serenely - Vivaciously •Sx/Str Quartet •TCP

HAUBRUCK, Joachim
Compositeur allemand.
5 Touken (1993) •Ssx/Electr. Bass •INM

HAUCK, Fr.
Neue Saxophonschule •Sch

HAUDEBERT, Lucien (1877-1963)
Compositeur et organiste français, né à Fougères, le 18 IV 1877; mort
à Paris, le 24 II 1963. Travailla avec G. Fauré.

"Haudebert a clairement défini, par les caractéristiques de son style,
l'idée qu'il se fait du beau musical: il est toute sobriété, toute pondération, en même temps que toute ferveur et toute effusion; sans être
emphatique ni grandiloquente sa musique se veut éloquente, et elle
l'est un peu à la façon de Franck." (R. BERNARD)

"He followed in his music the traditions of César Franck, preferring
large sonorities and clear tonal harmonies. He stood aloof from modern
developments in France and had little recognition even among traditional musicians, despite praise from Romain-Rolland." (BAKER)
Quatuor (1926) •SATB
Souvenir d'Armor (1960) •Asx/Pno

HAUPTMANN, Moritz (1792-1868)
Trio (EVERTSE) •3 Sx: SAT •Lis

HAUSER, Miska (1822-1887)
Chanson villageoise •Asx/Pno •CF

HAUTA-AHO, Teppo (1941)
Contrebassiste et compositeur finlandais.

"As a composer Teppo Hauta-Aho has always been his own teacher,
basing his technical knowledge on his wide practical musicianship as
an orchestral player, chamber and jazz musician. Along with modern
techniques his sources of inspiration include all the previous stylistical
periods in European music, impulses from oriental music and—of
course—jazz." (H. WESSMAN)
For Charles M. (1980) (15') •Tpt/Asx/Trb/Bass/Perc •FMIC

HAUTVAST
Meister Perlen •SATB •TM

HAVEL, Christophe (1956)

Compositeur, saxophoniste, et professeur français, né le 11 XII 1956, à Paris. Travailla avec J-M. Londeix, M. Fusté-Lambezat, et Christian Eloy. Enseigne actuellement l'électroacoustique au Conservatoire de Bordeaux.

"Après des études d'ingénieur en électronique, Christophe Havel commence ses études musicales par l'apprentissage du saxophone, puis par celui de l'écriture traditionnelle et de l'électroacoustique." "Musique éminemment française dans laquelle l'électronique se mêle intimement à l'acoustique, toute faite de clarté, de raffinement, de délicatesse, de tendresse même." (H. LERIC)

AER (la danse) (1994) (10') (to l'Ensemble Proxima Centauri) •Picc/SnoSx/Celesta/Perc •adr
Amers I (1992) (12') (to J-M. LONDEIX) •12 Sx: SnoSSAAATTTBBBs/2 Perc •adr
Amers II (1992) (12') (to J-M. LONDEIX) •12 Sx: SnoSSAAATTTBBBs •adr
L'canton'ier (1990) •Soprano Voice/Ssx/Harp •adr
Oxyton (1990) (9') (to M-B. CHARRIER) •Bsx Solo •adr
RamDam (1992) (15') (Commande de l'Etat) (to l'Ensemble Proxima Centauri) •Fl/1 Sx: S+B/Perc/Pno/Transformation électroacoustique •adr
S (1993) •Tsx/Computer •INM
Xaps (1991) (to M-B. CHARRIER) •Ssx/Transformation électroacoustique •adr

HAVELAAR, Anton

Quatuor (1991) (10') •SATB •Don

HAVER, Bruno

Compositeur allemand.
Flip und flap - Foxtrott (1938) •Asx/Pno •CH
Goldregen - Walzerintermezzo •Asx/Pno

HAWES, Charles

Crossover (to F. HEMKE) •Sx/Band

HAWKER, John

Compositeur australien.
Checkmate (1976) (to P. CLINCH) •Asx/Pno

HAWKINS, Coleman "Bean" (1904-1969)

Saxophoniste (ténor) de jazz américain, né à Saint-Joseph (Missouri), le 21 XI 1904; mort à New York, le 19 V 1969.

"Fut le premier grand spécialiste du saxophone-ténor dans le jazz et demeura le leader incontesté de l'instrument jusqu'à l'apparition de Lester Young."

Warm-up (Book) •Tsx/Pno •MCA

HAWORTH, Frank (1905)

Compositeur canadien d'origine anglaise, né à Liverpool, le 13 I 1905.

Kernwood Suite (1972) (12') 1) Allegro 2) Andante 3) Con moto 4) Allegro moderato •SATB •FHM/CMC
Vesperal Suite (1972) (5') (to P. BRODIE) 1) Allegro 2) Andante con moto 3) Allegretto graciozo •Ssx/Pno

HAWTHORNE, Allan (1909)

Whispering Hope (BRIEGEL) •2 Sx: AA/Pno or AATB •Bri

HAYAKAWA, Masaaki

Compositeur japonais.
Four Little Poems (1979) (9'30) •4 Sx: SATB/Soprano Voice/Harp/Perc •SFC

HAYDN, Franz Joseph (1732-1809)

Adagio (Piano sonata) (GEIGER) •Fl/Ob/Asx/Bsn •CF

Adagio No. 39 (SPEETS) •2 Sx: AT/Fl/Cl (or Ob) •TM/HE
Andante (from *Concerto*) •Bsx/Pno •JS
Andante No. 6 (SPEETS) •2Sx: AT/Fl/Cl (or Ob) •TM/HE
Ariette variée •Bb Sx/Pno •Mil
Concerto •Bb Sx/Pno •Mol
Finale (HERVIG) •AATB •Rub
Flötenuhr (1793) (2 volumes) (T. SCHÖN) •SATB •ApE
Gratias (SPEETS) •Eb Sx or Bb Sx/Pno •TM
Gypsy Rondo (TEAL) (Album) •Asx/Pno •GSch
Minuet (TEAL) (Album) •Asx/Pno •GSch
3 Movements (JOHNSON) •AATB •Rub
Oxen Minuet •2 Sx:AA/Pno or Fl (or Cl)/Asx/Pno •CF
Quartet, op. 76, no. 3 (STANTON) •SATB •Eto
Quatuor en Fa mineur, op. 20, no. 5 (21') (D. WALTER) •SATB •Bil
Quartet No. 84, op. 77 no. 1 (KOVAL) •SATB
Recueil de Quatuors classiques (CLERISSE) •SATB •Mar
Les Saisons (MULE) •Asx/Pno •Led
La 7me paroile du Christ (STRAUWEN) •Bb Sx/Pno •Sch
Sérénade •Bb Sx or Eb Sx/Pno •Mol
Serenade (WIENANDT) •Asx/Pno •South
Thema con variazoni (CLUWEN) •Bb Sx/Pno •Mol
The Witches Canon (SKOLNIK) •2 Sx: AT •Mus

HAYES, Gary (1948)

Compositeur canadien, né à Hamilton (Ontario), le 14 XII 1948. Travailla avec J. Beckwith et J. Weinzweig.
Concertino •Asx/Pno •ACA
4 Jouets (1977) (15') •SATB •ACA

HAYES, Jack

Concertino (to R. GARI) •Asx/Orch or Pno

HAYLAND, Marc

Compositeur canadien, né au Québec.
Paraphrase sur un thème de George Gershwin •Asx/Pno

HAZON, Roberto (1930)

Cantata spirituale (1955) •Contralto Voice/4 Sx/Org/Str
Pezzi (1959) •Sx

HAZZARD, Peter Peabody (1949)

Compositeur américain né à Poughkeepskie (New York), le 31 I 1949.
Massage •3 Voices (SAB)/3 Perc/Fl/Cl/Hn/Sx/Trb •SeMC

HEATH, David (1956)

Compositeur anglais.
"Out of the Cool" (1980) (5') (to J. HARLE) •Asx /Pno
Rumania (1979) (10') (to J. HARLE) •Ssx/Pno

HEBBLE, Robert

Dance (to F. HEMKE) •Asx/Pno

HECK, Armand (1878-1947)

Professeur et compositeur belge, mort à Nancy (France), le 22 VIII 1947.
Concertino en Sol Majeur, op. 41 (1940) (4') (to M. MULE) •Asx/Pno •Com

HECKMANN, Heinz (1932)

Compositeur allemand., né à Trier, le 11 VII 1932. Travailla avec H. Konietzny et O. Messiaen.
Kmk •SATB •adr
Thema und variationen über "Chevaliers de la Table ronde" (1981) •SATB •adr

HEDSTROM, Ase (1950)

Close by (1980) •Fl/Cl/BsCl/Ssx/Vln/Vcl •NMI

HEDWALL, Lennart (1932)

Chef d'orchestre, organiste, et compositeur suédois, né à Gothenburg, le 16 IX 1932.

"In recent years he has written a large number of organ compositions and lieder." "Admittedly, I wonder sometimes why I go on writing lieder in an age which seems to have neither the time nor the interest for the peaceful or intimate aspects of existence... It still feels like a challenge, trying to invest them with sound and musical form—not a 'supplementation' in music but a counterpoint of experience... Romanticism—yes, perhaps, but not escapism!" (SJ)

Une petite musique du soir (1984) (21') •Fl+Picc/Ob+EH/Cl+BsCl/ Asx/Hn/Bsn •SMIC/WIM

HEEGAARD, Lars

Compositeur danois.
Kwartet (1991) •SATB

HEESBEKE, G. van

Dyptique •Asx/Pno
Suite •Asx Solo

HEGVIK, Arthur (Ted)

Saxophoniste et professeur américain.
Modern Course for the Saxophone (1971) •HE
Scales and Arpeggios (1973) •HE
Tombeau de Mireille •SATB

HEIDEN, Bernhard (1910)

Compositeur américain, d'origine allemande, né à Frankfürt, le 24 VIII 1910. Travailla avec P. Hindemith. Aux U.S.A. depuis 1935.

"His music is neo-classical in general outline, and his contrapuntal idiom follows Hindemith's precepts." (BAKER) "Heiden is a highly accomplished and prolific composer, and his engaging musicality is best displayed in the many chamber works and sonatas. Initially he was strongly influenced by Hindemithian neo-classicism, but his music has become more concerned with sonority, and his use of texture, colour and register has grown more diversified and individual, as has his structural inventiveness." (W. SCHWINGER)

Diversion (1943) (7') •Asx/Band or Pno •Eto
Fantasia Concertante (1988) (12') •Asx/Wind Orch/Perc (or Pno) •Eto
Four Movements (1976) 1) Moderato 2) Allegro molto 3) Lento con espressione - Allegro alla marcia •4 Sx: SATB/Timp •Eto
Intrada (1970) (10') - Sextet •Fl/Ob/Cl/Asx/Hn/Bsn •South
Solo (1969) (6') (to E. ROUSSEAU) •Asx/Pno •AMP/B&B
Sonate (1937) (18') (to L. TEAL) 1) Allegro 2) Vivace 3) Adagio-Presto •Asx/Pno •Sch/AMP
Sonatina •Fl/Cl/Tsx/Hn/Trb/Harp/Vibr/Pno/Bass/Perc •MJQ

HEIDER, Werner (1930)

Compositeur allemand, né à Furth (Bavière), le 1er I 1930. Travailla avec W. Spilling et Höller.

"Ses oeuvres de tendance post-sérielle et de style assez éclectique, témoignent d'une réelle fantaisie." (Cl. ROSTAND)

"In his music he emphasizes structural factors, in which thematic elements follow serial organisation." (BAKER) "He includes Stravinsky, Webern and Stockhausen among his models; he became familiar with serial and aleatory music at Darmstadt summer courses, but he has not followed any specific system. Many of his compositions have originated from an interest in exploiting all the sound possibilities of an instrument." (W. SCHWINGER)

Edition (1985) •5 Sx: AAATB •Pet
Sax - 3 Stücke (1983-87) (10') 1) Jogging 2) Relaxing 3) Demonstration •Asx Solo •Pet
Sonata in jazz (1959) (11') (to J. de VRIES) (3 movements) •Asx/Pno •A&S

Typen (1957) (6') 1) Enjoué 2) Sentimental 3) Tendre 4) Bavard •Asx/Orch (2222/432/Perc/Harp/Str) or Pno •A&S
Verheissung (1988) •Asx Solo

HEILMANN, Harald (Arthur) (1924)

Compositeur allemand, né le 9 IV 1924, à Aue/Sachsen (Saxonie). Travailla avec Martin.
Pastorale (1991) (5') •Asx/Org •Tong
Sonata breve (1982) (7') •Asx/Org •Tong

HEILNER, Irwin (1908)

The Ghost of Amsterdam •Sx/Tape
My Lai •Sx/Narr
The Old Moonshiner (1984) •Asx/Pno
When our Children March •Sx/Narr

HEIM, Norman (1929)

Compositeur et clarinettiste américain. Professeur à l'University of Maryland.
Elegy Saxophonia, op. 66 •6 Sx: SAATTB •Nor
Essays, op. 82 (1984) (8') •Asx/Cl •Nor
Mosaics, op. 76 •6 Sx: SAATTB •Nor
Suite, op. 83 (1984) (13') (to R. JACKSON) •Asx/Pno •Nor

HEINICK, David

Compositeur américain.
Later, When I Dream (1987) (8') (to W. STREET) •Asx/Pno •adr

HEININEN, Paavo Johannes (1938)

Compositeur et pianiste finlandais, né le 13 I 1938, à Helsinki. Travailla avec Zimmermann, Merikanto, puis avec A. Zimmermann et Persichetti.

"Heininen's earliest works were influenced by Hindemith and Bartok. From 1963 new elements have gradually been appearing in his works. Restricted aleatory fieldtype textures have gained some importance, along with a thematic use of melodic and harmonic ideas." (I. ORAMO) "Heininen's musical language was based on dodecaphony from the outset and this is true of his 'easier' as of his more 'difficult' pieces. From the technical viewpoint, the way in which he adapts 12-tone technique to his ends is highly intricate: an analysis of the constellations of noterows reveals a multitude of possibilities." (J. KAIPAINEN)

Quintetto, op. 7 (1961) (18') •Fl/Sx/Pno/Vibr/Perc •Tie/FMIC
Discantus III, op. 33 (1976) (13') (to P. SAVIJOKI) •Asx Solo •FMIC
Concerto, op. 50 (1983) (30') (to P. SAVIJOKI) •Asx/Orch (2222/222/ Perc/Pno/Celesta/Str) •FMIC

HEINIO, Mikko (1948)

Compositeur finlandais, né le 18 V 1948.
"... in spe" - Diaphony (1984) (8'30) •Asx/Marimba+Vibr •JO/ FMIC

HEINKEL, Peggy

Chregalis •SATB •WWS
Concertino •Asx/Pno •DP

HEINS, John

Serenade 1) Allegro 2) Andante 3) Allegro molto 4) Allegro moderato •SATB

HEJDA, T.

Musicien polonais.
Méthode •B&H

HEKSTER, Walter (1937)

Compositeur néerlandais.
Between two worlds (1977) (12') (to E. BOGAARD) •Asx/Orch •Don
Monologues et conversation (1970-78) (4') •Asx/Vcl •Don

Of mere being (1982) (12') •Asx/Fl/Ob/Cl/2 Tpt/Perc/Electr. Guit
    •Don
Setting II (1982) (7') •Sx Solo •Don
Setting V (1985) (8') •Ob+EH/Cl+BsCl/Asx/Bsn •Don
Setting VII (1985) (9') •Sx/Perc •Don
Setting VIII (1986) (10') (for Amsterdam Saxophone Quartet)
    •SATB •Don
A song of peace •Voice/Cl/Asx/Vcl/Perc •Don
Windsong II (1970) (8') •Fl/Asx/Tpt •Don

HELDENBERG, Arthur
Improvisata •Tsx/Pno •WWS
Quatuor •SATB

HELFRITZ, Hans (1902)
Compositeur allemand, né le 25 VII 1902, à Hilbersdorf.
Concerto (1945) •Tsx/Orch or Pno •Sch

HELINEK, H.
3 Blue Sketches •Asx/Wind Group •EMod

HELLAN, Arne (1953)
Compositeur norvégien.
Sextet (1981) •Tpt/2 Sx/2 Guit/Perc •NMI

HELLER, Richard (1954)
Compositeur autrichien, né le 19 IV 1954 à Wien. Travailla avec A.
Kubizek et E. Urbanner.
Dialog •BsCl+Asx/Vibr+Marimba •adr
5 Stücke, op. 21/1-5 Prelude - Toccata - Hymn - Intermezzo - Fugue
    •Asx/Pno

HELLER, Stéphane (1814-1888)
Capriccio, Scherzetto, Canzonetta, op. 16 •SATB

HELLERMAN, William
Compositeur américain.
Circle Music I •Any 4 instruments •ACA
Circle Music II •Any 2 or more instruments •ACA
Circle Music III •Any 6 instruments •ACA
Round and About •Any 2 or more instruments •ACA/Bou

HELSIP, G.
West 10th •Sx/Perc

HEMKE, Frederick (1935)
Saxophoniste virtuose, concertiste, et professeur américain, né à
Milwaukee (Wisconsin). Travailla à Paris avec M. Mule (1er Prix du
Conservatoire). Doctorat de Musique à l'Université du Wisconsin.
New Directions in Saxophone Technique (1971) •Selm
Suite (1966) 1) Prelude 2) Chorale 3) Scherzo •SATB •adr

HEMMER, René (1919)
Compositeur luxembourgeois, né à Rodange (Luxembourg), le 27
XII 1919.
Coup de dés (1990) •SATB
Petite suite (1959) (7') •SATB •adr
Saxophonie (6 Pièces) (1984) •SATB

HEMPHILL, Julius
Last Supper at Uncle Tom's Cabin/The Promised Land - Ballet •6
Sx

HENDRICKS, Duane
The MacKenzie River Suite (1979) (to M. ECKROTH) •SATB

HENDRY, James
Compositeur anglais.
Lamentation, op. 8 (1989) (5'45) •SATB

HENDZE, Jesper (1955)
Percussionniste et compositeur de jazz danois. Travailla aux U.S.A.
The Beauty of the Beast (1990) (9'30) •SATB •Kon

HENNESSY, Swan (1866-1929)
Compositeur américain, né à Rodford (Illinois), le 24 XI 1866; mort
à Paris, le 26 VIII 1929.
   "Has was the son of an American-Irish settler. He wrote about 70
compositions, several of which are derived from Irish folk melodies;
his technical equipment was thorough; his idiom, impressionistic."
(BAKER)
2 Morceaux, op. 68 (1926) (to R. LAURENT) 1) Pièce celtique 2) Jazz
    •Asx/Pno •ME
4 Morceaux, op. 71 1) Fox-trot 2) Tango 3) Chanson de l'émigrant
    4) Lever de soleil dans les Hébrides •Asx/Pno •ME
Sonatine celtique, op. 62 (LAURENT) •Asx/Pno •ME

HENNING, Karl (1845-1914)
59 Duets •2 Sx •South

HENNING, Roslyn (see BROGUE, Roslyn)

HENNINGER, Richard (1944)
Compositeur canadien d'origine U.S.A., né à Pasadena (California).
Travailla avec K. Korn, T. Beversdorf, et R. Cedere, puis avec J.
Weinzweig et G. Ciamaga. Vit au Canada depuis 1967.
Evolutions: Music (1971) (to P. BRODIE) •Asx Solo •CMC

HENRY, Jean-Claude
Deux pièces (1956) (to Quatuor Desloges) •SATB

HENRY, Otto Walker (1933)
Compositeur américain, né à Reno (Nevada), le 8 V 1933. Travailla
avec G. Read et H. Norden.
The Cube (1974) (11') (to J. HOULIK) •Tsx/Pno •adr
New Adventures (1982) (to B. FOLEY) 1) Cenotaph 2) Caravan
    3) Escape 4) Coral Islands 5) Jungle Anne •Ob/Asx/Tape
    •RKM
Omnibus II •Asx/Pno •MP

HENTON, H. Bennie (1867-1938)
Clarinettiste et saxophoniste américain, né à Shelbyville. Appartint
en tant que saxophoniste au célèbre Sousa Band.
Laverne - Valse caprice (1910) •Asx/Pno •CF
Nadine - Valse caprice •Asx/Pno •CF

HEPPENER, Robert (1925)
Compositeur néerlandais né à Amsterdam, le 9 VIII 1925. Travailla
avec J. Ode, J. Boogert, et B. van Lier.
   "His work is noted particulary for strong melodic movement and for
a rather complex, clearly defined rhythmic structure; the harmony is
tonal." (J. WOUTERS)
Canzona (1969) (4') (to Limburgs Saxophone Quartet) •SATB
    •Don

HERBERG, Perig
Pevar benveg ("4 instruments") (to P. PAREILLE) Lent et caressant -
    Intense - Tempo primo •Ob/Cl/Asx/Bsn

HERBERT, Victor (1859-1924)
Gypsy Love Song (BUCHTEL) •1 Sx: T or A/Pno •Kjos
Gypsy Love Song (HARRIS) •2 Sx: AA/Pno or AAT/Pno •Lud
Ocean Breezes (BRIEGEL) •AATB •Bri

HERBIN, René (1911-1953)
Compositeur français, mort le 2 IX 1953.
Danse (1952) (3') •Asx/Pno •PN

HERFURTH, C. P.
A Tune a Day •Asx/Pno •Bos

HERMAN, N.
Wedgewood •Asx Solo •WWS

HERMAN, William
Expressions (1982) •3 Sx

HERMANN, Ralph
Compositeur américain.
Concertino (1969) •4 Sx: SATB/Str Orch

HERMANS, Nico
4 Impressions (1983) (12') •Tsx/Pno •Don

HERMANSSON, Christer (1943)
Compositeur suédois.
Aggjakten (1979) •Narr/Tsx/Trb/Guit/Bass/Perc •STIM
Rumba (1979) •Narr/2 Sx: ST/Trb/Guit/Pno/Bass •STIM

HERMSEN, Pieter
Compositeur néerlandais.
3 Movements (1986) (7') •SATB •Don

HEROLD, Louis Joseph (1791-1833)
Zampa (ROMBY) •Asx/Pno •PB

HERRER, P.
Saxophone Tutor •B&H/MB

HERSANT, Philippe (1948)
Compositeur français.
Extraits (to Quatuor d'Anches Français) •Ob/Cl/Asx/Bsn •adr

HERTZE, R.
Everybody Twostep Rag (SIBBING) •5 Sx: SAATB

HERTZOG, Christian
Compositeur américain.
Angry Candy (1989) (7') (for B. McKELVEY) •1 Performer: MIDI
   Wind Controller with Sampler, Squencer, MIDI Mapper, and
   FM Synthesizer •adr
The Cry of Those Being Eaten by America •Sx/Pno •adr

HERVIG, Richard
Divertimento No. 3 •AATB •Rub

HERZBERG, Max
Lament d'amor (1925) •Asx/Pno •Wie

HERZOG, Alfred
Compositeur et professeur français.
Quatuor (1978) (to Quatuor de Saxophones de Paris) •SATB

HESPOS, Hans-Joachim (1938)
Compositeur allemand, né le 13 III 1938, à Emden. Autodidacte.
   "C'est vers des méthodes spécifiques à chaque oeuvre que semble se
diriger un compositeur comme Hans-Joachim Hespos qui insiste sur la
nécessité singulière de la forme devant trouver à se matérialiser dans
une instrumentation et à travers un traitement des moyens sonores
intransposables." (D. J-Y. BOSSEUR) "Hors de tout système, auteur
d'une musique viscérale, issue de Varèse et du free jazz. Pour Hespos
il est temps que 'nous rêvions l'audace de nos rêves,' car nous
étouffons dans le tâtonnement aveugle du progrès. Et nous voici au
bord de l'impasse apocalyptique." (J-N. von der WEID)
   "His music belongs to no school or movement but shows links with
Schoenberg—more closely with his atonal phase than with his 12-note
serial music." (C. GOTTWALD)

Break •Ob/3 Tpt/2 Sx: TB/Vcl/Bass/Trb/Pno/Perc •EMod
Conga (1979) (15'30) •Tsx/5 Congas/2 Vln/2 Vla/2 Vcl/Bass •Hes
Druckspuren - geschattet (1970) (7'30) •Fl/Eb Cl/Asx/Bsn/2 Tpt/
   Trb/Bass •EMod
Dschen (1968) (11') •1 Sx: T+B/Str Orch (6321)
Einander - dedingenden (1966) (12-13') •Fl/Cl/Guit/Tsx/Vla
   •EMod
En-Kin das fern-nahe (1970) (5'30) Ssx/Cl/Bsn/Bass/Perc •EMod
Frottages •Asx/Vcl/Harp/Mandolin/Perc •EMod
Ika (1984) (5') (to D. KIENTZY) •Asx Solo
J. Lomba Trio (1980) (11') (to D. KIENTZY) - Théâtre musical •3 Sx:
   TTBs •Hes
Ka (1972) (8'30) •Bsx Solo/Bass Solo/Orch •EMod
Keime und male (9') •Picc/Fl/2 Cl/Asx/Hn/Guit/Vln/Vla/Bass/3 Perc
   •JJ
Passagen (1969) (9') •Cl/Asx/Tpt/Trb/Vla/Bass/Perc •EMod
Pico (1978) (4') (to D. KIENTZY) •Sx Solo: CBs or Sno
Profile (1972) (11') •Fl/Ob/Cl/Ssx/Bsn/Hn •EMod
Ragato (1986) (25') (to D. KIENTZY) •CBsSx/Bass/2 Perc/Instrumen-
   tal Ensemble

HESS, Nigel
Compositeur anglais.
"I can do anything..." (1981) (4') (for C. GRADWELL) •Sx/Pno

HETZEL
Photographic Fingering Chart •Pres

HEUBERGER, Richard (1850-1914)
Midnight Belles (KREISLER-LEIDZEIN) •2 Sx: AA/Pno or AAT •CFI

HEUMANN, Hans A.
Slavonic Fantasy (VOXMAN) •Asx/Pno •Rub

HEUSSENSTAMM, George (1926)
Compositeur américain, né à Los Angeles. Travailla avec L. Stein.
Canonograph 1 •Any 3 Winds: Fl/Ob/Cl/Sx/Bsn •SeMC
Dialogue, op. 77 (1984) (13') •Asx/Tuba •DP
Double Quintet, op. 83 (1985) (8') •10 Asx (3 double Ssx)
Duo, op. 71 (1981) (11') (to B. SPARKS) •Asx/Perc •DP
Duo, op. 89 (1988) •Sx/Perc •DP
Four Miniatures, op. 57 (1975) (9') (to R. GREENBERG) •Tsx/Fl/Ob/
   Vln •DP
Music for 12, op. 86 (1986) (13'30) (to J-M. LONDEIX) •12 Sx:
   SnoSSAAATTTBBBs
Periphony No. 3, op. 70 (1980) (18') •16 Sx: 4 x SATB/4 Perc •DP
Playphony, op. 56 (1975) (12') (to E. ERVIN) •Asx/Perc •DP
Quartet No. 1, op. 78 (1984) (13') •SATB •DP
Saxoclone, op. 42 (1971) (11') (to K. DORN) •1 Sx: A+T/Tape
   •SeMC
Saxophonium, op. 82 (1985) (10') •1 Sx: A+S/Euphonium
Score, op. 46 (1972) (15') (to my wife Mary) •16 Sx: 4 x SATB
   •SeMC

HEUTBERG, Cortland
Improvisation and electronic variation instrument •Any Instrument/
   Tape

HEVER, S.
Saxophone Tutor •Musi

HEWITT, Harry Donald (1921)
Compositeur américain, né le 4 III 1921. Travailla avec H. Lagassey,
   J. Barone, et E. Murray.
Adornments (1971) (20') (to K. & S. DORN) Sx/Tape •DP
Concerto No. 1 in C (1972) (20') Asx/Orch (2222/232/Perc/Str) •adr
Concerto No. 2 (1972) (15') •Asx/Orch (2222/232/Perc/Str) •adr

I Want My Karma (1971) (8') (to K. & S. Dorn) •Sx/
  Actress+Singer/Dancer •DP
34 Preludes, op. 439 (1972) (90') •Pno/Guit/Perc/Sx •DP
Saxercises, op. 438, no. 5 (1971) (60') •Sx/Tape •DP
Venus in Transit (1971) (15') (to K. & S. Dorn) •Sx/Tape •DP

HEYN, Thomas (1953)
Jazz Inspirierte Miniaturen (1989) •SATB

HEYN, Volker (1938)
Compositeur allemand.
Blues two (1983) •Voice/Vcl/Sx/Perc •Br&Ha
Buon natale, fratello Fritz (1984/85) (12') (to D. Kientzy) •Sx Solo:
  S+T •Br&Ha
Sandwich Gare de l'Est (1986) (12'30) (to D. Kientzy) •1 Sx:
  Sno+CBs/2 Hn/2 Tpt/2 Trb •Br&Ha

HIAN, Ben
Three Songs •2 Sx/Pno or Tsx/Pno •Pet

HICKMAN, David R.
Music Speed Reading (1979) •WM

HIGGINS, Dick (Richard C.) (1938)
Compositeur américain, d'origine anglaise, né à Cambridge, le 15 III
1938. Travailla avec J. Cage.
  "In his production he pursues the objective of total involvement in
which music is verbalized in conceptual designs without or expressed
in physical action." (Baker)
Clown Garden •14 Sx: SSAAAAATTTBBBBs
Suggested by Small Swallows - Theatre piece •Sx/Actress •DP

HIGUET, Nestor
Compositeur belge.
Thème, variations et fugue (to Quatuor Belge) •SATB

HIJMAN, Julius (1901-1969)
Compositeur et pianiste néerlandais, né à Almelo, le 25 I 1901; mort
à New York, le 6 I 1969. Travailla avec D. Schaeffer, puis, à Vienne.
Vit actuellement aux U.S.A.
Sonatine (1934) 1) Allegro 2) Moderato 3) Allegro con brio •Asx/
  Pno

HILDEMANN, Wolfgang (1925)
Compositeur allemand, né le 17 VI 1925, à Eger. Travailla avec F.
Finke, J. Keilberth, et A. Nowakowski.
Concerto coreografico (1976) (22') (to F. Daneels) •Asx/Orch
  (3333/3331/Perc/Harp/Str) •adr
Farben und Klänge (1982) •Asx/Str Quartet •adr
Jeux saxophoniques à quatre 1) Introduction 2) Air 3) Interlude
  4) Cadence 5) Finale •SATB •PJT
Partita coloratura (1978) Tempo 130 - Invention - Arioso - Tempo
  G-Dur Invention •Asx/Org (or Harp or Pno) •Mau
Pier fiali VII - Glimpser (1989) (6') •Asx Solo •adr
Psalmodia III (1973) Intonation - Cantus - Organum - Cantus -
  Motetus - Cantus - Jubilus •Asx/Org/Chorus •MV

HILGEMANN, P.
Compositeur américain.
Sonata (1960) •Asx/Pno

HILL, Dorothy
Concert •Asx/Orch

HILL, Jackson
Entourage •SATB •SeMC

HILLBORG, Anders (1954)
Compositeur suédois, né à Stockholm, le 31 V 1954. Travailla avec
G. Bucht puis, aux U.S.A., avec M. Feldman.
  "In 1980 Hillborg went on an educational visit to the U.S.A., where
he was confronted with 'minimalism' a tendency which he has subse-
quently disavowed." (H-G. P.)
Variations (1991) •Soprano Voice/Mezzo Soprano Voice/Fl/Sx/
  Perc/Vla/Bass •SMIC

HILLE, Wolfgang
Compositeur allemand.
Es wäre besser, es gäbe keine Nächte (1993) •Sx/Voice •INM

HILLER, Lejaren (1924)
Compositeur américain, né à New York, le 23 II 1924. Etudia la
chimie avant de se consacrer à la musique. Travailla avec Sessions et
Babbitt.
  "C'est en 1956 qu'est réalisée la première oeuvre de composition
entièrement automatique, et programmée, la *Suite Illiac*, du nom de
l'ordinateur qui la calcula. C'était un essai de Lejaren Hiller, qui se
trouve donc être le père ou tout au moins le véritable précurseur de la
composition automatique dans le monde." (J. & B. Massin)
  "His investigation of computer applications led him to experiment in
composition with computers working in collaboration with Leonard
Isaacson." (G. Chase)
Quartet (1984) (for the Amherst Saxophone Quartet) 1) Presto
  furioso 2) Adagio espressivo - andantino •SATB

HILLIARD, Jimmy
Compositeur américain.
Saxonata (1958) (3'30) •AATB •MCA

HILLIARD, John
Compositeur américain.
Fantasy (1976) (to S. Mauk) •Ssx/Pno

HILMY, Steven Cambel
Compositeur américain.
Sonata (1987) (to C. Leaman) •Asx/Pno •adr

HINDEMITH, Paul (1895-1963)
Compositeur, altiste, chef d'orchestre, et théoricien allemand, né à
Hanau (Hesse), le 16 XI 1895; mort à Frankfürt, le 28 XII 1963.
Professeur de composition à la Hochschule für Musik de Berlin (1927),
collègue de Gustave Bumcke, il intéressa nombre de ses élèves au
saxophone (S. Karg-Elert, H. Brehme, B. Heiden, E. von Borck, G.
Bialas, H. Gensmer, W. Glaser, E. Dressel, etc.).
  "Ennemi des effusions romantiques et de l'expressionnisme autant
que de l'impressionnisme, indifférent à la qualité du matériau sonore,
rejetant l'harmonie traditionnelle, usant volontiers d'un langage vigoureux, aux contrastes hardis et violents, Hindemith apparaît comme
un créateur volontaire et conscient de vastes architectures sonores, où
la beauté naît davantage de la forme que du fond. Ses oeuvres exemptes
de tout message sensible, s'adressent moins au coeur qu'à l'intelligence." (Ferchault) "Sa doctrine est fondée sur l'atonalité, mais avec
des bases infiniment plus logiques, moins conventionnelles que celles
de Schoenberg. Ayant supprimé les préséances de la gamme, il fonde
son harmonie sur les résonances harmoniques naturelles." (P. Wolff)
"Nulle place n'est faite chez lui à l'académisme. C'est tout simplement
un musicien qui crée de la musique ainsi qu'un arbre porte des fruits,
sans le moindre propos philosophique." (A. Einstein) "Voulant rompre
avec le chromatisme de Wagner et de Strauss, et retrouver la musique
pure, Hindemith prend comme point de départ lointain, Brahms auquel
il est relié par un chaînon intermédiaire: Max Reger." (P. Collaert)
"Hindemith est incontestablement l'un des principaux chef de file de
la musique de son époque, l'un de ceux qui a le plus contribué à doter

la musique d'un style, d'un langage et d'une esthétique réellement nouveaux." (R. BERNARD) "Paul Hindemith s'est trouvé à la tête de la nouvelle génération musicale allemande qui s'est efforcée de se dégager du subjectivisme passionnel des Romantiques et de renouer avec l'école classique." (L. GAUDRAN) "Il a été la grande personnalité musicale entre les deux guerres. D'abord traditionaliste, il est vite passé à l'avant-garde avec quelques scandales pendant les années 20; il est ensuite revenu en pente douce vers la tradition, pour finir dans l'académisme. Sa production est, avec celle de Darius Milhaud, l'une des plus considérables de l'époque. Et son influence, non moins considérable, s'est très fortement fait sentir, surtout dans les pays germaniques et alémaniques, ainsi qu'en Scandinavie et aux Etats-Unis." (Cl. ROSTAND)

"An exceptionally prolific composer, Hindemith has written works in all genres and for all instrumental combinations including a series of sonatas for each orchestral instrument with piano. Hindemith's style may be described as a synthesis of modern, Romantic, Classical and archaic principles, a combination saved from the stigma of eclecticism only by Hindemith's superlative mastery of technical means. As theorist and pedagogue, Hindemith has developed a self-consistent method of presentation derived from the acoustical nature of harmonic combinations." (BAKER) "Despite its originality, or perhaps because of its consistency, Hindemith's music has exerted no significant influence on composers of later generations. Yet its authentic sound and consummate technique assures its status both as a body of finished works of art of unassailable integrity and as a fitting monument to the neo-classical ideals of the 20th century." (G. GELLES)

Konzerstück (1933) (11'30) (to S. RASCHER) •2 Sx: AA •MM
Sonate (1943) (8'30) 1) Ruhig bewegt 2) Lebhaft 3) Sehr langsam 4) Lebhaft •Alto Hn (Mellophone) or Hn or Asx/Pno •Sch
Trauermusik (1936) (HUNT) •Asx/Pno
Trio, op. 47 (1928) I) 1-Solo 2-Arioso 3-Duett II) 1-Allegro 2-Vivo 3-Allegro 4-Espressivo •Pno/Vla/Heckelphone (or Tsx) •ME/Sch

HINE, Charles
Compositeur anglais.
Evagations (1972) (15'30) (to London Saxophone Quartet) •SATB

HINES, Malcolm (1948)
Saxophoniste canadien.
Quartet •SATB •adr

HIRANUMA, Yuri
Compositeur japonais.
Tiki Tika-Ta •Asx/Electr. Org

HISCOTT, James (1948)
Compositeur canadien
Ballad No. 1 (1978) (14') •Fl/Cl/Sx/Perc/Accordion/Pno •CMC
Mac Crimmon Will Never Return (1977) (4'30) •Asx/Accordion •CMC
Midnight Strut (1978) (13') •Asx Solo •CMC
Variations on O. Célestin's "My Josephine" (1978) (9') •Fl/Cl/Sx/Perc/Pno •CMC

HLOBIL, Emil (1901-1987)
Compositeur tchécoslovaque, né à Meziimosti, le 11 X 1901; mort le 25 I 1987. Travailla avec J. Kricka, V. Novak, et J. Suks à Prague.
"During the German occupation he evolved a synthesis of techniques introduced during the 1920s and 1930s, while at the same time his music came to express more intense nationalist feelings; but after the war he simplied both the form and expression of his work." (M. KUNA)
Canto pensieroso (1976) (8') •Tsx/Pno •CHF
Marcato di danza (1979) (2'30) •SATB •Praha

Quartetto, op. 93 (1974) (12') (to S. RASCHER) 1) Allegro 2) Grave 3) Allegro •SATB •CHF

HO, Wai On (1946)
Quartet (1974) •SATB

HOAG, Charles Kelso (1931)
Compositeur américain, né le 14 XI 1931. Travailla avec P. Bezanson et D. Milhaud.
An Elegy in Troubled Times (1972) (4') (to R. STANTON) •Asx/Org •adr

HOBBS
Sextet •Tsx/Fl/Ob/Cl/Hn/Bsn •DP

HOCK, Franj van
Compositeur néerlandais.
Burlesque (1979) •SATB

HOCK, James
Compositeur américain.
3 Expressions •Sx •SeMC

HOCK, Peter
Phrasen für Sax Quartet (1973) •SATB

HOCKETT, Charles F.
Compositeur américain.
Vocalise •Ssx/Pno

HODEIR, André (1921)
Critique musical, écrivain, arrangeur, et compositeur français , né à Paris, le 22 VI 1921. Travailla avec O. Messiaen. Fondateur (1954) du "Jazz Group de Paris" et de la revue *Jazz Hot.*
"Il écrit des oeuvres ambitieuses qui le classent comme l'un des plus audacieux parmi les orchestrateurs soucieux d'élargir le langage du jazz." (A. CLERGEAT) "Il a adhéré au dodécaphonisme mais non pas au principe sériel, ce qui, en d'autres termes, équivaut à dire qu'il pratique l'atonalisme." (R. BERNARD)
"In his writings he offers bold theories and startling evaluations. His book *Since Debussy* aroused much controversy on account of its iconoclastic attitude towards recognized modern composers and immoderate praise for purported young geniuses." (BAKER) "His writings are devoted mainly to jazz, especially its formal problems and the relationship between composing and improvisation. The bold ideas he has expounded on contemporary art music have inevitably aroused controversy." (C. SPIETH)
Ambiguité II (8') •3 Sx: ATB/2 Tpt/Trb/Bass/Perc •MJQ
Bicinium (3') •3 Sx: ATB/2 Tpt/Trb/Bass/Perc •MJQ
Cadenze (4') •Bsx/Tpt/Trb/Pno/Bass/Perc •MJQ
Evanescence (4') •3 Sx: ATB/2 Tpt/Trb/Vibr/Bass/Perc •MJQ
Jazz cantata (10') •Soprano Voice/3 Sx: ATB/2 Tpt/Trb/Vibr/Bass/Perc •MJQ
Oblique (3'30) •2 Sx: AT/Trb/Pno/Bass/Perc •MJQ
On a scale (5'30) •3 Sx: ATB/2 Tpt/Trb/Vibr/Bass/Perc •MJQ
Osymetrios (3') •Tpt/Tsx/Trb/Pno/Bass/Drums •MJQ
Palais idéal (12'30) •3 Sx: ATB/2 Tpt/Trb/Vibr/Bass/Perc •MJQ
Paradoxe I •Tsx/Trb/Bass/Perc •MJQ
Tension - détente (3'30) •3 Sx: ATB/2 Tpt/Trb/Vibr/Bass/Perc •MJQ
Triade (5'30) •3 Sx: ATB/2 Tpt/Trb/Vibr/Bass/Perc •MJQ
Trope à St-Trop •Tpt/Tsx/Trb/Pno/Bass/Drums •MJQ

HODKINSON, Sidney Phillip (1934)
Compositeur américain né à Winnipeg (Manitoba, Canada), le 17 I 1934. Travailla avec B. Rogers, R. L. Finney, et G. B. Wilson.
"In his music he pursues advanced techniques employing serial and

aleatory resources." (BAKER)

Another Man's Poison (1970) (6'30) •1 Sx: A or T/Orch (1212/
  2000/Pno/Str) •adr

Armistice (1966) (6') •Any group of instruments (any Sx) •RMI

Dissolution of the Serial (1967) (8') (to P. REHFELDT) •Asx/Pno •adr

Edge of the Olde One (1977) •Asx (or EH)/Chamber Orch (2 Perc/
  Str) •Pres

Funks - Improvisation (1969) (5') •7 Jazz Musicians: 4 Sx: AATB/
  Guit/Bass/Perc •adr

Interplay (1966) (12'30) •Fl+Picc/Cl/Asx/Perc/Bass •CMC

Three Dance Preludes (1981) (13') (to J. SAMPEN) 1) Bop:
  Risolutissimo - in memoriam Charlie Parker 2) Ballad: as a
  melancholy dance - for Lee Konitz 3) Riff Remnants: Molto
  Vivace - in memoriam Jimmy Dorsey •Asx/Pno •DP/NP

Trinity (1971) (to T. STACY) •Sx Solo (A or T or B) •adr

HODY, Jean

Dialogue •Asx/Pno •Chou
Souvenirs d'enfant •2 Sx •Bil
Une révérence •Asx/Pno •Chou

HOFFER, Bernard

Compositeur américain.

Concerto (1980) (32') (for A. REGNI) •Asx/Wind Orch •Shir

Preludes and Fugues (1977) (25') (to New York Saxophone Quartet)
  •4 Sx: SATB/Brass Quintet •Shir

Quartet I (1992) (to New York Saxophone Quartet) •SATB

The River - Symphony (1984) (30') (for M. LANG) •4 Sx: SATB/
  Large Perc Ensemble •Shir

Three Diversions for Doubling (1975) (19') (to New York Saxophone Quartet) •SATB •NYSQ

Variations on a Theme of Stravinsky (1974) (10') (to New York
  Saxophone Quartet) •SATB •NYSQ

HOFFMAN

Cavatine & Polacca (from *Armin*) (H. LUREMAN) •Bb Sx/Pno •TM

HOFFMANN, Adolf G.

Alborada •Eb Sx/Pno •Bel
Jota aragonesa •Eb Sx/Pno •B&H
Sérénade basque •Eb Sx/Pno •Bel

HOFFMAN, Allan

Duo •Sx/Narr •DP
6 Versions •Asx/Bass/Vibr

HOFFMAN, Norbert

Compositeur luxembourgeois.

Capriola •Eb or Bb Sx/Pno •Scz
Rapsodie champêtre •Eb or Bb Sx/Pno •Scz
1st song without words •Eb or Bb Sx/Pno •Scz
2nd song without words •Eb or Bb Sx/Pno •Scz
Suite concertante (1980) •2 Sx: AA/Band

HOFFMANN, Robin

Compositeur allemand.

Inquisition I (1993) •Asx/1 Performer obbligato •INM

HOFMANN, Thomas (1958)

Compositeur allemand.

Suite (1986) (9') •Asx/Orch (2222/2221/Perc/Str)
Konzertantes (1988) (20') •Pno/Asx/Str Orch

HOFMANN, Wolfgang (1922)

Compositeur allemand, né à Karlsruhe, le 6 IX 1922.

Concertino (1982) (to J. BOITOS) •Asx/Str Orch

HOIBY, Lee

Compositeur américain.

Three Monologues (15') (to K. RADNOFSKY & K. BEARDSLEY)
  •Soprano Voice/Asx/Pno •AMP

HOLBROOKE, Joseph (1878-1958)

Compositeur anglais, né à Croydon, le 5 VII 1878; mort à Londres,
le 5 VIII 1958.

"Joseph Holbrooke a composé des oeuvres fortement influencées par
R. Strauss." (N. DUFOURCQ) "Artiste combatif et original fait preuve de
vigueur et d'un sens de la couleur assez rare chez ses compatriotes." (E.
VUILLERMOZ) "Champion d'un style néo-romantique anglais, à grand
orchestre." (FASQUELLE) "Holbrooke appartient à une nouvelle génération de musiciens, la première, à laquelle a été réservée la tâche
d'édifier la musique du XXe siècle, une musique qui puisse revendiquer sa nationalité anglaise." (Cl. SAMUEL) "Outre le surnom de
'Wagner anglais,' on donna également à Joseph Holbrooke ceux de
'Moussorgsky anglais,' 'Strauss anglais,' 'Berlioz anglais'… Ce dernier qualificatif provient sans doute de la propension d'Holbrooke à
utiliser des masses instrumentales énormes et des instruments inusités.
En fait, en bon anglais, il tira souvent son inspiration du *folk song*." (G.
GEFEN) "Son oeuvre immense, actuellement redécouverte, le situe au
premier plan de la renaissance musicale britannique au début du
siècle." (M. FLEURY)

"Although he composed prolifically, and had many ardent admirers
of his music, he never succeeded in establishing himself as a representative British composer. Perhaps this was owing to the fact that he stood
aloof from modernistic developments of European music, and preferred to write for a mass audience, which, however, failed to materi-
alize at the infrequent performances of his music." (BAKER)

Concerto in B flat "Tamerlaine," op. 115 (1939) (15') (to W. LEAR)
  1) Allegro grazioso 2) Allegretto 3) Con brio
  •Cl+Asx+Tsx+Ssx/Orch (2222/2210/Perc/Str) or Pno •B&H/
  Klen

Cyrene, op. 88 (1925) (4'30) •Asx/Pno •Klen

Sonata, op. 99 (1928) •Asx/Pno

HOLCOMBE, Bill

Compositeur américain.

Stephen Foster Revisited (1991) (to the Empire Saxophone Quartet)
  •4 Sx: SATB/Orch •Gaz

HOLE, Rob

Toby and Pooh Bear (1993) •Tsx/Perc •INM

HOLEWA, Hans (1905)

Compositeur suédois d'origine autrichienne, né à Vienne, le 26 V
1905. Travailla avec Busoni et J. Heinz. Etabli en Suède depuis 1937.

"Holewa's starting point as composer was Mahler. He has also
received decisive impulses from Alban Berg and his circle. In his
compositions he has shown a strict 12-tone technique." "He began to
use 12-note techniques in 1939, but not until 1959 did he make a mark
as a composer in Sweden. Thereafter his intense and strongly disciplined music gradually acquired an increasingly striking lyricism." (R.
HAGLUND) "His compositions are never lengthy, but rather concise and
quintessential, even though during the years he has passed from
aphoristic disparate outlines to fuller, airier movements." (H-G. P.)

Lamenti (1976) (5') (3 pieces) •Asx/Hn/Bsn •STIM

HOLLAND, Dulcie Sybil (1913)

Compositeur australien, né à Sydney, le I V 1913. Travailla avec A.
Hill, R. Agnew, et J. Ireland.

Aria (1952) (5') (to C. AMADIO) •Asx/Str Orch •adr
Musette and Gigue (1958) (4') •Sx Solo •adr
Sax-happy (1958) (3') (to C. AMADIO) •Sx Solo •adr
Sky one (1958) (3') (to C. AMADIO) •Sx Solo •adr

Sonata (1953) (11'30) (to C. AMADIO) •Asx/Pno •adr
Summer serenade (1961) (4') •Sx Solo •adr
Waltz-lament (1960) (4') •Sx Solo •adr

HOLLFELDER, Waldram (1924)

Compositeur allemand.
Divertimento (1982) (5'30) 1) Allegro 2) Presto 3) Tranquillo
4) Vivo •SATB •VDMK
Quartett (1989) (7') 1) Toccata 2) Fantasie 3) Finale •SATB

HOLLIDAY, Kent

Sonata 1) Invocation 2) Elegy 3) Tarantella •Asx/Pno

HOLLOWAY, Laurie

Running Buffet (1981) (to the English Saxophone Quartet) •SATB
•LM

HOLLOWAY, Robin (Greville) (1943)

Compositeur anglais, né à Leamington Spa, le 19 X 1943. Travailla
avec Goehr.
"Holloway veut le tonal, ce qui signifie: 'réaliser des choses qui ont
été faites avant lui, mais à ma propre façon.' " (J-N. von der WEID)
"Robin Holloway est resté proche du style rapsodique d'un Schumann
ou d'un Brahms. Nombre de ses pièces témoignent d'un néo-romantisme violent et sincère." (G. GEFEN)
"Later works, have seen an attempt to synthesize his harmonic gains
of the 1970s with his gestural vigour of the 1960s, with remarkable
polymetric results." (B. NORTHCOTT)
Double Concerto (1987) •Cl/Asx/Orch

HOLMBERG, Gunnar (1931)

Compositeur suédois.
Schizofreni no. 1 - Avantgardistik etyd, op. 15 (1990) (3') Bsx Solo
•SMIC

HOLMBERG, Peter (1948)

Musica alta e bassa (1979) (12') •Fl/Tpt/Bsx/Tuba/Vln/Vcl •STIM

HOLMES, G. E. (1873-1945)

Saxophoniste, professeur, et compositeur américain, né le 14 II 1873,
à Baraboo (Wisconsin); mort à Chicago, le 10 II 1945. Travailla avec
G. Mitchell, W. Heath, Lattimer, et Weldon.
Ariel - Valse caprice •Eb Sx/Pno •CF
Auld Lang Syne (HARTMANN) •Eb Sx/Pno •CF
Ben Bolt •Eb Sx/Pno •CF
Christmas Medley •SATB or AATB •Ken
Cosette - Valse caprice (1929) •Eb Sx/Pno •Bar
Coventry Carol •SATB or AATB •Ken
Little Lone Waltz •AATB •Bar
Master Builder March •AATB •Bar
Memories of Stephen Foster •AATB •Bar
Primrose Intermezzo •AATB •Bar
Saxophone Symphony Album •AATB •Rub
Sextette - Spiritual fantasie •6 Sx •Rub
Spiritual Fantasie •AATB •Rub
Symphony Ensemble Series (LONG) •AATB •Bar
Tyrolean Fantasia •Bb Sx or Eb Sx/Pno •CF
Zayda - valse caprice (1929) •Bar

HÖLSKY, Adriana (1953)

Pianiste et compositeur allemand, d'origine roumaine, né le 30 VI
1953 à Bucarest. Travailla à Stuttgart, Siena, et Darmstadt.
Flux - Reflux (1981) (10'30) •Asx Solo •adr

HOLST, Gustav (1874-1934)

Dargason (from *St. Paul's Suite*, op. 29, no. 2) (1912) (SIBBING) •Sx
Ensemble

HOLSTEIN, Jean-Paul (1939)

Pianiste et compositeur français.
Chanson de flûte (4 Volumes) •Asx/Pno
5 Enigmes (d'après Lao Tseu) (1980) (24') (to Quatuor Deffayet)
•SATB •EMRF
Porcelaine de Sax •Asx/Pno •Lem
Saxophone en larmes •Asx/Pno •Lem
Suite en bleu (1991) •Asx/Pno/Perc/Ondes martenot (ad lib.) •Bil
Suite irrévérencieuse (1982) (to J-Y. FOURMEAU) 1) Trépidation (à
Paris chez Stravinsky) 2) Valse (à Vienne avec Schoenberg)
3) Langueurs (à Montfort l'Amaury, chez Ravel) 4) A la
recherche de l'âme populaire (en Europe centrale, avec Bartok et
Kodaly) 5) Improvisation (aux Champs-Elysées, avec
Gershwin). •Asx/Pno •Lem

HOLVICH, Karl

Sarabande •2 Sx/Band

HOLZMANN, Rodolfo (1910)

Compositeur, professeur, ethnomusicologue, et hautboïste péruvien
d'origine allemande, né à Breslau, le 27 XI 1910. Travailla avec Vogel
à Berlin, H. Scherchen à Strasbourg, et Rathaus à Paris.
"As a composer he kept abreast of European trends: the suites of the
1940s embedded Spanish or Peruvian melodies in orchestral eider-
down, but later works, such as the powerful *Dodedicata* are stark, serial
pieces. His many composition pupils include Iturriaga, Garrido Lecca
and Pinilla." (R. STEVENSON)
Divertimento (1936) •Fl/Cl/Sx/Hn/Bsn
Sarabande y Toccata (1934) •Asx/Pno
Sonata •Asx/Pno
Suite (1933) •Asx/BsCl/Tpt/Pno
Suite (1934) •Asx/Pno
Suite a tres temas •Asx/Tpt/Cl/Pno/Bongos

HONEGGER, Arthur (1892-1955)

Concerto da camera (1948) (12'30) (LONDEIX) •Fl (or Ssx)/Asx (or
EH)/Str Orch or Pno •Sal
Petite suite n° 1 (1934) (2'30) •2 Sx (parties en ut)/Pno •CDM

HOOK, James (1746-1827)

Adagio and Allegretto, op. 83 (GEE) •3 Sx: AAA or AAT or TTT
•South
Andante and Rondo, op. 83, no. 3 •3 Sx: AAA or AAT or TTT
•CPP
Andantino (VOXMAN & BLOCK) •3 Sx: AAT •South
Engelse Sonat (JOOSEN) •Bb Sx/Pno •Mol
6 Trios (VOXMAN) •3 Sx: AAT •Rub

HOOVER, Katherine (1937)

Suite (1980) (for the Amherst Saxophone Quartet) 1) "Going to
London" 2) Count Off 3) Ka's Tune 4) Honk! •SATB

HOPKINS, Bill (1943-1981)

Compositeur et critique musical anglais, né le 5 VI 1943 à Prestbury,
mort en 1981. Travailla avec Nono, Rubbra, Wellesz, puis avec O.
Messiaen et J. Barraque.
"His music proceeds particularly from the work of Boulez and
Barraqué, on both of whom he has written with keen insight. *Sensation*
has passages of tense, ecstatic writing, which have some parallel in
Barraque's *Sequence*, before feeling is withdrawn towards the chill
settings of Beckett's French poems at the close." (P. GRIFFITHS)
Sensation (1965) •Soprano Voice/Tsx/Tpt/Harp/Vla •Sch

HORIUCHI, Toshio (1953)

Compositeur japonais.
Fantasy (1975) (to K. UEDA) •2 Sx: AA/Pno

HORN, Art

Professeur américain.
Modern Method for Saxophone (1925) •NM

HORNOFF, G. Alfred (1902)

Compositeur allemand, né à Dresden, le 8 II 1902. Travailla avec Pellegrini et G. Schumann.
Variations über da Volklied •SATB

HOROVITZ, Joseph (1926)

Pianiste, chef d'orchestre, et compositeur anglais né à Vienne (Autriche), le 26 V 1926. Travailla avec N. Boulanger.
"He is a composer of remarkable versatility, graceful with an enviable ability to communicate, whether in his refreshingly light or more serious styles." (E. Bradbury)
Variations on a Theme of Paganini (1977) (8') (to English Saxophone Quartet) •SATB •RSC

HORVIT, Michael (1932)

Compositeur américain, né le 22 VI 1932 à Brooklyn (New York). Travailla avec W. Piston, A. Copland, G. Read, et L. Foss.
Antiphon (1971) 1) Recitativo - mosaicus 2) Mysterium 3) Cantus contrapunctus 4) Ostini 5) Epilogus •Asx/Tape •DP

HORWOOD, Michael S.

Compositeur canadien.
Facets (1974) (20') •Narr/Sx/Tpt/Hn/Trb/Pno/Accordion/Electr. Bass/2 Electr. Guit •CMC
For David and Johannes (1985) (to D. Mott) •Bsx Solo
Interphases (1975) (13') •Fl/Sx/Accordion (or Org)/Pno/2 Perc •CMC
Microduet No. 6 (1978) (2'30) •Sx/Perc •CMC

HOUBEN, Guido

Compositeur allemand.
Sax mit Worten (1993) •Baritone Voice/Tsx •INM

HOUDY, Pierrick/Pierre (1929)

Compositeur canadien, d'origine français, né à Rennes, le 18 I 1929. Travailla avec D. Milhaud et J. Rivier. Installé au Canada.
Cassation (1991) •SATB •CMC
Chemin (1977) (9') (to Quatuor Bourque) 1) Etude 2) La découverte 3) De multiples chemins - Final •SATB •Bil
5 Caractères en forme d'étude (1988) (8'30) •2 Sx: AA •CMC
Kastchentamoun (1974) (to Cl. Brisson) •Asx/Pno
Largo et toccata (1968) •Asx/Pno
Romanesca (1964) (2'30) •Asx/Pno •Led

HOUKOM, Alf S. (1935)

Compositeur américain né au Minnosota.
Shadows (1984) (7') (to W. Street) •Asx/Pno

HOULIK, James (1942)

Saxophoniste concertiste et professeur américain, né à Bay Shore (New York), le 4 XII 1942. Travailla avec W. Willett, S. Rascher, et W. Coggins.
"James Houlik has been a leader in establishing the tenor saxophone as an accepted solo voice for the performance of serious music." (H. Gee)
Two Lyric Pieces •Tsx/Pno •South

HOUNSELL

Showcase for Saxes •5 Sx/Pno/Bass/Perc •TMPI

HOUSKOVA, R.

Compositeur tchèque.
Music for Four Saxophones •SATB

HOUSTON, Rudy

Avant Garde Duets •2 Sx: AA or TT •DP

HOVEY, Nilo

Compositeur américain.
Daily Exercices (A. Pares) (1950) •Bel
Pratical Studies (1933) (2 Volumes) •Bel
Rubank Elementary Method •Rub

HOVHANESS, Alan (1911)

Compositeur américain, d'origines écossaise et arménienne, né à Somerville (Massachusetts), le 8 III 1911. Travailla avec B. Martinu et Fr. Converse.
"Ses oeuvres sont inspirées de la musique religieuse et de la musique populaire arménienne, notamment ses choeurs religieux et ses pages symphoniques." (Larousse) "Hovhaness s'est intéressé aux musiques indiennes et arméniennes." (Fasquelle) " Les ouvrages de Hovhaness séduisent à la fois par la beauté du matériel mélodique, la pureté de l'inspiration et l'originalité de l'écriture." (Cl. Samuel) "Hovhaness compose selon les techniques des premiers temps de la chrétienté de la musique médiévale et de l'art moderne arménien." (V. Thomson)
"Its tranquility and gentleness is still too alien to an age predominantly dissonant and rhetorical; but sooner or later so large and distinguished an output should find its way into the general concert world, even if only for its contrast and exotic value." (P. Glanville-Hicks) "While mastering the traditional technique of composition, he became fascinated by Indian and other Oriental musical systems; from his earliest works, he made use of Armenian melorythmic patterns. As a result, he gradually evolved an individual type of art, in which quasi Oriental cantillation and a curiously melodic texture became the mainstay. By dint of easeless repetition of themes and relentless dynamic tension, a definite impression is created of originality; the atmospheric effects often suggest Impressionistic exoticism." (Baker) "Hovhaness attained a considerable reputation in the 1950s, a decade during which he travelled widely and embarked on a third stylistic period. This combined elements of the first two periods as well as various experimental and international procedures. These international tendencies continued in a fourth period, begining around 1960, where Far Eastern elements, particularly Japanese and Korean predominate." (A. Rosner)
After Water •3 Cl/3 Tpt/3 Asx/Perc/Harp/Pno •ACA
Concerto (1981) (to G. Scudder, P. Cohen, & K. Radnofsky) •Ssx/Str •Pet
The Flowering Peach, op. 125 (1954) (21') 1) Overture 2) a) Lifting of Voices b) Building the Ark 3) Intermezzo 4) Rain 5) Love Song 6) Sun and Moon 7) Rainbow Hymn •Asx+Cl/Vibr/Perc/Harp (or Pno) •AMP
Is This Survival? (*King Vahaken*), op.59 (1949) •4 Cl/Asx/4 Tpt/Perc
Soliloquy •Asx/Pno •Ken
Suite, op. 291 (1976) (7') 1) Adagio espressivo 2) Senza misura - Allegro - Allegro - Vivace 3) Andante espressivo •Asx/Guit •adr
The World Beneath the Sea, op. 133/1 (1953) •Asx/Harp/Vibr/Timp/Gong

HOWARD, Robert

Compositeur américain.
Soliloquy •Asx Solo •Ken
Trilogue •Asx/Vla/Harp •Art

HOWLAND, Dulcie (1926)

Compositeur australien.
Saturday Stroll (to P. Clinch) •Asx/Pno •Allans

HOWLAND, Russel S. (1908)

Clarinettiste, saxophoniste, professeur, et compositeur américain, né à Novinger (Missouri), le 19 VII 1908.

1st Quartet (1962) 1) Slow - Moderately fast 2) Slow and quiet 3) Lively •SATB •Yb
Quartet No. 2 1) Allegretto 2) Sarabande 3) Scherzo •SATB •WWS/Shir
Quartet No. 3 (1976) (to J. WYTKO) •SATB •WHi
Quartet No. 4 (1976) (to E. ERVIN) •SATB •WHi
Quartet No. 5 (1977) •SATB •WHi
Quartet No. 6 (1978) •SATB •WHi
Quartet No. 7 (1979) •SATB •WHi
Quartet No. 8 (1981) •SATB •WHi
Quartet No. 9 (1982) •SATB •WHi

HOWRANI, Walid (1948)

Compositeur américain, né à New York. Travailla avec W. Albright.

Concerto (1990) (to the Harir Foundation) (Introduction, tempo di Marcia, Humoresque, Andante Dolorosa, Dolorosa, Vivace) •Asx/Str/Perc
Exotica (1982) 1) Reminiscence 2) The Horrors of Wars 3) Hope and Celebration •Asx/Pno

HRISANIDE, Alexandru Dumitru (1936)

Compositeur roumain, né à Pétrila, le 15 VI 1936. Travailla avec P. Constantinescu, T. Ciortea, Z. Vancea, M. Jora, A. Mendelsohn, et N. Boulanger à Paris.

"In his composition he employs the most novel means (abundant and inventive effects of timbre, employment of sound masses and of electronics) in an essentially romantic spirit." (V. COSMA)

M. P. 5 (1967) •Tsx+Cl/Vln/Vla/Vcl/Pno •IMD

HUANG, An-Lun

Compositeur chinois.

Chinese Rhapsody No. 3, op. 46 (1989) (to P. BRODIE) •Asx/Pno •DP

HUBERT, Eduardo (1947)

Compositeur italien.

"Por las Americas" (1992) (13') (to A. DOMIZI) •Asx/Orch

HUBERT, Nikolaus A. (1939)

Compositeur allemand.

"Aus Schwerz und Trauer" (1982) (15') •Asx Solo (or Cl Solo) •Br&Ha

HUBERT, Roger

Elégie •Bb Sx/Pno •Mar
Un soir (to L. MASSE) •Asx or Bb Sx/Pno •Mar
Les tourbillons - Caprice •2 Sx: SA •Mar

HUDADOFF, Igor (1926)

Compositeur américain, né le 25 XII 1926, à Rochester (New York)

24 Saxophone Quartets •AATB •PA

HUFFNAGLE, Harry

Junior Miss •Asx/Pno
Streamlined Etudes (2 Volumes) •DG
White Satin •SATB

HUGGENS, Ted

Air nostalgique (1979) (4') •Asx/Harmonie •Mol

HUGGLER, John Stillman (1928)

Compositeur américain né à Rochester (New York), le 30 VIII 1928.

Elaboration, op. 69 (1967) (10') (to D. SINTA) •Asx/Orch (2222/4331/Harp/Perc/Str) or Band or Pno •CFE/ACA

HUGHES, Eric (1924)

Compositeur et pianiste anglais, né à Llandudno. Etudie l'électronique à l'université de Wales Bangor. Travailla dans un laboratoire de recherche puis avec F. Reizenstein et A. Bush à la Royal Académie.

Rhapsodie (1973) (to J. DENMAN) •Asx/Pno
Scherzo Laconica (1970) (5'30) (to London Saxophone Quartet) •SATB

HUGOT, Eugène (1819-1903)

25 Grandes études (BRUYANT) •Bil

HUMBERT-CLAUDE, Eric

Eux (1983) •Asx/Fl/Cl/Vln/Vcl/Pno

HUMMEL, Berthold (1925)

Compositeur allemand, né le 27 XI 1925, à Hüfingen (Baden). Travailla avec H. Genzmer.

Drei Stücke (1979) (10') 1) Monolog 2) Gegensalslicher 3) Presto •Sx Solo •adr
Musik for 4, op. 88f (1990) (8') •SATB •adr

HUMMEL, Johann Nepomuk (1778-1837)

8 Variations (CORROYER) •2 Cl/2 Sx: TB •Buf

HUMPERDINCK, Engelbert (1854-1921)

Children's Prayer (JOHNSON) •AATB •Rub

HUNT, Frederick

Larghetto •Sx Ensemble

HUNT, Ted

Chaconne (1962) •Asx/Pno
Larghetto •Asx/Pno
Modern Syncopation (1934) •Rub

HUNT, Wynn (1910)

Compositeur anglais.

Sonate, op. 60 (1930-70) (10') •Asx/Pno •BMIC

HUNTERHOFER, Heinrich

Minneflug (to Quatuor Italiano di Sassof.) •SATB •Ru

HURÉ, Jean (1877-1930)

Compositeur, pianiste, organiste, et professeur français, né à Gien (Loiret), le 17 IX 1877; mort à Paris, le 27 I 1930.

"Excellent musicien, il a laissé un grand souvenir près de ceux qui l'ont connu." (FASQUELLE) "Oeuvres d'un style néo-franckiste." (Cl. ROSTAND)

"His music shows a rare harmonic adventurousness. Debussy praised the formal solidity and the orchestration of his *Prélude symphonique*." (GROVE)

Andante (1915) (to E. HALL) •Asx/Orch (Str/2 Harp/Timp/Org) or Pno •South
Concerstuck (1910) (to E. HALL & J. VIARD) •Asx/Orch (Fl/Ob/Hn/Str) or Pno •South
1er Sextuor •6 Sx
2me Sextuor •Tpt/2 Bugle/Cl/BsCl/Sx

HUREL, Philippe (1955)

Compositeur et animateur français. Après des études universitaires à Toulouse et musicales à Paris, il travaille au département de Recherches Musicales de l'IRCAM (1985-86, 1989-90). Il est pensionnaire à la Vialla Médicis à Rome de 1986 à 1988.

Bacasax (1990) (3'30) •Asx/Pno •Bil
Opcit (1984) (7'15) (to Cl. DELANGLE) •Tsx Solo •Bil
"Pour l'image" •Fl/Ob/Cl/Asx/Hn/Tpt/Trb/Perc/Str Quintet

HURREL, Clarence E. Jr.

Echo of Romany •Bsx/Pno •Rub
Summer Serenade •Tsx/Pno •Rub

HUSA, Karel (1921)

Compositeur américain d'origine tchécoslovaque, né à Prague, le 7 VIII 1921. Travailla avec N. Boulanger et A. Honegger. Aux U.S.A. depuis 1954.

"Lors de son séjour à Paris, il s'est donné un style très personnel, d'une modalité qui lui est propre. Son ordonnance des douze sons se crée en gammes originales, réalisées par des altérations qui donnent la couleur de ses thèmes, et se conservent dans le développement, dans de souples mutations, vibrantes sans être rauques. Son contrepoint rythmique est vivant et souplement articulé." (P. WOLFF) "Il a conservé le sens de la musique nationale tchèque." (Cl. ROSTAND)

"There are other striking qualities in Husa's music, the most notable a formal precision employing the free use of twelve tones in a framework of tonality and terseness of expression. In addition, each of the woodwind instruments seems to be treated almost as a flexible human voice." (B.S.) "Its rhythmic intensity and dramatic strength arouse immediate enthusiasm." (S. TOMSIG) "Though far from his native Czechoslovakia, and under the spell of contemporary music, the composer does not deny the characteristic rhythm of a musicianship rooted in folklore." (H. HAUPTMANN) "He is of the most forceful and original of today's composers." (Fl. CROCHE) "Husa's musical rhetoric, while structurally classical in orientation, is nevertheless fresh and individual. His rhythms are powerful and his use of dramatic ostinato patterns reflects the influences of Honegger and Bartok." (E. GALKIN)

Concerto (1967) (20') 1) Prolog 2) Ostinato 3) Epilog •Asx/Wind Ensemble or Pno •AMP
Elégie et rondeau (1960) (10') (to S. RASCHER) •Asx/Orch (2222/ 220/3Perc/Pno/Str) or Pno •Led

HUTCHESON, Jere

Interplay (1983) (15') •Asx/Marimba/Vibr •NP

HUUCK, Reinhard (1943)

Compositeur allemand.
3 Choräle (1968) (6') •SATB •MR

HWANG, Serra Mijeun

Duet (1989) (12') (to C. Rochester YOUNG & F. MEZA) Gold Sun/ Silver Moon - Coo Coo - In the Time of the First Cricket Song •Asx/Marimba •adr

HYLA, Lee (1952)

Compositeur américain.
For Tenor Saxophone (3'30) (to K. RADNOFSKY) •Tsx Solo •adr
Pre-Amnesia (1'45) (to K. RADNOFSKY) •Asx Solo •adr
We Speak Etruscan (8'30) (to K. RADNOFSKY) •BsCl/Bsx •adr

HYMANN , Julius (see HIJMAN)

HYMAS, Anthony

Compositeur anglais.
Blues and Waltz (1978) (10') •SATB

IANNACCONE, Anthony (1943)

Compositeur américain, né le 14 X 1943, à Brooklyn (New York). Travailla avec V. Giannini, D. Diamond, et S. Adler.

Bicinia (1975) (to R. HILL & M. PLANK) 1) Libero 2) 108-116 •Fl/Asx •CF
Invention •2 Sx
Remembrance (1973) (3') •Asx/Pno •Pres

IASSILLI, Gerardo (1880-19xx)

Compositeur, chef d'orchestre, et saxophoniste américain, né en Italie, le 10 XI 1880. Aux U.S.A. depuis 1904. Soliste au New York Philharmonique, au Carnegie Hall concert.

Estrellita - Mexican Serenade (PONCE) •CF
Goldie - Valse Brillante •2 Sx/Pno •CF
Modern Conservatory Method (2 parts) •CF
27 Virtuoso Studies (BASSI) •CF

IBERT, Jacques (1890-1962)

Compositeur français, né le 15 VIII 1890 à Paris où il est mort, le 5 II 1962. Travailla avec Gedalge. Grand Prix de Rome (1919). Directeur de la Villa Médicis à Rome (1936-1962). Membre de l'Institut de France.

"Musicien de la joie, de la clarté, de la bonne humeur; poète de la nature, de la jeunesse, dans tout ce qu'elle a de santé, de force, d'élan dionysiaque, de verve, de sensibilité spontanée, plus exubérante qu'approfondie. Foncièrement français, Jacques Ibert demande à la musique d'être un art à la fois psychologique et sensuel; il en écarte toute préoccupation idéologique, aussi bien qu'il répugne au pathétique délibéré, c'est-à-dire qui n'est pas strictement conditionné par une impulsion irrésistible." (R. BERNARD) "Fuyant les outrances d'écriture et de pensée, il sait échapper à la fadeur. Il ne se refuse pas l'humour." (P. WOLFF) "Son écriture est toujours caractérisée par la clarté, l'élégance et la distinction." (FASQUELLE) "Encore que camarade d'A. Honegger et de D. Milhaud, il ne les a pas toujours suivis dans leurs audaces les plus extrêmes; bien qu'il s'exprime dans un langage pimenté en surface d'un certain modernisme, il conserve en profondeur le souci de la tradition. Science, élégance, ingéniosité, sont les caractéristiques de cette production considérable, qui sollicite tous les genres." (Cl. ROSTAND) "Libre, distinguée, sobre et raffinée, la musique de Jacques Ibert jouit de toutes les qualités d'une pensée française à la fois équilibrée dans ses proportions, subtile dans sa psychologie et recherchée dans ses couleurs. Proche d'Honegger et de Poulenc, esprit épris de clarté il est digne héritier de Ravel." (G. CANTAGREL)

"In his music Ibert combines the most felicitous moods and techniques of Impressionism and Neo-classicism; his harmonies are opulent; his instrumentation is coloristic; there is an element of humour in lighter works." (BAKER) "As a whole his work is stylistically difficult to define because the elements are, like the output itself, extremely diverse. 'All systems are valid,' he said, 'provided that one derives music from them.' He wished to be free from compulsive influences, and was never interested in passing fashions. Inspiration was a vital spark that appeared unbidden and was only one per cent of the totality of creation. He summed up his general approach as follows: 'I want to be free—independent of the prejudices which arbitrarily divide the defenders of a certain tradition and the partisans of a certain avant garde.' " (D. COX)

L'Age d'or (*Le Chevalier Errant*) •Asx/Pno •Led
Aria en Réb (1930) •Asx/Pno •Led

Concertino da camera (1935) (11') (to S. RASCHER) 1) Allegro con moto 2) Larghetto - Animato molto •Asx/Orch (1111/110/Str) or Pno •Led
Histoires... (MULE) 1) La meneuse de tortues d'or 2) Le vieux mendiant 3) Dans la maison triste 4) Le palais abandonné 5) Bajo la mesa 6) La cage de cristal 7) La marchande d'eau fraiche •Asx/Pno •Led
3 Histoires... (CLERISSE) 1) La meneuse de tortues d'or 2) A Giddy Girl 3) Bajo la mesa •SATB •Led
Mélopée •Bb Sx/Pno •Lem

ICHIYANAGI, Toshi (1933)

Compositeur et pianiste japonais né à Kobe, le 4 II 1933. Travailla avec Ikenouchi. Influencé par les idées de J.Cage.

Trichotomy (1978) (to R. NODA) •Asx/Pno/Perc

IDO

Concerto •Asx/Orch •Lem

IKEGAMI, Satoshi

Compositeur japonais.

Métaphore (1987) (to K. UEDA) •Asx/Pno

ILLASOVAY, Elsor von

2 Songs •Soprano Voice/Asx/Vibr/Perc •IMD

ILYINSKY, Alexander A. (1859-1920)

Lullaby (BUCHTEL) •Tsx/Pno •Kjos

INDY, Vincent d' (1851-1931)

Compositeur et professeur français, né le 27 III 1851 à Paris, où il est mort, le 2 XII 1931. Travailla avec C. Franck.

"Un des plus grands musiciens que la France ait produits" (P. DUKAS) "Ses premières admirations allèrent aux grands maîtres allemands. Son enseignement, fondé sur le développement historique de la musique, exerça son rayonnement sur la France, l'Europe et l'Amérique." "Le trait dominant de sa personnalité est l'amour de l'ordre, un sentiment intérieur de la discipline pouvant freiner l'expansion de la sensibilité. Croyant fervent, sa foi reste l'un des éléments principaux de sa personnalité morale et artistique. Il était très attaché au chant populaire, qu'il a largement utilisé. La construction de l'oeuvre, la forme avaient pour lui une importance capitale. D'Indy se réclame de son maître Franck, dont chez lui, la forme cyclique fusionne étroitement avec l'influence de Wagner." (P. LE FLEM) "La spiritualité et les fortes convictions confessionnelles de d'Indy l'ont tout naturellement conduit à réduire systématiquement dans la création artistique l'intervention de l'instinct et celle de la sensualité de l'oreille." (E. VUILLERMOZ) "Son importance doctrinale et polémique, son rôle à la Schola Cantorum ont fait oublier l'oeuvre du compositeur. Cette oeuvre est pourtant considérable: 105 opus, avec des oeuvres de musique de chambre qui restent encore à découvrir." (J. & Br. MASSIN) "Sa production n'est en rien novatrice, mais ne mérite nullement le dédain—sinon le mépris—dont on l'accable aujourd'hui." (H. HALBREICH) "La flamme créatrice ne trouve son véritable aliment que dans l'amour, et dans le fervent enthousiasme pour la beauté, la vérité et le pur idéal." (V. d'INDY)

"His very powerful effect on French music and his pedagogic influence, which was immense both in Europe and America, began to diminish after about 1920, and they have by this time almost wholly disappeared. They were of a nature not to be understood without a close consideration of Vincent d'Indy's reserved and yet radiant personality in its relations to French musical life of the late 19th and more especially the early 20th century." (L. VALLAS) "Both as teacher and creative artist d'Indy continued the traditions of C. Franck. Although he cultivated almost every form of composition, his special talent seemed to be in the field of the larger instrumental forms. His style rests on Bach and Beethoven; however, his deep study of Gregorian Chant and the early contrapuntal style added an element of severity, and not rarely of complexity, that renders approach somewhat difficult, and has prompted the charge that his music is lacking in emotional force." (BAKER) "His earliest works do not wear well and, as Rolland pointed out, he always preferred assimilation to elimination." (R. ORLEDGE)

Choral varié, op. 55 (1903) (9') (to E. HALL) •Asx/Orch (2222/413/ Perc/Str) or Pno •Dur

Choral varié, op. 55 (GEE) •1 Sx: A or T/Pno •MMB

INGALLS, Jeremiah (1764-1828)

Northfield (1800) (HARTLEY) •1 Voice/5 Sx: BsBsBsBsBs

INGHAM, Richard

Clarinettiste, saxophoniste, et compositeur anglais.

Still Life (1992) (7') •Sx+Yamaha WX7 MIDI Wind Controller/Tape

INKYUNG, Inkyung

Compositeur allemand.

Spiel auf E. (1993) •Asx/Cl •INM

IOACHIMESCU, Calin

Musique spectrale (1985) (12') •1 Sx: S+Bs/Tape

IPPOLITOV-IVANOV, Mikhail (1859-1935)

Procession of the Sardar (from *Caucasian Sketches*) (BONNEL) •AATB •PAS

IRADIER, Sébastien de (1809-1865)

La paloma •Asx/Pno •Mol

IRIK, Mike

Interaction III (1983) (to BOK & LE MAIR) •Sx+Cl/Marimba+Vibr

IRINO, Yoshiro (1921-1980)

Compositeur japonais né à Vladivostok, le 13 XI 1921. Travailla avec S. Moroi.

"His works distinguished him as the first Japanese to use 12-note methods as his major tool, and at the same time he applied his comprehensive knowledge of the music of the past in such works." (M. KANAZAWA)

Quintette (1958) •Cl/Asx/Tpt/Vcl/Pno •OE

IRONS, Earl D.

Echoes from "The Painted Desert" •Tsx/Pno •CF
Song of the Pines •Tsx/Pno •Chart

ISAAC, Heinrich (1450-1517)

Der Hund (G. PRIESNER) •3 Sx: SAB •VW

ISABELLE, Jean Clément (1948)

Compositeur canadien.

Duo concertant, op. 5 (1982) (to F. R. CANTIN, peintr) 1) Introduction (lento) 2) Adagio trés expressif 3) Allegro •Asx/Pno •Led
Mienne (1973) (15') (to R. MÉNARD) •Ssx/Pno
Quatuor (1973) (15') (to R. MÉNARD) 1) Allegro ben ritmato e deciso 2) Andante doloroso 3) Allegro con brio •SATB
Quintet, op. 4 (1981) (to Quatuor Bourque) •4 Sx: SATB/Pno DP
Sonate (1974) (to R. MÉNARD) •Ssx/Pno

ISACOFF, Stuart

Jazz Time (Album) (1990) •Asx/Pno - Tsx/Pno •B&H

ISAKSSON, Madeleine (1956)

Compositeur suèdois.

Capriola (1989) •Bsx (or Trb) •SMIC

ISELE, David Clark

Compositeur américain

Progations (to D. BAMBER) •Asx/Pno

ISHIHARA, Taduoki (1939)

Compositeur japonais.

Successions (1980) (to K. MUNESADA) •Asx/6 Perc

ISHII, Maki (1936)

Compositeur et chef d'orchestre japonais né à Tokyo, le 28 V 1936. Travailla avec Ikenouchi, puis à Berlin, avec Blacher et Rufer.

"His works show an awareness of the newest Western techniques and great skill in the manipulation of sound." (M. KAZAWATA)

Black intention (1978) (8') (to R. NODA) •Sx Solo

ISHIKETA, Mareo (1916)

Compositeur et professeur japonais né à Wakayama, le 26 XI 1916. Travailla avec Kan'ichi Shimofusa.

Révélation (1972) •2 Sx: AT

ISHIMARU, Kan (1922)

Compositeur japonais.

2 Pièces (1958) •Asx/Chamber Orch

ISRAEL, Brian (1951-1986)

Compositeur américain.

Arioso e Canzona (for S. RASCHER - May 15, 1985) (1985) (2'30) •6 Sx: SAATBBs
Concertino (1982) (6'30) (for M. TAGGART) 1) Waltz 2) Elegy 3) Festival •7 Sx: SAATTBBs •Eth
Double Concerto (1984) (3 movements) •2 Sx: SnoBs/Band
Sonata (1980) (to M. TAGGART) 1) Cakewalk 2) Blues 3) Contrapunctus Interruptus •Asx/Pno

ISRAEL, Hovav

Compositeur israélien.

No name for it... (1985) •Asx/Perc •adr

ISTVAN, Miloslav (1928)

Compositeur tchécoslovaque, né à Olomouc, le 2 IX 1928. Travailla avec Kvapil.

"Istvan had now established his pluralist technique, and his creative potency increased greatly, despite the fact that his works were receiving few performances as he was no longer a member of the Composer's Union." (A. NEMCOVA)

Concertino pro Barok jazz quintet (1982) (13') •Ob/Cl+Asx/BsCl/ Perc/Pno

ITO, Yasuhito

Compositeur japonais.

Concerto (1987) (9'15) (2 parts) •Asx/Orch or Pno •Lem
Mouvement supplémentaire à "Zweiisamkeit" (1986) •Asx/Pno
Quartet II •SATB
Tableau (1987) •Sx Orch

ITURRALDE, Pedro (1929)

Saxophoniste de jazz professeur et compositeur espagnol, né à Falees (Novarra), le 3 VII 1929.

Airs Roumains et Suite Hellénique •Asx/Pno •Lem
Los armonicos en el saxofon (1986) •MSA
Ballada •6 Sx: SAATTB •adr
Escalas, arpegios y ejercicios diatonicos (1991) •MSA
324 Escalas para la improvisacion del jazz (1990) •Ot
Like Coltrane (1972) •Asx Solo •Mun
Pequena czarda (1982) •Asx/Pno or 4 Sx: SATB •RME
Suite de jazz •SATB
Suite hellénique 1) Kalamatianos 2) Fonky 3) Valse 4) Kritis •SATB •Lem

IVANOV, Vladimir.

Compositeur russe.

Etudes (1991) •Ivanov
26 Etudes techniques (1991) •Mu/Ivanov
Pièces de compositeurs russes transcrites (1992) •Asx/Pno •Ivanov

IVE, Joanna
Compositeur anglais.
Confrontations (1993) •Asx/Pno •INM

IVES, Charles Edward (1874-1954)
Compositeur américain, né à Danbury (Connecticut), le 20 X 1874; mort à New York, le 19 V 1954.

"Il est pour l'Amérique ce que Schoenberg et Stravinsky sont pour l'Europe." "Peut être considéré comme un autodidacte en même temps qu'un précurseur, car dans la plupart de ses oeuvres, il se lance à l'exploration des possibilités extrêmes de la musique de son temps, dans un isolement absolu. Son oeuvre dont la complication l'obligea à chercher quelquefois une nouvelle notation, n'est jamais vulgaire, même lorsqu'il s'appuie sur la musique populaire de la Nouvelle-Angleterre." "C'est une des figures les plus singulières, les plus originales de la musique du XXe siècle, l'un des pionniers les plus intrépides du langage sonore de son temps. C'est l'un des plus profondément américains des compositeurs américains." (Cl. Ros-TAND) "L'art sort directement du coeur de l'expérience de la vie et de la réflexion sur la vie, la vie vécue." (Ch. Ives)

"The role of Charles Ives in American music is unique; he was a true pioneer of a strong national art, and at the same time he applied methods and techniques that anticipated by many years the advance of modern music elsewhere in the world. Virtually every work he wrote bears relation to American life, not only by literary association, but through actual quotation of American musical sources, from church anthems to popular dances and marches. He experimented with dissonant harmonies, simultaneous conflicting rhythms and fractional intervals, such as quarter-tones, and combined simple diatonic tunes with chromatically embroidered counterpoints resulting in a highly complex polytonal and polyrhythmic texture. In some of his works he introduced an element of improvisation, in the manner of village musicians playing a constant refrain in a free style. In his orchestration, he often indicated interchangeable instrument and optional parts, so that same work is availaible in several versions. Ives possessed an uncommon gift for literary expression; his annotations to his works are trenchant and humorous." (BAKER) "For long a mysterious, elusive, almost unknown factor in American music, Charles Ives showed every sign of coming to be realized for what he was, the archetypal ancestor of much that is peculiarly American in the present-day American school of composers. His works are full of vigour, imagination and the many rugged and homely musical elements that today appear all over the U.S.A. as 'Americana' of one kind or another." (P. GLANVILLE-HICKS)

Over the Pavements, op. 20 (1906-13) •Picc/Cl/Bsx (or Bsn)/Tpt/3 Trb/Perc/Pno •PIC
Tun Street (1921) •Fl/Tpt/Bsx/Pno

IVEY, Hean-Eichealberger (1923)
Compositeur américain né à Washington (D.C.), le 3 VII 1923.
"Her compositional style has evolved through the integration of influences, rather than through innovation." (DESMOND)
Triton's horn (1982) (9') (to J. CUNNINGHAM) •Tsx/Pno •DP

IWAMOTO, Wataru
Compositeur japonais.
Image (1990) •2 Sx: AA/Tape

IWASHIRO, Taro
Compositeur japonais..
Colors (1992) (12') (to K. I. MUTO) •Asx/Orch

JACOB, Gordon (Percival Septimus) (1895-1984)

Compositeur anglais, professeur, et écrivain né à Londres, le 5 VII 1895.

"Musicien raffiné, soucieux de la forme concise, habile orchestrateur." (LAROUSSE) "Ecriture élégante, sobrement raffinée, ouvrages qui ont le mérite de la concision." (R. BERNARD)

"His style was formed at a time when romantic impulse was suspect and the general flavour of his music is astringent, though his robust counterpoint, ingenious rhythms and his willingness to repeat crisp figures *ostinato*-fashion, rarely result in the aggressiveness that characterized so much music after the 1st World War." (F. HOWES) " 'I dislike an *academic* outlook,' he has written, 'but my style is deeply rooted in the traditions in which I was trained and which, by inclination, I followed.' Everything he composes is marked by sterling craftsmanship and by clarity, economy and directness. Jacob is a composer who has done much to demonstrate the importance of high professional standards." (F. HOWES)

Miscellanies (1976) (13') (to P. HARVEY) 1) Scalic prelude 2) Folk song 3) Molto perpetuo 4) Interlude 5) Gavotte 6) Dirge 7) Quick march •Asx/Band or Str Orch
Quartet No. 1 (1972) (11') (to London Saxophone Quartet) 1) Allegro moderato 2) Scherzo 3) Adagio 4) Alla marcia con spirito •SATB •JE
Rhapsody (1948) (9') (to J. de VRIES) •EH or Asx/Str or Pno •Mills
Variations on a Dorian Theme (1972) (to S. TRIER) •Asx/Pno •JE

JACOBI, Wolfgang (1894-1972)

Compositeur et professeur allemand, né à Bergen, le 25 X 1894. Travailla avec F. E. Koch.

Aria (9') (to J. de VRIES) •Asx/Orch
Barcarole (1964) (to S. RASCHER) •2 Sx: AA/Pno
Cantata •Soprano Voice/Asx/Pno
Concerto (1962) •Asx/Orch
Niederdenkscher Tanz (1936) •SATB
Pastorale (1936) •Soprano Voice/Asx/Pno
Serenade and Allegro (1961) (11') (to S. RASCHER) Asx/Orch or Pno
Sonata (1932) (10'30) (to S. RASCHER) 1) Allegro ma non troppo 2) Sarabande 3) Allegro •Asx/Pno •Bou

JACOBS, Ivan

Trio •Soprano Voice or (Ssx)/Vln/Pno
Learn to Play the Saxophone (2 Volumes) •Alf

JACQUE-DUPONT

Bercement ("Petites pièces trés faciles") (1974) •Asx/Pno •Zu

JACQUES, Thilo (1967)

Compositeur allemand.
Sechs Duos (1979) (12') 1) Song I 2) Song II 3) Miniatur 4) Heiterkeit in Dur 5) Themenspiel 6) Abgesang •Hei

JADASSOHN, Salomon (1831-1902)

Noturno (from *Serenade*) •Eb Sx/Pno •CF

JAECKEL

Largo and Allegretto •Tsx/Pno •WWS

JAECKER, Friedrich

Compositeur allemand.

Flöte, Saxophon (1993) •Ssx/Fl •INM

JAEGER, Robert Edward (1939)

Compositeur américain, né à Binghamton (New York), le 25 VIII 1939.
Concerto (1967) (20') (to F. HEMKE) 1) Andante sostenuto - Allegro 2) Adagio 3) Allegro - Volk energico •Asx/Brass/Perc •adr
Concerto No. 2 (1977) (11'30) (to N. BRIGHTMAN) •Asx/Band •Volk/ CPP
Quintet (1969) •Asx/Vln/Vla/Vcl/Harp •adr
Three Pieces (1967) (6'30) (to G. ETHERIDGE) 1) Allegro molto vivace 2) Andante moderato 3) Allegro energico •Asx/Vln/Vla/ Vcl/Harp or Pno •adr

JAEGGI, Oswald (1913-1963)

Dum clamarem (1961) •Ob/EH/Cl/3 Sx/3 Tpt/3 Trb

JAHR, New

Froloc of the Keys •3 Sx: SAT or AAT/Pno •Bri
Scherzo (1979) (to MICHAÏLOV) •2 Sx: SB/Perc

JAKMA, Fritz Sr.

Cavatine •Bb Sx/Pno •TM
2° Concertino •Bb Sx/Pno •TM
8 Mélodies célèbres (2 Volumes) •SATB •TM
Novelette •Asx/Pno •TM
Parade des Olifanten •1 Sx: T or B/Pno •Mol
Sancta Lucia - Air varié •Eb Sx or Bb Sx/Pno •Mol
Starlight Dreams •Bb Sx/Pno •TM
Valse caprice •Asx/Pno •TM

JAMES

20 Christmas Carols •3 Sx: A A+T B •Sha
22 Masterworks •3 Sx: A A+T B
20 Traditional Melodies •3 Sx: A A+T B •Sha

JAMES, Lewis

Compositeur américain.
Music, op. 9 (1955/85) (9'30) •Asx/Orch (Str/Perc/Pno/Guit) •MMI

JANONE, René

Compositeur français.
Poême (1979) 1) Prélude 2) Cadence 3) Finale •Asx/Pno

JANSEN, Guus

Compositeur néerlandais.
Juist daarom (1981) (7') •Ob/Cl/Ssx/Vcl/Pno •Don

JANSSEN, Werner (1899)

Compositeur et chef d'orchestre américain, né à New York, le 1er VI 1899. Travailla avec F. Converse, Friedheim, et Chadwick, puis en Europe, avec Weingartner et H. Scherchen. Prix de Rome (1930).

"Werner Janssen ne s'est pas spécialisé dans le style du jazz et a écrit de la musique de chambre." (R. BERNARD) "S'est consacré presque exclusivement à la musique de film." (A. GAUTHIER)

"As a composer, Janssen tends towards illustrative representation of modern life. His most spectacular work of this nature is *New Year's Eve in New York*, a symphonic poem for large orchestra with jazz instruments." (BAKER) "As a composer he began by contributing numbers for the Ziegfeld Follies and other revues. In general his music incorporates descriptive effects and the idioms of jazz, which he considers as modern folk music, within traditional structures." (G. REESE)
Obsequies of a Saxophone (1929) •6 Wind Instruments/Snare Drum

JANSSON, Gunnar (1944)

Violoniste et compositeur suèdois, né à Helsingborg, le 8 IX 1944.
Sinfonia concertante (1991) (25') •4 Sx: SATB/Orch •Tons

JÄRNEFELT, Armas (1869-1958)

Berceuse •Bsx/Pno •Bel
Praeludium (THOMSON) •AATB •Alf

JARNIAT, Raymond

Compositeur français.

Andante et danse •Asx/Band •adr

JAROSKAWSKA, Joanna (1952)

Compositeur polonais, né le 26 III 1952, à Wroclaw. Travailla avec B. Schaffer.

Espressioni liriche (1977) •Ssx/Pno

JAY, Charles (1911)

Compositeur français, né à Anvers, le 29 V 1911. Travailla avec Caussade, Pech, et H. Busser.

Andante (1971) (8'40) (to P. PAREILLE) •Asx/Pno •Lem
Aria et Scherzetto •Asx/Pno •Lem
Complainte et rondo (1980) (to M. GET) •Asx/Pno •Lem
Divertissements agrestes (9') •Asx/Pno •adr
Fantaisie burlesque (1962) (7') (to P. PAREILLE) •Asx/Pno •Com
Lied (1942) (6') (to P. PAREILLE) •Asx/Pno •Com

JEAN, André

Compositeur belge.

Oriental suite •6 Sx: SAATTB •adr
Quatuor •SATB •adr
Sax battle •Jazz Tsx/4 Sx: SATB •adr
Saxologie •5 Sx: AATTB •adr

JEANJEAN, Paul (18xx-1929)

Capriccio (KLICKMAN) •Tsx/Pno •Alf
Heureux temps (COMBELLE) •Asx/Pno •Bil
Rêverie de printemps (COMBELLE) •Asx/Pno •Bil

JEANNEAU, François (1935)

Clarinettiste et saxophoniste de jazz français, né le 15 VI 1935.

Algorythmus •SATB •adr
Amybe •SATB •adr
8 Thèmes et improvisation •Sx Solo •Sal
Monodie •Ssx Solo •adr
Suite (to Quatuor G. Pierné) •SATB •Lem
Une anche passe (10'30) (to J-P. CAENS & Quatuor A Piacere) •SATB •adr

JELINEK, Hanns (1901-1969)

Compositeur et professeur australien, né le 5 XII 1901 à Vienne où il est mort le 27 I 1969. Travailla avec A. Schoenberg.

"In the 1930s he adopted the 12-tone method." (BAKER) "Jelinek's jazz-influenced compositions begin with the *Second Symphony*, op. 6 (1929, rev. 1949), which bears bears the description 'Sinfonia ritmica for big band and large orchestra.' In 1956 came the *Three Blue Sketches* for jazz soloists, pieces that are at once composed jazz and 12-note music of the most intricate facture." (W. SZMOLYAN)

Blue Sketches, op. 25 (1956) •Fl/Cl/2 Sx: AB/Tpt/Trb/Vibr/Bass/ Perc •EMod

JEMNITZ, Sandor (1890-1963)

Compositeur, chef d'orchestre, et critique musical hongrois, né à Budapest, le 9 VIII 1890; mort à Balatonfüred, le 8 VIII 1963. Travailla avec Reger, Koessler, et Schoenberg.

"Il a toujours suivi une voie très personnelle qui a quelquefois des analogies avec certaines tendances de la musique allemande contemporaine et avec celle de la jeune école hongroise." (FASQUELLE) "Musique d'un intérêt soutenu, où l'abstraction se tempère d'un courant musical spontané." (R. BERNARD)

"His chosen idiom represents a cross between the contrapuntal style of M. Reger (with whom he took a few lessons in 1916) and the radical language of atonality, modelled after Schoenberg's early works." (BAKER) "As composer Jemnitz remained to the end of his life faithful to the spirit of his two great teachers: his tightly woven, elaborate textures are rooted in Regerian counterpoint, but he was also quite strongly influenced by the expressionist Schoenberg of the 1910s." (V. LAMPERT)

Sonata, op. 28 (1934) •Asx/Banjo

JENKINS, John (1592-1678)

Fantasy No. 1 (GRAINGER) •5 Sx: SSATB •PG

JENNEFELT, Thomas (1954)

Compositeur suèdois, né à Huddinge, le 24 IV 1954. Travailla avec G. Bucht et A. Mellnäs.

"His style has developed in a dramatic direction and also towards increasing psychological insight and introspection." (SJ)

Stones (1981) •Ob/Cl/Asx/Tpt/Guit/2 Perc

JENNI, Donald

Compositeur américain.

Allegro for Brass Choir •4 Hn/4 Tpt/3 Trb/Tuba/2 Bsx •Pio

JENNY, Albert (1912)

Compositeur suisse, né à Soleure, le 24 IX 1912. Travailla avec Ph. Jarnach.

"Dans sa très grande majorité, la production d'Albert Jenny est d'inspiration religieuse." (R. BERNARD) "Albert Jenny avoue que c'est à la personnalité et à l'oeuvre d'Honegger qu'il doit le stimulant nécessaire à la poursuite de son travail." (Assoc. des Mus. Suisses) "Il a surtout subi les influences de Honegger et Fr. Martin, tout en ne méconnaissant pas, cependant, les apports de Schoenberg, Bartok et Hindemith. Il demeura attaché au système tonal, et utilise fréquemment les modes d'église dans une production dont la moitié au moins est d'inspiration religieuse." (Cl. ROSTAND)

Rhapsodie (1936) •Asx/Str Orch or Pno •adr

JENTZSCH, Wilfried (1941)

Compositeur allemand, né à Dresden, le 31 III 1941. Travailla avec Cilensek et Wagner-Regeny, puis à Paris.

"He aims at a combination of serial and diatonic, static and dynamic elements." (GROVE)

Maquam (1983-92) (12') (to G. PRIESNER) •Asx Solo •adr
Recitativo, Canzonetta e Fuga (1985) (7') •SATB •adr
Sonate (1978) (to G. PRIESNER) •Asx Solo •adr

JERGENSON, Dale

5 Little Duets •2 Sx: AA •SeMC

JESTL, Bernhard

Compositeur allemand.

5 Clownesken (12'30) •SATB •ECA
Isaak (1993) •1 Sx: S+A/Perc •INM
Rhapsodie •Asx/Orch •ECA

JETHS, Willem

Compositeur néerlandais.

Concerto (1985) (15') •Asx/Str Orch •Don

JETTEL, Rudolf (1903-1981)

Clarinettiste, professeur, et compositeur autrichien.

Figaro-saxophone (1937) (folio) (4 pieces) •Asx/Pno •Hof
Meine solomappe (1939) (6 pieces) •Asx/Pno •Hof
Method •Mol
Neue Saxophon Studien •BCM
Saxophon-Studien (2 volumes) •ApE
Schmetterling (1963) •Asx/Pno •Kli

Serenata (1963) •Asx/Pno •Kli
Spanischer Ständchen (1963) •Asx/Pno •Kli
Spielereien (1941) (4 pieces) •Asx/Pno •Hof

JEVERUD, Johan (1962)

Compositeur suèdois.
Bedtime near (1985) (4') •Tsx/Pno •SMIC
Chimaira (1984) •BsCl/Tsx/Trb/3 Vcl/Pno •SMIC
Introduktion (1986) (4') •SATB •SMIC
Människa svämmar över (1989/90) (9') •SATB •SMIC
2 Pieces in Black and White (1992) •Fl/Asx/Perc •SMIC

JOACHIM, Otto (1910)

Compositeur, altiste, et professeur canadien d'origine allemande, né le 13 X 1910, à Düsseldorf. Travailla avec Zitzmann.
"Joachim's 12-note music is characterized by a tonal orientation (achieved through frequent octave doublings, pedal points, ostinatos and note repetitions), rhythmic vitality, textual clarity and economy." (U. KASEMETS)
Interlude (1960) (3') •SATB •CMC

JOHANSON, Sven Eric (Emanuel) (1919)

Compositeur suédois., né à Västervik, le 10 XII 1919. Travailla avec Melchers et Rosenberg.
"Having made intensive studies of Gregorian chant and Palestrinian polyphony, he found the basis for his own work in Hindemith's counterpoint. This he gradually developed in an individual manner, applying the 12-note technique first loosely in the *Sinfonia ostinata* and the saxophone sonata, then rigorously in such pieces." (E. WAHLSTROM) "He has always been exploring new paths and producing music of every kind, from the popular to the electro-acoustic." (SJ)
Caccia (1968) •Fl/Cl/Tsx •STIM
5 Expressioner (1950) (5') (to J. de VRIES) (5 movements) •Asx/Pno •STIM/Ehr
Sonate (1949) (12') (to J. de VRIES) (3 movements) •Asx/Pno •SMIC/Ehr

JOHNER, Hans-Rudolf (1934)

Professeur et compositeur allemand, né à Schaffhausen, le 28 IX 1934.
Diskussion (1981) •SATB •adr

JOHNSEN, Hallvard Olav (1916)

Compositeur et flûtiste norvégien, né à Hamburg, le 27 VI 1916. Travailla avec Steenberg, Brustad, Fjeldstad, puis avec K. Andersen et Holmboe.
"His compositional style, at first influenced by folk music, has evolved into free atonality." (P. A. KJELDSBERG)
Quartet, op. 65 (1974) (9') •SATB •NMO

JOHNSON, Allen

Compositeur américain.
Nightsong (6') (to K. RADNOFSKY) •Asx/Chamber Orch or Pno •adr
Quartet (to K. RADNOFSKY) •AATB •adr

JOHNSON, Barry

Compositeur américain.
Concerto •Tsx/Orch •Reg
Slyndian •Sx Solo
Three Preludes •Sx Choir

JOHNSON, Clair W.

Scene Forestal (1938) •Bsx/Pno •Rub
Waltz Moods •Tsx/Pno •Rub

JOHNSON, J.

Chamber Music •Ssx/Pno

JOHNSON, J. J. (1924)

Tromboniste de jazz, né à Indianapolis, le 22 I 1924.
Turnpike (5') •Fl/Cl/3 Sx: ATB/Trb/Harp (or Guit)/Pno/Bass/Perc •MJQ

JOHNSON, Roger

Fantasy •Asx/Perc/Bass •DP

JOHNSON, Tom

Critique musical américain.
Rational Melodies (1982) (2' to 25') •Saxophone au choix solo

JOHNSON, William Spencer (1883-19xx)

Professeur et compositeur américain, né à Athol (Massachusetts). Travailla avec Reinecke et Rieman.
Chorale Fantasy •AATB •Fit
Concert Overture •6 Sx: AAATBBs •Bel/B&H/TM
Impromptu •AATB •B&H/Bel/TM
Mignonne •AATB •Bel/B&H/TM
National Melodies (2' to 25') •Sx Solo
Pastorale •AATB •Bel/B&H/TM

JOHNSTON, Benjamin Burwell (1926)

Compositeur américain, né à Macon (Georgia), le 15 III 1926. Travailla avec D. Milhaud, H. Partch, et J. Cage "whose influences are evident in, respectively, his use of just intonation and microtones (combined with serialism in the first two string quartets, for example) and his occasional indeterminate procedures." (GROVE)
Casta •Asx/Pno •MP

JOHNSTON, David (1931)

Compositeur américain, né à New York.
Ballade (1984) (to O. VRHOVNIK) •Asx/Wind Ensemble •Kf
Duo (1980) (11') 1) Allegro 2) Adagio con molta espressione 3) Allegro vivace •Asx/Pno
Konzert (1982) (To O. VRHOVNIK) •Asx/Orch
Tut suite (1983) (To O. VRHOVNIK) •7 Sx: SnoSATBBsCBs

JOHNSTON, Merle (1897-1978)

Saxophoniste (ténor) et professeur américain. Free-lance studio musician à New York.
"Merle Johnston was the first American saxophonist to teach the regulated jaw vibrato and was the founder of the New York school of saxophone playing." (GEE)
Blue Streak (1928) •Asx/Pno •Rob
Crystal Suite (BONNELL) (1936) •AATB •PAS
Deep River (BONNELL) (1937) •AATB •SH&MC
Liebestraum (1945) •AATB •PAS
Morning Glory (1928) •Asx/Pno •Rob
My Old Kentucky Home (1945) •AATB •PAS
Procession of the Sardar (BONNELL) (1937) •AATB •SH&MC
36 Staccato Exercices (1930) •MJ
36 Technical Exercices (1930) •MJ
36 Time and Rhythm Exercices for Daily Practice (1930) •MJ
Tip Toes (1928) •Asx/Pno •Rob
Valse Élégante (1928) •Asx/Pno •Rob

JOLAS, Betsy (1926)

Compositeur et professeur français, né à Paris, le 5 VIII 1926. Travailla aux U.S.A., puis à Paris avec D. Milhaud et O. Messiaen.
"C'est aux Etats-Unis que Betsy Jolas acquiert un goût jamais assouvi pour le chant et singulièrement pour la musique ancienne, notamment la Renaissance italienne." (C. GLAYMAN) "Rapidement inscrite dans la tendance post-sérielle, elle a aussitôt attiré l'attention par une invention très riche, un sentiment poétique raffiné et un style d'une extrême élégance dans le maniement des évènements sonores.

Dans toutes l'école musicale du XXe siècle, il n'y a guère eu de femmes compositeurs aussi solidement et richement douées que Betsy Jolas." (Cl. ROSTAND) "Sa réticence à l'égard du sérialisme fait qu'elle échappe à toute tendance musicale de son époque; son attrait pour la virtuosité et la magie du son, tout en étant déterminants dans sa composition, ne marquent pourtant pas le point de départ de l'acte créateur. L'intention formelle initiale subit, au cours de l'élaboration, toute une série d'éliminations qui aboutiront à clôturer la forme définitive. La primauté que Jolas accorde au vocal reste prégnante même dans l'écriture instrumentale. Cela lui permet d'intégrer dans sa musique des modalités expressives diversifiées qui dépassent toute obéissance à un système préalable." (D. J-Y. BOSSEUR) "Elle n'a jamais été tentée par le sérialisme: 'c'était pour moi comme un purgatoire, je me demandais s'il était tout à fait nécessaire d'y faire son temps.' Elle n'a guère souci non plus de formes 'ouvertes' ou d''aléatoire.' Sa pensée est orientée d'abord vers un univers sonore, vers une magie sonore, qu'il lui importe de tenter de traduire hors de son rêve." (J. & B. MASSIN) "Elle s'attache aux propriétés et sonorités de certains instruments, ainsi de la série des *Episodes*." Ecrites pour les formations les plus diverses, ses oeuvres expriment une force, une énergie d'esprit baroque, foisonnant, on les structures rigides du sérialisme sont délaissées au profit d'un système complexe d'échelles de hauteurs et d'une métrique souple et polyrythmique." (G. CANTAGREL)

"In her music, Jolas has shown a special predilection for the voice, or more generally, for a vocal mode of writing, and she has been particularly concerned with the relationships between word and music. Throughout her career, Jolas has been influenced by serial procedures without completely subscribing to them. Summarizing her experience, Jolas essays a synthesis between different aspects and meanings of song. The aesthetic and philosophical achievement, accomplished with lucidity and sensitivity, is deeply moving." (A. BOUCOURECHLIEV)

Episode 4me (1983) (8'15) •Tsx Solo •Led
Plupart du temps II (sur des poèmes de P. REVERDY) (1989) (10')
    •Tenor Voice/Tsx/Vcl •Led
Points d'or (1981) (23') (commande de l'AsSaFra [commissioned by the French Saxophonist's Association]) •1 Sx: S+A+T+B/Orch (2 Vla/2 Vcl/Bass/2 Cl/BsCl/2 Tpt/2 Trb/Pno/2 Perc •Ric

JOLIVET, André (1905-1974)

Compositeur français, né à Paris, le 8 VIII 1905; mort à Paris, le 20 XII 1974. Travailla avec E. Varèse. Membre du groupe 'Jeune France.'

"Je veux rendre à la musique son sens original antique, lorsqu'elle était l'expression magique et incantatoire de la religiosité des groupements humains." (A. JOLIVET) "Dans la première période de sa production, il s'efforce de trouver une musique qui soit l'expression magique et incantatoire de la religiosité des groupes humains; dans la seconde, son art se fait plus humain; dans une troisième, se manifeste le souci de recherches de langage (modes exotiques) et de timbres." (N. DUFOURCQ) "Plutôt que de diviser sa production en 'période incantatoire' et 'période humaine' comme on a voulu le faire, il semble bien que l'on puisse rattacher les oeuvres d'autrefois et d'aujourd'hui à ce même sentiment du 'religieux' qui a d'abord attiré Jolivet vers les musiques rituelles avant de généraliser les conquêtes qu'il avait faites en ce domaine." (R. STRICKER) "L'influence d'E. Varèse domine dans des pages écrites dans la liberté et l'enthousiasme, qui évoquent les cérémonies d'initiation des peuples primitifs, pages profondes, mystérieuses et étranges." (P. WOLFF) "Pour Jolivet le passé ce n'est ni l'impressionnisme, ni le romantisme, ni le classicisme ni même l'époque médiévale. C'est la musique primitive à l'art brut, l'incantation magique." (illustré par la Fantaisie-Impromptu) (B. GAVOTY) "Chez Jolivet le mysticisme chrétien se joint d'une façon curieusement harmonieuse à l'idéologie fondée sur la magie." (R. BERNARD) "André Jolivet révèle librement son tempérament de novateur ingénieux; dans chacun de ses ouvrages, l'instrument ou la voix adopte un accent insolite qui soutient constamment l'intérêt, car l'effet 'instrumental ou

vocal' n'est jamais gratuit, mais demeure en conformité avec l'esprit de la partition." (Cl. SAMUEL)

"As the avowed object of such music is to cast, as it were, a spell upon the listener, the composer has evolved a musical language of great harmonic freedom, largely atonal and relying on a wide range of rhythmic and dynamic effects to produce in the hearer an appropriate frame of mind." (R. MYERS) "Jolivet injected his empiric spirit into his music, making free use of polytonality and asymmetric rhythms, also experimenting with new sonorities produced by electronic instruments, despite these esoteric preoccupations, Jolivet's music is primarily designed to please and impress." (BAKER) "He never used the serial principle, and remained opposed to the subtle art of Webern while valuing the refinements of other composers, Debussy above all. Among the original techniques introduced in his music are the employment of pivotal chords, and the 'partial modes' that Jolivet used melodically and harmonically. As for the spirit of his art, he retained his concern with the elementary nature and expression of man, with the primordial forces revealed in human dance; this relates to his occasional reference to exoticism." (A. HOEREE)

Fantaisie-Impromptu (1953) (3'45) •Asx/Pno •Led

JOLLET, Jean-Clément (1956)

Compositeur français.

Amuse-gueules (1988) (10'30) 1) Java 2) Sarabande 3) Swing •Ob/ Asx/Vcl •Bil
15 Etudes (1986) •Bil
Trois pour quatre (1989) (6'30) 1) Gavotte 2) Aria 3) Java •SATB •Bil
Wales Song (1987) (2') (to Ph. LECOCQ) •Asx/Pno •Bil

JOLY, Denis (1906)

Compositeur français, né à Monthléry, le 12 V 1906.. Travailla avec P. Dukas.

Cantilène et danse (1949) (to A. BEAUCAMP) •Asx/Pno •Led

JOLY, Suzanne (1906)

Compositeur français.

Séquences - Musique pour un court métrage (1972) (12') (to Quatuor J. Desloges) 1) Générique et atelier de l'artiste 2) Modèles et rapins 3) Mobile 4) Exotique 5) Cortège •SATB •EFM

JONAS, Emile (1827-1905)

Compositeur israélite français, né à Paris, le 5 III 1827; mort à Saint-Germain en Laye, le 22 V 1905. Travailla avec Carafa. Prix de Rome (1849). Professeur de solfège puis d'harmonie au Conservatoire de Paris et directeur de la musique à la Synagogue.

Prière (1861) (to A. SAX) •SATB or 6 Sx: SAATTB •Marg
Quatuor •SATB •Sax
Sextuor •6 Sx: SSAATB •Sax

JONES, David

Compositeur américain.

Motor Music (1988) (7'30) Freeway (presto) - Pacific Coast Highway (Andante) •5 Sx: SAATB •Com

JONES, Hilton (1945)

Going Out (1974) •Asx/Pno

JONES, Kelsey (1922)

Compositeur canadien, d'origine américaine, né à South Norwalk (Connecticut), le 17 VI 1922. Travailla avec E. MacMillan, H. Willan, L. Smith, et, à Paris, avec N. Boulanger.

Three Preludes and a fugue (1982) •SATB •CMC

JONES, Kenneth V. (1924)

Compositeur anglais.

Quaquaverse (1978) (13') (to Myrha Saxophone Quartet) 1) Allegro moderato - vivo 2) Lento espressivo 3) Allegro giocoso •SATB •adr

JONES, Martin Edwin Mervyn (1940)
Pianiste et compositeur anglais, né à Witney, le 44 II 1940.
Quartet (To London Saxophone Quartet) •SATB •adr
Quintet •4 Sx: SATB/Pno •adr

JONES, Robert W.
Divertimento •Fl/Ob/Cl/Asx/Hn •WWS
Three by Three •3 Bb or 3 Eb Sx

JONG, Hans de (1957)
Saxophoniste, compositeur, et chef d'orchestre néerlandais.
Le rêve et la folie (5') •Asx Solo

JONG, Marinus de (1891-1984)
Sonata (1968) •Asx/Pno

JONGBLOED, D.
Romance •SATB •Lis/TM

JONGEN, Joseph (1873-1953)
Compositeur et organiste belge, né à Liège, le 14 XII 1873; mort Sart-lez-Spa, le 12 VII 1953. Prix de Rome (1897).

"Son oeuvre abondante révèle un tempérament traditionaliste, proche des idéaux scholastiques, au service d'une inspiration noble." (H. HALBREICH) "Joseph Jongen subit à la fois l'influence de C. Franck et de Debussy, et fut l'ami des musiciens français ses contemporains (Fauré, d'Indy)." (FASQUELLE) "Si son harmonie reflète l'esprit de la 'Schola', il sait se garder des modulations systématiques et il ne demeure pas étranger aux recherches de l'art contemporain." (E. MEYNAERTS-WATHELET) "Son écriture a une élégance patricienne et, si elle recourt souvent à des procédés typiquement debussystes ou raveliens, elle n'en baigne pas moins dans une autre atmosphère: son lyrisme a plus de spontanéité et d'abandon, il est beaucoup plus sentimental et imprégné de romantisme." (R. BERNARD)

"While not pursuing extreme modern effects, Jongen succeeded in imparting an original touch to his harmonic style." (BAKER) "Joseph Jongen was one of the best-known Belgian composers of the early 20th century. He excelled in chamber music, but his personality was not strong enough to enable him to form a personal style." (H. VANHULST)
Méditation, op. 21 (1901) (7') •Asx/Pno •Mur
Quatuor en forme rhapsodique libre, op. 122 (1942) (15') •SATB •CBDM/Ger

JONGEN, Léon (1885-1969)
Compositeur et pianiste belge, frère du précédent, né le 2 III 1885, à Liège; mort à Bruxelles, el 18 XI 1969. Prix de Rome (1913).

"Ses voyages à travers le monde lui inspirèrent des pages d'un exotisme très coloré." (H. HALBREICH)
Concours de lecture (1944) •Asx Solo
Divertissement (1937) (8'30) •SATB •CBDM
Piccoli (1931) (8') 1) Pseudo valse 2) Pseudo rag •Asx/Pno •An/Ger

JONGHE, Marcel de
Compositeur belge.
3 Bagatelles (1982) 1) Allegro grazioso 2) Allegro giocoso •SATB
Trio (1980) •Asx/Tpt/Trb

JOPLIN, Scott (1868-1917)
Antoinette (VOIRPY) (3'30) •SATB •Lem
Bethena - Valse concert (C. VOIRPY) •SATB •Lem
The Cascades (J-M. LARCHÉ) •SATB •Mart
The Easy Winners (DOMIZI) •Ob/Cl/Asx/Bsn
Elite, Bethena, Palm Leaf Rag •Asx/Pno •Lem
The Entertainer (AXWORTHY) •2 Sx: ST/Hn/Bsn/Perc •DP
The Entertainer (J-P. CAENS) •SATB •Mar
Euphonic sounds (AXWORTHY) •5 Sx: SATBBs or SATBB •DP/TVA
Let's Rag... Sax Collection (U. HEGER) •1 Sx: A or T/Pno •NoE
Maple Leaf Rag (AXWORTHY) •1 Sx: S or A or T/Harp (or Pno) •DP/TVA
Maple Leaf Rag (J-M. LARCHÉ) •SATB •Mar
Maple Leaf Rag - Solace - Swipesy (WEHAGE-FERGUSSON) •Asx/Pno •Lem
Original Rags (C. VOIRPY) •SATB •Lem
Pineapple Rag (AXWORTHY) •5 Sx: SATBBs or SATBB •DP/TVA
3 Ragtimes (LONDEIX) 1) Ragtime dance 2) The Entertainer 3) The Cascades •12 Sx: SnoSSAAATTTBBBs •Fuz

JORDAN, Paul (1939)
Rhapsody and Waltz (1979) (to A. HAMME) •Tsx/Pno

JÖRNS, Helge (1943)
Organiste et compositeur allemand, né le 18 III 1943, à Mannheim. Travailla avec D. Manicke, Kelterborn, Klebe, etc.
Zwei Kadenzen zu Raumblöke II & III (1980) •SATB •EMod

JORRAND, André
Compositeur français. Travailla avec H. Dutilleux, M. Ohana, et M. Mihalovici.

"Bien que traditionnel, son langage se complète d'atonalisme, de modalismme avec des accords bâtis sur la gamme pentatonique mais sensibilisés par des mutations chromatiques qui affectent aussi bien la mélodie que les agrégats."
Quatuor (1956) (to M. MULE) •SATB
Quatuor dans le style ancien (1981) (to Quatuor J. Desloges) •SATB

JOUBERT, Claude-Henry
Compositeur, écrivain, et animateur français.
Baroco (1988) (6') •Asx/Pno •Com
Chanson de Thibaut (3') •1 Sx: A or T/Pno •Com
Les malheurs de Juliette (1986) (3') •Asx/Pno •Mar

JOY, Jérôme (1961)
Compositeur de musique instrumentale et de musique électroacoustique français, né à Nantes, le 26 XII 1961. Travailla avec Michel Fusté-Lambezat et Christian Eloy.
Départ errance retour (1992) (13') •Fl/Asx/Transf. du son en direct/Tape

JU, Yong-Su
Winterliche Impressionen (1993) •Ssx/Vibr •INM

JUELICH, Raimund (1949)
Compositeur allemand.
Amok (1993) •Sx/Perc •INM
In-formation (1981) (12') •Ob/Cl/Asx/Bsn •adr
Werkstück 4 (1988) (11') •Sx Solo •Peer

JUGUET, Henri-Pierre
Compositeur français.
Macles (to M. JÉZOUIN) •SATB
Pierre de lune (1985) (to M. JÉZOUIN et F. BOURDIN) •Fl/Ssx
Trio suite (1986) (to M. JÉZOUIN) 1) Prélude 2) Refrain I 3) Allemande 4) Refrain II 5) Sarabande 6) Gavotte 7) Refrain IV •Ssx/Vla/Pno

JULLIEN-ROUSSEAU
10 petites esquisses poétiques •SATB

JUNGK, Klaus (1916)
Compositeur allemand né le 1 V 1916 à Stettin. Auteur de musiques

de films.
Kleine Suite (1985) (8') •SATB

JURANVILLE, Frédéric (1957)

Saxophoniste et professeur français, né à Sandillon (Loiret). Travailla avec D. Deffayet.

Grands Exercices Journaliers de Mécanisme d'après Taffanel et Gaubert (1992) •Sx •Led

JUSTEL, Elsa

Compositeur français.

Sikxo (1989) (11') (to D. KIENTZY) •Bsx/Tape •INM

JUTRAS, A.

Nocturne •2 Asx (or EH)/Pno •Do

KABALEVSKY

Sonatina, op. 13 (GEE) •1 Sx: A or T or B/Pno •South

KABELAC, Miloslav (1908-1979)

Compositeur tchécoslovaque, né le 1 VIII 1908 à Prague, où il est mort, le 17 IX 1979. Travailla avec K. B. Jirak.

"Miloslav Kabelac est la personnalité la plus importante de sa génération. D'inspiration forte et sombre, d'un souffle réellement ample et d'une grande maîtrise architecturale, ascétique jusqu'à la nudité parfois, il est habile à bâtir de longues et saisissantes progressions, et possède un tempérament de symphoniste. Même dans ses oeuvres relativement avancées, une parenté bartokienne demeure dans sa musique." (Cl. ROSTAND) "L'intégration dans l'oeuvre de Miloslav Kabelac des techniques tour à tour dodécaphonique, sérielle, aléatoire puis électronique manifeste non seulement l'éclectisme de sa pensée, mais aussi son souci de trouver, pour chaque composition, un procédé différent dépouillé de prescriptions dogmatiquement préétablies." (D. J-Y BOSSEUR) "Miloslav Kabelac réunissait en ses oeuvres les influences de Aloïs Haba et de Schoenberg (un véritable modèle pour lui). Depuis 1968 jusqu'à sa mort, il ne fut plus fait mention de lui en son pays." (J. & B. MASSIN)

"His works derive from a very wide range of interests: he played a part in the rediscovery of early music in Czechoslovakia, and he was also deeply concerned with Chinese, Japanese and Indian music, heading the committee for non-European music of the Oriental Society. In addition he maintained a lively interest in new musical trends. Kabelac's music is distinguished by great skill in instrumentation and the exploitation of often unusual sonorities." (A. SIMPSON)

Dechovy Sextet, op. 8 (1940) (17') •Fl/Ob/Cl/Asx/Hn/Bsn •CHF/ JMD/SHF

Suite, op. 39 (1959/1972) (9') •Asx/Pno •CHF

KACINSKAS, Jeronimas (1907)

Compositeur américain d'origine lithuanienne, né le 17 IV 1907 à Vidukle. Travailla avec son père puis avec J. Kricka et A. Haba.

"His music reflects the influences of Scriabin and French Impressionists." (BAKER)

Quartet (to D. SINTA) 1) Allegretto 2) Adagio 3) Moderato •SATB •adr

KADERAVEK, Milan

Introduction e Allegro (1963) •SATB •Pres/Uni

KAGEL, Mauricio (1931)

Compositeur argentin, né à Buenos Aires, le 24 XII 1931. Travailla avec Ginastera puis à Darmstadt. Installé en Allemagne depuis 1957.

"C'est un des tempéraments les plus puissants et les plus audacieux de sa génération, mais ses productions sont inégales. Influencé à ses débuts par Stockhausen, il est l'un de ceux qui ont le plus efficacement contribué à rechercher l'incorporation de la musique électro-acoustique au matériel sonore traditionnel. Il est également l'un des premiers à avoir exploré le domaine de la musique aléatoire, et il y est allé fort loin. Il est également l'un de ceux qui cherchent à déborder la musique de concert vers une tendance que l'on désigne par l'expression 'théâtre musical,' domaine dans lequel Kagel est l'un des plus aventureux supporters du néo-dadaïsme qui fleurit depuis les années 60." (Cl. ROSTAND) "Le Buster Keaton de la nouvelle musique ou son Pirandello? Un bricoleur ou un horloger de génie? Un provocateur négatif ou un compositeur de bonne race? C'est que l'art—on voudrait dire plutôt l'activité pertubatrice—de Kagel se situe à la frontière du cirque, de la prestidigitation, du théâtre de l'absurde, de la démonstration de gadgets et de la musique de chambre, avec à la fois une dure naïveté et un humour cruel à vous donner froid dans le dos. Si, par hasard, une certaine tendresse se glisse ici ou là, elle est insensiblement figée par un rictus caricatural. Mais, attention! La pureté de l'univers kagélien n'est ni réaliste ni simpliste et absolument pas idéologique. Sous l'évidence théâtrale, sous la provocation plus ou moins néo-dadaïste, sous le dénuement poussé jusqu'au silence, je vois moins 'la formulation esthétique d'une force destructive dirigée contre l'existence, la seule force dans laquelle soit aujourd'hui toute l'espérance du monde' qu'une approche tâtonnante et inquiète du global et de l'ambigu, à la fois fiévreuse et détachée, comme chez Cage et Stockhausen auxquels, en dépit de l'originalité de ses propres moyens, Kagel doit beaucoup." (M. FLEURET) "Kagel post-moderne? Ce en quoi Kagel se distingue, c'est plutôt son retour d'affection à l'égard des traditions musicales. Autrement dit, une façon de couver aujourd'hui avec bienveillance ce qu'on s'employait jusqu'alors à saper méthodiquement." (J-E. FOUSNAQUER) "De son installation en Allemagne—1957, va s'édifier peu à peu une oeuvre qui sonne comme un défi, qui se veut souvent pluridisciplinaire, qui est faite d'humour, qui relève parfois de l'absurde, qui se veut dérision, et qui refuse tous les enfermements, toutes les catégories établies, les esthétiques limitatives et répertoriées, pour devenir une grande dramaturgie du monde décrite à l'aide des sons et de la musique." (J. & B. MASSIN) "Mauricio Kagel s'intéresse à une musique de pauvreté et d'erreur. Ses oeuvres demandent des techniques inhabituelles, de grossières déformations du talent d'exécution, l'utilisation d'instruments extraordinaires—autant de moyens employés pour accentuer les effets visuels, dramatiques et musicaux. Les oeuvres de ce genre révèlent un sens provocant du comique et sans aucun doute entre-t-il dans les intentions de Kagel de créer des effets d'humour bizarre. Au-delà, se trouvent les questions posées par une intelligence critique—questions sur le niveau de virtuosité, sur la nécessité et le rôle de la musique, sur l'éthique d'une culture fondée sur la production de déchets, sur l'excès des chefs-d'oeuvre du passé qui pèsent sur la civilisation occidentale." (P. GRIFFITHS)

" 'Instrumental theatre,' of which Kagel has been the most determinant and influential exponent, proposes a music in which the actions of performers contribute as much as their sound. He has objected to being labelled a 'dadaist,' an 'anti-composer' or on the other hand an innovatory 'modernist,' the questioning of accepted values is one of the most significant impulses behind his work, directed to making doubt and negation fruitful. Kagel's rampant fantasy, the vast range of his humour and his love of the recondite and arcane, all have made his work the stimulus of much distaste, disturbance and protest." (J. HAÜSLER)

Acustica III (1968-70) (25') •2-5 Woodwind instruments/Perc •Uni

Atem (1970) (25') •1 Wind instrument/Tape •Uni

2 Akte - Grand duo (1988-89) •Asx/Harp •Pet

Musik aus diaphonie (1962-64) (12' minimum) •6-10 Instrumentalists or singers/diapositives •Uni

KAHAL & RASKIN

If I Give Up The Saxophone (WOLFE) •Voice/Ssx/Pno/Tuba (optional) •Ron

KAI, Akira (1947)

Compositeur japonais.

5 Pièces (1982) (to K. UÉDA) •SATB

KAINZ, Walter (1907)

Compositeur autrichien, né à Graz, le 21 II 1907.

Bläser Quintet, op. 12 (1935) 1) Allegro 2) Andante 3) Fugue-Presto •Fl/Cl/Asx/Hn/Bsn •adr

Sonate, op. 11 (1935) 1) Allegro moderato 2) Andante sostenuto
    3) Allegro •Asx/Pno •LK

KAIPAINEN, Jouni (1956)

Compositeur finlandais, né le 24 XI 1956.

"To his music Kaipainen is a humanist. He does not subscribe to any particular school, preferring to draw on the expressive material revealed as world's interest.

Far from home, op. 17 (1981) (10') •Fl/Asx/Guit/Perc •WH

"... la chimère de l'humidité de la nuit?," op. 12b (1978) (8') •Asx Solo •WH

KAIVULA, Kari (see KOIVULA)

KAJITAMI, Osamu

Compositeur japonais.

Jisoku - Trio •Ssx/Pno/Bonsho

KALAF, Jerry

3 Movements (1979) •Asx/Perc

KALED, Emil

Isomorphica (to Adirondack Saxophone Quartet) •SATB

KALINKOVISC, H.

Compositeur russe.

Concert caprice alla Paganini (13') 1) Pavane 2) Concert tango
    3) Tarentella •Asx/Pno •ECP

Tarentello •Asx/Pno

KALLSTENIUS, Edvin (1881-1967)

Compositeur suédois, né à Filipstadt, le 29 VIII 1881; mort à Stockholm, le 22 XI 1967.

"A pioneer of novel techniques in Sweden, he developed a pungent harmony, organized in later works by an adapted 12-note method. This harmonic style, demanding a constantly flexible tempo, caused difficulties in performance: not until the mid-1960s was he able to hear his music played to his satisfaction." (R. HAGLUND) "Kallstenius adhered to an individual, rigorous style which was full of renewal. He avoided getting bogged down in a monolithic tonal language by exploiting the intensity of melody, which he reinforced by broadening his harmony and by alternating between introspective romanticism and heavier, more expressionist gestures." (SJ)

Lyrische Suite, op. 55 (1960-62) (18') •Fl/Asx/Cl •STIM/EFM

KALLSTROM, Michael

Time Converging •2 Sx: AT/Pno

KAMALDINOV, G.

Compositeur russe.

Russian Melody •5 Sx: SAATB/Pno/Bass

KALMANN, Menno

Co + Menno's music + Co de Kloet (1986) (17') 1) Aria 2) Ticino
    3) Goyang Pantat 4) The stacker (de stapelaar) 5) Run to the
    Eyry ('t Hoentje) •Asx/Pno •Mol

KALOGERAS, Alexandra (1961)

Compositeur grec. Travailla avec O. Messiaen, L. Nono et T. Takemitsu.

Hors tempérament (1990) (9') (to S. BERTOCCHI) •Bsx Solo

KAMIMURA, Junko

Compositeur japonais.

Soumon •Asx/Pno

KAMIOKA, Yôichi

Compositeur japonais.

Ballade (1987) •Asx/Pno

KANE, Jack

Concerto •Asx/Orch

KANEFZKY, Franz (1964)

Compositeur allemand.

Leiche duette (1990) •2 Sx •Hag

KANEKO, S.

Compositeur japonais.

Damnoen sakuak floating market (14') •Sx/Perc

KANITZ, Ernest (1894-1978)

Compositeur américain d'origine autrichienne, né à Vienne, le 9 IV 1894; mort à Menlo Park (California), le 7 IV 1978. Travailla avec R. Heuberger et F. Schreker. Aux U.S.A. depuis 1938.

Interlude •Asx/Band

Intermezzo Concertante (1948/53) •Asx/Orch or Band or Pno •USC

Introduction and Allegro (1963) •SATB •Uni/Pres

Little Concerto (1970) (to H. PITTEL) •Asx Solo •Art

Phantastic Intermezzo •Asx/Pno

Pieces (to H. PITTEL) •Asx Solo

Serenade •Asx/Wind group •USC

Sonata Californiana (1952) •Asx/Pno •CFE

KANZLEITER, Dieter

Compositeur allemand.

Les mouvements de l'eau (1993) •Asx/Vcl •INM

KAPLAN, D.

Gotham Collection of Duets •2 Sx •JS/SPM

KAPPEY, Jacob Adam (1826-1907)

27 Exercices and 15 Cadenzas (DE VILLE) •CF

11 Progressive Studies •CF

KARAI, Jozsef (1927)

Compositeur hongrois, né le 8 XI 1927, à Budapest.

Sonatina •Asx/Pno •B&H

KAREL, Leon C.

Cypress Song (1955) •Tsx/Pno •B&H

Hewaphon (to A. RACLOT) •Tsx/Pno •South

Metrax (to A. RACLOT) •Tsx/Pno •South

Quintra (1965) (To A. RACLOT) •Tsx/Pno •South

KAREVA, Hilar

Compositeur russe.

Concerto No. 1, op. 25 •Asx/Orch or Pno

Sonate, op. 19 (1976) •Asx/Pno

KARG-ELERT Sigfrid (1877-1933)

Compositeur, organiste, et théoricien allemand, né à Oberndorf am Neckar, le 21 XI 1877; mort à Leipzig, le 9 IV 1933. Travailla avec Homeyer, Jadassohn, Reinecke, et Wendling.

"Etonnant personnage aujourd'hui par trop méconnu, de son vrai nom Siegfried Theodor Karg (alias Teo von Oberndorff, ou encore Dr. O. Bergk). Il succéda à Max Reger, trois ans après la mort de celui-ci, au Conservatoire de Leipzig (1919). Son activité de professeur ne l'empêcha pas de mener une brillante carrière de concertiste (hautbois, harmonium et orgue), qui le conduisit, peu de temps avant sa mort aux Etats-Unis (1931-32). L'oeuvre de Karg-Elert mériterait vraiment, dans son ensemble, d'être enfin et tout simplement reconnue." (G. CANTAGREL)

"As composer he developed a brilliant style, inspired by the music of the Baroque, but he embellished this austere and ornamental idiom with Impressionistic devices; the result was an ingratiating type of music with an aura of originality." (BAKER) "Whatever the chosen form may be, the music is intensely alive and expressive." (H. GRACE) "Like Reger, Karg-Elert was greatly influenced by Bach. With Reger he must be counted one of the major organ composers of the 20th century." (J. CLARK)

Atonal Sonata, op. 153b (1929) 1) Allegro con moto 2) Scherzo demoniaco 3) Larghetto malinconico 4) Toccata-Finale •Asx Solo •Zim

25 Capricen, op. 153a (1929) (2 books) •Asx Solo •Zim/South

KARKOFF, Ingvar (1958)

Compositeur suédois, né à Stockholm, le 14 IX 1958. Fils de Maurice Karkoff. Travailla avec G. Johansson, V. Söderholm, G. Bucht et, la musique électronique avec P. Lindgren.

2 Danses exotiques (1990) •Asx/Perc •STIM
Konsert (1988) (17') (to J. PETTERSSON) •Asx/5 Perc •SUE
Madrigale (1990) •Asx/Pno •SvM
Meditations - 3 pieces (1989/92) •Asx/Pno •SvM
Ricercare (1988) (9') •SATB •STIM
Suite (1989/93) •Asx Solo •SvM

KARKOFF, Maurice (1927)

Compositeur et professeur suédois, né à Stockholm, le 17 III 1927. Travailla avec L. E. Larsson et, plus tard avec Blomdahl, E. von Koch, Holmboe, Jolivet, N. Boulanger, et Vogel.

"His technique is based on the serial method of composition, but he adheres to classical forms." (BAKER) "Many works show his involvement with contemporary social and political issues." (R. HAGLUND) "Karkoff's music is characterized by an expressive style which combines lengthy melodic lines and concise phrases with powerful climaxes. His instrumental music clearly indicates a developed sense for colour and nuance and his melodic lines are sensitively constructed." (H-G. P.)

Ballada quasi une fantasia, op. 164 (1988) (17') •Asx/Pno •STIM
Concertino, op. 15 (1955) (13') Asx/Str Orch/Perc or Pno •Sue
Djurens Karneval (1974) (15') •Fl/Picc/2 Cl/Tsx/Bsn/Perc •STIM
Drömmeri/Poem, op. 165 (1988) (17') •Cl/Vla/Asx/Pno
Ernst und Spass, op. 156 (1984) (9'30) (to Rascher Quartet) Overtura - Elegia - Scherzo capriccioso - Finale •SATB •STIM
Kontrate, op. 155 (1984) (10') •3 Sx: SAB •STIM
The Lord is My Shepherd: pastorale, op. 196c (1992) •Fl/Ssx •SMIC
Poem, op. 166 (1989) •Bsx/Pno •STIM
Profilen, op. 157 (1984) (10') •2 Sx: AB •STIM
Quartett (1984) •SATB •WIM
Rapsodisk fantasi, op. 8a (1953) (6') (to J. de VRIES) •Asx/Pno •Ehr/SMIC/STIM
Reflexionen, op. 160 (1986) (to Rascher Quartet) •SATB •SMIC
8 Solominiatyrer, op. 8b (1953) (6'30) (to J. de VRIES) 1) Allegro risoluto 2) Adagio 3) Allegro burlesco 4) Andante espressivo 5) (Alla tango) Moderato 6) Moderato 7) Con moto 8) Allegro •Asx Solo •Ehr/STIM
Sonatine, op. 159 (1985-86) (10') 1) Toccata 2) Varianter 3) Burla •Asx/Pno •SMIC
4 Stycken, op. 4 (1952-53) 1) Liebeslied 2) Unter Jean Wasses 3) Abendlied 4) Elegy •Asx/Pno •SMIC/Ehr

KARLINS, M. William (1932)

Compositeur et professeur américain né à New York, le 25 II 1932. Travailla avec S. Wolpe, V. Gianinni, P. Bezanson, et F. Piket.

Blues (1965) (3'30) •AATB •TP/Pres/CFE/JB
Catena II (1982) (10') (to J. WYTKO) •Ssx/Brass Quintet •ACA
Concerto (1981-82) (22') (to R. BLACK) 1) Adagio 2) Allegro Moderato 3) Largo •Asx/Orch (Picc12EbCl11CBsn/2220/Timp/2 Perc/Str) •ACA

Fantasia (1978-79) (9'30) (to D. & C. HAWES) 1) Toccata 2) Cantelina •Tsx/Perc •ACA/NP
Graphic Mobile (1970) •Any 3 or more instruments •MP
Impromptu (12') •Asx/Org (or Electr. Pno or Pno) •ACA
Introduction and Passacaglia (1990) (10') •2 Sx: AT/Pno •ACA
Music (8') •Asx/Pno •South
Music (1969) (13') (to F. HEMKE) •Tsx/Str Quartet (or Pno) •South
Nostalgie (1991) (to J-M. GOURY and J-M. LONDEIX) •12 Sx: SnoSSAAATTTBBBs •adr
Quartet No. 1 (1966-67) (7') 1) Moderato 2) Slow 3) Fast •SATB •SeMC
Quartet No. 2 (1975) (to R. BLACK) (12 variations and cadenza) •SATB •adr
Quintet (1973-74) (15') (to F. HEMKE) (3 movements) •Asx/Str Quartet •SeMC
Reflux - Concerto (1970) •Amplified Bass/3 Sx •adr
Saxtuper (1989) (9') •1 Sx: A+S/Tuba/Perc •ACA
Seasons (1987) (13') (to F. HEMKE) Spring - Summer - Autumn - Winter •Sx Solo: S+A+T •TP
Sonata (to F. HEMKE) •Tsx/Pno •CFE
Variations (1962-63) •Ssx/Vln/Vla/Vcl •SeMC

KARPEN, Richard

Compositeur américain.
Saxonomy •1 Sx: A+T+B/Tape

KARPMAN, Laura (1958)

Compositeur américain, né à Los Angelès.
Capriccio (1981) (8'35) (to L. HUNTER & B. CONNELLY) •Asx/Pno •DP
Matisse and Jazz (1987) (18') (to L. HUNTER) •Voice/1 Sx: S+A/Perc/Pno •Eto
Saxmaniac (1988) (to L. HUNTER) •Asx Solo •MMB
Song Pictures (1989) (8') (to L. HUNTER) Running - Become Blue - Sound is Fading... - Become White - Ghost Dance •2 performers: Yamaha WX7 MIDI wind controller/Yamaha TX81Z tone generator/Sequencer/Soprano Voice •MMB

KARREN, Léon

Menuet marquise (1891) •Ssx/Pno

KASEMETS, Udo (1919)

Compositeur, pianiste, et chef d'orchestre canadien d'origine estonienne, né à Tallinn, le 16 IX 1919. Travailla à Darmstadt.

"His early works reflect his Estonian provenance. Later he espoused dodecaphony according to the strict Schoenbergian doctrine. Beginning in 1960 he progressed toward total serialism, became editor of *Canavangard* an annotated catalogue of works by Canadian avantgarde composers." (BAKER) "By the late 1960s Kasemets had reached a point where the live process of bringing a realization into being was more important to him than the 'work.' And so later pieces often take the form of 'lecturessays' (on such problems as the cultivation of sensitivity, or pollution) or 'combination scores,' where several basic schemes are set off simultaneously." (J. BECKWITH)

Calcolaria (1966) •Sx/Actress •BMI
Cascando-Poem (1965) •Vcl/Asx
Cascando-Solo (1965) •Asx Solo
Contactics (1966) •Sx/Actress •BMI
Cumulus (1964) •Any solo ensemble/2 Tape Recorders
Timepiece (1964) •1 Performer using any singular or multiple instruments
Trigon (1963) •1, 3, or 9 Performers •BMI

KASHLAYEV, M.

Compositeur russe.
Concerto (1975) •Asx/Orch

Concerto pour orchestre de jazz (1975)

KASPAR, Edward Anthony (1947)

Compositeur américain, né le 30 IX 1947, à Falmouth (Massachusetts). Travailla avec E. P. Diemente et E. Miller.
Abyss (1971) (5') (to K. DORN) •Asx/Vibr •adr
Quartet (1972) •2 Sx: AT/Vibr/Tuba •adr
Within and Beyond (1970) (5') •Asx/Pno •SeMC

KASPERSEN, Jan

Compositeur danois.
Quartet (1989) (7') •SATB

KASSAP, Sylvain

Saxophoniste et clarinettiste de jazz, d'origine d'Europe centrale.
Bolkanique (1993) (3'15) •Asx •Mis

KASTNER, Jean-Georges (1810-1867)

Théoricien, écrivain, et compositeur français, né à Strasbourg, le 9 III 1810; mort à Paris, le 19 XII 1867. Travailla avec Reicha et H-M. Berton. Membre de l'orchestre de la Garde Nationale à Strasbourg.
"His strongest interest was in wind music and he was particularly enthusiastic about Sax's instruments; his two compositions for the saxhorn and a set of variations for the alto saxophone were among the earliest works for those instruments." (T. LA MAY)
Grand sextuor (1844) •6 Sx: SAATBBs •Sax/DP/Eth
Méthode complète et raisonnée de saxophone - Famille complète et nouvelle d'instruments de cuivre à anche (1862) •Sax
Variations brillantes (1847) •Asx/Pno •Sax

KAT, Jack (1955)

Compositeur hollandais.
Convulsions (1979) (3') •SATB •Don

KATAYEV, Igor

Compositeur russe.
Sonata (1976) (to L. MIKHAILOV) •Asx/Pno
Concerto (1977) •Asx/4 Sx: SATB/Orch

KATAYEV, Vitaly

Compositeur russe, fils du précédent.
Concerto (1980) (to J-M. LONDEIX) 1) Allegro energico 2) Molto sostenuto 3) Allegro finale •Asx/Orch

KAUFMANN, Armin

Konzert für Tàrogato, op. 91 1) Moderato 2) Larghetto 3) Presto •Ssx/Chamber Orch •Dob

KAUFMANN, Dieter (1941)

Compositeur autrichien.
"Dieter Kaufmann a fondé son propre groupe de 'théâtre musical': K. und K. Experimental Studio," pour être à même de présenter devant de larges publics ses oeuvres multi-médias. Par ailleurs, il donne une impulsion nouvelle à la musique électro-acoustique." (J. & Br. MASSIN)
Genius compact - 6 Bagatellen (1992) (8') (to Wiener Saxophone Quartet) •SATB •ApE

KAUFMANN, Serge (1930)

Ecrivain et compositeur français. Travailla avec D. Lesur.
Rhapsodie (2') (Album) •Asx/Pno •Bil

KAUFMANN, Waldemar

Compositeur allemand.
Sein Weg (1993) •Bsx/Voice •INM

KAUFMANN, Walter

Meditation (1982) •Asx/Pno •Eto

KAUN, Hugo (1863-1932)

Compositeur et chef de choeur allemand, né le 21 III 1863 à Berlin, où il est mort, le 2 IV 1932. Travailla avec F. Kiel.
"He composed a great deal of music in every genre. His operas are Wagnerian in style, and the Wagnerian harmonic language pervades all of his larger compositions." (W. GUDGER)
"Aus den Bergen" - Suite (1932) (to S. RASCHER) •Asx/Pno

KAVANAUGH, Patrick (1954)

Debussy-variations No. 5 (1977) (to W. STREET) •Asx or other Sx •CF
Hommage to C. S. Lewis (1978) •Fl/Ob/Cl/Asx/Hn/Bsn
Quintus rotus (1980) (to W. STREET) •Asx/Tape

KAWAKAMI, Tetgo (1950)

Compositeur japonais.
Arabesque (to Y. SASAKI) •Asx/Pno

KAWAMOTO, Itaru

Compositeur japonais.
Nayuta (1993) •Asx/Cl •INM

KAZANDJIEV, Vasil Ivanov (1934)

Compositeur et chef d'orchestre bulgare, né à Marten le 19 IX 1934. Travailla avec Iliev, Vladigerov, et Simeonov.
"One of the most gifted Bulgarian composers of his generation, he has used 12-note, aleatoric and other novel means together with rhythmic and metric ideas from Bulgarian folk music." (L. BRASHOVANOVA)
Double concerto (1962) 1) Allegro non troppo 2) Andante espressivo 3) Allegro con moto •Asx/Pno/Orch

KAZIM, Necil

Allegro feroce (STATZER & WLIDGANS) (1932) •Asx/Pno •Uni

KEANE, David (1943)

Compositeur canadien d'origine américaine né dans l'Ohio. Installé au Canada depuis 1967.
Saxophonies (1987/90) (13') •Ssx/Computer •CMC

KECHLEY, David (1947)

Compositeur américain.
Concerto (1983) (to F. BONGIORNO) •Asx/Chamber Orch
In the Dragon's Garden (1992) (15'55) 1) Songs from the Wind; Islands in the Sand; The Sea of Stones; Beyond the Wall; Dancing between the Rocks •Asx/Guit •PV
Music for Saxophones (1985) (25') (to F. BONGIORNO) 1) Funky Music 2) Funeral Music 3) Fast Music •Asx/4 Sx: SATB •PV
Stepping Out (1989) (15') (to Saskatoon Saxophone Quartet) Minimum Overdrive - Midnight Reflection - Anonymous & An Easy Burden •SATB •PV
Tsunagari (1988) (15') (to F. BONGIORNO) 1) Strong 2) Timeless 3) Satirical 4) Intense 5) Quick •Ssx/4 Sx: AATB •PV

KEEFE, Robert

Relentless •Asx/Pno

KEFALA-KERR, John

Compositeur américain.
Motorola •SATB

KEIG, Betty (1920)

Compositeur américain, né à Defiance (Ohio), le 1er XII 1920.
After the Circus (1972) (10') •Sx/Tape/Pno •adr
Episodes (1990) (to K. L. FARRELL) •Ssx/Pno

KEISER, Henk (1960)

Compositeur néerlandais.

Syncopen (1982) (13') (to Quatuor Sax) •SATB •Don
V.S.O.P. (1984) (14') •Ob/Cl/Asx/Bsn •Don

KELER , Béla (18920-1882)
Lustspiel (HOLMES) •AATB •Bar

KELKEL, Manfred (1929)
Compositeur français, d'origine allemande, né à Siersburg, le 15 I 1929. Travailla avec J. Rivier et D. Milhaud.

"Ses compositions, d'une facture très solide, se situent sur le versant néo-classique." (Cl. ROSTAND) "Attiré par le mystérieux, le fantastique, Kelkel assignerait volontiers à l'oeuvre musicale un rôle quasiment *magique*. Il s'est forgé une langue musicale personnelle, partant d'une conception très libre de la tonalité pour aboutir à un chromatisme poussé, mais où l'usage des modes hiérarchisés maintient des centres d'attraction perceptibles. Le recours sporadique à la série s'inscrit dans cette perspective et ne donne jamais lieu à un système." (J. VIRET)
Concertino (1961) (16') (to M. PERRIN) •Asx/Orch
Lanterna magica (to M. PERRIN) •Asx/Perc/Pno
Musique funèbre (1960) (9') (to M. PERRIN) •Asx/Orch
Rhapsodie, op. 12 (1961) (18') (to M. PERRIN) •Asx/Orch (1111/210/Perc/Harp/Pno/Str) or Pno •Ric

KELTERBORN, Rudolf (1931)
Compositeur et chef d'orchestre suisse né à Bâle, le 3 IX 1931. Travailla avec G. Bialas, W. Fortner, et I. Markevitch, puis à Darmstadt.

"He began to adopt 12-note writing, and later serialism, but without employing these procedures rigorously. Subsequently he took up the imagery of avant-garde music, but throughout his path has been an independent one, more concerned with appeals to the listener's feelings than with careful structuring, although Kelterborn's music is always structurally clear. Typical of his early work is a certain raggedness of shape, bordering on the fantastic, together with humming, fluttering patterns that are often brilliantly and artfully orchestrated. A deliberate pictorialism has remained a feature of his music." (F. MUGGLER)
Quartet (1978-79) (10') (to I. ROTH) •AATB •Hug

KEMNER, F. Gerald (1932)
Compositeur américain.
Quiet Music (20') (to F. HEMKE) •Ssx/Str/Brass

KENNEDY, Amanda
Star of the Sea (HUMMEL) •Asx/Pno •Rub
Star of Hope - Rêverie •2 Sx: AA or AT/Pno •Cen

KENNELL, Richard
Compositeur américain.
Lamentations •Sx/Harp

KERGOMARD, Henri
Anem (1989) (8') (to D. KIENTZY) •Ssx/Tape

KERJULLOU (see PARIS-KERJULLOU)

KERN, Jerome (1885-1945)
Smoke Gets in your Eyes •5 Sx: AATBBs
Famous Song •Asx/Pno
All the Things You Are (M. ALBAM) •SATB/Orch
All the Things You Are (L. NIEHAUS) •SATB

KERN, Matthias (1928)
Compositeur allemand, né à Neuendettelsau, le 31 V 1928. Travailla avec S. Reda.
Erstes •SATB •adr

KERSHAW, David
Compositeur anglais.
Four Bagatelles 1) A Flourish 2) Fantasia 3) Sarabande 4) Rondoletto •SATB

KERSHNER, Brian
Chamber Concerto (1994) (to D. HASTINGS) 1) Introspections and Ballade 2) Outer Limits 3) Heads or Tales •Asx/Chamber Orch

KESNAR, Maurits (1900-1957)
Violoniste et compositeur américain, né à Amsterdam (Hollande), le 8 VII 1900; mort à Carbondale (Illinois), le 22 II 1957.
Capriccio •4 Sx: AATB or Asx/Pno •CBet
Pastorale •Asx/Pno •CBet
Un petit rien •2 Sx: AA/Pno •WWS

KESSNER, Daniel
Compositeur néerlandais.
Arabesque (1983) (to BOK & LE MAIR) •Sx/Vibr

KETELBEY, Albert W. (1875-1959)
In a Persian Market •Asx/Pno •Bel

KETTING, Otto (1935)
Compositeur néerlandais, né à Amsterdam, le 3 IX 1935. Travailla avec son père Piet Ketting et K. A. Hartmann.

"His music his highly individual, unconventional and well-crafted." (M. STARREVELD-BARTELS)
Mars (1974) (3'30) •4 Cl/4 Sx: AATT or 8 Sx: AATT AATT •Don
Musik zu einen Tonfilm (1982) (15') •2 Sx/Tpt/Trb/Perc/Pno/2 Vln •Don
Praeludium (1989) (to E. BOGAARD) •12 Sx: SnoSSAAATTTBBBs •Or
Symphony (1977-78) (30') (to Netherlands Saxophone Quartet) •4 Sx: SATB/Orch (0000/6561/Str/Pno/Perc) •Don

KEULEN, Geert van (1943)
Compositeur néerlandais.
Fingers is characterized by a breathtaking drive in the saxophone, throughout all registers of the instrument. Virtuosity is the key of the piece in the obstinate sense. Van Keulen wanted to create a piece that was rebellious to any idea of romanticism. That's why its use of the instrument at some instances is rough. Starting off with repetitive patterns in the saxophone the instrument grows in melodic ideas and gets interweaved with the orchestra or the piano. Towards the end, in a choral-like passage, the saxophone has lost all its rhythm and plays only melodic snatches." (M. Nieuwenhuizen)
Concert (1990) •Asx/Pno •Don
Fingers - Concerto (1991) (19') (To A. BORNKAMP) •Tsx/Chamber Orch (2222/2 Perc/2200/Str) or Pno •Don
Kwartet (1987) (7') (to Rijmond Saxophone Quartet) •SATB •Don
Onkruid (1981) (5') •Ob/Cl/2 Sx: AT/Bsn/Hn/Tpt/Trb/Vln/Vla/Pno •Don

KEURIS, Tristan (1946)
Compositeur néerlandais, né à Amsterdam, le 3 X 1946. Travailla avec Ton de Leeuw.

"He has already developed a daring, and at the same time controlled, style with a feeling for innovations in sound and clear formal structures." (GROVE)
Concerto (1971) (11') (to E. Bogaard) •Asx/Orch (3232/4221/Perc/Pno/Str) •Don
Music (1986) (17') (to Rascher Quartet) •SATB •Don/Nov
Quatuor (1970) (8') (to Netherlands Saxophone Quartet) •SATB •Don

KEVRE
Duo •Asx/EH

KEY, Francis Scott (1779-1843)
Star Spangled Banner •6 Sx: AATTBBs

KEYES
Trio •3 Sx: ATB

KHALADJI, Iwan
Solstice (1986) •Asx/Guit

KHATCHATURIAN, Aram (1903-1978)
Danse du sabre •Asx/Pno •MCA
Sabre Dance •Bsx/Pno •Lee

KHRENNIKOV, Tikhon (1913)
Serenade (SEDOV) •Asx/Pno

KIANOVSKY, Raphael
Quintet (1972) (to F. HEMKE) •Asx/Str Quartet

KIBBE
Divertimento •Ob/EH (or Asx)/Bsn •Sha

KIDD, Brian
Concerto (1988) (to D. UNDERWOOD) •Asx/Band

KIEFER, W.
Elena Polka •2 Sx: TT or AT/Pno •Bar

KIELLISH, F.
Serenade Impromptu •4 Sx: AATT/Pno •Ken

KIENTZY, Daniel (1951)
Saxophoniste, virtuose français né à Périgueux. Travailla avec R. Decouais et D. Deffayet. Docteur es Esthétique-Sciences et Technologie des Arts (1990).
Les sons simultanés aux saxophones (1982) •Sal

KIKUCHI, Yukio
Saxophones' Studies (3 movements) (1985) •SATB

KILAR, Wojciech (1932)
Compositeur et pianiste polonais, né à Lwow, le 17 VII 1932. Travailla avec Markiewiczowna, Woytowicz, et N. Boulanger.
"He began his compositional career as a neo-classicist, equally at ease in writing the strict polyphony he had learned with Woytowicz and in the complex harmonic style of the Sinfonia concertante. After 1962 he began to make use of novel technique, texture and vocal production." (B. SCHÄFFER)
1 Dla 3 (1963) •Asx/Vibr/Bass

KING, Karl L.
A Night in June •2 Sx: AA or TT/Pno •Bar

KINKELDER, Dolf de
Compositeur néerlandais.
De Verloedering (1985) (10') •SATB •Don

KINNINGTON, Alan
Sonare No. 1 •Sx Solo

KINYON, John (1918)
Breeze Easy Recital Pieces •Tsx Solo •Wit

KIPS, René
Compositeur belge.
Esquisse Orientale •Asx/Pno •An/HE/Ger

KIRCHSTEIN, Harold Manfred (1906)
Compositeur allemand d'origine américaine, né le 29 XII 1906 à New York.
Musik für Junggesellen Suite (20') •Asx/Orch •adr

KIRCK, George Thomas (1948)
Saxophoniste, compositeur américain, né le 13 IV 1948 à Mount Vernon (New York). Travailla le saxophone avec Donald Sinta.
The Reed Guide - A Handbook for Modern Reed Working for all Single Reed Woodwind Instruments (1983) •Reed
Resultants •SATB •DP
Song to Wind (1971) (10') •Asx/Perc/Tape •adr

KIRSCHENMANN, Mark
Compositeur américain.
Paradigm Shift (1993) •Ssx/Str Quartet •INM

KISZA, Stanislaw
Compositeur polonais.
Szkice (1964-65) •1 Sx: A or T/Pno •PWM

KITAZUME, Michio
Compositeur japonais.
Air (1992) (8') •Asx/Pno •Lem
Sérénade (1979) •SATB

KITTEL, Tilo
Compositeur allemand.
Saxgasse (1993) •Asx/Pno •INM

KITTLER, Richard
Compositeur autrichien.
Divertimento, op.163 (1992) (11') •SATB •CA
Phonosignale (10') •SATB •CA

KIYOSHI, Keiji (1933)
Compositeur japonais.
Sonatina (1977) (to K. UÉDA) •2 Sx: S+A/A

KLAMMER, David
Compositeur allemand.
Erwartingen oder Liebesdialog (1993) •Vln/Sx •INM

KLAUSS, Noah
Aria •Tsx/Pno •Ken
Night Song •SATB •Cap

KLEBE, Giselher (1925)
Compositeur allemand, né le 28 VI 1925, à Mannheim. Travailla avec K. von Wolfurt, Rufer, et B. Blacher.
"Au lendemain de la IIme Guerre mondiale, il s'est imposé comme l'une des natures les plus douées de la jeune école allemande de cette époque, collectionnant les prix de toutes sortes et donnant des oeuvres sérielles d'un accent très personnel et d'une vive invention." (Cl. ROSTAND)
"An experimenter by nature, he has written music in widely ranging forms, from classically conceived instrumental pieces to highly modernistic works; his technique is basically dodecaphonic; the chief influences being Schoenberg and Anton Webern; coloristic themes play an important role in his music (BAKER) "Klebe has, together with Henze, taken a leading part in the development of opera since 1955 and in bringing the genre to a somewhat unexpected importance in the history of music since World War II. Influenced by Blacher, he had written striking, rhythmically sharp, unsentimental music whose formal clarity and resolution at once surprised and rebuked traditional expectations. The knowledge of 12-note serialism that he gained from Rufer enabled him to broaden the sound spectrum he had used hitherto;

taking Berg as his example, he has always held himself open to particular expressive ideas." (H. KRELLMANN)
Gratullations - tango, op. 40a •Asx/Tpt/Pno/Perc •B&B

KLEIN, Georg
Compositeur allemand.
Nuit du visage (1993) •1 Sx: S+T/Live electronics •INM

KLEIN, Immanuel (1960)
Compositeur néerlandais.
Liederen voor rietrries (1991) •12 Sx: SnoSSAAATTTBBBs •Don

KLEIN, Jonathan
Hear O Israel •Soprano Voice/Alto Voice/Sx/Hn/Pno/Perc/Bass •SeMC

KLEIN, Lothar (1932)
Compositeur canadien d'origine allemande, né le 27 I 1932 à Hanovre. Travailla avec G. Petrassi, B. Blacher et L. Nono.
"His music is basically tonal; its esthetical premises are both neo-classical and neo-romantic. In his more abstract compositions he applies various species of serialism." (BAKER)
6 Exchanges (1972) (6') (to P. BRODIE) •Sx Solo •Pres/CMC/Ten
Vaudeville (1979) (12') •Ssx/Fl/Ob/Cl/Hn/Bsn •CMC

KLEINSINGER, George (1914)
Compositeur et chef d'orchestre américain, né à San Bernardino (California), le 13 II 1914.
"Kleinsinger played piano in dance bands, served as music director in youth camps, and traveled through the country. He acquired a taste for simple American songs and rhythms; sophisticated pieces or native subjects, often with a satiric purpose, and with colorful instrumental effects, became his specialty." (BAKER)
Street Corner Concerto (1953) 1) Dance of the City Kids 2) Sleeping City 3) Hustle Bustle •Asx/Orch (3222/3321/Perc/Harp/Str) or Pno •Chap

KLERK, Joseph de (1885-19xx)
Chef d'orchestre, chanteur, et compositeur néerlandais, né à Merxem (Belgique), le 8 I 1885.
Intrada •2 Sx or Bb Sx/Cl •Mol
Kleine Partita •2 Sx •Mol

KLETSCH, Ludwig
Ballade •1 Sx: A or T/Orch or Pno •Fro
Das Lachende Saxophon •Asx/Pno •Fro

KLICKMANN , F. Henry
Smiles and Chuckles (GEE) •SATB or AATB •Ron
Smiles and Chuckles (NASCIMBEN) •SATB
Sweet Hawaiian Moonlight •2 Sx/Pno •McK
Trail to Long Ago •2 Sx/Pno •McK

KLIER, Gottfield (1949)
Saxophoniste, arrangeur, et compositeur allemand, né le 18 I 1949 à Zittau.
25 Saxophone Quartets •4 Sx: ATTB or SATB •adr

KLING, Henri (1842-1918)
Olifan en mug •2 Sx •Mol

KLINGSOR, Tristan (1874-1966)
Sérénade •SATB •CBDM

KLOBUCAR, Andelko (1931)
Compositeur yougoslave. Travailla avec A. Jolivet.
Canzona (1982) (Album) •Asx/Pno •DSH/HG

Sonate (1981) (to D. SREMEE) Allegro - Largo - Vivace •Asx/Pno •DSH/HG

KLOIBER, Anton
Compositeur allemand.
Bekenntnisse eines Liebenden (1993) •Soprano Voice/Bsx •INM

KLOSE, Hyacinthe Eleonore (1808-1880)
Clarinettiste, concertiste, et pédagogue français, né à Corfou (Grèce), le 11 X 1808; mort à Paris, le 29 VIII 1880. Professeur de clarinette au Conservatoire de Paris. Etudia le saxophone avec Adolphe Sax.
Daniel d'après E. Depas - Fantaisie chromatique (1869) •Asx/Pno •Led
Le désir d'après Schubert - Fantaisie (1880) •Asx/Pno •Led
Duettino concertante (1876) •Cl/Asx/Pno •Led
15 Etudes chantantes (CAPELLE) (1883) •Led
Etudes de genre et de mécanisme (JEANJEAN) (1928) •Led
25 Daily Exercises for Saxophone •CF
25 Daily Exercises (GEE) •DP
25 Etudes de mécanisme (CAPELLE) (1881) •Led
25 Exercices journaliers (CAPELLE) (1928) •Led
Method (BUIJZER Jr.) •Mol
Méthode complète (1866-1910) •Led
Semiramis - Fantaisie •Asx/Pno •Led
Solo (1858) (to A. SAX) •Led
Solo (1859) (to ESCUDIÉ) •Sx Solo: A or S •Sax
La Somnambule •Cl/Asx/Pno •Bil

KLOTZMAN, Dorothy
Concerto (12') •Asx/Orch (3021/4331/Perc/Str)

KLOUMAN, Carsten (1923)
Compositeur norvégien.
Divertimento (1976) •SATB

KLUGHART, August (Friedrich-Martin) (1847-1902)
Romanze •Bsx/Pno •JS

KLUSAK, Jan (1934)
Compositeur tchécoslovaque né à Prague, le 18 IV 1934. Travailla avec Ridky et Borkovec.
"His music has developed from a complex, tonal neo-classicism to 12-note serial writing of spontaneous invention, rhythmic freshness and imaginatively varied texture. The yearning, lyrical character of his work has something in common with the music of Berg and of Mahler." (B. LARGE)
Suita (1983) (8') •SATB •CHF

KNAIFEL, Alexandre Aronovitch (1943)
Compositeur russe, né à Tachkent (Ouzbékistan). Travailla avec M. Rostropovich et B. Arapov.
"Il expérimente dès ses débuts toutes les possibilités offertes par les techniques occidentales: post-sérialisme, aléatoire, collage 'free-jazz'... Il recherche des formes nouvelles, des timbres nouveaux, selon une démarche compositionnelle influencée par les mathématiques. Il intro-duit dans la musique soviétique un état d'esprit frondeur, burslesque, fantasque qui lui manque fort. Son imagination sonore est extrême-ment séduisante; il n'y a dans son oeuvre, malgré la variété des moyens employés, aucun retour nostalgique à un style du passé." (J. di VANNI)
Agnus Dei (1985) (120-150') •Sx/Orch/Perc/Tape

KNAKKERGARD, Martin
Compositeur danois.
Monrovida discount replacement (1989) (15') •Tsx/Marimba

KNIGHT, Morris (1933)
Compositeur américain né à Charleston (South Carolina), le 25 XII

1933.

Concerto (1962) (12') (to C. Leeson) (7 short movements) •Asx/Str
   Orch •adr

Quartet No. 1 (1964) (10') (to C. Leeson) •AATB •adr

Quartet No. 2 (1968) (12') (to C. Leeson) Deliberately - Lightly -
   Broadly - Driving - Languidly - Declamatory - Reflectively -
   Dynamically - Nostalgic Cadenza •AATB •South

Sonata (1964) (20') (to C. Leeson) 1) Passacaglia 2) Chaconne
   3) Ayres 4) Differencia 5) Introduction e tarantella •Asx/Pno
   •South

KNORR, Ernst Lothar von (1896-1973)

Compositeur, violoniste, et professeur allemand, né à Eitorf, le 2 I
1896, mort à Heidelberg, le 30 X 1973.

"His works reflect his academic background." (K. Neumann)

Chamber Concerto (to S. Rascher) •Asx/Pno/Chamber Orch •adr

Introduction für drei Saxophone (1932) (5') (to S. Rascher) •3 Sx:
   AAT •TTF

Sonate (1932) (15'30) (to S. Rascher) 1) Fantasia 2) Allegro
   3) Allegretto scherzando 4) Signal •Asx/Pno •GrB

KNOSP, Erwin

Compositeur français.

Divertissement 1) Allegro 2) Lent 3) Scherzo 4) Allegro •SATB
   •adr

Introduction, Allegro, Rondo finale •4 Sx: AAAA •adr

Pièce concertante •SATB •adr

KNOX, Thomas

Arrangeur et compositeur américain.

Cascades (1972) •4 Sx: AATB/Band

KNUTSEN, Thorbjörn (1904-1987)

Compositeur norvégien.

Quartet (1974) (14') (to Oslo Saxophone Quartet) •SATB •NMI

KOBAYASHI, Hidéo (1931)

Compositeur japonais né à Tokyo.

Invention (1970) •SATB •adr

3 Pièces brèves (1970) (to A. Sakaguchi) •Sx Solo •adr

KOBLENZ, Babette

Grey Fire (1981) •Cl/2 Sx: AT/Tpt/Electr. Bass/Electr. Pno/Perc
   •adr

KÖBNER, Andreas (1951)

Compositeur allemand, né le 11 X 1951 à Mannheim.

E-Musik •SATB •adr

KOCH, Erland von (1910)

Compositeur, chef d'orchestre, et pianiste suédois, né à Stockholm,
le 26 IV 1910. Élève de son père, il eut très jeune ses premiers succès
de compositeur.

"Son style qui s'alimente aux sources folkloriques, est rigoureux, son
lyrisme généreux et contrôlé." (R. Bernard) "Sa musique est souvent
de caractère léger et populaire. L'influence étrangère et un caractère
rythmique et dramatique sont plus évidents dans ses compositions
récentes." (B&H)

"These varied experiences might quite well have led him to adopt the
cosmopolitan and rather impersonal style that is sometimes noticeable
in the younger Swedish composers; but his work shows that successful
combination of the romantic spirit with new ideas which is an essential
part of the Swedish temperament." (R. Carritt) "Erland von Koch is
one of the most versatile Swedish composers. His fulfillment and
renewal of the popular music tradition have earned him a special
position within his generation." (H-G. P.)

Bagatella virtuosa (1978) (2') (to S. Rascher) •Asx/Pno •STIM

Birthday Music for Sigurd Rascher (1987) (9') •2 Sx: AA •DP

Cantelina (1978) (3') (to S. Rascher) •Optional solo instrument in
   Bb with or without accompaniment •CG

Cantelina e vivo (1978) (3') (to S. Rascher) •SATB •CG/SMIC

Concerto (1958) (17') (to S. Rascher) 1) Allegro moderato 2) Andante sostenuto 3) Allegro vivo •Asx/Str Orch or Pno •Mt/Peer

Concerto piccolo (1962-76) (13') (to C. Peters) •1 Sx: S+A/Str
   Orch •Br&Ha

Danse n° 2 (1938-67) (2') •1 Sx: S+A/Pno •STIM

Dialogue (1975-77) (5') (to S. Rascher) •2 Sx: SA •DP

Melos (1982-83) (2'30) •Optional solo instrument •STIM

Miniatyrer (1970) (11') (to S. Rascher) 1) Intermezzo lirico
   2) Marchia piccola 3) Fantasia svedese 4) Rondo giocoso
   •SATB •Br&Ha/AMP

Moderato e Allegro (1981) (9') (to S. Rascher) •11 Sx:
   SSAAAATTBBBs •Eth

Monolog n° 4 (1975) (5'30) (to S. Rascher) •Sx Solo •CG

Rondo (1983) •Asx or EH/Str Orch •DP

Saxophonia: Concerto (1976) (18') (to Rascher Quartet) •4 Sx:
   SATB/Wind Orch (2232/0221/Bass) •STIM

Sonata (1985-87) (12'30) 1) Allegro moderato 2) Andante sostenuto
   - Molto vivace •Asx/Pno •STIM

Vision (1950) (6') (to Bergman) •Asx or EH/Str Orch •STIM

KOCH, Frederick (1923)

Compositeur américain né à Cleveland (Ohio), le 4 IV 1923. Travailla avec H. Ellwell, H. Cowell, et B. Rogers.

Anaclets •SATB •SeMC

Concertino (1964-65) (15') (to S. Rascher & D. Sinta) 1) Allegro
   2) Lento 3) Con moto •Asx/Orch (2222/3220/Pno/Perc/Harp/
   Str) or Band •SeMC/MCA

Three Dance Episodes (1971) (to K. Dorn) •Asx/Tape •SeMC

Soundings (1974) (to E. Apper) •Asx/Band •Mau

KOCKELMANS, Gérard

Compositeur néerlandais.

Suite (1956) (7') •SATB •Don

KOECHLIN, Charles (1867-1950)

Compositeur, théoricien, et pédagogue français, né à Paris, le 27 XI
1867; mort au Canadel (Var), le 31 XII 1950. Etudes à l'Ecole
polytechnique. Travailla la composition avec Massenet, Gedalge, et G.
Fauré.

"Véritable humaniste musical, il se penche sur tous les problèmes
relatifs à l'évolution de la musique (forme, langage, écriture, etc.) et
trouve des solutions qu'il met lui-même en pratique dans ses propres
compositions. Il semble que sa nature l'ait porté vers une harmonie de
caractère modal et un emploi fréquent de la polytonalité, emploi
d'ailleurs précoce dans la chronologie du XXe siècle, car il fut l'un des
premiers à la pratiquer à côté de Stravinski et de Milhaud. Koechlin a
eu une influence très profonde sur les musiciens des générations qui lui
ont succédé." (Cl. Rostand) "Indépendant au sens le plus absolu et le
plus noble du terme, d'une parfaite indifférence aux modes et aux
jugements de ses contemporains, Koechlin édifia une oeuvre considérable." (F. R. Tranchefort) "Ce doux polytechnicien égaré dans la
musique avant gardé de sa formation mathématique le goût de la
rigueur. Son art dense demande un contact prolongé avant qu'on en
saisisse la grande beauté. Lignes pures d'esprit souvent pastoral,
teintées d'une vive sensibilité, avec d'inattendus relents de romantisme." (P. Wolff) "Modalité, tonalité, polytonalité, atonalité ne sont
pas pour Charles Koechlin des langages différents, mais bien des
aspects, des tournures diverses d'un langage unique, et qui se présen-
tent à son esprit en fonction des nécessités expressives." (A. Collaert)
"Musicien considérable, un de ceux qui sont la conscience d'une
époque… Derrière cette hyperbole demeure une observation qui peut

fort bien se soutenir, en ce sens que Koechlin a tout compris et tout assimilé de ce qui s'est fait dans des époques antérieures, qu'il n'a rien ignoré des aspirations, des inquiétudes des victoires et des échecs, des espoirs et des impasses de son temps et que chez lui, comme chez le maître d'Eisenach, amour et science étaient les deux versants d'une seule et même réalité." (R. Bernard) "Sa curiosité inlassable l'amènera à pratiquer, sur les bases d'une écriture traditionnelle, la polytonalité et l'atonalité, et à introduire dans ses oeuvres l'usage des modes anciens. Koechlin laisse auprès de ceux qui l'ont connu le souvenir d'un personnage original, capable d'une générosité sans limites, mais aussi d'un compositeur doué et débordant d'imagination—il a laissé plus de 200 oeuvres qui méritent mieux que leur actuel oubli!" (J. & Br. Massin) "...Charles Koechlin me disait que certains accords inhabituels sonneraient mieux si un ou deux de leurs constituants étaient accordés un *comma* plus haut ou plus bas. Puis il allait à son piano et jouait avec un toucher doux et précis et un très expressif soulignement de chaque changement d'harmonie, mais habituellement peu ou pas de souci du tempo, du rythme et du mètre." (F. Goldbeck)

"In his own compositions he created a style that is unmistakably French in its clarity and subtlety of nuance and dynamics; although highly sympathetic to all innovation, he stopped short of crossing the borders of perceptible tonality and coherent rhythmic patterns; he was a master of orchestration." (Baker) "If Koechlin's music can be said to show any influences at all, that of Fauré would no doubt be the most easily discernible; but what most distinguishes him from his contemporaries is the very individual and personal idiom in which he always expressed himself. He never adhered to any 'system' or school; each of his works is composed in the idiom it seemed to him to demand. This eclecticism led him to experiment in a great variety of styles as well as forms and media, and his works cover an immense field." (R. Myers) "His fresh, effectively scored pieces, often using folk melody, have made him one of the most popular Swedish composers abroad. With the years his treatment of tonality has broadened, and he has developed a skilful ability in the rhythmic and contrapuntal variation of peasant music." (R. Haglund) "Koechlin's polytonal music is never at all cerebral in its conception for all its skilled craftsmanship; it shows balanced concern for vertical and horizontal effect that is often lacking in Milhaud." (R. Orledge)

24 Duos, op. 186 (1942) •2 Sx: SA or AA •ME

Epitaphe de Jean Harlow, op. 164 (1937) •Fl/Asx/Pno •ME

15 Etudes, op. 188 (1942-44) •Asx/Pno •EFM/Bil

24 Leçons de solfège - Duos •2 Sx: AA or TT •Bil

Pièce en Lab (1921) (Th. Doney) •Asx/Pno •Led

7 Pièces, op. 180 (1942) (30'30) A) 5 pièces: 1) Andante presque adagio 2) Adagio 3) Adagio 4) Andante con moto 5) Presque adagio B) 2 pièces: 1) Andante très doux 2) Andante calme et doux •Ssx/Pno

Le repos de Tityre, op. 216 (1948) (J. Desloges) •Ssx Solo •ME

Septuor d'instruments à vent, op. 165 (1937) (11'30) (to P. Collaert) 1) Monodie 2) Pastorale 3) Intermezzo 4) Fugue 5) Sérénité 6) Fugue •Fl/Ob/EH/Cl/Asx/Hn/Bsn •Oil

Sonatine n° 1, op. 194a (1942) 1) Andante quasi adagio 2) Andante con moto 3) Andante assez allant 4) Andante con moto 5) Allegro moderato •Oboe d'amour or Ssx/Chamber Orch (2010/000/2 Vln/2 Vla/2 Vcl/Clav) or Pno •ME

Sonatine n° 2, op. 194b (1943) 1) Andante très calme 2) Andante con moto 3) Presque adagio 4) Final •Oboe d'amour or Ssx/ Chamber Orch (2010/000/2 Vln/2 Vla/2 Vcl/Clav) •ME

KOEPKE, Paul

Intermezzo •Tsx/Pno •Rub

Recitative and Rondino •Bsx/Pno •Rub

Recitativo and Allegro •Asx/Pno •Rub

Reminiscence •Tsx/Pno •Rub

KOERBLER, Milivoj (1930)

Compositeur yougoslave, né le 3 V 1930. Président de l'Association des Musiciens de Jazz.

Varijacije (1956) •Asx/Jazz Orch •adr

KÖHLER, Ernesto (1849-1907)

Papillon (Conklin) •Asx/Pno •CF

KÖHLER, Theodor

Compositeur allemand.

Les songes d'un été (1993) •Asx/Pno •INM

KÖHLER, Wolfgang (1956)

Guitariste et compositeur allemand, né le 26 X 1956 à Heillbronn.

Morgen hol'ich mir die Rosen (1986) (3'30) •Voice/Sx/Perc/Synth •adr

Schwerenöters Liä-song (1986) (2'50) •Cl/Sx/Electr Guit/Guit/Synth •adr

KOHN, Karl (1926)

Compositeur, pianiste, et professeur américain d'origine autrichienne, né à Vienne, le 1 VIII 1926. Emigra aux U.S.A. en 1939. Travailla avec W. Piston, I. Fine, R. Thompson, et E. Ballantine.

"In his music he uses a chromatic and sometimes quasi-serial pitch vocabulary mixed with triadic sonorities. The resulting pitch contexts for both melodic and harmonic succession are flexible and generate powerful musical structures." (R. Swift)

Paranymus II (3 movements) •Asx/Pno

Quartet •SATB •WWC

KOIVISTIONEN, Eero (1946)

Compositeur et saxophoniste de jazz finlandais, né à Helsinki, le 13 I 1946. Travailla avec E. Linnala et A. Sallinen.

"Eero Koivistionen is a versatile, creative wizard and his tastes range from pithy sax solos to large-scale compositions." (T. Tommola)

Northern Lights (1987) (6') •Asx/Orch •FMIC

Runoelma - Elegy (1975) (6') •Ssx/Str Orch •FMIC

KOIVULA, Kari (1951-1988)

Compositeur finlandais.

Nox (1982) •Ob or Ssx •FMIC

KOJEDNIKOV

Compositeur russe.

Concertino •Asx/Orch •ECP

KOLASCH, Harald

The House of the Rising Sun (H. Kolasch) •Asx/Band •Hal

KOLB, Barbara

Related Characters (1980) (12') (to K. & M. Faricy) Tranquillo - Ritmico - Lirico - Esplosivo •Asx/Pno •B&H

KOLDITZ, Hans (1923)

Compositeur allemand.

Concertino (1979) (12') •Asx/Harmonie •adr

KOMAZA, K.

Märchen und Volkslieder (Hotz) •SATB •Sim

KOMEI, Abe (1911) (see ABE, Komei)

KOMIVES, James (1932)

Compositeur français, d'origine hongroise, né à Budapest. Travailla avec Z. Kodaly, F. Farkas, Somogy, et D. Milhaud. Fixé en France depuis 1956.

"Il compose à l'écart de tout système et dans une indépendance esthétique complète." (Cl. Rostand)

Spiralis (1974) (to L'Ensemble de Saxophones Français) •16 Sx: 4 X SATB

KOMOROUS, Rudolf (1931)

Compositeur, professeur, et bassoniste canadien d'origine tchécoslovaque, né à Prague le 8 XII 1931. Travailla avec P. Brkovec. Vit au Canada depuis 1971.

"Taking up ideas from the pre-war Czech avant garde, in particular from the surrealists." (C. SCHOENBAUM)

Dingy yellow (1972) (to P. BRODIE) •Ssx/Pno/Tape •CMC

KONAGAYA, Sôichi

Compositeur japonais.

Masquerade - Suite 1) The curtain rises 2) Still in the night 3) Grief days 4) The ball dance 5) The devil's dance 6) Prophecy in dream 7) Final dance •Cl Choir/4 Sx: SATB

Message •SATB

KONDO, Jo

Compositeur japonais.

A Crow (1978) (10') (to R, NODA) •Fl/Ssx

KONIETZNY, H.

Isometrisch-Isorhytmisch •2 Woodwinds •B&H

KONOE, Hidétaké (1931)

Compositeur japonais.

Concertino (1970) •Asx/Orch or Pno

Les Insectes •SATB

Poésie lyrique japonaise •SATB

Quintet (1968) (to A. SAKAGUCHI) •Sx/Vln/Vla/Vcl/Bass

Sonata caprice (1970) •Asx/Vln/Vla/Vcl/Bass

KONT, Paul (1920)

Compositeur autrichien. Travailla avec Lechthaler, Krips, et Swarowsky, puis à Paris, avec Milhaud, Honegger, et O. Messiaen.

"In the early 1950s he began to use 12-note methods." (J. CLARK)

Kammertanzsuite (10') •SATB •CA

Konzertante Symphonie (15') •Bsx/Str Orch •CA

5 Sketches •SATB •ECA

KOPELENT, Marek (1932)

Compositeur tchécoslovaque né à Prague le 28 IV 1932. Travailla avec J. Ridky.

"Actuellement une des personnalités les plus intéressantes et les plus dynamiques de son école nationale. Il a vite échappé à l'esthétique du réalisme socialiste et folklorisant pour évoluer vers les techniques nouvelles sans pourtant en assimiler complètement l'esprit." (Cl. ROSTAND) "Ses oeuvres récentes mettent en jeu le phénomène du spectacle; ainsi, à propos de *Voix errantes* (1970), il déclare: 'la voix, le jeu des instruments, le son de la bande magnétique, le film, la lumière, les changements de robe de l'actrice, tout est soumis à la loi du temps et au principe du mouvement—construction et émotion' ".

"The music of Webern had a decisive influence on him when he first discovered it about 1960; his own works use serial procedures within forms and textures of great delicacy. Of Czech composers of his generation, he is one of the best known in Western Europe." (O. PUKL)

Hkairy (1974) •Asx/Orch (2300/1531/Perc/Celesta/Pno/Zimbalon/ Guit/Bass)

Plauderstündchen (1974-75) (22') •Asx/Orch (22300/0531/2 Perc/ Vcl/Bass/Pno) •Br&Ha

Snehah (oriental) (1967) •Soprano Voice/Asx/Tape

KÖPER, Heinz-Karl (1927)

Compositeur allemand, né le 13 V 1927 à Hannover.

Dekaphonie (9') •4 Cl/Sx •adr

For four (10') •SATB •adr

Musik für fünf Bläzinstrumente und Kontrabass •Fl/Cl/Asx/Tpt/Trb/ Bass •EMBA

Triga (1976) (6') •3 Sx: ATB/Wind Orch •adr

KOPKA, Ulrico (1910)

Compositeur allemand, né le 17 VI 1910, à Bromberg.

Sonata da chiesa (12'30) •Tsx/Org •Asto

KOPP, Frederick Edward (1914)

Chef d'orchestre et compositeur américain, né le 21 III 1914 à Hamilton (Illinois).

Terror Suite •Brass/Sx/Timpani/3 Perc •SeMC

KOPPEL, Hermann David (1908)

Compositeur et pianiste danois, d'origine polonaise, né à Copenhague le 1er X 1908. Travailla avec Bangert, Hansen, Henrichsen, et Simonsen.

"D'abord influencé par C. Nielsen puis par Stravinsky quant à la vitalité rythmique et par Bartok quant au goût d'incorporer à la musique savante des éléments empruntés à la musique populaire." (Cl. ROSTAND)

"He retained tonality as a basic principle, but employed serial devices within an experimentally freer tonal framework." (W. REYNOLDS)

Ternio n° 2, op. 92 (1973) (to Ch. GRON) 1) Fantasia 2) Variazioni piccoli 3) Toccata-Vivace •Asx Solo

KOPROWSKI, Peter Paul (1947)

Compositeur canadien d'origine polonaise, né à Lodz, le 24 VIII 1947. Travailla avec B. Woytowica, N. Boulanger à Paris, et J. Weinzweig.

Vigoresque (1967) (8') •Asx/Vcl •MPC/CMC

KORBAR, Leopold (1917)

Compositeur tchécoslovaque.

Valse triste per trio (1978) (5') •Vln (or Fl or Ob or Cl or Ssx)/Vcl (or Bsn or Tsx)/Pno •CHF

KORDE, Shirish (1945)

Constellations (1973-74) (9') (To K. RADNOFSKY & the Boston Saxophone Quartet) •SATB •DP

KORN, Peter Jona (1922)

Compositeur et chef d'orchestre américain d'origine allemande, né à Berlin le 30 III 1922. Aux U.S.A. depuis 1941. Travailla avec Rubbra, Wolpe, Schoenberg, et I. Dahl.

"The resulting style of composition ultimately adopted by Korn is that of pragmatic romanticism marked by polycentric tonality in the framework of strong rhythmic counterpoint." (BAKER)

Concerto, op. 31 (1956) (16'30) (to S. RASCHER) •Asx/Orch (2222/ 4000/Perc/Str) or Pno •Sal-Hire

Passacaglia und Fuge (1952-86) (8') •8 Sx:SAAATTBB

Ruft uns die Stimme, op. 81 (1985) (to G. PRIESNER) Tsx (or Ssx)/Org •adr

KORNDORFF, Nikolaïs

Compositeur russe.

Monologue et ostinato •Asx/Pno •ECS

La musique primitive (1981) (23') (to J-M. LONDEIX) •12 Sx: SnoSSAAATTTBBBs

KORTE, Karl (1928)

Compositeur américain né à Ossining (New York), le 25 VIII 1928. Travailla avec P. Mennin, V. Persichetti, W. Bergsma, O. Luening, et A. Copland.

"*Matrix* does not have the stamp of stiff conformity which has blighted so much music in the past decade. This piece takes its own 'trip' and carries the listener along, through fascinating turnings and to

surprising points of arrival. It sounds exceptionally secure for a relatively young composer." (L. Trimble) "His music shows many influences, including serialism and jazz." (J. Rosen)
Dialogue (1969) (19') (to Hamm) •Asx/Tape •Ga/DP
Facets (1970) •SATB •SeMC
Matrix (1968) (16') •Fl/Ob/Cl/Asx/Hn/Bsn/Pno/Perc •GSch
Study •Asx/Tape (2 channels) •SeMC
Symmetrics (1973) (to A. Regni) •Asx/4 Perc •SeMC

KORTH, Thomas A. (1943)
Compositeur américain. Travailla avec Lawrence Moss.
Disparities II (1974) (to M. Sigmon) •Asx/Tape •adr
Elegy (1968) (11'30) (to the memory of R. Silverblatt) •Asx/Pno •adr

KOSCHATT, Thomas (1845-1914)
Forsaken •Eb Sx/Pno •CF

KOSTECK, Gregory (1937)
Compositeur américain, né à Plainfield (New Jersey). Travailla avec L. Bassett et R. L. Finney.
Chromatic Fantasy (1979) (7') (to J. Dawson) •Sx Solo •DP
Concerto (to J. Houlik) •Tsx/Orch
Mini - variations (1967) (to J. Houlik) •Tsx/Pno •RPS/MP
Music (to J. Houlik) •Tsx/Pno
Serious Developments: Music (1979) (to J. Dawson) Motivic Theme and Variations: Fantasy - Scherzo - Motet - Adagio - Finale •SATB
Summer Music- trio (to J. Houlik) •Ob/Cl/Tsx •RPS/DP
Three Lollipops for Harold •AATB
Two Songs (to J. Houlik) •Tsx/Pno

KOSUGI, Takehisa (1922)
Compositeur japonais né à Tokyo.
"Takehisa Kosugi qui organisa les premiers happenings à Tokyo en 1960 avec le groupe Ongaku, souhaite 'étendre la conscience de l'interprète en ce qui concerne le processus de fabrication des sons' par des 'Scores events' où la dimension temporelle, par exemple le ralentissement aussi radical que possible d'un mouvement habituel, joue un rôle pivot." (D. J-Y. Bosseur)
Mano-dharma with Takeda III •Asx/Cl/Tape

KOSUT, Michal
Honeymoon (1981) (to H. Bok et E. Le Mair) •Sx/Marimba+Vibr

KOTONSKI, Wladzimierz (1925)
Compositeur français d'origine polonaise, né à Varsovie, le 23 VIII 1925. Travailla avec Rytel et Szeligowsky.
"His early works are derived from native music; his style then changed to neo-classicism and finally to constructivism." (Baker)
Selection I (1962) •Electr. Guit/2 Sx: AT/Cl •PWM
Selection for 4 Jazzmen •Guit/2 Sx: AT/Cl •B&H

KOUMANS, Rudolf
Compositeur néerlandais.
Quartet, op. 37 •SATB

KOUTZEN, Boris (1901-1966)
Violoniste et compositeur américain, né à Uman (Russie), le 1er IV 1901; mort à New York en 1966. Aux U.S.A. depuis 1923. Travailla avec Gliere.
"Koutzen's style of writing is almost exclusively polyphonic. Explaining the complexities present in his writing, he insists that they are merely the tonal base of his work; but he also insists that the effect on the listener must be that of spontaneous expression. Like most other composers, Koutzen's ambition is to write works of the greatest possible simplicity." (D. Ewen)

Music trio (1940) •Asx/Vcl/Bsn •Bro/AMP

KOUZAN, Marien
Nyaya •Ob/Cl/Asx/Bsn

KOVARIK, Jàn
if (her Word = "Ay me!") (1993) •Asx/Perc •INM

KOX, Hans (1930)
Compositeur néerlandais né à Arnhem, le 19 V 1930. Travailla avec H. Badings.
"Kox's music from these early years until 1963 is marked by classical forms and by the harmonic influences of Berg, Mahler and Badings." (J. Wouters)
Concertino (1982) (to E. Bogaard) •Asx/Picc/2 Fl/BsCl/2 Hn/2 Tpt/Trb •Don
Concerto (1978) •Asx/Orch •Don
Face to Face (1992) (20') •Asx/Str Orch •Don
Quartet (1985) (10') •SATB •Don
Quartet No. 2 (1987-88) (17') •SATB •Don
Sonata (1982) (17') •Tsx/Pno •Don
Sonate (1985) (12') •Asx/Pno •Don
The Three Chairs (1989) (20') •3 Sx: ATB •Don
Through a Glass, Darkly (1989) (10') •Asx/Pno •Don

KOZELUH, Leopold Anton (1747-1818)
Allegro (Meriot) •Asx/Pno •Phi

KRAEMER, Ira
Petite Suite (1987) Prelude - Nocturne - Vaudeville •SATB

KRAFT, Leo (1922)
Compositeur et professeur américain, né le 24 VII 1922 à Brooklyn. Travailla avec Rathaus, R. Thompson et, à Paris, avec N. Boulanger.
"His early music is marked by the neo-classical attitudes of his teachers and the basic diatonicism of Hindemith. Since the 1960s his work has been freely atonal, though the neo-classical influence can occasionally be heard in his rhythm." (B. Saylor)
Encounters IX (1982) (to D. Hastings) •Asx/Perc
Five For One (1971) (6') (to K. Dorn) •Sx Solo •GMP
Pentagram (1971) •Asx Solo
Three Pieces (1977) (to P. & M. Delibero) •Asx/Pno •DP

KRAFT, William (1923)
Arietta Da Capo (1982) (3'30) (to M. Kupferman) •Ssx Solo •Don

KRAMER, Martin (1907)
Saxophoniste et professeur américain, né à Philadelphia (Pennsylvania), le 3 III 1907. Travailla avec M. Johnston.
Concerto (1933) (26') •Asx/Orch or Pno
Lawd •7 Sx: AAATTBBs •SC
Swing Fugue (1938) •3 Sx •Pro
Waltz Allegro (1938) (to C. Leeson) •Asx/Pno •SC

KRANTZ, A.
Tourbillon (Gurewich) •Asx/Pno •CF

KRATOCHWIL, Heinz
Compositeur autrichien.
Attacken, op. 163 •SATB •ApE
Fantasie, op. 148 •SATB •Dob/ECA/ApE

KRAUS, Marco
Compositeur luxembourgeois.
Suite concertante •1 Sx: Sno+S+A+T+B/Orch

KREIN, Michael (1908-1966)
Clarinettiste, saxophoniste, arrangeur, et chef d'orchestre anglais.

Serenade in A (1960) •Asx/Pno •NWM
Valse caprice (1930) (5') •SATB •NWM

KREINES, Joseph (1936)
Compositeur américain.
Prélude and Presto (1981) •Ssx

KREISLER, Fritz (1875-1962)
After Refrain (Gurewich) •Asx/Pno •Sch
Caprice Viennois (Gurewich) •Asx/Pno •Sch
Liebesfreud (Gurewich) •Asx/Pno •Sch
Liebeslied (Gurewich) •Asx/Pno •Sch
Midnight Bells (Leeson) •Asx/Pno •ChFo
Miniature Vienne March (Liedzen) •Asx/Pno •ChFo
Old Refrain (Gurewich) •Asx/Pno •ChFo
Rondino (Leeson) •Asx/Pno •ChFo
Schön Rosmarin (Gurewich) •Asx/Pno •ChFo/Sch
Two Impressions •Asx/Pno •South

KRELL, W. H.
Mississippi Rag (Frackenpohl) •AATB •Ken

KREMENLIEV, Boris (1911)
Ethnomusicologue et compositeur américain d'origine bulgare, né à Razlog, le 23 V 1911. Aux U.S.A. depuis 1929. Travailla avec La Violette et Hanson.

"He experimented with electronics and other new means, but then returned to a simpler style, colourful, rhythmically intense, terse and texturally unconventional; a shared cultural background led to some similarity with the music of Bartok." (W. T. Marrocco)
Quartet •SATB •adr
Tune •Asx/Hn/Str •adr

KREMP, Uwe
Klangverwesung (1991) (6') •SATB

KREUTZ, Arthur (1906)
Fantasy (1983) (to L. Gwozdz) •Asx/Pno
Saxonata (1979) (to L. Gwozdz) •Asx/Pno

KREUTZER, Léon (1817-1868)
Critique musical, écrivain, et compositeur français, né à Paris le 23 IX 1817; mort à Vichy, le 6 X 1868. Travailla avec Benoist.

"Epris d'un amour passionné pour l'art pur." (Fetis) "Un autodidacte ennemi de l'art frivole." (Larousse)
1ère partie de Quatuor (185x) •SATB •Sax

KRICKEBERG, Dieter (1932)
Compositeur allemand.
Chaconne (198x) (10') •SATB
Zummara (1987-88) (8') •Tsx/Harp

KRIEGER, Edino (1928)
Compositeur, violoniste, chef d'orchestre, et critique musical brésilien, né le 17 III 1928, à Brusque-Santa Catarina. Travailla avec Koellreutter, et A. Copland.

"Krieger began composing in a late Romantic and impressionist manner. Koellreutter's influence turned him to the 12-note technique of such works, but about 1952 he abandoned serialism for a slightly nationalist, neo-classical style. The most original work of this period is *Brasiliana*.
Brasiliana (1960) •Asx (or Vla)/Str Orch
Melopéia (1949) •Soprano Voice/Ob/Tsx/Trb/Vla

KRIEGER, Johann (1652-1735)
Suite •SATB •Mol

KRIEGER, Ulrich
Compositeur allemand.
Oktette (1989) (8') •8 Sx

KRIPS, Henry (1912)
Compositeur australien d'origine autrichienne, né à Vienne, le 10 II 1912.
Southern Intermezzo (1956) (5') •Asx/Pno •adr

KRISTENSEN, Kuno Kjaerbye
Compositeur danois.
Kwartet I (1989) (10') •SATB
Kwartet II (1990) (11') •SATB

KRIVITSKI, D.
Compositeur russe.
December Song (1976) •Baritone Voice/Ssx/Vcl/Pno

KROEGER, Karl
Professeur et compositeur américain.
Banchetto Musicale (1993) (to D. Gordon) 1) Prelude 2) March 3) Scherzo 4) Nocturne 5) Dance •8 Sx: SnoSAATTBBs
Concerto •Asx/Band

KROL, Bernhard (1920)
Compositeur et corniste allemand, né à Berlin, le 24 VI 1920. Travailla avec Mohr et Rufer.
Antifona, op. 53a (7') (to M. Perrin) •Asx/Org •B&B
Aria & Tarentella, op. 37 (1953-68) (11') (to M. Perrin) Asx/Orch (1110/2 Hn/Str) or Pno •AMP/Sim
Choral fantasia •Asx (or blookfl.) •HV
Elegia passionata, op. 69a (1979) (9') (to M. Perrin) Adagio - Andante tranquillo - Lento - Andante - Siciliano - Allegro - Lento semplice •Asx/Org •B&B
Intermezzo amabile, op. 79 (1980) (5'30) (to M. Perrin) Asx/Pno •DP/B&B
Litania pastorale, op. 62 (to M. Perrin) •Ssx/Org •B&B
Sonata, op. 17 (1956) (13') (to J. de Vries) 1) Presto 2) Maestoso, patetico 3) Allegro assai •Asx/Pno •Hof
Suite •Vln/Asx/Vcl/Pno •adr

KRÖLL, Georg
Compositeur allemand.
Fünf Versetten (1986) (16') •SATB
Quartett (1993) •Bsx/Vcl/Tuba/Pno

KROLL, Nathan
Four Pieces •5 Sx: AATTB •AMP

KROMMER
Partita (Schaefer) •6 Sx: SAAATB •WWS

KRSTO, Odak
Divertimento •Asx/Str Orch •YUC
Duvachi sekstet •YUC

KRUMLOVSKY, Claus (1930)
Compositeur et chef d'orchestre luxembourgeois, né à Luxembourg, le 24 XII 1930.
Divertissement, op. 3 1) Allegretto 2) Lento-Espressivo 3) Allegro 4) Vif •SATB •UGDAL
Concertino (1963) (10') (to G. Gourdet) •Asx/Orch (2222/220/Perc/Str) or Pno •Led
Concerto •Asx/Orch •adr
Sonate (1965) (7') (to G. Gourdet) 1) Allegro 2) Lent 3) Vif •Asx/Pno •UGDAL

KRUSE, Bjorne Howard (1946)

Clarinettiste, saxophoniste, et compositeur norvégien.

Colors (1979) Nordic yellow - American blue -Spanish red •SATB
•NMI

Metal (1984) (10') •Voice/Tsx/Jazz Perc/Orch •NMI

Reflections (1976) (4') (to the Oslo Saxophone Quartet) •SATB
•NMI

Statement (1975) (10') (to the Oslo Saxophone Quartet) •SATB
•NMI

KRUYF, Ton de (1937)

Compositeur hollandais, né le 3 X 1937, à Leerdam. Travailla avec
W. Fortner.

"After 1970, or thereabouts, 12-note serialism gave place to a freer
technique in which timbre has taken an increasingly important function." (J. Wouters)

Musica portuensis (1983) (17') 1) Genova 2) Siracusa 3) Heraklion
4) Alexandria 5) Haifa 6) Rhodos 7) Piracus 8) Genova…
•SATB •Don

KUBINSKY, Richard

2 Pièces (1934) 1) Pièce de concert 2) Mélodie •Asx/Pno •ME

Invention •2 Sx: AT/Pno/Vibr •NYPL

KUBIZEK, Augustin

Saxophonia, op. 60/2 (1989) (12') (to Wiener Saxophone Quartet)
Affetuoso (libero) - Lento misterioso - Vivace •SATB •CA

KUCHARZYK, Henry

Compositeur canadien.

One for the Underdog (1981) •Tpt/Sx/Pno/Bass/Perc •CMC

KUERGEL, Hannes (1906)

Compositeur autrichien.

Rhapsodie •Asx/Orch or Pno •NYPL/Krenn

Konzert (to O. Vrhovnik) •Asx/Winds/Male Choir

KUESTER, Herbert (1909-1986)

Compositeur allemand, né le 4 X 1909, né à Berlin-Schöneberg et
mort le 22 II 1986 à München.

Kentucky Serenade (1970) (3'52) •Asx/Str Orch

KUHLAU, Friederich (1786-1832)

Adagio (Meriot) •Asx/Pno •Phi

Menuet (Buchtel) •1 Sx: A or T/Pno •Kjos

Three Concert Duets (Teal) •2 Sx: AA or TT •Pres

KÜHMSTEDT, Paul

Compositeur allemand.

6 Arabesken (1988) 1) Sehr lebhaft 2) Allegro quasi fantasia
3) Allegro molto 4) Allegretto ironico 5) Ziemlich rasch
6) Allegro •SATB •GB

KÜHN, Carl Theodor (1865-1925)

Adagio ("Concerto militaire") •Eb Sx/Pno •CF

KUHN, Charles

Compositeur américain.

Sonata (1969-70) (to C. Leeson) •Asx/Pno

KÜHNE, Stephan

Compositeur autrichien.

Alla marcia dolente (1993) •Asx/Pno •INM

Fünf lettische Bauerntänze des 19 Jahrh. (1993) •Ssx/Pno •INM

Just for fun (1991) (2'30) •SATB •ApE

KUHNERT, Rolf (1932)

Pianiste et compositeur allemand, né à Berlin, le 4 III 1932. Travailla

avec H. Tiessen, Y. Lefebure, et H-E. Riebensahm.

2 Temperamente (1987) •SATB •KuD

3 Temperamente (1985) (7'30) 1) Cholerisch 2) Melancholisch
3) Sanquinisch •Asx Solo •KuD

KULESHA, Gary (1954)

Compositeur canadien.

Concertante music (1980) (to P. Brodie) •Asx/Woodwind Quintet
•CMC

Invocation and Ceremony (5') •Sx Solo •CMC

Journey into Sunrise (1987) •4 Sx: ATBBs/Orch (2222/4231/Timp/2
Perc/Str) •CMC

KULLMANN, Wilton (1926)

Compositeur allemand, né le 28 V 1926, à Bad Kreuznach.

Sentimental saxos (1983) •Sx/Band •adr

KUNDRATS, Vilnis

Emotions in Seconds (1993) •Sx/Electronics •INM

KUNUGIYAMA, Hideki (1947)

Compositeur japonais.

Steam (1982) •Asx/Pno

KUNZ, Ernst (1891-19xx)

Compositeur et chef d'orchestre , né à Berne, le 2 VI 1891. Travailla
à Munich avec Klose et Kellermann, puis avec Busoni.

"A prolific composer in a late Romantic style."

Nachtkonzert •3 Sx/Vla/Guit

25 pezzi per varie formazioni: Stück n° 3 (1962) •Asx/Bass/Perc

25 pezzi per varie formazioni: Stück n° 6 (1963) •Vcl/3 Sx/Bsn

KUPFERMAN, Meyer (1926)

Clarinettiste et compositeur de jazz américain, né à New York, le 8
VII 1926.

In Two Bits (1967) (2'30) •Asx/Pno •GMP

Jazz Cello Concerto (1962) (25') (3 Movements) •Vcl/3 Sx/Bass/
Perc •GMP

Jazz Infinities Three (1961) (90') (to H. Estrin) (5 Movements)
•Asx/Pno/Bass/Perc •GMP

Seven Inventions (1967) (15-21') 1) Prelude 2) Boomerang 3) Junks
4) Clockwork 5) Pelican 6) Mephisto's Journey 7) Conjecture
•Tsx Solo •GMP

Sound Phantoms No. 7 (1980) •Ssx/Perc

Three Pieces in Slow Motion (1967) (2'30) •Asx/Pno •GMP

KUPKOVIC, Ladislav (1936)

Compositeur et chef d'orchestre slovaque né à Bratislava, le 17 III
1936. Vit en Allemagne.

"Compose en autodidacte."

"In more conventional compositions he has been concerned principally with the filtering, alienation and analytical illumination of works
of the past and with reforming orchestral playing." (M. Lichtenfeld)

Interpretation einer Kritik (15') •Any instruments •Uni

Weniger und Mehr (15') •Any 6 groups of instruments •Uni

KURACHI, Tatsuya

Compositeur japonais.

2 Paroles tissées •SATB

KURTAG, György (1926)

Compositeur hongrois, d'origine roumaine, né à Lugoj, le 19 II 1926.
Travailla avec Eisikovits, Veress, et Farkas, puis, à Paris, avec Milhaud
et O. Messiaen. Vit en Hongrie depuis 1946.

"Il s'est très vite détaché du peloton des folkloristes socialistes pour
se faire l'un des rares représentants du style post-webernien en Hongrie. Il n'est pas un extrémiste du sérialisme et semble rechercher un

style de synthèse." (Cl. Rostand) "La musique de Kurtag est si pure et si forte dans sa brièveté ordinaire, si subtile et si naïve à la fois, d'une poésie si concentrée surtout qu'elle pousse irrésistiblement à l'émotion, à la tendresse, et qu'on rêve de lui donner un visage, comme on rêverait d'avoir connu personnellement Bartok, Schubert ou Monteverdi. Lorsqu'un art est à ce point pétri d'humanité, il paraît certain qu'on ne pourrait être déçu par l'artiste." (M. Fleuret) "L'univers de Kurtag n'est pas géographique mais tout intérieur. L'homme est introverti. Il travaille lentement, éternel insatisfait, et les oeuvres auquel il aboutit sont—sauf rare exception—des miniatures. Hongrois de l'intérieur, il n'a joué aucun rôle décisif dans les bagarres modernes d'après-guerre. Il n'est pas davantage le promoteur de révolutions formelles ou techniques dont la portée serait universelle. Non, l'apport de Kurtag est complètement étranger à cette idée de modèle ou de courant: il figure entièrement sous le signe de l'intimité et restaure une émotion éliminée du répertoire moderne." (C. Leblé) "Le minimalisme de Kurtag consiste à remplir de petits espaces musicaux d'un maximum d'expression et d'imagination, dans la lignée des miniatures atonales de Webern. Un minimalisme de l'audace, capable de renoncer aux articles d'ameublement que sont les échelles ou au confort de la familiarité. C'est une musique où chaque note compte, et où une expression directe et tendue résout d'un seul coup les problèmes apparemment insurmontables de la communication musicale." (P. Griffiths) "Il est l'auteur d'une création homogène, d'inspiration sérielle, libre et personnelle, qui prédilecte les microstructures rassemblées en grandes formes. Musique d'une pudeur extrême, parfois d'une inouïe violence: irremplaçable—et sans filiation directe." (J-N. von der Weid)

"His music employs pitch complementarity and other non-serial 12-note procedures; his approximately 12-note themes are sometimes close to Bartok or to the 'free atonal' works of Schoenberg, Berg and Webern." (G. Kroö)

Interrogation (1983) (11'30) (to D. Kientzy) •1 Sx: T+Bs+CBs/ Tape •Sal

KURTZ, Arthur Digby (1929)

Compositeur américain, né à Chicago. Travailla avec N. Boulanger.

Duets, op. 6 •2 Different instruments •adr

Isaiah VI, op. 31 (1971) (7'30) (to K. Dorn) •Narr/Asx/Pno/Perc •adr

KURZ, Karl-Wieland (1961)

Compositeur allemand né à Wetzlar, le 25 I 1961. Travailla avec R. Riehm, S. Zehr, et B. Kontarsky.

Teichlandschaft mit Erlen und Weiden (1992) •12 Sx •adr

KUSHIDA, Testurosuke (1935)

Compositeur japonais.

The Ancient poem in Asuka (1985) (15') (to Tokyo Saxophone Ensemble) 1) Fantastico 2) Adagio con espressivo 3) Animato 4) Lento 5) Allegro •SATB

Bugaku (1988) •Sx Orch

Fantasia (1990) 1) Jo, introduction 2) Fu-maï, la danse du vent 3) San Jo, l'éparpillement d'affection 4) Kargu, le fleuve de fleurs 5) Byaku-ya, le soleil de minuit •Ssx/Pno

KUSMYCH, Christina

Shapes and Sounds IV (1983) •Asx/Pno

KUTSCH, B.

Saxophon Klange •Asx/Pno •Zim

KUZCER, Bernardo

Even… the loudest sky (1981) (10') •4 Sx

KYLE, Mattews

Compositeur américain.

Thief (1987) (6') (for Charles Rochester Young) •Ssx/Pno •adr

KYNASTON, Trent (1946)

Saxophoniste, concertiste, professeur, et compositeur américain, né le 7 XII 1946. Travailla avec J-M. Londeix.

Concerto (1976) (19') (to Bird, Trane, Cannonball) (Introduction - Variations - Canonizations) •Asx/Orch (Picc2222/4331/Pno/4 Perc/Str) or Wind Orch or 2 Pno/Perc •DP

Corybant-Bleu (1980) (to J-M. Londeix) •12 Sx: SnoSSAAATTTBBBs

Daily Studies •DP

Dance Suite, op. 15 •Asx Solo •WIM

Espejos (1975) •Asx Solo

Sonata Duet •Asx/Cl •WIM

LABANCHI, Gaetono
33 Concert Etudes (3 Volumes) (Iasilli) •CF

LABATE, Bruno
Villanella •Tsx/Pno •CF

LABITZKY, Auguste (1832-1903)
Träum des Sennerin •Eb Sx/Pno •CF

LABOLE, Pierre (1863-1943)
Les Tourbillons - Caprice •2 Sx: SA •Mar

LABORDA, José Maria Garcia (1946) (see GARCIA LABORDA)

LABURDA, Jiric (1931)
Compositeur tchèque, né le 3 IV 1931. Travailla à Prague.
Dixie Quintetto (1990) (14') •Cl/Asx/Tpt/Trb/Pno •Com
Sonatina (11') •Asx/Pno •Cz

LA CASINIERE, Yves de (1887-1971)
Compositeur français, né à Angers, mort à Paris, le 26 X 1971. Travailla avec M. d'Ollone, N. Boulanger, et Caussade. Grand Prix de Rome (1925).
Ronde (1954) (2'30) •Asx/Pno •PN

LACERDA, Osvaldo (Costa de) (1927)
Compositeur brésilien, né le 23 III 1927 à Sâo Paulo. Travailla avec E. Kierski, C. Guarnieri, V. Giannini, et A. Copland.
"Lacerda's music incorporates a subtle national idiom into a modern harmonic context. His intimate knowledge of Brazilian popular and folk music is best shown in several pieces."
Variacoes sobre "o cravo brigou con a rosa" (1979) •Sx/Marimba

LACHARTE, Nicole
La Geste inachevée (1980) •Fl/Cl/Sx/Tpt/Trb/Pno/Perc/Vln/Vla/Vcl

LACK, Theodore (1846-1921)
Idilio •1 Sx: A or T/Pno •Cen

LACOME, Paul (1838-1920)
Rigaudon (Andraud) •Asx/Pno •South

LACOUR, Guy (1932)
Saxophoniste et compositeur français, né à Soissons (Aisne), le 8 VI 1932. Travailla le saxophone avec Marcel Josse puis avec Marcel Mule dont il fit partie du quatuor (1961-1967).
"Autodidacte, Guy Lacour utilise indifféremment un langage tonal, atonal, sériel ou modal adapté à chacune de ses oeuvres essentiellement destinées à son instrument dont il met bien en valeur les possibilités lyriques et techniques."
Belle époque - Evocation (1986) (2'15) •1 Sx: A or T/Pno •Bil
Cantilude (1993) (2'30) •1 Sx: A or T/Pno •Bil
Chanson modale (1992) (2'30) •1 Sx: A or T/Pno •Bil
100 Déchiffrages (en forme de petites études mélodiques et rythmiques) (to R. Weber) (1968) •Sx Solo •Bil
Divertissement (1968) (13') (to D. Deffayet) 1) Prélude (Sx Solo) 2) Intermède (Perc Solo) 3) Improvisation et presto •Asx/1 or 6 Perc •Bil

Etude de concert (1964) (2'35) (to R. Druet & G. Gourdet) •Sx Solo •Bil
8 Etudes brillantes (1963) (to M. Mule) •Led
24 Etudes atonales faciles (1975) •Bil
28 Etudes sur les modes à transpositions limitées d'O. Messiaen (1971) (to D. Deffayet) •Bil
50 Etudes faciles et progressives (1972) (to M. Josse) (2 Volumes) •Bil
Hommage à Jacques Ibert (1972) (13') (to J-M. Londeix) 1) Allegro 2) Berceuse et Vif •Asx/Orch (1121/010/Str) or Pno •Bil
Mélonade (1993) (2'30) •Tsx/Pno •Bil
Noctilène (1984) (3'20) •1 Sx: A or T/Pno •Bil
Octophonie (1991) (4'40) (to G. Gourdet) •1 Sx: A or T/Pno •Bil
Pièce concertante (1975-76) (8'30) •1 Sx: T or A/Str Orch or Wind Orch (2222/2001/2 Perc/Bass) or Pno •Bil
Précis sur l'étude des gammes (1968) •Bil
Prélodie (1994) (3') •Asx/Pno •Bil
Quatuor (1969) (11') (to MM. Arnoult, Gourdet & Pareille) 1) Elegie 2) Scherzo 3) Rondo final •SATB •Bil
Suite en duo (1971) (10'30) (to MM. Melzer & Audefroy) 1) Allegro 2) Aria 3) Petite fugue 4) Largo puis scherzetto •2 Sx: AA or TT •Bil
Tendre mélodie (1977) (3'30) •Eb Sx or Bb Sx/Pno

LACROIX, Eugène (1858-1957)
Compositeur et organiste français, né à Eshen (Angleterre), le 13 IV 1858. Travailla avec E. Gigout.
Pan •Asx/Orch or Pno

LACY, Steve
Quatuor (1986) (to Quatuor "A piacere") •SATB

LAJTHA, Làszlô (1892-1963)
Compositeur et ethnomusicologue hongrois, né le 30 VI 1892, à Budapest, où il est mort, le 16 II 1963. Travailla à Paris avec V. d'Indy.
"Spécialiste du folklore (chef de la section musicale du musée ethnographique de Budapest), son oeuvre de compositeur, qui s'alimente autant aux sources de la Transylvanie, de la Hongrie qu'aux sources françaises, vaut par la netteté de la ligne, la transparence de l'orchestration, l'ampleur de la mélodie, la solidité des structures, l'accent dramatique." (N. Dufourcq) "Son esthétique justifie pleinement la déclaration qu'il faisait au micro de la radio, d'employer son temps 'à la recherche de la beauté perdue.' " (J. Vigue) "Il s'exprime dans un style faisant la synthèse entre terroir hongrois et harmonie debussyste." (Cl. Rostand) "Lajtha apparaît profondément marqué par le XVIIIe siècle français. Comme Bartok, Lajtha devient un familier de nos clavecinistes et désormais il ne concevra guère de musique de chambre qui ne soit oeuvre de divertissement dans l'esprit même de l'art baroque." (M. Fleuret)
"Like Bartok and Kodaly, his activities have not been confined to creative and scientific work, but also included teaching: in this respect his influence is felt in the particular outlook of certain younger musicians. His main distinguishing characteristic, on the other hand, is his attachment to French—and generally to Latin—culture in sensibility and taste, discernible above all in the quality of his musical inspiration and in the manner of its expression." (J. Weismann) "As composer, he follows disparate trends; with Hungarian national melodies as focal strength; his formal influences were from German music, but prolonged contact with modern French developments left a trace in his harmonic idiom, which shows Impressionistic characteristics." (Baker) "In Lajtha's late period the assertion of melodic values was his main concern. Seeking to display them in a suitable formal disposition prompted him to investigate the designs of Italian and French 17th- and 18th-century composers. The conspicuous simplification of musical grammar, concurrently with and in consequence of a superior technical

accomplishment, produces in these works an equilibrium between transparency of expression and range of emotional sensibility, between technique and inspiration: a classical art in the truest sense of the word." (J. S. BERLASZ)

Intermezzo, op. 59 (1954) (5'30) •Asx/Pno or 4 Sx: SATB •Led

LAKE, Larry

Compositeur canadien.

Filar il tuono (1989) •Cl/3Sx: ATB/Bsn/Tpt/Trb/Marimba •CMC

LAKE, Mathew Lester (1879-1955)

Among the Roses •Eb Sx or Bb Sx/Pno •CF
Andantino •5 Sx: AATTB •Lud
Annie Laurie •2 Sx: AA or TT/Pno •CF
Cleveland March •5 Sx: AATTB •Lud
Iron Mountain •5 Sx: AATTB •Lud
Long, Long Ago •5 Sx: AATTB •Lud
Louisiana •5 Sx: AATTB •Lud
Madeline •5 Sx: AATTB •Lud
Nadia •Asx/Pno •Lud
Oloha-Oe & Like No-a-like (Two Hawaiian songs) •Eb Sx or Bb Sx/ Pno •CF
Wiedoeft's Rubato (1925) •Asx/Pno •CF

LAKEY, Claude (1910)

Saxophoniste et compositeur américain, né le 21 VIII 1910, à San Augustine (Texas). Travailla avec M. Lohson, J. Allard, et L. Maggio.

Five Saxets (1958) •5 Sx: SAATB •South

LALO, Edouard (1823-1892)

Chants russes (MULE) •Asx/Pno •Led
Chants russes (VIARD) •Asx/Pno •Sal
Le Roi d'Ys - Aubade et Air •Bb Sx or Eb Sx/Pno •Mol

LAMB, John David (1935)

Cenotaph (1987) (30') 1) Lamentation 2) Cursus Terrestris 3) In Memoriam •13 Sx: SSSAAAATTTBBBs/2 Perc
Concerto "Cloud Cuckoo Land" (1970) (to S. RASCHER) •Asx/Orch
Madrigal (1972) (to K. DEANS) •3 Sx: S (or A) AT •AMP/B&B
Night Music (1956) (to S. RASCHER) •Sx Solo
Romp •Bsx/Pno •DP
Six Barefoot Dances (1962) (8') (for S. RASCHER) 1) Firm 2) Swing- ing 3) Walking 4) Lively 5) Jaunty 6) Brisk •2 Sx: AA or TT •Gi&Ma
Three Antique Dances (1961) (to S. RASCHER) 1) Estampie 2) Pavanne •Asx/Perc
Three Flourishes (1961) (to C. PETERS) •2 Sx: AA
Three Pieces (1963) •Bsx/Pno

LAMB, Marvin L. (1946)

Compositeur américain, né le 12 VII 1946, à Jacksonville (Texas).
A Ballade of Roland (1979) (to N. RAMSAY) •Asx Solo •DP
Concerto (to J. HOULIK) •Tsx/Pno
Final Roland (1979) (to N. RAMSAY) •Asx/Pno •DP
In Memoriam, Benjy (1972) (6') •SATB •MP
Serenade for Unknown friends (to J. HOULIK) •Tsx/Ob/Cl/Pno •DP

LAMBERTO, Lugli

Compositeur italien.
Stefy (1993) (to R. MICARELLI) •Asx Solo
Vi, Ro, La (1992) •Asx/Pno

LAMBIJ, Ton

Symphonic verses (1991) (27') •SATB •Don

LAMBRECHT, Homer (1943)

Compositeur américain.

Metaphrases (1973) (to F. HEMKE) •1 Sx: S+A/Cl/BsCl/Bass

LAMON, Rune

Sonatine (to J. de VRIES) •Asx/Pno

LAMOTE, Raymond

Compositeur français.
Caprice, op. 34 (1985) (3'30) •Asx/Pno •Bil
Chant lyrique (1979) (5') (to A. BEUN) •Asx/Pno •Bil

LAMOTE de GRIGNON, Juan (1872-1949)

Canço de Maria (AMAZ) •1 Sx: T or A/Pno •UME
Rêverie (AMAZ & BAYER) •1 Sx: T or A/Pno •UME

LAMOTTE, Antony

18 Etudes (d'après MAZAS, KREUTZER, RODE, etc.) •Bil

LAMPERSBERG, Gerhard

Compositeur allemand.
Eulennacht (1985) (10') •SATB •ECA

LAMPROYE, André

Organiste et compositeur belge.
Messe de St Hadelin (1988) (16') (to J-P. RORIVE) 1) Entrée solennelle 2) Méditation 3) Offertoire 4) Communion 5) Com- munion 6) Sortie •Ssx/Org

LANCEN, Serge (1922)

Compositeur et pianiste français, né à Paris, le 5 XI 1922. Travailla avec Tony Aubin. Prix de Rome (1950).

"Sa tendance générale est clairement affirmée par l'éviction systéma- tique de tous les éléments de la technique contemporaine inassimilable, ou du moins inassimilée par la majorité du public, et par une nette volonté de composer une musique simple, avenante, enjouée, em- preinte de bonne humeur, de malice et de gaieté." (R. BERNARD) "Serge Lancen est resté attaché aux traditions françaises d'équilibre, de clarté, de modération. On peut cependant trouver, dans certaines de ses oeuvres, une affinité avec les romantiques allemands. Ses goûts le portent vers le style folklorique dont il aime la fraîcheur et la simpli- cité." (A. SIBERT) "Serge Lancen ne craint pas les envolées lyriques et ne laisse pas la rigidité scholastique prendre le pas sur l'esthétique." (W. LANDOWSKI) "Ecriture claire qui ne s'égare jamais en digressions inutiles." (Cl. CHAMFRAY) "Déborde d'humour." (P. TABET)

L'auteur cet inconnu •Asx/Pno •Bil
Confidences (1968) (2') •Bb Sx/Pno •Chap
Contraste (1992) (8'45) (to D-C. LUINI) •Asx/Pno •Lem
Dedicace (1984) (9'15) (a la mémoire d'A. SAX) •Asx/Wind Ensemble (113 BsCl 1/111/2 Sx:AT/Trb/BsTrb/Bass/Perc) or Pno •Mol
Espièglerie •Tsx/Pno •HE
Farniente (1968) (2'10) •Asx/Pno •Led
Four Somes •SATB •Chap
Intermède I (1974) (4') •SATB •Mol
Intermède II (1974) (3') •SATB •Mol
Intimité (1968) (3'30) •Bb Sx/Pno •Mol
Introduction et Allegro giocoso (1965) (5'30) •Bb Sx/Pno •Mol
Légende heureuse (1965) (3'45) •Asx/Pno •Bil
Jeunes musiciens (1979) 1) Choral et variation 2) Clément Marot 3) Marche 4) Canotage 5) Farandole 6) Simple mélodie 7) Danse russe 8) Jazz •3 voice: instrumentation variable •Mol
Les jumeaux (the twins) (1963) (5'30) 1) Le sommeil 2) Le lever 3) Bonne humeur 4) Pousser-couler 5) Calypso •2 Sx: AA or TT •Pet/Hin
Music for flexible wind (1978) (24 pieces) •3 voice: instrumentation variable •Mol
Pastorale •Tsx/Pno •HE

Petit concert (1984) (8 pièces) •3 voice: instrumentation variable/ Perc •Mol
Prélude et Rondo (1964) (4') •Asx/Pno •Bil
Prélude et Scherzo (1981) (8'30) (to D. Deffayet) •Asx/Pno •Bil
Quatre par quatre (1990) (10 pièces) •4 instruments de même nature •Mar
Quiètude - Nocturne (1965) (3'30) •Asx/Pno •EFM
Romance •Tsx/Pno •HE
Romance pour Nicolas (1984) (2'30) •Asx/Pno •Bil
Rondo-caprice (1975) (5'30) •SATB •Mol
Saxophonie (1964) (3'30) •Asx/Pno •Bil
Si j'étais... (1980) (6'30) 1) Haendel 2) Rameau 3) Brahms •Asx/ Pno •Led
Si j'étais... (1980) (5'30) 1) Vivaldi 2) Franck 3) Schumann •1 Sx: S or T/Pno •Led
Souvenirs (1989) (10') 1) Aubade de printemps (2'40) 2) Rêverie d'été (2'35) 3) Chanson d'automne (2') 4) Jeux d'hiver (2'45) •Asx/Pno •Mol
Trois Pièces (1963) (7') 1) Romance 2) Pastorale 3) Espièglerie •Bb Sx/Pno •Mol
Twelve old French songs - 12 pièces faciles •3 Sx: AAA or TTT •Hin/Pet
Variances (1982) (12'30) •Asx/Pno •Bil

LANCHANTEC, Maniannig
Harpiste et compositeur français.
Mosaïque (to J. Batteau) Andante - Vif - Andante - Allegro

LANDER, Joseph
Compositeur américain.
Passacaglia and Dance •Asx/Pno

LANDINI, Carlo Alessandro
Compositeur italien. Travailla avec R. Dionisi et B. Bettinelli, puis avec I. Xenakis, G. Ligeti, C. Halffter, I. Malec, et Cl. Ballif.
Incantation "non sempre i saxi sepolcuali a templi" (1984) (10') (to C. Delangle) •Asx Solo •Led

LANE, Richard B. (1933)
Compositeur et professeur américain, né le 11 XII 1933.
A Few Bits and Pieces (1972) •Asx/Pno
Nocturne (1988) (1'45) (for O. Klingenschmid) •Asx/Pno
Quartet (1982) (10') (to the Rhode Island Saxophone Quartet) 1) Prelude 2) Waltz 3) Fugue-like 4) Lament 5) Finale •SATB •TTF
Suite (1961) (9') (to H. Wood) 1) Prelude 2) Song 3) Conversation 4) Lament 5) Finale •Asx/Pno •TTF
Suite (1970) (7'30) (to J. Houlik) •Tsx/Band or Pno •B&H
Trio (1973) (to J. Houlik) •Ob/Tsx/Cl

LANERI, Roberto
Compositeur italien.
Canoni (vari.) (1978/84) •Variable instrumentation •adr
Sonora crossroads (1980) •SATB •adr

LANG, Rosemary (1920-1988)
Saxophoniste américaine, née le 29 IV 1920, à Weisburg (Indiana); morte à Indianapolis, le 5 II 1985. Travailla avec N. Hovey et E. Michelis.
Saxophone: Beginning Studies in the Altissimo Register (1970) •LMP

LANGE, Gustav (1830-1888)
Blumenlied •2 Sx: AT/Pno •Cen
Flower Song (Brooke) •AATB •CF

LANGENUS, Gustave (1883-1957)
Clarinettiste et compositeur américain, d'origine belge, né à Malines, le 6 VIII 1883, mort à New York, le 30 I 1957.
Practical Transposition •CF

LANGESTRAAT, Willy
Quartet for a Celebration (6') •SATB •Mol
Tribute to Rudy Wiedoeft (1934) (3') •Asx/Pno •Mol

LANGEY, Otto (1851-1922)
Practical Tutor (Fitzgerald) •B&H
The Saxophone •Mol
Saxophone Tutor (Fischer) •CF

LANGLOIS, Théo
Compositeur belge.
Facetie (to Fr. Daneels) •Asx/Pno •PC

LANSIÖ, Tapani (1953)
Compositeur finlandais.
Una lettra al amico mio in forma di domino (1984) •Asx Solo •FMIC

LANTIER, Pierre (1910)
Professeur et compositeur français, né à Marseille, le 30 IV 1910. Travailla avec Caussade et H. Busser. Prix de Rome.
"Pierre Lantier possède une technique éprouvée. Il écrit avec soin une musique aimable, sans se soucier de s'écarter des préceptes qui lui ont été inculqués et sans se poser de problèmes (R. Bernard)
Allegro, Arioso et Final (1963) (7'30) (to M. Mule) •Asx/Pno •Lem
Andante et scherzo (1942) •SATB •Bil
Euskaldunak-sonate (1954-61) (11') (to P. Maurice ma femme chérie) 1) Andante tranquillo 2) Andante - Final •Asx/Pno •Bil
Fugue jazz (1944) (3') •2 Cl/2 Sx: AT/Bsn/Tpt/Trb/Perc
Quatuor (18') 1) Allegro 2) Andante 3) Menuet 4) Final •SATB
Sicilienne (1943) (5') •Asx/Pno •Led

LANTOINE, Louis
Professeur et compositeur français.
Quatuor d'anches •Ob+EH/Cl+BsCl/1 Sx: A+S/Bsn •adr

LANZA, Alcides (1929)
Compositeur, chef d'orchestre, pianiste, et professeur canadien d'origine argentine, né à Rosario, le 2 VI 1929. Travailla à Buenos Aires avec J. Bautista et A. Ginastera, puis, avec O. Messiaen, R. Malipiero, A. Copland, B. Maderna, V. Ussachevsky, et R. Kinsky. Depuis 1971 il est à Montréal professeur de composition et de musique électronique à la McGill University.
"His major preoccupation has been electronic music—its composition, notation, recording and so on. The piece employs quarter-tone tuning, special coloured lights and contact microphones for the strings." (S. Salgado)
Interferences III (1983-84) •Fl/Cl/Sx/Guit/Pno/Perc •ShP
Modulos III (1983) •Guit/Tsx/Vln/Vcl/Perc/Pno/Tape •CMC

LAPARRA, Raoul (1876-1943)
Compositeur français, né à Bordeaux, le 13 V 1876, mort à Suresnes lors d'un bombardement, le 4 IV 1943. Travailla avec Massenet, Gedalge, et G. Fauré. Prix de Rome (1903).
"Laparra a surtout composé pour le théâtre, utilisant fréquemment dans ses oeuvres des thèmes folkloriques, principalement basques et espagnols." (Larousse) "Son réalisme bénéficie d'un coloris ibérique assez conventionnel (malgré l'utilisation, si contestable, de thèmes folkloriques). (R. Bernard)
"He was at his own in music inspired by Spanish subjects." (Baker)
"Laparra's music was characterized by an elective use of Spanish and Basque rhythms, and he was always his own librettist." (R. Myers)

Prélude valsé et Irish reel (5') •Asx/Pno •Led

LAPHAM, Claude (1890-19xx)

Compositeur américain. Vécut plusieurs années au Japon.
Concerto in Ab (to C. LEESON) •Asx/Orch (1121/4231/Perc/Harp/Str) or Pno •Lee

LA PORTA, John (1920)

Clarinettiste, saxophoniste américain, né à Philadelphie, le 1er IV 1920.

"John LaPorta is an active musician, performing with his own quartet around Boston, and as a member of the Berklee Saxophone Quartet, which includes Charlie Mariano. He has also written several stage band arrangements and has recorded both jazz and a Brahms chamber work with his own groups." (J. LEWIS)
Concertino •Asx/Orch (1121/1420/Perc/Str) or Pno
14 Jazz Rock Duets •2 Sx: AA or AT or TT •Ken
Miniature •Bsx/Pno

LA PRESLE, Jacques Sauville de (1888-19xx)

Compositeur français, né à Versailles, le 5 VII 1888. Travailla avec P. Vidal. Prix de Rome (1921).

"Compositeur traditionaliste." (R. STRICKER) "Style élégamment académique." (Cl. ROSTAND)

"He is successful in works conceived on a vast scale as in the most delicate sketches. The depth and richness of his work is equally well expressed in nobly flowing melody as in the subtlety of atmosphere impregnated with poetry." (F. RAUGEL)
Orientale (1930) (7') •Asx/Pno •Led

LARA, Augustin (1900-1969)

Granada •Tsx/Pno •PIC

LARMANJAT, Jacques (1878-1952)

Compositeur français, né le 19 X 1878, à Paris où il est mort, le 7 XI 1952.

"C'est sous le signe de la bonne humeur, d'une ironie narquoise et sans fiel, et d'une vivacité désinvolte que se place l'oeuvre de Jacques Larmanjat. Si le mot n'était pris en mauvaise part, on pourrait dire de lui qu'il fut un fantaisiste." (R. BERNARD)
4 Pièces en concert (1951) (9') 1) Prélude 2) Chacone 3) Air varié 4) Perpetuum mobile •Asx/Pno •Dur

LAROCQUE, Jacques

Saxophoniste, professeur, et quartettiste canadien.
Sonate (1966) •Asx/Pno •adr

LA ROSA, Michael (1948)

Compositeur américain, né à Hartford (Connecticut), le 26 VII 1948.
Coming in Glory (1974) 1) Prelude of Darkness 2) Triumph of the Light •Asx/Trb/Vibr •SeMC

LARSEN, Libby

Aubade (1991) •Asx Solo

LARSEN, Lindorff E.

Concerto (1954) •Asx/Orch or Pno •WH

LARSSON, Häkan (1959)

Compositeur suédois.
Farleder - 4 pieces (1993) •Fl/Tsx/Trb/Electr. Guit/Electr. Bass/Pno/Perc •SvM
Gester av en gest (1990) •Tsx/Str Orch •SMIC

LARSSON, Lars Erik (1908-1986)

Compositeur et professeur suédois, né à Akarp, le 15 V 1908; mort le 27 XII 1986, à Helsingborg. Travailla à Vienne avec A. Berg.

"Ne s'adonne à une fantaisie espiègle, subversive que sporadique-ment: plus souvent, il suit un penchant pour le lyrisme et pour une atmosphère néo-romantique. D'un style plus familier surtout plus acidulé, dans une intention de désinvolte fantaisie, il a donné un concerto pour saxophone." (R. BERNARD) "Lars Erik Larsson possède un don évident, mais un don 'à facettes.' En effet, il fut séduit dans sa jeunesse par une expression post-romantique avant de découvrir un art de notre époque grâce aux conseils d'Alban Berg. Larsson est revenu ensuite à un style plus conventionnel en adoptant les voies du néo-classicisme." (Cl. SAMUEL) "Larsson évolua du néo-classicisme léger de ses débuts vers un romantisme fortement national et se dirigea ensuite vers des dissonances plus audacieuses sous l'influence d'Hindemith." (H. HALBREICH)

"Larsson has continually oscillated between Nordic Romanticism, neo-classicism and more unconventional styles (serialism and polytonality)." (G. BERGENDAL) The neo-classicist who wrote the well-known Concertino series with its twelve compositions for solo instrument and orchestra; the steadfast artist who nurtured the classical tradition and imparted his belief in precision and expressive restraint to many of his pupils—Lars Erik Larsson's significance can be described in many ways." (SJ)
Konsert, op. 14 (1934) (20') (to S. RASCHER) 1) Allegro molto moderato 2) Adagio 3) Allegro scherzando •Asx/Str Orch or Pno •KG/CG

LARSSON, M.

Whirls in crouching positions (1990) •Sx/Marimba

LARSSON, Mats (1965)

Compositeur suédois.
Gopak (1989) (5'30) •SATB •SMIC
Sonatine n° 1 (1982) •Asx/Pno •SMIC
Sonatine n° 2 (1987) •Asx/Pno •SMIC

LASAGNA, Marco

Saxophoniste et compositeur italien. Travailla avec A. Guarnieri et G. Manzoni.
"Il nastro delle tredici lune" •Asx/Tape

LASEROMS, Wim

Saxorella (1977) (4') - Trio •3 Sx: AAT/Band or Fanfare •TM

LASNE, George, dit Vauquelin le Trouveur (1905-1972)

Organiste et compositeur français, né le 8 VII 1905, à Falaise (Calvados), où il est mort le 8 V 1972. Travailla avec les abbés P. Bigard et Beliard.

"Musique sincère, d'une délicate émotion."
Ballade française (1971) - Octuor •Fl/Ob/2 Cl/Asx/2 Tpt/Trb
Berceuse dans le deuil (1963) (6') •SATB
Choeur élégiaque (1948) •6 Sx: SAAATB
Divertissement (1969) •5 Sx: SAATB
Divertissement champêtre (1963) (5'30) •3 Sx: SAT
Duo en Lab inspiré de Baustetter •2 Sx: AA
Dyptique (1968) (6') 1) Impromptu 2) Aria •SATB
2 Esquisses à la mémoire de Schubert (1946) Andante pastoral •Asx (or Ssx)/Org (or Pno)
Lied-choral en do mineur (1968) (4'30) •SATB
Promenade de Noël avec Pachelbel (1963) •3 Sx: AAA

LASSEN, Eduard (1830-1904)

At Devotions (OSTRANDER) •Asx/Pno •Mus

LASTRA, Erich Eder de

Compositeur autrichien.
Divertissement (1974) (to S. FASANG) 1) 75 2) Langsam tempo di gigue 3) Monolog 4) Presto •Asx/Bsn •adr

3 Tempi (to E. Bogaard) •Tsx/Pno •adr

LATEEF, Yusef
Quintet No. 1 •5 Sx: AATTB
Sonata (1989) 1) 138 2) Moderato 3) Finale •Asx/Pno •FaM

LATHAM, William Peters (1917)
Compositeur et professeur américain, né à Shreveport (Louisiana), le 4 I 1917. Travailla avec E. Goossens et H. Hanson.
Concertino (1968) (to J. Giordano) •Asx/Orch •DP
Concerto Grosso (1960) (18') (to S. & C. Rascher) Allegro giusto - Andante molto moderato - Gavotte - Siciliano - Allegro non troppo •2 Sx: SA/Orch or Band
Ex tempore (1978) (to M. Moore) •Asx Solo •DP
Sisyphus (1971) (to Fr. Daneels) •Asx/Pno •Bil

LATHROP, Gayle
Pieces 4-5 •Asx/Tpt/Vcl/Bass/Perc •CAP

LATRAILLE, Gregory
Lyric Concerto (1972-78) (to J. Wytko) •Ssx/Chamber Ensemble

LAUBA, Christian (1952)
Compositeur français, né à Sfax (Tunisie), le 26 VII 1952. Travailla à Bordeaux avec M. Fusté-Lambezat, fortement influencé par la musique de Fr. Rossé et de Ligeti.

"Réalise la synthèse des musiques savantes et populaires—plus particulièrement d'Afrique du Nord où il a passé son enfance—et reste attentif à tous les genres musicaux y compris le rock et le jazz, trouvant dans l'écriture d'avant-garde les moyens de fixer une pensée libre de tout préjugé. C'est un artiste authentique plus libre qu'indépendant, qui refuse les interdits et les conventions, rejetant toute doctrine ou tout système. Chaque oeuvre le trouve disposé à exprimer avec le saxophone l'expression la plus achevée de sa pensée créative, ne craignant pas pour cela d'utiliser des langages nouveaux. Son imagination musicale paraît sans limite, chaque partition découvrant une facette inconnue de sa riche personnalité." (S. Piton) "Un authentique 'inventeur' du saxophone; une des personnalités des plus douées, des plus remarquables, des plus attachantes de sa génération." (H. Jarret) "Musique généreuse et triomphante, dans laquelle le populaire se mêle intimement au savant, *Hard* est sans doute l'oeuvre musicale la plus authentiquement dionysiaque que je connaisse. L'inspiration communicative du compositeur porte littéralement l'interprète à exalter la jouissance d'être, le conduisant à une sorte d'ivresse qu'un cri ultime libère. Musique débordante d'enthousiasme dans laquelle le plaisir de jouer provoque irrésistiblement la joie." (d'une interview de J-M. Londeix)

"He makes a synthesis between 'classical' contemporary music and popular music (especially music from North Africa where he lived) and is profoundly attracted by all musical genres including Rock, Jazz, etc. Refusing all doctrines, he endeavors to achieve the most complete expression of his creative thought, not fearing to create new languages. His musical imagination is boundless and each new work shows an unknown side of his personality (S. Piton) "He considers himself a free artist rather than an independent one and refuses all conventions and forbidden trends." (L. Garnier) "He is genuine 'inventor' of the saxophone and reveals himself one of the most gifted, remarkable and engaging personalities of his generation." (H. Jarret) "In his generous and triumphant music, 'learned' and popular music intimately mingle. *Hard* is undoubtedly the most authentically Dionysian work I ever heard. The composer's communicative inspiration induces the interpreter to glorify the joy of living and brings him to a sort of ecstasy ending with a final shout. This music bubbles over with vitality and the pleasure of interpreting *Hard* irresistibly provokes the highest delight." (J-M. Londeix)
Adria (1985) (12') (to F. Mondelci) •2 Sx: AA •Fuz

Atlantis (1990) (14') •Fl (+ Tam)/Tsx/2 Guit
Atlas (1984) (20') •1 Sx:A+B/Pno/Perc/Bass •adr
Autographie (1985) •Asx/Perc/Electr. Pno/Synth/Tape •adr
Chott 2 (1992) (11') (to Christoph Hansen) •Ssx Solo •adr
Dies Irae (1990) (12'30) (to J-M. Londeix) •Ssx/Org or Orch (2222/ 221/BsTrb/Tuba/3 Sx: ATB/2 Perc/Harp/Str: 22241) •B&N
Douar (1991) (16'30) (to J-P. Caens) •Ob/Cl/Asx/Bsn •adr
Dream in the bar (1992) (14'30) (to M-B. Charrier) •Bsx/Perc •Bil
Etudes (1992-94) •Asx •adr
Hard (1988) (8') (to J-M. Goury) •Tsx Solo •Fuz
La Forêt perdue (1983) (9') (to J-M. Londeix) 12 Sx: SnoSSAAATTTBBBs •adr
Les 7 îles (1988) (18') (to J-M. Londeix) •Pno Solo/12 Sx: SnoSSAAATTTBBBs •adr
Mutation-Couleurs IV (1985) (12') (to J-M. Londeix) •12 Sx: SnoSSAAATTTBBBs •Fuz
Parcours (1986) (2'30) (to M. Jézouin) •Asx/Perc •Bil
Passage •2 Sx/Perc •adr
Pulsar (1985-90) (8') (to J-M. Londeix) •Ssx/Org •adr
Ravel's raga (1993) (15') (to J-M. Lamothe) •Vln/Cl/Asx/Bsn/Pno •adr
Reflets (1986) (12') •SATB •Fuz
Rif (1991) (14') •Fl/2 Sx: SA/Pno/Perc •Fuz
Steady study on the boogie (1993) (to J-Y. Fourmeau) •Asx Solo •Bil
Sud (1986) (10') (to I. Roth) •Asx/Pno •Fuz
Variation-Couleurs (1986) (to M. Jézouin) •Ssx/Vcl (or Bass)/Perc •adr

LAUBE, P.
Alsacian Dance •Fl/Ob/Asx/Bsn (or Hn)/Pno •CF

LAUBER, Anne
Compositeur canadien.
5 Eléments (1972) (6'15) •Fl/Ssx/Vln/Bsn/Tuba •CMC
Mouvement (1990) •4 Sx/2 Pno •CMC

LAUER, Arthur
Concerto Grosso (3 movements) •SATB/Orch

LAUERMANN, Herbert
Compositeur autrichien.
Bagatellen •SATB •ECA/ApE

LAUREAU, Jean-Marc (1946)
Compositeur et chef d'orchestre français. Après des études supérieures et un diplôme de biochimie, travailla avec J-P. Henri, P. Lantier, M. Bitsch, J. Casterede, et I. Malec.
Connexions I (1985) (3-6') (Rossé-Rolin-Lejet) •Asx Solo •Sal
Etat limite (1981) (to Quatuor Contemporain) •SATB

LAURENDEAU
Collection of 25 Gospel Hymns (Laurendau) •SATB •CF

LAURENT, Léo
King-saxo (1939) (2'30) (to M. Mule) •Asx/Jazz Orch or Pno •Cos
Nouvelle méthode pratique •Sal
Le Saxophone jazz •Sal

LAURETTE, Marc
Kaléidoscope •Cl/Bsn/2Sx: SB/Hn/Vla/Bass/Vibr

LAUTH, Wolfgang (1931)
Pianiste et compositeur allemand, né le 15 V 1931 à Ludwigshafen.
Concertino in F (1958) (14') •Tsx/Trb/Fl/Perc •adr

LAUWRENCE
Contentment (9'30) (Newsom) •Asx/Band •Ken

LAUZURICA, Antonio

Compositeur espagnol.

El movimento de los astros (1991) •4 Sx: SATB/Perc

LAVAINNE

Souvenir et regrets - ballade (193x) (to A. LESPILLEZ) •Asx/Pno
•Gras

LAVAL, Philippe (1963)

Compositeur né à Bordeaux. Travailla avec M. Fusté-Lambezat.

1,0544876 (1992) •Soprano Voice/2 Sx: AT/Guit/Vibr

LAVENDA, Richard

Compositeur américain.

Illuminations (1988) (to L. HUNTER) •Asx/Pno
The Weary Man Whispers (1985) •Tenor Voice/Asx/Trb/Perc/Pno
•Eto

LAWES, William (1602-1645)

Fantasy and Air No. 1 (GRAINGER) •6 Sx: SSAABBs or SSATBB
•PG

LAYENS, Gilbert

Saxophonie •Asx/Pno •Cham

LAYZER, Arthur

Inner and Outer Forms •2 Sx/3 Brass/2 Perc

LAZARIN, Branko

Compositeur croate.

3 Movements (1982) •Asx Solo •DSH/HG

LAZARO, J.

Compositeur espagnol.

Juego n° 8 •SATB

LAZARUS, Daniel (1898-1964)

Compositeur israélite français, né le 13 XII 1898 à Paris, où il est
mort, le 26 VI 1964. Travailla avec Diemer, Leroux, et Vidal.

4 Mélodies •Contralto Voice/Fl/Cl/Asx/Bsn/Str Quintet
Sonate (1949) (8') (to M. MULE) 1) Allegro agitato 2) Air et
variations 3) Rondeau •Asx Solo •Dur

LAZARUS, Henry (1815-1895)

Grand Artistic Duets (TRAXLER) •2 Sx: AA or TT •Bel

LEAHY, Georges

Compositeur canadien, né au Québec.

Diderot-Québec (1988) •Asx Solo

LEANDRE, Joëlle

Duo n° 1 (6') •Asx/Bass

LEBIERRE, O.

Airs bohémiens •Bb Sx/Pno •TM
Styrienne •4 Sx •TM

LE BOUCHER, Maurice (1882-1964)

Fantaisie concertante (MULE) •Asx/Pno •Led

LEBOW, Leonard S. (1929)

Trompettiste et compositeur américain, né à Chicago, le 25 II 1929.

Four Movements •SATB

LEBRUN, G.

Shepherd's Song •Asx/Pno •HE

LECAIL, G.

Fantaisie Concertante (VOXMAN) •Asx/Pno •Rub

LECLAIR, Jean-Marie (1697-11764)

Adagio (MULE) •Asx/Pno •Led
Adagio, Allemande et Gigue (MULE) •Asx/Pno •Led
Adagio et Aria (MULE) •Asx/Pno •Led
Andante (MULE) •Asx/Pno •Led
Aria (MULE) •Asx/Pno •Led
Danse provençale (SMISM) •1 Sx: A or T/Pno •Mus
Gavotte et vivace (MULE) •Asx/Pno •Led
Gigue (MULE) •Asx/Pno •Led
Largo et vivace (MULE) •Asx/Pno •Led
Musette (LONDEIX) •Asx/Pno •Lem
Musette (MULE) •Asx or Bb Sx/Pno •Led
Sonata in G minor (GORNER) •Asx/Pno •South
Sonate en Ut (LONDEIX) •2 Sx: SS or AA or TT •Led
Sonate en Ré (LONDEIX) •2 Sx: SS or AA or TT •Led
Sonate en Fa (LONDEIX) •2 Sx: SS or AA or TT •Led

LECLERC, Michel

Compositeur belge.

Au coeur de la cité Ardente (1988) •Ssx/Pno
Rythmes et couleurs •Asx/Pno
Variations sur Harbouya (to J-P. RORIVE) •Ssx/Org

LECLERCQ, Edgard

Compositeur belge.

Caprice oriental (5') (to Fr. DANEELS) •Asx/Pno
Charmeuse •Asx/Pno •EMB
Concertino (1934) (to M. van GUTCHE) Allegro moderato - Largo -
Allegro molto •Asx/Pno •Braun
Happy moment •1 Sx: A or T/Pno •HE
Impression romantique (5') (to Quatuor Belge de Saxophones)
•SATB
Instant élégiaque •1 Sx: A or T/Pno •An
Intimité •Tsx/Pno •HE
Introduction et Scherzo capricioso (5') (to Quatuor belge de
Saxophones) •SATB •Mau
Prélude et mouvement perpétuel (4') (to Quatuor Belge de Saxo-
phones) •SATB •Mau
Tendresse •Asx/Pno •EMB

LECLERE, François (1950)

Périphéria (1977) (to M. JÉZOUIN) •SATB

LECUONA, Ernesto (1896-1963)

Andalucia (KLICKMANN) •AATB •EMa
Andalucia - Suite •2 Tpt/Trb/3Sx: AAT/2 Vln/Vcl/Bass
Malaguena (KLICKMANN) •AATB •EMa

LECUSSANT, Serge

Compositeur français.

Yesterday, Today and Forever (1979) (to G. LACOUR) •Tsx/Pno

L'ECUYER, Christian

Compositeur canadien.

Soleil 1) Rhapsodie 2) Rondo 3) Dance •SATB

LEDERER, Dezsö

Poème hongrois n° 2 •Vln Solo (or Sx)/Harmonie

LEDUC, Jacques (1932)

Compositeur belge, né le 1er III 1932, à Jattes-St-Pierre. Travailla
avec J. Absil.

Rhapsodie (to Fr. DANEELS) •Asx/Pno •Sch
Sortilèges africains (1967) (10') (to Quatuor Belge de Saxophones)
1) Abandon 2) Cet instant-là 3) Accords 4) La servante 5) Au
plus profond des terres •4 Sx: SATB or Voice/Sx/Pno/Perc

Suite, op. 15 (1964) (12') (to Quatuor Belge de Saxophones)
1) Marche 2) Berceuse 3) Gavotte et Musette 4) Saltarelle
•SATB •Sch

LEE, Chol-Woo
Compositeur allemand.
Meditation II (1993) •Tsx/Perc •INM

LEE, Hope (1953)
Compositeur canadien.
Jygge... somebody's (1987) (12') •2 Sx: SA •CMC

LEE, Sebastian (1805-1887)
Studies •CF

LEE, Thomas Oboe (1945)
Compositeur américain.
The MacGuffin (10') (to K. RADNOFSKY) •1 Sx: S+A/Perc •adr
Louie MCLV (8') (to K. RADNOFSKY) •SATB •adr
Piece for Viola (15') •SATB •adr
Saxxologie...A Sextet (11') (to K. RADNOFSKY) •6 Sx: SSATTB •adr
Sourmash (1978) (to K. RADNOFSKY) •Asx/Pno •DP

LEENEN, Ulrich Jakob (1964)
Compositeur allemand, né le 8 I 1964 à Meerbusch-Büderich.
Travailla avec G. Cornmann.
14 Duets (1989) (62') •Asx/Pno •adr
Magic exercise (1'39) •Sx/Pno •adr
Musical love-letter (2'35) •Sx/Pno •adr
Odyssey in 7/4, jazz (5'35) •Sx/Pno •adr
Rope-dancer (1982) (7'45) •Asx/Pno •adr
Suite fantastique (1986/87) (8'30) •Sx/Pno •adr
We'll meet next century (2'35) •Sx/Pno •adr

LEESON, Cecil Burton (1902-1989)
Saxophoniste concertiste, professeur, et compositeur américain, né le 16 XII 1902, à Candon (North Dakota), mort à Muncie (Indiana), le 17 IV 1989. Commença à donner des concerts en 1925.

"A development in which as the principal American pioneer of concert saxophone playing he has had so large a part." "From a man who has devoted most of his lifetime to the improvement of playing standards, literature, and acceptance of the saxophone, comes this extremely idiomatic work for the alto saxophone. It is written not just to flatter the solo, but through flattery, to express in absolute music a message for which the saxophone is best suited as narrator." (J. PAYNTER) "Cecil Leeson has been the greatest stimulus for the enrichment of the saxophone repertory, and I am most grateful for having been chosen a contributor to the repertory." (F. HEMKE) "He is regarded as one of the pioneers of the saxophone as a legitimate concert instrument. He was the first saxophonist to give a concert at New York City's Town Hall (5 II 1937), and he went on to concertize, teach, and inspire composers to write for the saxophone." (B. AYSCUE)
The Basics of Saxophone Tone Production - A Critical and Analytical Study
Concertino (1948) •Asx/Winds or Chamber Orch •South
Concertino (1957) (to N. G. DEHNBOSTEL) 1) Dialogue 2) Song and Recitation 3) In a fairly fast four •Asx/Wind Symphonette or Pno •Enc
Concerto No. 1 (1947) •Asx/Orch or Pno
Concerto No. 2 (1948-1960) •Asx/Orch or Pno
Concerto No. 3 (1952) •Asx/Orch or Pno
Concerto for Tenor Saxophone (1960) •Tsx/Orch or Pno
Sonata No. 1 (1953-79) (to my dear wife Louise) 1) Moderately fast 2) Slowly with feeling 3) Scherzo 4) Theme and variations •Asx/Pno •SMC/South
Sonata No. 2 (1966) •Asx/Pno

Three Children's Pieces (1946) •Asx/Pno

LEEUWENBERG, Boudewijn
Compositeur néerlandais.
Magic moments (1975) (5') •Asx/Pno •Don

LE FANU, Nicola (Frances) (1947)
Compositeur anglais, née à Wickham Bishop (Essex), le 28 IV 1947. Fille d'Elisabeth Maconchy. Travailla avec Petrassi, puis M. Davies.
"Son oeuvre abondante, où l'on peut percevoir l'influence de ses maîtres, a abordé tous les genres." (G. GEFEN)
"Her music is distinguished above all by its linear qualities: the melodic line of the contrapuntal, serially organized earlier works and of the monodic pieces; and the splintered line, the complex instrumental gestures, of her late writing." (G. LARNER)
Moon over the Western Ridge, Mootwinge (1985) (12'45) (to Rascher Quartet) •SATB

LE FASSE, Roger
Le biniou et le labo •Sx/Tape

LEFEBVRE, E-A.
Annie Laurie - Rock'd in the Cradle •Eb Sx/Pno •CF
Chant du soir - Maria's Song •Eb Sx/Pno •CF
The Last of Summer •Eb Sx/Pno •CF

LEFEBVRE, Pierre & R. GOFFIN
De la technique du son •Led

LEFEVRE, Charles (1843-1917)
Andante et Allegro (CAILLIET) •Asx/Pno •South

LEFEVRE
20 Melodious Studies (SAVINA) •Ric

LEFKOFF, Gerald
A Troubador's Rhapsody (1991) (3 movements) •Sx Solo •Gly
20 Rhythmic Etudes (1994) •Gly
Tapestries (4 movements) •SATB •Gly

LEGIDO, Jose Maria
Compositeur espagnol.
Skets for jazz (1991) (to M. MIJAN) •Asx/Pno

LEGLEY, Victor (1915)
Compositeur et violoniste belge, né le 18 VI 1915 à Hazebrouck. Travailla avec J. Absil. Prix de Rome (1943).
"L'une des personnalités de l'école flamande. D'abord influencé par Reber et son maître Absil, il est ensuite allé vers un néo-classicisme Hindemithien dans lequel il ne manque pas de vigueur et de sens architectonique." (Cl. ROSTAND) "Sa musique se meut dans le monde de l'atonalité, mais elle se refuse à obéir aux lois rigoureuses de la dodécaphonie sérielle. Sans renoncer pour autant à une dignité de langage, il s'efforce d'écrire une musique accessible. De même, il a voulu écrire aussi une musique qui puisse être exécutée par d'autres interprètes que les virtuoses." (R. WANGERMEE)
"In 1941 he took courses with Jean Absil, who became influential in shaping Legley's style. Later Legley adopted some devices of atonal music, without adhering to integral dodecaphonism." (BAKER) "Although clearly influenced by Absil in his early music, Legley has steadily developed an individual style in which highly charged emotion is kept in check by firm technique and refined taste. After 1952 he made particular efforts to reach the public, but without sacrificing his dignity and his individuality." (C. MERTENS)
Cinq miniatures, op. 54 (1958) (8') (to Quatuor Belge de Saxophones) 1) Danse 2) Lied 3) Fughetto 4) Berceuse 5) Marche •SATB •CBDM

Concert d'automne, op. 85 (1975) (11'15) (to Fr. DANEELS) •Asx/
Orch or Pno •CBDM/Bil
Concerto grosso (1976) (to E. APPER) 1) Allegro 2) Andante
3) Allegro •Vln/Asx/Chamber Orch •Bil/Mau
Hommage à Jean Absil (1980) •SATB/Band
Parade II, op. 93 (1978) (to Saxofonia ensemble) 1) Allegro grazioso
2) Scherzo 3) Molto adagio 4) Mesto 5) Alla marcia •6 Sx:
SAATTB •Sch

LEGRADY, Thomas (1920)
Concertino grossino (1977) •SATB/Band •CMC

LEGRAND, Michel (1932)
Compositeur, chanteur de variété, chef d'orchestre et pianiste français, né le 24 II 1932 à Paris. Travailla avec H. Chaland et N. Boulanger.
"Le jazz de Michel Legrand n'a rien de farouchement 'New Orleans,'
il ne se pique pas de pureté, il ne fait pas appel aux effets spectaculaires
d'une partition de Bernstein, il accepte le virus de tendresse d'un trois
temps à la Van Parys, il parle un langage musical de tous les jours,
comme une chanson." (M. FLEURET)
"Very soon his activities as composer, conductor and arranger were
directed towards jazz and light music. His international career began in
1954-55 when he conducted at Maurice Chevalier's shows in Paris and
New York. He has written scores for numerous films." (D. AMY)
Porcelaine de Sax (1958) (3') •6 Sx: SnoSATBBs (or Eb Cl/Cl/3 Sx:
ATB/Bsn) Trb/Bass/Perc •Mills

LEGRON, Léon
Compositeur français.
Canzonetta (1976) •Asx/Pno •Bil
Rêverie (1976) •Asx/Pno •Bil

LEGUAY, Jean-Pierre (1939)
Compositeur et organiste français, né à Dijon, le 4 VII 1939.
Travailla avec G. Litaize, S. Plé-Caussade, et O. Messiaen.
Flamme (1972-76) (6'30) •Sx Solo •Uni
Madrigal 6 (1985) •SATB
Scabbs (1984) (to M. JÉZOUIN) •Asx/Bass (or Bsx) •Lem
Sève (1974) (to R. DECOUAIS) •Asx/Pno •Lem

LEHAR, Franz (1870-1948)
La veuve joyeuse (ROMBY) •Asx/Pno •PB

LEHMAN
Intro Song Gigue •Asx/Band •DP

LEHMANN, Hans Ulrich (1937)
Compositeur et professeur suisse, né à Biel (Berne), le 4 V 1937.
Travailla avec P. Müller, Boulez, et Stockhausen.
"In the course of the 1960s Lehmann moved away from strict serial
writing to a style that is rich in contrast and contains many playful
elements." (J. STENZL)
Monodie (1970) (10') •Sx Solo: A or T •AVV

LEHMANN, Markus (1919)
Compositeur allemand, né le 31 III 1919 à Böhmisch Leipa (Cêskà
Lipa). Travailla avec W. Maler et P. Hindemith.
Concertino, op. 24a (1956) 1) Allegretto scherzando 2) Moderato
assai 3) Allegro vivo 4) Grottesco •Tsx/Pno •adr
Concerto (10'10) •Tsx/Orch •Asto
Cortidiana (17') •SATB •Asto
Elegie (1989) (8') •Asx/Org •Asto
Werke •SATB •adr

LEHNERT, Wolfgang
Kleine Suite •SATB •SRu

LEIBOWITZ, René (1913-1972)
Compositeur, chef d'orchestre, professeur, théoricien, et écrivain
français d'origine polonaise, né à Varsovie, le 17 II 1913; mort à Paris,
le 29 VIII 1972. Fixé en France depuis 1925. Travailla avec A.
Schoenberg et A. Webern, ainsi qu'avec M. Ravel pour l'orchestration.
"L'un des principaux représentants, en France, de la musique dodécaphonique." (N. DUFOURCQ) "Contrairement à ses cadets, il est resté
rigoureusement fidèle à l'orthodoxie schönbergienne." (Cl. ROSTAND)
"Cet ascète de l'atonalisme devait apprendre aux jeunes qui se con-
fiaient à lui toutes les ressources d'une technique rude qui refuse le
charme (P. WOLFF) "C'est un musicien complet, en même temps qu'un
homme modeste, discret, réfléchi." (M. FLEURET) "René Leibowitz eut
très vite à Paris une influence considérable dans l'immédiat après-
guerre. Il participa aussi, à partir de 1948, aux cours d'été internatio-
naux pour la musique nouvelle organisés au Kranuschsteiner Institut
de Darmstadt en Allemagne, institués deux ans plus tôt, en 1946." (J.
& Br. MASSIN)
"His compositions are close to Schoenberg and Berg in their classical
serial procedures, displaying a certain intellectualism which also
marked his work as a conductor (he advocated a conscientious faithful-
ness to the score based on close analysis)." (D. JAMEUX)
Variations, op. 84 (1969) (12') (to Quatuor de Lyon) Introduction -
Thema et 9 variations - Finale •SATB •JJ

LEICHTLING, Alan
Fantasy Piece IV (1978) •Asx •SeMC

LEIDZEN, Erik (1894-1962)
Chef d'orchestre, professeur, et compositeur américain, né à Stoc-
kholm, le 25 III 1894; mort à New York, le 20 XII 1962. Aux U.S.A.
depuis 1915.
Bourne Trio Album •3 Sx: •Bou
Four Leaf-Clover •AATB •Bou
The Foursome •AATB •Bou

LEINERT, Friedrich Otto (1908)
Compositeur et chef d'orchestre allemand, né à Oppeln (Haute-
Silésie), le 10 V 1908. Travailla avec A. Schoenberg.
Sonate (1952) (12'30) (to J. de VRIES) 1) Allegro moderato
2) Larghetto 3) Allegro con brio •Asx/Pno •Br&Ha

LEISTNER-MAYER, Roland (1945)
Compositeur allemand né à Graslitz (Böhmen), le 20 II 1945.
Travailla avec G. Biallas.
Quartetto agitamento e scemando (1984) (8') •SATB •Tong

LEJET, Edith (1941)
Compositeur français, né à Paris, le 19 VII 1941. Travailla avec J.
Rivier, D. Milhaud, et A. Jolivet.
Aube marine (1982) (8') (to Quatuor Contemporain) •SATB •Lem
Cérémonie (1986) (to C. DELANGLE) •Sx Orch: SATB •Lem
Connexions I (1985) (3-6') (LAUREAU-ROLIN-ROSSÉ) •Asx Solo •Sal
Emeraude et rubis (1984) (3') (to M. JÉZOUIN) •2 Sx •ET
Jade (1981) (3'30) (to M. JÉZOUIN) •Asx/Perc •Sal
Musique pour Quatuor (1973-74) (12') (to Quatuor Deffayet) (5
movements) •SATB •EFM
Quatre petits poèmes chinois (12') (to P. PAREILLE) •Soprano Voice/
Ob/Cl/Asx/Bsn •adr
Saphir (1982) (4'30) (to M. JÉZOUIN) •Bsx/Pno •Sal
Trois Petits préludes (1986) (4') (to C. DELANGLE) 1) Nostalgico
2) Andante 3) Moderato •Asx/Pno •Lem

LE JEUNE, Claude (16th century)
La bel'Aronde (GRAINGER) •6 Sx: SAATTB •PG

LELEU, Jeanne (1898)

Pianiste et compositeur français, né à Saint-Michel, le 29 XII 1898. Travailla avec Caussade, Widor, et Busser. Prix de Rome (1923).

"Connaissant son métier à la perfection, écrivant une musique aux lignes nettes et vigoureuses, elle a le courage d'être elle-même, c'est-à-dire une femme douée d'une sensibilité spécifiquement féminine." (R. BERNARD) "Ton volontaire, hardi, où la décision l'emporte parfois sur l'émotion." (R. STRICKER)

"In style her compositions belong to no school. Clear, rhythmically alive, adventurous in harmony." (D. Cox)

Danse nostalgique (1956) (3'30) (to M. MULE) •Asx/Pno •Lem

LELOUCH, Emile

Compositeur français.
Boutade (1990) (3') •Asx/Pno •Comb
Burlesque (1991) (3'50) •Asx/Pno •Comb

LEMAIRE, Félix (1926)

Compositeur français, né à Metz, le 4 IV 1926.
Ballade N° 2 (1973) (4'30) (to H. PRATI) •Asx/Pno •Led
Concertino (12') •Asx/Str Orch •adr
Entre chien et loup (1980) (to Quatuor Contemporain) •6 Sx/Pno
Mon premier récital (10 pieces) •Asx/Pno •Bil
3 Pièces (1980) (to H. PRATI) 1) Conte 2) Légende 3) Petit prélude •Asx/Pno •Bil
6 Strophes •Asx/Brass ensemble (4431/Perc) •adr
Suite brève (1980) (to H. PRATI) •Asx/Pno •Bil
Trio, op. 106 (1982) (to J. CHARLES) •Ob/Sx/Vcl •adr

LEMAIRE, Jean (1927)

Compositeur français.
Musiques légères (1969) (7') 1) Hispano 2) Gipsy 3) Duetto 4) Aria •Asx/Pno •Led
Quatuor (1982) (to Quatuor Deffayet) •SATB/Orch
Septuor •7 Sx

LE MAISTRE, MATTHEUS (1505-1577)

Dominus noster castellum (EVERTSE) •3 Sx: AAT •Lis/TM

LEMARE, Edwin Henry (1865-1934)

Andantino •2 Sx: AA or AT/Pno •CF
Andantino (LONG) •Bb Sx/Pno •Volk
Andantino (TRINKAUS) •Bb Sx/Pno •PMH
Andantino (TRINKAUS) •Sx/Tpt (or Trb)/Pno •CF
Cathedral Meditation •2 Sx: AA or AT/Pno or 3 Sx: AAT or ATT/Pno •Cen

LEMAY, Robert (1960)

Compositeur québécois (Canada) né à Montréal, le 13 II 1960. Travailla avec F. Morel, L. Andriesson, B. Ferneyhough, D. Erb, et M. Longtin.

"La musique de Robert Lemay se caractérise par une utilisation de l'espace scénique, une attention particulière, un comportement des interprètes et une exploration de la technique des instrumentistes." (L. RAMERT)

Konzertzimmermusic (1992) (30') •Ssx/3 Perc/Chamber Orch •CMC
Les yeux de la solitude (1987) (16') (to D. & Fr. GAUTHIER) •Asx/Perc •CMC
Vagues vertiges (1989) (21') (to J-M. LONDEIX) •12 Sx: SnoSSAAATTTBBBs/1 Perc •CMC
"Vous ne faites que passer... S.V.P. frappez fort" (1991) (durée variable [variable duration]) •5 Sx égaux et participation du public •CMC
Tryptique écarlate (1991) (18') (to D. GAUTHIER) •1 Sx: S+T+B/Harp/Perc •CMC

LEMELAND, Aubert (1932)

Compositeur français, né à La Haye du Puis (Manche), le 19 XII 1932.

"Je suis un indépendant s'exprimant en toute liberté."
Arioso, op. 24 (1972) (6') (to Quatuor de Saxophones de la Garde Républicaine) •SATB •adr
Capriccio, op. 68 (1979) (6') •Asx Solo •Bil
Concertino (1980) (to Quatuor Contemporain) •SATB •adr
Divertissement n° 1, op. 45 (9') •Fl/Asx/Cl •Bil
Divertissement n° 2 (10') •Fl/Asx/Cl •Bil
Epilogue nocturne, op. 22 (1971) (8'15) (to Quatuor de la Garde Républicaine) •SATB •Bil
Epitaph to John Coltrane, op. 86 (1979) (5') Andantino - Vivo e ritmico - Lento espressivo •Ssx/Pno •Bil
Figures qui bougent un peu..., op. 79 (10') •Asx/Vla/Vibr/Guit •adr
Mouvement concertant n° 3 (7'30) •Asx/Vla/Vcl •Bil
Noctuor, op. 93 (1983) (9') •SATB •Bil
Nocturne, op. 10 (1970) (9'40) (to P. PAREILLE) •Ob/Cl/Asx/Bsn •EFM
5 Portraits, op. 49 (1977) (7') 1) Reveno 2) Flegmatique 3) Capricieur 4) Elégiaque 5) Triomphal •Cl/Asx •Bil
Quatuor (1979) •SATB •adr
Quintette, op. 37 (1978) (15'30) •Asx/Str Quartet •adr
Terzetto, op. 69 (1974) (8') (to A. BEUN) •Ob/Cl/Asx •adr
Terzetto, op. 106 (1982) (10') (to J. CHARLES) •Ob/Cl/Asx •Bil
Trio, op. 98 (1979) (8') •Ssx/Cl/Hn •adr
Variations •SATB •adr
Walkings, op. 105 (8'30) (to J-F. BARAGLIOLI) •Ssx/Vibr •Bil

LENFANT, Patrick (1945)

Compositeur français, né à Paris.
"Lenfant s'efforce de sensibiliser le synthétiseur au jeu instrumental, et d'assouplir la dimension de l'électronique en l'associant à des plages de relative liberté." (D. J-Y BOSSEUR)
Sequencadenza IV (1986) •Sx/Synth

LENNERS, Claude (1956)

Compositeur luxembourgeois, né à Luxembourg. Après des études d'informatique, travailla avec A. Müllenbach.
Frammenti fugativi (1987) •Ssx/2 Guit •adr
Melisma (1986) •SATB •adr
Monotaurus (1988) (to P-S. MEUGÉ) •Asx Solo •Lem
Zenit - Fantasia (1990) •Fl/Ob/Ssx •Lem

LENNON, John & Paul MCCARTNEY

When I'm Sixty-Four (RICKER) •SATB or AATB •Ken
Yesterday (RONKIN) •MIDI Wind Controller/Pno •adr

LENNON, John Anthony (1950)

Compositeur américain, né à Greensboro (North Carolina). Travailla avec L. Bassett, W. Bolcom, E. Kurtz, et M. Crooks.
Distances Within Me (1979) (for J. FORGER) •Asx/Pno •DP
Symphonic Rhapsody (1985) (to D. SINTA) •Asx/Orch (1/Picc/21/BsCl/1/CBsn/4221/2Perc/Timp/Harp/Pno/Str) •Pet

LENON, C.

Lullaby •Asx/Pno •CBet

LENOT, Jacques (1945)

Compositeur français, né le 29 VIII 1965, à St. Jean d'Argels. Autodidacte.
"Comme pour plusieurs compositeurs de sa génération, les incidences poétiques sont extrêmement prégnantes dans son oeuvre." (D. J-Y BOSSEUR) "S'inscrivant hors de tout système, tendant à s'individualiser à l'extrême, Jacques Lenot veut traduire par une maîtrise indiscutable 'une expressivité proche des oeuvres virtuoses du passé.' " (J. & B.

Massin)
Pièce •Soprano Voice/Asx/Ob/Cl/Bsn •adr

LENTZ, Daniel (1943)

Compositeur américain, né le 10 III 1943, à Latrode (Pennsylvania). "...exploring ground which no one has yet really mapped out." (Vermeulen)
Aeolian Funk (1972) (10') •adr
Pound for Pound (1971) (10-30') •Asx/Actress/50-100 dogs •DP

LEONARD, Clair (1901)

Professeur et compositeur américain, né à Newton (Massachusetts). Travailla à Paris avec N. Boulanger.
Recitativo and Abracadabra (1962) (for S. Rascher) •Asx/Pno •Bou

LEONARD, J. Michael (1962)

Extended Technique for the Saxophone •adr

LEONCAVALLO, Ruggiero (1858-1919)

Arioso (Grooms) (*Pagliacci*) •1 Sx: T or A/Pno •Cen
Mattinnata (Barnes) •Asx/Pno •Lud

LEONTOVITCH, Nikolaï (1877-1921)

Two Ukrainian Songs (Voxman & Block) •AATB •South

LERIT, Vladimir

Compositeur israélien.
Capriccio (1993) •AATB •INM

LEROUX, Félix

Cavatine sans parole (1883) •Asx/Pno
Fantaisie sur "La Colombe" de Gounod (1891) •Asx/Pno
Faribole - Cavatine (1885) •Asx/Pno
1ère fantaisie sur Carmen (1892) •Asx/Pno
1ère fantaisie sur Mireille (1892) •Asx/Pno

LEROUX, Philippe

Phonice douce (1991) •Ob/Asx/Vcl •Bil

LEROUX, Xavier (1863-1919)

1ère Romance en La mineur (Mule) •Asx/Pno •Led
2me Romance en La majeur (Mule) •Asx/Pno •Led

LERSTAD, Terje Bjorn (1955)

Compositeur norvégien.
Concerto No. 1, op. 104 (1978) (24') •Tsx/Orch •NMI
Concerto No. 2, op. 171 (1984) (20') •Asx/Cl Choir •NMI
Fantasy, op. 39 (7') •Asx Solo •NMI
Improvisation & tarentella, op. 128 (1979) •BsSx Solo •NMI
Jubilee fanfare, op. 133 •9 Sx •NMI
Lamento, op. 168b (1984) •Tsx Solo •NMI
2 Pièces, op. 79 (1975) (7') •SATB •NMI
Quartet No. 1, op. 94 (1976) •SATB •NMI
Quartet No. 2, op. 97 (1976) (6') •SATB •NMI
Quartet, op. 110 •Ssx/2 Tpt/Fluegelhorn •NMI
Sonata, op. 117 (1978) (16') •Bsx/Pno •NMI

LERSY, Roger Raymond (1920)

Compositeur français, né à Lille, le 2 IV 1920. Travailla avec N. Gaillon et A. Girard.
"Humour, pudeur, volonté de communiquer." "Raymond Lersy possède à un haut degré le goût et le talent du coloris sonore. Il charme son auditoire tant ses trouvailles sont ingénieuses."
3 Esquisses en deux couleurs (1971) (7'30) 1) Agressif 2) Lamento 3) Deux dames de bonne compagnie •Asx/Vcl •adr
Kandinsky (1973) (to P. Pareille) •Asx/Bass/Perc/Pno •adr

Pérégrination (1969) (8') (to Quatuor d'Anches Paul Pareille) 1) Assez lent 2) Andante 3) Vivace •Ob/Cl/Asx/Bsn •adr
Vitraux (1972) (35') (514 séquences) •Cl/Asx/Vcl/Perc •adr

LESAFFRE, Charles

Mon premier blues •Ssx/Pno •Bil

LE SIEGE, Annette

Ordinary Things •Voice/Fl/Sx/Vibr/Vcl/Pno •SeMC
Suite (1979) (to M. Sigmon) 1) Praeludium 2) Allemande 3) Lachrymae Pavan 4) Galiarda 5) Fantasia •Asx/Pno •SeMC

LESIEUR, Emile (1910)

Chef d'harmonie et compositeur français, né à Hirson (Aisne).
Deux pièces brèves (1984) (3'15) •Asx/Pno •Bil
Prélude et rondo (1964) (4') •Asx/Pno •Bil
Rêverie •Asx/Pno •Mar
Rêverie et danse •Asx/Pno •Mar
Sarabande et menuet •Asx/Pno •Bil

LESKO, Ladislav (1932)

Intrada (1982) (to O. Vrhovnik) •7 Sx: SnoSATBBsCBs

LESSER, Jeffrey

Last Saxophone on Earth (1979) (to F. Miller) •Asx/Brass Quintet
Quartet (1979) (to F. Miller) •SATB •Pres
Suite for Clyde (1979) (to F. Miller) •Ssx/Pno •DP/WWS

LESSING, Walter

Concertino (1953) (to J. de Vries) •Asx/Pno/Chamber Orch

LESTER, L.

Easy Trios •3 Sx •Bel
50 Rambles •CF

LETASSEY, Laurent

Sempre tutti (1991) (17') (to G. Gourdet) •Asx Ensemble/8 Voices •Bil

LETELLIER, Llona Alfonso (1912)

Compositeur chilien, né à Santiago-du-Chili, le 4 X 1912. Travailla avec Allende.
"From the early 1950s his music became less attached to nationalism and more to the esthetics and methods of the Second Viennese School, using these with great freedom and individuality." (J. A. Orrego-Salas)
Cuarteto, op. 28 (1963) •SATB

LETELLIER, Robert (1918)

Saxophoniste français né à St-Omer. Travailla avec Marcel Mule.
Ballade (to J. Lecompte) •Asx/Pno •Mar
14 nouveaux duos et trios •2 or 3 Sx •Mar/Mol
38 etudes faciles pour le style et l'interprétation •Mar
40 etudes de style •Mar/Mol
Gammes majeures, mineures, etc. •Mar/Mol
Melancholy Song •Asx/Pno •Mar
Methode nouvelle •Mar/Mol
Pièce récréative d'après Gluck •3 Sx: AAA or TTT •Mar
Tablature pour tous les saxophones •Mar

LE THIERE, C.

Beneath Sky Window - Serenade •Bb Sx/Pno •CF

LETOREY, Omer (1888-19xx)

Compositeur français. Travailla avec Th. Dubois.
Faunes et Nymphes •SATB •Marg

LETOREY, Pierre

Compositeur français.

Papotages (1944) (4'30) (to M. Mule) •Asx/Pno •Bil

LEUCHTER, Heibert (1954)

Compositeur et saxophoniste allemand, né le 19 IV 1954, à Aachen.
Contemplativo (1993) •1 Sx: A+B/Accordion •INM
Diamonds in the water (1981) (5'30) •Asx/Bs Guit/Perc •adr

LEVAL, Charles (1908)

Saxophonia (1983) (to M. Jézouin) •SATB

LEVEL, Pierre-Yves

Cheminements •Fl/Ob/Cl/Asx/Hn/Bsn •Lem

LEVIN, Gregory

Compositeur canadien.
Corina (1971) •Asx/Pno •CMC

LEVIN, Todd

Compositeur américain.
Serenade Express (1987) •SATB

LEVINAS, Michael (1949)

Compositeur et pianiste français, né à Paris. Travailla avec Y. Loriod, O. Messiaen, puis Stockhausen. Suit des stages d'électro-acoustique.
"Pour Michael Levinas, la logique doit pouvoir provenir de la compréhension du matériau musical, 'une logique organique de sonorités et de formes analogues aux nécessités organiques des systèmes harmoniques.' Il s'agira généralement moins de composer son par son que de mettre en présence des jeux de forces sonores après en avoir évalué la densité." (D. J-Y. Bosseur) "Michael Levinas privilégie sur des sons purs, lisses, entraînant les trames harmoniques dans leurs sillages, les sons inclassables, impurs, 'sales' comme on a pu les appeler." "Michael Levinas a étudié les transitoires dans *Les rires du Gilles*—pour cinq instrumentistes et bande magnétique—et notamment le transitoire d'attaque, 'moment névralgique et décisif du son instrumental.' " (J-N. von der Weid)
Les rires du Gilles (1981) (7') •Ssx/Tape •Sal

LEVITIN, Jurij Abramovic (1912)

Concerto (1951) •Asx/Tpt/Orch de variété

LEVY, Frank (1930)

Violoncelliste et compositeur américain, d'origine française, né à Paris, le 15 X 1930.
Adagio and Scherzo •SATB •SeMC

LEVY, Matthew

Compositeur américain.
Quartet 1) Largo 2) Scherzo •SATB

LEWIS

Forlhney Duets •2 Sx •WWS
Lament and Caprice •2 Sx •WWS
Saxophone Trios •3 Sx: SAT •WWS
Quartet •SATB •WWS
Three Inventions •2 Sx •WWS

LEWIS, Arthur (1935)

Artiste et compositeur américain, né le 30 X 1935 à Philadelphia (Pennsylvania).
Pieces of Eight •Fl/2 Ob/3 Cl/Bsn/2 Tsx/Hn/Baritone Hn/Perc •CAP
Sonata (1982) (to P. Brodie) •Sx Solo •CMC

LEWIS, J.

Tampanera (1976) •Sx/Perc

LEWIS, John Aaron (1920)

Pianiste de jazz américain, né à La Grange, le 3 V 1920.
"In 1952 he organized the Modern Jazz Quartet."

Bel (Belkis) (4') •Tsx/Tpt/Trb/Pno/Bass/Perc •MJQ
Django (1954) (5') •Tsx/Tpt/Trb/Pno/Bass/Perc •MJQ
Little David's Fugue (5'30) •Fl/Cl/3 Sx: ATB/Trb or Tpt/Harp or Pno/Bass/Perc •MJQ
The Milanese Story (20') •Fl/Tsx/Guit/Pno/Bass/2 Vln/Vla/Vcl/Perc •MJQ
Milano (5') •Tsx/Tpt/Trb/Pno/Bass/Perc •MJQ
N.Y. 19 (7') •Tsx/Tpt/Trb/Pno/Bass/Perc •MJQ
The Queen's Fancy (4') •Fl/Cl/Tsx/Bsn/Hn/Trb/Harp/Bass/Perc •MJQ
Sun Dance (4') •Fl/Cl/3 Sx: ATB/Trb/Harp or Guit/Bass/Perc •MJQ
2 Degrees East, 3 Degrees West (8'30) •Tsx/Tpt/Trb/Pno/Bass/Perc •MJQ

LEWIS, Malcolm

Compositeur américain.
Elegy for a Hollow Man (1972) (4') •Asx/Band or Ssx/Pno
Poem (1976) (to S. Mauk) 1) Molto lento 2) Rapidly-rhythmic •Ssx/Pno •DP

LEWIS, Robert Hall (1926)

Compositeur américain, né à Portland (Oregon), le 22 IV 1926. Travailla avec N. Boulanger, puis avec H. E. Apostel.
"His musical style owes allegiance to no particular trend: although his earlier works were concerned with linear developmental processes using serial methods, he has abandoned this approach in favour of larger and more varied gestures. Textural invention, subtle contrasts of timbre and rhythm, structural flexibility and the interaction between continuity and discontinuity are features of his present style." (S. Di Bonaventura)
Combinazioni VI (1986) (8') •SATB
Monophony V (1982) (to J. Cunningham) 1) With frowing motion 2) Adagio 3) Cadenza-Allegro fantastico •Asx Solo •Pet

LEYBACH, Ignace (1817-1891)

5th Nocturne in G •2 Sx: AA or AT/Pno or 3 Sx: AAA or ATT/Pno •Cen

LHOMME, Charles

Menuet en sol majeur (to R. Letellier) •SATB •Marg

LIADOV, Anatole (1855-1914)

A Musical Snuff-box (Herger) •5 Sx: AATTB •Band

LIAGRE, Dartagnan

Souvenir de Calais •Bsx/Pno •Bil

LIANG, Lei

Peking Opera Soliloquy (1993) •Asx Solo

LIANG, Ming Yue

Compositeur américain d'origine chinoise.
Three Studies on Chinese Folk Song (1988) (to J. Cunningham) •Asx/Pno

LIBERO, Phillip de (see DELIBERO, Phillip)

LIC, Leslaw

Compositeur et professeur de saxophone polonais.
Koncerto (1973) (to J-M. Londeix) 1) Allegro 2) Lento 3) Presto •Asx/Orch or Pno •adr
Quasi improvisando •Asx Solo •adr
Uniwersalny skarbesyk •1 Sx: A or T/Pno •PWM

LIDDLE, Samuel

How Lovely are thy Dwellings (Glenn) •Asx/Pno •B&H

LIEB, Dick (1930)

Compositeur américain, né le 7 III 1930, à Gary (Indiana).
Short Ballet (1971) (12') (to A. Lawrence) •1 Sx: A or S/Band
•Ken

LIEBERMANN, Rolf (1910)

Compositeur, chef d'orchestre, et directeur de théâtre suisse, né à Zurich, le 14 IX 1910. Travailla avec H. Scherchen, W. Vogel, et Ascona.

"Est rattaché au mouvement dodécaphoniste par ses maîtres." (Larousse) "S'orienta rapidement vers le dodécaphonisme dont il a toujours usé sans rigueur, mais avec un tempérament très fort en même temps qu'une ingéniosité raffinée." (Cl. Rostand) "Affectionne les atmosphères de violence tant dans le tragique que dans la bouffonnerie. Il a 'démocratisé' le langage sériel." (H. Halbreich)

"He studied with Wladimir Vogel; became an adherent to the 12-tone method of composition, although without following the strict technique of the Schoenberg school. His interest lies chiefly in the modern musical theater and radio; his dramatic works often bear an allegorical significance." (Baker) "Liebermann used 12-note technique in a free and individual way, with a predilection for bitonality and with tonal references." (P. Ross)

Petit Rondo en Fa (1952) (6') (to E. Cohanier) •Asx/Pno

LIEBMAN, David (1946)

Saxophoniste de jazz américain, né le 4 IX 1946.
Developing a Personal Saxophone Sound (1989) •DP
The Grey Convoy •SATB •AdMu
A Moody Time (1975) •SATB •DP
Remembrance •Solo Instrument/Woodwind Quartet •AdMu
Untitled Duet (1993) •Ssx/Vla •INM

LIESENFELD, Paul (1908)

Chef de musique et compositeur français.
Sérénade (1965) (4') (to J-M. Londeix) •Asx/Woodwind Quintet or
Pno •adr

LIFSCHITZ, Max

Concerto (1992) (to P. Cohen) •Asx/Chamber Orch

LIGNET, Félix (18xx-18xx)

Air célèbre de Stradella (1897) •Asx/Pno •Mil
Thème suisse varié •Asx/Pno •Mil

LILJEHOLM, Thomas (1944)

Compositeur suédois.
Strata (1989) •Asx Solo •SMIC
Turnings (1989) (11') •Asx/4 Perc •SMIC

LILLYA

Album of Favorite Saxophone Solos (Isaac) •Sx Solo •Rub

LIMA, Candido (1939)

Compositeur portugais né à Viana do Castelo, le 22 VIII 1939. Travailla avec Stockhausen, Xenakis, Kagel, et Ligeti.

"His compositional style has evolved from impressionism through 12-note serialism to embrace later techniques." (J. Carlos Picoto)
Cantica II (1987) •Sx/Cl/Perc

LIMBERG, Hans Martin

Compositeur allemand.
L'arrivée (1990) •Tsx/Org •Eres
Quatre pieces (1990) •Tsx/Org •Eres
Saxophonietta (1992) •Asx/Pno •Eres

LIMNANDER de NIEUWENHOVE, Armand (1814-1892)

Compositeur belge, né à Ghent, le 22 V 1814; mort à Moignanville (près de Paris), le 15 VIII 1892. Travailla avec Fetis.
Quintette •5 Sx: SSATB •Sax

LINCKE, Paul (1866-1946)

The Glow Worm (Glenn) •Asx/Pno •Kjos/Rub

LINDBERG, Magnus (1958)

Compositeur et pianiste finlandais, né le 27 VI 1958, à Helsinki. Travailla avec P. Heininen, puis avec Donatoni, Ferneyhough, G. Grisey, V. Globokar, et I. Xenakis.

"Art tout de contraste et de dynamisme sonore. Magnus Lindberg appartient à cette génération de compositeurs pour qui la musique ne peut se situer qu'à mi-distance du sérialisme et du spectralisme." "Se proposant 'd'associer l'hypercomplexe et le primitif,' Magnus Lindberg préoccupé de 'l'harmonie sous toutes ses formes' manifeste dans sa musique une énergie, une diversité et une vitalité de langage remarquables." "La musique faite de masses limpides, précises et rationnelles, dénuée de chantonnements romantiques, le rapproche de Xénakis." (J-N. von der Weid)
Linea d'ombra (1981) (15') •Fl/Asx/Guit/Perc •WH/FMIC

LINDBERG, Nils (1933)

Compositeur suédois.
Dalasvit (1988) (15') •SATB •CG
Progression (1985) (28') •Fl/Ob/Cl/Hn/Bsn/Jazz Group: 2 Sx: SA/
Pno/Bass/Drum •SMIC
Torn-Eriks visa •SATB

LINDELL, Rolf (1929)

Compositeur suédois.
Kalejdoskopisk suite (1973) (15') •5 Sx: SAATB •STIM

LINDEMAN, Peter Brynie (1858-1930)

Organiste et professeur norvégien, né le 1er II 1858 à Christiana; mort à Oslo, le 1er I 1930. Travailla avec son père, Ludwig Mathias.
Gloxinta : Impression •Vln/Cl/Tsx/Pno

LINDEMANN, Henry & Harold BLANCHARD

18 Modern Hot Saxophone Solos •Mills
The Henry Lindemann Method •Mills
In schoen Nacht •Asx/Pno
Nocturno
Pimiento •Asx or Bb Sx/Pno •Sal
Quicksilver •Asx or Bb Sx/Pno •Sal
Wistaria •Asx or Bb Sx/Pno •Sal

LINDEMUTH, William (1915)

Pavane for a Japanese Princess •Asx/Pno •Ka
Rapture •Asx/Pno •Ka

LINDEN, N. van de

Chinese Mars (Lemarc) •4 Sx: SATB or SAAT •TM

LINDEN, Robert E. van de

Compositeur hollandais.
Quartet (1979) •SATB

LINDROTH, Scott

Chasing the Trane out of Darmstadt •Tsx/Pno •WWS
Two Pieces •Asx/Vln/Vla/Vcl/Pno •DP

LINDWALL, Christer

Compositeur suédois.
Cut up (1992) (8') •SATB

LINKE, Norbert (1933)

Compositeur, musicologue, et professeur allemand, né le 5 III 1933, à Steinau-Oder (Silésie). Travailla avec Klussmann.

"In this work the composer abandoned a serial pre-formation of the material to develop a method of composing intended to suspend the perception of time by means of a 'renunciation of any striving towards a goal or sense of direction' so attaining a 'wider mobility' that 'makes possible a direct interaction between presentation in time and placing in space.' (DIBELIUS) "Linke has sought to abolish the barriers between 'serious' and 'light' music." (R. LÜCK)

Matinée de jazz (12') 1) Begin the matinee 2) Twelve-Tone tune
  3) Youth blues 4) The way going at home •Asx/Pno/Perc •adr

LINKOLA, Jukka (1955)

Compositeur et pianiste de jazz finlandais, né le 21 VII 1955.

"The musical idiom of Jukka Linkola is individual and complex. He freely combines different musical elements with no concern for the conventional stylistic principles that tend to restrict expression. His music has always been characterized by the richness of its rhythms and his complex use of percussion instruments, particularly evident in his orchestral work." (A-M. JOENSUU)

Alta (1983) (8') •Vocal group (SATBs)/Octet (2 Sx: AT/Tpt/Trb/
  Pno/Bass/Drums/Perc) •FMIC
Crossings (1983) (33') •Tsx/Orch (3333/4221/Perc/Pno/Celesta/Str)
Joutsen - Swan (1979) (3') •Ssx/Pno •FMIC
Sketches from Karelia •Fl/2 Sx: ST/Str/Perc

LINN, Robert (1925)

Compositeur américain, né à San Francisco. Travailla avec D. Milhaud, H. Stevens, et R. Sessions.

Concerto (1991) (to K. FISCHER) 1) Broad 2) Moderate 3) Slow
  4) Quick 5) Unhurried 6) Fast •Ssx/Wind Ensemble
Prelude and Dance (1964) •SATB •WIM/AvMu
Quartet (9') •SATB •WIM/AvMu
Saxifrage Blue (1977) (to M. WATTERS) (2 movements) •Bsx/Pno
Suite •SATB

LIONCOURT, Guy de (1885-1961)

Compositeur et professeur français, né à Caen, le 1er XII 1885; mort à Paris, le 24 XII 1961. Travailla avec A. Roussel et V. d'Indy.

"Ses oeuvres témoignent d'une fraîcheur d'inspiration alliée à un souci d'équilibre dans l'écriture et la construction." (N. DUFOURCQ) "On lui doit des oeuvres de musique religieuse d'une noble inspiration." (R. BERNARD) "Inspiration médiévale et religieuse, dans un style très traditionnel." (Cl. ROSTAND)

"His music is that of a stalwart of the Schola; in particular, he placed a high value on plainsong and produced a large body of liturgical works." (P. GRIFFITHS)

3 mélodies grégoriennes, op. 60 (1923) •Asx/Org •SAE

LIPTAK, David (1949)

Compositeur américain.

Fantasy (1980) (to J. FORGER) •Asx/Pno •DP
Red Shift (1988) (16') (to J. FORGER) •Asx/Ensemble (Fl+Alto Fl/
  Ob+EH/Cl+BsCl 0/1000/Pno/Perc/Str) •adr
Statements (1971) 1) Adagio 2) Allegretto 3) Recitativo 4) Allegro
  •SATB •WWS

LIST, Andrew

Compositeur américain.

Concerto (1990) (to K. RADNOFSKY) (2 movements) •Asx/Orch •adr

LISZT, Franz (1811-1886)

Chant d'amour (ROMBY) •Asx/Pno •PB
Dream of Love •4 Sx: AATB/Pno ad lib. •Bri
Liebesträum (BONNEL) •AATB •Selm

Liebesträum (SMITH) •2 Sx: AA or AT/Pno •Bar
Liebesträume - Notturno n° 3 (BICHLER) •Asx/Pno •Zim
Phantasie un fuge "Ad nos, ad salutarem undam" (SAVOIE) •12 Sx:
  SnoSSAAATTTBBBs
Poème d'amour (VIARD) •Asx/Pno •Sal
Rêve d'amour (CHAUVET) •Asx/Pno •Cou
2me Rhapsodie hongroise (ROMBY) •Asx/Pno •PB
Rhapsodie hongrioise n° 11 (HOLMES) •AATB •Bar

LITTLE, David

Stonehenge Study 12 (1991) (10') •Tsx Solo •Don

LITTLE, Lowell

Great Duets (2 volumes) •PA
*Know Your Saxophone: Prerequisite Study for Mastery of the
  Instrument* •PA

LLANAS, Albert

Compositeur espagnol.

Contexto V 1) Misterioso 2) Giusto 3) Dolente, senza tempo
  4) Meccanico •SATB

LLEWELLYN, Edward

My Regards (LILLYA) •1 Sx: A or T/Pno •CF/Rem/DP

LLOPIS, Miguel V. BERNAT

Saxophoniste, clarinettiste, et professeur espagnol.

El saxofon - Metodo progressivo de iniciacion (1986) •UME
El saxofon classico - Metodo par saxofon y oboe (1987) •UME

LLOYD, Cy (1950)

Compositeur anglais.

Saxophone Quartet (1969) •SATB •adr

LLOYD, Jonathan (1948)

Compositeur anglais.

John's Journal (1980) (15') (to J. HARLE) Sunday - Monday -
  Tuesday -Wednesday - Thursday - Friday - Saturday (Sunday)
  •1 Sx: S+A/Pno •B&H

LLOYD, Richard G. (1952)

Compositeur américain, né à Utica (New York).

Breath Baby (1984-85) •Bsx/Amplified Pno
Stitched (1984) (13') (to L. N. FONTAINE) •Bsx Solo

LOBL, Karl Maria

Compositeur autrichien.

Quintette (1941) •Asx/Pno
Suite No. 1 in G Major •Asx/Pno •Eto
Suite No. 2 in C Major •Asx/Pno •Eto

LOCATELLI, Pietro (1695-1764)

Sonata in E Minor •2 Sx: AA or TT •EK

LOCHE, Henri

Arioso (1990) •Asx/Pno •Bil
Humoresque •Asx/Pno •Bil

LOCHU, Eric

Deguy jazz •SATB •SL
Lucky sax et Quart sax (1990) •SATB •Com

LOCKLAIR, Dan (1949)

Cavartine (1975) (to E. GREGORY) •Asx/Pno
Concerto (1976) (to E. GREGORY) •Asx/Wind Ensemble

LOCKWOOD, Harry

Compositeur américain.

Lyric Piece •Asx/Tpt/Vla/Tuba

Sonata •Asx/Pno

LOEFFLER, Charles Martin (1861-1935)

Compositeur et violoniste américain d'origine alsacienne, né à Mulhouse (France), le 30 I 1861; mort à Medfield (Massachusetts), le 19 V 1935. Travailla à Paris avec E. Guiraud. Fixé aux U.S.A. depuis 1881.

"C'est en grande partie grâce à lui que les compositeur américains parvinrent à s'affranchir de la tutelle germano-romantique et à considérer la création musicale, non plus comme une imitation plus ou moins servile de glorieux modèles, mais bien comme une tentative de découvrir un monde nouveau, inexploré, et qui soit conforme à leur génie national propre. Le rôle qu'il a joué dans l'évolution de la musique américaine est certainement plus considérable qu'on ne l'imagine communément." (R. BERNARD) "Sa production fortement teintée d'impressionnisme, reflète aussi le tempérament mystique de son auteur, ainsi que ses connaissances en matière de musique médiévale religieuse." (N. DUFOURCQ) "Son oeuvre, essentiellement française d'esprit et de syntaxe, a profondément influencé la première décade du siècle et puissamment contribué à la rupture avec le style académique." (A. GAUTHIER)

"Loeffler's participation in American music is unique: he was brought up under many different national influences, Alsatian, French, German, Russian and Ukrainian. His esthetic code was entirely French, with definite leanings toward Impressionism; the archaic construction that he sometimes affected, and the stylized evocations of 'ars antiqua,' are also in keeping with the French manner. He was a master of colourful orchestration; his harmonies are opulent without saturation; his rhapsodic forms are peculiarly suited to the evocative moods of his music. His only excursion into the American idiom was the employment of jazz rhythms in a few of his lesser pieces." (BAKER) "He defies precise classification. The strong feeling for line as wall as for colour in his music renders somewhat inaccurate the grouping of him with the French impressionists. A bold and individual harmonist, he treated dissonances as the outcome of a free polyphony rather than arbitrarily as discord for its own sake. Modal influences derived both from the music of the Russian liturgy and from plainsong play an important part in his style. While his music was never influenced by the country of his adoption, it variously reflects the idioms of Russia, Ireland and Spain. In an era of virtuoso orchestration his instrumentation commanded special admiration." (GROVE)

Ballade carnavalesque (1904) (to E. HALL) •Fl/Ob/Asx/Bsn/Pno •South

Divertissement espagnol (1900) (8') (to E. HALL) •Asx/Orch (2222/223/Perc/Harp/Str) •South

The Lone Prairée (c. 1930) (4') •Vla d'amore (or Vla)/Tsx/Pno •TTF

Rhapsodie (to E. HALL) •Asx/Pno

LOEILLET, Jean-Baptiste (1680-1730)

Adagio and Allegro (VOXMAN & BLOCK) •Tsx/Pno •South
Gavotte (LONDEIX) •Asx/Pno •Lem
Siciliana (LONDEIX) •Asx/Pno •Lem
Sonata (MERRIMAN) •Asx/Pno •South
Sonata, op. 3, no. 3 •Ssx/Pno
Trio (HORNIBROOK) •2 Sx: ST/Pno •Eto

LOGOTHETIS, Anestis (1921)

Compositeur autrichien d'origine grecque, né à Pyrgos. Travailla avec A. Uhl et E. Ratz. Vit à Vienne.

"Il s'est d'abord manifesté dans un style wébernien, dont il a rapidement débordé la rigueur pour aller vers un art apparenté à celui de John Cage et faisant appel à des éléments aléatoires. Il utilise des signes graphiques de notation musicale extrêmement personnels et originaux—fort décoratifs d'ailleurs. Une très vive imagination sonore

se dégage de ses compositions." (Cl. ROSTAND)

"Before 1959 he composed a number of 12-note and serial works in traditional notation. Then, aiming at greater fluidity of form, he gradually turned to graphic methods, developing what he has termed 'integrating' notation." (G. S. LEOTSAKOS)

Impulsion (1956) - Composition variable - Série rouge. Cahier 34 •Uni

LOGRANDE, L. A.

Compositeur américain.

An Appeal Amid the Razing (1994) (7') (to A. WEN & M. REYNOLDS, Commissioned by the University of Arkansas at Monticello) •Asx/Band •CI

Apparitions From Experience (1990) (5') •Asx Solo •CI
Harlequin of the Union (1993) (6'30) •2 Sx: SA •CI
ie, integrity eclipsed (1993) (6') (to A. WEN) •Ssx Solo •CI

LOLINI, Ruggero (1932)

Compositeur italien. Travailla avec Fr. Poulenc et D. Milhaud.

Molto riflesso (1975) •SATB
Nel cantore del vento (1985) (to F. MONDELCI) •Asx Solo
Onan e l'obbedieuza •4 Sx: Sno+S ATB/Pno
Solitudini declinate (1985) (8'10) (to F. MONDELCI & M. MAZZONI) •2 Sx: Sno+A B
Spirale •3 Sx: SAT
Stanze d'Ambra (1984) (to Quatuor d'Ance italiano) •Ob/Cl/Asx/Bsn
Tutti i colori dell'alba (1986) (to F. MONDELCI et G. GIULIODORI) •Asx/Pno

LOMANI, Borys Gregorz (1893-1975)

Compositeur polonais, né à Rydz, le 11 IV 1893; mort à Varsovie le 11 VII 1975. Travailla à Saint Pétersbourg avec A. Glazounov.

Concertino, op. 118 (1958) 1) Andante non troppo 2) Tempo di valsa 3) Vivo-Andante-Vivo •Asx/Pno •PWM/B&H
3 Miniatures (1964) 1) Sad romance 2) Little waltz 3) Song •Asx/Pno •PWM
3 Pièces, op. 133 (1961) 1) Song without words 2) Melody 3) Brazilian song •Asx/Pno •PWM

LOMBARDO, Robert Michael (1932)

Compositeur américain, né l e 5 III 1932, à Hartford (Connecticut).

Cantabile (1980) (to Thomas SMIALEK) •Asx/Vibr •adr
Fantasy Variations No. 4 •Asx Solo
Piece (1982) •Asx/Pno •adr

LONARDONI, Markus (1961)

Compositeur allemand, né le 16 XII 1961 à Esslingen. Travailla avec N. J. Schneider.

Modal interchange (1987) (6') •Sx/Perc/Pno/Guit/Bass

LONDEIX, Jean-Marie (1932)

Saxophoniste concertiste, professeur, animateur, et arrangeur français, né à Arveyres (Gironde), le 20 IX 1932. Travailla avec son père, P. Ferry, F. Oubradous, et M. Mule. Enseigna aux conservatoires de Dijon (1953), Bordeaux (1971), et, entre temps, à l'Université du Michigan (1968).

A la découverte des maîtres du 18e siècle (1975) (3 Collections) •Asx/Pno •Lem
A la découverte des maîtres du 18e siècle (1975) (3 Collections) •Bb Sx/Pno •Lem
Beau Dion (1976) (2') •Tsx/Pno •Comb
Ciné-Max - Hommage à Max Linder (1983) (18') 1) Sketches 2) Burlesque •12 Sx: SnoSSAAATTTBBBs •adr
Les classiques du saxophone Sib (1974) •Bb Sx/Pno •Led
De l'intonation (1981) •2 Sx: AA or TT or AT •Led

Le Détaché, Staccato (1967) •Lem

Eclesia II (Negro Spirituals, PURCELL, MOZART, BACH, etc.) •1 Sx: A or S/Org or Pno •Fuz

Etudes à douze d'après Chopin, Debussy (1993) •12 Sx: SnoSSAAATTTBBBs •adr

8 Etudes techniques, op. 8 (1960/92) •Sx Solo •Com

Exercices d'intonation - tous niveaux et tous saxophones [all levels and all saxophones] (1993) •Led

Exercices mécaniques (3 volumes) (1960-1965) •Lem

Exercices pratiques (1983) •4 to 12 Sx •Led

Les Gammes conjointes et en Intervalles (1962) •Lem

Gammes et modes d'après Debussy, Ravel et Bartok (2 Volumes) (1968) •Led

Méthode de rythme à l'usage des instrumentistes (3 Volumes) (1972) •Led

125 ans de musique pour saxophone (1958-1969) •Led

Music for Saxophone Volume II (1985) •Ron

Nouvelles études variées - avec suraigu (1983) •Led

Playing the Saxophone (Translation [Traduction] S. TRIER) (2 Volumes) (1973-76) •Lem

Il sassofono nella nuova didattica (Translation [Traduction] A. DOMIZI) (1986) (2 Volumes) •Ber

El Saxofon ameno (Translation [Traduction] M. MIJAN) (1988) (2 Volumes) •AE

Saxophon spielend leicht (Translation [Traduction] G. PRIESNER) (3 Volumes) (1978) •BFS

Le Saxophone en Jouant (4 Volumes) (1962-1971) •Lem

Tablature des doigtés comparés des notes suraigües du Saxophone alto (1974) •Led

Tableaux aquitains, op. 10 (1973) (5'30) 1) Bachelette 2) La gardeuse de porcs 3) Le traverseur de landes 4) Le raconteur d'histoires •Asx/Pno •Led

Die Tonleiter in Tonfolge und in Intervallen (1962-80) •Lem

LONDON, Edwin Wolf (1929)

Compositeur américain, né le 16 III 1929, à Philadelphia (Pennsylvania). Travailla avec L. Dallapiccola et D. Milhaud.

Balls (1985) (to H. SMITH) •Asx/Pno

Pressure Points (1972) (10') (to J. YANNATOS & H. SMITH) •Asx/Orch (2222/4331/Pno/Perc/Str) •adr

LONG, Duncan (1949)

Compositeur américain, né le 6 II 1949, à Smith Center (Kansas).

Future past perfect (1971) (8'30) •Sx/Tape •adr

Weep dark flame (1976) (to E. GREGORY) •Asx/Tape •adr

LONG, Newell H.

Undercurrent - Theme & Variations •Bsx/Pno •Rub

LONGY, George Léopold (1868-1930)

Hautboïste français, né à Abbeville, le 29 VIII 1868; mort à Mareuil (Dordogne), le 29 III 1930.

Impression (1902) (to E. HALL) •Asx/Orch or Pno

Rhapsodie - Lento (1906) (to E. HALL) •Harp/Bass/2 Cl/Bsn/Asx/ Timp or Asx/Pno •South

LONQUE, Armand Joseph (1908)

Compositeur belge.

Morceau de concours, op. 56 (1953) •Asx/Pno •HE/EMB

LONQUE, Georges (1900-1967)

Compositeur belge, né à Gand, le 8 XI 1900, mort à Bruxelles, le 3 III 1967. Travailla avec L. Moeremans, E. Mathieu, et M. Lunssens. Prix de Rome (1929).

"Strongly influenced by Franck in his early works, he remained a romantic." (H. VANHULST)

Images d'Orient, op. 20 (1935) (11') (to V. GUTCHE) •Asx/Orch (2222/222/Perc/Harp/Str) or Pno •Led

LOPEZ, CALVO

Compositeur espagnol.

Tema con variaciones •SATB

LOPEZ, Jose Susi

Compositeur espagnol.

Diàlogos (1993) •Ssx/Pno •INM

LOPEZ, Tom (1965)

Compositeur américain, né à Cincinnati. Etudes de musique électronique à l'Oberlin College.

"In what far part of the world" (1994) (to D. LOPEZ) •Soprano Voice/Asx

LOPEZ-LOPEZ, José-Manuel (1956)

Compositeur espagnol, né à Madrid. Travailla avec L. Nono, F. Donatoni, L. Hiller, C. Halffter, et P. Boulez.

Con cadencia de eternidad (1989) (9') (to D. KIENTZY) •Bsx/Tape

LOPEZ MA, Jorge

La palabra (1983) (to VILLAFRUELA) •Sx Solo

LORDERO, Rogue

Soliloques N° 2 •Sx Solo •Meri

LORENTZEN, Bent (1935)

Compositeur danois, né le 11 II 1935 à Stenvad. Travailla avec K. Jeppesen et J. Jersild.

"Lorentzen a commencé très tôt à travailler avec les principes sériels, et à travers les années 1970, il y ajouta de plus en plus de paramètres. Depuis 1980, on perçoit aussi nettement la présence dans sa musique de rythmes d'Amérique latine."

"Experience gained in the electronic field was further exploited in the late 1960s and early 1970s in instrumental compositions." (J. BRINCKER)

Concerto (1986) (23') (to D. PITUCH) •Sx/Wind Orch (2222/221/ BsTrb/Tuba/Pno/Perc) •WH

Farbentiegel •Asx/Pno

Lines (7'45) •SATB

Round (1981) (6') (to D. PITUCH) •Sx Solo •WH

LOSEY, F. H.

Woodland Whispers (KLICKMANN) •2 Sx: AA •EMa

LOTICHIUS, Erik

Compositeur néerlandais.

Kwartet (1980) (8') •SATB •Don

LOTTER, Adolph

Rouge et noir •1 Sx: A or T/Pno •B&H

LOTTERIE, G.

Petite pièce d'examen (2'30) •Tsx/Pno •Bil

LOTTI, Antonio (1667-1740)

Arietta (MAGANINI) •1 Sx: A or T/Pno •Mus

Vere languorus (EVERTSE) •3 Sx: AAT •Lis

Vere languores e Dominus noster castellum (EVERTSE) •3 Sx: SAT or AAT •TM

LOTZENHISER, George William (1923)

Poco Waltz •Asx/Pno •Bel

LOUIGUY

Cherry Pink and Apple Blossom White •Asx/Pno •WWS

LOUKIANOV, G.
Compositeur russe.
Quatuor en Si •SATB

LOUP, Félix (1906)
Pavane à un héros disparu (1939) (8'10) (to Quatuor M. Perrin) •SATB

Quatuor en Sol mineur (to C. François) 1) Cantilène 2) Rêverie 3) Cavalcade •SATB •Mar

LOUVIER, Alain (1945)
Compositeur français, né à Paris. Travailla avec T. Aubin et O. Messiaen.

"Classé parmi les sujets les plus prometteurs de la jeune école au niveau de l'avant-garde." (Cl. Rostand) "Musiques de gestes instrumentaux."

"His own music reveals a lively and adventurous personality." (A. Girardot)

5 Ephémères (1981) (7') (Commande de l'AsSaFra) •Ssx/Pno •Led

Hydre à cinq têtes •Asx/Pno •Led

Le jeu des sept musiques (1986) (10') 1) "Free jazz" 2) Récitatif d'opéra 3) Constellations 4) Frileuses 5) Valse mécanique 6) Marche militaire 7) Les 7 musiques 8) Anathème 9) Trompettes 10) Vagues 11) Valse interrompue 12) Jericho 13) Sortie des artistes •Asx/3 Sx: STB •Led

5 Portraits et une image (1973) (to P. Pareille) Le Fantasque - Le Fugitif - Le Sage - Le Frénétique - Le Mélancolique et une Image •Ob/Cl/Asx/Bsn •Led

LOVE, Randy
Passerine aria (1981) (to D. Masek)

LOVEJOY, Michel
Compositeur anglais.

"Je suis un compositeur heureux d'écrire de la musique tonale." (M. Lovejoy)

Sonatine lyrique (1974) (to J. Denman) •Asx/Pno

LOVELOCK, James
Compositeur australien.

Konzert (1970) (to P. Clinch) •Asx/Str Orch

LOVELOCK, William (1899)
Compositeur et organiste australien d'origine anglaise, né à Londres, le 13 III 1899. Vit en Australie depuis 1956.

Concerto (1973) (to P. Clinch) •Asx/Orch or Pno

Final •SATB

Quartet (1977) (to P. Clinch) •SATB

Sonata (1974) (18') (to P. Clinch) 1) Adagio sempre liberamente e rubato - Allegro 2) Molto vivo allegro 3) Adagio liberamente - Allegro •Asx/Pno

Suite (1978) Allegro - Andante - Presto - Finale •SATB •APRA

LOVREGLIO, Eleuthère (1900-198x)
Compositeur français d'origine italienne né à Naples, le 22 II 1900.

"Musique claire, prudemment écrite, orchestrée avec beaucoup de goût et de soin." (P. Le Flem) "Ecriture aristocratique." (L. Roggero) "Equilibre fait de sécurité et de majesté, une expression rayonnante et individuelle." (R. Doire)

"Lovreglio, who lives in France, is said to have composed after several months spent in a Buddhist Monastery in China. His work has originality, unusual tonal effects, and achieves a definite atmospheric purpose." (Star and Times)

Andante (1938) (4') (to M. Mule) •SATB •EFM

Concerto (1938) •SATB/Orch •Heu

Humoresque (1962) (6') (to M. Mule) •Asx/Pno •Com

Jacareros (1935) (9') •SATB

Quatuor (1937) (28') (to Quatuor Mule) •SATB

Variations sur un thème breton (1937) (7') •SATB

LOWDEN, Bob
Easy Play-Along Solos •Eb or Bb Sx/Recorded Accompaniment •Ken

LOWRY, Richard (1951)
Compositeur français d'origine anglaise, directeur de conservatoire.

Pièce (1982) •Asx/Org

LUBAT, Bernard
Musicien de jazz français.

Deux temps s'entend sans temps (1982) Lent - Vif •SATB

LUBIN, Ernest Viviani (1916)
Compositeur et pianiste américain, né le 2 V 1916 à New York.

Gavotte •SATB •adr

Lady of the Lake •SATB •adr

LUC, Francis (1948)
Compositeur français né à Paris. Travailla avec F. Vandenbogaerde, puis avec Stockhausen, Ligeti, Lutoslawski, Dutilleux, Xenakis, et Kagel.

Concerto (1981) (15') (to D. Kientzy) •1 Sx: Sno+A+T+B/Tape

Eliantheme (8') •Asx/Harp/Tape

LUCAS, Leighton (1903-1982)
Compositeur et chef d'orchestre anglais, né le 5 I 1903 à Londres, où il est mort en 1982.

Sonatina concertante (1939) •Asx/Chamber Orch

LUCIER, Alvin
Music for solo performer •Any solo instrument

LUCKEY, Robert A. (1948)
Saxophoniste de jazz américain, né à Dunbar (Pennsylvania). Travailla avec L. Rocereto et B. Cerilli, D. Borst, R. Lloyd, W. Willett, P. Swanson, D. DiCicco, N. Koval, et N. Davis.

Saxophone Altissimo (1992) •OMP

LUDWIG, J.
Stenogramme •Fl/Tsx/Trb/Bass/Vibr/Harps/Perc •EMod

LUEDEKE, Raymond (1944)
Compositeur canadien.

Accrostic (1976) •4 Sx: SATB/Pno •CMC

Concerto (1977) (33') •SATB/Orch (2222/4231/Timp/Str) •CMC/ ACA

Fancies and Interludes (1979) (20'30) Fancy I Interlude I - Fancy II Interlude II - Fancy III Interlude III - Fancy IV •Asx/Pno •ACA

Garbage Delight (1988) (29') •5 Sx: SATBBs •CMC

"Of him I love day and night" & "A noiseless, patient spider" •Chorus (SATB)/4 Sx: SATB/Bass/2 Perc

LUFT, J. Heinrich (1813-1868)
24 Etudes (Bleuzet) •Bil

24 Etudes in duets (Bleuzet) •2 Sx •CFE

LUGLI, Lanfranco
Compositeur italien.

A la page (1992) (8') •2 Sx: AT/Pno 4 hands (à 4 main)

LUKAS, Zdenek (1928)
Compositeur tchèque, né à Prague, le 21 VIII 1928. Travailla avec Modr et Ridky.

"With the two sinfoniettas (1957, 1962) Lukas developed a polyphonic manner close to Martinu, and then he followed directions suggested by the work of Kabelac, employing the newest techniques. Particularly in the later concertante pieces, Lukas' music derives from minimal initial material." (O. Pukl)

Koncert (1963) (22') •Ssx/Orch (3232/42311/Perc/2 Harp/Str) •CHF

Rondo, op. 70 (1970) (12') (to S. Rascher) •SATB •CHF

Legenda (1972) (9') •Tsx/Pno •CHF

Raccontino (1980) (10') (to L. Bangs) •1 Sx: B or T/2 Perc •CHF

2 + 2 (1982) (14') (to H. Bok & E. Le Mair) •Sx+BsCl/ Marimba+Vibr

LUKASIK, Joseph

Compositeur américain.

Concertino (1992) (16') (for M. Myer) 1) A few opening remarks 2) Nocturne 3) Moto perpetuo •Asx/Computer

LUKIJNOV, German

Compositeur russe.

Quartet in Bb (to Michailov Quartet) •SATB

LULLY, Jean-Baptiste (1632-1687)

Air tendre et Courante (Mule) •Asx/Pno •Led

Ballet du roi - Sarabande et gavotte (Londeix) •Bb Sx/Pno •Led

Dances for the King (Felix) •Bb Sx/Pno •Mus

Gavotte (Mule) •Asx/Pno •Led

Menuet (Le Bourgeois Gentilhomme) (Mule) •Asx/Pno •Led

Overture to Armide •6 Sx: SAATTB •WWS

Phaeton (Mule) •Bb Sx or Eb Sx/Pno •Led

LUNDE, Ivar Jr. (1944)

Quartet, op. 54 (1975) •SATB •DP

Sonata in One Movement, op. 49 (1973) (15') •Asx/Pno •DP

LUNDE, Lawson (1935)

Compositeur américain, né le 22 XI 1935, à Chicago. Travailla avec V. Rieti et R. Delaney.

A Trip to Pawtucket (O. Shaw) (1964) (1') (to B. Minor) •Asx/Pno •NSM

Alsacian Serenade, op. 31 (1969) (4') (to B. Minor) •Asx/Vcl •adr

Celtic pasan, op. 36 (1969) (4') (to B. Minor) •Asx/Vcl •adr

Hommage to Shostakovich, op. 35 (1969) (4') (to B. Minor) •Asx/ Vcl •adr

Meditation, op. 32 (1969) (5') (to B. Minor) •Asx/Vcl •adr

Music, op. 21a (1964) (10') (to B. Minor) (from *Sonata*, op. 21)
1) Moderato 2) Allegro marcato 3) Allegro molto 4) Comodo •Asx Solo •NSM

Scherzo, op. 38a (from *Sonata*, op. 38) (1970) (4') •Bsx/Pno •adr

Sonata No. 1, op. 12 (1959) (to C. Leeson, B. Minor & J. Bestman)
1) Allegro 2) Andante cantabile 3) Allegro vivace •Asx/Pno •NSM/South/SMC

Sonata, op. 21 (1964) (16') (to B. Minor) 1) Allegro assai
2) Comodo 3) Allegro molto 4) Moderato 5) Allegro marcato
6) Toccata: Allegro molto •Asx Solo •NSM/South

Sonata - Duet, op. 25 (1967) (10') (to C. Leeson) 1) Allegro giocoso
2) Moderato 3) Alla breve •2 Sx: AT •SMC

Sonata, op. 30 (1968) (15') (to C. Leeson) 1) Molto moderato
2) Allegro vivace 3) Theme and variations •Tsx/Pno •adr

Sonata "Alpine", op. 37 (1970) (8') (to J. Horency) 1) Allegro
moderato 2) Vivo •Ssx/Pno •TTF

Sonata No. 2, op. 38 (1970) (12') (to C. Leeson) 1) Allegro marziale
2) Scherzo: allegro non troppo 3) Giocoso •Asx/Pno •adr

Suite, op. 11 (1959) (8') (to C. Leeson) 1) Prelude 2) Five-Tones
3) Eclogue 4) Interlude 5) Finale •SATB or AATB •TTF

LUNDEN, Lennart (1914-1966)

Compositeur suédois, né à Ytterlännes, né le 11 IX 1914, mort, le 18 XI 1966.

Quadrille •2 Fl/2 Cl/Sx/Bsn •Che

Queen Christina's Song •2 Fl/2 Cl/Sx/Bsn •Che

LUNDER, Hans

Konsertino •Asx/Orch

LUNDIN, Dag (1943)

Compositeur suédois.

Concerto dorico (1979) (16') •Asx/Chamber Orch (2021/3000/Str) •STIM

LUNDQUIST, Torbjörn Iwan (1920)

Chef d'orchestre et compositeur suédois, né à Stockholm, le 30 IX 1920. Travailla avec Dag Wiren.

"Lundquist has incorporated many different modes of expression and stylistic devices in his work to achieve the synthesis he aims for: music in traditional guise, modern and avant-garde elements and jazz-influenced outbursts are confronted with one another." (Sj)

Alla prima (1989) (10') •SATB •SMIC

Concitato (1980) (4'30) (to B. Olsson) •SATB •STIM/SMIC

LUOLAJAN-MIKKOLA, Vilho (1911)

Compositeur finlandais, né le 22 XII 1911.

Elokuisessa Helsingissä (1984) •Asx/Pno •FMIC

LUQUE, Francisco (1954)

Compositeur espagnol, né le 6 II 1954. Travailla avec R. Cochini et H. Vaggione.

Saxofonia (1989) (7') (to D. Kientzy) •1 Sx: Sno+B/Tape

LUROT, Jacques

Compositeur français.

Sextuor (to P. Pareille) •Ob/Cl/Asx/Bsn/2 Women's Voices: SA

LURYE, Peter

Elegy (to P. Cohen) •Asx/Pno

LUSTGARTEN, Dan

De l'écriture de Dieu (1979) •Asx/Pno

Parole de Dieu (1982) (25') •Sx au choix/Dispositif électron.

Variations sur la Parole (1983) •Asx/2 Cl

LUSTIG, Leila

The Language of Bees (1983) (to Amherst Saxophone Quartet) •SATB

LUTTMANN, Reinhard

Compositeur allemand.

Méditation II (1972-77) •Asx/Org •Led

LUTYENS, Elisabeth (1906-1983)

Compositeur anglais, né à Londres, le 9 VII 1906. Travailla à Paris avec Caussade.

"Son oeuvre relève de la technique dodécaphonique." (Larousse) "Lutyens est inféodée au système dodécaphonique, ce qui est assez rare dans son pays." (R. Bernard) "Son style néo-classique révèle une personnalité extrêmement poétique." (Cl. Rostand) "Le représentant le plus pur et le plus dur de la seconde Ecole viennoise *in partibus* fut sans doute une femme, Elisabeth Lutyens." (G. Gefen)

"Elisabeth Lutyens has been a pioneer of 12-tone music in England and, with H. Searle, has laid the foundations for an English national school of 12-note composers. Although not so widely known as that of her comparable contemporaries, such as Rawsthorne and Tippett, her music commands a high regard among musicians for its integrity, its expressive power and the highly imaginative variety of its conceptions and invention… The chamber music and the various chamber concertos are inevitably more subtle, but not less eloquent in their statement of the emotional and musical convictions on which this composer's art is based." (C. MASSON) "As a composer, she progressed from an early Romantic style to an intense Expressionist idiom, with the application of a *sui generis* dodecaphonic technique; with this consummation, she discarded her music written before 1935." (BAKER)

Akapotik Rose, op. 64 (1966) (18') •Soprano Voice/Picc/Fl/Cl/Bsn/
    Cl+Tsx/Vln/Vla/Vcl/Pno
Chamber Concerto, op. 8/2 (1940-41) •Cl/Tsx/Pno/Str •Che
Fantasia, op. 114 (1977) •Asx/10 instruments
Islands, op. 80 (1971) •2 Narr: ST/Picc/Fl/Cl/BsCl/Tsx/Hn/Pno/
    Celesta/Vln/Vla/Vcl/2 Perc

LUTZ-RIJEKA, Wilhelm
Compositeur allemand.
Psy (1993) •Tsx/Computer •INM

LUYO, C.
Geometriche etudie (1981) (to I. MARCONI) •Asx/Org

LUYPAERTS, Guy
Compositeur belge.
Un bon petit diable (1979) •Asx/Harmonie or Pno •Bil
Carnavalesca •SATB •adr
Escapade (1988) (to J-P. RORIVE) •Ssx/Pno •adr

LYON, L. L.
Professeur américain.
How to Play Tones Above the Regular Saxophone Register (1922)

LYNE, Peter (1946)
Compositeur suédois d'origine anglaise, né à Northampton le 21 VII 1946. Travailla avec E. Rubbra et K. Leighton puis, à Stockholm, avec I. Lidholm, avec Lutoslawski, enfin.

"His experience inhibited his creativity for a number of years, the process was a necessary one and his inspiration returned towards the mid-1970s. He does not consider himself avant-garde, but he is amenable to new ideas. He is strongly rooted in tradition, but firmly opposes neo-romantic tendencies." (SJ)

Stampede (1985) (7') •SATB •STIM

LYONS
New Alto Sax Solos (2 Volumes) •Asx/Pno •USC
New Tenor Sax Solos (2 Volumes) •Tsx/Pno •USC

MABIT, Alain

Compositeur français.

Fragment pour un tombeau imaginaire (1992) (to Quatuor de Saxophones d'Aquitaine) •4 Sx: SATB/Org

MABRY, Drake

Compositeur américain.

Ceremony I (1993) (11'45) 1) Preparation 2) Search 3) Meditation •Asx Solo •Lem

7.20.88 (1988) (12') •4 Sx •adr

9.10.89 (1989) (17') •Ssx/Electr. Guit/Bass Guit/Synth/Perc

12.15.89 (1989) (to J. Sampen) •Ssx/Chamber Orch (2 Fl/Picc/111/1111/Pno/2 Perc/Str) •adr

MACBETH, Allan (1856-1910)

Intermezzo 'Forget me not' (Brooke) •AATB •CF

Intermezzo 'Forget me not' (Harris) •2 Cl/Asx/Bsn (or BsCl) •CF

MACBRIDE, Robert Guyn (1911)

Professeur, compositeur, clarinettiste, et saxophoniste américain, né à Tucson (Arizona), le 20 II 1911. Travailla avec O. Luening.

"Avant d'être professeur, Robert MacBride s'était fait une réputation pour les titres insolites de ses partitions, puis traversa l'expérience du jazz, et en vint, enfin, à des formes plus traditionnelles." (A. Gauthier)

"His compositions are mostly of a programmatic nature, often on American themes with jazz material." (Baker) "The titles of his works as well as their musical idiom reflect his extensive experience in jazz and theatrical music." (S. Gilbert)

Boogie (1943) (3') •Asx/Pno •ACA

Concerto for Doubles (14') •Asx+Cl/Orch (111 BsCl/0/5 Sx/1341/Harp/Guit/Pno/Str) •ACA

Let Down - Trio •Asx/EH (or Ob)/Pno

Parking on the Parkway •Pio

Warm Up •Sx Solo

The World is Ours •Asx/Pno •ACA/CFE

MACCALL

Two Spirituals •AATB •Lud

Valse Elise •3 Sx: AAT or AAA/Pno •Lud

MACCATHREN (1924)

Chef d'orchestre, clarinettiste américain, né à Gary (Indiana), le 6 VII 1924.

Daily Routine •Lebl

The Saxophone Book (1954) •Lebl

MACCHI, Egisto (1928)

Compositeur italien, né le 4 VIII 1928 à Grosseto. Travailla avec Vlad et Scherchen.

"After an isolated attempt at serialism, Macchi adapted himself to newer techniques, immediately reassessing the formal stability and expressive exuberance that had, in a traditional manner, characterized his previous compositions." (Cl. Annibaldi)

Schemi (1960) •2 Vln/2 Pno/Asx

MACCHIA, Salvatore

Cantando le canzoni d'una stella •Bsx Solo •DP

Concerto (1984) (to L. Klock) •Asx/Wind Ensemble

Duo •Asx/Bass

In a Dark Time (1980) (to L. Klock) •Asx/Pno

Profiles •Asx/Pno

MACCONNELL, Ray

Fantasia •Asx/Pno

MACDOWELL, Edward Alexander (1861-1908)

An Old Garden (Rex) •6 Sx: SAATBBs •WWS

Song (from *Sea Pieces*), op. 55, no. 5 (L. Patrick) •SATB

To a Wild Rose •Eb or Bb Sx/Pno •CF

To a Wild Rose •6 Sx: AATTBBs

To a Wild Rose (Buchtel) •Asx/Pno •Kjos

To a Wild Rose (Blaauw) •Asx or Bb Sx/Pno •Mol

To a Wild Rose (Coggins) •Asx/Pno •BM

To an Old White Pine (Rex) •9 Sx: SAAAATTBBs •WWS

Two Woodland Sketches (Patrick) 1) A Deserted Farm 2) From Uncle Remus •AATB •Pres

MACERO, Teo Attilio Joseph (1925)

Compositeur et saxophoniste (ténor) jazz américain, né à Glens Falls (New York) le 30 X 1925.

Canzona No. 1 •Tpt/4 Sx: AATB •Pres

Canzona No. 1 •2 Vln/Asx/Vcl/Tpt •Pres

Exploration •Asx/Cl/Bass/Perc/Accordion

Structure No. 4 •3 Sx: ATB/Tpt/Trb/Tuba/Perc •ACA

MÁCHA, Otmar (1922)

Compositeur tchèque, né à Ostrava, le 2 X 1922. Travailla avec Hradil et de Rychlic.

"Artiste réfléchi et concentré, il compose lentement, mais on lui doit des oeuvres denses." (Cl. Rostand)

"His early compositions, from the end of World War II, are deeply romantic." (B. Large)

Plâc saxofonu (1968) (6'30) (to S. Rascher) •Asx/Pno •CMIC

Saxophone's Lament •Asx/Pno •CMIC

The Weeping of the Saxophone (1968) (to S. Rascher) •Asx/Pno •CMIC

MACHAJDIK, Peter

Melodie (1993) •Sx/Pno •INM

MACHAUT, Guillaume de (ca. 1305-1377)

Ballade no. 17 (Grainger) •3 Sx: SAA or TTB or 6 Sx: SAATTB •PG

Kyrie (Axworthy) •SATB •DP

Messe de Notre Dame (Axworthy) •SATB •DP/TVA

MACHE, François-Bernard (1935)

Compositeur français, né à Clermont-Ferrand, le 4 IV 1935, dans une famille de musiciens. Normalien, professeur agrégé de lettres et diplômé d'Etudes supérieures d'archéologie grecque. Travailla avec E. Passani et O. Messiaen, puis au Groupe de recherche musicales de l'O.R.T.F. (1955-1963).

"Dans les démarches même expérimentales de François-Bernard Mache, c'est toujours un poète qui s'exprime, avec une imagination audacieuse, dynamique et parfois malicieuse." (Cl. Rostand) "Ses modèles de musique, François-Bernard Mache les emprunte tout aussi bien à un poème de Sapho, de Séféris ou d'Eluard qu'à un tambour de Nubie et, surtout, à la langue bantoue *xhosa*, aux cris des baleines, aux crissements des crevettes, aux piaulements d'un étourneau drogué, aux grognements d'un verrat faisant la cour à une truie, etc., —toutes choses que l'on retrouvera, d'une oeuvre à l'autre, dans la bande mère, dans la matrice musicale du 'cycle mélanésien' auquel Mache travaille." (M. Fleuret) "François-Bernard Mache reste très attaché à une vision relationnelle du réel, situant la musique 'à un point de rencontre entre la pensée et le réel sonore,' et vise ainsi à dissiper les frontières entre nature et culture, entre son brut et son musical." (D. J-Y. Bosseur)

"Tout en réduisant, dans ses oeuvres, la bande magnétique au rang de support de sons naturels enregistrés et conservés tels quels, il s'inspire de cette nouvelle écoute pour faire produire aux instruments, jouant en direct par-dessus cette bande, des commentaires ou des imitations stylisées de ces mêmes sons. Cette démarche s'inscrit dans une problématique de la nature et de la culture et dans une conception visant à arracher la musique au modèle rétrécissant du 'langage.' " (J. & Br. Massin) "En musique un des rares représentants du courant 'naturaliste.' Il s'efforce de mettre en lumière les rapports de structures entre les lois de l'univers et les formes sonores, des plus élémentaires aux plus complexes." (J-N. von der Weid)

"The example of Varèse, that formed the basis for Mache's creative work, which took him in a direction independent of both the serial school and the *musique concrète* group. Essential to his outlook is the belief that any sound may be perceived and used musically, but that the fundamental musical unit is not a sound object, rather a relationship. This openness with regard to material has led to a number of very diverse works, sometimes drawing on non-European music." (G. J. Faccarello)

Aulodie (1983) (11') •Ssx/Tape •Dur

MACHOVER, Tod (1953)

Compositeur et violoncelliste américain né à New York. Travailla avec E. Carter, R. Sessions, et L. Dallapiccola. Directeur de la Recherche Musicale à l'IRCAM-Paris.

"La musique de Tod Machover représente une application très personnelle des technologies mises au point à l'IRCAM." "Une de ses principales préoccupations est le rôle de l'ordinateur dans la musique, et spécialement son utilisation dans les exécutions 'live.' Son oeuvre cherche à créer un langage musical expressif et personnel basé sur les contrastes et les juxtapositions entre les éléments musicaux très différenciés mais cependant liés par des principes unificateurs fondamentaux."

Valise's Song (1989) (5') •1 Sx: S+T/Electr. Guit/Perc/Electr. Bass/ Computer tape •Ric/adr

MACHUEL, Thierry-Joël

Compositeur français.
France-Télécom (1991) •1 Sx: B+S

MACINTYRE, David

Compositeur américain.
Pantomime (1979) •Asx/Pno

MACINTYRE, Hal

Sax Rears its Ugly Head (Matthews) •Asx/Pno •Mut

MacLEAN, John T.

Duo (1982/92) •Tsx/Vcl

MACPHERSON, Ian

Compositeur anglais.
Suite (1978) (15') (to London Saxophone Quartet) •SATB

MACY, Charleton

Compositeur américain.
Connections (1986) (to J. Sampen) •Vln/Asx/Pno

MADDIRK, Daniel Scott

Quartet •SATB

MADDOCKS, David Scott (1932)

Compositeur anglais.
Threnody for Benjamin Britten (1977) (5'30) •SATB
Octet for Nicholas: "O Christi Pieta" (1977) •4 Sx: SATB/Tape (SnoATBs)

MADDOX, Arthur

Tanguitos de los Osos 1) Romanza 2) Tanguito Duo 3) Tanguito Solo 4) Milonga •Cl/Sx/Pno

MADERNA, Bruno (1920-1973)

Compositeur et chef d'orchestre italien, né à Venise, le 21 IV 1920. Travailla avec G. F. Malipiero et H. Scherchen.

"Avec Luigi Nono et Luciano Berio, il complète le grand trio de l'avant-garde italienne au lendemain de la Seconde Guerre Mondiale." (Cl. Rostand) "Bruno Maderna qui a su très tôt concilier une réflexion sur les méthodes nouvelles de composition avec son enracinement dans les traditions occidentales des polyphonistes flamands, considère le système sériel comme 'seul capable de réaliser une synthèse linguistique intégrale' et, en conséquence, de pouvoir prétendre se substituer au principe tonal." (D. J-Y. Bosseur) "Contemporain majeur, Bruno Maderna est probablement celui qui, parmi le Groupe de Darmstadt, est demeuré le plus fidèle aux idéaux d'une jeunesse radicale. La rigueur est le trait majeur de sa production." (C. Glayman)

"He played an unequalled part in the early postwar development of Italian music, presiding, as teacher and conductor, over the early careers of Nono, Berio, Donatoni, Aldo Clementi and others." (Cl. Annibaldi)

Dialodia (1972) (2'15) •2 Like instruments [instruments semblables] •Ric

MAEDA, Satoko

Compositeur japonais.
Anapana (10') •Asx Solo

MAEGAARD, Jan (Carl Christian) (1926)

Compositeur et musicologue danois, né le 14 IV 1926 à Copenhagen. Travailla avec Jeppesen, Schierbeck, Jersild, Larsen, et Schiorring.

"Maegaard has been decisively influenced as a composer by the music of Schoenberg, which has also been his main concern as a musicologist." (J. Brincker)

Musica riservata II (1976) •Ob/Cl/Sx/Bsn

MAERTENS, J.

Compositeur belge.
Moments tristes •Asx/Pno •CBDM

MAES, Jef (1905)

Compositeur belge né à Anvers, le 5 IV 1905. Travailla avec Candael.

"His music is light, though not vulgar." (C. Mortens)

Saxo-scope (10'30) •SATB •CRA

MAGANINI, Quinto (1897-1974)

Flûtiste, compositeur, et chef d'orchestre américain, né à Fairfield (California), le 30 XI 1897, mort à Greenwich (Connecticut), le 10 III 1974. Travailla la composition avec Nadia Boulanger.

"Romantic in spirit, his music is richly melodic and ingeniously contrived. It is freely written, but always based on strict classic forms. Maganini goes his own way, not being particularly concerned about contemporary trends in composition." (D. Ewen)

Ancient Greek Melody (Album) •Bb Sx/Pno •Mus
Beginner's Luck (6 pieces) •AATB •Mus
Canonico Expressivo •2 Sx •Mus
Clair de lune •Eb Sx/Pno •CF
Concert Album (12 pieces) •Tsx/Pno •Mus
Double Canon •4 Sx: AATB or AATT •Mus
In the Beginning (15 pieces) •2 Sx •Mus
Petite suite classique •2 Sx: AT •Mus
Rêverie (Harris) •Fl or Cl/Ob or Cl/Asx/Bsn or BsCl •CF
La Romanesca •Tsx/Guit or Harp •Mus
Song of a Chinese Fisherman •Bb Sx or Asx/Pno •Mus

Stars - valse caprice •Eb Sx/Pno •CF
Three Little Kittens •3 Sx •Mus
Triple Play •3 Sx •Mus
Troubadours •3 Sx: AAT •Mus

MAGNANENSI, Giorgio
Compositeur italien.
Color temporis (1992) (15') •1 Sx: A+B/Pno

MAGNANI, Aurelio (1856-1921)
30 Articulations Studies

MAHDI, Salah (1925)
Professeur, musicien, et écrivain tunisien, né à Tunis, le 9 II 1925. Etudia la musique occidentale à l'Ecole italienne de Tunis et la musique orientale en Tunisie, Egypte, et Syrie. Est le compositeur de l'hymne national tunisien.
Nuit d'Interloken (E. Scerri) (to J-M. Londeix) •Asx/Pno •adr

MAHIN, Bruce
Synapse •MIDI Wind Controller/Computer

MAHLER, Gustav (1860-1911)
A Rückert Song (Hemke) •Asx/Pno •South

MAHY, Alfred (1883-196x)
Compositeur belge, né le 4 VII 1883.
Aubade •Asx/Pno •Mol
Bourrée, cadenze e finale •Bb Sx/Pno •Mol

MAIER SCHANZ, Josef
Compositeur allemand.
Verletzte Gefühle •Sx/Ensemble •INM

MAIGUASHCA, Mesias (1938)
Compositeur équatorien, né à Quito, le 24 XII 1938. Etudia avec Ginastera avant de venir en Allemagne travailler à Darmstadt et Cologne au studio de musique électronique, puis à Paris, à l'IRCAM.
"Some of Maiguashca's early works reveal an interest in Ecuadorian folk music, but it was the contact with Stockhausen that decisively determined his compositional orientation." (G. Béhague)
Lindgrend (1985) (13') •Bsx/Tape
Vorwort zu solaris (1989) (19') (to D. Kientzy) •1 Sx: S+B/
Instrumental ensemble

MAILLOT, Jean (1911)
Chef de musique militaire français, né à Calsi, le 8 VII 1911.
Prélude et divertissement (1969) (4'30) •Asx/Pno •ET
Trio (13'10) 1) Sérénité 2) Sur un air de ronde •3 Sx: ATB •EFM

MAIMAN, Bruce
Quartet No. 1 (1979) (to J. Wytko) •SATB

MAIS, Chester L.
Compositeur américain.
Gossamer Piece (1981) (to M. Taggart) •Ssx/Pno •adr
Licksody (1980) (to M. Taggart) •Asx/Pno
Poem (1974) •Asx/Chorus •adr

MAJOS, Guilio di
Compositeur italien.
Passacaglia per 7 strumenti •Fl/Asx/Hn/Guit/Vibr/Pno/Bass •Sch

MAKRIS, Andreas (1930)
Violoniste et compositeur américain, né en 1930. Prix du Conservatoire de Salonique avant de poursuivre ses études de composition aux U.S.A., puis à Paris avec N. Boulanger.
Fantasy and Dance (1974) (12') (to M. Sigmon) •Asx/Pno •MeP

MALAQUIN, Maurice
Fantaisie •SATB

MALEC, Ivo (1925)
Compositeur croate, né à Zagreb, le 30 III 1925. Travailla avec Cipra, Zaun, O. Messiaen, puis au Groupe de Recherches de Musique Concrète de Paris. Installé en France depuis 1954. De 1972 à 1991, professeur de composition au Conservatoire de Paris.
"C'est l'un des musiciens les plus puissamment doués de sa génération, l'un de ceux qui ont le plus richement et le plus poétiquement tiré parti des acquisitions techniques les plus récentes. Il se développe tout en même temps dans le style électro-acoustique et dans la musique pour instruments traditionnels, combinant à l'occasion les deux langages, suscitant des influences réciproques de ces deux techniques parallèles." (Cl. Rostand) "A travers une double carrière de musicien concret et d'architecte de la voix et des instruments, Malec est parvenu à une maîtrise incomparable. Son art est celui de l'exactitude, de la mesure, de l'équilibre et de l'efficacité. Mais c'est également celui d'une invention jaillissant qui éclabousse et illumine constamment la logique intérieure des constructions musicales." (M. Fleuret) "Après une période purement concrète, puis une période électro-acoustique, Ivo Malec se tourne depuis 1963 vers la musique instrumentale et vocale, associée ou non à la bande magnétique, mais en projetant, dans sa méthode d'approche, une attitude identique à celle pratiquée en laboratoire: mettre en valeur la complexité de la matière sonore elle-même et, à cette fin, avoir 'recours aux diverses manières d'improvisation, avec l'intention de retrouver, dans l'orchestre, les échos de ce 'hasard calculé' que les manipulations aux magnétophones savent parfois si bien justifier.' " (D. J-Y. Bosseur)
"Greatly influenced by the Parisian avant-garde milieu, Malec was one of the first Yugoslav composers to make an international reputation for his use of the new techniques of the 1950s. He has continued to apply the latest compositional practices." (K. Kovacevic)
Lumina (1968-89) (Lauba/Malec) •12 Sx: SnoSSAAATTTBBBs/
Tape •Sal

MALECKI, Maciej (1940)
Compositeur polonais, né à Varsovie. Travailla avec K. Sikorskiego.
Elegia (1988) (5') (to C. Gadzinic) •Asx Solo •AAR

MALEZIEUX, Georges Ernest (1872-1945)
Romance sans parole •Asx/Pno •Sal
Mélodie religieuse •Asx/Pno •Sal
Sur le lac •Asx/Pno •Sal

MALHERBE, Claudy
Non-sun (1984-85) (10') (to D. Kientzy) •Picc/Tsx/Ob/Cl/Bsn

MALIPIERO, Gian Francesco (1882-1973)
Compositeur et musicologue italien, né à Venise, le 18 III 1882, mort à Triseo, le 1 VIII 1973.
"Un amoureux passionné des sonorités étranges et des rythmes rares…" (P. Wolff) "Doué d'une fantaisie très fine, jamais à court d'idées, il excelle dans les courtes notations. C'est surtout par le jaillissement mélodique que vaut sa musique." (P. Collaert) "Peut être considéré comme le Saint-Saëns de la musique contemporaine italienne." (A. Hodeir) "Violent, tourmenté, agressif, éclectique et fécond." (M. Hofmann) "Sous l'influence du renouveau musical français et des antiques traditions de la Renaissance italienne, il lutta entre le vérisme pour imposer un art pur et digne. Il est novateur dans la tradition." (Cl. Rostand). "L'histoire retiendra, outre son intense activité éditoriale (Monteverdi et contemporains), qu'il fut le professeur de Nono et Maderna—fait symptomatique du passage de témoin qui est en train de s'accomplir dans les années quarante et cinquante." (J-E. Fousnaquer)
"Although very uneven, and less influential than Casella and Pizzetti,

he was the most original and inventive Italian composer of his generation." (J. WATERHOUSE) "His absorption in old Italian music determines the principal current of his own works, which are unmistakably national in essence, while cosmopolitan in technique." (BAKER) "Malipiero's earliest compositions, most of them destroyed by him, reveal an essentially romantic nature and, to put it more exactly, a northern romanticism with its love of the supernatural and of nocturnal mystery; and this trait has remained noticeable in his late works, even where the musical expression tends towards pre-romantic modes and styles, and where the composer's whole aesthetic outlook becomes an act of rebellion against 19th-century music..." (G. GATTI)

Canto nell'infinito (MULE) •Asx/Pno •Led

Serenissima - 7 canzoni neveziane (1961) (21') •Orch (3322/420/Perc/Pno/Harp/Str)/Asx concertante •Uni

MALLIE, Loïc (1947)
Compositeur et organiste français, né à La Baule. Travailla avec O. Messiaen.

Sextuor (1989) •Fl/Cl/Asx/Pno/Guit/Perc

MALMBORG, Paula (1962)
Compositeur suédois.

Yakuzi (1992-93) •SATB •SvM

MALMFORS, Ake
Compositeur suèdois.

Quatuor •SATB •ACS

MALMGREN, Jens Ole
Compositeur danois.

Trio (1972) (to Ch. A Grøn) •Fl/Ob/Asx

MALONEY, Michael (1958)
Compositeur américain.

Music (1982) (to C. FORD) •Fl/Asx/Tape

MALOTTE, Albert Hay (1895-1964)
The Lord's Prayer (LAKE) •1 Sx: A or T/Pno •GSch

MALTBY
Heather on the Hill •Asx/Pno •Ken

MALYJ, Katherine
Compositeur américain.

Altarpiece (1993) •Asx/Pno •INM

MAN, Roderik de
Compositeur néerlandais.

Discrepancies (1990) (8') •Don

MANAS, Roger (1897-1965)
Two Pieces •SATB

MANA-ZUCCA (1887-19xx)
Compositeur, pianiste et actrice américaine, née à New York, le 25 XII 1887. Travailla à Berlin avec Busoni.

Walla-Kye, op. 115 (1936) (to C. LEESON) •Asx/Pno •Lee

MANCINI, Henry (1924-1994)
The Pink Panther (DOMIZI) •Ob/Cl/Asx/Bsn
The Pink Panther (FRACKENPOHL) •AATB •Ken

MANDANICI, Marcella
Compositeur italien.

Extraits I (1989) (to E. FILIPPETTI) •Tsx/Fl/Cl/Pno/Perc/Vln/Vla/Vcl •adr

Extraits II (1990) (5') (to E. FILIPPETTI) •Tsx Solo •adr

Nelle lettere di mi (1991) (5') (to E. FILIPPETTI) •Bsx Solo •adr

MANEN, Christian
Dans la forêt •Asx/Pno •Com

MANGELSDORFF, E.
Anleitung zur improvisation •Bb Sx/Pno •Sch

MANIERE, Léon (1885-1954)
Impromptu •SATB •Gras
Canzonetta •SATB
Sicilienne •SATB

MANIET, R.
Habanera (RULST) •2 Cl/2 Sx: AT •EMB

MANNEKE, Danièl (1939)
Organiste et compositeur hollandais, né à Kruiningen, le 7 XI 1939. Travailla avec Van Dijk et De Leeuw.

Vice versa (1979) (14') •5 variable instruments •Don

MANOURY, Philippe (1952)
Compositeur français né à Tulle. Travailla avec G. Condé, M. Deutsch, Ivo Malec, P. Barbaud, et M. Philippot. Collaborateur de l'IRCAM.

"Consacre une large part de son temps au travail sur l'ordinateur. Son oeuvre, instrumentale jusqu'en 1980, s'infléchit vers la pratique de l'électronic-live." (J. & B. MASSIN) "Le reproche que Philippe Manoury adresse aux musiques qui cherchent avant tout à exhorter ceux qui les écoutent à se laisser 'engloutir dans les sons' est très significatif; pour lui, cette attitude n'est pas une innocente démarche d'ordre esthétique mais bien une prise de position idéologique. Une idéologie qui tend à rien moins que plonger les auditeurs dans la plus complète passivité, à détruire en eux tout sens critique, et à les amener à cet état de non-pensée où 'tout est possible', d'où la faiblesse d'investissement intellectuel qui lui est inhérente." (D. J-Y BOSSEUR) "D'une manière générale, Manoury se déclare favorable à 'une musique qui conserve la mémoire de ce qui l'a précédé, tout en étant en perpétuelle évolution.' Loin des années cinquante et soixante, années radicales, Manoury prend son bien là où il le trouve, c'est-à-dire, parfois, dans des directions qui, en leur temps, furent antinomiques. Ce qui le préoccupe surtout, c'est le résultat musical, qui peut fort bien provenir de préceptes différents, qu'il s'agisse des sériels ou de Xenakis. Il ajoute: 'Je ne fais pas de la musique expérimentale mais prends le stade expérimental comme un moment de la composition.' " (C. GLAYMAN) "L'un des rares compositeurs de sa génération à se défier de l'alléchante tentation de l'épigonisme. Manoury choisit une synthèse entre deux esthétiques qui semblaient autrefois incompatibles: celle, du détail, de l'aphorisme; celle, globale, d'un Ligeti ou d'un Xénakis." (J-N. von der WEID)

Etude automatique 1 •Fl/Tpt/Sx/Tuba/Harp/Vln/Vla/Vcl/Bass

MANSHIP, Munch
Dance Suite No. 3 1) Tango 2) Waltz 3) Hop, Hop, Hop, Skip 4) Samba •MIDI Wind Controller/Synth •PBP

Four Songs •Bb or Eb Sx/Pno/Bass/Drums •PBP

MANZIARLY, Marcelle de (1899)
Pianiste et compositeur français, né à Kharkov (Russie), le 13 X 1899. Travailla avec Nadia Boulanger.

"Marcelle de Manziarly semble être la seule vraie disciple en France de Stravinski. Depuis les années 1920, elle a évolué du néo-classicisme à l'assimilation, et, à nouveau, à la variation des motifs de l'avant-garde." (F. GOLDBECK) "Marcelle de Manziarly connaît toutes les ressources de son métier et semble particulièrement curieuse des problèmes rythmiques. Elle a le don de la mélodie, une mélodie capricieuse et asymétrique, qui sourit plus volontiers qu'elle ne se pâme." (R. BERNARD) "Elle est restée soumise au système tonal jusque vers 1940 et s'en est dès lors écartée peu à peu tout en restant libre et indépendante dans le choix de ses moyens d'expression." (Cl. RosTAND)

"Marcelle de Manziarly is one of the most intelligent and independent followers of Stravinsky's doctrine of 'objective composition': her scores are devised to solve many problems of harmonic and contrapuntal syntax in their relation to form, and her solutions are often ingenious and always elegant." (F. GOLDBERG)

Concertino (to M. MULE) •4 Sx/Orch

MANZO, Silvio (1923)

Compositeur italien, né le 11 IX 1923.

2 tempi •4 Sx: SATB/Timp ad lib. •Pet

MANZONI, Giacomo

Compositeur italien.

To planets and to flowers (1990) (7') •SATB

MARACZEK, F.

Sommerabend am Berg, Impressionen •Asx/Orch or Pno •HD

MARBE, Myriam Lucia

Compositeur hollandais.

Concerto pour Daniel Kientzy (33') (to D. KIENTZY) 1 Sx: B+A+Sno/Orch (3333/4231/3 Perc/Harp/Str) •EMu

Hell, Klar, Glanzend (10') (to D. KIENTZY) •Sx/Mezzo Soprano Voice

Überrzeitliches God (1993) •Soprano Voice+Perc/Ssx

MARC, Edmond (1899)

Compositeur français, né à Gouvieux (Oise), le 29 VIII 1899.

"Edmond Marc révèle un don peu commun de ce que l'on pourrait appeler le sens descriptif psychologique." (P. I.)

Pierrot et Colombine (1945) (8') (to M. MULE) •Asx/Pno •Bil

MARCELLO, Allessandro (1684-1750)

Andante and Allegro (VOXMAN) •Bsx/Pno •Rub

Concert in C moll (JOOSEN) •Bb Sx/Pno •Mol

Concerto (ROSSI) •5 Sx: SAATB •DP

Concerto in C Minor (MOROSCO) •Ssx/Pno •DP

Concerto in C Minor (NIHILL) 1) Allegro moderato 2) Andante e spiccato 3) Allegro •Asx/Pno

MARCHAL, Dominique (1952)

Compositeur français.

Bonus est dominus (1980) (5') (to M. PEZZLA/M. PERRIN) •Soprano Voice/Asx/Org •adr

Jesus dulcis memoriam •Soprano Voice/Asx/Choir/Str •adr

Mouvement V (GAMMA) •Asx/Str •adr

Sonatine (1981) (8'40) •Asx Solo •adr

MARCHAND, Jean-Christophe

Hêtraies (1987) (10') •Asx/Str •adr

Sonate •Asx/Pno •adr

MARCHAND, Joseph (16xx-1747)

Air tendre (LONDEIX) •Asx or Bb Sx/Pno •Lem

MARCHETTI, Filippo (1931-1902)

Fascination (HURRELL) •Eb Sx or Bb Sx/Pno •Rub

MARCO, Tomàs (1942)

Compositeur espagnol, né à Madrid, le 12 IX 1942. Travailla avec P. Boulez, Stockhausen, Maderna, Ligeti et Adorno.

"Les fonctions psychologiques peuvent devenir l'élément moteur d'une oeuvre. Tomàs Marco qui ne semble pas concevoir 'un art sans existence physique indépendant du temps' livre les résultats de ses recherches sur les faits psychologiques de l'écoute musicale en une expérience sensorielle ménagée par la plus stricte discipline intellectuelle." (D. J-Y. BOSSEUR)

"His works display a fluid approach, using modern means to create music which is often dreamlike in its progress and resonance." (GROVE)

Anna Blume (1967) •2 Narr/Fl/Ob/Cl/Sx/Tpt/2 Perc

Car en effet... (1965) (10') •3 players: Cl+Sx •Sal

Espejo de viento (1988) (to J-M. LONDEIX) 12 Sx: SnoSSAAATTTBBBs

Jabberwochy (1967) •Voice/Tsx/Pno/4 Perc/Tape

Kwaïdan (1988) (to M. MIJAN) •Asx/Pno

Paraiso mecanico (1988) (13') •SATB •Lem

MARCONI - BRAMUCCI

Indian metamorphosis •Ssx

MARCOUX, Isabelle (1961)

Compositeur canadien, né le 30 V 1961 à Québec. Travailla avec F. Brouw, A. Gagnon, Fr. Morel, B. Cherney, B. Mather, et N. Parent.

Ofaeruffoss (1992) (12') •Ssx/Harp or Pno or 2 Vibr •adr

MARCUSSEN, Kjell (1952)

Compositeur norvégien.

Quartet (1983) •Ob (or Ssx)/Vln/Vcl/Pno •NMI

MARE, Corrado

Sonatina (Lento - Allegretto) •3 Sx: SAB

MARECZEK, Fritz

Sommerrabend am Berg [*Summer Evening on the Mountain*] •Asx/Pno •Zim/Pet

MAREZ OYENS-WANSINK, Tera de (1932)

Compositeur et pianiste néerlandais, né à Velsen, le 5 VIII 1932. Travailla avec J. Ode, H. Henkemans, et G. Koenig.

Kwartet (1985) (to Het Rijnmond Saxophone Quartet) •SATB

Mahpoochah-Lamentation II (1978) (8') •7 or more instruments •Don

Mandala (1988) (16') •Asx/Pno •Don

Powerset (1986) (9'30) •SATB •Don

Sound and silence •Sx/Actress •Don

Trajectory (1985) (8') •SATB •Don

MARGONI, Alain (1934)

Compositeur français, né à Neuilly-sur-Seine, le 13 X 1934. Travailla avec T. Aubin, J. Fourestier, H. Challan, M. Martenot, et O. Messiaen.

Cadence et danses (1974) (to D. DEFFAYET) •Asx/Pno •EFM

In memoriam (1982) •Asx/Org •Bil

Promenades romaines I, II et III (1993-94) 1) A l'aube sur la voie Appienne 2) Sur le Palatin 3) Nuit de Noël au Tastevere •Asx/Pno •Bil

1er Quatuor (1990) (11'40) (to Quatuor Fourmeau) 1) Chaconne 2) Intermezzo 3) Réjouissance •SATB •Bil

2me Quatuor (1991) •SATB

Sonate (1976) (to J. LEDIEU) •Bsx/Pno

Triple fugue (1981) •2 Sx: AB/Org

MARI, Pierrette (1929)

Compositeur, critique musical et musicologue français, née à Nice, le 1er VIII 1929. Travailla avec Tony Aubin et O. Messiaen.

"Son style, à prédominance tonale, donne une importance majeure aux problèmes de la forme la plus stricte." (HEUG)

Badinerie (3'20) •Asx/Pno •ET

La comète tenue en laisse (1987) •1 Sx: A or T/Pno •Bil

Corollaire d'un songe (1976) (to J. DESLOGES) •Bb Sx/Pno •Arp

De trois à quatre (1974) (to Quatuor Desloges) •SATB •adr

Fleur de crainte sauvage •Asx/Pno •adr

Jacasserie (1960) (to J. DESLOGES) •Ssx/Pno •Com

Paysage nocturne (1961) (4') (to J-M. Londeix) •Asx/Org •adr
Pièce (1959) (6') (to J-M. Londeix) •Asx/Pno •adr
Trio pour saxophones (1956) (to J. Desloges) •3 Sx: SAT •adr

MARIASY, David
Compositeur américain.
Private Eye (1982) (to J. Sampen) •Ssx/Tape

MARIE, E.
La tyrolienne - Air varié (to L. Mayeur) •Asx/Pno •Marg

MARIETAN, Pierre (1935)
Compositeur et chef d'orchestre suisse, né le 23 IX 1935, à Monthey. Travailla avec Marescotti, Zimmermann, Koenig, Boulez, et Stockhausen. A fondé en 1966 à Paris, le Groupe d'Etude et de Réalisation Musicales (GERM).

"Pierre Marietan compare son travail à celui du chimiste qui invente des formules mais ne fournit pas de modèle. A partir d'une formule, un enchaînement d'effets se propage. La présentation d'une *Initiative* est assouplie par rapport à certaines partitions verbales où la stimulation poétique reste primordiale; le projet n'est pas vraiment fixé par un texte définitif, inamovible mais soumis plutôt comme aide-mémoire." (D. J-Y. Bosseur)

"In his creative work he quickly overcame the appreciable influence of Boulez and, in close contact with instrumentalists, turned to composing sketch-scores and guidelines for improvisation, some of the former being intended for amateurs and children. He is also deeply concerned with ideas for new forms of concert in which past and contemporary music might be fused." (F. Muggler)
Concert III (1989) (7') (to D. Kientzy) •1 Sx: Sno+S/Magnétoph. multipistes
Concert IV (1989) (8') (to D. Kientzy) •1 Sx: Sno+S+T+B+Bs+CBs/Instrumental ensemble
Duo (1985) (to D. Kientzy) •1 Sx: Sno+A+T+B+Bs+CBs/Tape
La rose des vents (1982-83) (16') (to D. Kientzy) •Sx/Lyricon/Tape or 7 Sx: SnoSATBBsCBs/Tape
13 en concert (1983) (15') •1 Sx: Sno+S+B/Cl/Bsn/Trb/Vcl/2 Bass/Pno

MARIN, Amadeo (1955)
Compositeur espagnol, né le 3 VII 1955, à Castello de la Plana. Travailla avec L. de Pablo.
Quintet •Fl/Ob/Tsx/Vcl/Trb
Typologies (1977) •Tsx/Pno

MARIN, Jorge Lopoz
Compositeur cubain.
La Palabra (to M. Villafruela) 1) La palabra dura 2) La palabra dulce 3) L'ultima palabra •Sx Solo

MARINE, Sebastian
Compositeur espagnol.
Sic (1990) (to M. Mijan) •Asx/Pno

MARINUZZI, Gino (1920)
Compositeur et chef d'orchestre italien, né à New York, le 7 IV 1920. Travailla avec Paribeni et R. Rossi.
"His *Concertino* for piano, saxophone, oboe and strings was performed when he was 16."
Concertino (1936) •Pno/Ob/Sx/Str Orch

MARION, Alain (1938)
Flûtiste virtuose français.
50 duos progressif •2 Indentical [semblables] Sx

MARIOTTI, Christian
Resurgence (1991) •Ssx/Vibr

MARISCHAL, L.
Pour le plaisir •SATB •Chap

MARKOVITCH, Ivan (1929)
Professeur, chef de choeur et compositeur serbe, né à Belgrade, le 7 VII 1929. En France depuis 1960.
Appels (1985) (15') (to J-P. Fouchécourt) •1 player: Sx+Chanteur [Singer]/Tape
Aulodisation (1990) (to J-P. Caens & Quatuor Aulodia) •Ob/Cl/Asx/Bsn
Complainte et danse (1964) (5') (to J-M. Londeix) •Asx/Pno •Led
Petite marche (1963) (4') (to Sextuor à vent de Dijon) •Fl/Ob/Cl/Asx/Hn/Bsn
Variations (1964) (8') (to Sextuor à vent de Dijon) •Fl/Ob/Cl/Asx/Hn/Bsn

MAROCCHINI, Enrico
Compositeur italien.
Quartetto, op. 26 no. 1 (1990) (8') (to Quatuor Aquilano) •SATB •adr

MAROS, Miklos (1943)
Compositeur suédois d'origine hongroise, né à Pécs, fils du compositeur Rudolf Maros. En Suède depuis 1968. Travailla avec I. Lidholm, F. Szabo, et G. Ligeti.
"His music originates as the result of his continual endeavour to use and reinforce the instruments' own technical characteristics. Maros is very particular to preserve sound craftsmanship and his individual style is a combination of well-grounded traditional concepts and experiments with the newer techniques of our time." (H-G. P.)
Clusters for cluster (1981) •Fl/Ssx/Guit/Perc •SMIC
Coalottino (1969) (5') •Bsx/Electr. instrum./2 Pno/Harps/2 Vln/Vla/2 Vcl •STIM
Concerto (1990) (22') •Asx/Orch (2222/2221/Perc/Str) •SMIC
Concerto grosso (1988) •4 Sx: SATB/Orch •SMIC
Ondulations (1986) (8'30) (to J-E. Kelly) •Asx/Pno •SMIC
Quartet (1984) (10') (to Rascher Quartet) •SATB •SMIC

MARRA, James (1949)
To Suffer in Rhythm (1978) (11') (to V. Marcusson) •Tsx/Pno/2 Perc •DP
Legacy of the Four Winds (1978) (7') (to J. Cunnigham) •Sx Solo: S+T •DP

MARREN, Louis (1821-xxxx)
Petit conte breton •5 Sx

MARSAL
Grande fantaisie •2 Sx: SA •Mar

MARSH, Roger (1949)
Compositeur anglais.
Chamber Music (1981) (to J. Steele) •Asx/Soprano Voice

MARSHALL, Jack W.
The Goldrush Suite (1959) 1) Sweet Betsy from Pike 2) The Days of '49 3) Joe Bowers and California Bank Robbers 4) California Stage Coach 5) Used Up Man •SATB •Mar

MARTEAU
Morceau vivant •Asx/Pno •WWS

MARTELLI, Henri (1895-1980)
Compositeur français, né à Bastia (Corse), le 25 II 1895; mort à Paris, le 15 VIII 1980. Travailla avec Caussade et Widor.
"Henri Martelli parle le langage rigoureusement contrapuntique, et est peu préoccupé de séduire." (R. Stricker) "Art plein de rigueur dans

l'expression comme dans la forme, qui reflète le travail et la réflexion, qui n'est pas ennemi d'une certaine austérité de style. L'écriture est fréquemment contrapuntique, et dans ce domaine Henri Martelli montre une science singulière et ne redoute pas les audaces de langage. Compositeur volontiers intellectuel, d'une grande exigence envers lui-même, c'est un néo-classique qui sait ne pas tomber dans la convention ni dans la formule toute faite, et il se renouvelle avec souplesse au gré de ses exigences expressives." (Cl. Rostand) "Son style néoclassique ne dédaigne pas la polytonalité."

"In his compositions he attempted to recreate the spirit of old French music in terms of modern counterpoint." (Baker) "In his numerous compositions Martelli appears as a virtuoso of contrapuntal writing, with a taste, uncommon in out-and-out polyphonists, for briskness and gaiety, for every form of *divertimento*… This music is perfect in its somewhat restricted domain: stylized without loss of spontaneity, half puppet-show, half *commedia-dell'arte*, it displays the pleasant stiffness of masks and is never devoid of a sort of dry Florentine charm." (F. Goldberg) "His neo-classical style sometimes touches a certain austerity." (A. Girardot)

Cadence, Interlude et Rondo, op. 78 (1952) (to M. Mule) Asx/Pno •ME

Cinq Duos (1979) (8'30) •Cl/Sx •Bil

Trois esquisses, op. 55 (1943) (to M. Mule) 1) Préambule 2) Lied 3) Rythmé •Asx/Pno •ME

MARTHINSEN, Niels
Compositeur danois.
Burst (1990) •Asx/Perc
Sax 'n drums (1990) (6') (To P. Egholm) •Asx/Pno

MARTIN, David L. (1926)
Compositeur canadien, né à Toronto. Travailla avec S. Lancen, L. Menini, T. Canning, A. Hovhaness, et W. Barlow.
Jazz Rhapsody (1968) •Asx/Band •CMC

MARTIN, Frank (1890-1974)
Compositeur suisse, né à Genève, le 15 IX 1890, mort à Naarden (Pays-Bas) le 21 XI 1974. Travailla avec J. Laubert, puis à Zürich, Rome, et Paris.

"L'une des personnalités importantes de la musique de ce siècle. Beaucoup plus qu'un néoclassique à l'images d'autres musiciens, F.M. est un 'néomoderne.'" (C. Glayman) "L'évolution esthétique de Frank Martin laisse apparaître un musicien tiraillé entre les traditions française et germanique et, surtout, un compositeur en quête d'un langage original et moderne." (Cl. Samuel) "Passionnée et douloureuse, la recherche expérimentale d'un langage qui lui appartînt en propre devait conduire Fr. M. à l'atonalité (1940), puis au dodécaphonisme, dont il entendit toutefois se servir en toute indépendance, au point de l'accommoder avec le système tonal." (A. Chatelain) "La musique ne pourra vraiment bénéficier des enrichissements apportés par la technique de Schoenberg que dans la mesure où ses disciples n'appauvriront pas du même coup l'esprit du compositeur de toutes les richesses accumulées par des siècles de richesses et de trouvailles. Chacun doit façonner cette technique suivant son tempérament, et garder vis-à-vis de ces règles une pleine liberté d'action, se réserver le droit d'en violer tout ou partie dès que l'esprit l'exige." (Fr. Martin) "La synthèse de l'harmonie impressionniste (ravélienne principalement) et du chromatisme atonal viennois, aboutit à un langage harmonique extraordinairement raffiné et expressif. Il est capable de la véhémence tragique la plus haute, du souffle épique nécessaire à l'édification de vastes fresques chorales et religieuses, voire d'un humour très particulier et quelque peu sardonique." (H. Halbreich) "Son langage évolua avant de se définir par un style personnel, la cinquantaine venue: style de synthèse entre éléments germaniques et latins, entre acquis fondamentaux de la tonalité et exploitation originale, très libre, du dodécapho-

nisme." (H. Halbreich)

"His early music shows the influence of Franck and French Impressionists; but soon he succeeded in creating a distinctive style supported by a consummate mastery of contrapuntal and harmonic writing, and a profound feeling for emotional consistency and continuity; in later works he adopted a modified 12-tone method. He has also demonstrated his ability to stylize folksong material in modern harmonies with incisive, but always authentically scanned rhythms." (Baker) "It is especially noticeable that they often appear as harmonic foundations in the bass—a conception of the system that is entirely alien to Schoenberg—as in the following instance. The 12-tone series, moreover, is here broken up into harmonically related, sequential sections, a procedure that is likewise characteristic of Martin's technique. Also, the series are often built up over pedal basses. Used in this way, the 12-tone technique assumes a functional harmonic significance; and this is Martin's decisive contribution to the history of modern music." (K. von Fischer)

Ballade (1938) (15') (to S. Rascher) •Asx/Str Orch/Pno/Timp or Pno •Uni

Ballade (1940) (8') •Tsx/Orch (2222/222/Perc/Pno/Str) or Pno •Uni

MARTIN, Frédérick
Concerto - 2 Titres •Sx successifs/Orch

MARTIN, Robert (1898)
Saxopaline •Asx/Pno •Mar
Sérénade à Corinne •Asx/Pno •Mar

MARTIN, Vernon (1929)
Compositeur américain, né le 15 XII 1929, à Guthrie (Oklahoma). Travailla avec H. Kerr.
Concerto (1953) •Piano (4 hands)/Sx/Orch •adr
Contingencies (1969) •Asx/Tpt/Trb/Perc/Tape •CAP

MARTIN, Victor (1921)
Compositeur français.
Orbitales III (1982) (8') (to A. Bouhey) •Asx/Org

MARTIN, William
Compositeur américain.
One Movement (c. 1980) (6') •Asx/Pno

MARTIN RODRIGUEZ
Impromptu •SATB

MARTINEAU, Christine
Compositeur français.
Soprani-une-ni-deux (1989) •Voice/Sx/Tape

MARTINEZ FERNANDEZ, Julian
Compositeur espagnol.
Hacia la desconocido (1993) (to J. Escribano) •Sx Solo: S+Bs+T
Mijanianas (1993) (to M. Mijan) •Asx/Pno

MARTINI, Jean-Paul (1741-1816)
Plaisir d'amour •Eb Sx/Pno •Mol
Plaisir d'amour (Maganini) •2 Sx: AT/Pno or Tsx/Pno •Mus
Plaisir d'amour (Mule) •Asx/Pno •Led
Plaisir d'amour (Overveld) •Eb Sx or Bb Sx/Pno •TM
Plaisir d'amour (Viard) •Asx or Bb Sx/Pno •Sal

MARTINI, Padre Giovanni-Battista (1706-1784)
Canzona •Bb Sx/Pno •Mol
Gavotte (Rascher) •Asx/Pno •Chap
Gavotte des moutons (Meriot) •Asx/Pno •Phi
Les moutons (Mule) •Asx/Pno •Led

MARTINO, Donald (1931)

Compositeur américain, né à Plainfield (New Jersey), le 16 V 1931. Travailla avec Bacon, Sessions, et Babbitt, puis avec Dallapiccola.

"Martino's [music] has been characterized as expressive, dense, lucid, romantic, all of which are applicable. But it is his ability—as he engages himself in a world of virtuoso music-making—to conjure up for the listener a world of palpable musical presences and conceptions, which perseveres in intensity from the beginning to the end of one piece and from one piece to another, that seems most remarkable." (E. BARKIN)

Concerto (1986) (23') (to J. SAMPEN, J. FORGER, & K. RADNOFSKY) •Asx/Orch (1212/2120/Pno/2 Perc/Str) or Pno •MDM

MARTINON, Jean (1910-1976)

Chef d'orchestre et compositeur français, né à Lyon, le 10 I 1910, mort à Paris, le 1er III 1976. Travailla avec A. Roussel, Ch. Münch, et R. Desormiere.

"Jean Martinon compose dans un style néo-classique nettement influencé par Roussel et Bartok." (Cl. ROSTAND) "Le *Concerto lyrique* de 1944, originalement écrit pour quatuor à cordes et orchestre, fut transcrit en 1976 par le compositeur avec l'aide de D. Deffayet, pour quatuor de saxophones."

Concerto lyrique, op. 38 (1944/76) (21') •SATB/Orch or 2 Pno •EFM

MARTIRANO, Salvatore (1927)

Compositeur américain, né à Yonkers (New York), le 12 I 1927. Travailla avec Elwell, Rogers, et Dallapiccola.

"During the 1950s Martirano followed the prevailing 12-note trend, but by 1958 he had developed an individual style in *O, O, O, O, that Shakespeherian Rag.* This work marked a turning point in its assimilation of popular elements (later conspicuous in *Cocktail Music* and the *Ballad*) and in its inventive sound effects. *Underworld* had already introduced computer-generated sound to his work, and it also displayed a more open organization, involving stage action." (G. CHASE)

Ballad (1966) •Amplified club singer/Ensemble
O, O, O, O, That Shakespearian Rag (1958) •Chorus/ensemble
Underworld (1959) •4 Actors/Tsx/4 Perc/2 Bass/2 Track tape

MARVUGLIO, M.

Modal Etudes (1982) •DP

MASCAGNI, Pietro (1863-1945)

Intermezzo ("Cavalleria") •Eb Sx/Pno •CF
Intermezzo (HOLMES) •AATB •Bar
Siciliana •Tsx/Pno •Rem
Siciliana (SCHAFFER) •Asx/Pno •MPHC

MASETTI, Enzo (1893-1961)

Compositeur italien.
Divertimento •SATB

MASINI, Fabio

Compositeur et chef d'orchestre italien.
"Nuvole e colori forti" (1992) (18') •Fl/1 Sx: S+A/BsCl/Fl/Ob/Cl/ Bsn/2 Vln/Vla/Vcl/Harp

MASLANKA, David

Compositeur américain.
Heaven to clear when day did close •Tsx/Str Quartet
Sonata (1988) (33') (commissionned by the North American Saxophone Alliance) •Asx/Pno •NASA

MASON, Benedict

Compositeur allemand.
Coulour and information (1993) •Fl/Ob/Sx/Bsn/Hn/Tpt/Trb/Tuba/ Perc/Electr. Bass

MASON, Lucas

Compositeur canadien.
Canonic Dances (1970) 1) Energetically 2) With a lilt 3) Smoothly - not too fast 4) Sprightly - separated 5) Slowly but with enough motion - Quickly, slowly again 6) Lively •2 Sx: AA or TT •adr
Lay-Alla-Allah (1972) (to L. WYMAN) •Soprano Voice/Asx/Fl/Pno •adr
Quartet (1971) •SATB •adr
A Quilt of Love (1971) •Soprano Voice/Asx/Fl/Vln/Bsn/Trb/Vcl •adr
Romance (1978) (for L. WYMAN) •Asx/Guit •DP
Song and Dance (1982) (to L. WYMAN) •Sx Solo

MASON, Steven

Chamber Music (to P. COHEN) •5 Sx

MASON, Thom David

Saxophoniste de jazz et compositeur américain. Travailla la composition avec L. Stein, A. Donato, et A. Stout.

"Thom David Mason is a former saxophonist who understands the instrument and is able to exploit its possibilities in his compositions. His writing exhibits a sense of what is new and experimental in music and his writing for the saxophone exhibits these qualities. His concepts are challenging but necessary to the contemporary saxophonist." (F. H.)

Canzone da sonar (1970) •Asx/Pno •South
The City (1965) 1) The Hub 2) The Structures 3) A Park with Children •SATB
The Multiphonic Resources of the Saxophone

MASON, William (1725-1797)

Dance Antique (GEE) •5 Sx: SAATB •Sha

MASON - HARRISON

Nom de plume d'un couple de compositeurs anglais: John Harrison et sa femme Géraldine Mason.
Kaleidoscope (to J. DENMAN) •Asx/Pno

MASSA, Enrico

Compositeur italien.
Preludio, Duetto e Rondo •2 Sx: AT/Pno

MASSELLA, Thomas

Changing Times (10') (to S. POLLOCK) •Tsx/Pno •Marc
Pieces of April (1986) (8') (to R. DRISCOLL & C. EBLI) 1) Water Ribbons 2) Chasing Rainbows •2 Sx: SA (or Ob/EH) •Marc
Romance (1993) (4') (to R. FAUB) •Asx/Pno •Marc
Songs for a Poet (1987) (10') (to J. BOATMAN & S. POLLOCK) 1) If Wishes Could 2) Wings of a Whim •2 Sx: AT/Pno •Marc

MASSENET, Jules (1842-1912)

Air de ballety (THOMPSON) •AATB •Alf
Angelus ("Scènes pittoresques") •AATB •Alf/Rub
Elegy •Tsx/Pno •Cen
Elegy •Bsx/Pno •Bel
Elegy (TRINKAUS) •2 Sx: AA or AT/Pno •Pres
Elegy (WILSON) •Asx/Pno •MPHC
Fête bohémienne (THOMPSON) •AATB •Alf
Hérodiade (PONCELET-BARWOLF) •Asx/Pno •Led
Herod's Air (Hérodiade) •Asx/Pno •Mus
Last Slumber of the Virgin (HARRIS) •2 Cl/Asx/Bsn (or BsCl) •CF
March (THOMPSON) •AATB •Alf
Meditation from "Thais" (WORLEY) •Asx/Pno •DP
Mélodie - Elégie (MULE) •Asx/Pno •JJ
Phèdre (JOHNSON) •6 Sx: AAATTB •Rub
Sous les tilleuls (LEONARD) •1 Sx: A or T/Pno •Pres

Under the Lindens (Sous les Tilleuls) (LEONARD) •Ob or Cl/1 Sx: A
 or T/Pno •Pres
Valse des esprits (GRISELIDIS) •Asx/Pno •Mus
Virgin's Last Slumber •Bb Sx/Pno •CBet

MASSET-LECOQ, Roselyne
2 Pièces brèves (1977) (to Quatuor de Saxophones de Paris) •SATB
3 Pièces (1977) •Cl/Asx/Hn/Bsn

MASSIAS, Gérard (1933)
Compositeur français, né à Paris, le 25 V 1933. Travailla avec D.
Lesur.

"Toutes les techniques l'intéressent, et il conserve la liberté d'employer celle qui convient plus spécialement à l'oeuvre qu'il élabore.
Pourtant, quelques préoccupations essentielles assurent l'unité de son
style: une extrême économie thématique; l'importance primordiale
qu'il accorde à la forme; la plasticité des éléments linéaires et le souci
de leur situation. Il affectionne en outre les ensembles restreints et son
style, sévère et abstrait, refus de tout recours ou allusion à la littérature
ou à l'ésotérisme." (HEU)
Dialogues (1956) (6') (to J. DESLOGES & J. ARNAUD) 1) Prélude, lent
 et douloureux 2) Trés librement rêveur 3) Interlude, troisième
 dialogue 4) Rapide 5) Postlude •Asx/BsCl or 2 like Sx
 [identiques] •Bil
Laude (1961) (11') (to R. DUVAL) •Asx/Str Orch or Pno •Bil
Suite monodique (1954) (11') (to G. GOURDET) 1) Modéré, souple et
 libre 2) Vif, âpre et cursif 3) Lent, rêveur et chantant 4) Allegro,
 ironique et dansant 5) Animé, capricieux et rythmé •Asx Solo
 •Bil
Variations (1955) (11') (to Quatuor d'Anches Français) •Ob/Asx/Cl/
 Bsn •Bil

MASSIS, Amable (1893-1980)
Compositeur, chef d'orchestre, altiste français, né à Cambrai, le 2 VI
1893. Travailla avec Gedalge et M. Dupré.

"Je suis attaché à la forme classique, estimant inutile d'écrire pour
faire du bruit et ne rien dire. L'agressivité en musique n'est pas ma
formule." (A. MASSIS) "Massis ne recherche pas les effets faciles et son
art est d'une probité sans défaillance." (R. BERNARD)
Poème (1942) (18'30) •Asx/Orch (2232/4231/Harp/Perc/Str) •Bil
Six Etudes caprices (1954) (to M. MULE) •Led

MASSON, Gérard (1936)
Compositeur français né à Paris, le 12 VIII 1936. Travailla avec
Stockhausen, H. Pousseur, et E. Brown.

"L'une des personnalités les plus saillantes de la nouvelle génération
post-boulézienne." (Cl. ROSTAND) "Se dirigeant vers des méthodes
spécifiques à chaque oeuvre, Gérard Masson insiste sur la nécessaire
singularité de la forme devant trouver à se matérialiser dans une
instrumentation et à un traitement des moyens sonores intransposables."
(D. J-Y. BOSSEUR) "Poursuivant un chemin très solitaire, Gérard
Masson pense une musique large, volontiers symphonique, au caractère grave et raffiné. Berlioz, Varèse et Stockhausen ont été à la source
de sa réflexion de compositeur. Il lui arrive aussi de se référer aux
anciens pour la combinaison instrumentale." (J. & B. MASSIN)

"His music is influenced less by Stockhausen and Earle Brown than
by the French tradition extending from Debussy to Boulez. His works
have a graceful and decorative surface, and the attractive textures do
not prevent Masson from achieving moving effects." (D. AMY)
Minutes de St Simon (1989) (12') (to J. KELLY) (7 movements) •Asx/
 Pno •Sal

MASUDA, Kozo (1936)
Compositeur japonais. Travailla à Paris avec H. et N. Gallon.
Pièce brève (1977) (5') (to K. SHIMOJI) •Asx Solo
Quatuor (1975) •SATB

MASUY, Fernand
Compositeur belge.
Etude du saxophone (2 Volumes) (1955) (10 difficult etudes,
 including 2 duets [10 études difficiles, dont 2 duos]) •EMB/HE
10 Studies of medium difficulty •HE

MATHER, Bruce (1939)
Compositeur canadien, né à Toronto, le 9 V 1939. Travailla avec
Morawetz, Beckwith, D. Milhaud, O. Messiaen, et L. Smith.

"He writes in neo-classical forms, but his idiom is tinged with acrid
atonality." (BAKER) "His music has something of the opulent sonority
of Berg, the sensitive control of Debussy and the fine, graceful lyricism
of the later Boulez. Often it is elaborated in 'fields' generated from a
chromatic mode of six or seven notes, the rhythmic technique being
supple and mobile." (P. GRIFFITHS)
Elegy (1959) (6') (to P. BRODIE) •Asx/Str Orch or Pno •Wa/CMC

MATHEY, Paul
Quatuor •SATB
Trois Pièces, op. 19 (9') •Asx/Pno

MATITIA, Jean (1952)
Compositeur français, né à Tunis.
Chinese Rag (1985) (2'30) (to Cl. DELANGLE) •SATB •Lem
Devil's Rag (1985) (4'30) (to J-M. LONDEIX) •12 Sx:
 SnoSSAAATTTBBBs •Ron
Las Americas (1985/93) (21') (to J-M. LONDEIX) 1) Samba do diabo
 2) Rumba triste 3) Happy blues 4) Devil's Rag •12 Sx:
 SnoSSAAATTTBBBs •adr
Samba do diabo (1992) (8') (to J-M. LONDEIX) •12 Sx:
 SnoSSAAATTTBBBs •adr

MATOT, Pierre
Compositeur belge.
Spleen (to J-P. RORIVE) •Asx/Org

MATSUDAIRA, Roh (1938)
Compositeur japonais.
Quintette (1968) (to A. SAKAGUCHI) •Asx/Vln/Vla/Vcl/Bass

MATSUDAIRA, Yori-Aki (1931)
Compositeur japonais.
Gestaphony (1979) (to R. NODA) •Sx Solo

MATSUMOTO, Hinoharu
Compositeur japonais.
Archipose IV (1979) (to R. NODA) •Sx Solo

MATSUO, M.
Compositeur japonais.
Phono •Sx/Perc

MATSUSHITA, Isao (1951)
Compositeur japonais né à Tokyo. Travailla avec H. Minami et T.
Mayuzumi, puis à Berlin, avec I. Yun.
Ashi no sho II (1981) •Ob/Cl/Asx/Bsn
Atoll I (1982) (13') •SATB
Atoll II (1982-83) (6') (to R. NODA & D. BENSMANN) •Asx/Pno
 •B&B
Grand Atoll (1992) (13') •4 Sx: SATB/Orch

MATTEI, Tito (1841-1914)
The Mariner (WALTERS) •Bsx/Pno •Rub

MATTHESON, Johann (1681-1764)
Menuet •Asx/Pno •Bil

MATTHESSENS, Marcel

Short Habanera •Asx/Pno •Scz

MATTHEWS, David (1946)

Compositeur américain.

Chantefleur •SATB
Octet •8 Sx: SSAATTBB
Suite (1987) (to New York Saxophone Quartet) •SATB

MATTON, Roger (1929)

Compositeur canadien, né à Granby (Québec), le 18 V 1929. Travailla avec Champagne, N. Boulanger, O. Messiaen, et Vaurabourg-Honegger.

"L'un des compositeurs les plus intéressants de sa génération." (A. DESAUTELS)

"Folk music has played a significant, though decreasingly substantial, part in his work. His style is lyrical and conventional, though employing a wide range of techniques. An interest in jazz is evident in the insistent rhythms of his music, further accentuated by the use of large percussion forces in his orchestral scoring." (M. SAMSON)

Concerto (1948) •Asx/Pno/Perc/Str •Comp

MAUK, Steven

Saxophoniste et professeur américain.

Medici Masterworks Solos (2 Volumes) •MMP
Practical Guide for Playing the Saxophone: *for class or individual instruction* (1987) •adr

MAURAT, Edmond (1881-19xx)

Compositeur français.

Petites inventions, op. 21 n° 1 (1966) (18'30) (a la mémoire de ses fils François et Louis) 1) Entrelacs 2) Phantasme 3) Thrène 4) Enigme 5) Leurre •Asx/Pno •ME

MAURE

Christmastime International •SATB •WWS

MAURICE, Paule (1910-1967)

Compositeur français, né le 29 IX 1910 à Paris où elle est morte, le 18 VIII 1967. Travailla avec H. Busser. Epouse de Pierre Lantier.

Tableaux de Provence (1954-59) (12') (to M. MULE) 1) Farandole des jeunes-filles 2) Chanson pour ma mie 3) La bohémienne 4) Des Alyscamps mon âme soupira 5) Le cabridan •Asx/Orch (2221/210/Perc/Str) or Pno •Lem
Volio (1967) (3') •Asx Solo •Bil

MAURICE, R.

Aurore •SATB •Mau

MAURY, Lownder (1911)

Compositeur américain, né le 7 VII 1911, à Butte (Montana). Travailla avec W. La Violette et A. Schoenberg.

Cock of the Walk (1949) (5') (Molto vivace - Più tranquillo - Molto vivace) •4 Sx •AvMu
5th Contest Solo (KLICKMANN) •1 Sx: T or B/Pno •Alf

MAUSION, Octave

L'Aveu - cavatine, op. 60 (1893) •Asx/Pno

MAXFIELD, Richard (Vance) (1927-1969)

Compositeur américain, né à Seattle (Washington), le 2 II 1927, mort à Los Angeles, le 27 VI 1969. Travailla avec Babbitt, puis avec Dallapiccola et Maderna.

"His own works are for the most part designed for electronic instruments." (BAKER)

Domenon (suite from ballet) (1961) •Fl/Sx/Pno/Vibr/Vln/Bass/Tape
Perateia •Asx/Vln/Pno/Tape

Wind •Sx/Tape

MAXWELL

Acousma IV •Tsx/Perc/Pno •DP

MAY, Stephen

Sonatinissima (1979) (to M. TAGGART) •Asx/Pno

MAYERUS, A. G.

Compositeur belge.

Tarentelle •Asx/Pno •Ger/An

MAYEUR, Louis (1837-1894)

Saxophoniste et clarinettiste français d'origine belge, né à Menin le 21 III 1837, mort à Cannes. Travailla avec H. Klosé et A. SAX. Soliste à l'Opéra de Paris. Chef d'orchestre des Concerts du Jardin d'Acclimatation.

Cavatine du Barbier de Séville de Rossini (1878) •Asx/Pno
Don Pasquale de Donizetti - Récréation (1878) •Asx/Pno
10 Duos •2 Sx •G&F
10 Duos (revue par [revised by] P. de VILLE) (1907) •CF
21 Etudes
Fantaisie brillante sur Lucrèce Borgia de Donizetti (1877) (to P. MAYEUR) •Asx/Pno
1ère Fantaisie originale (1877) •Bsx/Pno
Fantaisie sur Bélisario de Donizetti (1878) •Asx/Pno
Fantaisie sur Cinq-Mars de Gounod (1878) •Asx/Pno
Fantaisie sur des mélodies de Cressonnois (1872) Asx/Pno •Led
Fantaisie sur Don Juan de Mozart (1872) •Asx/Pno
2me fantaisie sur Don Juan de Mozart (1879) •Asx/Pno
Fantaisie sur Les Noces de Jeannette de Massé (1876) •Asx/ Musique militaire or Pno
Fantaisie sur les Puritains de Bellini (1878) •Asx/Pno
Fantaisie sur Robert le Diable de Meyerbeer, op. 41 (1877) •Asx/ Pno
La Fleurance - Caprice (1885) •Asx/Pno
Grande fantaisie brillante sur "Le Carnaval de Venise" (1869) •Asx/Pno •Led
Grande fantaisie de concert sur La Somnambule de Bellini (1878) •Asx/Pno
Grande fantaisie de concert sur Freyschütz, op. 42 (1878) •Asx/Pno •ES
Grande fantaisie de concert sur Rigoletto de Verdi, op. 42 (1877) •Asx/Pno
Grande fantaisie sur Norma de Bellini, op. 15 (1869) Asx/Pno
Grande méthode complète de saxophone (1878) •G&F
Impromptu •SATB
Nouvelle grande méthode (revue par [revised by] M. PERRIN) (1963) •Led
Nuevo y Gran método de saxofon (1896) •E/S
Récréation sur des motifs de La Favorite (1877) •2 Sx: SA/Pno
Récréation sur des motifs du Trouvère (1877) •2 Sx: AT/Pno
Récréation sur La Favorite de Donizetti (1877) •Tsx/Pno
Solo de concert •Cl or Asx/Pno •Es

MAYS, Walter (1941)

Compositeur américain, né à Tennessee. Travailla avec J. Takacs, F. Labunski, et J. Cage.

Concerto (1974) (14') (to J. SAMPEN) (Senza mesura - Lointain - Rapid - Violent) •Asx/Chamber Orch (0111/0110/Pno/Org/Perc/ Str Quintet) or Pno •BM
Duet (1976) •2 Sx: SS

MAYUZUMI, Toshiro (1929)

Compositeur japonais, né à Yokohama, le 20 II 1929. Travailla à Tokyo au Studio de musique expérimentale, d'après les modèles de

Paris et de Cologne, avec Ikenouchi et Ifukube puis à Paris avec Tony Aubin, avant de revenir dans son pays.

"Après une première période hésitante, s'est bientôt classé parmi les personnalités les plus saillantes de l'avant-garde de son pays dans la tendance post-sérielle." (Cl. ROSTAND) "Au studio de musique concrète N.H.K. de Tokyo, Toshiro Mayuzumi fait rapidement dévier la musique concrète vers les techniques électro-acoustiques qui entremêlent les apports électroniques et concrets et leur permettent de tirer parti des sources instrumentales ou vocales." (D. J-Y. BOSSEUR)

"Mayuzumi has consistently experimented with new ideas and techniques in his compositions; he introduced almost all of the new trends in postwar European music into Japan. He has used 12-note, serial and aleatory methods, so that almost every one of his pieces has its own style. Nevertheless, it is possible to identify in his work a predominant interest in the unique sonorities of instruments and voices. This has led him to employ such unexpected combinations as 'claviolin,' electric guitar and vibraphone or five saxophones, piano and musical saw (in *Tone Pleromas 55*)." (M. KANAZAWA)

Metamusic (1961) (trio with conductor [avec chef]) •Pno/Vln/Asx •Pet
Sphenogramme (1951) •Contralto Voice/Fl/Asx/Marimba/Vln/Vcl/ Pno 4 hands [à 4 mains]
Tone Pleromas 55 (1955) •5 Sx/Musical saw [Scie musicale]/Pno •Saw

MAZELLIER, Jules (1879-1959)

Chef d'orchestre et compositeur français, né le 6 IV 1879, à Toulouse, où il est mort, le 6 II 1959. Travailla avec G. Fauré. Prix de Rome (1909).
Dix Fugues •SATB •EV
Fantaisie ballet (1944) (7') (to M. MULE) •Asx/Pno •Led
Quick et Spleen (1953) (to M. MULE) •Asx/Pno •Lem
Scherzo et Canter •SATB
Thème varié languedocien •Asx/Pno •Sal

MAZUREK, Micezyslaw

Ewokacje (1986) (8') •Asx/Vibr/Perc
Trio (1988) (11-12') •Fl/Asx/Pno

MAZUREK, Ron

Compositeur américain.
Focusing •Asx •SeMC

MAZZAFERRO, Dominico

Compositeur italien. Travailla avec T. Tesei.
Fluxi (1990) (6') •6 Sx: SAAATB

MAZZANTI, Alessandra

Compositeur et chef d'orchestre italien.
Liebes melodie (1992) (4') •8 Sx: SAAAATTB

McBRIDE, David

Inner Voices (to P. COHEN) •Asx/Tpt

McBRIDE, Robert Guyn (see MACBRIDE)

McCALL, H.

Annie Laurie •4 Sx: AATB/Pno •Lud
Two Spirituals •4 Sx: AATB/Pno •Lud

McCARTHY, Daniel

Sonata •1 Sx: S+A/Pno/Tape •adr

McCARTY, Frank (1941)

Compositeur américain, né le 10 IX 1941. Travailla avec I. Dahl, R. Erickson, et K. Gaburo.
Five Situations (1969) (15') (to R. ERICKSON) •4 Sx: SATB or SAAT •Art

Saxim Mixas (1972) (8') (to L. LIVINGSTON) •5 Sx (may be recorded or live)/Optional live electronic processing •adr

McCLAIN, Floyd A.

A Little Joke •Tsx/Pno •South

McCLINTOCK, Robert Bayles (1946)

Compositeur américain, né à Reno (Nevada), le 3 IV 1946. Travailla avec J. Adair, D. Kingman, et G. Hatton.
"In *Music* the two instruments are in hearty agreement throughout, and each has a brief, provocative few measures alone." (A. H. J.)
Duo •Asx/Harp •adr
Music (1971) (7') •Asx/Harp •adr
Music No. 2 (1972) (10') •Asx/Harp •adr

McCUALEY, William (1917)

Compositeur canadien.
5 Miniatures (4'30) •SATB •CMC

McFARLAND, Gary

Night Float (4'30) •3 Sx: ATB/Tpt/Hn/Guit/Pno/Bass/Drums •MJQ

McGEE, A.

Improvisation Sax •HD
Modal Studies •HD

McGUIRE, Edward (1948)

Compositeur anglais.
Five Small Pieces (1971) •SATB
Music for Saxophone(s) (1976) (10') •1 to 4 Sx (SATB)/Tape •SMPL

McINTOSH, Diana

Compositeur canadien. Travailla avec M. Colgrass.
Dance for Daedaluss (1989) (14') •Asx/Pno •CMC

McKAY, George Frederick (1899-1970)

Compositeur américain, né à Harrington (Washington), le 11 VI 1899, mort à Stateline (Nevada), le 4 X 1970. Travailla avec Palmgren et Sinding.
American Panorama •any 4 equal Sx •CF
American Street Scenes (1935) •Cl/Tpt/Asx/Bsn/Pno or 4 Sx/Pno •CAP
Amigos •3 Sx AAA or AAT/Pno •Bar
Anita •3 Sx: AAT/Pno •Bar
Arietta and Capriccio •Asx/Pno •NA
Berceuse (REX) •7 Sx: SAAATTB •WWS
Buckboard Blues •Asx/Pno •Bar
Carmela •3 Sx: AAA or AAT/Pno •Bar
Chiquita •3 Sx: AAA or AAT/Pno •Bar
Concert Solo Sonatine •Asx Solo •NA
Dream waltz •Asx/Pno •Bar
Fiesta Mejicana •4 equal Sx •CF
Halloween Time •3 Sx: AAT/Pno •Bar
Hernando's Holiday, The Powdered Wig •Asx/Pno •Bar
Instrumental Duo Suite •2 Woodwinds/Pno •WIM
Ten for Jeanine, Ye Traveling Troubadour •Asx/Pno •Bar
Three Cadets •3 Sx: AAA or AAT/Pno •Bar
Three Jesters •3 Sx: AAA or AAT/Pno •Bar

McKEE, Richard E.

Compositeur américain.
Quartet (1982) •SATB

McKINLEY, Thomas William

Tenor Rhapsody (1989) •Tsx/Orch
Emsdettener Totentanz •3 Voices/Str Quartet/4 Sx: SATB/2 Perc

McKINNEY, Kevin
Similarities •Asx/Pno

McLEAN, Barton (1938)
Dimensions III/IV (1979) (to A. REGNI) •Asx/Tape

McMILLAN, Nancy
Elegie and Rondo •Asx/Pno

McNEAL, L. B.
Professeur américain.
McNeal's Modern Preparatory Studies (1925) •F&U/Rub

McPEEK, Ben (1934-1981)
Compositeur canadien.
Canadian Audubon Suite (1977) (15') •SATB •CMC
Trillium - suite (1979) (to P. BRODIE) 1) The First Crocus 2) Forsythia (Harbinger of Spring) 3) The Enigmatic Pussy-Willows 4) The Proudest Hibiscus (the Rose of Sharon) •Ssx/Fl/Cl/Vln/Vcl/Pno

McTEE, Cindy
Compositeur américain.
Etudes (1992) (to D. RICHTMYER) 1) Filigree 2) Night Song 3) Filigree •Asx/Tape

MEACHAM, F. W.
American Patrol (HUMMEL) •Asx/Pno •Rub

MEAD, Andrew
Compositeur américain.
Concerto (1987) (to C. LEAMAN) •Asx/Chamber ensemble of 12 •adr

MEDINGER, Jean
Chanson slave •Asx/Pno •PB
Fantaisie-Sax •Asx/Pno •PB
Halt au swing •Asx/Pno •PB
Karacho •Asx/Pno •PB
Ma bergère (NIVELET) •Asx/Pno •Led
L'obsession •Asx/Pno •PB
Le rémouleur •Asx/Pno •PB
Le roi Dagobert •Asx/Pno •PB
Sax-swing •Asx/Pno •PB
Souvenir de vacances •Asx/Pno •PB
Les tricoteuses •Asx/Pno •PB
Une rose •Asx/Pno •PB
Valse allégresse •Asx/Pno •PB

MEFANO, Paul (1937)
Compositeur et chef d'orchestre français, né à Bassorah en Irak, le 6 III 1937. Travailla avec D. Milhaud, O. Messiaen, P. Boulez, K. Stockhausen, et H. Pousseur. En 1972, il est l'un des fondateurs de l'Ensemble 2E2M (Etudes/Expressions des Modes Musicaux) de Champigny.

"Non conformiste doué d'une solide formation de base, est un des plus inspirés de la jeune génération." (Cl. ROSTAND) "Il écrit des 'oeuvres ouvertes' aussi bien que des pièces où tout est prévu. Il s'est intéressé à la création collective. Toujours intéressantes, ses oeuvres dénotent une parfaite maîtrise de la matière instrumentale et une imagination en perpétuel bouillonnement." (P-L. SIRON) "L'oeuvre de Paul Mefano manifeste la volonté, d'une part, d'approcher divers modes de perception du temps, par un jeu sur plusieurs types d'écriture, et, d'autre part, d'assumer l'instabilité des systèmes, soulignant la relativité de toute pensée musicale… Loin de n'être que des spéculations de nature formelle, les préoccupation de Paul Mefano proviennent essentiellement d'une réflexion sur la matière musicale, souvent stimulée par une vision poétique. Il s'agit, en effet, pour lui d'être 'le plus abstrait sans sacrifier le moins du monde un matériau extrêmement

sensuel et physique et de s'ouvrir à des champs ambigus de significations." (D. J.-Y. BOSSEUR) "Tempérament fougueux, très ouvert à toutes les formes nouvelles de la musique, il se meut à l'aise sur les terres expérimentales. Les oeuvres sont nombreuses, éclectiques, souvent inattendues, toujours généreuses dans leur souffle." (J. & B. MASSIN) "Mes affirmations sur le couplage *énergie/interprétation* dérivent d'une expérience privilégiée tentée grâce à Paul Mefano. Avec *Périple* Mefano a mis dans le mille. A ma connaissance, il n'existe aucune oeuvre dans le répertoire du saxophone qui soit plus excitante, plus tonique pour l'interprète que ces redoutables lignes de navigation ou que ces circuits hérissés de difficultés. Et cette réussite, justement, il me semble qu'elle procède avant tout de la richesse de l'invention énergétique du compositeur. Il y a quelque chose d'oriental dans un tel raffinement, dans ces passages quasi instantanés du plus grand calme à l'extrême agressivité." (J-L. CHAUTEMPS)

"His very attractive Boulezian early works established his reputation, and he soon found a much more individual style, marked by a clear feeling for drama and lyricism and a predilection for setting large sound blocks in conflict." (D. JAMEUX)

Périple (1978) (14') (Pour J-L. CHAUTEMPS) •Tsx Solo •Sal
Quatuor (1980) (4') •SATB
Scintillante, Mémoire de la porte blanche, Dragonbass (1993) •Bass Voice/2 Sx
Tige (1986) (1'40) •Sx Solo •Sal

MEHKE, Ferd
Caricature •Asx/Pno

MEHUL, Etienne (1763-1817)
Rondeau basque (MULE) •Asx/Pno •Led

MEIER-BÖHME, Alfons
Humoresque •AATB •Fro
Vier Bummelanten •AATB •Fro

MEIER, Daniel (1934)
Compositeur français, né à Pau, le 22 II 1934. Travailla avec Mme A. Honegger, H. Dutilleux, et M. Ohana.
Epi (1973) (11') (to Quatuor Mériot) •SATB •EFM
Kuklos (to Quatuor d'Anches Français) (12') (Yin - Yang - Fecondation) •Ob/Cl/Asx/Bsn •EFM

MEIJERING, Chiel (1954)
Compositeur hollandais, né à Amsterdam, le 15 VI 1954.
Background-music for non-entairtainment (1988-90) (9') •SATB •Don
De heift van de lengte is nog lang genoeg (1986) (8') •SATB •Don
De navoer verstijfd in 't tochtige hol van 't geborgte (1983-89) (6') •Sx/Pno •Don
Everybody's Busy (1983) (7'50) •SATB •Don
Frequente Contacten (1985) (9') •Sx/Marimba •Don
Het ontblote feit (1988-90) (8'30) •2 Fl/3 Sx: ATB/2 Hn/Tpt/Trb/ Perc/Pno/Electr. Guit •Don
I Hate Mozart (1979) (4') •Fl/Asx/Harp/Vln •Don
I Like Rats, But I Don't Like Haydn (1981-83) (6') •SATB •Don
Jearus' val (1989) (6') •Asx/Pno •Don
Kwane dampen (1990) (10') •SATB
Meine Lippen die küssen so heiss (1984) (10') •Fl/Ob/Asx/Pno/Perc •Don
'N haar op 'N hoofd (1987-89) (8'30) •SATB •Don
Niet doorslikken (1985) (5') •Bsx/Vln •Don
Onderwerping (1986) (18') •Asx/Orch •Don
The pizza-connection (1989) (7') •Asx/Pno •Don
Sax sox (1991) •12 Sx: SnoSSAAATTTBBBs •Don
Schudden voor gebruik (1985) (8') •Asx/Perc/Pno/Harp •Don
7000 Days of the Zebra (1987) (9') •SATB •Don

Tripppette trippetic (1976) (15') •Variable sextet •Don
The Ugly Howling Monkey (1978) (7') •Vln/Bsx •Don

MELBY, John
Compositeur américain.
Rhapsody (1987) •Asx/Tape

MELILLO, Peter
Diane Piece •Ssx/Tape

MELIN, Sten (1957)
Compositeur suédois.
Källarbacksvariationerna (1993) •SATB •SvM

MELLE, R. del
Largo religioso (D. SPEETS) •SATB •TM

MELLÉ, Patrick (1957)
Compositeur français, né à Bourg-sur-Gironde, le 21 VIII 1957. Travailla avec M. Fusté-Lambezat.
"Compositeur mettant souvent en scène, musique, théâtre, et musique électroacoustique"
Arche d'anches (1990) (11') (to J-M. LONDEIX) •12 Sx: SnoSSAAATTTBBBs
Moments profanes et Lieu sacré (1986) (15') (to J-M. LONDEIX) •12 Sx: SnoSSAAATTTBBBs
Seriotis, op. 4 (1985) (10') •2 Sx: TB/Men's chorus [Choeur d'hommes]/Soprano Voice Solo/Perc/Pno/Synth/Tape
Verbiages d'un métal osseux (1992) (13') •Soprano Voice/Bsx/ Transf. en direct/Tape

MELLISH
Drink To Me •AATB •Bri

MELLNÄS, Arne (1933)
Compositeur et professeur suédois, né le 30 VIII 1933 à Stockholm. Travailla avec L. Larson, K. B. Blomdahl, B. Blacher, et G. Ligeti.
"In subsequent works he has used the newest compositional developments, which he has studied during the course of frequent travels. He was one of the first Swedes to introduce aleatory and deliberately theatrical elements into instrumental music. Mellnäs has also composed pieces that are popular with schools and amateurs." (R. HAGLUND)
"The important position that Arne Mellnäs holds as a technical innovator and introducer of avant-garde styles to Swedish music can hardly be overestimated. The results of his explorative energy during the expansive 1960's have crystallized into a personal musical language full of diverse moods." (H-G. P.)
Drones (1967) (8') •Fl/Cl/3 Sx: ATB/Tpt/Perc/Vcl/Bass •STIM
Fragile (1973) •Any instrument, any number •STIM
Gestes sonores (1964) •Any instrument, any number •STIM
No roses for Madame F. (1991) (3') •SATB •STIM
Per caso (1963) (5'30) •Asx/Trb/Vln/Bass/2 Perc •SeMC
Quartet (1984) (7') •SATB •STIM

MELNIK
Birthstones •Asx/Pno •ABC

MELROSE
Saxophone moderne solos •Asx/Pno •Mol

MENCHERINI, Fernando (1949)
Compositeur italien, né à Cagli. Travailla avec W. Branchi.
Ambra e Spunk (1985) (to F. MONDELCI) •Sx Solo
Caravan trio (1989) (to M. *Mazzoni*) •SnoSx/BsCl/Pno
Divaricanto 3 (1992) (to M. *MAZZONI*) •Bsx/Pno
Playtime IV (8'30) (to MM. *Mondelci - Mazzoni*) •2 Sx: ST

MENDELSSOHN, Arnold Ludwig (1855-1933)
Soldier's March (BUCHTEL) •Asx/Pno •Kjos

MENDELSSOHN, Félix (1809-1847)
Abenlied (VEKEN) •2 Bb Sx/Pno •TM
Adagio •5 Sx: SATBBs •WWS
Agitato (MULE) •SATB
Allegro No. 2 (REX) •Eb Sx or Bb Sx/Pno
Andante (MULE) •Asx/Pno •Led
Andante No. 6 (REX) •Eb Sx or Bb Sx/Pno
Andante du concerto (CHAUVET) •Asx/Pno •Com
Auf flüggeln der Gesanges (CLUWEN) •Bb Sx/Pno •Mol
Capriccio brillant •Bb Sx/Pno Mil
Chanson de printemps (MULE) •Asx or Bb Sx/Pno •Led
Chanson de printemps (ROMBY) •Asx/Pno •PB
Chanson de printemps (VIARD) •Asx/Pno •Sal
Evening Song •2 Sx: TT •TM
Faith, op. 102/6 •4 Sx: AATB/Pno ad lib. •Bri
Fileuse (2') (MULE) •SATB •Bil
Fragment du concerto •Bb Sx/Pno •Mil
Frühlingslied •Bb Sx or Eb Sx/Pno •Mol
Ich wollt' meine Liebe ergösse sich (VEKEN) •2 Bb Sx/Pno •TM
Maiglockchen und die Blümelein •2 Sx: AA or SS/Pno •Elk/TM
Marche nuptiale (ROMBY) •Asx/Pno •PB
Nocturne •AATB •MM
Noturno (TRINKAUS) •Bb Sx/Pno •EMH
Noturno (TRINKAUS) •2 Sx: AA or AT/Pno •CF
On Wings of Song (BUCHTEL) •1 Sx: A or T/Pno •Kjos
On Wings of Song (TRINKAUS) •1 Sx: A or T/Pno •CF
Romance sans parole •Bb Sx or Eb Sx/Pno •CF
2 Romances sans parole •Bb Sx/Pno •Mil
Romance sans parole (MAYEUR) •Asx/Pno •CF
Romance sans parole n° 1 (MULE) •Asx/Pno •Led
Romance sans parole n° 3 (MULE) •Asx/Pno •Led
Romance sans parole n° 20 (MULE) •Asx/Pno •Led
Rondo capriccioso (TEAL) •SATB •Eto
Song without words (GUREWICH) •Asx/Pno •Mills
Souvenir de Félix Mendelssohn (P. CLUWEN) •4 Sx: SATB or SAAT or SATT or SAAB •TM
Spinnerlied, op. 67, no. 4 (SAKAGUCHI) •SATB •EFJM
Spinning Song (TEAL) •SATB •Eto
Spring Song •2 Sx: AT/Pno •Cen
Spring Song (BROOKE) •AATB •CF
War March of the Priests (JOHNSON) •AATB •Rub

MENENDEZ, Julian (1895)
Clarinettiste et compositeur espagnol, né à Santander, le 28 V 1895.
Estudio de concerto (1985) (6'30) •1 Sx: A or T/Pno •RME
Lamento y tarentela (1958) (11') •Asx/Pno •AMP/UME

MENEYROL, Georges
Bazasax (1982) (2'30) •Tsx/Pno •Bil

MENGELBERG, Misha (1939)
Compositeur néerlandais.
Dressoir (1977) (10') •Fl/3 Sx: S+A A T/2 Tpt/Hn/2 Trb/Tuba/Pno •Don

MENGOLD, Paul
Miniatures •Asx/Pno •EV
Quartette •Vln/Vcl/Asx/Pno

MENICHETTI, François (1894-1969)
Chef de musique et compositeur français, né à Bastia (Corse). Travailla avec Caussade.

Bouquet oriental (1934) (5'30) 1) Chamya-menuet 2) La voix du désert - complainte •SATB •Mar

MENSING, Eberhard (1942)
Compositeur allemand.
Tennis ist toll (1978) (44') •Cl/Sx/Perc •adr

MERANGER, Paul (1936)
Compositeur français.
Amoroso •SATB
Andante (1977) •Asx/Pno •Com
Berceuse •Asx/Pno •Bil
Chanson russe •Asx/Pno •Bil
Concerto, op. 20 (1977) (15') 1) Allegro moderato 2) Andante 3) Allegro •Asx/Str Orch or Pno •Bil
Dialogue (1982) •Tsx/Pno
Diptuka, op. 15 (1976) (to B. BEAUFRETON) 1) Cadence-reflets 2) Tourbillons •Tsx/Pno
Historiette (1986) (2'30) •Asx/Pno •Com
Petite suite pittoresque (1973) (to J. DESLOGES) •SATB
1er Quatuor d'anches (1977) (to Quatuor d'Anches de Paris) •Ob/Cl/Asx/Bsn
Quatuor d'automne (1978) (to Quatuor Desloges) •SATB
Solo 24 (1981) (to G. PORTE) •Asx Solo •Bil
Tenerezza (1977) •Asx/Pno •Com

MERCADANTE, Saverio (1795-1870)
Testa di Bronzo (VERROUST) •Sx Solo •Bil

MERCURE, Pierre (1927-1966)
Compositeur canadien, né le 2 II 1927, à Montréal, mort à Avallon, le 29 I 1966. Travailla avec N. Boulanger et Dallapiccola.
"He had turned to a spontaneous lyrical expression in traditional forms, influenced by Stravinsky, Milhaud and Honegger, and also by popular American music and jazz. The rhythms are explicit, the orchestration shimmers. Mercure returned to Europe in the summer of 1962 to familiarize himself with new developments in electronic and other music in Paris, Darmstadt and Darlington. In *Tetrachromie* for instruments and electronic sounds (1963), Mercure produced a work on the four seasons and the four ages of man, symbolically represented by the colours green, yellow, red and white." (L. RICHER-LORTIE)
Tetrachromie (1963) •Cl/Asx/BsCl/Perc/Tape •CMC

MERILÄINEN, Usko (1930)
Compositeur finlandais, né le 27 I 1930. Travailla avec Merikando et Vogel.
"He was one of the first Finnish composers to use the 12-note method, and serial thinking led to an enrichment of texture in such works, but the rational control inherent in serial writing proved alien to his aspirations." (I. ORAMO)
Simultanus for four (1979) (16') (to P. SAVIJOKI) •Fl/Asx/Guit/Perc •Pan/FMIC
Sonata (1982) (13') (to P. SAVIJOKI) •Asx/Pno •FMIC

MERIOT, Michel (1928)
Saxophoniste français, né le 6 V 1928, à St Pierre de Maillé (Vienne). Travailla avec M. Mule. 1er Prix du Conservatoire de Paris, et J. Falk.
A l'ombre du micocoulier (1986) (2'15) •1 Sx: A or T/Pno •Com
Campanule, op. 33 (1984) (1'30) •1 Sx: A or T/Pno •Com
Comme un dimanche (1990) (3') •Asx/Pno •Com
En vacances (1983) (2') (to D. MASSÉ) •Asx/Pno •Com
Evasion (1990) (2'30) •1 Sx: A or T/Pno •Com
Grisaille, op. 39 (1985) (3') •1 Sx: A or T/Pno •Com
Le saxophoniste (Method) (1964) (to M. MULE) •Com
Légende poitevine (1988) (2'45) •Asx/Pno •Com
Les couleurs de l'Aube (1992) (2'45) •Asx/Pno •Com

12 Monodies atonales (des 32 pièces) •Sx Solo •Com
Le nouveau saxophoniste classique (4 volumes) •Com
15 Petites pièces en forme d'études (1981) •Com
28 pièces variées (2 Volumes), op. 36 •Com
32 pièces variées en différentes tonalités •Sx Solo •Com
Révérence (1986-87) •Asx/Pno •Com
Romance •Asx/Pno •Phi
Simplement (1992) (2'30) •Asx/Pno •Com
Solitude (1988) (2'30) •1 Sx: A or T/Pno •Com
Street song (1993) (3'10) •Asx/Pno •Com

MERK, Ulrike
Compositeur allemand.
Metamorphose (1993) •Asx/Pno •INM

MERKU, Pavle (1929)
Compositeur yougoslave, né à Trieste, le 12 VII 1929. Travailla avec I. Grbec et V. Levi.
"A prolific composer, he always aims for a refined and delicate style, particularly in his chamber music. He has little interest in folk music and has investigated new techniques, choosing only those elements that are compatible with clarity of expression and beauty of sound, and preferring a moderate approach." (N. O'LOUGHLIN)
Tiare •Baritone Voice/Sx/11 wind instruments [instruments à vent] •Piz

MERLET, Michel (1939)
Compositeur français né à Saint-Brieuc, le 26 V 1939. Travailla avec T. Aubin et O. Messiaen.
Variations, op. 32 (1982) (to Quatuor Desloges) (Theme & 9 variations) •SATB •Led

MERRELLI, Flavio
Il libro •3 Sx: SAB

MERRIMAN
Baroque Studies •Sx •Sha

MERSSON, Boris E. (1921)
Compositeur suisse, né à Berlin, le 6 X 1921, de parents suisses d'origine russe. Travailla avec son père puis avec I. Karr, H. Stierlin-Vallon, A. Denereaz, A. Fornerod, et H. Scherchen.
"Compositeur fort adroit bénéficiant à la fois d'une culture musicale classique et d'une grande expérience de la musique divertissante."
Concerto, op. 25 (1966) (to E. COHANIER) (Allegro ma non troppo svelto - Andante sostenuto e misterioso - Allegro comodo) •Asx/Band •adr
Fantaisie, op. 37 (1979) (to I. ROTH) •Asx/Pno •Ku
Sound for seven, op. 24 (12') •Ob Solo/Jazz Sx Quartet •adr
Suite, op. 17 (1960) (to E. COHANIER) 1) Conversation 2) Méditation 3) Soliloque •SATB •Br&Ha
Suite, op. 20 (1961) •SATB •adr

MESANG, T. L.
Pleasant Thoughts •Tsx/Pno •SBC

MESSAGER, André (1853-1929)
Chant birman (VIARD) •Asx/Pno •Sal

MESSIERI, Massimiliano
Compositeur italien.
Espressione I (1993) •Asx/Live Tape •INM

MESSINA-ROSARYO, Antonio (1945)
Compositeur, saxophoniste, et chanteur d'origine italienne, né à Giarre, le 29 IX 1945. Vit en Allemagne.
Buria (7') •Picc/Asx •Asto
Danza del demonio - ballet (1984) (35') •SnoSx/Orch •Asto

Dialogo (5') •Sx/BsTrb •Asto
Erlkönig - Suite (21'30) •Asx/Pno •Asto
Fantasia capricciosa (1984) (7'30) •3 Sx •Asto

MESTRAL, Patrice (1945)

Compositeur et chef d'orchestre français, né à Paris, le 7 VIII 1945. "Though he had no composition teacher, his association, beginning in 1961-2, With Eloy, Amy and others was of decisive importance: through them he came to a knowledge of the Boulezian techniques he has used in his work." (P. GRIFFITHS)
Alliages (1969) •Tpt Solo/Fl/Cl/Asx/2 Trb/2 Perc/Pno/Org/Bass

METEHEN

Fedora •Asx/Pno •Mar

METRAL, Pierre

Percussioniste et compositeur suisse.
Sonatine No. 2 (1976) (to R. CUNDIFF) •Asx/Perc •SeMC

MEULEMANS, Arthur (1884-1966)

Compositeur et chef d'orchestre belge né le 19 V 1884 à Aarschot, mort à Bruxelles, el 29 VI 1966. Travailla avec E. Tinel.
"Sans s'opposer au climat d'austérité mystique qui caractérise le style de son maître E. Tinel, Arthur Meulemans ne s'est pas moins affranchi de ce que cette religion sévère détient d'inconciliable avec le génie flamand, son dynamisme, son réalisme sensuel, son amour de la vie." (R. BERNARD) "Créateur d'une belle fécondité, dans un style post-impressionniste qui doit à Ravel, et qui est mis en valeur par une virtuosité orchestrale de premier ordre." (H. HALBREICH) "Arthur Meulemans s'exprime avec un accent néo-romantique affirmé et avec une fécondité impressionnante." (Cl. ROSTAND)
"He wrote a great deal and demonstrated a brilliant orchestral technique considerably influenced by French impressionism, although there is individuality in the descriptive nature of some of the symphonic poems that were stimulated by the naturalism of Flemish Renaissance painters." (C. MERTENS)
Concertino (1962) (14') (to Quatuor belge de Saxophones) •SATB/Orch (Fl/Ob/Tpt/Str/Perc) •CBDM
Concerto grosso (1958) (13'30) 1) Andante 2) Allegro 3) Sostenuto 4) Allegro •SATB/Orch (Perc/Harp/Str) •CBDM
Pièces •SATB •Ger
Quatuor (1953) (14') (to Quatuor belge de Saxophones) 1) Moderato 2) Poco lento e rubato 3) Andante 4) Allegro spiritoso •SATB •CBDM
Rapsodie - Quintette (1961) •3 Cl/BsCl/Asx •CBDM
Rhapsodie (1942) (5'30) •Asx/Orch (2222/430/Perc/Harp/Str) or Pno •Ger/An/CBDM

MEULEN, Henk van der

Compositeur néerlandais.
De profondis I (1986) (15') •Fl/3 Sx: S+T A A/Hn/3 Tpt/2 Trb/BsTrb/Bass/Pno •Don
Desert journey (1982) (15') •2 Sx: AT/Perc •Don
Introduction (1981) (4') •2 Sx: SA •Don
Quintet - Ballet (1981/84) (48') •2 Sx: SA/3 Perc •Don

MEULINK, Cor

Valse élégante •Asx/Pno •VAB

MEUNIER, R.

Metamorphosis (1982) •Sx/Perc

MEURICE, Félicien (1888-19xx) (see RUNGIS,

René)

MEYER, Alexandre Henri (1896-1968)

Pianiste et compositeur français, né à Mulhouse où il est mort. Travailla à Bâle et Strasbourg, ainsi qu'à Munich.
"Langage atonal, voire sériel"
Sonate Lab-Sib-Ré (1948-49) 1) Modéré 2) Valse lente 3) Rondo •Tsx/Pno

MEYER, Jean-Michel (1910)

Compositeur français, né le 19 VII 1910 à Paris. Travailla avec Noèl-Gallon.
"Pièces instrumentales en général d'un caractère alerte et enjoué." (SWANN) "Oeuvres d'un discret modernisme laissant à l'auditeur l'impression de la spontanéité." (A. ROCHE)
Divertissement (1975) 1) Prélude 2) Ronde 3) Minuetto 4) Final •SATB •Bil
Genêts et bruyères (1966) (2'45) (to R. BONNINGUE) •Asx/Pno •Led
Nocturne et Gigue •3 Sx: AAT •adr
Novelette (1962) (6') (to J-M. LONDEIX) •Asx/Pno •Sch
Romance sans parole (1968) •Asx/Pno •GD

MEYER, Krzysztof (1943)

Compositeur et pianiste autrichien d'origine polonaise, né à Krakau, le 11. VIII 1943. Travailla avec K. Penderecki puis, à Paris, avec Nadia Boulanger. Vit en Allemagne depuis 1987.
Quartet, op. 65a (1986) (12') (to Rascher Saxophone Quartet) •SATB •CA

MEYER, Lucien (1870-1932)

Compositeur français.
Assomption, Andante religioso (to Mlle LAROUSSE) •Asx/Org (or Pno) •ES
Méditation (to M. de l'ARGENTIÈRE) •Asx/Pno •ES
Morceau de concours (PENNEQUIN) •Asx/Pno •BC

MEYERBEER, Giacomo (1791-1864)

Cantiques (from *L'Africaine*) (W. HEKKER) •4 Sx: SATB or AATB •TM
Coronation March (HARRIS) •2 Cl/Asx/Bsn (or BsCl) •CF
Coronation March (HOLMES) •AATB •Rub
Coronation March (HOLMES) •AATB/Pno •Rub
Coronation March (TRINKAUS) •2 Sx: AA or AT/Pno •CF
Marche des flambeaux (ROMBY) •Asx/Pno •PB

MICHAEL, Edward (1921)

Nocturne (to M. PERRIN) •Asx/Pno/Perc
Pièce brève (1967) (9') (to M. PERRIN) •Asx/Orch or Pno

MICHAEL, Frank (1943)

Compositeur allemand, né le 3 II 1943 à Leipzig.
Kmk •Fl/Ssx/Trb/Vln/Vla/Vcl •adr

MICHALSKY, Donal

Compositeur américain.
Three Times four... •SATB •DP

MICHANS, Carlos

Compositeur néerlandais.
Quartetto (1989) (10') •SATB •Don

MICHEL, Bernard

Avant, pendant, après... (to J-P. CAENS) •SATB

MICHEL, Paul Baudoin (1930)

Compositeur belge né le 7 IX 1930, à Haine St-Pierre. Travailla avec O. Messiaen, B. Maderna, P. Boulez, et G. Ligeti, ainsi qu'avec J. Absil.

Arcs (1974) (10') (to Fr. DANEELS) •SATB •adr
Masscom (1983) (11') (to BOCK and LE MAIR) •Sx/Vibr •adr
Mouvement intérieur (1977) •Asx/Harp •adr
Mouvements (1977) (6'30) •Asx/Pno •adr
Quatuor (to Quatuor belge de Saxophones) 1) Prélude 2) Slow
   3) Allegro •SATB
Ultramorphoses (1965) (12-15') •Fl/Cl/Asx/Perc/Pno/Vln/Vla/Vcl
   •CBDM

MICHEL-FREDERIC, Félix (1956)

Saxophoniste français d'origine martiniquaise.
Micro-climat (1981) (Moderato - Lent - Scherzo) •2 Sx: AB/Tpt/Trb

MIDDELEER, Jean de (1908)

Compositeur belge, né à Molenbeek-St-Jean, le 24 II 1908. Travailla
avec P. Gilson et M. Dupre.
Recitativo e allegro (1970) (4') •Asx/Pno

MIELENZ, Hans (1909)

Compositeur allemand de musique de variétés.
Festklänge •AATB •Fro
Im Frühling •AATB •Fro
Rondo •AATB •Fro
Scherzo (VOXMAN) •AATB •Rub

MIEREANU, Costin (1943)

Compositeur français d'origine roumaine, né à Bucarest. Naturalisé
en 1977. Travailla avec Stockhausen, G. Ligeti, et E. Karkoschka.
Codirecteur avec Paul Mefano de l'ensemble 2E2M.
"Adepte de la 'théorie des catastrophes' de René Thom."
Aksax (1984) (5'35) •Sx Solo: Bs or CBs Solo •Sal
Boléro des Balkans (1984) (13') •1 Sx: CBs+Bs+T+S+Sno/Perc/
   Tape •Sal
Clair de biche (1986) (11') •Fl/Picc/Cl/1 Sx: Sno+S+T/Brass
   Quintet [de cuivres]/5 Perc •Sal
La colline bleue (1984) (8') (to F. BOTH) 1 to 6 Sx/Matériel électr.
   •Sal
Distance zero (1987) (10') •1 Player: Cl+Asx ad lib./Perc •Sal
Do-Mi-Si-La-Do-Ré (1980-81) (16'30) (to D. KIENTZY) •1 player:
   Cl+BsCl+Sx/Tape or 5 Sx: SATBBs/Tape •Sal
Doppelkammerkonzert (1985) (17') •1 Sx: Sno+A+T+Bs/Perc Solo/
   Orch •Sal
Jardins retrouvés (1985) (20') (to D. KIENTZY) •Electr. Ssx/Vcl/Perc/
   Harp/Tape •Sal
Kammer-koncert n° 1 (1984-85) (16') (to D. KIENTZY) •1 Sx:
   Sno+A+T+Bs/Orch (1010/000/1001/Guit/Mandolin/Harp/Perc
   •Sal
Miroir liquide (1986) (11') •1 Sx: Sno+S+A+T/Bsn/Perc/Harp/Pno/
   Bass •Sal
Ondes (1986) (6') •Asx Solo •Sal
Polymorphies 5 X 7 B (1969-70) (9-10') •Fl+Picc/Cl/Tsx/Pno/Vln/
   Vla/Vcl/Bass •Sal
Ricochets (1989) •1 Sx: Sno+S+A+T+B/Electr. Guit/Bass Guit/
   Synth/Perc/Régie électr. •Sal
Tercafeira (1984-85) (16') (to D. KIENTZY) •3 Sx Players: Sno+S+A,
   S+A+T, S+A+T+B/Tape
Variants - Invariants (1982) (14') (to D. KIENTZY) •1 Sx: A or S/
   Echo Chamber •Sal

MIGNION, René (1907-1981)

Chef de musique français, né à Montmedy, le 13 IX 1907. Travailla
avec G. Balay-Caussade, P. Lamirault et E. Mignion.
Andante et Gavotte (1980) •Bb Sx/Pno •Bil
Anémone (1980) •Ob/Asx/Vcl
Aurore (1976) •Asx/Pno •Bil
Camelia - Trio •Ob/Asx/Vcl

Colombine et Pierrot (1979) •Asx/Pno •Bil
Complainte et divertissement •Bb Sx/Pno •Bil
Diane en forêt (1976) •Asx/Pno •Bil
Eglogue (1976) •Bb Sx/Pno •Bil
Elégie pastorale (1972) (3'45) •Asx/Pno •Bil
Floralie (1980) 1) Larghetto 2) Adagio 3) Andantino •Ob/Asx/Vcl
Fugue bretonne (1977) •4 Sx: SATB/Pno •Bil
Les Glycines (Largo - Larghetto - Andantino - Moderato) •Ob/Asx/
   Vcl
Invocation et marche miniature (1973) (3') •Asx/Pno •Bil
Lamento e consolato (1980) •Asx/Pno •Bil
Perce-neige •Ob/Asx/Vcl
Pervenche (1980) •Ob/Asx/Vcl
Petit enfant (1977) 1) Reveil 2) Promenade 3) Cache-cache
   4) Berceuse •SATB •Bil
Petites esquisses •Asx/Pno •Bil
Pièces brèves (1980) •Bb Sx/Pno •Bil
Primerose •Asx/Pno •Bil
Roseraie (1980) •Ob/Asx/Vcl
Santa Marie-Lou (1979) •Asx/Pno •Bil

MIGOT, Georges (1891-1976)

Compositeur français, né le 27 II 1891, à Paris, où il est mort, le 5 I
1976. Travailla avec Widor, Gedalge, et d'Indy.
   "Esprit cultivé et très religieux, Georges Migot poursuit une oeuvre
sévèrement contrapuntique, animée par la mystique des nombres, en se
tournant fréquemment vers un passé musical français qui remonte aux
troubadours." (R. STRICKER) "L'Importance que revêt la voix humaine
dans son oeuvre, témoigne d'une vive création contre le chromatisme
systématique des écoles d'Europe centrale et d'un retour aux origines
chantantes de la musique occidentale." (M. HONEGGER) "Sa tendance au
dépouillement, sa recherche toute intérieure, sa liberté rythmique,
l'énorme souffle religieux qui inspire presque toutes ses pages, tout
semble indiquer qu'il occupe une place de choix en notre temps." (A.
SURCHAMP) "Anticonformiste et solitaire, il a recherché pour son
compte personnel et en marge de son époque un renouvellement du
langage et des formes, tout en s'appuyant sur les plus anciennes
traditions de la musique médiévale. Son art est essentiellement horizontal. Il témoigne de subtiles recherches dans les domaines de la
mélodie et du rythme, le tout se déroulant dans un climat généralement
modal." (Cl. ROSTAND) "Dans ses oeuvres, le musicien pose généralement un motif ou deux; il les laisse évoluer librement et suit attentive-
ment la trace de leur sillage. Ces 'sillages sonores' réagissent entre eux,
en fonction des pôles d'attraction que le musicien contrôle et ordonne.
Le compositeur pense avant tout en musicien, et ce n'est qu'à la
dernière note que la forme apparaît dans son ensemble. L'audition ne
laisse pas le souvenir d'une mosaïque d'éléments accolés, juxtaposés,
mais donne au contraire l'impression d'un tout dans lequel chaque
partie a trouvé naturellement sa place et sa nécessité dans cet accom-
plissement." (M. PINCHARD)
   "In his style, he attempts to recapture the old French spirit of
polyphonic writing, emphasizing the national continuity of art." (BAKER)
"In many aspects Migot seems to stand aloof from the main stream of
contemporary music, and it is with good reason that he has been dubbed
by a modern critic (HENRION) 'the spiritual brother of Guillaume de
Machaut,' with whose contrapuntal style, especially, his music has
great affinities. Thinking polyphonically he is chiefly concerned with
weaving arabesques of several independent parts moving at different
levels which engender their own harmony—hence, his predilection for
chamber and, above all, vocal combinations, especially *a capella*" (R.
MYERS) "The flowing quality of Migot's music sets it in the tradition
of Couperin, Rameau and Debussy. Migot moulded his thought on
biblical philosophy, particularly that of the New Testament, sometimes
using his own texts based on the Gospels. His independent poetry, too,
is concerned principally with spiritual themes. He insisted on a close

spiritual link between text and music, scorning simplistic word-painting, but even in his secular and instrumental works the loftiness of thought is unmistakable." (M. HONEGGER)

2 Stèles de Victor Segalen (1925) (15') •Voice (or Asx)/Celesta/ Bass/Perc •Led

Quatuor (1955) (17'30) (to M & G. HUESSER) 1) Allant-Mouvt. de valse 2) Choral-Berceuse 3) Final •SATB

MIHAJLO, Zivanovic
Balada •Asx/Pno •YUC
Invenaja •Asx/Pno •YUC
Rapsodija •Asx/Orch •YUC

MIHALOVICI, Marcel (1898-1985)
Compositeur français d'origine roumaine, né à Bucarest le 22 X 1898. Fixé à Paris depuis 1919, où il est mort en 1985. Travailla avec V. d'Indy. A fait partie de l'*Ecole de Paris.*

"Une des personnalités que l'école française peut s'honorer d'avoir en son sein et dont la stature se dégage nettement dans le paysage musical européen… L'art de Mihalovici unit la tradition et la nouveauté: tradition nationale dont la saveur imprègne certaines de ses oeuvres sans folklore indiscret, tradition des grandes formes instrumentales dans la descendance de Brahms et de Reger, tradition de clarté française; mais le poids de toutes ces traditions n'a jamais fait de lui un néo-classique ni un éclectique. Son style est bien de lui; cette grande culture classique est sans cesse tournée vers l'avenir et le renouvellement après avoir subi les influences de voisinages, comme ceux de Schoenberg, Stravinski, Prokofiev et Bartok, sans oublier celle de son compatriote Enesco. Son instinct le portait naturellement vers la syntaxe tonale avant même qu'il eût connu les réalisations de l'école de Vienne, et c'est dans ce climat qu'il s'exprime après avoir fait une magistrale synthèse des acquisitions de son temps." (Cl. ROSTAND) "Il utilise volontiers les modes folkloriques, ainsi que des modes qui lui sont personnels, les combinant avec un chromatisme poussé jusqu'aux limites de la tonalité et faisant souvent des incursions dans le domaine de l'atonalité, sans jamais perdre le souvenir de sa foi diatonique." (LAROUSSE)

Chant premier, op. 103 (1973) (12') (to G. LACOUR) •Tsx/Orch or Pno •Heu

MIJAN, Manuel
Saxophoniste virtuose et professeur espagnol. Travailla avec J-M. Londeix. Professeur au Conservatoire de Madrid.
Tecnica de base (1983)

MIKHAILOV, Lev (1928)
Saxophoniste russe; premier professeur de saxophone au Conservatoire de Moscou (1971)
Ecole du saxophone (Method) (1975)
Pièces de compositeurs soviétiques

MIKULSKA, Anna (1951)
Compositeur polonais, né le 10 I 1951, à Tarnow.
Fantaisie (1977) (10') •Bb Sx/Pno

MILES & ZIMMERMANN
Anchors Aweigh (WIEDOEFT) •Asx/Pno •Rob

MILETIC, Miroslav (1925)
Compositeur et violoniste yougoslave, né à Sisak.
Noveleta (1981) (to V. MACAN) •Asx/Pno •DSH
Sonate (1982) •Asx/Pno

MILHAUD, Darius (1892-1974)
Compositeur français, né à Aix-en-Provence, le 4 IX 1892, mort à Genève, le 22 VI 1974. Travailla avec P. Dukas, Gedalge et V. D'Indy. Membre du 'Groupe des Six.'

"Protée de la musique du vingtième siècle, Darius Milhaud l'a été, aussi bien par la quantité des oeuvres qu'il a produites que par son attitude: nonchalance, indolence, 'vie heureuse,' mais aussi puissance, diversité des genres qu'il a d'ailleurs pratiquement tous abordés. Milhaud où le tri s'impose, sous réserve qu'on le connaisse dans son ampleur et sa diversité, marque plus la fin d'une conception musicale que l'inauguration d'une nouveauté dont *la Création du monde*, son oeuvre la plus célèbre, aurait pu donner à croire." (C. GLAYMAN) "Lorsque je commençai à écrire de la musique, je sentis tout de suite les dangers qu'il y avait à suivre les sentiers de la musique impressionniste. Tant de flou, de brises parfumées, de fusées de feux d'artifice, de parures étincelantes, de fumées, d'alanguissements marquaient la fin d'une époque dont la mièvrerie me donnait un insurmontable dégoût." (D. MILHAUD) "Musicien robuste, de tempérament foncièrement classique." (E. VUILLERMOZ) "Darius Milhaud est un lyrique méditerranéen utilisant tous les procédés de langage actuellement connus, mais ennemis de tout système. Sa production est l'une des plus considérables de l'histoire de la musique. Elle touche aux genres les plus différents et s'y manifeste avec la même fécondité. On ne peut donc qu'opérer un choix dans le catalogue de celui qui est le plus grand lyrique français de notre époque. Darius Milhaud a employé la polytonalité depuis le début de sa carrière, mais il ne cherche pas à rompre avec l'univers tonal. Son style, rendu homogène et constant, d'une originalité incomparablement personnelle au surplus, est cependant, à l'analyse, d'une certaine complexité. Il révèle d'abord ses origines provençales et juives, ce qui en fait à l'origine le type même du lyrique méditerranéen." (Cl. ROSTAND) "De tous les musiciens français, Darius Milhaud est le plus méditerranéen. Tout ce qui est la mer latine, tout ce qui vit entre Constantinople et Cadix, entre Rio-de-Janeiro et les Antilles est présent dans sa musique, s'y exprime entièrement." (P. COLLAERT) "Milhaud est d'une fécondité surprenante; il nous apparaît comme une force de la nature, avec tout ce que cette notion peut impliquer, à la fois de puissant, de désordonné et d'excessif." (R. BERNARD) "*La Création du Monde* est une de ses plus belles réussites. Thèmes, rythmes, harmonies se construisent, s'assemblent pour nous, en un mystère lointain, traversé d'appels polytonaux étranges, en un bouillonnement cosmique qui, petit à petit s'exalte, s'organise. Dynamisme puissant et inspiré." (P. WOLFF) Son oeuvre qui illustre tous les genres, est absolument gigantesque: on a d'ailleurs souvent reproché à Milhaud sa prolixité; mais sa musique qui porte l'empreinte de la culture provençale, est lumineuse et claire. Son invention mélodique, intarissable, est à la fois originale, pure lyrique, chaude et profonde—au point que Paul Collaert a pu comparer Milhaud à un poète lyrique qui s'exprime en musique." (A. de PLACE) "*Caramel mou*, op. 68 'mouvement de shimmy' représente pour Alfred Cortot 'une évocation curieusement précise des premières manifestations de jazz et de l'atmosphère des dancings de Harlem et de Manhattan.' "

"He was the first to exploit polytonality in a consistent and deliberate manner; has applied the exotic rhythms of Latin America and the West Indies in many of his lighter works; Brazilian movements are also found in his *Scaramouche*; in some of this works he has drawn upon the resources of jazz. Despite this variety of means and versatility of forms, Milhaud has succeeded in establishing a style that is distinctly and identifiably his own; his melodies are nostalgically lyrical or vivaciously rhythmical, according to mood; his instrumental writing is of great complexity and difficulty, and yet entirely within the capacities of modern virtuoso technic; he has arranged many of his works in several versions each." (BAYER) "Each composition is based on a technique suited to it alone or at worst to similar works—and Milhaud has rarely produced works that show marked similarities. While his choice of medium is astonishingly diversified—the incidental music for almost every play is differently scored—his resources of composition may draw upon anything from jazz, folksong or exotic popular music to involved polyphonic complexities. He is particularly skilled in the handling of polytonal counterpoint and knows how to interweave melodic strands in different keys in such a way that the result strikes the ear as perfectly reasonable as well as invariably lucid." (E. BLOM) "He was one of the 20th century's most industrious composers, impelled to expend himself in unceasing productivity in such a way that his creativity diffused itself over a vast area of heterogeneous works. Potentially he was one of the best composers of his generation: there are few pieces that do not contain something of value, though not many people have the time or energy to sift through vast quantities of chaff in quest of the isolated grain of wheat." (Ch. PALMER)

Caramel mou, op. 68 (1921) (5') (to G. Auric) •Bb Sx (or Voice)/Cl/Tpt/Trb/Pno/Perc •ME

La Création du Monde (1923) (16') •Asx/2 Vln/Vcl/Bass/2121/121/Pno/Perc •ME

La Création du Monde - Suite (LONDEIX) (14') 1) Prélude 2) Fugue 3) Romance 4) Scherzo 5) Final •2 Vln/Asx/Vcl/Bass/Perc/Pno •ME

Danse (1954) (2') •Asx/Pno •PN

Etude poétique, op. 333 (1954) •2 Sx/Voice/Orch/Tape

Scaramouche (1937) (9'30) •Asx/Orch (2222/222/Perc/Str) or Pno •Sal

Scaramouche (LONDEIX) •Asx Solo/11 Sx: SnoSSAAAATTBBBs •Sal

Scaramouche (D. STEWART) •Asx/Fl/Ob/Cl/Hn/Bsn •Sal

MILICEVIC, Mladen

Solo (1986) (8') (to D. KIENTZY) •Ssx/Tape

MILIVOJ, Koerbler (1930)

Compositeur croate, né à Zagreb, le 3 V 1930. Président de l'Association des Musiciens de Danse et de Musique de jazz de Croatie (1961-63).

Varijacije (1956) •Asx •YUC

MILLER, Dennis

Compositeur américain.

Three Recitativi amorosi (1976) (4') •Sx Solo •adr

MILLER, Edward Jay (1930)

Compositeur américain, né le 4 VIII 1930, à Miami.

Fantasy-concerto (1971) (10') (To D. SINTA) (3 movements) •Asx/Band •ACA

Quartet Variations •Any 4 instruments

Two Pieces (1990) •Asx/Pno

MILLER, Ralph Dale

Compositeur américain.

The Modern Right-Way, Self Introduction •MCA

Quartet No. 2, op. 16 •AATB •Pro

MILLER, Robert

Instrumental Course (J. SKORNIKA) •Eb Sx •B&H

Instrumental Course (J. SKORNIKA) •Tsx •B&H

MILLER, Roy

Compositeur américain.

Uintah (Winter) (to L. TEAL) •Asx/Band

MILLS, Charles (1914)

Compositeur américain, né à Ashville (North Carolina), le 8 I 1914. Travailla avec A. Copland, R. Harris, et R. Sessions.

"His compositional style reflects his belief in the continued validity of traditional forms (fugue and sonata) and the diatonic system. There are often perceptible influences from his experience, both musical (the spirituals and folksongs heard during his childhood in South Carolina, and the jazz music of the dance orchestras in which he played as a young man) and spiritual: he was a convert to Roman Catholicism in 1944, and his work carries a sense of piety and contemplation." (B. HAMPTON)

Music •Sx/Bass •Pio

Music for Recorder •Sx/Bass •CFE/ACA

Paul Bunyan Jump (Jazz Quintet) (1964) •Asx/Pno/Tpt/Bass/Perc •ACA

MILLOCKER, Karl (1842-1899)

Herinneringer •SATB •Mol

MILOVIC, Janko

Metallochronie (1980) •Asx/Perc

MIMET, Anne-Marie

Ar foren Têg (1981) •Asx/Pno •Bil

Complainte •Asx/Harp or Pno •Bil

Le départ du roi Cafier - airs gaulois •Asx/Harp or Pno •Bil

Fanfare et divertissement •Fl/Ob/Cl/Bsn/3 Sx: SAT/Tpt/Trb/Tuba

Hiraeth (1981) (to R. PIERNY) •Asx/Harp or Pno •Bil

Y galon drom (1983) •Asx/Harp or Pno •Bil

MINAMIKAWA, Mio (1958)

Compositeur japonais, né à Kobé, le 14 VIII 1958. Travailla avec L. Takashi. Prix Concours Marcel Josse (1981).

Crystal shapar (1983) (to Y. HASHIZUMÉ) •Tsx/Pno •adr

Diptyque (1988) (11') •Asx/Pno •adr

Métaplasm (1982) •12 Sx: SnoSSAAAATTTBBBs/2 Perc •adr

Objet shop (1983) (to K. UÉDA) •2 Sx •adr

Ondulation (1981) •Asx/Ob/Vcl •adr

MINCIACCHI, Diego

Il nostro rapido viaggio (1992) •Sx Orch

MINDLIN, Adolfo

Blues song (1987) (2') (to F. MORETTI) •Asx/Pno •Led

Le forgeron (1985) (1'45) (to J. LEDIEU) •Asx/Pno •Led

Le petit soldat (1987) (to G. CANDEL) •Asx/Pno •Led

MINGUS, Charles

Jelly Roll •4 Sx: SATB or AATB •WWS

MINTCHEV, Gueorgui

Compositeur bulgare. Président de l'Union des compositeurs bulgares.

Musique de concert (1985) (10'30) (to J-M. LONDEIX) •12 Sx: SnoSSAAATTTBBBs •adr

MIRANDA, Ronaldo

Compositeur cubain.

Fantasia (to M. VILLAFRUELA) •Asx/Pno

MISTAK, Alvin F.

Compositeur américain.

Quartet •SATB •Eto

MITCHELL, John

Compositeur anglais.

Pod (1975) (5'30) (to London Saxophone Quartet) 1) Perambulation 2) Pastorale 3) Pagodas •SATB •BMIC

Pot-pourri (1976-77) (7'30) •SATB •BMIC

MITCHELL, William John (1906-1971)

Musicologue et professeur américain, né à New York, le 21 XI 1906, mort à Binghamton (New York) le 17 VIII 1971. Travailla à Vienne.

"His main area of interest was music theory; he devised the curriculum in this subject as an academic discipline at Columbia University, and wrote a wide variety of works on the theory and historical practice of harmony and structure." (GROVE)

Song of the City (1967) (to V. ABATO) •Asx/Band or Pno •CC

MITI, Luca

Compositeur italien.

One for Bill (1993) •2 Sx: AT •INM

MITREA-CELARIANU, Mihai (1935)

Compositeur roumain, né à Bucarest.

Convergence "quatre" •Sx Solo •Sal
Eté (1989) (9') •SATB
Ouverture -Valse centrale •Asx/Bass/Perc •Sal

MIYAGAWA, Tadatoshi (1948)

Compositeur japonais.

Quatuor (1975) •SATB
Das Spiel (Le Jeu) •SATB

MIYAMAE, Chieko (1951)

Compositeur japonais née à Osaka, le 26 III 1951. Travailla avec A. Yashiro et A. Miyoshi.

Poèlégie (1976) •Asx/Pno •Chou

MIYAZAWA, Kazuto (1952)

Compositeur japonais né à Tokyo le 11 XI 1952.

Paragraphen (1988) •Asx/Vibr/Harp or Asx/Pno
Polyphonie (1978) •SATB
Quartet No. 2 ("Zur ewigen stille") (1986) •SATB
Quartet No. 3 ("Ein hörbares fractal") (1990) •SATB
Versuch über fractal (1987) (8') (to J-M. LONDEIX) •12 Sx:
 SnoSSAAATTTBBs

MOBBERLEY, James

Spontaneous Combustion •1 Sx:S+A/Tape

MOEREMANS, Jean H. B. (186x-1922)

Saxophoniste belge virtuose. Installé aux U.S.A. il fut soliste du United States Marine Band. Réalisa de nombreux disques.

Swell of the Day - Air & Variations (1906) •Asx/ Pno

MOESCHINGER, Albert (1897)

Compositeur suisse, né à Bâle, le 10 I 1897. Travailla avec W. Courvoisier.

"Un des compositeurs suisses alémaniques les plus solides." (N. DUFOURCQ) "Perméable aux courants artistiques les plus divergents, il a écouté la leçon de Debussy et de Ravel tout autant que celle de Schoenberg et que celle de Hindemith." (R. BERNARD) "De formation germanique, Albert Moeschinger doit peut-être l'âpreté et la vigueur de son style au cadre des Alpes valaisannes, où il vit retiré depuis 1943." (H. HALBREICH) "Il s'agit toujours de compositions d'un esprit indépendant et scrutateur qui ne se laisse jamais aller à la facilité, mais exprime avec passion sa profonde sensibilité. Il n'est pas rare (et c'est là un trait bien bâlois) qu'un humour tout particulier y éclate en allégeant la densité de la phrase. Grave, âpre, souvent triste et obstiné, et même opiniâtre, plongé dans de rêveuses pensées, telles sont les caractéristiques de sa musique toujours pleine d'imagination." (Assoc. des Mus. Suisses) "Formé à l'école du post-romantisme germanique, il en a conservé la trace en accueillant les suggestions rythmiques de Stravinski et en y mêlant la rigueur de contraintes formelles empruntées au classicisme. Style assez éclectique en définitive." (Cl. ROSTAND)

"In his works he shows influences of German neo-Romanticism and French Impressionism." (BAKER) "Moeschinger brought about a distinctive and personal synthesis of German and French elements: his extensive oeuvre, numbering more than 200 works, is rooted in the chromaticism of Reger and also in the sound world of Debussy. Although the influence of Schoenberg, Moeschinger made no closer approach to that composer, not even when, from 1956, he began to make an independent use of 12-note procedures." (H. OESCH)

Concerto lyrique, op. 83 (1958) (15') (to S. RASCHER) •Asx/Orch
 (2122/220/Perc/Harp/Str) or Pno •B&H
Images - Quatuor mixte, op. 85 (1958) (18') •Fl/Vln/Asx/Vcl •Bil
Quatuor antherin •SATB

MOEVS, Robert (1920)

Compositeur américain, né à La Crosse (Wisconsin), le 2 XII 1921. Travailla avec W. Piston et N. Boulanger.

"His music is marked by sonorous exuberance and rhythmic impulsiveness; his use of percussion is plagent." "His broad musical structures are logical and balanced, with an extremely impassioned content; he is a master of the orchestra, and writes particularly skilfully for percussion." (B. ARCHIBALD)

Paths and Ways (1970) (4') (to K. DORN) •Sx/Dancer •DP

MOFFAT, J.-G.

Gavotte (RASCHER) •Tsx/Pno •Bel

MOHR, Gerhard

Compositeur allemand.

Douce espérance (1928) (to P. BOHRMANN) •Asx/Pno •Zim
Morning, Mister Plane (Fox-trot) (1928) •Asx/Pno •Zim

MOHR, Jean-Baptiste Victor (1823-1891)

Compositeur français.

1ère partie de Quatuor (1864) (to Ad. SAX) •SATB •Sax

MOHR, Ralph W.

3 Pieces •Sx Solo

MOLAND, Eirik (1959)

Compositeur norvégien.

Trio (1982) •Fl/Asx/Accordion •NMI

MOLINO, Andréa

Unité K (7') (to D. KIENTZY) •1 Sx: S+B/Tape

MOLLER, Kai

Rhapsodie (1953) •Asx/Str or Pno •WH

MOLLOY, James Lyman (1837-1909)

Kerry Dance (HARRIS) •2 Cl/Asx/Bsn (or BsCl) •CF
Love's Old Sweet Song •2 Sx/Pno •Mck
Love's Old Sweet Song •4 Sx: AATB/Pno (ad lib.) •Bri
Love's Old Sweet Song, Alice (RASCHER) •Eb Sx/Pno •CF
Love's Old Sweet Song (BLAAUW) •Bb Sx/Pno •Mol

MOLS, Robert

Compositeur américain, né à Buffalo. Travailla avec H. Hanson et W. Barlow, puis au Mozarteum de Salzburg.

Enchainment (1981) (for the Amherst Saxophone Quartet) •SATB
Mosaics (1987) (for the Amherst Saxophone Quartet) •SATB
Twenty Modern Duets •2 Sx •Ken

MOLTENI, Marco

Saturna pyri (1986) (6') •1 Sx: A+Bs/Tape

MONDELLO, Nuncio Francis (1911)

Compositeur et saxophoniste américain, né à Boston (Massachussets), le 14 VIII 1911. Travailla avec Ch. Paul, J. Schillinger, W. Riegger, et P. Creston.

"Nuncio Mondello is already known to the music world as one of the jazz giants of the swing era. He has constantly expanded with studies under Schillinger, Riegger and Creston. There is little doubt that his fluency with complex rhythms owes its authenticity to his varied and definitive background."

Introduction and Allegro (1959) •Asx/Str Orch •adr
Quartet •AATB •adr
Selected Studies (by Joe VIOLA) 1) Interval study 2) Varied studies
 •DP
Suite (1956) (to V. ABATO) 1) Prelude 2) Adagio 3) Toccata •Asx/2
 Fl/Ob/Cl/Bsn/2 Hn/Tpt/Trb/Perc •adr

Suite (1961) (to J. Trongone) 1) Prelude 2) Sarabande 3) Variations
•AATB •adr

MONDONVILLE, Cassanea de (1711-1772)
Sonata No. 6 (Hemke) •Asx/Pno •South
Tambourin (Mule) •Asx/Pno •Led

MONETTI, Gilberto
Il solista moderno - Metodo per saxofono (1990) •CoMu

MONFEUILLARD, René (1886-1958)
Compositeur français.
Deux Pièces (1938) (6'30) (to M. Mule) 1) Nocturne 2) Dialogue
joyeux •Asx/Pno •Led

MONNET, Marc (1947)
Compositeur français né à Paris.
"Je me veux un metteur en scène qui compose des images avec des
bruits." (M. Monnet) "Hors de tout dogmatisme, Marc Monnet après
avoir centré son travail sur les données visuelles et gestiques du jeu
instrumental, s'affronte parfois aux problèmes d'une 'relecture' du
système préétabli de la tonalité, 'non comme effet passéiste mais
comme autre face possible du non-système dans lequel nous sommes
aujourd'hui,' et de la radicalisation d'un système imaginé et varié.
Certaines pièces semblent sous-entendre le sujet physique de l'action,
la main, le bras ou le coude comme principe moteur de chaque
évènement sonore." (D. J-Y Bosseur) "L'une des personnalités les plus
originales du moment, Marc Monnet n'appartient à aucun des deux
courants majeurs de la musique française contemporaine: il n'est ni
post-sériel ni apparenté à la tradition harmoniste et coloriste des émules
de Messiaen. Deux traits caractérisent sa musique: d'abord un 'grain'
instrumental (sens des alliages sonores sombres et rugueux, pétrissant
la matière sonore avec un talent et une vigueur rares); ensuite le
caractère dramatique de ses partitions. Aux complexes structures
préétablies, cet amateur de Schumann et de Janacek préfère les tracés
libres et éruptifs." (J-E. Fousnaquer) "A le souci de pousser à l'extrême
le jeu instrumental. L'intérêt pour l'instrument, pour les nouvelles
sonorités, entraîne aussi sa curiosité vers l'utilisation d'instruments
insolites." (J. & Br. Massin)
Cirque (1986) (7') (to D. Kientzy) •CBsSx Solo •Sal
L'exercice de la Bataille (1991) (45') •2 Vln/2 Bsn/2 MIDI Sx/MIDI
Guit/MIDI Pno

MONROE, Samuel F.
Compositeur américain.
Rhapsodie •Tsx/Pno •Bel

MONSIGNY, Pierre-Alexandre (1729-1817)
Les Aveux indiscrets (Mule) •Asx/Pno •Led
La Reine de Golconde (Mule) •Asx/Pno •Led

MONTAGNE, Roger (1xxx-1969)
Compositeur français.
Berceuse, Pavane, Marche miniature •SATB
Chanson bretonne •SATB
Chanson d'octobre •SATB
Gambados •SATB
Habanera et seguedille •SATB
Menuet rustique •SATB
La petite classe (sur des thèmes enfantins) •SATB
Ronde joyeuse •SATB
Saltarelle •SATB
Scherzetto, Spleen, Avril •SATB

MONTALTO, Richard
Compositeur américain.
Reflection (1990) (4'30) •1 Sx: A or T/Pno •adr

MONTANES, Jose Manuel
Compositeur canadien, né en Espagne.
Cuarteto, op. 14 (1989) (to Quatuor de Stockholm) •SATB •CMC

MONTESINOS, Williams
Pièce (1992) (10') •SATB

MONTFORT, Robert (1884-1941)
Compositeur français.
1ère sonate •Asx/Pno
2me sonate •Asx/Pno
Trio •Ob/Asx/Pno

MONTGOMERY, James
Compositeur canadien.
Ritual I : The White Goddess (1980) (14') •Fl/Cl/Bsx/Koto (or
autoharp) •CMC

MONTI, Vittorio (1868-1922)
Czarda (Roberts) •Bb Sx/Pno •CF

MOODY, Ivan
Compositeur polonais.
Evocaczon de Silves (1993) •Asx/Vcl •INM

MOORE, David
"Le Rêve" (d'après une peinture de H. Rousseau) (1980) (to M.
Gersma) •Asx/2 Perc •WWS
Sicut cervus •2 Sx: AT/Org •WWS

MOORE, Edward Colman (1877-193x)
Critique musical américain, né à Fond-du-Lac (Wisconsin), le 22 I
1977.
The Moore Band Course (Method) •CF

MOORE, Keith
Hiatus Pitch •Sx Solo

MOORE, Thomas (1779-1852)
Poem •Fl/Sx/Pno •AMC

MOORTEL, Arie van de (1918-1976)
Capriccio •Asx/Pno •Mau
Nocturne, op. 18 (1956) •Cl/Asx/Vla/Vcl/Pno •Mau

MOQUÉ, Xavier (1911)
Compositeur français, né à Lugon, le 9 II 1911.
Intermezzo •SATB •adr
Danse Ukrainienne •SATB •adr

MORAN, Robert Leonard (1937)
Compositeur américain, né à Denver (Colorado), le 8 I 1937.
Travailla avec L. Berio, D. Milhaud, et H. E. Apostel.
"His music is written in graphic notation and is animated by surreal-
istic imagination and wit." (Baker) "In his music he seeks the involve-
ment of the performer through indefinite notation and mixed media
situations." (D. Walker)
Elegant Journey With Points of Interest (1965) (Indeterminate
duration) •Any ensemble •SS
Interiors (1964) (Indeterminate notation) •Any ensemble •Pet
L'après-midi de Dracoula (1966) (Indeterminate duration) •Any
sound-producing instrument •SS

MORATIN
Quintette •5 Sx •Mar

MOREAU, Léon (1870-1946)
Compositeur français, né à Brest, le 13 VII 1870, mort à Paris, le 11
IV 1946. Travailla avec Leneepveu. Prix de Rome (1899).

Pastorale (1903) (to Mme E. Hall) 1) Chanson 2) Idylle 3) Danse
 •Asx/Orch (2222/423/Perc/Str) or Pno •Led
Evocations rythmiques (Mule) •Asx/Pno •Led
Fête païenne (1933) 1) Cortège 2) Danse •Asx/Pno •HS

MOREE, L. de
Serenade •Asx/Pno •TM

MOREL
Norwegian Cradle Song •2 Sx: AT/Pno •Cen

MOREL, Jean-Marie
Compositeur français.
Trilude (1992) (2') (to J-P. Fouchécourt) •3 Sx: AAA •Fuz

MORGAN, David Sydney (1932)
Compositeur anglais.
Brilliant bagatelle (1971) (2'30) •SATB •BMIC

MORITZ, Edvard (1891-19xx)
Compositeur américain, d'origine allemande, né à Hambourg, le 23 VI 1891. Travailla avec P. Juon et C. Flesh.
Andante •AATB •Merc
Concerto, op. 97 (1939) (to C. Leeson) •Asx/Orch •Merc
Divertimento (trio) (1952) •2 Cl/Sx or 2 Sx/Cl or 3 Sx: SAA or 3 Sx: SAT •Merc
Intermezzo (from *Sonata No. 2*) •Asx/Pno •South
Quartet (1962) (C. Leeson) •AATB •South
Quartet, op. 181 (to C. Leeson) •AATB •SMC
Quintette, op. 99 (1940) (to C. Leeson) •Asx/Str Quartet •South
Sonata No. 1, op. 96 (1938) (to C. Leeson) 1) Allegro molto 2) Molto andante 3) Scherzo 4) Finale •Asx/Pno •South
Sonata No. 2, op. 103 (1940) (to C. Leeson) 1) Allegro 2) Molto andante 3) Un poco presto 4) Vivace •Asx/Pno •South
Sonata No. 1 (1963) (to C. Leeson) •Tsx/Pno •South
Trio Sonata (1963) (to C. Leeson) •Vln/Asx/Pno

MORLEO, Luigi
Compositeur italien.
Verty (1992) •Asx/Pno

MORLEY, Thomas (1557-1602)
April Is In My Mistress' Face (Harvey) •SATB •Che

MOROSCO, Victor (1936)
Saxophoniste et professeur américain. Travailla avec V. Abato, D. Bonade, et J. Allard. Membre du Los Angeles Saxophone Quartet.
Blue Caprice •Sx Solo •DP
Six Contemporary Etudes in Duet Form (1974) 2 Sx: AA •Art/AMu
Song "Song for R. Cole" •Asx/5 Sx: SATBBs or SATBB

MORRA
Nocturnal Serenade •Bb Sx/Pno •CF
Romantique •Bb Sx/Pno •CF

MORRILL, Dexter
Compositeur américain.
Getz Variations (1984) (22') (for S. Getz) 1) Echoes 2) The Lady From Portola 3) Windows •Tsx/Electron. tape •CVMP
Six Studies and an Improvisation 1) Window 2) Mysterioso 3) Ischl 4) Love Song 5) Weaving 6) Soliloque 7) Improvisation •Tsx/Tape

MORRIS, Jonathan
Compositeur américain.
Rumination (1983) •Asx Solo
Up the Street March •Sx Ensemble

MORRISSEY, John
Nightfall •Asx/Band •WWS/TM

MORRISSON, Julia
Compositeur américain, né à Minneapolis (Minnesota). Travailla avec D. Newlin.
De profundis •Asx/Vcl/Voices •CFE
Full Account (1970) (4'30) •Asx/Pno •CFE
John I, 19-23 •Alto Voice/Asx/Celesta •CFE
Julia Street (1969) (12') •Asx/Pno/Bass •CFE
Long John Brown and Little Mary Bell •Asx/Pno/Bass Voice •CFE
The Memorare •Asx/Bsn/Harp/Alto Voice •CFE
October Music (1969) (5') •Asx/Pno/Bass •CFE
Past the Solstice (1970) (3'30) •Asx/Pno •CFE
Psalm 29 •Fl/Tsx/Voices •CFE
Psalm 122 •Baritone Voice/Asx/Vcl •CFE
Psalm 130 •Alto Voice/Baritone Voice/Asx/Vcl •CFE
Psalm 131 •Baritone Voice/Asx •CFE
Subjective Objective (1970) (6') •Tsx/Bass/Electr. Guit •CFE
Yes, Yes, Yes (1970) (2'30) •Asx/Pno •CFE

MORTARI, Virgilio (1902)
Compositeur italien, né près de Milano, le 6 XII 1902. Travailla avec Pizetti qui eut sur lui une profonde influence.
"Virgilio Mortari a affirmé précocement une personnalité équilibrée et traditionaliste." (R. Bernard)
"In his works he betrayed the influence of Pizetti: they are distinguished by clarity of writing, a tendency towards folk melody and at times a spirit of humour." (G. Gatti) "His music was influenced at first by Pizetti, but he later adopted a principally neo-classical style, with frequent humorous touches and a tendency to use popular tunes." (A. Pironti)
Melodia (1954) (1'30) •Asx/Pno •Led

MORTHENSON, Jan W. (1940)
Compositeur et théoricien suédois, né à Örnsköldsvik, le 7 IV 1940. Travailla avec Mangs, Lidholm, et Metzger et la musique électronique avec Koenig.
"In his book *Nonfigurative Musik* (1966) he argued that developments in composition have rendered music of directed movement impossible, since the breakdown of tonal harmony has been followed by similar processes of neutralization in instrumentation, presentation and form. His works take note of the far-reaching consequences of this point of view." (R. Haglund) "Morthenson has not been interested in creating stylistic uniformity in his works. Despite Morthenson's changes of style, there are nevertheless special points that continually return and give him a particular identity in Swedish music." (H-G. P.)
Hymn (1987) (3'35) •SATB •SMIC
Koral (1987) (4') •SATB •Steim/SMIC
Scena (1990) (17') •4 Sx: SATB/Synth

MORTON, Jack
Rondo (1969) (to A. Hamme) •Sx/Rhythm

MORYL, Richard (1929)
Compositeur américain, né le 23 II 1929, à Newark (New Jersey). Travailla avec A. Berger et B. Blacher.
"Moryl displays a considerable instrumental fantasy and is a composer who should be better known, his works being handled with great skill and direction." (E. Salzman) "The subtle sense of order that this writer hears in all of Moryl's music is the result of rigorous application of principles of rigor, i.e., a constant-defined pitch area operating over a spectrum of combined *plucking, zapping and zonking*. The latter are not perceived as sound effects versus a row, but as unity and diversity, perceptually and psychologically." (C. Whittenberg)
Chamber II (1972) (11') •Asx/Tape •ACA

Sunday Morning (1971) (12') •Asx/Perc/Tape •CFE/ACA

MOSER, Roland (1943)

Compositeur suisse, né à Berne, le 16 IV 1943. Travailla avec S. Veress et W. Fortner, ainsi qu'au studio de musique électronique de Cologne.

Wal (1980-83) (26') •5 Sx: SATTB/Orch •HM

Wortabend (1979) (21'30) •2 Voices/Ensemble of 13 instruments including [dont] 1 Asx

MOSKOWSKI, Moritz (1854-1925)

Guitarre (Cunningham) •SATB •DP

Spanish Dance (Harger) •5 Sx: AATTB •Band

MOSS, Lawrence Kenneth (1927)

Compositeur américain, né le 18 XI 1927, à Los Angeles (California)

Evocation and Song (1972) (9'45) (to G. Etheridge) •Asx/Tape •Ron

Saxpressivo (1992) (8'10) (to R. Navarre) •Asx/Tape •Ron

Six Short Pieces (1993) (8') (to R. Jackson & J. Krasch) 1) Rounds 2) Blur 3) Broadway Boogie-Woogie 4) Chinese Lullaby 5) Introduction 6) Jazzy •Asx/Pno •Ron

MÖSS, Piotr (1949)

Compositeur polonais, né le 13 V 1949 à Bydgoszcz. Travailla à Varsovie avec P. Perkowski, puis à Paris avec N. Boulanger.

Angst und Form (1988) (33') (to K. Herder)

Avant le départ (1982) (10') •Ssx/Perc •Bil

4 Poèsies (1983) (23'30) (J. di Girolamo) 1) Lento 2) Lento misterioso 3) Allegro Dramatica 4) Allegro molto, quasi presto 5) Lento •Asx/Harp

Quartetto (1981) (10') •SATB •PNS

MOTZ, Wolfgang

Compositeur allemand.

Goranî-gazîn (1993) •Asx/Accordion •INM

MOULAERT, Raymond (1875-1962)

Compositeur, pianiste, et professeur belge, né le 4 II 1875 à Bruxelles, où il est mort, le 18 I 1962. Professeur au Conservatoire de Bruxelles et à la Chapelle Musicale de la Reine Elisabeth.

"Fut dans le domaine de la composition, volontairement un autodidacte." "Compositeur d'affinités françaises." (H. Halbreich) "C'est presque en vain qu'on essayerait de rattacher Raymond Moulaert à une esthétique d'aujourd'hui." (P. Moulaert)

"As a composer, he excelled in songwriting, and his best work in the genre recalls Fauré." (H. Vanhulst)

Andante, Fugue et Final (1907) (8') •SATB •CBDM

Tango-caprice (1942) (7') •Asx/Orch (2121/211/Perc/Str) or Pno •CBDM/EMB

MOUQUET, Jules (1867-1946)

Compositeur français, né le 10 VII 1867, à Paris, où il est mort, le 25 X 1946. Travailla avec X. Leroux et Th. Dubois. Prix de Rome (1896)

Rapsodie, op. 26 (1907) (to E. Hall) •Asx/Pno •Led

MOURANT, Walter

Compositeur américain.

Quartet 1) Lento deliberato 2) Vivace 3) Andantino lyrico 4) Allegro moderato •SATB •Pio

Scherzo •SATB •CFE

MOURZINE

Compositeur russe.

Burlesque - Humoresque •3 Sx: AAA

MOUSSART

Oboe - mazurka •Ssx/Pno •Mar

MOUSSORGSKY, Modeste (1839-1881)

Au Village (Londeix) •Asx/Pno •Lem

Ballet of the Chicks in their Shells •5 Sx: AAATB •Mus

Bilder einer Austellung - Teils I/II (Th. Schön) •SATB •ApE

En Crimée (Londeix) •Asx/Pno •Lem

Mushrooms •4 Sx: AATB or AATT •Mus/EM

The Old Castle (Gee) •Asx/Pno •EBMM

The Old Castel (Teal) •Asx/Pno •GSch

Pictures at an Exhibition (W. Schmidt) •9 Sx: SAAATTBBBs •DP

MOUTET, Joseph & André-Jean DERVAUX

Nocturne en Saxe (1955) •Asx/Orch or Pno •Com

MOWER, M.

Academicians •AATB •WWS

Building •SATB or AATB •WWS

Crillon Controller •SATB or AATB •WWS

Easter Islander •SATB or AATB •WWS

Financially Disturbed •SATB •WWS

Folly •SATB or ATTB •WWS

Ford Fiasco •SATB or AATB •WWS

Full English Breakfast •SATB or ATTB •WWS

Für Dich •SATB or ATTB •WWS

Hiatus •SATB or ATTB •WWS

Lovely Once You're In •SATB or AATB •WWS

Mower •SATB •WWS

Not the Boring Stuff •AATB •WWS

Quark •SATB or ATTB •WWS

Seven Pounds Fifty •SATB •WWS

Svea Rike •SATB •WWS

Terenga •SATB •WWS

This Morning •SATB or ATTB •WWS

Wal's •SATB or AATB •WWS

Woe •SATB or AATB •WWS

Yuppieville Rodeo •SATB or AATB •WWS

MOYLAN, William (1956)

Compositeur et Professeur américain.

Future Echoes from the Ancient Voices of Turtle Island (1992) (14') (to B. Ronkin) •MIDI Wind Controller/Pno •Ron

Solo Sonata (1978) (16-18') (to J. Cunningham) 1) Introduction 2) Adagio 3) Cadenza 4) Finale •1 Sx: S+A+T •SeMC/DP

Suite for Baritone or Alto Saxophone and Narrated Tape (1979) (13') (to J. Cunningham) 1) Cezanne 2) An Old Man 3) From a Poem in Memory of Wilfred Owen 4) Reiteration: Ennui •1 Sx: B or A/Tape •SeMC/DP

Two Suspended Images (1990) (8') (to B. Ronkin) •Solo MIDI Wind Controller (Yamaha WX11 with WT11 Synth) •Ron

MOZART, Leopold (1719-1787)

Four Short Pieces •2 Sx •Elk

MOZART, Wolfgang Amadeus (1756-1791)

Adagio (Rochon) •Bb Sx/Pno •Mol

Adagio in F, K. 580a (Gee) •5 Sx: SAATB •Sha

Adagio and Gigue, K. 411/K. 574 (Gee) •SAATB •Ron

Adagio and Menuet •4 Sx •Elk

Adagio et Menuetto (Voxman) •Tsx/Pno •Rub

Adagio and Romance (Hautvast) •Bb Sx/Pno •TM

Air de Chérubin (Chauvet) •Asx/Pno •Com

Allegro (from *Piano Sonata in C*) •4 Sx •Elk

Aria (from *The Magic Flute*) •Bsx/Pno •Bel

Ave Verum •4 Sx •Bri

Ave Verum •4 Sx: SATB or AATB •TM

Ave Verum (Dyck) •SATB •Braun

Ave Verum Corpus •2 Sx: AT/Pno •Mus

Ave Verum Corpus •3 Sx: AAT •Mus
Ave Verum Corpus, K. 618 (Gee) •AATB •DP
Berceuse •SATB •Mol
Célèbre larghetto (Dias) •Asx/Pno •Cos
Célèbre motet (Wittmann) •9 Sx: SSAATTBBBs •E&S
Ceremonial Adagio, K. 580A (Gee) •Asx/Pno or Org •adr
Concert-rondo (Kling) •Asx/Pno •South
Concert-rondo, K. 371 (Sansone) •Asx/Pno •South
Concerto, K. 191 (Smim) •Asx/Pno •Mus
Concerto pour clarinette - Adagio (Mule) •Asx or Bb Sx/Pno •Led
Divertissement en Ré - Menuet (Londeix) •Bb Sx/Pno •Led
12 Duos (Simon) •2 Sx •EM
Ein Andante für eine Walze in einer kleinen Orgel, K.V. 616 (T. Schön) •SATB •ApE
Ein Orgelstück für eine Uhr, K.V. 608 (T. Schön) •SATB •ApE
Ein Stück für ein Orgelwerk in einer Uhr, K.V. 594 (T. Schön) •SATB •ApE
Eine kleine Nachtmusik (Lang) •AATB •LMP
Eine kleine Nachtmusik (Navarre) •SATB •Ron
Marche turque (Romby) •Asx/Pno •PB
Mariage de Figaro (Thompson) •AATB •Alf
Meister Perien (Hautvast) •SATB •Lis
Menuet (Chauvet) •Asx/Pno •Com
Menuetto (Hautvast) •4 Sx: SATB or SAAT or SATT or AATT •TM
Menuet favorit •SATB •Mol
Minuet (from *Symphony in E*) (Stephens) •2 Cl/Asx/Bsn (or BsCl) •CF
Minuet, K. 334 (Teal) •Asx/Pno •GSch
Minuet (Voxman) •Asx/Pno •Rub
Nozze di Figaro - Ouverture (Muller) •SATB •GB
Papageno's Aria (from *The Magic Flute*) (Rascher) •1 Sx: T or B/ Pno •Bel
Per questo bella mano, K. 612 •Bsx/Pno •Spr
Petite musique de nuit (Classens-Meriot) •SATB •Phi
Les Petits riens - Gavotte (Mule) •Bb Sx or Asx/Pno •Led
1ère partie du concerto (Tourneur) •Asx/Pno •Led
Priester aria (from *Zauberflöte*) (Evertse) •Bsx/Pno •TM
Quartet, K. 370 (Bongiorno) •SATB •adr
Quintet, K. 406 (Sibbing) •5 Sx: SAATB •Eto
Quintet, K.515 (Sibbing) •5 Sx: SAATB •RS
Quintet for Strings, K.593 (Sibbing) •5 Sx: SAATB •RS
Quintet in C Minor, K.406 (Sibbing) •5 Sx: SAATB •RS
Recueil de quatuors (Clerisse) •SATB •Mar
Rondo in D (Teal) •Asx/Pno •GSch
Rondo (Toll) •2 Cl/Asx/Bsn (or BsCl) •CF
Sonate •SATB •Mol
19me sonate (Mayeur) •Asx/Pno
Sonate - thème varié •Asx or Bb Sx/Pno •Mil
Sonatine •3 Sx: SAT •Mil
Sonatine (de Kort) •3 Sx: SAT •TM
Sonatina (Webb) •Asx/Pno •Bel
Sonatine (Scheifes) •2 Cl/Bsx •Mol
Trio •2 Sx: ST/Bass (or Trb) •Mil
5 Trios (Mayeur) •3 Sx: ATB •ES
Valse favorite (Meriot) •Asx/Pno •Phi

MUCI, Italo Ruggero (1922)
Compositeur italien.
Quartetto (1981) •Cl/Tsx/Trb/Bass

MUCZYNSKI, Robert (1929)
Compositeur américain d'origine polonaise, né à Chicago, le 19 III 1929. Travailla avec A. Tcherepnine et W. Knupfer.
"His style follows the trend of French neo-classicism without chro-

matic elaboration but containing some polytonal usages." (Baker) "Muczynski's music is very melodic in an Aaron Copland fashion, and very rhythmic and percussive—an American Bela Bartok if you will. The unique combination of these two disparate styles, along with the regular use of jazz harmonic structures, combine to create Muczynski's style."
Concerto, op. 41 (1981) (17') (to T. Kynaston) 1) Allegro energico 2) Andante Maestoso 3) Andante espressivo-Allegro giocoso •Asx/Chamber Orch (1111/1100/Str/Pno) or Pno •Pres
Fuzzette - The Tarantula (1962) (12') •Narr/Fl/Asx/Pno
Sonata, op. 29 (1970) (9') (to T. Kynaston) 1) Andante maestoso 2) Allegro energico •Asx/Pno •GSch

MUELLER, Florian Frederick (1904)
Professeur et compositeur américain, né à Bay City (Michigan), le 15 VI 1904.
Duets in Various Meters •2 Sx •adr
Easy Duets •2 Sx •UMM
Preludium, Choral, Variations and Fugue •Asx/Pno •Mus
Sonata (to L. Teal) 1) Allegro moderato 2) Andante lento 3) Allegro •Asx/Pno •UMM
Sonatina in One Movement •Asx/Pno •UMM/CFE

MUELLER, Frederick A. (1921)
Compositeur américain d'origine allemande, né à Berlin, le 3 III 1921. Travailla avec S. Sachsse, E.V. Dohnanyi, et B. Rogers.
25 Caprices und Sonate •Sx Solo •adr
Dance Suite (1971) (9') 1) Air 2) Air 3) Swing 4) Largo 5) Saltarelle •Asx/Dancer •DP
Five Etudes •3 Sx: ATB
Sonata (1975) •Asx/Pno •adr
Suite for Four •Ssx (or Fl or Ob or Cl)/Tsx (or Ob or Cl)/Asx (or Cl)/Bsn (or BsCl) •Uni
Trio •3 Sx: ATB

MULDERMANS, Jules (18xx-18xx)
Fantaisie brillante (185x) (9') •Asx/Pno •Mar
Fantaisie variée •Asx/Pno •Lud

MULDOWNEY, Dominic (1952)
Compositeur anglais, né à Southampton, le 19 VII 1952. Travailla avec Birtwistle, Rands, et Blake.
Concerto (1984) (18') (for J. Harle) 1) Prélude 2) Développement 3) Danses macabres •Asx/Chamber Orch •Uni
An Heavyweight Dirge (1971) (25') •Voice/Fl/Asx/Perc/Pno/2 Vln/ Vla/Vcl •Nov
Five Melodies (1978) (16'30) •SATB •Nov
...In a Hall of Mirrors (1979) •Asx/Pno •Uni
Love Music for Bathsheba Everdene & Gabriel Oak (1974) (20') •Fl/Ob/Cl/Asx/Hn (or Trb) •Nov

MULE, Marcel René Arthur (1901)
Saxophoniste virtuose et professeur français, né à Aube (Normandie), le 24 VI 1901. Travailla le saxophone sous la direction de son père, ensuite le violon et le piano, puis l'harmonie avec Caussade. Instituteur (1920). Soliste à la Garde Républicaine (1923). Crée avec ses camarades en 1928 un quatuor de saxophones qui prendra successivement les noms de: "Quatuor de la Garde Républicaine," "Quatuor de Saxophones de Paris," puis de "Quatuor Marcel Mule." Concerts en France et à l'étranger. Nombreux enregistrements.
Est chargé en 1942, par Claude Delvincourt alors directeur de recréer la classe de saxophone au Conservatoire de Paris (1942-1968).
"Peut être considéré comme l'un des principaux fondateurs de l'école classique du saxophone." "Marcel Mule a transcrit de nombreuses oeuvres classiques pour son instrument et favorisé l'ascension constante de celui-ci dans le domaine symphonique." (N. Dufourcq)

Etudes variées dans toutes les tonalités, d'après Dont, Mazas,
   Paganini, etc. •Led
24 Etudes faciles, d'après Samie (1942) •Led
48 Etudes, d'après Ferling, augmentées de 12 Etudes originales
   (1946) •Led
53 Etudes, d'après Boehm, Terschak, Furstenau, etc. (1946) •Led
Exercices journaliers, d'après Terschak (1944) •Led
18 Exercices ou études, d'après Berbiguier (1943) •Led
30 Grands exercices ou études, d'après Sousmann (1944) •Led
Gammes (3 Volumes) (1944-1946) •Led
Tablature de la gamme chromatique (1943) •Led
Traits difficiles (3 volumes) (1943-1945) •Led
A large number of transcriptions for [Un grand nombre de transcriptions pour] Asx/Pno, Bb Sx/Pno, Sx Quartet: SATB

MULLER, Anders
   Compositeur danois.
Kvartet (1991) (8') •SATB

MÜLLER, Gottfried (1914)
   Professeur et compositeur allemand né à Dresden, le 8 VI 1914.
Agnus dei (1948) (5'30) •Sx Solo •KuD
Aria (1988) (to Nürnberg Saxophone Trio) •3 Sx: SAB •adr
Capriccio (1988) •3 Sx: SAB •adr
Dorische partita (1986) (to Akademie Quartet Nürnberg) •SATB
   •adr
Fantasie 1) Adagio 2) Allegretto leggiero •Asx/Str Quartet •adr
Interludium (1988) (4') (to Nürnberg Saxophone Trio) •3 Sx: SAB
   •adr
Kyrie (1986) •SATB •adr
Lacrimosa dies illa (1986) (to Akademie Quartet Nürnberg) •SATB
   •adr
Quartett (1984) 1) Recitativo 2) Canzonetta 3) Fuga 4) Recitativo
   •SATB •adr
Rezitativo, canzonetta e fuga (1984) (10') (to G. PRIESNER) •SATB
   •KuD
Sonate (1948) (16') 1) Grave-Andante 2) Allegretto scherzando
   3) Largo con moto flessibile, quieto •Sx Solo •Sik

MULLER, Iwan (1786-1854)
Concertante •Ob or Cl/Asx/Pno •Bil

MÜLLER-GOLDBOOM, Gerhardt
Exkurse (1988) (34') •SATB
Impromptu (1992) (14') (to J. ERNST) •Tsx Solo

MULLER VON KULM, Walter (1890-1967)
Concertino, op. 81 (1964-65) •Asx/Str Orch

MULS, André Jean (1935)
   Musicien de jazz belge.
Sax battle (1980) •Asx Solo

MUNDRY, Isabel
   Compositeur allemand.
Komposition (1992) •Asx/Band

MURAKI, Hirono
   Compositeur japonais.
Fantaisie •Asx/Pno

MURGIER, Jacques (1912-1986)
   Violoniste, chef d'orchestre, et compositeur français, né à Grenoble,
   le 30 IX 1912, mort, le 12 X 1986. Travailla avec J. Gallon et Max
   d'Ollone. Fondateur du "Trio à cordes de Paris."
   "Le Concerto pour saxophone et cordes écrit dans un esprit roussélien,
   affranchi de tous éléments pittoresques ou descriptifs, bien construit,

clair, inspiré, marque en dépit des nombreuses variations ou altérations
rythmiques des deux derniers mouvements une surprenante unité de
style." (J. B.) "Facture classique, déroulement précis pourtant, l'élément de surprise sans cesse renouvelé (tantôt le rythme, tantôt l'ironie
percutant d'un thème sautillant) donne à ce Concerto une originalité
souriante, un intérêt sans cesse renouvelé." (R. B.)
Chant sans paroles (Album) (1974) (1'30) •Asx/Pno •Zu
Concerto (1960) (23') (to J-M. LONDEIX) 1) Allegro giocoso
   2) Allegretto con variazoni 3) Final •Asx/Str Orch or Pno •ET
2 Pièces brèves (4') 1) Berceuse 2) Habanera •Asx/Pno •Lem
Suite française (1984) (21') (to J-M. LONDEIX) 1) Ouverture
   2) Courante 3) Passacaille et Variations 4) Menuet 5) Sarabande
   6) Rigaudon 7) Postlude •12 Sx: SnoSSAAATTTBBBs

MURPHY, Lyle
Cadenzas and Recitative •SATB •WWS
Notturno •3 Sx: ATB •WIM
Prelude and Canon •SATB •WIM
Rondino (1957) •SATB •AvMu
Suite (1967) (10') •SATB •WIM

MUSSEAU, Michel
Les paupières rebelles (1993) (40') •Fl/Cl/Ssx/Hn/Tpt/Trb/Tuba
   •Ed. Visage

MUSSER, Christian
   Compositeur autrichien.
Germ (1993) •Tsx/Pno •INM

MYERS, Robert (1941)
   Compositeur américain, né à Fredericksburg (Virginia), le 20 VIII
   1941. Travailla avec B. Rogers et N. Boulanger.
   "I was led into music by an early interest in jazz. This interest is
   sustaining me presently as well." (R. MYERS)
Concerto (1967) (to J. KRIPL & D. SINTA) •Asx/Band •adr
Contrast (1970) (7') •Tsx/Pno/Trb •Art
Fantasy Duos (1968) (to J. KRIPL) •Asx/Perc •Art
Instructions (1971) (5-7') •Jazz Ensemble
Movements (1967) (14') (to J. KRIPL) (Slowly - Allegro - Slowly -
   Allegro - Andante - Lento) •Ssx/Orch or Pno •Art
Quartet (1966) (Moderato - Andante non troppo - Presto) •Fl/Asx/
   Bsn/Vcl •SeMC/AMu
Quartet No. 1 (1966-67) (5'30) •SATB •adr
Quartet No. 2 •SATB •adr
Reprise •Asx/Pno •Art
Three Inventions (1971) (5') •Asx/Bsn •SeMC
Three Short Pieces (1967) (to J. KRIPL) 1) Cantando 2) Scherzando
   3) Lento sostenuto •Asx/Pno •Art
Three Songs Without Words •adr
Trio (1965) (8') •Asx/Bsn/Vcl •Art

MYERS, Theldon
Impromptu (1972) •Asx/Pno •adr
Sonatine •Asx/Pno •CAP
Two Inventions for Three (5') (to J. BRISCUSO) (Andante sostenuto -
   Moderato) •2 Sx: SA/Pno •DP
Vocalise (1986) (6'30) •Soprano Voice/Asx/Pno •DP

MYSLIVECEK, J.
   Compositeur tchèque.
Sinfonia •SATB

NAGAN, Zvi
Serenade for Lisa •3 Sx: AAA •ASM

NAGATA, Takanobu
Compositeur japonais.
Achse •Asx Solo

NAGEZY, Hans Georg (1773-1836)
Joys of Life (RASCHER) •Asx/Pno •Bel

NAGY-FARKAS, Peter
Sonatine (to P. DELIBERO & M. SMELLIE) •Asx/Pno •DP

NAKAGAWA, Ataru
Compositeur japonais.
Quartet (to Passereaux Saxophone Ensemble) •SATB

NAKAMURA, Hitoshi
Compositeur japonais.
Gradation (1993) •Tsx/Perc •INM

NAKAMURA, Koya (1958)
Compositeur japonais.
Hida (1980) (to K. SHIMOJI) •Asx/Str Quartet
Nenyo (1981) •Asx/Pno
Spiritual Song from Small Island (1982) (to Ensemble de Tokyo)
    •SATB

NAKATA, Mami
Compositeur japonais.
Distance (1990) •2 Sx: SA

NAKAZAWA, Michiko
Compositeur japonais.
Amber •Asx/Marimba

NASH, Ted
Studies in High Harmonics (1946) •Lee

NATANSON, Tadeus (1927)
Compositeur polonais, né le 26 I 1927, à Varsovie.
Kincert Podwojny - Double concerto (1959) Asx/Tsx/Orch •AAW/
    AMP
3 Pictures for 7 Instruments (1960) •Ob/Cl/Asx/Trb/Vcl/Tpt/Bsn/
    Pno/Perc •AMP
Trio (1977) (11'30) •Asx/2 Vcl •AAW

NÄTHER, Gisbert
Oktett (1990) (8') •8 Sx •adr
Quartettino (1988) (Allegro - Vivace - Andantino - Allegro vivace)
    •SATB •PMV

NAUDE, Jean-Claude (1933)
Compositeur français.
Sun - Sand - Sea - Sax (to A. BEUN) •5 Sx: SAATB

NAULAIS, Jérôme
Tromboniste, compositeur, et arrangeur français.
Atout sax (1987) (to Quintette à vent de Paris) •5 Sx: SAATTB
    •Arp
Coconotes (1991) (1'20) (to J-Y. FOURMEAU) •Asx/Pno •Bil

Concerto (1991) •Asx/Orch d'harmonie
Frissons (1991) (10'30) •Asx/Wind Orch or Pno •Bil
Kansax-City (1991) (2'20) (to J-Y. FOURMEAU) •Asx/Pno •Bil
Mise à sax •5 Sx: SATTB/Pno/Bass/Drums •Arp
Pain d'épice (1993) (1'15) •1 Sx: A or T/Pno •Mar
Patchwork •SATB •Arp
Vingt Etudes récréatives •Sx Solo •Arp

NAUMANN, Johann Gottlieb (1741-1801)
Petit duo •2 Sx •Mol

NAVARRE, Randy (1951)
Compositeur et saxophoniste américain.
Concertmusic for Solo Saxophone (1980) (8') •Sx Solo •Ron
Saxophone Quartet •SATB
Two Shorts for Two Saxes (1992) 1) Softly and gently 2) Moderately
    •2 Sx •Ron

NEGRE, Christophe
Improvisation au saxophone (Method) (1988) •Com

NELHYBEL, Vaclav (1919)
Compositeur et chef d'orchestre américain, d'origine tchécoslova-
que, né le 4 IX 1919, à Prague. Il travailla en Europe, avant d'aller à
New York (1957). Naturalisé Américain en 1962.
"His music is couched in linear modal counterpoint in which the-
matic notes, rhythms and intervals become serially organized. The
harmonic idiom is freely dissonant with all melorhythmic components
gravitating towards tonal centers." (BAKER)
Adagio and Allegro (1986-88) (to M-S. BERNANDO) •1 Sx: S+A/Orch
    •JCCC
Allegro (1966) (to D. SINTA) •Asx/Pno •Heu/GMP
Concert Piece •Asx/Pno •WWS
Concerto Spirituoso No. 2 (1976) •Ensemble/Baritone Voice/Pno
    •CM
Fantasia II (1987) (to M-S. BERNARDO) •4 Sx: SATB/Pno •JCCC
Four Duos •Any wind instruments •Heu
Golden Concerto •Tsx/Pno •Mus
Quartets (3 books) •AATB •FC
Ricercare •4 Sx: AATB/5 Cl •Lebl
Three Miniatures (1968) (3') 1) Allegro con bravora 2) Lento molto
    espressivo quasi rubato 3) Molto vivo •AATB •FC

NELSON, Oliver
Patterns for Improvisation •HD
Patterns for Saxophone •HD

NELSON, Ronald
Compositeur américain.
Danza Capriccio (1988) (to K. R. YOUNG) •Asx/Band or Pno

NEMESCU, Octavian
Compositeur roumain.
Metabyzantiniricon (1983-84) (19') (to D. KIENTZY) •Asx/Tape
Septuor (1983) •Fl/Cl/Trb/Tsx/Pno/Bass/Perc

NESSLER, Victor E.
Der Rattenfänger von Hameln (H. LUREMAN) •Bsx/Pno •TM
Young Werner's Parting Song, My Heaven (NEUMANN) •Eb Sx/Pno
    •CF

NESTICO, Sammy
The Basic Nestico Lead Sax Book (Count BASIE) (9 Pieces)
Persuasion •Asx/Band
A Study in Contrasts (3'20) 1) The Demure 2) The Delightful
    •SATB •Ken

NETTING, Frederick
Romance •8 Sx: AAAATTBBs
Shadows •7 Sx: AAATTBBs

NEUKOMM, Sigismund (1778-1858)
Aria (KAPLAN) •Bb Sx/Pno •JS

NEUWIRTH, Gösta
Compositeur allemand.
Gestern und Hente (1988) (to J. ERNST) •Asx Solo

NEVIN, Ethelbert (1862-1901)
Narcissus (HUMMEL) •Asx/Pno •Rub
Narcissus (THOMPSON) •AATB •Alf
Le rosaire (GUREWICH) •Asx/Pno •Bil

NEWELL, Robert
Synthesis (1965) (15') (to M. TAYLOR) •Asx/Pno

NEWHOUSE, Dana
Compositeur américain.
Sonata Sentimentale (1979) (to B. RONKIN) •Asx/Pno/Perc

NEWMAN, Ronald
Compositeur américain.
Music (1979) (to J. LULLOFF) •Asx/Pno
Quartet (1988) •SATB

NEWTON, Rodney Stephen (1945)
Compositeur anglais, né le 31 VII 1945, à Birmingham (United Kingdom)
Fantasies on Middle Eastern Themes (1976) (to A. HOVHANESS)
1) Senza mesura - In tempo molto moderato 2) Andante
3) Allegro moderato 4) Lento quasi senza misura 5) Allegro
grazioso 6) Senza misura. •SATB •adr

NICHIFOR, Serban
Compositeur roumain.
Chimaera (1993) (18') (to D. KIENTZY) •Asx/Vibr •INM

NICHOLLS, Charles
Professeur américain.
How To Conduct Saxophone Bands (1921)

NICHOLS, Red (1905-1965)
Holiday for Woodwinds (LAWSON-GOULD) •Picc/214BsCl/1/4 Sx:
AATB •GSch

NICKLAUS, Wolfgang (1956)
Compositeuir allemand, né le 2 XI 1956 à Lehnin.
Die Antwort (1986) (7'30) •Cl/Asx/2 Perc/Pno/Vln/Vcl/Bass •adr
Der Priwall (1984) (9') •Voice/Asx/Perc/Cl/Vcl •adr

NICOLAO, G.
Ave Maria; The light beyond (BARRETT) •Eb Sx/Pno •CF

NICOLAS, René (Mickey) (1926)
Saxophoniste, compositeur, et chef d'orchestre, né à Laon, le 18 I
1926. Travailla le saxophone avec M. MULE. Compositeur autodidacte. Chef d'orchestre au célèbre cabaret Le Lido.
Magnitude (1993) (7'45) 1) Moderato 2) Andantino 3) Prestissimo
•5 Sx: SAATB •Lem
Passim (1973) (8'45) (to Quatuor de la Garde Républicaine)
1) Gadget 2) Andantino 3) Fileuse •SATB

NICOLAU, Dimitri (1951)
Compositeur italien, d'origine grecque.
Alla donna di fondo, op. 80 (1987) •Fl/Asx/Pno •EDP
La Casa nuova, op. 82 (1988) (8') •3 Sx: SAB •EDP

Concerto per Pianoforte e Orch di sassofoni & Perc, op. 77 (1988)
•Pno/12 Sx: SnoSSAAATTTBBBs/Perc •adr
Mondelci's Songs, op. 75 (Scherzo musicale) •Asx Solo •EDP
Nel sogno une rosa, op. 57 - Raconto musicale (1985) (10') (to F.
MONDELCI) •2 Sx: AB/Pno •EDP
Pour le sax, op. 107 (1991) (10') •Tsx Solo
Quarta sinfonia, op. 70 (1987) (10') (to Ensemble Italiano di Sassof.)
•Sx Orch: SnoSSAAATTTBBBs/Soprano Voice/Perc
Quartetto III, op. 110 (1991) 1) Rock time 2) Dance time 3) Blues
time 4) Greek time •SATB
Reponses à l'avantgarde histérique - Sonata, op. 76 (1987-89) (18')
(to F. MONDELCI) •Asx/Pno •EDP
Saxquartett n° 2, op. 34bis (transcritto dal 4° Quartet per archi)
(1980/89) (13') •SATB •adr
Saxquartet, op. 61 (1986) (to Ensemble Italiano di Sassof.) •SATB
•EDP
Sonata (1991) •Asx/Pno
Strassenmusik n° 7, op. 51-7 (1985) (10'30) (to MONDELCI &
MAZZONI) •2 Sx: Eb or Bb •EDP
Strassenmusik n° 8 (1989) •1 Sx: A+T+S/Perc

NICOLAUS, Louis
Compositeur grec.
Concerto (1963) (to Cl. RICARD) 1) Andante 2) Allegro 3) Largo
4) Allegro moderato •Asx/Str Orch or Pno •adr

NICULESCU, Stefan (1927)
Compositeur roumain.
"L'une des figures saillantes de la première génération de compositeurs roumains de l'après-guerre." "Auteur d'opéras, de musique de
chambre, ayant étudié les musiques archaïques européennes et
extraeuropéennes, Niculescu trouve dans le symphonisme son terri-
toire de prédilection." (C. GLAYMAN)
Cantos (1984-85) (22') (to D. KIENTZY) •1 Sx: Sno+A+T+B/Orch
(3000/3431/3Perc/Str [14 12 10 8 6])
Chant-son (1989) (6') (to D. KIENTZY) •Sx Solo: S+A
Octoplum (1985) (10') (to D. KIENTZY) •1 Sx: S+A/Ensemble (1010/
000/00101/Guit/Mandolin/Perc)

NIEDER, Fabio
Lega (1983) (to BOK & LE MAIR) •Sx/Marimba

NIEHAUS, Lennie
Bee's Knees (3') •AATB •Ken
Christmas Jazz Favorites No. 1 •4 Sx: SATB or AATB
Cleanin' Up (3') •AATB •Ken
Developing Jazz Concepts for Saxophone
Down by the Riverside •AATB
A Dozen and One Sax Duets •2 Sx: AA or TT •WIM
Fanflares •Asx/Pno
Fugue •SATB •WWS
Fusion •SATB •WWS
Half-Past Sax •AATB
Halloween Fantasy •AATB
Heads Up •AATB
Jazz Conceptions (4 Volumes) •HD
Jazz Mosaics (No. 1, 2, & 3) •4 Sx: S(A)ATB •Ken
Jazz Improvisation
Just For Show •AATB
Making the Change •AATB
Miniature Jazz Suite Nos. 1-4 - in Four styles 1) Wingin' it (moder-
ate swing) 2) Sapphire skies (ballad) 3) Pocket change (waltz)
4) Tuffenuff? (blues) •AATB •Ken
No Need To •AATB
Of Days Remembered (1966) •Asx/Pno •WIM
One For All •AATB •Ken

Palo Alto •Asx/Band or Pno •WIM
Romantic Sketch •AATB
Rondolette •4 Sx: SATB or AATB •WWS
Saxability •AATB
Saxafrass •AATB
Saxism •AATB
Sir Sax •AATB
Six Jazz Duets Volume 2 •2 Sx: AA or AT or TT •WWS
Small Fry •AATB
So Little Time •Asx/Pno
Speed Reading •SATB
The Storm •AATB
Summer Nocturne •AATB
Symphonette •AATB
Swing Shift (2'30) •4 Sx: SATB or AATB •Ken
Ten Jazz Inventions •2 Sx: Eb or Bb •Ken
Theme and Variations • AATB
Waltzing the Blues Away (1966) •Asx/Pno •WIM
When the Saints go Marching In •AATB

NIEHAUS, Manfred (1933)

Compositeur allemand, né à Cologne, le 18 IX 1933.

"He has worked intensively in amateur music, and he has championed the deritualization of performance through 'open' concert forms and communal musical activities." (M. LICHTENFELD)

Concertino (1981) (18') •2 Sx: SS/Orch (2222/2221/Str/Perc) •adr
Saxophonquartett (1981) (Presto - Allegro molto - Molto lento - Allegro - Allegro molto) •SATB

NIELSON, Lewis (1947)

Compositeur américain.

Ain't Misbehavin' (1980) (9') (to K. FISCHER) •Sx/Perc •ACA
Dialectical Fantasy (1981) (to K. FISCHER) •Fl/Ob/Cl/Tsx/Hn •ACA
Fantasies (1983) (17'30) (to K. FISCHER) 1) Imminence 2) Remember 3) Homage (Little birds) •Ssx/Tape •ACA
Surrealistic Portraiture (1993) (to K. FISCHER and M. THOMAS) 1) Francisco Goya 2) Max Ernst 3) Alice Neel 4) Rene Magritte •Ssx/Pno

NIHASHI, Jun-ichi (1950)

Compositeur japonais, né le 2 I 1950, à Shizvoka. Travailla à Tokyo, puis à Paris. Prix Concours Marcel Josse (1981).

Banka - chant funèbre (1981-86) (12') •Ob/Cl/Asx/Bsn •Led
Invenzione della onda (1992) (7') •2 Sx: AA
Pratinade •Sx/6 Perc/Tablas
Third Adagio (1984) (to K. MUNESADA) •Asx/Pno

NIKIPROWETZKY, Tolia (1916)

Compositeur et ethnomusicologue français d'origine russe, né en Crimée, le 25 IX 1916. Travailla avec S. Plé-Caussade et R. Leibowitz.

"Il a tout d'abord été attiré par l'écriture modale, a utilisé quelque temps la technique sérielle, pour n'en plus conserver ensuite que de libres suggestions, aux quelles il joint certains apports électro-acoustique." (Cl. ROSTAND)

Auto-stop - Mini opéra (20') •Soprano Voice/Tenor Voice/Perc/Vcl/ 1 Sx: A+S •adr
Tetraktys (1976) (to J. DESLOGES) •1 Sx: S+A+T+B/Chamber Orch •adr

NILLNI, Ricardo

Compositeur argentin.
Spin (1988) (7') •5 Sx: SAATB

NILOVIC, J.

Métallochromie (1986) (6'40) •Asx/Perc •SL

NILSSON, Anders (1954)

Compositeur suédois.

"His scores show meticulous attention to detail as well as considerable refinement in his use of individual instruments. He regards himself as a practician, unaffected by academic schooling." (S. M.)

Cadenze (1992) •Fl/Ob/Cl/Bsn/Sx
Krasch! (1993) •4 Sx: SATB/6 Perc/Tape •SMIC

NILSSON, Bo (1937)

Compositeur suédois, né à Skelleftehamm, le 1er V 1937. Travailla avec M. Pedersen.

"Essentiellement autodidacte, son isolement de jeunesse en Laponie ne l'a pas empêché d'assimiler avec une très curieuse et très saillante originalité les influences pointillistes post-weberniennes de Boulez et de Stockhausen… C'est un imaginatif et un visionnaire audacieux, raffiné." (Cl. ROSTAND)

"Largely autodidact, he experimented with new techniques of serial composition and electronic sonorities." (BAKER) "Nilsson's compositions of the late 1950s, though often indebted to Boulez in instrumentation and to Stockhausen in technique… In *Entrée* (1962) Nilsson had returned to late Romanticism, and later in the 1960s he wrote film and television scores of a simple Swedish lyricism. Nilsson is certainly one of the most enigmatic and highly gifted Swedish composers of postwar years." (H. ASTRAND) "His musical language is characterized by a fervent intensity and impetuous affection. The forms he uses seldom contain a gradual build-up to a climax." (H-G. P.)

La Bran - Anagramme sur Ilmar Laaban (1963-76) (16') •Sx Solo: S+A/Chorus/Orch (4002/0441/Perc/Pno/Tape/Electr.) •STIM
Frequenzen (1957) •Fl/Picc/Ob/EH/Cl/BsCl/Tsx/Bsn •Uni
20 Gruppen (1958) •3 or more instruments
Ormhuvud I + II (Tête de serpent) - Concerto (1974) •Asx/Orch
Portrait de femme n° 2 (1976) •Asx/Str •SMIC
Szene IV (1975) •Jazz Sx/Chorus
Zeiten im Umlauf, op. 14 (1957) (3') •Fl/Ob/EH/Cl/BsCl/Tsx/Bsn •Uni
Zeitpunkte (1960) (5') •Fl/Alto Fl/Ob/EH/Cl/BsCl/2 Sx: AT/Bsn/ CBsn

NILSSON, Ivo (1966)

Compositeur suédois.
Agnosi (1988) (9') •Ob/Asx/Tpt/Harp/2 Vln/Vla/Vcl •STIM
Passad (1988) •Ssx/Trb •STIM
Per-cept: sestetto (1989-91) •Fl/Ob+EH/1 Sx: S+A/Trb/Pno/ Vln+Vla •SMIC
To no (1991) •Asx/Trb •SvM

NIN, Joaquin (1879-1949)

Chercheur, musicologue, compositeur et pianiste cubain, d'origine espagnole, né le 29 IX 1879, à La Havane où il est mort le 24 X 1949. Travailla à Paris, avec Moszowsky et D'Indy.

"L'interprète doit aller à la salle de concert la musique sous le bras et l'humilité dans le coeur." (J. NIN) "L'occasion lui fut donnée de fonder un conservatoire à La Havane; puis il vécut principalement à Bruxelles et à Paris—qu'il quitta en 1939 lors de déclaration de la guerre, pour regagner définitivement son pays. Si ses harmonisations de chants populaires anciens espagnols—de véritables re-créations— restent aujourd'hui de référence, c'est sur ses travaux en faveur d'une juste réhabilitation de maîtres du clavier que porte principalement son action." (Fr. TRANCHEFORT) "*Le Chant du veilleur*: comme en fait foi la couverture originale de ce trio, le saxophone a été initialement demandé par le compositeur avant le violon. Il est alors incompréhensible que cette partie ait été imprimée quarante ans après les autres…" (J-M. L)

"His enthusiasm for the Spanish Baroque is evident in his compositions, which also show the strong influence of French impressionism."

(A. Menendez-Aleyxandre)
Le chant du veilleur (1933) (4') (to E. Rykens) •Mezzo Soprano
Voice/Asx (or Vln)/Pno •ME

NINOMIYA, Tami
Compositeur japonais. Travailla à Paris. Epouse de I. Nodaïra.
Aya (1988) (1') •2 Sx: AA

NIRO, Pietro
Compositeur italie.
Parafrasi seconda (1992) •Asx/Pno

NISHIKAZE, Makiko
Compositeur japonais.
Liebeslied (1993) •Soprano Voice/Ssx •INM

NITTMAR, Zbigniew
Compositeur tchèque.
Piton (1993) •Ssx/Synth •INM

NIVELET, Victor (1829-1903)
Ma bergère (Medinger) •Asx/Pno •Led

NIVERD, Lucien (1879-1967)
Directeur de conservatoire, chef d'orchestre, et compositeur français.
Air simple (1974) •Asx/Pno •Zu
Crépuscule d'automne •Asx/Pno •GD
Insouciante •1 Sx: A or S/Pno •Bil/Mar
Intermezzo •Asx/Pno •Bil
Légende •Bsx/Pno •Braun
6 Petites pièces brèves 1) Grazioso 2) Cantabile 3) Giocoso 4) Allegro vivo 5) Intermezzo 6) Scherzetto •Asx/Pno •Com
6 Petites pièces de style 1) Hymne 2) Romance sentimentale
3) Complainte 4) Historiette dramatique 5) Chant mélancolique
6) Scherzetto •Asx/Pno •Bil

NIXON, Dohamain
Suite •Asx/Orch

NODA, Ryo (1948)
Compositeur et saxophoniste japonais, né à Nishinanima-cho, Amagasaki, le 17 X 1948. Travailla avec A. Sakaguchi, O. Kita, F. Hemke, W. Karlins, J-M. Londeix, et M. Fusté-Lambezat.
Atoll II (1982) •Asx/Pno •adr
Don Quichotte, op. 2 (to J-M. Londeix) •Asx Solo
Fantaisie et danse (1976) (3'45) (to J. Ledieu) •Bsx Solo •Led
Fourth Side of the Triangle (1983) (to J. Sampen) •2 Sx/Pno
Fushigi no basho (1985) (to J. Sampen) •2 Sx: AA/Pno
Gen concerto (1974, Revised 1979-81) •Asx/Str Orch/Pno/Perc
•Led
Guernica - Hommage à Picasso, op. 4 (1973) (to J-M. Londeix)
•Asx/Perc/Speaking Voice
Improvisation I (1972) (3'30) (to J-M. Londeix) •Asx Solo •Led
Improvisation II (1973) (2'30) (to J-M. Londeix) •Asx Solo •Led
Improvisation III (1974) (3') (to J-M. Londeix) •Asx Solo •Led
Maï (1975) (7') •Asx Solo •Led
Murasaki no Fushi - Duo (1981) (8') (to F. Hemke) •2 like Sx or
Shakuhachi •Led
Phoenix - Fushicho (1983) (a ma mère) •Asx Solo •Led
Pulse + - (1972-82) (15') (to M. Noda) •Ssx Solo •Led
Requiem - Shin-en (1979) (10') (to Yoshiro Irino) •Tsx Solo (or
Asx) •Led
Sextuor (1980) (12') •6 Sx: SATTBB •adr
Sketch (1973-76) (2'30) (to F. Hemke) 1) Invention 2) Fantaisie
•SATB
Symphonie rhapsody Maï II (1980) •Sx Solo •adr
Temple (1976) •Asx/Pno •adr

Tori - Oiseaux (Hommage à J. Ibert) (1977) (12') •SnoSx+Oriental
Flutes
W 1988 D (1988) •1 Sx: S+A/Pno •adr

NODAÏRA, Ichiro (1953)
Compositeur et pianiste japonais né à Tokyo. Vit en France. Travailla la composition avec G. Ligeti, G. Grisey, P. Eörvös, Fr. Donatoni et, l'électroacoustique avec G. Reibel.
Arabesque II (10') (to K. I. Muto) •Sx Solo •Lem
Arabesque III (1980-81) (13') •Asx/Pno •Lem
Quatuor (1985) (16') (to Quatuor Sax) •SATB •Lem

NOÈL-GALLON (1891)
Professeur et compositeur français, né le 11 IX 1891 à Paris. Travailla avec Lavignac et H. Rabaud. Grand Prix de Rome (1910).
"Ses oeuvres sont empreintes d'un charme et d'une distinction proches du style fauréen." (N. Dufourcq)
"As a composer, he was influenced by his brother (Jean G.) who was his first tutor in music." (Baker)
Essor (1953) (3'30) •Asx/Pno •PN

NOMURA, Mikiko
Compositeur japonais
In the rain (1993) •Tsx/Marimba

NONO, Luigi (1924-1990)
Compositeur italien, né à Venise, le 29 I 1924. Mort le 17 V 1990. Travailla avec Malipiero, H. Scherchen, et B. Maderna. A épousé la fille de Schoenberg.
"A côté de Boulez et de Stockhausen, l'un des trois grands ténors du mouvement post-wébernien né au lendemain de la Seconde Guerre mondiale. Il est un lyrique, un tempérament subjectif et dramatique, en cela bien italien. Son orchestre, mobile et plein de couleurs, fait une large place à la percussion, utilisée dans un dessein purement expressif. Parmi ses oeuvres instrumentales, il faut citer: *Polifonica-Monodia-Ritmica* d'une écriture encore assez rigoureusement wébernienne." (Cl. Rostand) "Parti des dernières oeuvres de Webern, il se situe à la pointe de la musique nouvelle. Une densité et une concentration extrêmes s'allient chez lui à une flamme et une sensibilité toutes latines. Nullement prisonnier d'un système, Nono utilise d'une manière personnelle le langage sériel." (N. Dufourcq) "Tout un groupe d'oeuvres à l'écriture concise et à la polyphonie somptueuse, qui n'excluent pas le lyrisme, affirment mieux encore sa personnalité." (P. Pitton). La limite vers le pointillisme a rarement été atteinte, du moins dans la musique européenne, sauf peut-être par Luigi Nono dans *Polifonica-Monodia-Ritmica*." (D. J-Y. Bosseur) "Avec Nono la musique contemporaine a eu enfin son grand artiste engagé politiquement, l'un de ceux qui, comme les constructivistes russes, ont mis l'avant-garde esthétique au service de la révolution bolchevique. Dans nos pays occidentaux le défi a eu un certain sens… et des résultats." (C.Glayman) "L'un des compositeurs les plus radicaux et le plus géniaux de notre temps." (H. Halbreich)
""He is the leader of the 'committed' wing of new Italian music, whose dissenting use of recent techniques is functional to an explicit relationship between artistic progressiveness and political militancy. A major clue to Nono's music is suggested in his first composition, the *Variazioni canoniche*, which aims at combining a strict classical 12-note serial technique with the claims of a music capable of becoming, impassioned social testimony. Such a suggestion is emphasized in the immediately succeeding works, whose uneven results essentially depend on a still-imperfect balance between procedural severity and ideological commitment. The former dominates the instrumental works, whose expressive urge, however, even involves an occasional surrender to a taut nostalgia for melody (as in the central section of *Polifonica-monodia-ritmica*)." (E. L. Will)

Polifonica, Monodia, Ritmica (1951) (10') •Fl/Cl/BsCl/Asx/Hn/4 Perc •AVV

NOON, David (1946)

Compositeur américain.

Ars Nova, op. 67 (1982) (6') (for J. BISHOP & A. PAULSSON) 1) Adagio 2) Allegro coda •Ssx/Pno •TTF

Coda, op. 39 (1976) (2') (to J. BISHOP) •SATB •TTF

Hymn Variations, op. 108 (1991) (7') (to P. COHEN) •Ssx/Vln/Vcl/Pno •TTF

Partita, op. 103b (1989) (8') 1) Preludio 2) Musette 3) Pastorale 4) Rigadoon •Ssx/Guit •TTF

NORDENSTEN, Frank Tveor (1955)

Compositeur norvégien.

Sample and hold (1978) (14') •Fl+Picc/Cl+BsCl/1 Sx: S+T/Vln+Vla/Vcl/Pno/Perc

NORGÂRD, Per (1932)

Compositeur danois, né à Gentofte, le 13 VII 1932. Travailla avec Holmboe et, à Paris, avec N. Boulanger.

"Per Norgârd parle de 'musique dans la musique' à travers une quête des possibilités latentes contenues dans les modèles du passé, desquelles peuvent découler des conséquences insoupçonnées en fonction des techniques compositionnelles apparues au cours de ce siècle." (D. J-Y. BOSSEUR)

"In his earliest works Norgård explored a Nordic style deriving from Sibelius. In the early 1970s Norgård reached the point of focussing the procedures and concepts with which he had experimented into a stylistic synthesis which employs a variety of modes, including pentatonic, 7-note, 12-note and microtonal scales." (W. H. REYNOLDS)

Protens (1983) (to BOK & LE MAIR) •Sx/Perc

NORHOLM , Ib (1931)

Compositeur danois, né le 24 I 1931 à Copenhagen. Travailla avec Bentzon et Hoffding.

" 'A Patchwork in Pink' existe en deux versions qui toutes deux comprennent un piano et, l'une avec quatuor d'anches et l'autre avec quatuor de saxophones."

"Norholm became a significant participant in the movement called 'the new simplicity' which emerged in Denmark in the mid-1960s. The term was applied to music in which simplicity (of conception and performance requirements or for the listener—is an important factor, and the movement represented a reaction against the extreme complexity of some avant-garde works." (W. H. REYNOLDS)

Kvartet , op. 122 (1992) (12'30) 1) Udvikling I 2) Snapshot 3) Udvikling II •SATB •Kon

A Patchwork in pink, op. 109 (1989) (12') •SATB

NORIKURA, Masaki

Compositeur japonais.

Etude de concert •Asx/Pno

NORTON, Christopher

Microjazz (1988) (Album - 14 pieces) •Asx/Pno - Tsx/Pno •B&H

NOSSE, Carl E. (1933)

Compositeur américain, né le 8 I 1933, à Irwin (Pennsylvania).

Sonnet (1978) (to P. MEIGHAN) •Asx/Guit •DP

NOTT, Douglas

Rhapsodic Song •Asx/Pno •Sha

NUIX, Jep

Compositeur espagnol.

Pièce (1992) (10') •Asx/2 Vln/Vla/Vcl

NUNES, Fazio

Jazz saxes solo •HD

NUNEZ, Adolfo (1954)

Compositeur espagnol né à Madrid.

Cambio de saxo (1989) (6') (to D. KIENTZY) •1 Sx: B+S/Tape

NUYTS, F.

Compositeur belge.

La sale mère, le boeuf et le crampon (1981) •SATB

NUYTS, Gaston

Bar-o-kjana •SATB •Sez

NYKOPP, Lauri (1957)

Compositeur finlandais, né le 10 IX 1957.

Hengen henki •3 Sx: AAA •FMIC

New music for Roma Saxophone Quartet (14-40') •4 Sx/Tape •FMIC

"... sillä ei ole nimeä" •7 Sx •FMIC

Tutuola music (1979) •4 Sx

NYORD, Morten

Compositeur danois.

Saxo (1989) (8') •SATB

NYQUIST, Morine A.

Echo Lake •Asx/Pno •Bel

NYVANG, Michael

Compositeur danois.

Kwartet (1991) •SATB

Tre korte karakterstykker (1988) (7') •Bsx/Pno

OAKES, Rodney (1937)

Compositeur américain, né le 15 IV 1937, à Rome (New York).
Introspectum in Six Refractions •Any number of musicians, audience and conductor •CAP
Six By Six •Any 6 instruments •CAP

OBERGEFELL, Glenn

Lullaby (1993) (4') (to M. LIBERATORE) •Bsx/Pno •TTF

O'BRIEN, Eugene

Compositeur américain.
Concerto (1992) (to J. SAMPEN) (2 movements) •Asx/Orch

OCKENFELS, Helmut (1937)

Compositeur allemand, né à Ohlenberg, le 30 VII 1937. Travailla avec Löbner.
Opusculum (1980) (3 movements) •Tsx/Perc •adr

ODAK, Krsto (1888-1965)

Compositeur croate né à Siveric le 20 III 1888, mort à Zagreb, le 4 XI 1965. Travailla avec Hartmann.
"In his music he inclined towards polyphonic forms and folk elements. His harmony was enriched with some contemporary developments as well as with ancient modalities, but melody remained his primary expressive means." (K. KOVACEVIC)
Divertimento, op. 66 (1957) •Asx/Str Orch •YUC
Sextet, op. 68 (1959) •6 wind instruments including saxophone •YUC

ODGREN

H is for Hottentotte •5 Sx •WWS

ODSTRCIL, Karl

Compositeur allemand.
Transit •8 Sx/Perc

OETTINGER, Alan

Compositeur et pianiste américain.
Reflections (1979) (8'30) •Asx/Pno •Eth

O'FARRILL, Chico

Three Pieces (to New York Saxophone Quartet) •SATB

OFFENBACH, Jacques (1819-1880)

Barcarolle •2 Sx: AT or AA/Pno •Cen/CF/Mck/Kjos
Barcarolle •AATB •CF
Barcarolle •Bb Sx/Pno •CBet/Volk
La Musette •Bb Sx/Pno •CBet
Orpheus Overture •AATB •Bar
Waltz "La Périchole" •Asx/Pno •Kjos

OGANESYAN, Edgar Sergeevic (1930)

Compositeur arménien, né à Erivan, le 14 I 1930. Travailla avec Eghiazaryan et Khachaturian.
"In his music he has preferred an epic style.
Concerto en forme de variations, op. 21 (1961-62) •Asx/Symphonic Jazz Orch •SOC/SK

OGATA, Toshiyuki (1955)

Compositeur japonais.

Bleu (1984) (to K. MUNESADA) •Asx Solo

OH, Don Je

Sonata (1982) •Asx/Pno

ÖHLUND, Ulf (1948)

Compositeur suédois.
Simplicity musik (1983) (10') •4 Perc/Ssx/Bass •STIM
Three Pieces for Woodwind Sextet (12') •Fl/Ob/Cl/Asx/Hn/Bsn •Tons/SMIC

OLAH, Tiberiu (1928)

Compositeur roumain né à Arpasel (Maramures), le 2 I 1928. Travailla avec D. Muresianu, M. Eisikovits, E. Messner, et D. Rogal-Levitski, puis avec G. Ligeti, Karkoschka, et A. Kontarsky.
"L'une des figures saillantes de la première génération de l'avant-garde roumaine des années 50".
"His concert music is marked by expressive clarity, formal balance and dramatic power, with liberal use of contrast. The percussion has an important place in his masterly orchestration, while the modality of the folk music of Transylvania and Tchango is at the base of his music." (V. COSMA)
Concerto notturno (1983) (to BOK & Le MAIR) •Sx+BsCl/ Marimba+Vibr
Obelisc pentru Wolfgang Amadeus (22') (to D. KIENTZY) •1 Sx: Sno+A+B/Orch (3333/433/Perc/Str)
Rimes (1985) (8') (to D. KIENTZY) •1 Sx: Sno+A/Matériel électr.

OLBRISCH, Franz-Martin (1952)

Compositeur allemand né à Mülheim/Ruhr le 5 XI 1952. Travailla à Berlin avec F. M. Beyer.
Cadenza (1988) (11'30) (D. BENSMANN) •Asx Solo •adr
"...Hu ha..." (Concerto) (1987) (20') •Asx/Orch (2222/2221/Harp/ Pno/Str) •adr
"Im Anfänglichen läuft keine Spur" (1989) (90') •Vln/Fl/Trb/Sx/ Perc/Electronics
Quintett (1989) 1) Allegretto 2) Andante 3) Largo 4) Adagio •EH+Ob/2 Sx: AT/Hn/Perc •adr
Trios (1984) (21') •Vln/Cl/Tsx/Pno •adr

OLCOTT, Chauncey

My Wild Irish Rose (BUCHTEL) •1 Sx: A or T/Pno •Bel/Rub

OLESEN, W.

Saxophonskole •WH
Six Saxophone Pieces •Asx or Bb Sx/Pno •WH/WWS

OLIVE, Vivienne (1950)

Music (1981) (to J. CHARLES) •2 Sx: AA/Orch •DP

OLIVER, John

Compositeur canadien.
Métalmorphose (1983) •Ob/Cl/Bsn/Sx/Tpt •CMC

OLIVEIRA, Willy Corrêa de (1938)

Compositeur brésilien, né le 11 II 1938 à Recife. Travailla avec O. Toni puis avec Henze, Stockhausen, P. Boulez, H. Pousseur, et L. Berio.
"After about 1961 he began working with 12-note and 'total serial' techniques, later developing an interest in aleatory procedures but maintaining a tight control of all parameters." (G. BEHAGUE)
Sugestoes (1971) •Ob/Asx/Bandoneon/Tuba/Bass/Perc

OLOFSSON, Kent

Compositeur suédois.
The voice of one who calls out in the desert: Tetramorf (1991-92) •Fl/Asx/Trb/Synth •Tons

OLSEN, Rovsing Poul (1922)

Compositeur et ethnomusicologue danois, né à Copenhagen, le 4 XI 1922. Travailla avec Jeppesen, N. Boulanger, et O. Messiaen.

"In early works Olsen's style reflected Bartok, Stravinsky and Nielsen. He used 12-note principles; subsequently he employed serial techniques in various ways. In the 1960s, his ethnomusicological research began to influence some of his compositional attitudes: rhythm became a primary feature, its simple organization (often based on non-Western formal concepts) presenting contrasts between free movement and patterns that are metrically complex and often long." (W. REYNOLDS)

Aria, op. 76 (1976) (to Ch. Gron) •Mezzo Sporano Voice/Asx/Pno

OLSEN, Sparre Carl Gustav (1903)

When Yuletide Comes (GRAINGER) •3 Sx: SAT •PG

OLSON, Roger

Compositeur américain.

Cobwebs (1983) (to K. GREGORY) •Narr/Guit/Asx/Vln

O'NEILL, Charles (1882-1964)

Compositeur et chef d'harmonie canadien, né à Glasgow, le 3 VIII 1882; mort à Québec, le 9 IX 1964.

Andante con moto •Asx/Pno
Canzona •Tsx/Pno
Intermezzo •Asx or Bb Sx/Pno
Melodie Phantasie •Asx/Pno
Rêverie •Asx/Pno

ONGARO, Michele dall' (1957)

Compositeur et chef d'orchestre italien né à Rome. Travailla avec A. Clementi, F. Ferrara, L. Markiz, et J. Bodmer.

Darstellüng (1987) (8') •Asx Solo •EDP

ONNA, Peter van (1966)

Compositeur hollandais, né à Hengelo, le 22 I 1966. Travailla avec T. Loevendie, L. Andriessen, et Klaas de Vries.

Crystal dreams (1991) (7') •Ssx/Pno •Don

OOSTERVELD, Ernst (1951)

Compositeur néerlandais.

Average music III (1979) (10') •SATB •Don
Graphic music loops (1983) (9') •Asx Solo •Don
Music loops II (1982) (5') •Sx Solo: A or T •Don
Music loops III (1982) (5') •Asx/Pno •Don
Omaga (1981/82) (19') •BsCl Solo/8 instruments including [dont] 1 Asx •Don

ORBAN, Marcel (1884-1958)

Compositeur belge naturalisé français, né à Liège, le 13 XI 1884; mort à Paris, le 7 XI 1958. Travailla avec V. d'Indy et A. Roussel.

Introduction, variations et Final (1938) •SATB
Scherzo •Asx/Pno

ORFE, John

Compositeur américain.

Three Movements (1991) (to J. SAMPEN) •Asx/Pno

ORLOFF, Eugene

Down Hall •SATB

ORNSTEIN, Leo (1892)

Compositeur et pianiste américain, d'origines russes, né à Kremenchug (Russie), le 11 XII 1892. Travailla avec B. Fiering Tapper.

"He has always worked in a wide range of musical styles, sometimes simultaneously, his choice dependent on the demands of each composition." (V. Perlis)

Ballade •Asx (or Vla)/Pno •DP

ORREGO SALAS, Juan (1919)

Compositeur et musicologue américain d'origine chilienne, né à Santiago du Chili, le 18 I 1919. Travailla avec P. H. Allende, D. Santa Cruz, A. Copland, et R. Thompson.

"The most powerful influence in musical life of his native country." (Tempo) "Orrego Salas is a musician of rich imagination and with a sensitive intuitive understanding of the demands of materials and the technical means of disposing them." (W. BERRY) "Orrego Salas is a great charmer; his music has regional sound to it, though its ease and polished craftsmanship bear testimony to a sophistication that preserves all the best elements of folk art without its limitations." (P. GRANVILLE-HICKS). A neo-classical craftsmanship, tempered by free invention." (G. R. BENJAMIN)

Concerto da camera (1987) (to E. ROUSSEAU) •Asx/Brass Quintet
Quattro Lirich brevi, op. 61 (1967) (17') (to E. ROUSSEAU)
  1) Elegiaca 2) Rapsodica 3) Semplice 4) Appassionata •Asx/ Chamber Orch or Pno •PIC

ORSI, Romeo (1843-1918)

Methodo populaire •Ric

ORTEGA, Sergio

Récit d'un naufragé (1990) (15') (Texte du compositeur d'après un récit de Gabriel Garcia Marquez) •Narr/7 Sx: SnoSATBBsCBs
Septuor de saxophones (1989) •7 Sx: SnoSATBBsCBs

ORTIZ, William

Housing Project (1985) (for the Amherst Saxophone Quartet) •SATB

ORTOLANI

More (from *Mondo Cane*) •Asx/Pno •WWS

ORTON, Richard (1940)

Compositeur et professeur anglais, né à Derby, le 1 I 1940. Travailla avec Mellers, Ridout, et Stockhausen.

"A highly gifted musician and always an adventurous composer, he has written successful examples of most sorts of progressive music, including repetitively patterned music." (G. LARNER)

Cycle (1967) •2 or 4 performers
Mythos (1980-81) (to J. STEELE) •Asx Solo

OSAWA, Kazuto (1926)

Compositeur japonais.

Sen (1973) (to A. SAKAGUCHI) •Sx Solo

OSSEÏTCHOUK, A.

Compositeur russe.

Travail des classiques du jazz (1987)

OSTENDORF, Jens-Peter (1944)

Compositeur allemand, né à Hamburg.

Johnny reitet westwärts - Alice in wunderland •Cl/2 Sx: AT/Perc/ Prepared Pno •Sik
Minnelieder (1987) 1) Agitato 2) Andante 3) Allegretto leggiero 4) Romance 5) Szene 6) Pastorale 7) 80 8) 58 9) 80 10) Fragmente 11) 72 12) 63 13) Hommage •Soprano Voice/ Tenor Voice/4 Sx: SATB •Sik
Monaden (1990) (10') •SATB •Sik

OSTERC, Slavko (1895-1961)

Compositeur slovène né à Verzej, le 17 VI 1895; mort à Ljubljana, le 23 V 1961. Travailla avec V. Novak, Janacek, et A. Haba.

"Osterc joue un rôle dans l'évolution de la musique slovène. Son style est caractérisé par l'application du principe atonal et mathématique par l'emploi d'une polyphonie très librement traitée, par l'étrangeté de son instrumentation."

"After some works in a late-Romantic style, he adopted new techniques, from atonality to athematicism and from 12-note writing to quarter-tone music. Within his wide stylistic range there are characteristic tendencies towards expressionism and neo-Baroque polyphony." (A. RIJAVEC)

Ave Maria (1930) •Soprano Voice/Vla/Ob/Cl/Sx

Sonate (1935) (to S. RASCHER) (Allegro moderato - Tranquillo-Presto) •Asx/Pno •DSS

OSTLING, Acton
Alto Saxophone Student
Duets (2 volumes) •2 Sx: AA •Bel
Quart-tet-à-tête •SATB •Bel
Tenor Saxophone Student
Tunes for Alto Saxophone - Technique
Tunes for Baritone Saxophone - Technique
Tunes for Tenor Saxophone - Technique

OSTRANDER, Allen
Sonate in G Minor •1 Sx: A or T/Pno •EM
Concert Piece in Fugal Style •Asx/Pno •Mus

OSTRANDER, Linda (1937)
Compositeur américain, né le 17 II 1937, à New York. Travailla avec J. Wood, R. Hoffman, A. Etler, B. Johnston, et G. Read.

"Concerning *Game of Chance*: A novel composition refreshing and imaginative with a fine sense of humour. About other compositions: imaginative and sensitive handling of sonorities. A sound spectrum ranging from the most exquisitely delicate to raucous thrusts of great excitement."

Game of Chance •Any small ensemble of 5-8 players •CAP
Tarot (to K. & S. DORN) 1) Patterns 2) Comments 3) Images 4) Changes 5) Rota •Asx/Narr+Dancer/Tape •DP

OSTRANSKY, Leroy (1918)
Compositeur américain, né à New York. Travailla avec Ph. James, Ph. Bezanson, et M. Rosenthal.

Ballet Impressions (1965) (3') •Tsx/Pno •Rub
Canzonetta and Giga (VOXMAN) •Asx/Pno •Rub
Contest Caprice •1 Sx: A or T/Pno •Rub
Contest Etude No. 1 •Bb Sx/Pno •Rub
Night Piece •Tsx/Pno •Rub
Peasant Dance •3 Sx: AAT •Rub
Poem and Dance •6 Sx: AAATTB •Rub
Prelude and Allegro •Tsx/Pno •Rub
Suite (1965) (5'30) 1) Prelude 2) Chaconne 3) Presto •Asx/Pno •Rub
Three Miniatures •3 Sx: AAT •Rub
Three Pieces •6 Sx: AAATTB •Rub
Two Portraits •3 Sx: AAT •Rub
Variations on a Theme by Schuman •Bb Sx/Pno •Rub

OSWALD, James (1711-1769)
Lento and Giga (L. PATRICK) •Asx/Pno •Eth

OTERO, Francisco
Compositeur espagnol.
Double suggestion (1981) (to M. MIJAN) •1 Sx: A+B/Pno

OTT, David (1947)
Compositeur américain.
Concerto (1987) (to D. RICHTMEYER) •Asx/Chamber Orch (222Asx/2110/Perc/Str) or Wind Ensemble or Pno •Eto
Concerto (1992) (24') (to J. HOULIK) •1 Sx: T or S/Orch (3222/4231/Timp/Perc/Str) or Pno
Essay (1983) (13') (To J. HOULIK) •Tsx/Band or Pno •Eto

OTT, Joseph (1929)
Compositeur américain, né le 7 VII 1929, à Atlantic City (New Jersey). Travailla avec H. Sachsse et R. Harris.
Quartet (1972) (9') •Asx Solo/Tape Recorder •DP

OTTEN, Ludwig (1924)
Compositeur néerlandais, né à Zandvoort, le 24 II 1924. Travailla avec H. Badings et S. Dresden.
Quartet (1969) (17'30) (to J. W. STCHTING) •SATB •Don

OTTOSON, David (1892-1970)
Compositeur suédois.
Svit (197x) (27') •AATB •STIM

OUBRADOUS, Fernand (1903-1985)
Bassoniste, professeur, et chef d'orchestre français, né le 15 II 1903 à Paris. Travailla avec J. Mazellier et Noël-Gallon.
Récit et variations (1938) •Asx/Pno •Led

OURGANDJIAN, Raffi
Chant élégiaque (1979) (to J-P. FOUCHÉCOURT) •Asx/Pno

OVANIN, Nikola (1911)
Compositeur américain d'origine croate, né à Sisek, le 25 XI 1911. Travailla avec C. Rhyclik, H. Elwell, A. Shepherd, E. Krenek, B. Rogers, et H. Hanson.
Dance Suite (1971) (14') (to S. & K. DORN) 1) Prelude 2) Jazz dance 3) Latin American dance 4) Oriental dance 5) Jazz dance 6) Postlude •Sx/Dancer •DP

OVERSTREET, W. Benton
That Alabama Jasbo Band (1918) (HOLMES) •4, 6 or 8 Sx
That Alabama Jazbo Band (1918) (GEE) •5 Sx: SAATB or AAATB

OWEN, Jerry
Diversion (1982) •2 Sx: AT/Band •DP

PAAKKUNAINEN, Seppo (1943)

Compositeur et saxophoniste de jazz finlandais, né à Tuusula, le 24 X 1943.

"Seppo 'The Baron' Paakkunainen can with all justification be called an allrounder in the field of light music, for during his career as musician and composer he has covered almost every type of Afro-American rhythm music. Yet one intrinsic feature of Paakkunainen's music has always been the folk music of the ancient Finns and the Lapps." (J. MUIKKU)

En voi unhoittaa sua pois •Asx/Pno
Le fratricide (1989) •Sx
Stereological monology •Sx

PABLO, Luis de (1930)

Compositeur espagnol, né à Bilbao, le 28 I 1930. Travailla avec M. Deutsch.

"Compositeur autodidacte, mais d'une culture générale encyclopédique, c'est au hasard de brefs passages de musiciens étrangers en Espagne, souvent Français du reste, ou par la lecture de livres importés (ceux de Leibowitz, entre autres) qu'il peut prendre connaissance des recherches musicales alors en cours." (J. & B. MASSIN) "Il a été l'un des premiers à tirer l'école espagnole de son étroit nationalisme pour lui donner une intonation universelle, mais aussi une des personnalités les plus saillantes de la musique actuelle dans le monde, grâce à l'impulsion qu'il a su donner aux techniques nouvelles et aux solutions personnelles et originales qu'il a trouvées pour exprimer un tempérament inventif et poétique exceptionnel. Car, dans toutes ces recherches l'homme est toujours derrière sa musique: c'est une présence qui lui est naturelle et à laquelle il tient" (Cl. ROSTAND) "De tous les chefs de file de l'avant-garde européenne, c'est bien Luis de Pablo qui a eu le plus d'importance historique, tant pour l'originalité, la constante qualité, l'abondance et la diversité de son oeuvre que pour le rôle qu'il a personnellement joué dans la diffusion de l'art actuel en Espagne, rôle assez comparable à celui de Pierre Boulez en France" (M. FLEURET) "L'écoute des oeuvres d'aujourd'hui suppose une nouvelle communication musicale, dépouillée d'habitudes perceptives d'ordre exclusivement psychologique; pour cela, l'auditeur doit nécessairement être impliqué dans le processus de jeu, s'inscrire dans la complicité du compositeur et de l'interprète" (L. de PABLO)

"Pablo's music developed from the influence of Stravinsky and Bartok to atonality in 1957, and shortly afterwards to serialism. By 1959 he had evolved an individual style within the mainstream of the European avant garde. Works of this period show a concern for abstract structure and for new possibilities of timbre and articulation. A preoccupation with aleatory forms led, around 1965, to his concept of 'modules,' interchangeable units considered as the smallest structures to have expressive value in their own right. In the later 1960s and early 1970s his interests extended to embrace electronics (tape and live), theatrical situations and the union of musical material from diverse cultures and times." (T. MARCO)

Elefant ivre •Ensemble of 15 musicians including 1 Sx •Sal
Oculto (1988) •Sx Solo
Polar, op. 12 (1963) •Vln/Ssx/BsCl/Xylophone/Trb/6 Perc •Tono/ SeMC
Une couleur (1988) (22') (to D. KIENTZY) •1 Sx: Sno+S+T+B+CBs/ Orch (3333/433/Perc/Pno/Celesta/Str) •SZ

PACALET, Jean

Compositeur français né à Chambéry.
Match (1987) •SATB •adr

PACHELBEL, Johann (1653-1706)

Canon and Gigue (FRASCOTTI) •4 Sx: AAAB •Ron
How lovely shines the morning star •3 Sx: SAT or 6 Sx: SATTBBs •RS
Three Fugues on the Fourth Tone •3 Sx: ATB •WWS

PACKER

Sea Breeze •2 Sx: AA/Pno •Ken

PADDING, Martijn

Compositeur néerlandais.
Ritorno (1988) (11') •SATB •Don
Ronk •SATB •Don

PADEREWSKI, Ignace (1860-1941)

Minuet (HOLMES) •AATB •Bar
Minuet à l'antique (TRINKAUS) •Bb Sx/Pno •FMH
Minuet à l'antique (TRINKAUS) •2 Sx: AA or AT/Pno or Sx/Tpt •CF

PADWA, Vladimir

Compositeur russe, né à Krivyaleino. Vit aux U.S.A.
Concertino •Asx/Guit •adr

PAGANINI, Nicolo (1782-1840)

Caprice, Op. 1, No. 24 (ROSSI) •Sx Solo •DP
Moto perpetuo (TEAL) •6 Sx: AATTBBs

PAGE, Eric

Quatuor (1984) •SATB

PAGGI

Caprice - mazurka •Bb Sx/Pno •Mil

PAICH, Marty

Toccata in F •4 Sx: SATB/Bass/Perc •Eto

PAINPARE, Hubert (18xx-192x)

Morceau de salon •Bb Sx/Pno •Mol

PAISIELLO, Giovanni (1740-1816)

Romance de Proserpine (CRESSONNOIS) •3 Sx: ATB •Marg

PAISNER, Ben

Compositeur américain.
Prelude to a Mood •Asx/Pno •GM
Swing Duets •2 Sx •DG

PALA, Johan (1895-1972)

Bonjour 1) Matin 2) Joli •Bb Sx/Pno •Mol
Fantasie •Asx/Pno •TM
Hulpgrepen •Ssx/Pno •Mol
3 Miniatures •2 Sx: TT •Mol/Elk

PALADILHE, Emile (1844-1926)

Concertante (VOXMAN) •Asx/Pno •Rub

PALAU BOIX, Manuel (1893-1967)

Compositeur et chef d'orchestre espagnol, né à Alfar del Patriarca (Valencia), le 4 I 1893, mort à Valencia, le 18 II 1967. Travailla à Paris avec Ch. Koechlin et M. Ravel.

"Ses premières compositions sont écrites dans un style très lyrique, influencé par le folklore de sa région. Il évolua ensuite vers une écriture symphonique impressionniste." (M. HONEGGER)

"His work did much to enliven the musical life of Valencia, and his music depicts the spirit of the region. There are elements of Mediterranean folk music in his style, and also some polytonality, atonality or modality." (A. RUIZ-PIPO)

Marcha burlesca "pour orchestra de saxofons filharmonica" (1936) (5'30) •10 Sx: SSAAATTTBBs/ophicleide

PALENICEK, Josef (1914)

Pianiste et compositeur tchèque, né à Travnik (Yougoslavie), le 19 VII 1914. Travailla à Paris avec A. Roussel.

Concerto (1966) (25') •Asx/Orch (0020/066/3 Sx/Perc/Pno/Str) •CHF

Masky (1957) (11') •Asx/Pno •CHF

PALESTER, Roman (1907)

Compositeur polonais, né à Sniatyn, le 28 XII 1907. Travailla avec Sikorski. Il fréquenta à Paris le 'Groupe des Six' et l'Ecole dite 'de Paris.'

"Roman Palester est l'une des personnalités les plus marquantes parmi les musiciens polonais contemporains." (FASQUELLE) "Musicien délicat, tout en nuances, et qui combine adroitement l'écriture horizontale, accueillante aux audacieuses rencontres de la polytonalité et une subtilité harmonique, voluptueusement imprécise et ambiguë, conciliant ainsi l'impressionnisme et ses détracteurs." (R. BERNARD) "Son influence reflète l'influence de Stravinsky et une soumission à la discipline classique." (Z. LISSA) "D'abord influencé par Szymanowski, puis par Stravinsky, il s'est ensuite développé dans un style néoclassique élargi où se manifeste un solide métier." (Cl. ROSTAND) "In his music Palester adopts the modernistic features of neoclassicism, in a lucid diatonic style, enlivened by a strong sense of rhythm." (BAKER) "Palester belongs to the most advanced group of Polish modernists. In his earlier works the influence of Szymanowsky and sometimes of Stravinsky is not to be overlooked. He was at first mainly interested in good effects of sound, but later problems of line and construction chiefly occupied his attention. His later mature works show that he has freed himself from the bondage of both cosmopolitanism and nationalism and bear traces of his attempts at finding a way of his own in expressing his musical ideas." (C. HALSKI) "The works of the period 1930-1945 show great feeling and vital linear writing, both recalling the mature Hindemith, but they are particularly notable for their folk character, expressed in the themes and also in the scoring." (B. SCHÄFFER)

Concertino (1938/78) (15') (to S. RASCHER & D. PITUCH) •Asx/Str Orch •CPWM

PALESTRINA, Giovanni Perluigi (1526-1594)

Adonamus te (D. SPEETS) •4 Sx: SATB or SATT •TM
Alma redemptoris (LETELLIER) •SATB •Mar
Christe eleison (LEMARC) •4 Sx: SATB or AATB or AATT •TM
Hodie Christus (REX) •12 Sx: SSAAAATTTTBB
Pueri Hebraerum (EVERSTE) •SATB •TM
Surge illuminare Hierusalem n° 28 (REX) •12 Sx: SSAAAATTTTBB

PALMER, E.

Serenade to an Empty Room •Ssx/Pno

PALMER, Glenn

Compositeur américain.
1990 Ballroom Blitz (1990) (10') (3 movements) •Asx/Perc •Ron

PALOMBO, Rudolphe (1931)

Compositeur français.
Quatuor (to Quatuor J. MELZER) •SATB

PANDELÉ, Thierry (1956)

Compositeur et pianiste français, né à Bordeaux. Travailla avec M. Fusté-Lambezat et Chr. Eloy. Etudes et recherches universitaires en archéologie (DEA) axées sur la musique égyptienne et mésopota-

mienne.
Le Fils apprête, à la mort, son chant (1993)(10') •Soprano Voice/Fl/Sx

PANELLA, Henri-François (1885-19xx)

Fantaisie sur "La Traviata" •Asx Solo •Sal
Fantaisie sur "Le Trouvere" •Asx Solo •Sal
Jack and Jill •2 Sx: AA/Pno •Volk
Jolly Two •2 Sx: AA/Pno •Volk
Tom and Jerry •2 Sx: AA/Pno •Volk
Two Bachelors •2 Sx: AA/Pno •Volk
Two Gnomes •2 Sx: AA/Pno •Volk
Two Lovers •2 Sx: AA/Pno •Volk

PANICCIA, Renzo

Compositeur italien.
Elegia, op. 6 (1985) (6') •Ssx Solo
Petit souffle du vent, op. 4 (1984) (9') •SATB
Ritimagici: Aleggiare delle sirenne, op. 8 (1985) (8') •Bsx Solo
Rusé, op. 5 (1984) (7') (to F. MONDELCI & M. MAZZONI) •2 Sx: AB
Sourires de clown, op. 7 (1985) (6') (to M. MAZZONI) •Bsx Solo
Study on sound variation, op. 3 (1983) (to F. MONDELCI & M. MAZZONI) •2 Sx: SB
Trilli esultanti, Dolci risonanze (1992) •2 Sx/Pno

PANOV, N.

Saxophoniste russe.
Travail des gammes et arpèges dans les classes spécialisées de saxophone (1986)

PANTALEO, L.

Six Virtuoso Caprices (IASILLI) •Sx Solo •CF

PANTON, David (Marshall) (1953)

Compositeur anglais.
Concerto (1965) •Asx/Orch •adr
Sonata 65 (1965) (8') •Asx/Pno •adr
Suites banalite's (1965) (10-15') •Asx/Pno •adr

PAPANDOPULO, Boris (1906)

Compositeur et chef d'orchestre croate né à Honnef, le 25 II 1906. Travailla avec Bersa.

"When he started composing he declared himself to be a follower of a national style, but he was one of the first Yugoslav composers to take an interest in neo-classicism. However, he quickly found a means of synthesizing such techniques with the rhythms and melodies of folksong. Papandopulo has employed different styles almost concurrently." (K. KOVACEVIC)

Concerto (198x) (to D. SREMEC) •Asx/Orch
6 Croquis (1992) •SATB

PAPE, Gérard (1955)

Compositeur américain, né à Brooklyn (New York). Travailla avec D. Winkler, G. Cacioppo, et W. Albright.
5 pieces •Asx/Pno
Pour un tombeau d'Anatole (poème de St. Mallarmé) (1985) •Soprano Voice/Perc/Sx Orch: SSAAATTTBBs

PAQUE, J.

Duo de "La Norma" n° 7 •2 Sx: TT/Pno •Sch

PAQUOT, Philippe (1877-1954)

10 Pièces mélodiques •1 Sx: A or T/Pno •Led

PARADIS, H.

Pastel Menuett (BUCHTEL) •Asx/Pno •Kjos

PARADIS, Maria Theresia von (1759-1824)
Sicilienne (PERCONTI) •Asx/Pno •Ron

PARASKEVAIDIS, Graciela
Compositeur uruguayen.
Saxsop (1993) •2 Sx: SS •INM

PARENT, Nil
Compositeur canadien.
Inter-modul-action (1973) (26') (to R. RENAUD) •4 Sx: SATB/Electr. equipment

PARERA, Antonio
El Cappo (WALTERS) •4, 5 or 6 Sx •Rub

PARES, Gabriel (1860-1934)
Chef de musique français, mort à Paris, le 2 I 1934.
Crépuscule •Eb Sx/Pno •Bil
Crépuscule (JUDY) •1 Sx: T or B/Pno •Braun/Rub
Daily Exercices and Scales •CFE
Fantaisie caprice (1911) •Asx/Pno •Bil
Méthode (1895) •Lem
Modern Pares Foundation Studies (WHISTER) •Rub
1er solo de concert (1897) •Asx/Pno •Mar

PARFREY, Raymond (1928)
Compositeur anglais.
Comedy Numbers (1979) •3 Sx: AAA •BMIC
Cosmo Allegro (1974) •Ssx/Pno •BMIC
Five Sketches (10') •SATB •BMIC
Quartet (1972) 1) Adagio 2) Allegro 3) Theme and variations 4) Finale •SATB •BMIC
Saxes Thro' the Centuries (8') •3 Sx: AAT •BMIC
Scherzo and Romance •SATB •BMIC
Two Pieces 1) Serenade 2) Sicilienne •Ssx/Pno •BMIC
Two Pieces (1979) •3 Sx: AAT •BMIC
Waltz Caprice (1974) •Ssx/Pno •BMIC

PARISI
40 Technical and Melodious Studies (IASILLI) (2 Volumes) •South

PARISI, Stephen (1955)
Compositeur américain, né le 11 XI 1955 à Buffalo. Travailla avec L. Smit.
Introduction and Capriccio (1980) (for the Amherst Saxophone Quartet) •SATB
Quintet (1988) (for the Amherst Saxophone Quartet) •Vln/4 Sx: SATB

PARIS-KERJULLOU, Ch.
Divertissement - Fantaisie concertante •Asx/Pno •Mar
Morceau de concert, op. 204 •4 Sx: SATB/Pno •Mar

PARKER, Charlie (1920-1955)
Jazz Master Series •Asx/Pno •MCA
Ornithology •SATB

PARKER, Phillip
Compositeur américain.
Sketches (1990) •Asx/Perc Ensemble

PARKS, Ron
Increments (1993) (to K. BROOKS & M. SPEDE) •Asx/Perc/Tape

PARME, F.
Serenade •Asx/Pno •CF

PARRIS, Herman (1903)
Physicien et compositeur américain d'origine russe, né le 30 X 1902 à Ekaterinoslav. Aux U.S.A. depuis 1905.
Suite •Asx/Pno •adr

PARSCH, Arnost (1936)
Compositeur tchèque né à Bucovice (Moravia) le 12 II 1936. Travailla avec J. Podesva, M. Istvan, et J. Kapr.
"In about 1970, he began to incorporate in his music more diverse ideas and techniques in collage structures containing frequent sharp confrontations of style." (M. STEDRON)
Ecce homo (Oeuvre collective) •Sx •CHF
Kure krakore (Chicken clucking) (Milos STEDRON) (1970) •Asx/Tape •DP

PARTCH, Harry (1901-1976)
Compositeur, facteur, et interprète américain, né à Oakland (California), le 24 VI 1901, mort à San Diego, le 3 IX 1976.
"Harry Partch a cherché à construire des instruments à clavier capables de contrôler des intervalles plus petits que le demi-ton; il va ainsi jusqu'à préconiser la division de l'octave en quarante-trois parties." (J. & B. MASSIN) "Il serait totalement excessif de faire de Harry Partch un génie universel ignoré, mais sa personnalité tellement américaine mérite qu'on prête une oreille à son univers sonore si particulier. Ancêtre revendiqué par toute une génération musicale de la côte Ouest, il incarne avec entêtement cette liberté d'action vénérée outre-Atlantique, ce *Do your own thing* inaliénable." (C. GLAYMAN) "Si le travail sur la notation appelle des rencontres avec les arts graphiques, il va sans dire que la construction de nouveaux objets sonores a été, de son côté, envisagée à des niveaux à la fois plastique et musical, nécessitant des collaborations avec sculpteurs et architectes. Harry Partch est considéré comme le fondateur de ce mouvement de 'sculpture sonore' qui doit conduire à une interaction des qualités visuelles et acoustiques des instruments inventés, afin d'engager la personnalité entière de l'individu, observateur ou actant, en une sorte de magie sonore et de rituel." (D. J-Y. BOSSEUR) "Sa théorie, le 'corporatisme,' invoque 'une trinité: la magie du son, la beauté visuelle, l'expérience-rituel." (J-N. von der WEID)
"Largely autodidact, he began experimenting with instruments capable of producing fractional intervals, which led him to the formulation of a 43-tone scale; he expounded his findings in his book *Genesis of a Music* (1949). He constructed new instruments… seeking intimate contact with American life. He wandered across the country, collected indigenous expressions of folk ways, inscriptions on public walls, etc., for texts in his productions." (BAKER) "Largely self-taught, he pursued independent researches into natural tunings of the past; these, together with a predominant concern with the physical 'corporeal' aspects of music, led him to reject all modern Western scales and techniques, necessitating the invention of his own tuning system and instruments, and the training of his own performing group, the Gate 5 Ensemble." (P. EARLS)
Ulysses at the Edge of the World (1955) •Vln/Tsx/Tpt/Perc

PARWEZ, Akmal
Chetna (1993) (to J. STOLTIE) (3 Movements) •Asx Solo
Punjab - Land of Five Rivers •Fl/Ob/Cl/Tsx/Bsn/Pno/Harp/Str/Perc •SeMC

PASCAL, Claude (1921)
Compositeur français, né à Paris, le 19 II 1921. Travailla avec T. Aubin et H. Busser. Grand Prix de Rome (1945).
"Très mélodieuse, la musique de Claude Pascal s'est toujours tenue à l'écart des courants qui agitent la musique contemporaine." (M. & I.) "Dans une esthétique traditionnelle et une écriture élégante, il resta solidement attaché au système tonal ainsi qu'à son esprit thématique." (Cl. ROSTAND)

"Pascal's music is traditional in style, adhering closely to classical forms and tonality; in its textural clarity and direct expression it shows some influence of Debussy and Ravel." (GROVE)
Impromptu (1953) (4') (to M. MULE) •Asx/Pno •Dur
Patchwork Ballet - 17 fresques musicales (1991) (40')
  I) Instrumental: Adage - Carnaval - Dinosaures - Invention - Introduction et marche des saltimbanques - Place au cirque! - Notturno II) Dansé: Adieu! - Burlesque - Danse des Martiens - Eveil - Passacaille - Procession - Squash ou Variation brillante - Repos des saltimbanques - Rodeo - Valse énigmatique •12 Sx: SnoSSAAATTTBBBs
Planetarium (1987) (2'30) •Asx/Pno •Com
Quatuor (1961) (17') (to Quatuor M. Mule) 1) Animé 2) Choral 3) Valse 4) Vif •SATB •Dur
Sonatine (1948) (8') (to M. MULE) •Asx/Pno •Dur

PASCAL, Michel
Bubble cooking (1990-91) (12') (to D. KIENTZY) •Sx/Instrumental Ensemble

PASCHEDAG
1st Ensemble (BUCHTEL) •AATB •Kjos

PASCUZZI, Gregory
Compositeur américain.
Concerto (1988) •Asx/Chamber Orch

PASQUALE, James Di (see DI PASQUALE, James)

PASQUALI, Nicolo (1718-1757)
Menuet (LONDEIX) •Asx/Pno •Lem

PASQUET, Luis
Compositeur finlandais.
3 Pièces 1) Conversation 2) Valse française 3) Tango •SATB

PATACHICH, Ivan (1922)
Compositeur hongrois, né le 3 VI 1922, à Budapest. Travailla avec Siklos, Viski, et Farkas.
"After a period influenced by Bartok and Kodaly he began to adopt new techniques, with which he came into contact at Darmstadt summer courses. Patachich pioneered electronic music in Hungary." (M. BERLASZ KAROLYI)
Concerto (20') •Asx/Str
Jeu 1+4 (1989) (12') •1 Sx: S+A+CBs/Instrumental Ensemble
Modsaxyn (1989) (9') (to D. KIENTZY) •Tsx/Tape
Patience (9') •Asx/Tape
Quartetino (1972) (to Rascher Quartet) 1) Allegro moderato 2) Moderato 3) Allegro •SATB •GMP
Sonata •Asx/Pno
Sonatina 1) Allegro 2) Andante 3) Allegro vivace •Bsx/Pno •SJ

PATCH, Marc
Compositeur canadien, né au Québec.
Le jardin féérique des jarres lipriconiennes •Asx/Pno
Magic spell (1992) •1 Sx: A+S/Str Quartet

PATRICK, Lee (1938)
Saxophoniste, compositeur, et arrangeur américain, professeur à l'université de Louisville.
Folk Song Miniatures (1981) 1) Meadowlands (Russia) 2) The Ash Grove (Wales) 3) The Lass from the low countree (U.S.A.) 4) Jack o' diamonds (U.S.A.) •3 Sx: ATB
Sea Songs (1980) •3 Sx: ATB
Tribute to JB (1980) •3 Sx: ATB

PATRIQUIN, Donald (1938)
Compositeur canadien.

Choo - Choo (1981) •SATB •CMC
Parodie (1982) •SATB
3 Mois (1982) •SATB •CMC

PATTEN, James (1936)
Compositeur anglais.
Trochee (1972) (5') (to London Saxophone Quartet) •SATB •BMIC
Two Short Pieces (1972) (2') (to London Saxophone Quartet) •SATB •BMIC

PATTERSON, Paul (1947)
Compositeur anglais, né le 15 Juin 1947, à Chesterfield. Travailla avec Stoker et Bennett.
"S'est beaucoup rapproché des compositeurs de l'école polonaise, en particulier de Penderecki et de Lutoslawski. Dans sa pièce pour orchestre Cracowian counterpoints, composée au début des années 1970, l'adhésion au sérialisme se manifeste sans ambiguïté. A partir des années 1980, ses oeuvres se signalent par un langage plus traditionnel." (G. GEFEN)
"A versatile composer, he was at first influenced by Bennett, employing serial procedures in a strictly orthodox fashion. At the same time this early music has a strong rhythmic interest that perhaps owes more to neo-classicism. His output of the early 1970s was the product of work with electronics and of a growing acquaintance with the music of Penderecki and Ligeti, manifested in a concern with unusual timbres, with space and with texture." (R. COOKE)
Diversions (1976) (12') 1) Gusty 2) Blowing blue 3) Sea breeze •SATB •adr

PAUL, Ernst (1907)
Compositeur, musicologue, et corniste autrichien, né le 18 XI 1907 à Vienne.
Kammerkonzert, op. 29 (1931) •Asx/Orch

PAUL, Gene
Estilian caprice •1 Sx: A or T/Pno •Rub

PAULET, Vincent (1962)
Compositeur et organiste français, né à Reims. Travailla avec J-Cl. Renaud, J-Cl. Henry, M. Merlet, S. Nigg, et G. Litaize.
Aeolian Voices (1990) (4'30) (to M. OBERLI & D. AUBERT) •SATB
Arabesque (1986) (2'30) •Asx/Pno •Com

PAULSON, Gustaf (1898-1966)
Organiste, pianiste, et compositeur suédois, né à Helsingborg, le 22 I 1898, mort le 17 XII 1966. Travailla à Paris avec Lortat, puis avec Gram.
"His music—influenced by Nielsen and Hindemith, and later employing 12-note serial techniques—is sometimes coloured by parody or bizarre humour. A feeling for timbre distinguishes the solo writing in his concertos and also his lively treatment of the orchestra." (J. RIDELL) "His music is rooted in that of Carl Nielsen and Paul Hindemith, but sometimes it also acquires touches of the Baroque and Renaissance." (SJ)
Konsert, op. 105 (1959) (15') •Asx/Orch (2222/2210/Tuba/Str) or Pno •Ton/STIM

PAUMGARTNER, Bernhard (1887-1971)
Musicologue, chef d'orchestre, et compositeur autrichien, né le 14 XI 1887 à Vienne, mort à Salzburg, le 27 VII 1971. Particulièrement influencé par Mandyczewski.
Divertimento •Picc/EH/Asx/Bsn/Hn/Tpt/Pno/Vla/Vcl/Perc •Uni

PAUR, Jiri
Slepici serenade (1988) (8') •SATB
Suite (1986) (8') •SATB

PAUWELS, M.
Andante et Allegro •1 Sx: A or T/Pno •HE/An

PAVEY
Gingerbread Man •Asx/Pno •Pip

PAVLENKO, Serguei (1952)
Compositeur russe, né à Moscou. Travailla avec H. Sidelnikov.
"Son oeuvre est surtout instrumentale et orchestrale. Elle s'inscrit dans la voie du post-sérialisme assez souple, qui n'exclue pas la rigueur et la concision." (J. di VANNI)
Concerto (1975) (15') •Asx/Orch (2222/343/3 Perc/Harp/Str) or Pno •adr
Concerto breve (1980) (13') (to J-M. LONDEIX) •12 Sx: SnoSSAAATTTBBBs •adr
Dedication (1989) (17') (to S. BICHON) 1) Andante tranquillo 2) Allegro scherzando 3) Tempo libro ma tranquillo 4) Tempo primo •Ob/Asx/Vcl
Intermezzo (1985) (12') •Asx/Harp/Perc
Pastorale (1988) (8') •5 Sx: S+A AATB •Com
Quartet (1976) (13') 1) Adagio 2) Allegretto 3) Lento 4) Presto •SATB •adr
Sonate (1975) (10') (Lento - Allegretto - Lento - Allegro - Lento) •Asx/Pno •adr

PAYNE, Frank Lynn
Compositeur américain.
Quartet •Asx/Tpt/Vla/Trb •SeMC
Sax Prepared Tape •Asx/Tape •NTS
Toccata •Asx/Pno •Sha

PAZ, Juan Carlos (1897-1972)
Compositeur argentin né le 5 VIII 1897, à Buenos-Aires, où il est mort le 25 VIII 1972. Travailla avec Gaito et Fornarini.
"Connaissant bien la technique sérielle de Schoenberg, auquel il a consacré un ouvrage, c'est à Juan Carlos Paz que l'on doit l'introduction en Argentine d'un esprit de recherche contemporain." (J. & B. MASSIN)
"Essentially he was self-taught in composition, and he remained an independent and isolated figure. He was drawn successively to Franck, to Stravinsky and to using jazz in art music, but, whatever the influence, the result was always highly individual." (S. SALGADO) "His early works are marked by strong polyphony in a neo-classical style. About 1927, he adopted atonal and polytonal procedures. In 1934 he began to compose almost exclusively in the 12-tone idiom. After 1950, he moderated his musical language and occasionally wrote pieces in simplified harmony." (BAKER)
Musica, op. 43 (1943) (18') •Fl/Sx/Pno •GSch
Trio, op. 36, no. 2 (1938) (16') •Cl/Tpt/Sx •GSch

PECK, Russell
Compositeur américain.
Drastic Measures 1) Poco adagio, molto espressivo 2) Allegro •SATB
Sonatina (1967) (to J. HOULIK) •Tsx/Pno •WIM
Time Being •Sx/Tape
The Upward Stream - Concerto (1985-86) (15') (to J. HOULIK) 1) Adagietto 2) Allegro-Adagietto 3) Allegro molto •Tsx/Orch

PEDERSEN, Jens Wilhelm
Compositeur de jazz.
Seks bagateller (1986) (7') •SATB

PEIKO, Nicholas (see PEYKO, Nicholas)

PEIXINHO, Jorge (Manuel Rosado MARQUES)

(1940)
Compositeur et pianiste portugais, né à Montijo, le 20 I 1940. Travailla avec Porena et G. Petrassi, puis avec Boulez, Stockhausen, Koenig et L. Nono. Il étudia également au studio de musique électroacoustique de Bilthoven.
Sax-Bleu (1982) (18') (to D. KIENTZY) •1 Sx: Sno+A/Echo Chamber •Sal
Concerto (1961) (20') •Sx/Orch (3222/223/3 Perc/Harp/Str)
Passage intérieur (1989) (16') (to D. KIENTZY) •1 Sx: Sno+S+A+T+B/Instrumental Ensemble

PELCHAT, André (1945)
Saxophoniste, clarinettiste, professeur, compositeur, et arrangeur canadien, né le 28 VIII 1945. Travailla avec F. Hemke et J-M. Londeix.
Exploration (1980) •SATB •CMC
Impro binantine •Ssx Solo •CMC

PELEMANS, Willem (1901)
Critique musical et compositeur belge, né à Anvers, le 6 IV 1901. Travailla l'harmonie et le contrepoint avec P. Lagye.
"Aborda la musique en autodidacte." "Willem Pelemans se réclame d'aucun système établi. Il nous propose une mélodie franchement tonale, sans forme préétablie, régie par des accords librement enchaînés, soutenue par un rythme simple et souvent populaire. C'est un romantique mûri, qui se contrôle, un chercheur qui parvient à exprimer sa nature puissante et souvent enjouée."
"Was essentially self-taught. His early music was sober, direct and little ornamented, though later works have a more lyrical and warm character, expressed principally in melody." (C. MERTEENS)
Concerto (1976) (to E. APPER) •Asx/Orch •Mau
Quatuor (1965) (12') 1) Allegro 2) Lento 3) Allegro •SATB •Mau

PELLEGRIN, Adrien (1881-1947)
Compositeur français, mort le 27 I 1947.
1ère Fantaisie appassionata de concours (to E. RATEZ) •Asx/Orch or Pno •Gras

PELLEGRINI, Ernesto
Divertimento a Due •2 Sx: SA
Duolog •Asx/Pno •WWS

PELLMAN, Samuel (1953)
Before the Dawn (1979) (to S. MAUK) •Ssx/Wind Ensemble
Concertpiece (1981) (to S. MAUK) •Ssx/Wind Ensemble
Horizon (1978) •Ssx/Wind Ensemble/Mixed Chorus/Narr
Pentacle (1976) (to E. GREGORY) •Asx/Tape •DP

PELUSI, Mario (1951)
Compositeur américain, né à Los Angeles. Travailla avec J. Hopkins, R. Linn, M. Babbitt, E. Cone, et C. Spies.
Concert Piece (1978) (12'30) (to M. WATTERS) •Bsx/Brass Quartet/Perc

PELZ, William
Ballad •2 Sx: AT •Bel
Portrait •Tsx/Pno •Bel

PENBERTHY, James (1917)
Compositeur australien, né le 3 V 1917, à Melbourne.
"For many years his style remained fairly conservative; since 1967, however, he has explored more advanced techniques including the use of serial and computer methods in some works." (D. SYMONS)
Concerto (1970) (10') (to P. CLINCH) •Asx/Orch (2232/331/Perc/Harp/Str) •adr
Scherzo and Lamentoso (1982) (to the Australian Saxophone Quartet) •SATB •adr

PENDERS, Joseph (1928)

Compositeur hollandais, né à Hoensbrock, le 21 X 1928.
Limburgse vla (1983) •Ensemble (variable instrumentation) •Mol
Rêverie (1985) (3'30) •Asx/Band

PENHERSKI, Zbigniew (1935)

Compositeur polonais, né le 26 I 1935 à Varsovie. Travailla avec S.
Poradowski et T. Szeligovski.
"In general, his compositions are lyrically melodic, rhythmically
effective and harmonically straightforward, though in later works he
has adopted novel techniques." (M. HANUSZEWSKA)
Jeux parties (1984) (11') (to D. PITUCH) •Asx/Perc •CPM

PENNEQUIN, Jean (16th century)

Morceau de concours (MEYER) •Asx/Pno •BC

PENNYCOOK, Bruce

Compositeur canadien.
3 Pièces (1982) (10') (to P. BRODIE) 1) Soprano alone 2) Alto and
Synclavier 3) Soprano and Tape •1 Sx: S+A/Tape •CMC

PENTLAND, Barbara (Lally) (1912)

Compositeur et pianiste canadien, né à Winnipeg, le 2 I 1912.
Travailla à Paris, avec Gauthiez, puis, aux U.S.A. avec Jacobi et
Wagenaar.
"Pentland's later works are economical, the textures swept clean of
the scales and arpeggios of her music of the 1940s. 12-note serialism
is a means of control, but not a rigid one: the series is treated quite freely
after its first presentation of the final notes; almost invariably the first
part of the series is emphasized while the remainder is obscured or
omitted." (S. E. LOOSLEY)
Variable Winds (1979) (5') •Fl (or Ob)/Asx/3 Tom-toms/Bongos
•CMC

PENTRENKO, M. F.

Compositeur russe.
Valse n° 1 (1960) •Asx/Pno •SK

PEPIN, Clermont (Jean-Josephat) (1926)

Compositeur, pianiste, et professeur canadien, né à St-Georges-de-
Beauce (Québec), le 15 V 1926. Travailla avec Champagne, Scalero,
et A. Walter, puis, à Paris, avec A. Jolivet, A. Honegger, et O.
Messiaen.
"It is perhaps through his association with physicists, mathemati-
cians and sociologists that Pepin has been able to view music in relation
to significant physical phenomena in the universe." (D. R. COOPER)
Pièces de circonstance (1967) •Childrens chorus/Fl/Ob/3 Cl/2 Sx/2
Hn •CMC

PEPPER, Richard

Compositeur anglais.
Quartet (1972) (5'30) (to London Saxophone Quartet) •SATB
Sounds for 2 Saxes •2 Sx: AT •Che

PEPPING, Ernst (1901)

Compositeur allemand, né le 12 IX 1901 à Duisburg. Travailla avec
Gmeindl.
"The continuing influence of 16th- and 17th-century music is already
evident, particularly in the use of cantus firmus technique, a tendency
to linearity, Baroque concerto forms and a broadening of tonality on the
basis of the church modes." (K. KIRCHBERG)
Suite (1925-26) •Tpt/Asx/Trb •Sch

PERDER, Kjell (1954)

Compositeur suédois.
Flexica (1985) (12') •5 Soloists: Fl-à-bec/Soprano Voice/Guit/Vcl/
Sx/Orch (variable instrumentation)

PEREZ-MASEDA, Eduardo (1953)

Compositeur espagnol, né à Madrid.
My echo, my shadow (1989) (10') (to D. KIENTZY) •1 Sx: S+B/Tape

PERFECT, Albert

Two Little Chums - Introduction and polka •2 Sx: AA/Pno •CF

PERGOLESE, Giovanni-Battista (1710-1736)

Nina (EPHROSS) •Asx/Pno •South
Se tu m'ami - Arietta (ELKAN) •1 Sx: A or T/Pno •HE
Sicilian Air •1 Sx: A or T/Pno •Mus
Sonata No. 12 (OSTRANDER) •Tsx/Pno •Mus

PERLONGO, Daniel

Aureole-quartet (1979) •SATB •Sha

PERNAIACHI, Gianfranco

Compositeur italien.
Realgar 1 & 2 (1984 & 1990) (8' + 5') (to G. SCHIAFFINI & E.
FILIPPETTI) •Trb and/or Tsx/Electr. •EDP

PERRAULT, Michel (1925)

Compositeur et chef d'orchestre canadien, né à Montréal, le 20 VII
1925. Travailla avec N. Boulanger, A. Honegger, et G. Dandelot.
"I am a classicist living in the wrong period. Dodecaphonism,
serialism or any other *ism* is not for me. I like a folktune and the
harmony that goes with it." (M. Perrault)
Esquisses québécoises 1) Envoyons de l'avant 2) J'entends le moulin
3) Isabeau s'y promène 4) Prélude, fugue et final sur 'J'ai tant
dansé' •SATB
Quatuor (1953) (to ROMANO) •SATB •PuB/CMC

PERRIER, Alain

Otinavari •Asx/Perc

PERRIER, Marius (1880-1948)

Prélude et allegro •Asx/Pno •Bil

PERRIN, Jean-Charles (1920)

Compositeur suisse, né le 17 IX 1920, à Lausanne.
Duo concertante (1974) (to I. ROTH) 1) Adagio 2) Allegro giocoso
•Asx/Pno •Bil

PERRIN, Marcel (1912)

Saxophoniste français, né à Alger, le 1er VI 1912. Travailla à Paris
avec M. Mule.
Agilité - étude chromatique (1951) (4') •GD
Arlequins (1943) (1'50) •Asx/Pno •Led
Badinage •Asx/Pno •GD
Bagatelle (1951) (3'10) •Asx or Bb Sx/Pno •Com/Phi
Berceuse (1941) (1'45) •Asx/Pno •Led
Caprice - étude atonale (1951) (4'50) •GD
Cinq Pièces (1941) •SATB •DP
Complainte - Trio (1951) (3'15) •2 Sx: SA/Tpt •Com
Duos •2 Sx
Elégie (1941) (2') •Asx or Bb Sx/Pno •GD
Esquisse (1983) (2'45) •Asx/Pno or Org •DP
Evocations (1958) •Asx Solo •DP
22 Exercices transcendants (1950) •Led
Fantaisie tzigane (1941) (5') •Asx/Orch or Band or Pno •GD
Mélodie (1941) (2') •Asx or Bb Sx/Pno •GD
Mélopée (2'30) •1 Sx: A or S/Pno
Mirage (1938) (2'30) •4 Sx: SATB or Asx/Orch (1122/20000Perc/
Harp/Str) or Pno •Led
Nocturne (1945) (7'30) •Asx/Orch or Org or Pno •GD
Nostalgie •Asx or Bb Sx/Pno •GD
Nouvelle méthode d'après Mayeur •Led

Poème (1942) (2'40) •Asx or Bb Sx/Pno •Led
Prière •Asx/Org •DP
Reflets (1983) (2'10) •1 Sx: S or A/Pno •DP
Rêves (1936) (2'45) (to M. MULE) •Asx/Pno •Led
Technique du saxophone (1957) •GD
Tourbillon - étude technique (1951) (4') •GD
Travail des gammes et des arpèges •Led

PERRON, Alain
Compositeur canadien.
Cycle 1 (1992) (8') •1 Sx: S+A+T+B/Perc

PERRUCCI, Mario (1934)
Compositeur italien.
Piccola serenata (1970) •2 Tsx/Timp/Pno

PERRY, David
Compositeur américain.
Piece (1988) •Asx/Pno

PERSICHETTI, Vincent (1915)
Compositeur, pianiste, et chef d'orchestre américain, né le 6 VI 1915, à Philadelphia. Travailla avec P. Nordoff et R. Harris.

"Il existe aux Etats-Unis, toute une catégorie de compositeurs reconnus (symphonistes pour la plupart) dont les oeuvres alimentent la vie musicale et les programmes des grands orchestres, et sur lesquels nous ne savons rien… Vincent Persichetti fait partie de ceux-là." (J-E. FOUSNAQUER)

"Persichetti's music is remarkable for its contrapuntal compactness, in a synthetic style, amalgamating the seemingly incompatible idioms of different historical epochs; the basis is tonal, but the component parts often move independently, creating polytonal combinations; the rhythmic element is always strong and emphatic; the melody is more frequently diatonic then chromatic or atonal." (BAKER) "Persichetti has written with fluency and facility in a wide variety of forms and styles: he has not allied himself to any school and his music may employ modal, tonal, polytonal or atonal structures, singly or in combination." (S. DI BONAVENTURA)
Parable XIII, op. 123 (7') (to B. MINOR) •Asx Solo •EV

PERSSON, Bob Anders (1937)
Compositeur suédois.
Om sommaren sköna II (1965) •Fl/BsCl/Trb/2 Perc/Vibr/Vcl/Tape/ Jazz Sx

PESSARD, Emile (Louis Fortuné) (1843-1917)
Professeur et compositeur français, né le 29 V 1843 à Paris, où il est mort, le 19 II 1917. Travailla avec Bazin et Carafa. Grand Prix de Rome (1866).
Andalouse (BUCHTEL) •Asx/Pno •Kjos
Andantino, op. 36 (188x) (to L. MAYEUR) •Asx/Pno •Led

PESSE, Maurice-Emile (1881-1943)
Au soir de la vie (MULE) •Asx/Pno •Led

PESTALOZZO
Ciribiribin •Asx/Pno •Kjos

PETER, H. A.
Bagatelle (to J. de VRIES) •Asx/Pno
Tempo de Minuetto (to J. de VRIES) •Asx/Pno

PETERSEN, Ted
Miniature Suite 1) March 2) Waltz 3) Andante 4) Allegro •AATB •Ken

PETERSMA, Wim (1942)
Compositeur néerlandais, né le 18 V 1942, à Dorssburg (Hollande).

Travailla avec de Goeuw.
Quatuor (1971) (8') (to Quatuor Néerlandais) •SATB •Don

PETIOT, André (1886-1973)
Hautboïste, arrangeur, compositeur, et chef d'orchestre français, né le 11 I 1886, mort à Paris, le 12 II 1973.
Concerto en Mib (GLAZOUNOV) •Asx/Pno •Led

PETIT, Alexandre-S.
1ère étude de concours (to G. PARÈS) •Asx/Pno •Bil

PETIT, Jacques (1946)
Saxorch (1976) (to Quatuor de Paris) •SATB
Swing sweet suite (1988) 1) Pop en Ré 2) Sicilienne blues 3) Be-bop sériel •SATB •Arp
Variations (1981) (3 Volumes) •4 Sx: AAAA •Bil

PETIT, Jean-Louis (1937)
Compositeur et chef d'orchestre français. Travailla avec S. Plé-Caussade et O. Messiaen, K. Sipush, L. Auriacombe, F. Ferrara, I. Markevitch, et P. Boulez.
La mort des autres (1980) •5 Sx: SAATB
Perceval (1985) (10') •SATB
Samu 92 (to A. BEUN) •5 Sx: SAATB •EMF
Trait multiple (1986) (4'15) •Asx Solo •Bil
Treize Passages - Duo contemporain (1985) •Asx/Vibr+Marimba

PETIT, Pierre (1922)
Compositeur et critique musical français, né à Poitiers, le 21 IV 1922. Travailla avec N. Boulanger, N. Gallon, et H. Busser. Grand Prix de Rome (1946).

"Son style traditionnel et d'une grande élégance, s'exprime avec une verve très diverse dans les compositions elles-mêmes les plus diverses." (Cl. ROSTAND) "Son style a quelque chose de racé et de subtil. Son niveau de culture est tout à fait exceptionnel." (R. BERNARD)
Andante et fileuse (1959) (7'30) (to M. MULE) •Asx/Pno •Led
Saxopéra (to FLAVIO) (1'30) •Asx/Pno •Led

PETTERSON, Allan (Gustav) (1911-1980)
Compositeur et violoniste suédois, né à Västra Ryd (Uppsala), le 19 IX 1911, mort à Stockholm le 20 VI 1980. Travailla avec A. Honegger et LEIBOWITZ.

"Petterson's music is remarkably independent: its most individual features are the frequently chromatic, triadic harmony and the complicated percussion patterns." (R. HAGLUND)
Symphony No. 16 (1979) (25') (to F. HEMKE) •Asx/Orch (3223/ 4330Tuba/Str) •STIM

PETTINE, Giuseppe
Professeur américain.
Modern Method for the Saxophone (1928) •RIM

PETTY, Byron W.
Introduction and Souvenir (1992-93) •Ssx/Pno

PETRIE, Henry-W.
Asleep in the Deep (BUCHTEL) •Bsx/Pno •Kjos
Asleep in the Deep (WALTERS) •Bsx/Band or Pno •Rub

PETROJ, Lionel
11 Actes (20') •Sx/Bass

PEUERL, Paul
Suite in Es-Dur (1992) •SATB •PMV

PEYKO, Nikolay Ivanovich (1916)
Compositeur et professeur russe né à Moscou, le 25 III 1916. Travailla avec Litinsky, Myaskovsky, et Rakov.

"His music has deep links with the Russian tradition, and in particular with the epic Russian symphony; in this he was at first a close follower of Myaskovsky. Subsequently, however, he was influenced by Stravinsky, Prokofiev and Shostakovitch, and in the 1960s he began working with 12-note methods, though still within a tonal framework. His orchestration is masterly." (G. GRIGOR'YEVA)
Fantaisie de concert (1977) •2 Sx: SA/Pno

PFENNINGER, Rik
Saxophoniste et professeur américain.
A Sequential Method for the Development of Basic Jazz Improvisation Skills •adr

PFLÜGER, Andreas
Compositeur tchèque.
Sogno d'estate •SATB

PHAN, P. Q.
Compositeur américain.
My Language (1988) •Asx/Pno •adr
Seagulls (1989) •SATB •adr

PHIFER, Larry
Construction II •3, 6 instruments

PHILIBA, Nicole (1937)
Compositeur français, née à Paris, le 30 VIII 1937. Travailla avec Tony Aubin et O. Messiaen.
"Musique onirique." (R. MANUEL) "Originale par le caractère incantatoire accusé de combinaisons rythmiques recherchées." (P. MARI)
Concerto (1962) (14') (to D. DEFFAYET) 1) Allegro moderato 2) Lento 3) Rondo final •Asx/Str Orch/Perc •Bil
Quatuor (1959) (16'30) (to Quatuor Deffayet) 1) Thème et variations 2) Lento 3) Rondo final •SATB
Sonate (1964) (17') (to D. DEFFAYET) 1) Allegro moderato molto marcato 2) Lento 3) Allegro molto •Asx/Pno •Bil
Trois Etudes (1966) (5'30) •Asx Solo

PHILIDOR, François-André (1726-1795)
Chant d'église (MULE) •Bb Sx or Eb Sx/Pno •Led
Ernelinnde - Rigaudon (MULE) •Asx/Pno •Led

PHILIPPI, Ronald
Compositeur néerlandais.
Trillingen (1987) (6') •Asx Solo

PHILIPS, Richard
Tarentelle et Fugue (1981) (2') •SATB •Com

PHILLIPS, Art
Compositeur canadien.
Tribute - to Leonard Bernstein (to Gerald Danovitch Saxophone Quartet) •SATB

PHILLIPS, Burril (1907)
Compositeur, pianiste, et professeur américain, né à Omaha (Nebraska), le 9 XI 1907. Travailla avec E. Stringham, H. Hanson, et B. Rogers.
"In the early 1960s Phillips began to work with free serial techniques, less sharply accented rhythms and an increasing sense of fantasy. Although he can in no sense be considered an imitator of earlier models, his works show a clarity of line and texture that reflects his great admiration for the music of Domenico Scarlatti and Purcell." (A. P. BASART)
Yellowstone, Yates and Yosemite (1972) •Tsx/Concert Band

PHILLIPS, Ivan C.
A Classical and Romantic Album •Asx/Pno •OUP

PHILLIPS, J.
2 Pieces diverses •Asx/Pno •WWS

PHILLIPS, Mark
Compositeur américain.
Night Visions (1988) (to A. D. REILLY) •Asx/Pno

PHILO
Etude •Tsx Solo •WWS
Piece in G Minor •Tsx Solo •WWS

PIAZZOLA, Astor (1921-1992)
Tango-études (1990) •Sx Solo •Lem
Histoire du tango (VOIRPY) (1991) (13') 1) Bordel 1900 2) Café 1930 3) Night club 1960 4) Concert d'aujourd'hui •SATB •Lem
Summit •Bandon./Sx/Picc

PIBERNIK, Zlatko (1926)
Compositeur serbe, né le 26 XII 1926 à Zagreb. Travailla avec K. Odak.
"Having written a number of neo-classical and folk-influenced pieces, he developed a strong expressionistic style. An imaginative series of five works with the title *Koncertantna muzika* shows his ability to develop his style in new directions. In these pieces the model of the modern chamber concerto is enlarged to include the use of reciters and tape, and the adoption and assimilation of many new techniques." (N. O'LOUGHLIN)
Koncertantna muzika (1956) •Fl/Sx/Harp/Orch •YUC

PICCOLOMINI, Marietta (1834-1899)
Play For Us •Bb Sx or Eb Sx/Pno •CF
The Soldier of the Cross •Bb Sx/Pno •CF

PICHAUREAU, Claude Roland Robert (1940)
Compositeur français, né le 30 V 1940, à Balla-Miré (I. & L.). Travailla avec R. Duclos, H. Challan, S. Pé-Caussade, T. Aubin, et M. Rosenthal.
Epilogue à Rafflésia (3'30) •Asx/Wind Orch or Pno or 4 Sx: SATB •Bil
Prélude à Rafflésia (1990) (5') •Asx Solo •Bil
Rafflésia (1970) (6'30) •Ssx/Wind Orch or Pno or 4 Sx: SATB •Bil
Saximini (1993) (3') •Tsx/Pno •Bil
Rafflésia, du Prélude à l'Epilogue •2 Sx: SA/Pno •Bil

PIECHOWSKA, Alina
Blanc, blanc, messager •Asx/Pno
Invitation à la méditation •Asx Solo

PIEPER, René (1955)
Compositeur néerlandais.
Chanson interrompue (1983) (6') •SATB •Don
Concerto (1984) (25') (for H. de JONG) 1) Introduzione lento 2) Lento capriccioso 3) Allegro con fuoco •Asx/Orch or Pno •Bil

PIERNÉ, Gabriel (Henri Constant) (1863-1937)
Compositeur et chef d'orchestre français, né à Metz, le 16 VIII 1863, mort à Ploujean (Finistère), le 17 VII 1937. Travailla avec Massenet et C. Franck. Grand Prix de Rome (1882). Membre de l'Institut (1924).
"La musique de Gabriel Pierné est empreinte des qualités qui ont caractérisé ce grand chef d'orchestre: la sensibilité, la grâce, la précision. La clarté de la virtuosité de son écriture, le charme délicat de ses harmonies font de lui l'un des artistes les plus représentatifs de sa génération." (Cl. NOËL) "Ecrit dans la tradition de Massenet." "Son oeuvre de compositeur touche à tous les genres, passe de la verve spirituelle à l'émotion pénétrante, allie la mesure châtiée du langage à la virtuosité de l'écriture et au chatoiement de la couleur orchestrale."

(G. Samazeuil) "Une inspiration généreuse, nuancée par l'émotion et l'humour." (P. Wolff) "Tout ce qu'il écrit est plein de finesse, de charme et d'esprit." (E. Vuillermoz) "Ecriture traditionnelle extrêmement élégante et inventive, et d'une science exemplaire d'orchestration." (Cl. Rostand) "Très soucieux d'ordre et de clarté, Pierné a toujours fait preuve d'adroites facultés d'adaptations." (G. Cantagrel)

"As composer of remarkable skill Pierné left an abundant and varied production in all branches of music." (Grove) "It was sometimes said that his willing absorption in so much music of other composers adversely affected his personal style—his compositions do give the impression of a cultivated synthesis of many tendencies in the French music of his time. Technically his work is always completely assured: he wrote easily, with virtuosity, always stylishly, and his touch was light even when the subject was serious or tragic—a very French characteristic." (D. Cox)

Introduction et variations sur un thème populaire (1937) (14'30) (to Quatuor Mule) •SATB •Led
Canzonetta, op. 19 (Gee) •1 Sx: S or T/Pno •South
Canzonetta (Mule) •Asx/Pno •Led
Canzonetta (Petiot) •Bb Sx/Pno •Led
Chanson d'autrefois (Mule) (2'30) •SATB •Led
Chanson de Grand-maman (2') (Mule) •SATB •Led
Guardian Angel (Nelson) •4 Sx: SATB or AATB •Lud
Marche des petits soldats de plomb (Mule) (2') •SATB •Led
Piece in G Minor (Gee) •1 Sx: S or T/Pno •South
Sérénade, op. 7 •Asx/Pno •Led
Sérénade, op. 7 (Gee) •Asx/Pno •South
Song of Grandmother (Nelson) •4 Sx: SATB or AATB •Lud
La Veillée de l'ange Gardien (Mule) •SATB •Led

PIERNÉ, Paul (1874-1952)

Professeur et compositeur français, cousin du précédent, né à Metz, le 30 VI 1874, mort à Paris, le 24 III 1952. Travailla avec Lenepveu et Caussade.

Concertino (1949) •Asx/Orch or Harmonie
Prélude et Scherzo (1944) (5') (to M. Mule) •Asx/Pno •Bil
Trois Conversations (to Quatuor de Paris) 1) Amusante 2) Sentimentale 3) Animée •SATB •Bil
Trois Pièces (to M. Mule) 1) Coquetterie 2) Scherzo 3) Le vol de la mouche •Asx/Pno •Bil

PIERRE - PETIT (see PETIT, Pierre)

PIERSON, Thomas Claude (1922)

Compositeur américain, né le 13 V 1922, à Houston (Texas).

Elegie (1974) (to D. Tofani) •Tsx/Band •adr

PIKOUL

Compositeur russe.

Concertino •Asx/Orch or Pno

PILATTI, Mario (1903-1938)

Inquiètude (Paquot) •Asx/Pno •Led

PILLEVESTRE (1837-1903)

Duos •2 Sx or Cl/Sx
Faune et Bacchante - Duo concertant (1896) •Sx/Cl/Pno
Idylle bretonne •Ob/Sx/Pno
Nocturne - Quintette •Fl/Ob/Cl/2 Sx: AB
Nuit d'été - Rêverie (1890) •Bb Sx or Eb Sx/Pno
2me Offertoire (1890) •Bb Sx or Eb Sx/Pno or Org

PILON, Daniel (1957)

Compositeur et saxophoniste canadien. Travailla avec R. Masino, M. Longtin, et S. Dion.

5 Arguments (1978-81) •SATB •adr

Bidoche et Patachon ou 7 épisodes dans la vie de nos petits mickeys préférés (1987-89) (23'30) (to D. Leboeuf) 1) Andante: Petzi chez la Castafiore 2) Allegro: Babar et le verre de lait hanté 3) Largo: Le cauchemar de Papa Talon 4) Moderato: Ze concombre masqué rides again 5) Larghetto: Compagnon Hilarion 6) Adagio: Les amours inavouées de Bécassine 7) Presto: Les Dalton en cavale. •12 Sx: SnoSSAAATTTBBBs •adr
Concerto n° 1 (1982) •10 Sx: SnoSSAATTBBBs •adr
Conversation sans issue (1978) (1er argument: modéré 2e argument: Lent 3e argument: Modéré 4e argument: Allegro moderato 5e argument: Allegro) •SATB •adr
3 Méditations (1982-83) (12') •Asx Solo •adr
10 Miniatures - sur un poème de J-G. Pilon (1979) •SATB •adr
Monochromies (1989) (for the Amherst Saxophone Quartet) •SATB •adr
Oleum perdidisti (1987-88) (21') (to M. Longtin & A. Prévost) 1) Adagio 2) Presto 3) Andante •4 Sx: SATB/Perc •adr
10 Sonances (1990-91) (28') (to M-J. Hudon) •SATB
Transparences (1985) (15') (to l'Ensemble Saxophone du Québec) •SATB •adr

PINARD, A.

Darling - Ballad •Eb Sx or Bb Sx/Pno •CF
Just a Little Song of Love •Eb Sx or Bb Sx/Pno •CF
Yearning •Eb Sx or Bb Sx/Pno •CF

PINOS-SIMANDL, Aloïs (1925)

Compositeur et théoricien tchécoslovaque, né à Vyskov (Moravie), le 2 X 1925. Travailla avec Blazek et Kvapil.

"In the 1960s they drew increasingly on the 'Second Viennese School' and the postwar avant-garde. In the late 1960s these detailed miniatures gave way to more complicated forms generated principally by tone colour. Pinos-Simandl has sometimes applied his theory of note groups to other parameters than pitch, and his use of chance is generally restricted to a choice in the ordering of controlled structures. Some of his music displays an ironic humour." (M. Strdron)

Ecce homo (Oeuvre collective) •CHF
Euforie (1983) (10') •Ob (or Fl)/Asx/Cl/BsCl/Pno/Perc/Bass •CHF
Geneze (1970) (8') •Vln/Asx/Vcl/Trb/Perc/Harp/Harps/Ionika •CHF

PINTO, Carlo

Compositeur italien.

Quartet (1985) (for the Amherst Saxophone Quartet) 1) Lento - Presto 2) Andante espressivo 3) Vivacisimo 4) Allegro - Andante - Tempo Primo •SATB

PIRSON, Al.

Adamanta (to D. Dispas) •Asx/Pno

PISATI, Maurizio

Compositeur italien.

"Calme, puis obsessionnel; de loin, et immédiatement tendrement fatigué; *AE*, sans signification, les deux lettres des cris ou des petites exclamations infantiles; sans respirer, même pendant les pauses; écrit dans les montagnes d'un rêve, debout dans les rochers, regardant vers le bas (M. Pisati)

AE (1987) (to J-S. Meugé) •Tsx Solo •Ric

PISHNY, Floyd Monte Keene (1941)

Five Canadian Soundscapes (1982) (to M. Eckroth) •SATB
Prelude, Aria, Fantasia (1985) (to M. Eckroth) •SATB

PISTONO, Piera

Compositeur italien.

Oasi (...un luogo o stato o tempo migliore rispetto ad altri che lo circondano...) (1988) (11') (to Quartet Sassof. Aquilano) •SATB

Dal fondo... la luce! (1990) (11') (to Quartet Sassof. Aquilano) •SATB

PITONI, Giuseppe Ottavio (1657-1743)

Cantate domino (D. SPEETS) •SATB •TM

PITTS

Church in the Wildwood •2 Sx: AT/Pno or 4 Sx: AATB/Pno (ad lib.) •Bri

PIZZI, Fulvio Delli (1953)

Compositeur italien. Travailla avec O. Greif, C. Zecchi, et R. Bianchini.

Hymmenaeus canonico modo (1986) (4'30) (to F. MONDELCI & M. MAZZONI) •2 Sx: AA

PLANEL, Robert (1908)

Compositeur français, né à Montélimar, le 22 I 1908. Travailla avec P. Vidal et H. Busser. Grand Prix de Rome (1933).

"Robert Planel s'exprime en un langage simple, clair, qui ne s'embarrasse pas de littérature." (M. & I.)

Burlesque (1942) (4'10) (to Quatuor Mule) •SATB

Prélude et saltarelle (1957) (7') •Asx/Pno •Led

Suite romantique (1944) (20'30) 1) Sérénade italienne 2) Danseuses 3) Chanson triste 4) Valse sentimentale 5) Conte de Noël 6) Chanson du miletier •Asx/Pno •Led

PLANK, Max

Saxophoniste, professeur, et compositeur américain.

Four Diversions •SATB

PLANQUETTE, Robert (1848-1903)

Cloches de Corneville •SATB •Mol

Fantaise sur 'Rip' (MOUSSARD) •Asx/Pno •Marg

PLATTI, Giovanni (1690-1762)

Sonata in G Major (ROUSSEAU) •Ssx/Pno •Eto

Sonata No. 3 (HERVIG) •Asx/Pno •Rub

Sonata No. 5 (HERVIG) •Asx/Pno •Rub

PLENEY, Bernard

Toccata •2 Sx: AB/Tpt/Trb

PLEYEL, Ignace (1757-1831)

Andante aus rondo, op. 48/1 •2 Cl/Asx/Bsn (or BsCl) •CF

PLUISTER, Simon

Compositeur néerlandais.

Cafe valencia - Suite (1978) (16') •Asx/Pno •Don

POLACCHI, Barbara

Ricerca (1992) (to R. SIEVER) •Asx Solo

POLANSKY, David

Compositeur américain.

Madness in 3 Episodes (8') (to K. RADNOFSKY) •Sx Solo •Ken

POLATSCHEK

40 More Hits of your Time (2 Volumes)

POLGAR, Tibor (1907)

Compositeur et chef d'orchestre d'origine hongroise, né à Budapest. Travailla avec Z. Kodaly. Vit au Canada depuis 1964.

Iona's Four Faces (1970) (12') (to P. BRODIE) 1) Her gentle face 2) Her capricious face 3) Her sad face 4) Her happy face •2 Sx: SA/Orch or Pno •CMC

POLIET, Lucien (1921)

Compositeur belge, né le 17 IV 1921 à Ixelles. Travailla avec P. Iranck et A. Souris.

Couques de Dinant (1971) •SATB •adr

Versailles suite (1960) (11') (to Quatuor Belge de Saxophones) 1) Pièce d'eau 2) Trianon 3) Le Hameau 4) Le musée de voitures •SATB •adr

POLIN, Claire (1926)

Compositeur américain, né à Merion (Pennsylvania), le 1 I 1926. Travailla avec V. Persichetti, R. Sessions, L. Foss, et P. Mennin.

"High point of the program... is a powerful musical statement, whispers, shouts, hisses of chorus... and saxophone's use of multiphonics, and pops, key slaps, harmonics all contribute to expressive effectiveness... and tremendous emotional impact. This is an important addition to 20th century music... Contributing by inherent musical value... to the advancement of the saxophone technique of our times." (M. SINDANOFF)

Aderyn pur (1972) (14') 1) Merula migratoria cyannospiza 2) Cardinalis cyanoctta cristata 3) Melospiza 4) (with tape) Coral yr Adar •Fl/Asx/Optional Tape •SeMC

Infinito - a requiem (1972) (23') (to K. DORN) •Soprano Voice/Asx/ Narr/Mixed chorus •SeMC

A Klockwork Diurnal (1977) (to L. KLOCK) •Asx/Bsn/Hn •DP

POLK, Marlyce

Compositeur américain.

Chromasia •Asx/2 Perc •SeMC

POLO, F. Fleta (see FLETA POLO, Francisco)

POLONIO, Eduardo

Compositeur espagnol.

Errance (1989) (8') (to D. KIENTZY) •Bsx/Tape

POMORIN, Sibylle (1956)

Flûtiste et saxophoniste de jazz, et compositeur allemande, née le 16 II 1956 à Altoberndorf.

Rabengold - Goldraben (1989) (80') •2 Sx: AT/Perc/Pno/Org/Vcl •adr

Zwei Lieder nach Anne Waldman (1989) (19') •Voice/Asx/Perc/Vcl/ Bass •adr

PONCE, Manuel-Maria (1882-1948)

Estrilla - Mexican Serenade (MAGANINI) •Eb Sx/Pno •CF

My Little Star (MAGANINI) •Eb Sx/Pno •CF

PONJEE, Ted (1953)

Compositeur néerlandais.

Autumn themes II (1986-91) (7') •Asx/Marimba •Don

Four saxes (1983) (10') •SATB •Don

Quatuor d'anches (1979) (9') •Ob/Cl/Asx/Bsn •Don

Saxuals songs (1981) (6') •Asx/Pno •Don

Sketches from invisible sounds (1988) (12') •SATB •Don

The square world (1984) (15') (to E. BOGAARD) •Asx/Orch or Pno •Don

POOLE, Geoffrey (1949)

Compositeur anglais.

Polter zeits (1975) •Vla/2 Cl/BsCl/2 Sx: AB/Prepared Pno •BMIC

Son of Paolo (1971) •Fl/Picc/Cl/BsCl/Tsx/2 Vln/2 Vcl/Prepared Pno •BMIC

POOT, Marcel (1901)

Compositeur belge, né à Vilvorde, le 7 V 1901. Travailla avec P. Dukas, P. Gilson. Fit partie du groupe des 'Synthétistes.'

"Son style refuse l'innovation, mais son oeuvres est bâtie sur une solide assise rythmique." (Cl. SAMUEL) "Exubérant, il retrouve dans sa verve l'atmosphère un peu débraillée des kermesses de son pays." (P. WOLFF) "Le tempérament vigoureux, la verve drue, une certaine rusticité qui ne s'encombre pas d'excessifs scrupules dans le choix des matériaux apparentent l'art de Marcel Poot à celui de Strauss et parfois à celui de Chabrier. Il y a chez lui une sorte d'humour, une truculence hardie qui confinent à la cocasserie et qui affrontent des envolées lyriques d'une générosité parfois grandiose." (R. BERNARD) "C'est un musicien sain, vigoureux, au style direct et sans apprêt, à la verve souvent truculente, au langage traditionnel pimenté de savoureux polytonalismes." (Cl. ROSTAND)

"The most striking element of his music is its rhythmic vivacity; he generally adheres to a basic tonal design, pursuing the aim of artistic utilitarianism." (BAKER) "He is a prolific composer, equipped with a splendid and refined technique, which is always at the service of a genuine artistic emotion, flavoured with a touch of irony. His real sense of humour makes him a valuable exception among his all too serious countrymen. His well-considered modernism clearly belongs to the sphere of thought of Stravinski or even more to that of Prokofiev. He may justly be considered as one of the most gifted Belgian composers of the 20th century and is doubtless one of the most intelligent artists of his generation." (A. CORBET) "Poot's brilliant and vigorous style—close to middle-period Stravinsky, or more particularly to Prokofiev—is often used to ironic or humorous effect, and has shown itself better suited to orchestral than to vocal music." (C. MERTENS)

Ballade (1948) (8') •Asx/Orch or Pno •Sch
Concertino (1962) (to Quatuor Belge de Saxophones) 1) Allegro deciso 2) Andantino 3) Allegro subito •SATB •CBDM
Concerto (14'15) (to Fr. DANEELS) •Asx/Orch or Pno
Impromptu (1931) (7') •Bsx/Pno •ME
Légende (1967) (8') •SATB •CBDM
Scherzo (1941) (5'30) •SATB •CBDM
Thema con variazioni (to Fr. DANEELS) •8 Sx

POPE, Peter

Compositeur anglais.
Fleet Street Concerto (1972) (17') 1) Editorial 2) Personal 3) Court circular 4) Agony column 5) Late-night final 6) Stop press •SATB
Quintet (1973) (20') •4 Sx: SATB/Pno

POPINEAU, François

Compositeur français.
Chi va piano va Saxo (1993) •Bsx/Pno •INM

POPOVICI, Fred

Heterosynthesis II (1986) (18') (to D. KIENTZY) •1 Sx: S+A+T/Orch (0000/3221/4 Perc/Celesta/Str)

POPP, André (1924)

Compositeur de musique légère français, né à Fontenay-le-Comte, auteur d'un grand nombre de chansons et de pièces à succès.
Berceuse noire •AATB
Le cirque Jolibois (1958) •Narr/4 Sx: SATB/Orch (2221/333/Tuba/Perc/Str)
Passeports pour Piccolo et Saxo (1957) •Narr/4 Sx: SATB/Orch (2221/333/Tuba/Perc/Str)
Piccolo Saxo et Cie (1956) (30') •Narr/4 Sx: SATB/Orch (2221/331/Tuba/Perc/Str)

PORCELIJN, David (1947)

Compositeur et chef d'orchestre néerlandais né à Achtkarspelen (Friesland), le 7 I 1947. Travailla avec Van Baaren et Van Vlijmen puis avec Tabachnik.
Pulverization II (1973) (15') (to E. BOGAARD) •Asx/Orch (22 winds/ 5 Perc/52 Str) •Don

PORCHET, E.

Solfège instrumental pratique •Mar

PORPORA, Nicola (1686-1768)

Sinfonia (RASCHER) •Tsx/Pno •MM

PORRET, Julien (1896-1979)

Chef de musique et compositeur français, mort à Bordeaux, le 11 I 1979.
Concertino n° 9 (to R. DRUET) •Asx/Pno •Mar
Concertino n° 10 (to P. FERRY) •Asx/Pno •Mar
Concertino n° 25 (to P. BOURIEZ) •Tsx/Pno •Mar
Concertino n° 26 (to A. KOZA) •Tsx/Pno •Mar
24 Déchiffrages manuscrits •Mar
25 Déchiffrages manuscrits •Mar
Dialogue, op. 237 (to P. ROMBY) •Asx/Pno •Mar
Dialogue-caprice •Asx/Pno •Mar
7e Duo de concours •2 Bb Sx/Pno •Mol
8e Duo de concours •Cl/Sx •Mol
12 Easy duos, op. 648 •2 Sx: AA or TT •HE/Mol
Ingres •2 Sx: AT/Pno •Mol
Intimité •SATB
Kleber (to P. CHEVALIER) •Asx/Cl/Pno •Mol
Lavoisier •Cl/Asx/Pno •Mol
Marivaux •Cl/Asx/Pno •Mol
Memento du saxophoniste •Mar
Nelson •Cl/Asx/Pno •Mol
Papillons - Caprice, op. 407 (to M. MULE) •Asx/Pno •Mar
Prélude et fugue d'après Frescobaldi •SATB
12 Progressive duets, op. 254 •2 Sx: AA or TT •HE
Senner •2 Sx: AT/Pno •Mol
17e solo de concours (to J. LACAZE) •Asx/Pno •Mar
18e solo de concours (to J-M. LONDEIX) •Asx/Pno •Mar
19e solo de concours (to R. DECOUAIX) •Tsx/Pno •Mar
20e solo de concours •Asx/Pno •Mar
Toccata (6') (to J-M. LONDEIX) 1) Allegretto 2) Larghetto 3) Allegro •Asx Solo
Villanelle fleurie, op. 406 (to J. COTTENET) •Asx/Pno •Mar

PORTA, Bernardo (1758-1829)

Two Duos •2 Sx: AA or TT •Pres
Studies in canon form

PORTER, Cole (1891-1964)

Just One of These Things •SATB

POSMAN, Lucien (1952)

Compositeur belge.
Marsyas' zwanezang (1988) (4'30) •Asx/Pno

POST, Jos

Compositeur néerlandais.
Litany (1983) (8') •SATB •Don

POTTER, Barbara Spence (see SPENCE POTTER)

POTTS, Albert III (1958)

Pianiste, chef d'orchestre, et compositeur américain.
Five Lyric Etudes (1983-84) (10') (to W. STREET) 1) Misterioso 2) Allegro •Asx/Pno

POULAIN, S.

Melody •Asx/Pno •HE

POULENC, Francis (1899-1963)

Capriccio (7') (LONDEIX) •12 Sx: SnoSSAAAATTBBBs •Sal
Sonata (from *Clarinet Sonata*) •Asx/Pno

Suite Française (J. Forsell) (13') •SATB

POUSSEUR, Henri (1929)

Compositeur, professeur et théoricien belge, né à Malmédy, le 23 VI 1929. Travailla avec A. Souris et P. Froibise.

"Le plus célèbre compositeur et le plus audacieux de la jeune école dans son pays, l'un des chefs de file les plus incontestés de l'avant-garde mondiale actuelle, aux côtés de Boulez, Stockhausen et Berio. Parti de l'exemple de Webern, il s'est imposé rapidement après avoir fait ses études aux Conservatoires de Liège et Bruxelles. Il avait également fait des stages dans les principaux studios électro-acoustiques européens… Parfois quelque peu problématiques, certaines de ses réalisations donnent une personnalité de chercheur à la fois lucide et sensible, d'une inlassable curiosité et d'une intelligence suraiguë." (Cl. Rostand) "Héritier spirituel de Webern, Henri Pousseur cherche par les techniques et les principes de l'aléatoire et par la combinaison de l'électronique avec les instruments traditionnels, à opérer un renouvellement du phénomène sonore." (M. Honegger) "Par une conception non dogmatique du sérialisme, Pousseur cherche à incorporer dans son oeuvre aussi bien les nouvelles dimensions de l'électronique que les principes des systèmes du passé dans ce qu'ils comportent de plus dynamique, sans en rester à l'effet du collage." (J. & B. Massin) "Ses extensions personnelles du sérialisme lui ont enfin permis d'intégrer une grande variété de styles harmoniques à sa musique." (P. Griffiths) "The development of Pousseur's work towards 'a richer, more complex musical expression, better adapted to today's relativist and pluralist reality' has been explained and discussed in several of his essays." (H. Vanhulst)

Vue sur les jardins interdits (1973) (to the memory of Bruno Maderna) •SATB •SZ

POWNING, Graham

Compositeur anglais.

Sonata (1984) (to C. Smith) •Asx/Pno
Three Pieces (1981) (to the Australian Saxophone Quartet) •SATB

PRADO, Almeida

Compositeur américain.

New York, east shert •Asx/Pno •SeMC

PRAETORIUS, Michael (1571-1621)

Bransle gentil (Harvey) •SATB •Che
Courante & Springdance (Harvey) •SATB •Che

PRÄSENT, Gerhard (1957)

Compositeur autrichien.

Solo für Saxophon (1978) (4') (to O. Vrhovnik) •Asx Solo

PRATI, Hubert (1939)

Saxophoniste et professeur français, né à Villerupt (M. & M.), le 25 VI 1939. Travailla avec M. Mule et D. Deffayet.

L'Alphabet du saxophoniste - Méthode pour débutants (1979) •Bil
Approche de la musique contemporaine (1985-86) (2 Volumes) 1) 15 Mosaïques 2) 13 Saxophonèmes •Bil
15 Bagatelles (1993) •Sx •Bil
Echelles modales (1987) •13 Sx •Bil
17 Etudes faciles et progressives (1980) •Bil
29 Etudes progressives trés faciles et faciles (1981) •Bil
Les Gammes conjointes, en 3ces, en arpèges •Bil
9 Negro Spirituals (1994) •4 Sx: AAAA or TTTT •Bil
Pièces en quatuor (1994) •4 Sx: AAAA •Bil

PRENDIVILLE, H.

Les bleus •Bb Sx/Pno •CF

PRESCOTT

Prescott Technique System

Universal Prescott Method

PRESCOTT, John

Transmigrations •Sx/Marimba

PRESLE, Jacques de la (see La Presle, J. de)

PRESSER, William (1916)

Compositeur américain, né le 19 IV 1916, à Saginaw (Michigan). Travailla avec R. Harris, B. Phillips, et B. Rogers.

Arioso (1980) •Ssx/Pno •Ten
Concerto (1965) (20') (to C. Leeson) •Tsx/Chamber Orch or Pno •adr
Partita (5'30) •Sx Solo •adr
Prelude (1966) (3') •Bsx/Pno •Pres/Ten
Prelude and Rondo (1962) (3'15) •Asx/Pno •Pres
Quartet (1969) (to C. Leeson) •AATB •adr
Rhapsody (3') •Tsx/Pno •Ten/Pres
Seven Duets •2 Sx: AA or TT •Pres
Sonatina (1979) (8') (to K. Deans) •Asx/Pno •Ten
Trio •3 Sx: AAT •Pres
Waltz and Scherzo (1962) (3'15) •AATB •South

PRESSL, Herman Markus (1939)

Compositeur autrichien.

N.N. 4/1 (1991) (4'30) (to D. Pätzol & Amtmann) •Asx/Org •INM
Sprang N.N. 6 (1992) •4 Sx: SATB/Org

PREVOST, André (1934)

Compositeur canadien.

'Il fait nuit lente' (Londeix) (16') •Chorus/10 Sx: SnoSSAATTBBBs

PRIBADI, Sinar

Djiwa •Asx Solo

PRICE, Deon Nielsen

Compositeur américain. Travailla avec L. Bassett et S. Adler.

"My style is rooted in Twentieth-Century harmony, timbre, and rhythm, with Nineteenth-Century-type melody." (D. N. Price)

Allegro barbaro (1980) •Vln/Ssx/Vla/Vcl
Augury (1980) (to K. & L. Gregory) •Vln/Asx/Pno •CCP
Mesurée (1979) (to D. Masek) •Ssx/Guit •DP
Vectoral Rhapsody (1981) (to D. Masek) •Asx/Pno

PRIESNER, Vroni (1946)

Professeur allemand.

Conversation (1974) (6') •Bsx/Perc
Divertimento (1986) (6') •3 Sx: AAA or TTT •VW
Gomringer (1988) •3 Sx: SAB/Darstelles (actors) •VW
Intrada-abläufe (1990) (15') •12 Sx: SnoSSAAATTTBBBs
Karussell (1992) (10') •SATB
Weg (1990) (7') •2 Sx: AA or TT •VW
"Wie du auch singst…" (1991) (6') •Asx-Speaker Solo
Zungenspiele (1989) (6') •3 Sx: AAA or TTT •VW

PRIEST, Barnaby (1954)

Compositeur anglais.

Quartet (1979) (10') (To Myrha Saxophone Quartet) •SATB

PRIETO, Claudio

Compositeur espagnol.

Divertimento (1984) (to M. Mijan) •Sx Solo •Ara

PRIN, Yves

Chef d'orchestre et compositeur français.

Quatuor d'anches - Suite en 3 parties (to P. Pareille) •Ob/Cl/Asx/Bsn

PRIOR, Claude (1918)
Compositeur français.
Konzertstück (1981) (to J-P. Fouchécourt) •Asx/Band

PRISS
Compositeur russe.
Concert •Asx/Orch or Pno

PROCACCINI, Teresa
Compositeurt italien.
Meeting (1988) (10') (to Quartet Sassof. Aquilano) •SATB

PROCOPIO, Joseph
Compositeur américain.
Three Variations (to J. Stoltie) •Sx Solo

PRODIGO, Sergio (1949)
Compositeur italien, né à Celano (Abruzzo). Travailla avec V. Bucchi et R. Vlad.
Concerto n° 9, op. 114 *"Omaggio a Gershwin"* (1992) •4 Sx/Orch
Quartetto V, op. 71b (1987-88) (13') (to Quartet Sassof. Aquilano) •SATB •adr
Sonata XXXIV, op. 106 (1991) (10') (to E. Filippetti & N. Carusi) •Asx/Pno •adr

PROHASKA, Miljenko (1925)
Compositeur yougoslave, né à Zagreb, le 17 IX 1925.
Dilemma (1964) •Asx/Jazz Orch •adr

PROKOFIEV, Sergei (1891-1953)
Five Melodies Without Words, op. 35 (15') (Radnofsky) •Asx/Pno •South
Kije's Wedding (Maganini) •1 Sx: T or A/Pno •EMa
Marche, op. 12, no. 1 (Dawson) •SATB •Ron
Romance and Troïka (Hummel) •Tsx/Pno •Rub
Romance and Troïka (Johnson) •AATB •Rub
Visions Fugitives (H. Harrisson) •Asx/Pno •B&H

PRONKO, Piotr
Saxophoniste et compositeur polonais.
Song of Love •2 Sx: AB/Pno

PRORVITCH, B.
Saxophoniste russe.
Base de technique du saxophone (1977)

PROVOST, Serge
Compositeur canadien, né au Québec.
Tétractys •Asx/Fl/Pno/Harp

PRUITT, Jay
Movement •Asx/Pno •NTS

PUCCINI, Giacomo (1859-1924)
Crisantemi (Stam) •SATB •Mol
Three Minuets (Stam) •SATB •Mol
Tosca Fantasy (Hermann) •Asx/Pno •PM

PUNES, Karel
Two Compositions •Asx/Pno •CMIC

PURCELL, Henry (1658-1695)
Dance Suite •Bb Sx/Pno •Mus
An English Suite •SATB •Ken
Fantasia No. 3 (Rosenthal) •3 Sx: ATB •Wim
Nymphs and Shepherds (Buchtel) •Bb Sx or Asx/Pno •Kjos
Rondeau (Fairie Queen) (Rascher) •Bsx/Pno •Bel
Sarabande (Kaplan) •Bb Sx/Pno •JS

Sonata in G Minor (Forst) •1 Sx: A or T/Pno •Mus
Suite en Fa (Maganini) •1 Sx: A or T/Pno •Mus
Two Bourrées (Rascher) •Asx/Pno •Bou

PUTET, Jean
Astrée •Asx/Orch or Pno •Doy

PUTSCHE, Thomas (1929)
Compositeur américain, né à Scarsdale (New York), le 29 VI 1929. Travailla avec Van Eps, Franchetti, Copland, et Babbitt.
Theme Song and Variations (1972) (14') •6 Sx: SAATTB •SeMC

PÜTZ, Eduard (1911)
Compositeur allemand, né le 13 II 1911, à Illerich-Cochem.
Blues •Asx/Str Quartet •adr
Cries in the dark (1993) •Asx/Str Quartet •Tong
Impressionen •SATB •adr
Kon-Takte - Jazz Cantata •Vocal Quartet (SATB)/Fl/Sx/Vibr/Guit/ Perc/Pno/Bass •SeMC

PÜTZ, Marco
Compositeur luxembourgeois.
Introduction, cadence et allegro •SATB
Septentrion •7 Sx: SnoSAATBBs

PYLE, Francis Johnson (1901)
Compositeur et chef d'orchestre américain, né à Bend (Indiana), le 13 IX 1901.
Edged Night and Fireworks •Asx/Pno •Br&Ha

QUANTZ, Johann Joachim (1697-1773)
Trio Sonata •2 Sx: SA/Pno

QUATE, Amy
Compositeur américain.
Ace of Swords (1992) •Sx/Perc
Light of Sothis (1982) (11') (to D. RICHTMEYER) 1) Grace 2) Passion
   3) Faith •Asx/Org or Pno •Led
Talking Pictures (1984) (15') 1) Water dance 2) Monet 3) Whirlgig
   4) Blues 5) Allegory •Ssx/Cl

QUELLE, Ernst-August (1931)
Pianiste et compositeur allemand, né à Herford, le 7 XII 1931.
"Kommissar Maigret-valse" (1964) (2'30) •Accordion/Sx/Perc/Str
   Orch •adr
Ragtime-company (1987) •SATB •GB

QUERAT, Marcel (1922)
Compositeur français, né à Paulnay (Indre), le 8 I 1922. Travailla
   avace H. Challan, W. Weber, et E. Bigot.
Andantino (1970) (2') •Asx/Pno •Phi
Lied et Canonica (1964) (3') •Fl (or Ob)/Asx •Phi
Magie (1979) (3') •Fl (or Ob)/Cl/Tsx •Bil
Petite suite (1982) (9'30) 1) Moderato 2) Allegretto 3) Andantino
   4) Deciso 5) Animato •Tsx/Pno •Bil
Quatuor d'anches (to P. PAREILLE) •Ob/Cl/Asx/Bsn •adr
Saxophonie 74 (1974) (to J-L. BOUSQUET) •Asx/Pno •adr

QUEYROUX, Yves (1946)
Compositeuir français.
Ellipse (1994) •Sx Solo •Mis
7 Jeux musicaux et 3 Promenades (1989) (to J-P. BARAGLIOLI) •Sx
   Solo: S or T or A •Lem
Sonate (to J-P. BARAGLIOLI) •Ssx/Perc

QUILLING, Howard (1935)
Compositeur américain, né à Enid (Oklahoma), le 16 XII 1935.
Travailla avec I. Dahl, R. Linn, et E. Kanitz.
Suite (1970) (to H. PITTEL & J. ROTTER) 1) Prelude 2) Pastorale
   3) Scherzo 4) Song 5) Finale •Asx/Wind Orch or Pno •Art

QUINET, Marcel (1915)
Compositeur et pianiste belge, né à Binche (Hainaut), le 6 VII 1915.
Travailla avec L. Jongen et J. Absil. Prix de Rome (1945).
   "Il s'exprime dans des cadres néo-classiques et un langage de
tendance atonale en des oeuvres objectives et très construites." (Cl.
ROSTAND) "Un constructeur et un atonaliste complexe et subtil." (H.
HALBREICH) "Polymélodique, sa musique s'exprime en un langage
atonal dépouillé, généralement respectueux des formes classiques."
   "Quinet's music is distinguished by formal clarity and the absence of
lyrical effusion; his objective art has affinities with that of Hindemith.
At first influenced by Absil, he began to evolve a more individual style
that shows his closeness to French music (particularly Ravel) and his
admiration for Bartok's orchestration. Evolving from polytonality to
atonality, his music has remained clear in timbre and texture." (H.
VANHULST)
Concerto grosso (to Quatuor Belge de Saxophones) •4 Sx: SATB/
   Orch •Bil

Pochades (1967) (6'30) (to Quatuor Belge de Saxophones)
   1) Marche 2) Havanaise 3) Rengaine 4) Galop •SATB •Bil

QUINT, Johannes
Compositeur allemand.
Mögliche Welten (1993) •1 Sx: S+B/Perc •INM

QUNTER, R.
Recitatif •Asx/Pno •Br & Ha

RAAFF, Anton (1714-1797)
Papillons •Asx/Pno •VAB

RABAUD, Henri (1873-1949)
Solo de concours (GEE) •Asx/Band or Pno •South

RABE, Folke (1935)
Compositeur et tromboniste suédois, né le 28 X 1935 à Stockholm. Travailla avec Blomdahl, Wallner, et G. Ligeti. Activités comme musicien de jazz.

"One aim of his music, as well as his teaching material *Ljudverkstad* ('Sound workshop') has been to sharpen awareness of the most subtle variations of sound." (R. HAGLUND)
Pajazzo for 8 jazz musicians (1964) •Tpt/Asx/Pno/2 BsCl/3 Perc •STIM

RABINOWITZ, Robert
Echoes for Forever (1983) (to J. WYTKO) •Asx/4 channel tape

RABINSKI, Jacek
Rosa dei venti (1993) •Asx/Harp •INM

RACHMANINOFF, Sergei (1873-1943)
Vocalise (MAGANINI) •1 Sx: A or T/Pno •Mus
Vocalise (5') (PFENNINGER) •SATB •Ron
Vocalise (TEAL) •Asx/Pno •GSch

RACKLEY-SMITH, Lawrence
Kay-Vee-Si-Si •2 Sx: AT/Pno/Bass/Perc/Tape

RACOT, Gilles (1951)
Compositeur français, né à Paris. Travailla avec P. Schaeffer et G. Reibel. Travailla au GRM et à l'IRCAM.
Anamorphées (1985) (to D. KIENTZY) •Ssx (acousmatique)
Exultitudes (1985) (20') •2 Sx/live electronics
Ité •Tsx/Tape
Jubilad'a (1985) (23'30) (to D. KIENTZY) •1 Sx: Bs+Sno/Vcl/Fl/6 Voices

RADDATZ, Otto (1917)
Compositeur allemand, né le 31 XII 1917 à Stettin.
Sehnsucht nach dem Frieden (1982) (3') •2 Hn/Asx •adr
Welcher Weg führt zum Frieden? (1982) (3') •2 Hn/Asx •adr

RADOVANOVIC, Vladan
Duet (1983) (to BOK & LE MAIR) •Sx+Cl/Marimba+Vibr

RADULESCU, Horatiu (1942)
Compositeur franco-roumain, né à Bucarest.

"Dans la lignée d'un Varèse, l'un des magnifiques novateurs de la musique du XX° siècle. Dès 1969 il développe la technique spectrale de composition, un système complet et clos, fondé, entre autres, sur ce que Radulescu appelle 'l'émanation de l'émanation,' c'est-à-dire la 'micro-spatialité' que le son développe grâce à l'activité de son propre timbre. Dans un univers neuf, il dépasse les quatre concepts historiques d'écriture (monodie, polyphonie, homophonie, hétérophonie) et remet à jour la millénaire interface art/science, ce qui lui permet d'entrer dans le son pour y 'retrouver l'océan de vibrations que Pythagore avait scruté il y a deux mille ans.' Alors que presque toutes les cultures musicales connues divisent le son en parties égales (½ ton, ¼ de ton, 1/

57 d'octave, etc.), la '*scordatura* spectrale' inventée par Radulescu utilise des intervalles à distances inégales et de plus en plus tassés vers l'aigu." (J-N. von der WEID)
Astray (1984-85) (23') (to D. KIENTZY) •1 Sx: Sno+S+A+T+B+Bs/ Prepared Pno or matériel électron.
Capricorn's nostalgic crickets (1974-83) (22') (to D. KIENTZY) •Asx/ matériel électron.
Sensual sky (1985) (to D. KIENTZY) •Asx/Trb/Vcl/Bass/Tape
Sky (1984-85) (to D. KIENTZY) •Sx/Cl/Fl/2 Bsn/2 Bass/Perc
X (1984-85) (to D. KIENTZY) •Sx/Cl/2 Bsn/2 Bass/Perc

RAE, James
Blue Saxophone •1 Sx: A or T/Pno
Easy Studies in Jazz and Rock •Sx Solo •Uni
Jazzy Saxophone I •Uni
Jazzy Saxophone Duets II •1 Sx: A or T/Pno •Uni
20 Modern Studies (1989) •Uni

RAFF, Joachim (1822-1882)
Cavatina •Eb Sx/Pno •CF
Cavatina (MOLENAAR) •Bb Sx/Pno •Mol
Cavatine (VIARD) •1 Sx: A or T/Pno •Sal
Quatuor (MULE) •SATB

RAGONE, Vincent
15 Melodious Duets •2 Sx •CF

RAHEB, Jeffrey
Compositeur australien
Quartet No. 1 (1980) (to the Australian Saxophone Quartet) •SATB

RAHN, John (1944)
Compositeur américain, né le 26 II 1944, à New York. Travailla avec M. Babbitt.
Games (1969) (8') (to M. TAYLOR) •Asx/Str Quartet •adr

RAITSCHEV, Alexander (1922)
Compositeur bulgare.
Sonate poeme (3 movements) •Asx/Pno

RALPH, Alan
Dance Band Reading and Interpretation •SF

RALSTON, Alfred
Compositeur anglais.
An Allegro (1973) (12') (to London Saxophone Quartet) •SATB

RAMAN, Gedert Gedertovic (1927)
Compositeur russe, né le 8 IX 1927, à Elgava.
Concerto (1964) •Asx/Str Orch/Pno/Perc •Mu

RAMEAU, Jean-Philippe (1683-1764)
Castor et Pollux - Menuet (MULE) •Asx/Pno •Led
Castor et Pollux - Passepied (MULE) •Asx/Pno •Led
Dardanus - Rigaudon (MAGANINI) •1 Sx: A or T/Pno •Mus
Dardanus - Rigaudon (MULE) •Asx/Pno •Led
Fête de l'Hymen (MULE) •1 Sx: A or T/Pno •Led
Hippolyte et Aricie (MULE) •Asx/Pno •Led
L'Indiscrète - Rondeau (MULE) •Asx/Pno •Led
Le temple de la gloire (MULE) •Asx/Pno •Led
Minuet (RASCHER) •Bb Sx/Pno •Bel
Ordre pour les festes des Grands ducs d'Occident (LONDEIX) •Fl/Ob/ Cl/Asx/Hn/Bsn
Rigaudon (BREHME-RASCHER) •Asx/Pno •Chap
Suite d'après Rameau (AMELLER) •Asx/Pno •ET
Tambourin (CRESSONNOIS) •SATB •Sax
Tambourin (MULE) •Asx or Bb Sx/Pno •Led

RAMSAY, Neal

Saxophoniste américain, né à Nashville (Tennessee). Travailla avec V. Abato.

Seven Solos (FAURÉ, BEETHOVEN, HANDEL, BACH, CHOPIN, etc.) •Asx/Pno •Sha

RAMSELL, Kenneth (1904)

Compositeur anglais.

Moorland Streams and Resthers River (1971) (4') (to London Saxophone Quartet) •SATB

Nocturne (1972) (5') •SATB

RAMSOE, Wilhelm (1837-1895)

Quartet No. 5 (VOXMAN) •AATB •Rub

RAN, Shulamit (1949)

Compositeur et pianiste israélite, né le 21 X 1949 à Tel-Aviv. Travailla avec Boskovich, Ben-Haim, et Dello Joio.

"In her music she has developed from the influence of Ben-Haim to make use of more novel techniques, including electronic music, which she studied with Badings in 1969." (W. Y. ELIAS)

Encounter (1979) (to F. HEMKE) •Asx/Perc

RANGER, A. R.

Country Gardens •Bb Sx or Eb Sx/Pno •CF

The Old Refrain - Viennese Popular Song •Bb Sx or Eb Sx/Pno •CF

A Wreath of Holly - 6 Christmas Songs •Eb Sx or Bb Sx/Pno •CF

RANIER, Tom

Rondo (1970) •SATB

RAOUKHVERGUER

3 Pieces (10') 1) Berceuse 2) Intermezzo 3) Impromptu •Asx/Pno

RAPEE, Erno (1891-1945)

Todlin' Sax (AXT) •Asx/Pno •Wie

RAPHAEL, Günter (1903-1960)

Compositeur allemand, né à Berlin, le 30 IV 1903, mort à Herford, le 19 X 1960. Travailla avec R. Kahn, M. Trapp, et K. Straube.

"As composer Raphael started from the post-romanticism of Brahms and Reger, but later the influence of Bach's music began to dominate his writing. He shows a predilection for counterpoint and aims at a simple, monumental style and at giving the instrumental body great transparency. His music is rooted in tradition, and he shows much skill in the use of rhythmic and harmonic effects, though the latter never overstep the boundaries of tonality." (K. BARLETT) "Raphael's last 15 years may be considered a third period, in which the new style crystallized and expanded to include some use of 12-note technique. The series is usually found as an ostinato." (W. D. GUDGER)

Concertino, op. 71 (1951) (16') (to J. de VRIES) •Asx/Orch (1101/111/Perc/Str) or Pno •Br&Ha

Divertimento, op. 74 (1952) (13'30) (to J. de VRIES) 1) Improvisation 2) Sérénade 3) Elegie 4) Scehrzo burlesque 5) Rondo Asx/Vcl •Br&Ha

Récitatif (1958) (4') (to J. de VRIES) •Asx/Pno •Led

Sonate - In memoriam E. Manz, op. 74a (1957) (9') 1) Con moto 2) Vivace 3) Allegro molto energico •Asx/Pno •PJT

RAPHLING, Sam (1910)

Compositeur et pianiste américain, né à Fort Worth (Texas), le 19 III 1910.

Concert Suite •4 Sx: AAAA •Mus

Duograms •2 Sx •Mus

Sonate No. 1 (1945) (to C. LEESON) 1) Moderately 2) Vivace 3) Lentamente 4) Vivace •Asx/Pno •South

Sonata No. 2 (1969) (to C. LEESON) •Asx/Pno •GMP

Square Dance •Tsx/Pno •Mus

Suite in Modern Style •3 Sx •Mus

RAPOPORT, Ricardo (1958)

Compositeur et bassoniste brésilien, né le 25 IX 1958 à Rio de Janeiro. Travailla avec G. Peixe, M. Ficarelli, Ch. Bochmann, et S. Ortega. Vit en France depuis 1984.

Pour quatuor de saxophones (1988) (8') •SATB

RARIG, John

Dance Episode •Asx/Orch or Pno

Night Song •Asx/Str Orch •DP

RASBACH, Oscar (1888-19xx)

Compositeur et pianiste américain, né à Dayton (Ohio), le 2 VIII 1888.

Trees •Asx/Pno •GSch

RASCHER, Sigurd (1907)

Saxophoniste virtuose américain, d'origine allemande, né à Elberfeld, le 15 V 1907. Commença une carrière de clarinettiste avant de se consacrer au saxophone. Travailla avec Ph. Dreisbach et H. Scherchen. Vit aux U.S.A. depuis 1939.

Est l'auteur de nombreuses transcriptions, et dédicataire d'oeuvres concertantes parmi les plus importantes de la première moitié du XXe siècle.

"Rascher is distinguished for his brilliant agility, sweetness of tone and musical sensibility." (G. GELLES)

Complete Chromatic Scale Chart •CF

24 Intermezzi (1954) •Asx/Pno •Bou

The Rascher Collection •WWS

Scales (1965) •Gi&Ma

158 Studies (1955-68) •Chap/WH

Top Tones (1941-61) •CF

RASQUIER, Hélène

Obsession (1993) (9'40) •Asx/Str Orch or Pno •Zu

RATHBURN, Eldon (1916)

Compositeur canadien, né le 21 IV 1916, à Queenstown (New Brunswick). Travailla avec H. Willan.

Two Interplays (1972) (7'30) 1) Andante 2) Allegro •SATB •CMC

RAUBER, Fr.

Pièce détachée •SATB

RAUCHVERGER, Milchail

Compositeur russe.

4 Pièces •Asx/Pno

RAULE, Renato

Compositeur italien.

Volo Vienna, Parigi, N-Y. •2 Sx: AT •Piz

RAVEL, Maurice (1875-1937)

Bolero •3 Sx: SAT •Dur

Five o'clock •1 Sx: A or T/Pno •Mus

Pavane (MAGANINI) •1 Sx: A or T/Pno •Mus

Pavane (SCHMIDT) •5 Sx: SAATB •DP

Pavane (VIARD) •Asx/Pno •Dur

Pavane (WALTERS) •Asx/Pno or 3 Sx: AAT/Pno •Rub

Pièce en forme de habanera (HOEREE) •Asx/Orch (2022/210/Perc/Harp/Str) •Led

Pièce en forme de habanera (MULE) •Asx/Pno •Led

Pièce en forme de habanera (VIARD) •Asx or Bb Sx/Pno •Led

Sonatine (TEAL) •Asx/Pno •GSch

RAWSON, Hector (1904)

Enseignement moderne du jazz, etc. •Lem
Méthode complète de tous les saxophones (1938) •Labbé

RAXACH, Enrique (1932)

Compositeur néerlandais d'origine espagnole, né le 15 I 1932 à Barcelone. Travailla à Paris, Zurich, Munich, Cologne, et Darmstadt, avant de s'installer définitivement aux Pays-Bas, en 1969.
Antevisperas (1986) (12'30) (to Rascher Quartet) •SATB •Don

RAYMOND, Fred (1900-1954)

Compositeur autrichien, né à Vienne, le 20 IV 1900, mort à Uberlingen, le 10 I 1954.
"Self-taught in composition, he worked as a bank official and began composing songs; in 1924 he became a professional cabaret entertainer, accompanying himself at the piano in his songs. He continued to compose for revues and for a series of operettas, having meanwhile settled in Berlin." (A. LAMB)
Design •Asx/Pno •WIM

RAYNAL, Gilles

Ombilic (1983) •Fl/Cl/Asx/Vln/Vcl/Pno
L'ordre et la lumière (6') •4 Sx: SATB/Choeur

REA, John (1942)

Compositeur et chef d'orchestre canadien, né le 3 VII 1942, à Toronto. Travailla avec S. Dolin.
"Sans nécessairement susciter une mise en parallèle des domaines plastiques et musicaux ni se traduire sous forme de notations graphiques, des concepts visuels peuvent être à l'origine de schémas compositionnels. *Treppenmusik* de John Rea s'inspire des dessins en boucle et des effets d'illusion du peintre hollandais M-C. Escher." (D. J-Y BOSSEUR)
La capra che suono (1986) •12 Sx: SnoSSAAATTTBBBs •CMC
Fantasies and Allusions (1969) (to P. SMITH) Prelude - Fantaisie ostinato - Fantaisie alea - Etude - Fantaisie canon - Fantaisie ranz des vaches: pastorale - Postlude •4 Sx: SATB/Perc ad lib. •CMC
Treppenmusik (1982) •4 Sx: SATB/4 Cl/Vln/Vla/Vcl/Bass •CMC

REA, Melvin

Compositeur allemand.
Goodbye Mr. Penguin (1993) •Asx/Bass •INM

READE, Paul Geoffrey (1943)

Compositeur anglais, né le 10 I 1943, à Liverpool.
Bienvenue prelude (1978) (2'35) •Mezzo Soprano Voice/Asx/Pno •adr
Cartoons (1980) (3') •Mezzo Soprano Voice/Asx/Pno •adr
Quartet (1979) (8'30) (to London Saxophone Quartet) 1) Toccata 2) Elegy 3) Contredanse 4) Finale •SATB •adr
Quintet (1976) (to S. TRIER) •Fl/Ob/Asx/Hn/Bsn •adr

REASER, Ronald (1954)

Liberare sonare (1978) (20') •Asx/Perc •WWS

REBEL, Meeuwis

Compositeur néerlandais.
Sextet à 5 (1984) (15') •4 Sx: SATB/Perc •Don

REBER, Napoléon-Henri (1807-1880)

Berceuse célèbre (FORET) •SATB •Bil

REBOTIER, J.

Compositeur français.
Le Bestiaire marin - Opéra pour choeur d'enfants amateur •Childrens Choir/4 Fl/4 Sx: SATB •Dur

RECK, David (1935)

Blues and Screamer (1965-66) •Fl+Picc/Harmonica/Asx/Bass/Perc •CPE
Number 1 for 12 Performers (15') •Fl/Cl/Tsx/Hn/Guit/Vibr/Pno/Bass/Perc •MJQ

REDDIE, Bill

Compositeur américain.
Concerto (16') •Asx/Orch
Gypsy Fantasy (3') •Asx/Orch or Pno

REDGATE, R.

Inventio •Asx/Ensemble •Lem

REDOLFI, Michel (1951)

Compositeur français, né à Marseille.
"Recherches sur la perception acoustique et de nombreuses expériences d'animations musicales, d'oeuvres 'participationnistes' provoquant le public. Notamment concerts 'subaquatiques,' à écouter immergé dans l'eau."
Swinging on a vine (1974) •Trb/Sx/Synth

REDOUTE, J.

Melody •Asx/Pno •HE

REED, Alfred (1921)

Compositeur et arrangeur américain, né le 25 I 1921, à New York. Travailla avec P. Yartin et V. Giannini.
Ballade (1956) (5'30) (for V. ABATO) •Asx/Band or Pno •South
Siciliana notturno (from *Suite Concertante*) (5') •Asx/Pno •Pied

REGI, A.

Ancient Melody (VOXMAN) •Bb Sx/Pno •Rub

REGT, Hendrik de (1950)

Compositeur néerlandais, né le 5 VII 1950. Travailla avec O. Ketting.
Musica, op. 8 (1971) (7-8') (to Netherland Saxophone Quartet) •SATB •Don
Musica, op. 9 (1971) (9-10') (to E. BOGAARD) •Asx/Pno •Don

REHL, Richard H.

Compositeur américain.
The Duchess - Valse Caprice (1928) •1 Sx: A or T/Pno •Rub
Nimble Fingers •Asx/Pno •Rub

REIBEL, Guy (1936)

Compositeur français né à Strasbourg.
"La seule solution pour adhérer à la réalité du matériau sonore consiste à faire le pas difficile mais décisif, qui amène à oublier l'origine des sons, pour ne s'attacher qu'à l'étude de leur perception; l'abandon des causalités et des descriptions physiciennes plonge au premier abord dans un état d''apesanteur,' de nature à inquiéter le musicien. C'est pourtant la condition indispensable pour pouvoir aborder l'univers des sons dans sa généralité et pour jeter les bases d'un nouveau solfège à la dimension de l'entreprise." (G. REIBEL)
Apogée (8') (to D. KIENTZY) •Sx Solo
Images élastiques (to J-M. GOURY) •Tsx/Pno
Sonate à deux (1988) (to J-M. GOURY & Y. JOSSET) •Tsx/Pno

REICH, Scott

Compositeur américain.
Trio for Duo (1980) (to L. HUNTER) •Ssx/Pno

REICH, Steve (1936)

Compositeur américain, né le 3 X 1936 à New York. Travailla avec D. Milhaud et L. Berio. Etudia la philosophie, particulièrement l'oeuvre de Wittgenstein.

"Toute une frange de compositeurs, non directement concernés par les discussions et palabres sur les problèmes d'écriture et de langage de leurs confrères européens, vont s'engager sur les voies précédemment ouvertes par Morton Feldman ou Earle Brown et, simplifiant à l'extrême les données de départ de la composition, créer un courant de musique dite 'répétitive,' qui ne désavoue pas la tonalité, se construit sur un principe rythmique, se déroule par variations imperceptibles, et où l'électronique prend souvent sa place, mêlée à l'instrumental. Les trois représentants les plus éminents de cette nouvelle école sont Terry Riley, Steve Reich et Philip Glass." (J. & B. MASSIN) "Pour Steve Reich adepte de la musique 'minimale,' le principe de répétition est un moyen privilégié de réaliser ce qu'il appelle la 'musique comme processus graduel.' Il lui importe 'que le processus de composition et la musique qu'on entend soient une seule et même chose.' Après les premières pièces réalisées à partir des principes de déphasage graduel et d'évolution progressive d'un matériau de base (1965-66), Steve Reich applique des techniques analogues au jeu instrumental. Il parvient à élaborer un système électro-acoustique quasiment autonome dont le développement ne dépend plus de la 'main-mise' des interprètes." (D. J-Y BOSSEUR) "Reich n'est pas né marginal. Il ne s'est enfermé ni dans une grotte ni dans une tour d'ivoire. Tout son travail le prouve, qui ne laisee aucune trace d'embarras ou d'ésotérisme." (C. LEBLÉ).

"As a composer he is interested in the possibilities of multiples of the same instrument, either live or contrived. He makes large pieces from minimal materials. He is particularly concerned with an extension or elaboration of canon, with identical lines proceeding as if recorded on tape loops at different speeds, starting together but gradually becoming separated, and the rhythms are finely and exactly imagined. Reich makes his music available for performance only by ensembles of which he is a member." (M. STEINBERG)

Reed Phase (1967) •Any reed instrument/2 channel tape or 3 reeds

REICHA, Anton (1770-1836)
Four Fugues (HARTLEY) •Sx Ensemble: SAATBBs •Eth

REICHARDT, Gustave (1797-1884)
The Image of the Rose •Eb Sx/Pno •CF

REICHEL, Bernard (1901)
Compositeur suisse, né le 3 VIII 1901 à Neuchâtel. Travailla avec H. Suter, J. Dalcroze et, à Paris, avec E. Levy.

"A écrit de nombreuses pages d'un caractère intime et attachant." (N. DUFOURCQ) "S'il a écouté la leçon du dodécaphonisme, il n'a pas été moins sensible à celle de Stravinski et, ces deux courants se neutralisant, sa personnalité qui est toute de naturel et de spontanéité, s'est trouvée préservée." (R. BERNARD)

"His music has been influenced by the rhythmic ideas of Jacques-Dalcroze, and it bears witness to a deep religious conviction. Sensible to the work of Honegger, Hindemith and Stravinsky, Reichel has retained an individual style, producing in his later years works of youthful spontaneity and expressive clarity." (P. MEYLAN)

Prélude •SATB

REIDLING, Jack
Compositeur américain.
Serenade in Sol (1988) (to L. W. POTTS) •Asx/Pno

REILLY, Allyn (1946)
Compositeur américain.
Spiral (1985) (7') (Fast - Slowly and freely - Very lively) •Asx Solo
Two Short Pieces (1973) 1) Quietly throughout 2) Very fast •Tsx/Pno •South

REINBERGER, Karl
Drei Miniaturen mit Introduktion und Coda (10') •SATB •CA

REINBOTHE, Helmut
Compositeur allemand.
Meditativer Monolog (1990) (6') •Sx Solo

REINER, Karel (1910-1979)
Compositeur et pianiste tchèque, né à Zatec, le 27 VI 1910, mort à Prague, le 17 X 1979. Travailla avec Haba.

"In his works he applies a modified 12-tone technique." (BAKER) "As a composer he closely identified himself at first with Haba, but later he followed a more independent path. In the 1960s he achieved a successful combination of ideas taken from Haba with new post-war techniques." (J. BEK)

Akrostichon e Allegro (1972) •Tsx/Pno
Dvé skladby (1967) •Asx/Pno •IMD/CHF
Hovory - Talks (1979) (11') •Fl/Bsx •CHF

REINER, Thomas (1959)
Compositeur australien, né le 12 VIII 1959 à Bad Homburg (Allemagne). Travailla avec W. Hufschmidt et H. W. Henze.
Moth and Spider (1988) (21') •Sx/Perc •AuMC
Movements in Time (1993) •Asx/Perc •INM/adr

RELMES, Léo
Lied •Asx/Pno •Bil

RENARD, Charles
Valse dramatique (1938) (from *The Decadence of Terpsichore*) •Asx/Pno •Carco

RENDINE, Sergio (1954)
Compositeur et professeur italien.
Januar - Polimetria IIIa (1985) (9') (to F. MONDELCI & M. MAZZONI) •2 Sx: S+A/B •EDP

RENDLEMAN, Richard
Compositeur américain.
Concertino (1992) (to J. HOULIK) •Tsx/Orch

RENERTS, Roland
5 Danses (pour un film de J. Delire sur A. Sax) (to Fr. DANEELS) •7 Sx: SnoSATBBsCBs

RENOSTO, Paolo (1935)
Compositeur italien, né le 10 X 1935 à Florence. Travailla avec Fragapane, Dallapiccola, et Lupi, puis avec Maderna.

"His music draws rather eclectically on the avant-garde developments of the 1950s and later, without being particularly radical; indeed, the influence of his friend Maderna may be discerned in his recourse to stylistic and formal methods not entirely foreign to tradition." (P. PETAZZI)

Dissolution •Vla/Vcl/Bass/Ob/Cl/BsCl/Sx/Hn/Perc

RESCHTNEFKI, Markus
Compositeur allemand.
Psychosomatik (1993) •Ssx/Harps •INM

REUCHSEL, Maurice (1880-1969)
Violoniste, organiste, et compositeur français, né à Lyon, le 22 XI 1880.
Syphax, op. 72 (1955) (to E. GAY) •Asx/Orch or Pno •Bil

REUTTER, Hermann (1900)
Compositeur et pianiste allemand, né le 17 VI 1900 à Stuttgart. Travailla avec W. Courvoisier.

"Cherche à concilier un lyrisme discret avec une atmosphère romantique." (P. WOLF) "Formé dans la tradition néo-romantique de Pfitzner, il a ensuite subi les influences de Hindemith et d'Honegger, mas sans un goût démesuré pour ce que ceux-ci lui offraient en fait de modernité, ce qui lui a permis de s'accommoder parfaitement du néo-classicisme recommandé pendant la période nazie." (Cl. Rostand)

"In this music Reutter follows the line of neo-classicism, and in his technical procedures comes close to Hindemith. The basic thematic material of many of his compositions is inspired by German folk music." (Baker) "It is in these works that his lyrical gifts are developed to the full, and even though many traces of romanticism and impressionism are to be found in his songs, his style here shows more personality and individuality than in most of his other works. Instrumental composition has not been neglected by Reutter, and it is not surprising that the pianoforte plays a predominant part in these works, the composer being an accomplished pianist." (K. Bartlett) "Reutter is among the most productive German composers of his generation, and the most traditionalist. The clarity of his music comes from Orff, the harmonic manner from Pfitzner and the tonal structure from Hindemith. His music is distinctly formed, and adapts itself equally to lyrical and dramatic modes." (H. Krellmann)

Elégie (1957) (3'30) •Asx/Pno •Led

Pièce concertante (1968) (11'30) (to J-M. Londeix) 1) Exposition 2) Berceuse 3) Combination •Asx/Pno •Sch

REVERDY, Michèle (1943)

Compositeur français née à Alexandrie. Travailla avec O. Messiaen.

"De tous les élèves de Messiaen, celle dont le style porte le plus l'empreinte du maître." (C. Leblé) Pour Michèle Reverdy, le travail de composition réside essentiellement dans l'épreuve de la forme, d'une forme qui ne se bâtirait point par juxtaposition de matières, mais qui naîtrait d'un matériau de base unique et se déroulerait par transformations progressives, par métamorphoses 'alchimiques,' en un continuum ouvert. "Je construis en organisant des matières, en découvrant des 'régions' sonores, en essayant de travailler sans cesse la même glaise d'origine pour en obtenir des effets kaléidoscopiques."

Cytrises (2'40) (Collect. Panorama) •Asx/Pno •Bil

REVUELTAS, Silvestre (1899-1940)

Violoniste, compositeur et chef d'orchestre mexicain, né à Santiago-Papasquiaro, le 31 XII 1899, mort à Mexico, le 5 X 1940. Travailla à Chicago avec F. Borowski.

"Son activité comme compositeur, tardive, le classe immédiatement après Chavez; il s'inspire du folklore national et utilise parfois les instruments populaires." (D. Devoto) "Sa verve et sa bonne humeur lui assurent une place de choix dans la musique du Nouveau-Monde." (N. Dufourcq) "Participa avec C. Chavez à la renaissance de la musique mexicaine."

"He possessed an extraordinary natural talent and intimate understanding of Mexican music, so that despite a lack of academic training in composition, he succeeded in creating works of great originality, melodic charm, and rhythmic vitality." (Baker) "Most of his music remains in manuscript, and for this reason it is rarely performed outside Mexico; but his importance for the development of national Mexican music in the modern idiom can hardly be exaggerated." (N. Slonimsky)

First Little Serious Piece (2'45) •Picc/Ob/Cl/Tpt/Bsx •MM/PIC/Peer

Second Little Serious Piece (1'15) •Picc/Ob/Cl/Tpt/Bsx •PIC/Peer

REX, Harley (1930)

Professeur de saxophone et compositeur américain, né le 29 III 1930, à Lehighton (Pennsylvania).

Andantino and Brillante (1982) (to D. Underwood) •Asx/Band or Pno •DP/WWS

Four Pastels •AATB •DP

Four Shades •4 Sx: AATB/Pno •Bou

Intrada and Fugato •Asx/Pno •WWS

Preludio and Movende (1960) •1 Sx: A or S/Band or Pno •adr

Saxophone Rhapsody (1941) •1 Sx: A or S/Band or Pno •adr

Shenandoah •4 Sx: AATB or 8 Sx: AAAATTTB •Mills

Tanz and Proportz (16th-century lute dance) •AATB •DP

Three Spirituals •8 Sx: AAAATTTB •DP

12-tone variations •3 Sx Solo: SSA/13 Sx: SAAAATTTTBBBsBs •DP

A Walk in the City •9 Sx: SAAAATTBBs •DP

Washington Sonata (1973) (12') (to J. Cunningham) •Asx/Band or Pno •DP

REYMAN, Randall G.

The Jazz Sax Primer (1982)

REYMOND, Roger (1920)

Compositeur français, né à Caluire, le 11 XI 1920. Travailla avec J. Bouvard et C. Geoffray.

Andante religioso (1972) (3'30) •SATB •adr

Cinq Pièces (1970) (13'30) 1) Obstination 2) Etrange 3) Médiéval 4) Fantaisie 5) Promenade rythmique •SATB •adr

Elégie (1972) •Tsx/Pno •adr

Tryptique (1971) (11') (to S. Bichon) 1) Charme 2) Insolite 3) Présence •Asx/Str Orch •adr

REYNAUD, Joseph-Félix (1841-1887)

Grande fantaisie •Asx or Bb Sx/Pno •Sal

Variations sur 'Ah! Vous dirai-je Maman' •1 Sx: A or S/Pno •Sal

REYNOLDS, Verne (1926)

Five Duos (1981) (to D. Hastings) •Asx/Perc

RHOADE, Mary R.

Compositeur américain.

Join the 20th Century - Suite 1) A Sultry Night in Bogota (Too Many Margaritas) 2) I Ain't Lazy, I'm Just Dreamin' Waltz 3) Dirty Dishes Blues 4) Beat, Beat, Who's Got the Beat? •Asx/Pno

RIBARI, Antal (1924)

Compositeur hongrois, né le 8 I 1924, à Budapest. Travailla avec R. Kokai et F. Szabo.

Dialogues •Asx/Orch •B&H

RIBAS, Rosa Maria Monné (1944)

Compositeur espagnol né à Barcelona. Travailla avec X. Montsalvage et J. Soler.

Cuarteto (1990) (8'30) 1) Andante espressivo 2) Scherzando 3) Molto affettuoso e vibrato •SATB •adr

Quatuor de viento (1981) (10') 1) Moderato 2) Dolce 3) Energico •Ob/Cl/Asx/Bsn •adr

Sonata (1980) (8') (to A. Ventas) 1) Allegretto 2) Legato espressivo 3) Allegro ritmico •Asx/Pno •Boi

Vitrall (1986) (10') •SATB •adr

RIBAULT, André

Barcarolle (1989) (1'45) •Asx/Pno •Mar

RIBOUR, Ph.

Quatuor •SATB

RICARD, Claude Ernest Roland (1929)

Compositeur français, né à Grand-Quevilly, le 28 XII 1929.

Badinerie (1962) (1'30) •SATB •South

Concerto sérénade •4 Sx: SATB/Harp/Str Orch •South

RICCO-SIGNORINI, Antonio (1867-1965)

Compositeur italien, né à Massalombarda (Ravena), le 22 II 1867, mort à Bologna, le 11 III 1965.

Divertissement (1926) (15') •4 Sx: SATB/Chamber Orch •Car

RICHARD, Charles (1620-1652)
L'alliance -Air varié •Asx/Pno •Sal
Le tour de France - Air varié •Asx/Pno •Sal

RICHARDS, J.
Triad •3 Sx: AAT/Pno •Bar

RICHARDSON, Alan (1904-1978)
Compositeur et pianiste écossais, né le 29 II 1904, à Edinburgh, mort à Londres, le 29 XI 1978.
Three Pieces, op. 22c (1975) 1) Prelude 2) Elegy 3) Alla burlesca •Asx/Pno •JE

RICHARDSON, Louis (1924)
Adagio (1984) (to L. WYMAN) •Asx/Pno
Variations on Four Notes •Asx/Pno

RICHARDSON, Neil
Compositeur anglais.
Jazz Suite (1978) (21'30) (to London Saxophone Quartet) •SATB

RICHENS, James
Compositeur américain, né à Memphis. Travailla avec S. Adler, L. Menin, B. Rogers, et W. Barlow.
Another Autumn (1976) (to S. Cochrau) •Asx/Band •Co

RICHER, Janine (1924)
Compositeur français, né à Candebec-en-Eaux, le 6 VI 1924.
Quatuor (1958) (14') (to Quatuor Desloges) 1) Fantaisie 2) Sérénade 3) Adagio 4) Presto •SATB

RICHMOND, Thomas
Compositeur américain.
Two Movements (1964) 1) Slow 2) Fast •Vln/Vla/Asx/Vcl

RICKER, Ramon
Saxophoniste et professeur américain.
The New Virtuoso Saxophonist (4 volumes: 1) Etudes on the diminished scales 2) Advanced chord studies 3) Jazz etudes on the pentatonic scale 4) Jazz etudes on familiar chord progressions) •Led
Solar Chariot •Ssx/Pno •DP

RIDDERSTRÖM, Bo (1937)
Compositeur suédois.
Saxofonkvartett (1984) (10') •SATB •STIM

RIEDEL, Georg (1934)
Compositeur suédois.
Concerto burlesco (1981) (17') •Asx/Jazz group/Orch •STIM
Reflexioner (1974) (8') •Woodwind Quintet/Jazz group (Cl+Asx/Pno/Bass) •SMIC

RIEDLBAUCH, Vaclav (1947)
Compositeur tchécoslovaque
Doslov (1983) (8') •SATB •CHF

RIEDSTRA, Tom (1957)
Compositeur néerlandais.
Bonk-kwartet (1985-90) (6') •SATB •Don

RIEHM, Rolf (1937)
Compositeur allemand né à Saarbrücken, le 15 VI 1937. Travailla avec Fortner.
Wie sind deine Schritte in den Sandalen Schon fürstliche Tochter •Sx/Actress

RIEMER, Franz (1953)
Compositeur allemand, né à Bamberg, le 20 XII 1953.

Reigen (1985) (17') (to J. ERNST) 1) Mäßig 2) Adagio 3) Allegro giocoso 4) Cantabile 5) Sehr frei 6) Agitato 7) Cantabile 8) 56 •Asx/Pno •adr

RIETI, Vittorio (1898)
Compositeur américain d'origine italienne, né à Alexandrie (Egypte), le 28 I 1898. Travailla à Rome avec Respighi.
A formé avec Massarani et Labroca un groupe appelé "I Tre," en imitation au "Groupe des Six."
"After early experiments with atonality, he evolved an idiom akin to neo-classicism, which remained his characteristic trait. He said in 1973: 'I maintain the same aesthetic assumptions I have always had; I have kept evolving in the sense that one keeps on perfecting the same ground.' His music has a natural, unaffected fluency, elegant charm, controlled feeling, sophisticated humour and impeccable technical mastery; his textures are clear and limpid, his orchestration transparent and sensitive." (B. SCHWARZ)
Sequence •Asx/Pno •DP

RIEU, Yannick
Saxophoniste canadien, né en Gaspésie. Travailla en France puis au Québec.
Improvisation •Asx Solo

RIEUNIER, Jean-Paul (1933-1992)
Compositeur français, né à Bordeaux, le 27 I 1933, mort à Paris, le 27 III 1992.
22 Déchiffrages instrumentaux •Led
Linéal (1970) (8') (to D. DEFFAYET) 1) Souple 2) Vif •Asx/Pno •Led
Volume 2 (1974) (to J. LEDIEU) •Bsx/Wind Ensemble •Led

RILEY, James R. (1938)
Visiones (1976) 1) = ca. 88 2) Drone and Lament 3) = 88 •SATB •South

RILEY, Terry (1935)
Compositeur, saxophoniste et pianiste américain, né à Colfax (California), le 24 VI 1935. Travailla avec S. Shifrin, W. Denny, et R. Erikson.
"Trente ans après leurs débuts, le divorce semble définitivement consommé entre les différents fondateurs de l'école 'répétitive.' Philip Glass et Steve Reich d'un côté, Terry Riley et LaMonte Young de l'autre illustrent dorénavant deux tendances, sinon antagonistes, du moins bien éloignées. Autant les premiers ont quitté leur simple défroque de minimalistes au profit d'habits plus rutilants, autant les seconds sont restés attachés à un idéal de dépouillement sonore et d'économie. Côté Reich et Glass, on produit une musique plutôt urbaine, brillante et agitée; côté adverse, une musique plus nonchalante et contemplative. Les premiers sont liés à la côte Est, et désormais ont les faveurs des grands orchestres; Riley vit reclus dans son ranch de la Sierra Nevada et LaMonte Young ne sort de sa retraite que pour de rares apparitions dans des galeries d'art." (J-E. FOUSNAQUER)
"In his music, Riley explores the extremes of complexity and gymnosophistical simplicity." (BAKER) "His is music in which the quality of sound, rather than thematic development, is of primary interest. The apparently static nature of the material focuses attention on acoustical properties, on perceptual shifts and on microscopic changes in sound quality and execution. In using repetition to a much greater extent than is usual in European classical music, Riley's work draws on aspects of jazz and blues instrumental playing, and has parallels in oriental traditions." (M. PARSONS)
Peppy Naggod's Phantom Band (1970) •Asx/Tape
Persian Surgery Dervishes (1971) •Sx/Perc/Tape
A Rainbow in Curved Air (1970) •Partly improvised Sx/Keyboards/Perc/Tapes

RIMMER, H. A.
Autumn Evensong (Rooij) •Ssx/Pno •Mol

RIMMER, William (1862-1936)
Saxonia •Asx/Pno •HE

RIMSKY-KORSAKOV, Nicolas (1844-1908)
Aimant la rose et le rossignol (Viard) •Mezzo Soprano Voice/Asx/
   Pno
Chant indou (Bumcke) •AATB •Belai
Chanson indoue (Classens) •Asx/Pno •Phi
Chanson indoue (Letellier) •Asx/Pno •Mar
Danse des bouffons (Londeix) •Fl/Ob/Cl/Asx/Hn/Bsn
Flight of the Bumble Bee (Davis) •Asx/Pno •Rub
Flight of the Bumble Bee (Isailli) •1 Sx: A or T/Pno •CF
Flight of the Bumble Bee (Leeson) •Asx/Pno •HilCol
Hummelflug (*Vol du bourdon*) (Lindeman) •8 Sx: SAAB ATTB •GB
Hymn to the Sun (Colby) •Asx/Pno •Rub
Le vol du bourdon (Londeix) •Asx/Pno •Lem
Le vol du bourdon (Mule) •SATB
Scherzo du 1er Quatuor, op. 12 (Mule) •SATB
Snégourotchka - Chanson de Lel (Londeix) •Asx/Fl/Ob/Cl/Hn/Bsn
Song of India (Barnby) •AATB •Rub
Song of India (Buchtel) •Eb Sx or Bb Sx/Pno •CF/Rub
Sweet and Low (Barnby) •AATB •Rub
The Young Prince and the Young Princess (Pickering) •6 Sx:
   AATTBBs •DG

RING-HAGER
Danse Hongroise (1923) (Wiedoeft) •Asx/Pno •Rob

RIOU, Alain
10 Duos d'étude (1986) •2 Sx •Bil
15 Etudes de style en duo •2 Sx •Bil

RIPOSO, Joe
Jazz Improvisation: A Whole-Brain Approach (1981/1994) •JR

RISSET, Jean-Claude (1938)
   Compositeur et théoricien français, né au Puy, le 13 III 1938.
Travailla avec S. Demarquez et A. Jolivet, puis aux U.S.A. avec
Mathews et Varese. Travailla à l'IRCAM.
   "Jean-Claude Risset qui collabore avec l'IRCAM, bénéficie déjà
d'années de pratique dans les laboratoires scientifiques américains.
Pionnier français de l'ordinateur, il utilise bien entendu les sons
synthétiques calculés à partir du programme *Music V*, mais aussi les
instruments ou la voix intégrés à ces nouveaux moyens sonores." (J. &
B. Massin)
Glissements (10'10) •3 melody instruments of choice [instruments
   monodiques au choix]/Perc/Pno/Tape
Saxatile •Ssx/2 Tapes •Sal
Voilements (1987) (14') •Tsx/2-track Tape (Bande à 2 pistes) •Sal

RITTER, George Thom (see GEORGE)

RITTER, Renée (1913)
Long Ago - Air varié •Bb Sx/Pno •Mol

RIVCHUN, A.
   Saxophoniste russe.
150 Exercices (1960)
Schola ingry na saksofone (1961)

RIVIER, Jean (1896-1987)
   Compositeur français, né à Villemomble (près de Paris), le 21 VII
1896, mort à La Penne-sur-Huveaune (près d'Aubagne), le 6 XI 1987.
   "L'effusion romantique, tour à tour rude et tendre, semble se faire

violence chez lui en adoptant un langage massif et ordonné, démarche
qui le rapproche un peu de Honegger, dont il n'a pas, cependant, la
communicative angoisse." (R. Stricker) "Une des personnalités les
plus séduisantes de l'école néo-classique française." (Cl. Rostand)
"Style d'un caractère rude et violent d'une part, tendre et sensible de
l'autre. Jean Rivier a le sens de l'architecture sonore." (Y. Hucher)
"Sait passer de la gravité au sourire sans abandonner la fermeté du
dessin." (A. Wolff) "L'intelligence a le pas, dans l'art de Rivier, sur
l'instinct; il est plus sensible à la construction qu'à l'ambiance, au
contrepoint qu'à l'harmonie, au rythme qu'au lyrisme." (R. Bernard)
"Ennemi de toute doctrine, recherchant avant tout l'équilibre entre
instinct et inspiration, Jean Rivier consacra surtout ses efforts à la
musique instrumentale." (E. Kocevar)
   "Rivier is exceptional among modern composers as an optimistic
unproblematic musician. Neither a revolutionary nor a reactionary
always an unexceptionable craftsman, he takes 'modern' dissonant
harmony and counterpoint for granted as the obvious and natural idiom
in which 20th century symphonic music should be couched. This
conciliatory and easy-going attitude has made him a bugbear to
ultramodernists and a favorite among organizers of festivals; but on the
whole his importance among the French composers of his generation,
the number of his works and the frequency of their performance, in
France and abroad, stand in inverse ration to the paucity of the
comments and discussions they call for." (F. Goldberg)
Aria (5') (J-M. Londeix) •1 Sx: S or A/Org •ET
Concertino (Mule) (1949) (14') 1) Allegretto 2) Adagio 3) Allegro
   vivo •Asx/Orch (1111/111/Perc/Harp/Str) or Pno •Sal
Concerto (1955) (17'30) 1) Allegro burlesco 2) Adagio
   3) Vivacissimo •Asx/Tpt/Str Orch •PN
Concerto (Decouais) •Asx/Tpt/Band •Bil
Grave et Presto (1938) (8') (to Quatuor Mule) •SATB •Bil

RIVIERE, Jean-Pierre (1929)
   Compositeur français, né à Bordeaux (Mérignac), le 22 VII 1929.
Travailla avec T. Aubin, N. Boulanger, et O. Messiaen. Prix de Rome
(1957).
Concertino •Asx/Orch or Pno
Parallèles (1982) (to Quatuor Deffayet) (Lent - Vif - Lent - Vif)
   •SATB
Variations (1956) •SATB

RIVOLTA, Renato
   Compositeur italien.
Solid machinery (1992) (10') •Asx/Chamber Orch

RIVTCHUN, Alexandre
   Saxophoniste et compositeur russe.
Concert étude (2'35) •Asx/Pno
Sonate •Asx/Pno

ROBBINS, David
Improvisation •Fl/2 Cl/Tsx/Bsn/Tpt/Trb/Vln/Vla/Vcl/Bass/Perc

ROBERT, C.
Concerto •Bb Sx/Pno •TM

ROBERT, Jacques
Chant sans parole (1983) (2'30) •Asx/Pno •Comb

ROBERT, Lucie (1936)
   Compositeur français, né le 3 X 1936, à Rennes. Travailla avec T.
Aubin, N. Gallon, et H. Challan.
Berceuse pour Rémi (1985) (5'30) •Asx/Pno •Bil
Cadenza (1974) (10') (to M. Nouaux) •Asx/Pno •Bil
Doppelchor (1993) (12') •8 Sx: SATB + SATB •adr

Double Concerto (1968) (28') (to G. Gourdet et Cl. Valmont)
1) Agitato - Andantino - Agitato 2) Cadence I 3) Prestissimo
4) Cadence II 5) Final •Asx/Pno/Orch (2222/2221/Timp/Perc/
Str) •Bil

Elégie •Asx/Pno •adr

Flammes et fumée, op. 53 (1982) (15'30) (to A. Beun) •5 Sx:
SnoSATB •Bil

Géométrie (1986) (12') •2 Sx: AB/Tpt/Trb/Perc •adr

Magheia (1976) (26') 1) Introduction et cantilène 2) Ronde 3) Récit I
4) Misterioso e quasi una fantasia 5) Récit II 6) Danse •4 Sx:
SATB/Pno •Bil

Magnetic I, II, III (1988) (12') (to M. Nouaux) •Asx/2 Pno •adr

Messanucté, op. 72 (1991) (18') (to l'Ensemble de Saxophones de
Lyon) (Carillon - Appel - Marche - Arrivée - Adoration -
Animation - Danse) •14 Sx •adr

Perpetuum mobile (1985) (14') (to A. Beun) •Asx Solo •adr

Pianaxo (1993) •Pno/12 Sx: SnoSSAAATTTBBBs •adr

Quintette (1960) (19') (to G. Gourdet) •Asx/Str Quartet •Bil

Rhapsodie (1977) (8'20) (to Cl. Delangle) •Asx Solo •DP

Rythmes lyriques (1982) (11'30) (to B. Beaufreton & A. Beun) •2
Sx: ST •Bil

Sonate (1967) (11') (to R. Le Bian) (Elegie - Poco a poco animato -
Allegro agitato - Choral) •Asx/Pno •Bil

Strophes (1978) (14'30) (to J-M. Londeix) (5 movements) •Asx/Pno
•DP

Supplications (1981) (10') (to Trio Evolution) •Asx/Ob/Vcl •DP

Tétraphone (1982) (16') •SATB •Bil

Tourbillons (1975) (18') (3 movements) •Asx/Pno •Bil

Trinôme (1982) (13') (to H. Saïto, K. Araki, & M. Saïto) •2 Sx:
SB/Pno •Bil

Variations (1977) (8'30) (to I. Roth) •Asx/Pno •Bil

Variations Diapason (1992) (14'20) •SATB •Bil

ROBERZNIK, Jure (1943)

Compositeur yougoslave, né à Ljubljana, le 23 VIII 1933.

Concertino (1965) •Tsx/Orch

ROBJOHN, William James (FLORIO, Caryl) (1843-1920)

Organiste et compositeur américain d'origine anglaise, né à Tavistock
(Devon), le 2 XI 1843, mort à Morganthon (North Carolina), le 21 XI
1920. Aux U.S.A. depuis 1858.

"Autodidacte."

"An inconsistent composer, he wrote some fresh, strong works
between 1860 and 1879." (B. Cantrell)

Allegro de concert •SATB

Introduction, Theme and Variations (1879) •Asx/Orch

Quintet •Pno/4 Sx

ROCCISANO, Joe

Compositeur américain.

Contrasts (1984) (for D. Underwood) •2 Sx: AT/Band or Pno

ROCERTO

Meditation (Morgan) •Bsx/Pno •Volk

ROCHBERG, George (1918)

Compositeur et professeur américain, né à Paterson (New York), le
5 VII 1918. Travailla avec Weisse, Szell, Mannes, et Menotti.

"His music of the late 1940s reveals a vigorous temperament with
strong affinities with the idioms of Stravinsky, Hindemith and, especially, Bartok (the *Capriccio*). Then in the early 1950s he plunged into
Schoenbergian serialism and felt his imagination liberated at last by a
language he took to be the inevitable culmination of historical developments." (A. Clarkson)

Capriccio (1949-57) Str/Perc/2 Sx: AT/Tpt/Hn/Pno/Perc •Pres

ROCHOW, Erich

Compositeur allemand.

Etüden I, II & III •Asx •FF

Handbuch der Saxophon Praxis •RB/FF

Konzert (1966) •Asx/Orch •FF

Saxophonie Schule •FF

Serenade •2 Sx/Pno •RB

RODBY, John (1944)

Concerto (1971) (to H. Pittel) •Asx/Orch

RODEN, Robert R.

Compositeur américain.

Sax-craft (1978) •4 Sx: SATB or AATB •South

RODGERS, Richard

Dancing on the Ceiling •4 Sx: SATB/Bass/Drums •DP

It Might as Well be Spring (Young) •SATB •Ron

My Funny Valentine (Young) •SATB •Ron

RODNEY

Calvary (Holmes) •AATB •Bar

RODRIGUEZ, Robert Xavier (1946)

Compositeur américain. Travailla avec H. Stevens, H. Johnson, J.
Druckmann, et N. Boulanger.

Sinfonia (1972) (to H. Pittel) •1 Sx: Sno+S/Orch •adr

Sonata in One Movement (1973) (to H. Pittel) •Ssx/Pno

RODRIGUEZ-PICO, Jesùs

Compositeur espagnol.

Sextet (1992) •Fl/2 Cl/2 Sx: AT/Bass

ROELENS, Alexandre (1881-1948)

Menuet vif (Mule) •Asx/Pno •JJ

ROELSTRAETE, Herman (1925)

Theme con variations (Jonehmans) •Sx Ensemble

ROERMEESTER

Introduction and Romance •Bb Sx/Pno •CBet

ROESGEN-CHAMPION, Marguerite (1894)

Claveciniste et compositeur français, né à Genève, le 25 I 1894.
Travailla avec E. Bloch et J. Dalcroze.

Scherzo (Mule) •SATB

Concert n° 1 •Asx/Bsn/Harps

Concert n° 2 (1945) •Asx/Bsn/Harps •FDP

ROGER, Denise (1924)

Compositeur français, né à Paris, le 21 I 1924. Travailla avec N.
Gallon et H. Busser.

"Oeuvres bien écrites et bien pensées pour les instruments." (M-Cl.
Clouzot)

Conversation (1989) (2') •1 Sx: A or T/Pno •Mar

Duo •Asx/Vcl •adr

Evocation (1982) (2'30) •1 Sx: A or T/Pno •Comb

3 mouvements (11') (to Quatuor d'Anches P. Pareille) 1) Lent -
Allegro - Lent - Allegro 2) Lent 3) Allegro •Ob/Cl/Asx/Bsn
•EFM

ROGERS, Lloyd

Alma redemptoris mater •Any 12 instruments

ROGERS, Rodney (1953)

Compositeur américain.

Lessons of the Sky •Ssx/Pno

The Nature of This Whirling Wheel (1987) (16'30) (to L. Hunter) •Asx/Orch

ROGISTER, Fernand (1872-1954)

Concertino (1946) •Asx/Orch or Pno •Bosw

ROIKJER, Kjell (1901)

Bassoniste et compositeur danois né à Malmö en Suède. Travailla avec K. Lassen, J. Andersen, H. Bull, et N. O. Rasted.

Divertimento n° 6, op. 72 (1978-90) (12'30) (Molto lento - Allegretto leggiero e con eleganza - Andante lento e mesto - Allegro risoluto e risvegliato) •SATB

ROIZENBLAT, Alain

Danse lointaine (1989) (1') •1 Sx: A or T/Pno •Bil
Musique pour rêver (1987) (1'50) •1 Sx: A or T/Pno •Bil

ROKEACH, Martin

Prelude and Fantasy •Asx/Orch •DP
Tango •Ob/Cl/Asx/Hn/Trb/Vcl •DP

ROLDAN, Ramon de SAMINAN

Compositeur espagnol.

Inter-relaciones (1984) (to M. Mijan) •SATB
Recitado a dos (1986) •Asx/Pno

ROLIN, Etienne (1952)

Compositeur français d'origines américaine et belge, né à Berkeley (California) le 12 VII 1952. Réside en Paris depuis 1974. Travailla avec N. Boulanger, O. Messiaen, et I. Xenakis. Prix du Concours Josse (1981). Professeur d'analyse musicale au Conservatoire de Bordeaux depuis 1985 et dirige l'atelier de jazz du Conservatoire de Montauban depuis 1989.

"La pluralité des modes d'expression, traités théoriques, notations, querelles esthétiques entre nations reflète pour Etienne Rolin notre situation présente, où le chaos peut aussi être considéré comme une marque de vie et de mouvement." (D. J-Y. Bosseur)

Adieu •13 Sx: SnoSSAAATTTBBBsCBs
Aphorismes VII - 10 pièces courtes à caractère pédagogique - Livre I (1982-83) (12') •Sx Solo •Lem
Aphorismes - Volume II (1988) •Sx Solo •Lem
Boogie con moto - Variations sur Mingus (1988) (8') •12 Sx •adr
Caccia (1991) (11') •2 Sx: AT/Echantilloneur [Sampler] •adr
Chants fleuris (1985) (23') (to J-M. Londeix) •Asx Solo/12 Sx: SnoSSAAATTTBBBs •adr
Connexions I (1985) (3-6') (Laureau-Rossé-Lejet) •Asx Solo •Sal
Dialogue (1985-86) (to M. Jézouin) •Asx/Vcl •Sal
Etude en bleu (1981) (3') •Ssx Solo •adr
Fantasy cycle (1985) (3') •Bsx Solo •adr
Figures et miniatures (1984) (to M. Jézouin) •SATB •adr
Jeu du trèfle - Trio (1981) (11') •Ob/Sx/Vcl •adr
Luce del fuoco (1992) (13') •40-60 Sx (ATBBs) •adr
Machine à sons (1990) (12') •12 Sx (solo bass)/Tape •adr
Maschera - Concerto (1980) (17') (to J. Charles and O. & C. Delangle) •Pno/1 Sx: A+S+B/13 instruments (1100/111/BsCl/CBsn/Pno/Perc •adr
Miniatures (1984) (4') (to M. Jézouin) •SATB •adr
Ost Schatten (1993) (10') •Ssx/Tape •adr
Passerelles (1989) (5') •Tsx Solo •ApE
Pulse - Puzzle (1989) (5'30) •Asx Solo •adr
Puzzle - Pulse (to R. Wolf) (1994) (5'30) •Asx Solo •SCo
Quasi un sol Nascente (1992) (8') (to M. Mucci) •2 Sx: SB/2 Pno •adr
Quatre Séquences (1983) (5') •SATB •adr
Quètes ancestrales (1989) (14') (to P. Méfano) •Tsx/Vla/2 Vcl/Bass/Harp/Marimba •Fuz

Rideau de feu - Double concerto (1993) (18') •2 Sx: ST/Orch (Synthophone/Double Str Quartet/2 Trb/2 Perc) •adr
Rotations - 11 duos (1990) (12-16') •2 Sx: SA/Improv. •adr
Rouages •Sx Solo •adr
Sablier (1984) (3'30) (to M. Jézouin) •SATB •Lem
Sax over seas (1992) (20') •4 Sx: SATB/Tape •adr
Sous les cieux (1993) (7') (to Fr. Ledroit) •Ssx/Org •adr
Still life (1983) (6') (to J. Charles & M. Jézouin) •2 Sx: SB •adr
Suite Poly-folique (1993) (10-15') •Tsx Solo •adr
Tandems - Jeux à deux (1987) (7') •Asx Solo/4 Sx: SATB •Lem
Teinte (to R. Wolf) (1994) (2') •2 Sx: AA •SCo
Tightrope (1979) (7') (to Quatuor Contemporain) •SATB •adr
Toile en trois couleurs (1976) (8') •Asx/Vcl/Pno •adr
Tourbillons (1981) (8') (to D. Kientzy) •1 Sx: S+A+T+B/Perc •adr
Tremplins (to Ph. Geiss) (1994) (3'30) •3 Eb Sx •SCo
Tressage - Concerto (1983-84) (10') •Ssx/5 instruments: Fl/Cl/Pno/Vln/Vcl or Pno •Lem
Tressage b (1986) (9') •Ssx/Pno •Lem
Vagues - pour commençants •SATB •adr
Vocalise II (1989) •Ssx/Pno/BsCl/Fl •adr
Wind flight (1986) •Free instrumentation including 1 Asx minimum [Instrumentation libre dont 1 Asx minimum] •Lem

ROLLE, Johann Heinrich (1716-1785)

Air varié •Asx/Pno •Sal
Concerto •Asx or Bb Sx/Pno •Sal

ROLLIN, Robert

Two Jazz Moods •Asx/Pno •SeMC
Song of Deborah •3 Sx: SnoSA/2 Tpt/Trb/Tuba/Perc/Str •SeMC

ROMANO, Edmond

Séquences alternées (1980) (to Quatuor Desloges) •SATB

ROMBY, Paul (1900)

Saxophoniste, arrangeur, et compositeur français, né à Le Nouvion (Aisne), le 26 XI 1900. Travailla avec Fr. Combelle. Soliste et membre du Quatuor de la Garde Républicaine, puis avec M. Mule du 'Quatuor de Saxophones de Paris.'

Andante cantabile •Asx/Pno •PB
Berger et bergère •Asx/Pno •PB
Cabrioles •Asx/Pno •PB
Ciel de Castille (Feret) •Asx/Pno •PB
Confidences d'une fleur •Asx/Pno •PB
Coteaux fleuris •Asx/Pno •PB
Fantaisie concertante •Asx/Pno •PB
Fantaisie suisse •Asx/Pno •PB
Fantaisie vénitienne •Asx/Pno •PB
Martinisax •Asx/Pno •PB
Méthode •Mar
Orientalisme •Asx/Pno •PB
Près du jardin (Mori) •Asx/Pno •PB
Primevères •Asx/Pno or 4 Sx: SATB •PB
Romance •Asx/Pno •PB
Saltarelle (Mori) •Asx/Pno •PB
Scènes champêtres (Delabre) •Asx/Pno •PB
Souvenir de Milan et du Pausilippe •Asx/Pno •PB
Trottade •Asx/Pno •PB
Vacances •SATB •PB
Valse romantique •Asx/Pno •PB

ROMERO

Compositeur espagnol.

Solo de Concurso •Tsx/Pno

ROMERO, Aldemaro (1951)

Chef d'orchestre et compositeur vénézuélien autodidacte.
Quartet (1976) (16'30) 1) Fandango 2) Serenata 3) Choro y tango
•SATB •Pag

ROMZA, Robert (1960)

Compositeur américain.
Quartet No. 2 (1993) 1) Moderato 2) Forceful 3) Allegro spirito
•SATB

RONKIN, Bruce (1957)

Professeur, éditeur, et saxophoniste américain, né à Mount Holly
(New Jersey), le 22 XI 1957. Travailla avec Reginald Jackson, William
Osseck, Ramon Ricker, et Eugene Rousseau.
Transient States (1993) (10'30) •MIDI Wind Controller/Pno •adr

RONKIN, Bruce & Robert FRASCOTTI

The Orchestral Saxophonist Volume I (1978) •Ron
The Orchestral Saxophonist Volume II (1984) •Ron

RCPARTZ, Guy (1864-1955)

Andante & Allegro (Buchtel) •Bb Sx/Pno •Kjos

ROQUIN, Louis (1941)

Compositeur français, né à Paris.
"Louis Roquin considère chaque élément du dispositif électro-
acoustique, bande magnétique, microphone, filtre modulateur, comme
susceptible d'être à l'origine de la composition musicale de manière
relativement indépendante; un tel matériel sera souvent exploité sous
son angle 'mécanique,' ce qui permet au compositeur d'introduire dans
son travail une certaine objectivité, tout en laissant l'interprète explorer
les propriétés acoustiques des éléments initialement choisis. L'intérêt
d'une telle approche réside dans le fait que rien n'est exclu a priori;
éliminer les 'impuretés' des évènements captés, rechercher une 'pro-
preté' somme toute stérilisée revient à se priver d'une zone particulièrement vivante de l'espace sonore." (D. J-Y Bosseur)
Machination VII (to D. Kientzy) •Sx Ensemble
Machination VIII (1983) (to D. Kientzy) •1 Sx: S+A+T+B+Bs/Tape
Soli, solo et solissimo (1984-85) (10') (to D. Kientzy) •1 Sx:
S+A+T+CBs/Tape

ROREM, Ned (1923)

Compositeur et essayiste américain, né à Richmond (Indiana), le 23
X 1923. Travailla avec V. Thomson, A. Copland, et L. Sowerby, puis
subit l'influence à Paris de F. Poulenc, A. Honegger, et D. Milhaud.
"Beginning in the late 1960s, his compositions are sometimes based
on various modified serial techniques while maintaining tonal har-
monic references." (J. Holms)
Picnic on the Marne (1983) (16'30) (to J. Harle) 1) Driving from
Paris 2) A Bend in the River 3) Bal Musette 4) Vermouth
5) Tense Discourse 6) Making Up 7) The Ride Back to Town
•Asx/Pno •B&H

RORIVE, Jean-Pierre

Saxophoniste belge. Travailla avec F. Daneels.
Diderius aurifaber - Etude concertante •Sx Solo
Novum monasterium •Ssx Solo

ROS, Pepito

Compositeur italien.
Maya e New dance •SATB

ROSA, Rich de

Matron of Children •Tsx/Orch

ROSARIO, Conrado del

Compositeur philippin.

Ringkaran (1990) •Asx Solo

ROSE

12 Rose Studies for Saxophone (Gee) •DP

ROSEN, Alex

Compositeur allemand.
Tensoren (1993) •1 Sx: S+B/Perc •INM

ROSEN, Jerome (1921)

Compositeur, saxophoniste, clarinettiste professeur américain, né à
Boston (Massachusetts), le 23 VII 1921. Travailla avec R. Sessions, W.
Denny et, à Paris, avec D. Milhaud.
"The highly chromatic, tonal, neo-classical language of his early
music has developed into a free chromaticism in which successive
tonal centres define the structure." (J. Bergsagel)
Concerto (1957) (18') (to P. Fromm) •Asx/Orch (2222/4230/Pno/
Perc/Str) or Band •CFE/ACA
Serenade (1964) (8') (to P. & A. Woodbury) 1) Prelude 2) Improvi-
sation 3) Nocturne 4) Improvisation 5) Finale •Asx/Soprano
Voice •ACA

ROSEN, Robert J.

Compositeur canadien.
Kikros II (1982) •Pno/2 to 4 Sx •CMC
Three Miniatures (1978) •2 Sx: SA/2 Vln/Vla/Vcl •CMC

ROSENBLOOM, David (1937)

Compositeur américain d'avant-garde, né à Fairfield (Iowa), le 9 IX
1937. Travailla avec S. Martirano, G. Binkerd, et L. Hiller.
"With esthetic background, his music was bound to be experimental
in nature; however, he also composed in classical forms. His scores are
notated in diagrams and engineering blueprints, with special symbols
for dynamics, tempi, etc." (Baker)
Pocket Pieces (1977) •Fl/Asx/Vla/Perc •SeMC
The thud, thud, thud of suffocating blackness (1966) •Sx/Electric
Vcl/Pno/Celesta/Perc/Tape/Lights •SeMC

ROSENTHAL, Manuel (1904)

Chef d'orchestre et compositeur français, né le 18 VI 1904, à Paris.
Travailla avec M. Hure et M. Ravel.
"Il est un des très rares élèves de Ravel. Il s'exprime dans un style
néo-classique, sur un ton vigoureux, non dénué d'humour." (Cl.
Rostand) "Ses compositions font valoir un don d'imagier musical
servi par une rare entente des timbres instrumentaux." (N. Dufourcq)
"Un orchestrateur brillant, un peu prolixe dans sa richesse, se laissant
aller à un humour imitatif parfois trop facile." (P. Wolff)
"Infallibly scored, Rosenthal's music is that of a superior refined and
vigorous craftsman, typically French in the tradition of Chabrier and
Ravel." (F. Goldberg)
Saxophon'marmelade (1929) (6') (to J. Viard) 1) Blues 2) Cadence
et stomp •Asx/Orch or Pno •ME
Trio •3 Sx

ROSS, Walter

Compositeur américain.
Didactic Duos - 16 duos •Sx/Cl (or Ob) •DP
Old Joe's Fancy: Variations on 'Old Joe Clark' •4 Sx: SATB/Band
•DP
Toward the Empyreans •Sx/Tape •DP

ROSS, William James

Compositeur américain.
Aria and Dance (1982) (to Michael) •Asx/Pno •South

ROSSARI, Gustavo

53 Etudes (Iasilli) (2 Volumes) •B&H/South

ROSSÉ, François (1945)

Compositeur français, né à Reichsoffen (Alsace), le 16 VI 1945. Travailla avec O. Messiaen, B. Jolas, et I. Malec, avant de s'installer à Bordeaux.

" *Cordée, Bachflussigkeit, Oem, Mod'son 1 à 7*, etc... s'induisent dans le rêve d'une mise en osmose d'espaces (du minéral au culturel) apparemment bien scindés. L'espoir de plénitude physique (et mentale) du geste instrumental est explicité dans les mouvements de *Mod'son 7* (1986)... une vieille quète archéo-gymnique... furtive perception de notre intégralité?" (F. Rossé) "Nourri d'une large et profonde culture musicale, François Rossé allant après certains auteurs comme Schumann ou Scelsi toujours plus loin vers l'essence de la musique, la genèse du phénomène sonore, l'origine de l'art... débouche sur des horizons nouveaux où le moindre son prend une valeur musicale singulière, parfois inouïe, riche de possibles libératoires extraordinaires. Un "découvreur" génial dont l'influence artistique est d'ores et déjà décisive." (G. Lachaud) "Dès 1979, les orientations compositionnelles de François Rossé dévient de la complexité acoustique "minérale" (micro-polyphonie ligetienne par exemple) pour cibler une complexité appartenant plutôt à l'ordre 'biologique,' 'anthropologique,' ou 'culturel.' Passant de Polyphonie à 'Sociologie,' le compositeur cherche à trouver des solutions dans la conception-même de la partition (rendue apte à engager à vif -in live- cette option) (A. Mermin) "Les oeuvres de François Rossé sont depuis les premiers opus d'une extraordinaire nouveauté. L'instinct y prime sur l'intellect, les rendant particulièrement accessibles malgré leur complexité." (J. Lenners). "A propos de *Mod'Son 7*, qui s'inscrit dans une série de pièces proposant un voyage hors des acquisitions spécifiques de notre civilisation musicale, le compositeur écrit: 'A travers les déambulations mentales et les différents retournements d'attitude jalonnant mon sentier musical, l'auditeur peut déceler une sympathie certaine avec une forme de primitivité, sorte de tentative de déshabillage limité provisoirement aux attitudes et matériaux musicaux. Au-delà de cette nudité culturelle, au niveau de la réflexion à la fois compositionnelle et pédagogique, j'entreprends de défricher mon propre chemin des découvertes à travers une forêt de questions élémentaires touchant à la nature, à la fonction, à la hiérarchisation, au contrôle, à l'organisation... en somme à la nécessité modale (ce mot pris dans un sens qui englobe tout) du fait musical.' "

Anchée (1987) (to J-P. Caens & Quatuor Aulodia) •Ob/Cl/1 Sx: S+A+B/Bsn •adr

Atemkreis (1990) (8') •Soprano Voice/Bsx •adr

Bachflüssigkeit (1985) (20') •15 instruments including [dont] 1 Sx:S+A+B+Bs (without conductor [sans chef]) •adr

Baiser de terre (1990) (51') •300 musicians including Sx [dont Sx] •adr

...ces berges voyantes (1988) (12') (to J-M. Goury) •Alto Voice/Baritone Voice/1 Sx: A+B/Prepared Pno/Tape •adr

Connexions I (1985) (3-6') (Laureau-Rolin-Lejet) •Asx Solo •Sal

Epiphanies (1990) (10') (to J-Cl. Dodin) •1 Sx: S+B+Bs/Dispositif électro-acoust. •adr

Etki en Droutzy (1986) (12') •1 Sx: S+B+Bs/1 Perc •adr

Etude en balance (to J-M. Londeix) •2 (or 4) like Sx [Sx semblables] •adr

La main dans le souffle (1985) (6') •Asx/Pno •Bil

Le frêne égaré (1978-79) (10') (to J-M. Londeix) •Asx Solo •Bil

Level 01-84 (1984) (to D. Kientzy) •Fl-à-bec/Fl/Asx/1 or 2 Synth/ Chambre d'écho & reverb. •adr

Lobuk constrictor (1982) (4') (to J-M. Londeix) •Asx Solo •Bil

Lombric (1985) (8') •2 Sx: AA/Pno •Lem

Mod'son 7 (1985) (12') (to Quatuor Contemporain) •SATB •CA

O yelp (1989) •3 Sx: SACBs/1 camion de pompiers - soliste & 9 camions tuttistes •adr

OEM (1988) (21') •Soprano Voice/1 Sx: S+Bs/EH/Accordion/Bass/ Jazz Guit/Pno/Dispositif électro-acoust. •adr

Ost Atem (1992) (8') (to T. Saïto) •Bsx/Tape •adr

Paléochrome (1988) (22') •Vla principal/2 Fl/Cl/BsCl/1 Sx: S+T/ EH/Bsn/Hn/4 Perc/Bass •adr

Quartz 01.83 - A la mémoire de Fr. Valonne (1982) (15') (to D. Kientzy) •3 Sx: Sno+A/A+B/A •Sal

Séaodie I (1985) (3') •Asx/Pno •Bil

Séaodie II (1985) (3') •Sx Solo: A or S •Bil

Séaodie III (1985) (3') •Asx/Harp •Bil

Shanaï (1992) (6') (to J-P. Caens & J-Cl. Dodin) •2 like Sx [Sx semblables]

Sonate en Arc (1982) (5-10') (to D. Kientzy) •1 Sx: S+A/1 other low Sx ad lib. [1 autre Sx grave ad lib.] •Sal

Spath (1981) (16') (to J-M. Londeix) 12 Sx: SnoSSAAATTTBBBs •Fuz

Triangle pour un souffle - Concerto (1980-81) (12') •Asx/Str Orch (70221) •Bil

UDEL 05.89 (1989) (12') •Melody instrument [Instrument monodique] (Ssx or SnoSx)/Tape •adr

Vestiges... (1993) •Vln/Pno/BsCl/Fl/Fl-à-bec/Sx/Orch •adr

3L19L501X (1993) (11') •Bsx/Vcl •B&N

ROSSELLE, Xavier

Saxophoniste et compositeur français.

La Marche dans le tunnel (after H. Michaux) •Sx/Inform. music.

ROSSI, Salomone (1570-1630)

Three Canzonets (Voxman & Block) •3 Sx: AAT or AAA •South

ROSSINI, Giacchino (1792-1868)

Basilio aria (*Barbier de Séville*) (Hekker) •Bsx/Pno •TM

Bologna Variations (Harvey) •Asx/Pno •Ron

Cavatine (*Sémiramis*) (Lemarc) •Asx or Bb Sx/Pno •TM

Danza •SATB •SL

Guillaume Tell (Romby) •Asx/Pno •PB

Inflammatus •Bb Sx/Pno •CBet

Italiener in Algiers •Bsx/Pno •TM

L'Italienne à Alger (Romby) •Asx/Pno •PB

Quartet No. 2 (Gee) •Fl/Cl/Sx/Bsn •DP

Rosine'aria •Asx/Pno •Lis

Rossini à la carte (Schneebiegl) •SATB •GB

Variations (Schmidt) •Ssx/Symphonic Winds •WIM

Village Dance (Rascher) •Asx/Pno •Bel

ROSSINYOL, Jordi

Compositeur espagnol.

Sax •SATB

ROT, Michael

8 miniaturen, op. 24 1/8 •SATB •ECA

Quartetto non troppo •SATB •ECA

ROTERS, Ernst (1892-1961)

Compositeur allemand, né à Oldenburg, le 6 VII 1892, mort à Berlin, le 25 VIII 1961. Travailla avec G. Schumann.

Trio, op. 26b (1926) •Vln/Asx/Vcl •Sim

ROTH, Iwan (1942)

Saxophoniste virtuose et professeur suisse, né à Bâle. Travailla avec M. Mule.

Schule für Saxophon •Hug

Tonleitern für Saxophon I - Gammes et Arpèges I •Hug

Tonleitern für Saxophon II - Gammes et Arpèges II (1988) •Hug

ROTH, Wolfgang

Compositeur allemand.

Drei Dialoge (1993) •Asx/Tpt •INM

ROTHBART, Peter
Compositeur américain.
Sonata (1988) •Ssx/Pno

ROUFFE, G.
Compositeur russe.
Concerto pour Quatuor •4 Sx: SATB/Orch

ROUGERON, Philippe (1928)
Compositeur français.
Choral et ballet (1985) (4'30) •1 Sx: A or T/Pno •Bil
Deux Pièces 1) Solitude 2) Vieil air •SATB •Com
Etude (1985) (2'10) •1 Sx: A or T/Pno •Bil
Mélodie •Asx/Pno •Bil

ROUGNON, Paul-Louis (1846-1934)
Professeur et compositeur français.
1er solo de concert (MEYER) •Asx/Pno •Gras/South
2me solo de concert •Asx/Pno •Gras

ROUND, H.
Long, Long Ago - Grand Fantasia •Eb Sx/Pno •CF
The Rosy Morn •Eb Sx/Pno •Mol
Scenes That Are Brightest (WALLACE) •Eb Sx/Pno •CF
Then You'll Remember Me (BALFE) •Eb Sx/Pno •CF

ROUSH, Dean
Nine Muses (1993) (to J. LANSING) •Asx/Pno

ROUSSAKIS, Nicolas
21 Quartets (1969) •AATB •CFE

ROUSSEAU, Eugene (1932)
Saxophoniste virtuose et professeur américain, né le 26 VIII 1932. Travailla aux U.S.A. avec E. J. Bengston, S. Meron, H. Voxman, puis à Paris, avec M. Mule. Professeur à Indiana Université (Bloomington, Indiana).
The Eugene Rousseau Saxophone Methods (2 Volumes) •Kjos
Marcel Mule: His Life and the Saxophone [*Marcel Mule: sa vie et le saxophone*] (1982) •Eto
Method for Beginning Students •Lebl
Practical Hints for the Alto Saxophonist •Bel
Practical Hints for the Baritone Saxophonist •Bel
Practical Hints for the Tenor Saxophonist •Bel
Saxophone High Tones (1978) •Eto
Solo Album for Alto Saxophone and Piano •Asx/Pno •Eto
Solo album for Tenor Saxophone and Piano •Tsx/Pno •Eto

ROUSSEAU, Jean (1919-1944)
Compositeur français. Travailla avec Ch. Koechlin.
"Musique dépouillée, réduite à l'essentiel" (Ch. Koechlin)
10 petites esquisses poètiques •SATB

ROWLAND, David
Doubles n° IV (1981) (12') •Asx/Pno •Don
Projections I (1987) (13') •Sx/Perc •Don

ROY, Camille (1934)
Pianiste et compositeur français, né aux Sables-d'Olonnes. Travailla avec Y. Nat et O. Messiaen.
Concerto (1991) (to D. KIENTZY) (Alternant I - Point - Alternant II - Trait - Variation) •Sx/Orch

ROY, Myke
Compositeur canadien.
Ne pas plier, brocher ou mutiler (1987) •4 Sx/8 Synth •CMC

ROYER, Alain
Sonate •Asx/Pno

ROZAS, Antonio
Compositeur espagnol.
Dos ensayos (1984) •SATB

ROZOV
Compositeur russe.
Imitation à la Benny Goodman •Asx/Pno
Valse •Asx/Pno

RUBBERT, Rainer (1957)
Compositeur allemand, né le 9 VI 1957, à Erlangen. Travailla avec H. Gollmitz et W. Szalonelz. Lauréat du concours Marcel Josse (1979).
Concertino (1989) (16') •Asx/Pno/Str Orch/Perc •adr
Kammerkonzert ("Serenade") (1990) •4 Sx: SATB/4 Vln/2 Vla/2 Vcl/Bass/Pno •adr
Obstacle 1087 (1992) (14') •Tsx/BsCl/Vln/Pno •adr
Trio "...le fou" (1979-88) (12') •Asx/Ob/Vcl •adr
Urban music (1993) •SATB •adr
Vision (Urban music II) (1993) •BsSx Solo •adr
Vocalise (1992) •Asx/Fl/Vcl/Perc/Pno •adr

RUBINSTEIN, Anton (1829-1894)
Célèbre mélodie en Fa (VIARD) •Asx/Pno •Sal
Fantasy for Three (WALTERS) •3 Sx: AAT/Pno •Rub
Mélodie •Eb Sx or Bb Sx/Pno •Mol
Melody in F •Eb Sx/Pno •CF
Romance (CHEYETTE) •Bb Sx/Pno •SF
Romance (LONG) •Bb Sx/Pno •Volk

RÜCKSTÄDTER, Hans
Compositeur allemand.
Saxonate (1993) •Asx/Pno •INM

RUCQUOIS, Jean
Andantino et chanson gaie •1 Sx: A or T/Pno •Bil
Petite berceuse et petite ronde •Asx/Pno •Mar
Petite gavotte (1979) •Bb Sx/Pno •Bil
Sax menuet •Bb Sx/Pno •Bil

RUDAJEV, Alexandre
Compositeur américain né à Prague de parents autrichiens et russes. Travailla avec Nadia Boulanger et O. Messiaen.
"Dans sa musique résolument tonale et d'une grande clarté de forme il montre un sens infaillible de la ligne mélodique." (P. WEHAGE)
Concerto (1990) (to C. DELANGLE) 1) Allegro 2) Andante 3) Allegro marciale •Ssx/Orch (222 BsCl 2CBsCl/0331/4 Perc/Str)
5 Episodes (1989) •Ob/Asx/Vcl •adr
Intermezzo (1991) •Bsx/Pno •adr
Sober aa ta bar ("Bar à Thé pour Alcooliques Anonymes Sobres") •5 Sx: SAATB •Com
Sonate (1990) (12'45) 1) Allegro 2) Adagio 3) Allegretto •Asx/Pno •adr
Variations et Thème (1991) (10') (5 movements) •Asx/5 Vcl •adr

RÜDENAUER, Meinhard (1941)
Compositeur autrichien, né à Vienne.
Dances and Sentimental Thoughts (13') •SATB •CA
Konzert (18') •Asx/Chamber Orch (Fl/Hn/2 Vln/Vla/Vcl/Bass) •CA
The Noble Sport (1973) (to S. FASANG) •Asx Solo

RUDIN, Richard
Compositeur américain.
Sonata for Alto Saxophone and Piano •Asx/Pno

RUDIN, Rolf (1961)

Compositeur allemand, né le 9 XII 1961 à Franfürt. Travailla avec H. Engelmann, B. Hummel, G. Wich, et Z. Gardonyl.

Nachtstücke, op. 9 (1988) (13') 1) Vision 2) Suche 3) Alptraum 4) Besinnung 5) Gegenüber 6) Be Freing 7) Versunken •Asx/Pno •B&B

RÜDINGER, Gottfried (1886-1946)

Compositeur et professeur allemand, né à Lindau, le 23 VIII 1886, mort à Cauting-Munich, le 17 I 1946. Travailla avec M. Reger.
"Much of Rüdinger's music shows the influence of Brahms and Reger." (B. Jacobson)

Divertimento, op. 75 (Allegro ma non troppo, risoluto - Andante sostenuto - Allegretto - Larghetto - Allegro risoluto) •Vla (or Cl)/Tsx/Pno •BAUS

RUEDA, Enrique

Compositeur espagnol.
La rosa magica (1990) (to R. Gil) •Sx/Pno
Cuarteto - Tocata (1992) (to Cuarteto Orpheus) •SATB
La otra zona (1992) (to M. Mijan) •Sx/Tape

RUEFF, Jeanine (1922)

Compositeur français, né le 5 II 1922, à Paris. Travailla avec H. Busser. Grand Prix de Rome (1948).
"Sens indéniable de l'architecture sonore." (P. Parisot) "Musicienne élégante, d'esprit, de finesse et parfois d'humour." (Cl. Rostand) "Musique généreuse, adroitement construite." (B. Gavoty).

Chanson et passepied (1951) (2'30) •Asx/Orch or Pno •Led
Concert en quatuor (1955) (17') (to Quatuor Mule) 1) Entrée 2) Fugue 3) Menuet 4) Passepied 5) Air 6) Final •SATB •Led
Concertino, op. 17 (1951-53) (15') (to M. Mule) 1) Allegro molto 2) Lent 3) Vif et bien rythmé •Asx/Orch (1111/110/Str) or Pno •Led
Mélopéa (1954) (3') •Asx/Pno •PN
Sonate (1967) (12'30) (to D. Deffayet) 1) Allegro 2) Adagio 3) Prestissimo •Asx Solo •Led
Trois pour deux (1982) (14'30) (to O. & J. Ledieu) 1) Allegro con fuoco 2) Assez lent et expressif 3) Rapide •Bsx/Pno

RUEGER, Christoph (1942)

Compositeur allemand.
Chansonabend Erich Mühsam (1975) (2 Std.) •Voice/Sx/Pno •adr

RUELLE, Fernand Jules (1921)

Compositeur belge né à Mons, le 20 III 1921. Travailla avec A. de Taeye.

A L'usine, op. 154 (1960) (12') (to Quatuor belge de Saxophones) 1) Au travail 2) La pause 3) Souvenirs de week-end •SATB •adr
Batifolages (1954) (3'30) (to Quatuor belge de Saxophones) •SATB •adr
Le Gille (1976) (to E. Apper) •Asx+Perc/Tsx+Perc/Pno •adr
Prélude, op. 80 (1954) (5') (to Quatuor belge de Saxophones) •SATB •Mau
Romance •Ssx/2 Cl •Mus
Ronde pastorale (1974) (to F. Daneels) •7 Sx: SnoSATBBsCBs •adr
Rondo giocoso, op. 107 (1955) (4') (to Quatuor belge de Saxophones) •SATB •adr
Scherzetto, op. 94 (1954) (4') (to Quatuor Belge de Saxophones) •SATB •adr
Trois Petites scènes, op. 95 (1954) (10') (to Quatuor Belge de Saxophones) 1) Galante 2) Mélancolique 3) Joyeuse •SATB •adr

Trois Tableautins (1955) (7'30) (to Quatuor Belge de Saxophones) 1) En badinant 2) En rêvant 3) En marchant •SATB •adr

RÜGER, Tobias

Compositeur allemand.
Festgesang (1993) •Tsx/Marimba •INM

RUGGERI, Gianluca

Percussionniste et compositeur italien. Travailla avec Stockhausen, N. Albarosa, et D. Gualtieri.
Esercizio dell'Attimo (1990) (13') (to E. Filippetti) •Ssx/Perc/Tape •adr

RUGGIERO, Charles H. (1947)

Compositeur américain.
Three Blues (1981) (to J. Forger) •SATB •DP
Interplay (to J. Luloff) •Ssx/Pno or Yamaha WX7 MIDI Wind Controller/Electronic Tape

RUGGIERO, Giuseppe (1909)

Andante & scherzo (1972) •3 Sx: AAT •Zan
16 Etudes de perfectionnement •Led
20 Etudes de perfectionnement •GZ
3 Pièces (1966) •2 Sx: AA •Led

RUHLMANN, J. J.

Jazzman français.
8 thèmes et improvisations •Sx •Sal

RUIZ, ESCOBES

Compositeur espagnol.
Solos de concurso •Asx/Pno

RUIZ, F.

Compositeur espagnol.
1° solo de concurso •Tsx/Pno •Tro
2° solo de concurso •Tsx/Pno •Tro

RUIZ, Manuel

Compositeur espagnol.
Faxce (1990) •SATB

RUIZ, Pierre (1940)

Compositeur américain d'origine colombienne, né le 30 X 1940 à Bogota. Travailla les Mathématiques et la Musique à l'Université de l'Illinois.
"Like so many of the best electronic pieces, even other electronic composers have trouble figuring out exactly what processor was used to put them together." (T. Johnson)
Another Lifetime (1972) (to K. & S. Dorn) •Asx/Tape •DP

RUNCHAK, Vladymyr (1960)

Compositeur ukrainien.
Concerto (15') •Asx/Chamber Orch
Contra spem spero ("J'espère, sans espoir") (1990) (to L. Oukraïnka) •SATB
Homo ludus (1992) (4') •Ssx Solo

RUNGIS, René (1895)

4 Pièces (Meurisse) 1) Caprice 2) Orientale 3) Scherzo 4) Sérénade •Asx/Pno •Lem

RUNSWICK, Daryl (1921)

Compositeur anglais.
Sonata •SATB •adr
Fantasia (1979) (8') •Tsx Solo/4 Sx: SATB/Jazz ensemble •adr
Family Group (1979) (15') (to English Saxophone Quartet) •SATB •adr

RUNYON, Alfred Santy (1907)

Saxophoniste, flûtiste, et professeur américain, né à Chanute (Kansas), le 18 IV 1907.
Dynamic Etudes (1949) •DG
Exotic (HUFFNAGEL) •Asx/Pno •DG
Santy Runyon's Modern Saxophone Studies (1944) •DG/Bay

RUSCH, Harold

Breath Control and Tuning and Intonation •CF

RUSHANT, Ian

This Side Up (1986) (15') •2 Sx: SA/Chamber ensemble

RUSHBY-SMITH, John

Compositeur anglais.
Quartet (1972) (13'30) (to London Saxophone Quartet) 1) Allegretto 2) Scherzo 3) Adagio 4) Finale •SATB •Sim

RUSSELL, Armand King (1932)

Compositeur américain, né le 23 VI 1932, à Seattle (Washington).
Particles (1954) (to S. RASCHER) 1) Allegro 2) Lento 3) Allegro moderato e barbaro 4) Andante 5) Allegro •Asx/Pno •Bou/DP
Transfluent Forms (1980) (to L. GWOZDZ) •Vln/Asx/Pno

RUSSO, William

Interplay (1987) (to A. RIPPE) •Asx/Chamber Orch

RUZDJAK, Marko (1946)

Compositeur croate, né à Zagreb. Travailla avec I. Malec et P. Scheffer.
Passamezzo (1986) •Asx/1 Perc (Tam-tam) •DSH/HG

RUZICKA, Rudolf (1941)

Compositeur tchécoslovaque, né à Brno. Cours à Prague de musique électro-acoustique.
Ecco homo - Oeuvre collective •CHF
Tibia I (1984) (11') (1er Prix au Concours Marcel Josse - 1984) •Ssx/Dispositif électro-acoustique

RYDBERG, Bo (1960)

Compositeur suédois.
Illuminated bodies (1985) (15') •1 Sx: T+S/Tape •SMIC
Link/Sequence (1990) •4 Sx: SATB/Computer/Live electronics •Tons

RYDIN, Alexandra

Fabliau (1987) (4'30) •Asx/Pno •Led
Hongroise (1987) (1') (for Annette) •Asx/Pno •Led

RYTTERKVIST, Hans (1926)

Compositeur suédois, né à Stockholm, le 31 VIII 1926. Travailla avec S-E. Bäck avant d'aller à Darmstadt.
"I presume the development I have gone through is limited to certain technical aspects. Being open-minded and assimilating as wide a musical field as possible is as axiomatic to me as assimilating everything essential to my particular personality. Since I find it right and relevant to go on working with the material, I have nothing more to add, beyond being allowed to regard my findings as a milestone along the road." (H-G. P.)
Lied ohne Worte (1968) •2 Vln/Vla/Vcl - Vln/Vcl/Harps - Bsx/Pno •SMIC

RZEWSKI, Frederick (1938)

Compositeur, pianiste, et compositeur américain d'avant-garde, d'origine polonaise, né à Westfield (Massachusetts), le 13 IV 1938. Travailla avec Thompson, Spies, Wagner, et Strunk.
"Frederick Rzewski s'évadera vite du sérialisme, pour chercher à exprimer une musique qui se veut 'plus proche du réel,' soit par l'approche de techniques d'improvisation, soit par son souci sociologique d'ouverture au monde contemporain." (J. & B. MASSIN) "Il a écrit de la musique instrumentale de chambre et des 'pièces en prose' (c'est-à-dire pour voix parlante) qui marquent son adhésion aux poétiques du geste et à la vitalité de Cage. En 1966, il a participé à Rome à la fondation de l'ensemble Musica Elettronica Viva, avec lequel il a étudié les possibilités de l'improvisation collective. Par la suite il a cherché un langage qui puisse refléter directement sa conception de l'engagement politique." (GARZANTI)
"IN 1966 he was a founder-member of the live electronic ensemble Musica Elettronica Viva (MEV) in Rome, where he lived until his return to New York in 1971." (E. MURRAY) "He pursues the vision of positivistic anti-music, mostly in free association for fluid ensembles with aleatory interludes." (BAKER)
Les moutons de Panurge (1969) •Soloist/Perc/Any ensemble

SABINA, Leslie
Compositeur américain.
Concerto •Ssx/Orch •adr

SABON, Edouard
Hautboïste français.
Nocturne (1889) •Cl or Ssx/Pno

SABON, Joseph-Pierre (1817-1893)
Compositeur français.
Autriche et Bohême - Fantaisie •Bb Sx/Pno •Mil
Les cloches bleues - Trio •Ob (or Fl or Cl)/Asx/Pno •Bil
12 études d'après Bochsa •Bil
Helvétie - Trio •Ob (or Fl or Cl)/Asx/Pno •Bil
La Hongroise •Bb Sx/Pno •Mil
Nocturne •Bb Sx/Pno •Mil
Noël •Asx or Bb Sx/Pno •Bil
Les Pibrochs écossais - Trio •Ssx/Cl (or Ob)/Pno •Mil

SACCHINI, Antonio (1730-1786)
Larghetto (MERIOT) •Asx/Pno •Phi

SADLER, Helmut (1921)
Professeur et compositeur allemand, né à Streitfort, le 23 VI 1921.
Quartet concertino •SATB •adr

SAEYS, Eugène (1887-19xx)
Pianiste et compositeur belge, né le 10 IX 1887, à Bruxelles. Travailla avec P. Gilson.
Intermède •Asx/Pno •HE/An
Poème, op. 199 •Asx/Pno •Ger/An
Romance •Asx/Pno •Mau

SAGVIK, Stellan (1952)
Compositeur suédois, né à Örebro, le 25 VII 1952. Travailla avec G. Bucht.
"He tidied up some of his earlier works, at the same time re-using a certain amount of old material. He is essentially an occasional composer, writing with the players in mind as opposed to positing theories and structural models." (S. J.)
Altosaxofonsymfoni, op. 128 (1984) •Sx ensemble •STIM
Det förlorade steget, op. 64 (1976) (20') •Fl/Cl+BsCl/Asx/Cnt/Trb/ Vln/Vla/Vcl/Perc •SMIC
Guenilles des jongleurs, op. 74 (1977) (7'30) •Fl/Ob/3 Cl/Asx/Bsn/ Cnt •STIM
Lamento, marsch & scherzo, op. 115 (1982) (11'30) •Ssx/Str Quartet •STIM
4 Miniatyrer ur baletten Eulidyke, op. 92 (1978) (4'30) •Fl/Ob/Cl/2 Sx: AT •STIM
Nocturne, op. 117d (1983) (6') •1 Sx: S or A/Vibr •STIM
Pastoral, op. 65 (1976) (4') •Asx/2 Vln/2 Vla/2 Vcl •STIM
Roughs from the wooden wind, op. 85 (1978) (7') •Ob/Cl/Asx/Bsn •STIM
Sma gyckelvisor till eu kort person, op. 112 (1981) (8') •Fl/2 Cl/ Asx/Mandolin/2 Perc •STIM
Suite circuler, op. 86 (1978) (10') (Alla turca - morena - hungara - romana) •Picc/Asx/Tpt/Hn/2 Trb/Perc/Bass •SMIC
Svensk concertino, op. 114 (1983) (9') •Asx/Str Orch •STIM

Tre Ballader, op. 112 (1983) (12') 1) Dis 2) Spegling 3) Gryning •Asx/Org or Guit •STIM

SAHL, Michael
Storms (1985) (for Amherst Saxophone Quartet) •4 Sx: SATB/2 Vln/Vla/Vcl

SAHORI, Aurelio (1946)
Compositeur et professeur italien.
Cadenze (1982) (to F. MONDELCI) •Asx/Pno

SAIN, James Paul
Dystopia 1) Emphatic 2) Languid 3) Flash •Asx/Pno

SAINT-AULAIRE, Roland (1886-1964)
Visages d'enfants (1938) (10'30) (to M. PERRIN) •SATB

SAINT-SAËNS, Camille (1835-1921)
Amour, viens aider (WHEAR) •Bb Sx/Pno •Lud
Andantino (BRANGA) •Asx/Pno •Dur
Aria (from *Samson et Dalila*) •Bb Sx/Pno •CBet
Le cygne (BERNARDS) •Asx/Pno •Dur
Le cygne •2 Sx: AT or AA or TT/Pno •Cen
The Elephant •Bsx/Pno •Bel
My Heart at thy Sweet Voice •Eb Sx or Bb Sx/Pno •CF
Rêverie du soir (BRANGA) •Asx/Pno •Dur
Romance (MAGANINI) •Asx/Pno •Mus
Sonate, op. 167 (TEAL) •Asx/Pno •Eto
The Swan (ROUSSEAU) •Asx/Pno •BM
The Swan (TRINKAUS) •Bb Sx/Pno •FMH
The Swan (TRINKAUS) •2 Sx: AA or TT/Pno •CF
Two Pavanes (FELIX) •1 Sx: A or T/Pno •Mus

SAITO, Takanobu (1926)
Compositeur japonais.
Quartet (1952) 1) Andante 2) Allegro moderato 3) Andante cantabile •SATB
2nd Quartet (1968) (to A. SAKAGUCHI) •SATB

SAKAGUCHI, Arata (1910)
Violoncelliste, saxophoniste, et professeur japonais, né à Tokyo, le 2 I 1910.
Method (1955) •ZOM
Scales for Saxophone (1979)

SALBERT, Dieter (1934)
Professeur et compositeur allemand, né à Berlin, le 2 VIII 1934.
3 Elegien (1989) (8') (Dunkel, Verhangen-ausdrucksvoll, schmerz-lich-dumpf, pochend) •1Sx: S+T+B/Org •adr
Saxophonia (1989) (10') 1) Poco dramatico 2) Con sentimente 3) Con ritmo •SATB •adr
Sinfonische Musik (1991) •12 Sx: SnoSSAAATTTBBBs •adr

SALCIANI
55 Masterpieces (IASILLI) •Tsx/Pno •Bel

SALIMEN-VLADIMIROV
Compositeur russe.
Scherzo •Asx/Pno •ECP

SALLUSTIO, Eraclio (1922)
Clarinettiste, saxophoniste, et compositeur italien. Travailla avec Vastucci et F. Di Donato.
Cralas 1) Moderato 2) Adagio 3) Allegretto •SATB
Gis N. 3 (1992) •Asx Solo
Lunaris (1980) (to I. MARCONI) •Asx/Str •adr
Saxologia 2 (1986) (to Quat. Aquilano) •SATB
Saxologia 5 (1992) •8 Sx: SAAAATTB

SALM, Andreas (1957)

Compositeur allemand, né à Bremen, le 30 III 1957.

Mah Jonhg (1993) •Asx/Vcl •INM

Momo-Musik, op. 3 (5 Jazz pieces) (1979-80) (29') •VDMK

Quartet and Strings, op. 30 (1991) •4 Sx: SATB/Orch

SALMON, Raymond (1917)

Compositeur français, né le 5 VIII 1917. Travailla avec M. Gennero et André Bloch.

Nonchalance (1970) (1'15) •Asx/Pno •Phi

Prélude et scherzo (1956) (8') (to Quatuor de la Garde Républicaine) •SATB

Quatuor en Sol mineur (1941) (15') 1) Allegro moderato 2) Andante 3) Presto •SATB

SALONEN, Esa-Pekka (1958)

Compositeur et chef d'orchestre finlandais, né le 30 VI 1958. Travailla avec Rautavaara et N. Castiglioni.

"In autumn 1980 Esa-Pekka Salonen went to Milan for his first extended period abroad. He studied with Niccolo Castiglioni and soon found himself composing his first large orchestral work, the *Concerto for saxophone and Orchestra*. It was eleven months before the work was completed, by which time Salonen has returned to Finland. The Saxophone *Concerto* reveals a completely new world. Modern Italian music has left its mark and Salonen's orchestral writing has clarity and control. On the other hand there are also traces of French Impressionism and in the middle movement of American minimal music style— admittedly in a European version, rather like Ligeti's *Three Pieces for Two Pianos*. Salonen himself once said of the orchestral thinking in Sibelius' seventh symphony: "It must inevitably influence any later composer using an orchestra." (R. NIEMINEN)

"...Auf den ersten Blick und ohne zu Wissen" - Concerto (1980-81) (17') (to P. SAVIJOKI) 1) 2) Attaca 3) •Asx/Orch (2222 4331/ Hrp/4 Perc/Str) •WH

SALTEN, Alfred

Concertino (14') •Asx/Orch

SALVATORE, Daniele (1956)

Compositeur italien.

Dal libro rosso del Signor Bagging (1987) (to Quart. d'Ance Italiano) •Ob/Cl/Asx/Bsn

SALVIANI, C.

Complete Method (from oboe) •Ric

Exercices in All the Pratical Keys (IASSILI) (1940) •CF

Studi dal Metodo per oboe (4 Volumes) (Giampieri) •Ric

SAMAMA, Leo (1951)

Compositeur néerlandais.

Capriccio (1976) (7') (to E. BOGAARD) •Asx/Pno •Don

Mémoires fanées (1992) •Asx Solo •Don

Soit que l'abîme, op. 19 (1983) (20') •5 Sx: SAATB/8 Perc •Don

Trio marchese, op. 24 (1984) (15') •Asx/Vla/Pno •Don

SAMAZEUILH, Gustave (1877-1967)

Compositeur et critique musical français, né à Bordeaux, le 2 VI 1877, mort à Paris, le 4 VIII 1967. Travailla avec E. Chausson, V. d'Indy, et P. Dukas.

"Il a relativement peu écrit, mais dans un style élégant qui, en dépit de sa formation, ne doit rien à la Schola et s'apparente au climat de certaines pages du premier Debussy et de Ravel." "Sa formation a certainement favorisé son adhésion à des courants esthétiques et des techniques contradictoires. Il dit fort bien, fort clairement, avec une grande lucidité, ce qu'il a à dire." (R. BERNARD)

"In his music he absorbed the distinct style of French Impressionism, but despite his fine craftsmanship, performances were few and far between." (BAKER) "Samazeuilh's music is notable for elegance and distinction, and for careful and excellent writing, and in spite of traces of those influences which belong to his period it reflects the composer's personality." (R. MYERS) "His music is small in quantity, but of a sustained quality; the style reflects the early works of Ravel and Debussy." (A. GIRARDOT)

Pièce dans le style ancien •SATB

SAMBIN, Victor (1834-1896)

Duo sur 'La Somnambule' de Bellini •2 Sx: ST/Pno •Sal

Méthode de saxophone

5 Quatuors brillants •SATB •Sal

30 Récréations musicales (1894) •Sx Solo •Sal

SAMIE, Auguste (18xx-1890)

24 études faciles (MULE) •Led

SAMMARTINI, Giovanni-Battista (1697-1775)

Allegro •Asx/Pno •HE

Vanto amoroso •Asx or Bb Sx/Pno •Mol

SAMONOV

Suite •Ob/Asx/Cl/Bsn

SAMORI, Aurelio

Compositeur italien.

Cadenze (1982) (13') (to F. MONDELCI) •Asx/Pno •adr

Solo (1985) (6'30) (to F. MONDELCI) •Asx Solo •adr

SAMUEL-ROUSSEAU, Marcel (1882-1955)

Romance (MULE) •Asx/Pno •Led

SAMUELSSON, Marie

Compositeur suédois.

Djup (1991) •SATB •Tons

SAMYN, Noël (1945)

Saxophoniste et compositeur belge né à Ménin, le 24 XII 1945. Installé au Canada depuis 1969. Travailla avec Fr. Daneels.

9 études transcendantes (1976) •Bil

Romance (1978) •Asx/Pno •Bil

Stratogy (1972) (to Fr. DANEELS) •Asx/Pno •adr

5 Trios (1976) •2 Cl/Asx •Bil

SANA, Paul

Compositeur belge.

Concerto (to A. CRÉPIN) •Asx/Orch or Band

SANCAN, Pierre (1916)

Pianiste et compositeur français, né à Paris. Travailla avec Y. Nat et H. Busser.

"S'exprime dans un langage traditionnel" (Cl. ROSTAND)

Lamento et rondo (1973) •Asx/Orch or Pno •Dur

SANCHEZ CANAS, Sebastian

Compositeur espagnol.

Nuevas diferencias (1990) (to M. MIJAN) •SATB

SANCO, Mario

Saxophoniste et compositeur italien.

Proposta (1978) (to W. KEFER) •Asx Solo •MS

SANDELL, Sten

Compositeur suédois.

Atanor (1988) •Asx/Pno •STIM

Procession n° I & II (1988) •Asx/Slagverk/Electr. Pno •STIM

SANDGREN, Joaklm
Jag fâr sâ ont i ögonen (1992) •SATB •SvM

SANDRED, Örjan
Compositeur suédois.
Skuggor (1989) (4') •SATB •STIM

SANDROFF, Howard (1949)
Compositeur américain.
Chorale •SATB
Concerto (1988) (to F. HEMKE) •Yamaha WX7 MIDI Wind
   Controller+Sx/Str Orch •adr
Eulogy (1988-91) (to the memory of Y. OMURO) •Asx/Pno •adr

SANDSTRÖM, Sven-David (1942)
Compositeur suédois né à Motala, le 30 X 1942. Travailla avec
Lindholm puis avec Ligeti et Norgard.
   "His music exploits the full range of serial and post-serial techniques,
as well as microtones and aleatory procedures." (T. STANFORD) "Des-
peration—security: these opposite relationships dominate his thoughts
on composition and make his works unusually existentially orientated.
Formally, his music is concentrated, often with complicated schemes
as bases of his works. His earlier works are characterized by a vague
and shadowy harmony caused by tuning in quarter-tones." (H-G. P.)
Concerto (1987) (23') •Asx/Str Orch •SMIC
Moments musicaux (1985) (14') (to Rascher Quartet) •SATB
   •SMIC

SANNELLA, Andy (1900-1961)
Musicien américain, né le 11 III 1900 à New York, où il est mort en
1961.
Intervals - studies (1932) •Asx/Pno •Ric
Jack and Jill (SHILKRET) •Asx/Pno
Saxannella (KLIKMAN) •Asx/Pno

SANNER, Lars-Erik (1926)
Compositeur suédois.
Sonatine (1954) (to J. de VRIES) •Asx/Pno •STIM/Ehr

SANSOM, Chris
Compositeur anglais.
5 Pieces (1975) (7'30) (to London Saxophone Quartet) •SATB

SANTIAGO, Armando
Quatuor (1988) (to Quatuor Bourque) •SATB

SAPIEYEVSKI, Jerzy (1945)
Compositeur polonais installé aux U.S.A.
   "Jerzy Sapieyevski combines both jazz and classical elements."
Air (1974) (10') (to M. SIGMON) •Asx/Str Quartet
Concerto (1976) (10') (to B. DUNHAM) •Asx/Str Ensemble (Vln/Vla/
   Vcl/Bass) or Pno •Merc

SARS, Gerard
Concertino (1989) •Asx/Str
Music (1992) •Asx/Org

SARY, Laszlö (1940)
Compositeur hongrois né à Györ, le 1er I 1940. Travailla avec
Szervansky.
   "After an early phase under the influence of Bartok, his interests
turned towards Boulez's music and in about 1970 he became ac-
quainted with Stockhausen's theories." (A. WILHEIM)
Incanto (1969) (7'30) •5 Sx: SAATB •Bri/MB

SASAMORI, Takefusa
Compositeur japonais.

Variations sur 'Taki's kojo no tski' (1963) (4'30) (to S. RASCHER)
   •Asx/Pno •PIC

SASONE, C.
Racconto •Asx/Pno •South

SATIE, Eric (1866-1925)
Gymnopédie I (GREENBERG) •SATB •WWS
Gymnopédies I (JAMIESON) •2 Sx/Pno •DP

SATO, Nabuhiro (1955)
Compositeur japonais.
Sonata (1975) (to A. SAKAGUCHI) •Asx/Pno

SATTERWHITE, Marc
Compositeur américain.
Aprilmourningmusic (1985) (10') (to M. MOORE) •Tsx/Pno
Nine Aphorisms •3 Sx

SAUCEDO, Victor (1937)
Compositeur américain né à Colton (California), le 20 VII 1937.
Travailla avec K. Stockhausen, R. Harris, et B. Kremenliev.
Four Bagatelles •2 Sx: AT/2 Pno/Perc •adr
Philolicia Comica (1971) (10') (to K. & S. DORN) •Ssx/Tape •adr

SAUCIER, Gene
An Impression •Asx/Pno •Ken
Two Pieces •AATB •DP

SAUGUET, Henri (1901-1989)
Compositeur français, né à Bordeaux, le 18 V 1901, mort à Paris, le
22 VI 1989. Travailla avec Ch. Koechlin, et appartint au groupe connu
sous le nom d'"Ecole d'Arcueil," patronné par Erik Satie.
   "J'ai appris à dédier tous mes loisirs à la musique, et elle reste pour
moi la récompense et le plaisir. J'en conserve une mentalité d'amateur
qui me garde je crois, de toute déformation professionnelle." (H.
SAUGUET) "Son art est celui d'un délicat romantique." (N. DUFOURCQ)
"Dans la majeure partie de son oeuvre, il fait preuve d'une telle
délicatesse dans l'agencement des tierces et des sixtes, que le jeu de ces
intervalles n'a jamais paru si suave ni si parfumé. Schoenberg avait
raison de dire qu''il y a encore beaucoup de choses à dire en Ut majeur.'
" (P. COLLAERT) "Ses tournures mélodiques, ses formules harmoniques,
ses habitudes rythmiques sont et restent éminemment personnelles."
(Cl. ROSTAND)
   "In conformity with the principles of utilitarian music, he wrote
sophisticated works in an outwardly simple manner." (BAKER) "Sauguet
never belonged to any clique or coterie; he has always been independent in his ideas as well as in his style of writing, and describes himself
as a 'traditionalist, though strongly anti-academic.' His music is above
all unpretentious and spontaneous; it does not seek to be profound, but
rather to please, which it does by its gracefulness and polish and its
unaffected melodiousness and simplicity of utterance." (R. MYERS)
"For him, the essentials are melody, harmony and rhythm, and he
develops his tonal or modal ideas in smooth curves, producing an art
of clarity, simplicity and restraint." (A. HOEREE)
Alentours saxophonistiques (1976) (10') •Asx/Wind Orch (2222/
   2000) •Chou
Concert à 3 pour Fronsac (1979) (12') 1) Feuillages 2) Ramages
   3) Ombrages •Fl/Asx/Harp •Fuz
L'arbre - Ballet (1976-80) (to J-M. LONDEIX) •10 Sx:
   SnoSSAATTBBBs
Oraisons (1976) (11') (to J-M. LONDEIX) •1 Sx: S+A+T+B/Org •Bil
Sonatine bucolique (1964) (13') (to J-M. LONDEIX) 1) Eglogue
   2) Chanson champêtre 3) Rondeau pastoral •Asx/Pno •Led
Une fleur (Album [Recueil]) (1984) (3') •Asx/Pno •Bil

SAUPE (18xx-1905)
Air varié •2 Sx •Mol

SAUTER, Eddie
Quartet No. 1 •SATB •Ken
Focus - Jazz Concerto •Asx/Orch

SAUTER, J.
Chanson joyeuse •Asx/Pno •Kjos

SAUTER, Otto
Quartett (1977) •AATB

SAVARD, Augustin (1861-1924)
Morceau de concours (MEYER) •Asx/Pno •Led

SAVARI, Jean-Nicolas (1786-1853)
Bassoniste, et chef de musique français au 34e Régiment d'Infanterie, né à Guise (Aisne), en Septembre 1786, mort à Paris le 9 II 1853.
Duo (to M. H. BERTHOUD) (Andante et allegro) •2 Sx: SA or TB •Sax
Fantaisie sur 'Le Freyschütz' (185x) (to A. AUCOUR) •Asx/Pno •Sax/Ron/Fuz
2me fantaisie sur un thème original (to Col. PINARD) •Asx/Pno •Sax
3me fantaisie sur un thème original (to J-B. SINGELÉE) •Bb Sx/Pno •Sax
Octuor (to M. le Ct MAREL) 1) Moderato 2) Andante 3) Allegro •8 Sx: SSAATTBB •Sax
Quatuor en 4 parties (17') (to M. le Gal MELLINET) 1) Allegretto 2) Allegretto quasi allegro 3) Andante quasi adagio 4) Final •SATB •Sax/Mol
Quintetto (to M-A. CAMBRIELS) 1) Allegretto 2) Andante 3) Pastorale 4) Final •5 Sx: SSATB •Sax
Septuor (to Gal FLEURY) •7 Sx: SSAATTB •Sax
Sextuor (to M. le Col. La PIQUEMAL) •6 Sx: SSAATB •Sax
Trio en 3 parties (to M. G. KASTNER) 1) Allegretto 2) Andante 3) Allegro moderato •3 Sx: SAB •Sax

SAVERINO, Louis
Compositeur américain.
Concertino petite (1946) (to K. DOUSE) •Asx/Orch or Pno •Mills

SAVOURET, Alain (1942)
Compositeur français, né au Mans.
"S'est affirmé comme une des imaginations les plus fertiles de l'électro-acoustique." (J. & B. MASSIN) "Venu du G.R.M., Alain Savouret fonde en 1969 avec Christian Clozier le groupe d'improvisation 'Opus N,' 'N' caractérisant la séance ou la manifestation à laquelle participent ou non d'autres musiciens improvisateurs; leur formation d'instrumentistes les a certainement déterminés dans la pratique de ce type d'action musicale, même si, à l'occasion de manifestations, 'ils s'entendent' à l'aide d'instruments et de matériel électroniques ou électro-acoustiques, créant sur scène, en direct, une musique de style électro-acoustique,' en utilisant soit une lutherie traditionnelle généralement électrifiée, violon et violoncelle électromécaniques, orgue électronique, vents, soit des instruments inventés par eux comme l'hydrophilus. Leur démarche s'apparente, à maints égards, à celle des musiciens de musique électronique vivante, ne serait-ce que dans leur manière de pratiquer l'improvisation, parfois en collaboration avec des musiciens de jazz, visant ainsi à reculer les cloisonnements entre catégories musicales." (D. J-Y. BOSSEUR)
Phil cello Joe Sax chez les trogloustiques •Asx/Vcl/Tape

SBACCO, Franco (1953)
Compositeur et chef d'orchestre italien. Travailla avec D. Guaccero, D. Paris, et G. Nottoli.

Equinst (1990) (13') (to Quatuor Aquilano) •4 Sx: SATB/Electron. •adr

SBORDONI, Alessandro (1948)
Compositeur italien, né à Rome. Travailla avec D. Guaccero, E. Macchi, G. Manzoni, et L-G. Bodin.
Cosi crescono i Girasoli (1992) (10') •Asx/Orch
Phaxes (1985) (5') (to F. MONDELCI & M. MAZZONI) 1) Molto libero 2) Liberamente improvisativo 3) Impetuoso •2 Sx: AA or TT

SCARLATTI, Alessandro (1660-1725)
Prelude and Fugue (SCHMIDT) •SATB •WIM

SCARLATTI, Domenico (1685-1757)
Scherzo (MULE) •SATB
Sonata No. 44 (HEMKE) •SATB •South
Sonata No. 66 (HEMKE) •SATB •South
Sonata Longo 104 •3 Sx: SAB •WWS
Sonata L. 129 Vivo (BRO) •SATB
Trois Pièces (PIERNE) •SATB

SCARMOLIN, Louis (1890-1969)
Compositeur et chef d'orchestre américain d'origine italienne, né à Schio, le 30 VII 1890, mort dans le New Jersey, le 3 VII 1969.
Duet Time •2 Woodwind instruments •Lud
Three Swingsters •3 Sx: AAT/Pno •IMD

SCELSI, Jacinto (1905-1988)
Compositeur italien, né à La Spezzia, le 8 I 1905, mort à Rome le 8 VIII 1988. Travailla avec Respighi et Casella avant de s'initier à la technique sérielle à Vienne avec W. Klein, dont il se détourna pour s'initier à la musique de Scriabine auprès d'un élève de ce dernier à Genève.
"Longtemps méconnu, Scelsi a effectué, après Debussy, le passage le plus conséquent, le plus radical du concept *note* au concept *son*, passage impliqué par un contact suivi avec les cultures musicales extra européennes. La musique de S. explore l'intérieur du son, elle se meut au-delà de la tonalité et du tempérament égal, elle se déploie dans la totalité du spectre sonore." (P. SZERSNOVICZ) "Compositeur, mais aussi poète, Jacinto Scelsi a orienté ses recherches, très influencées par sa connaissance des musiques asiatiques, vers les phénomènes de la perception sonore: 'celui qui ne pénètre pas à l'intérieur, au coeur du son, il se peut qu'il soit un parfait artisan, un grand technicien, mais jamais il ne sera un véritable artiste, un véritable musicien.' L'aventure prophétique de Scelsi passionne certains compositeurs de la génération suivante, en particulier Györgi Ligeti qui lui voue une profonde admiration. Personnage mystique, tenant d'une certaine musique statique, resté volontairement dans l'ombre, Scelsi demeure encore pour un large public un compositeur à découvrir." (J & B. MASSIN) "Ses oeuvres, pour la plupart instrumentales, sont aussi orientées vers des recherches d'ordre purement sonore se rattachant à celles de Varèse." (Cl. ROSTAND) "La musique de cet indépendant dérangeant, car libre de toute attache matérielle, de tout système, et en avance d'une génération au moins sur l'évolution générale, se trouvait totalement en porte-à-faux par rapport à l'esthétique sérielle des années 1950 et 1960." (F-R. TRANCHEFORT) "L'étape ultime du compositeur est probablement 'Chants du Capricorne,' véritable alphabet scelsien, pour Soprano accompagné de quelques percussions ou d'un saxophone. A l'écoute d'un tel 'poème de timbres,' absolument déconcertant, on mesure la proximité du compositeur italien avec John Cage. Tous deux ont porté l'oreille au-delà du monde occidental, conçu comme atelier où l'on fabrique des mélodies et des développements. Scelsi comme Cage, refusaient le nom de compositeur et se disait 'passeur de sons.' " (C. LEBLÉ) "Sa musique, profondément influencée par les philosophies de l'Orient (bouddhisme zen, taoïsme…) et par la conception orientale du son et de la durée, se situe en marge de toutes les esthétiques de la musique

contemporaine—alors même que la sienne propre fait de plus en plus école dans la jeune génération."

"The music is, for Scelsi, an intuitive link with the transcendental and involves the annulment of creative individuality, the countless changes in style contributing to the non-professional features of his vast output should be regarded as pure phenomena, which merely embody a spiritual process substantially unchanging. In surface characteristics his works up to the early 1950s submitted though with apparent difficulty, to the learned tradition of European music. Generally adopting a free atonality, he employed styles ranging from the modish 'machine music' of the 1920s, to the neo-romantic cast of such impromptu-type chamber pieces, and from the embryonic serialism, a partly parodistic homage to Webern, to the eclecticism. Having broken out of the old-fashioned esoteric attitude underlying his 'first-manner' works (an attitude with antecedents in the theosophical interests of Skryabin and Schoenberg), Scelsi's development in the last twenty years has disclosed an inner sympathy with the anti-rational tendencies of the new music." (Cl. ANNIBALDI)

Canti del Capricorno •Soprano Voice/Perc/Sx
I Presagi (1958) (9'30) •2 Hn/2 Tpt/Sx/2 Trb/2 Tuba/Perc •Sal
Ixor (1956) (4') •Ssx Solo •Sal
Kya (1959) (11') •Cl or Ssx/EH/Hn/BsCl/Tpt/Trb/Vla/Vcl/Bass •Sal
Maknongan (1976) (4') (to D. KIENTZY) •BsSx Solo •Sal
Pranam I •Asx/Orch (1EH11/1110/2 Vln/1 Vla/1 Vcl/Voice)/Tape
Tre pezzi (1961) (9'40) (3 movements) •Ssx Solo •Sal
Yamaon (1954-58) (10') •Bass Voice/2 Sx: AB/CBsn/Bass/Perc •Sal

SCHAAD, Roar (1941)
Compositeur américain d'origine norvégienne né à Oslo, le 30 X 1941.
Study (1972) (8'30) (to J. BOITOS & F. Bongiorno) •Asx/Tape
20:50 (1971) (20'50) (to K. & S. DORN) •Sx/Tape •DP

SCHAEFER, August H.
David's Dream •Bb Sx/Pno •FMH
The Soloist •Bb Sx/Pno •FMH
The Troubadors •2 Sx: AA •CF

SCHAEFFER, Don
Christmas Duets •2 Sx: AA/Pno •Pro
Duets are Fun •2 Sx •PMV
The Good Sound of Folk Song •Asx Solo
21 Rhythmic Duets •2 Sx •PMV

SCHAFFER, Boguslaw (1929)
Compositeur, théoricien et professeur polonais, né à Lwow, le 6 VI 1929. Travailla avec A. Malawski.

"La succession de ses compositions ne cesse de le confirmer comme l'une des personnalités les plus inventives de l'école moderne polonaise, toutes oeuvres principalement marquées par le souci d'exploiter les ressources pures du son et de constamment remettre en question les problèmes d'écriture et de forme." (Cl. ROSTAND) "Le théâtre musical fréquemment est envisagé par Boguslaw Schaffer comme un des moyens de soumettre à la musique des structures ambiguës, polyvalentes, susceptibles de déclencher une certaine marge d'indétermination. Ses 'musiques d'actions,' *Quartet SG* où la musique n'est en aucune manière subordonnée à une trame dramatique, se situent entre le voir et l'entendre." (D. J-Y. BOSSEUR)

"His early works are based on Polish folk music; later he turned towards constructivistic types of composition; devised a graphic notation indicating intensity of sound, proportional lengths of duration and position of notes in melodic and contrapuntal lines using methods of analytic geometry; in some of his scores he applies polychromatic optical notation." (BAKER) "Schaffer is an unusual figure in Polish music: his prolific creativity and the diversity of his activities are astonishing, but his originality lies in an ability to balance and benefit from the tensions involved in such abundant and multifarious occupations. The theorist supports and sometimes clashes with the composer; the strict, precise analyst contrasts with the intuitive musician of certain works; and a continual dialogue takes place between these and other 'characters' within the single personality. Even when considered solely as a composer, Schaffer appears to contain several isolable creative characters: the composer of music for conventional forces, the electronic composer and the creator of 'happenings.' But these are very often united or intertwined." (B. POCIEJ)

Collage and form n° 80 (1963) •8 Jazz players/Orch •AMP
Concerto per 6 e 3 n° 50 (1960) •Concerto pour 1 soliste changeant (Cl/Sx/Vln/Vcl/Perc/Pno)/3 Orch •PWM
Confrontations n° 148 (1972) •Any solo instrument/Orch •AMP
2 études n° 22 (1956) (3'20) •Asx •adr
Permutations n° 27 (1956) •Fl/Ob/Cl/Sx/Tpt/Trb/Vla/Perc/Harp/Pno •A&S
Proietto simultaneo (1983) (12') (to D. PITUCH) •Soprano Voice/Vln/ Pno/Ob/Sx/Tape
Quatuor SG.7 n° 112 (1968) •2 Pno or 4 Sx: SATB/2 optional instruments •AMP
S'alto n° 71 (1963) (15'30) •Asx/Chamber Orch (1121/121/2 Perc/ Harp/Pno/Str) •PWM
Sonatina n° 3 (1946) •Asx Solo •adr
Sound forms n° 58 (1961) (6') •Asx Solo •adr

SCHALLOCK, Ralf
Compositeur allemand.
So ach... chaos (1993) •Tsx/Tape •INM

SCHANKE, David
Five Mellow Winds (1959) (to the memory of G. Miller) •4 Sx: AATB/Cl •Chap

SCHARWENKA, Waver Franz (1850-1926)
Polish Dance (BROOKE) •AATB •CF

SCHATER, J.
Suite •Asx/Pno •Pres

SCHÄUBLE, Nikolaus
Compositeur allemand.
Ellington Medley (1990) (12') •SATB

SCHEDRIN, R.
Compositeur russe.
Nachahmung Albenis •Asx/Pno

SCHEIFES, Hans M.
Vier kleine Stücken alter Meister •3 Sx: SAT •TM

SCHENGOUNOV
Compositeur russe.
Blues-marche - 2 Inventions •Asx/Pno

SCHENK, Richard
Sometimes (1983) (to J. HILL) •Asx/Pno

SCHERR, Hans Jörg (1935)
Compositeur allemand.
Quartett n° 1 (1964) (Allegro giocoso - Scherzo - Presto) •SATB

SCHIAFFINI, Giancarlo (1942)
Compositeur et tromboniste italien, né à Roma. Autodidacte influencé par Stockhausen, Ligeti, et Globokar.
Aleune considerazioni sul sesso delle scale
Falsobordone (1984) (to Quatuor Gabriel Pierné) •SATB
Pieces d'April (1989) •Asx Solo

SCHIBLER, Armin (1920)

Compositeur suisse, né à Kreuzlingen, le 20 XI 1920. Travailla avec Müller, Frey, et Burkhard puis, en Angleterre, avec Rubbra et Tippett. A Darmstadt, il subit l'influence de Fortner, Leibowitz, Krenek, et Adorno.

"L'un des très féconds et des plus éclectiques compositeurs de l'école alémanique." (Cl. Rostand) "Souvent influencé d'I. Stravinsky."

"Schibler's lively interest in all contemporary music led him to an involvement with jazz. Through Adorno he became aware of the sociological implications of music, and this brought about his use of melodramatic techniques in drawing reciprocal relationships between words in music." (F. Muggler)

Konzertante fantaisie (1978) (to I. Roth) •Asx/Orch •Eul
Quartet (1978) (to I. Roth) 1) Lento, quasi senza tempo 2) Allegro vivace 3) Andante 4) Quasi presto •SATB

SCHIEMANN, Christian (1823-1915)

Seven Characteristic Studies •Mus

SCHIFFMANN, Harold (1928)

Compositeur américain.

Capriccio Concertante (1987) (to D. Underwood) •Asx/Wind ensemble or Pno
Concertino (1982) 1) Vivo 2) Lento e flessible 3) Preciso •Sx Ensemble

SCHIFRIN, Lalo (Boris) (1932)

Compositeur et musicien de jazz américain d'origine argentine. Travailla avec J. C. Paz et, à Paris, avec O. Messiaen. Installé aux U.S.A. depuis 1958.

Jazz Faust - ballet (1963) (20') •Asx/Tpt/Pno/Bass/Perc •MJQ
Mount Olive (3') •Asx/Guit/Pno/Bass/Perc •MJQ

SCHILLING, Hans Ludwig (1927)

Compositeur allemand, né le 9 III 1927, à Mayen (Rhenanie). Travailla avec Genzmer, Uetel, Gurlitt, Zenk, et Hindemith.

"His early compositions stand within the Brahms-Reger tradition, although the occasional use of modal structures, isorhythm and canon reveals his interest in medieval music. His first dodecaphonic works, written in the early 1950s, retain a harmonic relationship with Hindemith; later, as his employment of serial technique became more strict, the influence of Dallapiccola became evident. Schilling's most individual works were written after 1960, and they show a variety of means of juxtaposing musical materials. Jazz elements, quodlibet technique and instrumental contrast are all characteristic of his later style." (G. W. Loomis)

VII Bicinia serena (1968) (4') 1) Alla marcia-poco allegro 2) Arietta-Andantino 3) Allegro molto 4) Recitando-libero in tempo ma allegretto 5) Allegro vivace 6) Tempo di siciliano 7) Ben presto - Finale •2 Sx: AA or BB •B&B
Concerto für Saxophon Quartett (1986) (9') •SATB •B&B
Dialogue (1983) •Asx/Org
4 Dialoge (1976) (8') 1) Andante 2) Poco allegretto 3) Adagio amabile 4) Allegro vivace •Sx/Org •adr
Grande saxophonie - Quodlibet (1978) (to J-M. Londeix) •12 Sx: SAT + SATB + SATBBs •adr
Intonation und Partita "Erschienen ist der herrlich Tag" (1982) (12') •Asx/Org •B&B
Passions - Partita (1992) (10') •Asx/Org •adr
Sonatine (1978) (13'30) (to J-M. Londeix) 1) Ouverture 2) Allegretto 3) Ostinato 4) Allegro •Sx Solo •Bil
Suite nostalgique (1991) (10') 1) Adagio-Allegro vivace (Cl. Debussy-zitat) 2) Tristan lasst grussen! Andante (R. Wagner-zitat) 3) Allegretto-Presto (Stravinsky-zitat) 4) Adagio religioso (R. Strauss-zitat) 5) Allegro moderato (M. Ravel-zitat) •SATB

Trisax (1978) (12') (to J-M. Londeix) 1) Recitativo 2) Arietta 3) Choral 4) Rondetto •3 Sx: ATB •B&B

SCHILLING, Otto-Erich

Überall ist Wunderland •Voice/Fl/Cl/Sx/Tpt/2 Vln/Bass/Perc/ Accordion/Pno •SeMC

SCHILLINGER, Franz (1964)

Farbmodelle (10') •Asx Solo

SCHIMMEL, William

Quartet (1982) (to Amherst Saxophone Quartet) •SATB

SCHLAISH, Kennet

9'65 •Sx/Trb •SMIC

SCHLEI, Wolfgang (1941)

Compositeur allemand, né à Halle-au-der-Saale.

Invention (1986) (4') •SATB •Uni

SCHLIEPHACKE, Jan Jakob

Compositeur allemand.

Zwang (1993) •Asx/Perc •INM

SCHLOTHAUER, Burkhard

Compositeur allemand.

Something lost-töne (1993) •Ssx/Pno •INM

SCHLUMPF, Martin

Compositeur suisse.

Onyx (1983) •Asx/Vcl •Hug

SCHMADTKE, Harry (1929)

Contrebassiste et compositeur allemand, né le 14 XII 1929, à Berlin.

Joining Konzertstück (1980) (5') •Asx/Pno •adr
Monolog (1980) (10') •Tsx Solo •adr

SCHMALTZ, E.

Strictly for Saxes •5 Sx: AATTB •BD

SCHMELZER, August (1924-1982)

Organiste et compositeur allemand né le 8 VI 1924 à Ludwigshafen, où il est mort le 21 XI 1982.

Quartett (1981) (Andante - Allegro - Moderato - Allegretto) •SATB •adr

SCHMIDT, Arthur Paul (1846-1921)

Editeur américain, d'origine allemande, né le 1er IV 1846 à Altona (Allemagne), mort à Boston, le 5 V 1921.

2 Pièces •Asx/Pno •Mau

SCHMIDT, Joseph (17xx-1780)

Finale (from *Quartetto IV*) (Brink) •2 Cl/Tsx/Tuba or 4 Sx: SATB •Mol

SCHMIDT, William (1926)

Compositeur américain, né à Chicago, le 6 III 1926. Travailla avec H. Stevens et I. Dahl.

Concertino for Piano •Pno/4 Sx: SATB •WIM
Concerto (1981) (14') (to R. Greenberg) •Tsx/Wind Orch •WIM
Concerto (1983) (20') (to D. Masek) •Asx/Symphonic Wind Ensemble •WIM
Jazz Suite (3 movements) •2 Tsx/Perc •WIM
A Little Midnight Music (1970) (4') •Asx/Pno •WIM
Music for Unaccompanied Saxophone •Sx Solo •WIM
Prelude and Rondo •SATB •WIM
Rondoletto •Bsx/Pno •WIM
Sonata (1979) (to R. Greenberg) (3 movements) •Bsx/Pno •WIM

Sonatina (1967) 1) March 2) Sinfonia 3) Rondoletto •Tsx/Pno
•WIM
Suite (1963) (12') 1) Prelude 2) Capriccio 3) Pavane 4) Galliard
5) Finale •SATB •AvMu/WIM
Suite (1978) 1) Toccata 2) Waltz 3) Rhythmic study no. 2 •Sx Solo
Ten Contemporary Etudes (1963) •WIM
Twelve Concert Duets •2 Sx •WIM
Variations on a Theme of Prokofiev •2 Sx •WIM
Variegations (1973) (10') •Asx/Org •adr

SCHMIDT-HAMBROCK, Jochen (1955)

Compositeur allemand, né le 21 II 1955, à Wuppertal.
ARD - Sportschau (1984) (10') •Guit/Asx/Perc/Synth •adr
How could it happen (1983) (7') •Sx/Perc •adr
Ozie - Jazz waltz (1982) (10') •Sx/Guit/Perc •adr

SCHMIDT-MECHAU, Friedman

Compositeur allemand.
Differenz und begegnung (1993) •Tsx/Perc •INM

SCHMIT, Camille (1908-1976)

Compositeur et organiste belge, né à Aubarge, le 30 III 1908, mort à Lemelette, le 11 V 1976. Travailla avec J. et L. Jongen puis avec A. Souris.

"Camille Schmit a adopté dans plusieurs de ses compositions les moyens de l'écriture polytonale et celle du dodécaphonisme. Après quoi, cette discipline évoluera vers un mode d'expression qui utilise les ressources du total chromatisme."

"His creative output may be divided into two periods: in the first he was strongly influenced by Stravinsky, but in 1948 he turned, under Souris' influence, to 12-note serialism. In later works the constraints of serial writing did not inhibit Schmit's originality." (H. VANHULST)
Polyphonics (1970) (10') •SATB •CBDM

SCHMITT, Florent (1870-1958)

Compositeur français, né à Blâmant (Meurthe-et-Moselle), le 28 IX 1870. Mort à Paris, le 17 VIII 1958. Travailla avec Gedalge, Messager, et G. Fauré. Prix de Rome (1900). Membre de l'Institut (1936).

"Un musicien de grand tempérament, une généreuse nature, un artiste sans compromission." (Cl. ROSTAND) "Si, comme Berlioz il a ouvertement préféré la couleur à la nuance et s'est montré désarmé devant les sollicitations d'un matériau sonore pléthorique et des paroxysme frénétiques, son style s'est soudain amendé et s'est imprégné d'une sorte de sérénité enjouée souvent narquoise et capricieuse, mais d'un optimisme amène." "La *Légende*, op. 66, d'une intense couleur orientale annonce un des aspects de la magnifique musique de scène *Antoine et Cléopâtre*." (R. BERNARD) "Dans des pièces sollicitées en apparence par une donnée extérieure il conserve le sens d'un ordre voulu, purement musical, soutenu par une riche technique, et un sens profond de la poésie." (P. Le FLEM) "Il a le goût des chatoyances orientales… Une limpidité gracieuse, un classicisme équilibré, une discrétion et une éloquence de moyens qui rejoignent la tradition la plus pure des polyphonistes français." (P. WOLFF) "Classique par son art de la construction et la précision de son langage, romantique par son pouvoir de suggestion et sa fougue, réaliste par son amour de la vérité." (Y. HUCHER) "Un classique, un homme qui a utilisé le langage musical des compositeurs de son temps, mais avec une telle habileté qu'il semble parler une autre langue, une langue universellement appréciée et dont la portée a été très grande." (Cl. BRACH) "L'oeuvre, diverse, de Florent Schmit est celle d'un maître de l'orchestre—un symphoniste-né—, de même que de l'écriture instrumentale. Sa musique, à l'image de sa personnalité franche et assez rude, n'a guère subi d'influences,—bien que Schmit ait parfaitement connu les oeuvres d'un Debussy, d'un Stravinski ou d'un Schönberg; l'inspiration mélodique est généreuse, le langage harmonique riche jusqu'à la complexité." (F. R. TRANCHEFORT)

His formative years were spent in the ambient of French symbolism in poetry and Impressionism in music, and he followed these directions in his programmatically conceived orchestral music; but he developed a strong, distinctive style of his own, mainly by elaborating the contrapuntal fabric of his works and extending the rhythmic design to unprecedented asymmetrical combinations; he also exploited effects of primitivistic percussion, in many respects anticipating the developments of modern Russian music. He was not averse to humor; several of his works have topical allusions." (BAKER) "His invention is not particularly memorable, and it may be doubted whether much of his music will be often revisited except by way of curiosity; but the interest of connoisseurs in it will continue to be justified, not only because Schmitt's music differs from that of other French masters, but also because it has many positive qualities to recommend it; vigour, eloquence, passion, understanding of various media and masterly if at times too lavish orchestration to mention only some of the most immediately striking." (E. BLOM)
Andante religioso, op. 109 •SATB
Le songe de Coppelius (3') •Bb Sx/Pno •Lem
Légende, op. 66 (1918) (9') (to Mme E. HALL) •Asx/Orch (3333/434/Perc/Harp/Str) or Asx/Pno •Dur
Quatuor, op. 102 (1941) (to Quatuor M. Mule) 1) Avec une sage décision 2) Vif 3) Assez lent 4) Animé sans excès •SATB •Dur

SCHMUTZ, Albert Daniel (1887-1975)

Compositeur et professeur américain, né à Halstead (Kansas), le 11 X 1887.
Divertimento •Asx/Pno •WWS
Introduction, Recitativo and Choral •4 Sx: SATB or AATB •AMPC
Prelude and Final •4 Sx: SATB or AATB •AMPC
Sax-impro-ruba-sation •Asx/Pno
Sonata (1961) (to S. RASCHER) (Allegro - Andante sostenuto - Rondo) •Asx/Pno •SMP

SCHNEEBIEGEL, Rolf

Valse habelice (1987) •SATB •GB

SCHNEIDER, Catherine

Le Promeneur - 7 pièces pour les premières années (1993) 1) Le départ 2) En flânant 3) La pluie 4) Arc-en-ciel 5) Après la pluie 6) Hésitations sur le retour 7) Arrivée triomphale •Asx/Pno •Lem

SCHNEIDER, Stephan

Compositeur allemand.
Tripes de roche (1993) •Asx/Electr. Guit •INM

SCHNEIDERT, Arturo Eric (1929)

Instrumentiste argentin, né le 22 VIII 1929 à Santa Fe. Travailla à Buenos Aires avec J. Grisigrione et R. Lavecchia.
Coctel de ritmos (1954) •Asx/Pno

SCHOEMAKER, Maurice (1890-1964)

Compositeur belge, né à Anderlecht, le 27 XII 1890, mort à Bruxelles, le 24 VIII 1964. Travailla avec P. Gilson. Fit partie du groupe des "Synthétistes," au milieu desquels il sut, tout comme M. Poot, conserver ses caractéristiques proprement flamandes.

"Maurice Schoemaker a cherché tout de suite à rejoindre la tradition impressionniste établie par P. Gilson, et en intégrant les acquisitions de la musique de son temps." (A. CORBET)

"While assimilating the general European tendencies, Maurice Schoemaker drew for his thematic material on native folk music." (BAKER) "The rich orchestration and evocation nature of his orchestral music seek to express something of the Flemish character." (C. MERTENS)
Sinfonia da camera (1929) (20') •4 Sx: SATB/Orch •CBDM

SCHOENBERG, Arnold (1874-1951)

Von heute auf Morgen, op. 32 (Pennetier) •2 Voices/Cl/Asx/Pno

SCHOLLUM, Robert

Konzertstück, op. 106 (1978) •Asx/Pno •ApE

Elegie mit Unterbrechungen, op. 130 (1985) (to Rascher Quartet) •SATB •ECA/Dob/ApE

Veränderungen, op. 81a (1970) 1) Sehr ruhig 2) Sehr bewegt, scharf 3) Sehr langsam 4) Lebhafter marschzeitmass 5) Fliessend, doch im Charakter majestätisch 6) Sehr langsam 7) Höchst Lebendig und durchwegs mit 'drive' •2 Melodic instruments/Perc •Dob

SCHOLTENS

Claus fantasie •Bb Sx/Pno •TM

SCHÖNBACH, Dieter (1931)

Compositeur allemand né à Stolp (Pomeranie), le 18 II 1931. Travailla avec W. Fortner.

"Schönbach is, with Riedl, one of the foremost German exponents of mixed-media composition. Since 1960 he has engaged in collaborative ventures with visual artists, choreographers and film directors, and even in his 'pure' works he makes use of Kandinsky's theory of elements in pictorial form, disposing his materials as 'surfaces,' 'points,' 'silences' and 'curves.' Many of his pieces require graphic projections, sometimes prepared by other artists." (D. Gojowy)

Canzona (1970) •Asx/Band •adr

SCHÖNBERG, Stig Gustav (1933)

Organiste et compositeur suédois, né le 13 V 1933, à Norrköping. Travailla avec Larsson et Blomdahl puis, en Belgique, avec Peeters.

"His style radiates austerity and objectivity; the are no outpourings of feeling or temperament. In form, Schönberg inclines towards classical models, the less restricted, quasi-improvisatory forms of the Baroque (toccatas and preludes) and various models of moderate thematic development." (H-G. P.)

Sostetto per fiati, op. 85 (1979-80) (14') •Fl/Ob/Cl/1 Sx: S+A/Hn/Bsn •STIM

SCHONFELDER, Jorg (15th century)

Mich hat grob (Rippe) •3 Sx: ATB •DP

SCHONHERR, Max (1903)

Musicologue, chef d'orchestre, et compositeur autrichien, né à Marburg (Slovenie), le 23 XI 1903. Travailla avec H. Frisch et R. von Mojsisovics.

"He came to specialize in light music, and his radio performances of Viennese operetta and dance music displayed a rare sense of Viennese style." (T. Wohnhaas)

Appasionato, op. 48 •Asx/Pno •Hof

SCHOONENBEEK, Kees (1947)

Compositeur néerlandais.

Kwartet (1982) (13') (to Brabants Saxophone Quartet) 1) Koraal I-Allegro energico 2) Koraal II 3) Prelude en fuga 4) Koraal III 5) Finale •SATB •Don

Tournée (19'30) (for H. de Jong) 1) Andante-molto rubato 2) Allegro 3) Andante commodo 4) Allegro energico-corrente-Allegro energico 5) Andante misterioso 6) Allegro con brio •Asx/Orch •Don

Tre Capricci (1985) (10') •Asx/Pno •Don

SCHOSER, Brian

Traces •Ob/Cl/Asx/Bsn

SCHREIBER, Frederic C. (1895-19xx)

Compositeur américain d'origine autrichienne, né à Vienne, le 13 I 1895. Aux U.S.A. depuis 1939.

Concerto Grosso (1955) •2 Coloratura Soprano Voices/Asx/Tpt/Pno

SCHRIJVER, K. de

Compositeur flamand.

Caprice •Bb Sx/Pno •Scz

Concerto •Bb Sx/Pno •Scz

Drie-delige-suite •SATB •TM

Exotic pavane •Bb Sx/Pno •Scz

Miniatur concerto •Bb Sx/Pno •Scz

Quadrichromie •SATB •Scz

Romanza •Asx/Pno •Scz

Scherzo •Asx/Pno •Scz

SCHROEN

Russian Elegy •Bb Sx/Pno •CF

SCHROYENS, Daniel

Compositeur belge.

Rapsodie (1976) •SATB

SCHUBACK, Peter (1947)

Violoncelliste et compositeur suédois., né à Täby, le 31 III 1947. Travailla avec G. Gröndahl, S. Palm, et M. Tortellier à Paris.

"Peter Schuback became interested in new music and in questions relating to music and the function of musicians while he was still a student." (S J)

A Priori (1983) (45') •Sx/Trb/Perc/Vlc/Pno/Harps •Tons/SMIC

SCHUBERT, Franz (1797-1828)

Adieu (Klosé-Corroyez) •Tsx/Pno •Bel

Andante, op. 29 (Teal) •SATB •Eto

Arpeggione Sonate (Kelton) •Tsx/Pno

Ave Maria •2 Sx: TT/Pno •Elk

Ave Maria (Martin) •Asx or Bb Sx/Pno •Mar

The Bee (Leeson) •Asx/Pno •HiCol

Berceuse (Baudrier) •Asx or Bb Sx/Pno •HE/Mol

Célèbre marche militaire (Gilet) •SATB •Mar/Rub

Le Désir (Klosé) •Asx/Pno •Led

Du bist die Ruh' (Overveld) •Asx or Bb Sx/Pno •TM

The Erl King (Farewell) •Bb Sx or Eb Sx/Pno •CF

Impromptu (Londeix) •Bb Sx/Pno •Led

Marche militaire (Holmes) •5 Sx: AAATB •Rub

Menuetto, op. 78 •4 Sx: AATB or SATB •NW

Minuetto (Teal) (Album) •Bb Sx/Pno •GSch

Moment musical, op. 94 n° 3 •Bb Sx/Pno •Ric

Moment musical, op. 94 (Andreoni) •Asx/Pno •Ric

Moment musical (Thomson) •AATB •Alf

My sweet repose (Buchtel) •Bb Sx/Pno •Kjos

Rosamunde •Bb Sx/Pno •Mol

Rosamunde - Andante (Rascher) •Tsx/Pno •Bel

Salve Regina (Speets) •SATB •TM

Schubertiade (Londeix) •Fl/Ob/Cl/Asx/Hn/Bsn

Sei mir gegrusst •Bb Sx/Pno •Mol

Serenade •Eb Sx/Pno •CF

Serenade •2 Sx: AT/Pno •Cen

Serenade (Damm) •Bb Sx/Pno •CBet

Serenade (Holmes) •AATB •Bar

Sérénade (Mule) •Asx/Pno •Led

Sérénade (Segoin) •Asx/Pno •Bil

Sérénade d'amour (Viard) •Asx/Pno •Sal

Sonate "Arpeggione" (Shinn) •Asx/Pno •WWS

Ständchen (Overveld) •Asx or Bb Sx/Pno •TM

Suite de valses (Londeix) •Bb Sx/Pno •Led

Symphonic Theme (Ostling) •AATB •BM

Wandering Brooklet (Buchtel) •2 Sx: AT •Kjos

SCHUDEL, Thomas

Pentagram (1987) (14') 1) Intrada 2) Song 3) Scherzo 4) Elegy
    5) Finale •4 Sx: SATB/Perc •DP/CMC
Two Images (4') •Asx/Pno •Ken

SCHULER, Thomas Herwig (1961)

Compositeur autrichien, né à Vienne, le 18 I 1961.
Bagatelle, op. 13 (1992) (5') •12 Sx: SnoSSAAATTTBBBs •CA
Konzert, op. 8 (20') •Bsx/Str Orch •CA
Quartett, op. 5 (1991) (15') (to Vienna Saxophone Quartet) •SATB
    •CA

SCHULHOFF, Ervin (1894-1942)

Compositeur et pianiste tchèque, né à Prague, le 8 VI 1894, mort dans
un camp de concentration (Wülzbourg), le 18 VIII 1942. Travailla avec
M. Reger et Debussy.

"Il s'engagea d'abord dans une action d'avant-garde polytonale et
essaya d'incorporer le jazz à la musique traditionnelle." (Cl. ROSTAND)
"Ervin Schulhoff était issu d'une vieille famille juive pragoise. Ses
oeuvres des années 1930 sont pour l'essentiel marquées par son
penchant pour le jazz et la musique de danse moderne. Durant cette
période il interprétait avant tout de la musique nouvelle il devint en
outre un pianiste de jazz recherché. Il réussit à réaliser une synthèse du
jazz et des musiques occidentales traditionnelles. Ainsi devint-il le
modèle de nombreux compositeurs tchèques contemporains." (S.
BENSMANN)

"In his music he followed the modernistic ideas of the period between
the two wars emphasizing the grotesque and making use of atonal and
polytonal devices." (BAKER) "As a skilled and remarkably prolific
composer he showed surprising elasticity of style, having been influenced by the most recent tendencies of his time." (G. CHOUQUET) "As
a pianist he was the first to play the quarter-tone pieces of Hàba and his
pupil. From the early 1920s he was active as a jazz pianist, also using
jazz idioms in his compositions. A versatile composer, Schulhoff
readily responded to the trends of the day, from Germanic late
Romanticism to impressionism, expressionism, the use of jazz, neo-
classicism, socialist realism and Bartokian folklorism." (J. BEK)

Hot-sonate, op. 70 (1930) (15'30) (Der Funk-Stunde A.G. in Berlin)
    (4 movements) •Asx/Pno •Sch
Serenata •Asx/Pno •CF

SCHULLER, Gunther (1925)

Compositeur, professeur, corniste, et chef d'orchestre américain, né
à New York, le 22 XI 1925. Autodidacte, il fit du jazz avec le Modern
Jazz Quartet et, depuis 1959, se consacre à la composition.

"L'un des chefs de file de l'avant-garde américaine, avec Earle
Brown et Morton Feldman, mais de style infiniment moins rigoureux
et plus éclectique que ceux-ci. Son style a été sériel presque aussitôt.
Ses oeuvres inspirées par le jazz indiquaient une extrême habileté
(1944-1958) que l'on retrouve dans ses compositions de la seconde
période. Ses oeuvres témoignent souvent d'une grande virtuosité
orchestrale, mais aussi d'une rigueur de style parfois discutable en
raison de certaines concessions à l'effet facile." (Cl. ROSTAND) "C'est
un mérite, et non des moindres, d'avoir intégré sans heurt le jazz au
vocabulaire moderne. Il y a des lustres qu'on cherchait et que les
meilleurs ont échoué. Schuller, lui, a réussi cette idéale synthèse en
mettant toujours 'en situation' les éléments jazz de la partition et,
mieux en remontant aux sources de ce qui est commun au deux
langages." (M. FLEURET)

"As a composer Schuller is entirely self-taught. His interests cover
the Western tradition as well as modern art and popular forms; but,
though he draws on many sources, he is more syncretist than eclectic.
His aim appears to be, at least in part, the amalgamation of diverse
techniques, styles and aesthetics with a view to evolving hybrids
possessing a new viability, adaptability and communicative power. His

development was marked by a protean assimilation of styles and
genres, but especially of jazz, an unerring instinct for instrumental
technique and orchestration, a decreasing dependence on textures of
accompanied melody and a growing freedom in the modelling of sound
masses, and the movement from a somewhat self-conscious rhetoric to
a fuller integration of powerful gestures into the deeper structure." (A.
CLARKSON)

Abstraction (1959) (5') •Asx/Guit/Perc/2 Vln/Vla/Vcl/2 Bass •MJQ
Concerto (1983) (17') (to J. ALLARD, commissioned by the students
    of Joe Allard) (Allegro moderato - Molto adagio - Lively) •Asx/
    Orch (222BsCl2/4331/Harp/Perc/Celesta/Str) •AMP
Tribute to Rudy Wiedoeft (1978) (7'43) 1) Valse Erica 2) Saxarella
    3) Saxophobia •Asx/Band •CPP
12 by 11 (8'30) •Fl/Cl/Tsx/Hn/Trb/Vibr/Pno/Harp/Bass/Perc •MJQ

SCHULTE, Peter (1959)

Compositeur allemand, né le 22 IX 1959 à Hemer.
Du (Jazz ballade) (1983) (10') •Asx/Pno/Perc •adr
Samba für Birgit (Latin-jazz) (1983) (5-10') •Asx/Tpt/Perc/Pno •adr

SCHULZ, Johann Peter (1747-1800)

Little March (RASCHER) •Bsx/Pno •Bel

SCHULZ, Rüdiger

Compositeur allemand.
Herr Band - Herr Sax (1993) •Asx/Bandoneon •INM

SCHULZE, Werner

Compositeur allemand.
2 Duos (12') •Fl/Asx/Bsn •CA
Transplantazioni - 3 duos •Fl/Asx/Bsn •CA

SCHUMAN, William Howard (1910)

Quaterttino (RASCHER) •AATB •PIC/Peer

SCHUMANN, Gerrhard (1914)

Petite suite •Fl/Sx/EH/Cl •IMD

SCHUMANN, Robert (1810-1856)

Album pour la jeunesse (CAENS) 1) Le cavalier sauvage 2) Chanson
    populaire 3) Le gai laboureur 4) Chanson du nord 5) Premier
    chagrin 6) Chanson du faucheur 7) L'étranger •SATB •Mar
Andantino (MERRIMAN) •Tsx/Pno •South
Célèbre Rêverie (VIARD) •Asx/Pno •Sal
Chant du soir •Asx or Bb Sx/Pno •Mil
Chant du soir (CHAUVET) •Asx/Pno •Mar
Einsame Blumen •Bb Sx/Pno •JS
Fantasy Piece, op. 73, no. 3 (TEAL) •Asx/Pno •GSch
Fantasiestücke, op. 73 (1849) (MOORE) •Tsx/Pno
Folk Song (MERRIMAN) •Tsx/Pno •South
Four Short Pieces (RASCHER) •AATB •BM
Happy Farmer (RASCHER) •Bsx/Pno •Bel
Le gai laboureur (ROMBY) •Asx/Pno •PB
Die Lotusblume (CLUWEN) •Tsx/Pno •Mol
Pièces pour la jeunesse (MULE) •Asx/Pno •Led
Rêverie •Asx/Pno •CF
Rêverie (DYCK) •SATB •Braun
Rêverie (MOLENAAR) •Bb Sx/Pno •Mol
Romance (TEAL) (Album) •Bb Sx/Pno •GSch
Romance Nos. 1, 2, 3 (NIHILL) •Ssx/Pno •DP
Romance and Traumerei •Bb Sx/Pno •CBet
Scènes d'enfants - Rêverie (MULE) •Asx/Pno •Led
Song and March •4 Sx: AATB or SATB •Ken
Three Romances (HEMKE) •Asx/Pno •South
Traumerei •AATB •Alf
Traumerei (RASCHER) •Asx/Pno •Bel

Zwei Kinderszenen, op. 15, no. 8 & 9 (WILLIAMS) •5 Sx: SAATB
•South

SCHUST, Alfred (1915)

Pianiste et compositeur allemand, né le 29 IX 11915 à Berlin.
Travailla avec Blacher.

Trio (1984) •Fl/Asx/Trb •adr

SCHWANTNER, Joseph (1943)

Compositeur américain, né le 22 III 1943, à Chicago.

Diaphona intervallum (1966) (12') •Asx/Pno/Fl/Str sextet (2 Vln/
Vla/2 Vcl/Bass) •ACA

Concertino (Withdrawn by composer) •Asx/Chamber Orch •ACA

Entropy (1968) (to F. HEMKE) •Ssx/BsCl/Vcl •DP/ACA

SCHWARE

Fantasiestück •Asx/Harp •WWS

SCHWARTZ, Elliott (1936)

Compositeur américain né à Brooklyn (New York), le 19 I 1936.
Travailla avec J. Beeson et P. Creston, puis avec Brant, Chou Wen-
Cung, et Wolpe.

"Schwartz's large output of instrumental music displays a broad
knowledge of contemporary techniques; his colourful and everchanging
sonorities are not diffuse, but convey an almost romantic continuity of
line and expressiveness of design. An element of theatre entered into
much of his music after 1967." (B. ARCHIBALD)

Chamber Concerto IV (1981) (12') (to J. SAMPEN) •1 Sx: A+S/
Chamber Ensemble (001 Cl+BsCl 1/0110/3 Perc/Vln/Vla/Vcl
•adr

Cleveland Doubles (1981) (to H. SMITH) •1 Player: Asx+Cl/Wind
Ensemble •adr

Music for Soloist and Audience •Sx Solo •DP

SCHWARTZ, Francis

Daiamoni (5') (to D. KIENTZY) •Asx/Fl/Bass

Sex-Six-Sax (1990) (5') (to D. KIENTZY) •Asx/Dispositif électro-
acoust.

SCHWARTZ, George

International Folk Suite (1973) 1) In the town (France) 2) Carol of
the bagpipes (Sicily) 3) The Wassail song (England) 4) Summer
is icumen in (England) 5) Lovely moon (Germany)
6) Valencianita (Venezuela) •Tsx/Pno •South

SCHWARZ, Gunter

Compositeur allemand.

Nr. 37 (1993) •Sx/Gong •INM

SCHWARZ, Ira Paul

Sax serenade •AATB •Barn

Sax bleu (1985) (6') (to Cl. DECUGIS) •4 Sx: SATB/Band

Canzone •AATB •Rub

SCHWEIGER, Rudolph

Compositeur américain.

Concert suite •Asx/Pno

SCHWEINITZ, Wolfgang von (1933)

Compositeur allemand, né à Hamburg, le 7 II 1933. Travailla avec E.
G. Klussmann et G. Ligeti.

Musik für vier Saxophone, op. 25 (1986) (10'30) •SATB •B&H

SCHWERTSIK, Kurt (1935)

Compositeur et corniste autrichien, né le 25 VI 1935, à Vienne.
Travailla avec Marx et Schiske puis à Darmstadt.

"In his compositions he tries to bring the somewhat discredited
category of entertainment art back to a position of importance, as in pop

art or Viennese 'fantastic realism.' He deliberately uses well-worn
extracts from tonal (sometimes trivial) music, manipulating these with
irony and detachment as collage to make new and surprising constel-
lation." (M. LICHTENFELD)

Liebesträume, op. 7 (1963) •Asx/Trb/Pno/Vibr/Marimba/
Harmonium/Bass •EMod

Salotto romano, op. 5 (1961) •BsCl/Bsx/Bsn/Hn/Trb/Tuba/Perc/
Bass/Vcl/Guit •EMod

SCHWEYER, Bruno

Konzertstück (1983) •Tsx/Fl/Cl/Vln/Vcl/Pno

SCIORTINO, Patrice (1922)

Compositeur français, né à Paris, le 26 VII 1922. Travailla à la Schola
Cantorum, puis au Groupe de Recherche musicales de l'ORTF.

"Dans l'esprit d'un renouvellement du vocabulaire sonore, ses
propres recherches sont un peu marginales." (Cl. ROSTAND) "Musique
aux sonorités plutôt vives et tumultueuses d'où le pittoresque n'est pas
exclu."

Agogik (1974) (11') (to Quatuor de la Garde Républicaine) •SATB
•Chou

Danse païenne, op. 10 (1960) (4'30) (to G. NOUAUX) •SATB •Chou

Falw (1984) (7') •Bsx (or Asx or Tsx)/1 Perc (Cymbal/Temple
blocks/Toms) •Led

Flammes (1969) (to Quatuor d'Anches Français) •Ob+EH/Cl+Basset
Horn/1 Sx: A+B/Bsn+CBsn •adr

Moulin du temps •Vibr/Guit/Vla/Asx •adr

Rapsodique (to P. PAREILLE) •Ob/Cl/Asx/Bsn

Sapiaxono •Asx/Pno •adr

Sonances (1992) (18') 1) Souffle! 2) Prends 3) Frappe 4) Embrasse!
•Asx/Orch or Pno •Bil

3 Signatures (1978) •Ob/Cl/Asx •adr

SCIPIONE, Umberto

Compositeur italien.

Agressivo II •SATB

Miniature (1992) (6') 1) Folksong 2) Adagio 3) Allegro •SATB

SCLATER, James (1943)

Compositeur américain, né à Mobile (Alabama), le 24 X 1943.
Travailla avec M. Peter et W. Presser.

Suite (6'30) (to W. SMITH) 1) Prelude 2) Song 3) Dance •Sx Solo
•TP/Elk

SCOGNA, Flavio Emilio (1956)

Compositeur et chef d'orchestre italien, né à Savona. Travailla avec
G. Manzino, F. Ferrara puis avec L. Berio.

Duplum (to F. MONDELCI) •Asx Solo •BMG

Riflesi (1990) •SATB •BMG

SCOTT

Metodo para saxofono •UME

SCOTT, Andy

Hard to Please •5 Sx: AATTB or SATTB/Pno/Bass/Drums •PBP

Moving Low •5 Sx: AATTB or SATTB/Pno/Bass/Drums •PBP

One for the Tavern •5 Sx: AATTB or SATTB/Pno/Bass/Drums
•PBP

Rock Blues •5 Sx: AATTB or SATTB/Pno/Bass/Drums •PBP

Spring •5 Sx: AATTB or SATTB/Pno/Bass/Drums •PBP

Symphony for Saxophones •SATB or AATB •PBP

Travellin' Home •5 Sx: AATTB or SATTB/Pno/Bass/Drums •PBP

Waltz for the Devil •5 Sx: AATTB or SATTB/Pno/Bass/Drums
•PBP

Whithershins Waltz •5 Sx: AATTB or SATTB/Pno/Bass/Drums
•PBP

SCOTT, C.
Lotus Land, op. 47, no. 1 (5') •Asx/Orch or Pno

SCOTT, Cleve
Compositeur américain.
Rimes, rilles, rings (1988) (to J. SAMPEN) •Asx/Pno/Tape

SCOTT, Jack
Quartet •SATB

SCOTT, James (1886-1938)
Pianiste de jazz américain.
Frog Logs Rag •5 Sx: SAATB

SCOTT, Richard P. (1953)
Compositeur suédois.
En kloyenes morktchen (1984) •Asx/Org/Perc •STIM

SCOTT, Ronnie David (1927)
Saxophoniste-ténor de jazz anglais, né le 28 I 1927 à Londres.
Dark Flowers (1988) (13') (for E. WATERMANN) •Fl/Asx/Guit/Perc

SCOTT, Rupert (1945)
Compositeur anglais.
Quartet (1971) (13') (to London Saxophone Quartet) •SATB
Suite (1973) (14') (to Myrha Saxophone Quartet) •SATB

SCOTT, Tommy Lee (1912-1961)
Chanteur, guitariste, et compositeur américain, né à Toccoa (Georgia), le 28 V 1912, mort à New York, le 12 VIII 1961. Travailla avec H. Kerr et W. Riegger.
Lento (1953) •Asx/Str Orch or Pno

SCRIABIN, Alexander (1872-1919)
Etude, op. 8 n° 2 (DIERCKS) •Asx/Pno •BMP
Prélude, op. 9 n° 1 (DIERCKS) •Asx/Pno •BMP

SEAMARKS, Colin (1943)
Compositeur anglais.
Quartet (1971) (5') (to London Saxophone Quartet) •SATB

SEBASTIANI, Fausto
Compositeur italien.
Solo (1989) •Ssx Solo

SECO, Manuel (1958)
Compositeur espagnol.
Concierto de la Senda n° 4 (1988) (12') (to Sax Ensemble) •4 Sx: SATB/Pno/Perc
Tres Piezas (1989) (to M. MIJAN) •Asx/Pno

SEFFER, Yochk'o
Compositeur, saxophoniste, et instrumentiste français d'origine hongroise.
Alpha-gamma (1990) •Tsx improvised/5 Sx: SnoSATB/Bass/Perc
Dépression (1985) •Tsx improvised/4 Sx: SATB/BsCl/Bass/Perc
Dromüs (1991) •Pno/Cl/Perc/4 Sx: SATBs
Galère assymétrique (7'30) •4 Sx: SATB/Perc
Improvisation et modes (with A. BOUHEY) (1992) (Method) •Lem
Script et Orale - Galère assymétrique (1985-86) (40') 1) Torma 2) Danse de baptême 3) Danse profane •4 Sx: SATB/Pno
Self system •Tsx/Pno written or improvised
Szerkeset n° 1 - Sonate •Asx/Pno
Techouba - Le retour de Dieu ou la Repentance (Hommage à John Coltrane) •Tsx Solo/1 to 8 BsCl
Torma (7'30) •6 Sx: SnoSATBCBs/Perc
Trabla air •Ssx/Pno improvised

SEGERSTAM, Leif (1944)
Chef d'orchestre et compositeur finlandais, né le 2 III 1944, à Vasa.
"In his compositions he has always attached importance to the freedom and involvement of the performer, sometimes achieving this in what he calls a 'free pulsative style' in which the performer must decide the rhythmic interpretation at each point. He has eschewed the restraints of any system and has preserved an intuitive and coulourful idiom at the expense of formal stringency. An urge to make his musical message comprehensible has led him to give spoken introductions at concerts of his works." (E. WAHLSTRÖM)
Episode n° 7 (1979) (10') (to P. SAVIJOKI) •Asx/Perc •FMIC
Epitaph n° 2c (1977) (9') (to P. SAVIJOKI) •Asx/Pno •FMIC
Orchestral diary sheet n° 11h (1981) (13') •Asx Solo/Orch (1111/1110/Perc/Celesta/Str) •FMIC
Thoughts 1990 (1989) •4 Sx: SATB/Orch •FMIC

SEGOIN, P.
25 Etudes artistiques (2 volumes) •Bil
Méthode complète (1897) •G&F

SEIBER, Màtyàs (1905-1960)
Compositeur et professeur anglais d'origine hongroise, né à Budapest, le 4 V 1905, mort accidentellement à Johannesburg, le 24 IX 1960. Travailla avec Z. Kodaly.
"Arrivé en Grande-Bretagne en 1935, Màtyàs Seiber fut accueilli par la critique d'avant-garde comme le 'sauveur de la musique anglaise.' Ce musicien de talent prématurément disparu dans un accident en Afrique du Sud, pratiquait un subtil mélange d'écritures, juxtaposant tonalité et dodécaphonisme et y ajoutant le jazz, voire le *folk song*. (G. GEFEN)
"Seiber's early works are permeated with Hungarian idioms; later he expanded his melodic resources to include oriental modes and also jazz, treated as folk music; eventually he adopted the 12-tone method, with individual extensions." (BAKER) "Seiber's own music reflects both the breadth of sympathy and the insistence on craftsmanship that marked his teaching. Its range of expression and of intention is very wide—from ephemera like the successful pop song *By the Fountains of Rome* (1956), through much excellent incidental music, to chamber, orchestral and choral music of the highest calibre." (H. WOOD)
Dance Suite •Asx/Pno
Two Jazzolettes (1929-1933) •2 Sx/Tpt/Trb/Pno/Perc •WH

SEIDELMANN, Axel
Compositeur autrichien.
Variationen (8') •SATB •CA

SEKON, Joseph
Lemon Ice (1972) •Fl/Ob/Cl/2 Sx: ST/Bsn/Tpt/Trb/2 Perc/Vln/Vcl/Pno •adr

SELEN, Reinhold (1962)
Compositeur néerlandais.
Partita für 12 Saxophone und Becken (1989) (13'30) 1) Allegro 2) Largo 3) Finale •12 Sx: SnoSSAAATTTBBBs •Don
Quartett (1991) (9') •SATB •Don
Thema und Variationen (1987) •SATB •Don

SELESKI
Interlude romantique •Asx/Pno •WWS

SELLENICK, Adolphe-Valentin (1826-1893)
Chef de musique et compositeur français, né à Libourne (Gironde), mort aux Andelys. Chef de musique de la Garde Républicaine de 1873 à 1893.
Andante religioso (1861) •SATB •Marg

SELLNER, Joseph (1787-1843)
12 duos (BLEUZET) (4 volumes) •2 Sx: AA or TT •Cos
Etudes progressives (BLEUZET) •Braun
Méthode (BLEUZET) •Bil

SEMENOFF, Ivan K. (1917)
Compositeur français.
Gin-fizz (1953) (3') •Asx/Pno •PN

SEMLER-COLLERY, Armand (1912)
Chef de musique et compositeur français, né à Bourbourg (Nord). Travailla avec son père puis avec M. Pech.
Ave Maria (1956) (3'30) •SATB •adr
Canzonetta d'après Pierné (1957) •Cl/4 Sx: SATB •Led
Chantons Noël (1957) (3') •SATB •adr
Fantaisie d'après Meister (1966) •Cl/4 Sx: SATB •Marg
Lied (1969) •Asx/Pno •Bil
Notre Père (1958) (3'10) •SATB •adr
O salutaris hostia (1956) (2'50) •SATB •adr
Le p'tit quinquin (1958) (3') •SATB •adr
Petite suite (1965) (6') 1) Berceuse 2) Invention 3) Galant marquis •SATB •Marg
Le rationnel sensationnel (1939) •Asx/Pno •Braun
Stille Nacht - Vieux Noël (1958) (2'30) •SATB •adr
Tendresse sérénade (1956) (3'50) •SATB •adr

SEMLER-COLLERY, Jules (1902-1988)
Chef de musique et compositeur français, né à Dunkerque, le 17 IX 1902. Travailla avec P. Vidal et V. d'Indy.
"Ses oeuvres portent la marque de leur auteur: franchise et expression de la facture harmonique, écriture qui toujours 'sonne' net, enfin une belle science de la technique instrumentale." (J-G. MARIE)
Arlequinade (1950) (13') (to Quatuor Mule) •SATB •Marg
Barcarolle et danse (1968) (6'30) (to Fr. DANEELS) •Asx/Pno •ME
Cantabile (1956) (4') (to L. MONTAIGNE) •Bsx (or BsCl)/Pno •Dec
Cantilène (1958) (3') (to P. Semler-Collery) •Ssx (or Cl)/Pno •Dec
10 études concertantes (1964) (to M. MULE) •Asx/Pno (ad libitum) •ME
Elegia (1956) (6') (to P. TAILLEFER) •Asx (or EH)/Pno •Dec
Fantaisie caprice (1965) (7') (to M. MULE) •Asx/Orch or Pno •ME
Fantaisie de concert (1955) (10') •Tsx/Pno •Dec
Mélodie expressive •Asx or Bb Sx/Pno •ME
Petite marche burlesque (to E. COHANNIER) •SATB
Quatuor d'anches (1964) (9') (to Quatuor d'Anches Français)
1) Rêverie 2) Minuetto 3) Danse badine 4) Cantilène
5) Rondilette •Ob/Cl/Asx/Bsn
Récit et scherzando (1953) (6') (to L. NATTER) •Asx/Pno •Led
Rêverie •SATB •ME
Tarentelle (1948) (4') (to MASSPACHER) •Asx/Pno

SENAILLÉ, Jean-Baptiste (1687-1730)
Allegro Spiritoso (EPHROSS) •Tsx/Pno •South
Allegro Spiritoso (GEE) •Asx/Pno •South

SENERCHIA, R.
Street Music (for W. STREET) •Asx Solo

SENGSTSCHMID, Johann (1936)
Professeur et compositeur autrichien. Travailla avec O. Steinbauer.
"What has guided me in my artistic work was Mozart's principle that good music must appeal both to the ordinary listener as well as to the expert. That is why I maintain in my twelve-tone compositions a harmonic language pleasing to the ear: Josef Matthias Hauer's twelve-tone harmony, which is typified by intensified consonance or mild dissonance, was developed by my teacher Othmar Steinbauer into a dodecaphonic theory of music—equal to the theory of counterpoint

and harmony. This innovation was enlarged and developed further by me." (J. SENGSTSCHMID)
Meditation, op. 43c (1991) (4'30) •Asx/Org

SENON, Gilles (1949)
16 Etudes rythmo-techniques (1979) (to D. DEFFAYET) •Bil
26 petites études mélodiques (1978) •Bil
Flash-jazz (1982) •2, 3 or 4 Sx •Bil
Techni-Sax - 32 textes de vélocité (1987) •Asx/Pno •Bil

SEPOS, Charles
Breathless (1986) (to L. HUNTER) •Ssx Solo

SEREBRIER, José (1938)
Chef d'orchestre et compositeur urugo-américain, né à Montevideo, le 3 XII 1938. Travailla avec Ascone, Santorsola et, aux U.S.A., avec Giannini et Copland.
Cuarteto (1955) 1) Meditation 2) Danza 3) Caucion 4) Ronda •SATB •South/Peer/Meri

SERMILÄ, Jarno (1939)
Compositeur finlandais, né le 16 VIII 1939. Travailla avec J. Kokkonen en leçons privées à Prague.
"He begin his musical career as a jazz musician (in which role he is still active from time to time). In his music Sermilä has freely used various contemporary techniques, including aleatoric means and controlled improvisation together with strictly written structures. Timbre, rhythm and the enigma of time in music can be said to be his main points of interest."
Contemplation II (1978) (11') (to P. SAVIJOKI) •Asx/Tape •FMIC
Jean Eduard en face du fait accompli... (1986) (10') •SATB •FMIC

SEVRETTE, Danielle Henriette (1932)
Compositeur français, né à Paris, le 14 V 1932. Travailla avec J-E. Marie.
A peine ai-je entrevu les dessous du capitaine •Bsx Solo •adr
Azalaî (1972) (6') (to J-M. LONDEIX) •Asx/Pno •adr
Fadâa - Espaces (1974) (to L'Ensemble de Saxophones Français) •8 Sx: A+B/A+B/A+B/A+B/A+B/A+B/A+T/A+T
In diesem Brauss (1975) (to R. NODA) •Sx Solo •adr
L'innomé •Vln/Vcl/Asx/Org •adr

SEYRIG, François
Concert en trio •Asx/Tpt/Org

SHAFFER, Sherwood (1934)
Compositeur américain, né le 15 XI 1934, à Beeville (Texas). Travailla avec B. Martinu et V. Giannini.
Barcarolle •Tsx/Pno •adr
Charades •Vln/Tsx/Pno •adr
Concerto •Tsx/Orch •adr
Rhapsody (1987) •Tsx/Band •adr
Sicilienne (1991) (4') •Asx/Pno •adr
Sinfonia for Saxophone Quartet (to New Century Saxophone Quartet) •SATB •adr
Sonata: When Mountains Rising (1983) (15') (to S. POLLOCK) 1) bold and surging... 2) past singing springs... 3) to reach the stars... •Tsx/Pno •adr
Stargaze •Narr/Tsx/Orch •adr
Summer Nocturne (1981) (to J. HELTON) •Asx/Pno •adr
Vision of a Peacock - A Masque (1971) (15') (to K. & S. DURN) •Actress+Dancer/Asx/Tape (or 3 Asx)/Perc •DP/adr

SHALLITT, M.
Eili, Eili - Traditional Yiddish Melody •Eb or Bb Sx/Pno •CF

SHAPEY, Ralph (1921)

Compositeur, professeur et chef d'orchestre américain, né à Philadelphie, le 12 III 1921. Travailla avec Wolpe.

Se dit "traditionaliste radical".

"The term 'abstract expressionism' has been used to describe Shapey's highly complex, carefully organized textures." "In 1972 he ceased composing for a time in protest 'against all the rottenness' in the musical work today, and in the world in general." (Ch. HAUFMAN)

Concertante II (1988) (18') (to C. SIKER) (Variations - Rondo scherzo - Passacaglia) •Asx/Chamber Ensemble (12 players) •Pres/JJ

SHAW, Francis (1942)

Compositeur anglais.

Pages (1971) (4'30) (to London Saxophone Quartet) •SATB

SHAW, Oliver (1779-1848)

A Trip to Pawtucket (LUNDE) •Asx/Pno •NSM

SHCHETINSKY, Alexander

Compositeur ukrainien.

Crosswise (1993) •Asx/Vcl •INM

SHEHEDRIN, Rodion Konstantinovich (1932)

Dans le style d'Albeniz (MIKHAILOV) •Asx/Pno

SHELDON, R.

Compositeur américain.

Sarabande •SATB

SHEPHERD, Stu

Compositeur canadien.

Birthday Music III (1986) •1 Sx: A+T/Guit/Synth/Bass/Perc •CMC

SHEPPARD, James

Compositeur américain.

Bitter Ice •Tpt/Sx/Pno/Bass/Perc •SeMC

SHERMAN, Robert W. (1921)

Compositeur américain.

Sonata (1966) (to C. LEESON) 1) Slowly 2) Moderately 3) Moderately •Tsx/Pno •South

Trio Sonata (1963) (to C. LEESON) •Vln/Asx/Pno

Variations (1961) (to C. LEESON) •Asx/EH/Pno

SHIGERU, Kan-no

Keycoy (1993) •Tsx/Vla •INM

Mythos - Mosaik (1993) •Tsx/Pno •INM

Stück (1993) •Asx/Pno •INM

SHIMIZU, Hajime

Compositeur japonais.

Pour Saxophone-alto et piano (to Y. SASAKI) •Asx/Pno

SHINOHARA, Makoto

Compositeur japonais.

Situations (1993) •Asx/Electronics •INM

SHIPLEY, Edward (1941)

Compositeur anglais.

Quartet (1973) (4'30) (to Myrha Saxophone Quartet) •SATB

SHISHOV, Ivan Petrovitch (1888-1947)

Grotesque Dance (FELIX) •Asx/Pno •Mus

SHONO, Hirohisa (1959)

Professeur et compositeur japonais.

Bugaku (1985) (15') •2 Sx: ST/Pno

Toryanse-Paraphrase (1987) (16') •Asx/Pno

SHORES

Prelude for Eight •8 Sx: AAAATTBB

SHOSTAKOVICH, Dmitri (1906-1975)

Danses fantastiques (MAGANINI) •1 Sx: A or T/Pno •Mus

Prelude No. 7 •SATB •WWS

Satirical Dances (MAGANINI) •1 Sx: A or T/Pno •Mus

SHOUT, Vladislav

Compositeur polonais.

Metamorphosis (1979) 1) Adagio 2) Animato 3) Largo 4) Noire = 60 •Asx/Bass/Harp/Perc •ECS

SHREVE, Suzan

Music (1972) •Asx/Pno

SHROYER, Ronald

Reflections (1980) (to L. GWOZDZ) •Asx/Wind Ensemble

SHRUBSHALL, Peter & Catherine Shrubshall

Compositeurs anglais associés.

Valiant to the Last (to P. HARVEY) •SATB

SHRUDE, Marilyn (1946)

Compositeur américain, né à Chicago. Travailla avec W. Karlins et A. Stout.

"And they shall inherit..." (1992) •8 Sx: SSAATTBB •adr

Concerto (1994) (to J. UMBLE & Dana School of Music) •Asx/Wind ensemble •adr

Evolution V (1976) (14') (to J. SAMPEN) 1) Freely; quasi-improvisatory 2) Very sustained 3) Molto espressivo •Asx Solo/4 Sx: SATB •BMI

Masks (1982) (to J. SAMPEN) •4 Sx: SATB/Pno •adr

Music (1974) (to J. SAMPEN) (5 parts) •Ssx/Pno •adr

Music for Saxophone Choir (1992-93) •adr

Quartet (1971) (to J. SAMPEN) •SATB •South

Renewing the Myth (1988) (13') (to J. SAMPEN) •Asx/Pno •adr

Shadows and Downing (1982) •Ssx/Pno •adr

SHUEBUCK, R.

20 Duets •2 Sx: AA or TT •Shu

SHULMAN, Richard

Compositeur américain.

"Shulman Synthesized his musical style from many traditional genres; his melodies have a classical or folk favor while the rhythm of jazz, Latin and rock characterize much of his music."

Peace in Jerusalem (1984) (to Amherst Saxophone Quartet) (Allegro - Più allegro) •SATB

SIBBING, Robert V. (1929)

Professeur, saxophoniste, et compositeur américain, né à Quincy (Illinois), le 9 II 1929.

Alice Blue Jeans •5 Sx: SAATB

Aria •5 Sx: SAATB

Moments (1974) 1) Deciso 2) Lirico 3) Alla blues 4) Agitato •Sx/Bsn/Tuba (or Bass) •Eto

Pastiche •Sx/Hn •Pres

Sonata (1981) •Ssx/Pno •Eto

Vocalise (1980) •Asx/Pno •Eto

SIBELIUS, Jean (1865-1957)

Andante festivo (BEELER & ROPE) •AATB •PIC

Finlandia •4 Sx: AATB/Pno (ad libitum) •Bri

Swan of Tuonela (JOHNSON) •Asx/Pno •Bel

Valse triste (TRINKAUS) •Bb Sx/Pno •FMH

Valse triste (TRINKAUS) •2 Sx: AA or AT/Pno •CF

SICHLER, Jean
La mémoire de l'onde (1987) (3'30) •1 Sx: A or T/Pno •Led
Le passant des deux rives •Asx/Pno •Com
Promenades (1979) (1'30) (to S. Dubrulle) •SATB •Com
Sérénade (1979) (1') (to J-L. Rochon) •SATB •Com

SIEBERT, Robert Nicholas (1943)
Compositeur américain, né à Paterson (New Jersey), le 28 IV 1943.
"*Songs of Solomon*, a theatre piece, is based on the *Song of Solomon* from the Old Testament. Taking the form of dramatic narration, it unfolds the sensual personality of a woman's commitment to life. This composition is a marked departure from the music of the conservatives and the avant-garde. It rejects both of these established points of view as pedantic and negative. The *Songs of Solomon* was conceived with the idea that art is an illumination of life. As such, it is representative of the *new underground*, a return to the celebration of life, its joy and tragedy." (R. S.)
Songs of Solomon (1972) (20') •Asx/Pno/Actress •adr

SIEG, Jerry
Compositeur américain.
Fantasy (1985) (to K. Fischer) •Asx/Pno

SIEGEL, Arsene
Compositeur américain.
Pasquinade (1946) (7') (to S. Runyon) •1 Player: Cl+Asx/Pno •SeMC

SIEGMEISTER, Elie (1909)
Compositeur américain, né à New York, le 15 I 1909. Travailla avec S. Bingham, W. Riegger, et N. Boulanger (1927-1932).
"He began experimenting with jazz idioms and, after returning to the U.S.A., he determined to write music that would appeal to a broader audience than he had previously reached. Ives was an important stimulus. After a decade preoccupied with Americana, Siegmeister turned to a more individual and less direct style." (O. Daniel)
Around New York (1939) (to C. Leeson) •AATB
Down River (1970) •Asx/Pno •MCA

SIENNICKI, Edmund John (1920)
Compositeur américain, né le 11 IV 1920, à Cleveland (Ohio).
Ponytail Polka •3 Sx: AAA/Pno •Kjos

SIGEL, Allen
Compositeur et clarinettiste américain.
Homage to Gershwin •SATB •adr

SIGNARD, Pierre (1829-1901)
Chef de musique français du 37e Régiment d'Infanterie.
Air de Zelmira (1890) •Bb Sx/Pno •Mil
Cavatine d'Anna Bolena (1888) •Asx/Pno •Mil
Cavatine de Mahomet (1885) •Asx/Pno •Mil
Cavatine "Il Turco in Italia" (1887) •Bb Sx/Pno •Mil
Dolcissimo - air varié (1891) •Asx/Pno •Mil
Le vieux ménétrier (1892) •Ssx/Pno •Mil
Turco in Italia (1887) •Bb Sx/Pno •Mil

SILCHER, Friedrich (1789-1860)
Loreley Paraphrase (Harris) •2 Cl/Asx/Bsn (or BsCl) •CF

SILESU, Lao (1883-1953)
Son portrait - mélodie (1949) (3'30) •Asx/Pno •Sil

SILVA, Paulo
Preludio e fuga (1946) •SATB •IMD

SILVER, Horace (Ward Martin Tabares) (1928)
Pianiste de jazz noir et compositeur américain, né à Norwalk (Con-

necticut), le 2 IX 1928.
Peace •SATB

SILVERMAN, Faye Ellen (1947)
Compositeur américain, né le 2 X 1947, à New York. Travailla avec O. Luening, W. Sydeman, L. Kirchner, L. Foss, et V. Ussachewsky.
Shadings (1978) (to B. Street) •Vln/Vla/Bass/Fl/Ob/Asx/Bsn/Hn/Tuba
Showcase •Sx Solo
Three Movements (1971) (7') 1) Moderato 2) Andante 3) Allegretto •Ssx Solo •SeMC

SILVESTRI, J.
In Days of Knighthood - serenade •Eb Sx/Pno •CF

SIMEONOV, Blago
Compositeur canadien.
Sax-audience suite (1987) (7'30) •Asx Solo with audience participation •CMC

SIMEONOV, Dymyter
Compositeur bulgare.
Etudes (1973) •Wis
12 Etudes techniques (1974) •Wis

SIMIC, Vojislaw (1924)
Compositeur serbe, né à Belgrade, le 18 III 1924. Travailla avec P. Milosevic et S. Rajivic.
Balada (1959) •Bsx/Jazz Orch •adr

SIMMERUD, Patric
Compositeur suédois.
Lamento (1989) (3'30) •Asx Solo

SIMON, Jonathan
The Illegitimate Child •SATB •DP

SIMON, Robert
Echo! (1984) (3') •Asx/Pno •Led

SIMONIS, Jean-Marie (1931)
Compositeur belge, né à Mol, le 22 XI 1931. Travailla avec M. Quinet, A. Souris, R. Defossez, et E. del Puyo.
Boutades (1971) (12') (to Fr. Daneels) 1) Fantasque 2) Très lent - ironique 3) Improvisé - dynamique •SATB •Bil

SIMONS, Netty (1932)
Compositeur américain, né le 26 X 1932. Travailla avec P. Grainger et S. Wolpe.
"*Silver Thaw* had a sense of structure as well as beginning and ending with the minutest of sounds, relieved in the middle with a bit of violence… creating delicate and delectable sonorities." (*New York Times*)
Buckeye has Wings (1971) (indeterminate duration) (to K. Dorn) •1 to any number of players •Pres
Design Group No. 2 (1968) (8-10') (to B. Turetzky) •Duo for any combination of high and low pitched instruments •Pres
Silver Thaw (1969) (8') (to B. Turetzky) •Any combination of 1 to 8 players •Pres
Too Late – The bridge is closed (1972) (indeterminate duration) (to J. Fulkerson) •1 to any number of players •adr

SIMPSON, Kendall
Compositeur américain.
Rondo (1983) •Tsx/Pno

SIMS, Ezra (1928)
"Philosophical musician" américain, né à Birmingham (Alabama), le

16 I 1928. Travailla avec D. Milhaud et Kirchner.

"His instrumental works, many of them microtonal—he developed a microtonal keyboard in the late 1970s." (GROVES)

Sextet (1981) (22') (to K. RADNOFSKY) 1) Smooth-going 2) Slow 3) Quick •Cl/Asx/Hn/Vln/Vla/Vcl •ACA

Solo after Sextet (1982) (to K. RADNOFSKY) •Asx Solo •ACA

SIMS, Phil

Ellington-Medley (1982) (to Amherst Saxophone Quartet) •SATB

SINGELÉE, Jean-Baptiste (1812-1875)

Chef d'orchestre, violoniste, et compositeur belge, né à Bruxelles, le 25 IX 1812, mort à Ostende, le 29 IX 1875. Fit sa carrière musicale en France.

Adagio et Rondeau, op. 63 (1859) •Tsx/Pno •Sax/Ron

Caprice, op. 80 (1862) (to M. ELWART) •Ssx/Pno •Sax/Ron

Concertino, op. 78 (1861) (to M. J. DEMEUR) •Asx/Pno •Sax

Concerto, op. 57 (1858) (to Gen. de RUMIGNY) •Bb Sx/Pno •Sax

Concerto n° 2 (1858) •Eb Sx/Pno •Sax/Alf

Duo concertant, op. 55 (1858) (to G. KASTNER) 1) Risoluto 2) Andante 3) Allegretto •2 Sx: SA/Pno •Sax

Fantaisie, op. 50 (185x) (to Gen. FLEURY) •Bb Sx/Pno •Sax

Fantaisie, op. 60 (1858) (to Mme de CONTADES) •Bsx/Pno •Sax

Fantaisie, op. 89 (1863) (to M. COLBAIN) •Ssx/Pno •Sax/CF/Ron

Fantaisie, op. 101 (1864) •Tsx/Pno •Sax

Fantaisie, op. 102 (1864) (to M. PAULUS) •Ssx/Pno •Sax

Fantaisie brillante, op. 75 (1860) (to M. MATHIEU) •Tsx/Pno •Sax

Fantaisie brillante, op. 86 (1862) (to M. LIMNANDER) •Asx/Pno •Sax/Fuz

Fantaisie pastorale, op. 56 (1858) (to Gen. MALINE) •Bb Sx/Pno •Sax

Fantaisie sur 'La Somnambule', op. 49 (185x) •Bb Sx/Pno •Sax/CF

Fantaisie sur un thème suisse, op. 51 (185x) •Ssx/Pno •Sax

1er Quatuor, op. 53 (1858) 1) Andante-allegro 2) Adagio sostenuto 3) Allegro vivace 4) Allegretto •SATB (in Bb and Eb) •Mol

Quatuor, op. 79 (186x) •SATB •Sax

Solo de concert, op. 74 (1860) (to H. LITOLFF) •Asx/Pno •Sax

2e Solo de concert, op. 77 (1861) (to M. SAX père) •Bsx/Pno •Sax

3me Solo de concert, op. 83 (1862) •Bsx/Pno •Sax/Rub

4me Solo de concert, op. 84 (1862) (to M. SAVARI) •Tsx/Pno •Sax/Mol/Rub

5e solo de concert, op. 91 (1863) (to M. SELLENIK) •Asx/Pno •Sax

6e solo de concert, op. 92 (1863) (to M. H. KLOSÉ) •Tsx/Pno •Sax

7e solo de concert, op. 93 (1863) (to M. C. SAX fils) •Bsx/Pno •Sax/Ron

8e solo de concert, op. 99 (1864) •Bsx/Pno •Sax

9e solo de concert, op. 100 (1864) •Tsx/Pno •Sax

Souvenir de Savoie, op. 73 (1860) (to E. MAREUSE) •Ssx/Pno •Sax

SINGER, Malcolm (1973)

Compositeur anglais. Travailla avec N. Boulanger, F. Donatoni, et Ligeti.

Rat-rythme "A screed for Saxophone Quartet" (1977) (8') •SATB

SINGER, S.

Marionettes Modernes •Tsx/Pno •CF

Orientale •AATB •CF

Theme and Little Fugue •AATB •CF

SINQUIER, C.

Saxophonie (1976) •SATB

Six for Pleasure - duets •2 Sx: AT •South

SINTA, Donald & Denise Dabney

Voicing: An approach to the saxophone's third register •SiMC

SIPUS, Perislav

Compositeur yougoslave.

Sens (1976) •Asx Solo

SITSKY, Larry (1934)

Compositeur, professeur, et pianiste australien d'origine russe, né le 10 IX 1934, à Tientsin (China). En Australie depuis 1951. Travailla avec Petri.

"A diversity of influences and the radical stylistic contrasts in his music make Sitsky an unusually versatile and interesting figure among Australian composers. He has never lived in Europe, he has been profoundly influenced by European expressionism. Sitsky acknowledges a long-standing involvement with Chinese and Japanese gagaku music, joined later by an interest in the music of the Balinese gamelans." (E. WOOD)

Armenia a suite (1985) (to P. CLINCH) •Asx Solo •SeMC

SIVAK, Tom

Three Fugues Based on Beethoven •SATB

SIVERTSEN, Kenneth (1961)

Compositeur norvégien.

For ope hav II (1983) •Tsx/Str •NMI

Largo - December: in Bb minor (1981) •Tsx/Pno/Str •NMI

SIVIC, Pavel (1908)

Pianiste et compositeur slovène, né le 2 II 1908, à Radovljica. Travailla avec Osterc, Suk, Haba, et Kurz.

Notturno - evocazione (1964) •Asx/Pno •adr

SIVILOTTI, Valter

Improvisazione interrotta •1 Sx: A or B •Piz

SJÖHOLM, Staffan (1942)

Compositeur suédois.

Sommarlov for jazzgrupp (12') •Tpt/3 Sx/Tape •STIM

SKOLNIK, Walter (1934)

Compositeur américain, né à New York. Travailla avec B. Heiden.

Arioso and Dance •Ssx/Pno •WWS

Divertimento in Eb •SATB •DP

Four Improvisations(1971) (4'30) 1) Andante sostenuto 2) Allegretto pastorale 3) Lento 4) Presto •AATB •TP/Ten/Pres

Lullaby for Doria (1979) (2') •Asx/Pno •Pres

Meditation (1971) (4') •Tsx/Pno •TP/Ten/Pres

Saxoliloquy (1981) (3'30) (to J. COHEN) •Asx/Band or Pno •Ten

Sonatina (1962) (6'30) 1) Allegro molto 2) Lento 3) Allegro •Asx/Pno •TP/Ten/Pres

Three Canonic Tunes •3 Sx: AAT •Mus

SKORNICKA, Joseph (1902)

Compositeur et professeur américain, né à Birch Creek (Michigan), le 13 II 1902.

Intermediate Method •Rub

SKOUEN, Synne

Hva sa Schopenhauer...?: et partiturinnleg (1978) (8') •Narr/Fl/Cl+BsCl/Sx/Vln/Vcl/Perc •MNI

SKROWACZEWSKI, Stanislas (1923)

Chef d'orchestre et compositeur américain, d'origine polonaise né à Lvov, le 3 X 1923. Travailla avec R. Palester et N. Boulanger.

"He prefers not to conduct his own works, but he has continued to compose and is an advocate of contemporary music." (R. BERNAS)

Ricercari notturni (1977) (20') (to J. LUEDDERS) 1) Misterioso 2) Passacaglia 3) Drammatico •1 Sx: S+A+B/Orch or Pno •EAM

SLECHTA, T.
Father of Waters •2 Sx/Pno •CF

SLEEMAN, Anita
Cantilene and Dance •Asx/Pno

SLEICHIM, Eric (1958)
Saxophoniste et compositeur belge, né à Anvers. Fondateur du Blindam Kwartet, co-fondateur de Maximalist!

"Le saxophone induit chez Eric Sleichim un langage qui trouve son rythme dans les régularités et les irrégularités mécaniques et physionomiques intrinsèques au corps de l'instrument lui-même. Dans sa musique, le statut schizophrène du saxophone, déchiré physiquement entre une personnalité de bois et une personnalité de cuivre, est pleinement et sciemment exploité."

Lié / Délié (1988) (10'45) •SATB •adr
5 Movements for Beuys (1988) (30') •SATB •adr
Motus for choked saxophones (1991) •4 Sx mouthpieces [bouchés]: SATB •adr
Poortenbos (1989) (48') (3 mouvements et 9 portes) •SATB •adr
Verwikkelingen / Les Anamorphoses (1992) •SATB •adr
Visiting the sound (1985) •Asx Solo •adr

SLETTHOLM, Yngve (1955)
Compositeur norvégien.

Introduction og toccata (1981) (14') (to E. Tangvold) •Asx/Perc •NMI
4 Profiles, op. 3 (1978) (14') (to E. Tangvold) 1) Adagio 2) Allegro 3) Adagio con moto 4) Moderato - Allegro •Asx Solo •Ly
Symbiosis (1984-85) (3 movements) •4 Sx: SATB/Brass ensemble

SLEZAK, Milan (1941)
Compositeur tchécoslovaque.

3 Pisnê pro nizsi a Vyssi •Pno/Cymbals/Sx/Bass

SLONIMSKY, Sergei Mikhaylovich (1932)
Compositeur russe né à Leningrad, le 12 VIII 1932. Travailla avec A. O. Jevlakov et B. Arapov.

"D'abord influencé par Stravinski ('période russe'), il cultive l'humour, prétexte à des cocasseries instrumentales en souvenir des 'skomorokhi' (jongleurs-ménétriers de l'ancienne Russie pourchassés par le clergé orthodoxe pour leur esprit trop libre et l'usage des instruments). Manquant d'esprit critique, il compose actuellement dans un style hétéroclite faisant voisiner emprunts au folklore jazz, et musique pop, banalisant ainsi ses meilleures trouvailles." (J. di Vanni)

"Slonimsky was one of the first Soviet composers to adopt 12-note techniques, though undogmatically. 12-note serial principles, applied with varying degrees of freedom, are sometimes used with strict polyphonic forms, sometimes with improvisatory features. His ingenious use of sound often involves clusters, exotic percussion instruments, inside-piano sounds and unusual string effects. Slonimsky's instrumental writing is characterized by angularity of line, rhythmic energy and continuous impulse." (G. Orlov)

Suite exotique •2 Vln/Tsx Solo/Electr. Bass

SLUKA, Lubos (1928)
D-S-C-H- (1976) •Tsx/Pno

SMALL, J-L.
27 Melodious and Rhythmical Exercices •CF

SMART, Gary
Two Sound Pieces •Tsx/Pno

SMEDEBY, Sune (1934)
Compositeur suédois, né à Eskilstuna, le 3 IV 1934. Travailla avec L-E. Larsson, A. Udden, et K-B. Blomdahl puis avec G. Ligeti, et avec Miklos Maros enfin, à l'Electronic Music Studio de Stockholm.

"The composer has supplied the following characterisation of his style. 'The main emphasis is on choral compositions, most of them in a traditional, relatively plain style. None of them needs to be sung at the pitch in which it is written; the choir trainer decides the appropriate transposition, which in cyclical compositions of course has to be retained through out. The instrumental music varies immensely in structure, from exactly notated works to pieces affording a great deal of scope for improvisation, from a single instrument to 7,140, from flute to double bass. One of the electronic compositions is an adaptation of instrumental music, while the other is pure computer music.' " (H-G. P.)

Miniature (1988) (2') •Asx Solo •STIM

SMET, Robin de
The Good Old Days •6 Sx

SMETANA, Bedrich (1824-1884)
Polka (from *Bartered Bride*) (Harris) •2 Sx: TT/Pno •Lud

SMETSKY, J. de
March of the Spanish Soldiery (Whear) •AATB •Lud

SMIM, P.
Duet Album •2 Sx: AA or AT/Pno •Mus
Paris Soire •2 Sx: AT/Pno •Mus

SMIRNOV, Dimitry Nikolaïévitch (1948)
Compositeur russe, né à Minsk (Biélorussie), le 2 XI 1948. Travailla avec N. Sidelnicov et E. Denisov. Prix Marcel Josse (1981).

"Comme sa femme, le compositeur Eléna Firsova, Dimitry Smirnov adopte une écriture sérielle assez libre où certaines influences sont perceptibles (Stravinsky dernière manière, O. Messiaen)." (J. di Vanni)

Ballade •Asx/Pno •ECS
Canon humoresque •3 Sx •Mu
Fata morgana •Asx/Pno •adr
Mirages (1978) (9') 1) Andantino 2) Con moto 3) Adagio 4) Allegro 5) Lento •SATB •ECS
Poème •Bsx/Pno •ECS
Sérénade - Trio (1981) •Ob/Sx/Vcl •ECS
Suite de valses mélancoliques •Asx/Pno •Mu
Triple Concerto (1977) 1) Lento 2) Risoluto 3) Allegro •Asx/Pno/ Bass/Perc/Str Orch •adr

SMIT, Leo (1921)
Pianiste et compositeur américain, né à Philadelphia, le 12 I 1921. Travailla à Moscou avec D. Kabalevsky puis avec Nabokov.

"As a composer he has been particularly influenced by his contacts with Stravinsky, Copland and Fred Hoyle (librettist of his opera)." (Groves)

Tzadik (1983) (To Amherst Saxophone Quartet) •SATB

SMIT, Sytze
Double concerto •Vln/Asx/Orch •Don

SMITH, Charles W.
Compositeur américain.

Sonata I (1989) (11'30) (to R. A. Smith) 1) Moderately fast and gracefully 2) Very slowly 3) Moderately fast •Asx/Pno

SMITH, Claude T.
Fantasia (1983) (for D. Underwood) •Asx/Band •Wi&Ju
Suite (1988) (to G. Foster) •Fl/Cl/Asx

SMITH, Clay
Among the Sycamores •2 Sx: AT/Pno •Bar
Believe Me If All Those Endearing •2 Sx: AA or TT/Pno •CF
Call of the Sea •2 Sx: TT or AT/Pno •Bar

The Caribbean (HOLMES) •Bb Sx or Eb Sx/Pno •CF
De die in diem •1 Sx: A or T/Tpt (or Trb)/Pno •CF
Drink to Me (HOLMES) •Bb Sx or Eb Sx/Pno •CF
From Day to Day, Believe Me (HOLMES) •Bb Sx or Eb Sx/Pno •CF
Helen, Old Black Joe (HOLMES) •Bb Sx or Eb Sx/Pno •CF
Imogene •2 Sx: TT/Pno •Bar
Italiana (HOLMES) •2 Sx: AT or TT/Pno •Mar
Life's Lighter Hours (HOLMES) •2 Sx: AT or TT/Pno •Bar
Massa's in the Cold (HOLMES) •2 Sx: AT or TT/Pno •Bar
Milady's Pleasure •2 Sx: AT or TT/Pno •Bar
My Song of Songs •Bb Sx or Eb Sx/Pno •CF
Old Pleasure Bent •2 Sx: AT or TT/Pno •Bar
Rainbow Hues •2 Sx: AT or TT/Pno •Bar
Silver Threads (HOLMES) •2 Sx: AT or TT/Pno •Bar
Smithsonian •2 Sx: AT or TT/Pno •Bar
The Spirit, while the Fire •Bb Sx or Eb Sx/Pno •CF
Through Shadowed Vales (HOLMES) •2 Sx: AT or TT/Pno •Bar
The Trumpeter •2 Sx: AT or TT/Pno •Bar
The Wayfarer (HOLMES) •2 Sx: AT or TT/Pno •Bar

SMITH, Edwin

Compositeur américain.
Theme, Imitations, and Fugue •3 Sx: ATB •adr

SMITH, Glenn E. (1946)

Compositeur américain.
Mood Music 1 1) Fanfare for a lady in curlers 2) Almas' mater
    3) Who's in there any way? 4) Catchy tune 5) Passostéeone
    (1973) (7'35) •SATB •Eto
Mood Music 2 1) Bruin Hilda the Bear 2) A Walk Through the Red
    and Blue Forest 3) Polkabeams and Moondots 4) Same Place,
    Just a Different Way 5) Sad Flutterbyes 6) A Few Unquotables
    from Bartlett's (1980) •2 Sx: AA or SS or TT or BB •Eto

SMITH, Gregg

Compositeur américain.
Fugatto (1969) (to D. SINTA) •Asx Solo

SMITH, Howie (1943)

Saxophoniste de jazz et compositeur, né à Pottsville (Pennsylvania),
le 25 II 1943. Travailla avec D. Sinta, J. C. Borelli, et W. Coggins.
Helix III (1984) •Asx/Chamber Orch •Oa
Illoda (1965) •Sx/Wind Ensemble •Oa
Indian Orange •Tsx/Bass
Let the Games Begin (1983) •SATB •Oa
Life on Earth: coming soon •Sx/Amplified Vla/Electronics •Oa
Metaforest (1978) •Sx/Electronics/Tape •Oa
New York Still Life (1975) •2 Sx: SA •Oa
Passages (1981) •Asx/Str •Oa
Prelude, Post-prelude and Finale (1975) •SATB •Oa
Schizerzo (1983) •Sx/Tuba •Oa

SMITH, John Rushby (see RUSHBY-SMITH)

SMITH, Kent

Saxophoniste et compositeur américain.
Two Pieces (1974) •SATB

SMITH, Lawrence Rackley (see RACKLEY-SMITH)

SMITH, Linda Catlin

Compositeur canadien.
Periphery (1979) •Fl/Sx/Tpt/Marimba/Vibr/Chimes/Pno/Vln/Vcl/
    Bass •CMC

SMITH, Michael (1938)

Pianiste et compositeur suédois d'origine américaine, né à Tiline

(Kentucky), le 13 VIII 1938.
    "Melody is an essential element of Michael Smith's composition. He
has frequently developed the sound of the piano by using clubs, pieces
of glass and other objects. He derives frequent inspiration from
Oriental music. GEOMUSIC is his personal concept of an intensified
connection between musical imagination and terrestrial/cosmic awareness." (H-G. P.)
Elvira Madigan... and other dancer (Ballad - Thoughts on a found
    friend - Geomusic 3.715 - A face in a mirror I - II - Interaction)
    •Asx/Pno •SMIC

SMITH, Oscar (1951)

Symbols (1982) (5'30) (to N. RAMSAY) •Asx/Pno

SMITH, Stuart (1948)

Compositeur et organiste américain, né à Portland (Maine), le 16 III
1948.
    "Stuart Smith has a fabulous ear, a great sense of invention." (D.
PINKHAM)
A Fine Old Tradition (6-7') •Asx/Pno/Perc •MP
Hey, Did You Hear the One About... •Sx/Narr •adr
In Retrospect •Asx/Pno •SeMC
Legacy Variation No. 1 (1972) •3 Treble clef melody instruments
    •SeMC
Mute (5') •Sx Solo •SeMC
One for J. C. (6') •Asx/Bsn •SeMC
One for Two (6') •Asx/Org •SeMC
Organum Metamorphoses •Asx/Pno •SeMC
A Pool of Remembrances (1973) •Asx/Chorus •adr

SMITH, William O. (1926)

Compositeur et clarinettiste américain, né à Sacramento (California),
le 22 IX 1926. Travailla avec D. Milhaud, A. Copland, et R. Sessions.
    "His main compositional interest is in incorporating serial tech-
niques into a free jazz style." (W. T. MARROCCO)
Elegy for Eric •Fl/2 Sx: AB/Cl/Tpt/Trb/Vibr/Vln/Bass/Perc •MJQ
Schizophrenic Scherzo (1947) •Cl/Tpt/Asx/Trb

SMOLANOFF, Michael (1942)

Compositeur américain, né le 11 V 1941, à New York. Travailla avec
A. Copland et V. Persichetti.
Concertino, op. 16 •Asx/Band •EV
Parables (1972) (5') •Asx Solo •SeMC

SNAVELY, Jack (1929)

Clarinettiste, professeur d'instruments à vent américain, né le 11 III
1929 à Harrisburg (Pennsylvania). Directeur du Symphony-band de
l'Université du Wisconsin-Milwaukee.
Basic Technique for All Saxophones (1963) •Ken/DP
The Saxophone and its Performance •Her

SNOKE, Craig

Within a Dream (1990/93) •Soprano Voice/Sx/Pno

SNYDER, Randall (1944)

Compositeur américain, né à Chicago. Travailla avec L. Wagner et
H. Luckhardt.
Almagest •Asx/Fl/Ob/Cl/Hn/Bsn •DP
Quartet (to F. HEMKE) •SATB
Quintet (1972) (to F. HEMKE) •Asx/Str Quartet •DP
Seven Epigrams (1971) (to F. HEMKE) •Asx/Pno •South/SMC
Sonata (1966) (16'30) 1) Moderately fast 2) Slowly 3) Quickly •Asx/
    Pno •Pres/TP/Ten
Variations (1972) (5') •Sx Solo •Art

SÖDERLIND, Ragnar (1945)

Compositeur norvégien.

Eg hev funne min floysne lokkar att i mitt svarmerus, op. 35a (1982)
(9') •1 Soprano Voice/Fl+Picc/Ssx/Hn/Vln/Vla/Bass/Pno/Perc
•NMI
Legg ikkje ditt liv i mi hand, op. 39 n° 1 (1983) •1 Soprano Voice/Fl/
Sx/Hn/Vln/Vla/Bass/Pno/Perc •NMI

SÖDERLUNDH, Lille Bror (1912-1957)
Compositeur suédois, né à Kristinehamn, le 21 V 1912, mort, le 23
VIII 1957. Travailla avec T. Wilhhelmi et P. Möller.
"Many of these works still have a folk-music background." (S J)
2 Quatuors •SATB •ACS
Idea I & II (8') •4 Sx: SATB or AATB •HBus

SÖDERMANN, Johan August (1832-1876)
Bröllops-marsch (LEMARC) •SATB •TM
Swedish Wedding March (THOMPSON) •AATB •Alf

SODERO, Cesare (1886-1947)
Chef d'orchestre américain d'origine italienne, né à Naples, le 2 VIII
1886, mort à New York, le 16 XII 1947.
Morning Prayer (1933) •Fl/Ob/Cl/Tsx/Bsn •AMPC
Valse Scherzo (1933) •Fl/Ob/Cl/Tsx/Bsn •AMPC

SODOMKA, Karel (1929)
Compositeur tchécoslovaque.
Musica •SATB •CHF

SOEGIJO GUTAMA, P. (see GUTAMA SOEGIJO)

SOHAL, Naresh (Kumar) (1939)
Compositeur indou, né à Harsipind (Hoshiarpur district - Punjab), le
18 IX 1939. Après des études de science et mathématique travailla la
composition avec D. Roberts.
"He has developed an atonal non-serial style in which quarter-tones
have an important place and he has used them to build harmonies of
dark richness and strength, at the same time exploiting the increased
melodic subtlety they make possible. In all of this he has been
influenced less by his Indian heritage than by current Western concerns, though his finely spun decoration and the splendour of his
instrumental writing may hint at the exotic." (P. GRIFFITHS)
Shades I (1975) (4') •Ssx Solo •Nov

SOLAL, Martial (1927)
Pianiste et compositeur de jazz français, né à Alger, le 23 VIII 1927.
Travailla dans *Stress* avec Marius Constant, recherchant le mariage
de l'écriture et de l'improvisation issue du jazz. "Martial Solal dépas-
sera très vite la synthèse qu'il opérait en 1956-57 et 1962 entre les
esthétiques divergentes de Count Basie et Stan Kenton, pour aboutir à
une écriture reconnaissable entre toute: liberté tonale, fragmentation
des thèmes, goût des rythmes complexes associés à la pulsation
spécifique du jazz, opposition des timbres." (X. PREVOST) "Même
lorsqu'il cherche à créer des formes dans lesquelles puissent se mêler
la 'musique contemporaine' et le jazz, Martial Solal n'oublie jamais
que ce dernier doit swinguer." (J. & B. MASSIN)
"His best music has been made in a trio with bass and percussion, and
shows a grasp of form uncommon among improvisers. He has also
composed music for over 20 films." (M. HARRISON)
Ballade (1987) (5') (to A. BEUN) •5 Sx: SAATB/Perc ad lib. •Mar
Triptyque (1989) (55') (Fr. & J-L. MECHALI) (to Quatuor A Piacere)
•4 Sx: SATB/Jazz Trio (Pno/Bass/Perc)
Une pièce pour quatre (1985) (15') (to Quatuor A Piacere) •SATB
•Mar

SOLLFELNER, Bernd Hannes
Compositeur autrichien.
Tetralog (1992) (to Vienna Saxophone Quartet) •SATB •ApE

SOLLID, Torgrim (1942)
Compositeur norvégien.
Absurd gjenstand (1987) •5 Sx: SAATB •NMI

SOLOMAN, K.
Elegy and Dance •3 Sx: AAA •ASM

SOLOMON, Melvin (1947)
Compositeur américain.
Sonata (1982) 1) A la Beethoven 2) Calf Mountain 3) Presto •Asx/
Pno
Sonatina 1) Alla Mozart 2) A hymn to Andromeda 3) Dances •Ssx/
Pno •WWS

SOLVES, Jean-Pierre
Compositeur français.
A night maw (to Quatuor G. Pierné) •SATB

SOMERS, Harry
Compositeur canadien.
Limericks (1979) •Voice/Fl/Cl/Sx/Bsn/Tpt/Euphonium •CMC

SOMMERFELD, Willy (1904)
Violoniste et compositeur allemand, né à Danzig, le 11 V 1904.
Suite •Eb Sx Solo

SON, Yung Wha (1954)
Compositeur coréen, vivant aux U.S.A.
Song of Wishes (1987) (6') (to S. BERTOCCHI) •Ssx Solo

SØNSTEVOLD, Gunar (1912)
Compositeur norvégien.
Concerto (1955) (20') •Asx/Orch •NK

SONTAG, Henriette (1806-1854)
An Evening Serenade •Fl/1 Sx: A or T/Pno •CF

SOPRONI, Jozsef
Compositeur hongrois.
4 Pièces (1978) 1) Lento 2) Allegro animato 3) Andante sostenuto
4) Andante con moto •Asx/Pno •Min/Musi

SORENSEN
With the Colors (HOLMES) •AATB •Bar

SORG, Margarete (1960)
Compositeur allemand.
Cantica Catulliana (1986) (11') •Soprano Voice/Baritone Voice/
Tsx/Pno+Harps/Perc •adr

SOTELO, Mauricio (1961)
Compositeur espagnol, né à Madrid. Travailla avec Vienne avec F.
Burt, puis avec L. Nono.
Due voci (1990) •Tsx/BsCl+CBsCl/Orch •Uni
Nel suono indicibile - a Luigi Nono (1989) •1 Sx: A+T/BsCl+CBsCl/
Vcl/Live electronics •adr
Quando il cielo si oscura (1989) (18') (to M. WEISS) •Asx/Perc/Pno/
Vln/Vla/Vcl/Bass •ECA
Sax Solo (1988) (14'15) (to M. WEISS) •Asx Solo •ECA
IX +... - de substantiis separatis (1990) •Cl/Sx/Tuba/Vln/Vcl/Bass/
Pno/Schtagzeng with live electronics •adr

SOUALLE, Ali ben (18xx 18xx)
Saxophoniste français, né dans le Nord de la France. Se fit entendre
à Londres.
Caprice (1861) •Turcophone or Asx/Pno
Grande fantaisie variée sur "Lucie de Lammermoor" (1861)
•Turcophone or Asx/Pno

Le retour - Polka (1866) •Turcophone or Ssx/Pno
Souvenirs d'Irelande •Turcophone or Asx/Pno
Souvenirs de Java •Turcophone or Asx/Pno
Souvenirs de Shanghai - Loc-tee-kun-tzin - Air chinois (1861)
   •Turcophone or Ssx/Pno

SOUFFRIAU, Arsène (1926)

Compositeur belge, né le 26 II 1926, à Ixelles. Travailla avec Bourguignon.

"From his first works he employed serial procedures, and his interest in electronic means led him to establish his own studio in 1960." (H. VANHULST)

Concertino, op. 37 (5'30) (to V. GUTCHE) •Asx/Pno •EMB
Structures, op. 223 (1971) •Asx/Tape •adr
Temo 2856, op. 244 (1973) •SATB •adr

SOUKUP, Vladimir

Compositeur tchécoslovaque.
Concerto (1982) •Tsx/Orch

SOULE, Edmund F. (1915)

Compositeur américain, né le 4 IV 1915, à Boston. Travailla avec H. McDonald et R. Dorovan.

Concerto (1974) •Asx/Pno •adr
Quartet I •AATB •adr
Quartet II •AATB •adr
Serenade (1964) •Asx/Pno •Sha
Suite (1976) •2 Sx: SA •adr

SOUMAROKOV

Compositeur russe.
Incrustations (Lento rubato - Quasi presto - Tempo libro) •SATB •ECS

SOUSA, John Philip (1854-1932)

Belle Mahone (1885) (to J. MOEREMANS) •Asx/Pno
Stars and Stripes Forever (BUCHTEL) •1 Sx: A or T/Pno •Kjos
The Thunderer March (HERGER) •5 Sx: AATTB •Band
Untitled One-Step (1920s) (4') (to New York Saxophone Quartet) •Sx Ensemble: SAATTBBs •TTF

SOUSSMAN, Henri (1796-1848)

30 Grands exercices ou études (MULE) •Led
12 Light Pieces •2 Sx: AA or TT •Mus

SPAHLINGER, Mathias (1944)

Violoncelliste, saxophoniste de jazz, et compositeur allemand, né à Frankfürt. Travailla avec K. Lechner à Darmstadt, puis avec E. Karkoschka.

Aussageverweigerung-Gegendarstellung •Cl/Bsx/Bass/Pno / BsCl/ Tsx/Vcl/Pno •Peer

SPEAKS, Oley (1876-19xx)

Sylvia (LIEDZEN) •Asx/Pno •GSch

SPEARS, Jared (1936)

Compositeur américain, né le 15 VIII 1936, à Chicago. Travailla avec A. Stout, B. Owen, et A. Donato.

Basic Syncopation •South
Episode (1964) (5') (to F. HEMKE) •SATB •South
Quartet "66" (1966) (to Carla) 1) Allegro molto 2) Molto andante 3) Final •SATB •South
Ritual and Celebration (1981) (to K. KISTNER) •Bsx/Pno •South

SPEETS, D.

Klassiek kwartet •4 Sx: SATB or SAAT or SATT or SAAB •TM

SPENCE POTTER, Barbara

Compositeur canadien.
A Requiem for Lost Loves (1992) 1) Introit & Kyrie 2) Sanctus 3) Dies Irae 4) Lebera me 5) Lux aeterna •Asx/Pno

SPENCER, F.

Silvatones •2 Sx: AA/Pno •CF

SPIEWAK, Tomasz

Compositeur australien.
Quartet (1988) (to P. CLINCH) 1) Allegro molto 2) Chorale 3) Scherzo 4) Rondo •SATB
Sonatina (to P. CLINCH) •Asx/Pno

SPIJKER, Toon

Compositeur néerlandais.
Kwartet (1984) •SATB

SPINNLER, Victor

Compositeur allemand.
Russische Rhapsodie (1926) •Asx/Pno •Zim

SPINO, P.

Prelude of Woodwinds •2 Fl/Ob (ad lib.)/3 Cl/BsCl/Bsn (ad lib.)/4 Sx: AATB •StMu
Statement for Horn and Woodwinds •Hn Solo/2 Fl/Ob/3 Cl/BsCl/ Bsn/4 Sx: AATB •StMu

SPITZMÜLLER, Alexandre (-Harmersbach) von (1894-1962)

Compositeur autrichien, né à Vienne, le 22 II 1894, mort à Paris, le 12 XI 1962. Travailla avec A. Berg et Apostel avant de venir s'installer à Paris (1928).

"Venu assez tard à la composition, il s'est exprimé en un style généralement atonal, librement sériel et faisant une synthèse du néo-classicisme et des suggestions de l'école viennoise." (Cl. ROSTAND)

"Alexandre Spitzmüller a pris rang parmi les musiciens en possession d'un métier éprouvé et réfléchi." (R. BERNARD)

"His music embraces tonal and 12-note methods of organization, frequently reflecting his interest in Les Six." (J. MORGAN)

Etude en forme de variation (1960) •Asx/Pno
Quatuor •SATB

SPOHR, Ludwig (1784-1859)

Adagio (GEE) •Tsx/Pno •South

SPORCK, Georges (1870-1943)

Compositeur français d'origine Tchèque, né à Paris, le 9 IV 1870, où il est mort le 17 I 1943. Travailla avec Guiraud et V. d'Indy.

Chanson d'antan, op. 18 (to G. HOUSIEAUX) •Asx/Pno •Bil
Légende, op. 54 (1905) (to Mme E. HALL) •Asx/Orch or Pno •Bil
Lied •Asx/Orch or Pno •Bil
Méditation, op. 37 •Ssx/Pno •Braun
Novelette (to F. FORÊT) •Asx/Pno •Bil
Orientale •Asx/Pno •Bil
Virelai (COMBELLE) •Tsx/Pno •Bil

SPORCK, Jo (1953)

Pianiste et compositeur hollandais.
Poème (1981) (10') •SATB •Don

SPRATLAN, Lewis

Compositeur américain.
Penelope's Knees (1985) (23') •Asx Solo/Bass Solo/Chamber Orch (1+Picc01+BsCl0/1111/Pno/Perc/2 Vln/Vla/Vcl •MMI

SPROGIS, Eric

Comme une légère inexactitude (1992) •Asx/Hn/Tpt/Trb/Tuba/2 Perc

Comme un drame dérisoire (1992) •Asx/Harp

SPRONGL, Norbert (1892)

Compositeur autrichien, né à Oberrwarkersdorff, le 30 IV 1892.

Quintet, op. 124 (1958) •Ob/Asx/Tpt/Hn/Bsn •adr

STÄBLER, Gerhard (1949)

Compositeur allemand, né à Ravensburg, le 20 VII 1949. Travailla avec N. A. Huber et G. Zacher.

Traum 1/9/92 (1992) •Ssx/Vcl/Pno/Ensemble •Ric

STAEHLIN, Pierre (1912)

Compositeur et chef d'orchestre français.

Concertino (1986) 1) Décidé 2) Andante 3) Vif •Asx/Orch or Pno •adr

STAHMER, Klaus Hinrich (1941)

Compositeur allemand, né à Sczeczin (aujourd'hui en Pologne), le 25 VI 1941.

"De par une tradition solide, se reconnaît dans la succession d'Hindemith, Berg et Bartok."

Porcelain music (1983) (14') •Cl or Sx Solo •adr

Rhapsodia piccola (1976) (8') •Melodic instrument/Pno •Hei

STAIGERS, Del

Carnaval of Venise - Fantaisie brillante •Eb Sx/Band orPno •CF

Hazel - Valse caprice •Eb Sx/Pno •CF

STALLAERT, Alphonse (1920)

Compositeur et chef d'orchestre néerlandais, né à Helmond le 1er III 1920. Travailla avec Sir J. Barbiroli, A. Cluytens, et A. Honegger.

"Son oeuvre est caractérisée par un sens dramatique très prononcé."

"Cette musique est alimentée par une flamme que l'on ne rencontre pas toujours dans les compositions nordiques, surtout contemplatives." (W. L. LANDOWSKI)

Bestiaire (1966) (14') (to l'Institut néerlandais) 1) Le chat et le poisson rouge 2) Le paon et le miroir 3) Défilé des insectes: Thème - La mouche contre la vitre - Bourdon - Cafard - Puces et autres phlées - Grosse mouche - Couple de scorpions - Fourmis - Libellula depressa - Mante religieuse - Perce-oreille - Nuée de moustiques •Vcl/Asx •Bil

Quintette (1960) (19') (to G. GOURDET) 1) Introduction 2) Intermezzo 3) Scherzo 4) Finale •Asx/Str Quartet •Bil

STAMITZ, Anton (1754-1809)

Andante (KESNAR) •2 Cl/Asx/Bsn (or BsCl) •CF

STAMPFLI, Edward

Compositeur suisse.

5 Nocturnes (1983) (11') 1) Lent 2) Allant 3) Modéré 4) Assez animé 5) Sans hâte •Asx/Harp

STANDLEY

Bluebell Polka •SATB

STARER, Robert (1924)

Compositeur américain d'origine autrichienne, né à Vienne, le 8 I 1924. Installé aux U.S.A. depuis 1946.

"His music is direct in expression, using dissonance coherently within clear forms. Often he employs wedge-like harmonic progressions, parallel chords and quartal harmonies. Some work use 12-note serialism." (B. ARCHIBALD)

Light and Shadow (1977) (to Sigurd Rascher Quartet) •AATB •MCA

STAUDE, Christoph (1965)

Compositeur allemand, né à München, le 30 IX 1965. Autodidacte.

Memoire (1985) •Asx/Guit •adr

Obduktion (working title) (1988) (to J. ERNST) •Asx Solo

STEARNS, Peter Pindar (1937)

Compositeur américain, né le 7 VI 1931 à New York.

Chamber Set II •Asx/Vln/Tpt/Bass •ACA

Septet (1959) •Cl/Tsx/Hn/Vln/Vla/Vcl/Bass •Pio/ACA

STEDRON, Milos (1942)

Compositeur et musicologue tchécoslovaque, né à Brno, le 9 II 1942. Travailla avec Pinos, Istvan, et Kohoutek.

"His own music makes use of modality together with collage forms. Stedron's diverse compositional interests have included music for tape, collaboration with jazz bands and pop groups and work for the theatre, television and cinema." (J. FUKAC)

Chicken clucking (collab. PARSCH) (1970) •Sx/Tape

Ecce Homo (Oeuvre collective) •Sx

Jazz ma fin •Sx/Tape

STEEGMANS, Paul

Compositeur néerlandais.

Kwartet (1991) (11') (to Glazounov Saxophone Quartet) 1) Andante espressivo - più mosso 2) Largo - più mosso - largo 3) Allegro - più mosso - largo •SATB

STEEL, Robert

Compositeur américain.

Sonata •Asx/Pno

STEELE, Jan (1953)

Compositeur anglais.

Aesir (1963) (10') •Asx/Perc

Rhapsody spaniel (1976) (4') •Asx/Pno

Temporary farewell (1971) (5') •1 Sx: S+A/Electr. Guit/Pno/Bass/ Perc

STEFANI, Daniel

Compositeur espagnol.

Quinteto Burgalès (1980) (to M. MIJAN) •4 Sx: SATB/Pno •Alp

Elegia III (1989) (to M. MIJAN) •Asx/Pno

STEG, Paul

Kaleidoscope - Theater Concerto (1971) •Sx Solo/Woodwinds/ Brass/Perc/Celesta

STEIN, Leon (1910)

Chef d'orchestre, compositeur, et musicologue américain, né à Chicago (Illinois), le 18 IX 1910. Travailla avec L. Sowerby, H. Lange, F. Stock, et H. Butler.

"His music impresses one as being that of a real composer, enterprising rather then eccentric, leaning at no point upon the ready-made idioms or *schools of thought* of modernism. The orchestration is expert and original, and the themes are developed naturally from the feeling and imagination rather than from mechanical procedures..." (P. GRANVILLE HICKS)

Phantasy (1971) (12') (to B. MINOR) (Andante - Allegro moderato - Adagio -Allegro) •Asx Solo •DP

Quintet (1956) (25') (to C. LEESON) 1) Allegro 2) Andante-Allegro •Asx/Str Quartet •CFE/CP

Sextet (1958) (18') (to C. LEESON) 1) Allegro moderato 2) Adagio - Andante 3) Allegro •Asx/Fl/Ob/Cl/Hn/Bsn •CFE/CP

Sonata (1967) (to C. LEESON) 1) Allegro vivace 2) Adagio 3) Allegro •Tsx/Pno •South

Suite Quartet (1962) (to C. LEESON) 1) Allegro 2) Andante recitativo 3) Scherzo 4) Rondo - Allegro •AATB •South

Trio (1969) (20') (to B. Minor) 1) Allegro moderato 2) Adagio
  3) Scherzo 4) Allegro •Asx/Cl/Pno •DP
Trio Concertante (1961) (16') (to C. Leeson & B. Minor) 1) Allegro
  con brio 2) Siciliano 3) Scherzoso •Cl (or Vln)/Asx/Pno •CFE/
  ACA

STEINBACHER, Erwin

Blauer Schmetterling •Asx/Orch or Pno •Fro
Budenzauber •1 Sx: A or T/Orch or Pno •Fro
Canzonetta •1 Sx: A or T/Pno •Fro
Czardas •1 Sx: A or T/Orch or Pno •Fro
Die drei Grünschnäbel •3 Sx •Fro
Das eigensinnige Saxophon •Asx/Orch or Pno •Fro
Elegie appassionata •Asx/Pno •Fro
Horoskop •Asx/Orch or Pno •Fro
Lampenfieber •1 Sx: A or T/Orch or Pno •Fro
Saxophonschule und Sax-fidel •Asx/Pno •Fro
Der Schwarze Laüfer •Tsx/Pno •Fro
Spassvögel •AATB •Fro
Tarantelle •Asx/Pno •Fro

STEINBERG, Ben (1930)

Compositeur canadien.
Reflections in Sections (1984) •2 Sx: SA •CMC/DP
Suite Sephardi (1979) (to P. Brodie) •Ssx/Vln/Vla/Vcl •CMC
Trio (1972) (to P. Brodie) •3 Sx

STEINBERG, Jeffrey

Diary of Changes (1980) (to D. Sinta) •Asx/Pno
Tones (1978) (to D. Sinta) •Asx/Pno

STEINBERG, Paul

Troika (1983) (to J. Stoltie) •Asx/Tape •DP

STEINER, George (1900)

Compositeur et violoniste américain, né à Budapest, le 17 IV 1900.
Concerto (1955) (to V. Abato) •Asx/Orch •CC

STEINKE, Greg (1942)

Compositeur américain, né à Fremont (Michigan), le 2 IX 1942.
Travailla avec J. Wood, O. Reed, R. Hervig, P. Harder, et L. Moss.
Tricinium (1972) (8') (Hommage à Bach) •Tpt/Asx/Pno •SeMC
Episodes (1973) (8') (Hommage à A. Sax) (to K. Fischer) •Eb Sx or
  Bb Sx/Pno (ad lib.) •SeMC

STEINKE, Günter

Nachklang (10') •Bsx/Perc/Bass

STEINMAN, David WARD (see WARD-STEINMAN)

STEINMETZ, Hans

5 Studien (1971) 1) Accueil solennel 2) Magie des antennes 3) Bon
  voyage 4) Tarentelle 5) Toujours dans le rythme •4 Sx: AATB
  or AATT •OWR

STEKKE, Léon (1904)

Chef d'orchestre et compositeur belge, né à Soignnied, le 12 X 1904.
Prix de Rome (1931).
Fantaisie élégiaque, op. 20 (1940) •Asx/Pno •Ger/An
Nocturne •Asx/Pno •An/HE/Ger

STELZENBACH, Susanne

Compositeur allemand.
Imagination (1993) •Soprano Voice/Tsx

STEPALSKA, Joanna

Compositeur allemand.
Beregesave (1993) •Picc+Fl/Asx •INM

STEPANEK, Jiri

Concerto (1977) •Asx/Orch •FMT

STERN, Max (1947)

Compositeur israélien, né à New York. Immigré en Israel en 1947.
  "His work has attracted increasing attention due to its intrinsic
coherence, blend of vernacular and arcane elements, narrative forms,
and Hebrew ethnic influences."
Rainbow (1985) •7 Sx: SAATTBBs •adr

STERN, Theodore

Quartet (1971) 1) Allegro ma non troppo 2) Andante cantabile
  3) Allegro •SATB •Sha

STERNBERG

Variations on German Folk Songs (2 Volumes) •Sx/Bass/Guit/Pno/
  Perc •DV

STERNWALD

Lekmin •Asx/Pno

STEVEN, Donald

Compositeur canadien.
Just a few moments alone (1984) (4') •Ssx Solo •CMC
On the down side (1982) •2 Sx: AB/Trb/2 Perc/Pno/Electr. Bass
  •CMC
Straight on till morning (1985) •Fl/Cl/1 Sx: A+B/Electr. Pno •CMC

STEVENS, C.

Mourning his brother •Asx/Org

STEVENS, Halsey (1908)

Compositeur, musicologue et professeur américain, né le 3 XII 1908
à Scott (New York). Travailla avec W. Berwald et Bloch.
  "In his music, he uses vigorous rhythms, firm control of tonal centres
and brilliant instrumental writing. His many chamber works exhibit a
fine command of texture and proportion." (R. Swift)
Dittico (1972) (4'30) (to H. Pittel) 1) Notturno 2) Danza Arzilla
  •Asx/Pno •EH/DP

STEVENS, James (1930)

Compositeur anglais.
Girl in scena (1973) •Voice/Sx+Cl/Asx+Cl/Tsx+BsCl+Fl/Electr.
  Guit/Pno •BMIC

STEWART

Short Sonata •Asx/Pno •WWS

STEWART, Malcolm

Compositeur anglais.
Three (1971) (5') (to London Saxophone Quartet) •SATB

STIEL, Ludwig (1901-1988)

Compositeur allemand, né le 8 VII 1901, mort le 4 IV 1988 à Icking.
Musik (1953) (10') •Asx/Orch (2121/2210/Perc/Harp/Str)

STILL, William Grant (1895-1978)

Compositeur Noir américain, né le 11 V 1895 à Woodville, mort le
3 XII 1978 à Los Angeles. Travailla avec E. Varèse.
  "Réalise une tentative de synthèse entre les musiques de tradition
orale des Noirs et la musique symphonique." (J. & B. Massin)
  "Still became best known for his nationalist works, employing Negro
and other American folk idioms. After a period of avant-garde experiment he turned in a neo-romantic direction, with graceful melodies
supported by conventional harmonies, rhythms and timbres; his music
has a freshness and individuality that have brought enthusiastic response." (E. Southern)
Romance (1966) •Asx/Pno •Bou

STILLER, Andrew
Chamber Symphony (1982) (for the Amherst Saxophone Quartet)
1) Allegro 2) Mayn rue plats 3) Menuetto feroce 4) Presto
•SATB

STILLWELL, Richard (1942)
Visions of You - Reverie •Bb Sx or Eb Sx/Pno •CF

STINE, R.
Duo (1983) (6'30) •Asx/Perc

STOCK, David
Sax Appeal 1) Set Up 2) Blues 3) Sarabande 4) Jump •SATB

STOCKHAUSEN, Karlheinz (1928)
Compositeur et théoricien allemand, né à Attenberg, le 22 VIII 1928. Travailla avec D. Milhaud, O. Messiaen, P. Schaeffer, et Meyereppler.

"Pas de milieu, pas de mesure: il paraît qu'on l'adore ou qu'on le déteste et qu'on ne trouve pas de sentiment intermédiaire. Comme si nous en étions encore à discuter son génie. Je crois au contraire que toute l'habileté de Stockhausen est de susciter chez l'auditeur des réactions contradictoires et simultanées." (M. FLEURET) "Il représente l'avant-garde sans compromission, l'audace expérimentale, la puissance du travail et de l'invention, un goût de la spéculation intellectuelle très germanique une impulsion créatrice irrésistible, comme il en existe peu à ce niveau et qui donne même à ses recherches expérimentales la portée d'oeuvres d'art... Depuis un quart de siècle, il est la figure de proue de la musique dans le monde, sans défaillance, avec un déchet minime. C'est une des plus extraordinaires aventures de l'histoire de la musique: la musique, sortie de l'abstraction, retombe dans la vie, réalisant peut-être un siècle et demi plus tard, les rêves les plus fous des poètes romantiques allemands. C'est peut-être aussi un retour à une conception liturgique de la musique." (Cl. ROSTAND) "L'oeuvre de Stockhausen défie les bilans, sinon approximatifs: le temps seul, permettra d'en évaluer correctement l'importance, d'y démêler les coups de génie et les coups de bluff. Peu de musiciens ont à ce point conjugué la prolixité avec un lot de préoccupations techniques, spirituelles, philosophiques aiguës." (J-E. FOUSNAQUER)

"Stockhausen made a study of *musique concrète* and adopted an empiric method of composition which included highly complex contrapuntal formulas and uninhibited application of dissonance as well as the simplest procedures of tonal reiterations, all this in the freest of rhythms and a great variety of instrumental colors, with emphasis on percussive effects. He has also perfected a system of constructivist composition in which the subjective choice of the performer determines the succession of given thematic ingredients and their polyphonic simultaneities." (BAKER) "He has pioneered electronic music, new uses of physical space in music, open forms, live-electronic performance, 'intuitive music' and many other important developments in music after 1950. In his music and in his writings, he has evolved a uniquely coherent system of generalizations from the premises of total serialism, paying attention to aesthetic and philosophical consequences as well as to matters of technique and music theory. Each of his discoveries is compellingly demonstrated in his music." (G. W. HOPKINS)

Aus den 7 Tagen n° 26 (1968) (60') •Narr/1 Instrument (Improvised) •Uni

Expo für drei (1969-70) •3 Players •Uni

In Freundschaft - En toute amitié (1982) (10') •Asx Solo •Stv

Knabenduett (1980) (5') (extraits de Michaels Heimkeehuu) •2 Sx: SS •Stv

Linker Augentanz (1983) (Danse de l'Oeil gauche - Extrait de "Samstag aus light") •6 Sx: SSAA T+B Bs/1 Perc •Stv

Linker Augentanz (1990) •7 to 12 Sx: SS(S)AA(A)T(TT)B(B)Bs/1 Synth ad lib. •Stv

Plus Minus (1963) •2 X 7 Sx Solo •Uni

Pole für zwei (1969-70) •2 Players •Uni

Solo n° 19 (6 versions) (1965-66) (6-10') •1 Melody instrument •Uni

Spiral n° 27 (1969) (15') •1 Soloist/1 recepteur à O. C. •Uni

Tierkreiss - Zodiaque (1977) (11') (Wassermann - Fishe - Widder - Stier - Zwillinge - Krebs - Löwe - Jungfrau - Waage - Skorpion - Schütze - Steinbock) •1 Solo instrument/Pno ad lib. •Stv

STOCKMEIER, Wolfgang (1931)
Compositeur allemand.
Sonate (1981) (6') •Asx/Org •PJT/WWS

STOJANOVIC, Petar (1877-1957)
Compositeur et violoniste yougoslave né à Budapest, le 25 VIII 1877, mort à Belgrade, le 11 IX 1957. Travailla avec R. Fuchs et R. Heuberger.

"A prolific composer, he was at his best in concertante and, to a lesser extent, chamber pieces. The style is late-Romantic, except in same late works where more modern harmonies and jazz-like rhythms are introduced." (S. DURIC-KAJN)

Koncert, op. 74 (194x) •Asx/Orch •SKJ

STOKER, Richard (1938)
Compositeur anglais, né à Castleford (Yorkshire) le 8 XI 1938. Travailla avec E. Fenby et N. Boulanger.

"In his music he cultivates the 12-tone technique but derives it tonally from the quintal cycle of scales. Otherwise, he adheres to classical forms. As a believer in the universality of the arts, he writes utilitarian music for dilettantes, amateurs, musicasters and children." (BAKER) "Stoker's preference is for a serially orientated style maintaining a strict tonal centre." (R. TOWNSEND)

Four Dialogues, op. 12b (8') 1) Interview 2) Debate 3) Interrogation 4) Argument •2 Sx: AT

Little Suite (1966) 1) 1st little study 2) Canzone 3) 2nd little study 4) Invention 5) March •2 or more equal instruments •Hin

Music for Three, op. 12c (6') 1) Prelude 2) Ostinato 3) Canon •2 Sx: AB or ST

Quartet (1969) (6') 1) Prelude and fugue 2) Double canon 3) Finale •SATB •Hin

Rounds and Canons (1966) •2 Sx •Hin

STOKES, Eric (1930)
Compositeur américain, né le 14 VII 1930, à Haddon Heights (New Jersey). Travailla avec McKinley et Fleter.

Eldey Island: Homo sapiens in memoriam (1971) (8') •Sx/Tape •MP

Susquehanna (1985) (16') •2 Perc/Cl+Sx/Pno •HMC

Tag (1982) (5'35) (to R. DIRLAM) •Asx/Tape (or 2 assistant saxophonists off stage) •HMC

STOKES, Harvey (1930)
Values and Proposal VI (1988) (8'30) •7 Sx: SAATTBBs •SeMC

STOLL, Andre
Compositeur allemand.
Andy (1993) •Asx/Pno •INM

STOLL, Stefan
Compositeur allemand.
Chantimage (1993) •Asx/Pno •INM

STOLTIE, James (1937)
Saxophoniste et professeur américain né à Galesburq (Illinois), le 10 VII 1937.
Saxophone Orchestral Studies •adr

STOOP, Henk
Compositeur néerlandais.
Kwartet (1984) (20') •SATB •Don

STORE, Aurel
Orestia III (1985) (to D. KIENTZY) •1 Sx: Sno+S+A+B/8 Voices

STÖRRLE, Heinz (1933)
Compositeur allemand, né à Naila, le 5 II 1933.
Konzert (1990) (24') •4 Sx: SATB/Orch •adr

STOUFFER, P. M.
Duets - 10 Baroqual Compositions •2 Sx: AA or TT •HE

STOUT, Alan (1932)
Compositeur et professeur américain, né à Baltimore (Maryland), le 26 XI 1932. Travailla avec H. Cowell, W. Riegger, V. Holmboe, et J. Verrall.
"Works all couched in a non-aggressive, prudentially dissonant but harmonious vigesimosecular idiom." (BAKER) "His eclectic musical style displays a personal mixture of both experimental and traditional elements. An early innovatory feature is the use of large chromatic tone clusters, whose constant movement contributes to the overall form. A relaxed application of the 12-note system results in dissonant writing employing many 2nds and sounding closer to such American pioneers as Ruggles, Varese and Cowell than to the Viennese masters. Many of the composer's works since 1960 have a continuous rubato in which performers are free to mould micro-rhythms within strict metres." (D. C. GILLESPIE)
Canon in Four Voices •Any 4 instruments •ACA
Four Antiphonies •Fl/Trb/Asx/Org/Vln/Vla/Perc •CFE
Suite (1972) (6'45) (to J. SAMPEN) 1) Cantabile 2) Maestoso 3) Moderato 4) Con moto 5) Grave •Asx/Org •adr
Toccata (1965) (10') (to F. HEMKE & M. TAYLOR) •Asx/5 Perc •ACA

STOUT, Gordon
Compositeur américain.
Duo Dance-Song (1991) •Ssx/Marimba

STOYABNOV, Pentscho (1931)
Compositeur bulgare.
Scherzo •Ssx/Pno

STRADELLA, Alessandro (1644-1682)
Air célèbre (LIGNER) •Asx/Pno •Mil
Air d'église •Asx/Pno •Phi
Pieta Signore (SEGOIN) •Asx/Pno •Bil

STRADOMSKI, Rafal (1958)
Compositeur polonais. Travailla avec T. Paciorkiewicza.
DLA "R" (1987) •Tsx/Pno
MC XIII (1984) •Sx Solo
Per Gato (1988) (to D. PITUCH) •Asx (or Tsx)/Pno •DP
Sonata (1986-87) (17') (to K. HERDER & R. MATECKI) •Asx/Pno •AAR
Trio (1989) (9') (to S. BICHON) •Ob (or Ssx)/Asx/Vcl
555 (1988) (6') (to K. DORN) •5 Sx: SAATB •DP

STRAESSER, Joep (1934)
Compositeur hollandais né à Amsterdam, le 11 III 1934. Travailla avec De Leeuw.
Grand Trio (1984) (18') •Asx/Harp/Perc •Don
Intersections V (1977) (12') •Ob/Cl/Asx/Bsn •Don
Intersections V-1 (1974-79) (11'30) (to E. BOGAARD) •4 Sx: SATB or Ob/Cl/Asx/Bsn •Don
Points of contact II (1988) (11') •Sx/Perc •Don

Winter Concerto (1984) (18') •Ssx/Orch (2222/2220/3 Perc/Harp/Str) •Don

STRANDBERG, Newton (1922)
Fragments (1975) (10') (to J. CUNNINGHAM) •Asx/Pno

STRANDSJÖ, Göte
Compositeur suédois.
Liten svit, op. 15 (1954) (to J. de VRIES) •Asx/Str Orch or Pno •STIM/Ehr

STRANG, Gerald (1908)
Compositeur américain, né à Claresholm (Canada), le 13 II 1908. Travailla avec Ch. Koechlin, Toch, et Schoenberg.
"His music is strongly formalistic, with a technical idea determining the content." (BAKER)
Variations for Four •Any 4 instruments •ACA

STRANZ, Ulrich (1946)
Compositeur allemand, né le 10 V 1946 à Neumarkt. Travailla avec G. Bialas.
Erste Sinfonie "Grande ballade" (1979/90) (27') •4 Sx: SATB/Orch (122EH2BsCl2CFg/42311/3 Perc/Harp/Str)

STRATTON, Donald
Compositeur américain influencé par le jazz.
Nocturne (to New York Saxophone Quartet) •SATB
Onward Christian Soldiers •SATB •NYSQ
Small Symphony No. 2 (to New York Saxophone Quartet) •SATB
State Street Boogie Woogie (to D. DEMSEY) •Asx Solo •WS

STRAUSS, Johann (1825-1899)
Pizzicato-Polka (HOTZ) •SATB •Sim
Tritsch-Tratsch Polka (JOLLIFF) •Asx/Pno •Rub
Waltz 'Gypsy Baron' •Tsx/Pno •Kjos
Zueignung •Asx/Pno •Mus

STRAUSS, Oscar (1870-1954)
A Waltz Dream (HARRIS) •Asx/Pno •Lud

STRAUSS, Richard (1864-1949)
Allerseelen, op. 10/8 (WALTERS) •1 Sx: A or T/Pno •Rub
Fanfare (AXWORTHY) •22 Sx: SSSSAAAAAATTTTTBBBBBsBs/Timp •DP/TVA

STRAUWEN, Jean (1878-1947)
Compositeur belge, né à Lacken, le 22 III 1878, mort à Bruxelles, le 4 I 1947. Travailla avec E. Tinel.
Andante varié •1 Sx: A or T/Pno •EMB
Cavatine •Asx/Pno •Ger/An
Conte pastoral •Ssx/Pno •Sch

STRAVINSKY, Igor (1882-1971)
Berceuse (Firebird) •Bb Sx/Pno •Mus
Dance of the Princesses (Firebird) •Asx/Pno •Mus
Praeludium •Jazz Ensemble/Str •AMP
Suite No. 1 (TESEI) 1) Andante 2) Napolitana 3) Espanola - Balalaïka •Ob/Cl/Asx/Bsn

STRAWSER, Richard Alan
Compositeur américain.
Lamentation (1972) •Asx/Pno •adr

STRAYHORN, Billy (William) (1915-1967)
Noir américain compositeur de jazz, arrangeur, et pianiste.
"Strayhorn wrote or collaborated in more than 200 contributions to Ellington's repertory including the band's theme song." (J. HOSIASSON)
Lush Life •SATB

STREELS, René van

Compositeur belge.
Sonate I (to Fr. DANEELS) •Asx/Pno

STREET, Allan

Scales and Arpeggios (1977) •B&H

STRICKLAND, Lance

Compositeur américain.
Two Events •Asx/Pno •NTS

STRIETMAN, Willem

Compositeur néerlandais.
Musiquettes II (1981) (11') •SATB •Don

STRIMER, Joseph (1881-19xx)

Pianiste et compositeur russo-américain, né à Rostoy-sur-le-Don, le 28 X 1881. Travailla avec Rimsky-Korsakov, Liadov, Tcherepnine, et Glazounov. Aux U.S.A., depuis 1941, après avoir vécu en France pendant plus de 20 ans.
Orientale (1933) (to J. VIARD) •Asx/Pno •Led
Pastorale caucasienne (PAQUOT) •Asx/Pno •Dur
Sérénade (1933) (to J. VIARD) •Tsx/Pno •Led

STRINDBERG, Henrik (1954)

Instrumentiste (notamment saxophone) et compositeur suédois, né à Kalmar, le 28 III 1954.
Coming (1982) (6') •2 Sx: SA/BsCl/Tpt/Trb/2 Perc •SMIC
Hjärtats slag (1987) (7'10) •4 Sx: SATB/Fl •SMIC
Kommandez (1982-84) (6') •3 Sx: SAB/Tpt/Trb/2 Perc •SMIC/
WIM

STRINGFIELD, Lamar Edwin (1897-1959)

Chef d'orchestre, flûtiste, et compositeur américain, né à Raleigh (North Carolina), le 10 X 1897, mort à Asheville, le 21 I 1959.
"The source material of his music is largely derived from southern folklore." (BAKER) "His music dominated by folktunes and folklike material, is based in traditional harmony but overlaid with unconventional chord progressions, major-minor ambiguity and free dissonance." (D. R. NELSON)
To a Star (to J. HOULIK) •Tsx/Pno

STRMCNIK, Maks

Organiste et compositeur Yougoslave.
Recitativ in Aria (6'30) •Asx/Pno

STROBL, Otto

Poêmes (1978) •Asx/Pno •Dob

STROE, Aurel (1932)

Compositeur roumain, né à Bucarest, le 5 V 1932. Travailla avec Andricu, Ligeti, Stockhausen, et Kagel. Vit en Allemagne depuis 1972.
"Adepte de Darmstadt de 1966 à 1969, préoccupé par l'utilisation des ordinateurs dans le processus de composition, Aurel Stroe est l'auteur notamment de *La Cité Ouverte*, oeuvre écrite pour différents types de saxophones."
"Using all manner of contemporary techniques, Stroe carefully controls a range from powerful explosions of sound to the most delicate nuances; he has employed the mathematics of probability, deployed with the aid of computers, and timbre is of central importance in his music." (V. COSMA)
Aleph (1989) (7') •4 Sx
Colinda (1985) (to D. KIENTZY) •8 to14 Asx •Sal
La cité ouverte (1986) (9'30) •1 Sx: Sno+S+Bsx/Tape
Orestia III (60') •Voices (T/M-S/H-C)/Mixed choir of 6 voices/1 Sx:
Sno+A+B+CBs
Quatre chansons (10') (to D. KIENTZY) •Asx/Soprano Voice

Sonate (17') (to D. KIENTZY) •Sx/Perc

STROEYKENS, Armand

Compositeur belge.
Rapsodische Schetsen •SATB
Suite (1981) 1) Introduction 2) Scherzo 3) Finale •SATB

STROUD, Richard

Compositeur américain.
Capriccio •Fl/Ob/Asx/BsCl •SeMC

STUART

Saxophone Classics •AATB •WWS

STUBBE, TEGLBJAERG (see TEGLBJAERG STUBBE)

STUCKY, Steven

Notturno (1981) (to M. TAGGART) •Asx/Pno •ACA

STULTS, R. M.

The Sweetest Story •4 Sx: AATB/Pno ad lib. •Bri
The Sweetest Story Ever Told (HUMMEL) •Asx/Pno •Rub

SUBOTNICK, Morton (1933)

Compositeur et professeur américain, né le 14 IV 1933 à Los Angeles. Travailla avec D. Milhaud et L. Kirchner.
"In subsequent compositions, Subotnick has used instruments, films, lighting effects and taped electronic sounds. Pitch structures (both instrumental and electronic) are frequently derived from serial operations. Some compositions incorporate quasi-improvisational sections, while in recent works events may be derived from aspects of game theory." (R. SWIFT)
In Two Worlds - Concerto (1988) (25') (to SAMPEN, FORGER, &
RANDNOFSKY) •Asx/Computer/Orch (2+Picc 22 BsCl 2 CBsn/
4221/Timp/Perc/Str) or Yamaha WX7 MIDI Wind Controller/
Computer or Asx/Computer •EAM

SUCCARI, Dia (1938)

Compositeur, chef d'orchestre, et pédagogue français, d'origine syrienne, né à Alep. Travailla avec son père et M. Boricenko, puis, à Paris, avec H. Challan, N. Gallon, M. Bitsch, J. Rueff, T. Aubin, et O. Messiaen.
Fleurs d'un songe (1994) •Asx/Pno •Led
"Il est raconté" (1987) (11'35) (to Chr. OUTTIER) •Asx/Pno •Led

SUDLOW, Paul (1953)

Compositeur anglais.
Coming and Going (1978) (5-6') •Asx/Pno (4 hands)/Perc ad lib.
•adr
Meat and Three Veg (1978) (5-6') •Asx/Pno (4 hands)/Perc ad lib.
•adr
Untitled (1981) (for J. STEELE) •Asx/Pno •adr

SUENAGA, Ryuichi (1949)

Compositeur japonais.
Concerto (1982) (to Y. KHIKAWA) •Asx/Band
Romance (1981) (to Y. KHIKAWA) •Asx Solo

SULLIVAN, Arthur Sir (1842-1900)

Let Me Dream Again - The Palms (FAURÉ) •Eb Sx/Pno •CF
The Lost Chord •Eb Sx/Pno •Mol
The Lost Chord •2 Sx: AT/Pno •Cen

SULLIVAN, John

Six Sax Songs (1979) (to the Australian Saxophone Quartet) •SATB

SULPIZI, Fernando

Jeu du crépuscule •3 Sx: SAB

SULZER, Baldwin

Compositeur autrichien.

Suite (1974) (to S. FASANG) 1) Rezitativ 2) Diskussion 3) Lyrik 4) Tanz •Asx/Bsn

SUMAROKOV, Viktor (see SOUMAROKOV)

SUNDE, Helge

Compositeur norvégien.

The Thousand and Second Tale (1992) •SATB

SUPPE, Franz von (1819-1895)

Cavalerie légère (ROMBY) •Asx/Pno •PB
Light Cavalry Overture (HOLMES) •AATB •Bar
Poet and Peasant •6 Sx: AAATBBs •Rub
Poet and Peasant Overture (HOLMES) •AATB •Bar
Poète et paysan (ROMBY) •Asx/Pno •PB

SURIANU, Horia (1952)

Compositeur roumain, né le 3 VII 1952, à Timisoara. Vit en France depuis 1983. Travailla à Bucarest, puis à Paris.

Concerto (1984) (15') (to D. KIENTZY) •1 Sx: Sno+T/Orch (2222/ 100/Str: 64321) •Sal
Esquisse pour un clair obscur (1986) (11') •Ssx/Fl/Cl/Vln/Vcl/Pno •Sal
Vagues, ondes, contours (1984) (11') (to D. KIENTZY) •Asx/Tape or 6 Sx •Sal

SUSCHKE, Matthias

Compositeur allemand.

Meditation un Fughette (1992) •SATB •PMV

SUSI, Jose

Compositeur espagnol.

Cuarteto, op. 5 (1988) (to M. MIJAN) •SATB

SUTER, Robert (1919)

Compositeur suisse, né à St Gall, le 30 I 1919. Travailla avec W. Geiser.

"During the 1950s, Suter's attendance at the Darmstadt summer courses and his composition studies with Wladimir Vogel gave him an increasingly assured control over the compositional process. According to his own account, Suter endeavours to achieve unity in his music through a special differentiation of structural and expressive details. His intervallic structures indicate an intense preoccupation with Schoenberg's serial thought, but without their being completely serial." (R. HÄUSLER)

Conversazioni concertanti (1978) (18'15) (to I. ROTH) •Asx/Vibr/Str Orch or Pno
Estampida •Fl/Cl/Tsx/Hn/Tpt/Trb/Bass/Perc •EMod
Jeux à quatre (1976) (to I. ROTH) 1) Introduction 2) Monorythme 3) Canon 4) Mouvement perpétuel •SATB •HM

SUTHERLAND, Margaret (1897)

Compositeur et pianiste australien. Travailla avec F. Hart puis, à Londres avec Bax, à Vienne enfin.

"Her music at times betrays romantic warmth and often displays considerable strength of utterance and rhythmic vitality, although restraint, conciseness of expression and a strong taste for contrapuntal development must be considered basic qualities. Her chamber music shows a typically 20th-century interest in varied, often unusual instrumental combinations." (D. Symons)

Fantasy Sonatina (1935) •Asx/Pno
Quartet (1965) (to P. CLINCH) •Asx/Vln/Vla/Vcl
Sonata (1942) •Asx (or Vcl)/Pno

SUZUKI, Seiji (1926)

Compositeur japonais.

Sonata (1973) •Asx/Pno

SVENSSON, Reinhold (1919-1968)

Compositeur suédois.

Suite I (1981) (7') (Marsch - Valse - Tarantella) •5 Sx: AATTB •SR

SVOBODA, Tomàs (1939)

Compositeur américain, d'origine tchécoslovaque, né à Paris, le 6 XII 1939. Travailla avec Hlobil, Kabelac, et Dobiaj. Aux U.S.A. depuis 1964.

"His music is marked by broad melodic lines in economically disposed harmonies; there are elements of serialism in chromatic episodes." (BAKER)

Seven Short Dances •Fl/2 Cl/Asx/Trb/Vln/Bass/Pno/Perc

SWAIN, Freda (1902)

Pianiste et compositeur anglais, née à Portsmouth, le 13 X 1912.

Dance of the Satyr (1930) (5-6') •Asx/Pno •BMIC
Fantasy-march (1983) (to L. WYUREN) •Asx/Pno •BMIC
Naturo suite (1931) (6') •Any Sx Solo •BMIC
Shushan Waltz (1965) (1') •Asx/Pno •BMIC
The Tease (1965) (1'30) •Any Sx Solo •BMIC

SWANSON, Roy

Compositeur américain.

Locust Camp (1989) (6') (for C. R. YOUNG) •Asx/Pno •DP

SWANSON, Walter (1903)

Consolation (1930) (4') •Asx/Pno •BMIC

SWEELINCK, Jan Pieterzoon (1562-1621)

Angelus and Pastores (AXWORTHY) •7 Sx: SSAATBBs •DP/TVA
Variations on a Theme (RICKER) •SATB •DP

SWEENEY, William

Compositeur anglais.

Juno (to London Saxophone Quartet) •SATB

SYDEMAN, William (Jay) (1928)

Compositeur américain, né le 8 V 1928, à New York. Travailla avec Travis et Salzer puis avec Franchetti, Sessions, et Petrassi.

"His compositions are linear, motivic and intricately structured, employing complicated and free rhythms. Most of his music is freely atonal, but he has used tonal and serial techniques, and also aleatory episodes."

Duo (1977) •Cl/Tsx •SeMC
Trio (1965) •3 Treble [aigus] instruments •SeMC

SYMONDS, Norman (1920)

Compositeur canadien, né à Nelson (British Columbia), le 23 XII 1920.

Autumn Nocturne •Tsx/Str Orch •CMC
The Nameless Hour •Jazz Soloist/Orch •CMC
Sylvia (1974) •Narr/Jazz Quartet: Tsx/Fl/Pno/Bass •CMC

SYVERUD, Stephen L. (1938)

Compositeur américain.

Apotheosis (1972-74) (to F. HEMKE) •Asx/Tape
Field of Ambrosia (1975) (to J. WYTKO) •Asx/Tape
Fragile (1982) •SATB

SZALONEK, Witold (1927)

Compositeur polonais, professeur de composition à Berlin, né à Czechowice, le 2 III 1927. Travailla avec Woytowicz.

"His early works draw on the modality of Polish folk music; in later years he has followed other composers in developing new techniques.

At first he took Lutoslawski as a model, but he went on to incorporate impressionist and pointillist sonorities. Whatever the style, however, Szalonek displays high purpose and expressive intensity." (B. SCHÄFFER)

D. P.'s Ghoulish Dreams (1985-86) (7') (to D. PITUCH) •Asx Solo
•DP

SZEKELY, Endre (1912)

Compositeur hongrois, né à Budapest, le 6 IV 1912. Travailla avec Siklos.

"Up to 1970 Szekely made a gradual assimilation of the Bartok tradition and of the 12-note serialism of Schoenberg, Berg and Webern. He then began to admit more novel elements, including clusters and Pendereckian string effects, these being associated with an abandonment of 12-note serialism." (F. A. WILHEIM)

He Bem-Music (1982) (to BOK & LE MAIR) •Sx+Cl/Marimba+Vibr

SZEREMETA, Ryszard (1952)

Compositeur polonais. Travailla avec J. Patkowiski (musique électronique).

Agent Orange (1987) (13') •Sx/Synth
Amphora Snake Dance (1984) (to D. PITUCH) •Tsx/Tape
Trickstar (1989) (12') •Sx/Synth/Perc

TACHIBA

Introduction et allegro (1984) •SATB

TADA, Eiichi

Compositeur japonais.
Tonality (1993) •Asx/Perc •INM

TAFFANEL & GAUBERT

Grands exercices journaliers de mécanisme (JURANVILLE) •Led

TAGGART, Mark Alan (1956)

Saxophoniste et compositeur américain, né à Cleveland (Ohio), le 16 IX 1956. Travailla avec S. Rascher et L. Patrick.
Concerto (1981) (18') (to J. MOORE) •Tsx/Orch (Brass quintet/Harp/Pno/Perc/Str) •adr
Concerto for Chamber Ensemble (1983) (20') •Cl/Asx/Bsn/Tpt/Bass/Pno
Death (1978) (19') •Mezzo Voice/Sx/Vcl/Pno •adr
Lament and Credo (1984) (to K. DEANS) •11 Sx: SSAAAATTBBBs •adr
Red and White (1978) (10') •Tenor Voice/Sx/Vibr •adr
A Round o' Trios (1978-83) 1) A quotable quote (1981) 2) Wishful (1978) 3) A folk-song setting - 'Baby's first steps' (1981) 4) Lament in fears and doubts (1981) 5) Elegy for a slain leader - Anwar Sadat (1981) •3 Sx: ATB
Serenade (1981) (3') •AATB •adr
A Somewhat Sentimental Waltz (1992) •4 Sx: BsBsBsBs •adr
Two Sad Songs (1976) (8') (to L. PATRICK) 1) Prelude 2) Sarabande •10 Sx: SSAAATTBBBs •Eth
Welcome Traveler (1985) (to son of J. & A. MOORE) •Soprano Voice/Tsx •adr

TAILLEFERRE, Germaine (1892-19xx)

Compositeur français, né le 19 IV 1892, à Parc-St-Maur-des-Fossés. Travailla avec Caussade, Ch. Koechlin, E. Satie, et M. Ravel. Appartint au *Groupe des Six*, avec D. Milhaud, G. Auric, A. Honegger, F. Poulenc, et L. Durey.

"Elle se relie très directement à la tradition française du XVIIIe siècle. Son langage musical a de la verve et de la vigueur. Il ne craint pas certains frottements, certains acides harmoniques, mais ne cherche jamais l'agressivité comme ses confrères du groupe à leurs débuts. C'est un art qui n'essaie jamais d'être artificiellement masculin, mais s'il reste gracieux, il ne tombe pas dans la minauderie ou la sensiblerie. Germaine Tailleferre revendique l'influence de Chabrier, mais c'est celle de Satie qui est la plus visible dans ses premières oeuvres." (Cl. ROSTAND)

"The style she developed has the concision, incisiveness and mobility of Couperin or Domenico Scarlatti, together with a tenderness and humour. Her spontaneity, freshness and fantasy have remained as links with Satie and the original aesthetic of Les Six." (A. HOEREE)
Fox •2 Baritone Voices/2 Sx: SA •EFM

TAJINO, Masato (1948)

Compositeur japonais.
Collage mode key (8') •Asx/Perc
Quatre souffles (1981) •SATB

TAKÁCS, Jenö (1902)

Compositeur, ethno-musicologue, professeur, et pianiste autrichien d'origine hongroise, né le 25 IX 1902, à Siegendorf. Travailla avec J. Marx.

"In his works, he has made use of Hungarian and other folk musics in a contemporary tonal style which, over the years, has become more wide-ranging and involved." (J. DEMENY)
Two Fantastics, op. 88 (1969) (12'30) (to D. MASEK) 1) Tempo rubato 2) Tempo giusto •Asx/Pno •VD/HD/ApE

TAKEMITSU, Toru (1930)

Compositeur japonais, né le 8 X 1930, à Tokyo. Travailla avec Kiyose mais se considère comme un autodidacte.

"Le plus important des compositeurs japonais d'aujourd'hui, admirateur de Debussy et de Messiaen, il aime à mettre en contact dans une 'fertile antinomie' les instruments venus des deux cultures." (J. & B. MASSIN)

"Takemitsu's work is essentially independent. His music often gives an impression of spatial experience and of materials evolving freely of their own accord: each composition appears to fill its own acoustic space with a variety of sounds, which may be conventional, performed through some new device or recorded from everyday life, but always establishing a certain unity." (M. KANAZAWA)
Distance (1990) (10') (to S. BERTOCCHI) •Ssx Solo

TALENS PELLO, Rafael

Compositeur espagnol.
Introduction y danza (1983) •Asx/Pno •Piler/PEM
Soliloquio (1990) •Asx/Pno

TALLET, Eric (1949)

Compositeur français.
A.T.B. (1979) (11') (to D. KIENTZY) •3 Sx: SnoAT
Masques (1983) •1 Sx: Sno+S+T/2 Dancers

TALLET, Marc (1951)

Compositeur français.
Chrysalides (1984) (7') (to D. KIENTZY) •Asx/Harp
Estagari (12') •Fl/Asx/Trb/Vla/Guit
Mnémosyne et l'oubli (1982) (6'30) (to D. KIENTZY) •Asx/Chambre d'écho •Sal
Permutations pentatoniques (1977) (12') (to M. & D. KIENTZY) •Fl/Asx/Pno
Polyphonie •3 Sx: Sno (or S), A, T (or B)

TALLMADGE-LILLYA

56 Progressive Duets •2 Sx •Bel
Sextet I "Tchaikovsky" •6 Sx

TAMBA, Akira (1932)

Compositeur japonais, né à Kanagawa. Travailla à Paris.

"Japonais fixé en France, Akira Tamba a longuement étudié les 'Structures musicales du Nô,' sur lesquelles il a écrit un important ouvrage, et se situe personnellement à la convergence 'des recherches musicales actuelles en Occident et d'une tradition musicale japonaise, curieusement moderne bien qu'elle remonte au-delà du 13e siècle.' " (A. TAMBA) "Appartenant au théâtre musical, la musique de Akira Tamba devient le principal acteur quand la tension dramatique est à son paroxysme, mimant l'invisible et l'indicible." (D. J-Y. BOSSEUR)
Elemental II (1978) (to R. NODA) •Sx/Perc

TANABE, Tsuneya

Compositeur japonais.
Intermezzo 79 (1979-80) (to K. SHIMOJI) •Asx/Pno

TANAHASHI-TOKUYAM, Minako (1958)

Compositeur japonais, né à Osaka. Travailla avec T. Noda et Yun à Berlin.
Nocturne (1987) •Asx Solo •R&E

Trauma (1993) •Asx/Pno •INM

TANAKA, Akira (1947)
Compositeur japonais né le 7 I 1947, à Tokyo.
Au delà d'un rêve (3'15) (Album [Recueil]) •Asx/Pno •Bil
"... et l'été" •Asx/Pno

TANAKA, Katsuhiko (1940)
Compositeur japonais.
Jazz improvisation for Passereaux (1981) •SATB

TANAKA, Terumichi
Compositeur japonais.
The scene of silence (1992) (to T. SAÏTO) •Tsx Solo

TANAKA, Yoshifumi (1968)
Compositeur japonais.
Tros IV (1993) (8') (to T. SAÏTO) •Tsx Solo

TANENBAUM, Elias
Compositeur américain.
Consort •Fl/Hn/Asx/Electr. Guit/Vcl/Bass/Vibr/Jazz drums •ACA
Trios I, II, III •Fl/Ob/Cl/Vln/Vla/Vcl/Bass/Asx/Perc •ACA

TANIGAWA, Tadahiro
Compositeur japonais.
Quartett "Slix" •SATB

TANNER, David (1950)
Compositeur et saxophoniste canadien, né le 27 VII 1950, à Ottawa. Travailla avec G. Ciamaga.
Gathering no moss (1989) •5 Sx: SATBBs •CMC
Improvisation (1972) (4') •Asx Solo •adr
Lyric (1973) (5') •SATB •adr
Trois petits mals (1972) (7') 1) Marcato 2) Adagio 3) Playfully •SATB •CMC

TARANU, Cornel (1934)
Compositeur et chef d'orchestre roumain, né à Cluj, le 20 VI 1934. Travailla avec I. Muresianu, et Toduta puis, à Paris et à Darmstadt avec Ligeti, Stockhausen, Xenakis, et Bruno Maderna.
"In his music he has employed the *parlando rubato* cantelina and the rhythmic freedom and the folk-whistle sounds of Romanian peasant music; he has been particularly influenced by the innovations of Enescu. Taranu's instrumental works use improvisation and aleatory ideas, together with harshly acid harmonies and other material of a folklike modality." (V. COSMA)
Miroirs (1990) (18') (to D. KIENTZY) •1 Sx: S+T/Orch
Sonate sempre ostinato (1986) (7') (to D. KIENTZY) •Ssx Solo

TARAS, Yachshenko
Gobelin (1993) •Asx/Pno •INM

TARENSKEEN, Boudewijn (1952)
Compositeur hollandais.
Marchtelt suite (1978) (30') •4 Sx: AATT/Hn/2 Tpt/3 Trb/Bass •Don
Nonet (1982) (13') •Asx/Hn/BsCl/Accordion/Banjo/Harp/Vla/Vcl/Bass •Don

TARLOW, Karen Anne (1947)
Compositeur américain, né à Boston, le 19 IX 1947. Travailla avec R. Stern, P. Bezanson, F. Tillis, C. Fussel, et W. Fortner.
Music for Wind Quintet (1973) (12') •Fl/Ob/Cl/Asx/Hn •SeMC

TARP, Svend Erik (1908)
Compositeur danois, né à Thisted, le 6 VIII 1908. Travailla avec Jeppesen et Simonsen.

"Son style est marqué par une certaine influence française dans la tradition aimable et divertissante." (Cl. ROSTAND) "Svend-Erik Tarp poursuit la ligne suivie par Riisager celle d'un style léger, vivant, divertissant, d'esthétique 'française,' qui n'est pas sans évoquer celui de ses contemporains suédois Wiren et Larsson. Mais, ses oeuvres récentes marquent un approfondissement certain." (H. HALBREICH)
"Tarp has composed a number of works on Danish folk themes, and he has a fresh, melodious and accessible style." (GROVE) "Starting from the style of Nielsen, and in emphasizing a clearly arranged and entertaining concertante musical progression, Tarp represents the French-orientated neo-classical modernism of Denmark in the inter-war years. He composes music that is equally approachable and acceptable to listener and performer alike, without lapsing into banality and cliché. Rhythmic suppleness, polyphony on a tonal basis and ostinato formations are important elements in his style." (N. M. JENSEN)
Concertino (1932) (12') (to S. RASCHER) •Asx/Str Orch •adr

TARTINI, Giuseppe (1692-1770)
Grave (MULE) •Asx or Bb Sx/Pno •Led
Larghetto (REFF) •Tsx/Pno •HE

TASHJAN, Charmian
Antiphonies I (1976-77) (to J. SAMPEN) •Asx/Chamber ensemble

TATE, Phyllis (Margaret DUNCAN) (1911)
Compositeur anglais, né à Londres, le 6 IV 1911. Travailla avec H. Farjeon.
"She adopted a neo-classical style enlivened by modernistic dissonance and syncopated rhythms." (BAKER) "Her music is urbane in character and fastidious in expression, without being frivolous or insignificant. She delights in problems of craftsmanship presented by unusual chamber ensembles and excels in the solution of them... This accent is heard rather more strongly in the saxophone *Concerto* where the problem of writing something of just the right formal and musical weight for this symphonically still unassimilated instrument is admirably solved." (C. MASON) "Phyllis Tate provides perhaps the only example of the woman composer content to be herself and free from any suspicion of self-consciousness. Her music neither minces nor shorts. Grace and delicacy are there in plenty but without a hint of enervating prettiness; and the natural tone, whimsical humor and quiet, unostentatious tenderness of feeling suggest a confidence and relaxation of temperament which are as rare as they are welcome." (M. COOPER)
Concerto (1944) (22') 1) Air-Hornpipe 2) Canzonetta 3) Scherzo 4) Alla marchia-tarentella •Asx/Str Orch or Pno •B&H

TAUB, Bruce J.
Compositeur américain.
Serenade and Capriccio (1991) (4'15) (to W. KARLINS) •Asx/Pno

TAUTENHAHN, Günther (1938)
Compositeur américain, né en Lithuanie, le 22 XII 1938. Aux U.S.A. depuis 1956.
Concerto (1976) •Asx/Orch •SeMC
Dorn Dance (1971) (3') (to K. DORN) •Sx/Dancer •WIM
Elegy (1969) (2'30) •Tsx/Harp •SeMC
Sax Quartet (1976) •SATB •SeMC
Septet •Cl/Tpt/Tsx/Guit/Vcl/Pno/Perc •SeMC
Trio Sonata •Asx/Harp/Pno •SeMC

TAYLOR, Clifford O. (1923)
Compositeur américain, né à Avalon (Pennsylvania), le 20 X 1923. Travailla avec N. Lopatnikoff, W. Piston, et P. Hindemith.
"An intuitive composer with a disdain for mechanization, the tempo of his gestation periods has been unhurried." (G. DIEHL) "Based on skill alone Taylor ranks very high. He is not a militant avant-gardist like

Boulez or Stockhausen. He has rather gone back to the richest period of Arnold Schoenberg's orchestral works, just to give a point of reference... in four related movements, the variety and spicy density of a great orchestra sweeps upward at times toward a great outburst of lyrical feeling or some commanding image... a grand mosaic design almost compulsively kept staggered and off beat. One feels the great integrity of the material." (J. FELTON)

Duo (1964) (3'30) 1) Allegro 2) Larghetto sostenuto 3) Moderato energico •Asx/Trb •ACA

Quattro liriche (1970) (13') (from *Mattino dominicale* of W. Stevens) 1) Infanta Marina 2) Dominio del nore 3) L'uomo di Neve 4) Delusione alle dieci •Medium Voice/Asx/Pno •ACA

TAYLOR, Paul Arden

Compositeur anglais.

Bach Goes to Sea •3 Sx: SAB

TCHAIKOVSKY, Peter Ilyich (1840-1893)

Andante - Quatuor n° 1 (MULE) •SATB •Bil
Andante cantabile (GUREWICH) •Tsx/Pno •CF
Andante cantabile (HEMKE) •SATB
Canzonetta (CAILLIET) •Eb Sx/Pno •CF
Canzonetta (GEE) •Asx/Pno •South
Chanson triste •Bb Sx/Pno •Mol
Chanson sans paroles •Bb Sx/Pno •Mol
Chant sans paroles (LEMARC) •Bb Sx/Pno •TM
Chant sans paroles (TRINKAUS) •2 Sx: AA or AT/Pno •CF
Danse arabe (HURRELL) •Asx/Pno •Rub
Herzlied, op. 37 (LEMARC) •Asx/Pno •Lis/HE/TM
Impromptu •Bsx/Pno •Spr
Impromptu (SEAY) •Asx/Pno •JS
Lied ohne Worte •SATB •Mol
Melody, op. 213 (WIEDOEFT) •Asx/Pno •Rub
Nocturne •Bb Sx/Pno •Mol
Nuit bizarre •SATB •Mol
Quartet Album (ROUSSEAU) •SATB or AATB •Eto
Sextets Nos. 1 & 2 (TALLMADGE) •6 Sx: AATTBBs •Bel
Sweet Dreams (HARRIS) •3 Sx: AAT/Pno •Lud
Theme from Swan Lake •6 Sx: AATTBBs •WWS
Three Pieces - Album for Children •1 Sx: A or T/Pno •Mus

TCHEREPNINE, Alexandre (Nikolayevich) (1899-1977)

Compositeur et pianiste russe, né à Saint-Pétersbourg, le 20 I 1899, mort à Paris, le 29 IX 1977. Travailla sous la direction de son père puis de Liadov et de Sokolov, et enfin, à Paris, de Gedalge et de P. Vidal.

"Son style a de la vigueur, de la couleur, son écriture est soignée, efficace et souvent ingénieuse et, par-dessus tout, il a le sens de la vie, du mouvement." (R. BERNARD) "Sa musique—claire, positive, vitale, anti-impressionniste—unit les données classiques et populaires à celles de son époque, utilisant abondamment le modalisme russe, le pentatonisme oriental, ainsi qu'une échelle artificielle de neuf sons qu'il conçut lui-même: Do-Réb-Mib-Mi-Fa-Sol-Lab-La-Si." (A. LISCHKÉ)

"In his music Tcherepnine follows a neo-Romantic trend, using original means of expression within the framework of traditional forms. He adopted a 9-tone scale and applied it integrally in several of his instrumental works; at the same time he explored the latent resources of folk music; adjusted Oriental scales so as to utilize them in modern forms." (BAKER) "In the early works, the influence of Prokofiev is discernible (motor rhythms and a mordant though fundamentally good-tempered wit), as is that of contemporary French music (a sophisticated clarity and simplicity of texture); but Tcherepnine was also experimenting with new scales and a new species of counterpoint." (C. PALMER)

Sonatine sportive, op. 63 (1939) (6') 1) Lutte 2) Mi-temps 3) Course •Asx/Pno •Led
Sonatine sportive (E. YADZINSKI) •Asx/Ob/Cl/Bsn •Led

TCHEREPNINE, Serge (1941)

Compositeur américain d'origine russe, fils du précédent, né en France à Issy-les-Moulineaux, le 2 II 1941. Travailla avec son père puis avec N. Boulanger, H. Eimert, K. Stockhausen, P. Boulez, et E. Brown.

Morning After Piece (1965) •Sx/Pno •B&H

TCHUGUNOV, Y.

Compositeur russe.

Suite 1) Tango 2) Valse 3) Bossa-nova 4) Rag-time •Asx/Pno

TEAL, Laurence (Larry) (1905-1984)

Professeur, saxophoniste, flûtiste, et clarinettiste américain, né le 26 III 1905 à Midland (Michigan), mort à Ann Arbor (Michigan), le 11 VII 1984. Travailla avec A. Jacobson et M. Johnston.

The Art of Saxophonic Playing (1963) •SBC
Daily Studies for the Improvement of the Saxophone Technique •Eto
Program Solos - 12 transcriptions •Asx/Pno •Pres
The Saxophonist's Workbook - A Handbook of Basic Fundamentals (1958, revised 1976) •UMM
Solos for the Alto Saxophone Player •GSch
Solos for the Tenor Saxophone Player •GSch
Studies in Time Division •UMM

TEGLBAERG STUBBE, Hans Peter (1963)

Compositeur danois. Travailla avec J. Plaetner, N. Rosing-Schouw, et I. Norholm, puis en Suède et en France, ainsi que l'électroacoustique.

Skel (1986) (10'30) •SATB

TELEMANN, Georg Phillip (1681-1767)

Concerto (JOOSEN) •Ssx/Pno •Mol
Concerto in C (AXWORTHY) •Bb Sx/Pno •DP/TVA
Fantasy No. 6 in D Minor (PITTEL) •Ssx/Pno
Die kleine Kammermusik - Partirta n° 2 (AXWORTHY) •Bb Sx/Pno •TVA
Menuet and Polonaise (JOHNSON) •AATB •Rub
Overture Baroque (JOHNSON) •AATB •Rub
Overture Suite in F (SCHAEFER) •SATB •DP
Six Canonic Sonatas (TEAL) •2 Sx: Eb or Bb •Eto
Sonata in C Minor (VOXMAN) •Bb Sx/Pno •Rub
Sonate (LONDEIX) •Asx/Pno •Led

TELFER, Nancy

Compositeur canadien.

The Golden Cage (1979) •Mixed Choir/Fl/Cl/Sx/3 Perc/Pno

TEMPLE & SHAW

Vanity Fair Suite 1) Felicity 2) Audacity 3) Perplexity 4) Duplicity •Fl/Ob/4 Cl/BsCl/Asx/Str Quartet/Bass/Perc/Pno •Mills

TEMPLETON, Alec (1910-1963)

Pianiste et compositeur américain, né à Cardiff (Wales), le 4 VII 1910, mort à Greenwich (Connecticut), le 28 III 1963. Aux U.S.A. depuis 1935.

Elegie •Tsx/Pno •MCA

TENAGLIA, Antonio Francesco (1610-1661)

Aria Antica •Tsx/Pno •Mus
Aria (CHEYETTE) •2 Cl/Asx/Bsn (or Bsx) •Ga
Aria Antica (MAGANINI) •Asx/Pno •VAB

TENARO, L. (1889)

Trois Pièces 1) Chant du soir 2) Dans les bois 3) Romance •Asx/Pno •Led
Valse sentimentale •Asx/Pno •Led

TENNEY, James (1934)

Pianiste et compositeur américain, né à Silver City (New Mexico). Travailla avec E. Varese.

Sonata (1959-83) •10 Wind instruments (1 Asx)
Saxony (1978) •Sx Solo/Tape •CMC

TERAHARA, Nobuo

Compositeur japonais.

3 Fugues 1) Adagio 2) Allegro •SATB
Poème (1988) (to Y. Ichikawa) •Tsx/Pno

TERMOS, Paul

Concerto (1984) (15') •Asx/Chamber Orch •Don

TERRANOVA, Claude

Compositeur français.

Métamorphoses (to A. Beun) •5 Sx: SAATB

TERRENI, Ottavio

Xeres (1981) (to I. Marconi) •Asx/Org

TERRY, Peter

Compositeur américain.

Into Light: Concerto No. 1 (1986) (to J. Sampen) •Ssx/Chamber Orch (2011/2110/Pno/Perc/Vln/Vla/Vcl)/Computer generated tape •adr
Proanakrousna (1982) •Ssx/Pno •WWS
Spider Kiss •Asx/Electronic tape •adr
Strange Attractors (1992) •Asx/Pno
Windows Looking Nowhere •4 Sx: SATB/Pno/2 Perc •DP

TERSCHAK, Adolf (1832-1901)

Exercices journaliers (Mule) •Led
Wedding Procession •Eb Sx/Pno •CF

TERUGGI, Daniel (1952)

Compositeur français, d'origine argentine, né à La Plata. Travailla en Argentine puis en France. Membre du GRM, responsable de la pédagogie sur le système Syter.

"Il s'intéresse principalement à la composition de musique sur support, avec des incursions dans le domaine des musiques mixtes et transformées, le son acousmatique restant au centre de ses préoccupations." (Ph. de la Croix)

Xatys (1988) (18'30) (to D. Kientzy) •1 Sx: Bs+T+S/Dispositif électronique

TESEI, Tonino (1961)

Compositeur italien.

Controcontrasti (1993) •SnoSx/BsCl •INM
Gesta (1987) (8') •12 Sx: SnoSSAAATTTBBBs •EDP
5 Piccoli pezzi (1984) (7') (to Quatuor d'ance italiano) 1) Spirti 2) =168 3) =60 4) =100 5) Fugace •Ob/Cl/Asx/Bsn
Spleen (1985) (to A. Domizi) •Asx/Pno

TESSIER, Roger (1939)

Compositeur français né à Nantes. Participe à la fondation du groupe Itinéraire (1973).

"Pour Roger Tessier le son *vivant* ne doit pas déroger à sa prime définition, il engendre le *sonore* mais aussi la *vie*. Le son n'est pas seulement un objet de rapport/support à l'oeuvre d'art mais il est fondamentalement vecteur équipotentiel de communication." (M. Castanet)

Avaz (1975) (to J-Y. Fourmeau) •Asx/Pno
Concerto •Asx/Orch

THEBERGE, Paul

Compositeur canadien.

A Void Not Filled With Words (1983) (16'15) (to R. Massino) •Asx/Pno or Sx/Perc

THEIS, Ernst

Compositeur autrichien.

Slap (1992) •12 Sx: SnoSSAAATTTBBBs

THEOBALD, James

Compositeur américain.

Plane 5 •Asx/Vla/Pno/Perc •SeMC
Three Rapsodies (1980) •Asx/Perc/Orch
Lewis Carrolls (1983) (to Bok & Le Mair) •Sx+BsCl/Marimba+Vibr

THEOFANIDIS, Chris

Compositeur américain.

Concerto for Alto Saxophone and Orchestra "Netherland" (1994) (16') (Commissioned by World-Wide Concurrent Premieres and commissioning Fund) 1) Brutal, raging 2) A stream of pulses; labored, intense 3) Apocalyptic •Asx/Orch (2222/2211/Pno/Harp/2 Perc/Str) or Pno •adr

THEORIN, Håkan (1959)

Compositeur suédois.

Concertino (1987) (12') •Asx/Band •STIM

THIBAULT, Alain

Compositeur canadien, né au Québec.

E.L.V.I.S. (1984) (to R. Massino) •4 Sx: SATB/Tape

THIELS, Victor (1867-1925)

Saxophoniste français, soliste à la Garde Républicaine, mort à Paris, le 6 V 1925.

"Auteur de chansons à succès."

Méthode complète pour tous les saxophones (1903) •Lem

THIEME, Kerstin

Compositeur allemand.

Rapsodia festiva (22') (Fanfare e bandiere - Romanza notturna - Rondo di danza) •Asx/Orch or Pno •Asto

THILMAN, J.

Das kleine Requiem, op. 27 (1969) •EH/Asx/Vla/Pno •Bar

THINGHNAES, Frode (1960)

Compositeur norvégien.

Faces in motion (1976) •SATB

THIRIET, André (1906)

Compositeur français, né à Tarare (Rhône). Travailla avec V. d'Indy.

24 études d'expression (1966) •ET

THIRIET, Maurice (1906-1972)

Compositeur français, né à Meulan, le 2 V 1906, mort à Puys (Seine & Oise), le 28 IX 1972. Travailla avec Ch. Koechlin et Roland-Manuel.

"Je ne connais qu'une musique, une seule: celle qui vient du coeur et qui va au coeur." (M. Thiriet) "Clair, simple, sans détour, d'une généreuse invention mélodique, tel nous paraît le style de Maurice Thiriet" (R. Bernard)

"In his music, clearly and brilliantly orchestrated, bold and lyrical in feeling, he remained faithful to the orthodox standards of the Conservatoire." (D. Amy)

Adagio (1965) (5') •Asx/Pno •Led

THIRY, Albert (1866-1966)

Dimanche matin •Bb Sx/Pno •Mol
Promenade •Bb Sx/Pno •Mol

THOMAS, Ambroise (1811-1896)

Compositeur français, né à Metz, le 5 VIII 1811, mort à Paris, le 12 II 1896. Grand Prix de Rome 1832. Auteur notamment de *Mignon* (1866), *Hamlet* (1868), *Françoise de Rimini* (1882). Il fut comblé d'honneurs et de titres que la postérité n'a pas ratifiés.

Aria, Drinklied et Allegretto (from *Hamlet*) (LUREMAN) •Bb Sx/Pno •TM
Deux Chants de l'ancien Pérou (1865) (1'10) (to O. COMETTANT) •3 Sx: ATB •LMe
Mignon - sélection •Bb Sx/Pno •CBet
Polonaise (from *Mignon*) •Bb Sx/Pno •CF
Récitatif, aria, cavatine et Rondo (from *Raymond*) (LUREMAN) •Bb Sx/Pno •TM

THOMAS, John Charles (1891-1960)
Beautiful Isle, Old Dog Tray (FOSTER) •Eb Sx/Pno •CF

THOMAS, Robert
Compositeur anglais.
Study in White (1980) (5') (for J. STEELE) •Asx/Pno •adr

THOMAS, Ronald
Occasion •Ssx/Fl/Cl/Hn

THOMASSIN, A.
Compositeur français.
Om (1990) (to M. MIJAN) •SATB

THOME, François-Joseph (dit Francis) (1891-1909)
Fantaisie (MEYER) •Asx/Pno •Led
Pizzicato (HARRIS) •2 Cl/Asx/Bsn (or BsCl) •CF
Simple aveu •Asx/Pno •CF/Dur
Simple aveu •2 Sx: AT/Pno •Cen
Simple aveu (BLAAUW) •Bb Sx/Pno •Mol

THOMPSON, Kathryn E. (19xx-19xx)
Saxophoniste et professeur américain. Travailla avec E. A. Lefebvre.
Barcarolle •2 Sx: AT (in C)/Pno ad lib. •South
Bubble and Squeak •2 Sx: AT (in C)/Pno ad lib. •South/Volk
Carolyn - melodie •1 Sx: A or T (in C)/Pno •South
Londonderry Air •AATB •Alf
Practical Studies •South
Progressive Method •South
The Ragtime Saxophone •South
Song of Spring •2 Sx: AA or TT/Pno •Volk
Swing Low, Sweet Chariot •AATB •Alf
Valse caprice •1 Sx: A or T (in C)/Pno •South
Valse Minah •2 Sx: AA or TT/Pno •Volk

THOMPSON, Terence J. (1928)
Compositeur anglais.
Bach to Bach (2'30) •SATB
Brother Anansi and Peacock (1977) (25') •SATB
Comedy Flick (1977) •2 Sx: AA/Orch
Sometime Blue (2') •SATB
Three Stately Dances (3'30) •SATB

THOMSON, B.
Temple Song •Sx/Perc/Pno

THOMYS, Alojzy
Compositeur polonais.
10 miniatures dans différents styles (1968) •Asx/Pno •PWM

THON, Franz (1910)
Compositeur allemand, né le 30 VI 1910 à Cologne.

Humoresque •AATB •Fro
Meissner Porzellan •AATB •Fro
Polonaise (1940) •Asx/Pno •Fro

THORENSEN, Lasse
Narrative (1988) (27') •SATB •NMI

THORNTON, William
Compositeur américain.
Sonata (198x) (for E. CARINCI) 1) Variations with canon 2) March 3) Soliloquy and waltz 4) Allegro molto - final •Asx/Pno •South

THOU, Franz von
Suite (1941) •SATB •Fro

THOUIN, Lise
Compositeur canadien.
Joie •SATB •CMC

THÜRAUER, Franz
Compositeur autrichien.
Aria (A souvenir for Duke) (1991) •SATB •ApE
Mosaik (15') •SATB •CA

TICHELI, Frank
Compositeur américain.
Backburner (1988) (to C. LEAMAN) •SATB •adr

TIEDEMANN, Hans-Joachim
Compositeur allemand.
Mixed Pickles oder Allerlei von zwei bis drei (1993) •Asx/Pno •INM

TILLING, Lars (1940)
Compositeur suédois.
Konsert (1979) (18') •Asx/Orch

TILSTONE-ELLIS, John (1929)
Ollersett Suite (1978) (to English Saxophone Quartet) •SATB •BMIC

TIPPS, Greg
Compositeur américain.
Serio I (1976) •15 Sx: 3 x SATB/TTB

TIPTON, Clyde
Three Whitman Songs on Death •Bass Voice/Tsx

TISNÉ, Antoine (1932)
Compositeur français, né à Lourdes, le 29 XI 1932. Travailla avec D. Milhaud et J. Rivier.

"Il revendique une absolue indépendance de langage et réalise avec éclectisme une synthèse de tous les moyens d'expression actuellement en usage. Ses nombreux séjours à l'étranger, notamment aux Etats-Unis, au Danemark, en Espagne et en Grèce, ont considérablement enrichi ses horizons expressifs et c'est de cette gamme de moyens que résulte un art qui se veut lyrique et émotionnel avant tout." (Cl. ROSTAND) "L'attrait qu'exerça la philosophie de Teilhard de Chardin sur Antoine Tisné fut déterminant dans sa conception musicale; la plupart de ses oeuvres traduit son sentiment de faire corps 'avec la matière, avec tout le mouvement cosmique,' et témoigne de sa fascination pour les problèmes métaphysiques que pose l'Univers." (D. J-Y. BOSSEUR) "Il y a du peintre chez Antoine Tisné, un peintre qui peindrait avec des notes. Musicien indépendant et souvent solitaire, il est en réalité l'habitant d'un univers invisible, non seulement parce qu'il le porte en lui, mais surtout parce qu'il est trop immense ou trop petit pour être vu. Ce qu'il veut atteindre, c'est la force ou l'énergie qui meut les choses, et la musique, d'abord propagation d'ondes, en devient l'écho ordonné vers un sens. Son propos est de nous mener loin au-delà de nous, parfois hors du temps, aux limites de l'univers, là où notre regard se pose pour contempler, écouter l'Eternité. En cela, la musique d'Antoine Tisné est universelle parce qu'elle propose de réconcilier l'humain avec les forces vives de la Création. Des civilisations les plus reculées aux plus lointaines galaxies, de l'infiniment petit à l'infiniment grand." (D. NIEMANN) "Dès ses premières oeuvres la métaphysique et les mystères du cosmos fondent son inspiration; ses titres révèlent cette volonté de s'intégrer au tout par la spiritualité." (X. DARASSE)

"Making use of diverse contemporary techniques, including 12-note serialism and aleatory forms, his music is carefully constructed, has a powerful dramatic sense and shows a strong feeling for melody and richly coloured ideas. His writing for wind instruments is particularly fine." (A. HOEREE)

Alliages I & II (1971) (15') (to Quatuor Deffayet) •SATB •Bil
Dolmen (1976) (30') •Fl/Cl/Asx/Hn/Tpt/Trb/Tuba/Pno •adr
Duo (1990) •2 Sx: AA •adr
Duo 2 d'après le poème "Sur le Sol" de D. Niemann (1991) (9'30) (to S. BERTHOMMÉ & J. BAGUET) •2 Sx: SB •Fuz
Espaces irradiés (1978) (24'30) (to S. BICHON) 1) Lent et comme une improvisation 2) Récité et libre, dans le caractère d'une mélopée incantatoire, sans lenteur 3) Lunaire 4) Statique et libre •Asx/Pno •Chou
Hymne pour notre temps (1989) (17') •15 Sx: Sno+S SAAAATTTTBBBBBs •adr
Music for Stonehenge (1975) (16') 1) Extatique 2) Monologue 3) Scandé 4) Fugace 5) Dynamique 6) Volubile •Asx/Pno •Chou
Ombres de feu (1988) (18') (to K. HERDES) •Asx/Pno •adr
Point fixe (1982) •1 Player: BsCl+Asx/Perc à claviers •adr

TISO, Marco
Compositeur italien.
Piccola suite 1) Tango 2) Ragtime 3) Pavane 4) Tarantella •SATB

TITL, Anton Emil (1809-1882)
Serenade •Eb Sx/Pno •CF/Bet

TITTLE, Steve (1935)
Compositeur canadien.
The Dragon Doesn't Live Here Anymore (1989) •SATB •CMC
Sonata (1967) (12'30) •Asx/Pno •CMC

TOBANI, Theodore Moser (1855-1933)
Hearts and Flowers •Bb Sx or Eb Sx/Pno •CF

TOBIS, Boris
Compositeur russe.
Aria (1977) (to L. MICHAILOV) •Asx/Pno
2 Pieces (to L. MICHAILOV) •Asx/Pno •ECS

TODARO, Bruno
Saxophoniste français.
Apprendre seul à jouer du saxophone (1989) •JL

TODENHOFT, Walter
Danny Boy (TRADITIONAL) •SATB or AATB •Ron

TOEBOSCH, Louis (1916)
Compositeur, chef d'orchestre, et organiste néerlandais, né à Maestricht, le 28 III 1916. Travailla à Utrecht puis à Liège, avec H. Hermans et Ch. Hens.
"His music combines the polyphonic style of the Renaissance with modern techniques; he applies the 12-tone method of composition even in his sacred music." (BAKER)

Thema met variaties ous "Heflied van Hertog Jan", op. 42 (1953) (6') •3 Sx •Don

TOECHI
Music •Asx/2 Pno

TOENSING, Richard (1940)
Compositeur américain, né à St-Paul (Minnesota). Travailla avec R. L. Finney et L. Bassett.
Concerto (1990) (to M. MYER) •Asx/Synth •CF
For Saxophone Alone (1985) (4') (to D. PITUCH) •Sx Solo •PNS

TOEPLITZ, Kasper (1960)
Compositeur polonais, né à Varsovie. Vit en France depuis 1970. Autodidacte.
"Influencé autant par les compositeurs comme Scelsi ou Lévinas que par des groupes de Rock comme Godflesh ou Brötzmann, son langage utilise largement le chromatisme ou les micro-intervalles en une idée de 'grosse note' dont l'ambigus peut dépasser une quinte, mais aussi la virulence et l'urgence venues des guitares électriques dans un répertoire qui va de la musique de chambre au grand orchestre."
Anachorete (1991) (5') (to D. KIENTZY) •Ssx Solo •Saer/Ric
Johnny Panic et la bible des rêves (25') •1 Sx: T+CBs/Mezzo Soprano Voice/2 Fl/2 Cl/Hn/2 Vln/2 Vla/Perc/Tape

TOKUNAGA, Hidenori (1924)
Compositeur japonais. Travailla avec H. Takeochi.
Barcarolle (from *Epitaph*) (1964) (2') (to R. NODA) •Asx/Pno •adr
Columnation (1972-73) (to F. HEMKE) (Thema - Monophon I & II - Polyphony - Thema •Sx Solo: A or T •adr
Eidos (to F. HEMKE) •1 Sx: S+A+T+B/Tape •adr
Quartet (1970) (21') (to F. HEMKE) 1) Molto lento 2) Vivace 3) Andante 4) Allegro moderato 5) Vivace - Andantino 6) Andante moderato 7) Moderato 8) Larghetto rubato 9) Andantino 10) Adagio tranquillo 11) Allegro assai •SATB •South/SMC

TOLAR, J. K.
Compositeur tchèque.
Balette à 4 •SATB

TOLDRA, Eduardo (1895-1962)
Ave Maria (AMAZ & BAYER) •1 Sx: A or T/Pno •UME
Dels 4 vents (AMAZ & BAYER) •1 Sx: A or T/Pno •UME
La Font (AMAZ & BAYER) •1 Sx: A or T/Pno •UME
Oracio al maig (AMAZ & BAYER) •1 Sx: A or T/Pno •UME
Soneti de la rosada (AMAZ & BAYER) •1 Sx: A or T/Pno •UME

TOMASI, Henri (1901-1972)
Compositeur et chef d'orchestre français, d'origine corse, né à Marseille, le 17 VIII 1901, mort à Paris, le 13 I 1972. Travailla avec P. Vidal et V. d'Indy. Prix de Rome (1927).
"Style néo-classique des plus éclectiques où les influences les plus diverses sont discernables." (Cl. ROSTAND) "L'idéal de ce musicien est à base de lyrisme; ayant accepté les lois du théâtre en musique, il s'est créé un langage très personnel grâce à sa sincérité sans détours, à son indépendance et à son sens de la grandeur." (N. DUFOURCQ) "Henri Tomasi est un musicien de l'impression sensorielle, ce qui le sauve de l'académisme d'indyste, malgré un certain traditionalisme." (R. STRICKER)
"His music is intensely direct in feeling, occasionally dissonant and highly coloured; he absorbed influences from his French contemporaries (chiefly Ravel) while retaining an individual voice." (A. HOEREE)
Ballade (1939) (14') (to M. MULE) •Asx/Orch (2222/222/Perc/Harp/Str) or Pno •Led
Chant corse (1932) •Asx or Bb Sx/Pno •Led
Concerto (1949) (18'30) (to M. MULE) 1) Andante et Allegro 2) Final - Giration •Asx/Orch (3333/4332/Perc/Harp/Str) or Pno •Led

Evocations (1968) (4') (to D. DEFFAYET) •Asx Solo •Led
Introduction et danse (1949) (5') •Asx/Orch (1000/000/Harp/Str) or Pno •Led
Printemps (1963) (10') (to Sextuor de Dijon) 1) Réveil des oiseaux 2) Chant d'amour 3) Danse des oiseaux •Fl/Ob/Cl/Asx/Hn/Bsn •Led

TOMASSETTI, Benji
Quartet (1989) •SATB

TOMASSON, Haukur (1960)
Compositeur islandais, né à Rejtjavik. Travailla avec A. Heima Sveinsson, T. Sugarbjorssln, et T. de Leeuw.
Octette (1987) •Fl/Cl/Asx/Hn/Vla/Vcl/Pno/Perc (Vibr+Gong) •IMIC

TOMLINSON, Ernest (1924)
Compositeur anglais, né à Rawtenstall, le 19 IX 1924.
"He is a prolific composer, chiefly of light music." (Ch. PALMER)
Concerto (1965) (18') •5 Sx: AATTB/Orch •adr
Saxophone Ensemble (1976) •SATB •adr

TOMMASO, Bruno
Compositeur italien.
I virtuosi di noci •Asx/Jazz Orch

TONT, Patrice (1960)
Compositeur autodidacte français, né à Versailles, le 18 VIII 1960.
Aride sax (1988) (5') (to S. BERTOCCHI) •Asx Solo
Citharède (1990) (6') (to S. BERTOCCHI) •Bsx Solo
De ceux qui fréquentent l'altitude - Offertoire et Pie Jesu (1990) (10') (to S. BERTOCCHI) •1 Sx: S+B
Kiki song (1990) (to S. BERTOCCHI) •Tsx Solo
Sax requiem (to Quatuor Ars Gallica) •SATB
Tête oreille (1991) (to S. BERTOCCHI) •Bsx Solo

TONTELIES
Elegy •Asx/Pno

TON-THAT, Tiêt (1933)
Compositeur vietnamien, né à Hué. Travailla avec J. Rivier et A. Jolivet.
"Sa musique se réfère à la philosophie chinoise." (J. & B. MASSIN)
Moments rituels (1991) •Tsx/Marimba/Synth

TORBJÖRN, Iwan Lundgvist (1920)
Compositeur suédois.
Concitato (1980) (to B. OLSSON) •Sx Solo

TORRE, Salvador G.
Bira (1987) (15') (to D. KIENTZY) •Asx/Tape

TORREBRUNO, Leonida
Scemiary •Asx/Perc

TORSTENSSON, Klas (1951)
Compositeur suédois, né le 16 I 1951 à Nässjö.
"Klas Torstensson's compositions are frequently based on thoughts about form, volume and perspective, as can be educed from such titles. His pieces are based on an extensive abstract imagination coupled with a feeling for sound and spontaneous force. Any additional concepts applicable to his music are bound to include architecture and expansion of harmony and texture, for example." (H-G. P.) "Klas Torstensson's music is characterized by elaborate musical structures which have a strong emotional impact and probe extremes at every level for the performer and for the listener."

Licks and Brains (1987-88) 1) Solo (10') (BsSx Solo) 2) Licks and Brains I (19') (SATB) 3) Licks and Brains II (25'30) (Sx Quartet/Large ensemble •Don
Spâra (1984) (13') •3 Sx/3 Bs Guit/2 Electr. Pno/4 Perc •Don

TOSELLI, Enrico (1883-1926)
Célèbre sérénade (PIGUET) •Asx/Pno •GD
Serenade, op. 6 (GUREWICH) •Asx/Pno •Bos
Serenade (HARGER) •5 Sx: AATTB •Band

TOSI, Daniel (1953)
Compositeur né à Perpignan. Travailla avec I. Malec, P. Schaeffer, G. Reibel et F. Ferrera.
Multiphony III (1986) (6'30) •Fl/Cl/Asx/Pno/Vln/Vcl
Multitude II (1984-85) (to D. KIENTZY) •1 Sx: S+A+T/Fl/Vibr/Tape/2 Perc - 3 soloists
Multitude III (1984) (20') (to D. KIENTZY) •Fl/Asx/Vibr
Surimpressions II - Miroir aux cinq méditations (1982) (15') (to D. KIENTZY) •1 Sx: A+T+B+S/Synth/Tape •Sal

TOSTI, Francesco Paolo (1846-1916)
Goodbye •2 Sx: AT/Pno •Cen

TOULON, Jacques
3 Opuscules (1990) (2'30) 1) Badinage 2) Affable 3) Mascarade •Asx Solo •Mar

TOURNIER, Franz-André (1923)
Compositeur français, né à Vannes, le 29 IX 1923. Travailla avec T. Aubin et O. Messiaen.
"Musique claire, thèmes directs, contrepoint assez poussé pour devenir naturel."
Prélude et scherzo (1962) (5'30) •Asx/Pno •RR
Prophéties (1982) (10') (to A. BOUHEY) •Asx/Org •adr
Quatuor (1954) (16'15) 1) Allegro 2) Lent et très expressif 3) Presto 4) Lento-Presto •SATB •DP
Quatuor d'anches (1964) (14') (to Quatuor d'Anches Français) 1) Allegro giocoso 2) Lento 3) Allegro con brio •Ob/Cl/Asx/Bsn •RR
Trio (1953) (17') 1) Modéré 2) Allegro 3) Récit-sostenuto 4) Presto •3 Sx: ATB •DP
Variations sur un thème de Cl. Le Jeune (1955) (3'30) •Asx/Pno •Led

TOWER, Joan
Compositeur américain.
Wings (1991) •Asx

TOWNER, Ralph
Compositeur américain.
Icarus •Asx/Vibr

TOYAMA, Yuzo (1930)
Compositeur japonais.
Sérénade (1968) (to A. SAKAGUCHI) •Asx/Pno

TOYOZUMI, Tastshi
Compositeur japonais.
Sinphonic Suite (1992) (to K. MUNESADA) •Asx/Pno

TRAJNOVIC, Vlatimir (1947)
Compositeur croate, né à Belgrade. Travailla avec Mokranjac, W. Lutoslawski, et O. Messiaen.
Air et danse (Album [Recueil]) (2'30) •Asx/Pno •Bil

TRAN, Fanny
Majowka (1981) (7') •7 to 15 Sx
Warszawian Echoes (1981) (11') (for D. PITUCH) •Sx Solo •DP

TRAVERSA, Martino

Compositeur italien.
Fragment (1992) •Ssx/Live electronics

TRAXLER, A. (1xxx-19xx)

Clarinettiste, professeur, et compositeur américain.
Grand Artistic Duets •2 Sx •Bel
Grand Virtuoso Saxophone Studies (1928) •Bel
Romance •Asx/Pno •Bel

TREBINSKY, Arkadi (1897)

Compositeur et pianiste français, d'origine russe, né à Ir Kléeff (Poltava), le 9 IV 1897. Travailla avec R. Lenormand.
"Musicien délicat et probe, qui poursuit avec une discrétion anachronique une carrière de compositeur, jalonnée de partitions symphoniques et de musiques de chambres réfléchies, sensibles et équilibrées." (R. BERNARD)
Concertino, op. 7 (1945) (16') (to M. MULE) 1) Allegro 2) Lento 3) Allegro vivace •Asx/Str Orch •adr
Deux mouvements (to Quatuor d'Anches Français) •Ob/Cl/Asx/Bsn •adr
Double quatuor (1977) (to Quatuor Deffayet) •4 Sx: SATB/Str Quartet •adr
Quatuor, op. 25 (1956) (18') (to Quatuor Mule) 1) Allegro 2) Adagio 3) Presto possibile •SATB •adr
Sonatine, op. 7 (1945) (16') (to M. MULE) 1) Allegro 2) Lento 3) Allegro vivace •Asx/Pno •adr

TREMBLAY, George (1911)

Compositeur et pianiste américain d'origine canadienne, né à Ottawa, le 14 I 1911. Travailla avec son père puis avec D. Patterson et A. Schoenberg. Aux U.S.A. depuis 1919.
"In his work he has made use of 'cycles' of serial forms with the aim of producing integrated structures." (B. HAMPTON)
Epithalamium (1962) •Fl/Ob/Cl/Sx/Bsn/Hn/Tpt/Trb/Tuba/Perc •CFE
Piece •Fl/Ob/Cl/Tsx/BsCl

TRIEBERT, Charles-Louis (1810-1867)

Air pastoral •Bb Sx/Pno •Mil
Doglianza - Mélodie •Bb Sx/Pno •Mil
L'illusion valse •Bb Sx/Pno •Mil
Rêverie •Bb Sx/Pno •Mil

TRIMBLE, Lester

Compositeur américain.
Panels I (1973) (6') •Picc/Bsx/Vln/Vla/Vcl/Bass/2 Perc/Electr. Guit/ Electr. Org/Electr. Harp •Pet

TRINKAUS, G.

Lament •Bb Sx/Pno •FMH
Lament •2 Sx: AA or AT/Pno •CF
World's Best-Known Pieces •2 Woodwinds/Pno •CF

TRORY, Robert

Compositeur anglais.
David's Lament (1970) (2') •SATB
Quartet (1970) (4') (to London Saxophone Quartet) •SATB

TROUILLARD, Raymond

Compositeur français.
Divertissemnt sur des airs populaires •SATB •adr
Enfantillages •SATB •adr
Les anches s'amusent •SATB •adr

TROWBRIDGE, Luther (1892)

Compositeuir américain, né à Delta (Ohio).

Albumblatt •Asx/Pno •VAB
Album Leaf (1947) (3'15) •Asx/Pno •SeMC
In Retrospect (1946) (3'15) •Asx/Pno •SeMC
Organum Metamorphoses (1946) (3') •Asx/Pno •SeMC

TRUAX, Bert

Trompettiste et compositeur américain.
Romance and Burlesque (1985) (15') (to D. RICHTMEYER) •Ssx/Tpt/ Pno

TRUILLARD, Robert

Compositeur français.
Sérénade (1983) (1'30) •Asx/Pno •Com

TRUMBAUER, Frank (1901-1956)

Compositeur et saxophoniste américain, né à Carbondale (Illinois), le 30 V 1901, mort à Kansas City, le 11 VI 1956.
Trumbology •Asx/Pno •RoMu

TRYTHALL, Gil

Rima's Song (1994) (to P. SCEA) •MIDI Wind Controller/Computer

TSCESNOKOV

Salvation Belongeth to our God (WORLEY) •8 Sx: SAAATTBBs •DP

TSOUPAKI, Calliope

Kentavros (1991) (17') •3 Sx/Pno/Bass •Don

TUBIN, Eduard (1905-1982)

Compositeur et chef d'orchestre estonien, né à Kallaste, le 8 V 1905, mort à Stockholm, le 17 XI 1982. Travailla avec H. Heller. Installé à Stockholm depuis 1944.
"His music often combines propulsive rhythm with expansive melody, orchestrated in a clear and expressive manner." (H. OLT) "Emulating Kodàly, he studied at the Museum of Ethnography in Tartu so as to acquaint himself with Estonian folk music. His music has an insistent rhythmic beat, clarity of structure and imaginative, colourful orchestration. And yet to the end, he received quite niggardly treatment in his new country." (SJ)
Sonate (1951) (14') (to J. de VRIES) 1) Allegro 2) Adagio 3) Allegro vivace •Asx/Pno •STIM/SMIC

TUFILLI, W.

Random Reverie •Tsx/Pno •Bel
Rose Blush •AATB •BM

TULL, Fisher (1934)

Compositeur américain, né à Waco (Texas). Travailla avec S. Adler.
Colloquy (1982) (to D. HASTINGS) •Asx/Perc
Concertino da camera (to M. JACOBSON) •Asx/Brass quintet •South
Cyclorama II •12 Sx
Dance Suite (1976) •Asx/Pno
Dialogue (1987) (for the 80th birthday of Sigurd Rascher) •2 Sx: AT •South
Sarabande and Gigue (1976) (5'30) (to K. DEANS) •Asx/Pno •B&H
Threnody (1984) (to K. DEANS) •Asx Solo

TUONG, van Nguyen (see VAN TUONG, Nguyen)

TUREK, Ralph

Piece (1982) •Asx/Tape
Precis (1979) •Asx/Tape

TUREWICZ, Kazimierz

Compositeur polonais.
Miniatures rythmiques (1962) 1) Amethyst 2) Golden butterfly 3) Street in roses •Asx/Pno •PWM

TURINA, Joaquin (1882-1949)
Oracion del Torero •SATB

TURKIN, Marshall W.
Compositeur américain.
Sonata (1958) (to S. Rascher) 1) Allegro con moto 2) Adagio
   3) Allegro con spirtito •Asx/Pno •Pres

TURNER, Malcolm (1964)
Weasels Try Harder (1992) •Asx/Pno

TURNER, Robert (1920)
Compositeur canadien, né à Montréal. Travailla avec D. Clarke, C.
  Champagne, G. Jacob, H. Howells, R. Harris, et O. Messiaen.
Nostalgie (1972) (6'30) (to P. Brodie) •Ssx/Pno •CMC

TURNER, Thomas
Fantasy (to J. Houlik) •Tsx/Pno •SeMC

TURNHOUT, Gerard de (1520-1580)
Motet (Evertse) •SATB •TM

TUROK, Paul (1929)
Chef d'orchestre, critique, et compositeur américain.
Improvisation (1988) (15'30) (to J. Umble) •Vln/Asx/Pno •SeMC
Sonata, op. 72 (1988) (17') (to J. Umble) •Asx/Pno •SeMC

TUSTIN, Whitney
30 Duets (2 volumes) •2 Bb Sx or 2 Eb Sx •PIC

TUTHILL, Burnett Corwin (1888-19xx)
Compositeur, chef d'orchestre, écrivain, et clarinettiste américain,
  né le 16 XI 1888, à New York.
  "My music is on the whole conservative. I have always been a
protagonist for the contemporary composer, and I have tried to study
all the new music that has been written. All this study does not convince
me that the effort to get away from the classic forms and principles has
created a new art that will stand the test of time. For atonality I have no
use, nor for harmony that is merely distortion. My own work tries to
seek expression through rhythms that are not ordinary, and to create an
atmosphere through the modern use of church modes and the newer
harmonic juxtapositions which adherence to these scales creates." (B.
Tuthill)
Concerto, op. 50 (1965) (20') (to C. Leeson) •Tsx/Orch (0000/0330/
  Perc/Str) or Pno •South
Quartet, op. 52 (1966) (18') (to C. Leeson) •AATB •South
Sonata, op. 20 (1939) (16') (to C. Leeson) 1) Allegro giocoso
  2) Andante, un poco adagio 3) Presto, molto vivace •Asx/Pno
  •South
Sonata, op. 56 (1968) (16') (to C. Leeson) •Tsx/Pno •South

TWEED, Andrew
Compositeur anglais.
PR Girl •SATB

TWINN, S.
Old English Songs •2 Sx •Pet
Three Dialogues - Duo (1963) •2 Sx •Hin

TYLE, Teddy
Whodnit •Sx Ensemble

TYSSENS, Albert
Saxophoniste et compositeur belge.
Derogation (1982) •Asx/Pno •adr
4 Etudes sur les graphismes musicaux contemporains •Ty
8 Etudes classiques •Ty
12 Etudes de concours (d'après Bach et Handel) •Ty

2 Excerpts from 'Opus numerus clausus' (1984) 1) Méditation -
  Thème principal 2) Contestation •adr
3 Excerpts from 'Phantasmes' (1983) •Asx/Voice/Tape •adr
Fantaisie irlandaise (1982) •Asx/Pno •adr
Poclades (1988) •2 Sx •adr
Saxo superstar (1988) (to J. Selmer) •Asx/Pno •adr
Singeries (1982) •Asx Solo •adr
Toccata (1980) •Sx •adr

UBER, David
First Saxophone Quartet (1977) (to F. MILLER) •SATB •Sha/Pres

UCHIMOTO, Yoshio
Compositeur japonais.
Afro-blue (1993) •1 Sx: S+T/Bass •INM

UDELL, Budd
Compositeur américain.
Elegie and Ecossaise (1990) (to K. L. FARRELL) •Ssx/Pno

UDOW, Michael (1949)
Compositeur américain, né le 10 III 1949, à Detroit.
Sandsteps I (1989) (15') (for C. Rochester Young) •Asx/Marimba •adr
Understanding (1969) (15') •6 Unspecified instruments/8 Perc/Tape •MP

UEDA, Keiji (1953)
Saxophoniste japonais, né à Yamagushi, le 27 XII 1953. Travailla avec Keizo Inoue, A. Sakaguchi, et J-M. Londeix.
Ohanashi (1990) •Sx Solo

UHLMANN, Thomas
Compositeur allemand.
Die Eintagsfliege (1993) •Tsx/Banjo •INM

ULBEN, Denize
Compositeur américain.
Concertino (1985) (15') (to P. COHEN) (3 movements) •1 Sx: A+Sno/ Orch (Winds/Brass/Perc/Str) •adr

ULLMAN, Viktor
Slovanic Rhapsody (1940) •Sx/Orch •LCM

ULRICH, Jürgen (1939)
Professeur et compositeur allemand, né le 21 XI 1939, à Berlin. Travailla avec J. Driessler et G. Klebe.
5 Duets (1966) •2 Sx •WH
Spiel (1974) (5') •Fl/Ob/Cl/Bsn/Sx/Hn/Tpt/Trb/Tuba •VDMK

UNEN, Kees van (1955)
Compositeur hollandais.
...and the world doesn't own me... (12'20) 1) ...that leaves you, you'll have to do it... 2) ...fair warning... 3) ...it's only just a song... •Asx Solo
Rhombi (1981) (8') •SATB •Don

UNGVARY, Tamas (1936)
Chef d'orchestre et compositeur suédois d'origine hongroise, né le 12 XI 1936, à Kalocsa. Travailla à Salzbourg avec D. Dixon, Jean Martinon, A. Simon et G. Wimberger avant d'aller à Darmstadt étudier avec G. Ligeti et I. Xenakis. En Suède, depuis 1970.
"He has taken a close interest in the psychological and social problems arising in the chain of communication between composer and listener, and between composer and computer. Ungvary's music represents a fascinating synthesis of the extremes of contemplative/ aggressive and protracted/compact." (SJ)
Pignon, Paul Olarra (1983) (10') •Ssx/Live computer •SMIC
Sonologos •2 Sx

URATA, Kenjiro (1941)
Compositeur japonais. Travailla avec M. Ishigeta.
Sonata (1968) (to Y. SASAKI) •Asx/Pno

URBANNER, Erich (1936)
Compositeur et professeur autrichien, né à Innsbruck. Travailla avec W. Fortner, K. Stockhausen, et B. Maderna.
Concerto (1989) (20') •4 Sx: SATB/Str Orch •CA
Concerto XIII (1989-90) (18') •4 Sx: SATB/Orch (Ob/Cl/3 Perc/ Vln/Vla/Vcl/Bass) •CA
Emotionen (1984) (9') (to Rascher Quartet) •SATB •CA/ApE

USMANBAS, Ilham (1921)
Compositeur turc, né à Istanbul, le 28 IX 1921. Travailla avec H. Ferit Alnar, puis avec Dallapiccola.
"Usmanbas is the main Turkish advocate of new musical procedures. The influences of Bartok, Stravinsky and Hindemith, seen in his earlier neo-classical works, has given way to an individual style which embraces 12-note technique." (F. YENER)
Quartet (1979) •SATB

USSACHEVSKY, Vladimir (1911)
Compositeur américain, d'origine russe, né à Hailar (Manchourie), le 21 X 1911. Aux U.S.A. depuis 1931.
"En 1953 s'ouvre aux U.S.A., dans le cadre de l'Université de Columbia (New York) un Laboratoire de musique expérimentale joint au département de musique et dont les pionniers sont les professeurs Luening et Ussachevsky." (J. & B. MASSIN) "L'activité de Vladimir Ussachevsky se déploie globalement axée sur les ressources de l'enregistrement et de ses traitements sur bande magnétique."
"Ussachevsky's works divide into two principal genres: the electronic and the choral. He was brought up in the Russian Orthodox Church and has acknowledged a profound influence from Russian liturgical music. In his electronic works Ussachevsky has consistently maintained a flexible attitude towards sound: recordings of live sounds, analogue studio and computer-generated material all feature in his works." (C. WUORINEN)
Mimicry (1982) (to J. SAMPEN) •Asx/Tape

UYTTENHOVE, Yolande (1925)
Compositeur belge.
Le cygne d'or, op. 109 (1984)) (to H. GEE) •Asx/Pno
Sonata, op. 113 (1985) (to H. GEE) •Asx/Pno

VACHEY, Henri
Pastorale (Album [Recueil]) (1974) •Asx/Pno •Zu

VADALA, Kathleen
Sea Change (1988) •1 Sx: A or T/Pno •South

VAGGIONE, Oracio (1943)
Compositeur argentin.
Thema (1985) (10') (to D. Kientzy) •BsSx/Dispositif électroacoust.
•Sal

VALEK, Jiri (1923)
Compositeur tchécoslovaque.
Symphony III - Speranza (1963) (28') •2 Sx Solo: ST/Narr/Orch
(3332/4331/Harp/Perc/Str) •CHF

VALENTI, William
Duo •Asx/Bass

VALK, Adriaan (1943)
Saxophoniste, professeur, et compositeur autodidacte néerlandais.
Appris d'un clown - 20 duos (1987) •2 Sx •TM
Circles - Impressions (Niels Le Large) (1979) •Asx/Perc •BVP
Dialogue (1980) •Asx/Vcl •BVP
20 Duos - L'homme au chapeau melon (1984) •2 Sx: Eb or Bb •TM
20 Interpretations libres (1978) •HZ
4 Miniatures (1988) •Cl/Asx/Voice ad lib. •TM
Movements (1988) •SATB •Mol
5 Paintings (1988) •SATB •TM
7 Pieces for sax n° 635 (1976) •Asx Solo •HZ/WWS
Saxophone I, II, III, IV - Method in 4 volumes •BVP

VALKARE, Gunnar (1943)
Compositeur suédois.
Passage 3, 5 (1993) •Asx Solo •SMIC

VALLIER, Jacques (1922)
Compositeur français, né le 7 I 1922, à Paris. Travailla avec D.
Milhaud et A. Honegger.
Andante (1967) (1'30) (to Quatuor de l'Ile-de-France) •SATB •adr
Concertino, op. 78 (5'30) •Asx/Str Orch or Pno •adr
Deux pièces (1964) (2'30) 1) Andantino 2) Scherzando •2 Sx: AA or
TT •Phi
Divertissement (1982) •Asx/Pno •VCD
Duo, op. 196 (5') •Asx/Pno •adr
Fantaisie, op. 157 (1979) •Asx/Pno •VCD
Improvisation •Asx Solo •CANF
Suite, op. 59 (1960) (6') (to M. Perrin) 1) Andantino 2) Andantino
3) Allegro •Asx/Pno •Com

VAN APPLEDORN, Mary-Jeanne
Liquid Gold (1982) (to D. Underwood) •Asx/Pno •DP

Van BALKOM, Joost
Compositeur hollandais.
Cataract (1993) •Bsx/Pno •INM

VAN BELLE, A.
Koan V (to N. Nozy) •Sx Solo

VAN BEURDEN, Bernard
Compositeur français.
Concertino (1984) (15') •4 Sx: SATB/Orch (Str/Harp/Pno/Perc)
•Don
Überwindung des toten Punktes (1993) •1 Sx: S+A+T/Tuba •INM

VAN CLEEMPUT, Werner
Fiori •SATB •Sez

VAN DAM, Herman
Rage, rage, against the dying of the light - In memorian G. M. Blok
(1984) (8') •SATB •Don

VAN DELDEN, Lex (see DELDEN)

VANDELLE, Romuald (1895-19xx)
Compositeur français, né à Beaune. Travailla avec Ch. Koechlin, V.
d'Indy, et A. Schoenberg.
Prélude et gigue (1958) (5') (to M. Mule) •Asx/Pno •Led

VAN de MOORTEL (see MOORTEL)

VANDENBOGAERDE, Fernand (1946)
Compositeur français, né à Roubaix. Collaborateur de Jean-Etienne
MARIE depuis la fondation du C.I.R.M.
"Le travail électro-acoustique accompli par Fernand Vandenbogaerde
à partir de sources instrumentales, répond, dans la multiplicité de ses
directions, à un souci manifeste d'échapper à l'exclusive d'une option
esthétique particulière." (D. J-Y. Bosseur)
Tezcatlipoca I (1986) •7 Sx: SnoSATBBsCBs/Tape •Mor
Tezcatlipoca II (1986) •1 Saxophonist playing 3 Sx/Tape •Mor

VANDERCOOK, Hale A.
Colombine, Daisies, Hyacinthe (Buchtel) •1 Sx: A or T/Pno •Kjos
Ivy, Lily, Magnolia, Marigold (Buchtel) •1 Sx: A or T/Pno •Kjos
Morning glory, Peony, Tulip (Buchtel) •1 Sx: A or T/Pno •Kjos

VAN DER LINDEN, Robert E.
Compositeur hollandais.
Quadra •SATB

VANDERMAESBRUGGE, Max (1933)
Compositeur belge. Travailla avec J. Absil, A Souris, et M. Quinet.
Saxofolies, op. 40 (1974) (to Fr. Daneels) •7 Sx: SnoSATBBsCBs

VAN DER MEULEN, Henk (see MEULEN)

VAN DIJK, Jan (see DIJK)

VAN DIJK, Rudi M. (see DIJK)

VAN DOORN, Franz
Compositeur hollandais.
Ballade (1981) •Asx/Pno

VAN DOREN, T.
Album Leaf •Asx/Pno •HE

VAN GOENS, Daniel (1904)
Elegie •Eb Sx/Pno •CF
Romance sans paroles •Eb Sx/Pno •CF

VAN HAUTE, Anna
Compositeur belge.
Lucioles (1980) (to Saxofonio Ensemble) (Moderato - Lente
espressive - Allegro vivo) •SATB
Visions (1980) •6 Sx: SAATTB

VAN HULTEN, Lex (1957)
Guitariste et compositeur hollandais.

Kwartet (1982) •SATB

VAN MAELE, Gérard (1907)

Saxophoniste et compositeur français d'origine belge, né à Ménin, le 7 X 1907. Travailla avec M. Niverd.

Aria et allegro (1969) (4'15) •Asx/Pno •adr
Caprice en forme de bourrée (1950) (3') •5 Sx: AATTBs •adr
Concertino (to M. Sieffert) •Asx/Orch (1111/1110/Harp/Str)
Conte de Grand-mère (1944) (3') •5 Sx: AATTBs •adr
Effervescente (1986) (7'30) (to B. Jeannenot) •8 Sx: S S+A AATTBBs
Etincelante (1982) (4'30) (to B. Jeannenot) •8 Sx: SAAATTBB •adr
Etudes (1950) (7'30) 1) Allegro risoluto - Andante cantabile 2) Allegro vivace •Sx Solo •adr
Octuor •8 Sx: SAAATTBBs •adr
Scarabée - Divertissement (6'30) •Asx/Orch or Pno •adr

VAN RICKSTAL, J.

Compositeur belge.
45 Daily Studies •Sez

VAN TUONG, Nguyen

Synthese (1975) (to R. Noda) •Asx/Tape

VAN UNEN, Kees (see UNEN)

VAN VACTOR, David (1906)

Andante and Allegro (1972) (to C. Leeson) •Asx/2 Vln/Vla/Vcl

VARTKES, Baronjian (1933)

Compositeur croate, né le 23 IV 1933 à Belgrade. Travailla avec P. Milosevic.
Sonatina (1957) •Sx/Pno •YUC

VASSENA, Nadir

Compositeur suisse.
Nocturnes I - II - III (1993) •Asx/Pno •N&B

VASSILENKO, Sergei Nikiforovitch (1872-1959)

Rhapsodie orientale •Tsx/Pno •Mus

VASSILIADIS, Anastassios

Compositeur grec.
Kyklorythmia II (1993) •Asx/Marimba •INM

VAUBOURGOIN, Jean-François (1880-1952)

Organiste, compositeur, et professeur français, né le 29 XII 1880 à Bordeaux, où il est mort, le 27 XI 1952. Travailla avec Pennequin.
Introduction et allegro (1952) •Asx/Pno

VAUBOURGOIN, Marc (1907-1983)

Compositeur et professeur français, fils du précédent, né à Caudéran-Bordeaux, le 19 III 1907. Travailla avec son père, puis avec Gedalge, B. Gallon, et P. Dukas. Prix de Rome (1930).

"Style traditionnel très vivant. Dans sa musique, on retrouve toujours l'élégance et le raffinement harmonique qu'il inculque à ses élèves." (Cl. Rostand) "Consacre son oeuvre à la musique symphonique et à la musique de chambre, où il se montre préoccupé des leçons de Paul Dukas." (R. Stricker)

"His own music has qualities of elegance and refined nobility." (A. Girardot)

6 Petites pièces (1951) (11') (to M. Mule) 1) Modéré sans traîner 2) Mouvement de valse 3) Vif et léger 4) Très rythmé 5) Modéré expressif 6) Animé •Asx/Orch (2222/2200/Harp/Perc/Bass) or Pno •EFM

VAUGHAN WILLIAMS, Ralph (1872-1958)

Compositeur anglais, né à Down Ampney (Gloucestershire), le 12 X 1872, mort à Londres, le 26 VIII 1958. Travailla à Berlin avec M. Bruch puis avec M. Ravel à Paris.

"Considéré dans son pays comme le compositeur le plus éminent depuis Purcell. Son langage est plus modal que tonal, et son art va de la méditation la plus intérieure à l'âpreté la plus amplement tragique, son évolution ne cessant de se personnaliser tout en restant toujours de saveur nationale." (Cl. Rostand) "Vaughan Williams a cherché avec passion de retrouver dans le folklore principalement, la tradition nationale de la musique anglaise, perdue depuis le milieu du XVIIIe siècle." (M. Cross) "Comme Charles Koechlin, Vaughan Williams a écrit des pages audacieuses et parfois téméraires, et d'autres où il cherche la sérénité et l'équilibre." (P. Collaert) "Romantique attardé, pur produit de l'Angleterre victorienne, Vaughan Williams a insufflé à son langage symphonique une force nouvelle qui le place, sporadiquement, aux côtés d'un Sibelius ou d'un Martinu." (J-E. Fousnaquer)

"In his later works, Vaughan Williams adopted an advanced technique of harmonic writing, with massive agglomerations of chordal sonorities; parallel progressions of triads are especially favoured, but there is no intention of adhering to any uniform method of composition; rather, there is a great variety of procedures integrated into a distinctively personal and thoroughly English style. A parallel with Sibelius may plausibly be drawn; both are proponents of nationalism without isolationalism, and stylistic freedom without eclecticism." (Baker) "His music though so personal in idiom that it can be recognized in the space of a few bars, has arisen out of the life of the community and the spirit of the time to which he belongs, and as is the way of art so begotten and so nourished, it reveals the abiding and the essential in the local and the temporary—which is the way of the prophets throughout history." (F. Howes)

Household Music - 3 preludes (1940-41) 1) Crug-y-bar - Fantasia 2) St-Denis - Scherzo 3) Aberystwyth - Variations •3 Sx: SAA or diverse combinations with Vln/Vcl/Ob/Cl/Bsn/Tpt/Trb •B&H
Six Studies in English Folksong (1926) (Transcription) •Asx •SB

VAUGHN, John J.

Gorges (1991) •BsSx/Pno

VAUTE, Maurice

Compositeur belge.
Cantilène variée •Asx/Pno •CBDM
Divertissement (to Quatuor Belge de Saxophones) •SATB •CBDM
Impromptu (to Quatuor Belge de Saxophones) •SATB •CBDM

VAZZANNA, Anthony

Quartet •SATB
8 Studi (1978) (Preambolo - Strali - Gioco) •Asx Solo

VECCHI, Orazio (1550-1605)

The Cricket (Maganini) •AATB •Mus

VEERHOFF, Carlos Heinrich (1926)

Compositeur allemand d'origine argentine, né à Buenos-Aires, le 3 VI 1926. Travailla à Berlin avec Grabner et Blacher puis avec Thomas et Scherchen.
Dialogues (1967) (to J. Kripl) •Asx/Pno •IMD
Moments musicaux, op. 50 •Asx/Accordion/Perc

VEHAR, Persis (1937)

Compositeur américain.
A Day Off •Asx/Vln/Pno
Cakewalk •Sx Ensemble
Four Pieces (1975) (to M. Ried) •Asx/Pno •Pres/Ten
Quintus Concertino (1981) (to M. Ried) •Asx/Wind Ensemble

Sounds of the Outdoors (1984) (7'40) 1) Call of the birds 2) On the water 3) Back-tracking 4) Dusk 5) Chase homeward •Asx Solo •Ken

VELLONES, Pierre (1889-1939)

Compositeur français, né le 29 III 1889, à Paris, où il est mort, le 17 VII 1939. Travailla avec J. H. Louvier et L. Maingueneau.
"Docteur en médecine, autodidacte en musique, écrit dans les formes traditionnelles." (LAROUSSE) "Musicien fin et délicat, qui a le goût du rare et de l'exquis." (R. BERNARD)

A Cadix, op. 102 (1938) (4') •3 Sx/2 Ondes Martenot/Bass/Harp/ Perc

Au Jardin des bêtes sauvages - 8 pièces enfantines, op. 26 (1929) (35') 1) Les dauphins 2) Les pingouins 3) L'oiseau-lyre 4) La méduse 5) L'autruche 6) La biche 7) L'hippopotame 8) L'amadryas •SATB •Dur

Le bal Binetti - divertissement persan, op. 60 (1934) (4') •SATB •Chou

Castillanes, Argentines (de l'op. 23) •SATB •JJ

Les Cavaliers andalous, op. 37 (1930) (5'15) •SATB •Lem

Cinq poèmes de Mallarmé, op. 24 (1929) (28') •High Voice/4 Harp/ 2 Sx: AT/Bass •Lem

Concerto en Fa, op. 65 (1934) (25') (to M. MULE) 1) Introduction et allegro 2) Alla marcia e andante sostenuto •Asx/Orch (3334/ 434/Perc/Harp/Str) or Pno •Lem

Deux Pièces pour Colombia, op. 67 (1935) (6'30) 1) Split 2) Vitamines •2 Fl/4 Sx/Pno/Bass/Perc/Ondes Martenot •Sal

Fête fantastique, op. 83 (1937) (18') •2 Sx: AT/3 Ondes Martenot/ Pno/Fl/2 Cl/Bsn/3 Tpt/2 Trb/Tuba/2 Bass/Perc/Exotic Perc

Les Gauchos •SATB •Lem

Planisphère, op. 23 - 4 pièces pour jazz symph. (1930) 1) Castillanes 2) Argentines 3) Ouled Nails 4) Mittel Europa •2 Sx: AT/Cl/2 Tpt/Trb/Bass (or Tuba)/Perc/Pno •JJ

Prélude et fables de Florian, op. 28 (1930) •Tenor Voice/3 Sx: SAB/2 Tpt/Trb/Tuba/Banjo •Dur

Prélude et rondo français, op. 89 (1937) (4'15) •SATB •Lem

Rapsodie - Trio, op. 92 (1937) (4'30) •Asx/Harp/Celesta or Asx/Pno •Lem

Rastelli - Poème symphonique, op. 82 (1936) (20') •4 Sx: SATB/ Orch •Lem

Scherzo tarentelle, op. 42 •SATB •Chou

Sévillanes, op. 66 (1934) (3'30) •SATB •Lem

Valse chromatique, op. 41 (1931) (3'30) •SATB •Lem

VENTAS, Adolfo (1927)

Professeur de saxophone et compositeur espagnol.

Concerto d'Amposta (1991) •Asx/Orch d'harmonie •adr

Concierto •Cl Solo/4 Sx: SATB •adr

Cuevas de Nerja - Suite andaluza (1979) 1) Bulerias 2) Guajira flamenca 3) Noturno 4) Martinete 5) Zapateado •SATB •adr

3 danzas (1980) (to J-M. LONDEIX) (des Etudes caprices) 1) Exotica 2) Tarantela 3) Oriental •SATB or Asx/Pno •adr

12 duets, op. 11 (to J-M. LONDEIX) •2 Sx: AA or TT •adr

Etudes caprices •adr

Mélancolia (1980) •SATB •adr

VERACINI, Antonio (1659-1733)

Gavotte (FELIX) •Tsx/Pno •Mus

Two Classic Dances •Tsx/Pno •Mus

VERBEY, Theo

Compositeur hollandais.

Passamezzo •SATB

VERBIEST, R.

Compositeur belge.

Ballad for Marleen •SATB

VERDI, Giuseppe (1813-1901)

Anvil Chorus (from *Il Trovero*) •AATB •Bar

Celeste Aïda •2 Sx: AT/Pno •Cen

Celeste Aïda •AATB •CF

Grand Air (from *The Masked Ball*) •Asx/Pno •Mus

La Donna e mobile •2 Sx: AT/Pno •Cen

La Traviata (PANELLA) •Asx Solo •Sal

Le Trouvère (PANELLA) •Asx Solo •Sal

March (from *Aïda*) (LAKE) •Bb Sx/Pno •GSch

Miserere (from *Il Trovero*) •Bb Sx/Pno •CF

Miserere (from *Il Trovero*) •2 Sx: AT/Pno •Cen

Miserere (HOLMES) •AATB •Bar

Pilgerchor (from *I Lombardi*) (EVERTSE) •SATB •TM

Quartet (from *Rigoletto*) •4 Sx: AATB or 2 Cl/Asx/Bsn (or BsCl) •CF

Rigoletto (HOLMES) •AATB •Bar

Slavenkoor (from *Nabucco*) (LEMARC) •SATB •TM

Traviata fantaisie •SATB •Mol

VERDI, Luigi

Compositeur italien.

Organum (1990) •12 Sx: SnoSSAAATTTBBBs

VERDI, Ralph Carl (1966)

Compositeur américain, né le 24 IX 1966, à New York.

Strong Song •4 Sx: SATB/Wind Ensemble •adr

VEREECKEN, Benjamin (18xx-19xx)

Saxophoniste américain.

Admirations (1908) •Asx/Pno •Bar

Autumn Life - Blue Bells of Scotland •Eb Sx or Bb Sx/Pno •CF

Bouquet de fleurs (1908) •Asx/Pno •Bar

Cheerfulness (1908) •Asx/Pno •Bar

Complete Chart for all Saxophones •CF

Cupid's Courting - Narrative East •Eb Sx or Bb Sx/Pno •CF

Foundation to Saxophone Playing (1917) •CF

Junior Saxophone Method •Rub

Last Rose of Summer - Mocking Bird •Eb Sx or Bb Sx/Pno •CF

Love's Declaration - Fading Blossoms •Eb Sx or Bb Sx/Pno •CF

The Saxophone Virtuoso (1919) •CF

A Shepherd's Dream (1908) •Asx/Pno •Bar

16 Artistic Duets •2 Sx: AA or TT •Rub

Song of the Desert - Queen of the Night •Eb Sx or Bb Sx/Pno •CF

Waternymphs (1908) •Asx/Pno •Bar

VERHAEGEN, Mark (1943)

Compositeur belge.

Etchings (1982) (to BOK & LE MAIR) •Sx+Cl/Marimba+Vibr

Intrada e Allegro (1984) (10') •Asx/Pno

VERHIEL, Ton (1956)

Saxophoniste et professeur hollandais, né à Heerlen, le 4 I 1956. Travailla avec N. Nozy et W. Kersters.

Aria (1985) •Fl/4 Sx: SATB or AATB

Berceuse (1987) (to MIRJA) •Ssx/Pno

Brie bagatellen (1990) (1'40) •Asx/Guit

A Collection of trios (1989) (Hymne - Andante - Mars - Scherzo - Wals - Volkdans - Swing - Blues) •3 Sx: AAT

Drei miniaturen (1983) 1) Alla marcia 2) Elegie 3) Vivo •4 Sx: SATB or AAAT

An Easy overture (1984) 1) Maestoso 2) Andante moderato 3) Allegro •7 Sx: SAAATTB

Experiment 1 (1992) (2') (to S. WELTERS) •Asx Solo

Experiment 2 (1992) (2') (to N. NOZY) •Asx Solo

Experiment 3 (1992) (2') (to R. Noda) •Asx Solo
3 Folkdances (1989) 1) Popetdance 2) Where has my love gone
    3) Jig •Asx/Guit
Impromptu miniature (1985) •Bsx/Pno
Introduktie en scherzo (1990) (2'30) •Asx/Guit
Kinderstücke (1989) 1) Kleine Marsch 2) Kinderlied 3) Scherzo
    4) Intermezzo 5) Final •Asx/Vibr
Kleine suite n°2 (1980) (to Roman & Mirja) 1) Prelude 2) Menuet
    3) Arietta 4) Gavottes •Asx/Pno
Meditation (1984) (3'50) •Asx/Org •Eres
Partita breve (1990) (7'15) (to J-M. Londeix) 1) Prelude 2) Menuet
    3) Hymne 4) Gigue •Asx/Org •Eres
3 Pièces (1978) 1) Prélude et valse 2) Berceuse 3) Marche •3 Sx:
    AAT
3 Pieces in popular style 1) Prelude 2) Song 3) Little rock-theme •4
    Sx: SAAT
4 Pièces (1988-89) 1) Intrada-moderato 2) Menuet vif 3) Arioso -
    Andante 4) Gavotte - Allegretto •3 Sx: SAT
Prelude and rondo (1985) •7 Sx: SAATTB
Prelude, folksong and dance (1990) (2'45) •Asx/Pno
14 Studies in various styles (1992) (to K. Fischer) •Asx Solo •Run
Sonatine (1984) 1) Allegro moderato 2) Andante 3) Allegro •Asx/
    Pno
Song and little waltz (1990) (2'10) •Asx/Pno
Suite (1982) (for Jocelÿn) 1) Marche d'entrée 2) Prière - Berceuse
    3) Finale •Ssx/Pno or Org
Trio en Fa mineur (1978) 1) Allegro 2) Andante moderato
    3) Fughetto •3 Sx: AAT
Vivace (1986) •4 Sx: SAAT

VERMET, Ernest (1930)

Professeur de clarinette et de saxophone français, né à Dunkerque, le
I VIII 1930.
Gammes et exercices (1968) •HE/An

VERRALL, John (1908)

Compositeur et professeur américain, né à Britt (Iowa), le 17 VI
1908. Travailla avec R. O. Morris, Z. Kodaly, puis avec D. Ferguson,
Copland, Harris, et F. Jacobi.
"Since the late 1940s, he has used as the tonal basis for his compositions a nine-note scale consisting of two tetrachords on either side of
a central note, itself alterable. This material lends itself to symmetrical
harmonic formations and melodic contours which, with equivalent
rhythmic and metrical construction, generate the global pitch and
rhythmic relations in his music." (R. Swift)
Eusebius Remembered - Fantasy Sonata (1976-82) (to H. Gee) •Tsx/
    Pno •ACA

VERROUST, Stanislas Louis Xavier (1814-1863)

24 Etudes, op. 65 (2 volumes) •Bil
Ranz des vaches, op. 40 (Segoin-Dias) •1 Sx: S or T/Pno •Bil
Solo (S. Simon) •Asx/Orch militaire
12e solo •Bb Sx/Pno •Mol

VERSCHRAEGEN, G.

Compositeur belge.
Danse espagnole •Asx/Orch
Humoresque •Asx/Pno

VERSCHRAEGEN, Herman (1936)

Concerto (1981) (to W. Demey) •Asx/Orch or Pno

VESCOVO, Italo

Compositeur italien.
Cadenza (1988) (to Fr. Salime) •Asx Solo

VIARD, Jules (1890-1935)

Hautboïste, saxophoniste, arrangeur, et compositeur français.
Douce berceuse •Asx/Pno •Sal
Grande méthode (1935) •Sal
Jota, Sicilienne, Tarentelle •Asx/Pno •Sal
La dernière rose d'été (1935) •Asx/Pno •Sal
Rondo et Capriccio •Asx/Pno •Sal
Scherzetto, Menuet, Ecossaise (1935) •1 Sx: A or T/Pno •Sal
Slap and Laugh •Asx/Pno •Sal
Variations sur "Le carnaval de Venise" •Asx/Pno •Sal

VICTORY, Gerard (1921)

Compositeur irlandais, né le 24 VII 1921, à Dublin.
"Victory is notable for the ease and fluency of his style, and
successive works of his often show a different techniques, either
traditional, serial or post-serial, according to the dictates of form and
subject." (A. Fleischmann)
Sonatine (1973) (to S. Egan) •Asx/Pno •adr

VIDAL, Paul (1863-1931)

Mélodie (Mule) •Asx/Pno •Led

VIDENSKY, Jan (1947)

Compositeur tchécoslovaque.
Kwartet (1985) (8'15) 1) Preludium 2) Andante 3) Rondo 4) Lento
    5) Presto 6) Adagio7) Allegro assai - Fuga •SATB
Ranni rosa (1986) (1'15) •SATB
Vyznani (1986) (5'30) •SATB

VIERA, Joe

Saxophone im Jazz •HD

VIERU, Anatol (1926)

Compositeur roumain, né à Iasi, le 8 VI 1926. Travailla avec
Constantinescu, Klepper, Rogalski, Dragoi, Brauner, et Silvestri, puis,
à Moscou, avec A. Khatchaturian et Rogal-Levitsky.
"Une des figures saillantes de la première génération de composi-
teurs roumains de l'après-guerre."
"In early compositions the folk elements were combined with a
modal technique, but he grew dissatisfied with this about 1964 and
developed a sound block of 61 notes based on his previous works. He
has compared his creative work with that of a sculptor." (V. Cosma)
Diathlon (20') (to D. Kientzy) •Sx/Perc
Double duos (1983) (to Bok & Le Mair) •Sx+Cl/Marimba+Vibr
Doux polyson (1984) (7') •Asx Solo •Sal
Giusto (1989) (10') (to D. Kientzy) •Asx/Instrumental ensemble
Metaksaks (1984) (4') (to D. Kientzy) •1 Sx: A or T/suiveur
    d'enveloppe •Sal
Narration II (1985) (17') (to D. Kientzy) •1 Sx: S+B/Orch (2111/
    220/Perc/Str) •Sal
Quartett (1990) (10') •SATB
Siehe du bist Schoen (8') •Mezzo-Soprano Voice/Asx

VIGELAND, Nils

Classical Music (1986) (for Amherst Saxophone Quartet) 1) Sonata
    2) Scherzo 3) Aria 4) Rondo variations •4 Sx: SATB/2 Vln/Vla/
    Vcl

VIGNERON, Josée

Quatuor •SATB

VILEN, Asko (1946)

Compositeur finlandais, né le 21 V 1946.
Sonata (1976) •Asx/Pno •FMIC

VILLA-LOBOS, Heitor (1887-1959)

Compositeur brésilien, né le 5 III 1887, à Rio-de-Janeiro, où il est mort, le 17 XI 1959. Travailla avec son père puis avec Fr. Braga. Joua de la guitare, du saxophone et divers autres instruments populaires.

"Sa formation est presque uniquement autodidacte. Il se forma un style folklorique qu'il n'abandonnera plus, bien qu'ayant subi les influences de d'Indy et de Debussy, puis de Stravinski, influences qui restèrent très extérieures et qu'il ne sut pas assimiler en profondeur. Il se créa une certaine célébrité en faisant connaître "une nouvelle forme de composition musicale synthétisant les différentes modalités de la musique brésilienne, indienne et populaire." (Cl. ROSTAND) "Les *Chôros* sont une nouvelle forme de composition musicale qui synthétise les différentes modalités de la musique brésilienne, indienne et populaire." (VILLA-LOBOS) "Prolifique, précoce, autodidacte et fantasque: ces quatre adjectifs renferment toutes les qualités et les défauts de son oeuvre. Riche et prolixe, primesautier et irréfléchi, anti-académique et naïf, heureux et biscornu, Villa-Lobos est tout cela tour à tour, sinon en même temps. Dans sa production, très vaste, trop de bonnes choses sont noyées, ne fut-ce que dans leur propre abondance." (D. DEVOTO) "La chronologie est cruelle: toutes les 'grandes' oeuvres de Villa-Lobos, des *chôros* aux *Etudes pour guitare*, appartiennent aux années d'avant-guerre. La série des *Bachianas brasileiras*, appelée à lui apporter l'essentiel de sa popularité, touche à sa fin en 1945. Aussi faut-il nécessairement retourner en arrière pour trouver, au sein d'un fouillis au demeurant inextricable, quelques véritables joyaux. Telle la *Bachianas brasileiras n°2* pour orchestre, avec ses solos lascifs, brûlants, de saxophone et de violoncelle: vingt minutes qui comptent peut-être (avec le premier *Chôros* pour guitare) parmi les plus suaves qu'ait jamais écrites Villa-Lobos" (J-E. FOUSNAQUER) "Ce compositeur surabondant offre l'exemple d'une synthèse accomplie entre deux cultures fort distantes l'une de l'autre,—celle de la musique populaire brésilienne, celle de la musique savante occidentale." (F-R. TRANCHEFORT)

"Villa-Lobos is one of the most original composers of the 20th century. His lack of formal academic training, far from hampering his development, compelled him to create a technique all his own, curiously eclectic, and yet admirably suited to his musical ideas. An ardent patriot, he resolved from his earliest steps in composition to use Brazilian song materials as the exclusive source of thematic inspiration. Occasionally he uses actual quotations from folksong; much more often he wrote melodies in an authentic Brazilian style, but of his own invention. In his desire to relate Brazilian folk resources to universal values, he has written a series of unique works, *Bachianas Brasileiras*, in which Brazilian melorhythms are treated with Bachian *Chôros*, a popular dance marked by incisive rhythm and songful ballad-like melody. Villa-Lobos expanded the *Chôros* to embrace a wide variety of forms, from an instrumental solo to a large orchestral work with chorus." (BAKER)

Bachianas Brasileiras n° 2 (1930) •Chamber Orch (including [dont] 1 Tsx) •Ric

Bachianas Brasileiras No. 5 - Aria (BONGIORNO) •Ssx Solo/4 Sx: AATB •adr

Chôros n° 3 - Pica-Pào, op. 189 (1925) (6') (to T. & O. de ANDRADE) •Cl/Asx/Bsn/3 Hn/Trb •ME

Chôros n° 7 - Settiminio, op. 186 (1924) (10') (to A. GUINLE) •Fl/Ob/Cl/Asx/Bsn/Vln/Vcl/Tam-tam •ME

Fantasia, op. 630 (1948) (10') (to M. MULE) 1) Animato 2) Lento 3) Trés animé •Ssx/Orch (3 Hn/Str) or Pno •SMPC/PIC/Peer

Nonetto, op. 181 (1923) (18') (to O. G. PENLEADO) •Fl/Ob/Cl/1 Sx: A+B/Bsn/Perc/Celesta/Harp/Pno/Mixed Chorus •ME

Quatuor, op. 168 (1921) (20') (to Mme SANTOS LOBO) 1) Allegro con moto 2) Andantino (avec voix de femmes) 3) Allegro deciso •Fl/Asx/Celesta/Harp •ME

Sexteto mistico, op. 123 (1917) (9') •Fl/Ob/Asx/Guit/Celesta/Harp •ME

Song of the Black Swan (SIMON) •Asx/Pno •EBMM

VILLA-ROJO, Jésus (1940)

Compositeur espagnol né à Brihuega (Guadalajara). Directeur fondateur du Laboratoire d'Interprétation Musicale de Madrid.

Divertimento III (1992) (to M. MIJAN) •2 Sx: AA

Eclipse (1982) (7') (to M. MIJAN) •Any Sx Solo •EMEC

Lamento (1989) (8'15) (to D. KIENTZY) •Tsx/Tape

Lineas convergentes (1984) (to M. MIJAN) •SATB

Quatuor (1984) (to M. MIJAN) •SATB

VILLETARD, Albert (1883-1934)

Sous les ombrages •Asx/Pno •Bil

VILLETTE, Pierre

Compositeur français.

Arabesque (1986) (8'30) (to J-M. LONDEIX) •Asx/Pno •Led

VINCENT, Herman

Tunes for Tenor Saxophone Technique •Bel

VINCENT-DEMOULIN, Jean (1905)

Compositeur français, né à Dijon, le 24 VIII 1905. Travailla avec L. Dumas, N. Boulanger, et P. Dukas.

"C'est dans la tradition provençale et dans le folklore bourguignon que Jean Vincent-Demoulin puise le plus souvent sont inspiration." (R. BARTHALAY)

Petite suite gaélique (1949) (12') (to S. BICHON) •Asx/Str Orch or Pno •adr

Quatuor (14') •SATB •adr

Sonatine •Asx/Pno

Suite pastorale (1972) •Asx/Pno •adr

VINCI, Leonardo (1696-1730)

Sonata (FLEURY-PRZYSTAS) •Asx/Pno •PWM

VINTER, Gilbert (1909-1969)

Compositeur anglais.

Concerto burlando (1954) (14') (to M. PERRIN) •Asx/Orch (2222/4230/Harp/Perc/Str) •BMIC

Little March •SATB

VIOLA, Joseph

Professeur américain.

The Technique of the Saxophone (1963) •BP

VIOLAU, Rémy (1919)

Saxophoniste et compositeur français, né à Coussay (Vienne), le 29 XII 1919. Travailla avec M. Mule.

Suite chinoise (1964) (5') 1) Introduction et danse 2) Chants de la pagode 3) Promenade en pousse-pousse •SATB or AATB •Bil

VISONI, L.

Doux propos •1 Sx: A or T/Pno

VISSER, Peter (1939)

Compositeur néerlandais.

Orient express (1982) (12') •Sx+Cl/Vla/Pno •Don

VISVIKIS, Demis (1951)

Compositeur de nationalité Hellénique né le 20 X 1951 au Caire. Travailla à Paris, avec E. Richepin, M. Beugnier, J. Lacour, puis J. Falk.

Cascades de feu (1990) (12'45) (to Quatuor de Versailles) •SATB

Cercles (1989) (10') (to E. RICHEPIN & D. DEFFAYET) •Asx/Pno •Bil

VITAKIS, Manolis

Compositeur allemand.

Stück (1992) •Asx/Vcl •INM

VIVALDI, Antonio (1678-1741)
Concerto "alla rustica" (PATRICK) •10 Sx: SSAAAATTBBs
Concerto en La Mineur (OSTRANDER) •Asx/Orch •Mus
Concerto in A Major (FREDRIKSON) •10 Sx: SSAAAATTBBs
Concerto Grosso in D minor (REX) •8 Sx: SSAATBBBs •WWS
Giga (MAGANINI) •AATB •Mus
Ouverture (FOURMEAU) •SATB •SL
Rain (FELIX) •Asx/Pno •Mus
Sonata in G Minor (MARX) •Asx/Pno •DP
Sonata in Bb Minor (RIDDELL) •Asx/Pno
Sonata, op. 1, no. 7 (F. HUNT) •Asx/Pno
Sonata No. 6 (BODKY-RASCHER) •Tsx/Pno •MM
Suite in C Minor •1 Sx: A or T/Pno •Mus

VIVIER, Claude (1948-1983)
Compositeur canadienne à Montréal, et mort à Paris. Travailla avec Gilles Tremblay, puis avec Stockhausen.

"*Pulau Dewata*, oeuvre d'instrumentation variable, évoque l'univers du gamelan balinais pars ses ostinati rythmiques, l'articulation polyphonique de ses formules mélodiques." (D. J-Y. BOSSEUR) "La musique de Claude Vivier est très exceptionnelle. Il y a chez cet artiste une inspiration d'une rareté épurée, un extrême sens de l'économie, une nostalgie générale et lyrique que l'on peut comparer aux qualités de György Kurtag." (C. GLAYMAN) "Claude Vivier s'est construit peu à peu un style très personnel, à la recherche d'une simplicité expressive au ton très authentique. Son oeuvre, déjà importante, faisait de lui un des espoirs les plus brillants de la jeune musique canadienne. Claude Vivier a été assassiné à Paris, il allait avoir 35 ans." (J. & B. MASSIN)
Palau Dewata (1979) (to Quatuor Bourque) •SATB •CMC
Pulau Dewata (SAVOIE) •12 Sx: SnoSSAAATTTBBBs

VIVIER, F.
Enchantress •Eb Sx/Pno •CF

VLADIGEROV, Pantscho (1899-1978)
Compositeur bulgare.
Rêverie •Asx/Pno

VLAHOPOULOS, Sotireos (1926)
Compositeur américain.
Petite Partita (1984) (to G. LOUIE & C. STIER) 1) Prelude 2) Gavotte 3) Sarabande 4) Rondeau •Cl/Asx

VLAHOS, James P.
Exclamation Points! (1983) (2'30) (to R. CARAVAN) 7 Sx: SAATTBBs •Eth

VLIET, Brtus van der
Sax action (1987) •Asx/Pno •Mol

VOGEL, Ernst
Compositeur autrichien.
Konzert (1979) (23') (to F. FUCHS) 1) Bewegt 2) Sehr ruhig 3) Tänzerisch •Asx/Orch (3323/424/Perc/Str) or Pno •Dob

VOGEL, Roger G.
Compositeur américain.
Concerto (1986) (to K. FISCHER) •Asx/Wind Ensemble •DP
Divertimento (1978) (9') (to L. GWOZDZ) •11 Sx: SSAAAATTBBBs •SeMC
One Flesh (1988) (to K. FISCHER) •Ssx/Bass Voice/Pno •adr
Partita (1977) (to L. GWOZDZ) 1) Allegro 2) Lento 3) Scherzo-Allegro 4) Berceuse: dolce con tenerezza 5) Vivace •Asx Solo •TP
Quartet (1980) (to K. FISCHER) •SATB •DP
Temporal Landscape No. 5 (1981) (to K. FISCHER) •Asx/Pno •DP

VOGEL, Wladimir (1896)
Compositeur suisse, d'origine russe, né à Moscou, le 29 II 1896. Travailla avec Scriabine, puis avec Busoni. Fixé à Ascona, depuis 1934.

"Esprit curieux, éclectique avec rigueur et choix, ouvert à toutes les tendances nouvelles, ayant subi entre autres l'influence de Schoenberg, mais n'en faisant pas un système, c'est un musicien d'une grande distinction et d'une rare culture." (Cl. ROSTAND) "Son oeuvre 'Wagadu' est de la grande musique, trop peu connue, digne de prendre rang parmi les productions les plus belles de notre temps." (P. COLLAERT)

"His music reveals influences of Scriabin and Schoenberg; in some of his works he applied the 12-tone method of composition; he is very much preoccupied with philosophical expression in music." (BAKER) "In contrast with the abstract world of sound represented by his instrumental music there are very powerfully impressive choral works. Making use of a rhythmically speaking chorus he achieves novel effects of a grandiose, often almost nerve-racking gloom; but such dark passages are relieved by incidents of great sensuous beauty." (K. von FISCHER)
La Ticinella quintette (1941) (to Mme D. SPOERRY) 1) "Quel Granellin di riso" - Introduction 2) "Girumeta de la muntagna" - Pastorale 3) "Il cucu" - In modo della ritmica scherzosa 4) "Addio alla caserna" - In modo della ritmica ostinata •Fl/Ob/Cl/Asx/Bsn •SZ
Wagadu's Untergang durch die Eitelkeit (1930) •Soli Voices (Soprano/Alto/Bass-Baritone)/Singing Chorus/Speaking Chorus/5 Sx: SAATB •adr

VOGT, Gustave
Adagio religioso •2 Cl/Asx •Bil
Boat song - Dream waltz - Remembrance •1 Sx: A or T/Pno •Cen
Sax-O-man - Saxonade - Saxonola •1 Sx: A or T/Pno •Cen

VOGT, Hans (1911)
Pianiste, violoncelliste, chef d'orchestre, compositeur, et professeur allemand, né à Danzig, le 4 V 1911. Travailla avec G. Schumann.
Sieben Stücke (12') •Asx/Pno

VOIRPY, Alain (1955)
Compositeur et chef d'orchestre français. Travailla avec O. Messiaen.
Méditation sur un sanctus (1982) (4'30) (to A. BOUHEY) •Asx/Org •Lem
Motum V (1981) (9') (to Cl. DELANGLE) •Asx Solo •Lem
Offrandes (1982) •Ssx/Perc/Pno •Lem
Sylphe (1983) (10') (to J-M. LONDEIX) •12 Sx: SnoSSAAATTTBBBs •adr

VOLLEMAN
Improvisation et allegro •Asx/Pno •Mau

VON KNORR, Ernst Lothar (1896)
Compositeur allemand.
Suite fantaisie (Allegro - Allegretto - Scherzando - Signal) •Ssx/Pno

VOORMOLEN, Alexander (1895)
Compositeur néerlandais.
La Sirène (1949) (8') •Asx/Orch (2300/210/Perc/Harp/Str) •Don

VOORN, Joop
Compositeur néerlandais.
Sonata (1984) (20') •Asx/Pno •Don

VORONOV
Compositeur russe.
Scherzo •Asx/Pno •ECS

VOSK, Jay

Compositeur américain.

Caliopsis (8') •SATB
Chimera (1983) •2 Sx: AT/Marimba •DP
Concerto (1987) •Asx/Chamber Orch (2222/2211/Perc/Str) or Pno
  •DP
Deep River Variations (1991) (9'45) (to the Sonora Quartet) •SATB
Diversions •2 Sx: AA •SeMC
Le Nid •Ssx/Vibr/Guit/Vln/Bass •SeMC
Midnight Passacaglia (1984) •Sx Choir: SSAATTBBs •DP
Saxophone Spirituals (1990) (8') 1) Evocation 2) Dance •SATB
Sky-Island (1993) (10'20) •SATB
Three Sonoran Desertscapes (1983) •SATB •DP
Whirling Dervishes (1988) •Asx Solo •DP

VOTQUENNE, Victor

Barcarolle - Fioriture •Asx/Pno •HE
New technic (Volume I: Scales, Intervals, chords) •HE
New technic (Volume II: Rhythms, Velocity, Virtuosity) •HE
Serenata •Asx/Pno •HE/An

VOUILLEMIN, Sylvain (1910)

Compositeur et chef d'orchestre belge, né le 21 II 1910 à Charleroi.
Membre de l'Académie de Belgique.

Divertimento sur des chants populaires (1983) (8'30) 1) Deciso
  2) Largo 3) Allegro ritmico •Ssx/2 Vln/Vla/Vcl/Bass/Perc or
  Ssx/Pno •Led

VOUSTINE, Alexandre

Compositeur russe.

3 Pièces (1979) •Asx/Pno

VOXMAN, Hymie

Professeur et arrangeur américain.

Advanced Method (2 volumes) •Rub
At Christmas Time (Arrangments) 1) The first Noël 2) God rest ye
  merry, Gentlemen 3) Good Christian me, Rejoice (1986)
  •AATB •South
Chamber Music Series •3 Sx: AAT •Rub
Concert and Contest Collection •Asx/Pno •Rub
Contemporary Recital Pieces •Sx Solo •Rub
First Book of Saxophone Quartets (Arrangements) (1986) •AATB
  •South
Lament and Tarentella •Asx/Pno •Char
Quartet Repertoire (13 pieces) •AATB •Rub
Selected Duets (2 volumes) •2 Sx: AA or TT •Rub
Two Ukrainian Songs (Arrangements) (1986) •AATB •South

VRANA, Frantisek (1914-1975)

Compositeur tchécoslovaque.

Rapsody (1971) (12') (to P. Brodie) •Ssx/Pno •CHF/B&H

VRIEND, Huub de

Compositeur néerlandais.

Psycho (1984) (13') •Bsx/Pno or Orgue à bouche •Don

VRIES, Klaas de (1944)

Compositeur néerlandais, né le 14 VII 1944. Travailla avec O.
Ketting et M. Kelemen.

2 Koralen (1974) (6') (to Netherland Saxophone Quartet) •SATB
  •Don
March (1972) (5') •Tsx/Pno •Don
Moeilijkheden - Difficulties (1977) (15') •Fl/2 Sx: AT/Hn/2 Tpt/3
  Trb/Pno •Don

VRIONIDES, Christos (1894)

Compositeur et chef d'orchestre crétois, né à Khania, le 12 I 1894.

Travailla à Athène, puis aux U.S.A. où il dirige de nombreux concerts
et chorales.

Theme and Variations •4 Sx: SATB/Orch (2222/3231/Perc/Str)
  •ACA

VUATAZ, Roger (1898-19xx)

Compositeur, organiste, maître de chapelle, chef d'orchestre suisse,
né le 4 I 1898 à Genève. Travailla avec J. Dalcroze.

"Sans s'affilier à une école ou à une chapelle, Vuataz a coqueté avec
l'atonalité et le dodécaphonisme, pour les rejeter ensuite. Il en est arrivé
à limiter volontairement ses moyens d'expression en choisissant, pour
telle de ses compositions, un groupe déterminé de notes, une gamme
arbitraire, un accord type." (Ams)

"His works embrace practically all the categories of music. If some
are not without a certain artificiality of construction, his sense of
instrumental, particularly orchestral sounds is remarkable." (H. Ehinger)

*Destin - Symphony à trois pour un drame de T. S. Eliot ("La Réunion
  de famille"),* op. 91 (1954) (23') •Harp/Asx/Perc
Impromptu, op. 58/4 (1941) (7') •Asx/Orch (2222/4231/Perc/Harp/
  Str) or Pno •Henn
Incantation, op. 58/6 (1953) (2'30) •Asx/Pno •PN
Nocturne et danse, op. 58/2 (1940) (7'30) •Asx/Orch (2222/4230/
  Perc/Harp/Str) or Pno

VUSTIN, Alexander

Compositeur russe.

Autumn sonatina (1978) (to L. Michailov) •Asx/Pno •ESC

WAELE de
Quintette •5 Sx •Mar

WAGEMANS, Peter-Jan (1952)
Compositeur hollandais.
Quartet, op. 8 (1975) (10') 1) Allegro 2) Allegro •SATB •Don

WAGENAAR, Diderik (1946)
Compositeur hollandais.
Kaleïdofonen I (1969) (8') •Asx/Pno
Metrum (1981-84) (18') •4 Sx: SATB/Orch •Don

WAGENDRISTEL, Alexander (1965)
Flûtiste et compositeur autrichien, né le 23 III 1965 à Vienne. Travailla avec F. Neumann, H. Gattermeyer, et E. Urbaner.
Und (und ohne und), op. 32 (32b) •SATB •CA

WAGNER
Sonata •Ssx/Pno •WWS

WAGNER, Franz
Solo - waltzer •Asx Solo

WAGNER, Joseph (1900)
Chef-d'orchestre, compositeur, et professeur américain, né à Springfield (Massachusetts). Travailla avec F. Converse, N. Boulanger, A. Casella, et F. Weingartner.
"The most undiscovered among American composers. This style as enlightened romanticism and aggressive modernism… that has a tremendous driving force." (N. SLONIMSKY) "Great refinement of musical perception." (L.A.H.E.) "He has all the techniques of his art and uses them with so much imagination that he must be credited with additions to the expressive vocabulary of music." (W.T.H.)
Monologue (1971) (6') •Asx Solo •DP

WAGNER, Richard (1813-1883)
Album Leaf - Elsa's Dream - Pilgrim's Chorus •Eb Sx/Pno •CF
Bridal Chorus (from *Lohengrin*) •2 Sx/Pno •Mck
Evening Star (BUCHTEL) •Bb Sx/Pno •Kjos
Lohengrin: Brant-char (DÖMÖTÖR) •SATB •K&D
March (from *Tannhauser*) (GORDON) •AATB •Kjos
Pilgrim's Chorus (GORDON) •AATB •Kjos
Prize Song (LEESON) •Eb Sx/Pno •Hil Col
Romance (from *Tannhauser*) •2 Sx: AT/Pno •Cen
Song to Evening Star (TRINKAUS) •Bb Sx/Pno •FMH
Song to Evening Star (TRINKAUS) •2 Sx: AA or AT/Pno •CF
Song to the Evening Star •Eb or Bb Sx/Pno •CF
Tannhauser March (HOLMES) •AATB •Bar
Walter's Prize Song (BUCHTEL) •Bb Sx/Pno •Kjos
Walter's Prize Song (TRINKAUS) •Bb Sx/Pno •FMH
Walter's Prize Song (TRINKAUS) •2 Sx: AA or AT/Pno •CF

WAGNER-LEBENSLAUF, Wolfram (1962)
Compositeur autrichien, né le 28 IX 1962, à Vienne. Travailla avec E. Urbanner et F. Burt, puis avec R. Saxton à Londres et H. Zender à Frankfurt, avant d'aller à Darmstadt.
Drei Studien (1992) •12 Sx: SnoSSAAATTTBBBs •ApE
Konzert (1988) (12') (Preludium - Kadenz - Largo - Finale) •SATB •CA
Konzert (1990) •4 Sx: SATB/Str Orch/Perc •ApE

Konzert (1992) (15') 1) Lento 2) Con moto 3) Kanon: lento 4) Scherzando 5) Vivace •12 Sx: SnoSSAAATTTBBBs •CA

WAHLBERG, Rune (1910)
Pianiste, chef d'orchestre, et compositeur suédois, né le 15 III 1910 à Gävle.
"Conducting has given him a knowledge of the immense tonal potentialities of the orchestra." (H-G. P.)
Prisma (1961) (12'30) 1) Syncopation 2) Arioso 3) Alla gavotta - Uruppf •SATB •STIM

WAIGNEIN, André
Compositeur belge.
Feeling (1970) (to W. DEMEY) •Eb Sx/Pno •Scz
Pièces pour saxes (1981) 1) Technical part which shows the virtuosity of the soloists 2) Romantic Melody - Solo for alto saxophone 3) Two dances: Folklore dance; A la Brubeck •SATB
Scherzando (1971) (to W. DEMEY) •Asx/Pno

WALCKIERS, E.
Rondo (HARRIS) •2 Cl/Asx/Bsn (or BsCl) •CF

WALDEN, D. E.
Compositeur canadien.
Soguante (1972) •Asx/Pno •adr

WALENTYNOWICZ, Wladyslaw
Compositeur polonais.
Concerto •Asx/Pno

WALKER, "Singin' Billy" (1809-1875)
Hallelujah (1835) (HARTLEY) •1 Voice/5 Sx: BsBsBsBsBs •adr

WALKER, Gregory (1951)
Compositeur américain.
Four Sketches (1982) (to R. KNUESEL) •Asx Solo
Sonatine (1981) (to R. KNUESEL) •Asx/Tpt

WALKER, James (1937)
Recitative in Transition (1966) (to F. HEMKE) •SATB

WALKER, James J. (1881-1946)
Avocat et musicien américain, né le 9 VI 1881, à New York, où il est mort, le 18 XI 1946.
Chamber Concerto •Asx/Fl/Ob/Cl/Hn/Bsn
Prelude and Polka •SATB
Quartet •SATB

WALKER, Richard (1940)
Compositeur américain né le 18 1940, à Lexington (North Carolina).
Ballade •Asx/Pno •Ken
Four Fancies •AATB •Bel/BM
Reminiscence •Asx/Pno •PA
Suite •AATB •Ken
Waltz Casual •Tsx/Pno •Bos

WALKER, Robin
HB TO HB (11') •3 Sx/Harp

WALLACE, William (1933)
Compositeur canadien.
Free Soliloquy (1975) (7'10) (to P. BRODIE) •Sx Solo •CMC
Introduction and Chaconne (1977) (9') (to P. BRODIE) •SATB •CMC
Quartet No. 1 (1962) 1) Slow - moderately fast 2) Slow and quiet 3) Lively •SATB •CMC

WALLACE, William V. (1860-1940)

Only a Dream - Ave Maria •Eb Sx/Pno •CF
Scenes that are Brightest (*Round*) •Eb Sx/Pno •CF

WALLACH, Joelle

Quartet (1980) •SATB
Sweet Briar Elegies •Ssx/Vcl Ensemble

WALLIN, Peter (1964)

Compositeur suédois.
Harmony family (1987) (7'30) •Sx Solo •SMIC
Scäövu po màrrànànn eller vem satte... (1989) •Asx/2 Perc •SMIC

WALLNER, Alarich (1922)

Compositeur autrichien.
Fünf Ludi (1991) (18') (to D. Pätzold) •Asx/Org
Konzert (to D. Pätzold) •1 Sx: A+B/Org
Musik •Asx/Pno
Siciliana (1992) •4 Sx: SATB/Org

WALTER

Ballad •Asx/Pno •WWS
Quintalism (Transition - Finale) •SATB •WWS

WALTER, Caspar J.

Studie 9 (10') (to D. Kientzy) •Bsx Solo

WALTER, Civitaraele

Compositeur belge.
Aubade •Asx/Pno
Un soir à Moscou •Tsx/Orch

WALTER, D.

Hauboïste et compositeur français.
Deux Silhouettes (1975) •Ob/Cl/Asx/Bsn

WALTER, Douglas

Saxophoniste et compositeur américain.
Quartet No. 1 •SATB •Ken

WALTER, Richard

Compositeur anglais.
Jazz Suite (1979) (10') •SATB •adr
Little People (1978) (4') •SATB •SM

WALTER, Wolfgang

Compositeur allemand.
La cité de la douleur, Trois visages de Sarajewo (1993) •1 Sx: A+T+B/Guit •INM

WALTERS, David L. (1923)

Compositeur américain, né le 19 II 1923, à Youngstown (Ohio).
Andante and Scherzo (1982) •Asx/Pno •South
Episode (1968) (5'30) (Lento - Allegro - Lento - Allegro) •Asx/Pno •South

WALTERS, Harold L.

Fair and Warmer •AATB •Rub
Fantasy for Three - Jim Dandies •3 Sx: AAT •Rub
40 Fathoms •Bsx/Pno •Rub
I'm On My Way •AATB •Rub
Moonrise •6 Sx: AAATTB •Rub
Pizza Party - I'm On My Way •AATB •Rub
Spiritual Contrasts •AATB •Rub
Tarantelle •Tsx/Pno •Lud
Three Kings •Bb Sx/Pno •Rub

WALTON, William Sir (1902-1983)

Compositeur anglais, né à Oldham (Lancashire), le 29 III 1902, où il est mort à Ischia, le 8 III 1983. Travailla avec E. Dent et Busoni.

"Il a attiré l'attention dès sa dix-septième année avec un quatuor à cordes (influencé par Brahms et Fauré), qui sera suivi de *Façade*, oeuvre qui raffermira cet intérêt par son caractère satirique assez audacieux (texte de Sitwell)." (Cl. Rostand) "A quelques exceptions près, Walton n'a composé qu'une oeuvre dans chaque genre, mais on sent qu'il y a réalisé son idéal de perfection." (N. Dufourcq) "Les dénominateurs communs de son écriture: mélodies amples; harmonies et contrepoints très fouillés; rythmes complexes; et, par-dessus tout, facture essentiellement aristocratique." (M. Cross) "Avec M. Tippett et B. Britten, des trois plus grands compositeurs de leur temps. *Façade*, s'inspirait manifestement du Groupe des Six et l'exemple français de *Parade* ou des *Mariés de la Tour Eiffel*. Oeuvre brillante et provocatrice qui lui valut à l'époque l'enthousiasme de quelques-uns et l'indignation de beaucoup d'autres." (G. Gefen) "Walton a su concilier l'humour avec le lyrisme le plus sincèrement romantique. L'expression franche et vigoureuse de sa musique, qui ne considère pas le modernisme comme une fin en soi, lui a valu dès le départ une large audience, en Angleterre, mais aussi de par le monde." (M. Fleury)

"Walton has established himself in the front rank of English composers outstanding in his generation; and his music, which has never followed any school of musical thought and has been more concerned with the evolution of accepted forms than finding new modes of expression, shows an unusual and consistently high standard of work maintained by his severe self-criticism and slow output." (K. Avery) "On June 12, 1923, his amusing and original work, *Façade* to poems by Edith Sitwell, created something of a sensation in London. However, the somewhat impish wit displayed in *Façade* is but one aspect of Walton's creative personality; in his later works, there is evident a deep emotional strain, a fine eloquence, and a definitely English melodic style; the sense of tonality is strong in the modern harmonic structure; and the formal design is invariably clear. Walton's temperament lends itself to great versatility; he is successful both in lighter music, and compositions of an epical character." (Baker)

Façade (1922/26, revised 1942) (34'30) (to T. B. Strong) 1) Fanfare-Hornpipe 2) En famille 3) Mariner Man 4) Long Steel Grass 5) Tango-Pasodoble 6) Lullaby for Jambo 7) Black Mrs. Behemoth 8) Tarentella 9) A Man from Far Country 10) By the Lake 11) Country Dance 12) Polka 13) Four in the Morning 14) Something Lies Beyond the Scene 15) Valse 16) Jodelling Song 17) Scotch Rhapsody 18) Popular Song 19) Fox-Trot "Old Sir Faulk" 20) Sir Beelzebub •2 Narr/Fl+Picc/Cl/BsCl/Asx/Tpt/Vcl/Perc •OUP

WARD, David (1917)

Compositeur américain.
An Abstract (1963) (4'30) •Asx/Pno •South
Concert Piece (1978) (to D. Underwood) •Asx/Band •DP
Encore (1974) (to D. Underwood) •Asx/Band
Prelude and Rondo •Asx/Pno
Seven Miniatures •SATB or AATB
Suite •Asx/Pno

WARD, Robert (1917)

Compositeur et professeur américain, né à Cleveland, le 13 IX 1917. Travailla avec F. Jacobi, A. Stoessel, E. Schenkman, et A. Copland.

"His music tends to be eclectic and conservative; it has a strong rhythmic profile and a distinct dramatic flair." (R. Jackson)

Concerto (1983) (14'30) (to J. Houlik) 1) Allegro moderato 2) Lento 3) Allegro •Tsx/Orch or Pno •Ga
Quartet (to F. Hemke) •SATB

WARD-STEINMAN, David (1936)

Compositeur américain né à Alexandria (Louisiana), le 6 XI 1936. Travailla avec Boda, Phillips, Binkerd, et N. Boulanger.

"His earlier works are neo-classical, the later more adventurous." (K. Kroeger)

Golden Apples (1981) (to J. Rotter) •Sx/Fortified Pno

WARE, Peter (1951)

Compositeur canadien.

Libera me domine (1981) •2 Sx/3 Perc •CMC
4 Miniatures (1989) (6') •Sx Solo •CMC

WARGNEIN, A.

Compositeur belge.

Impressions •SATB

WARING, Kate

Collage (1985) (5') (to M. Jezouin) •4 Sx: SATB/Str Orch
Plainte (1985) (4') (to M. Jezouin) •1 Sx: S or A/Pno or Org
Psalmance (1978) (5') (to M. Jezouin) •Fl/Ssx/Guit/Perc
Ulterior motives (1984) (to M. Jezouin) •8 Sx: SAAAAAAT/Str Orch

WARNER, Scott

Compositeur américain.

To Pierce the Night (1988) (to C. Leaman) •Asx/Pno •adr

WARREN, B.

Compositeur américain, né à Boston. Travailla avec W. Piston, A. Copland, et N. Boulanger.

For Two Saxophones (Andantino - Pastorale - Presto) •2 Sx: SA
Quartet (Innocente - Cantabile - Energico - Final brilliante) •SATB

WARREN, David

Chorale Fantasy •1 Sx: A or T/Pno •Lud
Sonatina •Tsx/Pno •Lud

WARZECHA, Piotr

Compositeur polonais.

Dialoghi (1993) •Bsx/Bass •INM

WASHBURN, Gary (1946)

Compositeur américain, né à Tulsa (Oklahoma), le 14 I 1946. Travailla avec I. Dahl, J. Yuasa au Japon, et G. Read, M. Feldman, et D. Del Tredici.

Quintet I (1960) (6') •2 Bsx/2 Perc/Tape •SeMC
Quintet II •2 Bsx/2 Perc/Tape •SeMC
A Ride; A Moonbeam; Polka Dot (1974) (20') •Sx Solo: A+S+B •SeMC
Solitudes for Music (1974) (3 parts) •Tpt/1 Sx: S+A/Pno •SeMC

WASTALL, Peter

Concert Pieces (1979) •Asx/Pno •B&H
Learn as You Play Saxophone (1983) •Asx/Pno •B&H
Session Time (1988) •2 Sx: AT

WATANABE, Hiroshi

Compositeur japonais.

Q-I-love •4 Sx: AATB/Bass

WATERS, Dick

Compositeur anglais.

Two Pieces •SATB

WATERS, Renee Silas

Compositeur américain.

Concerto (to J. Waters) •Asx/Orch •adr
Meditation and Frenzy •Sx/Pno •adr

Quartet (1987) (to University of Georgia Saxophone Quartet) •SATB •Ron
The Scream •Sx/Pno •adr
Sonata (1986) 1) Slowly-Quickly 2) Slowly 3) Aggressively •Ssx/Pno

WATTERS, Cyril

Valse coquette (1961) •Asx/Pno •B&H

WATTERS, Mark E. (1955)

Saxophoniste et compositeur américain, né à Irving (Texas), le 25 V 1955. Travailla avec E. Haberkamp et H. Pittel.

Rhapsody - Concerto (1983) •Bsx/Orch or Band

WAYNE, Anthony

Compositeur américain.

Schisms and Schists (1983) (to J. Umble) •Asx/Pno

WEAGE, Bradley K.

Hexagram (1986) (to D. Schmidt) •Tsx/Pno

WEAVER, Gary

Compositeur américain.

A Tribute to Paul Desmond (1985) (to N. Ramsay) •Asx/Pno

WEBER

Deep River •Bsx/Pno •Bel
Elephant Dance •Bsx/Pno •Bel
Evening Shadows •1 Sx: B or T/Pno •Bel

WEBER, Alain (1930)

Compositeur français, né à Château-Thierry, le 8 XII 1930. Travailla avec T. Aubin et O. Messiaen. Grand Prix de Rome (1952).

"Style traditionnel de fond néo-classique." (Cl. Rostand) "Semble particulièrement à l'aise dans le domaine de la musique de chambre, où il montre des possibilités expressives qui, sans être outrées ni arbitraires, atteignent à une réelle intensité." (R. Bernard) "Son évolution musicale est jalonnée aussi bien par l'emploi d'une écriture tendant à un chromatisme total (n'excluant pas l'emploi épisodique de la série) que par un langage formé d'agrégats sonores, le tout s'inscrivant dans un besoin de couleurs instrumentales et de recherches formelles."

"In his works he evokes Ravel and Honegger." (Baker)

Assonances (1980) (to S. Bichon) •Asx/Ob/Vcl
Epitames (1974) (to Quatuor d'Anches de Paris) •Ob/Cl/Asx/Bsn
Epodes (1974) (to P. Pareille) •Ob/Cl/Asx/Bsn •EFM
Linéaire I (1973) (17') (to D. Deffayet) (Perpendiculaire - Hyperboles - Parallèles - Octogone) •Asx/Orch (2222/2210/Harp/Perc/Str) •EFM
Mélopée (1'45) •Asx/Pno •Led
Saxetto (3') •Asx/Pno •Led

WEBER, Carl-Maria von (1786-1826)

Concertino (Davis) •Asx/Pno •Rub
Der Freischütz (Thompson) •AATB •MPHC
Der Freischütz Selection (Holmes) •4 Sx: AATB/Pno •Rub
Le Freischütz -Valse (Mule) •Asx or Bb Sx/Pno •Led
Le Freischütz (Romby) •Asx/Pno •PB
Hunter's Chorus (from *Der Freischütz*) (Rascher) •Asx/Pno •Bel
Ländler (Meriot) •Asx/Pno •Phi
L'invitation à la valse (Romby) •Asx/Pno •PB
Oberon (Thompson) •AATB •Alf
Petite valse et Tyrolienne (Mule) •Asx/Pno •Led
Prayer (from *Der Freischütz*) •AATB •MPHC
Thème varié •Asx/Pno •Phi

WEBER, Fred

Andante et rondo (Decompe) •Asx/Pno •EMB

Concertino (Davis) •Asx/Orch or Pno •Rub

WEBER, Henri (18xx-19xx)
Saxophoniste de jazz américain.

Sax Acrobatix (1927) (The laugh - The bark - The slap tongue - The klack - The Gliss - To produce chords - The caw - To mute - The vibrato - The moan - The meow - Altissimo notes - Double and Triple tonguing - The volume - To rear - To talk- To tongue - The staccato - To auto horn - The cry - The yelp - The flutter tongue - The sneeze) •Bel

Tongue Gymnastix for the Development of Speed in Single, Double and Triple Tonguing (1927) •Bel

WEBERN, Anton (1883-1945)
Compositeur autrichien, né à Vienne, le 3 XII 1883, mort à Mittersill, le 15 IX 1945. Travailla avec A. Schoenberg.

"Un des plus grands génies du siècle." (Cl. Rostand) "Webern incarne le bonheur céleste, la paisible contemplation des joies supérieures." (Ph. Collaert) "Il se peut que la musique de Webern, tout comme la poésie de Mallarmé, ne devienne jamais aussi 'populaire' que celle de certains de ses contemporains; elle gardera néanmoins une force d'expression, une pureté dans l'exception, qui obligera toujours le musicien à prendre ses repères par rapport à elle, et cela d'une façon beaucoup plus aiguë que par rapport à toute autre musique." (P. Boulez) "On a qualifié cette musique de 'pointilliste' parce que chacun de ses instants sonores a une importance 'harmonique' égale, mais elle n'en constitue pas moins une solide réalisation des principes dodécaphoniques. Il est même possible qu'elle en représente l'état le plus avancé." (L. Pestalozza)

"Webern left relatively few works, and most of them are of short duration; but in his music he achieved the utmost subtilization of expressive means. He adopted the 12-tone method of composition almost immediately after its definitive formulation by Schoenberg (1924), and extended the principle of non repetition of notes to tone colors, so that in some of his works no instrument is allowed to play 2 successive thematic notes. Dynamic marks are also greatly diversified. Harmonic concepts are all but obliterated; counter-point (always dissonant) is deprived of imitation or canon; single motifs are extremely brief, and stand out as individual particles or lyric ejaculations. The impact of these works on the general public and on the critics was usually disconcerting, and upon occasion led to violent demonstrations; however, the extraordinary skill and novelty of technique, as well as inherent poetic quality made this music endure beyond the fashions of the times." (Baker) "Webern was a pure idealist, who allowed nothing to make him deviate from his chosen path. He was an inspired and painstaking teacher, always demanding the highest results from his pupils, and a brilliant and lucid lecturer. His personality was simple, direct and charming, and like Goethe he was a passionate student of nature. His death when still in the prime vigour of life was an irreparable loss to the music of his time." (H. Searle)

Quartet, op. 22 (1930) (8') 1) Sehrfsig 2) Sehr schwungvoll •Vln/Cl/Tsx/Pno •Uni

WEBERT & OSTLING (see OSTLING, Acton)

WEBSTER, Benjamin Francis (Ben) (1909-1973)
Saxophoniste et compositeur Noir américain, né à Kansas City (Missouri), le 27 III 1909, mort à Amsterdam, le 20 IX 1973. Appartint comme saxophone-ténor à l'orchestre Duke Ellington.

Sweet By and By, Old Folks at Home (Foster) •Eb Sx/Pno •CF

WEDDINGTON, Maurice
Compositeur allemand d'origine américaine, né à Chicago. En Allemagne, depuis 1975.

Fire in the Lake, op. 43 (1978) •4 Sx: SATB/Perc
Into that Goodnight (1979) •SATB

Quartett (1989) (8') •SATB

WEEKS, John (1934)
Compositeur anglais.

African Dance, op. 33 (1976) (for London Saxophone Quartet) •SATB

WEGNER, August Martin (1961)
Compositeur américain, né le 20 II 1961, à Saginaw (Michigan).

Something For... •Asx/Prepared Pno •SeMC

WEIDENAAR, Reynold (1945)
Compositeur américain.

The Stillness (1985) (12'45) (to M. Taylor) •Asx/Tape/Color video •adr

WEIGL, Karl (1881-1949)
Compositeur autrichien, né le 6 II 1881, à Vienne, mort à New York, le 11 VIII 1949. Travailla avec A. Door, Zemlinsky, et G. Adler. Naturalisé Américain depuis 1943.

"His music was admired by Strauss, Mahler, Schoenberg, Walter and Furtwängler. Representing the best of Viennese tradition in the melodiousness and the clarity of design of his works." (Ch. Erwin)

Love Song (1941-42) (4'30) •Asx/Pno •ACA

WEIGL, Vally (1899)
Compositeur autrichien, né le 11 IX 1899 à Vienne. Travailla avec K. Weigl, R. Robert, et G. Adler.

Old Time Burlesque (1937) (4'30) •Asx/Pno •ACA
Sir Voire (Harris) •2 Cl/Asx/Bsn (or BsCl) •CF

WEIL, Les
Odd Meter Studies •Asx •DP

WEILL, Kurt (1900-1950)
Die Dreigroschenoper (J. Harle) •SATB •Uni
L'Opéra de quat'sous (Londeix) •12 Sx: SnoSSAAATTTBBBs/Perc

WEINBERGER, Bruce
Various Quartets •SATB

WEINBERGER, Jaromir (1896-1967)
Compositeur américain d'origine tchèque, né à Prague, le 8 I 1896, mort à St. Petersburg (Florida), le 8 VIII 1967. Travailla avec Kricka, K. Hoffmeister, et M. Reger. Aux U.S.A. depuis 1939.

"The works from his American sojourn employ not only Czech but also Austrian, English and American folk or traditional tunes." (R. M. Longyear)

Concerto (1940/69) (to C. Leeson) 1) Andante rubato 2) Scherzo 3) Finale, con moto •Asx/Orch or Pno •South/SMC

WEINER, Lawrence
Etude (1984) •Tsx/Pno •South

WEINER, Stanley
Compositeur allemand.

Quartett, op. 55 (1982) (15') •SATB •R&E

WEINHORST, Richard
Trio Sonata (1963) (to C. Leeson) •Vln/Asx/Pno

WEINLAND, John David
Compositeur américain.

Quartet •SATB

WEINZWEIG, John (1913)
Compositeur et professeur canadien, né à Toronto, le 11 III 1913. Travailla avec H. Willan et B. Rogers.

"Musique post-webernienne."

"He was the first Canadian composer to employ the 12-tone technique and his wide range of compositions are marked by an individual application of its methods." (CMC) "His later works extend the control, economy and craftsmanship of his previous music. He has also been concerned with developing timbral resources, notably in the solo writing of the clarinet and saxophone divertimentos." (R. HENNINGER)
Divertimento No. 6 (1972 revised 1989/92) (13'10) (to P. BRODIE)
  •Asx/Str Orch •CMC

WEIRAUCH, Peter
Compositeur allemand.
Concertino (1993) •Asx/Orch or Pno •INM

WEISGARBER, Elliott (1919)
Compositeur canadien d'origine américain, né le 5 XII 1919, à Pittsfield (Massachusetts).
Netori (1974) (to D. PULLEN) •Asx/Orch (2 Hn/Perc/Harp/Str) or Pno •CMC

WEISS, Adolph (1891-1971)
Compositeur et bassoniste américain, né à Baltimore, le 12 IX 1891, mort à Van Nuys (California), le 2 II 1971. Travailla avec A. Schoenberg.
"He used 12-note serial techniques." (R. STEVENSON)
Tone Poem •2 Sx/Brass/Perc •ACA

WEISS, Ferdinand (1933)
Chef d'orchestre, flûtiste, et compositeur autrichien, né à Vienne.
Méditation et danse (1982) (to BOK & LE MAIR) •Sx/Vibr
Quattro-fonia (1988) (11'30) (to Vienna Saxophone Quartet) (Preambolo - Piccolessa giocosa - Cantilena malinconia - Fuga burlesca) •SATB •ECA
Ragtime und Boogie (1'40 + 0'45) •SATB •CA
20 Virtuosenetüden (1992) •Sx •ApE

WEISSING, Matthias
Compositeur allemand.
La ville non nommée (1993) •1 Sx: S+T+B/Pno •INM

WELANDER, Svea (1898)
Compositeur suédois.
Liten Fuga über B-A-C-H (1976) •SATB
Preludium (1961) •3 Sx: AAA •SMIC

WELANDER, Waldemar (1899-1984)
Organiste et compositeur suédois, né à Gödelöv, le 26 VIII 1899, mort le 2 I 1984. Travailla avec L-E. Larsson.
"Waldemar Welander belonged to the Scanian circle of composers and his music has had great difficulty in penetrating the rest of the country. However, his Concertino for saxophone acquired some currency. Such are the qualities of his music that it should have a good chance of earning wider popularity." (SJ)
Arietta (1947) (4'30) (to S. RASCHER) •Asx/Orch or Pno •CF
Due pezzi ur concertino (1963-64) (8') (to S. RASCHER) 1) Andante 2) Allegretto •Asx/Orch •STIM

WELLS, Thomas
Pianiste et compositeur américain.
Comedia (1978) (to J. HILL) •Sx/Fl/Tpt/Vcl
Music (1978) •Asx/Pno
Nocturne (1985) (to J. HILL) •Sx/Computer generated sound
Recitative and Aria (1979) (to J. HILL) •Asx/Pno

WELSH, Wilmer Hayden
Compositeur américain.
Hymn and Fuging Tune (1988) •Asx/Pno
Mosaic Portraits II: The Golden Calf (1982) (to C. KELTON) •4 Sx/ Org/Narr

Mosaic Portraits IV •2 Sx: SA/Pno
One Language, One Speech (1992) •2 Sx: SA/Pno
Passacaglia (1983) •1 Sx: S+A+T+B/Pno

WENDEL, Eugen (1934)
Compositeur allemand, d'origine Roumaine, né le 18 XII 1934, à Valea Rea.
Diason (15') (to D. KIENTZY) •Asx/Perc •adr
Saphonospir (15') (to D. KIENTZY) •Asx/Fl/Cl/Ob/Tpt/Trb/2 Vln/ Vla/Vcl/Bass/2 Perc •adr

WENDLAND, Waldemar (1873-1947)
Compositeur allemand, né à Liegnitz, le 10 V 1873, mort à Zeitz, le 15 VIII 1947. Travailla avec Humperdinck.
Twin Stars •2 Sx: AA/Pno •Volk

WENTING, Victor (1948)
Compositeur néerlandais.
Raderwek, met trage en snelle delen... (1973) (30') •4 wind or string instruments/Sx/Vln/Pno/Radio electronic

WERDER, Felix (1922)
Compositeur australien d'origine allemande, né à Berlin, le 22 II 1922.
"Werder's musical vocabulary appears to have drawn extensively on two principal sources: first, the modality and cantillation of Hebrew chant, and second, the major currents that appeared in central European, and more particularly Austro-German, music since 1920, including neo-Romanticism, Hindemithian counterpoint, dodecaphony, serialism, 'point' technique, clusters in the manner of Ligeti and Penderecki, aleatory means and the use of space." (A. D. MCCREDIE)
Dramaturgy (to P. CLINCH) •Asx/Orch •adr
Komposition (1987) (10') •4 Sx/Perc •adr
Sax Consort Music (1985) (6') •SATB •adr
Saxtronic, op. 135 (1973) (18') (to P. CLINCH) •Asx/Chamber Orch •adr
Unisax (to P. CLINCH) •Asx/Pno •adr

WERLE, Floyd
Arrangeur et compositeur américain.
Partita (1972) •4 Sx: SATB/Band •Bou

WERNER, Jean-Jacques (1935)
Compositeur, chef d'orchestre, pédagogue, et instrumentiste français. Travailla à Strasbourg puis à Paris.
"Jean-Jacques Werner s'est forgé un langage personnel, libre plus encore qu'indépendant, en ce qu'il est conscient de ses refus d'allégeance autant que de ses acceptations. Toute son oeuvre libère le souffle secret d'une ferveur intérieure, transfigure une réflexion que le compositeur nourrit de lectures, de contemplations, d'échanges." (P. GERMAIN)
Cahier d'inventions (1992) •Asx/Pno •CDM

WERNER, Milt
Vibrato Tone Studies (1946) •HP

WERNER, S. E.
Compositeur danois.
Lettres de voyage (1987) (17') •Sx/Vibr

WERTS, Daniel (1948)
Compositeur américain. Travailla avec M. Babbitt.
Sigmonody - 9 variations (1972) (7') (to M. SIGMON) •Asx Solo •DP

WESLEY-SMITH, Martin (1945)
Compositeur australien, né le 10 VI 1945, à Adélaïde.
"His compositional interests were at first centered on educational music, but from the early 1970s he concentrated on electronic music-

theatre." (M. T. RADIC)
Doublets II (1974) (8') (to H. SMITH) •Asx/Tape
For Alto Saxophone and Tape (1988) •Asx/Tape

WESTBROOK, Mike
Compositeur américain.
Bean Rows and Blue Shoots (1991) (30') (to J. HARLE) •Ssx/
Chamber Orch •Matisse Music

WESTBROOKE, Simon
Masque in D •Ob/Ssx/Pno

WESTENDORF
I'll Take You Home Again •2 Sx: AA/Pno or 4 Sx: AATB/Pno ad
lib. •Bri

WESTON, Norman
Compositeur américain.
Skyscraper (1988) (10'30) •SATB

WESTPHAL, Herwarth
Monolog in Dunkel •AATB •Fro

WESTRUP, Jack Allan (1904-1975)
Musicologue, chef d'orchestre, professeur, et compositeur anglais,
né le 26 VII 1904 à Londres, mort le 21 IV 1975, à Headley (Hants.).
Divertimento (1948) 1) March 2) Romance 3) Waltz •Tsx/Vcl/Pno
•Ga

WETTGE, Gustave (1844-1909)
Fantaisie variée (BLAAUW) •Bb Sx or Asx/Pno •Mil/Mol
2e Fantaisie de concert •Asx/Pno •Mil

WETZEL, Richard
Vignettes of a Fable Land (1983) •Asx/Pno •South

WHEELER, Kenneth
Compositeur anglais.
By My Self (1978) (4') •SATB •adr
The Way We Were (1978) (4') •SATB •adr

WHITE, Andrew N. III
Concerto for Alto Saxophone
Symphony No. 1 •8 Sx: SSSAAATT
Symphony No. 2 •8 Sx: SSSAAATT

WHITE, Donald (1921)
Concertino (1971) (to H. GEE) •Cl/4 Sx: AATB/Woodwind
ensemble/Perc •Lud

WHITE, Gene
Two Moods of Winter •Asx/Band

WHITE, Keith
9th Floor •Sx/Dancer

WHITE WILLIAM, C. (1881-1964)
Universal Scales, Chords and Rhythmic Studies •CF

WHITICKER, Michael (1954)
Compositeur anglais, né à New South Wales. Travailla avec W.
Szalonek.
"He views each new work as an opportunity to explore an untried
aspect of his potential. Because of this each composition, although
stamped with his own idiosyncratic gestures, sounds refreshingly new
and different."
Redror (1989) (to H. BOK & E. Le MAIR) •Asx/Perc

WHITNEY, Maurice C. (1909)
Hautboïste, pianiste, et compositeur américain, né à Glens Falls
(New York), le 25 III 1909.
Introduction and Samba (1950) (10') (to S. RASCHER) •Asx/Band or
Pno •Bou
Melancholy •1 Sx: A or T/Pno •JS
Rhumba (1949) (to S. RASCHER) •Asx/Band or Pno •Bou

WIBLÉ, Michel
Compositeur suisse.
Ballade (1970) •Asx/Pno •Henn

WIEDOEFT, Rudy (1893-1940)
Saxophoniste virtuose et compositeur de musique légère américain,
né le 3 I 1893 à Detroit, mort à Flushing (New York), le 18 II 1940.
D'abord clarinettiste avant de se consacrer plus particulièrement au
saxophone. Réalisa un nombre impressionnant d'enregistrements (1917-
1935).
Advanced Etudes and Studies (2 volumes) (1928) •Rob
Andantino (E. LIMARE) - *Londonderry Air* (traditional) •Asx/Pno
•Rob
Bitter Sweets - Valse Pamela - Rubenola (1929) •Asx/Pno •Rob
Blue Lotus - Cleo - Sax-O-Minute - Vera (1937) •Asx/Pno •Rob
Bupkis - Cloudy days - Grand and Noble (1919) •Asx/Pno •Rob
Carry Me Back to Old Virginny (J. BLAND) (1926) •Asx/Pno •Rob
Claraphobia (1935) •1 Sx: A or T/Pno •Rob
Collection of Famous Classic Transcriptions •Asx/Pno
Collection of Transcriptions of World Famous Love Songs (D.
SAVINO) •Asx/Pno
Complete Modern Method (1927) •Rob
Dans l'Orient (D. SAVINO) •1 Sx: A or T/Pno
A Dream - Sweetest Kiss of All (1926) •1 Sx: A or T/Pno •Rob
Fancies (L. WESLYN) (1920) •1 Sx: A or T/Pno •Rob
Folio of Easy Saxophone Solos (H. Frey)
Folio of Saxophone Solos and Duets (1931) •Rob
Forgotten (E. COWLES) (1926) •1 Sx: A or T/Pno •Rob
Jonteel (J. RICKY) (1920) •1 Sx: A or T/Pno
Just for Today (A. BERNARD) (1919) •Asx/Pno •Rob
Lightnin' - Valse Sonia •1 Sx: A or T/Pno •Rob
Lone Star (A. BERNARD) (1919) •1 Sx: A or T/Pno •Rob
Love o' Mine - Northern Lights - Oriental Blues (1919) •Asx/Pno
•Rob
Melodie (TCHAIKOVSKY) •1 Sx: A or T/Pno •Rob
Na-Jo (W. HOLLIDAY & G. O'NEIL) (1920) •1 Sx: A or T/Pno
Saxema (1920) •1 Sx: A or T/Pno •Rob
Sax-O-Doodle (H. FREY) •1 Sx: A or T/Pno
Saxophobia (1918) •1 Sx: A or T/Pno •Rob
Saxophone Blues (A. BERNARD) (1920) •1 Sx: A or T/Pno
Sax-O-Phun •1 Sx: A or T/Pno •Rob
Sax-O-Phun (SIBBING) •Asx Solo/5 Sx: SAATB
Sax-O-Trix (D. SAVINO) (1928) •1 Sx: A or T/Pno
Sax-Serene - Valse Mazanetta (1925) •1 Sx: A or T/Pno •Rob
Secret of Staccato for the Saxophone (1938) •Rob
Simplified Photographic Saxophone Chart
A Southern Sketch - Frolic (J. R. ROBINSON) (1932) •Asx/Pno •Rob
Souvenir (1924) •1 Sx: A or T/Pno •Rob
Strange Butterfly (CIOCIANO) (1933) •1 Sx: A or T/Pno •Rob
The Sweetest Story Ever Told (R. STULTS) (1926) •Asx/Pno •Rob
Ta-Hoe (C. FENTON & G. O'NEIL) (1920) •1 Sx: A or T/Pno
Tribute to Rudy Wiedoeft (1978) (7'43) (SCHULLER) 1) Valse Erica
2) Saxarella 3) Saxophobia •Asx/Band •CPP
Valse Erica (1917) (to Mrs. Erica NOLL) •Asx/Pno •Rob
Valse Erica (1917) (B. RONKIN) •SATB •Ron
Valse Marilyn •1 Sx: A or T/Pno •Rob
Valse Vanité - Waltz Llewellyn (1917) •Asx/Pno •Rob

Valse Yvonne - Saxarella - Vision d'amour (1923) •Asx/Pno •Rob
Very Soon - Karavan (Abe OLMAN) (1919) •1 Sx: A or T/Pno •Rob
Wee Bit of Love (D. RINGLE) (1922) •1 Sx: A or T/Pno

WIENER, Gaston (1896)
Compositeur français, né le 19 XII, à Paris.
Le saxo qui chante (1973) (2') (to J-M. LONDEIX) •Asx/Pno •adr

WIENHORST, Richard
Trio •Vln/Asx/Pno •ACF

WIER, Albert
Pièces •Asx/Tape •HaBr/AC

WIERNIK, Adam (1916)
Violoniste, chef d'orchestre, et compositeur suédois d'origine hongroise, né à Varsovie, le 4 I 1916. Travailla avec K. Sikorski, P. Perkowski et A. Malawski. En Suède, depuis 1969.
Feelings (1981) (11') •Ob/Cl/Asx/Bsn •STIM

WIGGINS
Conversation (6') •Asx/Band •Ken

WILBER
Waltz •Asx/Pno •WWS

WILBYE, John (1574-1638)
Adieu Sweet Amarillis (HARVEY) •SATB •Che

WILCOX, Joseph
T-bird Repents •Asx/Pno

WILDBERGER, Jacques (1922)
Compositeur suisse, né à Bâle, le 3 I 1922. Travailla avec V. Vogel.
"L'un des représentants les plus remarquables de l'avant-garde postwebernienne suisse... C'est un postsériel qui ne va pas jusqu'à la nouvelle école néo-dadaïst: un classique est en lui." (Cl. ROSTAND)
"Vogel taught him how to manipulate 12-note serial technique with assurance, but was also a lasting influence on his concern to find a meaningful relationship between music and speech. His personal contact with Boulez had important consequences in his music." (R. HÄUSLER)
Konzertante Szenen (to I. ROTH) •Asx/Orch or Pno
Portrait (1982) (7-8') (to I. ROTH) (Moderato - Cantando) •Asx Solo •Uni
Prismes (1975) (9') (to I. ROTH) 1) Polyphonie 2) Polarisations 3) Monodie 4) Polyphonie II (Reminiscences/Quolibet) •Asx Solo •Br&Ha/HG

WILDER, Alec (1907-1980)
Compositeur américain, né à Rochester (New York), le 16 II 1907. Travailla avec H. Inch et E. Royce.
"In the late 1930s he experimented with jazz compositions for unusual ensembles, including woodwinds and harpsichord." (J. G. ROR, Jr.)
Air for Saxophone •Asx/Brass Septet •WWS
Air for Saxophone (DEMSEY) •Asx/Pno •WWS
Concerto (1966) (to D. SINTA) •Asx/Orch or Pno •B&B/Marg
Concerto (1970) (to S. GETZ) •Tsx/Chamber Orch or Band or Pno •JB/WIM
If Someday Comes Eves Again (5'10) •Asx/Pno
I'll Be Around (4'30) •Asx/Pno
A Long Night (5') •Asx/Pno
Quartet 1) Moderato 2) Pastorale 3) Andantino 4) Allegro •SATB •DP
She'll Be Seven in May •Fl/Ob/Asx/2 Cl/BsCl/Bsn/Bass/Drums/Pno
Sonata (1969) (11'30) (to D. SINTA) (4 movements) •Asx/Pno •MMI/B&B

Stan Getz Piece I •Tsx/Pno •WWS
Suite (1964) •SATB •JB/WIM
Suite (3 movements) •Asx/Pno •LC
Suite •Bsx/Fl/Ob/Cl/2 Hn/Bsn/Bass/Drums
Suite No. 1 (1965) •Tsx/Str or Pno •JB/WIM
Summer is a-comin'in (4') •Asx/Pno
Three Ballads for Stan (1966) 1) Sempre libero e rubato 2) With passion, sempre rubato 3) Flowingly •Tsx/Str Orch or Pno •JB/WIM

WILEY, Frank
Ritual Music •Cl/Asx/Perc

WILLIAMS, Bert
That's A-Plenty (NAGLE) •SATB

WILLIAMS, Clarence (1893-1965)
Pianiste et compositeur de jazz Noir américain, né à Plaquemine (Louisiana), le 6 X 1893, mort à Queens (New York), le 6 XI 1965.
Saxophone Folio No. 1 •MCA

WILLIAMS, Clifton (1923)
Theme from Apartment •Asx/Pno •WWS
Pandean Fable (to J. HOULIK) •Tsx/Band

WILLIAMS, Jay
Looking at Number •Sx/Tape

WILLIAMS, Joan F.
Compositeur américain.
Etude from Moscow Idaho •Any instrument •ACA

WILLIAMS, V.
Artistic Duets •2 Sx: AA or TT •CC
Prelude and Beguine •AATB •CF

WILLIAMS, Vic
Compositeur américain.
Ballad and Waltz (1981) •AATB •South

WILLIAMSON, Kristina
Compositeur américain.
Ballade (1989) •Asx/Pno •NoMu

WILLIAMSON, Malcolm (1931)
Compositeur, pianiste, et organiste australien, né à Sydney, le 21 XI 1931. Installé en Angleterre au début des années 1950. Travailla avec Goosens et E. Lutyens.
"Organiste, converti au catholicisme, il a consacré à la musique religieuse chorale et à son instrument une partie de son oeuvre, marquée par l'exemple d'O. Messiaen. Sa personnalité déborde cependant largement ces influences et le cadre de l'écriture sérielle. Il est en outre l'auteur d'une oeuvre symphonique et concertante très intéressante qui illustre la manière dont la musique britannique sait adapter un langage venu du continent au lyrisme et à l'expressivité qui lui sont propres." (G. GEFEN)
"Williamson's obvious eclecticism has been held against him. But it seems that a greater bane is his immense facility. Like many extremely fluent artists he is not always self-critical, nor is he above allowing shoddy workmanship to pass under the banner of 'music-made-easy.' As for eclecticism, it may be no bad quality in an artist who can absorb many influences without losing everything essential to himself, as Williamson has seemed able to do." (S. WALSH)
Merry Wives of Windsor (1964) •Fl+Picc/Cl/Tsx/Tpt/Perc/Bass/Pno •JW

WILLIS, Richard (1929)
Compositeur américain, né le 21 IV 1929 à Mobile (Alabama).

Colloquy III (1982) (to D. Hᴀꜱᴛɪɴɢꜱ) •Asx/Perc •adr
Irregular Resolutions (to Baylor Chamber Players) •Fl/Ob/Cl/Asx/
    Bsn/Hn/Perc •adr
Metamorphoses (to M. Jᴀᴄᴏʙꜱᴏɴ) •Asx/Orch or Wind Ensemble
    •adr
Tetralogue •SATB

WILMAUT, Jean-Marie
3 Chronautes •Ob/Cl/Asx
La complainte de Vincent sur un poème de Prévert •Narr/Ob/Cl/Asx

WILSAM, J.
Floralie •Asx/Pno •HE

WILSON
Moonlight on the Hudson, op. 60 •1 Sx: A or T/Pno •Cen
The Wayside Chapel •1 Sx: A or T/Pno •Cen

WILSON, Dana
Compositeur américain.
Calling, Ever Calling •Ssx/Wind ensemble
Concerto (1990) 1) Persistantly 2) =60 3) =108 •Asx/Wind sym-
    phony
The Dream of Icarus (1985) (to S. Mᴀᴜᴋ) •Asx/Pno •Ken
Escape to the Center •SATB
Incantation and Ritual (1985) (to S. Mᴀᴜᴋ) •Tsx/Pno
Sati (1982) •Asx/Vcl/2 Perc •DP
Time Cries, Hoping Otherwise (1990) (17') (to L. Hᴜɴᴛᴇʀ) •Asx/
    Wind ensemble •Lud

WILSON, Donald M. (1937)
Compositeur américain, né le 30 VI 1937, à Chicago.
Sett •Any 3 instruments •ACA
Stabile II •Any combination of 2 or more high instruments/1 or more
    low instruments •ACA
Tetragon (1990) (to J. Sᴀᴍᴘᴇɴ) •Fl/Asx/Cl/Bsn

WILSON, G.
Theater Trio •Asx/Tpt/Pno

WILSON, Iain
Compositeur irlandais.
Drive •Sx/Pno

Wilson, J. Eric
Amazing Grace (Wɪʟꜱᴏɴ) •SATB or WW Quintet •SiMC

WILSON, Jeffery
Compositeur anglais.
Modes •SATB

WINKLER, Gerhard E. (1959)
Compositeur autrichien.
Aussenhäute (1989) •Cl/Vln/Bsx/Vcl •adr
Hybrid I (1992) (to M. Wᴇɪꜱꜱ) •Bsx Solo •adr

WINKLER, Wolfgang
Compositeur allemand.
Dankeschön (1992) •Asx/Cl •INM

WINSTRUP, Olesen
Six saxophone pieces - Book 1 1) The Platters dream 2) Infatuation
    3) Desertion 4) Devination 5) Incense 6) Rhythmic tale •Tsx/
    Pno •WH
Six saxophone pieces - Book 2 1) Etude 2) Duo Mosconi 3) Sonatine
    4) Embers 5) Skizze 6) Sunset •Tsx/Pno •WH

WINZENBURGER, Walter
Quartet •4 Sx: AATB/Perc •adr

WIRTH, Carl Anton (1912-1986)
Compositeur et chef d'orchestre américain, né à Rochester (New
York), le 24 I 1912.
"The music of Carl Anton Wirth encompasses many emotions,
moods and styles. His two year stay in Indonesia introduced him to a
musical tradition of great power and high spiritual aspirations. But after
all is said and done, one must personally hear this wonderful composer's
work to realize what a truly great man we had sojourn with is in Carl
Anton Wirth." (CAW Publ.)
Antiphon •Asx/Pno •adr
Ballad No. 1 •Asx/Pno •adr
Ballad No. 2 •Asx/Pno •adr
Ballad No. 3 •Asx/Pno •adr
Ballad No. 4 •Asx/Pno •adr
Ballad No. 5 •Asx/Pno •adr
Ballad No. 7 •Asx/Pno •adr
Ballad No. 8 •Asx/Pno •adr
Ballad and Final (from *Idlewood Concerto*) •Asx/Band •TP
Beyond the Hills (1965) (to S. Rᴀꜱᴄʜᴇʀ) •Asx/Pno •LeBl/CPP
Dark Flows the River (to S. Rᴀꜱᴄʜᴇʀ) •Asx/Pno •CPP
David - Triptych (1978) (to S. Rᴀꜱᴄʜᴇʀ) 1) David the Shepherd
    2) David's Lament 3) David Danced •Asx/Winds/Perc •adr
Diversions in Denim (16') 1) Excursion 2) Idlewood 3) Gallumphery
    4) Lornsome 5) Shindig •SATB •Eth
I Been Blue •Asx/Pno •adr
Idlewood Concerto (1954) (19') (to S. Rᴀꜱᴄʜᴇʀ) 1) Vista
    2) Scherzando 3) Ballad and Final •Asx/Orch (2222/4331/Perc/
    Str) or Pno •EV/Pres
Jephta (1958) (8') (to S. Rᴀꜱᴄʜᴇʀ) •1 Sx: A+S/Orch (Str/Pno/Perc)
    •Eth
A Keening •Asx/Pno •adr
Lazy Sunday •Asx/Pno
Only the Blues •Asx/Pno •adr
Pavan •Asx/Pno •adr
Petite Chaconne •Asx/Pno •adr
Portals - A Prelude (1971) •7 Sx: SAATTBBs •Eth
A Portrait •Asx/Pno •adr
Prelude •Asx/Pno •adr
Prelude (1971) •AATB
Prologue •Asx/Pno •adr
Puntjak (1972) •Asx/Pno
Serenade No. 3 •Ssx/Pno •adr
Sunrise on a Snowy Hill •Asx/Pno •adr
Three Indonesian Landscapes 1) Puntjak: Nightfall 2) Rice Field
    with Dancers 3) Isle of the Gods •Asx/Pno
Three Little Pieces 1) Whistling 2) Walking 3) Lullaby •Asx/Pno
    •adr
Two Adagios from Dong of the Sierra •Asx/Pno •adr

WISE, Loren E.
Compositeur hollandais.
Litany (1979) •SATB

WISHART, Peter (1921)
Professeur et compositeur anglais, né le 25 IV 1921, à Crowborough
(Sussex, United Kingdom).
Aquarella, op. 84 (1982) (to English Saxophone Quartet) •SATB
    •adr
Barcarolle (1982) (to English Saxophone Quartet) •SATB •adr

WISSMER, Pierre (1915-1992)
Compositeur, pédagogue, et critique musical français, d'origine
suisse, né à Genève, le 30 X 1915, mort à Paris en Octobre 1992.
Travailla avec Roger-Ducasse et D. Lesur. En France depuis 1958.
"Il a subi l'influence esthétique du groupe de la 'Jeune France' et son

style néo-classique recherche l'expression lyrique même dans ses oeuvres instrumentales." (Cl. ROSTAND) "Il cherche avant tout à écrire une musique facile d'accès, agréable à entendre, gaie, malicieuse et fringante." (R. BERNARD)

"He writes in the lucid neo-Classical style, and is particularly adept in writing for small instrument groups." (BAKER) "His music shows affinities with that of the 'Jeune France;' his moderately advanced style is distinguished by charming effects of sound, admirable instrumentation and a spirited musicality." (K. von FISCHER)

Quatuor (1956) (14'30) 1) Allegro 2) Moderato 3) Allegro •SATB •ET

WISZNIEWSKI, Zbigniew (1922)

Compositeur polonais né à Lwow, le 30 VII 1922. Travailla avec Sikorski.

"After an initial period of eclectic composition, he has made use of quasi-serial methods and electronic means." (M. HANUSZEWSKA)

Bicinium (1993) •Asx/Vcl •INM
Duo (1982) (12') (to BOK & Le MAIR) 1) Vorspid - Moderato 2) Langsam - Quasi lento 3) Geschwind - vivace 4) Tempo I° •Asx/Marimba
Duo (1983) (14') (to D. PITUCH) •Asx/Vcl

WOLF, Hans (1927)

Saxophoniste, clarinettiste, arrangeur, et compositeur allemand, né le 8 X 1927 à Hof.

Honey Polka (1971) (3') •Asx/Accordion/Perc •Figurata
Lady Style (1972) (3') •2 Asx/4 Trb/Perc •Moz
Lovely Lips (1966) (3') •Asx Solo/Str •Moz
Tip Kick - Swing Fox (1964) (3') •4 Sx/Tpt/Trb/Perc •Moz

WOLF, Hugo

Andante (GEE) •4 Sx: AATB or AATT •CPP
The Forsaken Maiden •Asx/Pno •WWS

WOLF, Jaroslav

Virgilia •Sx Solo

WOLFE, George W. (1948)

Saxophoniste américain, né à Corry (Pennsylvania) le 21 III 1948. Travailla avec E. Rousseau, R. Kemper, D. Baker, et D. Deffayet.

Five Scriabin Etudes (1985) •Kjos
Persian Dance (1982) •Asx/Picc/Bsn/Xylophone/Exotic Perc
Preparatory Method for the Saxophone (Volume 1: Classical Technique) (1985) •Ron
Randomization No. 1 (1982) •Ssx/Marimba/Perc

WOLFEREN, Gerhard von

Kwartet •SATB

WOLFF, Christian (1934)

Compositeur américain d'avant-garde, d'origine française, né à Nice, le 8 III 1934. Au U.S.A. depuis 1941. Travailla avec Cage, Brown, et Feldman.

"Jouez, faites des sons, en courts éclats, aux contours clairs la plupart du temps; tranquilles: deux ou trois fois, déplacez-vous vers les autres et jouez aussi fort que possible; mais dès que vous n'entendez plus ce que vous jouez vous-même ou ce qu'un autre joue, arrêtez-vous immédiatement. Laissez des intervalles variés entre les interventions (deux, cinq secondes, indéfinies); parfois faites chevaucher les évènements. Une deux, trois, quatre ou cinq fois, jouez un son long, un complexe ou une séquence de sons. Jouez parfois indépendamment, parfois en coordination: avec les autres (lorsqu'ils commencent ou s'arrêtent ou pendant qu'ils jouent ou qu'ils se déplacent) ou bien un instrumentiste doit jouer (commencer ou, avec des sons longs, commencer et s'arrêter ou juste s'arrêter) à un signal (ou pendant les deux à cinq secondes d'un signal) qu'il ne peut contrôler lui-même (il ne sait pas quand le signal va se produire). En certains points ou d'un bout à l'autre utiliser l'électricité." (Ch. WOLFF) "Les partitions de Christian Wolff comme celles de son maître Feldman dont il pousse à l'extrême les préoccupations, deviennent visuellement des sortes de 'cartes' qui permettent à chacun d'établir une stratégie de jeux dont les frontières ne sont pas délimitées à l'avance. Parce qu'elles appellent à la créativité, ces tentatives sont amenées à jouer leur rôle dans le contexte de la pédagogie et à élargir l'abord de la pratique musicale. Le fait qu'elles transgressent les séparations entre les différentes techniques artistiques, joue sur l'ambiguïté de leurs contenus." (J. & B. MASSIN)

"He evolved a curiously static method of composition using drastically restricted numbers of pitches. His only structural resources became arithmetical progressions of rhythmic values and the expressive use of rests." "Wolff's later work (after 1966) provides material and rules that are still less determinate, permitting a wide scope for improvisation. He has summarized the convictions behind such music under four headings: a composition must make possible the freedom and dignity of the performer; it should allow both concentration and release; no sound or noise is preferable to any other sound or noise; and the listeners should be as free as the players." (W. BLAND)

For 1, 2 or 3 People (1964) •Any 1, 2 or 3 instruments •Pet
For 5 or 10 People (1962) •Any instruments •Pet
In Between Pieces (1963) •Any 3 players •Pet
Pairs (1968) •2, 4, 6, or 8 players •Pet
Septet (1964) •Any 7 instruments •Pet
Tilbury 2 and 3 (1969) •Any instruments (instruments amplified ad lib.) •Pet

WOLPE, Stefan (1902-1972)

Compositeur israélien, allemand de naissance, naturalisé américain avant de rejoindre Israël, né à Berlin, le 25 VIII 1902; mort à New York, le 4 IV 1972. Travailla avec Busoni, Webern, et Scherchen.

"A écrit des études théoriques, préconisant notamment une conception personnelle du dodécaphonisme basé sur ce qu'il appelle les 'zones harmoniques.' " (R. BERNARD)

"One of the most remarkable of living composers… his music is strikingly original… some pounding natural force brings it forth and gives it reality… Wolpe is definitely someone to be discovered." (A. COPLAND) "His music shows traces of many successive influences: folk music, jazz, Hebrew and oriental melodies, atonality and modified 12-tone technique." (BAKER)

Quartet No. 1 (1950) •Tpt/Tsx/Perc/Pno •Gi&Ma/MM

WONG, Vincent

Compositeur américain.
Music (1983-84) (to J. UMBLE) •Asx/Tape

WOOD, Gareth

Compositeur anglais.
Sinfonietta (1976) (8') (to London Saxophone Quartet) 1) Prelude 2) Toccata 3) Scherzo 4) Fantasia •SATB

WOOD, Haydn (1882-1959)

Let 'er Go •2 Sx: AA or AT/Pno •Cen
Roses of Picardy (BLAAUW) •Tsx/Pno •Mol

WOOD, James (1953)

Compositeur anglais.
Sonata for Four (1971) (20') (to London Saxophone Quartet) •SATB

WOOD, Jeffrey

Moortown Elegies (to N. RAMSAY) •Asx/Pno

WOOD, Nigel

Compositeur anglais.
Schwarzer Tanzer •5 Sx: S+A ATTB

WOOD, Sam B.
Alllamada - Fantaisie •Eb Sx/Pno •Mol

WOODBURN, James Alexander
Compositeur anglais.
Aubade (1976) •Asx/Pno •adr
Piece in Three Sections (1976) •Asx/Bsn •adr
Scherzo (1982) (to S. MAUK) •Ssx/Pno
Threnodie (1982) (to S. MAUK) •Ssx/Pno

WOODBURY, Arthur (1930)
Bassoniste, saxophoniste, et compositeur américain, né à Kimball (Nebraska), le 20 VI 1930.
"His early works are written in a traditional modern idiom; later he branched out as a composer of experimental music, cultivating electronic and aleatory techniques." (BAKER)
Between Categories •Asx/Pno
Hommage J.S.: Variations and Improvisation on a well known chord progression (1982) •Sx/Pno
Remembrances (1968) (16'30) (to the New Music Ensemble) •Asx/Vln/Vibr •CPE

WOODCOCK, Robert (16xx-1734)
Concerto No. 2 (V. WÜRTH) •1 Sx: S or A/Pno or Org •VW

WOODS, Phil (1931)
Musicien de jazz.
Sonata (1980) (16') (to V. MOROSCO) 1) Allegro 2) Slowly 3) Moderato 4) Bluesy and free •Asx/Pno •Ken
Three Improvisations (1981) (to New York Saxophone Quartet) 1) Presto 2) Broadly 3) Part III •SATB •Ken

WOODWARD, Gregory
Compositeur américain.
Concerto (1983) (to S. MAUK) •Asx/Wind ensemble
Parapter (1976) (to S. MAUK) •Asx Solo

WOOLLETT, Henri Edouard (1864-1936)
Compositeur et professeur français d'origine anglaise, né le 13 VIII 1864 au Havre, où il est mort, le 9 X 1936. Travailla avec R. Pugno, Massenet. A. Caplet, et A. Honegger ont notamment été ses élèves.
Sibéria (1909) (5'30) (to E. HALL) •Asx/Orch or Pno •South
Danses païennes (19xx) •2 Fl/Asx/Vcl/Harp
Octuor n° 1 (1911) (to E. HALL) •Ob/Cl/Asx/2 Vln/Vla/Vcl/Bass •South

WORIGNEIN, André
Compositeur belge.
Pieces for saxes •SATB

WORLEY, Daniel (1967)
To Tame the Beast (1992) •Asx/Pno

WORLEY, John Carl (1919)
Compositeur américain né le 2 IX 1919 à Waltham (Massachusetts). Travailla avec P. Monteux, J. Gardnet Iennof.
Adagio and Scherzo •SATB •DP
All Through the Night (traditional) •AATB or SATB •DP
Annie Laurie (traditional) •AATB or SATB •DP
Apple Strudel Rag •SATB •DP
The Ash Grove (traditional) •SATB •DP
Black is the Color of my True Love's Hair (traditional) •AATB or SATB •DP
Blueberry Cobbler Blues •SATB •DP
Boston Harbor (traditional) •AATB or SATB •DP
Chocolate Mousse Waltz •SATB •DP

Claremont - Concerto (1962) (22') (to S. RASCHER) •Asx/Orch or Pno
A Coastal Sonata •Asx/Pno •DP
Comin' Through the Rye (traditional) •SATB •DP
Deep River (traditional) •AATB or SATB •DP
Four Sketches •3 Sx: ATB •DP
Gute Nacht (traditional) •AATB or SATB •DP
If I Had the Wings of a Dove (traditional) •AATB or SATB •DP
John Peel (traditional) •SATB •DP
Lyric Piece •AATB or SATB •DP
Old Joe Meets Tom Turkey (traditional) •SATB •DP
Oneonta Quartet (1970) (to S. RASCHER) •AATB
Owl's Head Sonatina •Tsx/Pno •DP
Pemaquid Sonatina •Asx/Pno •DP
Penobscot Suite •Asx/Pno •DP
Pop Goes the Weasel (traditional) •SATB •DP
Quintet •SAATB •DP
Raspberry Torte Swing •SATB •DP
Samoset Concerto (withdrawn by composer) (1972) (to J. HOULIK) •Tsx/Orch
Second Sonata •Asx/Pno •DP
September Sonata II (1985) •Tsx/Pno •DP
Simple Gifts (traditional) •SATB •DP
Six Dances •Ssx/Pno •DP
Ski Trail Through the Birches •Ssx/Pno •DP
Sonata (1974) (to S. RASCHER) 1) Andante moderato 2) Adagio - Dolce espressivo 3) Freely with exhilaration - Allegro con brio •Asx/Pno •CF
Sonata •Tsx/Pno •DP
Sonata "Pleasant Bay" (1992) 1) Andante 2) Largo 3) Allegro moderato •Bsx/Pno •DP
Sonatina (1978) (Allegro moderato - Andante simplice - Allegro con brio) •Bsx/Pno •DP
Suite •Ssx/Pno •DP
Sweet Betsy (traditional)/*Darling Clementine* (traditional) •SATB •DP
Tempo di Viennese (1982) •10 Sx: SSAAAATTBBs •DP
Trio (1983) (to L. GWOZDZ) •Vln/Sx/Pno
Twilight Pine Shadows •1 Sx: B or Bs/Pno •DP
We Gather Together (traditional) •SATB •DP
What Shall We Do With a Drunken Sailor? (traditional) •SATB •DP
White Morning Stillness •Tsx/Pno •DP
Windswept Snowscapes •Asx/Pno •DP

WREDE, Bert
Compositeur allemand.
Miniature (1993) •Asx/Vln •INM

WRIGHT, Rayburn
Verberations •Ssx/Perc

WROCHEM, Klaus von
Oratorium meum plus praeperturi •3 Voices/2 Vln/Vla/Vcl/Asx/Tpt/Perc •CAP

WUENSCH, Gerhard (1925)
Compositeur canadien d'origine autrichienne, né à Vienne. Travailla avec P. A. Pisk et K. Kennan. Vit au Canada depuis 1964.
Sonata, op. 59 (1971) (19') (to P. BRODIE) 1) Fast and with energy 2) Recitative - Vivace - Fast and light •Ssx/Pno •CMC

WUORINEN, Charles (1938)
Compositeur, pianiste, chef d'orchestre, et professeur américain, né le 9 VI 1938, à New York. Travailla avec O. Luening, J. Beeson, et V. Ussachevsky.
"The flexibility of Wuorinen's serial technique is demonstrated in

his later music, where repetition and registral duplication of pitches play an ever larger role. In the 'new' composition, the richness and subtlety of live music allowed the composer to shape his material differently." (R. Swift) "About 'Divertimento,' the composer has forsworn the writing or discussion of program notes and prefers that the 'listener should simply listen' to the music and enjoy the experience. One might mention, however, that the composition's macrocosmic construction is one of gradual growth in density, speed and intensity."
Divertimento (1982) (10') (to C. Ford) •Asx/Pno •Pet

WURMSER, Lucien (1877-1967)

Pianiste et compositeur français, né le 23 V 1877, à Paris, où il est mort.

Bagatelle - Barcarolle - Esquisse •Asx/Pno •Bil
Fantasia (5') •Asx/Pno •ET
Frivole - Pochade •Asx/Pno •Bil
Petit solo de concours •Tsx/Pno •Bil
Solo de concours - Tendre mélodie •Bsx/Pno •Bil
Tristesse •Asx/Pno •Phi

WÜRTH, Volker (1968)

Compositeur allemand.
Meditation I (1988) (2') (to Petra) •Bsx Solo •VW

WYATT, Scott A.

Compositeur américain.
Counterpoints (1992) •Ssx/Tape •adr
Vignettes (1989) (to J. Lulloff) 1) Ballad 2) Spritz 3) Waltz
    4) Turnabout 5) Blues •MIDI Wind Controller/Tape •adr

WYDEVELD, Wolfgang

Sarabande du roi •Asx/Orch or Pno

WYMAN, Laurence (1935)

Saxophoniste américain, né à Elgin (Illinois), le 26 XI 1935. Travailla avec S. Rascher et O. Kiltz.
Deltangi (1964) •Asx/4 Vcl •adr
Gjiwa (1971) •Asx Solo •adr
Rainfall (1972) •Tsx/Pno •adr
Saxophone Abstractions •Sx/Laser beam/Prepared audience

WYSOCKI, Zdzislaw

Movimenti, op. 47 (1991) 1) Improvisazione-Moderato 2) Silenzio-Lento 3) Furioso vivace non troppo •SATB •ApE

WYSTRAETE, Bernard

Alphonic (1985) (2'30) •Asx/Pno •Led
Petite pièce (1993) •Bb or Eb Sx/Pno •Led
Saxaubade (1982) (2'30) •Asx/Pno •Led

XANTHOUDAKIS, Charis
Les visages de la nuit (1989) (8') (to D. Kientzy) •CBsSx/Tape

XENAKIS, Iannis (1922)

Compositeur français d'origine grecque, né à Braïla, le 29 V 1922, en Roumanie. Fixé à Paris depuis 1947. Travailla avec Honegger, Milhaud, Messiaen, et H. Scherchen. D'autre part, il a travaillé et collaboré pendant dix ans avec Le Corbusier.

"Il est actuellement l'un des plus audacieux explorateurs du temps et de l'espace sonores, par des itinéraires très personnels et des procédés très originaux: son action se situe en marge—et peut-être en avant—de l'aventure sérielle, qu'il a toujours estimée dépassée. Pour organiser le vocabulaire nouveau, Xenakis va se fonder sur les théories mathématiques des probabilités et des évènements en chaîne (musique stochastique), la théorie des jeux (musique stratégique), ainsi que sur la théorie des ensembles et la logique mathématique (musique symbolique). Tout cela a amené le musicien à élargir considérablement le domaine du son musical traditionnel, à explorer les ressources inusitées des instruments classiques et à utiliser les sons considérés comme bruits. C'est là que Xenakis se place dans un univers proche de celui qui a été précédemment exploré par Edgard Varèse. Il est difficile de ne pas être frappé par la grandeur et la puissance de son éloquence, par le spectacle auditif des impressionnantes murailles de sons dont les blocs et les arêtes suggèrent l'interprétation de phénomènes géologiques et dont l'effet ne manquera pas d'être sensible à ceux qui se sont aperçus que, depuis Beethoven, Berlioz, Stravinski ou Milhaud, la beauté peut être ailleurs que dans la grâce." (Cl. Rostand) "Tard venu à la composition, totalement indépendant de tous les courants issus de l'Ecole de Vienne, immédiatement original dans ses principes et théories de composition, Iannis Xenakis est aujourd'hui un des tout plus importants compositeurs de cette seconde moitié du XXme siècle, celui qui par son cheminement solitaire a ouvert des voies absolument nouvelles au développement de la musique." (J. & B. Massin) "Avec Iannis Xenakis, se dégage une pensée musicale qui manifeste une réelle autonomie vis-à-vis des systèmes existants, en particulier du système sériel. Le déterminisme du sérialisme lui apparaît comme un cas particulier d'une logique plus générale, dont la limite serait le hasard pur. Iannis Xenakis pose, pour ainsi dire, un principe d'incertitude à l'égard de tout système compositionnel, choisissant ainsi d'introduire les lois universelles susceptibles d'élever le discours musical à un plus haut degré de généralité.". (D. J-Y. Bosseur)

"The techniques used by Xenakis involve the handling of extremely large numbers of elements, but the complicated calculations needed may be facilitated by the use of a computer. The computer can both undertake the mechanical calculations required and explore fields of possibilities among which the composer can choose. Unlike other workers in computer music, Xenakis has not used composition or sound-generating programmes, although in the mid-1970s he began to investigate the latter. Although Xenakis' employment of mathematical and physical models might suggest that his work is highly abstract, it is rather the expression of a profound humanity, even a thinly veiled romanticism. His often expressed aim to find 'a new open path to man' is most evidently the driving force in the choral works, among them several which return to the origins of western culture for their texts." (M. Philippot)

Xas (1987) (10') (to Rascher Quartet) •SATB •Sal

YAMANOUCHI, Tadashi (1940)

Compositeur japonais.
Correlation (1979) (to K. Munesada) •Marimba/Asx/Bass
Epistoraphe (1968) (to A. Sakaguchi) •Asx/Marimba/Vibr/Vcl

YASINITSKY, Gregory W. (1953)

Saxophoniste, compositeur, et professeur américain. Travailla avec J. Schwantner, W. Peterson, L. Harrison, S. Adler, et R. Morris.
Four Short Pieces (1990) (8'30) (to R. Ricker) 1) A Tear for Leonardo 2) Family Business 3) This One's for Anton 4) Pulse •Tsx/Pno
On Wings of Angels (1992) (4') (to my wife) •Sx Solo
Sixth Sense (1985) (7') 1) Dynaflow 2) Say it Softly •Asx/Pno •DP

YATES, Ronald (1947)

Compositeur américain né à Michigan. Travailla avec Applebaum et D. Andrus.

"His *Triune* abandons tonality and melody and its shape is derived from different rates of change of textures… The range which each instrument played was important as well as the patterns of voice overplays."
Concerto (1970) (14') (to J. Rotter) •Asx/Orch (Str/Perc) •adr
Triune (1971) •Asx/Vla/BsTrb •adr

YEOMANS, Will

Compositeur anglais.
Composition •Ssx/Pno

YERGEAU, Liette

Compositeur canadien.
Dans les spirales du silence (1992) •Ssx/Tape

YOCAPETTA

Largo •5 Sx: AATBBs

YODER, Paul (1908)

Compositeur et arrangeur américain, né à Tacoma (Washington), le 8 X 1908.
Dry Bones •AATB •Kjos
Jericho •AATB •Kjos
Relax •AATB •Kjos

YOI, Hisayasu

Compositeur japonais.
Asukanite •Asx/Pno

YONEKURA, Yuki

Compositeur japonais.
After the Rain (1992) •2 Sx: AA

YORKO, Bruce

Night Dances (1982) (to R. Greenberg) •SATB

YOSHIBA, Susumu (1947)

Compositeur japonais.

"Susumu Yoshiba représente déjà une nouvelle génération de jeunes compositeurs japonais, mais dans ses premières oeuvres il cherche à établir un lien avec des sources d'inspiration populaire japonaise." (J. & B. Massin)
Erka •Fl/Ob/Sx/Tpt/Trb/Perc/Vcl/Guit/Pno

YOSHIMATSU, Takashi (1953)

Compositeur japonais.

"Yoshimatsu absorbs all types of music—classical, serialism, tone cluster, jazz, rock, and traditional music. He does not, however, imitate or simply mix different styles but rather integrates them to form his own unique creations." (K-I. ISODA)

Fuzzy Bird Sonata (1991) (22') (to N. SUGAWA) 1) Run, Bird 2) Sing, Bird 3) Fly, Bird •Asx/Pno •Bil

YOSHIOKA, Emmett Gene (1944)

Compositeur, flûtiste, chanteur, et saxophoniste américain, né à Honolulu, le 19 III 1944. Travailla avec I. Dahl, H. Stevens, et R. Linn. Membre du "Los Angeles Saxophone Quartet."

Aria and Allegro (1968) (8') •SATB •Art
Arioso (1969) (10') (to H. PITTEL) •Asx/Harp/Str Orch •Art
Duo Concertino (to H. PITTEL) •Asx/Band or Pno •adr
Intermezzo (1966-68) •Ssx/Band or Pno •adr
Sonata (1973) (to H. PITTEL) •Asx/Pno •adr

YOUNES, Nicole

Compositeur autrichien.
Sapere audes (1992) •1 Sx: S+A/Pno •INM

YOUNG, Charles Rochester (1965)

Saxophoniste et compositeur américain. Travailla avec R. Willis.

Big o'blues (1987) •Sx/Jazz ensemble
Concerto (1990) (to D. SINTA) •Asx/Wind Orch •adr
Diversions (1986) •1 Sx: S or T/Pno
Excursions (1989) (6') (to F. MEZA) •Asx/Marimba •adr
Farewell (1986) •Sx/Jazz ensemble
Horizons (1986) •Sx/Jazz ensemble
October in the Rain (1989) (5') (to J. Pendell) •MIDI Wind Controller/Hn/Pno/Synth/Perc •adr
Quartet (1989) (7') (to Texas Saxophone Quartet) (Fantasie - Ritual - Incantations) •SATB •adr
Reflections (1986) •Sx/Jazz ensemble
Sahib Supreme •SATB •SiMC
Slam Funk (1987) •Sx/Jazz ensemble
Sonata (1987) (9') (to C. Rasmussen) 1) Recitative 2) Nocturne 3) Tarentelle •Ssx/Pno •DP
Winter Echoes •Sx/Jazz ensemble

YOUNG, Gordon (1919)

Compositeur et organiste américain, né à McPherson (Kansas), le 15 X 1919. Travailla à Paris avec J. Bonnet.

Contempora Suite (1956) (for L. SMITH) 1) Prelude 2) Allemande 3) Sarabande 4) Gigue •Asx/Pno •Bel

YOUNG, Jeremy (1948)

Compositeur américain.

Concerto (1973-83) (9') (to W. STREET) •Asx/Orch (222 3 Sx: STB 0/2221/4 Perc/Str)
Family Portraits (1988) 1) Easter '87 2) Christmas '87 3) Family Reunion '88 •2 Sx: S+A+T/A+B/Pno
Hassle (1970-79) (to W. STREET) •Sx Solo
Rondeau à Bordeaux (1979) (to W. STREET) •Asx/Fl

YOUNG, Lynden de (1923)

Chamber Music: Quintet (1972) (to F. HEMKE) •Asx/Bsn/Ob/Pno/ Vibr •SeMC
Introduction, Blues and Finale •2 Sx: AT/Pno •DP
Transformation (1981) 1) Recitative 2) Air (in the style of Johnny Hodges) 3) Variations •Asx/Pno

YOUNG, Wha Son (see SON, Yung Wha)

YUASA, Joji (1929)

Compositeur japonais, né à Koriyama, le 12 VIII 1929.

"In composition he is self-taught, yet his music shows an exceptional sensitivity to sonority and an intellectual approach to the handling of materials. His compositional attitude is, however, quite unconventional, which may be due in part to his medical interest in auditory physiology; he is particularly skilled in distributing sounds of various tone-colours in a 'space' without attempting any logical formal arrangement." (M. KANAZAWA)

Not I, but the wind (1976) (11') (to R. NODA) •Amplified Asx Solo

YUNG, Karl

Piece •Asx/Pno

YUSTE, M.

Solo de concours •Tsx/Pno •UME

YUYAMA, Akira (1932)

Compositeur japonais. Travailla avec T. Ikenouchi.
Divertimento (1968) (9') •Asx/Marimba •JCC/B&B

ZAAGMANS, J.
Abenderzählung (Conte du soir) •SATB •TM
Scherzo •SATB •TM

ZAGARYN, Arthur
Compositeur russe.
Ballade •Asx/Band

ZAJAC, Elaine (1940)
Saxophoniste, professeur, et compositeur américain, né le 12 VI 1940, à Detroit (Michigan). Travailla avec L. Teal.
Elaborations (1976) •Asx/Pno
Five Miniatures (1970) (to L. TEAL) 1) Allegro moderato 2) Andante 3) Allegretto 4) Lento 5) Allegro marcato •SATB •Eto

ZAJDA, Edward M. (1941)
Compositeur américain, né à Chicago, le 15 X 1941.
Brass and Weed (1972) (6-7') (to my wife) •Asx/Pno •adr

ZAKREVSKY, Vadim
Compositeur russe.
Softmusic (1992) •Asx/Vibr •INM

ZALACZEK, Roman W.
Canzona ebraica (1982) (8') 1) Preludio 2) Canzona •SATB

ZAMACOIS, Joaquin (1894-1976)
Serenada d'hivern (AMAZ) •1 Sx: A or T/Pno •UME

ZAMBARANO, Alfred
Compositeur américain.
Napolitan tarantella •Asx/Pno •Sha

ZAMECNIK
Polly •Bb Sx/Pno •SF

ZANDER, Heinz Joachim (1920)
Pianiste, chef d'orchestre, et compositeur allemand, né à Breslau, le 29 XI 1920.
Fantasie für Saxophonquartett (1986) (13') •SATB •adr
Rhapsodie •Asx/Pno •adr

ZANETTOVICH, Daniele (1950)
Compositeur italien.
Prima sonata (1966-68) •Asx/Pno •Piz
Second sonata •Tsx/Pno •Piz
Tango in Nero (1992) (6') (to A. DOMIZI) •12 Sx: SnoSSAAATTTBBBs

ZANINELLI, Luigi (1932)
Autumn Music •Asx/Pno •Sha
Misterioso (1978) (to K. DEANS) •Asx/Pno

ZEBINGER, Franz
Compositeur allemand.
Sopra... Fünf Anachronismen (1992) •Asx/Org •INM
Weill noch das Lämpchen (1992) •Asx/Org •INM

ZEBRE, Demetrij (1912)
Compositeur et chef d'orchestre yougoslave, né le 22 XII 1912 à Ljubljana. Travailla avec J. Suk.

Intermezzo saxofonico •Asx/Pno •YUC

ZECCHI, Adone (1904)
Compositeur, chef d'orchestre, et professeur italien, né le 23 VII 1904, à Bologna. Travailla avec Alfano, Nordio, et Casella.
"His early works were neo-classical, but later he approached dodecaphony." (A. PIRONTI)
Recitativi ed arie (1983) (7') •Asx/Pno •CoMu

ZECHLIN, Rutj (1926)
Compositeur et professeur allemand, né à Grossharmanndorf (Sax), le 22 VI 1926. Travailla avec D. Straube et Ramin.
"As a composer she is best known for her three symphonies, a number of cantatas, and chamber works." (H. SEEGER)
7 Versuche und 1 Ergebnis (1988) (17') •SATB •R&E

ZELLER, Fredrik
Compositeur allemand.
Geteiltes Lied ist halbes Lied (1992) •Bsx/Electr. Guit

ZELLER, Karl (1842-1898)
Schenkt man sich Rosen in Tirol •Asx/Pno •Mol

ZEMP, Joseph (1915)
Compositeur français, né à Belfort, le 12 XII 1915. Travailla avec L. Debraux et E. Mavet.
Air scandinave (1972) •4 Sx: SATB or 5 Sx: AATTB •Mar
Prélude et fugue •SATB •Mar
Souffle printanier •Fl/Ob/Cl/4 Sx: SATB •adr

ZENDER, Hans (1936)
Compositeur et chef d'orchestre allemand, né le 22 XI 1936, à Wiesbaden. Travailla avec Fortner, B. A. Zimmermann, et E. Picht-Axenfeld.
"His own compositions are intricate, tasteful and finely crafted in a somewhat Boulezian mold." (GROVE)
Konzertino, op. 5 (1952) (15') (to J. de VRIES) 1) Allegro moderato 2) Andante tranquillo 3) Allegro •Asx/Orch (2101/020/Perc/Str) or Pno •Br&Ha
Stephen Climax (1979-84) •3 Sx •adr

ZENONI
Sinfonia a tre •3 Sx •WWS

ZIELENSKI, Nikolaj (15xx-1611)
Da pacem domine (D. STREETS) •4 Sx: SATB or AATB •TM

ZIMMERMAN, A.
Rip-torn (1980) (to I. MARCONI) •Asx/Pno

ZIMMERMAN, Keith
Saxophoniste et compositeur américain.
The Paradoxes of Love (1987) (7') •Soprano Voice/Ssx •adr
Reflections (1985) (6'30) •Ssx Solo •adr

ZIMMERMANN, Kai-Otto
Compositeur allemand.
Die Zehn Gebote (1993) •Tsx/Pno •INM

ZIMMERMANN, Walter (1949)
Compositeur allemand, né à Schwabach.
In der Welt sein (1982) (9') •Tsx Solo

ZINDARS, E.
Quiddity •2 Sx: AA/Pno •AMC

ZINN, Michael (1947)
Compositeur américain, né le 23 VIII 1947, à New Haven (Connecticut). Travailla avec H. O. Reed, P. Harder et C. Wittenberg.

Suspensions (1973) (to K. FISCHER) •Asx/Bsn/Vibr •SeMC

ZITEK, F.

Saxophone Studies, op. 3

ZIVANOVIC, Mihajlo (1928)

Clarinettiste et compositeur yougoslave, né à Belgrade, le 17 II 1928.

Balada (1957) •Asx/Jazz Orch •YUC

Inveneija (1957) •Asx/Jazz Orch •YUC

Rapsodija (1965) •Asx/Orch •YUC

ZLATIC, Smlavko (1910)

Compositeur yougoslave, né le 1 VI 1910 à Pula (Sovinjak). Travailla avec B. Bersa.

Balum (1936) •Ob/EH/Asx/Bsn •UKH

ZLATO, Pibernick

Compositeur yougoslave.

Koncertantna musika •Fl/Sx/Harp/Str •YUC

ZOBEL, Edgar H.

Spruce Shadows •Tsx/Pno •Kjos

ZONN, Paul Martin (1938)

Compositeur, clarinettiste, et chef d'orchestre américain, né à Boston (Massachusetts).

"My compositions have always been concerned with the very new and the old and the integration of diverse elements. I use the many languages of world music and try to bind them together with a common syntax. Oftentimes my jazz background will influence the rhythmic detailing and melodic partitioning of a set." (P. M. ZONN)

Canzoni, Overo sonate concertare conserere (1977) (14') •Ob Solo or Ssx •ACA

Desmond Dream (1991) (24') (to J. LULLOFF) 1) The Salt Garden 2) Boundary Walker 3) Mirrors and Windows 4) Monotones 5) Whisper Once More •Asx/Pno •ACA

Midnight Secrets (1992) (20') (to D. RICHTMEYER) 1) Well-spring of the Temptress 2) 1st Interlude 3) Moondance 4) 2nd Interlude 5) Flat Light Rising •Ssx/Vln/Vla/Vcl •ACA

Nimbus III (1994) •Asx/Cl/Ob

Voyage of Columbus (1974) (13') (to D. HICKMAN) •Tpt Solo/Fl/Ob/ Ssx/Hrn/Trb/2 Perc/Pno/Vln/Bass •ACA

ZOURABICHVILI, Nicolas de Pelken (1936)

Compositeur français, d'origine russe, né à Paris. Travailla avec N. Boulanger et M. Deutch.

Pointillés (1974) (to J-P. CAENS) •Asx/Tape •adr

Winterleid (1984) (18') (to Quatuor d'Anches Aulodia) (2 movements) •Ob/Cl/Asx/Bsn

ZSCHUPPE, Frank

Compositeur allemand.

Sonatine (1992) •Asx/Pno •INM

ZUCKERT, Leon (1904)

Compositeur et chef d'orchestre canadien d'origine russe.

Doina (1967-70) (4'30) (to P. BRODIE) •Ssx/Pno •CMC

Indian Lullaby (1969-70) (3'30) (to P. BRODIE) •Ssx/Pno •CMC

Sur le lac Baptiste-Ontario (1972) (9') (to P. BRODIE) 1) Ete 2) Hiver •Ssx/Pno •CMC

Index By Instrumentation

Sopranino Saxophone

Also see Unspecified Instrumentation (Voir aussi instruments non déterminés), page 422 and Saxophone and Tape (Saxophone et Bande magnétique), Page 416.

BABBITT, Milton - *Images* (1979) (10'30) •1 Sx: Sno+S+A/Synth Tape •adr

BRABANT, Eric - *Saxodrome* (1982) (22') 1 Sx: Sno+S+A+T+B/Tape

BRINDUS, Nicolae - *Kitsh II-N* (20') •1 Sx: Sno+S+A+T+B/Tape

CAVANA, Bernard - *Goutte d'or blues* (1985) (7') •1 Sx: Sno+S/Tape or 12 Sx •Sal

CHIHARA, Paul - *Concerto* (1980) (13'30) •1 Sx: Sno+S+A/Orch

CONDÉ, Gérard - *Monarch...* (1983) (22') •1 Sx: Sno+S+A+T+B+Bs

DONATONI, Franco - *Hot* (1989) (14') •1 Sx: T+Sno/Cl+Eb Cl/Tpt/Trb/Perc/Bass/Pno •Ric

FOURCHOTTE, Alain - *Disgression I* (1981) (5') •Sno Sx Solo •Sal

GARCIN, Gérard - *Enfin...* (1981) (13') •Sno Sx/Tape •Sal

GINER, Bruno - *Entrechocs I* (1985) (14') •1 sx: Sno+S+B/Tape/Synth

GIULIANO, Giuseppe - *Tempi della mente* (1986) (11') •1 Sx: Sno+S/Tape

GRIMAL, A. - *Bravura...* (1879) •SnoSx/Pno •Mil

GUNSENHEIMER, Gustav - *Concertino n° 4* (1986) (10') •1 Sx: Sno+S+A/Str Orch •VF

HESPOS, Hans-Joachim - *Pico* (1978) (4') •Sx Solo: CBs or Sno

ISRAEL, Brian - *Double Concerto* (1984) •2 Sx: SnoBs/Band

KRAUS, Marco - *Suite concertante* •1 Sx: Sno+S+A+T+B/Orch

LUC, Francis - *Concerto* (1981) (15') •1 Sx: Sno+A+T+B/Tape

LUQUE, Francisco - *Saxofonia* (1989) (7') •1 Sx: Sno+B/Tape

MARBE, Myriam - *Concerto* (33') •1 Sx: B+A+Sno/Orch •EMu

MARIETAN, Pierre - *Concert III* (1989) (7') •1 Sx: Sno+S/Magnétoph. multipistes

Concert IV (1989) (8') •1 Sx: Sno+S+T+B+Bs+CBs/Instrumental ensemble

Duo (1985) •1 Sx: Sno+A+T+B+Bs+CBs/Tape

13 en concert (1983) (15') •1 Sx: Sno+S+B/Cl/Bsn/Trb/Vcl/2 Bass/Pno

MESSINA-ROSARYO, Antonio - *Danza del demonio* (1984) (35') •SnoSx/Orch •Asto

MIEREANU, Costin - *Doppelkammerkonzert* (1985) (17') •1 Sx: Sno+A+T+Bs/Perc Solo/Orch •Sal

Kammer-Koncert n° 1 (1984-85) (16') •1 Sx: Sno+A+T+Bs •Sal

NICULESCU, Stefan - *Cantos* (1984-85) (22') •1 Sx: Sno+A+T+B/Orch

OLAH, Tiberiu - *Obelisc pentru...* (22') •1 Sx: Sno+A+B/Orch

Rimes (1985) (8') •1 Sx: Sno+A/Matériel électr.

PABLO, Luis de - *Une couleur* (1988) (22') •1 Sx: Sno+S+T+B+CBs/Orch •SZ

PEIXINHO, Jorge - *Sax-Bleu* (1982) (18') •1 Sx: Sno+A/Echo Chamber •Sal

Passage intérieur (1989) (16') •1 Sx: Sno+S+A+T+B/Instrumental Ensemble

RADULESCU, Horatiu - *Astray* (1984-85) (23') •1 Sx: Sno+S+A+T+B+Bs/matériel électron. (or Prepared Pno)

RODRIGUEZ, Robert Xavier - *Sinfonia* (1972) •1 Sx: Sno+S/Orch •adr

STROE, Aurel - *La cité ouverte* (1983) (9'30) •1 Sx: Sno+S+B/Tape

SURIANU, Horia - *Concerto* (1984) (15') •1 Sx: Sno+T/Orch •Sal

ULBEN, Denize - *Concertino* (1985) (15') •1 Sx: A+Sno/Orch •adr

Solo Soprano Saxophone

Also see Unspecified Instrumentation (Voir aussi instruments non déterminés), page 422 and Saxophone and Tape (Saxophone et Bande magnétique), Page 416.

ANDERSON, Tommy Joe - *Impromptu*, op. 29 •DP

ARCHER, Violet - *Three Essays* (1988) •Sx Solo: S+A •CMC

ARMA, Paul - *3 Contrastes* (1971) (6') •Sx Solo •Chou

ARTIOMOV, Vyatcheslav - *Recitative I* (1978)

BATTISTA, Tonino - *Narcisso* (1989/91) •1 Sx: S+B/Live Electron.

BERNARD, Jacques - *6 Miniatures* (1978) (8'30) •An

BIANCHINI, Laura - *NO.DI* (1987/88) (10') •1 Sx: S+A+T/Computer "Fly" •adr

BOONE, Ben - *Election Year* (1994) •Sx Solo: S or A or T or B •INM

BORTOLOTTI, Mauro - *Luogo...* (1985/90) •Sx Solo: S+A •adr

BOURLAND, Roger - *Fire From Fire* •ECS

BRIZZI, Aldo - *De la transmutazione del Metalli* (1983-86) (9') •Sx Solo: S+T

BROWN, Robert - *Ken's Patience*

BUCKINX, Boudewin - *Clink of Sounds...* •Ssx/Actress •AMP

CAMPANA, José - *Acting out* (1982) •Sal

CONDÉ, Gérard - *Monarch...* (1983) (22') •1 Sx: Sno+S+A+T+B+Bs

COSMA, Edgar - *Soliloque* (1984) (10')

COUTU, Jacques - *Etude de comportement...* (1983) (12'30) •CMC

DAKIN, Charles - *The Tarots of Marseille* (1981) (17')

Debussy, Claude - *Syrinx* (LONDEIX) (2'45) •Sx Solo: A or S •JJ

Syrinx (REID) •Ken

DIEDERICHS, Yann - *Pieces*

ERDMANN, Dietrich - *Saxophonata* •Sx Solo: S+A+T •R&E

ERNST-MEISTER, Sigrid - *"E... Staremo Freschi!"* (1992) (8') •Sx Solo: S+T

FEILER, Dror - *Don't walk out on me* (1984) •SMIC/Tons

Hallel (1984) •SMIC/Tons

FINNISSY, Michael - *Moon's...* (1980) (8') •Voice or Ssx Solo •Uni

FOURCHOTTE, Alain - *Disgressions II* (1981-82) (5') •Sal

GAGNEUX, Renaud - *Babel* (1978) (7') •1 Sx: A+S/Dispositif électro-acoustique simple

GISSELMAN, Philippe - *Série L.* (4'30) (to S. BERTOCCHI) •adr

GLASS, Philip - *8 for John Gibson* (1968)

GRAEF, Friedemann - *Karorak 7Z* (14') •adr

GROOT, Rokus de - *Kontur* (1982) (25') •Sx Solo: S or A •Don

HARTLEY, Walter - *Prelude and Finale* (1966) (5') •RMP

HAVEL, Christophe - *Xaps* (1991) •Ssx/Transformation électroacoustique •adr

HEYN, Volker - *Buon natale...* (1984/85) (12') •Sx Solo: S+T

HOLLAND, Dulcie - *Pieces* •adr

ISHII, Maki - *Black intention* (1978) (8')

JEANNEAU, François - *Monodie* •adr

JOHNSON, Tom - *Rational Melodies* (1982) (2' to 25')

KARLINS, M. William - *Seasons* (1987) (13') •Sx Solo: S+A+T •TP

KAVANAUGH, Patrick - *Debussy-variations No. 5* (1977) •CF

KLEIN, Georg - *Nuit...* (1993) •1 Sx: S+T/Live electronics •INM

KOECHLIN, Charles - *Le repos de Tityre*, op. 216 (1948) •ME

KOIVULA, Kari - *Nox* (1982) •Ob or Ssx •FMIC

KOSTECK, Gregory - *Chromatic Fantasy* (1979) (7') •DP

KRAFT, William - *Arietta Da Capo* (1982) (3'30) •Don

LAUBA, Christian - *Chott 2* (1992) (11') •adr

LOGRANDE, L. A. - *ie, integrity eclipsed* (1993) (6') •CI

MACHUEL, Thierry-Joël - *France-Télécom* (1991) •Sx Solo: B+S

MARCONI-BRAMUCCI - *Indian metamorphosis*

MARRA, James - *Legacy...* (1978) (7') •Sx Solo: S+T •DP

MARTINEZ FERNANDEZ, Julian - *Hacia la desconocido* (1993) •Sx Solo: S+Bs+T

MIEREANU, Costin - *Variants - Invariants* (1982) (14') •Asx or Ssx/ Echo Chamber •Sal
MOYLAN, William - *Solo Sonata* (1978) (16-18') •1 Sx: S+A+T •SeMC/DP
NICULESCU, Stefan - *Chant-son* (1989) (6') •1 Sx: S+A
NODA, Ryo - *Pulse +* - (1972-82) (15') •Led
Paganini, Nicolo - *Caprice*, Op. 1, No. 24 (ROSSI) •Sx Solo •DP
PANICCIA, Renzo - *Elegia*, op. 6 (1985) (6')
PELCHAT, André - *Impro binantine* •CMC
QUEYROUX, Yves - *7 Jeux musicaux et 3 Promenades* (1989) •Sx Solo: S or T or A •Lem
RACOT, Gilles - *Anamorphées* (1985)
RADULESCU, Horatiu - *Astray* (1984-85) (23') •1 Sx: Sno+S+A+T+B+Bs/matériel électron. (or Prepared Pno)
ROLIN, Etienne - *Etude en bleu* (1981) (3') •adr
RORIVE, Jean-Pierre - *Novum monasterium*
ROSSÉ, François - *Epiphanies* (1990) (10') •1 Sx: S+B+Bs/Dispositif électro-acoust. •adr
    Séaodie II (1985) (3') •Sx Solo: A or S •Bil
RUNCHAK, Vladymyr - *Homo ludus* (1992) (4')
SCELSI, Jacinto - *Ixor* (1956) (4') •Sal
    Tre pezzi (1961) (9'40) •Sal
SCLATER, James - *Suite* (6'30) •TP/Elk
SEBASTIANI, Fausto - *Solo* (1989)
SEPOS, Charles - *Breathless* (1986)
SEVRETTE, Danielle - *In diesem Brauss* (1975) •adr
SILVERMAN, Faye Ellen - *Three Movements* (1971) (7') •SeMC
SOHAL, Naresh - *Shades I* (1975) (4') •Nov
SON, Yung Wha - *Song of Wishes* (1987) (6')
STEVEN, Donald - *Just a few moments alone* (1984) (4') •CMC
SWAIN, Freda - *Naturo Suite* (1931) (6') •Any Sx Solo •BMIC
    The Tease (1965) (1'30) •Any Sx Solo •BMIC
TAKEMITSU, Toru - *Distance* (1990) (10')
TARANU, Cornel - *Sonate sempre ostinato* (1986) (7')
TERUGGI, Daniel - *Xatys* (1988) (18'30) •1 Sx: Bs+T+S/Dispositif électronique
TOEPLITZ, Kasper - *Anachorete* (1991) (5') •Saer/Ric
TONT, Patrice - *De ceux qui fréquentent...* (1990) (10') •1 Sx: S+B
WASHBURN, Gary - *A Ride; A Moonbeam; Polka Dot* (1974) (20') •Sx Solo: A+S+B •SeMC
ZIMMERMAN, Keith - *Reflections* (1985) (6'30) •adr

Soprano Saxophone and Piano

Also see Soprano Saxophone and Orchestra or Band
(Voir aussi saxophone soprano et orchestre ou band),
Page 290.

ANDERSEN, Michael - *Sonata* (1976)
ANDERSON, Gerry - *Pastiche* (1993) •INM
ANDERSON, Tommy Joe - *Liebeslied*, op. 20 (1975)
    Sonate No. 3, op. 30 (1988) (14'15) •1 Sx: S+A/Pno •Ron
ARMA, Paul - *Phases contre Phases* (1978) (13') •Lem
Aubert, Esprit - *Angela Aria* •1 Sx: S or A/Pno •TM
BABAYAN, Yahram - *Mantra*, op. 63 (1986) (7') •Led
BANTER, Harald - *Phönix* (1989) •B&B
BARILLER, Robert - *Fan'Jazz* (3') •1 Sx: A or S/Pno •Led
BEDARD, Denis - *Fantaisie* (1984) (6'30) •Do
BEERMAN, Burton - *Passager* (1985)
BEHRENS, Jack - *Music from Wawerfree* (1972) (8') •CMC
BENNETT, Richard Rodney - *Sonata* (18'30)
BENTZON, Niels Viggo - *Sonata*, op. 478 (1985) (14') •WH
Berlin, Irving - *Cheek to Cheek* (POLANSKY) •Ssx/Pno •Lem
BERTOCCHI, Serge - *Axolotl* (1987) (4') •Ssx/Synth

Blavet, Michel - *Sonata no. 5* (WOLFE) •Ron
    Sonatine en Sib •Bb Sx/Pno •Mol
BOIS, Rob du - *Herman's Hide-Away* (1976) •Don
BOMBERG, David - *Interactions* (1980) •WWS
BONNARD - *Sonate*, op. 1, no. 1 (1954/71) (15') •EFM
    Villancico, op. 47 •adr
Brahms, Johannes - *Intermezzo in A*, op. 118, no. 2 •Ron
    Pieces •Bb Sx/Pno
BURNETTE, Sonny - *Winter Wind* (1993) •Ron
CALHOUN, William - *Sonata* (1982) •DP
CARAVAN, Ronald - *Quiet Time* (1980) •1 Sx: S+T/Pno •Eth
CARRE-CHESNEAU, Thierry - *2 Pièces* (1979) •1 Sx: S+A/Pno
CONTE, David - *Sonata* (1979)
CORBIN, A. - *Tout le long du Rhin - Valse caprice* (1890) •Marg
COSSABOOM, Sterling - *Fragments*
COSTE, Napoléon - *Regrets...*, op. 36 (1880) •Bb Sx/Pno •Mil
COWLES, Colin - *Recitative and Air* (3') •Ssx/Harp or Pno
    Sarabande (2') •adr
    Sopsonare (1973) (12') •adr
CREPIN, Alain - *Sicilienne* •1 Sx: A or S/Pno •HM
CUNLIFFE - *Farewell to Peace* •WWS
CUNNINGHAM, Michael G. - *Sonata* •SeMC
DEASON, David - *Blues-Walk* (1984) •1 Sx: S+A+T/Pno
    Epigrams •DP
DELGUIDICE, Michel - *Saxboy* •1 Sx: S or A or T/Pno •Mar
DELIO, Thomas - *Gestures* •DP
DELVINCOURT, Claude - *Scapin joué* (3'30) •1 Sx: S or T/Pno •Lem
DEMERSSEMAN, Jules - *Fantaisie pastorale* •Bb Sx/Pno •Bil
    Introduction et Variations... •Bb Sx/Pno •Marg
    1er solo (1865)
    2me Solo (1866)
DI SALVO - *Rhapsody* (1973)
DOBBINS, Bill - *Sonata* (1991) (13') •1 Sx: S or T/Pno •AdMu
DUBOIS, Pierre-Max - *Triangle* (1974) (19') •1 Sx: S+A+T/Pno •RR
Du Parc - *4 Love songs* (DAVIS) •WWS
DUTKIEWICZ, Andrzzei - *Danse triste* (1977) (13') •Bb Sx/Pno •DP
DWYER, Benjamin - *Tiento* (1993) •INM
DYCK, Vladimir - *Invocation to Euterpe* •Bb Sx/Pno •WA
    2me légende hébraïque (1936) •Bil
EHLE, Robert - *Sonata*
ERB, Donald - *I "Mixed-Media": Fission* (1968) (13') •Ssx/Pno/Tape •adr
FELD, Jindrich - *Elegie* (1981) (6') •Led
    Sonate (1982) (14') •Led
FINNEY, Ross Lee - *Two Studies* (1980) (10') 1 Sx: A+S/Pno •Pet
FLEMING, Robert - *Threo* (1972) •CMC
FLETA POLO, Francisco - *Impromptu n° 7a*, op. 69 (1979)
FONTAINE, Louis-Noël - *Scherzo* (1992) (8') •Capri
FONTYN, Jacqueline - *Fougères* (1981) (5') •1 Sx: S+A/Pno or Harp •Sal
    Mime III (1980) (5') •1 Sx: S+A/Pno •Sal
FORD, Clifford - *5 Short pieces...* (1971) (6') •CMC
FUERSTNER, Carl - *Incantations*, op. 45 •Eto
GARLICK, Antony - *Pièces* •SeMC
GEE, Harry - *Festival Solo* •1 Sx: S or T/Pno •DP
GELLER, Gabriel - *Osculum infame* (1993) •Ssx/Pno+Synth •INM
GENZMER, Harald - *Sonate* (1982) (14') •R&E
GERHARD, Fritz - *Rhapsodie* (1980)
GERHARDT, Frank - *Geschichten vom Erwachen* (1993) •INM
GLICK, Srul - *Suite hebraique* (1968) (14'45)
GOULD, Tony - *Introduction for Two Players* (1988)
GOWER - *Elegy and Presto* •WWS
GRAINGER, Percy - *The Lonely Desert Man...* (1949-54) •Ssx/ Chamber Group or Pno •GSch
    The Power of Love (1922-41-50) •PG

GRILLAERT, Octave - *Sopran song*, op. 9393 (1978) (2'30)
HAIDMAYER, Karl - *Romanesca 10* (4'20); *Sonate n° 1*
Handel, Georg-Friedrich - *Pieces*
HARTLEY, Walter - *Divsersions* (1979) (7'30) •Eth
    The Saxophone Album (1974) •DP
HAWORTH, Frank - *Vesperal Suite* (1972) (5')
HEATH, David - *Rumania* (1979) (10')
HILLIARD, John - *Fantasy* (1976)
HOCKETT, Charles - *Vocalise*
IBERT, Jacques - *Mélopée* •Bb Sx/Pno •Lem
ISABELLE, Jean Clément - *Mienne* (1973) (15')
    Sonate (1974)
JAROSKAWSKA, Joanna - *Espressioni liriche* (1977)
JOHNSON, J. - *Chamber Music*
Karren, Léon - *Menuet marquise* (1891)
KEIG, Betty - *Episodes* (1990)
KOCH, Erland von - *Danse n° 2* (1938-67) (2') •1 Sx: S+A/Pno
    •STIM
KOECHLIN, Charles - *7 Pièces*, op. 180 (1942) (30'30)
KOMOROUS, Rudolf - *Dingy yellow* (1972) •Ssx/Pno/Tape •CMC
KÜHNE, Stephan - *Fünf lettische Bauerntänze...* (1993) •INM
KUSHIDA, Testurosuke - *Fantasia* (1990)
KYLE, Mattews - *Thief* (1987) (6') •adr
LANCEN, Serge - *Confidences* (1968) (2') •Bb Sx/Pno •Chap
    Intimité (1968) (3'30) •Bb Sx/Pno •Mol
    Introduction et Allegro giocoso (1965) (5'30) •Bb Sx/Pno •Mol
    Si j'étais (1980) (5'30) •1 Sx: S or T/Pno •Led
    Trois Pièces (1963) (7') •Bb Sx/Pno •Mol
LASNE, George - *2 Esquisses...* (1946) •Asx (or Ssx)/Org (or Pno)
LECLERC, Michel - *Au coeur de la cité Ardente* (1988)
LEMELAND, Aubert - *Epitaph...*, op. 86 (1979) (5') •Bil
LESAFFRE, Charles - *Mon premier blues* (2'30) •Bil
LESSER, Jeffrey - *Suite for Clyde* (1979) •DP
LEWIS, Malcolm - *Elegy...* (1972) (4') •Asx/Band or Ssx/Pno
    Poem (1976) •DP
LINKOLA, Jukka - *Joutsen - Swan* (1979) (3') •FMIC
LLOYD, Jonathan - *John's journal* (1980) (15') •1 Sx: S+A •B&H
Loeillet, Jean-Baptiste - *Sonata*, op. 3, no. 3
LOPEZ, Jose Susi - *Diàlogos* (1993) •INM
LOUVIER, Alain - *5 Ephémères* (1981) (7') •Led
LUNDE, Lawson - *Sonata "Alpine"*, op. 37 (1970) (8') •TTF
LUYPAERTS, Guy - *Escapade* (1988) •adr
MAIS, Chester - *Gossamer Piece* (1981) •adr
Marcello, Allessandro - *Concerto in C Minor* (MOROSCO) •DP
MARI, Pierrette - *Jacasserie* (1960) •Com
    Corollaire d'un songe (1976) •Bb Sx/Pno •Arp
McCARTHY, Daniel - *Sonata* •1 Sx: S+A/Pno/Tape •adr
Monti, Vittorio - *Czarda* (ROBERTS) •Bb Sx/Pno •CF
Moussart - *Oboe - mazurka* •Mar
NIELSON, Lewis - *Surrealistic Portraiture* (1993)
NIVERD, Lucien - *Insouciante* •1 Sx: A or S/Pno •Bil/Mar
NODA, Ryo - *W 1988 D* (1988) •1 Sx: S+A/Pno •adr
NOON, David - *Ars Nova*, op. 67 (1982) (6') •TTF
ONNA, Peter van - *Crystal dreams* (1991) (7') •Don
PALA, Johan - *Hulpgrepen* •Mol
PALMER, E. - *Serenade to an Empty Room*
PARFREY, Raymond - *Cosmo Allegro* (1974) •BMIC
    Two Pieces •BMIC
    Waltz Caprice (1974) •BMIC
PERRIN, Marcel - *Mélopée* (2'30) •1 Sx: A or S/Pno
    Reflets (1983) (2'10) •1 Sx: S or A/Pno •DP
    Pieces •Asx or Bb Sx/Pno
PETTY, Byron W. - *Introduction and Souvenir* (1992-93)
Pierné, Gabriel - *Pieces* (GEE) •1 Sx: S or T/Pno •South
PILLEVESTRE - *2me Offertoire* (1890) •Bb Sx or Eb Sx/Pno or Org

Platti, Giovanni - *Sonate in G Major* (ROUSSEAU) •Eto
PRESSER, William - *Arioso* (1980) •Ten
REICH, Scott - *Trio for Duo* (1980)
Reynaud, Joseph-Félix - *Pieces* •Sal
RICKER, Ramon - *Solar Chariot* •DP
Rimmer, H. A. - *Autumn Evensong* (ROOIJ) •Mol
RODRIGUEZ, Robert Xavier - *Sonata in One Movement* (1973)
ROGERS, Rodney - *Lessons of the Sky*
ROLIN, Etienne - *Tressage b* (1986) (9') •Lem
ROTHBART, Peter - *Sonata* (1988)
RUGGIERO, Charles - *Interplay*
Sabon, Edouard - *Nocturne* (1889) •Cl or Ssx/Pno
SCHLOTHAUER, Burkhard - *Something lost-töne* (1993) •INM
SCHMITT, Florent - *Le songe de Coppelius* (3') •Bb Sx/Pno •Lem
Schumann, Robert - *Romance Nos. 1, 2, 3* (NIHILL) •DP
    Pieces •Bb Sx/Pno
SEFFER, Yochk'o - *Trabla air* •Ssx/Pno improvised
SEMLER-COLLERY, Jules - *Cantilène* (1958) (3') •Ssx (or Cl)/Pno
    •Dec
SHRUDE, Marilyn - *Music* (1974) •adr
    Shadows and Downing (1982) •adr
SIBBING, Robert - *Sonata* (1981) •Eto
SIGNARD, Pierre - *Pieces* •Mil
SINGELEE, Jean-Baptiste - *Caprice*, op. 80 (1862) •Sax/Ron
    Fantaisies •Sax/CF/Ron
    Souvenir de Savoie, op. 73 (1860) •Sax
SKOLNIK, Walter - *Arioso and Dance* •WWS
SOLOMON, Melvin - *Sonatina* •WWS
SOUALLE, Ali ben - *Pieces* (186x)
SPORCK, Georges - *Méditation*, op. 37 •Braun
STEINKE, Greg - *Episodes* (1973) (8') •Eb Sx or Bb Sx/Pno (ad lib.)
    •SeMC
STOYABNOV, Pentscho - *Scherzo*
STRAUWEN, Jean - *Conte pastoral* •Sch
TCHEREPNINE, Serge - *Morning After Piece* (1965) •Sx/Pno •B&H
Telemann, Georges-Philippe- *Concerto* (JOOSEN) •Mol
    Fantasy No. 6 (PITTEL)
    Pieces •Bb Sx/Pno
TERRY, Peter - *Proanakrousna* (1982) •WWS
TURNER, Robert - *Nostalgie* (1972) (6'30) •CMC
UDELL, Budd - *Elegie and Ecossaise* (1990)
VERHIEL, Ton - *Berceuse* (1987)
    Suite (1982) •Ssx/Pno or Org
VON KNORR, Ernst - *Suite fantaisie*
VOUILLEMIN, Sylvain - *Divertimento...* (1983) (8'30) •Ssx/2 Vln/
    Vla/Vcl/Bass/Perc or Ssx/Pno •Led
VRANA, Frantisek - *Rapsody* (1971) (12') •CHF/B&H
WAGNER - *Sonata* •WWS
WARING, Kate - *Plainte* (1985) (4') •Ssx or Asx/Pno or Org
WATERS, Renee Silas - *Sonata* (1986)
WEISSING, Matthias - *La ville...* (1993) •1 Sx: S+T+B/Pno •INM
WELSH, Wilmer - *Passacaglia* •1 Sx: S+A+T+B/Pno
WIRTH, Carl Anton - *Serenade No. 3* •adr
WOODBURN, James - *Pieces* (1982)
WORLEY, John - *Pieces* •DP
WUENSCH, Gerhard - *Sonata*, op. 59 (1971) (19') •CMC
YEOMANS, Will - *Composition*
YOUNES, Nicole - *Sapere audes* (1992) •1 Sx: S+A/Pno •INM
YOUNG, Charles - *Diversions* •1 Sx: S or T/Pno
    Sonata (1987) (9') •DP
ZUCKERT, Leon - *Doina* (1967-70) (4'30) •CMC
    Indian Lullaby (1969-70) (3'30) •CMC
    Sur le lac Baptiste-Ontario (1972) (9') •CMC

Soprano Saxophone
and Orchestra or Band

Orchestra unless otherwise indicated (Orchestre, sauf indication contraire).

ANTONINI, Félix - *Concertino baroque* •Ssx/Band •adr
BANTER, Harald - Konzert (1979) (16') •Ssx/Jazz Orch •adr
BARNES, Milton - *Medley* (1979) •1 Sx: A+S/Str Orch •CMC
BARREL, Bernard - *Concerto*, op. 29 •Ssx/Str Orch •BMIC
BERTAIN, Jules - *Mazurka pastorale* (1900) •Cl or Ssx/Military Orch or Pno
BETTS, Lorne - *Concertino* (1972) •CMC
BLATNY, Pavel - *Dialogue* (1959/64) •Ssx Solo/Jazz Orch •DP
   Pour Ellis (1966) •Tpt/Ssx/Jazz Orch •IMD
BORÄNG, Gunnar - *Estimerat val* (1984) (8') •Tons/Smic
BÖRJESSON, Lars-Ove - *Sipapu*, op. 36 (1983) (16') •STIM
BORRIS, Siegfried - *Konzert* (1966)
BOURLAND, Roger - *Double Concerto* (1983) (11') •Ssx/Bsn •ECS
BOTTENBERG, Wolfgang - *Fa-Sol-La-Si-Do-Ré* (1972) (21') •Ssx/Str Orch •CMC
CASTRO, Dino - *Concerto* (1978) •1 Sx: S+A+B/Chamber Orch
CELERIANU, Michel - *Aus* (1985) •1 Sx: S+Bs/Ensemble/Choir
CERHA, Friedrich - *Concertino*
CHEN, Qijang - *Feu d'ombres* (1990) (16'30) •Bil
CHIHARA, Paul - *Concerto* (1980) (13'30) •1 Sx: Sno+S+A
COULEUVRIER, Alphonse - *Andante religioso n° I* (1897) •Ssx/Fanfare or Pno •Cos
COWLES, Colin - *Elegy* (1973) (12') •Ssx/Str Orch •adr
DEASON, David - *Gossamer Rings* (1982) •Ssx/Wind ensemble
DELDEN, Lex van - *Concerto*, op. 91 (1967) •2 Ssx •Don
DJEMIL, Enyss - *Concerto* (1974) (16') •1 Sx: S+A+T •adr
DRESSEL, Erwin - *Concerto* (1965) •2 Sx: SA/Orch
EISENMANN, Will - *Konzert* (1962) (12') •2 Sx: SA/Orch
ERDMANN, Dietrich - *Konzert* •1 Sx: A+S/Orch •R&E
ERICKSON, Nils - *Konsert* (1980) (17') •Ssx/Str Orch •STIM
ESCUDIER, H. - *4me fantaisie*, op. 55 (1880) •Ssx/Harmonie or Fanfare •Mol
ESHPAY, Andrei - *Concerto* (1988) •ECP
FELD, Jindrich - *Concerto* (1980) •1 Sx: S+A+T/Orch or Band •Kjos
FISCHER-MÜNSTER, Gerhard - *Fantasiestücke* (1977) (8') •Tarogato Solo or Ssx Solo/Orch •adr
FRANCAIX, Jean - *Concerto* (1959-92) •EH or Ssx •ET
FREEDMAN, Harry - *Celebration* (1977) •1 Sx: S+B •CMC
GLASER, Werner - *Canto* (1970) (6') •Ssx/Str Orch •STIM
   Konsert (1980) (17') •Ton
GRAINGER, Ella - *Honey Pot Bee* (1948) •Voice or Ssx/Chamber Orch •GS
GUNSENHEIMER, Gustav - *Concertino n° 3* (1982) (10') •Ssx/Str Orch •VF
   Concertino n° 4 (1986) (10') •1 Sx: Sno+S+A/Str Orch •VF
HARRISON, Jonty - *CQ* (1989) (16') •1 Sx: S+B/Instrumental Ensemble •adr
HARVEY, Paul - *Concertino* (1973) (15') •Mau
HOLBROOKE, Joseph - *Concerto in Bb*, op. 115 (1939) (15') •Cl+Asx+Tsx+Ssx/Orch •B&H
HOVHANESS, Alan - *Concerto* (1981) •Ssx/Str •Pet
HUBERT, Eduardo - *"Por las Americas"* (1992) (13')
JOLAS, Betsy - *Points d'or* (1981) •1 Sx: S+A+T+B •Ric
Kaufmann, Armin - *Konzert*, op. 91 •Dob
KEMNER, F. Gerald - *Quiet Music* (20') •Ssx/Str/Brass
KOCH, Erland von - *Concerto piccolo* (1962-76) (13') •1 Sx: S+A/Str Orch •Br&Ha
KOECHLIN, Charles - *Sonatine Nos. 1 & 2*, op. 194 (1942/43) •Ssx/Chamber Orch •ME

KOIVISTIONEN, Eero - *Runoelma* (1975) (6') •Ssx/Str Orch •FMIC
KRAUS, Marco - *Suite concertante* •1 Sx: Sno+S+A+T+B/Orch
LATHAM, William - *Concerto Grosso* (1960) (18') •2 Sx: SA/Orch or Band
LATRAILLE, Gregory - *Lyric Concerto* (1972-78) •Ssx/Chamber Ensemble
LAUBA, Christian - *Dies Irae* (1990) (12'30) •Ssx/Org or Orch •B&N
LEMAY, Robert - *Konzertzimmermusic* (1992) (30') •Ssx/3 Perc/Chamber Orch •CMC
LIEB, Dick - *Short Ballet* (1971) (12') •1 Sx: A or S/Band •Ken
LINN, Robert - *Concerto* (1991) •Ssx/Wind Ensemble
LUKAS, Zdenek - *Koncert* (1963) (22') •Ssx/Orch •CHF
MABRY, Drake - *12.15.89* (1989) •Ssx/Chamber Orch
MAIGUASHCA, Mesias - *Vorwort zu solaris* (1989) (19') •1 Sx: S+B/Instrumental ensemble
MARIETAN, Pierre - *Concert IV* (1989) (8') •1 Sx: Sno+S+T+B+Bs+CBs/Instrumental ensemble
MYERS, Robert - *Movements* (1967) (14') •Art
NELHYBEL, Vaclav - *Adagio and Allegro* (1986-88) •1 Sx: S+A •JCCC
NIEHAUS, Manfred - *Concertino* (1981) (18') •2 Sx: SS/Orch •adr
NIKIPROWETZKY, Tolia - *Tetraktys* (1976) •1 Sx: S+A+T+B/Chamber Orch •adr
NILSSON, Bo - *La Bran - Anagramme sur Ilmar Laaban* (1963-76) (16') •Sx Solo: S+A/Chorus/Orch/Tape/Electr. •STIM
OTT, David - *Concerto* (1992) (24') •1 Sx: T or S/Orch
PABLO, Luis de - *Une couleur* (1988) (22') •1 Sx: Sno+S+T+B+CBs •SZ
PASCAL, Michel - *Bubble cooking* (1990-91) (12') •Sx/Instrumental Ensemble
PATACHICH, Ivan - *Jei 1+4* (1989) (12') •1 Sx: S+A+CBs/Instrumental Ensemble
PEIXINHO, Jorge - *Passage intérieur* (1989) (16') •1 Sx: Sno+S+A+T+B/Instrumental Ensemble
PELLMAN, Samuel - *Before the Dawn* (1979) •Ssx/Wind Ensemble
   Concertpiece (1981) •Ssx/Wind Ensemble
   Horizon (1978) •Ssx/Wind Ensemble/Mixed Chorus/Narr
PICHAUREAU, Claude - *Rafflésia* (1970) (6'30) •Ssx/Wind Orch or Pno or 4 Sx: SATB •Bil
POPOVICI, Fred - *Heterosynthesis II* (1986) (18') •1 Sx: S+A+T/Orch
REX, Harley - *Preludio and Movende* (1960) •1 Sx: A or S/Band •adr
   Saxophone Rhapsody (1941) •1 Sx: A or S/Band •adr
RODRIGUEZ, Robert Xavier - *Sinfonia* (1972) •1 Sx: Sno+S/ •adr
ROLIN, Etienne - *Maschera* (1980) (17') •1 Sx: S+A+B/Pno/Chamber Orch •adr
   Rideau de feu (1993) (18') 2 Sx: ST/Orch •adr
Rossini, Giacchino - *Variations* (SCHMIDT) •Ssx/Symphonic Winds •WIM
RUDAJEV, Alexandre - *Concerto* (1990)
SABINA, Leslie - *Concerto* •Ssx/Orch •adr
SCHWARTZ, Elliott - *Chamber Concerto IV* (1981) (12') •1 Sx: A+S/Chamber Ensemble •adr
SKROWACZEWSKI, Stanislas - *Ricercari notturni* (1977) (20') •1 Sx: S+A+B •EAM
STÄBLER, Gerhard - *Traum...* (1992) •Ssx/Vcl/Pno/Ensemble •Ric
STRAESSER, Joep - *Winter Concerto* (1984) (18') •Don
TARANU, Cornel - *Miroirs* (1990) (18') •1 Sx: S+T
TERRY, Peter - *Into Light...* (1986) •Ssx/Chamber Orch/Tape •adr
VALEK, Jiri - *Symphony III* (1963) (28') •2 Sx: ST/Narr/Orch •CHF
VIERU, Anatol - *Narration II* (1985) (17') •1 Sx: S+B •Sal
VILLA-LOBOS, Heitor - *Fantasia*, op. 630 (1948) (10') •SMPC/PIC/Peer

WESTBROOK, Mike - *Bean Rows and Blue Shoots* (1991) (30') •Ssx/
Chamber Orch •Matisse Music
WILSON, Dana - *Calling, Ever Calling* •Ssx/Wind Ensemble
WIRTH, Carl Anton - *Jephta* (1958) (8') •1 Sx: A+S/Orch
YOSHIOKA, Emmett - *Intermezzo* (1966-68) •Ssx/Band •adr

Solo Alto Saxophone

Also see Unspecified Instrumentation (Voir aussi
instruments non déterminés), page 422 and Saxophone
and Tape (Saxophone et Bande magnétique), Page 416.

ABRAHAMSEN, Hans - *Flush* (1974-79) •Gron
ABSIL, Jean - *Etude* (3'30) •Bil
ADAM, Adolphe - *Le Postillon de Longjumeau - Air* •Sx Solo
ADLER, Samuel - *Canto IV* (1970) •DP
ALIS, Romàn - *Ambitos*, op. 135 (1982) (10'30) •EMEC
AMELLER, André - *Capriccio* (1974) (7'30) •Com
   Entrée, Deux petites pièces Estudio (1961)
   Entrée et danse (1977) (4'30) •Com
   Gypsophile •Mar
ANDERSON, Tommy Joe - *24 Preludes*, op. 28
ANDERSSON, Magnus - *Gömma* (1989) •SMIC
ANDREWS - *Threnos* •Sha
ARCHER, Violet - *Three Essays* (1988) •Sx Solo: S+A •CMC
ARMA, Paul - *Comme une improvisation* (1978) (7'30) •DP
   3 Contrastes (1971) (6') •Chou
   6 Mobiles (1975) (12') •1, 2, 3, or 4 Sx
   Soliloque (1968) (10') •Bil
ARSENEAULT, Raynald - *Namo* (1980) (7') •Sx Solo •CMC
ARTIOMOV, Vyatcheslav - *Sonate all pongo* •ECS
AYSCUE, Brian - *Three Pieces* (1969) (5'30) •Art
Bach, Carl Philip Emanuel - *Sonate in A moll* (from Fl) •Ric
Bach, Johann Sebastian - *Suite I, III* (Vcl) (LONDEIX) •Lem
BÄCK, Sven-Erik - *Dithyramb* (1949/89) (4') •SMIC
BALLIF, Claude - *Solfegietto*, op. 36, no. 8 (1982) (12'30) •ET
BANASIK, Christian - *Melodien*
BARBER, Clarence - *Kiribilli* (1988) (5') •TTF
BAUER, Robert - *NB 911 WR* (1971) (2') •CMC
BAUMANN, Herbert - *Monodie* (1987) •B&B
BAUMGARTNER, Jean-Paul - *Séquence* (1983)
BAUZIN, Pierre-Philippe - *Esquisses*, op. 57 (1967-68) •adr
BAYLES, Philip - *Méditation* •Sx/Dancer
BECKER, Holmer - *Pieces*
BERGERON, Thom - *Pieces*
BERIO, Luciano - *Sequenza IXb* (1980) •Uni
BEYTELMAN, Gustavo - *Jardin mélancolique* (1990) (8')
BIANCHINI, Laura - *NO.DI* (1987/88) (10') •1 Sx: S+A+T/Computer
   "Fly" •adr
BLANK, Allan - *Around The Turkish Lady* (1991) •Ron
   Three Novelties (1971) •DP
BLICKHAN, Tim - *State of the Art* (1977) •DP
BLOCH, Augustin - *Notes for Saxophone* (1980) (6')
BOLCOM, William - *A Short Lecture...* (1979) •Asx+Narr
BONNEAU, Paul - *Caprice en forme de valse* (1950) (4') •Led
BOONE, Ben - *Election Year* (1994) •Sx Solo: S or A or T or B •INM
BOROS, Jim - *Shreds* (1986) •Asx Solo
BORSTLAP, Dick - *From here to eternity* (1966) (6') •Don
BORTOLOTTI, Mauro - *Luogo...* (1985/90) •Sx Solo: S+A •adr
BÖRTZ, Daniel - *Monologhi 7* (1979) (8') •SMIC/CG
BOZZA, Eugène - *Improvisation et Caprice* •Led
   Pièce brève (1955) •Led
BRANDOLICA, Ljubomir - *Improvizacija* (1959) •adr
BRENET, Thérèse - *Phoenix* (1984) (3') •Lem
BRINGS, Allen - *Ricercar* •SeMC

BRIXEL, Eugen - *Saxophonissimo* (1983) (6'30)
BRNCIC, Isaza - *Melodies* (1987)
BROSH, Thomas - *3 movements* (1985)
BUDD, Harold - *The Candy Apple Revision* (1970)
BUEL, Charles Samuel - *Reflections on Raga Todi* (1972) (6') •adr
BULOW, Harry T. - *Pieces* •Sil
BURNETTE, Sonny - *Stained Glass Window* •Asx Solo/Optional
Echo Delay •Ron
CAMILLERI, Charles - *Fantasia concertante no.6* (1974) (11') •Ram
CAMPANA, José Luis - *Acting-In* (1983) (16'15) •1 Sx: A+T •Sal
   Pezzo per Claudio (1985) (6') •Lem
CAPDEVIELLE, Pierre - *Exorcisme* (1936) (9'30) •Aug
CAPOËN, Denis - *Euphonie* (1987) (8-10') •1 Sx: T+B or A+T
CARAMAZZA, Filippo Maria - *Saxenty 115* (1992)
CARAVAN, Ronald - *Pieces* •DP/Eth/adr
CARRE-CHESNEAU, Thierry - *2 Etudes en ¼ de ton* (1975)
CASTELLANO, Mauro - *Vento di mare* (1992)
CHAILLY, Luciano - *Improvisation n° 10* (1978)
CHIHARA, Hideki - *Lied*
CHILDS, Barney - *Sonatina* (1958) (6'30) •TP
CHOPARD, Patrice - *3 Stücke* (1980) (7') •VDMK
CHOQUET, Patrick - *Aires* (1992) (4') •Sx Solo •Lem
CLELLAND, Kenneth P. - *Dream So Real* (1991) •Sx Solo •adr
CLEMENT, Nicole - *Sonata* (1983)
COCCO, Enrico - *Actings* (1990) (10') •1 Sx: A+B/Electronics •adr
CONDÉ, Gérard - *Monarch...* (1983) (22') •1 Sx: Sno+S+A+T+B+Bs
COPE, David - *Probe No. 3* •Asx/Actress+Dancer •DP
CORDERO, Roque - *Soliloquios No. 2* (1976) •Peer/SMPC
COREY, Kirk - *Three Vignettes* (1993) •Sx Solo
CORTES, Ramiro - *5 Studies* (1968) •USC
COUF, Herbert - *Introduction, Dance et Furioso* (1959) •Band
CROLEY, Randall - *Gli Occhi* (1984) (8'30)
CUNNINGHAM, Michael G. - *Rara Avis*, op. 19b (1966) (4') •Eto
DAM, Hermann van - *Rituals...* (1988) (8') •Sx Solo: A or T •Don
DAMAIS, Emile - *5 Divertissements* (1946) (17') •Bil
DAMASE, Jean-Michel - *Vacances* (1990) (2'30) •Bil
DANEELS, François - *4 Miniatures* •Sch
   Suite (1973) (7') •Sch
DARBELLAY, Jean-Luc - *Plages* (5')
DEASON, David - *Jazz Partita* (1983)
Debussy, Claude - *Syrinx* (LONDEIX) (2'45) •Sx Solo: A or S •JJ
DELAGE, Jean-Louis - *Climat* (1989) •Sx Solo: A or T
DEL BORGO, Elliott - *Canto* (1973) •DP
DELIO, Thomas - *Partial Coordinates* •DP
DELLI PIZZI, Fulvio - *Quinta bagatella* (1985)
DHAINE, Jean-Louis - *Sonate* (1983)
DIAZ, Rafael - *Perfil reflejado* (1986)
   3 Preludios del CEI (1984)
DIEDERICHS, Yann - *Pieces*
DIEMENTE, Edward - *Mirrors IV* (1974) •DP
DININNY, John Ernest - *Crab* (1972) (12'30) •Asx/Dancer •DP
DOBBINS, Bill - *Echoes Distant Land* •WWS
DOMAGALA, Jacek - *Impression* (5'30) •Asto
DOUGHERTY, William - *Seven Bagatelles* (1990) (12'-14') •Heil
DUBOIS, Pierre-Max - *Conclusions* (1978) (12') •Led
   Le Récit du chamelier (1964) (5') •Bil
   Sonate d'étude (1970) •Led
   Suite française (1962) (16') •Led
EGGLESTON, Anne - *6 Pieces in Popular Style* (1972) •CMC
EICHMANN, Dietrich - *Situations...* (1985) (30-40') •adr
EISMA, Will - *Non-lecture II* (1971) (7'15) •Don
ELLIS, Norman - *Before a D'BL Scherzo* (1971-72) •DP
ELOY, Christian - *Saxotaure* (1985) (8') •Com
ERDMANN, Dietrich - *Saxophonata* •Sx Solo: S+A+T •R&E
ESCOT, Pozzi - *Pluies* •WWS

EVERTT, Steven - *Interactive Electronics* •Asx+MIDI Wind Controller+Narr/Computer

EYSER, Eberhard - *Ghiribizzi* (1980) (12') •Sx Solo •EMa
Por los senderos del aire (1980) (13') •STIM

FEDIE, Jessie - *Room 120* (1975)

FEILER, Dror - *Antafada* (1988) •Asx/Electronics •Tons

FENNELLY, Brian - *Tesserae VIII* (1980) (6') •PRO/PNS

FERRANTE, Mauro - *Do-Mi-Si* (1985)

FLOTHUIS, Marius - *Impromptu, op. 76, no. 3* (1976) •Don

FONGAARD, Bjorn - *Solosonata, op. 117, no. 2* (1973) (9') •NMI
Sonata, op.125, no. 13 (1973) (7') •NMI

FOURCHOTTE, Alain - *Disgressions III* (1982) (5') •Sal

FOURNIER, Marie-Hèléne - *Horoscope* (1986) (3'30) •Com
Sétiocétine (1987) (3'30) •Com

FRACKENPOHL, Arthur - *Expressive Excursion...* •Ken
Rhapsody (1984) (3'30) •Ken
Waltz Ballad (1979)

FRANCO, Johan - *Sonata* (1964) •CFE

FRANK, Andrew - *Alto Rhapsody* (1973) •SMT

FROIO, Giovanni - *Vita* (1988)

GABUS, Monique - *Etude*

GAGNEUX, Renaud - *Babel* (1978) (7') •1 Sx: A+S/Dispositif électro-acoustique simple

GALAY, Daniel - *Exotique à l'envers* (1984) (5')

GASTINEL, Gérard - *Suite en 4 mouvements* (1982) (10')

GATES, Everett - *Incantation and Ritual* (1963) (4') •EG

GAY, Harry - *Soliloquy* (1968) (3'30) •Eri

GEDDES, Murray - *Inner time/in her time* (1980) (10') •Sx/Reverberant room •CMC

GELALIAN, Boghos - *2 Monodies orientales* (1990) (8'30)

GENEST, Pierre - *Saxolo* (1972) (4'30-5') •adr

GENTILUCCI, Armando - *La trame di un labirinto* (1986) (8') •Ric

GINGRAS, Guy - *Equistares...* (1989) (17') •Med

GLASER, Werner - *Solosonat* (1936) (10') •STIM
3 Sonaten im alten Stil (1934) (12') •STIM

GOODWIN, Gordon - *Anonymous V* (1971) (6') •SeMC

GOUGEON, Denis - *Mercure* (1992)
6 thèmes solaires •CMC

GRAEF, Friedemann - *Werke* •adr

GRAHN, Ulf - *Ballad* (1985) (8') •NGlani

GRIGORIOU, Lefteris - *Musique "Tu, toi, moi"* (1991)

GRIMS-LAND, Ebbe - *Thema des Tages II* (1977) (6-7') •STIM

GROOT, Rokus de - *Kontur* (1982) (25') •Sx Solo: S or A •Don

GROSS, Eric - *Three Bagatelles, op. 96* •Lee

GUAGNIDZÉ - *Solo* •ECS

GUIOT, Raymond - *Opium* (1976) (6'30) •Bil

HÂBA, Alois - *Partita, op. 99* (1968) (9') •FM/CMIC

HADER, Widmar - *Antizipation* (6') •Asto

HAIDMAYER, Karl - *Impromptu n° 1* (1980)

HALL LEWIS, Robert - *Monophony V* •Dob

HARREX, Patrick - *Passages III* (1972) (9-12') •DP

HARTLEY, Walter - *Petite Suite* (1961) (5'30) •Wi&Jo

HARVEY, Paul - *Damenesque* (1973) •Mau

HEESBEKE, G. van - *Suite*

HEIDER, Werner - *Verheissung* (1988); *Sax* (1983-87) (10') •Pet

HEININEN, Paavo - *Discantus III, op. 33* (1976) (13') •FMIC

HEKSTER, Walter - *Setting II* (1982) (7') •Don

HENNINGER, Richard - *Evolutions: Music* (1971) •CMC

Herman, N. - *Wedgewood* •WWS

HESPOS, Hans-Joachim - *Ika* (1984) (5')

HILDEMANN, Wolfgang - *Pier fiali VII - Glimpser* (1989) (6') •adr

HISCOTT, James - *Midnight Strut* (1978) (13') •CMC

HODKINSON, Sidney - *Trinity* (1971) •Sx Solo: A or T or B •adr

HOLLAND, Dulcie - *Pieces* •adr

HÖLSKY, Adriana - *Flux-Reflux* (1981) (10'30) •adr

HOWARD, Robert - *Soliloquy* •Ken

HUBERT, Nikolaus - *"Aus Schwerz und..."* (1982) (15') •Br&Ha

HUMMEL, Bertold - *Drei Stücke* (1979) (10') •adr

HYLA, Lee - *Pre-Amnesia* (1'45) •adr

ISHII, Maki - *Black intention* (1978) (8')

ITURRALDE, Pedro - *Like Coltrane* (1972) •Mun

JEANNEAU, François - *8 thèmes et improvisation* •Sal

JENTZSCH, Wilfried - *Sonate* (1978) •adr
Maquam (1983-92) (12') •adr

JOHNSON, Barry - *Slyndian*

JOHNSON, Tom - *Rational Melodies* (1982) (2' to 25')

JONG, Hans de - *Le rêve et la folie* (5')

JONGEN, Léon - *Concours de lecture* (1944)

JUELICH, Raimund - *Werkstück IV* (1988) (11') •Peer

KAIPAINEN, Jouni - *"...la chimère de l'humidité de la nuit ?,"* op. 12b (1978) (8') •WH

KANITZ, Ernest - *Pieces; Little Concerto* (1970) •Art

KARG-ELERT, Sigfrid - *Atonal Sonata, op. 153b* (1929) •Zim
25 Capricen, op. 153a (1929) •Zim/South

KARLINS, M. William - *Seasons* (1987) (13') •Sx Solo: S+A+T •TP

KARKOFF, Ingvar - *Suite* (1989/93) •Asx Solo •SvM

KARKOFF, Maurice - *8 Solominiatyrer, op. 8b* (1953) (6'30) •Ehr/STIM

KARPMAN, Laura - *Saxmaniac* (1988) •MMB

KASEMETS, Udo - *Calcolaria; Contactics* (1966) •Sx/Actress •BMI
Cascando-Solo (1965)

KASSAP, Sylvain - *Balkanique* (1993) (3'15) •Mis

KAVANAUGH, Patrick - *Debussy-variations No. 5* (1977) •CF

KINNINGTON, Alan - *Sonare No. 1* •Sx Solo

KLEIN, Lothar - *6 Exchanges* (1972) (6') •Pres/CMC/Ten

KOBAYASHI, Hidéo - *3 Pièces brèves* (1970) •adr

KOCH, Erland von - *Monolog n°4* (1975) (5'30) •CG

KOPPEL, Hermann David - *Ternio n°2, op. 92* (1973)

KOSTECK, Gregory - *Chromatic Fantasy* (1979) (7') •DP

KRAFT, Leo - *Five For One* (1971) (6') •GMP
Pentagram (1971)

KUHNERT, Rolf - *Drei Temperamente* (1985) (7'30) •KuD

KULESHA, Gary - *Invocation and Ceremony* (5') •Sx Solo •CMC

KUNDRATS, Vilnis - *Emotions...* (1993) •Sx/Electronics •INM

KYNASTON, Trent - *Dance Suite, op. 15* •WIM
Espejos (1975)

LACOUR, Guy - *Etude de concert* (1964) (2'35) •Bil

LAMB, John David - *Night Music* (1956)

LAMB, Marvin L. - *A Ballad of Roland* (1979) •DP

LAMBERTO, Lugli - *Stefy* (1993) Stefy

LANDINI, Carlo Alessandro - *Incantation...* (1984) (10') •Led

LANSIÖ, Tapani - *Una lettra al amico...* (1984) •FMIC

LARSEN, Libby - *Aubade* (1991)

LATHAM, William Peters - *Ex tempore* (1978) •DP

LAUBA, Christian - *Etudes* (1992-1994) •adr
Steady study on the boogie (1993) •Bil

LAUREAU, Jean-Marc - *Connexions I* (1985) (3-6') (LAUREAU-LEJET-ROLIN-ROSSÉ) •Sal

LAZARIN, Branko - *3 movements* (1982) •DSH

LAZARUS, Daniel - *Sonate* (1949) (8') •Dur

LEAHY, Georges - *Diderot-Québec* (1988)

LEFKOFF, Gerald - *A Troubador's Rhapsody* (1991) •Gly

LEGUAY, Jean-Pierre - *Flamme* (1972-76) (6'30) •Uni

LEHMANN, Hans Ulrich - *Monodie* (1970) (10') •Sx Solo: A or T •AVV

LEJET, Edith - *Connexions I* (1985) (3-6') (LAUREAU-LEJET-ROLIN-ROSSÉ) •Sal

LEMELAND, Aubert - *Capriccio, op. 68* (1979) (6') •Bil

LENNERS, Claude - *Monotaurus* (1988) •Lem

LENTZ, Daniel - *Pound for Pound* (1971) (10-30') •Asx/Actress/50-100 dogs •DP

LERSTAD, Terje Bjorn - *Fantasy*, op. 39 (7') •NMI

LEWIS, Arthur - *Sonata* (1982) •CMC

LEWIS, Robert Hall - *Monophony V* (1982) •Pet

LIANG, Lei - *Peking Opera Soliloquy* (1993)

LIC, Leslaw - *Quasi improvisando* •adr

LILJEHOLM, Thomas - *Strata* (1989) •SMIC

LOGRANDE, L. A. - *Apparitions From Experience* (1990) (5') •CI

LOLINI, Ruggero - *Nel cantore del vento* (1985)

LOMBARDO, Robert - *Fantasy Variations No. 4*

LOPEZ MA, Jorge - *La palabra* (1983)

LORDERO, Rogue - *Soliloques N° 2* •Meri

LORENTZEN, Bent - *Round* (1981) (6') •WH

LUNDE, Lawson -*Music*, op. 21a (1964) (10') •NSM
    Sonata, op. 21 (1964) (16') •NSM/South

MABRY, Drake - *Ceremony I* (1993) (11'45) •Lem

MAEDA, Satoko - *Anapana* (10')

MALECKI, Maciej - *Elegia* (1988) (5') •AAR

MARCHAL, Dominique - *Sonatine* (1981) (8'40) •adr

MAREZ OYENS-WANSINK, Tera de - *Sound...* •Sx/Actress •Don

MARIN, Jorge Lopoz - *La Palabru*

MASON, Lucas - *Song and Dance* (1982)

MASSIAS, Gérard - *Suite monodique* (1954) (11') •Bil

MASUDA, Kozo - *Pièce brève* (1977) (5')

MATSUDAIRA, Yori-Aki - *Gestaphony* (1979)

MATSUMOTO, Hinoharu - *Archipose IV* (1979)

MAURICE, Paule - *Volio* (1967) (3') •Bil

McKAY, George Frederick - *Concert Solo Sonatine* •NA

MEFANO, Paul - *Tige* (1986) (1'40) •Sal

MENCHERINI, Fernando - *Ambra e Spunk* (1985)

MERANGER, Paul - *Solo 24* (1981) •Bil

MERIOT, Michel - *12 Monodies atonales* •Com
    32 pièces variées... •Com

MIEREANU, Costin - *Ondes* (1986) (6') •Sal
    Variants - Invariants (1982) (14') •Asx or Ssx/Echo Chamber •Sal

MILIVOJ, Koerbler - *Varijacije* (1956) •YUC

MILLER, Dennis - *Three Recitativi amorosi* (1976) (4') •adr

MOEVS, Robert - *Paths and Ways* (1970) (4') •Sx/Dancer •DP

MOHR, Ralph - *3 Pieces*

MOORE, Keith - *Hiatus Pitch* •Sx Solo

MORRIS, Jonathan - *Rumination* (1983)

MOYLAN, William - *Solo Sonata* (1978) (16-18') •1 Sx: S+A+T •SeMC/DP

MUELLER, Frederick - *25 Caprices und Sonate* •adr

MÜLLER, Gottfried - *Agnus dei* (1948) (5'30) •KuD
    Sonate (1948) •Sik

MULS, André Jean - *Sax battle* (1980)

NAGATA, Takanobu - *Achse*

NAVARRE, Randy - *Concertmusic* (1980) (8') •Ron

NEUWIRTH, Gösta - *Gestern und Hente* (1988)

NICOLAU, Dimitri - *Mondelci's songs*, op. 75 •EDP

NICULESCU, Stefan - *Chant-son* (1989) (6') •1 Sx: S+A

NODA, Ryo - *Don Quichotte*, op. 2 (1972)
    Improvisations I, II, III (1972-74) •Led
    Maï (1975) (7') •Led
    Phoenix - Fushicho (1983) •Led
    Requiem - Shin-en (1979) (10') •Sx Solo: T or A •Led
    Symphonie rhapsody Maï II (1980) •adr

NODAÏRA, Ichiro - *Arabesque II* (10') •Lem

OGATA, Toshiyuki - *Bleu* (1984)

OLAH, Tiberiu - *Rimes* (1985) (8') •1 Sx: Sno+A/Matériel électr.

OLBRISCH, Franz-Martin - *Cadenza* (1988) (11'30) •adr

ONGARO, Michele dall' - *Darstellüng* (1987) (8') •EDP

OOSTERVELD, Ernst - *Graphic music loops* (1983) (9') •Don

Music loops II (1982) (5') •Sx Solo: A or T •Don

ORTON, Richard - *Mythos* (1980-81)

OSAWA, Kazuto - *Sen* (1973)

Paganini, Nicolo - *Caprice*, Op. 1, No. 24 (Rossi) •Sx Solo •DP

PANELLA, Henri-François - *Fantaisie sur "La Traviata"* •Sal
    Fantaisie sur "Le Trouvere" •Sal

PARWEZ, Akmal - *Chetna* (1993)

PEIXINHO, Jorge - *Sax-Bleu* (1982) (18') •1 Sx: Sno+A/Echo Chamber •Sal

PERRIN, Marcel - *Evocations* (1958) •DP

PERSICHETTI, Vincent - *Parable XIII*, op. 123 (7') •EV

PETIT, Jean-Louis - *Trait multiple* (1986) (4'15) •Bil

PHILIBA, Nicole - *Trois Etudes* (1966) (5'30)

PHILIPPI, Ronald - *Trillingen* (1987) (6')

PICHAUREAU, Claude - *Prélude à Rafflésia* (1990) (5') •Bil

PIECHOWSKA, Alina - *Invitation à la méditation*

PILON, Daniel - *3 Méditations* (1982-83) (12') •adr

POLACCHI, Barbara - *Ricerca* (1992)

POLANSKY, David - *Madness in 3 Episodes* (8') •Sx Solo •Ken

PORRET, Julien - *Toccata* (6')

PRÄSENT, Gerhard - *Solo* (1978) (4')

PRESSER, William - *Partita* (5'30) •adr

PRIBADI, Sinar - *Djiwa*

PRIETO, Claudio - *Divertimento* •Ara

PROCOPIO, Joseph - *Three Variations*

QUEYROUX, Yves - *Ellipse* (1994) •Sx Solo •Mis
    7 Jeux musicaux et 3 Promenades (1989) •Sx Solo: S or T or A •Lem

RADULESCU, Horatiu - *Astray* (1984-85) (23') •1 Sx: Sno+S+A+T+B+Bs/matériel électron. (or Prepared Pno)

RAE, James - *Easy Studies in Jazz and Rock* •Uni

REIBEL, Guy - *Apogée* (8')

REILLY, Allyn - *Spiral* (1985) (7')

RIEHM, Rolf - *Wie sind deine Schritte...* •Sx/Actress

RIEU, Yannick - *Improvisation*

ROBERT, Lucie - *Perpetuum mobile* (1985) (14') •adr
    Rhapsodie (1977) (8'20) •DP

ROLIN, Etienne - *Aphorismes VII* (1982-83) (12') •Lem
    Aphorismes - Volume II (1988) •Lem
    Connexions I (1985) (3-6') (LAUREAU-LEJET-ROLIN-ROSSÉ) •Sal
    Pulse - Puzzle (1989) (5'30) •adr
    Puzzle - Pulse (1994) (5'30) •SCo

RORIVE, Jean-Pierre - *Diderius aurifaber*

ROSARIO, Conrado del - *Ringkaran* (1990)

ROSSÉ, François - *Connexions I* (1985) (3-6') (LAUREAU-LEJET-ROLIN-ROSSÉ) •Sal
    Le frêne égaré (1978-79) (10') •Bil
    Lobuk constrictor (1982) (4') •Bil
    Séaodie II (1985) (3') •Sx Solo: A or S •Bil

RÜDENAUER, Meinhard - *The Noble Sport* (1973)

RUEFF, Jeanine - *Sonate* (1967) (12'30) •Led

SALLUSTIO, Eraclio - *Gis N. 3* (1992)

SAMAMA, Leo - *Mémoires fanées* (1992) •Don

SAMBIN, Victor - *30 Récréations musicales* (1894) •Sal

SAMORI, Aurelio - *Solo* (1985) (6'30) •adr

SANCO, Mario - *Proposta* (1978) •MS

SCHAEFFER, Don - *The Good Sound of Folk Song*

SCHAFFER, Boguslaw - *Sonatina n° 3* (1946) •adr
    Sound forms n° 58 (1961) (6') •adr

SCHIAFFINI, Giancarlo - *Pieces d'April* (1989)

SCHILLING, Hans Ludwig - *Sonatine* (1978) (13'30) •Bil

SCHILLINGER, Franz - *Farbmodelle* (10')

SCHMIDT, William - *Music for Unaccompanied Saxophone* •WIM
    Suite (1978)

SCHWARTZ, Elliott - *Music for Soloist and Audience* •DP
SCLATER, James - *Suite* (6'30) •TP/Elk
SCOGNA, Flavio Emilio - *Duplum* •BMG
SENERCHIA, R. - *Street Music*
SEVRETTE, Danielle - *In diesem Brauss* (1975) •adr
SIVILOTTI, Valter - *Improvisazione interrotta* •1 Sx: A or B •Piz
SIMEONOV, Blago - *Sax-audience suite* (1987) (7'30) •Asx Solo
       with audience participation •CMC
SIMMERUD, Patric - *Lamento* (1989) (3'30)
SIMS, Ezra - *Solo* (1982) •ACA
SIPUS, Perislav - *Sens* (1976)
SITSKY, Larry - *Armenia a suite* (1985) •SeMC
SLEICHIM, Eric - *Visiting the sound* (1985) •adr
SLETTHOLM, Yngve - *4 Profiles*, op. 3 (1978) (14') •Ly
SMEDEBY, Sune - *Miniature* (1988) (2') •STIM
SMITH, Gregg - *Fugatto* (1969)
SMITH, Stuart - *Mute* (5') •SeMC
SMOLANOFF, Michael - *Parables* (1972) (5') •SeMC
SNYDER, Randall - *Variations* (1972) (5') •Art
SOMMERFELD, Willy - *Suite*
SOTELO, Mauricio - *Sax Solo* (1988) (14'15) •ECA
STAUDE, Christoph - *Obduktion* (1988)
STEIN, Leon - *Phantasy* (1971) (12') •DP
STOCKHAUSEN, Karleinz - *In Freundschaft* (1982) (10') •Stv
STRADOMSKI, Rafal - *MC XIII* (1984)
STRATTON, Donald - *State Street Boogie Woogie* •WS
SUENAGA, Ryuichi - *Romance* (1981)
SWAIN, Freda - *Naturo Suite* (1931) (6') •Any Sx Solo •BMIC
   The Tease (1965) (1'30) •Any Sx Solo •BMIC
SZALONEK, Witold - *D. P.'s Ghoulish Dreams* (1985-86) (7') •DP
TANAHASHI, Minako - *Nocturne* (1987) •R&E
TANNER, David - *Improvisation* (1972) (4') •adr
TAUTENHAHN, Günter - *Dorn Dance* •Sx/Dancer •WIM
TOENSING, Richard - *For Saxophone Alone* (1985) (4') •PNS
TOKUNAGA, Hidenori - *Columnation* (1972-73) •Sx Solo: A or T
       •adr
TOMASI, Henri - *Evocations* (1968) (4') •Led
TONT, Patrice - *Aride sax* (1988) (5')
TORBJÖRN, Iwan - *Concitato* (1980)
TOULON, Jacques - *3 Opuscules* (1990) (2'30) •Mar
TRAN, Fanny - *Warszawian Echoes* (1981) (11') •DP
TULL, Fisher - *Threnody* (1984)
TYSSENS, Albert - *Singeries* (1982) •adr
   Toccata (1980) •adr
UEDA, Keiji - *Ohanashi* (1990)
UNEN, Kees van - *...and the world doesn't own me...* (12'20)
VALK, Adriaan - *7 Pieces for sax n° 635* (1976) •HZ/WWS
VALKARE, Gunnar - *Passage 3, 5* (1993) •SMIC
VALLIER, Jacques - *Improvisation* •CANF
VAN BELLE, A. - *Koan V*
VAZZANNA, Anthony - *8 Studi* (1978)
VEHAR, Persis - *Sounds of the Outdoors* (1984) (7'40) •Ken
VERHIEL, Ton - *Experiment 1, 2, 3* (1992)
   14 Studies in various styles (1992) •Run
VESCOVO, Italo - *Cadenza* (1988)
VIERU, Anatol - *Doux polyson* (1984) (7') •Sal
VOGEL, Roger - *Partita* (1977) •TP
VOIRPY, Alain - *Motum V* (1981) (9') •Lem
VOSK, Jay - *Whirling Dervishes* (1988) •DP
VOXMAN, Hymie - *Contemporary Recital Pieces* •Rub
WAGNER, Franz - *Solo - waltzer*
WAGNER, Joseph - *Monologue* (1971) (6') •DP
WALKER, Gregory - *Four Sketches* (1982)
WALLACE, William - *Free Soliloquy* (1975) (7'10) •CMC
WALLIN, Peter - *Harmony family* (1987) (7'30) •SMIC

WARE, Peter - *4 Miniatures* (1989) (6') •CMC
WASHBURN, Gary - *A Ride; A Moonbeam; Polka Dot* (1974) (20')
       •Sx Solo: A+S+B •SeMC
WERTS, Daniel - *Sigmonody* (1972) (7') •DP
WILDBERGER, Jacques - *Portrait* (1982) (7-8') •Uni
   Prismes (1975) (9') •Br&Ha/HG
WOLF, Jaroslav - *Virgilia*
WOODWARD, Gregory - *Parapter* (1976)
WYMAN, Laurence - *Gjiwa* (1971) •adr
   Saxophone Abstractions •Sx/Laser beam/Prepared audience
YUASA, Joji - *Not I, but the wind* (1976) (11')

Alto Saxophone and Piano

Selected repertoire (Choix sélectif).

Also see Alto Saxophone and Orchestra or Band
(Voir aussi saxophone alto et orchestre ou band), Pages
305 and 310.

AARON, Yvonne - *Fantaisie...* (1972) (13') •adr
ABSIL, Jean - *5 Pièces faciles*, op. 138 (1968) •Lem
   Sonate, op. 115 (1963) (8'30) •Lem
Achron, Joseph - *Impressions*, op. 32, no. 1 (GUREWICH) •Uni
Ackermans, Johann - *Pieces* •B&H/Led
Ackermans, H. - *Pieces* •Kr/Cra
Adams, Stephen - *The Holy City* (GLENN) •B&H
Adamski - *Feelin fine* •Sha
ADASKIN, Murray - *Daydreams* (1968-71) (2'40) •CMC
Akimenko, Fyodor Stefanovich - *Eglogue* (EPHROSS) •South
AKSES, Necil - *Allegro feroce* (1931) •Uni
Albeniz, Isaac - *Pieces*
ALBRIGHT, William - *Sonata* (1984) (20') •Pet
ALESSANDINI, Raymond - *Piazzolino* •Bil
ALESSANDRINI, Pierluigi - *Pieces* •Bil
ALIX, René - *Prélude fantasque et Impromptu* •Led
ALKEMA, Henk - *Sonatine* (1980) (8') •Don
Alter, Louis - *Manhattan Serenade* (WIEDOEFT) •Rob
ALTISENT, J. - *Soliloquio* •Boi
AMATO, Bruno - *Sonatella* (1977) •Rub
Ambrioso, Alfred d' - *Pieces* •GSch/Rub
AMDAHL, Magne - *Pieces* •NMI
AMELLER, André - *Pieces*
AMIOT, Jean-Claude - *Sérénade* (1969) •Mar
AMOS - *Compositae no. 11*
ANDERSON, Garland - *Sonata* (1966) •South
ANDERSON, Jean - *Pieces* •CMC
ANDERSON, Michael - *Sonata*
ANDERSON, Tommy Joe - *Sonata*, op. 10, no. 1 (1970) (4'30) •SMC
   Sonata no. 2, op. 17 (1973) •DP
   Sonate No. 3, op. 30 (1988) (14'15) •1 Sx: S+A/Pno •Ron
ANDRIEU, Fernand - *Pieces*
ANGULO, Manuel - *Bisonante* (1983) (8'30) •Mun
ANTONINI, Félix - *Pieces* •adr/Bil
APPLEDORN, Mary Jeanne van - *Liquid Gold* (1981) •DP
ARBAN, Joseph - *Caprice et Variations* (1861) •Ron/Sax
   Oberto, Air varié •1 Sx: A or T/Pno •Mol
ARCHER, Violet - *Sonata* (1972) (15'30) •BML
Ariosto, Attilio - *Gigue* (MULE) •Led
Arlt, Kurt - *Liebeswalzer* (H. KIRCHSTEIN) •Fro
Arnaud-Marwys & ADAM - *Saxolo* •ME
Arne, Thomas Auguste - *Finale* (MERIOT) •Phi
ARNOLD, André - *Védéa* (1971) (10') •Arp
ARNOLD, Jay - *Homeless - Romance* •CF
ARTIOMOV, Vyatcheslav - *Automne Sonata* (1977)

ARZOUMANOV, Valery - *7 Chansons russes* (1993) •INM
Ascher, Joseph - *Pieces* (MOLLOY) •CF
ATOR, James - *Three Pieces* (1970) •SeMC
Aubert, Esprit - *Angela Aria* (W. HEKKER) •1 Sx: S or A/Pno •TM
Aubert, Jacques - *Gigue* (MAGANINI) •1 Sx: A or T/Pno •Mus
AUBIN, Francine - *Pieces* •Mar
AUBIN, Tony - *Petite rêverie* (1980) •Mar
AUCLERT, Pierre - *Comme un vieux Noël* (1941/69) (1'30) •Bil
Audran, Edmond - *Fantaisie sur "La Mascotte"* (SOHIER) •Marg
AUSEJO, Cesar - *Sax-Fantasy* (1991) •Mun
AVIGNON, Jean - *Spiritual et Danse exotique* (1967) (4') •Bil
BABBITT, Milton - *Whirled Series* (1987) (13') •Pet
Bach, Carl Philip Emanuel - *Spring's Awakening* (GALLO) •1 Sx: A or T/Pno •CBet
Bach, Johann Christian - *Allegro Siciliana* (TRILLAT) •GD
Bach, Johann Sebastian - *Pieces*
Bachmann, Gottob - *Dance bretonne* (LEFEVRE) •CF
BÄCK, Sven-Erik - *Bagateller* (1961) •SMIC
  Elegie (1952) •SMIC/WH
BADINGS, Henk - *Cavatina* (1952) (5') •Don
  Largo cantabile (1983) (6') •Don
  La Malinconia (1949) (8') •Don
BAER, Walter - *Fragments of a Dream* (1991)
BAEYENS, Henri - *Pieces* •EMB/Ver
BAILLY, Jean-Guy - *Capriccio* •Sch
BAKER, Ernest - *Night Theme* (1980) (4'45) •BMIC
Balay, Guillaume - *Piece de Concours* (MEYER) •Led
BALBOA, Manuel - *Sombra Interrumpida* (1980) •EMEC
Balfe, Michael - *Pieces* •CF
BARAT, Joseph-Edouard - *Pieces* •HS/Led/Rub
BARCE, Ramon - *Largo viaje* (1988) (11')
BAREIS, Hermann - *When the Cock Crows* (1993) •INM
BARILLER, Robert - *Fan'Jazz* (3') •1 Sx: A or S/Pno •Led
BARLETT, J. C. - *A Dream* (HUMMEL) •Rub
BARNES, Clifford P. - *Saxophone Album* (1956) •B&H
BARON, Maurice - *Pieces* •GSch/MBCo
BARRAINE, Elsa - *Andante et Allegro* •Sal
  Improvisation (1947) •Bil
Barratt & Jenkins - *Sounds for Sax 1* •1 Sx: T or A/Pno •Che
BASSET, Leslie - *Duo Concertante* (1984) (17') •Pet
  Music (1967/69) (10') •Pet
BASTEAU, Jean-François - *Blue-Jean* (1993) (1'30) •1 Sx: A or T/Pno •Mar
BATAILLE, Prudent - *Badine badine* (1968) (2'30) •Bil
BAUMANN - *2° Solo; Fantaisie* •Sax
BAUMANN, Eric - *Sonate* •NoE
Baumann, P. - *Concert in the Forest* (RASCHER) •Bel
BAUR, Jürg - *Ballata romana* (1960-87) (11') •Br&Ha
BAUZIN, Pierre-Philippe - *Sonate*, op. 15 (1959) (15') •adr
Bazzini, Antonio - *Ronde des lutins*, op. 25 (MUTO) •Lem
BEALL, John - *Sonata* (1976) •South
BEAUCAMP, Albert - *Chant élégiaque* •Led
  Menuet d'Orphée •Led
  Tarentelle (1946) •Led
BECK, Conrad - *Nocturne* (1959) (3'30) •Lem
BEDARD, Denis - *Sonate* (1981) (11'30) •SEDIM/Do
BEDFORD, David - *Five Easy Pieces* (1987) •Uni
BEECKMANN, Nazaire - *Pieces*
BEERMAN, Burton - *Moment* (1978) •ACA
Beethoven, Ludwig van - *Pieces*
Beldon - *Feather River* •Bel
Bellini, Vincenzo - *Les Puritains* (MAYEUR) •Cos
BELLISARIO, Angelo - *Improviso* (1973) •Ber
Belon - *Fantaisie Hongroise* •Pre

BEN-HAIM, Paul - *3 Songs Without Words* (1952) (10') •1 Sx: A or T/Pno •MCA
BENNETT, David - *Modern* •CF
BENSON, Warren - *Cantelina* (1964) (2'30) •B&H
  Farewell (1964) (2') •MCA
BENTZON , Niels Viggo - *Emancipatio*, op. 471 (1985) (9'30) •WH
  Sonate, op. 320 (1973) (9')
  Sonatina, op. 498 (1986) (6'30) •WH
BENZIN, A. - *Caprice russe* •1 Sx: A or T/Pno •An
BERG, Gunnar - *Prosthesis* (1952) •adr
BERGH, Alja - *Motivationen* (1993) •INM
BERKELEY, Michael - *Keening* (1987) (10'30)
BERLIOZ, Gabriel-Pierre - *Air à danser* •Braun
Berlioz, Hector - *Pieces* •Cos/VAB
BERNAUD, Alain - *Final* •Chou
  Rhapsodie (1984) •Chou
BERNIER, René - *Capriccio* (1957) (2'30) •Led
BERTHELOT, René - *Pieces* •Led/Lem
BERTHOMIEU, Marc - *Pieces* •Com/Lem
BESWICK, Aubrey - *Six for Sax* (1986) •Uni
BEUGNIOT, Jean-Pierre - *Sonate* (1975) (14') •Bil
BEVELANDER, Brian - *Sonata* •WWS
BEVERIDGE, Thomas - *Alborada* (1980)
BEYDTS, Louis - *Romanesque* (1935) (3') •Led
BIALOVSKY, Marshall - *Fantasy Scherzo* •WIM
Bigot, Pierre - *Sicilienne* •Eb Sx or Bb Sx/Pno •Mar
Billault - *Grand solo de concert* •Mar
BILOTTI, Anton - *Sonata* (1939) •Pres
BIRD, Hubert - *Sonata* (1987) •HB
BISSELL, Keith - *3 Etudes* (1972) •CMC
BITSCH, Marcel - *Pieces* •Led
Bizet, Georges - *Pieces*
Blaauw, L. - *Pieces* •Lis/Mol/TM
BLANC, Jean-Robert - *Aubade et Impromptu*, op. 29 (1956) (4') •Bil
Blanchard, Harold - *Pieces* (LINDEMANN) •1 Sx: A or T/Pno •Sal
BLANK, Allan - *Concert Duo* •DP
BLANQUER, Amando - *Sonatina Jovenivola* (1986) •Piles/AE
Blavet, Michel - *Pieces*
Bleger, Adolphe - *Les Echos de Barcelone* •Mar
BLIN, Lucien - *Gentiment* •Phi
BLOCH, André - *Pieces* •Gras/PN
BLUMER, Theodor - *Zwei Lieder ohne Worte*, op. 67 •Zim
BOERLIN, Richard - *Elegy* •Sha
Bohm, Charles - *Laender* •Eb Sx/Pno •CF
Boïeldieu, François Adrien - *Le Calife de Bagdad* (ROMBY) •PB
BOLCOLM, William - *Lilith* (1984) (14'15) •EBMM
Boni, Pietro - *Largo and Allegro* (VOXMAN) •Rub
BORBOUSSE, P. - *Simple mélodie* •1 Sx: A or T/Pno •An
BORGHINI, Louis - *Romance* •ES
BORMANN, Emile von - *Valse Impromptu* •Fro
Borodin, Alexandre - *Intermezzo* (LONDEIX) •Lem
BORSARI, Amédée - *Blues* (1941) (4') •Bil
BORSCHEL, E. - *Pastell* •Fro
BOUCHARD, Marcel - *Pieces*
BOUDREAU, Walter - *Cocktail music* (1984) •CMC
BOUILLON, Pierre - *Pieces*
BOURGEOIS, César - *Rêverie, Introduction, et Andante* •Bes
BOURGUIGNON, Francis de - *Prélude et Ronde*, op. 72 (1941) (5') •Ger/An
Bournonville, Armand - *Danse pour Katia* (GEE) •South
BOURREL, Yvon - *Sonate*, op. 18 (1964) (14') •Bil
BOUTIN, Pierre - *Berceuse* (1985) •Com
BOUTRY, Roger - *Cadence et mouvement*
BOUVARD, Jean - *Pieces*
BOZZA, Eugène - *Pieces*

BRADY, Timothy - *Sonata* (1979) •CMC
BRAGA, Francisco - *Dialogue sonore ao lunar* •IMD
Braga, Gaetano - *Serenata* (BRANGA) •Dur
Brahe, May H. - *Bless This House* (GLENN) •B&H
Brahms, Johannes - *Pieces*
Brändle - *Pieces* •Fro
BRANDON, Seymour - *Pieces* •MaPu
Bräu, Albert - *Pieces* •Fro
BREARD, Robert - *1ère suite* (1928) (to V. GUCHTE) •Led
BREDEMEYER, Reiner - *Sonate*
BREHME, Hans - *Sonata*, op. 25 & 60 (1932-57)
BRIARD, Raymond - *Pastorale et Tarentelle* (193x) •Marg
BRINDEL, Bernard - *Autumnal Meditation* (1938) •MCA/Pro
    Suite (1938) (17') •Pres
BROEGE, Timothy - *9 Arias* (1978) •DP
Brooks, E. - *The Message* (BUCHTEL) •Kjos
BROUQIERES, Jean - *Pieces* •Bil/Mar
BROWN, Charles - *Arlequinade* (1969) (7'30) •Led
    Pieces •Lem/Phi
BROWN, Earle - *Sonata* •CAP
BROWN, Newel Kay - *Sonata* •SeMC
Brunard, Gaston - *Offertoire* •1 Sx: A or T/Org or Pno •Mil
Bruniau, Augistin - *Pieces* •Bil
BRUNNER, Hans - *2 oeuvres*, op. 19
BULL, Edward Hagerup - *Duo concertant*, op. 52b (1980) (13') •NMI
    Perpetuum mobile (1992) (2') •adr
    Sonatine, op. 59-2 (1986) (7'15) •adr
BUMCKE, Gustav - *Pieces*
BUOT, Victor - *Pieces* •ES
BURKHARDT, Joel - *Chanson* (1987) (1'30) •South
BURNETTE, Sonny - *Nuage Music* •Ron
BUSCH, Carl - *Valse élégiaque* (1933) •Wit
BUSSER, Henri - *Pieces* •Led
Buttstedt - *Aria* •WWS
CAILLIET, Lucien - *Andante and Allegro* (LEFEBVRE) •South
Caiola, A. - *You are the Soloist* •1 Sx: A or T/Pno •MCA
CALMEL, Roger - *Aria* (1950) •adr
    Nocturne (1961) (1'30) •Phi
    Sonate d'Automne (1991) (10'30) •Com
    Suite (1961) (8') •adr
CAMARATA, Salvador - *Rhapsody* (1949) •Mills
Campra, André - *Pieces* •Led/Lem
CAMPS, Pompeyo - *Fantasia*, op. 93 (1989) (7') •CIDEM
CANAT de CHIZY, Edith - *Saxy* (1985) (3'30) •Bil
CANIVEZ, L. - *Fantaisie de concert*, op. 127 •TM
CAPDEVIELLE, Pierre - *Schandh'Ebhen* •HS
CAPLET, André - *Légende* (1903) (13') •Fuz
Carago - *Dance of the Silhouettes* •Mills
CARDEW, P. - *Alto Reverie* •Ka
Carion, F. - *Elegy* •HE
Carle - *Enchantment* (WHEELER) •Volk
CARLES, Marc - *Cantilène* (1963) (2'30) •Led
    Cycliques (1976) •adr
CARLID, Göte - *Triad* (1950) (5'30) •STIM/Ehr
CARMICHAEL, John - *Introduction and Allegro*
CARRE-CHESNEAU, Thierry - *2 Pièces* (1979) •1 Sx: S+A/Pno
    Rencontres (1977)
CARSTE, Hans Friedrich - *Pieces* •Fro
Casadesus, Francis - *Romance et Danse pastorale* (MULE) •Lem
CASTEREDE, Jacques - *Pieces* •Led
Cavallini, Ernesto - *30 Caprices* (IASILLI) •CF
CECCARELLI, Luigi - *Koan II* (1989) (9') •adr
CECCONI, Monique-Gabrielle - *Ariette* (1962) (5') •Com/Phi
CHAILLEUX, André - *Andante et Allegro* (1958) (3') •Led
CHANDLER, Erwin - *Sonata*, op. 25 (1969)

CHARPENTIER, Jacques - *Gavambodi 2* (1966) (8') •Led
CHATILLON, Jean - *Sonate* (1966) •Reb
CHIC, Léon - *Tyrolienne variée* (1861) •Sax
CHLEIDE, Thierry - *Suite brève* (1991) (10') •An
CHO, Gene - *Sonata* (1971) (7'30) •South
Chopin, Frédéric - *Pieces*
CHRETIEN, Hedwige - *Allegro appassionato* •1 Sx: A or T/Pno •Mil
Christophe - *Les Petits oiseaux* •Eb Sx/Pno •TM
Christol - *Pieces* •Mil/Mol
CIBULKA, Franz - *Capriccio* (1980)
Cirri, Giovanni Battista *Arioso* (MAGANINI) •1 Sx: A or T/Pno •Mus
CIRY, Michel - *Capriccio*, op. 52 •Sch
CLARKE, Herbert - *Pieces* •CF
CLASSENS, Henri - *Pieces* •Com/Phi
Clear, Th. - *Romance* •ES
CLERISSE, Robert - *Pieces* •Braun/Led/Phi
CLINCH, Peter - *Inventions*
CLOSTRE, Adrienne - *Kalamar* (1954) (3') •PN
COFIELD, Frank - *Pieces* •Rub
COHANIER, Edmond - *Silhouette* •Bil
COITEUX, Francis - *Pieces* •Mar
Coleridge-Taylor, Samuel - *Demande et Réponse* (BISHOP) •B&H
COLIN, Charles - *Pieces* •Mil/South
COLLER, Father Jerome - *Sonatina*
COMBELLE, François - *Pieces*
COMBES-DAMIENS, Jean-René - *Fable du Souffle* (1990) (3') •Led
COME, Tilmant - *Capriccio* •Mau
Concone, Giuseppe - *Pieces* (SANSONE) •South
Confrey, Zez - *Dizzy Fingers* (POTTER) •Mills
CONSTANT, Franz - *2 Episodes*, op. 119 (1986) (5'30) •Bil
    Sonatine à deux, op. 136 (1992) •HM
    Tension (1976) •adr
COOLIDGE, Richard - *Weeping Dancer* •WWS
COOPER, Paul - *Four Impromptus* (1983) •WH
    Variants IV (1986) •Che
COPELAND, Eugene - *Petite suite*; *Sonatine* •DP
CORBIN, A. - *Pieces* •Marg
Corelli, Arcangelo - *Pieces*
CORIGLIANO, James - *Serenade and Rondo* (1977) (5'15) •Sha
CORIOLIS, Emmanuel de - *Pieces* •Bil/Led
COTTET, Jean-Marie - *Variations* (1976) •Chou
COULEUVRIER, Alphonse-Louis - *Andante relligioso n° 2* •Mar
Couperin, François - *Pieces* •Led/Phi
COURROYER, Bernard - *Improvisation* •HM
COWAN, Don - *Pieces* •B&H
COWLES, Colin - *Pieces* •Stu
Cox, J. S. - *Call Me Time Own* •Eb Sx/Pno •CF
CREPIN, Alain - *Pieces* •HM/Lem
CRESSONNOIS, Jules - *Fantaisie d'après Mayeur* •Cos
CRESTON, Paul - *Rapsodie*, op. 108b •Sha
    Sonata, op. 19 (1939) (13') •Sha
    Suite, op. 6 (1935) (10') •Sha
CROUSIER, Claude - *Pieces* (1991) •Fuz
Cui, César - *Pieces* •CF/Led/Mills
CUNEO, Angelo Francesco - *Capriccio* •Ric
CUNNINGHAM, Michael - *The Nightingale* (1964) (4') •DP
    Sonata, op. 50 (1972) (10') •SeMC
CURTI, Guido - *Pieces* •Col
CURTIS-SMITH, Curtis - *Unisonics* (1976) (14') •Pres
CUSHING, Charles - *Hommage à A. Roussel* (1954) (3') •PN/Bil
DACHEZ, Christian - *Pieces* •1 Sx: A or T/Pno •Led
Dahm - *Concert Album of French Classics* •1 Sx: A or T/Pno •Mus
    Paris soir •1 Sx: A or T/Pno •Mus
DAIGNEUX, A. - *Sinuosity* •Sez
DAKIN, Charles - *Sonata da camera* •DP

DAM, Hermann van - *Who's afraid of black...* (1988) (35') •Don
DAMASE, Jean-Michel - *Pieces* •Bil/Comb/Sal/Zu
Dancla, Jean-Baptiste - *Rêverie et Polka* •Mol
DANDELOT, Georges - *Sonatine* (1967) (7') •ME
DANEAU, N. - *Piasaxo* •TM
D'ANGELO, Nicholas - *Five Mobiles* (1972) (15') •adr
DAUTREMER, Marcel - *Pieces* •Led/Zu
Dawes, Charles G. - *Melody* (SEARS) •Rem
DEASON, David - *Blues-Walk* (1984) •1 Sx: S+A+T/Pno
Debaar, Mathieu - *Prélude et Humoresque* •EMB
De Bueris, John - *Miami Moon - Valse brillante* •CF
Debussy, Claude - *Rapsodie* (ROUSSEAU) •Eto
    Pieces
DECOUAIS, René - *3 Pièces de concert* (1983) (8') •Bil
DECRUCK & BREILH - *Pieces*
DEDRICK, Rusty - *A Tune for Christopher* •Ken
DEFAYE, Jean-Michel - *Ampélopsis* (1976) •Led
De Fesch, Willem - *Sonata* •WWS
DEFOSSEZ, René - *Mélopée et Danse* •Asx/Pno or Fl/Ob/Cl/Asx/Bsn
    •An
DEGEN, Helmut - *Sonate* (1950) •Sch
DELAGE, Jean-Louis - *Illusions, Rêves et Caprices* (1990) (12')
    •Asx/Pno/Synth/Perc or Asx/Pno •Bil
Delannoy, J. - *The Last Thought of Weber* •HE
DELAUNAY, René - *Pieces* •Bil
DEL BORGO, Elliot - *Elegy II* (1989)
    Sonata nos. 1 & 2 •Sha
DELDEN, Lex van - *Sonatina*, op. 36 (1952) (6'45) •Don
DELERUE, Georges - *Prisme* (1977) •ET
DELGUIDICE, Michel - *Saxboy* •1 Sx: S or A or T/Pno •Mar
    Pieces •Bil/Led
Delhaye, Alyre - *5 Bagatellen* •Sez
Delibes, Léo - *Coppélia* (DAVIS) •Rub
Delmas, Marc - *Pieces* •Bil
DE LUCA, Joseph - *Pieces* •CF
DELVINCOURT, Claude - *6 Croquembouches* (1946) (14') •Led
Demaret, R - *Habanera* •Che
DEMERSSEMAN, Jules - *Pieces*
DEMILLAC, Francis - *Pieces* •Com
DEMUTH, Norman - *Sonata* (1955) •adr
DENISOV, Edison - *Deux Pièces brèves* (1974) (5'10) •Led
    Sonate (1970) (12') •Led
DENNEHY, Donnacha - *Contingency, Irony...* (1993) •INM
DEPELSENAIRE, Jean-Marie - *Pieces*
DERKSEN, Bernard - *Kapriolen - Waltz*, op. 28 •EB/AMP/B1B
De Rose, Peter - *Deep Purple* (WIEDOEFT) •Rob
DERR, Ellwood - *One in Five in One*, op. 10 (1955-65) •UMM/DP
DERVEAUX, André-Jean - *Pieces* •Bil/Marg
DESCHAMPS, Jean-Henri - *Danse arabe* (1970) (4') •Bil
DESENCLOS, Alfred - *Prélude, Cadence et Finale* (1956) (11') •Led
DESLOGES, Jacques - *Pieces* •Com/Mar
DESPORTES, Yvonne - *Les trois demeures* (15'15) •DP
    Pieces •Com/Bil
DESSAU, Paul - *Suite* (1935) (8') •B&B
Destouches, André - *Issé - Pastorale et passepied* (MULE) •Led
De Swert, Jules - *Ballade* •Eb Sx/Pno •CF
DEVEVEY, Pierre - *Arabesque* •ELC
DeVille, Paul - *Pieces* •CF
DEVOGEL, Jacques - *Pieces* •Com/Mar
D'HAEYER, Frans C. - *Introduction et Allegro* (1953) •Met/An
DIAMOND, David - *Duo concertante; Sonata* (1984)
DI BIASE, Paolo - *Pieces* •PT
DI DOMENICA, Robert - *Sonata* (1967) (5'30) •MJQ
DI DONATO, Vincenzo - *Pastorale* •DS
DIEMENTE, Edward - *Mirrors VI* (1974) •DP

Response (1969) (4'30) •OKM/SeMC
DIERCKS, John - *Suite* (1972) (6'30) •Pres/TP/Ten
DIJK, Jan van - *Sonate* (1953) (9') •Don
DIJK, Rudi Martinus van - *Sonata movement* (1960) •CMC
DILLON, Henry - *Sonate* (1949) (7') •Sal
DINDALE, E. - *Pieces* •HE/Sch
DINESCU, Violeta - *Méandre* (1993) •INM
DOERR, Clyde - *Saxophone Moods* •Asx/Pno or SATB •Sal
DOMAGALA, Jacek - *Ballade* (1986) (15') •adr
DONDEYNE, Désiré - *Pieces* •Mar
Donizetti, Gaetano - *Pieces* •Cos/Led
DONORA, Luigi - *5 X 5 - Canoni* •Piz
DORAN, Matt - *Lento and Allegro* (1962) •AvMu/WIM
DÖRFLINGER, Kurt - *Illusion* •Fro
DORSEY, Jimmy - *Pieces*
DORSSELAER, Willy van - *Pieces* •Bil/Lem/Met/adr
Douane, Jules-Albert - *Capriccio* (1960) (4') (to M. MULE) •Lem
Doullon - *Pieces* •Mil
DOURSON, Paul - *Allegretto grazioso* (1993) •Eb or Bb Sx/Pno •Led
DOURY, Pierre - *Caprice en Rondeau* (2'10) (Recueil 1) •Bil
DOUSE, Kenneth - *Cynthia* (1939) •CF
DRESSEL, Erwin - *Pieces* •RE
Drigo, Riccardo - *Pieces*
DRUET, Robert - *Pieces* •Bil
DUBOIS, Pierre-Max - *Pièces caractéristiques* (1962) (16'30) •Led
    Sonate (1956) (20') •Led
    Sonate fantaisie (1979) (13'30) •Bil
    Pieces •Led/RR/Bil
DUCLOS, René - *Pièce brève* (1950) (2'30) •Led
DUFLOT, Raoul - *Lido* (1991) (1') •Com
DUHA, Isabelle - *Scherzo* (1981) (2'30) •Bil
DUIJK, Guy Christian - *Contest + 5* •An
Dukas, Paul - *Alla gitana* (MULE) •Led
DUKE, Lewis - *Variations on a Tone Row* (1952/70) (13'30) •BPb
DUNKEL, Elmar - *B / S new* (1993) •INM
DUPONT, Jacques - *Bercement* (Recueil [Album]) (1974) (3'30) •Zu
DURAND, Pierre-Hubert - *Saxovéloce* (1989) (4'30) •1 Sx: A or T/
    Pno •Com
Dussekk, Johann Ludwig - *Andante* (MERIOT) •Phi
Duval, François - *Rondeau* (LONDEIX) •Lem
DUYCK, Guy - *Introduction et Danse* •Mau
DUYSBUTG, F. - *Prélude et Danse* •EMB
Dvorak, Anton - *Pieces* •CF/GSch/VAB
DYCK, Vladimer - *1ère Légende hébraïque* (1936) •Bil
Eccles, Henry - *Sonata* (RASCHER) •ElVo/Pres
ECKARD, Walter - *Highlights of Familiar Music* (46 pieces) •Pres
EDELSON - *Night Song* •Mus
EFFINGER, Cecil - *Solitude* (1960) (3'30) •Pres
EISENMANN, Will - *Pieces* •CF/Ken
EITHLER, Estaban - *Pieces* •EMBA/BBC
ELBE, Carl - *Giocondita* •Fro
Elgar, Edward - *Salut d'amour* (STABER) •Sch
ELIASSON, Anders - *Poem* (1986-88) (10') •SMIC/STIM
ELLIS, James - *Napoli* •WWS
ENDRESEN, R. M. - *Indispensable Folio* (11 pieces) •Rub
Enesco - *Concertstück* •Eno
ENGELMANN, Hans Ulrich - *Intégrale*, op. 14a •A&S
Erdna - *6 Pieces Swing* •1 Sx: A or T/Pno •Sal
ESCAICII, Thierry - *8 Pièces* (1992) •Mis
ESCUDIER, H. - *Pieces* •Mar
ESHPAY, Andrei - *Danse russe* (3') (Recueil [Album]) •Bil
    Miniature •ECP
Espejo, César - *Complainte andalouse* (MULE) •Lem
ETTORE, Eugene - *L. T. the kid* •CAP
EVANS, O. A. - *Jazz-Intermezzo* •Zim

Evans, Tolchard - *Lady of Spain* (KLICKMANN) •SF
Evartt, R. - *Eleonora* •Me/An
Exaudet, André Joseph - *Tambourin* (LONDEIX) •Lem
EYCHENNE, Marc - *Sonate* (1963) (11') •Bil
Farigoul, Joseph-Marie - *Arioso* •And
Farina, Carlo - *Fragmento verdo musimo* •SeMC
Farnaby, Giles - *Pieces* •WWS
Faulx, J. B. - *Pieces* •HE/EMB
Fauré, Gabriel - *Pièce* (DONEY) •Led
Fauré, Jean-Baptiste - *The palms, Let me dream* (SULLIVAN) •CF
FELD, Jindrich - *Sonate* (1989-90) (21') •Led
Felix - *Pieces*
FENIGSTEIN, Victor - *Memento et épitaphe* (1980) (8') •Ku
FENNELLY, Brian - *Corollary II* (1988) (8') •NP/ACE
Ferling, Wilhelm-Franz - *4 Etudes* (GEE) •PA
Fesca, Alexander - *The Wanderer* •Eb Sx/Pno •CF
Fesch, Willem de - *Sonata in F* (R. JONES) •Eto
FIALA, George - *Sonata* (1970) (14') •CMC
FICHE, Michel - *Pieces* •Bil/Comb
FIEVET, Paul - *Pieces* •Com/GD
FINNEY, Ross Lee - *Sonata* (1971) (13'30) •Pet
   Two Studies (1980) (10') 1 Sx: A+S/Pno •Pet
FINZI, Graciane - *De l'un à l'autre* (1977) (2'30) •Led
Fiocco, Joseph-Hector - *Pieces* •Bou/DP
FISCHER, M. - *Saxonetta* •Fro
FLAMENT, Edouard - *Romance* (MULE) •Led
Flegier, André-Ange - *Pieces* •CF/VAB
FLETA POLO, Francisco - *Impromptu n° 8*, op. 79 (1979) •Cil
   Sonata, op. 62 (1978) •Cil
FLOTHUIS, Marius - *3 Moments musicaux*, op. 82 (1982) (12') •Don
Flotow, Friedrich von - *Pieces* •Mol/PB
FOARE, Charles - *Doux espoir - Romance* (1893) •Vcl or Asx/Pno
FOISON, Michèle - *10 Variations...* (1966) (8') (Album) •Bil
FONTAINE, Louis Noël - *Divertimento* (1992) (10') •Capri
FONTYN, Jacqueline - *Dialogues* (1969) (13') •Chou
   Fougères (1981) (5') 1 Sx: S+A/Pno (or Harp) •Sal
   Mime III (1980) (5') 1 Sx: S+A/Pno •Sal
FORESTIER, J. - *Solo* •Mol
FORET, Félicien - *Pieces* •Bil/Dur
FORSSELL, Jonas - *Mia* (1981) (10') •STIM
FORSYTH, Malcolm - *Breaking Through* (1991) (5'15) •Ric
FORTINO, Mario - *Prelude and Rondo* •TP
Foster, Stephen - *Pieces* •CF
Fote, R. - *Waltz for Juliet* •1 Sx: A or T/Pno •WWS
Fouque, Octave - *Pieces* •Mil
FOX, Frederick - *Annexus* (1981) (10')
Fox, Oscard - *Pieces* •Bel/CF
FRACKENPOHL, Arthur - *Variations* (1969) (7') •Sha/RPS
   Pieces •Ken
FRANCAIX, Jean - *5 Danses exotiques* (1962) (6') •Sch
FRANCHETTI, Arnold - *Sonata* (1970) (14') •Led
Franck, César - *Pièce* (MULE) •Led
FRANCK, Marcel G. - *Légende* (3') •EMa
FRANGKISER, Carl - *Moraine* •Bel
FRICKER, Peter Racine - *Aubade* (1951) (4') •Sch
FRID, Geza - *Kleine Suite*, op. 88 (1975) (10') •Don
FROMIN, Paul - *Le Grand Canyon - Air de chasse* •Cham
Fucik, Julius - *Entrée des Gladiateurs* •Sal
GABAYE, Pierre - *Printemps* (1959) (2'30) •Led
GABELLES, Gustave - *Pieces* •Bil/Cham/Gras
Gabriel-Marie - *Pieces* •Bil/Cos/Mar/Rub
GAGNON, Alain - *Fantaisie lyrique*, op. 28 (1982) (9'30) •Led
GAILLARD, Marius François - *Note sobre o Tejo* (1934) (3') •Bil
GALLAHER, Christopher - *Impressions of Summer* (1960) (5') •South
   Sonatina (1968) (7') •SP

GALLET, Jean - *Pieces* •Bil
GALLOIS-MONTBRUN, Raymond - *6 Pièces...* (1954) (16'30) •Led
   Pieces •Com/Led
GARDNER, Samuel - *From the Canebrake* •GSch
Garique - *Mélodie* •Mil
GARLICK, Antony - *Pieces* •SeMC
GARRIGUENC, Pierre - *N. O. Rhapsody* •EP
GASTINEL, Gérard - *Improvisation II* (1976) (12'30) •Chou
GAUBERT, Philippe - *Intermède champêtre* (MULE) •Led
GAUJAC, Edmond - *Funambule* •Bil
Gautier, Leonard - *Le secret* (DAVIS) •Rub
GEE, Harry - *Pieces* •DP/Ken/adr
GEISER, Walther - *Danza notturna*, op. 36a (1947) •B&N
GENIN, Paul Agricol - *Pieces* •Bil
GENZMER, Harald - *Sonate* (1985) (12') •R&E
   Sonatine •R&E
GEORGE, Thom Ritter - *Introduction and Dance*, op. 150
   Suite in homage to J. S. Bach (1963-76) (19') •South
GERBER, René - *Sonate* (15')
GERSCHEFSKI, Edwin - *Workout*, op. 10 (1933) •ACA
Gershwin, George - *Pieces*
GHIDONI, Armando - *Pieces* •Led/Ma
Giazotto - *Adagio in G minor on a theme of Albinoni* •Ric
Gillet, Ernest - *Caprice, Gavotte* (LEFEBRE) •CF
GILSON, Paul - *Pièces romantiques* (1933-36) (32') •An
Giordani, Giuseppe - *An 18th Century Air* •Eb Sx or Bb Sx/Pno •Mus
GIORDANO, John - *Fantasy* (1968) (5') •South
GIOVANNINI, Caesar - *Romance* (1988) (4') •1 Sx: B or A/Pno
                         •South
GIRNATIS, Walter - *Sonate* (1962) •Sik
GLASER, Werner Wolf - *Allegro, Cadenza e Adagio* (1950) (9')
                         •STIM
   Duo (1985) (12') •STIM
   Pieces •Chap/Pres
Glazounov, Alexander - *Sérénade espagnole* (LEESON) •Hil/Col
GLICK, Srul Irving - *Sonata* (1992) (10')
Glinka, Mikhaïl - *The Lark - Romance* (BELLINI) •CF
Glover, Sarah Ann - *Rose of Tralee* •Mol
Gluck, Christoph - *Pieces* •Led/Mus
GOCHT, J. - *Impressions 65* •AMP
Goddard, Benjamin - *Pieces* •Kjos/Mol
GOEYENS, Alphonse - *Pieces* •EMB/HE
GOEYENS, F. - *Solitude* •Scz
GOLBERG, Johann Gottlieb - *Le Chardonneret* (ROMBY) •PB
GOLDBERG, Theo - *Anti thesis* (1974) •Asx/Pno or Tape
Goldman, Edwin Franco - *Air and Variations* (BELLINI) •Eb Sx/Pno
                         •CF
Golterman, George - *Pieces*
GORNSTON, David - *Valses* (HANSON) •Eb Sx/Pno •CF
Gossec, François - *Pieces* •Led/South
GOTKOVSKY, Ida - *Brillance* (1974) (12') •EFM
   Sonate •Bil
   Variations pathétiques (1983) (28') •Bil
Gottwald - *Friendship* (SANSONE) •South
Gounod, Charles - *Pieces*
GRAINGER, Percy - *Molly on the Shore* (4') •PG/TTF
Granados, Enrique - *Pieces* •GSch/Mol/UME
GRANDERT, Johnny - *Etyd* (1990) (5'30) •SMIC
Granom, Lewis - *Sicilienne* (MERIOT) •Phi
GRETCHANINOFF, Alexandre - *2 Miniatures*, op. 145 (4') •Led
   Pieces •Rub
Grieg, Edvard - *Pieces* •BM/GSch/Sch
GRILLAERT, Octave - *Fantaisie variée*, op. 1531 •Met/HE
GRISONI, Renato - *Pieces* •Cur/Pet
GROFÉ, Ferde - *Pieces* •Rob

GROHNER, Franz - *Koboldsprünge - Foxtrott* •CH
GROSSE-SCHWARE, Bernhard - *Drei Kleine Stücke* (1993) •INM
GROVLEZ, Gabriel - *Sarabande et allegro* •Led
GUACCERO, Domenico - *Esercizi* (1965) (9') •1 Sx: A+S/Pno
      •CRM
GUICHERD, Yves - *Pieces* •Bil
Guilhaud, Georges - *Pieces* •Bil/Rub
GUILLAUME, Eugène - *Andante et scherzo* •EMB
GUILLAUME, Georges - *Humeurs* (1986) (5'15) •Bil
GUILLONNEAU, Christian - *Evocation et Danse* (1993) (4') •1 Sx:
      A or T/Pno •Mar
GUILLOU, René - *Sonatine* (1946) (5') •Led
GULLY, Michel - *Conte* (1983) (1'30) •Com
Gundlach, Eric - *Elfentraum* (LÖBEL) •Rot
GURBINDO, Jose Fermin - *Sonatina* •RCSMM
GUREWICH, Jascha - *Sonata*, op. 130 (1928) •CF
   Pieces •CF/GHS/GSch/Ric/SF
GUYENNON, Bernard - *100 chansons à jouer* •Mar
HAAS, Hans - *Mixtura* •IMD
Haddad - *Andante and allegro* •Sha
HALETZKI, P. - *Vater und Sohn* •WWS
Halévy, Jacques - *Pieces* •CF/Mus
Handel, Georg-Friedrich - *Pieces*
HANSEN, Ted - *Elegy* (1978) •SeMC
HARBISON, John - *Sonata* (1995) (15') •AMP
HARLE, John - *Sax Album - to Baker Street and Bach* (1985) •B&H
HARRIS, Floyd - *Pieces* •Lud
HARRISON, Jonty - *EQ* (1980) (13'30) •Ssx/Tape dispositif acoustique
      or Asx/Pno •adr
HARTL, Heinrich - *Sonate im Jazz Stil*, op. 32 (1991) (7') •Hag
HARTLEY, Walter - *Duo* (1964) (5'30) •TP/Ten
   The Saxophone Album (1974) •DP
   Sonata Elegiaca (1987) (13'45) •TP
   Song (1972) (3') (from *Southern Tier Suite*) •Ten/Pres
   Sonorities IV (1976) (3') •DP
   Valse Vertigo (1978) (3'40) •DP
Hartmann, John - *Pieces* •CF/Mol
HARTZELL, Doug - *Pieces*
HARVEY, Paul - *Saxophone Solos* (2 Volumes) •Che
   The Singing Saxophone (1989) •1 Sx: A or T/Pno •SMC
Hatton, John - *Goodbye, Sweetheart, Goodbye* •Eb Sx/Pno •CF
HAUDEBERT, Lucien - *Souvenir d'Armor*
HAUSER, Miska - *Chanson villageoise* •CF
HAVER, Bruno - *Flip und flap - Foxtrott* (1938) •CH
Haydn, Franz Joseph - *Pieces*
HAYES, Gary - *Concertino* •ACA
HECK, Armand - *Concertino en Sol Majeur*, op. 41 (1940) (4') •Com
HEIDEN, Bernhard - *Solo* (1969) (6') •AMP/B&B
   Sonate (1937) (18') •Sch/AMP
HEIDER, Werner - *Sonata in jazz* (1959) (11') •A&S
HEIM, Norman - *Suite*, op. 83 (1984) (13') •Nor
HEINICK, David - *Later, When I Dream* (1987) (8') •adr
HEINKEL, Peggy - *Concertino* •DP
HENNESSY, Swan - *Morceaux*, op. 68 & 71 •ME
   Sonatine celtique, op. 62 (LAURENT) •ME
HENRY, Otto - *Omnibus II* •MP
HENTON, H. Bennie - *Pieces* •CF
Herbert, Victor - *Gypsy Love Song* (BUCHTEL) •1 Sx: T or A/Pno •Kjos
HERBIN, René - *Danse* (1952) (3') •PN
Herfurth, C. P. - *A Tune a Day* •Bos
Herold, Louis Joseph - *Zampa* (ROMBY) •PB
HERZBERG, Max - *Lament d'amor* (1925) •Wie
Heumann, Hans A. - *Slavonic Fantasy* (VOXMAN) •Rub
HINDEMITH, Paul - *Sonate* (1943) (8'30) •Sch
HODKINSON, Sidney - *Dissolution of the Serial* (1967) (8') •adr

Three Dance Preludes (1981) (13') •DP/NP
HODY, Jean - *Pieces* •Chou
Hoffmann, Adolf G. - *Pieces* •Bel/B&H
HOFFMAN, Norbert - *Pieces* •Eb or Bb Sx/Pno •Scz
HOLBROOKE, Joseph - *Cyrene*, op. 88 (1925) (4'30) •Klen
   Sonata, op. 99 (1928)
HOLLAND, Dulcie - *Sonata* (1953) (11'30) •adr
HOLMES, G. E. - *Pieces* •Eb Sx/Pno •Bar/CF
HOLSTEIN, Jean-Paul - *Suite irrévérencieuse* (1982) •Lem
   Pieces •Lem
HOLZMANN, Rodolfo - *Sarabande y toccata* (1934)
   Sonata
   Suite (1934)
HOUDY, P. - *Pieces*
HOVHANESS, Alan - *Soliloquy* •Ken
HOWLAND, Dulcie - *Saturday Stroll* •Allans
HUANG, An-Lun - *Chinese Rhapsody No. 3*, op. 46 (1989) •DP
HUNT, Wynn - *Sonate*, op. 60 (1930-70) (10') •BMIC
HUREL, Philippe - *Bacasax* (1990) (3'30) •Bil
IANNACCONE, Anthony - *Remembrance* (1973) (3') •Pres
IBERT, Jacques - *L'Age d'or* (*Le Chevalier Errant*) •Led
   Aria en Réb (1930) •Led
   Histoires... (MULE) •Led
Indy, Vincent d' - *Choral varié*, op. 55 (GEE) •1 Sx: A or T/Pno •MMB
Iradier, Sébastien de - *La paloma* •Mol
ISABELLE, Jean Clément - *Duo concertant*, op. 5 (1982) •Led
ISACOFF, Stuart - *Jazz Time* (1990) •Asx/Pno - Tsx/Pno •B&H
ISRAEL, Brian - *Sonata* (1980)
ITURRALDE, Pedro - *Airs Roumains et Suite Hellénique* •Lem
   Pequena czarda (1982) •Asx/Pno or 4 Sx: SATB •RME
IVANOV, Vladimir - *Pièces de compositeurs russes...* (1992) •Ivanov
IVE, Joanna - *Confrontations* (1993) •INM
JACOB, Gordon - *Variations on a Dorian Theme* (1972) •JE
JACOBI, Wolfgang - *Sonata* (1932) (10'30) •Bou
JACQUE-DUPONT - *Bercement* (1974) •Zu
Jadassohn, Salomon - *Noturno* (from *Serenade*) •Eb Sx/Pno •CF
Jakma, Fritz - *Pieces* •Mol/TM
JAY, Charles - *Pieces* •Com/Lem/adr
Jeanjean, Paul - *Pieces* •Bil
JETTEL, Rudolf - *Pieces* •Hof/Kli
JOHANSON, Sven Eric - *5 Expressioner* (1950) (5') •STIM/Ehr
   Sonate (1949) (12') •SMIC/Ehr
JOHNSTON, Benjamin - *Casta* •MP
JOHNSTON, Merle - *Pieces* •Rob
JOLIVET, André - *Fantaisie-Impromptu* (1953) (3'45) •Led
JOLLET, Jean-Clément - *Wales Song* (1987) (2') •Bil
JOLY, Denis - *Cantilène et danse* (1949) •Led
JONGEN, Joseph - *Méditation*, op. 21 (1901) (7') •Mur
JONGEN, Léon - *Piccoli* (1931) (8') •An/Ger
Joplin, Scott - *Pieces* •DP/Lem/NoE/TVA
JOUBERT, Claude-Henry - *Pieces* •Com/Mar
Kabalevsky - *Sonatina*, op. 13 (GEE) •1 Sx: A or B/Pno •South
KABELAC, Miloslav - *Suite* (1959/72) (9') •CHF
KAINZ, Walter - *Sonate*, op. 11 •LK
KALINKOVISC, H. - *Concert caprice alla Paganini* (13') •ECP
KALMANN, Menno - *Co + Menno's music...* (1986) (17') •Mol
KANITZ, Ernest - *Sonata Californiana* (1952) •CFE
KARAI, Jozsef - *Sonatina* •B&H
KARKOFF, Ingvar - *Madrigale* (1990) •SvM
   Meditations (1989/92) •SvM
KARKOFF, Maurice - *Ballada...*, op. 164 (1988) (17') •STIM
   Rapsodisk fantasi, op. 8a (1953) (6') •Ehr/SMIC/STIM
   Sonatine, op. 159 (1985-86) (10') •SMIC
   4 Stycken, op. 4 (1952-53) •SMIC/Ehr
KARLINS, M. William - *Music* (8') •South

KARPMAN, Laura - *Capriccio* (1981) (8'35) •DP
KASPAR, Edward - *Within and Beyond* (1970) (5') •SeMC
KASTNER, Jean-Georges - *Variations brillantes* (1847) •Sax
KAUFMANN, Serge - *Rhapsodie* (2') (Album) •Bil
KAUFMANN, Walter - *Meditation* (1982) •Eto
KAUN, Hugo - *"Aus den Bergen"* (1932)
Kazim, Necil - *Allegro feroce* (STATZER & WLIDGANS) (1932) •Uni
Kennedy, Amanda - *Star of the Sea* (HUMMEL) •Rub
KESNAR, Maurits - *Pieces* •CBet
Ketelbey, Albert - *In a Persian Market* •Bel
KEULEN, Geert van - *Concert* (1990) •Don
Khatchaturian, Aram - *Danse du sabre* •MCA
KIPS, René - *Esquisse Orientale* •An/HE/Ger
KISZA, Stanislaw - *Szkice* (1964-65) •1 Sx: A or T/Pno •PWM
KITAZUME, Michio - *Air* (1992) (8') •Lem
KITTEL, Tilo - *Saxgasse* (1993) •INM
Kletsch, Ludwig - *Das Lachende Saxophon* •Fro
KLOBUCAR, Andelko - *Canzona* (1982) (Album) •DSH/HG
    Sonate (1981) •DSH/HG
KLOSE, Hyacinthe - *Pieces* •Led
KNIGHT, Morris - *Sonata* (1964) (20') •South
KNORR, Ernst Lothar von - *Sonate* (1932) (15'30) •GrB
KOCH, Erland von - *Bagatella virtuosa* (1978) (2') •STIM
    Danse n° 2 (1938-67) (2') •1 Sx: S+A/Pno •STIM
    Sonata (1985-87) (12'30) •STIM
KOECHLIN, Charles - *15 Etudes*, op. 188 (1942-44) •EFM/Bil
    Pièce en Lab (1921) (Th. DONEY) •Led
Koepke, Paul - *Recitativo and Allegro* •Rub
Köhler, Ernesto - *Papillon* (CONKLIN) •CF
KÖHLER, Theodor - *Les songes d'un été* (1993) •INM
KOHN, Karl - *Paranymus II*
KOLB, Barbara - *Related Characters* (1980) (12') •B&H
KORNDORFF, Nikolaïs - *Monologue et ostinato* •ECS
KORTH, Thomas - *Elegy* (1968) (11'30) •adr
Koschatt, Thomas - *Forsaken* •Eb Sx/Pno •CF
KOX, Hans - *Sonate* (1985) (12') •Don
    Through a Glass, Darkly (1989) (10') •Don
Kozeluh, Leopold Anton - *Allegro* (MERIOT) •Phi
KRAFT, Leo - *Three Pieces* (1977) •DP
KRAMER, Martin - *Waltz Allegro* (1938) •SC
Krantz, A. - *Tourbillon* (GUREWICH) •CF
KREIN, Michael - *Serenade in A* (1960) •NWM
Kreisler, Fritz - *Pieces*
KROL, Bernhard - *Intermezzo amabile* (1980) (5'30) •DP/B&B
    Sonata, op. 17 (1956) (13') •Hof
KRUMLOVSKY, Claus - *Sonate* (1965) (7') •UGDAL
KUBINSKY, Richard - *2 Pièces* (1934) •ME
Kuhlau, Friederich - *Pieces* •Kjos/Phi
Kühn, Carl Theodor - *Adagio* ("Concerto militaire") •Eb Sx/Pno •CF
KÜHNE, Stephan - *Alla marcia dolente* (1993) •INM
KUPFERMAN, Meyer - *Pieces* •GMP
Kutsch, B. - *Saxophon Klange* •Zim
Labitzky, Auguste - *Träum des Sennerin* •Eb Sx/Pno •CF
LABURDA, Jiric - *Sonatina* (11') •Cz
LA CASINIERE, Yves de - *Ronde* (1954) (2'30) •PN
Lack, Theodore - *Idilio* •1 Sx: A or T/Pno •Cen
Lacome, Paul - *Rigaudon* (ANDRAUD) •South
LACOUR, Guy - *Pieces* •Bil
LAJTHA, Làszlô - *Intermezzo*, op. 59 (1954) (5'30) •Led
LAKE, Mathew - *Pieces* •CF/Lud
Lalo, Edouard - *Pieces* •Led/Mol/Sal
LAMB, Marvin - *Final Roland* (1979) •DP
LAMOTE, Raymond - *Pieces* •Bil
Lamote de Grignon, Juan - *Pieces* •1 Sx: T or A/Pno •UME
LANCEN, Serge - *Variances* (1982) (12'30) •Bil

    Pieces •Bil/EFM/Led/Lem/Mol
LANE, Richard - *Suite* (1961) •TTF
LANGESTRAAT, Willy - *Tribute to Rudy Wiedoeft* (1934) (3') •Mol
LANGLOIS, Théo - *Facetie* •PC
LANSIÖ, Tapani - *Una lettra al amico mio...* (1984) •FMIC
LANTIER, Pierre - *Allegro, Arioso et Final* (1963) (7'30) •Lem
    Euskaldunak-sonate (1954-61) (11') •Bil
    Sicilienne (1943) (5') •Led
LAPARRA, Raoul - *Prélude valsé et Irish reel* (5') •Led
LA PRESLE, Jacques Sauville de - *Orientale* (1930) (7') •Led
LARMANJAT, Jacques - *4 Pièces en concert* (1951) (9') •Dur
LARSSON, Mats - *Sonatine 1, 2* (1982, 1987) •SMIC
Lassen, Eduard - *At Devotions* (OSTRANDER) •Mus
LATEEF, Yusef - *Sonata* (1989) •FaM
LATHAM, William - *Sisyphus* (1971) •Bil
LAUBA, Christian - *Sud* (1986) (10') •Fuz
LAVAINNE - *Souvenir et regrets - ballade* (193x) •Gras
LAYENS, Gilbert - *Saxophonie* •Cham
Le Boucher, Maurice - *Fantaisie concertante* (MULE) •Led
Lebrun, G. - *Shepherd's Song* •HE
Lecail, G. - *Fantaisie Concertante* (VOXMAN) •Rub
Leclair, Jean-Marie - *Pieces*
LECLERCQ, Edgard - *Pieces* •An/Braun/EMB/HE
LEDUC, Jacques - *Rhapsodie* •Sch
LEE, Thomas Oboe - *Sourmash* (1978) •DP
LEESON, Cecil - *Sonatas 1 & 2*
LEEUWENBERG, Boudewijn - *Magic moments* (1975) (5') •Don
Lefebvre, E.-A. - *Pieces* •Eb Sx/Pno •CF
Lefevre, Charles - *Andante et Allegro* (CAILLIET) •South
LEGRON, Léon - *Canzonetta* (1976); *Rêverie* (1976) •Bil
LEGUAY, Jean-Pierre - *Sève* (1974) •Lem
Lehar, Franz - *La veuve joyeuse* (ROMBY) •PB
LEINERT, Friedrich Otto - *Sonate* (1952) (12'30) •Br&Ha
LEJET, Edith - *Trois Petits préludes* (1986) (4') •Lem
LELEU, Jeanne - *Danse nostalgique* (1956) (3'30) •Lem
LELOUCH, Emile - *Boutade* (1990) (3') •Comb
    Burlesque (1991) (3'50) •Comb
LEMAIRE, Félix - *Pieces* •Bil/Led
LEMAIRE, Jean - *Musiques légères* (1969) (7') •Led
Lenon, C. - *Lullaby* •CBet
LENNON, John Anthony - *Distances Within Me* (1979) •DP
LEONARD, Clair - *Recitativo and Abracadabra* (1962) •Bou
Leoncavallo, Ruggiero - *Pieces* •Cen/Lud
Leroux, Xavier - *Romances* •Led
LE SIEGE, Annette - *Suite* (1979) •SeMC
LESIEUR, Emile - *Pieces* •Bil/Mar
LETELLIER, Robert - *Ballade*; *Melancholy Song* •Mar
LETOREY, Pierre - *Papotages* (1944) (4'30) •Bil
LEVIN, Gregory - *Corina* (1971) •CMC
LIC, Leslaw - *Uniwersalny skarbesyk* •1 Sx: A or T/Pno •PWM
Liddle, Samuel - *How Lovely are thy Dwellings* (GLENN) •B&H
LIGNET, Félix - *Pieces* •Mil
LIMBERG, Hans Martin - *Saxophonietta* (1992) •Eres
Lincke, Paul - *The Glow Worm* (GLENN) •Kjos/Rub
LINDEMUTH, William - *Pavane*; *Rapture* •Ka
LIPTAK, David - *Fantasy* (1980) •DP
Liszt, Franz - *Pieces*
Llewellyn, Edward - *My Regards* (LILLYA) •1 Sx: A or T/Pno •CF/
                       Rem/DP
LOBL, Karl Maria - *Suites* •Eto
LOCHE, Henri - *Arioso* (1990); *Humoresque* •Bil
LOEFFLER, Charles Martin - *Rhapsodie*
Loeillet, Jean-Baptiste - *Pieces* •Lem/South
LOMANI, Borys - *Concertino*, op. 118 (1958) •PWM/B&H
    Pieces •PWM

LONDEIX, Jean-Marie - *Tableaux aquitains* (1973) (5'30) •Led
    Pieces •Fuz/Lem
LONGY, George Léopold - *Rhapsodie - Lento* (1906) •South
LONQUE, Armand Joseph - *Morceau de concours*, op. 56 •HE/EMB
Lotter, Adolph - *Rouge et noir* •1 Sx: A or T/Pno •B&H
Lotti, Antonio - *Arietta* (MAGANINI) •1 Sx: A or T/Pno •Mus
Lotzenhiser, George - *Poco Waltz* •Bel
Louiguy - *Cherry Pink and Apple Blossom White* •WWS
LOUVIER, Alain - *Hydre à cinq têtes* •Led
LOVREGLIO, Eleuthère - *Humoresque* (1962) (6') •Com
LUEDEKE, Raymond - *Fancies and Interludes* (1979) (20'30) •ACA
Lully, Jean-Baptiste - *Pieces* •Led
LUNDE, Ivar - *Sonata in One Movement*, op. 49 (1973) (15') •DP
LUNDE, Lawson - *A Trip to Pawtucket* (1964) (1') •NSM
    Sonata No. 1, op. 12 (1959) •NSM/South/SMC
    Sonata No. 2, op. 38 (1970) (12') •adr
LUOLAJAN-MIKKOLA, Vilho - *Elokuisessa...* (1984) •FMIC
Lyons - *New Alto Sax Solos* (2 Volumes) •USC
MACBRIDE, Robert - *Pieces* •ACA/CFE
MacDowell, Edward - *Pieces* •CF/Kjos/Mol
MÁCHA, Otmar - *Plâc saxofonu* (1968) (6'30) •CMIC
    The Weeping of the Saxophone (1968) •CMIC
MACHAJDIK, Peter - *Melodie* (1993) •INM
Macintyre, Hal - *Sax Rears its Ugly Head* (MATTHEWS) •Mut
MAERTENS, J. - *Moments tristes* •CBDM
MAGANINI, Quinto - *Pieces* •CF/Mus
MAHDI, Salah - *Nuit d'Interloken* •adr
Mahler, Gustav - *A Rückert Song* (HEMKE) •South
MAHY, Alfred - *Aubade* •Mol
MAILLOT, Jean - *Prélude et divertissement* (1969) (4'30) •ET
MAKRIS, Andreas - *Fantasy and Dance* (1974) (12') •MeP
Malezieux, Georges - *Pieces* •Sal
MALIPIERO, Gian Francesco - *Canto nell'infinito* •Led
Malotte, Albert - *The Lord's Prayer* (LAKE) •1 Sx: A or T/Pno •GSch
MALTBY - *Heather on the Hill* •Ken
MALYJ, Katherine - *Altarpiece* (1993) •INM
MANA-ZUCCA - *Walla-Kye*, op. 115 (1936) •Lee
MANEN, Christian - *Dans la forêt* •Com
MARC, Edmond - *Pierrot et Colombine* (1945) (8') •Bil
Marchetti, Filippo - *Fascination* (HURRELL) •Eb Sx or Bb Sx/Pno •Rub
MARCO, Tomàs - *Kwaïdan* (1988)
Mareczek, Fritz - *Sommerraabend am Berg* •Zim/Pet
MAREZ OYENS-WANSINK, Tera de - *Mandala* (1988) (16') •Don
MARGONI, Alain - *Pieces* •EFM/Bil
MARI, Pierette - *Pieces* •Bil/ET/adr
MARIE, E. - *La tyrolienne - Air varié* (to L. MAYEUR) •Marg
MARKOVITCH, Ivan - *Complainte et danse* (1964) (5') •Led
MAROS, Miklos - *Ondulations* (1986) (8'30) •SMIC
MARTEAU - *Morceau vivant* •WWS
MARTELLI, Henri - *Cadence, Interlude et Rondo*, op. 78 (1952) •ME
    Trois esquisses, op. 55 (1943) •ME
MARTIN, Robert - *Saxopaline; Sérénade à Corinne* •Mar
Martini, Padre - *Pieces* •Chap/Led/Phi
Martini, Jean-Paul - *Pieces* •Led/Mol/TM/Sal
Mascagni, Pietro - *Pieces* •CF/MPHC
MASLANKA, David - *Sonata* (1988) (33') •NASA
MASON, Thom David - *Canzone da sonar* (1970) •South
MASSELLA, Thomas - *Romance* (1993) (4') •Marc
Massenet, Jules - *Pieces*
MASSON, Gérard - *Minutes de St Simon* (1989) (12') •Sal
MATSUSHITA, Isao - *Atoll II* (1983) (6') •B&B
Mattheson, Johann - *Menuet* •Bil
MATTHESSENS, Marcel - *Short Habanera* •Scz
MAURAT, Edmond - *Petites inventions* (1966) (18'30) •ME
MAYERUS, A. G. - *Tarentelle* •Ger/An

MAYEUR, Louis - *Pieces* (187x) •Led/ES
MAZELLIER, Jules - *Pieces* •Led/Lem/Sal
McINTOSH, Diana - *Dance for Daedaluss* (1989) (14') •CMC
McKAY, George Frederick - *Pieces* •Bar/NA
Meacham, F. W. - *American Patrol* (HUMMEL) •Rub
Medinger, Jean - *Pieces* •Led/PB
Mehul, Etienne - *Rondeau basque* (MULE) •Led
MEIJERING, Chiel - *Pieces* •Don
MELNIK - *Birthstones* •ABC
MELROSE - *Saxophone moderne solos* •Mol
Mendelssohn, Arnold Ludwig - *Soldier's March* (BUCHTEL) •Kjos
Mendelssohn, Félix - *Pieces*
MENENDEZ, Julian - *Pieces* •RME/AMP/UME
MENGOLD, Paul - *Miniatures* •EV
MERANGER, Paul - *Pieces* •Bil/Com
MERILÄINEN , Usko - *Sonata* (1982) (13') •FMIC
MERIOT, Michel - *Pieces* •Com/Phi
MERK, Ulrike - *Metamorphose* (1993) •INM
MERSSON, Boris - *Fantaisie*, op. 37 (1979) •Ku
Messager, André - *Chant birman* (VIARD) •Sal
MESSINA-ROSARYO, Antonio - *Erlkönig - Suite* (21'30) •Asto
METEHEN - *Fedora* •Mar
MEULINK, Cor - *Valse élégante* •VAB
MEYER, Jean-Michel - *Pieces* •GD/Led/Sch
MEYER, Lucien - *Pieces* •BC/ES
Meyerbeer, Giacomo - *Marche des flambeaux* (ROMBY) •PB
MIGNION, René - *Pieces* •Bil
MIHAJLO, Zivanovic - *Balada; Invenaja* •YUC
Miles & Zimmermann - *Anchors Aweigh* (WIEDOEFT) •Rob
MILETIC, Miroslav - *Noveleta* (1981) •DSH
MILHAUD, Darius - *Danse* (1954) (2') •PN
    Scaramouche (1937) (9'30) •Sal
MIMET, Anne-Marie - *Pieces* •Bil
MINDLIN, Adolfo - *Pieces* •Led
MIYAMAE, Chieko - *Poèlégie* (1976) •Chou
MOHR, Gerhard - *Pieces* •Zim
Molloy, James - *Love's Old Sweet Song...* (RASCHER) •Eb Sx/Pno •CF
MONDONVILLE, Cassanea de - *Sonata No. 6* (HEMKE) •South
    Tambourin (MULE) •Led
MONFEUILLARD, René - *Deux Pièces* (1938) (6'30) •Led
MONTALTO, Richard - *Reflection* (1990) (4'30) •1 Sx: A or T/Pno
    •adr
Monsigny, Pierre-Alexandre - *Pieces* •Led
MOORTEL, Arie van de - *Capriccio* •Mau
MOREAU, Léon - *Evocations rythmiques* (MULE) •Led
    Fête païenne (1933) •HS
MOREE, L. de - *Serenade* •TM
MORITZ, Edvard - *Sonatas 1 & 2* (1938 & 1940) •South
MORLEO, Luigi - *Verty* (1992)
MORRISSON, Julia - *Pieces* •CFE
MORTARI, Virgilio - *Melodia* (1954) (1'30) •Led
MOSS, Lawrence - *Six Short Pieces* (1993) (8') •Ron
MOUQUET, Jules - *Rapsodie*, op. 26 (1907) •Led
Moussorgsky, Modeste - *Pieces* •EBMM/GSch/Lem
Mozart, Wolfgang - *Pieces*
MUCZYNSKI, Robert - *Sonata*, op. 29 (1970) (9') •GSch
MUELLER, Florian - *Sonata* •UMM
    Pieces •Mus/UMM/CFE
MULDERMANS, Jules - *Fantaisies* •Lud/Mar
MULDOWNEY, Dominic - *...In a Hall of Mirrors* (1979) •Uni
MURGIER, Jacques - *Pieces* •Lem/Zu
MYERS, Robert - *Pieces* •Art
MYERS, Theldon - *Sonatine* •CAP
Nagezy, Hans Georg - *Joys of Life* (RASCHER) •Bel
NAGY-FARKAS, Peter - *Sonatine* •DP

NIVERD, Lucien - *Pieces* •Bil/Mar/Com/Zu

NAULAIS, Jérôme - *Coconotes* (1991) (1'20) •Bil

   Kansax-City (1991) (2'20) •Bil

   Pain d'épice (1993) (1'15) •1 Sx: A or T/Pno •Mar

NELHYBEL, Vaclav - *Allegro* (1966) •Heu/GMP

   Concert Piece •Asx/Pno •WWS

Nessler, Victor - *Young Werner's...* (NEUMANN) •Eb Sx/Pno •CF

Nevin, Ethelbert - *Pieces* •Bil/Rub

Nicolao, G. - *Ave Maria; The light beyond* (BARRETT) •Eb Sx/Pno •CF

NICOLAU, Dimitri - *Reponses à l'avantgarde histérique - Sonata*, op. 76 •EDP

NIEHAUS, Lennie - *Pieces* •WIM

Nivelet, Victor - *Ma bergère* (MEDINGER) •Led

NIVERD, Lucien - *Pieces* •Bil/Com/GD/Mar/Zu

NODA, Ryo - *Atoll II* (1982); *Temple* (1976) •adr

   W 1988 D (1988) •1 Sx: S+A/Pno •adr

NODAÏRA, Ichiro - *Arabesque III* (1980-81) (13') •Lem

NOËL-GALLON - *Essor* (1953) (3'30) •PN

NORTON, Christopher - *Microjazz* (1988) •B&H

NOTT, Douglas - *Rhapsodic Song* •Sha

Nyquist, Morine A. - *Echo Lake* •Bel

OETTINGER, Alan - *Reflections* (1979) (8'30) •Eth

Offenbach, Jacques - *Waltz "La Périchole"* •Kjos

Olcott, Chauncey - *My Wild...* (BUCHTEL) •1 Sx: A or T/Pno •Bel/Rub

OOSTERVELD, Ernst - *Music loops III* (1982) (5') •Don

Ortolani - *More* (from *Mondo Cane*) •WWS

OSTERC, Slavko - *Sonate* (1935) •DSS

OSTRANDER, Allen - *Pieces* •EM/Mus

OSTRANSKY, Leroy - *Pieces* •Rub

Oswald, James - *Lento and Giga* (L. PATRICK) •Eth

OTERO, Francisco - *Double suggestion* (1981) •1 Sx: A+B/Pno

OUBRADOUS, Fernand - *Récit et variations* (1938) •Led

PAISNER, Ben - *Prelude to a Mood* •GM

PALA, Johan - *Fantasie* •TM

PALENICEK, Josef - *Masky* (1957) (11') •CHF

Paquot, Philippe - *10 Pièces mélodiques* •1 Sx: A or T/Pno •Led

Paradis, H. - *Pastel Menuett* (BUCHTEL) •Kjos

Paradis, Maria Theresia von - *Sicilienne* (PERCONTI) •Ron

PARES, Gabriel - *1er solo de concert* (1897) •Mar

   Pieces •Bil

PARIS-KERJULLOU, Ch. - *Divertissement...* •Mar

Parker, Charlie - *Jazz Master Series* •Asx/Pno •MCA

PARME, F. - *Serenade* •CF

PASCAL, Claude - *Sonatine* (1948) (8') •Dur

   Pieces •Com/Dur

Pasquali, Nicolo - *Menuet* (LONDEIX) •Lem

Paul, Gene - *Estilian caprice* •1 Sx: A or T/Pno •Rub

PAULET, Vincent - *Arabesque* (1986) (2'30) •Com

PAUWELS, M. - *Andante et Allegro* •1 Sx: A or T/Pno •HE/An

Pavey - *Gingerbread Man* •Pip

PAVLENKO, Serguei - *Sonate* (1975) (10') •adr

PAYNE, Frank - *Toccata* •Sha

PELLEGRINI, Ernesto - *Duolog* •WWS

Pennequin, Jean - *Morceau de concours* (MEYER) •BC

PENTRENKO, M. F. - *Valse n° 1* (1960) •SK

Pergolese, Giovanni-Battista - *Pieces* •HE/Mus

Perrier, Marius - *Prélude et allegro* •Bil

PERRIN, Jean-Charles - *Duo Concertante* •Bil

PERRIN, Marcel - *Pieces* •Com/DP/GD/Led

PESSARD, Emile - *Andalouse* (BUCHTEL) •Kjos

   Andantino, op. 36 (188x) •Led

Pesse, Maurice-Emile - *Au soir de la vie* (MULE) •Led

Pestalozzo - *Ciribiribin* •Kjos

Petiot, André - *Concerto en Mib* (GLAZOUNOV) •Led

PETIT, Alexandre-S. - *1ère étude de concours* •Bil

PETIT, Pierre - *Pieces* •Led

PHAN, P. Q. - *My Language* (1988) •adr

PHILIBA, Nicole - *Sonate* (1964) (17') •Bil

Philidor, François-André - *Pieces* (MULE) •Led

Phillips, Ivan C. - *A Classical and Romantic Album* •OUP

PHILLIPS, J. - *2 Pieces diverses* •WWS

Piccolomini, Marietta - *Play For Us* •Bb Sx or Eb Sx/Pno •CF

Pierné, Gabriel - *Pieces* •Led/South

PIERNÉ, Paul - *Pieces* •Bil

Pilatti, Mario - *Inquiètude* (PAQUOT) •Led

PINARD, A. - *Pieces* •Eb Sx or Bb Sx/Pno •CF

PLANEL, Robert - *Prélude et Saltarelle* (1957) (7') •Led

   Suite romantique (1944) (20'30) •Led

Planquette, Robert - *Fantaise sur 'Rip'* (MOUSSARD) •Marg

Platti, Giovanni - *Sonatas* (HERVIG) •Rub

PLUISTER, Simon - *Cafe valencia - Suite* (1978) (16') •Don

Ponce, Manuel-Maria - *Pieces* (MAGANINI) •Eb Sx/Pno •CF

PONJEE, Ted - *Saxuals songs* (1981) (6') •Don

PORRET, Julien - *Pieces* •Mar

Poulain, S. - *Melody* •HE

PRADO, Almeida - *New York, east shert* •SeMC

PRESSER, William - *Prelude and Rondo* (1962) (3'15) •Pres

   Sonatina (1979) (8') •Ten

Prokofiev, Sergei - *Pieces* •B&H/EMa/South

Pruitt, Jay - *Movement* •NTS

Puccini, Giacomo - *Tosca Fantasy* (HERMANN) •PM

PUNES, Karel - *Two Compositions* •CMIC

Purcell, Henry - *Pieces* •Bou/Kjos/Mus

PYLE, Francis Johnson - *Edged Night and Fireworks* •Br&Ha

QUERAT, Marcel - *Pieces* •Phi/adr

QUNTER, R. - *Recitatif* •Br & Ha

Raaff, Anton - *Papillons* •VAB

Rachmaninoff, Sergei - *Vocalise* •GSch/Mus

RAE, James - *Blue Saxophone* •1 Sx: A or T/Pno

   Jazzy Saxophone Duets II •1 Sx: A or T/Pno •Uni

Raff, Joachim - *Pieces* •CF/Sal

Rameau, Jean-Philippe - *Pieces* •Chap/ET/Led/Mus

Ramsay, Neal - *Seven Solos* •Sha

Ranger, A. R. - *Pieces* •CF

Rapee, Erno - *Todlin' Sax* (AXT) •Wie

RAPHAEL, Günter - *Récitatif* (1958) (4') •Led

   Sonate (1957) (9') •PJT

RAPHLING, Sam - *Sonatas 1 & 2* (1945 & 1969) •South/GMP

RASBACH, Oscar - *Trees* •GSch

RASCHER, Sigurd - *24 Intermezzi* (1954) •Bou

Ravel, Maurice - *Pieces* •Dur/Led/Mus/Rub

RAYMOND, Fred - *Design* •WIM

Redoute, J. - *Melody* •HE

REED, Alfred - *Siciliana notturno* (5') •Pied

REGT, Hendrik de - *Musica*, op. 9 (1971) (9-10') •Don

REHL, Richard - *The Duchess* (1928) •1 Sx: A or T/Pno •Rub

   Nimble Fingers •Rub

Reichardt, Gustave - *The Image of the Rose* •Eb Sx/Pno •CF

REINER, Karel - *Dvé skladby* (1967) •IMD/CHF

RELMES, Léo - *Lied* •Bil

RENARD, Charles - *Valse dramatique* (1938) •Carco

REUTTER, Hermann - *Elégie* (1957) (3'30) •Led

   Pièce concertante (1968) (11'30) •Sch

REVERDY, Michèle - *Cytrises* (2'40) (Collect. Panorama) •Bil

REX, Harley - *Intrada and Fugato* •WWS

Reynaud, Joseph-Félix - *Grande fantaisie* •Asx or Bb Sx/Pno •Sal

   Variations sur 'Ah! Vous dirai-je Maman' •1 Sx: A or S/Pno •Sal

RIBAS, Rosa Maria - *Sonata* (1980) (8') •Boi

RIBAULT, André - *Barcarolle* (1989) (1'45) •Mar

Richard, Charles - *Pieces* •Sal
RICHARDSON, Alan - *Three Pieces*, op. 22c (1975) •JE
RIETI, Vittorio - *Sequence* •DP
RIEUNIER, Jean-Paul - *Linéal* (1970) (8') •Led
RIMMER, William - *Saxonia* •HE
Rimsky-Korsakov, Nicolas - *Pieces*
Ring-Hager - *Danse Hongroise* (1923) (WIEDOEFT) •Rob
ROBERT, Jacques - *Chant sans parole* (1983) (2'30) •Comb
ROBERT, Lucie - *Berceuse pour Rémi* (1985) (5'30) •Bil
    Cadenza (1974) (10') •Bil
    Elégie •adr
    Sonate (1967) (11') •Bil
    Strophes (1978) (14'30) •DP
    Tourbillons (1975) (18') •Bil
    Variations (1977) (8'30) •Bil
Roelens, Alexandre - *Menuet vif* (MULE) •JJ
ROGER, Denise - *Conversation* (1989) (2') •1 Sx: A or T/Pno •Mar
    Evocation (1982) (2'30) •1 Sx: A or T/Pno •Comb
ROIZENBLAT, Alain - *Pieces* •1 Sx: A or T/Pno •Bil
Rolle, Johann Heinrich - *Pieces* •Sal
ROLLIN, Robert - *Two Jazz Moods* •SeMC
ROMBY, Paul - *Pieces* •PB
ROREM, Ned - *Picnic on the Marne* (1983) (16'30) •B&H
ROSS, William - *Aria and Dance* (1982) •South
ROSSÉ, François - *Pieces* •Bil
Rossini, Giacchino - *Pieces*
ROUGERON, Philippe - *Pieces* •Bil
Rougnon, Paul-Louis - *Solos de concert* •Gras/South
Round, H. - *Pieces* •Eb Sx/Pno •CF
ROUSSEAU, Eugene - *Solo Album* •Eto
ROWLAND, David - *Doubles n° IV* (1981) (12') •Don
Rubenstein, Anton - *Pieces* •CF/Mol/Sal
RÜCKSTÄDTER, Hans - *Saxonate* (1993) •INM
RUCQUOIS, Jean - *Pieces* •Bil/Mar
RUDAJEV, Alexandre - *Sonate* (1990) •adr
RUDIN, Rolf - *Nachtstücke*, op. 9 (1988) (13') •B&B
RUEFF, Jeanine - *Mélopéa* (1954) (3') •PN
Rungis, René - *4 Pièces* (MEURISSE) •Lem
RUNYON, Santy - *Exotic* (HUFFNAGEL) •DG
RUSSELL, Armand - *Particles* (1954) •Bou
RYDIN, Alexandra - *Pieces* •Led
Sacchini, Antonio - *Larghetto* (MERIOT) •Phi
SAEYS, Eugène - *Pieces*
Saint-Saëns, Camille - *Pieces* •CF/Dur/Eto/Mus
SALIMEN-VLADIMIROV - *Scherzo* •ECP
SALMON, Raymond - *Nonchalance* (1970) (1'15) •Phi
SAMAMA, Leo - *Capriccio* (1976) (7') •Don
Sammartini, Giovanni-Battista - *Pieces* •HE/Mol
SAMORI, Aurelio - *Cadenze* (1982) (13') •adr
Samuel-Rousseau, Marcel - *Romance* (MULE) •Asx/Pno •Led
SAMYN, Noël - *Romance* (1978) •Bil
SANDELL, Sten - *Atanor* (1988) •STIM
SANDROFF, Howard - *Eulogy* (1988-91) •adr
Sannella, Andy - *Pieces*
SANNER, Lars-Erik - *Sonatine* (1954) •STIM/Ehr
SASAMORI, Takefusa - *Variations...* (1963) (4'30) •PIC
SASONE, C. - *Racconto* •South
SAUCIER, Gene - *An Impression* •Ken
SAUGUET, Henri - *Sonatine bucolique* (1964) (13') •Led
    Une fleur (Album [Recueil]) (1984) (3') •Bil
SAUTER, J. - *Chanson joyeuse* •Kjos
Savard, Augustin - *Morceau de concours* (MEYER) •Led
SAVARI, Jean-Nicolas - *Pieces* •Sax/Ron/Fuz
SCHATER, J. - *Suite* •Pres
SCHMIDT, Arthur - *2 Pièces* •Mau

SCHMIDT, William - *A Little Midnight Music* (1970) (4') •WIM
SCHMITT, Florent - *Légende*, op. 66 (1918) (9') •Dur
SCHMUTZ, Albert - *Sonata* (1961) •SMP
SCHNEIDER, Catherine - *Le Promeneur* (1993) •Lem
SCHOLLUM, Robert - *Konzertstück*, op. 106 (1978) •ApE
SCHONHERR, Max - *Appasionato*, op. 48 •Hof
SCHOONENBEEK, Kees - *Tre Capricci* (1985) (10') •Don
SCHRIJVER, K. de - *Pieces* •Scz
Schubert, Franz - *Pieces*
SCHUDEL, Thomas - *Two Images* (4') •Ken
SCHULHOFF, Ervin - *Hot-sonate*, op. 70 (1930) (15'30) •Sch
    Serenata •Asx/Pno •CF
Schumann, Robert - *Pieces*
SCIORTINO, Patrice - *Sapiaxono* •adr
Scriabin, Alexander - *Pieces* (DIERCKS) •BMP
SEGERSTAM, Leif - *Episode n° 7* (1979) (10') •FMIC
    Epitaph n° 2c (1977) (9') •FMIC
Seleski - *Interlude romantique* •WWS
SEMENOFF, Ivan K. - *Gin-fizz* (1953) (3') •PN
SEMLER-COLLERY, Armand - *Pieces* •Bil/Braun
SEMLER-COLLERY, Jules - *Pieces* •Dec/Led/ME
Senaillé, Jean-Baptiste - *Allegro Spiritoso* (GEE) •South
SENON, Gilles - *Techni-Sax - 32 textes de vélocité* (1987) •Bil
SHAFFER, Sherwood - *Sicilienne* (1991) (4') •adr
    Summer Nocturne (1981) •adr
Shallitt, M. - *Eili, Eili...* •Eb or Bb Sx/Pno •CF
Shaw, Oliver - *A Trip to Pawtucket* (LUNDE) •NSM
SHIGERU, Kan-no - *Stück* (1993) •INM
Shishov, Ivan Petrovitch - *Grotesque Dance* (FELIX) •Mus
Shostakovich, Dmitri - *Pieces* •1 Sx: A ot T/Pno •Mus
SHRUDE, Marilyn - *Renewing the Myth* (1988) (13') •adr
SIBBING, Robert V. - *Vocalise* (1980) •Eto
Sibelius, Jean - *Swan of Tuonela* (JOHNSON) •Bel
SICHLER, Jean - *Pieces* •Com/Led
SIEGMEISTER, Elie - *Down River* (1970) •MCA
SIGNARD, Pierre - *Pieces* •Mil
SILESU, Lao - *Son portrait - mélodie* (1949) (3'30) •Sil
Silvestri, J. - *In Days of Knighthood* •Eb Sx/Pno •CF
SIMON, Robert - *Echo!* (1984) (3') •Led
SINGELÉE, Jean-Baptiste - *Pieces* •Sax/Ron/Fuz
SKOLNIK, Walter - *Lullaby for Doria* (1979) (2') •Pres
    Sonatina (1962) (6'30) •TP/Ten/Pres
SMIRNOV, Dimitry - *Ballade* •ECS
    Fata morgana •adr
    Suite de valses mélancoliques •Mu
SMITH, Clay - *Pieces* •CF
SMITH, Michael - *Elvira Madigan...* •SMIC
SMITH Stuart - *In Retrospect; Organum Metamorphoses* •SeMC
SNYDER, Randall - *Seven Epigrams* (1971) •South/SMC
    Sonata (1966) (16'30) •Pres/TP/Ten
SOPRONI, Jozsef - *4 Pièces* (1978) •Min/Musi
SOUALLE, Ali ben - *Pieces*
SOUFFRIAU, Arsène - *Concertino*, op. 37 (5'30) •EMB
SOULE, Edmund F. - *Serenade* (1964) •Sha
Sousa, John Philip - *Belle Mahone* (1885) (to J. MOEREMANS)
    Stars and Stripes Forever (BUCHTEL) •1 Sx: A or T/Pno •Kjos
Speaks, Oley - *Sylvia* (LIEDZEN) •GSch
SPIEWAK, Tomasz - *Sonatina*
SPINNLER, Victor - *Russische Rhapsodie* (1926) •Zim
SPITZMÜLLER, Alexandre - *Etude en forme de variation* (1960)
SPORCK, Georges - *Pieces* •Bil
Staigers, Del - *Hazel - Valse caprice* •Eb Sx/Pno •CF
STEINBACHER, Erwin - *Pieces* •Fro
STEINKE, Greg - *Episodes* (1973) (8') •Eb Sx or Bb Sx/Pno (ad lib.)
    •SeMC

STEKKE, Léon - *Pieces* •Ger/An/HE

STEVENS, Halsey - *Dittico* (1972) (4'30) •EH

STEWART - *Short Sonata* •WWS

STILL, William Grant - *Romance* •Bou

Stillwell, Richard - *Visions of You - Reverie* •Bb Sx or Eb Sx/Pno •CF

STOLL, Andre - *Andy* (1993) •INM

STOLL, Stefan - *Chantimage* (1993) •INM

Stradella, Alessandro - *Pieces* •Bil/Mil/Phi

STRADOMSKI, Rafal - *Sonata* (1986-87) (17') •AAR

Strauss, Johann - *Pieces* •Mus/Rub

Strauss, Oscar - *A Waltz Dream* (HARRIS) •Lud

Strauss, Richard - *Allerseelen* (WALTERS) •1 Sx: A or T/Pno •Rub

STRAUWEN, Jean - *Pieces* •EMB/Ger/An

Stravinsky, Igor - *Dance of the Princesses* (*Firebird*) •Mus

STRICKLAND, Lance - *Two Events* •NTS

STRIMER, Joseph - *Pieces* •Dur/Led

STROBL, Otto - *Poêmes* (1978) •Dob

STUCKY, Steven - *Notturno* (1981) •ACA

Stults, R. M. - *The Sweetest Story Ever Told* (HUMMEL) •Rub

SUCCARI, Dia - *"Il est raconté"* (1987) (11'35) •Led
   Fleurs d'un songe (1994) •Led

Sullivan, Arthur - *Let Me Dream Again - The Palms* •Eb Sx/Pno •CF
   The Lost Chord •Eb Sx/Pno •Mol

Suppe, Franz von - *Pieces* •PB

SWAIN, Freda - *Pieces* •BMIC

SWANSON, Roy - *Locust Camp* (1989) (6') •DP

SWANSON, Walter - *Consolation* (1930) (4') •BMIC

TAKÁCS, Jenö - *Two Fantastics*, op. 88 (1969) (12'30) •VD/HD/ApE

TALENS PELLO, Rafael - *Introduction y danza* (1983) •Piler/PEM

TANABE, Tsuneya - *Intermezzo 79* (1979-80)

TANAHASHI-TOKUYAM, Minako - *Trauma* (1993) •INM

TANAKA, Akira - *Au delà d'un rêve* (3'15) (Album [Recueil]) •Bil

TARAS, Yachshenko - *Gobelin* (1993) •INM

TAYLOR, Clifford - *Quattro liriche* (1970) (13') •ACA

Tchaikovsky, Peter Ilyich - *Pieces*

TCHEREPNINE, Alexandre - *Sonatine sportive*, op. 63 (1939) (6')
   •Led

TEAL, Laurence - *Program Solos* •Pres

Telemann, Georg Phillip - *Sonate* (LONDEIX) •Led

Tenaglia, Antonio - *Aria Antica* (MAGANINI) •VAB

Tenaro, L. - *Pieces* •Led

Terschak, Adolf - *Wedding Procession* •Eb Sx/Pno •CF

THIRIET, Maurice - *Adagio* (1965) (5') •Led

Thomas, John - *Beautiful Isle, Old Dog Tray* (FOSTER) •Eb Sx/Pno •CF

Thome, François-Joseph - *Pieces* •CF/Dur/Led

THOMPSON, Kathryn - *Pieces* •1 Sx: A or T (in C)/Pno •South

THOMYS, Alojzy - *10 miniatures...* (1968) •PWM

THON, Franz - *Polonaise* (1940) •Fro

THORNTON, William - *Sonata* •South

TIEDEMANN, Hans-Joachim - *Mixed Pickles...* (1993) •INM

TISNÉ, Antoine - *Espaces irradiés* (1978) (24'30) •Chou
   Music for Stonehenge (1975) (16') •Chou
   Ombres de feu (1988) (18') •adr

Titl, Anton - *Serenade* •Eb Sx/Pno •CF/Bet

TITTLE, Steve - *Sonata* (1967) (12'30) •CMC

Tobani, Theodore - *Hearts and Flowers* •Bb Sx or Eb Sx/Pno •CF

TOBIS, Boris - *2 Pieces* •ECS

Toldra, Eduardo - *Pieces* (AMAZ & BAYER) •1 Sx: A or T/Pno •UME

TOMASI, Henri - *Chant corse* (1932) •Asx or Bb Sx/Pno •Led

Toselli, Enrico - *Pieces* •Bos/GD

TOURNIER, Franz-André - *Prélude et scherzo* (1962) (5'30) •RR
   Variations sur un thème de Cl. Le Jeune (1955) (3'30) •Led

TRAJNOVIC, Vlatimir - *Air et danse* (Album [Recueil]) (2'30) •Bil

Traxler, A. - *Romance* •Bel

TREBINSKY, Arkadi - *Sonatine*, op. 7 (1945) (16') •adr

TROWBRIDGE, Luther - *Pieces* •SeMC/VAB

TRUILLARD, Robert - *Sérénade* (1983) (1'30) •Com

TRUMBAUER, Frank - *Trumbology* •RoMu

TUBIN, Eduard - *Sonate* (1951) (14') •STIM/SMIC

TULL, Fisher - *Dance Suite* (1976)
   Sarabande and Gigue (1976) (5'30) •B&H

TUREWICZ, Kazimierz - *Miniatures rythmiques* (1962) •PWM

TURKIN, Marshall - *Sonata* (1958) •Pres

TUROK, Paul - *Sonata*, op. 72 (1988) (17') •SeMC

TUTHILL, Burnett - *Sonata*, op. 20 (1939) (16') •South

UYTTENHOVE, Yolande - *Sonata*, op. 113 (1985)

VACHEY, Henri - *Pastorale* (Album [Recueil]) (1974) •Zu

VADALA, Kathleen - *Sea Change* (1988) •1 Sx: A or T/Pno •South

VALLIER, Jacques - *Pieces* •Com/VCD/adr

VAN APPLEDORN, Mary-Jeanne - *Liquid Gold* (1982) •DP

VANDELLE, Romuald - *Prélude et gigue* (1958) (5') •Led

Vandercook, Hale - *Pieces* (BUCHTEL) •1 Sx: A or T/Pno •Kjos

Van Doren, T. - *Album Leaf* •HE

Van Goens, Daniel - *Pieces* •Eb Sx/Pno •CF

VASSENA, Nadir - *Nocturnes I - II - III* (1993) •N&B

VAUTE, Maurice - *Cantilène variée* •CBDM

VEERHOFF, Carlos - *Dialogues* (1967) •IMD

VEHAR, Persis - *Four Pieces* (1975) •Pres/Ten

VELLONES, Pierre - *Rapsodie - Trio*, op. 92 (1937) (4'30) •Asx/
   Harp/Celesta or Asx/Pno •Lem

Verdi, Giuseppe - *Grand Air* (from *The Masked Ball*) •Mus

VEREECKEN, Benjamin - *Pieces* •Bar/CF

VIARD, Jules - *Pieces* •Sal

VICTORY, Gerard - *Sonatine* (1973) •adr

Vidal, Paul - *Mélodie* (MULE) •Led

VILEN, Asko - *Sonata* (1976) •FMIC

Villa-Lobos, Heitor - *Song of the Black Swan* (SIMON) •EBMM

Villetard, Albert - *Sous les ombrages* •Bil

VILLETTE, Pierre - *Arabesque* (1986) (8'30) •Led

Vinci, Leonardo - *Sonata* (FLEURY-PRZYSTAS) •PWM

VISVIKIS, Demis - *Cercles* (1989) (10') •Bil

Vivaldi, Antonio - *Pieces* •DP/Mus

Vivier, F. - *Enchantress* •Eb Sx/Pno •CF

VLIET, Brtus van der - *Sax action* (1987) •Mol

VOGEL, Roger - *Temporal Landscapes No. 5* (1981) •DP

Vogt, Gustave - *Pieces* •1 Sx: A or T/Pno •Cen

VOLLEMAN - *Improvisation et allegro* •Mau

VOORN, Joop - *Sonata* (1984) (20') •Don

VORONOV - *Scherzo* •ECS

VOTQUENNE, Victor - *Pieces* •HE/An

VOXMAN, Hymie - *Pieces* •Char/Rub

VUATAZ, Roger - *Incantation*, op. 58/6 (1953) (2'30) •PN

VUSTIN, Alexander - *Autumn sonatina* (1978) •ESC

Wagner, Richard - *Album Leaf - Elsa's Dream...* •Eb Sx/Pno •CF

WAIGNEIN, André - *Pieces* •Scz

Wallace, William V. - *Pieces* •Eb Sx/Pno •CF

WALKER, Richard - *Ballade; Reminiscence* •Ken

WALTER - *Ballad* •WWS

WALTERS, David - *Pieces* •South

WARD, David - *An Abstract* (1963) (4'30) •South
   Prelude and Rondo; Suite

WARD-STEINMAN, David - *Golden Apples* (1981) •Sx/Fortified
   Pno

WARING, Kate - *Plainte* (1985) (4') •1 Sx: S or A/Pno or Org

WARREN, David - *Chorale Fantasy* •1 Sx: A or T/Pno •Lud

WASTALL, Peter - *Pieces* •B&H

WATTERS, Cyril - *Valse coquette* (1961) •B&H

WEBER, Alain - *Mélopée* (1'45); *Saxetto* (3') •Led

Weber, Carl-Maria von - *Pieces*

Weber, Fred - *Andante et rondo* (DECOMPE) •EMB

Webster, Benjamin - *Sweet By and By...* (Foster) •Eb Sx/Pno •CF
WEIGL, Karl - *Love Song* (1941-42) (4'30) •ACA
WEIGL, Vally - *Old Time Burlesque* (1937) (4'30) •ACA
WELSH, Wilmer - *Hymn and Fuging Tune* (1988)
WERDER, Felix - *Unisax* •adr
WERNER, Jean-Jacques - *Cahier d'inventions* (1992) •CDM
Wettge, Gustave - *Fantaisies* •Mil/Mol
WETZEL, Richard - *Vignettes of a Fable Land* (1983) •South
WHITNEY, Maurice - *Melancholy* •1 Sx: A or T/Pno •JS
WIBLÉ, Michel - *Ballade* (1970) •Henn
WIEDOEFT, Rudy - *Pieces* •Rob
Wilber - *Waltz* •WWS
WILDER, Alec - *Sonata* (1969) (11'30) •MMI/B&B
    Suite •LC
    Pieces
WILLIAMS, Clifton - *Theme from Apartment* •WWS
WILLIAMSON, Kristina - *Ballade* (1989) •NoMu
WILSAM, J. - *Floralie* •HE
WILSON - *Pieces* •1 Sx: A or T/Pno •Cen
WILSON, Dana - *The Dream of Icarus* (1985) •Ken
WIRTH, Carl Anton - *Pieces* •LeBl/CPP/adr
Wolf - *The Forsaken Maiden* •WWS
Wood, Sam B. - *Alllamada - Fantaisie-* •Eb Sx/Pno •Mol
WOODBURY, Arthur - *Between Categories*
Woodcock, Robert - *Concerto No. 2* (V. Würth) •1 Sx: S or A/Pno or
    Org •VW
WOODS, Phil - *Sonata* (1980) (16') •Ken
WORLEY, John - *Sonata* (1974) •CF
    Pieces •DP
WUORINEN, Charles - *Divertimento* (1982) (10') •Pet
WURMSER, Lucien - *Pieces* •Bil/ET/Phi
WYSTRAETE, Bernard - *Pieces* •Led
YASINITSKY, Gregory - *Sixth Sense* (1985) (7') •DP
YOSHIMATSU, Takashi - *Fuzzy Bird Sonata* (1991) (22') •Bil
YOSHIOKA, Emmett - *Sonata* (1973) •adr
YOUNES, Nicole - *Sapere audes* (1992) •1 Sx: S+A/Pno •INM
YOUNG, Gordon - *Contempora Suite* •Bel
Zamacois, Joaquin - *Serenada...* (Amaz) •1 Sx: A or T/Pno •UME
ZAMBARANO, Alfred - *Napolitan tarantella* •Sha
ZANETTOVICH, Daniele - *Prima sonata* (1966-68) •Piz
ZANINELLI, Luigi - *Autumn Music* •Sha
ZEBRE, Demetrij - *Intermezzo saxofonico* •YUC
ZECCHI, Adone - *Recitativi ed arie* (1983) (7') •CoMu
ZELLER, Karl - *Schenkt man sich Rosen in Tirol* •Mol
ZONN, Paul Martin - *Desmond Dream* (1991) (24') •ACA
ZSCHUPPE, Frank - *Sonatine* (1992) •INM

Alto Saxophone and Orchestra

Orchestra unless otherwise indicated (Orchestre, sauf
indication contraire).

AATZ, Michel - *Frühling* (11')
ABE, Komei - *Divertimento* (1951-53)
ABSIL, Jean - *Ballade*, op. 156 (1971) •Asx/Chamber Orch
    Berceuse (1932) (5') •1 Sx: A or T •An/Ger
    Fantaisie-Caprice, op. 152 (1971) (5') •Asx/Str or Band or Pno
        •Lem
    Sicilienne (1950) (9') •1 Sx: A or T •An/Ger
ALBERT, Eugen d' - *Saxophon Musik* (193x)
ALBERTH, Rudolf - *Saxophonmusik* (1950) (19') •adr
ALESSANDRO, Raffaele d' - *Serenade*, op. 12 •Asx/Str Orch
AMELLER, André - *Concertino*, op. 125 (1959) (12'30) •Asx/Str
        Orch et Fl obligée •Phi
    Suite d'après Rameau (1960) (9') •Asx/Str •ET

AMIROV, Fikret - *Concerto* (1974)
    Poème Symphonique (1977)
AMRAM, David - *Ode to Lord Buckley (Concerto)* (1980) (30') •Pet
ANCELIN, Pierre - *Saxophonie* (1983) (8') •Asx/Str Orch •Bil
ANDERBERG, Carl Olof - *Konsert* (1969) •FS
ANDRIESSEN, Juriaan - *Concertino* (1966/67) •Don
APOTHELOZ, Jean - *Sérénade* (1951) •adr
ATWOOD, Charles - *Alienated Thing* (1989) •Asx/Electr.Vln •CMA
BADINGS, Henk - *Concerto* (1951) (20') •Don
BAGOT, Maurice - *Concerto* (1951)
BAILY, Jean - *Ballade* •Asx/Str •HM
BAKER, Michael - *Capriccio* (1986) CMC
BALAKAUSKAS, Osvaldas - *Polilogas* (1991) (20') •Asx/Str •PWM
BARBIER, René - *Pièce concertante*, op. 95 (1958) (10') •CBDM
BARCK, Ed. - *Konzert*, op. 6
BARDI, Benno - *Musik* (1931) •Asx/Chamber Orch
BARILLER, Robert - *Rapsodie bretonne* (1953) (12') •Led
BARNES, Milton - *Concerto* (1975) •Asx/Str Orch •CMC
    Medley (1979) •1 Sx: A+S/Str Orch •CMC
BAUMANN, Herbert - *Variationen über ein englisches Volkslied*
        (1968) (13'45) •Asx/Str Orch •MV
BAUZIN, Pierre-Philippe - *1er Concerto*, op. 18 (1959) (16') •adr
    2me Concerto, op. 55 (1966) (18') •Asx/Str Orch •adr
    Poême, op. 20 (1960) (14') •adr
BEALL, John - *Concerto* (1991) •adr
BEAUME - *Suite*
BECKER, Günter - *Correspondances* (1966/68) •Eb Cl/BsCl/Asx/
        Chamber Orch •HG/IMD
BEERS, Jacobus - *Concerto* •Voice/Asx
BELL, Derek - *Honest Pleasures* (1981) •Asx/Chamber Ensemble
BENSON, Warren - *Aeolian Song* (5') •Asx/Orch or Band or Pno
        •MCA
    Concertino (1955) (13') •Asx/Orch or Band or Pno •MCA
    Star Edge (1966-67) (18') •Asx/Orch or Band •MCA
BENTZON, Jorgen - *Introduction, Variations and Rondo* (1938) (17')
        •Asx/Str Orch •SOBM
BERGHMANS, José - *Concerto lyrique* (1974) (14') •EFM
BERGSTRÖM, Harry - *Suite* (1936) •FMIC
BERNIER, René - *Hommage à Sax* (1958) (10') •Asx/Orch or Band
        or Pno •Led
BIENVENU, Lily - *Symphonie concertante* •adr
BIGOT, Eugène - *Prélude et danses* (1961) (10') •Led
BILIK, Jerry - *Concertino* (1973) (11') •Asx/Orch or Band or Pno •CL
BILOTTI, Anton - *Concerto*
BINGE, Ronald - *Concerto* (1956) (14') •IAC
BINNEY, Oliver - *Conecrt Suite* (1964) (10') •Asx/Str Orch •adr
BIRUKOFF, Andrei - *Concerto* (1975)
BODART, Eugen - *Concertino* (14') •Hen
    Sonatina (10'30) •Hen
BOGULAWSKI, Edward - *Muisica concertante* (1988) •PWM
BOND, Victoria - *Concerto* (1993)
BONNEAU, Paul - *2 Caprices en forme de valse* (1950-80) •Led
    Concerto (1944) (15'30) •Led
    Pièce concertante dans l'esprit jazz (1944) (10') •Led
    Suite (1944) (7') •Led
BORCK, Edmund von - *Concerto*, op. 6 (1932) (16') •EK
BORISOV, Lilcho - *Concertino* (1983)
BORSARI, Amédée - *Concerto* (1947) (18') •Asx/Str Orch •Bil
BORSCHEL, E. - *Kubanishes Liebeslied* •1 Sx: A or T •Fro
BOSSE, Denis - *...d'un léger souffle cosmique* (1987) (10') •Sx Solo
        B+A+S/Str
BOURLAND, Roger - *Minstrel* (1982)
BOUTRY, Roger - *Divertimento* (1964) (9') •Asx/Str Orch •Led
    Sérénade (1961) (14') •Sal
BOZZA, Eugène - *Concertino* (1938) (15') •Led

BRACHT, Thomas - *Concertino* (1982) (15') •Asx/Str Orch

BRANDON, Seymour - *Bachburg Concerto No. 2* (1978) •Asx/Pno/
Orch •adr

BRANT, Henry - *Concerto* (1941) (20') •CFE

BRÄU, Albert - *Leichte Kost* •Fro

BRENTA, Gaston - *Saxiana* (1962) (7'30) •Asx/Str Orch •Led

BREVER, Karl - *Atonalyse II* (1957) •5 Soloists: Tpt/Cl/Vln/Vla/Sx/
Str Orch •Led

BROWN, Anthony - *Beyond Oblivion* •Asx/Chamber Orch orTape
•SeMC

BROWN, Tony - *Concerto*, op. 18 (1968)

BRUNNER, Hans - *Fantaisie* •Asx/Str Orch •Kneu

BUHR, Glenn - *The Ebony Tower* (1986) •CMC

BULL, Edward Hagerup - *Concerto*, op. 52a (1980) (17') •NMI
3 Morceaux brefs (1955) (11'30) •ET

BULOW, Harry - *Concerto* (1985) •adr

BUMCKE, Gustav - *Concertino*, op. 95 (1961) •Asx/Chamber Orch
or Wind Ensemble •R&E

Pieces

BUONO, Michel - *Concertino* (1942) (11')

BUSCH, Adolph - *Nocturne*, op. 58a (1932)

BUSSER, Henri - *Au pays de Léon et de Salamanque*, op. 116 (1943)
(4'30) •Led

CABUS, Peter - *Facetten* (1974) •Asx/12 Str •Mau

CALMEL, Roger - *Concertino* (1952) (11') •Heu/Led
Concertino (1958) (14') •Asx/Chamber Orch •Heu/Led
Concerto (1972) •Chou

CALTABIANO, Ronald - *Concerto* (1983) (22') •MeM

CAMILLERI, Charles - *Suite* (1960) •Wa/Che

CARISCH - *Concertino* (1940) •Car

CARLES, Marc - *3 Chants incantatoires* (1965) (14'30) •Asx/Str
Orch •ET

CARPENTER, Kurt - *The Marlboro Concerto* (1971-72) (12'30)
•Asx/Str Orch •adr

CARVALHO, F. Urban - *Song and Dance* (1970) •Asx/Orch or Band
or Pno •Pres

CASTRO, Dino - *Concerto* (1978) •1 Sx: S+A+B/Chamber Orch

CENTEMERI, Gian Luigi - *Concerto* (1964) •Asx/Str

CHALLAN, René - *Concerto* (1946) (20') •Led

CHARPENTIER, Jacques - *Concert n° 5* (1974) (23') •Asx/Str Orch
•Led

CHEVREUILLE, Raymond - *Double Concerto*, op. 34 (1946) (21')
•Pno/Asx •CBDM

CHIHARA, Paul - *Concerto* (1980) (13'30) •1 Sx: Sno+S+A

CIBULKA, Franz - *Kaleidoscop* (1981) (4'30); *Saxophonic* (1981)

CLERISSE, Robert - *Chanson à bercer* (4') •adr

COATES, Eric - *Saxo-Rhapsody* (1936) (11') •Asx/Orch or Band or
Pno •B&H

COHN, Arthur - *Variations* (1945) •Cl/Asx/Str Orch •EV

CONSTANT, Franz - *Concerto*, op. 13 (1963) (13') •Met
Fantaisie, op. 41 (12') •Bil

CONSTANT, Marius - *Concertante* (1978-79) (20') •Ric
Musique de concert (1954) (10') •Led

COOPER, Paul - *Concertino* (1982) (18') •Sal

CORNIOT, René - *Eglogue et Danse pastorale* (1946) (14') •Led

COSMA, Edgar - *Invocation*

COWELL, Henry - *Air and Scherzo* (1961) •Asx/Chamber Orch
•AMP/ACA

COWLES, Colin E. - *Rhapsody* (1977) (10') •Asx/Str Orch •adr

COYNER, Lou - *Solo...* (1985) •Asx/Ensemble

CRAGUN, J. Beach - *Concerto No. 1*, op. 21 (1925) •Rub

CRESTON, Paul - *Concerto*, op. 26 (1941) (17') •Asx/Orch or Band
or Pno •GSch

CUNNINGHAM, H. - *Concerto* (1960)

DAMAIS, Emile - *Esquisse symphonique* (1944) (10') •Bil

DAMASE, Jean-Michel - *Concertstück*, op. 16 (1950) (9'30) •Led

D'ANGELO, Nicholas - *Capriccio...* (1967) (8') •adr
Introduction and Fantasy (1967) (10') •Asx/Chamber Orch •adr

DARIJAN, Bozii - *Concert* •YUC

DAUTREMER, Marcel - *Concerto*, op. 61 (1962) (12'30) •Asx/Str
Orch •Lem

DAVID, Karl Heinrich - *Concerto* (1947) •Asx/Str Orch

DEBUSSY, Claude - *Rapsodie* (1904) (10') •Dur

DECADT, Jean - *Concerto 1* (1973) •CBDM

DEFAYE, Jean-Michel - *Concerto* (1983) •SL

DEFOSSE, Henry - *Elégie* (1952) (6')
Sicilienne et Gavotte (1940/42) (3'30);

DEL BORGO, Elliot - *Concertino* (1972) •Asx/Str Orch

DENISOV, Edison - *Concerto* (1986-92) (25') •Led

DEPELSENAIRE, Jean-Marie - *Concertino* (1969) (9') •Ob/Asx
•Chou
Dialogue (1966) (6'30) •Tpt/Asx •ET
Suite concertante (1971) (10') •ET

DERR, Elwood - *Elegy* (1963) •adr

DERVAUX, André-Jean - *Nocturne en Saxe* (1955) •Com

DESPALJ, Pavle - *Concerto* (1966) (11') •South

DIJK, Jan van - *Concertino* (1953) (9') •Don

Dinicu, Grigoras - *Hora Staccato* (HEIFETZ) •1 Sx: A or T •CF

DJEMIL, Enyss - *Concerto* (1974) (16') •1 Sx: S+A+T •adr

DMITRIEV, Gueorgui Petrovitch - *Labyrinth* (20') •adr

DOERR, Clyde - *Valse Impromptu*

DONDEYNE, Désiré - *Symphonie concertante* (1970-71) (16'30)
•Chou

DRESSEL, Erwin - *Capriccio*, op. 45 (9') •Asx/Str Orch
Concerto, op. 27 (1932) (24') •RE
Concerto (1965) •2 Sx: SA

DUBOIS, Pierre-Max - *Concerto* (1959) (17') •Asx/Str Orch •Led
Concertstück (1955) (10') •Led
Divertissement (1953) (10') •Led
Le Lièvre et la tortue (1957) (4'30) •Led
Moments musicaux (1985) (17'30) •Bil
Sonatine (1966) (8') •Led

DUIJK, Guy - *Introduction et Danse* (10') •Mau

EINFELD, Dieter - *Imaginationen II* (1980-81) (19')

EISENMANN, Will - *Concertino*, op. 69 (1962) (11') •Asx/Chamber
Orch •adr
Concerto, op. 38 (1937) (14') •Asx/Str Orch •Uni
Concerto da camera (1945-48) (15') •Asx/Str Orch •Uni
Konzert (1962) (12') •2 Sx: SA

EITHLER, Esteban - *Concertino* (1953) •Asx/Str Orch
3 Canciones

ELBE, Carl - *Konzert* (1936) (15') •HR/Fro

ELIASSON, Anders - *Sinfonia concertante* (1989) (27') •SMIC

ERDMANN, Dietrich - *Konzert* •1 Sx: A+S •R&E
Konzertstück •Asx/Chamber Orch •R&E

ERICKSON, Nils - *Concerto* (1952) (23') •STIM

ERIKSSON, Joseph - *Konsert* (1959) (14') •Asx/Orch or Band •Ton

EYCHENNE, Marc - *Concerto* (1966) •Asx/Str Orch/Perc •adr

FAITH, Walter - *Divertimento* (1951) •Asx/Pno/Tpt •adr

FARBERMAN, Harold - *Concerto* (1965) (10'30) •Asx/Str Orch

FELD, Jindrich - *Concerto* (1980) •1 Sx: S+A+T/Orch or Band •Kjos

FENNELLY, Brian - *Concerto* (1982-84) (32') •Asx/Str Orch/Perc
•EPN

FERNANDEZ, Oscar - *Noturno*
Sombra suave •Asx/Str Orch

FERRE, Stephen - *From Her Husband's Hand...* (1990)

FINNEY, Ross Lee - *Concerto* (1974) •Asx/Orch or Band or Pno •Pet

FISCHER, Eric - *Concerto* (1982)

FISCHER, Clare - *Rhapsody* •Asx/Chamber Orch •adr

FLIARKOVSKI - *Concerto* •ECP

FLOTHUIS, Marius - *Sinfonietta concertante*, op. 55 (1954-55) (15') •Cl/Asx •Don

FONGAARD, Bjorn - *Concerto*, op. 120, no. 11 (1976) (17') •NMI

FORSYTH, Malcolm - *Tre vie* (1992) (20') •Ric

FRANCESCONI, Luca - *Trama* (1987) (20') •Ric

FRANCHETTI, Arnold - *Seven Little Steps on the Moon* (1976) •Asx/Chamber Ensemble •adr

FREEDMAN, Harry - *Scenario* (1970) •Asx/Electr. Bs Guit •CMC

FREUND, J. - *Concertino*

FROSCHAUER, H. - *Rhapsody*

GAL, Hans - *Suite*, op. 102b (1949) (18') •Asx/Chamber Orch •WWS

GASTINEL, Gérard - *Assonance* •Asx/Str Orch
  Concerto (1984) •Asx/Str Orch

GAUBERT, Philippe - *Poême élégiaque* (1911) (8') •South

GENZMER, Harald - *Konzert* •R&E

GERHARD, Fritz - *Concerto breve* (14') •Asx/Str Orch •Sal

GILSON, Paul - *1er Concerto* (1902) (11'30) •Ger/An
  2me concerto (1902) (10'30) •RTB

GIMENO, J. - *Caprici*

GIRARDIN, Jean-Paul - *L'Insolitude* (1983) •Asx/Vibr/Str Orch

GLASER, Werner - *Concertino* (1935) •STIM
  Suite No. 3, op. 16 (1935) (8') •Asx/Str Orch •STIM

GLAZOUNOV, Alexander - *Concerto en Mib* (1934) (14') •Asx/Str Orch •Led

GLICK, Srul Irving - *Lament and Cantorial Chant* (1985) •Sx/Str Orch •CMC

GODZINSKY, George de - *Pièce romantique* (1966) (4'15) •FMIC
  Sxysrunoelma (1969) (4'30) •FMIC

GORBUISKIA, Vladimir - *Concerto* •Asx/Jazz Orch

GORBULSKIS, Benjaminas - *Concerto* (1969)

GÖRNER, Hans Georg - *Concertino*, op. 31 (1957) •2 Sx: AT •Hof

GOTKOVSKY, Ida - *Concerto* (1966) (16'30) •ET

GOTLIB, A. - *Concerto*

GROSSE, Erwin - *Capriccio*, op. 43 (1954) (5'); *Concerto* •adr

GROVLEZ, Gabriel - *Suite* (1915) (16') •Fuz/South

GRUND, Bert - *Triple-Konzert*

GRUNDMAN, Claire - *Concertante* (1972) •Asx/Orch or Band or Pno •B&H

GULDA, Friedrich - *Music...* (triple concerto) •Trb/Bugle/Sx

GUNAROPULOS, George - *Concerto No. 1* (1935) (22') •FBC/FMIC
  Concerto No. 2 (1946) (22') •FBC/FMIC

GUNSENHEIMER, Gustav - *Concertino n° 4* (1986) (10') •1 Sx: Sno+S/A/Str Orch •VF

GUREWICH, Jascha - *Concerto*, op. 102 (1926) •Rub

HAIDMAYER, Karl - *Concerto n° 2* (1981)
  Popludium IV (1988/91) •Asx/Str Orch

HAÏK-VANTOURA, Suzanne - *Visages d'Adam* (1966) (20') •adr

HALFFTER, Ernesto - *Cavatine sobre...* •ME

HALSTENSON, Michael - *Ballade* (1984) (13')

HARTLEY, Walter - *Concerto No. 2* (1989) (10'30) •DP

HASQUENOPH, Pierre - *Concertino*, op. 20 (1960) (10'30) •Heu
  Concerto, op. 43a (1982) (14') •Asx/Str •ME

HATORI, Ryoichi - *Concerto* (1948)

HAYES, Jack - *Concertino*

HEIDER, Werner - *Typen* (1957) (6') •A&S

HEININEN, Paavo - *Concerto*, op. 50 (1983) (30') •FMIC

HEKSTER, Walter - *Between two worlds* (1977) (12') •Don

HEWITT, Harry - *Concerto No. 1* (1972) (20') •adr
  Concerto No. 2 (1972) (15') •adr

HILDEMANN, Wolfgang - *Concerto coreografico* (1976) (22')

HILL, Dorothy - *Concert*

HODKINSON, Sidney - *Another Man's Poison* (1970) (6'30) •1 Sx: A or T •adr
  Edge of the Olde One (1977) •Asx/Chamber Orch •Pres

HOFMANN, Thomas - *Suite* (1986) (9')

Konzertantes (1988) (20') •Pno/Asx/Str Orch

HOFMANN, Wolfgang - *Concertino* (1982) •Asx/Str Orch

HOLBROOKE, Joseph - *Concerto in Bb*, op. 115 (1939) (15') •Cl+Asx+Tsx+Ssx •B&H

HOLLAND, Dulcie - *Aria* (1952) (5') •Asx/Str Orch •adr

HOLLOWAY, Robin - *Double Concerto* (1987) •Cl/Asx

HOWRANI, Walid - *Concerto* (1990) •Asx/Str/Perc

HUBERT, Eduardo - *"Por las Americas"* (1992) (13')

HUGGLER, John - *Elaboration*, op. 69 (1967) (10') •Asx/Orch or Band or Pno •CFE

HURÉ, Jean - *Andante* (1915) •South
  Concerstuck (1910) •South

HUSA, Karel - *Elégie et Rondeau* (1960) (10') •Led

IBERT, Jacques - *Concertino da camera* (1935) (11') •Led

IDO - *Concerto* •Lem

INDY, Vincent d' - *Choral varié*, op. 55 (1903) (9') •Dur

ISHIMARU, Kan - *2 Pièces* (1958) •Asx/Chamber Orch

ITO, Yashuhito - *Concerto* (1987) (9'15) •Lem

IWASHIRO, Taro - *Colors* (1992)

JACOB, Gordon - *Miscellanies* (1976) (13') •Asx/Band or Str Orch
  Rhapsody (1948) (9') •Asx/Str •Mills

JACOBI, Wolfgang - *Aria* (9'); *Concerto* (1962)
  Serenade and Allegro (1961) (11')

JAMES, Lewis - *Music*, op. 9 (1955/85) (9'30) •MMI

JENNY, Albert - *Rhapsodie* (1936) •Asx/Str Orch •adr

JESTL, Bernhard - *Rhapsodie* •ECA

JETHS, Willem - *Concerto* (1985) (15') •Asx/Str Orch •Don

JOHNSON, Allen - *Nightsong* (6') •Asx/Chamber Orch •adr

JOHNSTON, David - *Konzert* (1982)

JOLAS, Betsy - *Points d'or* (1981) •1 Sx: S+A+T+B •Ric

KANE, Jack - *Concerto*

KANITZ, Ernest - *Intermezzo concertante* (1948/53) •Asx/Orch or Band or Pno •USC

KAREVA, Hilar - *Concerto No. 1*, op. 25

KARKOFF, Maurice - *Concertino*, op. 15 (1955) (13') •Asx/Str Orch/Perc •Sue

KARLINS, M. William - *Concerto* (1981-82) (22') •ACA

KASHLAYEV, M. - *Concerto* (1975)

KATAYEV, Vitaly - *Concerto* (1980)

KAZANDJIEV, Vasil - *Double concerto* (1962) •Asx/Pno

KECHLEY, David - *Concerto* (1983) •Asx/Chamber Orch

KELKEL, Manfred - *Concertino* (1961) (16')
  Musique funèbre (1960) (9')
  Rhapsodie, op. 12 (1961) (18') •Ric

KERSHNER, Brian - *Chamber Concerto* (1994) •Asx/Chamber Orch

KEURIS, Tristan - *Concerto* (1971) (11') •Don

KIRCHSTEIN, Harold - *Musik für Junggesellen Suite* (20') •adr

KLEINSINGER, George - *Street Corner Concerto* (1953) •Chap

KLOTZMAN, Dorothy - *Concerto* (12')

KNAIFEL, Alexandre Aronovitch - *Agnus Dei* (1985) (120-150') •Sx/Orch/Perc/Tape

KNIGHT, Morris - *Concerto* (1962) (12') •Asx/Str Orch •adr

KOCH, Erland von - *Concerto* (1958) (17') •Asx/Str Orch •Mt/Peer
  Concerto piccolo (1962-76) (13') •1 Sx: S+A/Str Orch •Br&Ha
  Rondo (1983) •Asx/Str Orch •DP
  Vision (1950) (6') •Asx/Str Orch •STIM

KOCH, Frederick - *Concertino* (1964-65) (15') •Asx/Orch or Band •SeMC/MCA

KOERBLER, Milivoj - *Varijacije* (1956) •Asx/Jazz Orch •adr

KOIVISTIONEN, Eero - *Northern Lights* (1987) (6') •FMIC

KOJEDNIKOV - *Concertino* •ECP

KOLDITZ, Hans - *Concertino* (1979) (12') •Asx/Harmonie •adr

KONOE, Hidétaké - *Concertino* (1970)

KOPELENT, Marek - *Hkairy* (1974)
  Plauderstündchen (1974-75) •Br&Ha

KORN, Peter Jona - *Concerto*, op. 31 (1956) (16'30) •Sal

KOX, Hans - *Concerto* (1978) •Don
   Face to Face (1992) (20') •Asx/Str Orch •Don

KRAMER, Martin - *Concerto* (1933) (26')

KRAUS, Marco - *Suite concertante* •1 Sx: Sno+S+A+T+B

KREMENLIEV, Boris - *Tune* •Asx/Hn/Str •adr

KRIEGER, Edino - *Brasiliana* (1960) •Asx/Str Orch

KROL, Bernhard - *Aria & Tarentella*, op. 37 (1953-68) (11') •AMP/
   Sim

KRSTO, Odak - *Divertimento* •Asx/Str Orch •YUC

KRUMLOVSKY, Claus - *Concertino* (1963) (10') •Led
   Concerto •adr

KUERGEL, Hannes - *Rhapsodie* •NYPL/Krenn

KUESTER, Herbert - *Kentucky Serenade* (1970) (3'52) •Asx/Str Orch

KYNASTON, Trent - *Concerto* (1976) (19') •Asx/Orch or Wind Orch
   •DP

LACOUR, Guy - *Hommage à Jacques Ibert* (1972) (13') •Bil
   Pièce concertante (1975-76) (8'30) •1 Sx: T or A/Str Orch or Wind
      Orch •Bil

LACROIX, Eugène - *Pan*

LAMB, John David - *Concerto* (1970)

LAPHAM, Claude - *Concerto in Ab* •Lee

LA PORTA, John - *Concertino*

LARSEN, Lindorff E. - *Concerto* (1954) •WH

LARSSON, Lars Erik - *Konsert*, op. 14 (1934) (20') •Asx/Str Orch
      •KG/CG

LATHAM, William Peters - *Concertino* (1968) •DP
   Concerto Grosso (1960) (18') •2 Sx: SA/Orch or Band

LAURENT, Léo - *King-saxo* (1939) (2'30) •Asx/Jazz Orch •Cos

LEESON, Cecil - *Concerti No. 1, 2, 3* (1947) (1948-60) (1952)
   Concertino (1948) •Asx/Winds or Chamber Orch •South

LEGLEY, Victor - *Concert...*, op. 85 (1975) (11'15) •CBDM/Bil
   Concerto grosso (1976) •Vln/Asx/Chamber Orch •Bil/Mau

LEMAIRE, Félix - *Concertino* (12') •Asx/Str Orch •adr

LENNON, John Anthony - *Symphonic Rhapsody* (1985) •Pet

LEVITIN, Jurij - *Concerto* (1951) •Asx/Tpt/Orch de variété

LIC, Leslaw - *Koncerto* (1973) •adr

LIFSCHITZ, Max - *Concerto* (1992) •Asx/Chamber Orch

LIPTAK, David - *Red shift* (1988) (16') •adr

LIST, Andrew - *Concerto* (1990) •adr

LOEFFLER, Charles Martin - *Divertissement...* (1900) (8') •South

LONDON, Edwin Wolf - *Pressure Points* (1972) (10') •adr

LONGY, George Léopold - *Impression* (1902)

LONQUE, Georges - *Images d'Orient*, op. 20 (1935) (11') •Led

LOVELOCK, James - *Konzert* (1970) •Asx/Str Orch

LOVELOCK, William - *Concerto* (1973)

LUCAS, Leighton - *Sonatina concertante* (1939) •Asx/Chamber Orch

LUNDER, Hans - *Konsertino*

LUNDIN, Dag - *Concerto...* (1979) (16') •Asx/Chamber Orch •STIM

LUTYENS, Elisabeth - *Chamber Concerto*, op. 8/2 (1940-41) (triple
      concerto) •Cl/Tsx/Pno/Str •Che

MACBRIDE, Robert Guyn - *Concerto...* (14') •Asx+Cl •ACA

MAIER SCHANZ, Josef - *Verletzte Gefühle* •Sx/Ensemble •INM

MALIPIERO, Gian Francesco - *Serenissima* (1961) (21') •Uni

MARACZEK, F. - *Sommerabend am Berg, Impression* •HD

MARBE, Myriam - *Concerto* (33') •1 Sx: B+A+Sno •EMu

MARCHAL, Dominique - *Mouvement V* •Asx/Str •adr

MARCHAND, Jean-Christophe - *Hêtraies* (1987) (10') •Asx/Str •adr

MARINUZZI, Gino - *Concertino* (1936) (triple concerto) •Pno/Ob/
      Sx/Str Orch

MAROS, Miklos - *Concerto* (1990) (22') •SMIC

MARTIN, Frank - *Ballade* (1938) (15') •Asx/Str Orch/Pno/Timp
      •Uni

MARTIN, Frédérick - *Concerto - 2 Titres* •Sx successifs/Orch

MARTINO, Donald - *Concerto* (1986) (23') •MDM

MASSIAS, Gérard - *Laude* (1961) (11') •Asx/Str Orch •Bil

MASSIS, Amable - *Poème* (1942) (18'30) •Bil

MATHER, Bruce - *Elegy* (1959) (6') •Asx/Str Orch •Wa/CMC

MATTON, Roger - *Concerto* (1948) •Asx/Pno/Perc/Str •Comp

MAURICE, Paule - *Tableaux de Provence* (1954-59) (12') •Lem

MAYS, Walter - *Concerto* (1974) (14') •Asx/Chamber Orch •BM

MEIJERING, Chiel - *Onderwerping* (1986) (18') •Don

MERANGER, Paul - *Concerto*, op. 20 (1977) (15') •Bil

MEULEMANS, Arthur - *Rhapsodie* (1942) (5'30) •Ger/An/CBDM

MICHAEL, Edward - *Pièce brève* (1967) (9')

MIEREANU, Costin - *Kammer-Koncert n° 1* (1984-85) (16') •1 Sx:
      Sno+A+T+Bs •Sal

MIHAJLO, Zivanovic - *Rapsodija* •YUC

MILHAUD, Darius - *Scaramouche* (1937) (10') •Sal

MOESCHINGER, Albert - *Concerto...*, op. 83 (1958) (15') •B&H

MOLLER, Kai - *Rhapsodie* (1953) •Asx/Str •WH

MONDELLO, Nuncio Francis - *Introduction and Allegro* (1959)
      •Asx/Str Orch •adr

MOREAU, Léon - *Pastorale* (1903) •Led

MORITZ, Edvard - *Concerto*, op. 97 (1939) •Merc

MOULAERT, Raymond - *Tango-caprice* (1942) (7') •CBDM/EMB

MOUTET & DERVAUX - *Nocturne en Saxe* (1955) •Com

MUCZYNSKI, Robert - *Concerto*, op. 41 (1981) (17') •Asx/Chamber
      Orch •Pres

MULDOWNEY, Dominic - *Concerto* (1984) (18') •Asx/Chamber
      Orch •Uni

MULLER VON KULM, Walter - *Concertino*, op. 81 (1964-65) •Asx/
      Str Orch

MURGIER, Jacques - *Concerto* (1960) (23') •Asx/Str Orch •ET

NATANSON, Tadeus - *Kincert Podwojny* (1959) •2 Sx: AT •AAW/
      AMP

NELHYBEL, Vaclav - *Adagio and Allegro* (1986-88) •1 Sx: S+A
      •JCCC

NICOLAUS, Louis - *Concerto* (1963) •Asx/Str Orch •adr

NICULESCU, Stefan - *Cantos* (1984-85) (22') •1 Sx: Sno+A+T+B

NIKIPROWETZKY, Tolia - *Tetraktys* (1976) •1 Sx: S+A+T+B/
      Chamber Orch •adr

NILSSON, Bo - *La Bran - Anagramme sur Ilmar Laaban* (1963-76)
      (16') •Sx Solo: S+A/Chorus/Orch/Tape/
      Electr. •STIM
   Ormhuvud I + II (1974)
   Portrait de femmes n° 2 (1976) •Asx/Str •SMIC

NIXON, Dohamain - *Suite*

NODA, Ryo - *Gen concerto* (1974/1979-81) •Asx/Str Orch/Pno/Perc
      •Led

O'BRIEN, Eugene - *Concerto* (1992)

ODAK, Krsto - *Divertimento*, op. 66 (1957) •Asx/Str Orch •YUC

OGANESYAN, Edgar - *Concerto*, op. 21 (1961-62) •Asx/Symphonic
      Jazz Orch •SOC

OLAH, Tiberiu - *Obelisc pentru...* (22') •1 Sx: Sno+A+B

OLBRISCH, Franz-Martin - *"...Hu ha..."* (1987) (20') •adr

OLIVE, Vivienne - *Music* (1981) •2 Sx: AA •DP

ORREGO SALAS, Juan - *Quattro Lirich brevi*, op. 61 (1967) (17')
      •Asx/Chamber Orch •PIC

OTT, David - *Concerto* (1987) •Asx/Chamber Orch or Wind En-
      semble or Pno •Eto

PALENICEK, Josef - *Concerto* (1966) (25') •CHF

PALESTER, Roman - *Concertino* (1938/78) (15') •Asx/Str Orch
      •CPWM

PANTON, David - *Concerto* (1965) •adr

PAPANDOPULO, Boris - *Concerto* (198x)

PASCUZZI, Gregory - *Concerto* (1988) •Asx/Chamber Orch

PATACHICH, Ivan - *Concerto* (20') •Asx/Str
   Jei 1+4 (1989) (12') •1 Sx: S+A+CBs/Instrumental Ensemble

PAUL, Ernst - *Kammerkonzert*, op. 29 (1931)

PAULSON, Gustaf - *Konsert*, op. 105 (1959) (15') •Ton/STIM
PAVLENKO, Serguei - *Concerto* (1975) (15') •adr
PEIXINHO, Jorge - *Concerto* (1961) (20')
    Passage intérieur (1989) (16') •1 Sx: Sno+S+A+T+B/Instrumental Ensemble
PELEMANS, Willem - *Concerto* (1976) •Mau
PELLEGRIN, Adrien - *1ère fantaisie appasionata...* •Gras
PENBERTHY, James - *Concerto* (1970) (10') •adr
PERRIN, Marcel -*Fantaisie tzigane* (1941) (5') •Asx/Orch or Band or Pno •GD
    Mirage (1938) (2'30) •Led
    Nocturne (1945) (7'30) •GD
PETTERSON, Allan - *Symphony No. 16* (1979) (25') •STIM
PHILIBA, Nicole - *Concerto* (1962) (14') •Asx/Str Orch/Perc •Bil
PIEPER, René - *Concerto* (1984) (25') •Bil
PIERNÉ, Paul - *Concertino* (1949) •Asx/Orch or Harmonie
PIKOUL - *Concertino*
PONJEE, Ted - *The square world* (1984) (15') •Don
POOT, Marcel - *Ballade* (1948) (8') •Sch
    Concerto (14'15)
POPOVICI, Fred - *Heterosynthesis II* (1986) (18') •1 Sx: S+A+T
PORCELIJN, David - *Pulverization II* (1973) (15') •Don
PRISS - *Concert*
PROHASKA, Miljenko - *Dilemma* (1964) •Asx/Jazz Orch •adr
PUTET, Jean - *Astrée* •Doy
RAMAN, gedert - *Concerto* (1964) •Asx/Str Orch/Pno/Perc •Mu
RAPHAEL, Günter - *Concertino*, op. 71 (1951) (16') •Br&Ha
RARIG, John - *Dance Episode*; *Night Song* •DP
RASQUIER, Hélène - *Obsession* (1993) (9'40) •Asx/Str Orch •Zu
Ravel, Maurice - *Pièce en forme de habanera* (HOEREE) •Led
REDDIE, Bill - *Concerto* (16'); *Gypsy Fantasy* (3')
REDGATE, R. - *Inventio* •Asx/Ensemble •Lem
REUCHSEL, Maurice - *Syphax*, op. 72 (1955) •Bil
REYMOND, Roger - *Tryptique* (1971) (11') •Asx/Str Orch •adr
RIBARI, Antal - *Dialogues* •B&H
RIEDEL, Georg - *Concerto burlesco* (1981) (17') •Asx/Jazz group/Orch •STIM
RIVIER, Jean - *Concertino* (MULE) (1949) (14') •Sal
    Concerto (1955) (17'30) •Asx/Tpt/Str Orch •Bil
RIVIERE, Jean-Pierre - *Concertino*
RIVOLTA, Renato - *Solid machinery* (1992) (10') •Asx/Chamber Orch
ROBERT, Lucie - *Double Concerto* (1968) (28') •Asx/Pno •Bil
ROBJOHN, William - *Introduction, Theme and Variations* (1879)
ROCHOW, Erich - *Konzert* (1966) •FF
RODBY, John - *Concerto* (1971)
ROGERS, Rodney - *The Nature...* (1987) (16'30)
ROGISTER, Fernand - *Concertino* (1946) •Bosw
ROKEACH, Martin - *Prelude and Fantasy* •DP
ROLIN, Etienne - *Maschera* (1980) (17') •1 Sx: S+A+B/Pno/Chamber Orch •adr
ROSEN, Jerome - *Concerto* (1957) (18') •CFE/ACA
ROSENTHAL, Manuel - *Saxophon' marmelade* (1929) (6') •ME
ROSSÉ, François - *Triangle...* (1980-81) (12') •Asx/Str Orch •Bil
ROY, Camille - *Concerto* (1991)
RUBBERT, Rainer - *Concertino* (1989) (16') •Asx/Pno/Str Orch/Perc •adr
RÜDENAUER, Meinhard - *Konzert* (18') •Asx/Chamber Orch •CA
RUEFF, Jeanine - *Chanson et passepied* (1951) (2'30) •Led
    Concertino, op. 17 (1951-53) (15') •Led
RUNCHAK, Vladymyr - *Concerto* (15') •Asx/Chamber Orch
RUSSO, William - *Interplay* (1987) •Asx/Chamber Orch
SAGVIK, Stellan - *Svensk concertino*, op. 114 (1983) (9') •Asx/Str Orch •STIM
SALLUSTIO, Eraclio - *Lunaris* (1980) •Asx/Str •adr

SALONEN, Esa-Pekka - *"...Auf den ersten Blick..."* - Concerto (1980-81) (17') •WH
SALTEN, Alfred - *Concertino* (14')
SANA, Paul - *Concerto* •Asx/Orch or Band
SANCAN, Pierre - *Lamento et rondo* (1973) •Dur
SANDROFF, Howard - *Concerto* (1988) (to F. HEMKE) •Yamaha WX7 MIDI Wind Controller+Sx/Str Orch •adr
SANDSTRÖM, Sven-David - *Concerto* (1987) (23') •Asx/Str Orch •SMIC
SAPIEYEVSKI, Jerzy - *Concerto* (1976) (10') •Asx/Str Ensemble •Merc
SARS, Gerard - *Concertino* (1989) •Asx/Str
SAUTER, Eddie - *Focus* - Jazz Concerto
SAVERINO, Louis - *Concertino petite* (1946) •Mills
SBORDONI, Alessandro - *Cosi crescono i Girasoli* (1992) (10')
SCELSI, Jacinto - *Pranam 1* •Asx/Orch/Tape
SCHAFFER, Boguslaw - *Concerto per 6 e 3 n° 50* (1960) •PWM
    S'alto n° 71 (1963) (15'30) •Asx/Chamber Orch •PWM
SCHIBLER, Armin - *Konzertante fantaisie* (1978) •Eul
SCHMITT, Florent - *Légende*, op. 66 (1918) (9') •Dur
SCHOONENBEEK, Kees - *Tournée* (19'30) •Don
SCHULLER, Gunther - *Concerto* (1983) (17') •AMP
SCHWANTNER, Joseph - *Concertino* •Asx/Chamber Orch •ACA
SCHWARTZ, Elliott - *Chamber Concerto IV* (1981) (12') •1 Sx: A+S/Chamber Ensemble •adr
SCIORTINO, Patrice - *Sonances* (1992) (18') •Bil
SCOTT, C. - *Lotus Land*, op. 47, no. 1 (5')
SCOTT, Tommy Lee - *Lento* (1953) •Asx/Str Orch
SEGERSTAM, Leif - *Orchestral diary sheet...* (1981) (13') •FMIC
SEMLER-COLLERY, Jules - *Fantaisie caprice* (1965) (7') •ME
SHAPEY, Ralph - *Concertante II* (1988) (18') •Asx/Chamber Ensemble •Pres/JJ
SKROWACZEWSKI, Stanislas - *Ricercari notturni* (1977) (20') •1 Sx: S+A+B •EAM
SMIT, Sytze - *Double concerto* •Vln/Asx •Don
SMITH, Howie - *Helix III* (1984) •Asx/Chamber Orch •Oa
    Passages (1981) •Asx/Str Orch •Oa
SØNSTEVOLD, Gunar - *Concerto* (1955) (20') •NK
SOTELO, Mauricio - *Quando il cielo si oscura* (1989) (18') •Asx/Chamber Orch •CA
SPORCK, Georges - *Légende*, op. 54 (1905) •Bil
    Lied •Bil
SPRATLAN, Lewis - *Penelope's Knees* (1985) (23') •Asx/Bass/Chamber Orch •MMI
STAEHLIN, Pierre - *Concertino* (1986) •adr
STEINBACHER, Erwin - *Pieces* •Fro
STEINER, George - *Concerto* (1955) •CC
STEPANEK, Jiri - *Concerto* (1977) •FNT
STIEL, Ludwig - *Musik* (1953) (10')
STOJANOVIC, Petar - *Koncert*, op. 74 (194x) •SKJ
STRANDSJÖ, Göte - *Liten svit*, op. 15 (1954) •Asx/Str Orch •STIM
SUBOTNICK, Morton - *In Two Worlds* - Concerto (1988) (25') •Asx/Computer/Orch or Yamaha WX7 MIDI Wind Controller/Computer or Asx/Computer •EAM
TARP, Svend - *Concertino* (1932) (12') •Asx/Str Orch •adr
TASHJAN, Charmian - *Antiphonies I* (1976-77) •Asx/Chamber Ensemble
TATE, Phyllis - *Concerto* (1944) (22') •Asx/Str Orch •B&H
TAUTENHAHN, Günter - *Concerto* (1976) •SeMC
TERMOS, Paul - *Concerto* (1984) (15') •Asx/Chamber Orch •Don
TESSIER, Roger - *Concerto*
THEOBALD, James - *Three Rapsodies* (1980) •Asx/Perc/Orch
THEOFANIDIS, Chris - *Concerto* (1994) (16') •adr

THIEME, Kerstin - *Rhapsodia festiva* (22') •Asto
THOMPSON, Terence - *Comedy Flick* (1977) •2 Sx: AA
TILLING, Lars - *Konsert* (1979) (18')
TOMASI, Henri - *Ballade* (1939) (14') •Led
 Concerto (1949) (18'30) •Led
 Introduction et danse (1949) (5') •Led
TREBINSKY, Arkadi - *Concertino*, op. 7 (1945) (16') •Asx/Str Orch
 •adr
ULBEN, Denize - *Concertino* (1985) (15') •1 Sx: A+Sno •adr
ULLMAN, Viktor - *Slovanic Rhapsody* (1940) •LCM
VALLIER, Jacques - *Concertino*, op. 78 (5'30) •Asx/Str Orch •adr
VAN MAELE, Gérard - *Concertino*
 Scarabée -Divertissement (6'30) •adr
VAUBOURGOIN, Marc - *6 Petites pièces* (1951) (11') •EFM
VELLONES, Pierre - *Concerto en Fa*, op. 65 (1934) (25') •Lem
VERSCHRAEGEN, G. - *Danse espagnole*
VERSCHRAEGEN, Herman - *Concerto* (1981)
VINCENT-DEMOULIN, Jean - *Petite suite gaélique* (1949) (12')
 •Asx/Str Orch adr
VINTER, Gilbert - *Concerto burlando* (1954) (14') •BMIC
Vivaldi, Antonio - *Concerto en La Mineur* (OSTRANDER) •Mus
VOGEL, Ernst - *Konzert* (1979) (23') •Dob
VOORMOLEN, Alexander - *La Sirène* (1949) (8') •Don
VOSK, Jay - *Concerto* (1987) •Asx/Chamber Orch •DP
VUATAZ, Roger - *Impromptu*, op. 58/4 (1941) (7') •Henn
 Nocturne et danse, op. 58/2 (1940) (7'30)
WATERS, Renee Silas - *Concerto* •adr
WEBER, Alain - *Linéaire I* (1973) (17') •EFM
Weber, Fred - *Concertino* (DAVIS) •Rub
WEINBERGER, Jaromir - *Concerto* (1940/69) •South
WEINZWEIG, John - *Divertimento No. 6* (1972 revised 1989/92)
 (13'10) •Asx/Str Orch •CMC
WEIRAUCH, Peter - *Concertino* (1993) •INM
WEISGARBER, Elliot - *Netori* (1974) •CMC
WELANDER, Waldemar - *Arietta* (1947) (4'30) •CF
 Due pezzi ur concertino (1963-64) (8') •STIM
WERDER, Felex - *Dramaturgy* •adr
 Saxtronic, op. 135 (1973) (18') •Asx/Chamber Orch •adr
WHITE, Andrew - *Concerto for Alto Saxophone*
WHITE, Gene - *Two Moods of Winter*
WILDBERGER, Jacques - *Konzertante Szenen*
WILDER, Alec - *Concerto* (1966) •B&B/Marg
WILLIS, Richard - *Metamorphoses* •Asx/Orch or Wind Ensemble
 •adr
WIRTH, Carl Anton - *Idlewood Concerto* (1954) (19') •EV/Pres
 Jephta (1958) (8') •1 Sx: A+S
WOLF, Hans - *Lovely Lips* (1966) (3') •Asx Solo/Str •Moz
WOOLLETT, Henry - *Sibéria* (1909) (5'30) •South
WORLEY, John - *Claremont - Concerto* (1962) (22')
WYDEVELD, Wolfgang - *Sarabande du roi*
YATES, Ronald - *Concerto* (1970) (14') •adr
YOSHIOKA, Emmett - *Arioso* (1969) (10') •Asx/Harp/Str Orch •Art
YOUNG, Jeremy - *Concerto* (1973-83) (9')
ZENDER, Hans - *Konzertino*, op. 5 (1952) (15') •Br&Ha
ZIVANOVIC, Mihajlo - *Pieces* •YUC
ZLATO, Pibernick - *Koncertantna* •Fl/Sx/Harp/Str •YUC

Alto Saxophone and Band

Band unless otherwise indicated (Band, sauf
indication contraire).

ABSIL, Jean - *Fantaise-Caprice*, op. 152 (1971) (5') •Asx/Str or Band
 or Pno •Lem
ALBRIGHT, William - *Heater* (1977)

AMRAM, David - *Ode to Lord Buckley (Concerto)* (1980) (30') •Pet
ANDERSON, Garland - *Concerto* •DP
ANDERSON, Tommy Joe - *Concerto* (1976) •WWS
ARGERSINGER, Charles - *Doxology Variations* (1983)
BAJUS, Louis - *Prélude et Allegretto* (1935) •Asx/Harmonie or
 Fanfare
BARBER, Clarence - *New York Concerto* (1993) (12') •TTF
BARLOW, Wayne - *Concerto* (1969) (14') •Tem
BEALL, John - *Concerto* (1991) •adr
BENCRISCUTTO, Frank - *Serenade* •adr
BENNETT, David - *Latinata* •CF
 Saxophone Royal •South
BENSON, Warren - *Aeolian Song* (5') •Asx/Orch or Band or Pno
 •MCA
 Concertino (1955) (13') •Asx/Orch or Band or Pno •MCA
 Images •adr
 Star Edge (1966-67) (18') •Asx/Orch or Band •MCA
BERNIER, René - *Hommage à Sax* (1958) (10') •Asx/Orch or Band
 or Pno •Led
BILIK, Jerry - *Concertino* (1973) (11') •Asx/Orch or Band or Pno •CL
BINGE, Ronald - *Romance* (from *Concerto*) •MMC
BORGULYA, Andràs - *Burlesque* (1966) •Asx/Fanfare
BRANT, Henry - *Concerto* (1941) (20') •CFE
Breedam, J. van - *Ecoutez-moi* •1 Sx: A or T/Band •An
BUESS, Alex - *Audio konstrukt...* (1990) •Asx/Band/Syst. électron.
BUMCKE, Gustav - *Concertino*, op. 95 (1961) •Asx/Chamber Orch
 or Wind Ensemble •R&E
 Pieces
BUNTON, Eldridge - *Alto Mood* (1966) (4') •Ken
 Theme from Lushabye •DP
BUOT, Victor - *Morceau d'élévation* (1880) •Asx/Org (or Pno or
 Harmonie) •ES
CACAVAS - *Montage* •DP
CADWALLADER, Rex - *Rhapsody* (1987) •adr
CAIAZZA, Nick - *Portraits* •DP
CALMEL, Roger - *Concertino* (1974) •Chou
CARVALHO, F. Urban - *Song and Dance* (1970) •Asx/Orch or Band
 or Pno •Pres
CASKEN, John - *Kagura* (1972-73) (15') •Sch
CHATTAWAY, Jay - *Double Star* (1985) •2 Sx: AT
 Nocturne and Ritual Dance (1976)
 The Prize (1988) •Sx/Jazz Ensemble
CHILDS, Barney - *Bayonne Gum and Barrel Cie* •ACA
COATES, Eric - *Saxo-Rhapsody* (1936) (11') •Asx/Orch or Band or
 Pno •B&H
COOKE, Anthony - *Pictures at Hemke's Exhibition*
CORVALHA, Urban - *Song and Dance* (1971)
CREPIN, Alain - *Saxoflight* •Asx/Orch d'harmonie or Pno •Scz
CRESTON, Paul - *Concerto*, op. 26 (1941) (17') •Asx/Orch or Band
 or Pno •GSch
DAHL, Ingolf - *Concerto* (1949/53) (19') •EAM
DAVIS, Rick - *Concerto* (1966) •Electronic Asx/Jazz Band
DELAMARRE, Pierre - *Rhapsodie* (1979) (5') •adr
DEL BORGO, Elliot - *Soliloquy and Dance* (1978) •DP
DEMUTH, Norman - *Concerto* (1938) (12') adr
Dinicu, Grigoras - *Hora Staccato* (ZAJAC)
DUSCHINGER, Jean - *Escapade* (1982) •Asx/Orch d'harmonie
EDMONDSON, John - *Essay in Blue* (1981) •Ken
ERB, Donald - *Concert Piece no. 1* (1966)
ERICKSON, Frank - *Concerto* (1960) (14') •Bou
ERIKSSON, Joseph - *Konsert* (1959) (14') •Asx/Orch or Band •Ton
ESCUDIER, H. - *3me fantaisie*, op. 46 (1878) •Asx/Harmonie or
 Fanfare •Mol
Everaarts, Mathieu - *Solo* •Asx/Harmonie •TM

FAILLENOT, Maurice - *Rapsodie occitane* (1992) (9'30) •Asx/Orch d'Harmonie or Pno •Mar
FELD, Jindrich - *Concerto* (1980) •1 Sx: S+A+T/Orch or Band •Kjos
Fibich, Zdenko - *Poème* (BUCHTEL) •Kjos/Eto
FILIPOVITCH, Remy - *Stück* (10') •adr
FINNEY, Ross Lee - *Concerto* (1974) •Asx/Orch or Band or Pno •Pet
FISCHER, Clare - *Rhapsody Nova* (1988) •1 Soloist: Fl+Cl+Asx/Band •adr
FRANCHETTI, Arnold - *Canti* (1969) (12') •SeMC
   Concertino (1960) •adr
FROMIN, Paul - *Ballade pour Angèle* •Asx/Orch d'harmonie •Mar
   Le petit orchestre (1985) •Asx/Orch d'harmonie •Mar
GADENNE, G. - *Marjolaine - Mazurka* (1946) •Asx/Fanfare •BC
GOEYENS, Alphonse - *Introduction et Polonaise* •Asx/Harmonie •An
GOODE, Jack - *Rondino* (1962) (5'30) •Kjos
GOTKOVSKY, Ida - *Concerto* (1966) (16'30) •Asx/Orch or Orch d'Harmonie or Pno •ET
GRAINGER, Percy - *The Annunciation Carol* •PG
GRUNDMAN, Claire - *Concertante* (1972) •Asx/Orch or Band or Pno •B&H
GUILLONNEAU, Christian - *Rapsodie occitane* (1992) (9'30) •Asx/Harmonie •Mar
HACKBARTH, Glen - *Metropolis* (1979) (18') •DP
Hagen, Earl - *Harlem Nocturne* (HARING) •SB
HAIDMAYER, Karl - *Concerto n° 1* (1980)
HARTLEY, Walter - *Concerto* (1966) (12') •Pres
   Saxophrenia (1976) (2'30) •DP
HEIDEN, Bernhard - *Diversion* (1943) (7') •Eto
   Fantasia Concertante (1988) (12') •Eto
HOFFER, Bernard - *Concerto* (1980) (32') •Shir
HOFFMAN, Norbert - *Suite concertante* (1980) •2 Sx: AA/Band
HOLVICH, Karl - *Sarabande* •2 Sx/Band
HUGGENS, Ted - *Air nostalgique* (1979) (4') •Asx/Harmonie •Mol
HUGGLER, John - *Elaboration*, op. 69 (1967) (10') •Asx/Orch or Band or Pno •CFE
HUSA, Karel - *Concerto* (1967) (20') •AMP
JACOB, Gordon - *Miscellanies* (1976) (13') •Asx/Band or Str Orch
JAEGER, Robert - *Concerto* (1967) (20') •Asx/Brass/Perc •adr
   Concerto No. 2 (1977) (11'30) •Volk/CPP
JARNIAT, Raymond - *Andante et danse* •adr
JOHNSTON, David - *Ballade* (1984) •Kf
KANITZ, Ernest - *Interlude*
   Intermezzo... (1948/53) •Asx/Orch or Band or Pno •USC
KIDD, Brian - *Concerto* (1988)
KOCH, Frederick - *Concertino* (1964-65) (15') •Asx/Orch or Band •SeMC/MCA
   Soundings (1974) •Mau
KOERBLER, Milivoj - *Varijacije* (1956) •Asx/Jazz Orch •adr
KOLASCH, Harald - *The House of the Rising Sun* •Hal
KOLDITZ, Hans - *Concertino* (1979) (12') •Asx/Harmonie •adr
KROEGER, Karl - *Concerto*
KUERGEL, Hannes - *Konzert* •Asx/Winds/Male Choir
KULLMANN, Wilton - *Sentimental saxos* (1983) •adr
KYNASTON, Trent - *Concerto* (1976) (17') •Asx/Orch or Wind Orch •DP
LACOUR, Guy - *Pièce concertante* (1975-76) (8'30) •1 Sx: T or A/Str Orch or Wind Orch •Bil
LANCEN, Serge - *Dedicace* (1984) (9'15) •Mol
LATHAM, William - *Concerto Grosso* (1960) (18') •2 Sx: SA/Orch or Band
LAURENT, Léo - *King-saxo* (1939) (2'30) •Asx/Jazz Orch •Cos
LAUWRENCE - *Contentment* (9'30) •Ken
Lederer, Dezsö - *Poème hongrois n° 2* •Vln Solo or Sx/Harmonie

LEESON, Cecil - *Concertino* (1948) •Asx/Winds or Chamber Orch •South
   Concertino (1957) •Enc
LEHMAN - *Intro Song Gigue* •DP
LEMAIRE, Félix - *6 Strophes* •Asx/Brass Ensemble/Perc •adr
LEWIS, Malcolm - *Elegy for a Hollow Man* (1972) (4')
LIEB, Dick - *Short Ballet* (1971) (12') •1 Sx: A or S/Band •Ken
LOCKLAIR, Dan - *Concerto* (1976)
LOGRANDE, L. A. - *An Appeal Amid the Razing* (1994) (7') •CI
LORENTZEN, Bent - *Concerto* (1986) (23') •WH
LUYPERTS, Guy - *Un bon petit diable* (1979) •Asx/Harmonie •Bil
MACCHIA, Salvatore - *Concerto* (1984)
MARTIN, David L. - *Jazz Rhapsody* (1968) •CMC
MERSSON, Boris - *Concerto*, op. 25 (1966) •adr
MILLER, Edward - *Fantasy-concerto* (1971) (10') •ACA
MILLER, Roy - *Uintah*
MITCHELL, William John - *Song of the City* (1967) •CC
MORRISSEY, John - *Nightfall* •WWS/TM
MUCZYNSKI, Robert - *Concerto*, op. 41 (1981) (17') •Asx/Orch or Wind Orch •Pres
MUNDRY, Isabel - *Komposition* (1992)
MYERS, Robert - *Concerto* (1967) •adr
NAULAIS, Jérôme - *Concerto* (1991) •Asx/Orch d'harmonie
   Frissons (1991) (10'30) •Bil
NELSON, Ronald - *Danza Capriccio* (1988) •Asx/Band or Pno
NESTICO, Sammy - *Persuasion*
NIEHAUS, Lennie - *Palo Alto* •WIM
OTT, David - *Concerto* (1987) •Asx/Chamber Orch or Wind Ensemble or Pno •Eto
OWEN, Jerry - *Diversion* (1982) •2 Sx: AT/Band •DP
PENDERS, Joseph - *Rêverie* (1985) (3'30)
PERRIN, Marcel - *Fantaisie tzigane* (1941) (5') •Asx/Orch or Band or Pno •GD
PICHAUREAU, Claude - *Epilogue à Rafflésia* (3'30) •Asx/Wind Orch or Pno or 4 Sx: SATB •Bil
PIERNÉ, Paul - *Concertino* (1949) •Asx/Orch or Harmonie
PRIOR, Claude - *Konzertstück* (1981)
PROHASKA, Miljenko - *Dilemma* (1964) •Asx/Jazz Orch •adr
QUILLING, Howard - *Suite* (1970) •Art
Rabaud, Henri - *Solo de concours* (GEE) •South
REED, Alfred - *Ballade* (1956) (5'30) •South
REX, Harley - *Andantino and Brillante* (1982) •DP
   Preludio and Movende (1960) •1 Sx: A or S/Band •adr
   Saxophone Rhapsody (1941) •1 Sx: A or S/Band •adr
   Washington Sonata (1973) (12') •DP
RICHENS, James - *Another Autumn* (1976) •Co
Rivier, Jean - *Concerto* (DECOUAIS) •Asx/Tpt/Band •Bil
SANA, Paul - *Concerto* •Asx/Orch or Band
SAUGUET, Henri - *Alentours saxophonistiques* (1976) (10') •Chou
SCHIFFMANN, Harold - *Capriccio Concertante* (1987)
SCHMIDT, William - *Concerto* (1983) (20') •WIM
SCHÖNBACH, Dieter - *Canzona* (1970) •adr
SCHULLER, Gunther - *Tribute to Rudy Wiedoeft* (1978) •CPP
SCHWARTZ, Elliott - *Cleveland...* (1981) •1 Player: Asx+Cl •adr
SHROYER, Ronald - *Reflections* (1980)
SHRUDE, Marilyn - *Concerto* (1994) •adr
SKOLNIK, Walter - *Saxoliloquy* (1981) (3'30) •Ten
SMITH, Claude T. - *Fantasia* (1983) •Wi&Jo
SMITH, Howie - *Illudu* (1965) •Oa
SMOLANOFF, Michael - *Concertino*, op. 16 •EV
Staigers, Del - *Carnaval of Venise* •CF
STEG, Paul - *Kaleidoscope* (1971) •Sx Solo/Woodwinds/Brass/Perc/Celesta
SUENAGA, Ryuichi - *Concerto* (1982)
THEORIN, Häkan - *Concertino* (1987) (12') •STIM

TOMMASO, Bruno - *I virtuosi di noci* •Asx/Jazz Orch
VEHAR, Persis - *Quintus Concertino* (1981) •Asx/Wind Ensemble
VENTAS, Adolfo - *Concerto...* (1991) •Asx/Orch d'harmonie •adr
VOGEL, Roger - *Concerto* (1986) •DP
WARD, David - *Concert Piece* (1978) •DP
    Encore (1974)
WHITE, Gene - *Two Moods of Winter*
WHITNEY, Maurice - *Introduction and Samba* (1950) (10') •Bou
    Rhumba (1949) •Bou
WIEDOEFT, Rudy - *Tribute to Rudy Wiedoeft* (1978) (7'43) (SCHULLER)
    •CPP
WIGGINS - *Conversation* (6') •Ken
WILLIS, Richard - *Metamorphoses* •Asx/Orch or Wind Ensemble
    •adr
WILSON, Dana - *Time Cries, Hoping Otherwise* (1990) (17') •Lud
WIRTH, Carl Anton - *Ballad and Final* •TP
    David - Triptych (1978) •Asx/Winds/Perc •adr
WOODWARD, Gregory - *Concerto* (1983)
YOSHIOKA, Emmett - *Duo Concertino* •adr
YOUNG, Charles Rochester - *Concerto* (1990) •adr
    Pieces •Sx/Jazz Ensemble
ZAGARYN, Arthur - *Ballade*
ZIVANOVIC, Mihajlo - *Pieces* •Asx/Jazz Orch •YUC

Solo Tenor Saxophone

Also see Unspecified Instrumentation (Voir aussi
instruments non déterminés), page 422 and Saxophone
and Tape (Saxophone et Bande magnétique), Page 416.

BIANCHINI, Laura - *NO.DI* (1987/88) (10') •1 Sx: S+A+T/Computer
    "Fly" •adr
BOMBERG, David - *Music for Nürnberg* (1982)
BOONE, Ben - *Election Year* (1994) •Sx Solo: S or A or T or B •INM
BORENSTEIN, Daniel - *Eshet-Haïl* (1983) (8') •Sal
BRANDON, Seymour - *Micro Pieces* (1973) •MaPu
BRIZZI, Aldo - *De la transmutazione...* (1983-86) (9') •Sx Solo: S+T
BUDD, Harold - *The Candy Apple Revision* (1970)
CAMPANA, José Luis - *Acting-In* (1983) (16'15) •1 Sx: A+T •Sal
CAPOËN, Denis - *Euphonie* (1987) (8-10') •1 Sx: T+B or A+T
CARAVAN, Ronald - *Improvisation (Romani)* (1980) •Eth
CHARPILLE, Jean-Louis - *Lettrine* (1990)
CHARRON, Damien - *Vers tous les chemins* (1987-88) (5') •Dur
CHILDS, Barney - *Music for One Player* •ACA
CONDÉ, Gérard - *Monarch...* (1983) (22') •1 Sx: Sno+S+A+T+B+Bs
CORTES, Ramiro - *Five Studies* (1968) •USC
DAM, Hermann van - *Rituals...* (1988) (8') •Sx Solo: A or T •Don
DEASON, David - *Jazz Partita* (1983)
DECOUST, Michel - *Olos* (1983-84) (11') •Tsx/Dispositif électro-
    acoust. •Sal
DELAGE, Jean-Louis - *Climat* (1989) •Sx Solo: A or T
DIEDERICHS, Yann - *M.L.K.* (1981) (10'30) •1 Sx: S+A+T+B/
    Dispositif électro-acoust. ad lib.
ERDMANN, Dietrich - *Fantasia colorata* (1987) (6'50) •R&E
    Saxophonata •Sx Solo: S+A+T •R&E
ERNST-MEISTER, Sigrid - *"E... Staremo Freschi!"* (1992) (8') •Sx
    Solo: S+T
FRACKENPOHL, Arthur - *Rhapsody* (1984) (3'30) •Ken
GALAY, Daniel - *Le nom dernier* (1984) (4')
GINGRAS, Guy - *Perseides* (1993) •Med
HARREX, Patrick - *Passages III* (1972) (9-12') •DP
HEYN, Volker - *Buon natale...* (1984/85) (12') •Sx Solo: S+T
HODKINSON, Sidney - *Trinity* (1971) •Sx Solo: A or T or B •adr
HOLLAND, Dulcie - *Pieces* •adr
HUREL, Philippe - *Opcit* (1984) (7'15) •Bil

HYLA, Lee - *For Tenor Saxophone* (3'30) •adr
JEANNEAU, François - *8 thèmes et improvisation* •Sal
JOHNSON, Tom - *Rational Melodies* (1982) (2' to 25')
JOLAS, Betsy - *Episode 4me* (1983) (8'15) •Led
KARLINS, M. William - *Seasons* (1987) (13') •Sx Solo: S+A+T •TP
KAVANAUGH, Patrick - *Debussy-variations No. 5* (1977) •CF
Kinyon, John - *Breeze Easy Recital Pieces* •Wit
KLEIN, Georg - *Nuit...* (1993) •1 Sx: S+T/Live electronics •INM
KUPFERMANN, Meyer - *Seven Inventions* (1967) (15-21') •GMP
LAUBA, Christian - *Hard* (1988) (8') •Fuz
LEHMANN, Hans Ulrich - *Monodie* (1970) (10') •Sx Solo: A or T
    •AVV
LERSTAD, Terje Bjorn - *Lamento*, op. 168b (1984) •NMI
LITTLE, David - *Stonenhenge Study 12* (1991) (10') •Don
LUTZ-RIJEKA, Wilhelm - *Psy* (1993) •Tsx/Computer •INM
MANDANICI, Marcella - *Extraits II* (1990) (5') •adr
MARTINEZ FERNANDEZ, Julian - *Hacia la desconocido* (1993)
    •Sx Solo: S+Bs+T
MARRA, James - *Legacy...* (1978) (7') •Sx Solo: S+T •DP
MEFANO, Paul - *Périple* (1978) (14') •Sal
MOYLAN, William - *Solo Sonata* (1978) (16-18') •Sx Solo: S+A+T
    •SeMC/DP
MÜLLER-GOLDBOOM, Gerhardt - *Impromptu* (1992) (14')
NICOLAU, Dimitri - *Pour le sax*, op. 107 (1991) (10')
NODA, Ryo - *Requiem - Shin-en* (1979) (10') •Sx Solo: T or A •Led
OOSTERVELD, Ernst - *Music loops II* (1982) (5') •Sx Solo: A or T
    •Don
Paganini, Nicolo - *Caprice*, Op. 1, No. 24 (ROSSI) •Sx Solo •DP
Philo - *Etude; Piece in G Minor* •WWS
PISATI, Maurizio - *AE* (1987) •Ric
QUEYROUX, Yves - *7 Jeux musicaux et 3 Promenades* (1989) •Sx
    Solo: S or T or A •Lem
RADULESCU, Horatiu - *Astray* (1984-85) (23') •1 Sx:
    Sno+S+A+T+B+Bs/matériel électron. (or
    Prepared Pno)
ROLIN, Etienne - *Passerelles* (1989) (5') •ApE
    Suite Poly-folique (1993) (10-15') •adr
SCHMADTKE, Harry - *Monolog* (1980) (10') •adr
SWAIN, Freda - *Naturo Suite* (1931) (6') •Any Sx Solo •BMIC
    The Tease (1965) (1'30) •Any Sx Solo •BMIC
TANAKA, Terumichi - *The scene of silence* (1992)
TANAKA, Yoshifumi - *Tros IV* (1993) (8')
TERUGGI, Daniel - *Xatys* (1988) (18'30) •1 Sx: Bs+T+S/Dispositif
    électronique
TOKUNAGA, Hidenori - *Columnation* (1972-73) •Sx Solo: A or T
    •adr
TONT, patrice - *Kiki song* (1990)
ZIMMERMANN, Walter - *In der Welt sein* (1982) (9')

Tenor Saxophone and Piano

Selected repertoire (Choix sélectif).

Also see Tenor Saxophone and Orchestra or Band
(Voir aussi saxophone ténor et orchestre ou band), Pages
317 and 318.

Ackermans, H. - *Nordic Landscape* •1 Sx: A or T/Pno •HE
Albeniz, Isaac - *Mallorca, barcarola* (AMAZ) •UME
    Puerta de Tierra, bolero (AMAZ) •UME
Albinoni, Tomaso - *Adagio* (PICARD) •Phi
    Concerto in D moll, op. 9, no. 2 (JOOSEN) •Mol
ALKEMA, Henk - *Op avontuur* (1988) (10') •Don
AMELLER, André - *Pieces* •1 Sx: A or T/Pno •Com/Led/Mar/Phi
AMOS - *Compositae no. 12*

ANDERSON, Garland - *Sarabande* (1966) •adr
   Sonata (1968) •South
ANDRIESSEN, Louis - *Itropezione III* (1959) •2 Pno/Tsx •Don
ANDRIEU, Fernand - *Concertino n° 3* •Mus
   1er solo de concours •1 Sx: T or B/Pno •Alf
   Pièces •Mar
ARBAN, Joseph - *Oberto, Air varié* •1 Sx: A or T/Pno •Mol
   Perpetual Motion (1'30) (VANASEK) •Bb Sx/Pno •SC
ARNOLD, Hubert - *Anamesis* (1977)
Ascher, Joseph - *Alice, Where art Thou?* (BLAAUW) •Mol
Aubert, Jacques - *Gigue* (MAGANINI) •1 Sx: A or T/Pno •Mus
AUBIN, Francine - *Frédéri* (1990) (3') •1 Sx: A or T/Pno •Mar
AYSCUE, Brian - *The Place of Peace* (1972) (3'30) •adr
Bach, Carl Philip Emanuel - *Spring's Awakening* (GALLO) •1 Sx: A or T/Pno •CBet
Bach, Johann Sebastian - *Pieces*
BAEYENS, Henri - *Canzonetta* •Bb Sx/Pno •EMB
Balfe, Michael - *Killarmey* •Bb Sx/Pno •CBet
BARAT, Jacques - *Elégie dolente* •Map
BARAT, Joseph - *Chant slave* (album) •Bb Sx/Pno •GW
Barratt & Jenkins - *Sounds for Sax 1* •1 Sx: T or A/Pno •Che
Barret, Reginald - *The Light Beyond, Ave Maria* •Bb Sx/Pno •CF
BASTEAU, Jean-François - *Blue-Jean* (1993) (1'30) •1 Sx: A or T/Pno •Mar
BAUDRIER, Emile - *Pieces* •Bb Sx/Pno •Mol
Baumgart - *Ein Hauch Lavendel* •Dux
Baumgartner, Wilhelm - *Noch Sind...* (BLAAUW) •Bb Sx/Pno •Mol
Bazelaire, Paul - *Suite française* (7') (LONDEIX) •Sch
BECKLER, Stanworth - *Folksong Fantasy* •SeMC
BEDARD, Denis - *Fantasie* (1984) (6'30) •1 Sx: S or T/Pno •Bil
Beethoven, Ludwig van - *Pieces* •Bb Sx/Pno
Bellini, Vincenzo - *Pieces* •Bb Sx/Pno
BELLISARIO, Angelo - *Papillons* •adr
BELMANS, R. - *Pieces* •Bb Sx/Pno •Scz
Benda, Franz - *Introduction et Danse* (FELIX) •Mus
   Sonata in F Major •Mus
BEN-HAIM, Paul - *3 Songs...* (1952) (10') •1 Sx: A or T/Pno •MCA
BENZIN, A. - *Caprice russe* •1 Sx: A or T/Pno •An
Bergson, Michael - *Scène et air* •Asx or Bb Sx/Pno •Mol
Berlioz, Hector - *3 Songs* (CLARK) •Bb Sx/Pno •Mus
Besozzi, Jerome - *Sonata*
Bigaglia, Diogeno - *Pieces* •Bb Sx/Pno •Lem
Bigot, Pierre - *Sicilienne* •Eb Sx or Bb Sx/Pno •Mar
BINEGGER, Thomas - *Phoenix* (1993) •INM
BISSELINK, Piet - *Izegrim* •1 Sx: T or B/Pno •Mol
Bizet, Georges - *Pieces*
Blaauw, L. - *Pieces* •TM
Blanchard, Harold - *Pieces* •Sal
Blavet, Michel - *Sonatine en Sib* •Bb Sx/Pno •Mol
Bleger, Adolphe - *Souvenir de Valence - Air varié* •Bb Sx/Pno •Mol
Boccherini, Luigi - *Pieces* •Bb Sx/Pno •CBet/Led/Mol
Boisdeffre, Charles-Henri - *3 Pièces* (DAILEY) •Bb Sx/Pno •GW
BONNARD, Alain - *Sonate*, op. 10 •adr
Borbousse, P. - *Simple mélodie* •1 Sx: A or T/Pno •An
Borodin, Alexandre - *Polovetsian Dance* (WALTERS) •Asx or Bb Sx/Pno •Rub
BORSCHEL, E. - *Silberner Mond* •Fro
BOUILLON, Pierre - *La Pluie d'Or - Air varié* •Bb Sx/Pno •Mol
Boyce, William - *Moderato & Larghetto* •Bb Sx/Pno •TM
BRANCOUR, René - *Suite*, op. 99 (1923) •Tsx in C [en Ut] •ES
Brahms, Johannes - *Pieces* •Bb Sx/Pno •Bel/GSch/HE/Mol
Bright, W. W. - *Regrets d'amour* •Bb Sx/Pno •CF
BROUQIERES, Jean - *Côtes-d'Armor* (1992) (3') •1 Sx: A or T •Mar
Brunard, Gaston - *Pieces* •Mil
BURKHOLDER, Reed - *Sonata* (1975) •DP

Caiola, A. - *You are the Soloist* •1 Sx: A or T/Pno •MCA
Camidge, Mattew - *Sonatine in B* (JOOSEN) •Bb Sx/Pno •Mol
Campra, André - *Musette* (LONDEIX) •Asx or Bb Sx/Pno •Lem
CARAVAN, Ronald - *Quiet Time* (1980) •1 Sx: S+T/Pno •Eth
Chaminade, Cécile - *Pastorale enfantine* •Bb Sx/Pno •CBet
CHAMPAGNAC, René - *Eglogue* •Bb Sx/Pno •Bil
Chauvet, Georges - *Chant du soir* •Asx or Bb Sx/Pno •Com
Chedeville, Esprit - *La Chicane* (LONDEIX) •Bb Sx/Pno •Lem
CHENETTE, Edward Stephen - *Pieces* •Bel/CF
Cherubini, Luigi - *2° Sonate* (PALA) •Mol
Chopin, Frédéric - *Pieces*
CHRETIEN, Hedwige - *Allegro appassionato* •1 Sx: A or T/Pno •Mil
Christol - *Grand solo, Andante et Allegro* •1 Sx: A or T/Pno •Mil
Cimarosa, Domenico - *Sonate en Sib* (JOOSEN) •Bb Sx/Pno •Mol
Cirri, Giovanni - *Arioso* (MAGANINI) •1 Sx: A or T/Pno •Mus
CLARKE, Herbert - *Trixie Valse...* •Bb Sx or Eb Sx/Pno •CF
Clement - *Evening Zephyr* •Bb Sx/Pno •Bar
CLERISSE, Robert - *Pieces*
COHEN, Sol - *Introduction et Czardas* •Wit
COLIN, Charles Joseph - *Pieces*
COMBELLE, François - *1er Solo de concert* •1 Sx: B or T/Pno •Alf
Cooke, Charles - *Lazy Lute* •MBCo
COOLIDGE, Richard - *Ballade* (1993) •adr
COPE, David - *Clone* (1976) (7'30) •SeMC
Corelli, Arcangelo - *Pieces*
CORIOLIS, Emmanuel de - *Barcarolle* (1973) •1 Sx: A or T/Pno •Bil
Cosmey - *Louise* •Bb Sx/Pno •Rub
COSTANTINI, Andreina - *Nicht nur, noch nicht* (1988) (6') •adr
COSTE, Napoléon - *Regrets...*, op. 36 (1880) •Bb Sx/Pno •Mil
Couperin, François - *Pieces*
COWAN, Don - *Shadows* (1975) •B&H
COWLES, Colin - *Sonata* (1978) (18') •adr
   Pieces •DP
CRUFT, Adrian - *Chalumeau Suite* (1975) (6') •JP
Cui, César - *Pieces*
CUNNINGHAM, Michael - *French Fantasy* (1985)
   Pleasantries (1991)
   Trigon, op. 31 (1969) (10') •Eto
DACHEZ, Christian - *Melodi-lène* (1986) (2'10) •1 Sx: A or T/Pno •Led
   Saxorama (1986) (2') •1 Sx: A or T/Pno •Led
Dahm - *Pieces* •1 Sx: A or T/Pno •Mus
DAILEY, Dwight Morris - *12 Concert Pieces* (1950) •GW
Daillet - *Concert Pieces* •Mus
Dancla, Jean-Baptiste - *Pieces* •Bb Sx/Pno •Mol
DEASON, David - *Blues-Walk* (1984) •1 Sx: S+A+T/Pno
   Tenor-ventions (1980) •DP
Debussy, Claude - *Pieces*
De Koven, Henry - *Oh Promise Me* (LEIDZEN) •Tsx/Pno •ECS
DELAUNAY, René - *Au fil de l'eau* •Asx or Bb Sx/Pno •Bil/Braun
DELBECQ, Laurent - *Pieces* •Bb Sx/Pno •Mol
DELGUIDICE, Michel - *Saxboy* •1 Sx: S or A or T/Pno •Mar
   Pieces •Bil/Led
Delhaye, Alyre - *Silver Threads - Air varié* •Bb Sx/Pno •Mol
Delle-Haensch - *Modern Saxophonschule...* •Dux
De Long - *Sonate francese* •Ken
DE LUCA, Joseph - *Pieces* •CF
DELVINCOURT, Claude - *Scapin joué* (3'30) •1 Sx: S or T/Pno •Lem
DEMERSSEMAN, Jules - *Fantaisie pastorale* •Bb Sx/Pno •Bil
   Fantaisie pastorale - In Arcadie •Bb Sx/Pno •Mol
   Introduction et Variations... •Bb Sx/Pno •Marg
   1er Solo - Andante et Boléro (1866) •Sax/Ron
DESLOGES, Jacques - *Fabliau* (1984) (3') •1 Sx: A or T/Pno •Mar
DESPORTES, Yvonne - *L'Homme...* (6') •Tsx/Accordion or Pno •DP
   Le Noir et la Rose (5'30) •Tsx/Harp or Pno •DP

3 Petits contes (DAILEY) •Bb Sx/Pno •WA

Devienne, François - *Largo and Allegretto* (JAECKEL) •South

De Ville, Paul - *Happy be Thy Dreams* •Eb or Bb Sx/Pno •CF

DEVOGEL, Jacques - *Volupté* (1989) (2'30) •1 Sx: A or T/Pno •Mar

DHAINE, Jean-Louis - *Grave* (3') •Bb Sx/Org (or Pno)

Dhossche - *Invocation* •Bb Sx/Pno •South

DINDALE, E. - *Pieces* •1 Sx: A or T/Pno •HE

DI PASQUALE, James - *Sonata* (1967) (10') •South

DOBBINS, Bill - *Sonata* (1991) (13') •1 Sx: S or T/Pno •AdMu

DONDEYNE, Désiré - *Saturne* (1993) (1'30) •1 Sx: A or T/Pno •Mar

DORSSELAER, Willy van - *Andantino* (2') •Eb or Bb Sx/Pno •Lem
    Arabesque, op. 57 (1960) (4'30) •Met
    Solo de concours, op. 60 (1963) (4') •Braun

DOURSON, Paul - *Allegretto grazioso* (1993) •Eb or Bb Sx/Pno •Led

Drigo, Riccardo - *Pieces* •Bel/Cen/CF

DUBOIS, Pierre-Max - *2 Mini...* (1979) (5') •1 Sx: A or T/Pno •Bil
    Prélude et Rengaine (1979) •1 Sx: A or T/Pno •Bil
    Triangle (1974) (19') •1 Sx: S+A+T/Pno •RR
    Vieille chanson et Rondinade (1982) (3'30) •Bil

DUCKWORTH, William - *A Ballad in Time...* (1968) (3') •SeMC
    Pitt County Excusrsions (1972) •SeMC

Duport, Jean-Louis - *Romance* •Bb Sx/Pno •JS

DURAND, Emile - *1ère valse*, op. 83 •Bb Sx/Pno •CBet

DURAND, Pierre - *Saxovéloce* (1989) (4'30) •1 Sx: A or T/Pno •Com

DUTKIEWICZ, Andrzzei - *Danse triste* (1977) (13') •Bb Sx/Pno •DP

Dvorak, Anton - *Pieces* •Bb Sx/Pno

DYCK, Vladimir - *Invocation to Euterpe* •Bb Sx/Pno •WA

Elgar, Edward - *Pieces* •Bb Sx/Pno •CF/FMH

ERDMANN, Dietrich - *Akzente* (1989) (8'30)

Erdna - *6 Pieces Swing* •1 Sx: A or T/Pno •Sal

ERNST - *Elegie* •Bb Sx/Pno •CBet

Evans, Edwin - *Pieces* •Bb Sx/Pno •CF

Faillenor - *Air rustique* •WWS

Fasolo, Giovanni Battista - *Ballade* •WWS

Faulx, J. B. - *Pieces* •HE/EMB

Fauré, Gabriel - *Après un rêve* (Album) (DAILEY) •Bb Sx/Pno •WA

Felix - *3 Canzonettas of the 17th Century* •1 Sx: A or T/Pno

Field, John - *Notturno* •Bb Sx/Pno •Mol

Fillmore, Henry - *Ann Earl* •Bb Sx/Pno •FMH

Fiocco, Joseph-Hector - *Pieces* •DP/Ken/OMC

FISCHER - *Here I Sit in the Deep Cellar* •Ken

FISCHER, Eric - *Kephas a Antioche* (1984) (10') •Bil
    Sonate •adr

Flegier, André-Ange - *Vilanelle* (SMIM) •Asx or Bb Sx/Pno •VAB

Follman, G. - *3 Improvisations* •Bb Sx/Pno •Sez

FONTAINE, Louis-Noël - *Sonatine* (1992) (8') •Capri

Foster, Stephen - *Pieces* •HE/Mol

Fote, R. - *Waltz for Juliet* •1 Sx: A or T/Pno •WWS

FRACKENPOHL, Arthur - *Sonata* (1982)

FRANGKISER, Carl - *Theme from Alaskan Night* •Bel

Frank, M. - *Centurion* •WWS

GALLET, Jean - *Andante et Jeu* (1969) •Asx or Bb Sx/Pno •Bil

Galliard, Johann Ernst - *Pieces* •CPP/Gi&Ma/Lem/Pet

Gatti, Domenico - *Concertino in Bb Major* •CF

Gaubert, Philippe - *Deux Pièces* (PAQUOT) •Asx or Bb Sx/Pno •Led

GAUDRON, René - *Andante et allegretto* •Bil

GEE, Harry - *Festival Solo* •1 Sx: S or T/Pno •DP

German, Edward - *Pastorale et Bourrée* (VOXMAN) •Rub

Gershwin, George - *Pieces* •MPHC/WaB

GHIDONI, Armando - *Mélodie* (1991) (3'15) •1 Sx: A or T/Pno •Led
    Pièce brève (1994) •Bb or Eb Sx/Pno •Led

GILMORE, Cortland - *Martinello* •Rub

Giordani, Giuseppe - *An 18th Century Air* •Eb Sx or Bb Sx/Pno •Mus

GIOVANNINI, Caesar - *Rhapsody* (1977) •APC

Glinka, Mikhail - *Romance Melody* (SCHUMANN) •Bb Sx/Pno •JS

Gluck, Christoph Willibald - *Pieces* •Led/Mol/Mus

GNATTALI, Radamès - *Brasiliano n° 8* (1957) •Ric

Godard, Benjamin - *Pieces* •CF/Mol

GODFREY, Paul - *Sonata* (1979) (9') •BMIC

Godfroid - *Valsette* •Bb Sx/Pno •TM

GOEYENS, Alphonse - *English Melody* •1 Sx: A or T/Pno •HE

Goldman, Edwin Franco - *Pieces* •CF/ECS

Goltermann, George - *Concerto No. 4*, op. 65 (TEAL) •1 Sx: A or T/Pno

Gossec, François Joseph - *Sonata* •Bb Sx/Pno •Mol

Gounod, Charles - *Pieces* •CBet/Cen/Mol/Rub/TM

GRAINGER, Christian - *Sonata*

GRAINGER, Percy - *Sonata* •PG

Granados, Enrique - *Pieces* •GSch/UME

GRANT, Bruce - *Everything Comes from the Blues* (1978) (12')

Graupner (Johann) Christoph - *Intrada* •WWS

Greer - *Flapperette* •Bb Sx/Pno •Mills

Gretry, André-Modeste - *Panurge...* (LONDEIX) •Bb Sx/Pno •Led

Grieg, Edvard - *Pieces* •CBet/GSch/Mol

Grovlez, Gabriel - *Lamento et Tarentelle* (DAILEY) •Bb Sx/Pno •WA

GUENTZEL - *Mastodon* •Bb Sx/Pno •Mills

Guilhaud, Georges - *1er Concertino* (VOXMAN) •1 Sx: A or T/Pno •Rub

GUILLONNEAU, Christian - *Evocation et Danse* (1993) (4') •1 Sx:
    A or T/Pno •Mar

GUREWICH, Jascha - *Pieces* •SF

Halévy, Jacques - *Bright Star of Hope* (*L'Eclair*) •Bb Sx/Pno •CF

Handel, Georg-Friedrich - *Pieces*

HARRIS, David - *Moments*

HARRIS, Floyd - *Pieces* •Lud

HARTLEY, Walter - *Poem* (1967) (3'30) •Ten/Pres
    The Saxophone Album (1974) •DP
    Scherzino (1986) (1'15) •Tsx/Pno •Eth
    Sonata (1973-74) (10'30) •DP
    Sonorities VII (1985) (2') •Eth

Hartmann, John - *The Return* •Mol

HARTZELL, Doug - *Ballade for Young Cats* •WWS

HARVEY, Paul - *The Singing...* (1989) •1 Sx: A or T/Pno •SMC

Hasse, Johann Adolf - *Concert in G moll* (JOOSEN) •Bb Sx/Pno •Mol

HAWKINS, Coleman - *Warm-up* •MCA

Haydn, Franz Joseph - *Pieces*

HELFRITZ, Hans - *Improvisata* •WWS

HENRY, Otto Walker - *The Cube* (1974) (11') •adr

Herbert, Victor - *Gypsy Love Song* (BUCHTEL) •1 Sx: T or A/Pno •Kjos

HERMANS, Nico - *4 Impressions* (1983) (12') •Don

Hian, Ben - *3 Songs* •2 Sx/Pno or Tsx/Pno •Pet

HLOBIL, Emil - *Canto pensieroso* (1976) (8') •CHF

Hoffmann - *Cavatine & Polacca* (H. LUREMAN) •Bb Sx/Pno •TM

HOFFMAN, Norbert - *Pieces* •Eb or Bb Sx/Pno •Scz

HOLMES, G. E. - *Tyrolean Fantasia* •Bb Sx or Eb Sx/Pno •CF

Hook, James - *Engelse Sonat* (JOOSEN) •Bb Sx/Pno •Mol

HOULIK, James - *Two Lyric Pieces* •South

Hubert, Roger - *Pieces* •Mar

HURREL, Clarence - *Summer Serenade* •Rub

IBERT, Jacques - *Mélopée* •Bb Sx/Pno •Lem

Ilyinsky, Alexander A. - *Lullaby* (BUCHTEL) •Kjos

Indy, Vincent d' - *Choral varié*, op. 55 (GEE) •1 Sx: A or T/Pno •MMB

Irons, Earl - *Pieces* •CF/Chart

ISACOFF, Stuart - *Jazz Time* (1990) •Asx/Pno - Tsx/Pno •B&H

IVEY, Hean-Eichealberger - *Triton's horn* (1982) (9') •DP

Jaeckel - *Largo and Allegretto* •WWS

Jakma, Fritz - *Pieces* •Mol/TM

Jeanjean, Paul - *Capriccio* (KLICKMAN) •Alf

JEVERUD, Johan - *Bedtime near* (1985) (4') •SMIC

JOHNSON, Clair - *Waltz Moods* •Rub

Joplin, Scott - *Let's Rag...* (U. HEGER) •1 Sx: A or T/Pno •NoE

JORDAN, Paul - *Rhapsody and Waltz* (1979)

JOUBERT, Claude-Henry - *Chanson...* (3') •1 Sx: A or T/Pno •Com
Kabalevsky - *Sonatina*, op. 13 (GEE) •South
KAREL, Leon C. - *Cypress Song* (1955) •B&H
    Hewaphon; *Metrax*; *Quintra* •South
KARLINS, M. William - *Sonata* •CFE
KISZA, Stanislaw - *Szkice* (1964-65) •1 Sx: A or T/Pno •PWM
KLAUSS, Noah - *Aria* •Ken
Koepke, Paul - *Pieces* •Rub
KOSTECK, Gregory - *Mini-variations* (1967) •RPS/MP
    Music; *Two Songs*
KOX, Hans - *Sonata* (1982) (17') •Don
Kuhlau, Friederich - *Menuet* (BUCHTEL) •1 Sx: A or T/Pno •Kjos
Labate, Bruno - *Villanella* •CF
Lack, Theodore - *Idilio* •1 Sx: A or T/Pno •Cen
LACOUR, Guy - *Pieces* •Bil
LAKE, Mathew - *Pieces* •CF
Lalo, Edouard - *Le Roi d'Ys* •Bb Sx or Eb Sx/Pno •Mol
LAMB, Marvin - *Concerto*
Lamote de Grignon, Juan - *Pieces* •1 Sx: T or A/Pno •UME
LANCEN, Serge - *Confidences* (1968) (2') •Bb Sx/Pno •Chap
    Espièglerie •HE
    Intimité (1968) (3'30) •Bb Sx/Pno •Mol
    Introduction et Allegro giocoso (1965) (5'30) •Bb Sx/Pno •Mol
    Pastorale •HE; *Romance* •HE
    Si j'étais (1980) (5'30) •1 Sx: S or T/Pno •Led
    Trois Pièces (1963) (7') •Bb Sx/Pno •Mol
Lara, Augustin - *Granada* •PIC
LASTRA, Erich Eder de - *3 Tempi* •adr
Lebierre, O. - *Airs bohémiens* •Bb Sx/Pno •TM
Leclair, Jean-Marie - *Pieces*
LECLERCQ, Edgard - *Happy moment* •1 Sx: A or T/Pno •He
    Instant élégiaque •1 Sx: A or T/Pno •An
    Intimité •HE
LECUSSANT, Serge - *Yesterday, Today and Forever* (1979)
LEHMANN, Markus - *Concertino*, op. 24a •adr
Lemare, Edwin Henry - *Pieces* •Volk/PMH
Leoncavallo, Ruggiero - *Arioso* (GROOMS) •1 Sx: T or A/Pno •Cen
Le Thiere, C. - *Beneath Sky Window* - Serenade •Bb Sx/Pno •CF
LIC, Leslaw - *Uniwersalny skarbesyk* •1 Sx: A or T/Pno •PWM
Lindemann & Blanchard - *Pieces* •Sal
LINDROTH, Scott - *Chasing the Trane out of Darmstadt* •WWS
Llewellyn, Edward - *My Regards* (LILLYA) •1 Sx: A or T/Pno •CF/
    Rem/DP
Loeillet, Jean-Baptiste - *Adagio & Allegro* (VOXMAN & BLOCK) •South
LONDEIX, Jean-Marie - *Beau Dion* (1976) (2') •Comb
    Pieces •Led/Lem
Lotter, Adolph - *Rouge et noir* •1 Sx: A or T/Pno •B&H
LOTTERIE, G. - *Petite pièce d'examen* (2'30) •Bil
LUKAS, Zdenek - *Legenda* (1972) (9') •CHF
Lully, Jean-Baptiste - *Pieces* •Led/Mus
LUNDE, Lawson - *Sonate*, op. 30 (1968) (15') •adr
Lyons - *New Tenor Sax Solos* (2 Volumes) •USC
MacDowell, Edward - *Pieces* •CF/Mol
MAGANINI, Quinto - *Pieces* •Mus
MAHY, Alfred - *Bourrée, cadenze e finale* •Bb Sx/Pno •Mol
Malotte, Albert - *The Lord's Prayer* (LAKE) •1 Sx: A or T/Pno •GSch
MANGELSDORFF, E. - *Anleitung...* •Bb Sx/Pno •Sch
Marcello, Allessandro - *Concert in C moll* (JOOSEN) •Bb Sx/Pno •Mol
Marchand, Joseph - *Air tendre* (LONDEIX) •Asx or Bb Sx/Pno •Lem
Marchetti, Filippo - *Fascination* (HURRELL) •Eb Sx or Bb Sx/Pno •Rub
MARI, Pierrette - *La comète tenue en...* (1987) •1 Sx: A or T/Pno •Bil
    Corollaire d'un songe (1976) •Bb Sx/Pno •Arp
MARIN, Amadeo - *Typologies* (1977)
Martini, Padre - *Canzona* •Bb Sx/Pno •Mol
Martini, Jean-Paul - *Pieces* •Mus/Sal/TM

Mascagni, Pietro - *Siciliana* •Rem
MASSELLA, Thomas - *Changing Times* (10') •Marc
Massenet, Jules - *Pieces* •CBet/Cen/Pres
MAURY, Lownder - *5th Contest Solo* (KLICKMANN) •1 Sx: T or B/Pno
    •Alf
MAYEUR, Louis - *Récréation sur la Favorite de Donizetti* (1877)
McCLAIN, Floyd A. - *A Little Joke* •South
Mendelssohn, Félix - *Pieces*
MENENDEZ, Julian - *Estudio de concerto* (1985) (6'30) •1 Sx: A or
    T/Pno •RME
MENEYROL, Georges - *Bazasax* (1982) (2'30) •Bil
MERANGER, Paul - *Dialogue* (1982)
    Diptuka, op. 15 (1976)
MERIOT, Michel - *Pieces* •Com
MESANG, T. L. - *Pleasant Thoughts* •SBC
MEYER, Alexandre Henri - *Sonate Lab-Sib-Ré* (1948-49)
MIGNION, René - *Pieces* •Bil
MIHALOVICI, Marcel - *Chant premier*, op. 103 (1973) (12') •Heu
MINAMIKAWA, Mio - *Crystal shapar* (1983) •adr
Moffat, J.-G. - *Gavotte* (RASCHER) •Bel
Molloy, James - *Love's Old Sweet Song* (BLAAUW) •Bb Sx/Pno •Mol
MONROE, Samuel - *Rhapsodie* •Bel
MONTALTO, Richard - *Reflection* (1990) (4'30) •1 Sx: A or T/Pno
    •adr
Monti, Vittorio - *Czarda* (ROBERTS) •Bb Sx/Pno •CF
MORITZ, Edvard - *Sonate No. 1* (1963) •South
MORRA - *Nocturnal Serenade*; *Romantique* •Bb Sx/Pno •CF
Mozart, Wolfgang - *Pieces*
MUSSER, Christian - *Germ* (1993) •INM
NAULAIS, Jérôme - *Pain d'épice* (1993) (1'15) •1 Sx: A or T/Pno
    •Mar
NELHYBEL, Vaclav - *Golden Concerto* •Mus
Neukomm, Sigismund - *Aria* (KAPLAN) •Bb Sx/Pno •JS
NORTON, Christopher - *Microjazz* (1988) •B&H
Offenbach, Jacques - *Barcarolle*; *La Musette* •CBet/Volk
Olcott, Chauncey - *My Wild...* (BUCHTEL) •1 Sx: A or T/Pno •Bel/Rub
Olesen, W. - *Six Saxophone Pieces* •Asx or Bb Sx/Pno •WH/WWS
O'NEILL, Charles - *Pieces*
OSTRANDER, Allen - *Sonate in G Minor* •1 Sx: A or T/Pno •EM
OSTRANSKY, Leroy - *Pieces* •Rub
Paderewski, Ignace - *Minuet...* (TRINKAUS) •Bb Sx/Pno •FMH
Paggi - *Caprice - mazurka* •Bb Sx/Pno •Mil
Painpare, Hubert - *Morceau de salon* •Bb Sx/Pno •Mol
PALA, Johan - *Bonjour* •Bb Sx/Pno •Mol
Paquot, Philippe - *10 Pièces mélodiques* •1 Sx: A or T/Pno •Led
PARES, Gabriel - *Crépuscule* (JUDY) •1 Sx: T or B/Pno •Braun/Rub
Paul, Gene - *Estilian caprice* •1 Sx: A or T/Pno •Rub
PAUWELS, M. - *Andante et Allegro* •1 Sx: A or T/Pno •HE/An
PECK, Russell - *Sonatina* (1967) •WIM
PELZ, William - *Portrait* •Bel
Pergolese, Giovanni-Battista - *Pieces* •HE/Mus
PERRIN, Marcel - *Pieces* •Com/GD/Led/Phi
Philidor, François-André - *Chant...* (MULE) •Bb Sx or Eb Sx/Pno •Led
Piccolomini, Marietta - *Pieces* •Bb Sx or Eb Sx/Pno •CF
PICHAUREAU, Claude - *Saximini* (1993) (3') •Bil
Pierné, Gabriel - *Pieces* •Led/South
PILLEVESTRE - *Nuit d'été - Rêverie* (1890) •Bb Sx or Eb Sx/Pno
    2me Offertoire (1890) •Bb Sx or Eb Sx/Pno or Org
PINARD, A. - *Pieces* •Eb Sx or Bb Sx/Pno •CF
Porpora, Nicola - *Sinfonia* (RASCHER) •MM
PORRET, Julien - *Pieces* •Mar
Prendiville, H. - *Les bleuts* •Bb Sx/Pno •CF
PRESSER, William - *Concerto* (1965)
    Rhapsody (3') •Ten/Pres
Prokofiev, Sergei - *Pieces* •EMa/Rub

315

Purcell, henry - *Pieces* •JS/Kjos/Mus

QUERAT, Marcel - *Petite suite* (1982) (9'30) •Bil

Rachmaninoff, Sergei - *Vocalise* (MAGANINI) •1 Sx: A or T/Pno •Mus

RAE, James - *Blue Saxophone* •1 Sx: A or T/Pno
  Jazzy Saxophone Duets II •1 Sx: A or T/Pno •Uni

Raff, J. - *Pieces* (MOLENAAR) (VIARD) •Mol/Sal

Rameau, Jean-Philippe - *Pieces* •Bel/Led/Mus

Ranger, A. R. - *Pieces* •Bb Sx or Eb Sx/Pno •CF

RAPHLING, Sam - *Square Dance* •Mus

Ravel, Maurice - *Pieces* •Led/Mus

Regi, A. - *Ancient Melody* (VOXMAN) •Bb Sx/Pno •Rub

REHL, Richard - *The Duchess* (1928) •1 Sx: A or T/Pno •Rub

REIBEL, Guy - *Images élastiques*
  Sonate à deux (1988)

REILLY, Allyn - *Two Short Pieces* (1973) •South

REINER, Karel - *Akrostichon e Allegro* (1972)

REYMOND, Roger - *Elégie* (1972) •adr

Reynaud, Joseph-Félix - *Grande fantaisie* •Asx or Bb Sx/Pno •Sal

Rimsky-Korsakov, Nicolas - *Pieces* •CF/Rub

Ritter, Renée - *Long Ago - Air varié* •Bb Sx/Pno •Mol

ROBERT, C. - *Concerto* •Bb Sx/Pno •TM

Roermeester - *Introduction and Romance* •Bb Sx/Pno •CBet

ROGER, Denise - *Conversation* (1989) (2') •1 Sx: A or T/Pno •Mar
  Evocation (1982) (2'30) •1 Sx: A or T/Pno •Comb

ROIZENBLAT, Alain - *Danse...* (1989) (1') •1 Sx: A or T/Pno •Bil
  Musique pour rêver (1987) (1'50) •1 Sx: A or T/Pno •Bil

Rolle, Johann Heinrich - *Concerto* •Asx or Bb Sx/Pno •Sal

ROMERO - *Solo de Concurso*

ROPARTZ, Guy - *Andante & Allegro* (BUCHTEL) •Bb Sx/Pno •Kjos

Rossini, Giacchino - *Pieces* •CBet/TM

ROUGERON, Philippe - *Pieces* (1985) (4'30) •1 Sx: A or T/Pno •Bil

ROUSSEAU, Eugene - *Solo Album* •Eto

Rubenstein, Anton - *Pieces* •Mol/SF/Volk

RUCQUOIS, Jean - *Pieces* •Bil

RUIZ, F. - *Solos de concurso* •Tro

SABON, Joseph-Pierre - *Pieces* •Bil/Mil

Saint-Saëns, Camille - *Pieces*

Salciani - *55 Masterpieces* (IASILLI) •Bel

Sammartini, Giovanni-Battista - *Vanto amoroso* •Asx or Bb Sx/Pno •Mol

SATTERWHITE, Marc - *Aprilmourningmusic* (1985) (10')

SAVARI, Jean-Nicolas - *3me fantaisie...* •Bb Sx/Pno •Sax

SCHAEFER, August H. - *David's Dream* •Bb Sx/Pno •FMH
  The Soloist •Bb Sx/Pno •FMH

SCHMIDT, William - *Sonatina* (1967) •WIM

SCHMITT, Florent - *Le songe de Coppelius* (3') •Bb Sx/Pno •Lem

SCHOLTENS - *Claus fantasie* •Bb Sx/Pno •TM

SCHRIJVER, K. de - *Pieces* •Bb Sx/Pno •Scz

Schroen - *Russian Elegy* •Bb Sx/Pno •CF

Schubert, Franz - *Pieces*

Schumann, Robert - *Pieces*

SCHWARTZ , George - *International Folk Suite* (1973) •South

SEFFER, Yochk'o - *Self system*

SEMLER-COLLERY, Jules - *Fantaisie de concert* (1955) (10') •Dec
  Mélodie expressive •Asx or Bb Sx/Pno •ME

Senaillé, Jean-Baptiste - *Allegro Spiritoso* (EPHROSS) •South

SHAFFER, Sherwood - *Barcarolle* •adr
  Sonata (1983) (15') •adr

Shallitt, M. - *Eili, Eili...* •Eb or Bb Sx/Pno •CF

SHERMAN, Robert - *Sonata* (1966) •South

SHIGERU, Kan-no - *Mythos - Mosaik* (1993) •INM

Shostakovich, Dmitri - *Pieces* •1 Sx: A ot T/Pno •Mus

Sibelius, Jean - *Valse triste* (TRINKAUS) •FMH

SICHLER, Jean - *La mémoire...* (1987) (3'30) •1 Sx: A or T/Pno •Led

SIGNARD, Pierre - *Pieces* •Mil

SIMPSON, Kendall - *Rondo* (1983)

SINGELEE, Jean-Baptiste - *Pieces* •Sax/Mol/Ron

SINGER, S. - *Marionette Modernes* •CF

SKOLNIK, Walter - *Meditation* (1971) (4') •TP/Ten/Pres

SLUKA, Lubos - *D-S-C-H-* (1976)

SMART, Gary - *Two Sound Pieces*

SMITH, Clay - *Pieces* •CF

Sousa, John Philip - *Stars and Stripes Forever* (BUCHTEL) •1 Sx: A or T/Pno •Kjos

Spohr, Ludwig - *Adagio* (GEE) •South

SPORCK, Georges - *Virelai* (COMBELLE) •Bil

STEIN, Leon - *Sonata* (1967) •South

STEINBACHER, Erwin - *Pieces* •Fro

STEINKE, Greg - *Episodes* (1973) (8') •Eb Sx or Bb Sx/Pno (ad lib.) •SeMC

Stillwell, Richard - *Visions of You - Reverie* •Bb Sx or Eb Sx/Pno •CF

STRADOMSKI, Rafal - *DLA "R"* (1987)
  Per Gato (1988) •1 Sx: A or T/Pno •DP

Strauss, Johann - *Waltz 'Gypsy Baron'* •Kjos

Strauss, Richard - *Allerseelen* (WALTERS) •1 Sx: A or T/Pno •Rub

STRAUWEN, Jean - *Andante varié* •1 Sx: A or T/Pno •EMB

STRAVINSKY, Igor - *Berceuse (Firebird)* •Bb Sx/Pno •Mus

STRIMER, Joseph - *Sérénade* (1933) •Led

STRINGFIELD, Lamar Edwin - *To a Star*

Tartini, Giuseppe - *Pieces* •HE/Led

Tchaikovsky, Peter - *Pieces*

Telemann, Georg Phillip - *Pieces* •DP/Rub/TVA

TEMPLETON, Alec - *Elegie* •MCA

Tenaglia, Antonio Francesco - *Aria Antica* •Mus

TERAHARA, Nobuo - *Poème* (1988)

Thiry, Albert - *Dimanche matin; Promenade* •Bb Sx/Pno •Mol

Thomas, Ambroise - *Pieces* •Bb Sx/Pno •CBet/CF/TM

Thome, François-Joseph - *Simple aveu* (BLAAUW) •Bb Sx/Pno •Mol

THOMPSON, Kathryn - *Pieces* •Tsx (in C)/Pno •South

Tobani, Theodore - *Hearts and Flowers* •Bb Sx or Eb Sx/Pno •CF

Toldra, Eduardo - *Pieces* (AMAZ & BAYER) •1 Sx: A or T/Pno •UME

TOMASI, Henri - *Chant corse* (1932) •Asx or Bb Sx/Pno •Led

Triebert, Charles-Louis - *Pieces* •Bb Sx/Pno •Mil

Trinkaus, G. - *Lament* •Bb Sx/Pno •FMH

Tufilli, W. - *Random Reverie* •Bel

TURNER, Thomas - *Fantasy* •SeMC

TUTHILL, Burnett - *Sonata*, op. 56 (1968) (16') •South

VADALA, Kathleen - *Sea Change* (1988) •1 Sx: A or T/Pno •South

Vandercook, Hale - *Pieces* •1 Sx: A or T/Pno •Kjos

Vassilenko, Sergei - *Rhapsodie orientale* •Mus

Veracini, Antonio - *Gavotte* (FELIX); *Two Classic Dances* •Mus

Verdi, Giuseppe - *March* (LAKE) •Bb Sx/Pno •GSch
  Miserere •Bb Sx/Pno •CF

VEREECKEN, Benjamin - *Pieces* •Eb Sx or Bb Sx/Pno •CF

VERRALL, John - *Eusebius Remembered...* (1976-82) •ACA

Verroust, Stanislas - *Pieces* •Bil/Mol

VIARD, Jules - *Scherzetto, Menuet, ...* (1935) •1 Sx: A or T/Pno •Sal

Vivaldi, Antonio - *Pieces* •MM/Mus

VISONI, L. - *Doux propos* •1 Sx: A or T/Pno

Vogt, Gustave - *Pieces* •1 Sx: A or T/Pno •Cen

VRIES, Klaas de - *March* (1972) (5') •Don

Wagner, Richard - *Pieces* •CF/FMH/Kjos

WALKER, Richard - *Waltz Casual* •Bos

WALTERS, Harold - *Pieces* •Lud/Rub

WARD-STEINMAN, David - *Golden Apples* (1981)

WARREN, David - *Chorale Fantasy* •1 Sx: A or T/Pno •Lud
  Sonatina •Lud

WEAGE, Bradley - *Hexagram* (1986) •Tsx/Pno

Weber - *Evening Shadows* •1 Sx: B or T/Pno •Bel

Weber, Carl-Maria von - *Le Freischütz -Valse* (MULE) •Asx or Bb Sx/ Pno •Led

WEINER, Lawrence - *Etude* (1984) •South

WEISSING, Matthias - *La ville...* (1993) •1 Sx: S+T+B/Pno •INM

WELSH, Wilmer - *Passacaglia* •1 Sx: S+A+T+B/Pno

Wettge, Gustave - *Fantaisie...* (BLAAUW) •Bb Sx or Asx/Pno •Mil/Mol

WHITNEY, Maurice - *Melancholy* •1 Sx: A or T/Pno •JS

WIEDOEFT, Rudy - *Pieces* •Rob

WILDER, Alec - *Stan Getz Piece I* •WWS

WILSON - *Pieces* •1 Sx: A or T/Pno •Cen

WILSON, Dana - *Incantation and Ritual* (1985)

WINSTRUP, Olesen - *Six Saxophone Pieces* (2 Volumes) •WH

Wood, Haydn - *Roses of Picardy* (BLAAUW) •Mol

WORLEY, John - *Owl's Head Sonatina* •DP
  September Sonata II (1985); *Sonata* •DP
  White Morning Stillness •DP

WURMSER, Lucien - *Petit solo de concours* •Bil

WYMAN, Laurence - *Rainfall* (1972) •adr

WYSTRAETE, Bernard - *Petite pièce* (1993) •Bb or Eb Sx/Pno •Led

YASINITSKY, Gregory - *Four Short Pieces* (1990) (8'30)

YOUNG, Charles Rochester - *Diversions* •1 Sx: S or T/Pno

YUSTE, M. - *Solo de concours* •UME

Zamacois, Joaquin - *Serenada...* (AMAZ) •1 Sx: A or T/Pno •UME

Zamecnik - *Polly* •Bb Sx/Pno •SF

ZANETTOVICH, Daniele - *Second sonata* •Piz

ZIMMERMANN, Kai-Otto - *Die Zehn Gebote* (1993) •INM

ZOBEL, Edgar - *Spuce Shadows* •Kjos

Tenor Saxophone and Orchestra

Orchestra unless otherwise indicated (Orchestre, sauf indication contraire).

ABSIL, Jean - *Berceuse* (1932) (5') •1 Sx: A or T •An/Ger
  Sicilienne (1950) (9') •1 Sx: A or T •An/Ger

BAKER, David - *Concerto* (1987) (25') •Tsx/Chamber Orch •SOMI
  Ellingtones (1987) (2'30) •Dus

BENNETT, David - *Concerto in G Minor* (1939) (7') •CF

BORSCHEL, E. - *Kubanishes Liebeslied* •1 Sx: A or T •Fro

BOTTENBERG, Wolfgang - *Concertino* (1989) •CMC

BRANDON, Seymour - *Concerto* •adr

BUSCHMANN, Rainer - *Tenor Talen* (1965) (15') •Br&Ha

COPE, David - *Concerto* (1975) •adr

COWLES, Colin - *From the King's Chamber* •Tsx/Narr/Chamber Orch •adr
  In Memoriam (1976) (13') •Tsx/Str Orch adr

DE ROSSI RE, Fabrizio - *Aria di Strepito* (1992) (6')

Dinicu, Grigoras - *Hora Staccato* (HEIFETZ) •1 Sx: A or T •CF

DJEMIL, Enyss - *Concerto* (1974) (16') •1 Sx: S+A+T •adr

DONATONI, Franco - *Hot* (1989) (14') •1 Sx: T+Sno/Cl+Eb Cl/Tpt/ Trb/Perc/Bass/Pno •Ric

ERICKSON, Nils - *Konsert* (1981) (16') •STIM

EWAZEN, Eric - *Concerto* (1993) (22')

FELD, Jindrich - *Concerto* (1980) •1 Sx: S+A+T/Orch or Band •Kjos

Fiocco, Joseph-Hector - *Concerto* (LONDEIX) (15') •Sch

GLASER, Werner - *Concerto* (1981) (16') •Tsx/Str Orch •STIM

GÖRNER, Hans Georg - *Concertino*, op. 31 (1957) •2 Sx: AT •Hof

GOULD, Morton - *Diversions* (1990) (25') •GSch

GREEN, John - *Mine Eyes Have Seen* (1978) (37') •Tsx/ Tpt+Flugelhorn/Electr. Guit/Orch •B&H

Gretry, André - *Suite rococo* (8') (LONDEIX) •Tsx/Str Orch •Sch

HARTLEY, Walter - *Rhapsody* (1979) (6'15) •Tsx/Str Quartet or Str Orch •DP

HARVEY, Paul - *Concertino* (1974) (15') •Tsx/Chamber Orch or Band •Mau

HASQUENOPH, Pierre - *Concertino*, op. 34b (1976) (10'30) •Tsx/Str Orch •ME

HELFRITZ, Hans - *Concerto* (1945) •Sch

HESPOS, Hans-Joachim - *Dschen* (1968) (11') •1 Sx: T+B/Str Orch

HODKINSON, Sidney - *Another Man's Poison* (1970) (6'30) •1 Sx: A or T •adr

HOLBROOKE, Joseph - *Concerto in Bb*, op. 115 (1939) (15') •Cl+Asx+Tsx+Ssx •B&H

JOLAS, Betsy - *Points d'or* (1981) •1 Sx: S+A+T+B •Ric

JOHNSON, Barry - *Concerto* •Reg

KEULEN, Geert van - *Fingers* •Tsx/Chamber Orch •Don

KOSTECK, Gregory - *Concerto*

KRAUS, Marco - *Suite concertante* •1 Sx: Sno+S+A+T+B

LACOUR, Guy - *Pièce concertante* (1975-76) (8'30) •1 Sx: T or A/ Str Orch or Wind Orch •Bil

LARSSON, Häkan - *Gester av en gest* (1990) •Tsx/Str Orch •SMIC

LEESON, Cecil - *Concerto for Tenor Saxophone* (1960)

LEHMANN, Markus - *Concerto* (10'10) •Asto

LERSTAD, Terje Bjorn - *Concerto No. 1*, op. 104 (1978) (24') •NMI

LINKOLA, Jukka - *Crossings* (1983) (33')

LUTYENS, Elisabeth - *Chamber Concerto*, op. 8/2 (1940-41) (triple concerto) •Cl/Tsx/Pno/Str •Che

MARIETAN, Pierre - *Concert IV* (1989) (8') •1 Sx: Sno+S+T+B+Bs+CBs/Instrumental ensemble

MARTIN, Frank - *Ballade* (1940) (8') •Uni

McKINLEY, Thomas - *Tenor Rhapsody* (1989)

MIEREANU, Costin - *Kammer-Koncert n° 1* (1984-85) (16') •1 Sx: Sno+A+T+Bs •Sal

MIHALOVICI, Marcel - *Chant premier*, op. 103 (1973) (12') •Heu

NATANSON, Tadeus - *Kincert Podwojny* (1959) •2 Sx: AT •AAW/ AMP

NICULESCU, Stefan - *Cantos* (1984-85) (22') •1 Sx: Sno+A+T+B

NIKIPROWETZKY, Tolia - *Tetraktys* (1976) •1 Sx: S+A+T+B/ Chamber Orch •adr

OTT, David - *Concerto* (1992) (24') •1 Sx: T or S

PABLO, Luis de - *Une couleur* (1988) (22') •1 Sx: Sno+S+T+B+CBs •SZ

PECK, Russell - *The Upward Stream* (1985-86) (15')

PEIXINHO, Jorge - *Passage intérieur* (1989) (16') •1 Sx: Sno+S+A+T+B/Instrumental Ensemble

POPOVICI, Fred - *Heterosynthesis II* (1986) (18') •1 Sx: S+A+T

PRESSER, William - *Concerto* (1965) (20') •Tsx/Chamber Orch •adr

RENDLEMAN, Richard - Concertino (1992)

ROBERZNIK, Jure - *Concertino* (1965)

ROLIN, Etienne - *Maschera* (1980) (17') •1 Sx: S+A+B/Chamber Orch •adr
  Rideau de feu (1993) (18') 2 Sx: ST •adr

ROSA, Rich de - *Matron of Children*

SHAFFER, Sherwood - *Concerto* •adr
  Stargaze •Narr/Tsx/Orch •adr

SIVERTSEN, Kenneth - *For ope hav II* (1983) •Tsx/Str •NMI
  Largo... (1981) •Tsx/Pno/Str •NMI

SOTELO, Mauricio - *Due voci* (1990) •Tsx/BsCl+CBsCl •Uni

SOUKUP, Vladimir - *Concerto* (1982)

STEINBACHER, Erwin - *Pieces* •Fro

SURIANU, Horia - *Concerto* (1984) (15') •1 Sx: Sno+T •Sal

SYMONDS, Norman - *Autumn Nocturne* •Tsx/Str Orch •CMC

TAGGART, Mark Alan - *Concerto* (1981) (18') •adr

TARANU, Cornel - *Miroirs* (1990) (18') •1 Sx: S+T

TUTHILL, Burnett - *Concerto*, op. 50 (1965) (20') •South

VALEK, Jiri - *Symphony III* (1963) (28') •2 Sx: ST/Narr/Orch •CHF

WALTER, Civitaraele - *Un soir à Moscou*

WARD, Robert - *Concerto* (1983) (14'30) •Ga

WILDER, Alec - *Concerto* (1970) •Tsx/Chamber Orch or Band or Pno
JB/WIM
Suite No. 1 (1965) •Tsx/Str •JB/WIM
Three Ballads for Stan (1966) •Tsx/Str Orch •JB/WIM
WORLEY, John Carl - *Samoset Concerto* (1972)

Tenor Saxophone and Band

Band unless otherwise indicated (Band, sauf
indication contraire).

ABLINGER, Peter - *Escapse* (1989) •adr
Breedam, J. van - *Ecoutez-moi* •1 Sx: A or T/Band •An
CHATTAWAY, Jay - *Double Star* (1985) •2 Sx: AT
DANNENBERG, Torsten - *Skizze no. 1* (3'30) •Tsx/Big Band •SMIC
DUCKWORTH, William - *Fragments* (1967) (12') •Tsx/Wind Orch/
Perc •SeMC
FELD, Jindrich - *Concerto* (1980) •1 Sx: S+A+T/Orch or Band •Kjos
FOLLAS, Ronald - *Ballade and Allegro* (1985)
HARTLEY, Walter - *Concertino* (1977-78) (9') •DP
HARVEY, Paul - *Concertino* (1974) (15') •Tsx/Chamber Orch or
Band •Mau
LACOUR, Guy - *Pièce concertante* (1975-76) (8'30) •1 Sx: T or A/
Str Orch or Wind Orch •Bil
LANE, Richard - *Suite* (1970) (7'30) •B&H
OTT, David - *Essay* (1983) (13') •Eto
OWEN, Jerry - *Diversion* (1982) •2 Sx: AT/Band •DP
PHILLIPS, Burril - *Yellowstone, Yates and Yosemite* (1972)
PIERSON, Thomas - *Elegie* (1974) •adr
SCHMIDT, William - *Concerto* (1981) (14') •WIM
SHAFFER, Sherwood - *Rhapsody* (1987) •adr
WILDER, Alec - *Concerto* (1970) •Tsx/Chamber Orch or Band or Pno
JB/WIM
WILLIAMS, Clifton - *Pandean Fable*

Solo Baritone Saxophone

Also see Unspecified Instrumentation (Voir aussi
instruments non déterminés), page 422 and Saxophone
and Tape (Saxophone et Bande magnétique), Page 416.

Bach, Johann Sebastian - *Suites I, III, IV* •South
BATTISTA, Tonino - *Narciso* (1989/91) •1 Sx: S+B/Live Electron.
BEGLARIAN, Eve - *Getting to Know the Weather* •DP
BOONE, Ben - *Election Year* (1994) •Sx Solo: S or A or T or B •INM
CAPOËN, Denis - *Euphonie* (1987) (8-10') •1 Sx: T+B or A+T
COCCO, Enrico - *Actings* (1990) (10') •1 Sx: A+B/Electronics •adr
CONDÉ, Gérard - *Monarch...* (1983) (22') •1 Sx: Sno+S+A+T+B+Bs
DELAMARRE, Pierre - *Ballade* (1983) (7') •adr
DIEDERICHS, Yann - *M.L.K.* (1981) (10'30) •1 Sx: S+A+T+B/
Dispositif électro-acoust. ad lib.
DÜMKE, Ulrich - *1058* (1990) (6') •Wu
EITHLER, Estaban - *Congaja* •Lee/EMBA
FORSSELL, Jonas - *Den Kortaste natten...* (1979) •STIM
FOURCHOTTE, Alain - *Disgressions V* (1983) (5')
FRIEDMAN, Jeffrey - *Music for Solo Baritone* •DP
GINER, Bruno - *Io* (1992) (8')
GRAEF, Friedemann - *Facettes* (1992) •R&E
GRISEY, Gérard - *Anubis et Nout* (1992) •1 Sx: Bs or B •Ric
HAVEL, Christophe - *Oxyton* (1990) (9') •adr
HODKINSON, Sidney - *Trinity* (1971) •Sx Solo: A or T or B •adr
HOLLAND, Dulcie - *Pieces* •adr
HOLMBERG, Gunnar - *Schizofreni no. 1*, op. 15 (1990) (3') •SMIC
HORWOOD, Michael - *For David and Johannes* (1985)
JOHNSON, Tom - *Rational Melodies* (1982) (2' to 25')

KALOGERAS, Alexandra - *Hors tempérament* (1990) (9')
LLOYD, Richard - *Stitched* (1984) (13')
MACCHIA, Salvatore - *Cantando le canzoni...* •DP
MACHUEL, Thierry-Joël - *France-Télécom* (1991) •1 Sx: B+S
MANDANICI, Marcella - *Nelle lettere di mi* (1991) (5') •adr
MIEREANU, Costin - *Aksax* •Sal
MOLINO, Andréa - *Unité K* (7') •1 Sx: S+B/Tape
NODA, Ryo - *Fantaisie et danse* (1976) (3'45) •Led
Paganini, Nicolo - *Caprice*, Op. 1, No. 24 (Rossi) •Sx Solo •DP
PANICCIA, Renzo - *Ritimagici: Alleggiare delle...*, op. 8 (1985) (8')
Sourires de clown, op. 7 (1985) (6')
RADULESCU, Horatiu - *Astray* (1984-85) (23') •1 Sx:
Sno+S+A+T+B+Bs/matériel électron. (or
Prepared Pno)
ROLIN, Etienne - *Fantasy cycle* (1985) (3') •adr
ROSSÉ, François - *Epiphanies* (1990) (10') •1 Sx: S+B+Bs/Dispositif
électro-acoust. •adr
SEVRETTE, Danielle - *A peine ai-je vu les dessous du capitaine* •adr
SIVILOTTI, Valter - *Improvisazione interrotta* •1 Sx: A or B •Piz
SWAIN, Freda - *Naturo Suite* (1931) (6') •Any Sx Solo •BMIC
The Tease (1965) (1'30) •Any Sx Solo •BMIC
TONT, Patrice - *Citharède* (1990) (6')
De ceux qui fréquentent l'altitude (1990) (10') •1 Sx: S+B
Tête oreille (1991)
WALTER, Caspar - *Studie 9* (10')
WASHBURN, Gary - *A Ride; A Moonbeam; Polka Dot* (1974) (20')
•Sx Solo: A+S+B •SeMC
WINKLER, Gerhard - *Hybrid I* (1992) •adr
WÜRTH, Volker - *Meditation I* (1988) (2') •VW

Baritone Saxophone and Piano

Also see Baritone Saxophone and Orchestra or Band
(Voir aussi saxophone baryton et orchestre ou band), Page
319.

ALKEMA, Henk - *Rituelen II* (1987) (11') •Don
Alschausky - *Walser-Arie no. 2* •CBet
ANDERSON, Garland - *Sonata* (1976) •South
ANDRIEU, Fernand - *1er solo de concours* •1 Sx: T or B/Pno •Alf
BERNAUD, Alain - *Humoresque* (1982) •adr
BISSELINK, Piet - *Izegrim* •1 Sx: T or B/Pno •Mol
BRENET, Thérèse - *Incandescence* (1984) (8') •Lem
CADEE, J. L. - *Nocturnes* (1986) (14'30) •adr
CARNEY, Harry - *Warm-Up* •MCA
CLERISSE, Robert - *Prélude et Divertissement* •1 Sx: T or B/Pno •Bil
COMBELLE, François - *1er Solo de concert* •1 Sx: B or T/Pno •Alf
COOLS, Eugène - *Allegro de concert* •Bil
COWLES, Colin - *Pieces* •adr
DAVIS, William - *Variations on a Theme...* (1982) •South
DEMERSSEMAN, Jules - *1er solo* (1865); *2me solo* (1866)
DENHOF, Robert - *Orion* (1993) •B&N
DI BARI, Marco - *1° studio sugli oggetti...* (1989) (7') •Ric
Donjon, Johannes - *Invocation* •CBet
DUBOIS, Pierre-Max - *Fantaisie* •Led
Fasch, Johann - *Sonata* (RASCHER) •GiMa
Fesch, Willem de - *Canzonetto* •Spr
Fontaine, E, - *Interlude Melody* •PA
FONTAINE, Louis-Noël - *Sonate* (1993) (15') •Capri
FRANGKISER, Carl - *Canzona* •Bel
GENZMER, Harald - *Rhapsodie* (1987) (10') •R&E
GIOVANNINI, Caesar - *Romance* (1988) (4') •1 Sx: B or A/Pno
•South
GLASER, Werner - *Sonata* (1986) (15') •STIM
Gliere, Reinhold - *Russian Sailor's Dance* (HURRELL) •Rub

Godfrey-Harris - *Lucy Song* •CBet
Golterman, George - *Cantilena* (TEAL) •GSch
GRAETZER, Guillermo - *Divertimento* •Mus
GRILLAERT, Octave - *Spirito*, op. 9331 (1')
HAGI, Kyôko - *Par avion*
Handel, Georg-Friedrich - *Sound an Alarm* •Spr
HARTLEY, Walter - *Little Suite* (1974) (5'30) •DP
    The Saxophone Album (1974) •DP; *Sonata* (1976) (10'30) •DP
Hartmann - *Pieces*
HARTZELL, Doug - *The Egotistical Elephant* (1957) (3'30) •Sha
Haydn, Joseph - *Andante* •JS
HURREL, Clarence - *Echo of Romany* •Rub
ISAKSSON, Madeleine - *Capriola* (1989) •SMIC
Jakma - *Parade des Olifanten* •1 Sx: T or B/Pno •Mol
Järnefelt, Armas - *Berceuse* •Bel
JOHNSON, Clair - *Scene Forestal* (1938) •Rub
Kabalevsky - *Sonatina*, op. 13 (GEE) •1 Sx: A or B/Pno •South
KARKOFF, Maurice - *Poem*, op. 166 (1989) •STIM
Khatchaturian, Aram - *Sabre Dance* •Lee
Klughart, August - *Romanze* •JS
Koepke, Paul - *Recitative and Rondino* •Rub
LAMB, John David - *Romp* •DP; *Three Pieces* (1963)
LA PORTA, John - *Miniature*
LEJET, Edith - *Saphir* (1982) (4'30) •Sal
LERSTAD, Terje Bjorn - *Sonata*, op. 117 (1978) (16') •NMI
Liagre, Dartagnan - *Souvenir de Calais* •Bil
LINN, Robert - *Saxifrage Blue* (1977)
LLOYD, Richard - *Breath Baby* (1984-85) •Bsx/Amplified Pno
Long, Newell - *Undercurrent - Theme & Variations* •Rub
LUNDE, Lawson - *Scherzo*, op. 38a (1970) (4') •adr
MAGNANENSI, Giorgio - *Color...* (1992) (15') •1 Sx: A+B/Pno
Marcello, Allessandro - *Andante and Allegro* (VOXMAN) •Rub
MARGONI, Alain - *Sonate* (1976)
Massenet, Jules - *Elegy* •Bel
Mattei, Tito - *The Mariner* (WALTERS) •Rub
MAURY, Lownder - *5th Contest Solo* (KLICKMANN) •1 Sx: T or B/Pno •Alf
MAYEUR, Louis - *1ère Fantaisie originale* (1877)
MENCHERINI, Fernando - *Divaricanto 3* (1992)
Mozart, Wolfgang - *Pieces*
Nessler, Victor - *Der Rattenfänger von Hameln* (H. LUREMAN) •TM
NIVERD, Lucien - *Légende* •Braun
NYVANG, Michael - *Tre korte karakterstykker* (1988) (7')
OBERGEFELL, Glenn - *Lullaby* (1993) (4') •Bsx/Pno •TTF
OTERO, Francisco - *Double suggestion* (1981) •1 Sx: A+B/Pno
PARES, Gabriel - *Crépuscule* (JUDY) •1 Sx: T or B/Pno •Braun/Rub
PATACHICH, Ivan - *Sonatina* •SJ
Petrie, Henry - *Asleep in the Deep* (BUCHTEL) •Kjos
POOT, Marcel - *Impromptu* (1931) (7') •ME
POPINEAU, François - *Chi va piano va Saxo* (1993) •INM
PRESSER, William - *Prelude* (1966) (3') •Pres/Ten
Purcell, Henry - *Rondeau (Fairie Queen)* (RASCHER) •Bel
Rocerto - *Meditation* (MORGAN) •Volk
Rossini, Giacchino - *Pieces* •TM
RUDAJEV, Alexandre - *Intermezzo* (1991) •adr
RUEFF, Jeanine - *Trois pour deux* (1982) (14'30)
Saint-Saëns, Camille - *The Elephant* •Bel
SCHMIDT, William - *Rondoletto* •WIM
    Sonata (1979) •WIM
Schulz, Johann Peter - *Little March* (RASCHER) •Bel
Schumann, Robert - *Happy Farmer* •Bel
SEMLER-COLLERY, Jules - *Cantabile* (1956) (4') •Dec
SINGELÉE, Jean-Baptiste - *Fantaisie*, op. 60 (1858) •Sax
    2me Solo de concert, op. 77 (1861) •Sax
    3me Solo de concert, op. 83 (1862) •Sax/Rub

7me Solo de concert, op. 93 (1863) •Sax/Ron
8me Solo de concert, op. 99 (1864) •Sax
SMIRNOV, Dimitry - *Poème* •ECS
SPEARS, Jarde - *Ritual and Celebration* (1981) •South
Tchaikovsky, Peter Ilyich - *Impromptu* •Spr
Van BALKOM, Joost - *Cataract* (1993) •INM
VERHIEL, Ton - *Impromptu miniature* (1985)
VRIEND, Huub de - *Psycho* (1984) (13') •Bsx/Pno or Orgue à bouche •Don
WALTERS, Harold - *40 Fathoms* •Rub
Weber - *Deep River*; *Elephant Dance* •Bel
    Evening Shadows •1 Sx: B or T/Pno •Bel
WEISSING, Matthias - *La ville...* (1993) •1 Sx: S+T+B/Pno •INM
WELSH, Wilmer - *Passacaglia* •1 Sx: S+A+T+B/Pno
WORLEY, John Carl - *Sonata "Pleasant Bay"* (1992) •DP
    Sonatina (1978) •DP
    Twilight Pine Shadows •1 Sx: B or Bs/Pno •DP
WURMSER, Lucien - *Solo de concours* •Bil

Baritone Saxophone
and Orchestra or Band

Orchestra unless otherwise indicated (Orchestre, sauf indication contraire).

BENTZON, Niels Viggo - *Climatic Changes*, op. 474 (1985) (20') •Bsx/Pno •Hire/Sal
CASTRO, Dino - *Concerto* (1978) •1 Sx: S+A+B/Chamber Orch
COUINEAU, Patrice - *Mouvements volcaniques* (1992) (9') •Bsx/Orch •adr
FREEDMAN, Harry - *Celebration* (1977) •1 Sx: S+B •CMC
GASLINI, Giorgio - *Silver concert* (1992) (12')
GLASER, Werner Wolf - *Konzertstück* (1992) •Bsx/Str Orch •SMIC
HARRISON, Jonty - *CQ* (1989) (16') •1 Sx: S+B/Instrumental Ensemble •adr
HARTLEY, Walter - *Chamber Concerto* (1988) (9'30) •Bsx/Wind octet •DP
HARVEY, Paul - *Concertino* (1976) (15') •Bsx/Orch or Band or Pno •Mau
HESPOS, Hans-Joachim - *Dschen* (1968) (11') •1 Sx: T+B/Str Orch
    Ka (1972) (8'30) •Bsx/Bass •EMod
JOLAS, Betsy - *Points d'or* (1981) •1 Sx: S+A+T+B •Ric
KONT, Paul - *Konzertante Symphonie* (15') •Bsx/Str Orch •CA
KRAUS, Marco - *Suite concertante* •1 Sx: Sno+S+A+T+B
MAIGUASHCA, Mesias - *Vorwort zu solaris* (1989) (19') •1 Sx: S+B/Instrumental ensemble
MARBE, Myriam - *Concerto* (33') •1 Sx: B+A+Sno •EMu
MARIETAN, Pierre - *Concert IV* (1989) (8') •1 Sx: Sno+S+T+B+Bs+CBs/Instrumental ensemble
NICULESCU, Stefan - *Cantos* (1984-85) (22') •1 Sx: Sno+A+T+B
NIKIPROWETZKY, Tolia - *Tetraktys* (1976) •1 Sx: S+A+T+B/Chamber Orch •adr
OLAH, Tiberiu - *Obelisc pentru...* (22') •1 Sx: Sno+A+B
PABLO, Luis de - *Une couleur* (1988) (22') •1 Sx: Sno+S+T+B+CBs •SZ
PEIXINHO, Jorge - *Passage intérieur* (1989) (16') •1 Sx: Sno+S+A+T+B/Instrumental Ensemble
Petrie, Henry - *Asleep in the Deep* (WALTERS) •Bsx/Band •Rub
RIEUNIER, Jean-Paul - *Volume 2* (1974) •Bsx/Wind Ensemble •Led
ROLIN, Etienne - *Maschera* (1980) (17') •1 Sx: S+A+B/Pno/Chamber Orch •adr
SCHULER, Thomas - *Konzert*, op. 8 (20') •Bsx/Str Orch •CA
SIMIC, Vojislaw - *Balada* (1959) •Bsx/Jazz Orch •adr

SKROWACZEWSKI, Stanislas - *Ricercari notturni* (1977) (20') •1 Sx: S+A+B •EAM
SOTELO, Mauricio - *Due voci* (1990) •Tsx/BsCl+CBsCl •Uni
VIERU, Anatol - *Narration II* (1985) (17') •1 Sx: S+B •Sal
WATTERS, Mark - *Rhapsody* (1983) •Bsx/Orch or Band

Bass Saxophone

Also see Unspecified Instrumentation (Voir aussi instruments non déterminés), page 422 and Saxophone and Tape (Saxophone et Bande magnétique), Page 416.

AMELLER, André - *Kryptos* •BsSx/Pno •Pet
BERENGUER, José-Manuel - *Fuego* (1989) (8') •BsSx/Tape
CAVANA, Bernard - *Cache-sax* (1984) (10') •BsSx Solo •Sal
CELERIANU, Michel - *Aus* (1985) •1 Sx: S+Bs/Ensemble/Choir
CONDÉ, Gérard - *Monarch...* (1983) (22') •1 Sx: Sno+S+A+T+B+Bs
CRUZ, Zulema de la - *Chio* (1989) •BsSx/Tape
DI BETTA, Philippe - *Fissures* (1991) (3') •BsSx/Harp •adr
EBENHÖH, Horst - *Konzert*, op.76 (25') •BsSx/Orch •CA
FOURCHOTTE, Alain - *Disgressions VI* (1983-84) (5') •BsSx Solo
FRANGKISER, Carl - *Melody variante* •BsSx/Pno •Bel
GRISEY, Gérard - *Anubis et Nout* (1992) •1 Sx: Bs or B •Ric
HARTLEY, Walter - *Sonatina Giocosa* (1987) (5') •BsSx/Pno •TP
IOACHIMESCU, Calin - *Musique spectrale* •1 Sx: S+Bs/Tape
ISRAEL, Brian - *Double Concerto* (1984) •2 Sx: SnoBs/Band
KURTAG, György - *Interrogation* (1983) (11'30) •1 Sx: T+Bs+CBs/ Tape •Sal
LERSTAD, Terje Bjorn - *Improvisation & tarentella*, op. 128 (1979) •BsSx Solo •NMI
MARIETAN, Pierre - *Concert IV* (1989) (8') •1 Sx: Sno+S+T+B+Bs+CBs/Instrumental ensemble
Duo (1985) •1 Sx: Sno+A+T+B+Bs+CBs/Tape
MARTINEZ FERNANDEZ, Julian - *Hacia la desconocido* (1993) •Sx Solo: S+Bs+T
MIEREANU, Costin - *Pieces* •Sal
MOLTENI, Marco - *Saturna pyri* (1986) (6') •1 Sx: A+Bs/Tape
RADULESCU, Horatiu - *Astray* (1984-85) (23') •1 Sx: Sno+S+A+T+B+Bs/matériel électron. (or Prepared Pno)
ROQUIN, Louis - *Machination VIII* (1983) •1 Sx: S+A+T+B+Bs/ Tape
ROSSÉ, François - *Epiphanies* (1990) (10') •1 Sx: S+B+Bs/Dispositif électro-acoust. •adr
RUBBERT, Rainer - *Vision (Urban music II)* (1993) •BsSx Solo •adr
SCELSI, Jacinto - *Maknongan* (1976) (4') •BsSx Solo •Sal
TERUGGI, Daniel - *Xatys* (1988) (18'30) •1 Sx: Bs+T+S/Dispositif électronique
TORTENSSON, Klas - *Licks and Brains* 1) Solo (1987-88) (10') •Don
VAGGIONE, Oracio - *Thema* (1985) (10') •BsSx/Dispositif électroacoust. •Sal
VAUGHN, John J. - *Gorges* (1991) •BsSx/Pno
WORLEY, John - *Twilight Pine Shadows* •1 Sx: B or Bs/Pno •DP

Contrabass Saxophone

Also see Unspecified Instrumentation (Voir aussi instruments non déterminés), page 422 and Saxophone and Tape (Saxophone et Bande magnétique), Page 416.

CAVANA, Bernard - *La Villette* (1984-85) •1 Sx: S+T+CBs/Tape
FOURCHOTTE, Alain - *Disgressions VII* (1984) (5') •CBsSx Solo
Girard, L. - *Le sommeil de Polyphème* •CBsSx Solo

HESPOS, Hans-Joachim - *Pico* (1978) (4') •Sx Solo: CBs or Sno
KURTAG, György - *Interrogation* (1983) (11'30) •1 Sx: T+Bs+CBs/ Tape •Sal
MARIETAN, Pierre - *Concert IV* (1989) (8') •1 Sx: Sno+S+T+B+Bs+CBs/Instrumental ensemble
Duo (1985) •1 Sx: Sno+A+T+B+Bs+CBs/Tape
MIEREANU, Costin - *Aksax* (1984) (5'35) •Sx Solo: Bs or CBs •Sal
MONNET, Marc - *Cirque* (1986) (7') •CBsSx Solo •Sal
PABLO, Luis de - *Une couleur* (1988) (22') •1 Sx: Sno+S+T+B+CBs •SZ
PATACHICH, Ivan - *Jei 1+4* (1989) (12') •1 Sx: S+A+CBs/Instrumental Ensemble
ROQUIN, Louis - Soli, solo et solissimo (1984-85) (10') •1 Sx: S+A+T+CBs/Tape
XANTHOUDAKIS, Charis - *Les visages...* (1989) (8') •CBsSx/Tape

2 Saxophones

Also see Unspecified Instrumentation (Voir aussi instruments non déterminés), page 422.

Adams, Stephen - *The Holy City* •2 Sx/Pno •Kjos/Rub
Aldrich, Henry - *Love and Flowers* •AT/Pno
Amsden - *Practice Duets* •AA •WWS
ANDRAUD, Albert - *3 Duos concertants* •AA or TT
ANDRÉ, Paul - *Romance d'Automne* •AA/Pno •Braun
ANDRIEU, Fernand - *Impressions napolitaines* •SA or TB •Mar
APPLEBAUM, Terry - *Duets* •WWS
APPLEDORN, Mary Jeanne van - *Four Duos* (1985) (4'30) •AA •DP
Arditi - *Il Bacio* •AT/Pno •Cen
ARMA, Paul - *Divertimento no. 12* (1971) (15') •AA or TT •Chap
   6 Mobiles (1975) (12') •1, 2, 3, or 4 Sx
   Musique d'après des thèmes populaires... (1968) (12') •2 Sx
ARNOLD, Jay - *Easy Saxophone Solos or Duets* (1960) •Ams
ATOR, James Donald - *Duo* (1983)
Aubert, Jacques - *Suite* (LONDEIX) •Led
Bach, Johann Sebastian - *Ave Maria* (GOUNOD) •AT/Pno •Cen
   Canon no. 4 (SMIM) •AT •Rub
   4 Canons (MOROSCO) •ST & SB
   Duet Cantata 78 (SIBBING) •AA/Pno •Eto
   Duo Sonata •EM
   Duo Sonata •Mus
   Duos •Mil
   15 Inventions (TEAL) •AA or AT •Pres
   Kanon in der Oktave (T. SCHÖN) •AB •ApE
Bach, Wilhelm Friedmann - *6 Duets* (2 Vol.) •AA or TT •EK
BACHTISCHA, Michael - *Notation* (1993) •SA •INM
BAKER, David N. - *Duet* •AA
Barnhouse, C. - *Pieces* •AT/Pno •Bar
BEDARD, Denis - *Duetto* (1988) •AA
Beethoven, L. van - *Allegro and Minuet* •Mus
   Duo •Mil
   Minuet (TRINKAUS) •AA or AT/Pno •CF
   Minuet in G •AA or AT/Pno •CBet/CF
   Moonlight Sonata •AA or AT/Pno •Cen
   Seven Variations... (SAKAGUCHI) •IM
Bellini, Vincenzo - *Duet from "Norma"* •2 Sx/Pno •CF
BENNETT, Richard - *Conversations* (1983) •Uni
Bent - *Swiss Boy* •AA/Pno
Berbiguier, Benoît Tranquille - *6 Easy Duets* •Mus
BERNARDS, B. - *Pieces* •Zim
BERNAUD, Alain - *Sonate* (1974) (20'30) •SB •adr
BODA, John - *Perambulations* •AT/Pno
Boismortier, Bodin de - *2 Sonates*, op. 6 •EK
Borodin, Alexandre - *Solicitude* (MAGANINI) •AT/Pno •Mus
BOUVARD, Jean - *13 Chansons et danses...* •adr
   7 Duos faciles •adr
   21 Mini duetti (1979) •Bil
   Trio •SB/Pno •adr
Braga, Gaetano - *Angel's Serenade* •AT/Pno •CF/Cen
Brahms, Johannes - *Famous Waltz*, op. 39/15 •2 Sx/Pno •CF
Braun - *2 Grand duos*, op. 3 •Cos
Briegel, George - *Pieces* •2 Sx/Pno •Bri
BROWN, Rayner - *Suite* •WIM
Druniau, Augustin - *Toi et moi - Fantaisie duo* •SA •Bil
BRÜNINGHAUS, Rainer - *Minimal-paraphrasen* (1990) •B&B
Bucquet, P. - *Suites 1 & 2* •Mus
BUMCKE, Gustav - *38 Duette*, op. 43 •VAB
Butterfield, N. - *When you and I were young* •AT/Pno •Cen
BUTTERWORTH, Arthur - *Three Dialogues* (1962) •SS •Pet
CAGE, John - *Sonata* (1933) •Any 2 instruments •Pet
   Pieces •Pet

CARAVAN, Ronald - *Little Showpiece* (1985) •SnoBs •adr
   Three Modal Dances (1978) •Eth
CARDEW, Cornelius - *Solo* (1964) (10') •2 performers •Uni
CHAGRIN, Francis - *6 Duets* •Nov
CHARRON, Damien - *Vers tous les chemins* (1988) (3') •AA •Dur
CHATMAN, Stephen - *Music for Two Saxophones* •AA
Chauvet, Georges - *15 Grande études* (BARRET) •AB or ST •Com
Chedeville, Esprit - *Scherzo - Trio* (CLARK) •AT/Pno •Mus
CHESKY - *Contemporary Duets*
Chopin, Frédéric - *Minute Waltz* (BRIEGEL) •AT/Pno •Bri
CLERGUE, Jean - *Volutes et Primavera* (1965) (3') •Phi
Clodomir, Pierre - *12 Duos in B* •TT •Elk/Mol
COGGINS, Willis - *Duets* •Bel
COLLER, Jerome - *Trio* (1984) •AA/Pno
Conklin - *Handy Andy* •2 Sx/Pno •CF
CONLEY, Lloyd - *Christmas for Two* (1981) •Ken
CONSTANT, Marius - *Traits* (1991) (11') •2 Sx: Sno+S+A+B/ S+A+T+Bs
CORINA, John - *Partita* •AA
CORNU, Françoise - *Filigranes I & II* (1988) •AA
COSTE, Napoléon - *Fantaisie de concert* •Mil
COWELL, Henry - *Hymn and Fuguing Tune No. 18* (1964) •SA
   Hymn and Fuguing Tune No. 18 (1964) (4') •S CBs •TTF
COX, Rona - *A Saxophone* (1968) (6') •AT/Tape •adr
CRAGUN, J. Beach - *Eight Concert Duets* (1926) •Rub
CUNNINGHAMM, Michael - *Trio*, op. 59 (1974) •SA/Pno •Eto
DAKIN, Charles - *Mobiles* (1982) (11'15) •ST •DP
Danks, Hart - *Silver Threads Among the Gold* •AT/Pno or AATB/Pno
DEASON, David - *Glow* (1980) •AT •DP
DECRUCK, Fernande - *12 Duos* (1934) (2 Volumes) •AA •EP
Delamater, Eric - *Adeste Fidelis* •AA/Pno •Rub
DELBECQ, Laurent - *Pieces* •Mol
Delisse - *Pieces* •Mil
DEPELSENAIRE, Jean-Marie - *Le Dragon de jade* •SA/Pno •adr
DESCHAMPS, Jean-Henri - *Sonatine* •AA/Pno •Bil
DESPORTES, Yvonne - *Blablabla* (1971) (15') •AT/Pno •Dom
   Pour copie conforme (4') •AT •DP
Devienne, François - *6 Sonatas* (ANDRAUD) •AA •South
DHAINE, Jean-Louis - *Entrechants* (1978) (3') •AT •Fuz
DI BETTA, Philippe - *Passages* (1990) (12') •AA •adr
Di Capua, Eduardo - *O sole mio* •AT/Pno •Cen
DIEMENTE, Edward - *Dimensions II* •With Tape •SeMC
   Diary Part II (1972) •AA/Tape •DP
DIJOUX, Marc - *60 Duos sur des airs populaires* •AA •Mar
Donizetti, Gaetano - *Lucia de Lammermoor* •AT/Pno •Cen
Dorado - *Two Friends* (WHEELER) •AA or AT/Pno •Volk
Drigo, Riccardo - *Valse bluette* •AA/Pno •CF
DUBOIS, Pierre-Max - *Deux Caprices en forme d'études* (1964) •AA •adr
   Six Caprices (1967) •AA •Led
Dvorak, Anton - *Pieces* •2 Sx/Pno •Bri/Cen
EDLUND, Mikael - *Trio sol* (1980) (9') •SS/Pno •TIM
Elgar - *Salut d'amour* •AT/Pno
ELLIS, James - *Dixieland Duet* •WWS
Emmett, Daniel - *Dixie's Land* •2 Sx/Pno •McK
ENGEBRETSON, Mark - *An Arc in Solitude* (1991) (8') •AA •ApE
EYSER, Eberhard - *Duo 2D* (1989) (10') •2 Sx: S+T/A+B •EMa
Fabre, C. - *Pieces* •AA/Pno •CF
Fauré, Jean-Baptiste - *Les Rameaux* •AT/Pno •Cen
Feldman, M. - *Round I* •AA •Cen
FELICE, John - *An American Ceremony* •AA
Ferling - *Duo Concertante No. 1* (GEE) •AT •MMB
   Three Duos Concertants (GEE) •AA or AT •South
FERRARI, Luc - *Tautologos III* (1969)
Ferstl, Herbert - *15 Duette* (UHDE, DI LASSO, CASTOLDI, etc.) •AT

FLEISHER, Robert - *Oblique Motions* •2 Sx

FONTAINE, Louis Noël - *Duo pour les...* (1979) (6') •AB •Capri

Foster, Stephen - *Come Where my Love Lies...* •TT/Pno •CF

Fote, R. - *Amigos* •AA/Pno •Ken

FOURNIER, Marie-Hélène - *Oxydes* (1986) (3'40) •AA •Lem
  Quatre Duos (1988) (10') •AA •Com

FOX, Frederick - *Visitations* (1982) (10') •AA

Franck, César - *Aux petits enfants* (CLUWEN) •AA/Pno •TM

FRIEDRICHS, Günter - *Pas de deux* (1981-82) •AT •B&B

GARCIN, Gérard - *Dialogosax* (1971) •2 Sx
  6me Musique... (1984) (6') •1 to 7 Asx/Tape •Sal

GATES, Everett - *Odd Meter Duets* •SF

Gatti - *30 Progressive Duets* (IASILLI) •CF

Gearhart - *Duet Sessions Serious and Amusing* •AA or TT •Shaw

Gee, Harry - *16 Intermediate Duets* (various composers) •AT •CPP

GENZMER, Harald - *Sonatine; 10 Stücke* •SA •R&E

GILARDIN, Jean-Paul - *2 Danses yougoslaves* •ST/Pno •adr

GINGRAS, Guy - *3 Duos scabreux* (1987) •AA •Med

GLASER, Werner Wolf - *Ritornello* (1989) (7') •SMIC

GLASS, Philip - *Play* (1966) •2 Sx

GORNER, Hans Georg - *Concertino*, op. 31 (1957) •AT/Orch or Pno •Hof

Gossec, François Joseph - *Ouverture* •AA •Mol

Grieg, Edvard - *Pieces* •AT/Pno •Cen

GRISEY, Gérard - *2 Incantations* •AA •Ric

GUERIN, Roland - *Divertissement* (1976) •SB

Gurewich, J. - *17 Classic Duets* •CF

HAIDMAYER, Karl - *Duet* •SB

Handel, Georg-Friedrich - *Trio Sonata No. 1* (VOXMAN-HERVIG) •AA/Pno •South

Hänsel, Arthur - *Concertino*, op. 80 (SANSONE) •AT •South

Harris, F. - *Pieces* •AA or TT/Pno •Lud

HARTLEY, Walter - *Dance* (1990) (2') •2 like Sx •Eth
  Duet-Sonatina (1986) (4'40) •AT •Eth
  Three American Folk Hymns (1987) •2 like Sx •DP
  Trio Estatico (1991) (8'45) •AT/Pno •Eth

HARTZELL, Doug - *Two Rogues* (1968) (2'30) •AA or 1 Sx Solo/Pno •Tmp

HARVEY, Paul - *Bubble and Squeak* •SnoB •adr
  Concert Duets (1981) •AT •Ron
  Equal Partners (1988) •AT •CasM

HASENPFLUG, Curt - *Vater un Sohn* •2 Sx/Pno •Fro

HAUBENSTOCK-RAMATI, Roman - *Multiple V* (1969) (10') •Uni

Hawthorne, Allan - *Whispering Hope* (BRIEGEL) •AA/Pno •Bri

Haydn, Franz Joseph - *Pieces* •CF/Mus

Henning, Karl - *59 Duets* •South

Herbert, Victor - *Gypsy Love Song* (HARRIS) •AA/Pno •Lud

Heuberger, Richard - *Midnight Belles* (KREISLER-LEIDZEIN) •AA/Pno •CFI

Hian, Ben - *Three Songs* •2 Sx/Pno or Tsx/Pno •Pet

HINDEMITH, Paul - *Konzertstück* (1933) (11'30) •AA •MM

HODY, Jean - *Souvenirs d'enfant* •Bil

Honegger, Arthur - *Petite suite n° 1* (1934) (2'30) •2 Sx (parties en ut)/Pno •CDM

HORIUCHI, Toshio - *Fantasy* (1975) •AA/Pno

HOUDY, Pierre - *5 Caractères...* (1988) (8'30) •AA •CMC

HOUSTON, Rudy - *Avant Garde Duets* •AA or TT •DP

Hubert, Roger - *Les tourbillons - Caprice* •SA •Mar

IANNACCONE, Anthony - *Invention*

IASSILLI, Gerardo - *Goldie - Valse Brillante* •2 Sx/Pno •CF

ISHIKETA, Mareo - *Révélation* (1972) •AT

IWAMOTO, Wataru - *Image* (1990) •AA/Tape

JACOBI, Wolfgang - *Barcarole* (1964) •AA/Pno

JERGENSON, Dale - *Five Little Duets* •AA •SeMC

KALLSTROM, Michael - *Time Converging* •AT/Pno

KANEFZKY, Franz - *Leiche duette* (1990) •Hag

Kaplan, D. - *Gotham Collection of Duets* •JS

KARKOFF, Maurice - *Profilen*, op. 157 (1984) (10') •AB •STIM

KARLINS, William - *Introduction and Passacaglia* •AT/Pno •ACA

Kennedy, Amanda - *Star of Hope - Rêverie* •AA or AT/Pno •Cen

KESNAR, Maurits - *Un petit rien* •AA/Pno •WWS

Kiefer, W. - *Elena Polka* •TT or AT/Pno •Bar

KING, Karl - *A Night in June* •AA or TT/Pno •Bar

KIYOSHI, Keiji - *Sonatina* (1977) •S+A A

KLERK, Joseph de - *Intrada; Kleine Partita* •Mol

Klickmann, F. Henry - *Pieces* •2 Sx/Pno •McK

Kling, Henri - *Olifan en mug* •Mol

KOCH, Erland von - *Birthday Music...* (1987) (9') •AA •DP
  Dialogue (1975-77) (5') •SA •DP

KOECHLIN, Charles - *24 Duos*, op. 186 (1942) •SA or AA •ME
  24 Leçons de solfège •AA or TT •Bil

KONIETZNY, H. - *Isommetrisch-isorhytmisch* •B&H

Kuhlau, F. - *Three Concerts Duets* (TEAL) •AA or TT •Pres

Labole, P. - *Les tourbillons* •SA •Mar

LACOUR, Guy - *Suite en duo* (1971) (10'30) •AA or TT •Bil

Lake, Mathew - *Annie Laurie* •AA or TT/Pno •CF

LAMB, John David - *Six Barefoot Dances* (1962) (8') •AA or TT •Gi&Ma
  Three Flourishes (1961) •AA

LANCEN, Serge - *Les jumeaux* (1963) (5'30) •AA or TT •Pet

Lange, Gustav - *Blumenlied* •AT/Pno •Cen

LA PORTA, John - *14 Jazz Rock Duets* •AA or AT or TT •Ken

LASNE, George - *Duo en Lab inspiré de Baustetter* •AA

LAUBA, Christian - *Adria* (1985) (12') •AA •Fuz

Lazarus, H. - *Grand Artistic Duets* (TRAXLER) •AA or TT •Bel

Leclair, J-M. - *Sonates en Ut, en Ré, en Fa* (LONDEIX) •SS or AA •Led

LEE, Hope - *Jygge... somebody's* (1987) (12') •SA •CMC

LEGUAY, Jean-Pierre - *Scabbs* (1984) •Asx/Bass (or Bsx) •Lem

LEJETH, Edith - *Emeraude et rubis* (1984) (3') •ET

Lemare, Edwin - *Pieces* •AA or AT/Pno •Cen/CF

LETELLIER, Robert - *14 nouveaux duos et trios* •Mar/Mol

Lewis - *Pieces* •WWS

Leybach, Ignace - *5th Nocturne in G* •AA or AT/Pno •Cen

Liszt, Franz - *Liebesträum* (SMITH) •AA or AT/Pno •Bar

LITTLE, Lowell - *Great Duets* •PA

Locatelli, P. - *Sonata in E Minor* •AA or TT •EK

Loeillet, J-B. - *Trio* (HORNIBROOK) •ST/Pno •Eto

LOGRANDE, L. A. - *Harlequin of the Union* (1993) (6'30) •SA •CI

LOLINI, Ruggero - *Solitudini declinate* (1985) (8'10) •Sno+A B

LONDEIX, Jean-Marie - *De l'intonation* (1981) •AA or TT or AT •Led

Losey, F. H. - *Woodland Whispers* (KLICKMANN) •AA •EMa

Luft, J. Heinrich - *24 Etudes in duets* (BLEUZET) •CFE

LUGLI, Lanfranco - *A la page* (1992) (8') •AT/Pno 4 hands (à 4 main)

LUNDE, Lawson - *Sonata-duet*, op. 25 (1967) (10') •AT •SMIC

MADERNA, Bruno - *Dialodia* (1972) (2'15) •Ric

MAGANINI, Quinto - *Canonico expressivo* •Mus
  In the Beginning - 15 Pieces •Mus
  Petite suite classique •AT •Mus

MARION, Alain - *50 duos progressifs*

MARSAL - *Grande fantaisie* •SA •Mar

Martini, Jean-Paul - *Plaisir d'amour* (MAGANINI) •AT/Pno •Mus

MASON, Lucas - *Canonic Dances* (1970) •AA or TT •adr

MASSA, Enrico - *Preludio, Duetto e Rondo* •AT/Pno

MASSELLA, Thomas - *Pieces of April* (1986) (8') •SA •Marc
  Songs for a Poet (1987) (10') •AT/Pno •Marc

Massenet, Jules - *Elegy* (TRINKAUS) •AA or AT/Pno •Pres

MASSIAS, Gérard - *Dialogues* (1956) (6') •Asx/BsCl or 2 Sx •Bil

MAYEUR, Louis - *10 Duos* •CF/G&F
  Pieces (1877) •2 Sx/Pno

MAYS, Walter - *Duet* (1976) •SS
McGUIRE, Edward - *Music...* (1976) (8') •1 to 4 Sx (SATB)/Tape •SMPL
MENCHERINI, Fernando - *Playtime IV* (8'30) •ST
Mendelssohn, Félix - *Pieces*
MEULEN, Henk van der - *Introduction* (1981) (4') •SA •Don
Meyerbeer, Giacomo - *Coronation March* (TRINKAUS) •AA or AT/Pno •CF
MINAMIKAWA, Mio - *Objet shop* (1983) •adr
MITI, Luca - *One for Bill* (1993) •AT •INM
Molloy, James - *Love's Old Sweet Song* •2 Sx/Pno •Mck
MOLS, Robert - *20 Modern Duets* •Ken
MOREL - *Norvegian Cradle Song* •AT/Pno •Cen
MOROSCO, Victor - *Six Contemporary Etudes...* (1974) •AA •Art
Mozart, Leopold - *Four Short Pieces* •Elk
Mozart, Wolfgang - *Ave Verum Corpus* •AT/Pno •Mus
    12 Duos (SIMON) •EM
MUELLER, Florian - *Duets in Various Meters* •adr
    Easy Duets •UMM
MYERS, Theldon - *Two Inventions for Three* (5') •SA/Pno •DP
NAKATA, Mami - *Distance* (1990) •SA
Naumann, Johann Gottlieb - *Petit duo* •Mol
NAVARRE, Randy - *Two Shorts for Two Saxes* (1992) •Ron
NICOLAU, Dimitri - *Nel sogno*, op. 57 (1985) (10') •AB/Pno •EDP
    Strassemusik n° 7, op. 51-7 (1985) (10'30) •EDP
NIEHAUS, Lennie - *A Dozen and One Sax Duets* •WIM
    Six Jazz Duets Volume 2 •AA or AT or TT •WWS
    Ten Jazz Inventions •2 Sx: Eb or Bb •Ken
NIHASHI, Jun-ichi - *Invenzione della onda* (1992) (7') •AA
NINOMIYA, Tami - *Aya* (1988) (1') •AA
NODA, Ryo - *Fourth Side of the Triangle* (1983) •2 Sx/Pno
    Fushigi no basho (1985) •AA/Pno
    Murasaki (1981) (8') •Led
Offenbach, Jacques - *Barcarolle* •AT or AA/Pno •Cen/CF/Mck/Kjos
OSTLING, Acton - *Duets* •AA •Bel
PACKER - *Sea Breeze* •AA/Pno •Ken
Paderewski, I. - *Minuet à l'antique* (TRINKAUS) •AA or AT/Pno •CF
PAISNER, Ben - *Swing Duets* •DG
PALA, Johan - *3 Miniatures* •TT •Mol
PANELLA, Henri-François - *Pieces* •AA/Pno •Volk
PANICCIA, Renzo - *Rusé*, op. 5 (1984) (7') •AB
    Study on sound variation, op. 3 (1983) •SB
    Trilli esultanti, Dolci risonanze (1992) •2 Sx/Pno
PAQUE, J. - *Duo de La Norma n° 7* •TT/Pno •Sch
PARASKEVAIDIS, Graciela - *Saxsop* (1993) •SS •INM
PELLEGRINI, Ernesto - *Divertimento a due* •SA
PELZ, William - *Ballad* •AT •Bel
PEPPER, Richard - *Sounds for Two Saxophones* •AT •Che
PERFECT, Albert - *Two Little Chums* •AA/Pno •CF
PERRIN, Marcel - *Duos*
PEYKO, Nikolay - *Fantaisie de concert* (1977) •SA/Pno
PICHAUREAU, Claude - *Rafflésia...* •SA/Pno •Bil
PILLEVESTRE - *Duos* (18xx)
PITTS - *Church in the Wilwood* •AT/Pno •Bri
PIZZI, Fulvio - *Hymnaeus canonico modo* (1986) (4'30) •AA
POLGAR, Tibor - *Iona's Four Faces* (1970) (12') •SA/Orch or Pno •CMC
PORRET, Julien - *7me duo de concours* •SS or TT/Pno •Mol
    12 Easy Duos, op. 648 •AA or TT •Mol
    Ingres; Senner •AT/Pno •Mol
    12 Progressive Duets, op. 254 •AA or TT •HE
PORTA, Bernardo - *Two Duos* •AA or TT •Pres
PRESSER, William - *Seven Duets* •AA or TT •Pres
PRIESNER, Vroni - *Weg* •AA or TT •VW
PRONKO, Piotr - *Song of Love* •AB/Pno

Quantz, Johann - *Trio Sonata* •SA/Pno
RACOT, Gilles - *Exultitudes* (1985) (20') •2 Sx/live electronics
RAGONE, Vincent - *15 Melodious Duets* •CF
RAPHLING, Sam - *Duograms* •Mus
RAULE, Renato - *Colo Vienna, Parigi, N-Y.* •AT •Piz
RENDINE, Sergio - *Januar -Piletria IIIa-* (1985) (9') •S+A B •EDP
RIOU, Alain - *10 Duos d'étude* (1986) •Bil
    15 Etudes de style en duo •Bil
ROBERT, Lucie - *Rythmes lyriques* (1984) (11'30) •ST •Bil
    Trinome (1988) (13') •SB/Pno •Bil
ROCCISANO, Joe - *Contrasts* (1984) •AT/Band or Pno
ROCHOW, Erich - *Serenade* •2 Sx/Pno •RB
ROLIN, Etienne - *Caccia* (1991) (12') •AT/Echantilloneur [sampler] •adr
    Quasi un sol Nascente (1992) (8') •SB/2 Pno •adr
    Rotations (1990) (12-16') •S+A/Impro •adr
    Still life (1984) (7') •SB •adr
    Tandems (1988) (7') •A S+A+T+B •Lem
    Teinte (1994) (2') •AA •SCo
ROSSÉ, François - *Etude en balance* •AA or TT •adr
    Lombric (1985) (8') •AA/Pno •Lem
    Shanaï (1992) (6') •2 Like Sx •Bil
RUGGIERO, Giuseppe - *3 Pieces* (1966) •AA •Led
Saint-Saëns, Camille - *Pieces* •2 Sx/Pno •Cen/CF
SAMBIN, Victor - *Duo sur 'La Somnambule'* (188x) •ST/Pno
Satie, E. - *Gymnopédies I* •2 Sx/Pno •DP
SAUPE - *Air varié* •Mol
SAVARI, Jean-Nicolas - *Duo* (185x) •SA or TB •Sax
SBORDONI, Alessandro - *Phaxes* (1985) (5') •AA or TT
SCARMOLIN, Louis - *Duet Time* •2 Woodwind instruments •Lud
SCHAEFER, August - *The Troubadors* •AA •CF
SCHAEFFER, Don - *Christmas Duets* •AA/Pno •Pro
    Duets are Fun •PMV
    21 Rhythmic Duets •PMV
SCHILLING, Hans Ludwig - *VII Bicinia...* (1968) •AA or BB •B&B
SCHMIDT, William - *12 Concert Duets* •WIM
    Variations on a Theme of Prokofiev •WIM
Schubert, Franz - *Pieces*
Sellner, Joseph - *12 duos* (BLEUZET) (4 volumes) •AA or TT •Cos
SENON, Gilles - *Flash-jazz* (1982) •Bil
SHONO, Hirohisa - *Bugaku* (1985) (15') •ST/Pno
SHUEBUCK, R. - *20 Duets* •AA or TT •Shu
Sibelius, Jean - *Valse triste* (TRINKAUS) •AA or AT/Pno •CF
SINGELEE, Jean-Baptiste - *Duo concertant*, op. 55 (1858) •SA/Pno •Sax
SINQUIER, C. - *Six For Pleasure* •AT •South
SLECHTA, T. - *Father of Waters* •2 Sx/Pno •South
Smetana, Bedrich - *Polka* (Bartered Bride) (HARRIS) •TT/Pno •Lud
SMIM, P. - *Pieces* •Mus
SMITH, Clay - *Pieces* •CF/Bar/Mar
SMITH, Glenn - *Mood Music 2* (1980) •AA or SS or TT or BB •Eto
SMITH, Howie - *New York Still Life* (1975) •SA •Oa
SOULE, Edmund - *Suite* (1976) •SA •adr
Soussman, Henri - *12 Light Pieces* •AA or TT •Mus
SPENCER, F. - *Silvatones* •AA/Pno •CF
STEINBERG, Ben - *Reflections in Sections* (1984) •SA •CMC/DP
STOCKHAUSEN, Karlheinz - *Knabenduett* (1980) (5') •SS •Stv
STOKER, Richard - *Four Dialogues*, op. 12b (8') •AT
    Music for Three, op. 12c (6') •AB or ST
    Rounds and Canons (1966) •Hin
Stouffer, P. M. - *Duets* •AA or TT •HE
Sullivan, Arthur - *The Lost Chord* •AT/Pno •Cen
TALLMADGE-LILLYA - *56 Progressive Duets* •Bel
Tchaikowsky, P. - *Chant sans paroles* (TRINKAUS) •AA or AT/Pno •CF
Telemann, G-Ph. - *Six Canonic Sonatas* (TEAL) •Eto

Thome, François - *Simple aveu* •AT/Pno •Cen
THOMPSON, Kathryn - *Pieces* •2 Sx/Pno •South
TISNÉ, Antoine - *Duo* (1990) •AA •adr
    Duo 2 d'après le poème "Sur le Sol"... (1991) (9'30) •SB •Fuz
Tosti, F. - *Goodbye* •AT/Pno •Cen
Traxler, A. - *Grand Artistic Duets* •Bel
Trinkaus, G. - *Lament* •AA or AT/Pno •CF
    World's Best-Known Pieces •2 Woodwinds/Pno •CF
TULL, Fisher - *Dialogue* (1987) •AT •South
Twin, S. - *Old English Songs* •Pet
    Three Dialogues (1963) •Hin
TYSSENS, Albert - *Poclades* (1988) •adr
ULRICH, Jurgen - *5 Duets* (1966) •WH
UNGVARY, Tamas - *Sonologos*
VALK, Andriaan - *Appris d'un clown - 20 duos* (1987) •TM
    20 duos - L'homme au chapeau melon (1984) •TM
VALLIER, Jacques - *Deux pièces* (1964) (2'30) •AA or TT •Phi
VENTAS, Adolfo - *12 Duets*, op. 11 •AA or TT •adr
Verdi, Giuseppe - *Pieces* •AT/Pno •Cen
Vereecken, B. - *16 Artistic Duets* •AA or TT •Rub
VILLA-ROJO, Jesùs - *Divertimento III* (1992) •AA
VOSK, Jay - *Diversions* •AA •SeMC
Voxman, H. - *Selected Duets* (2 volumes) •AA or TT •Rub
Wagner, Richard - *Pieces* •2 Sx/Pno •Cen/CF/McK
WARREN, B. - *For Two Saxophones* •SA
WASTALL, Peter - *Session Time* (1988) •AT
WELSH, Wilmer - *Pieces* •SA/Pno
WENDLAND, Waldemar - *Twin Stars* •AA/Pno •Volk
Williams, Vic - *Artistic Duets* •AA or TT •CC
Wood, Haydn - *Let 'er Go* •AA or AT/Pno •Cen
YONEKURA, Yuki - *After the rain* (1992) •AA
YOUNG, Jeremy - *Family Portraits* (1988) •2 Sx: S+A+T A+B/Pno
YOUNG, Lynden de - *Introduction, Blues and Finale* •AT/Pno •DP
ZINDARS, E. - *Quiddity* •AA/Pno •AMC

3 Saxophones

Also see Unspecified Instrumentation (Voir aussi instruments non déterminés), page 422.

ALBRIGHT, William - *Doo-Dah* (1975) •AAA •DP
ALESSANDRINI, Pierluigi - *Sweetly* (1987) (2'30) •AAT •CoMu
    Trilogie (1991) •AAT •CoMu
    Improvisation & Sax in jazz; Notturno •ATB
ANDRIESSEN, Louis - *Song lines* (1989); *Widow* (1990) •TTB •JG
Arditi, Luigi - *Il Bacio* •AAA/Pno •Cen
ARMA, Paul - *6 Mobiles* (1975) (12') •1, 2, 3, or 4 Sx
AUDOIN, Jean-Claude - *Rue Descartes* (1981)
Bach, J. C. - *Trio in Two Movements* (CUNNINGHAM) •SAT •Eto
Bach, J. S. - *Bist du bei mir* •SAT or SAB or AAT or AAB •TM
    Fugue no. 21 •SAB •WIM
    Gavotte Favorite no. 2 (VITTMANN) •SAB •ES
    Invention no. 8 •SAB •Ken
    6 Sonates en trio (LONDEIX) •SAB •KuD
    Trio, op. 17, no. 3 (CUNNINGHAM) •ATB •DP
BARAT, Jacques - *Porcelaines de Saxe* •AAA •Chou
Barnard, George - *The Pals* (BUCHTEL) •AAA/Pno •Kjos
Barnes, C. - *Three Debonairs* •3 Sx/Pno •Kjos
BARREL, Bernard - *Suites* (1960) (4' + 4') •SSS
BARTHALAY, Raoul - *Mini-variations...* (1978) (2'15) •AAA •Bil
BAUZIN, Pierre-Philippe - *Divertimento* (1968) (26') •AAT •Lem
BECKER, Holmer - *"Lacht das Licht..."* (1988) (3') •SAB
Beethoven - *Adagio and Finale* (GEE) •AAT •MMB
    Allegro con brio (SIBBING) •AAB •Eto
    Fugue •AAT •Mus

    Trio, op. 87 (TEAL) •SAT or ATB •Eto
BELARDINELLI, Daniele - *Tris* (1992) •SAB
BERGER, Jean - *Divertimento* •SSS •Bou
Berlinski, Herman - *Canons and Rounds* (9 Pieces) •3 or 4 Sx •Pres
BERTOUILLE, Gérard - *Trio* (1955) (4') •SAB •CBDM
Bevin, Elway - *Browning* (RIPPE) •ATB •DP
Bizet, Georges - *Farandole de l'Arlésienne* (DELAMARRE) •ATB •adr
BLANK, Allan - *Music for Three* •Any instruments •ACA
Bond, C. - *I Love You Truly* •3 Sx/Pno •Kjos
BORRIS, Siegfried - *Sonatina per tre*, op. 45/1 •AAA •SV
Bourne-Leidzen - *Bourne Trio Album* •AAT •Bou
BOUVARD, Jean - *Pieces* •AAA or TTT •Bil/adr
BRENET, Thérèse - *Flânerie* •AAA or AAB •Phi
Briegel, George - *Pieces* •AAT/Pno •Bri
BROSH, Thomas - *Misterioso*; *Trio* (1967) •AAT
BROWN, Anthony - *Surface Textures* (1977) •AAT •SeMC
BUMCKE, Gustav - *Pieces*
BURGHARDT, Victor - *Pieces* (1986) •B&B
BUTTS, Carrol - *Chameleon* •SH&MC
    Moderato and Allegro •AAA •Ken
    Trio •Pro
BYRNE, Andrew - *Pieces* •3 or more instruments of equal pitch •Hin
Cabezon - *Prelude in the Dorian Mode* (GRAINGER) •SAT •PG
CAGE, John - *Pieces* •Any instruments •Pet
CARDEW, Cornelius - *Pieces* (1960) •Any instruments •Uni
CASKEN, John - *Visu for Three* •Any instruments •BMIC
CECCONI, Monique - *Aubade et Danse* (1964) (3') •AAA •Phi
CHALFONTE, Richard - *Suite* (1962) •adr
Cherubini, Luigi - *Canon* •SAT/Pno •Mol
CHILDS, Barney - *Operation Flabby Sleep* •3 or more instruments
    •ACA
Ciconia, Johannes - *O Padua* (AXWORTHY) •ATB •DP/TVA
Clark, Scotson - *Seicento - trio* •AAT •Mus
Clodomir, Pierre - *1er Trio* •SSA •Mol
Corelli, Arcangelo - *Chamber Sonata*, op. 2, no. 2 (SCHMIDT) •SAB
    •DP
COWELL, Henry - *Hymn and Fuguing Tune No. 4* (1945) •Any 3
    instruments (SAT) •ACA
    "60" (1942) (2') •SAB •TTF
Craen, Nikolauss - *Si ascendero in Caelum* (RIPPE) •ATB •DP
CRESSONNOIS, Jules - *Romance de Proserpine* (187x) •Sax
CUNNINGHAM, Michael - *Three Quaint Cameos* •ATB •SeMC
D'ANGELO, Nicholas - *Dimensions Three* (1965) (7') •ATB •adr
DELAMARRE, Pierre - *Trio n° 1* •SAT •adr
DELBECQ, Laurent - *Accord tripartite* (1983) (10') •AAA or TTT
    •Mar
DEPELSENAIRE, Jean-Marie - *Concertino* (1972) (9') •AAA/Orch
    •ET
    Trio de saxophones (1979) (3') •AAA or TTT •adr
DESCARPENTRIES, Hugues - *Braer* (1992) •SSS/Pno
Des Pres, Josquin - *La Bernardina* (GRAINGER) •AAA •PG
Devienne, François - *Trio* •2 Cl/Tsx or 3 Sx: TTB •Mol
Di Capua, Eduardo - *O sole mio* •AAT or AAA or ATT/Pno •Cen
DIEDERICHS, Yann - *Versants* (1985/88) (10'30)
DIEMENTE, Edward - *Dimensions I & II* •SeMC
Dorn, Kenneth - *Pieces* •ATB •DP
DUBOIS, Pierre-Max - *Trois Miniatures* (1981) •AAT •Ly
Dvorak, Anton - *Humoresque* •AAA or ATT or AAT •Cen
ESSL, Karlheinz - *Close the gap* (1990) (13') •TTT •adr
FOTEK, Jan - *Musiquette* (1983) (3') •AAA
FRANK, Fred - *Minka, Minka* •AAT/Band or Pno •Rub
Galuppi, Baldassaro - *Toccata* •AAA or TTT •Mus
GARCIN, Gérard - *Enfin, après, elle arriva* (1981) (14') •SnoSB •Sal
    6me Musique... (1984) (6') •1 to 7 Asx/Tape •Sal
GEE, Harry - *Fugue in Baroque Style* (1976) •AAT •CPP

12 Saxophone Trios (various composers, arr. GEE) •AAA or AAT •CPP

Gershwin, George - *Rhapsody in Blue* •AAT •Sal

Gibbons, Orlando - *Fantasia à 3* (ATHMANN) •SAB •K&D
  Fantasia for Three •AAT •Mus

GIBBS, Cecil Armstrong - *Harlequinade* •Pet

GINGRAS, Guy - *Trois duos scabreux* (1987) (7') •AAA •Med

Giuffre, Jimmy - *Four Brothers* •ATB

GLASER, Werner Wolf - *Trio* (1981) (10') •ATB •ECA
  Trio (1989) (14') •ATB/Pno •SMIC

GLEN, Rainer - *Einfach* (198x) •AAT •Schu

Gluck, Christoph - *Pièce récréative* (LETELLIER) •AAA or TTT •Mar

GOCA, Vladimir - *Etude* •SAT

GOLDMANN, Marcel - *Trio* (1985) (20')

GOODMAN, Alfred Grant - *Divertimento* (1950) (12') •AAT •RG

Grieg, Edvard - *To Spring* •AAA •Cen

GUYENNON, Bernard - *Jouons en trio* (NICOLLET) •Mar

Handel, Georg-Friedrich - *Trio C-Dur* (V. WÜRTH) •ATB •VW

Harris, Floyd - *Pieces* •AAT/Pno •Lud

HARTL, Heinrich - *Trio Concertante*, op. 41 (1989) (8') •SAB •VW

HARTLEY, Walter - *Trio* (1984) (11') •ATB •Pres

HASQUENOPH, Pierre - *Petite sérénade* (1952)

Hauptmann, Moritz - *Trio* (EVERTSE) •SAT •Lis

HERMAN, William - *Expressions* (1982)

HESPOS, Hans-Joachim - *J. Lomba Trio* (1980) (11') •TTBs •Hes

Hook, James - *Pieces* •AAA or AAT or TTT •CPP/Rub/South

Isaac, Heinrich - *Der Hund* (PRIESNER) •SAB •VW

JAHR, New - *Froloc* •SAT or AAT/Pno •Bri

James - *Pieces* •A A+T B •Sha

JONES, Robert - *Three by Three* •3 Bb Sx or 3 Eb Sx

KARKOFF, Maurice - *Kontrate*, op. 155 (1984) (10') •SAB •STIM

KARLINS, William - *Graphic Mobile* (1970) •MP

Keyes - *Trio* •ATB

KNORR, Ernst von - *Introduction...* (1932) (5') •AAT •TTF

KÖPER, Heinz Karl - *Triga* (1976) (6') •ATB/Wind Orch •adr

KOX, Hans - *The Three Chairs* (1989) (20') •ATB •Don

KRAMER, Martin - *Swing Fugue* (1938) •Pro

LAMB, John David - *Madrigal* (1972) •S (or A) AT •B&B

LANCEN, Serge - *Twelve Old French Songs* •AAA or TTT •Hin/Pet

LASEROMS, Wim - *Saxorella* (1977) (4') •AAT/Band or Fanfare •TM

LASNE, George - *Divertissement champêtre* (1963) (5'30) •SAT
  Promenade de Noël avec Pachelbel (1963) •AAA

Leidzen, Erik - *Bourne Trio Album* •Bou

Le Maistre, Mattheus - *Dominus noster...* (EVERTSE) •AAT •Lis/TM

Lemare, Edwin - *Cathedral Meditation* •AAT or ATT/Pno •Cen

Lester, L. - *Easy Trios* •Bel

LETELLIER, Robert - *Pieces* •Mar/Mol

Lewis - *Saxophone Trios* •SAT •WWS

Leybach, Ignace - *5th Nocturne in G* •AAA or ATT/Pno •Cen

LOLINI, Ruggero - *Spirale* •SAT

Lotti, Antonio - *Pieces* •AAT or SAT •Lis/TM

MAC CALL - *Valse Elise* •AAT or AAA/Pno •Lud

Machaut, Guillaume de - *Ballade no. 17* (GRAINGER) •SAA or TTB •PG

MAGANINI, Quinto - *Three Little Kittens* •Mus
  Triple Play •Mus
  Troubadours •AAT •Mus

MAILLOT, Jean - *Trio* (13'10) •ATB •EFM

MARCO, Tomàs - *Car en effet...* (1965) (10') •3 players: Cl+Sx •Sal

MARE, Corrado - *Sonatina* •SAB

MARI, Pierrette - *Trio* (1956) •SAT •adr

McGUIRE, Edward - *Music...* (1976) (8') •1 to 4 Sx (SATB)/Tape •SMPL

McKAY, George - *Pieces* •3 Sx/Pno •Bar

MERRELLI, Flavio - *Il libro* •SAB

MESSINA-ROSARYO, Antonio - *Fantasia...* (1984) (7'30) •Asto

MEYER, Jean-Michel - *Nocturne et Gigue* •AAT •adr

MIEREANU, Costin - *Tercafeira* (1984-85) (16') •3 Sx Players: Sno+S+A, S+A+T, S+A+T+B/Tape •Sal

MOREL, Jean-Marie - *Trilude* (1992) (2') •AAA •Fuz

MORITZ, Edvard - *Divertimento* (1952) •SAA or SAT •Merc

MOURZINE - *Burlesque - Humoresque* •AAA

Mozart, Wolfgang - *Pieces*

MUELLER, Frederick - *Pieces* •ATB

MÜLLER, Gottfried - *Pieces* •SAB •adr

MURPHY, Lyle - *Notturno* •ATB •WIM

NAGAN, Zvi - *Serenade for Lisa* •AAA •ASM

NICOLAU, Dimitri - *La casa nuova*, op. 82 (1988) (8') •SAB •EDP

NYKOPP, Lauri - *Hengen henki* •AAA •FMIC

Olsen, Sparre - *When Yuletide Comes* •SAT •PG

OSTRANSKY, Leroy - *Pieces* •AAT •Rub

Pachelbel, Johann - *How lovely...* •3 Sx: SAT or 6 Sx: SATTBBs •RS
  Three Fugues on the Fourth Tone •ATB •WWS

Paisiello, Giovanni - *Romance...* (CRESSONNOIS) •ATB •Marg

PARFREY, Raymond - *Comedy Numbers* (1979) •AAA •BMIC
  Saxes Thro' the Centuries (8') •AAT •BMIC
  Two Pieces (1979) •AAT •BMIC

PATRICK, Lee - *Folk Song Miniatures* (1981) •ATB
  The Songs •ATB
  Tribute to JB (1980) •ATB

PRESSER, William - *Trio* •AAT •Pres

PRIESNER, Vroni - *Divertimento* (1986) (4') •AAA or TTT •VW
  Gomringer (1988) •SAB/Actors •VW
  Zungenspiele (1989) •AAA or TTT •VW

Purcell, Henry - *Fantasia No. 3* (ROSENTHAL) •ATB •Wim

RAPHLING, Sam - *Suite in Modern Style* •Mus

Ravel, Maurice - *Bolero* •SAT •Dur
  Pavane (WALTERS) •Asx/Pno or 3 Sx: AAT/Pno •Rub

RICHARDS, J. - *Triad* •AAT/Pno •Bar

ROLIN, Etienne - *Tremplins* (1994) (3'30) •3 Eb Sx •SCo

ROSENTHAL, Manuel - *Trio*

ROSSÉ, François - *O yelp* (1989) •3 Sx: SACBs/1 camion de pompiers - soliste & 9 camions tuttistes •adr
  Quartz O1.83 (1982) (15') •Sno+A A+B A •Sal

Rossi, Salomone - *Three Canzonets* (VOXMAN & BLOCK) •AAT or AAA •South

Rubinstein, Anton - *Fantasy for Three* (WALTERS) •AAT/Pno •Rub

RUGGIERO, Giuseppe - *Andante & Scherzo* (1972) •AAT •Zan

SATTERWHITE, Marc - *Nine Aphorisms*

SAVARI, Jean-Nicolas - *Trio en trois parties* •SAB •Sax

Scarlatti, Domenico - *Sonata longo 104* •SAB •WWS

SCARMOLIN, Louis - *Three Swingsters* •AAT/Pno •IMD

Scheifes, Hans - *Vier kleine Stücken...* •SAT •TM

SCHILLING, Hans Ludwig - *Trisax* (1978) (12') •ATB •B&B

Schonfelder, Jorg - *Mich hat grob* (RIPPE) •ATB •DP

SIENICKI, Edmund - *Ponytail Polka* •AAA/Pno •Kjos

SKOLNIK, Walter - *Three Canonic Tunes* •AAT •Mus

SMIRNOV, Dimitry - *Canon humoresque* •Mu

SMITH, Edwin - *Theme, Imitations, and Fugue* •ATB •adr

SOLOMAN, K. - *Elegy and Dance* •AAA •ASM

STEINBACHER, Erwin - *Die Drei Grünschnäbel* •Fro

STEINBERG, Ben - *Trio* (1972)

SULPIZI, Fernando - *Jeu du crépuscule* •SAB

TAGGART, Mark - *A Round o' Trios* (1978-83) •ATB

TALLET, Eric - *A.T.B.* (1979) (11') •SnoAT

TALLET, Marc - *Polyphonie* •3 Sx: Sno (or S), A, T (or B)

TAYLOR, Paul Arden - *Bach Goes to Sea* •SAB

Tchaikowsky, Peter - *Sweet Dreams* (HARRIS) •AAT/Pno •Lud

THOMAS, Ambroise - *Deux Chants...* (1865) (1'10) •ATB •LMe

TOEBOSCH, Louis - *Thema met variaties...*, op. 42 (1953) (6') •Don
TOURNIER, Franz - *Trio* (1953) (17') •ATB •DP
VAUGHAN WILLIAMS, Ralph - *Household Music* (1940-41) •AAA
              or diverse combinations •B&H
VERHIEL, Ton - *Pieces*
Voxman, Hymie - *Chamber Music Series* •AAT •Rub
WALTERS, Harold - *Fantasy for Three* •AAT •Rub
   Jim Dandies •AAT/Pno •Rub
WELANDER, Svea - *Preludium* (1961) •AAA •SMIC
WORLEY, John - *Four Sketches* •ATB •DP
ZENDER, Hans - *Stephen Climax* (1979-84) •adr
ZENONI - *Sinfonia a tre* •WWS

4 Saxophones - SATB

Also see Unspecified Instrumentation (Voir aussi
instruments non déterminés), page 422.

ABBOTT, Alain - *Poême* (1969) (12'30) •Bil
Abel, Carl-Friedrich - *Andante* (BRINK) •Lis
ABELLAN, G. - *Pieces*
ABSIL, Jean - *Quatuor I* (1937) •Lem
  Suite d'après le folklore roumain (1956) (17') •CBDM
  Trois Pièces en Quatuor (1938) •Lem
ACHENBERG, David - *4 Portraits*
ADAMIS, Michalis - *Kalophonikon* (1989) (12') •4 Sx
ADAMS, Daniel - *Threshold* (1987) (6') •Ron
Adams, Stephen - *The Holy City* (A. LEMARC) •SATB or AATB •TM
ADLER, Samuel - *Line Drawings* (1978) •DP
AGER, Klaus - *Shigöpotuu* (1988) •ADE
AGNESENS, Udo - *Quartets 1, 2, 3* (1981, 1985, 1989) •adr
AHLBERG, Gunnar - *Mosaïk* (1964) (6') •STIM
Aichinger, Gregor - *Jubilate Deo* •WWS
ALBAM, Manny - *Quartet no. 1* (1964)
Albeniz, Isaac - *Pieces* (MULE) •Bil/Led
ALBERT, Karel - *Quatuor* (1960) •adr
ALBERT, Thomas - *Devil's Rain* (15')
Album of Celebrated Folk Songs and PatrioticAirs •CF
ALESSANDRINI, Pierluigi - *Pieces* •Ber/Piz
Alessandrini, R. - *Travelling Suite* •SL
ALKEMA, Henk - *Quartet* (1983-84) (10') •Don
ALLA, Thierry - *Offshore* (1990) (6') •Fuz
AMELLER, André - *Pieces* (1959)
AMIOT, Jean-Claude - *1er Quatuor* (1967)
AMOS - *Saxifrage*
ANDERSEN, Erling - *Movements* (1976)
APPERSON, Ronald - *Quartet* •TM
  Suite antique •Mol
APPLEBAUM, Terry - *Quartet* (1964) (4') •South
ARCHER, Violet - *Divertimento* (1979) •DP
Arend, A. den - *Quartet* •TM
Arend, Johann Krieger - *Boismortier Suite* •Mol
ARMA, Paul - *Divertissement 1600* (1960) (12'30)
  Petite suite (1972) (10'30) •Lem
  7 Convergences (1974) (14'30) •DP
  7 Transparences (1968) (13'30) •Lem
ARNOLD, André - *Quatuor*, op. 50 (1974) •MSC
ARNOLD, Hubert - *Dithyrambe* (1969) •Art
ARTIOMOV, Vyatcheslav - *Litania* (1979) •ECS
  Litania I (1982) •ECS
ASHFORD, Theodore - *American Folksong Suite* •South
ASHTON, John - *Dialogues, Discourses* (1975) •SeMC
ASTON, David - *Euphonium* (1977) (5')
ATOR, James - *Adagio* (1981) •WWS
Aubert, Esprit - *Prière* (W. HEKKER) •SATB or AATB

AYOUB, Nick - *Pieces* •DP
AYSCUE, Brian - *Quartet* (1982) •adr
Bach, Johann Christian - *Sinfonia en Sib* •Mol
Bach, Johann Sebastian - *Pieces*
BACULIS, Alphonse - *Six Pieces for Saxophone Quartet* (15')
BADAULT, Denis - *En effet* (1990) (8')
BADINGS, Henk - *Friere Trije; Gelderse Peerdesprong* •TM
  Hollande Boerenplof •TM
BAGOT, Maurice - *Quatuor* (1965)
  Saxofonie (1975) (9')
BAGUERRE, Francis - *Appolinaria* (1982) (10')
BAILEY, Judith - *Quartet* (1972) (15')
BAILLY, Jean-Guy - *Contraires II* •adr
BARAB, Seymour - *Quartet* (1978) (13'45)
BARAT, Jacques - *Descente sur la neige* (1972) •adr
  Karanguez (1972) (1'30) •adr
BARBER, Clarence - *Vignettes* (1993) (6') •4 Sx: A A+S TB •TTF
Barber, Samuel - *Adagio* (MARR)
BARREL, Joyce - *Quartet*, op. 47 (1973) (13')
BACKERATH, Alfred von - *6 Kleine Bilder* (1970) (9') •adr
Barber, Samuel - *Adagio* (MARR) •SATB
BARBIER, René - *Quatuor*, op. 99 (1961) (14') •CBDM
BARCE, Ramon - *Anabasis* •RME
BARKER, Warren - *Scherzo* •SATB or SSTB •Ken
  Voici le Quatuor... •Ken
BARRAUD, Henry - *Quatuor* (1973) (16') •B&H
BARREL, Joyce - *Quartet*, op. 47 (1973) (15')
BARRET, Richard - *Quartet* (1981) •BMIC
BARTHOLOMEE, Pierre - *Ricercar* (1974)
Bartok, Béla - *6 Bagatelles* (SCHMIDT) •DP
BASSI, Adriano - *Movie*
BATIAROV - *Rondo joyeux* •ECS
BAUDRIER, Emile - *Mes amis* (1965) •Mol
BAUER, Robert - *Pieces* •BML/CMC
BAUR, Jürg - *Cinque foglie* (1986) (17') •B&H
BAUZIN, Pierre-Philippe - *Quatuor*, op. 29 (1962) (20') •adr
BAVICCHI, John - *Quartette no. 4* •DP
BEAUME - *Suite*
BECERRA, Gustavo - *Quartetto* (1959)
BECHARD, René - *L'Orgue de Barbarie*
BECKER, Charles - *Triade* (1974)
BECKERATH, Alfred von - *6 Kleine Bilder* (1970) (9') •adr
BEDARD, Denis - *Suite* (1983) •Do
BEDFORD, David - *Fridiof kennings* (1980) (10')
BEEFTINCK, Herman - *Quartet* (1977) (5') •Don
Beethoven, Ludwig van - *Pieces*
BEINKE, Eckart - *Quartett* (1993) (14') •adr
BELDA, J. - *Cuarteto*
BENNETT, Richard - *Travel Notes* (1979) (4') •Nov
BENSON, Warren - *Quartet* •adr
  Wind Rose (1966) (7') •MCA
BERG, Olav - *Quartet* (1989) (12'45)
BERGMAN, Erik - *Etwas rascher*, op. 108 (1985) (17') •Nov
BERLIN, David - *Patterns*
BERNARD, Jacques - *Andante et Scherzo* (1965) (10'40) •adr
BERNARD, Robert - *Quatuor* (1931) •adr
BERNARDINI, Giampiero - *Quartet* (1992)
BERNAUD, Alain - *Quatuor* (24'30) •RR
BERNIER, René - *Serinette en guise de bis* (1974) (1') •Bil
  Suite pour le plaisir de l'oreille (1973) (13') •CBDM
Bernstein, Leonard - *West Side Story: America* (DÖMÖTÖR) •KuD
Berry, Hans - *Pieces*
BERTAINA, Pier Michele - *Pieces*
Berthomieu, Marc - *Rondo* (LETELLIER) •Elk
BERTOCCHI, Serge - *Quatrième méridien* (1986) (5')

BERTOMEU, Agustin - *Cuarteto romantico* (1990)
BERTOUILLE, Gérard - *Prélude et Fugue* (1955) (4') •CBDM
BETTA, Marco - *Mirrors*
BETTARINI, Luciano - *Sonata* (1959)
BEUGNIOT, Jean-Pierre - *Pièces en Quatuor* (1970) (11'30) •EFM
BEURDEN, Bernard van - *Psychophony* (1979) •Don
BEYER, Frank - *Sanctus* (1989) (12') •adr
BEYTELMAN, Gustavo - *Momentos*
BIALAS, Günter - *6 Bagatellen* (1985-86) (14') •Br&Ha
BIANCHINI, Riccardo - *Alberi* (1990)
BIELER, Helmut - *Sounding Colours* (1985) •adr
BIELAWA, Bruce - *Extended Dance Suite* (1993) •4 Sx •INM
BISCHOF, Rainer - *Nightwoods* •ECA/ApE
Bizet, Georges - *Pieces*
Blaauw, L. - *Pieces*
BLAIR, Dean - *Symphonette...* (1990) •CMC
BLANES, Luis - *Tres impresiones* (1990)
BLATNY, Pavel - *Kreis*
    Kruh-Circolo (1982) (5') •CHF
BLINKO, Timothy - *Sculptures*
BLOMBERG, Erik - *Melos* (1992) •SMIC
BLYTON, Carey - *Pieces* •adr
BOBILIOV, Leonid - *Sons de Forêt* (1980) •ECP
Boccherini, Luigi - *Pieces*
BODA, John - *Opus* (1984)
BOEDJIN, Gérard - *Badinage...*, op. 163 (1961) •Mol
BOEUF, Georges - *L'Image poursuivie* (1973) (12') •adr
    Parallèles (1967) (12') •CANF
Boiëldieu, François Adrien - *Souvenir...* (W. HEKKER) •TM
BOIS, Rob du - *The 18th of June* (1978) (12') •Don
Boismortier, Bodin de - *Suite* (AREND) •Mol
BOISSELET, Paul - *Quatuor* (1946) (12') •adr
Bokhove, H. - *Pro Musica* •TM
Bolzoni, Giovanni - *Minuetto* (MULE) •Bil
BON, Maarten - *Canzon Francese del principe display* •Don
BONDON, Jacques - *Movimenti* (1980) •ME
BONNARD, Alain - *Double invention et Fugue*, op. 18 •adr
    Stochateïs •adr
BONTEMPELI, Bruno - *Pieces*
BOOGARD, Bernard - *Kwartet* (1985) (12') •Don
BORCHARD, Adolphe - *Fileuse* •adr
BOREL, René - *Fugato in F* (1976) •Bou
BORIK, Reginald - *Last Dance* (1988)
BORMANN, Emile von - *Suite im alten Stil* •Fro
BORROFF, Edith - *Two Rags From the Old Bag*
BORSARI, Amédée - *Prélude et choral varié* (1943) •Bil
BOTTJE, Will Gay - *Quartet I* (1963) (13') •ACF
BOTYAROV, Yergeni - *A Merry Rondo*
BOUCHARD, Marcel - *Pieces* •adr/Bil
BOUDREAU, Walter - *Le Cercle gnostique* (1979) •CMC
    Chaleurs (1985-89) (40') •CMC
    Incantations I (1979) (23') •CMC
    L'Odyssée du soleil II (1979) •CMC
BOUILLAGUET, Gérard - *Quatuor* (1973)
BOURDIN, François - *Quatuor* (1985)
BOURQUE, Pierre - *Quatuor* (1970) (41') •CMC
BOUVARD, Jean - *Noëls* (1983) •Mar
    Suite française (1973) •Chou
    Variations sur un thème populaire tchèque •adr
BOUTRY, Roger - *Improvisations* (1978) •adr
BOWLES, Anthony - *Quartet* (1974) (15')
BOYLE, Rory - *Passacaglia* (1975) (3'30)
BOZZA, Eugène - *Andante et Scherzo* (1973) (7') •Led
    Introduction et Scherzo
    Nuages (1946) •Led

BRADY, Timothy - *Unison Rituals* (1991) (12') •CMC
Brahms, Johannes - *Célèbre valse* (MARTIN) •Mar
BRAMUCCI, Rodolfo - *Spiel* (1992)
BRANDMÜLLER, Theo - *Quatuor* (1987) (13')
BRANT, Henry Dreyfus - *From Bach's Menagerie* (1974) •adr
BRAUNFELS, Michael - *Encore* (1986) (3'); *4 X 4* (1985-86) (19')
BRENET, Thérèse - *Gémeaux I & II* •SATB or SSAATTBB •Lem
BREVILLE, Pierre - *Prélude, trois Interludes & Postlude* (1946)
BRINGS, Allen - *Three Fantasies* •SeMC
BROEKHUIJSEN, H. - *Pieces* •TM
BRONS, Carel - *Ballade '81* (1981) (12') •Don
BROTONS, Seler - *Planyment* (1980)
BROTT, Alexander - *Berceuse* (1962) •CMC
    Saxi-Foni-Saties (1972) (16') •CMC
    Three Actes for Four Sinners (1961) (11') •CMC
BROUWER, Leo - *Ludus metallicus* (1972)
Brown & Shrigley - *Bull Frog Blues* (GEE) •SATB or AATB •Ron
BROWN, Anthony - *Quartet* •SeMC
BROWN, Charles - *Quatuor* (1959) (20')
BROWN, John R. - *The Millet of Dee* (traditional) •SM
    The Squirrel •SM
BROWN, Rayner - *Fugues* •WWS
Brüll, Ignaz - *Bauerntanz* •TM
BRUN, François-Julien - *Fantaisie*
BRUNO, Mauro - *Pieces*
BUBALO, Rudolph - *Conicality* (1977)
Buckland, Rob - *Irish Air* •SATB or AATB •PBP
BULLARD, Alan - *Three Picasso Portraits*
BUMCKE, Gustav - *2 Quartette*, op. 23 (1908) •E&R
BURCH, John Robert - *Capriccio* (1966)
BURKE, John - *Near Rhymes* (1984) (14') •CMC
BUSCHMANN, Rainer - *Quartett n° I*
BUWEN, Dieter - *Nachtgedanken* (1990) (8') •CA
Byrd, William - *Pieces* (HARVEY) •Che
CADWALLADER, Rex - *Quartet* (1987) •adr
CAFARO, Sergio - *Sax* (1985)
CAILLIET, Lucien - *Pieces* •South
Caix d'Herveloix, Louis - *La Marche...* (CLASSENS-MERIOT) •Com
CALI, Giuseppe - *Pieces*
CALMEL, Roger - *Quatuor* (1957) •adr
    Quatuor méditerranéen (1982) •adr
    7 Séquences (12'15) •4 Sx: SATB or Ob/Cl/Asx/Bsn •EFM
CAMBRELING, Sylvain - *Facette I*
Canet, Jacques - *Suite brève*
CANNING, Thomas - *Two Chorales after Bach*
CAPPETO, Michael - *Quartet in 3 Movements*
CARAVAN, Ronald - *Four Miniatures* (1971) •adr
    Four Movements (1968) •adr
CARISI, John - *Quartet I* •NYSQ
CARL, Robert - *Duke Meets Mort* (1992) (9')
CARLES, Marc - *Quatuor* (1973) •adr
CARLOSEMA, Bernard - *L'eau* (1985) (5'30) •Fuz
CARRON, Willy - *Quartet* (1978) •CBDM
CASTEREDE, Jacques - *Trois Nocturnes* (1981) (5') •Led
CATEL, Charles-Simon - *Symphonie militaire* (FERSTL) •GB
CATURANO, Francesco - *Out of the Time* (1987) (10') •Ber
CAVANA, Bernard - *Quatuor* (1982)
CEKOW, André - *Etude en forme de fugue* (1971) (4'30)
CERVELLO, Garriga Jordi - *Shoshanna* (1979) •adr
CEUGNART, Robert - *Berceuse* •adr
CHALLAN, René - *Jacasserie*
CHAMBERS, Evan - *The Trouble With the Wind* (1991) (4')
CHAN, Francis - *Quartet* (1989) (14') •CMC
CHARLTON, Andrew - *Fantaisie on the Chaconne*
CHAUVET, Georges - *Quatuor concertant* •Bes

Chopin, Frédéric - *Chopin Favorite* (DEDRICK) •AATB or SATB
CHOQUET, Patrick - *Quatuor* (1974)
CHRISTENSEN, James - *Hey Ride!* •SATB or AATB •Ken
CIAPOLINO, R. - *Pieces*
CIBULKA, Franz - *Quartet n° 1* (1984) (12') •CA
   Saxophonquartett n° 3 (15')
CLAY, Carleton - *Lullaby for J.Y.C.* (1993)
Clementi, Muzio - *Canon* (EVERTSE) •Lis/TM
CLERISSE, Robert - *Pieces* •Led/Mar/adr
CODINA, M. A. - *Sélène* (12') •adr
Cohen, Paul - *The Renaissance Book II* (8') (COHEN) •TTF
COHEN, Steven - *Quartet* (1980) •DP
COLBORNE-VEEL, John - *Quartet* (1988)
COLEMAN, Randolph - *Divertimento*
COLIN, Jeanne - *Quatuor*
COLUMBRO, Carmelo - *Acedia*
CONSTANT, Franz - *Pieces* •CBDM/adr
COOPER, David - *Quartet* (1985)
COOPER, Kenneth - *Rondo*
COPELAND, Eugene - *Three Chorale Preludes* (6') •DP
COPPENS, Claude - *Quartet*
CORDELL, Frank - *Pieces* •NOV
Cordeiro, George - *Pieces* •DP
CORREGIA, Enrico - *Augenblick der Stille* (1985)
COSMA, Edgar - *Graphiques* (1981) (14'); *Quatuor*
   Sept Séquences (1963) (12'30) •Sen
COURTIOUX, Jean - *Opus market* (1983) •DP
COWLES, Colin - *Pieces*
COYNER, Lou - *Saxifrage II* •WWS
CRAS, Jean - *Danse* (1924) •Sen
CRAWLEY, Clifford - *Boutade* (1977) (4') •CMC
CRESSONNOIS, Jules - *Pieces* •Sax
CRESTON, Paul - *Suite* (1978) (15') •Sha
CRIVELLI, Carlo - *Nel buio del Mare* (1988) (12')
CROLEY, Randall - *Sette Momenti* (1967-72) •AEN
   Trè Expressioni (1969) •AEN
CUNCHE, Jean - *Introduction et Tarentelle* (1958) (6') •adr
CUNNINGHAM, Michael - *Pieces* •Eto/SeMC
DAKIN, Charles - *Pieces* •Pet/WWS
DALLINGER, Fridolin - *Suite* (7') •CA
DAM, Hermann van - *Rage* (1984) (8') •Don
DAMASE, Jean-Michel - *Quatuor* (1976) (11') •Lem
D'ANGELO, Nicholas - *Pieces* •adr
DARBELLAY, Jean-Luc - *Quatuor*
DARCY, Robert - *Four Movements*
DARLING, John - *Quatre de la famille* (1982) •Mar
DAUTREMER, Marcel - *Quatuor*; *Tetraventi* (1975)
DAVIA, Moises - *Dialogo* (1982); *Quatuor* (1981)
DAVIS, Michael - *Night Poem*
DEAK, Csaba - *Kvartett* (1988) (15') •SUE/SMIC
DEASON, David - *Pieces*
Debussy, Claude - *Pieces*
DECLOEDT, E. - *Entrée - Danse villageoise* •An
DECOUST, Michel - *Quatuor* (1980)
DECRUCK & BREILH - *Pieces* •EP
DE DECKER, George - *Quatuor*
DEDRICK, Chris - *Sensitivity* (6'15) •SATB or AATB •AMI/Ken
DEDRICK, Rusty - *The Modern Art Suite* (13') •Ken
   Saxafari •SATB/Optional Perc •Ken
De Fesch, Willem - *Sonata* (STANTON) •Eto
DEFONTAINE, M. - *Prélude, Menuet et Gigue*
DEFOSSE, Henry - *Bucolique nocturne* (1931) (7')
DEFOSSEZ, René - *Mouvemento perpetuo* (1973)
DEGASTYNE, Serge - *Quartet, op. 53* •FP
DEGEN, Johannes - *Canzone devota* (1981) (4') •STIM

DEJONCKER, Théodore - *Quatuor*
DE JONGHE, Marcel - *3 Bagatelles* (1982)
DEKKER, Dirk - *Obsessie* (1986) (10') •Don
DELA, Maurice - *Divertimento* (1972) (12') •CMC
DELAMARRE, Pierre - *Quatuor pour rire* (1977) (3') •Bil
DELAMONT, Gordon - *Three Entertaiments* (8'35) •Ken
DELBECQ, Laurent - *Pieces* •Mar
DEL BORGO, Elliot - *Quartet* (1987)
DELDEN, Lex van - *Tomba*, op. 112 (1985) (10') •Don
DELGIUDICE, Michel - *Quatuor* •adr
DELLI PIZZI, Fulvio - *Elegia per F.* (1982)
DE MAN, Roderik - *Discrepancies* (1993) •INM
DENHOFF, Michael - *Pieces* •GrB
DEOM, Michel - *Les pêcheurs d'ombres, op. 7* (1980) (16'30) •Bil
DEPELSENAIRE, Jean-Marie - *Pieces*
DEPRAZ, Raymond - *Quatuor n° 2* (1974) (17'15) •EFM
DE ROSSI RE, Fabrizio - *Allegro nero* (1986) (5') •EDP
DERVAUX, André-Jean - *Kopak et Ciolina* (4') •Phi
DESCHAMPS, Jean-Henri - *Pieces* •Bil/adr
DE SCHRISVER, K. - *Quadrochromie* •Scz
DESENCLOS, Alfred - *Quatuor* (1964) (15'30) •Led
DESLOGES, Jacques - *Prélude et danse* (1983) •4 Sx: SATB or Ob/
                       Cl/Asx/Bsn (or Vcl or Trb) •Arp
   Rondo (1972) •CANF
DESPARD, Marcel - *Quatuor*
DESPORTES, Yvonne - *Pieces*
DEVENIJNS, Gaston - *3 Mouvements*
DEVEVEY, Pierre - *Pieces* •ELC/adr
DE WOLF, Karel - *4 Easy Pieces* (2') •Scz
DHAINE, Jean-Louis - *Concertinos*
DIAZ, Rafael - *Nudos* (1981) (5'); *Quatuor* (1980)
DI BIASE, Paolo - *Sirio* (1993) (2') •PT
DIERGUNOV, Fevgen - *Dream in Blue of All Life*
DIESSEL, Karl - *Danse des spectres* •adr
DIJK, Jan van - *7 Bagatellen* (1982)
DIKKER, Loek - *Kwartet* (1989) (8'15)
DILLON, Robert - *Night Shade* (1956) •B&H
DINESCU-LUCACI, Violeta - *Pieces* •adr
DI NOVI, Eugene - *Blues* (1964)
DI PIETRO, Rocco - *Phantom Melos* (1981)
DMITRIEV, Gueorgui - *Pieces*
DMITRIEV, Sergej - *Fanfar* (1992) •SMIC
   Hâgrigar (Mirages) (1992) •SvM
DOERR, Clyde - *Saxophone Moods* •Asx/Pno or SATB •Sal
DOMAZLICKY, Frantisek - *Musica, op. 54* (12') •DHF
DONAL, Michalsky - *3 Time Four* (1928/1974) •Sha
DONATONI, Franco - *Rasch* (1990) (5'30) •Ric
DONDEYNE, Désiré - *Pieces* •SF/adr
DORFF, Daniel - *Fantasy, Scherzo, Nocturne* (1978) •Sha
DORSAM, Paul - *Sax Section*
DORWARD, David - *Quartet* (1979)
DOTT, Hans-Peter - *Sonanzen* (1984) (6') •adr
DOULIEZ, Victor - *Prélude et Scherzo*
DOURY, Pierre - *Quatuor*
DOUSA, E. - *Jazz tones*
D'RIVERA, Paquito - *Suite*
DROUET, Raymond - *Quatuor* •adr
DRUMHALLER, Jonathan - *Wednesday...* (1992) (6')
DUBOIS, Pierre-Max - *Quatuor* (1956) (17') •Led
   Pieces •Bil/adr
DUBUS, Georges - *Adagio, Larghetto et Largo* •adr
DUCHEMIN, Lucien - *Suite*
DUCKWORTH, William - *Real Music* (1970) •MP
DUFFAU, Lionel - *Pieces*
DULAT, Philippe - *Quatuor à l'enfant malade - Le Phénix* (1980)

DUPERIER, Jean - *3 Airs pour un soir de Mai* (1936) •Lem
DUPONT, Jacques - *Saxophonie*
DURAND, André - *Divertissement* •adr
DURAND, Pierre-Hubert - *A Piacere* (1984) (9')
DURRANT, Frederick - *Sonata for Saxophone Quartet* (1972) (20')
DURY, Martial - *Divertissement*, op. 5 •EMB
Du Tertre, Etienne - *Pavane and Gailliarde* (HARVEY) •Che
Dvorak, Anton - *Pieces*
EARLY, Judith - *Variations on a Theme...* (1972) (4')
EBENHÖH, Horst - *Saxzyklus*, op. 70/2 (20') •CA
   Short Tale, op. 70, no. 3 •CA/ApE
EDER de LASTRA, Erich - *Suite für vier Saxophone* (14') •ECA
EECHAUTE, Prosper van - *Quatuor*, op. 42 (1963)
EETVELDE, Van J. - *Quatuor* (1980)
EGEA, Jose Vincente - *Affa*
EGGLESTON, Anne - *Quartet* (1972) •CMC
EHLE, Robert - *Pieces*
EKLUND, Hans - *Omaggio a San Michele* (1980) (12') •STIM/SMIC
Elgar, Edward - *Land of Hope and Glory* •SATB or SAAT or SATT
        or SAAB
ELLIS, James - *Poems and Transitions* (1972) (30')
ELLIS, John Tilstone - *Ollersett Suite* (1978) (8') •BMIC
EMMERECHTS, Raymond - *Ferroluro* •adr
END, Jack - Two *Modern Saxophone Quartets* •Ken
ENDRICH, Tom - *Lifelines* (1983)
ENGEBRETSON, Mark - *Pieces* •ApE
ENSTRÖM, Rolf - *Vigil* (1993) •B&N
ERDMANN, Dietrich - *Resonanzen* (1984) (12'30) •Br&Ha
Erikson - *Pieces*
ESPOSITO, Patrizio - *Agressivo II*
ESTEBAN, C. - *3 Canciones alicantinas*
EVENSEN, Kristian - *Quartet* (1982-83) (10') •NMI
EYSER, Eberhard - *Pieces* •EMa/SvM
FALK, Julien - *Pieces* •adr
FANTICINI, Fabrizio - *Canto notturno* (1987) (8') •Ric
FARHART, H. - *Divertimento* •Lebl
Farmer, John - *Pieces* •Che/SM
Farnaby, Giles - *Sometime she would and sometime not* (HARVEY) •Che
FARNON, Dennis - *Bouquet of Barbed Wire* (1978-79) (3'30) •WOC
FAULKNER, Elizabeth - *Quartet* (1978) (12')
FAUSTIN, Jean-Jean - *Pieces* •HS
FEDELE, Ivan - *Magic* (1985)
FELD, Jindrich - *Quatuor* (1981) (26') •Led
FENZL, Helmut - *3 Bagatellen* (1985) (8')
FERM, Thomas - *Elegie*
FERRARI, Luc - *Tautologos III* (1969)
FERRERO, A. - *3 Piezas breves*
FIALA, George - *Quartets I, II, III* (1955-1983) •BML/CMC
FICHER, Jacobo - *Quartet*, op. 89 (1957)
FINNISSY, Michael - *N* (1969) (8-10') •Uni
FINZI, Graciane - *5 Séquences* (1982) (10'30) •Bil
FISCHER, Eric - *Pieces* •adr
FLETA POLO, Francisco - *Quartetto n° 13*, op. 79 (1980)
FLORENZO, Lino - *Süd America Suite* (1978) (10'30) •ME
FLOTHUIS, Marius - *Capriccio*, op. 86 •Don
FLYNN, George - *Quartet* (1982) •adr
FONGAARD, Bjorn - *Quartet*, op. 129, no. 5 (1975) (12') •NMI
FONTAINE, Fernand Marcel - *Concertino de Dinant* (1975) •CBDM
FONTAINE, Louis-Noël - *Pieces* •Capri/adr
FORAY, Claude - *Quatuor*
FORD, Andrew - *Four Winds* (1984) •Don
FORD, Trevor - *Suite* (1978) •Mol
FORENBACH, Jean-Claude - *Dialogues* (1982)
FORET, Félicien - *Célèbre berceuse de Reber* •Cos
FORSSELL, Jonas - *Tyst vår (Printemps silent)* (1986) (20') •STIM

FORTERRE - *Quatuor*
FORTIER, Marc - *Tempo I* (1968)
FOSS, Lukas - *Quartet* (1985) •Ron
FOURNIER, Marie-Hélène - *What's what* (1989)
FOX, Christopher - *Stone-Wind-Rain-Sun* (1990) (10')
FOX, Frederick - *Three Diversions*
FRACKENPOHL, Arthur - *Pieces* •Ken/Pres/RPS/Sha
FRANCAIX, Jean - *Petit quatuor* (1939) (7') •Sch
   Suite (1990) (16'30) •Sch
Franck, César - *Panis angelicus* (LEMARC) •SATB or AATB •TM
Frescobaldi, Girolamo - *Pieces*
FREUDENTHALER, Erland Maria - *Capriccios* (8'36)
FRIBERG, Tomas - *Längs ett oavslutat ögonblick* (1989) (8') •SMIC
FRICKER, Peter - *Serenade No. 3*, op. 57 (1969) (8')
FRIED, Alexej - *Sonate fÿur saxophonquartett* •Peer
FRIIS, Flemming - *Pieces*
Froberger - *Capriccio* •WWS
FROMIN, Paul - *Danceries* •Mar
GABBRIELLI, Michelangelo - *Sigla, Epigramma in 4 Aforismi*
GABELLES, Gustave - *Pieces* •Mar
Gabriel - *Canzona crequillon* •WWS
Gabrieli, Giovanni - *Canzona a 4* (BULOW) •Ron
   Canzona per sonare no. 2 (AXWORTHY) •DP
GAGNÉ, Marc - *Quatuor du petit Chaperon...* (1981) (16') •CMC
GAGO, José Garcia - *Pieces* •adr
GALANTE, Steven - *Saxsounds I "Sealed with a Kiss"* (1972) •DP
GALARINI, Marco - *Speculazioni* (1992) (10')
GALLAHER, Christopher - *Quartet No. 2*, op. 31 (1969) (9'30)
       •SATB or AATB •adr
   Three Thoughts (1961) (8') •adr
GAMSTORP, Göran - *Barnet i skogen...* (1987) (9'30) •SMIC
Gandolfo - *Pièce*
GARCIA, Russell - *Miniature Symphony* •EMod
GARCIA LABORDA, José Maria - *Paisaje biografico* (1991)
GARCIA ROMAN, José - *Musica para el otono* (1990)
GARNOT, Claude - *Quatuor* (1989) (14')
Gassman, Florian - *Rococo Quartet No. 2 in Bb* (AXWORTHY) •TVA
GASTINEL, Gérard - *Gamma 415* (1976) •Chou
GATES, Everett - *Declamation and Dance*
GAUJAC, Edmond - *Rêves d'enfant* (1957) (10') •Bil
GENEST, Pierre - *Pieces* •adr
GENZMER, Harald - *Quartets I, II, III* (1982-1992) •WWS/R&E
GEORGE, Graham - *Quartet* (1972) •CMC
GERAEDTS, Jaap - *Moto perpetuo* (1968) (4') •Don
GERARD, Marc - *Ouverture pour Clevremont*
GERHARD, Fritz Chr. - *Fantaisie...* (1970) (7') •AMP
GERHARD, Roberto - *Quartet*
GERIN, Roland - *Suite en concert* (1978)
Gershwin, George - *Pieces*
Gervaise, Claude - *Bransle Gay* (HARVEY) •Che
GHIDONI, Armando - *Pieces* •CoMu/adr
Gibbons, Orlando - *Fantazia* (HEMKE) •South
GIBSON, Kenneth - *Pieces* •SM
GILLET, Roger - *Pieces* •Mar
GILSON, Paul - *Quatuor* (unfinished [inachevé])
GINGRAS, Guy - *Pieces* •Med
GIORDANO, John - *Quatuor* (1966)
GLASER, Werner - *4 Phantasies* (1982) (12') •STIM
   Quartet (1984) (17'30) •STIM
GLAZOUNOV, Alexandre - *Quatuor*, op. 109 (1932) (24') •B&H
GLOBOKAR, Vinko - *Discours V* (1982) (22') •Pet
Gluck, Christoph - *Iphigénie en Tauride* (CLASSENS-MERIOT) •Com
GOCA, Vladimir - *Pieces*
GOLESTAN, Stan - *Divertissement champêtre*
GOODWIN, Gordon - *Quiet Canzona* (1978) •adr

GORDON, Jacob - Three *Movements* •Sha

GOTKOVSKY, Ida - *Quatuor* (1983) (26'30) •Bil

GOULD, Alec - *Swing Suite; Three Piece Suite* •SM

GRAEF, Friedemann - *Bearbeitungen* •adr
  Brandenburgische Messe (1989) (15') •adr
  Rondo (1985) (10'30) •R&E

Granados, Enrique - *Danza espanola no. 2* (SAKAGUCHI) •EFSM

GRANDERT, Johnny - *Kvartett n° 2* (1989-91) (16') •SMIC
  Quattro pareri (1983) (13'30) •SMIC

GREAVES, Terence - *Three Folk Songs* (1978) (7') •SM

GREEN, Stuart - *Consortium* (1976) (8')

Gretry, André - *Pieces* •Mol

GREY, Geoffrey - *Quartet* (1973) (14')

Grieg, Edvard - *Pieces* •DP/Sim

GRIFFITH, Oliver - *Prelude and Fugue...* •WWS/DP

GRILLAERT, Octave - *Suite baroque*

GRISONI, Renato - *Für Sigurd*, op. 60 (5'30) •Kneu

GROBA, Rogelio - *Tensiones - Quatuor n° 4* (1979) •adr

GROOME, Richard - *Variations*

GROOT, Hugo de - *Hasta la vista...* (1987) •Mol

GROSS, Eric - *Quartet No. 1* (1987)

GROUVEL, Pierre - *Les humeurs du jour* (1982)

GUALDA JIMENEZ, Antonio - *Soledades rojas* (1988)

GUERIN, Roland - *Suite* (1978)

GUERRINI, Guido - *Canzonetta e ballo Forlinese* (1938)
  Chant et danse dans un style rustique (1946)

GUIBERT, Alvaro - *Del aire* (1992) (10')

GUILLOU, René - *Pièce concertante*

GUILMAIN, Paul - *Espoir, Impatience*

GUTAMA SOEGIJO, Paul - *Pieces*

HÄBERLING, Albert - *Music für Saxophon* (1983)

HAIDMAYER, Karl - *Antispasmodium* (1990); *Quartet*

HALLBERG, Bengt - *Quatuor* (1992)

HALMRAST, Tor - *Fire Fall* (1984) •NMI

HAMMERTH, Johan - *Under tiden* (1993) •SvM

HAMPTON, Calvin - *Pieces* •TTF

Handel, Georg Friedrich - *Pieces*

HANDY, George - *Quartets Nos. 1 - 2 - 3* (1964)

HANNIKEN, Jos - *Blues & Scherzo*, op. 5a; *Variations* •An

HANSEN, Flemming Christian - *A la mémoire de Dali* (1989) (10'30)

HARDING, Taylde - *Quartet*

HARLE, John - *Foursquare for Saxophones* (1980) (13')

HARRISON, Jonty - *SQ* (1979) (17') •adr

HARTL, Heinrich - *Quartett*, op. 16 (1984) (8') •Tong

HARTLEY, Walter - *Suite* (1972) (11') •PhiCo
  Pieces

HARTMANN, Otto B. - *E-Musik ("L'Arlecchino")* •adr

HARTZELL, Eugene - *Divertimento* (1992) (7') •CA

HARVEY, Paul - *Pieces*

HASQUENOPH, Pierre - *Sonate à quatre*, op. 7 (1957) (18') ME

HATCHARD, Michael - *Quartet* (1977) (10'); *Quartet for the Bean* •SM

HAUBENSTOCK-RAMATI, Roman - *Enchaîné* (1987) (19')

HAUDEBERT, Lucien - *Quatuor* (1926)

Hautvast - *Meister Perlen* •TM

HAVELAAR, Anton - *Quatuor* (1991) (10') •Don

HAWORTH, Frank - *Kernwood Suite* (1972) (12') •FHM/CMC

Haydn, Joseph - *Pieces*

HAYES, Gary - *4 Jouets* (1977) (15') •ACA

HECKMANN, Heinz - *Kmk* •adr
  Thema und variationen... (1981) •adr

HEEGAARD, Lars - *Kwartet* (1991)

HEGVIK, Arthur - *Tombeau de Mireille*

HEINKEL, Peggy - *Chregalis* •WWS

HEINS, John - *Serenade*

HEKSTER, Walter - *Setting VIII* (1986) (10') •Don

HELDENBERG, Arthur - *Quatuor*

Heller, Stéphane - *Capriccio, Scherzetto, Canzonetta*, op. 16

HEMKE, Frederick - *Suite* (1966) •adr

HEMMER, René - *Pieces* •adr

HENDRICKS, Duane - *The MacKenzie River Suite* (1979)

HENDRY, James - *Lamentation*, op. 8 (1989) (5'45)

HENDZE, Jesper - *The Beauty of the Beast* (1990) (9'30) •Kon

HENRY, Jean-Claude - *Deux pièces* (1956)

HEPPENER, Robert - *Canzona* (1969) (4') •Don

HERMSEN, Pieter - *3 Movements* (1986) (7') •Don

HERZOG, Alfred - *Quatuor* (1978)

HEUSSENSTAMM, George - *Quartet*, op. 78 (1984) (13') •DP

HEYN, Thomas - *Jazz Inspirierte Miniaturen* (1989)

HIGUET, Nestor - *Thème, variations et fugue*

HILDEMANN, Wolfgang - *Jeux saxophoniques à quatre* •PJT

HILL, Jackson - *Entourage* •SeMC

HILLER, Lejaren - *Quartet* (1984)

HINE, Charles - *Evagations* (1972) (15'30)

HINES, Malcolm - *Quartet* •adr

HLOBIL, Emil - *Marcato di danza* (1979) (2'30) •Praha
  Quartett, op. 93 (1974) (12') •CHF

HO, Wai On - *Quartet* (1974)

HOCK, Franj van - *Burlesque* (1979)

HOCK, Peter - *Phrasen für Sax Quartet* (1973)

HOFFER, Bernard - *Preludes and Fugues* (1977) (25') •SATB/Brass
  quintet •Shir
  Quartet I (1992)
  Three Diversions (1975) (19') •NYSQ
  Variations sur un thème de Stravinsky (1974) (10') •NYSQ

HOLLFELDER, Waldram - *Pieces* •VDMK

HOLLOWAY, Laurie - *Running Buffet* (1981) •LM

HOLMES, G. E. - *Pieces* •Ken

HOLSTEIN, Jean-Paul - *5 Enigmes* (1980) (24') •EMRF

HOOVER, Katherine - *Suite* (1980)

HORNOFF, G. Alfred - *Variations über da Volklied*

HOROVITZ, Joseph - *Variations on a Theme...* (1977) (8') •RSC

HOUDY, Pierre - *Pieces* •Bil/CMC

HOUSKOVA, R. - *Music for Four Saxophones*

HOWLAND, Russel - *Pieces* •Yb/Shir/WHi

HUFFNAGLE, Harry - *White Satin*

HUGHES, Eric - *Scherzo Laconica* (1970) (5'30)

HUMMEL, Berthold - *Musik for 4*, op. 88f (1990) (8') •adr

HUNTERHOFER, Heinrich - *Minneflug* •Ru

HUUCK, Reinhard - *3 Choräle* (1968) (6') •MR

HYMAS, Anthony - *Blues and Waltz* (1978) (10')

Ibert, Jacques - *3 Histoires...* (CLERISSE) •Led

ISABELLE, Jean-Clément - *Quatuor* (1973) (15')

ITO, Yasuhito - *Quartet II*

ITURRALDE, Pedro - *Pequena czarda* (1982) •RME
  Suite de jazz
  Suite hellénique •Lem

JACOB, Gordon - *Quartet No. 1* (1972) (12') •JE

JACOBI, Wolfgang - *Niederdenkscher Tanz* (1936)

Jakma, Fritz - *8 Mélodies célèbres* (2 Volumes) •TM

JEAN, André - *Quatuor* •adr

JEANNEAU, François - *Pieces* •Lem/adr

JENTZSCH, Wilfried - *Recitativo, Canzonetta e Fuga* (1985) (7') •adr

JESTL, Bernhard - *5 Clownesken* (12'30) •ECA

JEVERUD, Johan - *Pieces* •SMIC

JOACHIM, Otto - *Interlude* (1960) (3') •CMC

JOHNER, Hans-Rudolf - *Diskussion* (1981) •adr

JOHNSEN, Hallvard - *Quartet*, op. 65 (1974) (9') •NMO

JOLLET, Jean-Clément - *Trois pour quatre* (1989) (6'30) •Bil

JOLY, Suzanne - *Séquences...* (1972) (12') •EFM

JONAS, Emile - *Pieces* •Marg/Sax
JONES, Kelsey - *Three Preludes and a fugue* (1982) •CMC
JONES, Kenneth - *Quaquaverse* (1978) (13') •adr
JONES, Martin - *Quartet* •adr
Jongbloed, D. - *Romance* •Lis/TM
JONGEN, Joseph - *Quatuor...*, op. 122 (1942) (15') •CBDM
JONGEN, Léon - *Divertissement* (1937) (8'30) •CBDM
JONGHE, Marcel de - *3 Bagatelles* (1982)
Joplin, Scott - *Pieces*
JÖRNS, Helge - *2 Kadenzen zu Raumblöke II & III* (1980) •EMod
JORRAND, André - *Pieces*
JUGUET, Henri-Pierre - *Macles*
JULLIEN-ROUSSEAU - *10 petites esquisses poétiques*
JUNGK, Klaus - *Kleine Suite* (1985) (8')
KACINSKAS, Jeronimas - *Quartet* •adr
KADERAVEK, Milan - *Introduction e allegro* (1963) •Uni
KAI, Akira - *5 Pieces* (1982)
KALED, Emil - *Isomorphica*
KANITZ, Ernest - *Introduction and Allegro* (1963) •Uni
KARKOFF, Ingvar - *Ricercare* (1988) (9') •STIM
KARKOFF, Maurice - *Ernst und Spass*, op. 156 (1984) (9'30) •STIM
    Quartett (1984) •WIM
    Reflexion, op. 160 (1986) •SMIC
KARKOV, Ingvar - *Ricercare* (1988) (10') •STIM
KARLINS, William - *Quartet No. 1* (1966-67) •SeMC
    Quartet No. 2 (1975) •adr
KASPERSEN, Jan - *Quartet* (1989) (7')
KAT, Jack - *Convulsions* (1979) (3') •Don
KAUFMANN, Dieter - *Genius compact* (1992) (8') •ApE
KECHLEY, David - *Stepping Out* (1989) (15') •PV
KEFALA-KERR, John - *Motorola*
KEISER, Henk - *Syncopen* (1982) (13') •Don
Kern, Jerome - *All the Things You Are* (L. NIEHAUS)
KERN, Mathias - *Erstes*
KERSHAW, David - *Four Bagatelles*
KEULEN, Geert van - *Kwartet* (1987) (7') •Don
KEURIS, Tristan - *Music* (1986) (17') •Don
    Quatuor (1970) (8') •Don
KIKUCHI, Yukio - *Saxophones' Studies* (1985)
KINKELDER, Dolf de - *De verloedering* (1985) (10') •Don
KIRCK, George Thomas - *Resultants* •DP
KITAZUME, Michio - *Serenade* (1979)
KITTLER, Richard - *Divertimento*, op.163 (1992) (11') •CA
    Phonosignale (10') •CA
KLAUSS, Noah - *Night Song* •Cap
Klickmann, F. Henry - *Smiles and Chuckles* (GEE) •SATB or AATB
                    •Ron
    Smiles and Chuckles (NASCIMBEN)
KLIER, Gottfield - *25 Saxophone Quartets* •ATTB or SATB •adr
KLINGSOR, Tristan - *Sérénade* •CBDM
KLOUMAN, Carsten - *Divertimento* (1976)
KLUSAK, Jan - *Suita* (1983) (8') •CHF
KNOSP, Erwin - *Divertissement* •adr
    Pièce concertante •adr
KNUTSEN, Thorbjörn - *Quartet* (1974) (14') •NMI
KOBAYASHI, Hidéo - *Invention* (1970) •adr
KÖBNER, Andreas - *E-Musik* •adr
KOCH, Erland von - *Cantelina e vivo* (1978) (3') •SMIC
    Miniatyrer (1970) (11') •Br&Ha
KOCH, Frederick - *Anaclets* •SeMC
KOCKELMANS, Gérard - *Suite* (1956) (7') •Don
KOHN, Karl - *Quartet* •WWC
Komaza, K. - *Märchen und Volkslieder* (HOTZ) •Sim
KONAGAYA, Sôichi - *Message*
KONOE, Hidéraké - *Les insectes*; *Poèsie lyrique japonaise*

KONT, Paul - *Kammertanzsuite* (10') •CA
    5 Sketches •ECA
KÖPER, Heinz Karl - *For Four* (10') •adr
KORDE, Shirish - *Constellations* (1973-74) (9') •DP
KORTE, Karl - *Facets* (1970) •SeMC
KOSTECK, Gregory - *Serious Developments: Music* (1979)
KOUMANS, Rudolf - *Quartet*, op. 37
KOX, Hans - *Quartet* (1985) (10') •Don
    Quartet No. 2 (1987-88) (17') •Don
KRAEMER, Ira - *Petite Suite* (1987)
KRATOCHWIL, Heinz - *Attacken*, Op. 163 •ApE
    Fantasie, op. 148 •Dob/ECA/ApE
KREIN, Michael - *Valse caprice* (1930) (5') •NWM
KREMENLIEV, Boris - *Quartet* •adr
KREMP, Uwe - *Klangverwesung* (1991) (6')
Kreutzer, Léon - *1ère partie de Quatuor* (185x) •Sax
KRICKEBERG, Dieter - *Chaconne* (198x) (10')
Krieger, Johann - *Suite* •Mol
KRISTENSEN, Kuno Kjaerbye - *Kwartet I* (1989) (10')
    Kwartet II (1990) (11')
KRÖLL, Georg - *Fünf Versetten* (1986) (16')
KRUMLOVSKY, Claus - *Divertissement*, op. 3 •UGDAL
KRUSE, Bjorne Howard - *Colors* (1979) •NMI
    Reflections (1976) (4') •NMI
    Statement (1975) (10') •NMI
KRUYF, Ton de - *Musica portuensis* (1983) (17') •Don
KUBIZEK, Augustin - *Saxophonia*, op. 60/2 (1989) •CA
KÜHMSTEDT, Paul - *6 Arabesken* (1988) •GB
KÜHNE, Stephan - *Just for fun* (1991) (2'30) •ApE
KUHNERT, Rolf - *2 Temperamente* (1987) •KuD
KURACHI, Tatsuya - *2 Paroles tissées*
KUSHIDA, Testurosuke - *The Ancient Poem in Asuka* (1985) (15')
LACOUR, Guy - *Quatuor* (1969) (11') •Bil
LACY, Steve - *Quatuor* (1986)
LAJTHA, Làszlô - *Intermezzo*, op. 59 (1954) (5'30) •Asx/Pno or 4 Sx:
                    SATB •Led
LAMB, Marvin L. - *In Memoriam, Benjy* (1972) (6') •MP
LAMBIJ, Ton - *Symphonic verses* (1991) (27') •Don
LAMPERSBERG, Gerhard - *Eulennacht* •ECA
LANCEN, Serge - *Four Somes* •Chap
    Intermèdes I & II (1974) (7') •Mol
    Rondo-caprice (1975) (5'30) •Mol
LANE, Richard - *Quartet* (1982) (10') •TTF
LANERI, Roberto - *Sonora Crossroads* (1980) •adr
LANGESTRAAT, Willy - *Quartet for a Celebration* (1985) (6') •Mol
LANTIER, Pierre - *Andante et Scherzo* (1942) •Bil
    Quatuor (18')
LARSSON, Mats - *Gopak* (1989) (5'30) •SMIC
LASNE, George - *Berceuse dans le deuil* (1963) (6')
    Dyptique (1968) (6')
    Lied-choral en do mineur (1968) (4'30)
LAUBA, Christian - *Reflets* (1986) (12') •Fuz
LAUERMANN, Herbert - *Bagatellen* •ECA/ApE
LAUREAU, Jean-Marc - *Etat limite* (1981)
Laurendeau - *Collection of 25 Gospel Hymns* •CF
LAZARO, J. - *Juego n° 8*
LEBOW, Leonard S. - *Four Movements*
LECLERCQ, Edgard - *Impression romantique* (5')
    Introduction et scherzo capricioso (5') •Mau
    Prélude et mouvement perpétuel (4') •Mau
LECLERE, François - *Périphéria* (1977)
L'ECUYER, Christian - *Soleil*
LEDUC, Jacques - *Sortilèges africains* (1967) (10')
    Suite, op. 15 (1964) (12') •Sch
LEE, Thomas Oboe - *Louie MCLV* (8'); *Piece for Viola* (15') •adr

LEFANU, Nicola - *Moon Over the Western Ridge* (1985) (12'45)
LEFKOFF, Gerald - *Tapestries* •Gly
LEGLEY, Victor - *Cinq Miniatures*, op. 54 (1958) (8') •CBDM
LEGUAY, Jean-Pierre - *Madrigal 6* (1985)
LEHMANN, Markus - *Cortidiana* (17') •Asto
   Werke •adr
LEHNERT, Wolfgang - *Kleine Suite* •SRu
LEIBOWITZ, René - *Variations*, op. 84 (1969) (12') •JJ
LEISTNER-MAYER, Roland - *Quartetto* (1984) •adr
LEJETH, Edith - *Aube marine* (1982) (8') •Lem
   Musique pour quatuor (1973-74) (12') •EFM
LEMELAND, Aubert - *Arioso*, op. 24 (1972) (6') •adr
   Concertino (1980) •adr
   Epilogue nocturne, op. 22 (1971) (8'15) •Bil
   Noctuor, op. 93 (1983) (9') •Bil
   Quatuor (1979) •adr
   Variations •adr
LENNERS, Claude - *Melisma* (1986) •adr
Lennon & McCartney - *When I'm Sixty-Four* (RICKER) •SATB or
                AATB •Ken
LERSTAD, Terje Bjorn - *2 Pièces*, op. 79 (1975) (7') •NMI
   Quartets Nos. 1 & 2 (1976) •NMI
LESSER, Jeffrey - *Quartet* (1979) •Pres
LETELLIER, Llona Alfonso - *Cuarteto*, op. 28 (1963)
LETOREY, Omer - *Faunes et Nymphes* •Marg
LEVAL, Charles - *Saxophonia* (1983)
LEVIN, Todd - *Serenade Express* (1987)
LEVY, Frank - *Adagio and Scherzo* •SeMC
LEVY, Matthew - *Quartet*
Lewis - *Quartet* •WWS
LEWIS, Robert Hall - *Combinazioni VI* (1986) (8')
LHOMME, Charles - *Menuet en sol majeur* •Marg
LIEBMAN, David - *The Grey Convoy* •AdMu
   A Moody Time •DP
LINDBERG, Nils - *Dalasvit* (1988) (15') •CG
   Torn-Eriks Visa
Linden, N. van de - *Chinese Mars* (LEMARC) •SATB or SAAT •TM
LINDEN, Robert E. van de - *Quartet* (1979)
LINDWALL, Christer - *Cut up* (1992) (8')
LINN, Robert - *Prelude and Dance* (1964) •WIM
   Quartet (9'); *Suite* •WIM
LIPTAK, David - *Statements* (1971) •WWS
LLANAS, Albert - *Contexto V*
LLOYD, Cy - *Quartet* (1969) •adr
LOCHU, Eric - *Deguy jazz* •SL
   Lucky sax et Quart sax (1990) •Com
LOLINI, Ruggero - *Molto riflesso* (1975)
LOPEZ, CALVO - *Tema con variaciones*
LORENTZEN, Bent - *Lines* (7'45)
LOTICHIUS, Erik - *Kwartet* (1980) (8') •Don
LOUKIANOV, G. - *Quatuor en Si*
LOUP, Félix - *Pavane à un héros disparu* (1939) (8'10)
   Quatuor en Sol mineur •Mar
LOUVIER, Alain - *Le jeu des sept musiques* (1986) (10') •Led
LOVELOCK, William - *Final & Quartet* (1977)
   Suite (1978) •APRA
LOVREGLIO, Eleuthère - *Andante* (1938) (4') •EFM
   Jacareros (1935) (9')
   Quatuor (1937) (28')
   Variations sur un thème breton (1937) (7')
LUBAT, Bernard - *Deux temps s'entend sans temps* (1982)
LUBIN, Ernest Viviani - *Gavotte*; *Lady of the Lake* •adr
LUKAS, Zdenek - *Rondo*, op. 70 (1970) (12') •CHF
LUKIJNOV, German - *Quartet in Bb*
LUNDE, Ivar Jr. - *Quartet*, op. 54 (1975) •DP

LUNDE, Lawson - *Suite*, op. 11 (1959) (8') •TTF
LUNDQUIST, Torbjörn Iwan - *Alla prima* (1989) (10') •SMIC
   Concitato (1980) (5') •SMIC
LUSTIG, Leila - *The Language of Bees* (1983)
LUYPAERTS, Guy - *Carnavalesca* •adr
LYNE, Peter - *Stampede* (1985) (7') •STIM
MacDowell, Edward - *Song* (from *Sea Pieces*), op. 55, no. 5
Machaut, Guillaume de - *Pieces* (AXWORTHY) •DP/TVA
MACPHERSON, Ian - *Suite* (1978) (15')
MADDIRK, Daniel - *Quartet*
MADDOCKS, David - *Threnody for Benjamin Britten* (1977) (5'30)
MAES, Jef - *Saxo-scope* (10'30) •CRA
MAIMAN, Bruce - *Quartet No. 1* (1979)
MALAQUIN, Maurice - *Fantaisie*
MALMBORG, Paula - *Yakuzi* (1992-93) •SvM
MALMFORS, Ake - *Quatuor* •ACS
MANAS, Roger - *Two Pieces*
Maniere, Léon - *Pieces* •Gras
MANZO, Silvio - *2 Tempi* •4 Sx: SATB/Timp ad lib. •Pet
MANZONI, Giacomo - *To planets and to flowers* (1990) (7')
MARCO, Thomas - *Paraiso mecanico* (1990) •Lem
MAREZ OYENS-WANSINK, Tera de - *Pieces* •Don
MARGONI, Alain - *1er Quatuor* (1990) (11'40) •Bil
   2me Quatuor (1991)
MARI, Pierrette - *De trois à quatre* (1974) •adr
MARISCHAL, L. - *Pour le plaisir* •Chap
MAROCCHINI, Enrico - *Quartetto*, op. 26 no. 1 (1990) (8') •adr
MAROS, Miklos - *Quartet* (1984) (10') •SMIC
MARSHALL, Jack - *The Goldrush Suite* (1959) •Mar
MARTIN RODRIGUEZ - *Impromptu*
MASETTI, Enzo - *Divertimento*
MASON, Lucas - *Quartet* (1971) •adr
MASON, Thom David - *The City* (1965)
MASSET-LECOQ, Roselyne - *2 Pièces brèves* (1977)
MASUDA, Kozo - *Quatuor* (1975)
MATHEY, Paul - *Quatuor*
MATITIA, Jean - *Chinese Rag* (1985) (2'30) •Lem
MATSUSHITA, Isao - *Atoll I* (1982) (13')
MATTHEWS, David - *Pieces*
Maure - *Christmastime International* •WWS
MAURICE, R. - *Aurore* •Mau
MAURY, Lownder - *Cock of the Walk* (1949) (5') •4 Sx •AvMu
MAYEUR, Louis - *Impromptu*
MAZELLIER, Jules - *Pieces* •EV
McCARTY, Frank - *Five Situations* (1969) (15') •SATB or SAAT
                •Art
McCUALEY, William - *5 Miniatures* (4'30) •CMC
McGUIRE, Edward - *Five Small Pieces* (1971)
McKEE, Richard - *Quartet* (1982)
McPEEK, Ben - *Canadian Audubon Suite* (1977) (15') •CMC
MEFANO - *Quatuor* (1980) (4')
MEIER, Daniel - *Epi* (1973) (11') •EFM
MEIJERING, Chiel - *Pieces* •Don
MELIN, Sten - *Källarbacksvariationerna* (1993) •SvM
Melle, R. del - *Largo religioso* (D. SPEETS) •TM
MELLNÄS, Arne - *No Roses for Madame F.* (1991) (3') •STIM
   Quartet (1984) (7') •STIM
Mendelssohn - *Pieces*
MENICHETTI, François - *Bouquet oriental* (1934) (5'30) •Mar
MERANGER, Paul - *Pieces*
MERLET, Michel - *Variations*, op. 32 (1982) •Led
MERSSON, Boris - *Suites* •Br&Ha/adr
MEULEMANS, Arthur - *Pièces* •Ger
   Quatuor (1953) (14') •CBDM
MEYER, Jean-Michel - *Divertissement* (1975) •Bil

MEYER, Krzysztof - *Quartet*, op. 65a (1986) (12') •CA
Meyerbeer, Giacomo - *Cantiques* (W. HEKKER) •SATB or AATB •TM
MICHALSKY, Donal - *Three Times four...* •DP
MICHANS, Carlos - *Quartetto* (1989) (10') •Don
MICHEL, Bernard - *Avant, pendant, après...*
MICHEL, Paul Baudoin - *Pieces* •adr
MIGNION, René - *Petit enfant* (1977) •Bil
MIGOT, Georges - *Quatuor* (1955) (17'30)
Millocker, Karl - *Herinneringer* •Mol
Mingus, Charles - *Jelly Roll* •SATB or AATB •WWS
MISTAK, Alvin - *Quartet* •Eto
MITCHELL, William - *Pieces* •BMIC
MITREA-CELARIANU, Mihai - *Eté* (1989) (9')
MIYAGAWA, Tadatoshi - *Pieces*
MIYAZAWA, Kazuto - *Pieces*
MOESCHINGER, Albert - *Quatuor antherin*
MOHR, Jean-Baptiste - *1ère partie de Quatuor* (1864) •Sax
MOLS, Robert - *Pieces*
MONTAGNE, Roger - *Pieces*
MONTANES, Jose Manuel - *Cuarteto*, op. 14 (1989) •CMC
MONTESINOS, Williams - *Pièce* (1992) (10')
MOQUÉ, Xavier - *Pieces* •adr
MORGAN, David - *Brilliant bagatelle* (1971) (2'30) •BMIC
Morley, Thomas - *April Is In My Mistress' Face* (HARVEY) •Che
MORTHENSON, Jan W. - *Pieces* •Steim/SMIC
Moskowski, Moritz - *Guitarre* (CUNNINGHAM) •DP
MÖSS, Piotr - *Quartetto* (1981) •PNS
MOULAERT, Raymond - *Andante, Fugue et Final* (1907) (8') •CBDM
MOURANT, Walter - *Pieces* •CFE/Pio
Moussorgsky, Modeste - *Bilder einer Austellung* (Th. SCHÖN) •ApE
MOWER, M. - *Pieces* •WWS
Mozart - *Pieces*
MULDOWNEY, Dominic - *Five Melodies* (1978) (16'30) •Nov
MULLER, Anders - *Kvartet* (1991) (8')
MÜLLER, Gottfried - *Pieces* •KuD/adr
MÜLLER-GOLDBOOM, Gerhardt - *Exkurse* (1988) (34')
MURPHY, Lyle - *Pieces* •AvMu/WIM/WWS
MYERS, Robert - *Quartets 1 & 2* •adr
MYSLIVECEK, J. - Sinfonia
NAKAGAWA, Ataru - *Quartet*
NAKAMURA, Koya - *Spiritual Song from Small Island* (1982)
NÄTHER, Gisbert - *Quartettino* (1988) •PMV
NAULAIS, Jérôme - *Patchwork* •Arp
NAVARRE, Randy - *Saxophone Quartet*
NESTICO, Sammy - *A Study in Contrasts* (3'20) •Ken
NEWMAN, Ronald - *Quartet* (1988)
NEWTON, Rodney - *Fantasies on Middle Eastern...* (1976) •adr
NICOLAS, René (Mickey) - *Passim* (1973) (8'45)
NICOLAU, Dimitri - *Pieces* •EDP/adr
NIEHAUS, Lennie - *Pieces*
NIEHAUS, Manfred - *Saxophonquartett* (1981)
NODA, Ryo - *Sketch* (1973-76) (2'30)
NODAIRA, Ichiro - *Quatuor* (1985) (16') •Lem
NOON, David - *Coda*, op. 39 (1976) (2') •TTF
NORHOLM, Ib - *Kvartet* , op. 122 (1992) (12'30) •Kon
    A Patchwork in pink, op. 109 (1989) (12')
NUYTS, F. - *La sale mère, le boeuf et le crampon* (1981)
NUYTS, Gaston - *Bar-o-kjana* •Sez
NYORD, Morten - *Saxo* (1989) (8')
NYVANG, Michael - *Kwartet* (1991)
O'FARRILL, Chico - *Three Pieces*
OOSTERVELD, Ernst - *Average music III* (1979) (10') •Don
ORBAN, Marcel - *Introduction, variations et Final* (1938)
ORLOFF, Eugene - *Down Hall*
ORTIZ, William - *Housing Project* (1985)

OSTENDORF, Jens-Peter - *Monaden* (1990) (10') •Sik
OSTLING, Acton - *Quart-tet-à-tête* •Bel
OTTEN, Ludwig - *Quartet* (1969) (17'30) •Don
Overstreet, W. Benton - *That Alabama Jasbo Band* (1918) (HOLMES)
    •SATB or AATB
PACALET, Jean - *Match* (1987) •adr
PADDING, Martijn - *Ritorno* (1988) (11'); *Ronk* •Don
PAGE, Eric - *Quatuor* (1984)
Palestrina, G. - *Pieces* •Mar/TM
PALOMBO, Rudolphe - *Quatuor*
PANICCIA, Renzo - *Petit souffle du vent*, op. 4 (1984) (9')
PAPANDOPULO, Boris - *6 Croquis* (1992)
PARENT, Nil - *Inter-modul-action* (1973) (26') •SATB/Electr. equip-
    ment
PARFREY, Raymond - *Quartet* (1972) •BMIC
    Pieces •BMIC
PARISI, Stephen - *Introduction and Capriccio* (1980)
Parker, Charlie - *Ornithology*
PASCAL, Claude - *Quatuor* (1961) (17') •Dur
PASQUET, Luis - *3 Pièces*
PATACHICH, Ivan - *Quartetino* (1972) •GMP
PATRIQUIN, Donald - *Pieces* •CMC
PATTEN, James - *Pieces* •BMIC
PATTERSON, Paul - *Diversions* (1976) (12') •adr
PAULET, Vincent - *Aeolian Voices* (1990) (4'30)
PAUR, Jiri - *Slepici serenade* (1988) (8'); *Suite* (1986) (8')
PAVLENKO, Serguei - *Quartet* (1976) (13') •adr
PECK, Russell - *Drastic Measures*
PEDERSEN, Jens Wilhelm - *Seks bagateller* (1986) (7')
PELCHAT, André - *Exploration* (1980) •CMC
PELEMANS, Willem - *Quatuor* (1965) (12') •Mau
PENBERTHY, James - *Scherzo and Lamentoso* (1982) •adr
PEPPER, Richard - *Quartet* (1972) (5'30)
PERLONGO, Daniel - *Aureole-quartet* (1979) •Sha
PERRAULT, Michel - *Esquisses québécoises*
    Quatuor (1953) •PuB/CMC
PERRIN, Marcel - *Cinq Pièces* (1941) •DP
    Mirage (1938) (2'30) •SATB or Asx/Orch •Led
PETERSMA, Wim - *Quatuor* (1971) (8') •Don
PETIT, Jacques - *Saxorch* (1976)
    Swing sweet suite (1988) •Arp
PETIT, Jean-Louis - *Perceval* (1985) (10')
PEUERL, Paul - *Suite in Es-Dur* (1992) •PMV
PFLÜGER, Andreas - *Sogno d'estate*
PHAN, P. Q. - *Seagulls* (1989) •adr
PHILIBA, Nicole - *Quatuor* (1959) (16'30)
PHILIPS, Richard - *Tarentelle et Fugue* (1981) (2') •Com
PHILLIPS, Art - *Tribute - to Leonard Bernstein*
PIAZZOLA, Astor - *Histoire du tango* (1991) (13') •Lem
PICHAUREAU, Claude - *Pieces* •Bil
PIEPER, René - *Chanson interrompue* (1983) (6') •Don
PIERNÉ, Gabriel - *Introduction et variations sur un thème populaire*
    (1937) (14'30) •SATB •Led
    Pieces •Led/Lud
PIERNÉ, Paul - *Trois Conversations* •Bil
PILON, Daniel - *Pieces* •adr
PINTO, Carlo - *Quartet* (1985)
PISHNY, Floyd - *Pieces*
PISTONI, Piera - *Pieces*
Pitoni, Giuseppe Ottavio - *Cantate domino* (D. SPEETS) •TM
PLANEL, Robert - *Burlesque* (1942) (4'10)
PLANK, Max - *Four Diversions*
Planquette, Robert - *Cloches de Corneville* •Mol
POLIET, Lucien - *Couques de Dinant* (1971) •adr
    Versailles suite (1960) (11') •adr

PONJEE, Ted - *Pieces* •Don
POOT, Marcel - *Concertino* (1962) •CBDM
    Pieces •CBDM
POPE, Peter - *Fleet Street Concerto* (1972) (17')
PORRET, Julien - *Intimité; Prélude et fugue d'après Frescobaldi*
Porter, Cole - *Just One of These Things*
POST, Jos - *Litany* (1983) (8') •Don
Poulenc, Francis - *Suite Française* (J. FORSELL) (13')
POUSSEUR, Henri - *Vue sur les jardins interdits* (1973) •SZ
POWNING, Graham - *Three Pieces* (1981)
Praetorius, Michael - *Pieces* (HARVEY) •Che
PRIESNER, Vroni - *Karussell* (1992) (10')
PRIEST, Barnaby - *Quartet* (1979) (10')
PROCACCINI, Teresa - *Meeting* (1988) (10')
PRODIGO, Sergio - *Quartetto V*, op. 71b (1987-88) (13') •adr
Prokofiev, Sergei - *Marche*, op. 12, no. 1 (DAWSON) •Ron
Puccini, Giacomo - *Crisantemi; Three Minuets* (STAM) •Mol
Purcell, Henry - *An English Suite* •Ken
PÜTZ, Eduard - *Impressionen* •adr
PÜTZ, Marco - *Introduction, cadence et allegro*
QUELLE, Ernst-August - *Ragtime-company* (1987) •GB
QUINET, Marcel - *Pochades* (1967) (6'30) •Bil
Rachmaninoff, Sergei - *Vocalise* (5') (PFENNINGER) •Ron
Raff, Joachim - *Quatuor* (MULE)
RAHEB, Jeffrey - *Quartet No. 1* (1980)
RALSTON, Alfred - *An Allegro* (1973) (12')
Rameau, Jean-Philippe - *Tambourin* (CRESSONNOIS) •Sax
RAMSELL, Kenneth - *Pieces*
RANIER, Tom - *Rondo* (1970)
RAPOPORT, Ricardo - *Pour quatuor de saxophones* (1988) (8')
RATHBURN, Eldon - *Two Interplays* (1972) (7'30) •CMC
RAUBER, Fr. - *Pièce détachée*
RAXACH, Enrique - *Antevisperas* (1986) (12'30) •Don
RAYNAL, Gilles - *L'ordre et la lumière* (6') •4 Sx: SATB/Choeur
REA, John - *Fantasies...* (1969) •4 Sx: SATB/Perc ad lib. •CMC
READE, Paul - *Quartet* (1979) (8'30) •adr
Reber, Napoléon-Henri - *Berceuse célèbre* (FORET) •Bil
REGT, Hendrik de - *Musica*, op. 8 (1971) (7-8') •Don
REICHEL, Bernard - *Prélude*
REINBERGER, Karl - *Drei Miniaturen...* (10') •CA
REYMOND, Roger - *Pieces* •adr
RIBAS, Rosa Maria Monné - *Pieces* •adr
RIBOUR, Ph. - *Quatuor*
RICARD, Claude Ernest Roland - *Badinerie* (1962) (1'30) •South
RICHARDSON, Neil - *Jazz Suite* (1978) (21'30)
RICHER, Janine - *Quatuor* (1958) (14')
RIDDERSTRÖM, Bo - Saxofonkvartett (1984) (10') •STIM
RIEDLBAUCH, Vaclav - *Doslov* (1983) (8') •CHF
RIEDSTRA, Tom - *Bonk-kwartet* (1985-90) (6') •Don
RILEY, James - *Visiones* (1976) •South
Rimsky-Korsakov, Nicolas - *Pieces* (MULE)
RIVIER, Jean - *Grave et Presto* (1938) (8') •Bil
RIVIERE, Jean-Pierre - *Pieces*
ROBERT, Lucie - *Tétraphone* (1982) (16'0 •Bil
    Variations Diapason (1992) (14'20) •Bil
ROBJOHN, William - *Allegro de concert*
RODEN, Robert R. - *Sax-craft* (1978) •SATB or AATB •South
Rodgers, Richard - *Dancing on the Ceiling* •SATB/Bass/Drums •DP
    It Might as Well be Spring (YOUNG) •SATB •Ron
    My Funny Valentine (YOUNG) •SATB •Ron
Roesgen-Champion, Marguerite - *Scherzo* (MULE)
ROIKJER, Kjell - *Divertimento n° 6*, op. 72 (1978-90) (12'30)
ROLDAN, Ramon de SAMINAN - *Inter-relaciones* (1984)
ROLIN, Etienne - *Tightrope* (1979) (7') •adr
    Pieces •adr

ROMANO, Edmond - *Séquences alternées* (1980)
ROMBY, Paul - *Primevères* •Asx/Pno or 4 Sx: SATB •PB
    Vacances •PB
ROMERO, Aldemaro - *Quartet* (1976) (16'30) •Pag
ROMZA, Robert - *Quartet No. 2* (1993)
ROS, Pepito - *Maya e New dance*
ROSSÉ, François - *Mod'son 7* (1985) (12') •CA
Rossini, Giacchino - *Pieces* •GB/SL
ROSSINYOL, Jordi - *Sax*
ROT, Michael - *8 miniaturen*, op. 24 1/8; *Quartetto non troppo* •ECA
ROUGERON, Philippe - *Deux Pièces* •Com
ROUSSEAU, Jean - *10 petites esquisses poètiques*
Rozas, Antonio - *Dos ensayos* (1984)
RUBBERT, Rainer - *Urban music* (1993) •adr
RÜDENAUER, Meinhard - *Dances and Sentimental...* (13') •CA
RUEDA, Enrique - *Cuarteto - Tocata* (1992)
RUEFF, Jeanine - *Concert en quatuor* (1955) (17') •Led
RUELLE, Fernand Jules - *Pieces* •Mau/adr
RUGGIERO, Charles - *Three Blues* (1981) •DP
RUIZ, Manuel - *Faxce* (1990)
RUNCHAK, Vladymyr - *Contra spem spero* (1990)
RUNSWICK, Daryl - *Pieces* •adr
RUSHBY-SMITH, John - *Quartet* (1972) (13'30) •Sim
RYDBERG, Bo - *Link/Sequence* (1990) •SATB/Computer/Live elec-
                    tronics •Tons
SADLER, Helmut - *Quarttet concertino* •adr
SAINT-AULAIRE, Roland - *Visages d'enfants* (1938) (10'30)
SAITO, Takanobu - *Quartet; 2nd Quartet*
SALBERT, Dieter - *Saxophonia* (1989) (10') •adr
SALLUSTIO, Eraclio - *Cralas; Saxologia 2* (1986)
SALMON, Raymond - *Prélude et scherzo* (1956) (8')
    Quatuor en Sol mineur (1941) (15')
SAMAZEUILH, Gustave - *Pièce dans un style ancien*
SAMBIN, Victor - *5 Quatuors brillants* •Sal
SAMUELSSON, Marie - *Djup* (1991) •Tons
SANCHEZ CANAS, Sebastian - *Nuevas diferencias* (1990)
SANDGREN, Joaklm - *Jag fâr sâ ont i ögonen* (1992) •SvM
SANDRED, Örjan - *Skuggor* (1989) (4') •STIM
SANDROFF, Howard - *Chorale*
SANDSTRÖM, Sven-David - *Moments musicaux* (1985) (14') •SMIC
SANSOM, Chris - *5 Pieces* (1975) (7'30)
SANTIAGO, Armando - *Quatuor* (1988)
Satie, Eric - *Gymnopédie I* (GREENBERG) •WWS
SAUTER, Eddie - *Quartet No. 1* •Ken
SAVARI, Jean-Nicolas - *Quatuor en 4 parties* (185x) (17') •Sax/Mol
SBACCO, Franco - *Equinst* (1990) (13') •SATB/Electron. •adr
Scarlatti, Alessandro - *Prelude and Fugue* (SCHMIDT) •WIM
Scarlatti, Domenico - *Pieces*
SCHAFFER, Boguslaw - *Quatuor SG.7 n° 112* (1968) •2 Pno or 4 Sx:
                    SATB/2 optional instruments •AMP
SCHÄUBLE, Nikolaus - *Ellington Medley* (1990) (12')
SCHERR, Hans Jörg - *Quartett n° 1* (1964)
SCHIAFFINI, Giancarlo - *Falsobordone* (1984)
SCHIBLER, Armin - *Quartet* (1978)
SCHILLING, Hans Ludwig - *Concerto* (1986) (9') •B&B
    Suite nostalgique (1991) (10')
SCHIMMEL, William - *Quartet* (1982)
SCHLEI, Wolfgang - *Invention* (1988) (4') •Uni
SCHMELZER, August - *Quartett* (1981) •adr
Schmidt, Joseph - *Finale* (BRINK) •2 Cl/Tsx/Tuba or 4 Sx: SATB •Mol
SCHMIDT, William - *Prelude and Rondo* •WIM
    Suite (1963) (12') •WIM
SCHMIT, Camille - *Polyphonics* (1970) (10') •CBDM
SCHMITT, Florent - *Andante religioso*, op. 109
    Quatuor, op. 102 (1941) •Dur

SCHMUTZ, Albert - *Pieces* •AMPC

SCHNEEBIEGEL, Rolf - *Valse habelice* (1987) •GB

SCHOLLUM, Robert - *Elegie*, op. 130 (1985) •ECA/Dob/ApE

SCHOONENBEEK, Kees - *Kwartet* (1982) (13') •Don

SCHRIJVER, K. de - *Pieces* •Scz/TM

SCHROYENS, Daniel - *Rapsodie* (1976)

Schubert, Franz - *Pieces*

SCHUDEL, Thomas - *Pentagram* (1987) (14') •SATB/Perc •DP/ CMC

SCHULER, Thomas Herwig - *Quartett*, op. 5 (1991) (15') •CA

Schumann, Robert - *Pieces* •Braun/Ken/Mar

SCHWEINITZ, Wolfgang von - *Musik...* (1986) (10'30) •B&H

SCIORTINO, Patrice - *Agogik* (1974) (11') •Chou

   Dans païenne, op. 10 (1960) (4'30) •Chou

SCIPIONE, Umberto - *Agressivo II*; *Miniature* (1992) (6')

SCOGNA, Flavio - *Riflesi* (1990) •BMG

SCOTT, Andy - *Symphony for Saxophones* •SATB or AATB •PBP

SCOTT, Jack - *Quartet*

SCOTT, Rupert - *Quartet* (1971) (13'); *Suite* (1973) (14')

SEAMARKS, Colin - *Quartet* (1971) (5')

SEIDELMANN, Axel - *Variationen* (8') •CA

SELEN, Reinhold - *Quartett* (1991) (9') •Don

   Thema und Variationen (1987) •Don

SELLENICK, Adolphe-Valentin - *Andante religioso* (1861) •Marg

SEMLER, COLLERY, Armand - *Pieces* •Marg/adr

SEMLER, COLLERY, Jules - *Pieces* •Marg/MEr

SEREBRIER, José - *Cuarteto* (1955) •South/Peer/Meri

SERMILÄ, Jarno - *Jean Eduard en face...* (1986) (10') •FMIC

SHAFFER, Sherwood - *Sinfonia for Saxophone Quartet* •adr

SHAW, Francis - *Pages* (1971) (4'30)

SHELDON, R. - *Sarabande*

SHIPLEY, Edward - *Quartet* (1973) (4'30)

Shostakovich, Dmitri - *Prelude No. 7* •WWS

SHRUBSHALL, Peter & Catherine - *Valiant to the Last*

SHRUDE, Marilyn - *Quartet* (1971) •South

SHULMAN, Richard - *Peace in Jerusalem* (1984)

SICHLER, Jean - *Pieces* •Com

SIGEL, Allen - *Homage to Gershwin* •adr

SILVA, Paulo - *Preludio e fuga* (1946) •IMD

SILVER, Horace - *Peace*

SIMON, Jonathan - *The Illegitimate Child* •DP

SIMONIS, Jean-Marie - *Boutades* (1971) (12') •Bil

SIMS, Phil - *Ellington-Medley* (1982)

SINGELEE, Jean-Basptiste - *Premier quatuor*, op. 53 (1958) •Mol

   Quatuor, op. 79 (186x) •Sax

SINGER, Malcolm - *Rat-rythme* (1977) (8')

SINQUIER, C. - *Saxophonie* (1976)

SIVAK, Tom - *Three Fugues Based on Beethoven*

SKOLNIK, Walter - *Divertimento in Eb* •DP

SLEICHIM, Eric - *Poortenbos* (1989) •adr

   Pieces •adr

SMIRNOV, Dimitry - *Mirages* (1978) •ECS

SMIT, Leo - *Tzadik* (1983)

SMITH, Glenn - *Mood Music I* (1973) (7'35) •Eto

SMITH, Howie - *Pieces* •Oa

SMITH, Kent - *Two Pieces* (1974)

SNYDER, Randall - *Quartet*

SÖDERLUNDH, Lille Bror - *Pieces* •ACS/HBus

Södermann, Johan August - *Bröllops-marsch* (LEMARC) •TM

SODOMKA, Karel - *Musica* •CHF

SOLAL, Martial - *Une pièce pour quatre* (1985) (15') •Mar

SOLLFELNER, Bernd Hannes - *Tetralog* (1992) •ApE

SOLVES, Jean-Pierre - *A night maw*

SOUFFRIAU, Arsène - *Temo 2856*, op. 244 (1973) •adr

SOUMAROKOV - *Incrustations* •ECS

SPEARS, Jared - *Episode* (1964) (5') •South

   Quartet "66" (1966) •South

Speets, D. - *Klassiek kwartet* •SATB or SAAT or SATT or SAAB •TM

SPIEWAK, Tomasz - *Quartet* (1988)

SPIJKER, Toon - *Kwartet* (1984)

SPITZMÜLLER, Alexandre - *Quatuor*

SPORCK, Jo - *Poême* (1981) (10') •Don

Standley - *Bluebell Polka*

STEEGMANS, Paul - *Kwartet* (1991) (11')

STERN, Theodore - *Quartet* (1971) •Sha

STEWART, Malcolm - *Three* (1971) (5')

STILLER, Andrew - *Chamber Symphony* (1982)

STOCK, David - *Sax Appeal*

STOKER, Richard - *Quartet* (1969) (6') •Hin

STOOP, Henk - *Kwartet* (1984) (20') •Don

STRAESSER, Joep - *Intersections V-1* (1974-79) (11'30) •Don

STRATTON, Donald - *Pieces*

Strauss, Johann - *Pizzicato-Polka* (HOTZ) •Sim

STRAYHORN, Billy - *Lush Life*

STRIETMAN, Willem - *Musiquettes II* (1981) (11') •Don

STROEYKENS, Armand - *Rapsodische Schetsen*; *Suite* (1981)

SULLIVAN, John - Six *Sax Songs* (1979)

SUNDE, Helge - *The Thousand and Second Tale* (1992)

SUSCHKE, Matthias - *Meditation un Fughette* (1992) •PMV

SUSI, Jose - *Cuarteto*, op. 5 (1988)

SUTER, Robert - *Jeux à quatre* (1976) •HM

Sweelinck, Jan Pieterzoon - *Variations on a Theme* (RICKER) •DP

SWEENEY, William - *Juno*

SYVERUD, Stephen - *Fragile* (1982)

TACHIBA - *Introduction et allegro* (1984)

TAJINO, Masato - *Quatre souffles* (1981)

TANAKA, Katsuhiko - *Jazz improvisation for Passereaux* (1981)

TANIGAWA, Tadahiro - *Quartett "Slix"*

TANNER, David - *Trois petits mals* (1972) (7') •CMC

TAUTENHAHN, Günther - *Sax Quartet* (1976) •SeMC

Tchaikovsky, Peter Ilyich - *Pieces* •Bil/Mol

TEGLBAERG STUBBE, Hans Peter - *Skel* (1986) (10'30)

Telemann, Georg Phillip - *Overture Suite in F* (SCHAEFER) •DP

TERAHARA, Nobuo - *3 Fugues*

THINGHNAES, Frode - *Faces in motion* (1976)

THOMASSIN, A. - *Om* (1990)

THOMPSON, Terence - *Pieces*

THORENSEN, Lasse - *Narrative* (1988) (27') •NMI

THOU, Franz von - *Suite* (1941) •Fro

THOUIN, Lise - *Joie* •CMC

THÜRAUER, Franz - *Aria* (1991) •ApE; *Mosaik* (15') •CA

TICHELI, Frank - *Backburner* (1988) •adr

TILSTONE-ELLIS, John - *Ollersett Suite* (1978) •BMIC

TISNÉ, Antoine - *Alliages I & II* (1971) (15') •Bil

TISO, Marco - *Piccola suite*

TITTLE, Steve - *The Dragon Doesn't Live...* (1989) •CMC

Todenhoft, Walter - *Danny Boy* (TRADITIONAL) •SATB or AATB •Ron

TOKUNAGA, Hidenori - *Quartet* (1970) (21') •South/SMC

TOLAR, J. K. - *Balette à 4*

TOMASSETTI, Benji - *Quartet* (1989)

TOMLINSON, Ernest - *Saxophone Ensemble* (1976) •adr

TONT, Patrice - *Sax requiem*

TORSTENSSON, Klas - *Licks and Brains I* (1987) (19') •Don

TOURNIER, Franz-André - *Quatuor* (1954) (16'15) •DP

TRORY, Robert - *David's Lament* (1970) (2'); *Quartet* (1970) (4')

TROUILLARD, Raymond - *Pieces* •adr

TREBINSKY, Arkadi - *Quatuor*, op. 25 (1956) (18') •adr

TURINA, Joaquin - *Oracion del Torero*

Turnhout, Gerard de - *Motet* (EVERTSE) •TM

TWEED, Andrew - *PR Girl*

UBER, David - *First Saxophone Quartet* (1977) •Sha/Pres
UNEN, Kees van - *Rhombi* (1981) (8') •Don
URBANNER, Erich - *Emotionen* (1984) (9') •CA/ApE
USMANBAS, Ilham - *Quartet* (1979)
VALK, Adriaan - *Movements* (1988) •Mol
   5 Paintings (1988) •TM
VALLIER, Jacques - *Andante* (1967) (1'30) •adr
VAN CLEEMPUT, Werner - *Fiori* •Sez
VAN DAM, Herman - *Rage, rage, against the...* (1984) (8') •Don
VAN DER LINDEN, Robert E. - *Quadra*
VAN HAUTE, Anna - *Lucioles* (1980)
VAN HULTEN, Lex - *Kwartet* (1982)
VAUTE, Maurice - *Divertissement; Impromptu* •CBDM
VAZZANNA, Anthony - *Quartet*
VELLONES, Pierre - *Pieces* •Chou/Dur/JJ/Lem
VENTAS, Adolfo - *Pieces* •adr
VERBEY, Theo - *Passamezzo*
VERBIEST, R. - *Ballad for Marleen*
Verdi, Giuseppe - *Pieces* •Mol/TM
VERHIEL, Ton - *Drei miniaturen* (1983) •SATB or AAAT
VIDENSKY, Jan - *Pieces*
VIERU, Anatol - *Quartett* (1990) (10')
VIGNERON, Josée - *Quatuor*
VILLA-ROJO, Jesus - *Lineas convergentes* (1984); *Quatuor* (1984)
VINCENT-DEMOULIN, Jean - *Quatuor* (14') •adr
VINTER, Gilbert - *Little March*
VIOLAU, Rémy - *Suite chinoise* (1964) (5') •Bil
VISVIKIS, Demis - *Cascades de feu* (1990) (12'45)
Vivaldi, Antonio - *Ouverture* (FOURMEAU) •SL
VIVIER, Claude - *Palau dewata* (1979) •CMC
VOGEL, Roger G. - *Quartet* (1980) (to K. FISCHER) •DP
VOSK, Jay - *Caliopsis* (8')
   Deep River Variations (1991) (9'45)
   Saxophone Spirituals (1990) (8')
   Sky-Island (1993) (10'20)
   Three Sonoran Desertscapes (1983) •DP
VRIES, Klaas de - *2 Koralen* (1974) (6') •Don
WAGEMANS, Peter-Jan - *Quartet*, op. 8 (1975) (10') •Don
WAGENDRISTEL, Alexander - *Und...*, op. 32 (32b) •CA
Wagner, Richard - *Lohengrin: Brant-char* (DÖMÖTÖR) •K&D
WAGNER-LEBENSLAUF, Wolfram - *Konzert* (1988) (12') •CA
WAHLBERG, Rune - *Prisma* (1961) (12'30) •STIM
WAIGNEIN, André - *Pièces pour saxes* (1981)
WALKER, James - *Recitative in Transition* (1966)
WALKER, James J. - *Prelude and Polka; Quartet*
WALLACE, William - *Introduction and Chaconne* (1977) (9') •CMC
   Quartet No. 1 (1962) •CMC
WALLACH, Joelle - *Quartet* (1980)
WALTER - *Quintalism* •WWS
WALTER, Douglas - *Quartet No. 1* •Ken
WALTER, Richard - *Jazz Suite* (1979) (10') •adr
   Little People (1978) (4') •SM
WARD, David - *Seven Miniatures* •SATB or AATB
WARD, Robert - *Quartet*
WARGNEIN, A. - *Impressions*
WARREN, B. - *Quartet*
WATERS, Dick - *Two Pieces*
WATERS, Renee Silas - *Quartet* •Ron
WEDDINGTON, Maurice - *Into that Goodnight* (1979)
   Quartett (1989) (8')
WEEKS, John - *African Dance*, op. 33 (1976)
Weill, Kurt - *Die Dreigroschenoper* (J. HARLE) •Uni
WEINBERGER, Bruce - *Pieces*
WEINER, Stanley - *Quartett*, op. 55 (1982) (15') •R&E
WEINLAND, John - *Quartet*

WEISS, Ferdinand - *Quattro-fonia* (1988) (11'30) •ECA
   Ragtime und Boogie (1'40 + 0'45) •CA
WELANDER, Svea - *Liten Fuga über B-A-C-H* (1976)
WERDER, Felix - *Sax consort music* (1985) (6')
WESTON, Norman - *Skyscraper* (1988) (10'30)
WHEELER, Kenneth - *Pieces* •adr
Wiedoeft, Rudy - *Valse Erica* (1917) (B. RONKIN) •Ron
Wilbye, John - *Adieu Sweet Amarillis* (HARVEY) •Che
WILDER, Alec - *Quartet* •DP
   Suite (1964) •JB/WIM
WILLIAMS, Bert - *That's A-Plenty* (NAGLE)
WILLIS, Richard - *Tetralogue*
WILSON, Dana - *Escape to the Center*
Wilson, J. Eric - *Amazing Grace* (WILSON) •SiMC
WILSON, Jeffery - *Modes*
WIRTH, Carl Anton - *Diversions in Denim* (16') •Eth
WISE, Loren E. - *Litany* (1979)
WISHART, Peter - *Pieces* •adr
WISSMER, Pierre - *Quatuor* (1956) (14'30) •ET
WOLFEREN, Gerhard von - *Kwartet*
WOOD, Gareth - *Sinfonietta* (1976) (8')
WOOD, James - *Sonata for Four* (1971) (20')
WOODS, Phil - *Three Improvisations* (1981) •Ken
WORIGNEIN, André - *Pieces for saxes*
WORLEY, John - *Pieces* •DP
WYSOCKI, Zdzislaw - *Movimenti*, op. 47 (1991) •ApE
XENAKIS, Iannis - *Xas* (1987) (10') •Sal
YORKO, Bruce - *Night Dances* (1982)
YOSHIOKA, Emmett Gene - *Aria and Allegro* (1968) (8') •Art
YOUNG, Charles Rochester - *Quartet* (1989) (7') •adr
   Sahib Supreme •SiMC
ZAAGMANS, J. - *Abenderzählung; Scherzo* •TM
ZAJAC, Elaine - *Five Miniatures* (1970) •Eto
ZALACZEK, Roman - *Canzona ebraica* (1982) (8')
ZANDER, Heinz Joachim - *Fantasie* (1986) (13') •adr
ZECHLIN, Rutj - *7 Versuche und 1 Ergebnis* (1988) (17') •R&E
ZEMP, Joseph - *Pieces* •Mar
Zielenski, Nikolaj - *Da pacem domine* (D. STREETS) •SATB or AATB
   •TM

4 Saxophones - AATB

Also see Unspecified Instrumentation (Voir aussi
instruments non déterminés), page 422.

Adams, Stephen - *The Holy City* (A. LEMARC) •SATB or AATB •TM
Album of Celebrated Folk Songs and Patriotic Airs •CF
ANDERSON, Garland - *Quartet* •adr
Arensky, Anton - *The Cuckoo* •AATB/(Pno ad lib.) •Bri
ARNOLD, Jay - *Saxophone Quartets* (1964) •Ams
Artot, J-B. - *12 Quartets* •CF
Aubert, Esprit - *Prière* (W. HEKKER) •SATB or AATB
Avril - *Introduction and Allegro* •WWS
AYOUB, Nick - *Joey's Place* •AATB/Rhythm Section •DP
Bach, Johann Sebastian - *Pieces*
Balfe, Michael William - *Bohemian Girl* •Bar
Barnby, Joseph - *Sweet and Low* •Alf
Bartok, Béla - *Three Folk Dances* •South
Beethoven, Ludwig van - *Pieces*
BENNETT, David - *Saxophone Symphonette* •CF
Bizet, Georges - *Pieces* •Bel/Rub
Boiëldieu, François Adrien - *Souvenir...* (W. HEKKER) •TM
BRANDON, Seymour - *Concert Overture* •PA/MaPu
Briegel, George F. - *Cathedrale echoes* •Bri
Brown & Shrigley - *Bull Frog Blues* (GEE) •SATB or AATB •Ron

Buckland, Rob - *Irish Air* •SATB or AATB •PBP

CAILLIET, Lucien - *Pieces* •LCP/South/Bel

CARAVAN, Ronald - *Canzona* (1978) •Eth

Casseday, A. - *Quartet in G minor* •Bou/WWS

Casto - *Heart Strings Intermezzo* (HOLMES) •Bar

Chaminade, Cécile - *The Flatterer* (THOMSON) •Alf

CHAUDOIR, James - *Textures* (1980) •DP

Cheyette, Irving - *Viennese Lullaby* •Sha

Chopin, Frédéric - *Chopin Favorite* (DEDRICK) •AATB or SATB

CHRISTENSEN, James - *Pieces* •Ken/Kjos

Clark, Scotson Frederick - *Belgian March* (WILLIAMS) •4 Sx: AATB
or 5 Sx •South

COHEN, Sol - *Novelette* •Bel

CONLEY, Lloyd - *Song and Caprice* •Ken

Cordeiro, George - *Christmas Folio* •4 Sx: AATB or SATB •DP

Corelli, Arcangelo - *Sarabande and Courante* (JOHNSON) •Rub

COWELL, Henry Dixon - *Quartet* (1946) (6') •PIC
Sailor's Hornpipe (4') •AATB •PIC
Sax-Happy (1949) (4') •PIC

Crequillon, Thomas - *Canzona* (REX) •DP

Dallin - *Aubade in Blue* (WESTPHAL) •Bel

DAWSON, Carl - *Quartet* (1968)

DEDRICK, Art - *Waltz for Four* •Ken

DEDRICK, Chris - *Sensitivity* (6'15) •SATB or AATB •AMI/Ken

DEGASTYNE, Serge - *Quartet* (1968)

DELAMONT, Gordon - *Three Entertainments* •Ken

Donizetti, Gaetano - *Lucia di Lammermoor* (DIETZE) •Rub

DUBOIS, Pierre-Max - *Petit Quatuor* (1980) (8'30) •Ly

Dvorak, Anton - *Pieces*

Elgar, Edward - *Salut d'amour* •Rub

ERICKSON, Frank - *Rondino* •Bel

Fauré, Jean-Baptiste - *The palms* (BROOKE) •CF

Ferstl, Emil - *Pieces* •Fro

FORTNER, Wolfgang - *Sweelinck Suite* (1930) •adr

Foster, Stephen - *Two Melodies* •Bri

FRANCHETTI, Arnold - *Quartetto* (1971) (10') •DP

Franck, César - *Pieces* •Bri/TM

FRANGKISER, Carl - *Pieces* •Bel/B&H

Frank, M. - *Conversation Piece* •Ken

FRANZEN, Olov - *Heptyk* (1987) (14'30) •SMIC

Gabriel-Marie - *Golden Wedding* •Alf

Gade, Niels Wilhelm - *Novelette*, op. 19 (GEE) •AATB or AATT •DP

GALLAHER, Christopher - *Quartet No. 2*, op. 31 (1969) (9'30)
•SATB or AATB •adr

Galuppi, Baldassaro - *Toccata* (MAGANINI) •Mus

GATES, Everett - *Foursome Quartet* (1957) (7') •TTF

German, Edward - *Pieces* •Alf

Glazounov, Alexander - *Pieces* •Bel/adr

Gluck, Christoph - *Air de ballet* (JOHNSON) •Rub

Godard, Benjamin - *Berceuse* (BROOKE) •CF

GOODE, Jack - *Petite Suite* (1964) •adr

Gounod, Charles - *Marche pontificale* •AATB/Pno ad lib. •Bri

Grieg, Edvard - *Pieces* •Alf/CF/Mills/Rub

GUERRINI, Guido - *Chant et danse dans un style rustique* (1946)

Handel, Georg-Friedrich - *Pieces*

HARRIS, Arthur - *Farewell to Cucullain; Four Heart Songs* •CF

HARRIS, Floyd - *Vesper Moods* •Lud

HARTZELL, Doug - *Potato Sax* (1965) •RM

HASENPFLUG, Curt - *Pieces* •Fro

HAUBIEL, Charles - *For Louis XVI* (1940) (6') •B&H

Hawthorne, Allan - *Whispering Hope* (BRIEGEL) •Bri

Haydn, Joseph - *Pieces* •Rub

Herbert, Victor - *Ocean Breezes* (BRIEGEL) •Bri

HERVIG, Richard - *Divertimento No. 3* •Rub

HILLIARD, Jimmy - *Saxonata* (1958) (3'30) •MCA

HOLMES, G. E. - *Pieces* •Bar/Ken/Rub

HUDADOFF, Igor - *24 Saxophone Quartets* •PA

Humperdinck, Engelbert - *Children's Prayer* (JOHNSON) •Rub

Ippolitov-Ivanov, Mikhail - *Procession of the Sardar* (BONNEL) •PAS

Järnefelt, Armas - *Praeludium* (THOMSON) •Alf

JOHNSON, Allen - *Quartet* •adr

JOHNSON, William Spencer - *Pieces* •Fit/Bel/B&H/TM

JOHNSTON, Merle - *Pieces* •PAS/SH&MC

KARLINS, William - *Blues* (1965) (3'30) •Pres

Keler , Béla - *Lustspiel* (HOLMES) •Bar

KELTERBORN, Rudolf - *Quartet* (1978-79) (10') •Hug

KESNAR, Maurits - *Capriccio* •CBet

Klickmann, F. Henry - *Smiles and Chuckles* (GEE) •SATB or AATB
•Ron

KNIGHT, Morris - *Quartet No. 1* (1964) (10') •adr
Quartet No. 2 (1968) (12') •South

KOSTECK, Gregory - *Three Lollipops for Harold*

Krell, W. H. - *Mississippi Rag* (FRACKENPOHL) •Ken

Lange, Gustav - *Flower Song* (BROOKE) •CF

Lecuona, Ernesto - *Pieces* (KLICKMANN) •EMa

LEIDZEN, Erik - *Four Leaf-Clover; The Foursome* •Bou

Lennon & McCartney - *When I'm Sixty-Four* (RICKER) •SATB or
AATB •Ken

Leontovitch, Nikolaï - *Two Ukrainian Songs* (VOXMAN & BLOCK)
•South

LERIT, Vladimir - *Capriccio* (1993) •INM

Liszt, Franz - *Pieces* •Bar/Bri/Selm

LUNDE, Lawson - *Suite*, op. 11 (1959) (9') •TTF

Macbeth, Allan - *Intermezzo 'Forget me not'* (BROOKE) •CF

Maccall - *Two Spirituals* •Lud

MacDowell, Edward - *Two Woodland Sketches* (PATRICK) •Pres

MAGANINI, Quinto - *Beginner's Luck; Double Canon* •Mus

Mancini, Henry - *The Pink Panther* (FRACKENPOHL) •Ken

Mascagni, Pietri - *Intermezzo* (HOLMES) •Bar

Massenet, Jules - *Pieces* •Alf//Rub

Meier-Böhme, Alfons - *Humoresque; Vier Bummelanten* •Fro

Mellish - *Drink To Me* •Bri

Mendelssohn - *Pieces*

Meyerbeer, Giacomo - *Pieces* •Rub

MIELENZ, Hans - *Pieces* •Fro/Rub

MILLER, Ralph Dale - *Quartet No. 2*, op. 16 •Pro

Mingus, Charles - *Jelly Roll* •SATB or AATB •WWS

Molloy, James - *Love's Old Sweet Song* •AATB/Pno ad lib. •Bri

MONDELLO, Nuncio Francis - *Quartet* •adr
Suite (1961) •adr

MORITZ, Edvard - *Andante* •Merc
Quartet (1962) •South
Quartet, op. 181 •SMC

Moussorgsky, Modeste - *Mushrooms* •AATB or AATT •Mus/EM

MOWER, M. - *Pieces* •WWS

Mozart, Wolfgang - *Pieces*

NELHYBEL, Vaclav - *Quartets* •FC
Three Miniatures (1968) (3') •FC

Nevin, Ethelbert - *Narcissus* (THOMPSON) •Alf

NIEHAUS, Lennie - *Pieces* •Ken

Offenbach, Jacques - *Pieces* •Bar/CF

OTTOSON, David - *Svit* (197x) (27') •STIM

Overstreet, W. Benton - *That Alabama Jasbo Band* (1918) (HOLMES)
•SATB or AATB

Paderewski, Ignace (1860-1941) - *Minuet* (HOLMES) •Bar

Palestrina, G. - *Christe eleison* (LEMARC) •SATB or AATB or AATT
•TM

Paschedag - *1st Ensemble* (BUCHTEL) •Kjos

PETERSEN, Ted - *Miniature Suite* •Ken

Pierné, Gabriel - *Pieces* (NELSON) •SATB or AATB •Lud

Pitts - *Church in the Wildwood* •AATB/Pno ad lib. •Bri
POPP, André - *Berceuse noire*
PRESSER, William - *Quartet* (1969) •adr
   Waltz and Scherzo (1962) (3'15) •South
Prokofiev, Sergei - *Romance and Troïka* (JOHNSON) •Rub
Ramsoe, Wilhelm - *Quartet No. 5* (VOXMAN) •Rub
REX, Harley - *Pieces* •DP
   Shenandoah •AATB or AAAATTTB •Mills
Rimsky-Korsakov - *Pieces* •Belai/Rub
RODEN, Robert R. - *Sax-craft* (1978) •SATB or AATB •South
Rodney - *Calvary* (HOLMES) •Bar
Roussakis, Nicolas - *21 Quartets* (1969) •CFE
SAUCIER, Gene - *Two Pieces* •DP
SAUTER, Otto - *Quartett* (1977)
Scharwenka, Waver Franz - *Polish Dance* (BROOKE) •CF
SCHMUTZ, Albert Daniel - *Introduction, recitativo and choral* •AMPC
   Prelude and Final •AMPC
Schubert, Franz - *Pieces* •Alf/Bar/BM/NW
Schuman, William - *Quaterttino* (RASCHER) •PIC/Peer
Schumann, Robert - *Pieces* •Alf/BM/Ken
SCHWARZ, Ira - *Pieces* •Barn/Rub
SCOTT, Andy - *Symphony for Saxophones* •SATB or AATB •PBP
Sibelius, Jean - *Pieces* •Bri/PIC
SIEGMEISTER, Elie - *Around New York* (1939)
SINGER, S. - *Orientale; Theme and Little Fugue* •CF
SKOLNIK, Walter - *Four Improvisations* (1971) (4') •Pres
Smetsky, J. de - *March of the Spanish Soldiery* (WHEAR) •Lud
SÖDERLUNDH, Lille Bror - *Idea I & II* (8') •SATB or AATB •HBus
Södermann, Johan August - *Swedish Wedding March* (THOMPSON) •Alf
Sorensen - *With the Colors* (HOLMES) •Bar
SOULE, Edmund - *Quartets I & II* •adr
STARER, Robert - *Light and Shadow* (1977) •MCA
STEIN, Leon - *Suite Quartet* (1962) •South
STEINBACHER, Erwin - *Spassvögel* •Fro
STEINMETZ, Hans - *5 Studien* (1971) •OWR
STUART - *Saxophone Classics* •WWS
Stults, R. M. - *The Sweetest Story* •AATB/Pno ad lib. •Bri
Suppe, Franz von - *Pieces* (HOLMES) •Bar
TAGGART, Mark - *Serenade* (1981) (3') •adr
Tchaikovsky, Peter Ilyich - *Quartet Album* (ROUSSEAU) •SATB or
   AATB •Eto
Telemann, Georg Phillip - *Pieces* (JOHNSON) •Rub
THOMPSON, Kathryn - *Londonderry Air; Swing Low...* •Alf
THON, Franz - *Humoresque; Meisner Porzellan* •Fro
Todenhoft, Walter - *Danny Boy* (TRADITIONAL) •SATB or AATB •Ron
Tufilli, W. - *Rose Blush* •BM
TUTHILL, Burnett - *Quartet*, op. 52 (1966) (18') •South
Vecchi, Orazio - *The Cricket* (MAGANINI) •Mus
Verdi, G. - *Pieces* •Bar/CF
VIOLAU, Rémy -- *Suite chinoise* (1964) (5') •Bil
Vivaldi, Antonio - *Giga* (MAGANINI) •Mus
Voxman, H. - *Quartet Repertoire* •Rub/South
Wagner, Richard - *Pieces* •Bar/Kjos
WALKER, Richard - *Four Fancies* •Bel/BM
   Suite •Ken
WALTERS, Harold - *Pieces* •Rub
WARD, David - *Seven Miniatures*
Weber, C-M. von - *Pieces* •Alf/NPHC
Westendorf - *I'll Take You Home Again* •2 Sx: AA/Pno or 4 Sx:
   AATB/Pno ad lib. •Bri
WESTPHAL, Herwarth - *Monolog in Dunkel* •Fro
Williams, V. - *Prelude and Beguine* •CF
WILLIAMS, Vic - *Ballad and Waltz* (1981) •South
WINZENBURGER, Walter - *Quartet* •AATB/Perc •adr
WIRTH, Carl Anton - *Prelude* (1971)

Wolf, Hugo - *Andante* (GEE) •AATB or AATT •CPP
WORLEY, John Carl - *Oneonta Quartet* (1970)
   Pieces •DP
YODER, Paul - *Dry Bones; Jericho; Relax* •Kjos
Zielenski, N. - *Da pacem domine* (STREETS) •TM

4 Saxophones - Diverse

Also see Unspecified Instrumentation (Voir aussi instruments non déterminés), page 422.

AMORÉ, Daniel - *Aux Quatre vents* (1988) •4 Sx: Sno+S ATB
Anonymous - *Pieces* (BIRTWISTLE & MULDOWNEY) •SSSS
APERGHIS, G. - *Signaux* (1978) •Quatuor d'instruments de même
   timbre et tessiture •Sal
ARMA, Paul - *6 Mobiles* •1, 2, 3, or 4 Sx
AUDOIN, Jean-Claude - *Hommage à Fr. Valonne* (1986) •4 like
   instruments
AYOUB, Nick - *Four of a Kind* •AAAA •WWS
BADINGS, Henk - *Friere trije* •SATT or SATB •TM
   Gelderse •SATT or SATB •TM
   Hollande Boerenplof •SATT or SATB •TM
BARBER, Clarence - *Vignettes* (1993) (6') • A A+S TB •TTF
BARKER, Warren - *Scherzo* •SATB or SSTB •Ken
BARTLING, Stefan - *Falsche Verse* (1991) (6') •AABB
BAUER, Robert - *Sokasodik* (1974) •Any 4 Sx •BML
Berlinski, Herman - *Canons and Rounds* (9 Pieces) •3 or 4 Sx •Pres
Blaauw, L. - *Humoreske* •SATB or SAAT or SATT or SAAB •TM
Bokhove, H. - *Pro Musica* •SATB or SAAT or SATT or SAAB •TM
BONNARD, Alain - *Menuet* (1985) (2'45) •AAAA •adr
BOUVARD, Jean - *Pieces* •AAAA •adr
BRESNICK, Martin - *Tent of Miracles* •Bsx Solo/3 Bsx
BROEKHUIJSEN, H. - *Glorification* •SATB or SAAB •TM
BROSH, Thomas - *Dialogue* •Several Asx (AAAA)
BUDD, Harold - *Pieces* •Any Sx
BUESS, Alex - *Hyperbaton* (1991) (7') •TTBB •adr
BURGSTALHER - *Quartet* •AAAA or TTTT
BYRNE, Andrew - *Pieces* •3 or more instruments of equal pitch •Hin
CAGE, John - *Pieces* •Pet
CARDEW, Cornelius - *Pieces* (1960) •Any instruments •Uni
CARTER, Elliott - *Canonic Suite* (1939) (6'30) •AAAA •Bro/ME
CHILDS, Barney - *Operation Flabby Sleep* •3 or more instruments
   •ACA
COSMA, Edgar - *Graphiques* (1981) •4 Sx
DELAMONT, Gordon - *Divertimento* •AATT •WWS
DESPORTES, Yvonne - *Pieces* •AAAB •Bil/VB
DILLENKOFER, Josef - *Junior - Music - Camp* •AATT •Zim
DUPRE, René - *Pieces* •AAAA •adr
Elgar, Edward - *Land of Hope and Glory* •SATB or SAAT or SATT
   or SAAB
Eymann - *Prelude and Fugue* •AAAA •CF
FERRARI, Luc - *Apparitions et disparitions...* (1979) •AAAA •ET
FONTAINE, Louis Noël - *Musique...* (1981) (9') •BBBB •Capri
Gade, Niels Wilhelm - *Novelette*, op. 19 (GEE) •AATB or AATT •DP
GLASER, Werner Wolf - *4 Kleine Stücke*, op. 8a (1934) (6') •SAAT
   •Pres
GUNJI, Takashi - *Quatuor* 1) Andante 2) 96 3) Final •4 Sx: S+A ATB
KLIER, Gottfield - *25 Saxophone Quartets* •ATTB or SATB •adr
KNOSP, Erwin - *Introduction, Allegro, Rondo finale* •AAAA •adr
LANCEN, Serge - *Quatre par quatre* (1990) •4 instruments de même
   nature •Mar
Linden, N. van de - *Chinese Mars* (LEMARC) •SATB or SAAT •TM
Liszt, Franz - *Dream of Love* •AATB/Pno ad lib. •Bri
LONDEIX, Jean Marie - *Exercices pratiques* (1983) •4 to 12 Sx •Led
MAGANINI, Quinto - *Double Canon* •AATB or AATT •Mus

McCARTY, Frank - *Five Situations* (1969) (15') •SATB or SAAT •Art

Mendelssohn, Félix - *Souvenir...* (CLUWEN) •SATB or SAAT or SATT or SAAB •TM

Moussorgsky, Modeste - *Mushrooms* •AATB or AATT •Mus/EM

MOWER, M. - *Pieces* •ATTB •WWS

Mozart, Wolfgang - *Menuetto* (HAUTVAST) •SATB or SAAT or SATT or AATT •TM

Pachelbel, Johann - *Canon and Gigue* (FRACOTTI) •AAAB •Ron

Palestrina, Giovanni - *Adonamus te* (D. SPEETS) •SATB or SATT •TM
  Christe eleison (LEMARC) •SATB or AATB or AATT •TM

Parera, Antonio - *El Cappo* (WALTERS) •4, 5 or 6 Sx •Rub

PETIT, Jacques - *Variations* (1981) (3 Volumes) •AAAA •Bil

PRATI, Hubert - *9 Negro Spirituals* (1994) •AAAA or TTTT •Bil
  Pièces en quatuor (1994) •AAAA •Bil

RAPHLING, Sam - *Concert Suite* •AAAA •Mus

Speets, D. - *Klassiek kwartet* •SATB or SAAT or SATT or SAAB •TM

STEINMETZ, Hans - *5 Studien* (1971) •4 Sx: AATB or AATT •OWR

TAGGART, Mark -*A Somewhat Sentimental Waltz* (1992) •BsBsBsBs •adr

VERHIEL, Ton - *Drei miniaturen* (1983) •SATB or AAAT
  Vivace (1986) •SAAT

Wolf, Hugo - *Andante* (GEE) •AATB or AATT •CPP

Zielenski, Nikolaj - *Da pacem domine* (D. STREETS) •SATB or AATB •TM

4 Saxophones and Piano or Organ

AKKERMANN, Michel - *"To be redreamed in colors pale but intense"* (1991) (10') •4 Sx: SATB/Tpt/Pno

ALBRIGHT, William - *From Dawn to Dusk in the Valley of Fire* (1989) (6'30) •SATB/Org •Hen/Pet

Bach, J. S. - *Koraalbewerking* •SATB/Org •Lis

BIRKNER, Rudolf - *Pastorale und Fughetta* (1992) •SATB/Org

BONNARD, Alain - *Quintette* (1976) •SATB/Pno •adr

BRENET, Thérèse - *Tetrapyle* (1978) (19') •SATB/Pno

CARAVAN, Ronald - *Lament...* (1979) •SATB/Pno •Eth

Danks, Hart Pease - *Silver Threads Among the Gold* •2 Sx: AT/Pno or AATB/Pno

Debussy, Claude - *La Fille...* (OOSTROM) •SATB/Pno •Mol

DENISOV, Edison - *Quintette* (1992) (15') •SATB/Pno

DESLOGES, Jacques - *6 Pièces faciles* (1978) •AAAA or TTTT/Pno •Bil

DIJK, Gijs van - *Quintette* (1986) (11'30) •4 Sx: SATB/Pno •Don

ESCUDIER, H. - *Quatuor - Andante* •SATB/Pno •Mar

Franck, César - *Panis angelicus* •AATB/Pno ad lib. •Bri

GASTINEL, Gérard - *Cinq poèmes anciens* (1974) •SATB/Voice/Pno •Chou

Gounod, Charles - *Marche pontificale* •AATB/Pno ad lib. •Bri

Grieg, Edvard - *Ase's Death* (from *Peer Gynt*) •AATB/Pno ad lib. •Bri

GRÖSCHKE, Heinz - *Quintett* (1935) •AATB/Pno •RE

HAIDMAYER, Karl - *Popludium III* (1991) (11') •SATB/Org

HANKS, Sybil - *Concertino*, op. 16 •AATT/Orch or Pno •WB

HARTLEY, Walter - *Antiphonal Prelude* (1984) (5') •SATB/Org •Eth
  Solemn Postlude (1985) (4'30) •SATB/Org •Eth
  Toccata Concertante (1984-85) (3'40) •SATB/Org •Eth

ISABELLE, Jean Clément - *Quintet*, op. 4 (1981) •SATB/Pno •DP

JONES, Martin - *Quintet* •SATB/Pno •adr

Kiellish, F. - *Serenade Impromptu* •AATT/Pno •Ken

LAUBER, Anne - *Mouvement* (1990) •4 Sx/2 Pno •CMC

Liszt, Franz - *Dream of Love* •AATB/Pno ad lib. •Bri

LOLINI, Ruggero - *Onan e l'obbedieuza* •Sno+S ATB/Pno

LUEDEKE, Raymond - *Accrostic* (1976) •SATB/Pno •CMC

MABIT, Alain - *Fragment...* (1992) •SATB/Org

McCall, H. - *Annie Laurie*; *Two Spirituals* •AATB/Pno •Lud

McKAY George - *American Street Scenes* (1935) •Cl/Tpt/Asx/Bsn/Pno or 4 Sx/Pno •CAP

Mendelssohn - *Faith*, op. 102/6 •AATB/Pno ad lib. •Bri

Meyerbeer, Giacomo - *Coronation March* (HOLMES) •AATB/Pno •Rub

MIGNION, René - *Fugue bretonne* (1977) •SATB/Pno •Bil

Molloy, James - *Love's Old Sweet Song* •AATB/Pno ad lib. •Bri

NELHYBEL, Vaclav - *Fantasia II* (1987) •SATB/Pno •JCCC

PARIS-KERJULLOU, Ch. - *Morceau de concert*, op. 204 •SATB/Pno •Mar

Pitts - *Church in the Wildwood* •AATB/Pno ad lib. •Bri

POPE, Peter - *Quintet* (1973) (20') •SATB/Pno

PRESSL, Hermann - *Sprang N.N. 6* (1992) •SATB/Org

REX, Harley - *Four Shades* •AATB/Pno •Bou

ROBERT, Lucie - *Magheia* (1976) (25') •SATB/Pno •Bil

ROSEN, Robert J. - *Kikros II* (1982) •Pno/2 to 4 Sx •CMC

SCHMIDT, William - *Concertino for Piano* •Pno/SATB •WIM

SECO, Manuel - *Concierto de la Senda n° 4* (1988) •SATB/Pno/Perc

SEFFER, Yochk'o - *Script et Orale - Galère assymétrique* (1985-86) (40') •SATB/Pno

SHRUDE, Marilyn - *Masks* (1982) •SATB/Pno •adr

Sibelius, Jean - *Finlandia* •AATB/Pno (ad libitum) •Bri

SOLAL, Martial - *Triptyque* (1989) (55') •SATB/Jazz trio (Pno/Bass/Perc)

STEFANI, D. - *Quinteto Burgalès* (1983) •SATB/Pno •Alp

Stults, R. M. - *The Sweetest Story* •AATB/Pno ad lib. •Bri

TERRY, Peter - *Windows Looking Nowhere* •SATB/Pno/2 Perc •DP

WALLNER, Alarich - *Siciliana* (1992) •SATB/Org

Weber, Carl -Maria von - *Der Freischütz* (HOLMES) •AATB/Pno •Rub

WELSH, Wilmer - *Mosaic Portraits II...* •4 Sx/Org/Narr

Westendorf - *I'll Take You Home Again* •2 Sx: AA/Pno or 4 Sx: AATB/Pno ad lib. •Bri

4 Saxophones and Orchestra or Band

ABSIL, Jean - *Divertimento* (1955) (20') •SATB/Orch •CBDM

ADLER, Samuel - *Concerto* (1985) (20') •SATB/Orch •Gravis

AGNESENS, Udo - *Aufbruch-Paradoxon* (1989) (8') •SATB/Str Quartet

ALBAM, Manny - *Eubie Medley* (1982) •SATB/Orch

BADINGS, Henk - *Quadruple concert* (1984) (20') •SATB/Orch or Band •Don

BARKER, Warren - *Capriccio* (1987) •SATB/Band •JP

BAUWENS, Alphonse - *London Concertino* (1974) (8') •SATB/Orch

BAUZIN, Pierre-Philippe - *Concerto*, op. 32 (22') •SATB/Str Orch •adr

BENCRISCUTTO, Franck - *Concerto Grosso* (1962) (8') •AATB/Band) •Sha

BENNETT, David - *Sax Soliloquy* •AATB or SATB/Band •B&H

Blake, Eubie - *Eubie Medley* (1982) (M. ALBAM) •SATB/Orch

BLAKE-ALBAM - *Eubie Medley* (1982) •SATB/Orch

BOUTRY, Roger - *Alternances* (1974) •SATB/Orch or Band •adr

BRUNO, Mauro - *California Concerto Grosso* •SATB/Band

CALMEL, Roger - *Concerto Grosso* (1956) (17') •SATB/Str Orch/Perc •Heu

CIBULKA, Franz - *Konzert* (1990) •SATB/Str Orch •ECA

DAKIN, Charles - *Suite Concertante* (1974) (25') •SATB/Str Orch •DP

DEMILLAC, Francis - *Concerto pour suite de 4 saxophones* (1975) (20') •SATB/Orch

DEPRAZ, Raymond - *2e Symphonie* (1973) (32'30) •SATB/Orch •EFM

DUBOIS, Pierre-Max - *Concertino* (1967) (12') •SATB/Chamber Orch •Led

10 Préludes imaginaires (1993) •SATB/Orch
EBENHÖH, Horst - *Konzert...*, op. 73 (25') •SATB/Orch •CA
GEDDA, Giulio - *Concerto* (1952) •SATB/Orch
GRISONI, Renato - *Kabbalah*, op. 58 (19'30) •SATB/Str Orch •CA
HALLBERG, Bengt - *Sax vobiscum* (1992) •SAATB or SATB/Orch •STIM
HAMPTON, Calvin - *Concerto* (1974) •SATB/Str Orch/Perc •NYSQ
HANKS, Sybil - *Concertino*, op. 16 •AATT/Orch or Pno •WB
HARTLEY, Walter - *Quartet Concerto* (1992) (12') •SATB/Orch or Wind ensemble •EK
HASQUENOPH, Pierre - *3me Symphonie concertante*, op. 12 (1954) (24') •SATB/Orch •Chou

4me Symphonie, op. 17 (1954-58) (30') •SATB/Orch •ET
HERMANN, Ralph - *Concertino* (1969) •SATB/Str Orch
HOFFER, Bernard - *The River - Symphony* (1984) (30') •SATB/Large Perc ensemble •Shir
HOLCOMBE, Bill - *Stephen Foster...* (1991) •SATB/Orch •Gaz
JANSSON, Gunnar - *Sinfonia concertante* (1991) (25') •SATB/Orch •Tons
KATAEV, Igor - *Concerto* (1977) •Asx/4 Sx: SATB/Orch
Kern, J. - *All the Things You Are* (ALBAM) •SATB/Orch
KETTING, Otto - *Symphony* (1977-78) (30') •SATB/Orch •Don
KNOX, Thomas - *Cascades* (1972) •AATB/Band
KOCH, Erland von - *Saxophonia: Concerto* (1976) (18') •SATB/Wind Orch •STIM
KULESHA, Gary - *Journey Into Sunrise* (1987) •ATBBs/Orch •CMC
LAUER, Arthur - *Concerto Grosso* •SATB/Orch
LEGLEY, Victor - *Hommage à Jean Absil* (1980) •SATB/Band
LEGRADY, Thomas - *Concertino grossino* (1977) •SATB/Band •CMC
LEMAIRE, Jean - *Quatuor* (1982) •SATB/Orch
LOVREGLIO, Eleuthère - *Concerto* (1938) •SATB/Orch •Heu
LUEDEKE, Raymond - *Concerto* (1977) (33') •SATB/Orch •CMC
MANZIARLY, Marcelle de - *Concertino* •4 Sx/Orch
MAROS, Miklos - *Concerto grosso* (1988) •SATB/Orch •SMIC
MARTINON, Jean - *Concerto lyrique*, op. 38 (1944/76) (21') •SATB/Orch or 2 Pno •EFM
MATSUSHITA, Isao - *Grand Atoll* (1992) (13') •SATB/Orch
MEULEMANS, Arthur - *Concertino* (1962) (14') •SATB/Orch •CBDM

Concerto grosso (1958) (13'30) •SATB/Orch •CBDM
PERRIN, Marcel - *Mirage* (1938) (2'30) •SATB/Orch •Led
POPP, André - *Pieces* •Narr/4 Sx: SATB/Orch
PRODIGO, Sergio - *Concerto n° 9*, op. 114 (1992) (13') •4 Sx/Orch
QUINET, Marcel - *Concerto grosso* •SATB/Orch •Bil
RICARD, Claude - *Concerto sérénade* •SATB/Harp/Str Orch •South
RICCO-SIGNORINI, Antonio - *Divertissement* (1926) (15') •SATB/Chamber Orch •Car
ROSS, Walter - *Old Joe's Fancy* •SATB/Band •DP
ROUFFE, G. - *Concerto pour Quatuor* •SATB/Orch
RUBBERT, Rainer - *Kammerkonzert ("Serenade")* (1990) •SATB/4 Vln/2 Vla/2 Vcl/Bass/Pno •adr
RUNSWICK, Daryl - *Fantasia* (1979) (8') •Tsx Solo/4 Sx: SATB/Jazz ensemble •adr
SAHL, Michael - *Storms* (1985) •SATB/2 Vln/Vla/Vcl
SALM, Andreas - *Quartet and Strings*, op. 30 (1991) •SATB/Orch
SCHOEMAKER, Maurice - *Sinfonia da camera* (1929) (20') •SATB/Orch •CBDM
SCHWARZ, Ira Paul - *Sax bleu* (1985) (6') •SATB/Band
SEGERSTAM, Leif - *Thoughts* (1990) •SATB/Orch •FMIC
STÖRRLE, Heinz - *Konzert* (1990) (24') •SATB/Orch •adr
STRANZ, Ulrich - *Erste Sinfonie* (1979/90) (27') •SATB/Orch

TORSTENSSON, Klas - *Licks and Brains* (1988) (25'30) •4 Sx/Large ensemble •Don
TREBINSKY, Arkadi - *Double quatuor* (1977) •SATB/Str quartet •adr
URBANNER, Erich - *Concerto* (1989) (20') •SATB/Str Orch •CA

Concerto XIII (1989-90) (18') •SATB/Orch •CA
VAN BEURDEN, Bernard - *Concertino* (1984) (15') •SATB/Orch •Don
VELLONES, Pierre - *Rastelli*, op. 82 (1936) (20') •SATB/Orch •Lem
VERDI, Ralph Carl - *Strong Song* •SATB/Wind Ensemble •adr
VIGELANDD, Nils - *Classical music* (1986) •SATB/Str quartet
VRIONIDES, Christos - *Theme and Variations* •SATB/Orch •ACA
WAGENAAR, Diderik - *Metrum* (1981-84) (18') •SATB/Orch •Don
WAGNER-LEBENSLAUF, Wolfram - *Konzert* (1990) •SATB/Str Orch/Perc •ApE
WARING, Kate - *Collage* (1985) (5') •SATB/Str Orch
WERLE, Floyd - *Partita* (1972) •SATB/Band •Bou

4 Saxophones and Tape

ABBOTT, Alain - *Le Tombeau de Bach* (1984) •SATB/Tape
BEGLARIAN, Eve - *Fresh Air* •SATB/Tape •NP
BIANCHINI, Laura - *Tra le voci* (1990) (15') •SATB/Tape •adr
BOTTJE, Will Gay - *Modalities* •AATB/Tape •AMA
BREGENT, Michel-Georges - *Mitzvot...* (1982) •SATB/Tape
BROWN, Anthony - *Quartet No. 2* •SATB/Tape •SeMC
DASKE, Martin - *Sisaxason* (1991) (13') •SATB/Tape
DIEMENTE, Edward - *Dimensions II* •Any 1 to 6 instruments/Tape •SeMC
GARCIN, Gérard - *Après, bien après, enfin...* (1981) •4 Reeds (SATB or other combinations)/Tape •Sal

6me Musique... (1984) (6') •1 to 7 Asx/Tape •Sal
HAJDU, Georg - *Die Stimmen...* (1990) (12') •4 Sx/Tape •Peer
HARRIS, Roger - *Sopwith Hemke* (1972) •SSSS/Tape •Bou
MADDOCKS, David - *Octet...* (1977) •SATB/Tape (SnoATBs)
McGUIRE, Edward - *Music...* (1976) (8') •1 to 4 Sx (SATB)/Tape •SMPL
NILSSON, Anders - *Krasch!* (1993) •4 Sx: SATB/6 Perc/Tape •SMIC
NYKOPP, Lauri - *New music...* (14-40') •4 Sx/Tape •FMIC
ROLIN, Etienne - *Sax over seas* (1992) (20') •SATB/Tape •adr
THIBAULT, Alain - *E.L.V.I.S.* (1984) •SATB/Tape

5 Saxophones

SAATB unless otherwise indicated (SAATB, sauf indication contraire). Also see Unspecified Instrumentation (Voir aussi instruments non déterminés), page 422.

Albinoni, Tomaso - *Sonata*, op. 2, no. 5 (SIBBING)
Avril - *Bicentennial Quintet* •WWS
Bach, J. S. - *Brandenburg Concerto No. 5* (REX) •SSATB/Pno •DP

Fugue no. 22 (SCHMIDT) •WIM

Fugue in G Minor "Little Fugue" (SCHMIDT)

O Mensch Bewein (GRAINGER) •SAABBs

Prelude and Fugue in B Minor (SIBBING)

Prelude and Fugue in Bb Minor (GEE) •Sha

Sicut Iocutus Est (GARCIA) •DP

3 Thèmes célèbres (BEUN & TERRANOVA) •AATTB •Mar
BACULIS, Alphonse - *Six Pieces for Five Saxophones*

Three Folk Songs •SAATB/Soprano Voice
BAKER, David - *Faces of the Blues* (1988) (8'49) •Asx Solo/SATB •MMB
BARRET, Eric - *Quintet Kavisilak* •Tsx Solo/SATB
Bartok, Béla - *Bear Dance* (Schmidt)

Brahms, Johannes - *Quintet*, op. 88, no. 1 (SIBBING)
BROEGE, Timothy - *Partita IV* (1975) (7') •adr
Brown, Tom - *Chicken Walk* (c. 1913) (2'30) (GEE) •Eto
BYRNE, Andrew - *Pieces* •3 or more instruments of equal pitch •Hin
CAGE, John - *Pieces* •Any instruments •Pet
CARDEW, Cornelius - *Pieces* (1960) •Any instruments •Uni
CAZDEN, Norman - *Six Discussions for Wind Ensemble No. 4* •5 Sx
•EK
CHILDS, Barney - *Operation Flabby Sleep* •3 or more instruments
•ACA
Clark, Scotson - *Belgian March* (WILLIAMS) •4 Sx: AATB or 5 Sx
•South
CLOEDT, Emile - *Dorpsdans* (1958) •SATBBs •An
Entrée - Dance villageoise •SATBBs •An
DAKEN, K. - *Cuckoo* •SAATB/Pno/Bass/Drums
Debussy, Claude - *Bruyères* (SIBBING)
DEFAYE, Jean-Michel - *Dialogues*
DELAMARRE, Pierre - *Détente* •AAAAA •adr
DHAINE, Jean-Louis - *9me Concertino* (1983-84) (17') •SnoSATB
•Fuz
DIEMENTE, Edward - *Dimensions II* •Any 1 to 6 instruments/Tape
•SeMC
Drdla, Franz - *Souvenir* (HARGER) •5 Sx: AATTB •Band
DUHAMEL, Antoine - *Hommage à Mingus* (12'30) •AATTB •EFM
DUPRÉ, René - *Pieces* (1967) •SATBBs, AAAABs, AAAAA •adr
EYSER, Eberhard - *Baroque* (1976) (8') •STIM
Quintette... (1988) (8') •EMa
Ferrabosco, Alfonso - *Four notes pavan* (GRAINGER) •SATTB •PG
FISCHER, Eric - *La force 50 - Musique de scène* •adr
FOURCHOTTE, Alain - *Pour K.* (1985) (6') •5 Sx
FRACKENPOHL, Arthur - *Tango and Two-Step* (1993) (8') •SSATB
•adr
Frescobaldi, Girolamo - *Fugue* (CARAVAN) •SATBBs •Eth
FURMANOV, V. - *Inspiration* •SAATB/Pno/Bass
GARCIN, Gérard - *6me Musique...* (1984) (6') •1 to 7 Asx/Tape •Sal
GAYFER, James McDonald - *Quintet concertante* (1972) (4') •CMC
GEE, Harry - *Prelude and Passacaglia* •DP
Gershwin, G. - *Summertime* (BEUN) •Mar
GIBSON, Kenneth - *Prologue and Epilogue* (1968) (5')
Gilson, Paul - *Fackelzug* (STRAUWEN) •5 Sx
GLASER, Werner Wolf - *Quintet* (1964-77) (15') •STIM
GODEL, Didier - *Quintette* (1975) •adr
GOODWIN, Gordon - *Heterophonie* •SATTB/Electr. Bass •adr
GRAINGER, Percy - *Lisbon* (1943) (3') •Sx Choir: SAATB •PG/TTF
Pieces (COHEN) •SAATB or SATBBs •TTF
GRANDERT, Johnny - *Kvintett* (1975) (6'30) •STIM
GRIBOJEDOV, A. - *Waltz* (3') •SAATB/Pno/Bass
GURILIOV, A. - *Nocturne* (5') •SAATB/Pno/Bass
HAENSCH, Gerhard Delle - *Andantino* •4 or 5 Sx •adr
HAIDMAYER, Karl - *Saxophone 10* (3'45)
HALLBERG, Bengt - *Sax vobiscum* (1992) •SAATB or SATB/Orch
•STIM
Harger, Earle - *Pieces* •AATTB •Band
HARTLEY, Walter - *Quintet* (1981) (10') •DP
HEIDER, Werner - *Edition* (1985) •AAATB •Pet
Hertze, R. - *Everybody Twostep Rag* (SIBBING)
HOUNSELL - *Showcase for Saxes* •5 Sx/Pno/Bass/Perc •TMPI
JEAN, André - *Sax battle* •Jazz Tsx/SATB •adr
Saxologie •AATTB •adr
Jenkins, John - *Fantasy No. 1* (GRAINGER) •SSATB •PG
JONES, David - *Motor Music* (1988) (7'30) •Com
Joplin, Scott - *Pieces* (AXWORTHY) •SATBBs or SATBB •DP/TVA
KAMALDINOV, G. - *Russian Melody* •SAATB/Pno/Bass
KECHLEY, David - *Music for Saxophones* (1985) (25') •Asx/4 Sx:
SATB •PV

Tsunagari (1988) (15') •Ssx/4 Sx: AATB •PV
Kern, Jerome - *Smoke Gets in your Eyes* •AATBBs
Kroll, Nathan - *Four Pieces* •AATTB •AMP
LAKE, Mathew Lester - *Andantino; Cleveland March* •AATTB •Lud
Iron Mountain; Long, Long Ago •AATTB •Lud
Louisiana; Madeline •AATTB •Lud
LAKEY, Claude - *Five Saxets* (1958) •South
LASNE, George - *Divertissement* (1969)
LATEEF, Yusef - *Quintet No. 1* •AATTB
LEMAY, Robert - *"Vous ne faites...* (1991) (variable duration) •5 Sx
égaux et participation du public •CMC
Liadov, A. - *A Musical Snuff-box* (HERGER) •AATTB •Band
LIMNANDER de NIEUWENHOVE, Armand - *Quintette* (188x)
•SSATB •Sax
LINDELL, Rolf - *Kalejdoskopisk suite* (1973) (15') •STIM
LONDEIX, Jean Marie - *Exercises pratiques* (1983) •4 to 12 Sx •Led
LUEDEKE, Raymond - *Garbage Delight* (1988) (29') •SATBBs
•CMC
Marcello, Allessandro - *Concerto* (ROSSI) •DP
Marren, Louis - *Petit conte breton* •5 Sx
MASON, Steven - *Chamber Music* •5 Sx
Mason, William - *Dance Antique* (GEE) •Sha
MAYUZUMI, Toshiro - *Tone Pleromas 55* (1955) •5 Sx/Musical saw
[Scie musicale]/Pno •Saw
McCARTY, Frank - *Saxim Mixas* (1972) (8') •5 Sx (may be recorded
or live)/Optional live electronic processing
•adr
Mendelssohn, Félix - *Adagio* •SATBBs •WWS
MIEREANU, Costin - *Do-Mi-Si-La-Do-Ré* (1980-81) (16'30) •1
player: Cl+BsCl+Sx/Tape or 5 Sx: SATBBs/
Tape •Sal
Moratin - *Quintette* •5 Sx •Mar
MOSER, Roland - *Wal* (1980-83) (26') •SATTB/Orch •HM
Moskowski, Moritz - *Spanish Dance* (Harger) •AATTB •Band
Moussorgsky, Modeste - *Ballet of the Chicks...* •AAAATB •Mus
Mozart, Wolfgang - *Adagio in F*, K. 580a (GEE) •Sha
Adagio and Gigue, K. 411/K. 574 (GEE) •Ron
Quintets (Sibbing) •Eto/RS
NAUDE, Jean-Claude - *Sun-Sand-Sea-Sax*
NAULAIS, Jérôme - *Atout sax* (1987) •SAATTB •Arp
Mise à sax •SATTB/Pno/Bass/Drums •Arp
NICOLAS, René (Mickey) - *Magnitude* (1993) (7'45) •Lem
NILLINI, Ricardo - *Spin* (1988) (7')
ODGREN - *H is for Hottentotte* •5 Sx •WWS
Overstreet, W. Benton - *That Alabama Jazbo Band* (1918) (GEE)
•SAATB or AAATB
Parera, Antonio - *El Cappo* (WALTERS) •4, 5 or 6 Sx •Rub
PAVLENKO, Serguei - *Pastorale* (1988) (8') •S+A AATB •Com
PETIT, Jean-Louis - *La mort des autres* (1980)
Samu 92 •ENF
Ravel, Maurice - *Pavane* (SCHMIDT) •DP
ROBERT, Lucie - *Flammes...*, op. 53 (1982) (15'30) •SnoSATB •Bil
RUDAJEV, Alexandre - *Sober aa ta bar* •Com
SAMAMA, Leo - *Soit que l'abime*, op. 19 (1983) (20') •SAATB/8
Perc •Don
SARY, Laszlö - *Incanto* (1969) (7') •Bri/MB
SAVARI, Jean-Nicolas - *Quintetto* (185x) •SSATB •Sax
SCHMALTZ, E. - *Strictly for Saxes* •AATTB •BD
Schubert, Franz - *Marche militaire* (HOLMES) •AAATB •Rub
Schumann, Robert - *Zwei Kinderszenen* (WILLIAMS) •South
SCOTT, Andy - *Pieces* •AATTB or SATTB/Pno/Bass/Drums •PBP
SCOTT, James - *Frog Logs Rag*
SIBBING, Robert - *Pieces*
SOLAL, Martial - *Ballade* (1987) (5') •SAATB/Perc ad lib. •Mar
SOLLID, Torgrim - *Absurd gjenstand* (1987) •NMI

Sousa, John Philip - *The Thunderer March* (HERGER) •AATTB •Band
STRADOMSKI, Rafal - *555* (1988) (6') •DP
SVENSSON, Reinhold - *Suite I* (1981) (7') •AATTB •SR
TANNER, David - *Gathering no moss* (1989) •SATBBs •CMC
TERRANOVA, Claude - *Métamorphoses*
TOMLINSON, Ernest - *Concerto* (1965) (18') •AATTB/Orch •adr
Toselli, Enrico - *Serenade* (HARGER) •AATTB •Band
VAN MAELE, Gérard - *Caprice...* (1950) (3') •AATTBs •adr
   Conte de Grand-mère (1944) (3') •AATTBs •adr
Villa-Lobos, Heiter - *Bachianas Brasileiras No. 5* - Aria (BONGIORNO) •Ssx Solo/4 Sx: AATB •adr
WAELE de - *Quintette* •5 Sx •Mar
WOOD, Nigel - *Schwarzer Tanzer* •S+A ATTB
Yocapetta - *Largo* •AATBBs
ZEMP, Joseph - *Air scandinave* (1972) •SATB or AATTB •Mar

6 Saxophones

SAATTB unless otherwise indicated (SAATTB, sauf indication contraire). Also see Unspecified Instrumentation (Voir aussi instruments non déterminés), page 422.

Albinoni, Tomaso - *Sonata*, op. 2, no. 5 (SIBBING)
ALLA, Thierry - *Météore* (1986) •SAATBBs/Perc •adr
ANDRIESSEN, Louis - *Song lines* (1989) •TTTTBB/Perc •JG
AYOUB, Nick - *Saxtet* •SAATTB/Bass/Drums •DP
Bach, J. C. - *Symphony No. 2* (AXWORTHY) •SAATBBs •TVA
Bach, J. S. - *Brandenburg Concerto No. 2* (REX) •SAATBBs •DP
   Brandenburg Concerto No. 6 (WESTERN) •AATTBBs
   Chorale "Ach Gott und Herr" (HARTLEY) •SAATBBs •adr
   Fugue No. 4 (GRAINGER) •SATTBBs •PG
   March (GRAINGER) •PG
   Ricercar No. 4 (AXWORTHY) •SAATBBs •TVA
BOUVARD, Jean - *Vive Henri IV!* •AAAATB •adr
Brahms, Johannes - *Chorale Preludes* •SAATBBs •Eth
BRIGHT, Greg - *Music of the Maze* (10') •6 woodwind instruments •EMIC
Byrd, William - *Fantasie* (AXWORTHY) •SSAATB/Optional Perc
Cabezon, Antonio - *Prelude in the...* (GRAINGER) •SnoSATBBs •PG
CABUS, Peter - *Preludium & Rondo* (1979) •Mau
CAGE, John - *Pieces* •Any instruments •Pet
CALENS, P. - *Prélude et Rondo*
CARAVAN, Ronald - *Declamation...* (1984) •SAATBBs •Eth
   Pastorale •SAATBBs •Eth
CARDEW, Cornelius - *Pieces* (1960) •Any instruments •Uni
Dallin - *Aubade in Blue* •AATTBBs •WWS
Debussy, Claude - *Pieces* •SAATBBs
DELAMARRE, Pierre - *Nazaireïdes* •Asx Solo/AAAAT •adr
DEPELSENAIRE, Jean-Marie - *Entre la vie...* •SnoSATBBs •adr
DEVOGEL, Jacques - *Suite enfantine* •SAATTB/Pno •Bil
DIEMENTE, Edward - *Dimensions II* •Any 1 to 6 instruments/Tape •SeMC
Dvorak, Anton - *1er mouvement* (JOHNSON) •AAAATB •Rub
FOSS, Lukas - *Music for Six* •Any 6 instruments •DP
FOURCHOTTE, Alain - *Disgressions IV - Multiples* (1984) (6') •Tsx Solo or 6 Sx: SnoSABBsCBs
FRACKENPOHL, Arthur - *Two Rags* •SAATBBs •Sha
GARCIN, Gérard - *6me Musique...* (1984) (6') •1 to 7 Asx/Tape •Sal
GEE, Harry - *Sextet* (1978) •adr
Gershwin, George - *Summertime* (TEAL) •AATTBB
GUENTZEL - *Indian Dance* •AATTBBs •Rub
Guilmant, Alesandre - *Cantilène pastorale* (TAYLOR) •AAAATB •Mills
HARLE, John - *Bonjour... triste dame* •SSSSSS
HARTLEY, Walter - *Aubade* (1985) (1'20) •SAATBBs •Eth

HEIM, Norman - *Elegy Saxophonia*, op. 66 •Nor
   Mosaics, op. 76 •Nor
HEMPHILL, Julius - *Last Supper at Uncle Tom's Cabin...* •6 Sx
HOLMES, G. E. - *Sextette - Spiritual fantasie* •6 Sx •Rub
HURÉ, Jean - *1er Sextuor* •6 Sx
ISRAEL, Brian - *Arioso e Canzona* (1985) (2'30) •SAATBBs
ITURRALDE, Pedro - *Ballada* •adr
JEAN, André - *Orientale suite* •adr
JOHNSON, William - *Concert Overture* •AAATBBs •Bel/B&H/TM
JONAS, Emile - *Prière* (1861) •SATB or SAATTB •Marg
   Sextuor •SSAATB •Sax
KASTNER, Jean-Georges - *Grand sextuor* (1844) •SAATBBs •Sax/DP/Eth
Key, Francis Scott - *Star Spangled Banner* •AATTBBs
Krommer - *Partita* (SCHAEFER) •SAAATB •WWS
LASNE, George - *Choeur élégiaque* (1948) •SAAATB
Lawes, William - *Fantasy and Air No. 1* (GRAINGER) •SSAABBs or SSATBB •PG
LEE, Thomas Oboe - *Saxxologie...A Sextet* (11') •SSATTB •adr
LEGLEY, Victor - *Parade II*, op. 93 (1978) •Sch
LEGRAND, Michel - *Porcelaine de sax* (1958) (3') •SnoSATBBs •Mills
Le Jeune, Claude - *La bel'Aronde* (GRAINGER) •PG
LEMAIRE, Félix - *Entre chien et loup* (1980) •6 Sx/Pno
LONDEIX, Jean Marie - *Exercices pratiques* (1983) •4 to 12 Sx •Led
Lully, Jean-Baptiste - *Overture to Armide* •WWS
MacDowell, Edward - *An Old Garden* (REX) •SAATBBs •WWS
   To a Wild Rose •AATTBBs
Machaut, Guillaume de - *Ballade no. 17* (GRAINGER) •PG
Massenet, Jules - *Phèdre* (JOHNSON) •AAATTB •Rub
MAZZAFERRO, Dominico - *Fluxi* (1990) (6') •SAAATB
MOROSCO, Victor - *Song...* •Asx/5 Sx: SATBBs or SATBB
NODA, Ryo - *Sextuor* (1980) (12') •SATTBB •adr
OSTRANSKY, Leroy - *Poem and Dance* •AAATTB •Rub
   Three Pieces •AAATTB •Rub
Overstreet, W. Benton - *That Alabama...* (1918) (HOLMES) •6 Sx
Pachelbel, Johann - *How lovely...* •3 Sx: SAT or 6 Sx: SATTBBs •RS
Paganini, Nicolo - *Moto perpetuo* (TEAL) •AATTBBs
Parera, Antonio - *El Cappo* (WALTERS) •4, 5 or 6 Sx •Rub
PUTSCHE, Thomas - *Theme Song and Variations* (1972) (14') •SeMC
Rimsky-Korsakov, Nicolas - *The Young Prince...* •AATTBBs •DG
SAVARI, Jean-Nicolas - *Sextuor* (185x) •SSAATB •Sax
SEFFER, Yochk'o - *Torma* (7'30) •SnoSATBCBs/Perc
SMET, Robin de - *The Good Old Days* •6 Sx
STOCKHAUSEN, Karlheinz - *Linker Augentanz* (1983) •SSAA T+B Bs/1 Perc •Stv
Suppe, Franz von - *Poet and Peasant* •AAATBBs •Rub
SURIANU, Horia - *Vagues, ondes, contours* (1984) (11') •Asx/Tape or 6 Sx •Sal
Tchaikowsky, Peter - *Sextets Nos. 1 & 2* (TALLMADGE) •AATTBBs •Bel
   Theme from Swan Lake •AATTBBs •WWS
VAN HAUTE, Anna - *Visions* (1980)
Walters, Harold - *Moonrise* •AAATTB •Rub
Wiedoeft, Rudy - *Sax-O-Phun* (SIBBING) •Asx Solo/5 Sx: SAATB

7 Saxophones

Also see Unspecified Instrumentation (Voir aussi instruments non déterminés), page 422.

Bach, J. S. - *Brandenburg Concerto No. 3* (WAID) •7 Sx
   Chorales (LEWIS) •SAATTBB •WWS
BARROLL, Edward - *Laf 'n Sax* (1924) •7 Sx

BLICKHAN, Tim - *Music for 7 Saxophones* (1979) •7 like saxophones •DP

CAGE, John - *Pieces* •Any instruments •Pet

CARDEW, Cornelius - *Pieces* (1960) •Any instruments •Uni

CERINO, Sandro - *Pieces* •7 Sx

CIBULKA, Franz - *Kaleidoscop* (1981) (4'30) •Asx/Orch or 7 Sx: AAATTBBs

COURROYER, Bernard - *Ventose* (1969) (10') •SnoSATBBsCBs •adr

GARCIN, Gérard - *6me Musique...* (1984) (6') •1 to 7 Asx/Tape •Sal

GRAINGER, Percy - *Ye Banks and Braes o' Bonnie Doon* (1932-37) •SAATTBBs •GSch

HAIDMAYER, Karl - *Saxophonie X* (1982) •SnoSATBBsCBs

HAUBENSTOCK-RAMATI, Roman - *Multiple III* (1969) (10') •Uni

ISRAEL, Brian - *Concertino* (1982) (6'30) •SAATTBBs •Eth

JOHNSTON, David - *Tut suite* (1983) •SnoSATBBsCBs

KRAMER, Martin - *Lawd* (193x) •AAATTBBs •SC

LEMAIRE, Jean - *Septuor* •7 Sx

LESKO, Ladislav - *Intrada* (1982) •SnoSATBBsCBs

LONDEIX, Jean Marie - *Exercises pratiques* (1983) •4 to 12 Sx •Led

MARIETAN, Pierre - *La Rose des vents* (1982-83) (16') •Sx/Lyricon/ Tape or 7 Sx: SnoSATBBsCBs/Tape

McKay, George - *Berceuse* (REX) •SAAATTB •WWS

NETTING, Frederick - *Shadows* •AAATTBBs

NYKOPP, Lauri - *"...sillä ei ole nimeä"* •7 Sx •FMIC

ORTEGA, Sergio - *Récit d'un naufragé* (1990) (15') •SnoSATBBsCBs/ Narr

Septuor (1989) •SnoSATBBsCBs

PÜTZ, Marco - *Septentrion* •SnoSAATBBs

RENERTS, Roland - *5 Danses* •SnoSATBBsCBs

RUELLE, Fernand - *Ronde pastorale* (1974) •SnoSATBBsCBs •adr

SAVARI, Jean-Nicolas - *Septuor* (185x) •SSAATTB •Sax

STERN, Max - *Rainbow* (1985) •SAATTBBs •adr

STOCKHAUSEN, Karlheinz - *Linker Augentanz* (1990) •7 to 12 Sx: SS(S)AA(A)T(TT)B(B)Bs/1 Synth ad lib. •Stv

STOKES, Harvey - *Values and Proposal VI* (1988) (8'30) •SAATTBBs •SeMC

Sweelinck, Jan Pieterzoon - *Angelus and pastores* (AXWORTHY) •SSAATBBs •DP

TRAN, Fanny - *Majowka* (1981) (7') •7 to 15 Sx

VANDENBOGAERDE, Fernand - *Tezcatlipoca I* (1986) •SnoSATBBs CBs/Tape •Mor

VANDERMAESBRUGGE, Max - *Saxofolies*, op. 40 (1974) •SnoSATBBsCBs

VERHIEL, Ton - *An Easy Overture* (1984) •SAAATTB

Prelude and Rondo (1985) •SAAATTB

VLAHOS, James - *Exclamation Points!* (1983) (2'30) •SAATTBBs •Eth

WIRTH, Carl Anton - *Portals - A Prelude* (1971) •SAATTBBs •Eth

8 Saxophones

Also see Unspecified Instrumentation (Voir aussi instruments non déterminés), page 422.

Adriet - *Mélodie* •8 or 10 Sx: SSAATTBBs •Marg

Bach, J. S. - *Choral Variations* (REX) •SAAATTBBs •DP

Chorale "Wachet Auf" (HARTLEY) •SnoSAATBBsCBs •DP

Bernstein, Leonard - *America* (WHITE) •SnoSAATTBCBs

BRENET, Thérèse - *Gémeaux I & II* •SATB or SSAATTBB •Lem

BRINDUS, Nicolae - *Saxonatina* (1985) •8 Sx

BUSSEUIL, Patrick - *Trans* (1982) •SSAATTBB

CAGE, John - *Pieces* •Any instruments •Pet

CARAVAN, Ronald - *Jubilate!* (1982) (4') •SSAATTBBs •Eth

CARDEW, Cornelius - *Pieces* (1960) •Any instruments •Uni

CARRE-CHESNEAU, Thierry - *Conduit* (1990) •8 Sx

CHANDLER, Erwin - *Sinfonia* (1982) •SSAATTBBs

Chopin, Frédéric - *Prelude*, op. 29, no. 20 (ROSSI) •SAATTTBBs •DP

DESPORTES, Yvonne - *Danses saxsonnantes* (6'30) •8 Sx •DP

Saxophonades (9') •8 Sx •DP

DONDEYNE, Désiré - *Variations sur un air tyrolien* (1971) (10') •SAATTBBBs •EMRF

DÜMKE, Ulrich - *Oktett* (1989) •SSAATTBB

ESPOSITO, Patrizio - *Attraverso* (1991) (6') •SnoSAATTBBs

EVANGELISTA, José - *Saxfolly* (1985) (12') •8 Sx

GALANTE, Steven - *Saxsounds II* (1975) (10') •SSAATTBB •adr

GLASER, Werner Wolf - *3 Fancies* (1982) (12') •SnoSSAATTB •STIM

GONZALES, Luis Jorge - *Israel Concertino* (1992) •SSAATTBBs

Partita para un Virrey Mestizo (1992) (12'30) •SSAATTBBs

HARTLEY, Walter - *Adagio* (1994) (2'40) •SAAATTBBs •adr

Octet for Saxophones (1975) (8'30) •SAAATTBBs •DP

ISRAEL, Brian - Concertino (1984) •SSAATTBbs

KETTING, Otto - *Mars* (1974) (3'30) •4 Cl/4 Sx: AATT or 8 Sx: AATT AATT •Don

KORN, Peter Jona - *Passacaglia und Fuge* (1952-86) (8') •SAAATTBB

KRIEGER, Ulrich - *Oktette* (1989) (8') •8 Sx

KROEGER, Karl - *Banchetto musicale* (1993) •SnoSAATTBBs

LONDEIX, Jean Marie - *Exercises pratiques* (1983) •4 to 12 Sx •Led

MATTHEWS, David - *Octet* •SSAATTBB

MAZZANTI, Alessandra - *Liebes melodie* (1992) (4') •SAAAATTB

NÄTHER, Gisbert - *Oktett* (1990) (8') •8 Sx •adr

NETTING, Frederick - *Romance* •AAAATTBBs

ODSTRCIL, Karl - *Transit* •8 Sx/Perc

Overstreet, W. Benton - *That Alabama...* (1918) (HOLMES) •8 Sx

POOT, Marcel - *Thema con variazioni* •8 Sx

REX, Harley - *Shenandoah* •AATB or AAAATTTB •Mills

Three Spirituals •AAAATTTB •DP

Rimsky-Korsakov, Nicolas - *Hummelflug* (LINDEMAN) •SAAB ATTB •GB

ROBERT, Lucie - *Doppelchor* (1993) (12') •SATB + SATB •adr

SALLUSTIO, Eraclio - *Saxologia 5* (1992) •SAAAATTB

SAVARI, Jean-Nicolas - *Octuor* (185x) •SSAATTBB •Sax

SEVRETTE, Danielle - *Fadâa - Espaces* (1974) •8 Sx: A+B/A+B/ A+B/A+B/A+B/A+B/A+T/A+T

SHORES - *Prelude for Eight* •AAAATTBB

SHRUDE, Marilyn - *"And they shall inherit..."* (1992) •SSAATTBB •adr

STOCKHAUSEN, Karlheinz - *Linker Augentanz* (1990) •7 to 12 Sx: SS(S)AA(A)T(TT)B(B)Bs/1 Synth ad lib. •Stv

STROE, Aurel - *Colinda* (1985) •8 to 14 Asx •Sal

TRAN, Fanny - *Majowka* (1981) (7') •7 to 15 Sx

Tscesnokov - *Salvation...* (WORLEY) •8 Sx: SAAATTBBs •DP

VAN MAELE, Gérard - *Effervescente* (1986) (7'30) •S S+A AATTBBs •adr

Etincelante (1982) (4'30) •SAAATTBB •adr

Octuor •SAAATTBBs •adr

Vivaldi, Antonio - *Concerto Grosso in D Minor* (REX) •SSAATBBBs •WWS

WARING, Kate - *Ulterior motives* (1984) (to M. JEZOUIN) •SAAAAAAT/Str Orch

WHITE, Andrew N. III - *Symphonies No. 1 & 2* •8 Sx: SSSAAATT

9 Saxophones

Also see Unspecified Instrumentation (Voir aussi instruments non déterminés), page 422.

Bach, J. S. - *Brandenburg Concerto No. 3* (GOINS) •SSAAAATTBB
  Jésus, que ma joie demeure (LONDEIX) •Asx Solo/8 Sx: SSAATTBB
Biber, Heinrich-Franz von - *Battalia* (LONDEIX) •SSAAAATTBB
Brahms, Johannes - *Varation & Fugue*, op. 24 (SCHAEFFER)
  •SnoSAAAATTBBs •DP
CAGE, John - *Pieces* •Any instruments •Pet
CARDEW, Cornelius - *Pieces* (1960) •Any instruments •Uni
Debussy, Claude - *Ballet* (WORLEY) •SnoSAAAATTBBs •DP
  Cortege (WORLEY) •SnoSAAAATTBBs •DP
  En Bateau (WORLEY) •SnoSAAAATTBBs •DP
  La Fille aux cheveux de lin (REX) •SAAATTTBBs •DP
  Menuet (WORLEY) •SnoSAAAATTBBs •DP
Guilmant, Alesandre - *Finale in E Major* (REX) •SAAAAATTTB •DP
Handel, Georg-Friedrich - *Concerto Grosso in C Major* •9 Sx: SAT +
  AATTBBs •WWS
LERSTAD, Terje Bjorn - *Jubilee fanfare*, op. 133 •9 Sx •NMI
LONDEIX, Jean Marie - *Exercises pratiques* (1983) •4 to 12 Sx •Led
MacDowell, Edward - *To an Old White Pine* (REX) •SAAAATTBBs
  •WWS
Moussorgsky, Modeste - *Pictures at an Exhibition* (SCHMIDT)
  •SAAAATTBBBs •DP
Mozart, Wolfgang - *Célèbre motet* (WITTMAN) •SSAATTBBBs •E&S
REX, Harley - *A Walk in the city* •SAAAATTBBs •DP
STROE, Aurel - *Colinda* (1985) •8 to 14 Asx •Sal
STOCKHAUSEN, Karlheinz - *Linker Augentanz* (1990) •7 to 12 Sx:
  SS(S)AA(A)T(TT)B(B)Bs/1 Synth ad lib.
  •Stv
TRAN, Fanny - *Majowka* (1981) (7') •7 to 15 Sx

10 Saxophones

Also see Unspecified Instrumentation (Voir aussi instruments non déterminés), page 422.

Adriet - *Mélodie* •8 or 10 Sx: SSAATTBBs •Marg
Bach, J. S. - *Brandenburg Concerto No. 2* (REX) •SAAAATTTBBs
  •WWS
BOEUF, Georges - *Tryptique* (1985) (15') •2 Sx/Group of 8 to 14 Sx
  •adr
BUMCKE, Gustav - *3 Fantasien*, op. 50 (1930-31) •SnoSAAAATTBBs
CAGE, John - *Pieces* •Any instruments •Pet
CARDEW, Cornelius - *Pieces* (1960) •Any instruments •Uni
CRAIG, Jack - *Slap 'n Sax* (1924)
Debussy, Claude - *Estampes* (LONDEIX) •SnoSSAATTBBBs
  Miniatures - 7 pièces (LONDEIX) •SnoSSATTBBBs
ELOY, Christian - *Quattrocento* (1991) (7') •SnoSSAATTBBBs •adr
Gabrieli, Giovanni - *Canzona XIV* (LONDEIX) •SSAAAATTBB •Fuz
GIPPS, Ruth - *Seascape*, op. 53 (1958) (6') •10 woodwind instruments
  •KP
Grieg, Edvard - *The Last Spring* (1880) (WORLEY) •SSAAAATTBBs
  Suite in Olden Style (WORLEY) •SSAAAATTBBs
HEUSSENSTAM, George - *Double Quintet*, op. 83 (1985) (8') •10
  Asx (3 double Ssx)
LONDEIX, Jean Marie - *Exercises pratiques* (1983) •4 to 12 Sx •Led
PALAU BOIX, Manuel - *Marcha burlesca* (1936) (5'30) •10 Sx:
  SSAAATTTBBs/ophicleide
PILON, Daniel - *Concerto n° 1* (1982) •SnoSSAATTBBBs •adr
Prevost, André - *'Il fait nuit lente'* (LONDEIX) (16') •SnoSSAATTBBBs/
  Chorus
SAUGUET, Henri - *L'arbre* (1976-80) •SnoSSAATTBBBs

STOCKHAUSEN (continued)

STOCKHAUSEN, Karlheinz - *Linker Augentanz* (1990) •7 to 12 Sx:
  SS(S)AA(A)T(TT)B(B)Bs/1 Synth ad lib.
  •Stv
STROE, Aurel - *Colinda* (1985) •8 to 14 Asx •Sal
TAGGART, Mark - *Two Sad Songs* (1976) (8') •SSAAATTBBBs
  •Eth
TRAN, Fanny - *Majowka* (1981) (7') •7 to 15 Sx
Vivaldi, Antonio - *Concerto "alla rustica"* (PATRICK) •SSAAAATTBBs
  Concerto in A Major (FREDRICKSON) •SSAAAATTBBs
WORLEY, John - *Tempo di Viennese* •SSAAAATTBBs •DP

11 Saxophones

Also see Unspecified Instrumentation (Voir aussi instruments non déterminés), page 422.

BOEUF, Georges - *Tryptique* (1985) (15') •2 Sx/Group of 8 to 14 Sx
  •adr
CAGE, John - *Pieces* •Any instruments •Pet
CARDEW, Cornelius - *Pieces* (1960) •Any instruments •Uni
DUBOIS, Pierre-Max - *Hommage à Hoffnung* (1980) (25')
  •SnoSSSAAATTBBBs/Perc •adr
GLASER, Werner Wolf - *3 Pieces* (1981) (12') •SSAAAATTBBBs
  •STIM
HARTLEY, Walter - *Sinfonia VI* (1984-85) (8'30) •SSAAAATTBBBs
  •Eth
KOCH, Erland von - *Moderato e Allegro* (1981) (9') •SSAAAATT
  BBBs •Eth
LONDEIX, Jean Marie - *Exercises pratiques* (1983) •4 to 12 Sx •Led
STOCKHAUSEN, Karlheinz - *Linker Augentanz* (1990) •7 to 12 Sx:
  SS(S)AA(A)T(TT)B(B)Bs/1 Synth ad lib.
  •Stv
STROE, Aurel - *Colinda* (1985) •8 to 14 Asx •Sal
TAGGART, Mark - *Lament and Credo* (1984) •SSAAAATTBBBs
  •adr
TRAN, Fanny - *Majowka* (1981) (7') •7 to 15 Sx
VOGEL, Roger - *Divertimento* (1978) (9') •SSAAAATTBBBs •SeMC

12 Saxophones

SnoSSAAATTTBBBs unless otherwise indicated (SnoSSAAATTTBBBs, sauf indication contraire). Also see Unspecified Instrumentation (Voir aussi instruments non déterminés), page 422.

ALESSANDRINI, Pierluigi - *Blues for Sax*
  Ellingtoniana (ELLINGTON)
ALLA, Thierry - *Polychrome* (1994)
ANDERSON, Garland - *Symphony* (1973) •12 Sx: ATB •adr
ANDROSCH, Peter - *Dr. Mabuse*
Berlioz, Hector - *Chant sacré* (LONDEIX) •Bil
Bizet, Georges - *L'Arlésienne* (25') (LONDEIX) •Kud
BOEUF, Georges - *Tryptique* (1985) (15') •2 Sx/Group of 8 to 14 Sx
  •adr
BOLIART I PONSA, Xavier - *5 X 12* (1993) (12') •adr
BOMBARDELLI, Umberto - *12 Sounds* (1988)
BOUDREAU, Walter - *Demain les étoiles* (1980) (14') •CMC
BRAUNEISS, Leopold - *2 Inventionen...* (1992) (7') •CA
BRIE, Jérôme - *"Comme la main gauche de Thelonious Monk"* (1994)
  (10') •12 Sx: SnoSx Solo/SSAAATTTBBBs
CAGE, John - *Pieces* •Any instruments •Pet
CARDEW, Cornelius - *Pieces* (1960) •Any instruments •Uni
CARLOSEMA, Bernard - *Azulejos* (1987) (6') •Fuz
Catel, charles-Simon - *Thermidor de l'An II* (LONDEIX)

CAVANA, Bernard - *Goutte d'or blues* (1985) (7') •1 Sx: Sno+S/Tape or 12 Sx: SnoSnoSnoSSSAAABBB •Sal

CHARRON, Damien - *Carrière d'étincelles* (1991) (10')

CIBULKA, Franz - *Saxophonic* (1981)

COURTIOUX, Jean - *Les Quatre éléments* (1980) •SnoSSAAATTT BBBs/Electric Pno/Perc/Bass

Dorham, Kenny - *Blue Bossa* (MOSCATELLI)

DUFFAU, Lionel - *Questions* (1985) (8')

DUPRÉ, René - *Canon chromatique à 12 voix* •12 Sx: 6 Asx/6 Tsx •adr

EKIMOVSKY, Victor - *Cantus figuralis*, op. 32 (1980) (25')

Ellington, Edward Kennedy (Duke) - *Ellingtoniana* (ALESSANDRINI)

ENGEBRETSON, Mark - *L'Idéal* (1987) (6')

FERRANTE, Mauro - *"In prossimità dell'evento"* (1992) (8')

FONTAINE, Louis-Noël - *Concertante* (1991) (13') •Asx Solo/11 Sx: SnoSSAATTTBBBs •Capri

Polymorphie (1992) (13') •Capri

FREUDENTHALER, Erland Maria - *Fata Morgana* (5'45)

Saxophon-Fanfare (1990) (1'30)

FUSTÉ-LAMBEZAT, Arnaud - *Blanc et noir* (1982) (12') •adr

FUSTÉ-LAMBEZAT, Michel - *Forme-couleurs* (1988) (18'30) •adr

Mouvements (1978-84) (13') •adr

Gabrieli, Giovanni - *Canzona XV* (LONDEIX) •Ron

GABRIELI, Mauricio - *Do.Dicis.Acs.* (1991) (8')

GARCIN, Gérard - *A Sax* (1991) •SnoSSAAATTTBBBs/Perc

Duel à la recherche du chant sacré (1988) (15')

Gershwin, George - *Suite American stories* (LONDEIX) (16')

GOTKOVSKY, Ida - *Golden symphonie* (1991) (26'30) •SSSAAATTT BBB •Bil

GUERRERO, Francisco - *Rhéa* (1988) (6')

GUILLONNEAU, Christian - *Sax promenade* (1989) (4')

HALL, Helen - *Ruisselle/Fluvial* (1988)

HAVEL, Christophe - *Amers I* (1992) (12') •SnoSSAATTTBBBs/2 Perc •adr

Amers II (1992) (12') •adr

HEUSSENSTAMM, George - *Music for 12*, op. 86 (1986) (13'30)

Joplin, Scott - *3 Ragtimes* (LONDEIX) •Fuz

KARLINS, M. William - *Nostalgie* (1991) •adr

KETTING, Otto - *Praeludium* (1989) •Or

KLEIN, Immanuel - *Liederen voor rietries* (1991) •Don

KORNDORFF, Nikolaïs - *La musique primitive* (1981) (23')

KURZ, Karl-Wieland - *Teichlandschaft mit Erlen...* (1992) •12 Sx •adr

KYNASTON, Trent - *Corybant-Bleu* (1980)

LAUBA, Christian - *La Forêt perdue* (1983) (9') •adr

Les 7 îles (1988) (18') •SnoSSAAATTTBBBs/Pno Solo •adr

Mutation-Couleurs IV (1985) (12') •Fuz

LEMAY, Robert - *Vagues vertiges* (1989) (21') •SnoSSAAATTT BBBs/1 Perc •adr

Liszt, Franz - *Phantasie un fuge "Ad nos, ad...* (SAVOIE)

LONDEIX, Jean-Marie - *Ciné-Max...* (1983) (18') •adr

Etudes à douze... (1993) •adr

Exercises pratiques (1983) •4 to 12 Sx •Led

MALEC, Ivo - *Lumina* (1968-89) •12 Sx: SnoSSAAATTTBBBs/Tape •Sal

MARCO, Tomàs - *Espejo de viento* (1988)

MATITIA, Jean - *Devil's Rag* (1985) (4'30) •Ron

Las Americas (1985/93) (21') •adr

Samba do diabo (1992) (8') •adr

MEIJERING, Chiel - *Sax sox* (1991) •Don

MELLÉ, Patrick - *Arche d'anches* (1990) (11')

Moments profanes et Lieu sacré (1986) (15')

Milhaud, Darius - *Scaramouche* (LONDEIX) •Asx Solo/11 Sx: SnoSSAAATTBBBs •Sal

MINAMIKAWA, Mio - *Métaplasm* (1982) •SnoSSAAATTTBBBs/2 Perc •adr

MINTCHEV, Gueorgui - *Musique de concert* (1985) (10'30) •adr

MIYAZAWA, Kazuto - *Versuch über fractal* (1987) (8')

MURGIER, Jacques - *Suite française* (1984) (21')

NICOLAU, Dimitri - *Concerto per piano*, op. 77 (1988) •SnoSSAAATTTBBBs/Piano Solo/Perc •adr

Quarta sinfonia, op. 70 (1987) (10') •Sx Orch: SnoSSAAATTT BBBs/Soprano Voice/Perc

Palestrina, Giovanni - *Pieces* (REX) •SSAAAATTTTBB

PASCAL, Claude - *Patchwork Ballet* (1991) (40')

PAVLENKO, Serguei - *Concerto breve* (1980) (13') •adr

PILON, Daniel - *Bidoche et Patachon...* (1987-89) (23'30) •adr

Poulenc, Francis - *Capriccio* (7') (LONDEIX) •Sal

PRIESNER, Vroni - *Intrada-abläufe* (1990) (15')

REA, John - *La Capra che suono* (1986) •CMC

ROBERT, Lucie - *Pianaxo* (1993) •Pno/12 Sx: SnoSSAAATTTBBBs •adr

ROLIN, Etienne - *Boogie con moto...* (1988) (8') •12 Sx •adr

Machine à sons (1990) (12') •12 Sx (solo bass)/Tape •adr

ROSSÉ, François - *Spath* (1981) (16') •Fuz

SALBERT, Dieter - *Sinfonische Musik* (1991) •adr

SCHILLING, Hans Ludwig - *Grande saxophonie - Quodlibet* (1978) •SAT SATB SATBBs •adr

SCHULER, Thomas - *Bagatelle*, op. 13 (1992) (5') •CA

SELEN, Reinhold - *Partita* (1989) (13'30) •Don

STOCKHAUSEN, Karlheinz - *Linker Augentanz* (1990) •7 to 12 Sx: SS(S)AA(A)T(TT)B(B)Bs/1 Synth ad lib. •Stv

STROE, Aurel - *Colinda* (1985) •8 to 14 Asx •Sal

TESEI, Tonino - *Gesta* (1987) (8') •EDP

THEIS, Ernst - *Slap* (1992) •12 Sx

TRAN, Fanny - *Majowka* (1981) (7') •7 to 15 Sx

TULL, Fisher - *Cyclorama II* •12 Sx

VERDI, Luigi - *Organum* (1990)

Vivier, Claude - *Pulau Dewata* (SAVOIE)

VOIRPY, Alain - *Sylphe* (1983) (10') •adr

WAGNER-LEBENSLAUF, Wolfram - *Drei Studien* (1992) •ApE

Konzert (1992) (15') •CA

Weill, Kurt - *L'Opéra de quat'sous* (LONDEIX) •SnoSSAAATTTBBBs/Perc

ZANETTOVICH, Daniele - *Tango in Nero* (1992) (6')

13 Saxophones

Also see Unspecified Instrumentation (Voir aussi instruments non déterminés), page 422.

BOEUF, Georges - *Tryptique* (1985) (15') •2 Sx/Group of 8 to 14 Sx •adr

CAGE, John - *Pieces* •Any instruments •Pet

CARDEW, Cornelius - *Pieces* (1960) •Any instruments •Uni

ESCAICH, Thierry - *Le chant des ténèbres* (1992) (18') •Ssx/12 Sx: SnoSSAAATTTBBBs •Bil

GROSSI, Daniel - *"Sur le tombeau de Florence"* (1986) (14') •SnoSSAAAATTTBBBs •adr

GROUVEL, Pierre - *Volcan* (1993) (16'15) •Sx Solo: A+T+B/12 Sx: SnoSSAAATTTBBBs/3 Perc

LAMB, John David - *Cenotaph* (1987) (30') •SSSAAAATTTBBBs/2 Perc

PRATI, Hubert - *Echelles modales* (1987) •13 Sx •Bil

ROLIN, Etienne - *Adieu* •SnoSSAAATTTBBBsCBs

Chants fleuris (1985) (23') •Asx Solo/SnoSSAAATTTBBBs •adr

STROE, Aurel - *Colinda* (1985) •8 to 14 Asx •Sal

TRAN, Fanny - *Majowka* (1981) (7') •7 to 15 Sx

14 Saxophones

Also see Unspecified Instrumentation (Voir aussi instruments non déterminés), page 422.

APPARAILLY, Yves - *Danse sacrée* (1980) •SnoSnoSSSAAAATT BBBs •adr
Bach, J. S. - *Jésus, que ma joie demeure* (JEZOUIN) •SnoSSAAAATTT BBBsBs
BOEUF, Georges - *Tryptique* (1985) (15') •2 Sx/Group of 8 to 14 Sx •adr
BULLARD, Alan - *Circular Melody* (1990) •14 Sx
CAGE, John - *Pieces* •Any instruments •Pet
CARDEW, Cornelius - *Pieces* (1960) •Any instruments •Uni
DI PASQUALE, James - *Radical Departures* •SSAAAAATTTBBBBs
GASTINEL, Gérard - *Sax appeal* (1988) (12'30) •SnoSSSAAAATTT BBBs
HIGGINS, Dick - *Clown Garden* •SSAAAAATTTBBBBs
ROBERT, Lucie - *Messanucté*, op. 72 (1991) (18') •14 Sx •adr
STOCKHAUSEN, Karlheinz - *Plus Minus* (1963) •2 X 7 Sx Solo •Uni
STROE, Aurel - *Colinda* (1985) •8 to 14 Asx •Sal
TRAN, Fanny - *Majowka* (1981) (7') •7 to 15 Sx

15 Saxophones

Also see Unspecified Instrumentation (Voir aussi instruments non déterminés), page 422.

BOEUF, Georges - *Tryptique* (1985) (15') •2 Sx/Group of 8 to 14 Sx •adr
BRUNO, Mauro - *Circus Saxophonius* (1990); *Happy Birthday Adolphe Sax*; *Saxes Strike Up* (1990); •SSAAAAAA TTTTBBBs
CAGE, John - *Pieces* •Any instruments •Pet
CARDEW, Cornelius - *Pieces* (1960) •Any instruments •Uni
CENSHU, Jiro - *Spring in the wind* (1992) •SSAAAAAAAATTBBB
TIPPS, Greg - *Serio I* (1976) •15 Sx: 3 x SATB/TTB
TISNÉ, Antoine - *Hymne pour notre temps* (1989) (17') •Sno+S S AAAATTTTBBBBBs •adr
TRAN, Fanny - *Majowka* (1981) (7') •7 to 15 Sx

16 Saxophones

Also see Unspecified Instrumentation (Voir aussi instruments non déterminés), page 422.

BOEUF, Georges - *Tryptique* (1985) (15') •2 Sx/Group of 8 to 14 Sx •adr
CAGE, John - *Pieces* •Any instruments •Pet
CARDEW, Cornelius - *Pieces* (1960) •Any instruments •Uni
HEUSSENSTAMM, George - *Periphony No. 3*, op. 70 (1980) (18') •16 Sx: 4 X SATB/4 Perc •DP
Score, op. 46 (1972) (15') •16 Sx: 4 X SATB •SeMC
KOMIVES, James - *Spiralis* (1974) •16 Sx: 4 X SATB
REX, Harley - *12-tone variations* •3 Sx Solo: SSA/13 Sx: SAAAATTTTBBBsBs •DP

19 Saxophones

Also see Unspecified Instrumentation (Voir aussi instruments non déterminés), page 422.

Bach, J. S. - *Toccata and Fugue in D Minor*, BWV 565 (MAEDA)
Bernstein, Leonard - *West Side Story* (Excerpts) (MAEDA)

22 Saxophones

Also see Unspecified Instrumentation (Voir aussi instruments non déterminés), page 422.

Strauss, Richard - *Fanfare* (AXWORTHY) •SSSS AAAAAA TTTTT BBBB BsBs/Timp •DP/TVA

58 Saxophones

Also see Unspecified Instrumentation (Voir aussi instruments non déterminés), page 422.

GARCIN, Gérard - *A la recherche du chant sacré* (1991) •58 Sx including [dont] 12 soloists

Saxophone Ensembles

Also see Unspecified Instrumentation (Voir aussi instruments non déterminés), page 422 and 5, 6, 7, 8, 9, 10, 11, 12, 13, 14, 15, 16, 19, 22, 58 Saxophones.

Bach, J. S. - *In Thou Be Near* (PATRICK) •Sx Ensemble
Jesu, Joy of Man's Desiring (CARAVAN) •Sx Ensemble: SATBBs
Ricercar a6 (PATRICK) •Sx Ensemble: SATBBs
Wie Schön leuchtet... (PATRICK) •Sx Ensemble: SATBBs
BARBER, Clarence - *A Lincolnshire Whimsy* (1991) (7') •Sx Ensemble: SSAATTBBs •TTF
Belssel - *God, Ruler...* (HARTLEY) •Sx Ensemble: SSAATTB •adr
BERTOCCHI, Serge - *Sphéroïde* (1989) (6') •Sx Ensemble
Berwald, Franz - *Hymn* (c. 1845) (HARTLEY) •Sx Ensemble: SAATBBs •Eth
BOEUF, Georges - *Tryptique* (1985) (15') •2 Sx/Group of 8 to 14 Sx •adr
Borodin, Alexandre - *Peasant's Chorus* (4') (MIDDLETON) •Sx Ensemble: SAATTBBs •TTF
BOROFF, Edith - *Mottos* (1989) •Sx Ensemble
BOUVARD, Jean - *Variations sur un thème de Haydn* •3 Sx Soloists/ Sx Ensemble •adr
CAGE, John - *Four 5* (1992) (8') •Sx Ensemble: SATB
COWLES, Colin - *Fweekout* •Sx Choir: SnoSATBBs •adr
CRAIG, Jack - *Slap 'n Sax* (1924) •Sx Ensemble
DARROW, Melissa - *Rites of Passage* (1992) •Sx Ensemble: SATBBs
Elgar, Edward - *Nimrod* (1899) (WORLEY) •Sx Ensemble
FICHER, Jacobo - *Rhapsodie*, op. 88 (1956) •Sx Ensemble: SATB
GENZMER, Harald - *Paergon* (14') •Sx Orch: SAATBBs/1 Perc •Pet
Gershwin, George - *Rhapsody in Blue* (WORLEY) •Pno/Sx Ensemble
GRAINGER, Percy - *The Annunciation Carol* (c. 1943) (4') •Sx Ensemble: SAATTBBs •TTF
The Immovable Do... (1933-39) •Sx Choir: SAATTBBs •GSch
Lisbon... (1943) (1') •Sx Choir: SAATB •PG/TTF
Grieg, Edvard - *Wedding Day at Troldhaugen*, op. 65, no. 6 (1897) (HEYBURN) •Sx Ensemble: SATBBs
Handel, Georg Friedrich - *Hornpipe* (1717) •Sx Ensemble: SATBBs
HARTLEY, Walter - *Overture, Interlude & Scherzo* (1988) (8'30) •Sx Orch: SSAAATTBBs •DP
Serenade (1991) (10') •Sx Ensemble: SAATBBs •Eth
Three "Sacred Harp" Songs (1987) •Sx Ensemble: SSATTBBs •DP
A William Billings Suite (1987) •Sx Ensemble: SAATBBs •DP
HARVEY, Paul - *Saxophone Spectrum* (1989) •Sx Ensembles •RSC
Holst, Gustav - *Dargason* (1912) (SIBBING) •Sx Ensemble
HUNT, Frederick - *Larghetto* •Sx Ensemble
ITO, Yasuhito - *Tableau* (1987) •Sx Orch
JOHNSON, Barry - *Three Preludes* •Sx Choir

KUSHIDA, Testurosuke - *Bugaku* (1988) •Sx Orch

LETASSEY, Laurent - *Sempre tutti* (1991) (17') •Asx Ensemble/8 Voices •Bil

MINCIACCHI, Diego - *Il nostro rapido viaggio* (1992) •Sx Orch

MORRIS, Jonathan - *Up the Street March* •Sx Ensemble

PAPE, Gérard - *Pour un tombeau d'Anatole* (1985) •Soprano Voice/ Perc/Sx Orch: SSAAATTTBBs

REICHA, Anton - *Four Fugues* (HARTLEY) •Sx Ensemble: SAATBBs •Eth

Roelstraete, Herman - *Theme con variations* (JONEHMANS) •Sx Ensemble

ROLIN, Etienne - *Luce del fuoco* (1992) (13') •40-60 Sx (ATBBs) •adr

ROQUIN, Louis - *Machination VII* •Sx Ensemble

SAGVIK, Stellan - *Altosaxofonsymfoni*, op. 128 (1984) •Sx ensemble •STIM

SCHIFFMANN, Harold - *Concertino* (1982) •Sx Ensemble

SOUSA, John Philip - *Untitled One-Step* (1920s) (4') •Sx Ensemble: SAATTBBs •TTF

TYLE, Teddy - *Whodnit* •Sx Ensemble

VEHAR, Persis - *Cakewalk* •Sx Ensemble

VOSK, Jay - *Midnight Passacaglia* (1984) •Sx Choir: SSAATTBBs •DP

Saxophone and Flute or Piccolo

2 Musicians

ARMA, Paul - *Divertimento no. 18* (1976) (13') •Fl/Asx
BAGUERRE, Francis - *Duo* (1977) •Fl/Asx
CHARLTON, Andrew - *Diversions* (1980) •Fl/Asx
CHRETIEN, Hedwige - *Duo* •Asx/Fl
DEASON, David - *Five Diversions* (1980) •Fl/Ssx •DP
 Two Studies (1980) •Ssx/Fl •DP
DI BETTA, Philippe - *Croquis* (1991) (6') •Fl/Asx •adr
HAMILTON, Tom - *Dialogue* •Asx/Fl
IANNACCONE, Anthony - *Bicinia* (1975) •Fl/Asx •CF
JAECKER, Friedrich - *Flöte, Saxophon* (1993) •Ssx/Fl •INM
JUGUET, Henri-Pierre - *Pierre de lune* (1985) •Fl/Ssx
KARKOFF, Maurice - *The Lord...*, op. 196c (1992) •Fl/Ssx •SMIC
KONDO, Jo - *A Crow* (1978) (10') •Fl/Ssx
MALONEY, Michael - *Music* (1982) •Fl/Asx/Tape
MESSINA-ROSARYO, Antonio - *Buria* (7') •Picc/Asx •Asto
NODA, Ryo - *Tori - Oiseaux* (1977) (12') •SnoSx/Oriental Flutes
POLIN, Claire - *Aderyn pur* (1972) (14') •Fl/Asx/Optional Tape •SeMC
QUERAT, Marcel - *Lied et Canonica* (1964) (3') •Fl (or Ob)/Asx •Phi
REINER, Karel - *Hovory - Talks* (1979) (11') •Fl/Bsx •CHF
STEPALSKA, Joanna - *Beregesave* (1993) •Picc+Fl/Asx •INM
YOUNG, Jeremy - *Rondeau à Bordeaux* (1979) •Asx/Fl

3 Musicians

ABLINGER, Peter - *Verkündigung* (1990) •Fl/Asx/Pno •adr
APPERSON, Ronald - *Concertino* •Fl/Asx/Bsn
Artot, J.-B. - *12 Trios* •Fl/Cl/Asx •DG
BARKIN, Elaine - Media speak (1981) •Fl/Asx/Bass/Tape
BARON, Maurice - *Elegy* •Fl/Asx/Harp (or Pno) •MBCo
Beethoven, Ludwig van - *Grand Trio*, op. 87 •Fl/Ob/Asx •Braun
 Trio, op. 87 •Fl/Ob/Asx •Bil
Bentley, Arnold - *16th Century Trios* •Fl (or Ob or Cl)/Ob (or Cl)/Sx •Chap
BOND, Victoria - *Ménage à trois* •Fl/Asx/Cl •SeMC
BOURDIN, François - *Rêverie* (1984) •Fl/Asx/Pno
Braga, Gaetano - *Angel's Serenade* •Fl/1 Sx: A or T/Pno •CF
BROCKMAN, Jane - *Divergencies* (1975) •Fl/Ssx/Pno
BUSSOTTI, Sylvano - *Trio "Voliera"* •Fl+Picc/Asx/Pno
CHALLULAU, Tristan - *Sur quelque étoile morte...* •Fl/Asx/Cl
DEPELSENAIRE, Jean-Marie - *Mosaïque* (1979) (2'30) •Fl/1 Sx: A+T+B/Harp •adr
DESROCHERS, Pierre - *5 Miniatures* •Fl/Tsx/Pno
DI BETTA, Philippe - *Vents pluvieux* (1992) (6') •Fl/Cl/Asx •Fuz
DIEDERICHS, Yann - *Prismes* (1983/88) (12'30) •Fl/Asx/Pno
DUBOIS, A. - *Trio* •Fl/Tsx/Pno •CDM
DUBOIS, Pierre-Max - *Les Tréteaux* (1966) (7'30) •Fl/Asx/Pno •Chou
 Trio •Fl/Tsx/Harp •adr
EHRLICH, Abel - *The Answer* (1970) •Tenor Voice/Fl/Sx
EIMERT, Herbert - *Tanzmusik* (1926) •Fl/Sx/Mechanical Instrum. •Br&Ha
 Der weisse Schwan (1926) •Fl/Sx/Mechanical Instrum. •Br&Ha
EITHLER, Estaban - *Trio* (1944) •Fl/Asx/Bass •BBC
 Trio (1945) •Fl/Ob/Asx •BBC
ELOY, Christian - *Archipel* (1990) •Fl/Asx/Guit •adr
ESCAICH, Thierry - *3 Intermezzi* (1994) •Fl/Cl/Sx •Bil
FURRER, Beat - *Trio* (1985) •Fl/Cl/Asx (or Ob) •Uni
Gattermann, Philippe - *Fantaisie concertante* •Fl (or Ob or Cl)/Asx/Pno •Bil
GLASER, Werner Wolf - *Triade* (1992) •Fl/Marimba/Bsx

GOLDSTEIN, Malcolm - *Ludlow Blues* (1963) (12') •Asx/Fl/Trb/Tape •adr
GUERRINI, Guido - *Dialogo sui Fiori* (1956) •Fl/Tsx/Pno
HALSTENSON, Michael - *Trio* (1984) (8') •Fl/Sx/Pno
HARVEY, Paul - *Trio* •Fl (or Ob)/Cl/Tsx •DP
Haydn, Franz Joseph - *Oxen Minuet* •Fl (or Cl)/Asx/Pno •CF
HEKSTER, Walter - *Windsong II* (1970) (8') •Fl/Asx/Tpt •Don
JEVERUD, Johan - *2 Pieces...* (1992) •Fl/Asx/Perc •SMIC
JOHANSON, Sven - *Caccia* (1968) •Fl/Cl/Tsx •STIM
JOY, Jérôme - *Départ errance retour* (1992) (13') •Fl/Asx/Tape
KALLSTENIUS, Edvin - *Lyrische Suite*, op. 55 (1960-62) (18') •Fl/Asx/Cl •STIM
KARKOFF, Ingvar - *The Lord is my shepherd: pastorale*, op. 196c (1992) •Fl/Ssx •SvM
KOECHLIN, Charles - *Epitaphe de Jean Harlow*, op. 164 (1937) •Fl/Asx/Pno •ME
LEMELAND, Aubert - *Divertissement no. 1 & 2* (9') (10') •Fl/Asx/Cl •Bil
LENNERS, Claude - *Zenit - Fantasia* (1990) •Fl/Ob/Ssx •Lem
MALMGREN, Jens - *Trio* (1972) •Fl/Ob/Asx
MAZUREK, Micezyslaw - *Trio* (1988) (11-12') •Fl/Asx/Pno
MOLAND, Eirik - *Trio* (1982) •Fl/Asx/Accordion •NMI
Moore, Thomas - *Poem* •Fl/Sx/Pno •AMC
NICOLAU, Dimitri - *Alla donna di fondo*, op. 80 (1987) •Fl/Asx/Pno •EDP
PANDELÉ, Thierry - *Le Fils apprête, à la mort, son chant* (1993)(10') •Soprano Voice/Fl/Sx
PAZ, Juan Carlos - *Musica*, op. 43 (1943) (18') •Fl/Sx/Pno •GSch
PIAZZOLA, Astor - *Summit* •Bandon./Sx/Picc
QUERAT, Marcel - *Magie* (1979) (3') •Fl (or Ob)/Cl/Tsx •Bil
SABON, Joseph-Pierre - *Pieces* •Ob (or Fl or Cl)/Asx/Pno •Bil
SAUGUET, Henri - *Concert à 3 pour Fronsac* (1979) (12') •Fl/Asx/Harp •Fuz
SCHULZE, Werner - *2 Duos* (12') •Fl/Asx/Bsn •CA
 Transplantazioni •Fl/Asx/Bsn •CA
SCHUST, Alfred - *Trio* (1984) •Fl/Asx/Trb •adr
SCHWARTZ, Francis - *Daiamoni* (5') •Asx/Fl/Bass
SMITH, Claude T. - *Suite* (1988) •Fl/Cl/Asx
Sontag, Henriette - *An Evening Serenade* •Fl/1 Sx: A or T/Pno •CF
TALLET, Marc - *Permutations...* (1977) (12') •Fl/Asx/Pno
TOSI, Daniel - *Multitude III* (1984) (20') •Fl/Asx/Vibr

4 Musicians

ADDERLEY, Mark - *Waver* (1986) •Fl/Cl/Tsx/Vln •NMI
AHO, Kalevi - *Quartet* (1982) (22') •Fl/Asx/Guit/Perc •FMIC
ATOR, James Donald - *Woodwind Quartet* (1969) (11') •Fl/Cl/Sx/Bsn •SeMC
BENTZON, Jörgen - *Raconto n° 1*, op. 25 (1935) (13') •Fl/Asx/Bsn/Bass •SOBM/BMCo
BERGMAN, Erik - *Mipejupa*, op. 96 (1981) (17') •Fl/Asx/Guit/Perc •FMIC
BERNAOLA, Carmelo - *Superficie n° 3* (1963) •Asx/Picc/Xylophone/Bongos •Alp
BOEUF, Georges - *Em Misma...* (1971) (10') •Vln/Fl/Cl/Asx •adr
BOIS, Rob du - *Stuleken* (1960) •Fl/Tsx/Vla/Perc •Don
BONNARD, Alain - *Bis*, op. 42 •Fl/Ob/Cl/Asx •Bil
BOUVARD, Jean - *3 Images* •Fl/Vln/Asx/Pno •Bil
BROWN, Newel - *Déjeuner sur l'herbe* (14') •Mezzo Voice/Fl/Sx/Pno •SeMC
DAILEY, Dwight - *Reflections in Gold...* (1982) •Sx/Fl/Cl/Pno
DANCEANU, Liviu - *Florilège* (15') •Sx/Fl/Fl-à-bec/Pno
DEPELSENAIRE, Jean-Marie - *Petit concert à quatre* (1973) (2') •Fl/Tpt/Asx/Cl •Phi/Com
DIJK, Jan van - *Concertino* •Vln/Fl/Cl/Asx •Don
EITHLER, Estaban - *Quartet* (1945) •Picc/Fl/Tpt/Sx

ENGELMANN, Hans - *Permutagioni* •Fl/Ob/Sx/Bsn •A&S

ERB, Donald - *Quartet* (1962) (7') •Fl/Ob/Asx/Bass •CMC

EYSER, Eberhard - *Edictus to the...* (1985) •Fl/Ssx/Cl/BsCl •STIM

GARIN, Didier-Marc - *Da caccia IV* (1992) •Fl/2 Sx: AT/Perc

GERSCHEFSKI, Edwin - *America*, op. 44, nos. 6 & 13 (1962) •Fl/Cl/
Asx/Bsn •CFE

GLASER, Werner Wolf - *5 Strukturer* •Soprano Voice/Fl/Sx/Vcl
•STIM

GOTTSCHALK, Arthur - *The Sessions* •Fl/Asx/Vibr/Bass •SeMC

GRANT, Jerome - *Classical Woodwind Quartet* (1966) (20') •Asx/Cl/
Fl/Bsn •adr

GREEN, Stuart - *Pipedreams* (1978) (7') •Fl/Asx/Ob/BsCl

HALETZKI, P. - *Father and Son* (1938) •Picc/Asx/Bsn/Pno •Sch

HAMBURG, Jeff - *Elegie* (1985-86) (9') •Fl/BsCl/Bsx/Perc •Don

HÄMEENIEMI, Aero - *Chamber Music Book* (1980) •Fl/Guit/Asx/
Perc •FMIC

HAVEL, Christophe - *AER (la danse)* (1994) (10') •Picc/SnoSx/
Celesta/Perc •adr

   RamDam (1992) (15') •Fl/1 Sx: S+B/Perc/Pno/Transformation
électroacoustique •adr

Haydn, Franz Joseph - *Adagio* (GEIGER) •Fl/Ob/Asx/Bsn •CF

   Pieces (SPEETS) •2 Sx: AT/Fl/Cl (or Ob) •TM/HE

HEUSSENSTAMM, George - *Four Miniatures*, op. 57 (1975) (9')
•Tsx/Fl/Ob/Vln •DP

IVES, Charles - *Tun Street* (1921) •Fl/Tpt/Bsx/Pno

KAIPAINEN, Jouni - *Far from home*, op. 17 (1981) (10') •Fl/Asx/
Guit/Perc •WH

LAUBA, Christian - *Atlantis* (1990) (14') •Fl (+Tam)/Tsx/2 Guit •adr

LAUTH, Wolfgang - *Concertino* (1958) (14') •Tsx/Trb/Fl/Perc •adr

LINDBERG, Magnus - *Linea d'ombra* (1981) (15') •Fl/Asx/Guit/
Perc •WH/FMIC

MAGANINI, Quinto - *Rêverie* (HARRIS) •Fl or Cl/Ob or Cl/Asx/Bsn
or BsCl •CF

MAROS, Miklos - *Clusters for cluster* (1981) •Fl/Ssx/Guit/Perc
•SMIC

MASON, Lucas - *Lay-Alla-Allah* (1972) •Soprano Voice/Asx/Fl/Pno
•adr

MEIJERING, Chiel - *I Hate Mozart* (1979) (4') •Fl/Asx/Harp/Vln
•Don

MERILÄINEN, Usko - *Simultanus for four* (1979) (16') •Fl/Asx/
Guit/Perc •Pan/FMIC

MOESCHINGER, Albert - *Images*, op. 85 (1958) (18') •Fl/Vln/Asx/
Vcl •Bil

MONTGOMREY, James - *Ritual I : The White Goddess* (1980) (14')
•Fl/Cl/Bsx/Koto (or autoharp) •CMC

MUCZYNSKI, Robert - *Fuzzette...* (1962) (12') •Narr/Fl/Asx/Pno

MYERS, Robert - *Quartet* (1966) •Fl/Asx/Bsn/Vcl •SeMC/AMu

OLOFSSON, Kent - *The voice of one who calls...* (1991-92) •Fl/Asx/
Trb/Synth •Tons

PROVOST, Serge - *Tétractys* •Fl/Asx/Pno/Harp

ROLIN, Etienne - *Vocalise II* (1989) •Ssx/Pno/BsCl/Fl •adr

ROSENBLOOM, David - *Pocket Pieces* (1977) •Fl/Asx/Vla/Perc
•SeMC

ROSSÉ, François - *Level 01-84* (1984) •Fl-à-bec/Fl/Asx/1 or 2 Synth/
Chambre d'écho & reverb. •adr

Rossini, Giacchino - *Quartet No. 2* (GEE) •Fl/Cl/Sx/Bsn •DP

SCHUMANN, Gerrhard - *Petite suite* •Fl/Sx/EH/Cl •IMD

SCOTT, Ronnie - *Dark Flowers* (1988) (13') •Fl/Asx/Guit/Perc

STEVEN, Donald - *Straight on till morning* (1985) •Fl/Cl/1 Sx: A+B/
Electr. Pno •CMC

STROUD, Richard - *Capriccio* •Fl/Ob/Asx/BsCl •SeMC

THOMAS, Ronald - *Occasion* •Fl/Ssx/Cl/Hn

VILLA-LOBOS, Heitor - *Quatuor*, op. 168 (1921) (20') •Fl/Asx/
Celesta/Harp •ME

WARING, Kate - *Psalmance* (1978) (5') •Fl/Ssx/Guit/Perc

WELLS, Thomas - *Comedia* (1978) •Fl/Sx/Tpt/Vcl

WILSON, Donald - *Tetragon* (1990) •Fl/Asx/Cl/Bsn

5 Musicians

ALLA, Thierry - *Aérienne* (1994) (8') •Fl/2 Sx/Pno/Perc/dispositif
électroacoustique

AMBROSINI, Claudio - *Trobar clar* (1982) •Fl/Ob/Cl/Tpt/1 Sx: S+A

ARCURI, Serge - *Prologue* (1985) •Fl/Ssx/Cl/Hn/Perc/Tape •CMC

ASCOUGH, R. - *Quintet* •Ssx/Fl/Ob/Cl/Bsn

AYSCUE, Brian - *Permutations I* (1972) (6'30) •Fl/Ob/Cl/Tpt/Tsx
•adr

BENHAMOU, Maurice - *Mouvement* (1979) •Fl/Sx/Vla/Vcl/Perc/
Tape

BROTONS, Soler - *Quinteto* (1978) •Fl/Ob/Asx/Hn/Bsn •EMEC

BROWN, Newel Kay - *Pastorale and Dance* •Fl/Cl/Asx/Tpt/Trb
•SeMC

BUCZKOWNA, Anna - *Hipostaza* (1984/85) (15') •1 Sx: S+A+T/Fl/
Vcl/Vibr/Soprano Voice

BUEL, Charles - *Chimera, Avatars and Beyond* (1972) (15-20') •Fl/
Ob/2 Sx: AT/Perc •adr

CAMPANA, José - *Insight* (1987) (18') •Fl/Voice/Sx/Bass/Perc/
Tape/Video •Bil

CARPENTER, Gary - *Dances for Mutilated Toys* (1970) (15') •Fl/Ob/
Cl/Asx/Bsn •BMIC

CELERIANU, Michel - *Janvier* (1983) •Ssx/Fl/2 Bass/Perc •Sal

CONTI, Francis - *Quintet* (1972) •Fl/Picc/1 Sx: A+S/Cl/Bsn •adr

CONYNGHAM, Barry - *Jazz Ballet* (1964) •Fl/Asx/Bass/Perc/Pno
•Uni

CUNNINGHAM, Michael - *Miro Gallery* •Fl/Ob/Cl/Asx/Bsn •SeMC

D'ANGELO, Nicholas - *The Seventh Star of Paracelsus* (1968) (16')
•Fl/Vln/Asx/Vcl/Pno •adr

DEFOSSEZ, René - *Mélopée et Danse* •Asx/Pno or Fl/Ob/Cl/Asx/Bsn
•An

DESPORTES, Yvonne - *Sonate pour un baptême* (1959) (18') •Fl/
Asx/Soprano Voice (or EH)/Perc/Pno •Bil

DUBOIS, Pierre-Max - *Sonatine* (1974) (7') •Fl/Cl/Asx/Tpt/Trb •adr

EYSER, Eberhard - *Baroque* (1987) •Fl/4 Sx: SATB

FIRSOVA, Elena - *Capriccio* (1976) (8') •4 Sx: SATB/Fl

FONTAINE, Louis-Noël - *Mauresque* (1992) (8') •Fl/Ssx/Cl/Vcl/
Perc •Capri

GHEZZO, Dinu - *Sound shapes* •Fl/Ob/Cl/Sx/Bsn •SeMC

HAERL, Dan - *Quintet* •Fl/Asx/Tpt/Trb/Bass •adr

HARTLEY, Walter - *Suite for 5 Winds* (1951) (7') •Fl/Ob/Cl/Asx/Trb
•Wi&Jo

HEININEN, Paavo - *Quintetto*, op. 7 (1961) (18') •Fl/Sx/Pno/Vibr/
Perc •Tie/FMIC

HESPOS, Hans - *Einander* (1966) (12-13') •Fl/Cl/Guit/Tsx/Vla
•EMod

HISCOTT, James - *Variations on O. Cèlestin's...* (1978) (9') •Fl/Cl/
Sx/Perc/Pno •CMC

HODKINSON, Sidney - *Interplay* (1966) (12'30) •Fl+Picc/Cl/Asx/
Perc/Bass •CMC

HOLZMANN, Rodolfo - *Divertimento* (1936) •Fl/Cl/Sx/Hn/Bsn

JONES, Robert - *Divertimento* •Fl/Ob/Cl/Asx/Hn •WWS

KAINZ, Walter - *Bläser Quintet*, op. 12 (1935) •Fl/Cl/Asx/Hn/Bsn
•adr

LAUBA, Christian - *Rif* (1991) (14') •Fl/2 Sx: SA/Pno/Perc •Fuz

Laube, P. - *Alsacian Dance* •Fl/Ob/Asx/Bsn (or Hn)/Pno •CF

LAUBER, Anne - *5 Eléments* (1972) (6'15) •Fl/Ssx/Vln/Bsn/Tuba
•CMC

LOEFFLER, Charles-Martin - *Ballade carnavalesque* (1904) •Fl/Ob/
Asx/Bsn/Pno •South

MALHERBE, Claudy - *Non-sun* (1984-85) (10') •Picc/Tsx/Ob/Cl/
Bsn

MARIN, Amadeo - *Quintet* •Fl/Ob/Tsx/Vcl/Trb
MEIJERING, Chiel - *Meine Lippen die...* (1984) (10') •Fl/Ob/Asx/
Pno/Perc •Don
MULDOWNEY, Dominic - *Love Music for Bathsheba...* (1974) (20')
•Fl/Ob/Cl/Asx/Hn (or Trb) •Nov
NIELSON, Lewis - *Dialectical Fantasy* (1981) •Fl/Ob/Cl/Tsx/Hn
•ACA
NILSSON, Anders - *Cadenze* (1992) •Fl/Ob/Cl/Bsn/Sx
OLBRISCH, Franz-Martin - *"Im Anfänglichen...* (1989) (90') •Vln/
Fl/Trb/Sx/Perc/Electronics
PILLEVESTRE - *Nocturne* •Fl/Ob/Cl/2 Sx: AB
READE, Paul - *Quintet* (1976) •Fl/Ob/Asx/Hn/Bsn •adr
RECK, David - *Blues and Screamer* (1965-66) •Fl+Picc/Harmonica/
Asx/Bass/Perc •CPE
REVUELTAS, Silvestre - *First Little Serious Piece* (2'45) •Picc/Ob/
Cl/Tpt/Bsx •MM/PIC/Peer
Second Little Serious Piece (1'15) •Picc/Ob/Cl/Tpt/Bsx •PIC/Peer
ROSSÉ, François - *Level 01-84* (1984) •Fl-à-bec/Fl/Asx/1 or 2 Synth/
Chambre d'écho & reverb. •adr
RUBBERT, Rainer - *Vocalise* (1992) •Asx/Fl/Vcl/Perc/Pno •adr
SAGVIK, Stellan - *4 Miniatyrer ur baletten Eulidyke*, op. 92 (1978)
(4'30) •Fl/Ob/Cl/2 Sx: AT •STIM
SODERO, Cesare - *Pieces* (1933) •Fl/Ob/Cl/Tsx/Bsn •AMPC
STRINDBERG, Henrik - *Hjärtats slag* (1987) (7'10) •Fl/4 Sx: SATB
•SMIC
SYMONDS, Norman - *Sylvia* (1974) •Narr/Tsx/Fl/Pno/Bass •CMC
TALLET, Marc - *Estagari* (12') •Fl/Asx/Trb/Vla/Guit
TARLOW, Karen - *Music...* (1973) (12') •Fl/Ob/Cl/Asx/Hn •SeMC
TREMBLAY, George - *Piece* •Fl/Ob/Cl/Tsx/BsCl
VERHIEL, Ton - *Aria* (1985) •Fl/4 Sx: SATB or AATB
VOGEL, Wladimir - *La Ticinella...* (1941) •Fl/Ob/Cl/Asx/Bsn •SZ
WOLFE, George - *Persian Dance* (1982) •Asx/Picc/Bsn/Xylophone/
Exotic Perc
WOOLLETT, Henri - *Danses païennes* (19xx) •2 Fl/Asx/Vcl/Harp

6 Musicians

Also see Wind Sextet (Voir aussi sextuor à vent),
page 368.

ABECASSIS, Eryck - *Dans 3 nuits* (1984) •Asx/Fl/Cl/Vln/Vcl/Pno
AMELLER, André - *Azuleros de Valencia* (1965) (13') •Fl/Ob/Cl/
Asx/Hn/Bsn
ASHEIM, Nils Henrik - *Midt iblant os...* (1978) •Fl/Asx/Vla/Vcl/
Bass/Perc •NMI
BARCE, Ramon - *Obertura fonética* (1968) (8'50) •Fl/Ob/Cl/Asx/
Tpt/Trb •EMEC
BENNETT, Richard Rodney - *Comedia I* (1972) •Fl/Asx/BsCl/Tpt/
Vcl/Perc •Uni
BERG, Paul - *To Teach His Own* (1984) (12') •Fl/Ob/Tsx/Trb/Vln/
Vcl/Tape •Don
BONDON, Jacques - *Sonate à Six* (1980) •2 Fl/2 Cl/2 Asx •ME
BOUDREAU, Walter - *Variations* (1975) •Ssx/Asx+Fl/Tsx+Picc/
Tuba/Pno+Celesta/Guit •CMC
Braun, R. - *Pieces* •Fl/3 Cl/2 Sx: AT •Yb
BRIGHT, Greg - *Music...* (10') •6 Woodwinds instruments •EMIC
CARLOSEMA, Bernard - *Radiance* (1988) (5'30) •Fl/Asx/Hn/Tpt/
Trb/Tuba •Fuz
CHINI, André - *Pieces* (1992) •Fl/Sx/2 Perc/Pno/Bass
DE MARS, James - *Premonitions...* (16'30) •Native American Fl/
African Perc/Asx/Vcl/Pno/Perc •adr
DINESCU-LUCACI, Violeta - *"Auf der Suche nach Mozart"* (1983)
(19') •Fl/Sx/Bsn/Hn/Vln/Pno+Celesta •adr
EISMA, Will - *Affairs no. 1* •Fl/Asx/Vibr/Pno/Bass/Perc •Don
ERB, Donald - *Hexagon* (1962) (6') •Fl/Asx/Tpt/Trb/Vcl/Pno •CMC

ERIKSON, Ake - *The rest is silence* (1971/73) •Fl/Asx/Cl/Pno/Bass/
Perc •SMIC
FERRO, Pietro - *Amphitrion divertimento* •2 Fl/2 Sx/CBsn/Perc •Ric
FUSTÉ-LAMBEZAT, Arnaud - *Catalogue d'étoiles* (1983) •Asx/Fl/
Cl/Vln/Vcl/Pno •adr
GARCIN, Gérard - *SA* (1986) •Asx/Fl/Cl/Vln/Vcl/Pno
GAUTHIER, Brigitte - *Like the Sweet Blonde* (1983) •Fl/Asx/Cl/Vln/
Vcl/Pno
GERSCHEFSKI, Edwin - *America*, op. 44, no. 14a •Fl/Cl/Asx/Tpt/
Bsn/Pno •CFE
GOEHR, Alexander - *Shadowplay*, op. 30 (1976) (20') •Actor+Tenor
Voice/Narr+Fl/Asx/Hn/Vcl/Pno •Sch
GOTKOVSKY, Ida - *Poème lyrique* (1987) •2 Voices: SB/Pno/Fl (or
Vln)/Asx (or Vla)/Bsn (or Vcl)
HAMBRAEUS, Bengt - *Kammarmusik for 6*, op. 28 (1950) (8') •Fl/
Ob/Cl/Asx/Vla/Harp •STIM/Ehr
HEDSTROM, Ase - *Close by* (1980) •Fl/Cl/BsCl/Ssx/Vln/Vcl •NMI
HISCOTT, James - *Ballad No. 1* (1978) (14') •Fl/Cl/Sx/Perc/Accor-
dion/Pno •CMC
HOLMBERG, Peter - *Musica alta e bassa* (1979) (12') •Fl/Tpt/Bsx/
Tuba/Vln/Vcl •STIM
HORWOOD, Michael - *Interphases* (1975) (13') •Fl/Sx/Accordion
(or Org)/Pno/2 Perc •CMC
HUMBERT-CLAUDE, Eric - *Eux* (1983) •Asx/Fl/Cl/Vln/Vcl/Pno
KÖPER, Heinz-Karl - *Musik...* •Fl/Cl/Asx/Tpt/Trb/Bass •EMBA
LANZA, Alcides - *Interferences III* (1983-84) •Fl/Cl/Sx/Guit/Pno/
Perc •ShP
LE SIEGE, Annette - *Ordinary Things* •Voice/Fl/Sx/Vibr/Vcl/Pno
•SeMC
LUNDEN, Lennart - *Quadrille; Queen Christina's Song* •2 Fl/2 Cl/Sx/
Bsn •Che
MALLIE, Loïc - *Sextuor* (1989) •Fl/Cl/Asx/Pno/Guit/Perc
MAXFIELD, Richard - *Domenon* (1961) •Fl/Sx/Pno/Vibr/Vln/Bass/
Tape
McPEEK, Ben - *Trillium* (1979) •Ssx/Fl/Cl/Vln/Vcl/Pno
MICHAEL, Frank - *Kmk* •Fl/Ssx/Trb/Vln/Vla/Vcl •adr
NILSSON, Ivo - *Per-cept* (1989-91) •Fl/Ob+EH/1 Sx: S+A/Trb/Pno/
Vln+Vla •SMIC
PENTLAND, Barbara - *Variable Winds* (1979) (5') •Fl (or Ob)/Asx/
3 Tom-toms/Bongos •CMC
RAYNAL, Gilles - *Ombilic* (1983) •Fl/Cl/Asx/Vln/Vcl/Pno
RODRIGUEZ-PICO, Jesùs - *Sextet* (1992) •Fl/2 Cl/2 Sx: AT/Bass
ROLIN, Etienne - *Tressage-Concerto* (1983-84) (10') •Ssx/Fl/Cl/
Pno/Vln/Vcl •Lem
SCHWEYER, Bruno - *Konzertstück* (1983) •Tsx/Fl/Cl/Vln/Vcl/Pno
SURIANU, Horia - *Esquisse pour un clair obscur* (1986) (11') •Ssx/
Fl/Cl/Vln/Vcl/Pno •Sal
TOSI, Daniel - *Multiphony III* (1986) (6'30) •Fl/Cl/Asx/Pno/Vln/Vcl
VILLA-LOBOS, Heitor - *Sexteto mistico*, op. 123 (1917) (9') •Fl/Ob/
Asx/Guit/Celesta/Harp •ME

7 Musicians

ADDERLEY, Mark - *The Worm and the Toothache* (1986) •Asx/Tsx/
Vln/Fl/Trb/Pno/Perc •NMI
ARGERSINGER, Charles - *Drastic Measures* •Fl/Ob/Cl/Asx/Bsn/
Hn/Perc
BJORKLUND, Terje - *Herbarium* (1982) •Fl/Ssx/Vln/Hn/Bass/Pno/
Perc •NMI
CANTON, Edgardo - *Phares et balises* •Fl/Ob/Sx/BsCl/Hn/Tpt/Trb
ESCAICH, Thierry - *Antiennes oubliées* (1994) •Vln/Fl/Asx/Tpt/Trb/
Vcl/Vibr •Bil
ESCOT, Pozzi - *Visione* (1964-87) •Fl/Asx/Vibr/Soprano Voice/
Bass/Perc/Narr
HAAS, Konrad - *Pieces* •Voice/Fl/Sx/Pno/Perc/Guit/Bass •Holz

HILLBORG, Anders - *Variations* (1991) •Soprano Voice/Mezzo Soprano Voice/Fl/Sx/Perc/Vla/Bass •SMIC

KARKOFF, Maurice - *Djurens Karneval* (1974) (15') •Fl/Picc/2 Cl/Tsx/Bsn/Perc •STIM

KOECHLIN, Charles - *Septuor*, op. 165 (1937) (11'30) •Fl/Ob/EH/Cl/Asx/Hn/Bsn •Oil

LARSSON, Häkan - *Farleder - 4 pieces* (1993) •Fl/Tsx/Trb/Electr. Guit/Electr. Bass/Pno/Perc •SvM

LUDWIG, J. - *Stenogramme* •Fl/Tsx/Trb/Bass/Vibr/Harps/Perc •EMod

MAJOS, Giulio di - *Passacaglia* •Fl/Asx/Hn/Guit/Vibr/Pno/Bass •Sch

MASON, Lucas - *A Quilt of Love* (1971) •Soprano Voice/Asx/Fl/Vln/Bsn/Trb/Vcl •adr

MIEREANU, Costin - *Polymorphies 5 X 7 B* (1969-70) (9-10') •Fl+Picc/Cl+Tsx/Pno/Vln/Vla/Vcl/Bass •Sal

MUSSEAU, Michel - *Les paupières rebelles* (1993) (40') •Fl/Cl/Ssx/Hn/Tpt/Trb/Tuba •Ed. Visage

NEMESCU, Octavian - *Septuor* (1983) •Fl/Cl/Trb/Tsx/Pno/Bass/Perc

NILSSON, Bo - *Zeiten im Umlauf*, op. 14 (1957) (3') •Fl/Ob/EH/Cl/BsCl/Tsx/Bsn •Uni

NORDENSTEN, Frank - *Sample and hold* (1978) (14') •Fl+Picc/Cl+BsCl/1 Sx: S+T/Vln+Vla/Vcl/Pno/Perc

PINOS-SIMANDL, Aloïs - *Euforie* (1983) (10') •Ob (or Fl)/Asx/Cl/BsCl/Pno/Perc/Bass •CHF

SAGVIK, Stellan - *Sma gyckelvisor...*, op. 112 (1981) (8') •Fl/2 Cl/Asx/Mandolin/2 Perc •STIM

SKOUEN, Synne - *Hva sa Schopenhauer...* (1978) (8') •Narr/Fl/Cl+BsCl/Sx/Vln/Vcl/Perc •NMI

SOMERS, Harry - *Limericks* (1979) •Voice/Fl/Cl/Sx/Bsn/Tpt/Euphonium •CMC

STOUT, Alan - *Four Antiphonies* •Fl/Trb/Asx/Org/Vln/Vla/Perc •CFE

WILLIAMSON, Malcolm - *Merry Wives of Windsor* (1964) •Fl+Picc/Cl/Tsx/Tpt/Perc/Bass/Pno •JW

WILLIS, Richard - *Irregular Resolutions* •Fl/Ob/Cl/Asx/Bsn/Hn/Perc •adr

ZEMP, Joseph - *Souffle printanier* •Fl/Ob/Cl/4 Sx: SATB •adr

8 Musicians

BERG, Olav - *Fragments* (1977) (8') •Fl/Cl/Asx/Vla/Vcl/Pno/2 Perc •NMJ

BIRTWISTLE, Harrison - *Medusa* (1969/70/78) •Fl/Cl/Ssx/Pno/Perc/Vln/Vla/Vcl/Tape

BLATNY, Pavel - *D-E-F-G-A-H-C* •Fl/3 Sx: ATB/Pno/Bass/Tpt/Trb •CMIC

BREGENT, Michel - *Melorytharmundi* (1984) •Fl/Cl/Sx/2 Perc/Pno/Vcl/Guit •CMC

BUMCKE, Gustav - *Suite G Dur*, op. 24 •Tenor Voice/Fl/Ob/Cl/Bsn/Hn/Bsx/Harp •VAB

CHATMAN, Stephen - *Outer Voices* (1978) •Fl/Cl/Asx/2 Perc/Celesta/Guit/Harp/Tape •CMC

DELAMARRE, Pierre - *La 8* (1981) (3') •Fl/Ob/Cl/Asx/Pno 4 hands [à 4 mains]/Bass/Perc •adr

DELIO, Thomas - *Congruent Formalizations* •Fl/3 Cl/4 Sx •DP

DEL PRINCIPE, Joseph - *Lyric Pieces for Octet* •Fl/Ob/Sx+Cl/BsCl/Tpt/Hn/Trb/Tuba •SeMC

ERNRYD, Bengt - *Rödingsjön II* (1967) •Fl+Picc/Trb/Tsx+Perc/Bsx+Perc/Vcl/Bass/2 Perc •SMIC

FONTYN, Jacqueline - *Cheminement* (1986) (15') •Soprano Voice/Fl/Cl/Hn (or Asx)/Vcl/Bass/Perc/Pno

FRANCESCONI, Luca - *Piccola trama* (1989) (14') •1 Sx: S+A/Fl/Cl/Guit/Perc/Vln/Vla/Vcl •Ric

FRANCO, Clare - *Four Winds...* •Asx/Harp/Vibr/Fl/Ob/Cl/Hn/Bsn

GARCIN, Gérard - *Encore plus tard* (1984) (12') •1 Sx: Sno+A+Bs/Fl/Cl/Bsn/Vla/Vcl/Bass/Perc/Tape •Sal

GHEZZO, Dinu - *Pontica II* •Fl/Sx/2 Tpt/2 Hn/Pno/Narr •SeMC

GUY, Georges - *Concerto en forme de jazz* •Asx Solo/Pno Solo/Fl/Ob/Cl/Hn/Bsn/Bass

HACHIMURA, Yoshiro - *Concerto per 8 soli* •Fl/Cl/Sx/Vibr/Vcl/Vla/2 Perc •OE

HARBISON, John - *The Flower-fed Buffaloes* (1976) •Voice/Cl/Tsx/Fl/Vcl/Bass/Pno/Perc

HEKSTER, Walter - *Of mere being* (1982) (12') •Asx/Fl/Ob/Cl/2 Tpt/Perc/Electr. Guit •Don

HESPOS, Hans - *Druckspuren - geschattet* (1970) (7'30) •Fl/Eb Cl/Asx/Bsn/2 Tpt/Trb/Bass •EMod

KORTE, Karl - *Matrix* (1968) (16') •Fl/Ob/Cl/Asx/Hn/Bsn/Pno/Perc •GSch

LASNE, George - *Ballade française* (1971) •Fl/Ob/2 Cl/Asx/2 Tpt/Trb

MANDANICI, Marcella - *Extraits I* (1989) •Tsx/Fl/Cl/Pno/Perc/Vln/Vla/Vcl •adr

MAYUZUMI, Toshiro - *Sphenogramme* (1951) •Contralto Voice/Fl/Asx/Marimba/Vln/Vcl/Pno 4 hands [à 4 mains]

MICHEL, Paul - *Ultramorphoses* (1965) (12-15') •Fl/Cl/Asx/Perc/Pno/Vln/Vla/Vcl •CBDM

NILSSON, Bo - *Frequenzen* (1957) •Fl/Picc/Ob/EH/Cl/BsCl/Tsx/Bsn •Uni

PERSSON, Bob - *Om sommaren sköna II* (1965) •Fl/BsCl/Trb/2 Perc/Vibr/Vcl/Jazz Sx/Tape

RADULESCU, Horatiu - *Sky* (1984-85) •Sx/Cl/Fl/2 Bsn/2 Bass/Perc

RIEDEL, Georg - *Reflexioner* (1974) (8') •Woodwind Quintet/Jazz group (Cl+Asx/Pno/Bass) •SMIC

SAGVIK, Stellan - *Guenilles des jongleurs*, op. 74 (1977) (7'30) •Fl/Ob/3 Cl/Asx/Bsn/Cnt •STIM

Suite circuler, op. 86 (1978) (10') •Picc/Asx/Tpt/Hn/2 Trb/Perc/Bass •STIM

SUTER, Robert - *Estampida* •Fl/Cl/Tsx/Hn/Tpt/Trb/Bass/Perc •EMod

TANENNBAUM, Elias - *Consort* •Fl/Hn/Asx/Electr. Guit/Vcl/Bass/Vibr/Jazz drums •ACA

TISNÉ, Antoine - *Dolmen* (1976) (30') •Fl/Cl/Asx/Hn/Tpt/Trb/Tuba/Pno •adr

TOMASSON, Haukur - *Octette* (1987) •Fl/Cl/Asx/Hn/Vla/Vcl/Pno/Perc (Vibr+Gong) •IMIC

VILLA-LOBOS, Heitor - *Chôros n° 7* (1924) (10') •Fl/Ob/Cl/Asx/Bsn/Vln/Vcl/Tam-tam •ME

9 Musicians

ALBRIGHT, William - *Introduction...* (14') •Pno/Fl/Cl/Asx/Hn/Tpt/Trb/Tuba/Perc •Pet

ALLGEN, Claude - *Adagio och Fuga* (25') •Fl/Ob/EH/Cl/BsCl/2 Sx: AB/Bsn/Hn •STIM

BOUVARD, Jean - *Choral dialogue* •3 Fl/3 Cl/3 Asx •adr

BUMCKE, Gustav - *"Der Spaziergang"*, op. 22 •Fl/Ob/EH/Cl/Bsn/Hn/BsTrb/Bsx/Harp

CLARK, Thomas - *Dreamscape* •Fl/Ob/Cl/Sx/Tpt/Trb/Pno/Perc/Bass •SeMC

COLE, Helen - *Serenade* •Fl/Ob/2 Cl/BsCl/Hn/Asx/2 Bsn

COX, Rona - *Two Expressions* (1968) •Fl/Ob/Cl/2 Sx: SB/Hn/Bsn/Bass/Perc •adr

DIEMENTE, Edward - *For Lady Day* •Fl/Ob/Cl/Tpt/Trb/Vln/Vla/Sx/Bsn/Tape •SeMC

FICHER, Jacobo - *Los invitados*, op. 26 •Fl/Cl/2 Sx: AT/2 Tpt/Tuba/Pno/Perc

GRAINGER, Ella - *To Echo* (1945) •Soprano Voice/Picc/Fl/Cl+Asx/Tsx/Vla/BsCl/Bass/Marimba •GS

GRANDERT, Johnny - *86 T* •Fl/EH/BsCl/Bsx/CBsn/2 Tpt/Perc/Pno
•STIM

IVES, Charles - *Over the Pavements*, op. 20 (1906-13) •Picc/Cl/Bsx
(or Bsn)/Tpt/3 Trb/Perc/Pno •PIC

JELINEK, Hanns - *Blue Sketches*, op. 25 (1956) •Fl/Cl/2 Sx: AB/Tpt/
Trb/Vibr/Bass/Perc •EMod

LEWIS, John Aaron - *Little David's Fugue* (5'30) •Fl/Cl/3 Sx: ATB/
Trb or Tpt/Harp or Pno/Bass/Perc •MJQ

The Queen's Fancy (4') •Fl/Cl/Tsx/Bsn/Hn/Trb/Harp/Bass/Perc
•MJQ

Sun Dance (4') •Fl/Cl/3 Sx: ATB/Trb/Harp or Guit/Bass/Perc
•MJQ

MANOURY, Philippe - *Etude automatique* 1 •Fl/Tpt/Sx/Tuba/Harp/
Vln/Vla/Vcl/Bass

MARCO, Tomàs - *Anna Blume* (1967) •2 Narr/Fl/Ob/Cl/Sx/Tpt/2
Perc

MELLNÄS, Arne - *Drones* (1967) (8') •Fl/Cl/3 Sx: ATB/Tpt/Perc/
Vcl/Bass •STIM

MULDOWNEY, Dominic - *An Heavyweight Dirge* (1971) (25')
•Voice/Fl/Asx/Perc/Pno/2 Vln/Vla/Vcl •Nov

NONO, Luigi - *Polifonica, Monodia, Ritmica* (1951) (10') •Fl/Cl/
BsCl/Asx/Hn/4 Perc •AVV

RACOT, Gilles - *Jubilad'a* (1985) (23'30) •1 Sx: Bs+Sno/Vcl/Fl/6
Voices

SAGVIK, Stellan - *Det Förlorade steget*, op. 64 (1976) (20') •Fl/
Cl+BsCl/Asx/Cnt/Trb/Vln/Vla/Vcl/Perc
•SMIC

SCHWANTNER, Joseph - *Diaphona intervallum* (1966) (12') •Asx/
Pno/Fl/2 Vln/Vla/2 Vcl/Bass •ACA

SILVERMAN, Faye - *Shadings* (1978) •Vln/Vla/Bass/Fl/Ob/Asx/
Bsn/Hn/Tuba

SÖDERLIND, Ragnar - *Eg hev funne...* (1982) (9'); *Legg ikkje ditt...*
(1983) •Soprano Voice/Fl+Picc/Ssx/Hn/Vln/
Vla/Bass/Pno/Perc •NMI

SVOBODA, Tomàs - *Seven Short Dances* •Fl/2 Cl/Asx/Trb/Vln/Bass/
Pno/Perc

TANENBAUM, Elias - *Trios I, II, III* •Fl/Ob/Cl/Vln/Vla/Vcl/Bass/
Asx/Perc •ACA

ULRICH, Jürgen - *Spiel* (1974) (5') •Fl/Ob/Cl/Bsn/Sx/Hn/Tpt/Trb/
Tuba •VDMK

WALTON, William - *Façade* (1922/26, 42) (34'30) •2 Narr/Fl+Picc/
Cl/BsCl/Asx/Tpt/Vcl/Perc •OUP

WILDER, Alec - *Suite* •Bsx/Fl/Ob/Cl/2 Hn/Bsn/Bass/Drums

YOSHIBA, Susumu - *Erka* •Fl/Ob/Sx/Tpt/Trb/Perc/Vcl/Guit/Pno

10 Musicians

ANDRIESSEN, Louis - *On Jimmy Yancey* (1973) (10') •Fl/2 Sx: AT/
Hn/Tpt/3 Trb/Bass/Pno •Don

BRANT, Henry - *Dialogue in the Jungle* (1964) (15') •Tenor Voice/
Fl/Ob/Cl/Bsx/2 Tpt/Trb/Hn/Tuba •adr

BUMCKE, Gustav - *Präludium und Fuge*, op. 20 (1903) •Fl/Ob/EH/
Sx/Cl/BsCl/2 Bsn/2 Hn

CHIARPARIN, Antonio - *Omaggio à Zoltan Kodaly* •2 Fl/6 Sx:
AAAATTB/Bugle (Flicorno)/BsTrb •Piz

COLE, Hugo - *Serenade...* (1965) (15') •2 Fl/Ob/2 Cl/Asx/2 Bsn/2 Hn

COSTEN, Roel van - *Prisma* (1984) (8') •Vla/Fl/Cl/Asx/BsCl/Trb/
Vcl/Bass/Perc/Pno •Don

CUNNINGHAM, Michael - *Linear Ceremony* •2 Fl/2 Ob/2 Cl/Sx/Hn/
2 Bsn •SeMC

Spring Sonnet •Fl/2 Cl/BsCl/2 Sx/3 Hn/Bass •SeMC

DEPELSENAIRE, Jean-Marie - *Dixtour* (1971) •2 Fl/2 Tpt/2 Sx/4 Cl
•adr

FORTNER, Jack - *SprING sur des poèmes de E. E. Cummings* (1966)
(11') •Mezzo Soprano Voice/Fl/Asx/Bsn/
Vla/Vcl/Bass/Vibr/Harp/Pno •JJ

GOODMAN, Alfred - *3 Gesänge für Gresang* •Soprano Voice/Fl/Ob/
Asx/Cl/Vla/Vcl/Prepared Pno/Guit/Perc •adr

GOUGEON, Denis - *Heureux qui comme...* (1987) •Soprano Voice/
Picc/EH/Bsx/2 Vln/Vla/Vcl/Bass/Perc
•CMC

GRAHN, Ulf - *Soundscape II* (1974) (7') •Fl/Cl/EH/Asx/2 Trb/2 Vln/
Vcl/Bass •SMIC

HARTLEY, Walter - *Double Concerto* (1969) (7'30) •Asx/Tuba/
Wind Octet (Fl/Ob/Cl/Bsn/Hn/2 Tpt/Trb)
•PhiCo

HEIDEN, Bernhard - *Sonatina* •Fl/Cl/Tsx/Hn/Trb/Harp/Vibr/Pno/
Bass/Perc •MJQ

JOHNSON, J. J. - *Turnpike* (5') •Fl/Cl/3 Sx: ATB/Trb/Harp (or Guit)/
Pno/Bass/Perc •MJQ

KOX, Hans - *Concertino* (1982) •Asx/Picc/2 Fl/BsCl/2 Hn/2 Tpt/Trb
•Don

LACHARTE, Nicole - *La Geste inachevée* (1980) •Fl/Cl/Sx/Tpt/Trb/
Pno/Perc/Vln/Vla/Vcl

LAZARUS, Daniel - *4 Mélodies* •Contralto Voice/Fl/Cl/Asx/Bsn/2
Vln/Vla/Vcl/Bass

LEWIS, John Aaron - *The Milanese Story* •Fl/Tsx/Guit/Pno/Bass/2
Vln/Vla/Vcl/Perc •MJQ

LINDBERG, Nils - *Progression* (1985) (28') •Fl/Ob/Cl/Hn/Bsn/2 Sx:
SA/Pno/Bass/Drums •SMIC

LUTYENS, Elisabeth - *Akapotik Rose*, op. 64 (1966) (18') •Soprano
Voice/Picc/Fl/Cl/Bsn/Cl+Tsx/Vln/Vla/Vcl/
Pno

MASON, Benedict - *Coulour and information* (1993) •Fl/Ob/Sx/Bsn/
Hn/Tpt/Trb/Tuba/Perc/Electr. Bass

MIMET, Anne-Marie - *Fanfare et divertissement* •Fl/Ob/Cl/Bsn/3 Sx:
SAT/Tpt/Trb/Tuba

NILSSON, Bo - *Zeitpunkte* (1960) (5') •Fl/Alto Fl/Ob/EH/Cl/BsCl/2
Sx: AT/Bsn/CBsn

PAUMGARTNER, Bernhard - *Divertimento* •Picc/EH/Asx/Bsn/Hn/
Tpt/Pno/Vla/Vcl/Perc •Uni

POOLE, Geoffrey - *Son of Paolo* (1971) •Fl/Picc/Cl/BsCl/Tsx/2 Vln/
2 Vcl/Prepared Pno •BMIC

SCHAFFER, Boguslaw - *Permutations n° 27* (1956) •Fl/Ob/Cl/Sx/
Tpt/Trb/Vla/Perc/Harp/Pno •A&S

SCHULLER, Gunther - *12 by 11* (8'30) •Fl/Cl/Tsx/Hn/Trb/Vibr/Pno/
Harp/Bass/Perc •MJQ

SMITH, Linda - *Periphery* (1979) •Fl/Sx/Tpt/Marimba/Vibr/Chimes/
Pno/Vln/Vcl/Bass •CMC

SMITH, William - *Elegy for Eric* •Fl/2 Sx: AB/Cl/Tpt/Trb/Vibr/Vln/
Bass/Perc •MJQ

SPINO, P. - *Prelude of Woodwinds* •2 Fl/Ob (ad lib.)/3 Cl/BsCl/Bsn
(ad lib.)/4 Sx: AATB •StMU

TREMBLAY, George - *Epithalamium* (1962) •Fl/Ob/Cl/Sx/Bsn/Hn/
Tpt/Trb/Tuba/Perc •CFE

VELLONES, Pierre - *Deux Pièces...*, op. 67 (1935) (6'30) •2 Fl/4 Sx/
Pno/Bass/Perc/Ondes Martenot •Sal

VRIES, Klaas de - *Moeilijkheden* (1977) (15') •Fl/2 Sx: AT/Hn/2 Tpt/
3 Trb/Pno •Don

WILDER, Alec - *She'll Be Seven in May* •Fl/Ob/Asx/2 Cl/BsCl/Bsn/
Bass/Drums/Pno

11 Musicians

ANDRIESSEN, Jurriaan - *Hommage à Milhaud* (1945) (8') •Fl/Ob/
Cl/Bsn/Hn/Tpt/Trb/Asx/Vln/Vla/Vcl •Don

BOIS, Rob du - *Springtime* (1978) •Picc/3 Sx/Hn/2 Tpt/2 Trb/Tuba/
Pno •Don

BORSTLAP, Dick - *Fanfare II* (1975) (6'); *Over de verandering...*
(1974) (5') •Fl/Picc/2 Sx: AT/Hn/Tpt/2 Trb/
BsTrb/Pno/Bass •Don

Vrijheidslied (1978) (2') •Picc/3 Sx: SAT/Hn/2 Tpt/2 Trb/Tuba/ Pno •Don

COLE, Bruce - *Pantomimes* (25') •Soprano Voice/Fl/Cl/BsCl/Ssx/ Perc/Pno/Guit/Vln/Vla/Vcl •B&H

HAZZARD, Peter - *Massage* •3 Voices (SAB)/3 Perc/Fl/Cl/Hn/Sx/ Trb •SeMC

MENGELBERG, Misha - *Dressoir* (1977) (10') •Fl/3 Sx: S+A A T/ 2 Tpt/Hn/2 Trb/Tuba/Pno •Don

MESTRAL, Patrice - *Alliages* (1969) •Tpt Solo/Fl/Cl/Asx/2 Trb/2 Perc/Pno/Org/Bass

MONDELLO, Nuncio - *Suite* (1956) •Asx/2 Fl/Ob/Cl/Bsn/2 Hn/Tpt/ Trb/Perc •adr

PÜTZ, Eduard - *Kon-Takte* •Vocal Quartet (SATB)/Fl/Sx/Vibr/Guit/ Perc/Pno/Bass •SeMC

SCHILLING, Otto-Erich - *Überall ist Wunderland* •Voice/Fl/Cl/Sx/ Tpt/2 Vln/Bass/Perc/Accordion/Pno •SeMC

SPINO, P. - *Prelude of Woodwinds* •2 Fl/Ob (ad lib.)/3 Cl/BsCl/Bsn (ad lib.)/4 Sx: AATB •StMU

TRIMBLE, Lester - *Panels I* (1973) (6') •Picc/Bsx/Vln/Vla/Vcl/Bass/ 2 Perc/Electr. Guit/Electr. Org/Electr. Harp •Pet

ZONN, Paul Martin - *Voyage of Columbus* (1974) (13') •Tpt Solo/Fl/ Ob/Ssx/Hrn/Trb/2 Perc/Pno/Vln/Bass •ACA

12 Musicians

BENNETT, Richard Rodney - *A Jazz Calender* (1963-64) (31') •Fl/ 3 Sx: ATB/2 Tpt/Hn/Trb/Tuba/Pno/2 Perc •Uni

CURTIS-SMITH, Curtis - *Sundry Dances* (1981) •Fl/Ob/Cl/3 Sx: SAB/Bsn/CBsn/Tpt/Trb/Tuba/Bass •adr

DUREY, Louis - *Feu la mère de Madame*, op. 49 (1945) (5') •Fl/Ob/ Asx/Bsn/Tpt/Tuba/Perc/2 Vln/Vla/Vcl/Bass •BRF

HASQUENOPH, Pierre - *Inventions* •2 Vln/Vla/Vcl/Bass/Fl/Ob/Cl/ Asx/Bsn/Hn/Tpt •Heu

LEWIS, Arthur - *Pieces of Eight* •Fl/2 Ob/3 Cl/Bsn/2 Tsx/Hn/Baritone Hn/Perc •CAP

MASINI, Fabio - *"Nuvole e colori forti"* (1992) (18') •Fl/1 Sx: S+A/ BsCl/Fl/Ob/Cl/Bsn/2 Vln/Vla/Vcl/Harp

MEIJERING, Chiel - *Het ontblote feit* (1988-90) (8'30) •2 Fl/3 Sx: ATB/2 Hn/Tpt/Trb/Perc/Pno/Electr. Guit •Don

RECK, David - *Number 1 for 12 Performers* (15') •Fl/Cl/Tsx/Hn/Guit/ Vibr/Pno/Bass/Perc •MJQ

ROBBINS, David - *Improvisation* •Fl/2 Cl/Tsx/Bsn/Tpt/Trb/Vln/Vla/ Vcl/Bass/Perc

SPINO, P. - *Prelude of Woodwinds* •2 Fl/Ob (ad lib.)/3 Cl/BsCl/Bsn (ad lib.)/4 Sx: AATB •StMU

TOEPLITZ, Kasper - *Johnny Panic...* (25') •1 Sx: T+CBs/Mezzo Soprano Voice/2 Fl/2 Cl/Hn/2 Vln/2 Vla/ Perc/Tape

13 Musicians

BENHAMOU, Maurice - *Musique pour 13 instruments* •Fl/2 Cl/ Harmonica/Sx/2 Vln/3 Guit/Pno 6 hands (à 6 mains)

EICHMANN, Dietrich - *George...* (1984) (35') •3 Fl/Cl/2 Sx: AT/2 Tpt/Trb/2 Perc/Pno/Bs Guit •adr

FINNISSY, Michael - *First sign a sharp white mons* (1974-67) (45') •2 Fl/2 Cl/Asx/CBsn/Hn/Accordion/Guit/ Vln/2 Vcl/Pno •BMIC

HESPOS, Hans - *Keime und male* (9') •Picc/Fl/2 Cl/Asx/Hn/Guit/Vln/ Vla/Bass/3 Perc •JJ

HUREL, Philippe - *"Pour l'image"* •Fl/Ob/Cl/Asx/Hn/Tpt/Trb/Perc/ 2 Vln/Vla/Vcl/Bass

MERKU, Pavle - *Tiare* •Baritone Voice/Sx/11 wind instruments •Piz

MEULEN, Henk van der - *De profondis I* (1986) (15') •Fl/3 Sx: S+T A A/Hn/3 Tpt/2 Trb/BsTrb/Bass/Pno •Don

SEKON, Joseph - *Lemon Ice* (1972) •Fl/Ob/Cl/2 Sx: ST/Bsn/Tpt/Trb/ 2 Perc/Vln/Vcl/Pno •adr

SPINO, P. - *Statement...* •Hn Solo/2 Fl/Ob/3 Cl/BsCl/Bsn/4 Sx: AATB •StMu

WENDEL, Eugen - *Saphonospir* (15') •Asx/Fl/Cl/Ob/Tpt/Trb/2 Vln/ Vla/Vcl/Bass/2 Perc •adr

14 Musicians

HARBISON, John - *Confinement* (1965) (15'15) •Fl/Ob/EH/Cl/BsCl/ Asx/Tpt/Trb/Vln/Vla/Vcl/Bass/Pno/Perc

HARVEY, Jonathan - *The Valley of Aosta* (1985) (13'30) •Fl/Ob/Ssx/ Tpt/2 Yamaha DX7 Synth/2 Harp/Pno/2 Vln/ Vla/Vcl/Perc •FM

MIEREANU, Costin - *Clair de biche* (1986) (11') •Fl/Picc/Cl/1 Sx: Sno+S+T/Brass Quintet/5 Perc •Sal

ROSSÉ, François - *Paléochrome* (1988) (22') •Vla principal/2 Fl/Cl/ BsCl/1 Sx: S+T/EH/Bsn/Hn/4 Perc/Bass •adr

15 Musicians

LUTYENS, Elisabeth - *Islands*, op. 80 (1971) •2 Narr: ST/Picc/Fl/Cl/ BsCl/Tsx/Hn/Pno/Celesta/Vln/Vla/Vcl/2 Perc

TEMPLE & SHAW - *Vanity Fair Suite* •Fl/Ob/4 Cl/BsCl/Asx/2 Vln/ Vla/Vcl/Bass/Perc/Pno •Mills

oOo

ALLA, Thierry - *La terre et la Comète* (1991) •Fl/Cl/Asx/Pno/Bass/ Synth/Perc/Tape/Children's Choir •adr

BELLEMARE, Gilles - *La chasse-galerie* (1981) •Narr/Choir/2 Fl/2 Recorder/2 Cl/2 Tpt/1 Sx

DHAINE, Jean-Louis - *Fantaisies...* •4 Fl/4 Cl/4 Sx: AATT/2 Tpt/2 Trb

MORRISSON, Julia - *Psalm 29* •Fl/Tsx/Voices •CFE

PEPIN, Clermont - *Pièces de circonstance* (1967) •Childrens chorus/ Fl/Ob/3 Cl/2 Sx/2 Hn •CMC

REBOTIER, J. - *Le Bestiaire marin* •Childrens Choir/4 Fl/4 Sx: SATB •Dur

TELFER, Nancy - *The Golden Cage* (1979) •Mixed Choir/Fl/Cl/Sx/ 3 Perc/Pno

VILLA-LOBOS, Heitor - *Nonetto*, op. 181 (1923) (18') •Fl/Ob/Cl/1 Sx: A+B/Bsn/Perc/Celesta/Harp/Pno/Mixed Chorus •ME

Saxophone and Oboe or English Horn

2 Musicians

BOURDIN, François - *Fugue* (1983) (2') •Asx/Ob

GRANT, Stewart - *Fantasia No. 2* (1982) •Ob d'amore or EH/Ssx •CMC

HENRY, Otto Walker - *New Adventures* (1982) •Ob/Asx/Tape •RKM

Kevre - *Duo* •Asx/EH

QUERAT, Marcel - *Lied et Canonica* (1964) (3') •Fl (or Ob)/Asx •Phi

ROSS, Walter - *Didactic Duos* •Sx/Cl (or Ob) •DP

3 Musicians

Beethoven, Ludwig van - *Grand Trio*, op. 87 •Fl/Ob/Asx •Braun Trio, op. 87 •Fl/Ob/Asx •Bil

Bellini, Vincenzo - *La Somnambule* •Ob (or Cl)/Asx/Pno •Bil

Bentley, Arnold - *16th Century Trios* •Fl (or Ob or Cl)/Ob (or Cl)/Sx •Chap

BEUGNIOT, Jean-Pierre - *Anamorphose* (1976) (11') •Ob/Hn/Bsx •adr

BONNARD, Alain - *Pieces* •Ob/Sx/Vcl •Chou/adr

BOUCHARD, Marcel - *Triade* (1970) (7'30) •Asx/Ob/Cl •Bil

BOUVARD, Jean - *4 Fabliaux* •Ob/Asx/Bsn •adr

BRANT, Henry - *Strength through Joy...* •Ob/Asx/Pno •adr

BUSSEUIL, Patrick - *Trio - Inertie* (1981) •Ob/Asx/Vcl

DUBOIS, Pierre-Max - *Trio* •Ob/Asx/Vcl •adr

EITHLER, Estaban - *Trio* (1945) •Fl/Ob/Asx •BBC

Gattermann, Philippe - *Fantaisie concertante* •Fl (or Ob or Cl)/Asx/Pno •Bil

GASTINEL, Gérard - *8 Pièces en trio* (1981) (8') •Asx/Ob/Vcl

GIRARD, Anthony - *Trio* (1981) •Ob/Asx/Cl •adr

GLASER, Werner Wolf - *Trio* (1981) (14') •Ob/Asx/Vcl •STIM

GUILLAUME, Marie-Louise - *Turquie* •Ob/Cl/Asx

HARRIS, Roger - *Concert Etudes* •Asx/Cl/EH •SeMC

HARTLEY, Walter - *Trio...* (1987) (10'30) •Ssx (or Ob)/Tsx (or Heckelphone)/Pno •DP

HARVEY, Paul - *Trio* •Fl (or Ob)/Cl/Tsx •DP

JOLLET, Jean-Clément - *Amuse-gueules* (1988) (10'30) •Ob/Asx/Vcl •Bil

Kibbe - *Divertimento* •Ob/EH (or Asx)/Bsn •Sha

KOSTECK, Gregory - *Summer Music* •Ob/Cl/Tsx •DP

LANE, Richard - *Trio* (1973) •Ob/Tsx/Cl

LEMAIRE, Félix - *Trio*, op. 106 (1982) •Ob/Sx/Vcl •adr

LEMELAND, Aubert - *Terzetto*, op. 69 (1974) (8') •Ob/Cl/Asx •adr
Terzetto, op. 106 (1982) (10') •Ob/Cl/Asx •Bil

LENNERS, Claude - *Zenit - Fantasia* (1990) •Fl/Ob/Ssx •Lem

LEROUX, Philippe - *Phonice douce* (1991) •Ob/Asx/Vcl •Bil

MACBRIDE, Robert - *Let Down* •Asx/EH (or Ob)/Pno

MALMGREN, Jens - *Trio* (1972) •Fl/Ob/Asx

Massenet, Jules - *Under the Lindens* (LEONARD) •Ob or Cl/1 Sx: A or T/Pno •Pres

MIGNION, René - *Pieces* •Ob/Asx/Vcl

MINAMIKAWA, Mio - *Ondulation* (1981) •Ob/Asx/Vcl •adr

MONTFORT, Robert - *Trio* •Ob/Asx/Pno

Muller, Iwan - *Concertante* •Ob or Cl/Asx/Pno •Bil

PAVLENKO, Serguei - *Dedication* (1989) (17') •Ob/Asx/Vcl

PILLEVESTRE - *Idylle bretonne* •Ob/Sx/Pno

QUERAT, Marcel - *Magie* (1979) (3') •Fl (or Ob)/Cl/Tsx •Bil

ROBERT, Lucie - *Supplications* (1981) (10') •Ob/Asx/Vcl •DP

ROLIN, Etienne - *Jeu de trèfle* (1981) (11') •Ob/Sx/Vcl •adr

RUBBERT, Rainer - *Trio "...le fou"* (1979-88) (11') •Ob/Asx/Vcl •adr

RUDAJEV, Alexandre - *5 Episodes* (1989) •Ob/Asx/Vcl •adr

SABON, Joseph-Pierre - *Pieces* •Ob (or Fl or Cl)/Asx/Pno •Bil

SCIORTINO, Patrice - *3 Signatures* (1978) •Ob/Cl/Asx •adr

SHERMAN, Robert - *Variations* (1961) •Asx/EH/Pno

SMIRNOV, Dimitry - *Sérénade - trio* (1981) •Ob/Sx/Vcl •ECS

STRADOMSKI, Rafal - *Trio* (1989) (9') •Ob (or Ssx)/Asx/Vcl

VAUGHAN WILLIAMS, Ralph - *Household Music* (1940-41) •Diverse combinations •B&H

WEBER, Alain - *Assonances* (1980) •Asx/Ob/Vcl

WESTBROOKE, Simon - *Masque in D* •Ob/Ssx/Pno

WILMAUT, Jean-Marie - *3 Chronautes* •Ob/Cl/Asx

ZONN, Paul Martin - *Nimbus III* (1994) •Asx/Cl/Ob

4 Musicians

Also see Reed Quartet (Voir aussi quatuor d'anches), page 367.

ALBERT, Thomas - *Sound Frames* (1968) (6') •Asx/Ob/Trb/Vibr •MP

ATOR, James - *Haikansona* (1974) (10') •Mezzo Soprano Voice/Ob/Asx/Vcl •SeMC

BLYTON, Carey - *Market* (1964) (30') •Ob/Asx/Harp/Vcl •adr

BONNARD, Alain - *Bis*, op. 42 •Fl/Ob/Cl/Asx •Bil

BOURDIN, François - *Choral en canon* •Ob/Asx (or Tsx)/Vcl/Bass

EMMER, Huib - *Koud zoud* (1984) (5') •Ob/Asx/Trb/Bass •Don

ENGELMANN, Hans - *Permutagioni* •Fl/Ob/Sx/Bsn •A&S

ERB, Donald - *Quartet* (1962) (7') •Fl/Ob/Asx/Bass •CMC

GREEN, Stuart - *Pipedreams* (1978) (7') •Fl/Asx/Ob/BsCl

HARTLEY, Walter - *Quartet 1993* (1993) (8'15) •Asx/Ob/Hn/Bsn •DP

Haydn, Franz Joseph - *Adagio* (GEIGER) •Fl/Ob/Asx/Bsn •CF
Pieces (SPEETS) •2 Sx: AT/Fl/Cl (or Ob) •TM/HE

HEUSSENSTAMM, George - *Four Miniatures*, op. 57 (1975) (9') •Tsx/Fl/Ob/Vln •DP

LAMB, Marvin - *Serenade for Unknown...* •Tsx/Ob/Cl/Pno •DP

MAEGAARD, Jan - *Musica riservata II* (1976) •Ob/Cl/Sx/Bsn

MAGANINI, Quinto - *Rêverie* (HARRIS) •Fl or Cl/Ob or Cl/Asx/Bsn or BsCl •CF

SCHUMANN, Gerrhard - *Petite suite* •Fl/Sx/EH/Cl •IMD

STRAESSER, Joep - *Intersections V* (1977) (12') •Ob/Cl/Asx/Bsn •Don

STROUD, Richard - *Capriccio* •Fl/Ob/Asx/BsCl •SeMC

THILMAN, J. - *Das kleine Requiem*, op. 27 (1969) •EH/Asx/Vla/Pno •Bar

WILMAUT, Jean-Marie - *La complainte...* •Narr/Ob/Cl/Asx

ZLATIC, Slmavko - *Balum* (1936) •Ob/EH/Asx/Bsn •UKH

5 Musicians

AMBROSINI, Claudio - *Trobar clar* (1982) •Fl/Ob/Cl/Tpt/1 Sx: S+A

ASCOUGH, R. - *Quintet* •Ssx/Fl/Ob/Cl/Bsn

ATOR, James - *Life Cycle* (1973) (18') •Mezzo Soprano Voice/Asx/Ob/Perc/Vcl •SeMC

AYSCUE, Brian - *Permutations I* (1972) (6'30) •Fl/Ob/Cl/Tpt/Tsx •adr

BARGSTEM, Joey - *Quintet for Winds* •Ob/Cl/Asx/Trb/Bsn •DP

BIRTWISTLE, Harrison - *Dinah & Nick's Love Song* (1972) (5') •3 Sx: SSS/EH/Harp •Uni

BROTONS, Soler - *Quinteto* (1978) •Fl/Ob/Asx/Hn/Bsn •EMEC

BUEL, Charles - *Chimera, Avatars and Beyond* (1972) (15-20') •Fl/Ob/2 Sx: AT/Perc •adr

BUMCKE, Gustav - *Quintet*, op. 23b •Cl/EH/Wald Horn/Bsn/Bsx

CARPENTER, Gary - *Dances for Mutilated Toys* (1970) (15') •Fl/Ob/Cl/Asx/Bsn •BMIC

CHANDLER, Erwin - *Concert Music* •Asx/Ob/2 Hn/Pno

CUNNINGHAM, Michael - *Miro Gallery* •Fl/Ob/Cl/Asx/Bsn •SeMC

DEFOSSEZ, René - *Mélopée et Danse* •Asx/Pno or Fl/Ob/Cl/Asx/Bsn •An

DESPORTES, Yvonne - *Sonate pour un baptême* (1959) (18') •Fl/Asx/Soprano Voice (or EH)/Perc/Pno •Bil

FERRITO - *Concertino* •Asx/Ob/2 Perc/Bass •DP

FLOTHUIS, Marius - *Kleine Suite* (1952) •Ob/Cl/Ssx/Tpt/Pno •Don

GASTINEL, Gérard - *Quintette* (1977) •Ssx/Ob/Cl/Hn/Bsn

GHEZZO, Dinu - *Sound shapes* •Fl/Ob/Cl/Sx/Bsn •SeMC

HARTLEY, Walter - *Suite for 5 Winds* (1951) (7') •Fl/Ob/Cl/Asx/Trb •Wi&Jo

ISTVAN, Miloslav - *Concertino...* (1982) (13') •Ob/Cl+Asx/BsCl Perc/Pno

JANSEN, Guus - *Juist daarom* (1981) (7') •Ob/Cl/Ssx/Vcl/Pno •Don

JONES, Robert - *Divertimento* •Fl/Ob/Cl/Asx/Hn •WWS

KRIEGER, Edino - *Melopéia* (1949) •Soprano Voice/Ob/Tsx/Trb/Vla

Laube, P. - *Alsacian Dance* •Fl/Ob/Asx/Bsn (or Hn)/Pno •CF

LOEFFLER, Charles-Martin - *Ballade carnavalesque* (1904) •Fl/Ob/Asx/Bsn/Pno •South

MALHERBE, Claudy - *Non-sun* (1984-85) (10') •Picc/Tsx/Ob/Cl/Bsn

MARIN, Amadeo - *Quintet* •Fl/Ob/Tsx/Vcl/Trb
MEIJERING, Chiel - *Meine Lippen die...* (1984) (10') •Fl/Ob/Asx/
Pno/Perc •Don
MERSSON, Boris - *Sound for seven*, op. 24 (12') •Ob Solo/Jazz Sx
Quartet •adr
MULDOWNEY, Dominic - *Love Music for Bathsheba...* (1974) (20')
•Fl/Ob/Cl/Asx/Hn (or Trb) •Nov
NIELSON, Lewis - *Dialectical Fantasy* (1981) •Fl/Ob/Cl/Tsx/Hn
•ACA
NILSSON, Anders - *Cadenze* (1992) •Fl/Ob/Cl/Bsn/Sx
OLBRISCH, Franz-Martin - *Quintett* (1989) •Ob+EH/2 Sx: AT/Hn/
Perc •adr
OLIVER, John - *Métalmorphose* (1983) •Ob/Cl/Bsn/Sx/Tpt •CMC
OSTERC, Slavko - *Ave Maria* (1930) •Soprano Voice/Vla/Ob/Cl/Sx
PILLEVESTRE - *Nocturne* •Fl/Ob/Cl/2 Sx: AB
READE, Paul - *Quintet* (1976) •Fl/Ob/Asx/Hn/Bsn •adr
REVUELTAS, Silvestre - *First Little Serious Piece* (2'45) •Picc/Ob/
Cl/Tpt/Bsx •MM/PIC/Peer
Second Little Serious Piece (1'15) •Picc/Ob/Cl/Tpt/Bsx •PIC/Peer
SAGVIK, Stellan - *4 Miniatyrer ur baletten Eulidyke*, op. 92 (1978)
(4'30) •Fl/Ob/Cl/2 Sx: AT •STIM
SCHAFFER, Boguslaw - *Proietto simultaneo* (1983) (12') •Soprano
Voice/Vln/Pno/Ob/Sx/Tape
SODERO, Cesare - *Pieces* (1933) •Fl/Ob/Cl/Tsx/Bsn •AMPC
SPRONGL, Norbert - *Quintet*, op. 124 (1958) •Ob/Asx/Tpt/Hn/Bsn
•adr
TARLOW, Karen - *Music...* (1973) (12') •Fl/Ob/Cl/Asx/Hn •SeMC
TREMBLAY, George - *Piece* •Fl/Ob/Cl/Tsx/BsCl
VOGEL, Wladimir - *La Ticinella...* (1941) •Fl/Ob/Cl/Asx/Bsn •SZ
YOUNG, Lynden de - *Chamber Music* (1972) •Asx/Bsn/Ob/Pno/Vibr
•SeMC

6 Musicians

Also see Wind Sextet (Voir aussi sextuor à vent),
page 368.

AMELLER, André - *Azuleros de Valencia* (1965) (13') •Fl/Ob/Cl/
Asx/Hn/Bsn
BACHOREK, Milan - *Inspirace* (1983) (12') •Ob/Asx/Cl+BsCl/Perc/
Pno/Electr. Guit •CHF
BARCE, Ramon - *Obertura fonética* (1968) (8'50) •Fl/Ob/Cl/Asx/
Tpt/Trb •EMEC
BERG, Paul - *To Teach His Own* (1984) (12') •Fl/Ob/Tsx/Trb/Vln/
Vcl/Tape •Don
BRANDON, Seymour - *Chaconne and Variations* •Ob/Asx/2 Hn/Trb/
Pno •MaPu
BRIGHT, Greg - *Music...* (10') •6 Woodwinds instruments •EMIC
BUMCKE, Gustav - *Sextet*, op. 19 (1903) •Cl/EH/Wald Horn/BsCl/
Sx/Bsn •Diem
Sextuor, op. 20 en Lab •2 Sx: AA/EH/Hn/BsCl/Bsn •VAB
GOTSKOSIK, Oleg - *Svit...* (1986) •Ob/Asx/Bsn/2 Vln/Pno •SMIC
HAMBRAEUS, Bengt - *Kammarmusik for 6*, op. 28 (1950) (8') •Fl/
Ob/Cl/Asx/Vla/Harp •STIM/Ehr
LUROT, Jacques - *Sextuor* •Ob/Cl/Asx/Bsn/2 Voices: SA
NILSSON, Ivo - *Per-cept* (1989-91) •Fl/Ob+EH/1 Sx: S+A/Trb/Pno/
Vln+Vla •SMIC
OLIVEIRA, Willy Corrêa de - *Sugestoes* (1971) •Ob/Asx/Bandoneon/
Tuba/Bass/Perc
PENTLAND, Barbara - *Variable Winds* (1979) (5') •Fl (or Ob)/Asx/
3 Tom-toms/Bongos •CMC
ROKEACH, Martin - *Tango* •Ob/Cl/Asx/Hn/Trb/Vcl •DP
VILLA-LOBOS, Heitor - *Sexteto mistico*, op. 123 (1917) (9') •Fl/Ob/
Asx/Guit/Celesta/Harp •ME

7 Musicians

ARGERSINGER, Charles - *Drastic Measures* •Fl/Ob/Cl/Asx/Bsn/
Hn/Perc
BERNARD, Jacques - *L'Opéra de l'espace* (1970) •Narr/Ob/Cl/BsCl/
1 Sx: S+A+B/Bsn/Perc •adr
CANTON, Edgardo - *Phares et balises* •Fl/Ob/Sx/BsCl/Hn/Tpt/Trb
EYCHENNE, Marc - *Petite suite* •Ob/Ssx/5 Hn •adr
JENNEFELT, Thomas - *Stones* (1981) •Ob/Cl/Asx/Tpt/Guit/2 Perc
KOECHLIN, Charles - *Septuor*, op. 165 (1937) (11'30) •Fl/Ob/EH/
Cl/Asx/Hn/Bsn •Oil
NILSSON, Bo - *Zeiten im Umlauf*, op. 14 (1957) (3') •Fl/Ob/EH/Cl/
BsCl/Tsx/Bsn •Uni
PINOS-SIMANDL, Aloïs - *Euforie* (1983) (10') •Ob (or Fl)/Asx/Cl/
BsCl/Pno/Perc/Bass •CHF
ROSSÉ, François - *OEM* (1988) (21') •Soprano Voice/1 Sx: S+Bs/
EH/Accordion/Bass/Jazz Guit/Pno/Disposi-
tif électro-acoust. •adr
WILLIS, Richard - *Irregular Resolutions* •Fl/Ob/Cl/Asx/Bsn/Hn/
Perc •adr
ZEMP, Joseph - *Souffle printanier* •Fl/Ob/Cl/4 Sx: SATB •adr

8 Musicians

BUMCKE, Gustav - *Suite G Dur*, op. 24 •Tenor Voice/Fl/Ob/Cl/Bsn/
Hn/Bsx/Harp •VAB
CHAGRIN, Francis - *Sarabande* (1951) (6') •Ob/Hn/Vln/Asx/Str
Quartet •ALC
DECOUST, Michel - *Ombres portées* (1986) (9') •2 Ob/Cl/2 Asx/
Harp/Pno/Perc •Sal
DELAMARRE, Pierre - *La 8* (1981) (3') •Fl/Ob/Cl/Asx/Pno 4 hands
[à 4 mains]/Bass/Perc •adr
DEL PRINCIPE, Joseph - *Lyric Pieces for Octet* •Fl/Ob/Sx+Cl/BsCl/
Tpt/Hn/Trb/Tuba •SeMC
FRANCO, Clare - *Four Winds...* •Asx/Harp/Vibr/Fl/Ob/Hn/Bsn
GUY, Georges - *Concerto en forme de jazz* •Asx Solo/Pno Solo/Fl/Ob/
Cl/Hn/Bsn/Bass
HEKSTER, Walter - *Of mere being* (1982) (12') •Asx/Fl/Ob/Cl/2 Tpt/
Perc/Electr. Guit •Don
KORTE, Karl - *Matrix* (1968) (16') •Fl/Ob/Cl/Asx/Hn/Bsn/Pno/Perc
•GSch
LASNE, George - *Ballade française* (1971) •Fl/Ob/2 Cl/Asx/2 Tpt/
Trb
NILSSON, Bo - *Frequenzen* (1957) •Fl/Picc/Ob/EH/Cl/BsCl/Tsx/
Bsn •Uni
NILSSON, Ivo - *Agnosi* (1988) (9') •Ob/Asx/Tpt/Harp/2 Vln/Vla/Vcl
•STIM
RIEDEL, Georg - *Reflexioner* (1974) (8') •Woodwind Quintet/Jazz
group (Cl+Asx/Pno/Bass) •SMIC
SAGVIK, Stellan - *Guenilles des jongleurs*, op. 74 (1977) (7'30) •Fl/
Ob/3 Cl/Asx/Bsn/Cnt •STIM
VILLA-LOBOS, Heitor - *Chôros n° 7* (1924) (10') •Fl/Ob/Cl/Asx/
Bsn/Vln/Vcl/Tam-tam •ME
WOOLLETT, Henri - *Octuor n° 1* (1911) •Ob/Cl/Asx/2 Vln/Vla/Vcl/
Bass •South

9 Musicians

ALLGEN, Claude - *Adagio och Fuga* (25') •Fl/Ob/EH/Cl/BsCl/2 Sx:
AB/Bsn/Hn •STIM
BORTOLOTTI, Mauro - *Studio per E.E. Cummings n° 2* (1964) •Vla/
Vcl/Bass/Ob/Cl/BsCl/Sx/Hn/Perc •adr
BUMCKE, Gustav - *"Der Spaziergang"*, op. 22 •Fl/Ob/EH/Cl/Bsn/
Hn/BsTrb/Bsx/Harp
CAPLET, André - *Impressions d'Automne* (1905) (3') •Asx/Ob/2 Cl/
Bsn/Harp/Org/2 Vcl
Légende (1903) (13') •Asx/Ob/Cl/Bsn/2 Vln/Vla/Vcl/Bass •Fuz

CLARK, Thomas - *Dreamscape* •Fl/Ob/Cl/Sx/Tpt/Trb/Pno/Perc/ Bass •SeMC

COLE, Helen - *Serenade* •Fl/Ob/2 Cl/BsCl/Hn/Asx/2 Bsn

COX, Rona - *Two Expressions* (1968) •Fl/Ob/Cl/2 Sx: SB/Hn/Bsn/ Bass/Perc •adr

DIEMENTE, Edward - *For Lady Day* •Fl/Ob/Cl/Tpt/Trb/Vln/Vla/Sx/ Bsn/Tape •SeMC

GRANDERT, Johnny - *86 T* •Fl/EH/BsCl/Bsx/CBsn/2 Tpt/Perc/Pno •STIM

MARCO, Tomàs - *Anna Blume* (1967) •2 Narr/Fl/Ob/Cl/Sx/Tpt/2 Perc

NATANSON, Tadeus - *3 Pictures for 7 Instruments* (1960) •Ob/Cl/ Asx/Trb/Vcl/Tpt/Bsn/Pno/Perc •AMP

RENOSTO, Paolo - *Dissolution* •Vla/Vcl/Bass/Ob/Cl/BsCl/Sx/Hn/ Perc

SCELSI, Jacinto - *Kya* (1959) (11') •Cl (or Ssx)/EH/Hn/BsCl/Tpt/ Trb/Vla/Vcl/Bass •Sal

SILVERMAN, Faye - *Shadings* (1978) •Vln/Vla/Bass/Fl/Ob/Asx/ Bsn/Hn/Tuba

TANENBAUM, Elias - *Trios I, II, III* •Fl/Ob/Cl/Vln/Vla/Vcl/Bass/ Asx/Perc •ACA

WILDER, Alec - *Suite* •Bsx/Fl/Ob/Cl/2 Hn/Bsn/Bass/Drums

YOSHIBA, Susumu - *Erka* •Fl/Ob/Sx/Tpt/Trb/Perc/Vcl/Guit/Pno

ULRICH, Jürgen - *Spiel* (1974) (5') •Fl/Ob/Cl/Bsn/Sx/Hn/Tpt/Trb/ Tuba •VDMK

10 Musicians

BRANT, Henry - *Dialogue in the Jungle* (1964) (15') •Tenor Voice/ Fl/Ob/Cl/Bsx/2 Tpt/Trb/Hn/Tuba •adr

BUMCKE, Gustav - *Präludium und Fuge*, op. 20 (1903) •Fl/Ob/EH/ Sx/Cl/BsCl/2 Bsn/2 Hn

COLE, Hugo - *Serenade...* (1965) (15') •2 Fl/Ob/2 Cl/Asx/2 Bsn/2 Hn

CUNNINGHAM, Michael - *Linear Ceremony* •2 Fl/2 Ob/2 Cl/Sx/Hn/ 2 Bsn •SeMC

GOODMAN, Alfred - *3 Gesänge für Gresang* •Soprano Voice/Fl/Ob/ Asx/Cl/Vla/Vcl/Prepared Pno/Guit/Perc •adr

GOUGEON, Denis - *Heureux qui comme...* (1987) •Soprano Voice/ Picc/EH/Bsx/2 Vln/Vla/Vcl/Bass/Perc •CMC

GRAHN, Ulf - *Soundscape II* (1974) (7') •Fl/Cl/EH/Asx/2 Trb/2 Vln/ Vcl/Bass •SMIC

HARTLEY, Walter - *Double Concerto* (1969) (7'30) •Asx/Tuba/ Wind Octet (Fl/Ob/Cl/Bsn/Hn/2 Tpt/Trb) •PhiCo

LINDBERG, Nils - *Progression* (1985) (28') •Fl/Ob/Cl/Hn/Bsn/2 Sx: SA/Pno/Bass/Drums •SMIC

MASON, Benedict - *Coulour and information* (1993) •Fl/Ob/Sx/Bsn/ Hn/Tpt/Trb/Tuba/Perc/Electr. Bass

MIMET, Anne-Marie - *Fanfare et divertissement* •Fl/Ob/Cl/Bsn/3 Sx: SAT/Tpt/Trb/Tuba

NILSSON, Bo - *Zeitpunkte* (1960) (5') •Fl/Alto Fl/Ob/EH/Cl/BsCl/2 Sx: AT/Bsn/CBsn

PAUMGARTNER, Bernhard - *Divertimento* •Picc/EH/Asx/Bsn/Hn/ Tpt/Pno/Vla/Vcl/Perc •Uni

SCHAFFER, Boguslaw - *Permutations n° 27* (1956) •Fl/Ob/Cl/Sx/ Tpt/Trb/Vla/Perc/Harp/Pno •A&S

TREMBLAY, George - *Epithalamium* (1962) •Fl/Ob/Cl/Sx/Bsn/Hn/ Tpt/Trb/Tuba/Perc •CFE

WILDER, Alec - *She'll Be Seven in May* •Fl/Ob/Asx/2 Cl/BsCl/Bsn/ Bass/Drums/Pno

11 Musicians

ANDRIESSEN, Jurriaan - *Hommage à Milhaud* (1945) (8') •Fl/Ob/ Cl/Bsn/Hn/Tpt/Trb/Asx/Vln/Vla/Vcl •Don

HESPOS, Hans - *Break* •Ob/3 Tpt/2 Sx: TB/Vcl/Bass/Trb/Pno/Perc •EMod

KEULEN, Geert van - *Onkruid* (1981) (5') •Ob/Cl/2 Sx: AT/Bsn/Hn/ Tpt/Trb/Vln/Vla/Pno •Don

MONDELLO, Nuncio - *Suite* (1956) •Asx/2 Fl/Ob/Cl/Bsn/2 Hn/Tpt/ Trb/Perc •adr

SPINO, P. - *Prelude of Woodwinds* •2 Fl/Ob (ad lib.)/3 Cl/BsCl/Bsn (ad lib.)/4 Sx: AATB •StMU

ZONN, Paul Martin - *Voyage of Columbus* (1974) (13') •Tpt Solo/Fl/ Ob/Ssx/Hrn/Trb/2 Perc/Pno/Vln/Bass •ACA

12 Musicians

CECCONI, Monique - *Hommage à...* •Ob/Cl/Asx/Bsn/4 Vln/2 Vla/2 Vcl •Phi

CURTIS-SMITH, Curtis - *Sundry Dances* (1981) •Fl/Ob/Cl/3 Sx: SAB/Bsn/CBsn/Tpt/Trb/Tuba/Bass •adr

DUREY, Louis - *Feu la mère de Madame*, op. 49 (1945) (5') •Fl/Ob/ Asx/Bsn/Tpt/Tuba/Perc/2 Vln/Vla/Vcl/Bass •BRF

HASQUENOPH, Pierre - *Inventions* •2 Vln/Vla/Vcl/Bass/Fl/Ob/Cl/ Asx/Bsn/Hn/Tpt •Heu

JAEGGI, Oswald - *Dum Clamarem* (1961) •Ob/EH/Cl/3 Sx/3 Tpt/3 Trb

LEWIS, Arthur - *Pieces of Eight* •Fl/2 Ob/3 Cl/Bsn/2 Tsx/Hn/Baritone Hn/Perc •CAP

MASINI, Fabio - *"Nuvole e colori forti"* (1992) (18') •Fl/1 Sx: S+A/ BsCl/Fl/Ob/Cl/Bsn/2 Vln/Vla/Vcl/Harp

SPINO, P. - *Prelude of Woodwinds* •2 Fl/Ob (ad lib.)/3 Cl/BsCl/Bsn (ad lib.)/4 Sx: AATB •StMU

13 Musicians

FINNISSY, Michael - *Babylon* (1971) (19') •Mezzo Soprano Voice/ Ob/Cl/Asx/Bsn/Guit/Harp/Pno/2 Perc/2 Vcl/ Bass •Uni

HUREL, Philippe - *"Pour l'image"* •Fl/Ob/Cl/Asx/Hn/Tpt/Trb/Perc/ 2 Vln/Vla/Vcl/Bass

SEKON, Joseph - *Lemon Ice* (1972) •Fl/Ob/Cl/2 Sx: ST/Bsn/Tpt/Trb/ 2 Perc/Vln/Vcl/Pno •adr

SPINO, P. - *Statement...* •Hn Solo/2 Fl/Ob/3 Cl/BsCl/Bsn/4 Sx: AATB •StMu

WENDEL, Eugen - *Saphonospir* (15') •Asx/Fl/Cl/Ob/Tpt/Trb/2 Vln/ Vla/Vcl/Bass/2 Perc •adr

14 Musicians

HARBISON, John - *Confinement* (1965) (15'15) •Fl/Ob/EH/Cl/BsCl/ Asx/Tpt/Trb/Vln/Vla/Vcl/Bass/Pno/Perc

HARVEY, Jonathan - *The Valley of Aosta* (1985) (13'30) •Fl/Ob/Ssx/ Tpt/2 Yamaha DX7 Synth/2 Harp/Pno/2 Vln/ Vla/Vcl/Perc •FM

MIEREANU, Costin - *Clair de biche* (1986) (11') •Fl/Picc/Cl/1 Sx: Sno+S+T/Brass Quintet/5 Perc •Sal

ROSSÉ, François - *Paléochrome* (1988) (22') •Vla principal/2 Fl/Cl/ BsCl/1 Sx: S+T/EH/Bsn/Hn/4 Perc/Bass •adr

15 Musicians

TEMPLE & SHAW - *Vanity Fair Suite* •Fl/Ob/4 Cl/BsCl/Asx/2 Vln/ Vla/Vcl/Bass/Perc/Pno •Mills

oOo

ANSIND, Caroline - *Het water...* (1986) (14'30) •Ob/Cl/2 Sx: AB/2 Trb/Perc/Pno/Choir •Don

PEPIN, Clermont - *Pièces de circonstance* (1967) •Childrens chorus/ Fl/Ob/3 Cl/2 Sx/2 Hn •CMC

VILLA-LOBOS, Heitor - *Nonetto*, op. 181 (1923) (18') •Fl/Ob/Cl/1 Sx: A+B/Bsn/Perc/Celesta/Harp/Pno/Mixed Chorus •ME

Saxophone and Clarinet

2 Musicians

ARCHER, Violet - *Moods* (10') •Cl/Asx •CMC
Bizet, Georges - *Prélude (8 Scènes bohémiennes)* •Asx/Cl •Mol
BOUSSAGOL, Emile - *Duo* •Cl/Asx
DELBECQ, Laurent - *Dans la montagne* •2 Bb Sx or Cl/Bb Sx •Mol
DI BETTA, Philippe - *Echantillons...* (1993) (9'30) •Cl/Asx •adr
Dobrzynski, Ignacy - *Duo* •Asx/Cl •WWS
EYSER, Eberhard - *Watermusic - Submarine* (1979-84) •1 Sx: A+T/ Cl+BsCl/Tape •STIM
FREEDMAN, Harry - *3 for 2* (1980) •Cl/1 Sx: S+A •CMC
GINER, C. - *Conversaciones* •Cl/Asx •Piles
HEIM, Norman - Essays, op. 82 (1984) (8') •Cl/Asx •Nor
INKYUNG, Inkyung - *Spiel auf E.* (1993) •Asx/Cl •INM
KAWAMOTO, Itaru - *Nayuta* (1993) •Asx/Cl •INM
KLERK, Joseph de - *Intrada* •2 Sx or Bb Sx/Cl •Mol
KOSUGI, Takehisa - *Mano-dharma...* •Cl/Asx/Tape
KYNASTON, Trent - *Sonata Duet* •Cl/Asx •WIM
LEMELAND, Aubert - *5 Portraits*, op. 49 (1977) (7') •Cl/Asx •Bil
MARTELLI, Henri - *Cinq Duos* (1979) (8'30) •Cl/Sx •Bil
PILLEVESTRE - *Duos* •2 Sx or Cl/Sx
PORRET, Julien - *8e Duo de concours* •Cl/Sx •Mol
QUATE, Amy - *Talking Pictures* (1984) (15') •Cl/Ssx
ROSS, Walter - *Didactic Duos* •Sx/Cl (or Ob) •DP
SYDEMAN, William - *Duo* (1977) •Cl/Tsx •SeMC
VALK, Adriaan - *4 Miniatures* (1988) •Cl/Asx/Voice ad lib. •TM
VLAHOPOULOS, Sotireos - *Petite Partita* (1984) •Cl/Asx
WINKLER, Wolfgang - *Dankeschön* (1992) •Asx/Cl •INM

3 Musicians

ANDERSON, Thomas - *Intermezzi* (1983) •Cl/Asx/Pno •B&B
Beethoven, Ludwig van - *Excepts from Rondo* •Cl/Asx/Bsn •CF
  Trios •2 Cl/Asx •Braun/Mol
Bellini, Vincenzo - *La Somnambule* •Ob (or Cl)/Asx/Pno •Bil
Bentley, Arnold - *16th Century Trios* •Fl (or Ob or Cl)/Ob (or Cl)/Sx •Chap
BERGERON, Thomas - *Magical Dances* •Cl/Sx/Pno
BERTHELEMY, Norbert - *Rondo pour rire* (2') •2 Cl/Tsx •Bil
BLIN, Lucien - *Grupettino* •Cl/2 Sx: AT •GD
BOND, Victoria - *Ménage à trois* •Fl/Asx/Cl •SeMC
Borodin, Alexandre - *Introduction* (AREND) •Cl/Asx/Pno •Mol
BOUCHARD, Marcel - *Triade* (1970) (7'30) •Asx/Ob/Cl •Bil
BOUCHARD, Marcel - *Triade* (1970) (7'30) •Asx/Ob/Cl •Bil
Bruch, Max - *Three Pieces*, op. 8 (GEE) •Cl/Sx/Pno •DP
CAVANA, Bernard - *Mariage* (1984) •1 Sx: Sno+S+T+Bs+CBs/Cl/ Pno/Voices
CHALLULAU, Tristan - *Sur quelque étoile morte...* •Fl/Asx/Cl
CHILDS, Barney - *The World from...* (1979) •Cl/Asx/Pno •CFE
CUNNINGHAM, Michael - *Serenade*, op. 13a (1961) (7') •Cl/Asx/ Bsn •SeMC
DEPELSENAIRE, Jean-Marie - *Trio surprise* (1975) (4') •Cl/Asx/ Tpt •Phi/Com
Devienne, François - *Trio* •2 Cl/Tsx or 3 Sx: TTB •Mol
DI BETTA, Philippe - *Vents pluvieux* (1992) (6') •Fl/Cl/Asx •Fuz
DUPRÉ, René - *Trio en canon* •Cl/Asx/Tpt •adr
ENGELMANN, Hans - *Inter-lineas*, op. 50b (1985) •Cl/Sx/Perc •Br&Ha
ESCAICH, Thierry - *3 Intermezzi* (1994) •Fl/Cl/Sx •Bil

EYSER, Eberhard - *Salinas nocturnas* (1979) (11') •Ssx/Cl/Vcl (or Bsn) •STIM
Fabre, C. - *Pieces* (HARRIS) •Cl/Sx/Pno or 2 Sx: AA/Pno •CF
FRANCIS, Mark - *Divertimento* •Cl/Asx/Perc
FURRER, Beat - *Trio* (1985) •Fl/Cl/Asx (or Ob) •Uni
Gattermann, Philippe - *Fantaisie concertante* •Fl (or Ob or Cl)/Asx/ Pno •Bil
GIRARD, Anthony - *Trio* (1981) •Ob/Asx/Cl •adr
GUILLAUME, Marie-Louise - *Turquie* •Ob/Cl/Asx
HARRIS, Roger - *Concert Etudes* •Asx/Cl/EH •SeMC
HARVEY, Paul - *Trio* •Fl (or Ob)/Cl/Tsx •DP
Haydn, Franz Joseph - *Oxen Minuet* •Fl (or Cl)/Asx/Pno •CF
JOHANSON, Sven - *Caccia* (1968) •Fl/Cl/Tsx •STIM
KALLSTENIUS, Edvin - *Lyrische Suite*, op. 55 (1960-62) (18') •Fl/ Asx/Cl •STIM
KLOSE, Hyacinthe - *Duettino concertante* (1876) •Cl/AsxPno •Led
  La Somnambule •Cl/Asx/Pno •Bil
KOSTECK, Gregory - *Summer Music* •Ob/Cl/Tsx •DP
LANE, Richard - *Trio* (1973) •Ob/Tsx/Cl
LEMELAND, Aubert - *Divertissement no. 1* (9') •Fl/Asx/Cl •Bil
  Divertissement no. 2 (10') •Fl/Asx/Cl •Bil
  Terzetto, op. 69 (1974) (8') •Ob/Cl/Asx •adr
  Terzetto, op. 106 (1982) (10') •Ob/Cl/Asx •Bil
  Trio, op. 98 (1979) (8') •Cl/Ssx/Hn •adr
LIMA, Candido - *Cantica II* (1987) •Cl/Sx/Perc
LUSTGARTEN, Dan - *Variations sur la parole* (1983) •2 Cl/Asx
MADDOX, Arthur - *Tanguitos de los Osos* •Cl/Sx/Pno
Massenet, Jules - *Under the Lindens* (LEONARD) •Ob or Cl/1 Sx: A or T/Pno •Pres
MENSING, Eberhard - *Tennis ist toll* (1978) (44') •Cl/Sx/Perc •adr
MORITZ, Edvard - *Divertimento* (1952) •2 Cl/Sx or 2 Sx/Cl or 3 Sx •Merc
Mozart, Wolfgang - *Sonatine* (SCHEIFES) •2 Cl/Bsx •Mol
Muller, Iwan - *Concertante* •Ob or Cl/Asx/Pno •Bil
PAZ, Juan Carlos - *Trio*, op. 36, no. 2 (1938) (16') •Cl/Sx/Tpt •GSch
PILLEVESTRE - *Faune et Bacchante* (1896) •Sx/Cl/Pno
PORRET, Julien - *Pieces* •Cl/Asx/Pno •Mol
QUERAT, Marcel - *Magie* (1979) (3') •Fl (or Ob)/Cl/Tsx •Bil
RÜDINGER, Gottfried - *Divertimento*, op. 75 •Vla (or Cl)/Tsx/Pno •BAUS
RUELLE, Fernand - *Romance* •Ssx/2 Cl •Mus
SABON, Joseph-Pierre - *Les Pibrochs...* •Ssx/Cl (or Ob)/Pno •Mil
  Pieces •Ob (or Fl or Cl)/Asx/Pno •Bil
SAMYN, Noël - *5 Trios* (1976) •2 Cl/Asx •Bil
SCIORTINO, Patrice - *3 Signatures* (1978) •Ob/Cl/Asx •adr
SMITH, Claude T. - *Suite* (1988) •Fl/Cl/Asx
STEIN, Leon - *Trio* (1969) (20') •Cl/Asx/Pno •DP
  Trio Concertante (1961) (16') •Asx/Cl (or Vln)/Pno •CFE/ACA
VALK, Adriaan - *4 Miniatures* (1988) •Cl/Asx/Voice ad lib. •TM
VAUGHAN WILLIAMS, Ralph - *Household Music* (1940-41) •Di- verse combinations •B&H
Vogt, Gustave - *Adagio religioso* •2 Cl/Asx •Bil
WILEY, Frank - *Ritual Music* •Cl/Asx/Perc
WILMAUT, Jean-Marie - *3 Chronautes* •Ob/Cl/Asx
ZONN, Paul Martin - *Nimbus III* (1994) •Asx/Cl/Ob

4 Musicians

Also see Reed Quartet (Voir aussi quatuor d'anches), page 367

ALSINA - *Rendez-vous* •Cl/Asx/Trb/Perc •Led
ADDERLEY, Mark - *Waver* (1986) •Fl/Cl/Tsx/Vln •NMI
Aspelmayer, Franz (1728-1786) - *Quatuor concertant* (CORROYER) •2 Cl/2 Sx: TB •Buff

ATOR, James Donald - *Woodwind Quartet* (1969) (11') •Fl/Cl/Sx/Bsn •SeMC

Bach, J. S. - *Air* (HEKKER) •3 Sx: ATB/Cl or 3 Cl/Bsx •WaB

Bagley - *Thistledown* (HARRIS) •2 Cl/Asx/Bsn •CF

BARBAUD, Pierre - *Arthémise...* (6'30) •Cl/Bsn/2 Sx •EFM

BOESWILLWALD, Pierre - *La vie des Saints...* (1989) (45') •2 Sx: AT/Cl/Tape/Comédienne

BOEUF, Georges - *Em Misma...* (1971) (10') •Vln/Fl/Cl/Asx •adr

BONNARD, Alain - *Bis*, op. 42 •Fl/Ob/Cl/Asx •Bil

BRIZZI, Aldo - *D'après une esquisse* (1987) (8') •1 Sx: A+S/Vln/Cl/Pno

CALLHOFF, Herbert - *Facetten* (1986) •Asx/BsCl/Cl/Perc •adr

Clementi, Muzio - *Canon* (EVERTSE) 2 Cl/2 Sx: AB •Lis/TM

COLIN, Jean-Marie - *L'homme cage* (1976) •Soprano Voice/2 Cl/Sx

Corelli, Arcangelo - *Gigue* (HARRIS) •2 Cl/Asx/Bsn (or BsCl) •CF

Cui, César - *Orientale* (HARRIS) •2 Cl/Asx/Bsn (or BsCl) •CF

DAILEY, Dwight - *Reflections in Gold...* (1982) •Sx/Fl/Cl/Pno

Denza, Luigi - Funiculi-Funicula (HARRIS) •2 Cl/Asx/Bsn (or BsCl) •CF

DEPELSENAIRE, Jean-Marie - *Petit concert à quatre* (1973) (2') •Fl/Tpt/Asx/Cl •Phi/Com

Dewit, A. - *Pieces* (HARRIS) •2 Cl/Asx/Bsn (or BsCl) •CF

DIJK, Jan van - *Concertino* •Vln/Fl/Cl/Asx •Don

Di Lasso, O. - *Matona...* (CHEYETTE) •2 Cl/Asx/Bsn (or Bsx) •Ken

DUBOIS, Pierre-Max - *Dessins animés* (1978) (16') •2 Sx: SA/Cl/BsCl •FroMu

EKSTRÖM, Lars - *Vargtimen* (1990) •Cl/Asx/Vln/Pno •STIM

EYSER, Eberhard - *Edictus to the...* (1985) •Fl/Ssx/Cl/BsCl •STIM

FUSTÉ-LAMBEZAT, Michel - *Polyphonies* (1975) (15') •Cl/Asx/Vla/Vcl •SeMC

GERMETEN, Gunnar - *Applaus* (1985) •Cl/Sx/Trb/Accordion

GERSCHEFSKI, Edwin - *America*, op. 44, nos. 6 & 13 (1962) •Fl/Cl/Asx/Bsn •CFE

GORTHEIL, Bernhard - *Die Kirmes* (1993) •3 Sx/Cl •INM

Glazounov, Alexander - *In modo religioso* (BETTONEY) •2 Cl/Asx/Bsn (or BsCl) •CF

GRANT, Jerome - *Classical Woodwind Quartet* (1966) (20') •Asx/Cl/Fl/Bsn •adr

GUACCERO, Domenico - *Quartetto* •Tsx/Cl/2 Voices: ST •DP

Handel, Georg-Friedrich - *3 Concertos* (CORROYEZ) •2 Cl/2 Sx: TB •Buff

Pieces (STANG) •2 Cl/Asx/Bsn (or BsCl) •CF

HARRIS, Floyd - *Pieces* •2 Cl/Asx/Bsn (or BsCl) •CF

Haydn, Franz Joseph - *Pieces* (SPEETS) •2 Sx: AT/Fl/Cl (or Ob) •TM/HE

Hummel, Johann - *8 Variations* (CORROYER) •2 Cl/2 Sx: TB •Buf

KARKOFF, Maurice - *Drömmeri/Poem*, op. 165 (1988) (17') •Cl/Vla/Asx/Pno •STIM

KOTONSKI, Wladzimierz - *Pieces* (1962) •Electr. Guit/2 Sx: AT/Cl •B&H/PWM

LAMB, Marvin - *Serenade for Unknown...* •Tsx/Ob/Cl/Pno •DP

LAMBRECHT, Homer - *Metaphrases* (1973) •1 Sx: S+A/Cl/BsCl/Bass

LERSY, Roger - *Vitraux* (1972) (35') •Cl/Asx/Vcl/Perc •adr

LINDEMAN, Peter - *Gloxinta* •Vln/Cl/Tsx/Pno

Macbeth, Allan - *Intermezzo* (HARRIS) •2 Cl/Asx/Bsn (or BsCl) •CF

MAEGAARD, Jan - *Musica riservata II* (1976) •Ob/Cl/Sx/Bsn

MAGANINI, Quinto - *Rêverie* (HARRIS) •Fl or Cl/Ob or Cl/Asx/Bsn or BsCl •CF

Maniet, R. - *Habanera* (RULST) •2 Cl/2 Sx: AT •EMB

Massenet, Jules - *Last Slumber...* (HARRIS) •2 Cl/Asx/Bsn (or BsCl) •CF

MASSET-LECOQ, Roselyne - *3 Pièces* (1977) •Cl/Asx/Hn/Bsn

MERCURE, Pierre - *Tetrachromie* (1963) •Cl/Asx/BsCl/Perc/Tape •CMC

Meyerbeer, Giacomo - *Coronation March* (HARRIS) •2 Cl/Asx/Bsn (or BsCl) •CF

Molloy, James - *Kerry Dance* (HARRIS) •2 Cl/Asx/Bsn (or BsCl) •CF

MONTGOMREY, James - *Ritual I : The White Goddess* (1980) (14') •Fl/Cl/Bsx/Koto (or autoharp) •CMC

Mozart, Wolfgang - *Pieces* (STEPHENS, TOLL) •2 Cl/Asx/Bsn (or BsCl) •CF

MUCI, Italo - *Quartetto* (1981) •Cl/Tsx/Trb/Bass

OLBRISCH, Franz-Martin - *Trios* (1984) (21') •Vln/Cl/Tsx/Pno •adr

Pleyel, Ignace - *Andante aus rondo*, op. 48/1 •2 Cl/Asx/Bsn (or BsCl) •CF

ROLIN, Etienne - *Vocalise II* (1989) •Ssx/Pno/BsCl/Fl •adr

Rossini, Giacchino - *Quartet No. 2* (GEE) •Fl/Cl/Sx/Bsn •DP

Schmidt, Joseph - *Finale* (BRINK) •2 Cl/Tsx/Tuba or 4 Sx: SATB •Mol

SCHUMANN, Gerrhard - *Petite suite* •Fl/Sx/EH/Cl •IMD

Silcher, Friedrich - *Loreley Paraphrase* (HARRIS) •2 Cl/Asx/Bsn (or BsCl) •CF

SMITH, William O. - *Schizophenic Scherzo* (1947) •Cl/Tpt/Asx/Trb

Stamitz, Anton - *Andante* (KESNAR) •2 Cl/Asx/Bsn (or BsCl) •CF

STEVEN, Donald - *Straight on till morning* (1985) •Fl/Cl/1 Sx: A+B/Electr. Pno •CMC

STRAESSER, Joep - *Intersections V* (1977) (12') •Ob/Cl/Asx/Bsn •Don

Tenaglia, Antonio - *Aria* (CHEYETTE) •2 Cl/Asx/Bsn (or Bsx) •Ga

THOMAS, Ronald - *Occasion* •Fl/Ssx/Cl/Hn

Thome, François - *Pizzicato* (HARRIS) •2 Cl/Asx/Bsn (or BsCl) •CF

Verdi, Giuseppe - *Quartet* •2 Cl/Asx/Bsn (or BsCl) •CF

Walckiers, E. - *Rondo* (HARRIS) •2 Cl/Asx/Bsn (or BsCl) •CF

WEBERN, Anton - *Quartet*, op. 22 (1930) (8') •Vln/Cl/Tsx/Pno •Uni

Weigl, Karl - *Sir Voire* (HARRIS) •2 Cl/Asx/Bsn (or BsCl) •CF

WILMAUT, Jean-Marie - *La complainte...* •Narr/Ob/Cl/Asx

WILSON, Donald - *Tetragon* (1990) •Fl/Asx/Cl/Bsn

WINKLER, Gerhard - *Aussenhäute* (1989) •Cl/Vln/Bsx/Vcl •adr

5 Musicians

ADAM, Adolphe - *Quintette* (185x) •3 Cl (Eb, Bb, Bs)/2 Sx

AMBROSINI, Claudio - *Trobar clar* (1982) •Fl/Ob/Cl/Tpt/1 Sx: S+A

ARCURI, Serge - *Prologue* (1985) •Fl/Ssx/Cl/Hn/Perc/Tape •CMC

ASCOUGH, R. - *Quintet* •Ssx/Fl/Ob/Cl/Bsn

AYSCUE, Brian - *Permutations I* (1972) (6'30) •Fl/Ob/Cl/Tpt/Tsx •adr

BARGSTEM, Joey - *Quintet for Winds* •Ob/Cl/Asx/Trb/Bsn •DP

BROWN, Newel Kay - *Pastorale and Dance* •Fl/Cl/Asx/Tpt/Trb •SeMC

BUMCKE, Gustav - *Quintet*, op. 23b •Cl/EH/Wald Horn/Bsn/Bsx

CARPENTER, Gary - *Dances for Mutilated Toys* (1970) (15') •Fl/Ob/Cl/Asx/Bsn •BMIC

CAVANA, Bernard - *Mariage* (1984) •1 Sx: Sno+S+T+Bs+CBs/Cl/Pno/Singers

CONTI, Francis - *Quintet* (1972) •Fl/Picc/1 Sx: A+S/Cl/Bsn •adr

CUNNINGHAM, Michael - *Miro Gallery* •Fl/Ob/Cl/Asx/Bsn •SeMC

DEFOSSEZ, René - *Mélopée et Danse* •Asx/Pno or Fl/Ob/Cl/Asx/Bsn •An

DUBOIS, Pierre-Max - *Sonatine* (1974) (7') •Fl/Cl/Asx/Tpt/Trb •adr

FLETA POLO, Francisco - *Divertimento 26* (1985) •Sx/Cl/Accordion/Bass/Timp

FLOTHUIS, Marius - *Kleine Suite* (1952) •Ob/Cl/Ssx/Tpt/Pno •Don

FONTAINE, Louis-Noël - *Mauresque* (1992) (8') •Fl/Ssx/Cl/Vcl/Perc •Capri

Musique (1978) (8') •Cl/2 Hn/2 Sx: AB •Capri

FREE, John - *A Wind of Changes* (1990) •Cl/Bsn/Sx/Perc/Pno •CMC

GASTINEL, Gérard - *Quintette* (1977) •Ssx/Ob/Cl/Hn/Bsn

GHEZZO, Dinu - *Sound shapes* •Fl/Ob/Cl/Sx/Bsn •SeMC

HALL, Neville - *For a Single Point* (1990) (11') •Cl/Tsx/Pno/Vla/Vcl •adr

HARTLEY, Walter - *Suite for 5 Winds* (1951) (7') •Fl/Ob/Cl/Asx/Trb •Wi&Jo

HEKSTER, Walter - *A song of peace* •Voice/Cl/Asx/Vcl/Perc •Don

HESPOS, Hans - *Einander* (1966) (12-13') •Fl/Cl/Guit/Tsx/Vla •EMod

En-kin das fern-nahe (1970) (5'30) •Ssx/Cl/Bsn/Bass/Perc •EMod

HISCOTT, James - *Variations on O. Cèlestin's...* (1978) (9') •Fl/Cl/Sx/Perc/Pno •CMC

HODKINSON, Sidney - *Interplay* (1966) (12'30) •Fl+Picc/Cl/Asx/Perc/Bass •CMC

HOLZMANN, Rodolfo - *Divertimento* (1936) •Fl/Cl/Sx/Hn/Bsn

Suite a tres temas •Asx/Tpt/Cl/Pno/Bongos

HRISANIDE, Alexandru - *M. P. 5* (1967) •Tsx+Cl/Vln/Vla/Vcl/Pno •IMD

IRINO, Yoshiro - *Quintette* (1958) •Cl/Asx/Tpt/Vcl/Pno •OE

ISTVAN, Miloslav - *Concertino...* (1982) (13') •Ob/Cl+Asx/BsCl/Perc/Pno

JANSEN, Guus - *Juist daarom* (1981) (7') •Ob/Cl/Ssx/Vcl/Pno •Don

JONES, Robert - *Divertimento* •Fl/Ob/Cl/Asx/Hn •WWS

KAINZ, Walter - *Bläser Quintet*, op. 12 (1935) •Fl/Cl/Asx/Hn/Bsn •adr

KÖHLER, Wolfgang - *Schwerenöters Liä-song* (1986) (2'50) •Cl/Sx/Electr Guit/Guit/Synth •adr

KÖPER, Heinz - *Dekaphonie* (9') •4 Cl/Sx •adr

LABURDA, Jiric - *Dixie Quintetto* (1990) (14') •Cl/Asx/Tpt/Trb/Pno •Com

LAUBA, Christian - *Ravel's raga* (1993) (15') •Vln/Cl/Asx/Bsn/Pno •adr

MACERO, Teo - *Exploration* •Asx/Cl/Bass/Perc/Accordion

MALHERBE, Claudy - *Non-sun* (1984-85) (10') •Picc/Tsx/Ob/Cl/Bsn

McKAY George - *American Street Scenes* (1935) •Cl/Tpt/Asx/Bsn/Pno or 4 Sx/Pno •CAP

MEULEMANS, Arthur - *Rapsodie* (1961) •3 Cl/BsCl/Asx •CBDM

MOORTEL, Arie van de - *Nocturne*, op. 18 (1956) •Cl/Asx/Vla/Vcl/Pno •Mau

MULDOWNEY, Dominic - *Love Music for Bathsheba...* (1974) (20') •Fl/Ob/Cl/Asx/Hn (or Trb) •Nov

NICKLAUS, Wolfgang - *Der Priwall* (1984) (9') •Voice/Asx/Perc/Cl/Vcl •adr

NIELSON, Lewis - *Dialectical Fantasy* (1981) •Fl/Ob/Cl/Tsx/Hn •ACA

NILSSON, Anders - *Cadenze* (1992) •Fl/Ob/Cl/Bsn/Sx

OLIVER, John - *Métalmorphose* (1983) •Ob/Cl/Bsn/Sx/Tpt •CMC

OSTENDORF, Jens-Peter - *Johnny reitet westwärts* •Cl/2 Sx: AT/Perc/Prepared Pno •Sik

OSTERC, Slavko - *Ave Maria* (1930) •Soprano Voice/Vla/Ob/Cl/Sx

PILLEVESTRE - *Nocturne* •Fl/Ob/Cl/2 Sx: AB

REVUELTAS, Silvestre - *First Little Serious Piece* (2'45) •Picc/Ob/Cl/Tpt/Bsx •MM/PIC/Peer

Second Little Serious Piece (1'15) •Picc/Ob/Cl/Tpt/Bsx •PIC/Peer

SAGVIK, Stellan - *4 Miniatyrer ur baletten Eulidyke*, op. 92 (1978) (4'30) •Fl/Ob/Cl/2 Sx: AT •STIM

SCHANKE, David - *Five Mellow Winds* (1959) •4 Sx: AATB/Cl •Chap

Schoenberg, Arnold - *Von heute auf Morgen*, op. 32 (PENNETIER) •2 Voices/Cl/Asx/Pno

SEMLER-COLLERY, Armand - *Pieces* •Cl/4 Sx: SATB •Led/Marg

SODERO, Cesare - *Pieces* (1933) •Fl/Ob/Cl/Tsx/Bsn •AMPC

TARLOW, Karen - *Music...* (1973) (12') •Fl/Ob/Cl/Asx/Hn •SeMC

TREMBLAY, George - *Piece* •Fl/Ob/Cl/Tsx/BsCl

VENTAS, Adolfo - *Concierto* •Cl Solo/4 Sx: SATB •adr

VOGEL, Wladimir - *La Ticinella...* (1941) •Fl/Ob/Cl/Asx/Bsn •SZ

6 Musicians

Also see Wind Sextet (Voir aussi sextuor à vent), page 368.

ABECASSIS, Eryck - *Dans 3 nuits* (1984) •Asx/Fl/Cl/Vln/Vcl/Pno

AMELLER, André - *Azuleros de Valencia* (1965) (13') •Fl/Ob/Cl/Asx/Hn/Bsn

BACHOREK, Milan - *Inspirace* (1983) (12') •Ob/Asx/Cl+BsCl/Perc/Pno/Electr. Guit •CHF

BAINBRIDGE, Simon - *People of the dawn* (1975) •Soprano Voice/Cl/Ssx/BsCl/Perc/Pno •UMPL

BARCE, Ramon - *Obertura fonética* (1968) (8'50) •Fl/Ob/Cl/Asx/Tpt/Trb •EMEC

BERLIOZ, Hector - *Chant sacré* (1843/44) •2 Tpt/Bugle/2 Cl/Bsx

BONDON, Jacques - *Sonate à Six* (1980) •2 Fl/2 Cl/2 Asx •ME

Braun, R. - *Pieces* •Fl/3 Cl/2 Sx: AT •Yb

BRIGHT, Greg - *Music...* (10') •6 Woodwinds instruments •EMIC

BUMCKE, Gustav - *Sextet*, op. 19 (1903) •Cl/EH/Wald Horn/BsCl/Sx/Bsn •Diem

CASANOVA, André - *Duo Canzoni* (1973) (10'30) •Asx/Cl/Tpt/Perc/Small Org/Electr. Bass Guit •adr

ERIKSON, Ake - *The rest is silence* (1971/73) •Fl/Asx/Cl/Pno/Bass/Perc •SMIC

FUSTÉ-LAMBEZAT, Arnaud - *Catalogue d'étoiles* (1983) •Asx/Fl/Cl/Vln/Vcl/Pno •adr

GARCIN, Gérard - *SA* (1986) •Asx/Fl/Cl/Vln/Vcl/Pno

GAUTHIER, Brigitte - *Like the Sweet Blonde* (1983) •Fl/Asx/Cl/Vln/Vcl/Pno

GERSCHEFSKI, Edwin - *America*, op. 44, no. 14a •Fl/Cl/Asx/Tpt/Bsn/Pno •CFE

GUINJOAN, Juan - *Musique intuitive - Diari* (1969) •Cl/Tsx/Tpt/Vln/Vcl/Pno

HAMBRAEUS, Bengt - *Kammarmusik for 6*, op. 28 (1950) (8') •Fl/Ob/Cl/Asx/Vla/Harp •STIM/Ehr

HEDSTROM, Ase - *Close by* (1980) •Fl/Cl/BsCl/Ssx/Vln/Vcl •NMI

HISCOTT, James - *Ballad No. 1* (1978) (14') •Fl/Cl/Sx/Perc/Accordion/Pno •CMC

HUMBERT-CLAUDE, Eric - *Eux* (1983) •Asx/Fl/Cl/Vln/Vcl/Pno

HURÉ, Jean - *2me Sextuor* •Tpt/2 Bugle/Cl/BsCl/Sx

KÖPER, Heinz-Karl - *Musik...* •Fl/Cl/Asx/Tpt/Trb/Bass •EMBA

LANZA, Alcides - *Interferences III* (1983-84) •Fl/Cl/Sx/Guit/Pno/Perc •ShP

LUNDEN, Lennart - *Quadrille; Queen Christina's Song* •2 Fl/2 Cl/Sx/Bsn •Che

LUROT, Jacques - *Sextuor* •Ob/Cl/Asx/Bsn/2 Voices: SA

MALLIE, Loïc - *Sextuor* (1989) •Fl/Cl/Asx/Pno/Guit/Perc

McPEEK, Ben - *Trillium* (1979) •Ssx/Fl/Cl/Vln/Vcl/Pno

MILHAUD, Darius - *Caramel mou*, op. 68 (1921) (5') •Bb Sx (or Voice)/Cl/Tpt/Trb/Pno/Perc •ME

RAYNAL, Gilles - *Ombilic* (1983) •Fl/Cl/Asx/Vln/Vcl/Pno

RODRIGUEZ-PICO, Jesùs - *Sextet* (1992) •Fl/2 Cl/2 Sx: AT/Bass

ROKEACH, Martin - *Tango* •Ob/Cl/Asx/Hn/Trb/Vcl •DP

ROLIN, Etienne - *Tressage-Concerto* (1983-84) (10') •Ssx/Fl/Cl/Pno/Vln/Vcl •Lem

SCHWEYER, Bruno - *Konzertstück* (1983) •Tsx/Fl/Cl/Vln/Vcl/Pno

SIMS, Ezra - *Sextet* (1981) (22') •Cl/Asx/Hn/Vln/Vla/Vcl •ACA

SURIANU, Horia - *Esquisse pour un clair obscur* (1986) (11') •Ssx/Fl/Cl/Vln/Vcl/Pno •Sal

TAGGART, Mark - *Concerto for Chamber Ensemble* (1983) (20') •Cl/Asx/Bsn/Tpt/Bass/Pno

TOSI, Daniel - *Multiphony III* (1986) (6'30) •Fl/Cl/Asx/Pno/Vln/Vcl

7 Musicians

ALLA, Thierry - *La terre et la Comète* (1991) •Fl/Cl/Asx/Pno/Bass/Synth/Perc/Tape/Children's Choir •adr

ARGERSINGER, Charles - *Drastic Measures* •Fl/Ob/Cl/Asx/Bsn/
Hn/Perc

BERNARD, Jacques - *L'Opéra de l'espace* (1970) •Narr/Ob/Cl/BsCl/
1 Sx: S+A+B/Bsn/Perc •adr

BOSSEUR, Jean-Yves - *43 Miniatures* (1992) •Vln/Cl/2 Sx: AB/
Harp/Pno/Perc

BROTT, Alexander - *7 for seven* (1954) (14'30) •Narr/Cl/Asx/Vln/
Vla/Vcl/Pno •CMC

CERHA, Friedrich - *Fantasies nach Cardw's Herbst 60* •Cl/BsCl/Tsx/
Vln/Vla/Vcl/Pno •EMod

DONATONI, Franco - *Hot* (1989) (14') •1 Sx: T+Sno/Cl+Eb Cl/Tpt/
Trb/Perc/Bass/Pno •Ric

HARVEY, Paul - *Concertino* (1973) (15') Ssx/Orch or Cl Choir (3 Bb/
Alto/Bs/CBs) or Pno •Mau

HESPOS, Hans - *Passagen* (1969) (9') •Cl/Asx/Tpt/Trb/Vla/Bass/
Perc •EMod

JENNEFELT, Thomas - *Stones* (1981) •Ob/Cl/Asx/Tpt/Guit/2 Perc

KARKOFF, Maurice - *Djurens Karneval* (1974) (15') •Fl/Picc/2 Cl/
Tsx/Bsn/Perc •STIM

KOBLENZ, Babette - *Grey Fire* (1981) •Cl/2 Sx: AT/Tpt/Electr. Bass/
Electr. Pno/Perc •adr

KOECHLIN, Charles - *Septuor*, op. 165 (1937) (11'30) •Fl/Ob/EH/
Cl/Asx/Hn/Bsn •Oil

LONGY, George - *Rhapsodie - Lento* (1904) •Harp/Bass/2 Cl/Bsn/
Asx/Timp •South

MIEREANU, Costin - *Polymorphies 5 X 7 B* (1969-70) (9-10')
•Fl+Picc/Cl+Tsx/Pno/Vln/Vla/Vcl/Bass •Sal

MUSSEAU, Michel - *Les paupières rebelles* (1993) (40') •Fl/Cl/Ssx/
Hn/Tpt/Trb/Tuba •Ed. Visage

NEMESCU, Octavian - *Septuor* (1983) •Fl/Cl/Trb/Tsx/Pno/Bass/
Perc

NILSSON, Bo - *Zeiten im Umlauf*, op. 14 (1957) (3') •Fl/Ob/EH/Cl/
BsCl/Tsx/Bsn •Uni

NORDENSTEN, Frank - *Sample and hold* (1978) (14') •Fl+Picc/
Cl+BsCl/1 Sx: S+T/Vln+Vla/Vcl/Pno/Perc

PINOS-SIMANDL, Aloïs - *Euforie* (1983) (10') •Ob (or Fl)/Asx/Cl/
BsCl/Pno/Perc/Bass •CHF

POOLE, Geoffrey - *Polter zeits* (1975) •Vla/2 Cl/BsCl/2 Sx: AB/
Prepared Pno •BMIC

RADULESCU, Horatiu - *X* (1984-85) •Sx/Cl/2 Bsn/2 Bass/Perc

SAGVIK, Stellan - *Sma gyckelvisor...*, op. 112 (1981) (8') •Fl/2 Cl/
Asx/Mandolin/2 Perc •STIM

SEFFER, Yochk'o - *Dromüs* (1991) •Pno/Cl/Perc/4 Sx: SATBs

SKOUEN, Synne - *Hva sa Schopenhauer...* (1978) (8') •Narr/Fl/
Cl+BsCl/Sx/Vln/Vcl/Perc •NMI

SOMERS, Harry - *Limêricks* (1979) •Voice/Fl/Cl/Sx/Bsn/Tpt/Eupho-
nium •CMC

SOTELO, Mauricio - *IX +... - de substantiis separatis* (1990) •Cl/Sx/
Tuba/Vln/Vcl/Bass/Pno/Schtagzeng with live
electronics •adr

STEARNS, Peter - *Septet* (1959) •Cl/Tsx/Hn/Vln/Vla/Vcl/Bass •Pio/
ACA

TAUTENAHN, Günther - *Septet* •Cl/Tpt/Tsx/Guit/Vcl/Pno/Perc
•SeMC

VILLA-LOBOS, Heitor - *Chôros n° 3 - Pica-Pào*, op. 189 (1925) (6')
•Cl/Asx/Bsn/3 Hn/Trb •ME

WILLIAMSON, Malcolm - *Merry Wives of Windsor* (1964) •Fl+Picc/
Cl/Tsx/Tpt/Perc/Bass/Pno •JW

WILLIS, Richard - *Irregular Resolutions* •Fl/Ob/Cl/Asx/Bsn/Hn/
Perc •adr

ZEMP, Joseph - *Souffle printanier* •Fl/Ob/Cl/4 Sx: SATB •adr

8 Musicians

ARMSTRONG, David - *The Protest* (1960) (9'30) •Cl/Trb/2 Asx/Tpt/
Perc/Pno/Bass •BMIC

BARCE, Ramon - *Concierto de Lizara V* (1977) (10'45) •Cl/Tsx/Tpt/
Trb/Harp/Pno/Vln/Vcl

BERG, Olav - *Fragments* (1977) (8') •Fl/Cl/Asx/Vla/Vcl/Pno/2 Perc
•NMJ

BIRTWISTLE, Harrison - *Medusa* (1969/70/78) •Fl/Cl/Ssx/Pno/
Perc/Vln/Vla/Vcl/Tape

BREGENT, Michel - *Melorytharmundi* (1984) •Fl/Cl/Sx/2 Perc/Pno/
Vcl/Guit •CMC

BUMCKE, Gustav - *Suite G Dur*, op. 24 •Tenor Voice/Fl/Ob/Cl/Bsn/
Hn/Bsx/Harp •VAB

CHATMAN, Stephen - *Outer Voices* (1978) •Fl/Cl/Asx/2 Perc/
Celesta/Guit/Harp/Tape •CMC

DECOUST, Michel - *Ombres portées* (1986) (9') •2 Ob/Cl/2 Asx/
Harp/Pno/Perc •Sal

DELAMARRE, Pierre - *La 8* (1981) (3') •Fl/Ob/Cl/Asx/Pno 4 hands
[à 4 mains]/Bass/Perc •adr

DELIO, Thomas - *Congruent Formalizations* •Fl/3 Cl/4 Sx •DP

DEL PRINCIPE, Joseph - *Lyric Pieces for Octet* •Fl/Ob/Sx+Cl/BsCl/
Tpt/Hn/Trb/Tuba •SeMC

EYSER, Eberhard - *3 Paraphrases* (1979) (8') 3 Sx: ATB/3 Cl/BsCl/
CBsCl •EMa

Petite suite [Liten suite für 8 blasure] (1978) (10') •3 Sx: SAB/2
Cl/Basset Horn/BsCl/CBsCl •STIM

Symphonie Orientale (1978) (18') •3 Sx: SAT/3 Cl/BsCl/CBsCl
•EMa

FERRAND-TEULET, Denise - *Octuor* (1975) •4 Sx: SATB/3 Cl/Bsn

FONTYN, Jacqueline - *Cheminement* (1986) (15') •Soprano Voice/
Fl/Cl/Hn (or Asx)/Vcl/Bass/Perc/Pno

FRANCESCONI, Luca - *Piccola trama* (1989) (14') •1 Sx: S+A/Fl/
Cl/Guit/Perc/Vln/Vla/Vcl •Ric

FRANCO, Clare - *Four Winds...* •Asx/Harp/Vibr/Fl/Ob/Cl/Hn/Bsn

GARCIN, Gérard - *Encore plus tard* (1984) (12') •1 Sx: Sno+A+Bs/
Fl/Cl/Bsn/Vla/Vcl/Bass/Perc/Tape •Sal

GUY, Georges - *Concerto en forme de jazz* •Asx Solo/Pno Solo/Fl/Ob/
Cl/Hn/Bsn/Bass

HACHIMURA, Yoshiro - *Concerto per 8 soli* •Fl/Cl/Sx/Vibr/Vcl/
Vla/2 Perc •OE

HARBISON, John - *The Flower-fed Buffaloes* (1976) •Voice/Cl/Tsx/
Fl/Vcl/Bass/Pno/Perc

HEKSTER, Walter - *Of mere being* (1982) (12') •Asx/Fl/Ob/Cl/2 Tpt/
Perc/Electr. Guit •Don

HESPOS, Hans - *Druckspuren - geschattet* (1970) (7'30) •Fl/Eb Cl/
Asx/Bsn/2 Tpt/Trb/Bass •EMod

KETTING, Otto - *Mars* (1974) (3'30) •4 Cl/4 Sx: AATT or 8 Sx:
AATT AATT •Don

KORTE, Karl - *Matrix* (1968) (16') •Fl/Ob/Cl/Asx/Hn/Bsn/Pno/Perc
•GSch

LAKE, Larry - *Filar il tuono* (1989) •Cl/3 Sx: ATB/Bsn/Tpt/Trb/
Marimba •CMC

LANTIER, Pierre - *Fugue jazz* (1944) (3') •2 Cl/2 Sx: AT/Bsn/Tpt/
Trb/Perc

LASNE, George - *Ballade française* (1971) •Fl/Ob/2 Cl/Asx/2 Tpt/
Trb

LAURETTE, Marc - *Kaleïdoscope* •Cl/Bsn/2 Sx: SB/Hn/Vla/Bass/
Vibr

MANDANICI, Marcella - *Extraits I* (1989) •Tsx/Fl/Cl/Pno/Perc/Vln/
Vla/Vcl •adr

MARIETAN, Pierre - *13 en concert* (1983) (15') •1 Sx: Sno+S+B/Cl/
Bsn/Trb/Vcl/2 Bass/Pno

MICHEL, Paul - *Ultramorphoses* (1965) (12-15') •Fl/Cl/Asx/Perc/
Pno/Vln/Vla/Vcl •CBDM

NICKLAUS, Wolfgang - *Die Antwort* (1986) (7'30) •Cl/Asx/2 Perc/
Pno/Vln/Vcl/Bass •adr

NILSSON, Bo - *Frequenzen* (1957) •Fl/Picc/Ob/EH/Cl/BsCl/Tsx/
Bsn •Uni

RADULESCU, Horatiu - *Sky* (1984-85) •Sx/Cl/Fl/2 Bsn/2 Bass/Perc

RIEDEL, Georg - *Reflexioner* (1974) (8') •Woodwind Quintet/Jazz group (Cl+Asx/Pno/Bass) •SMIC

SAGVIK, Stellan - *Guenilles des jongleurs*, op. 74 (1977) (7'30) •Fl/Ob/3 Cl/Asx/Bsn/Cnt •STIM

SPAHLINGER, Mathias - *Aussageverweigerung-Gegendarstellung* •Cl/Bsx/Bass/Pno/BsCl/Tsx/Vcl/Pno •Peer

SUTER, Robert - *Estampida* •Fl/Cl/Tsx/Hn/Tpt/Trb/Bass/Perc •EMod

TISNÉ, Antoine - *Dolmen* (1976) (30') •Fl/Cl/Asx/Hn/Tpt/Trb/Tuba/Pno •adr

TOMASSON, Haukur - *Octette* (1987) •Fl/Cl/Asx/Hn/Vla/Vcl/Pno/Perc (Vibr+Gong) •IMIC

VILLA-LOBOS, Heitor - *Chôros n° 7* (1924) (10') •Fl/Ob/Cl/Asx/Bsn/Vln/Vcl/Tam-tam •ME

WOOLLETT, Henri - *Octuor n° 1* (1911) •Ob/Cl/Asx/2 Vln/Vla/Vcl/Bass •South

9 Musicians

ALBRIGHT, William - *Introduction...* (14') •Pno/Fl/Cl/Asx/Hn/Tpt/Trb/Tuba/Perc •Pet

ALLGEN, Claude - *Adagio och Fuga* (25') •Fl/Ob/EH/Cl/BsCl/2 Sx: AB/Bsn/Hn •STIM

BORTOLOTTI, Mauro - *Studio per E.E. Cummings n° 2* (1964) •Vla/Vcl/Bass/Ob/Cl/BsCl/Sx/Hn/Perc •adr

BOUVARD, Jean - *Choral dialogue* •3 Fl/3 Cl/3 Asx •adr

BUMCKE, Gustav - *"Der Spaziergang"*, op. 22 •Fl/Ob/EH/Cl/Bsn/Hn/BsTrb/Bsx/Harp

CAPLET, André - *Impressions d'Automne* (1905) (3') •Asx/Ob/2 Cl/Bsn/Harp/Org/2 Vcl

Légende (1903) (13') •Asx/Ob/Cl/Bsn/2 Vln/Vla/Vcl/Bass •Fuz

CLARK, Thomas - *Dreamscape* •Fl/Ob/Cl/Sx/Tpt/Trb/Pno/Perc/Bass •SeMC

COLE, Helen - *Serenade* •Fl/Ob/2 Cl/BsCl/Hn/Asx/2 Bsn

COX, Rona - *Two Expressions* (1968) •Fl/Ob/Cl/2 Sx: SB/Hn/Bsn/Bass/Perc •adr

DIEMENTE, Edward - *For Lady Day* •Fl/Ob/Cl/Tpt/Trb/Vln/Vla/Sx/Bsn/Tape •SeMC

FICHER, Jacobo - *Los invitados*, op. 26 •Fl/Cl/2 Sx: AT/2 Tpt/Tuba/Pno/Perc

FISCHER, Eric - *Tango* (1982) •2 Cl/4 Sx: SATB/Mallet Perc [Perc à clavier]/Synth/Pno •adr

GRAINGER, Ella - *To Echo* (1945) •Soprano Voice/Picc/Fl/Cl+Asx/Tsx/Vla/BsCl/Bass/Marimba •GS

GUALDA JIMENEZ, Antonio - *Noneto Zarco* (1988) (16') •Vln/Vcl/Cl/2 Sx: SA/Vibr/Marimba/Guit/Pno

IVES, Charles - *Over the Pavements*, op. 20 (1906-13) •Picc/Cl/Bsx (or Bsn)/Tpt/3 Trb/Perc/Pno •PIC

JELINEK, Hanns - *Blue Sketches*, op. 25 (1956) •Fl/Cl/2 Sx: AB/Tpt/Trb/Vibr/Bass/Perc •EMod

LEGRAND, Michel - *Porcelaine de Sax* (1958) (3') •6 Sx: SnoSATBBs (or Eb Cl/Cl/3 Sx: ATB/Bsn) Trb/Bass/Perc •Mills

LEWIS, John Aaron - *Little David's Fugue* (5'30) •Fl/Cl/3 Sx: ATB/Trb or Tpt/Harp or Pno/Bass/Perc •MJQ

The Queen's Fancy (4') •Fl/Cl/Tsx/Bsn/Hn/Trb/Harp/Bass/Perc •MJQ

Sun Dance (4') •Fl/Cl/3 Sx: ATB/Trb/Harp or Guit/Bass/Perc •MJQ

MARCO, Tomàs - *Anna Blume* (1967) •2 Narr/Fl/Ob/Cl/Sx/Tpt/2 Perc

MELLNÄS, Arne - *Drones* (1967) (8') •Fl/Cl/3 Sx: ATB/Tpt/Perc/Vcl/Bass •STIM

NELHYBEL, Vaclav - *Ricercare* •4 Sx: AATB/5 Cl •Lebl

NATANSON, Tadeus - *3 Pictures for 7 Instruments* (1960) •Ob/Cl/Asx/Trb/Vcl/Tpt/Bsn/Pno/Perc •AMP

NONO, Luigi - *Polifonica, Monodia, Ritmica* (1951) (10') •Fl/Cl/BsCl/Asx/Hn/4 Perc •AVV

RENOSTO, Paolo - *Dissolution* •Vla/Vcl/Bass/Ob/Cl/BsCl/Sx/Hn/Perc

SAGVIK, Stellan - *Det Förlorade steget*, op. 64 (1976) (20') •Fl/Cl+BsCl/Asx/Cnt/Trb/Vln/Vla/Vcl/Perc •SMIC

SVOBODA, Tomàs - *Seven Short Dances* •Fl/2 Cl/Asx/Trb/Vln/Bass/Pno/Perc

TANENBAUM, Elias - *Trios I, II, III* •Fl/Ob/Cl/Vln/Vla/Vcl/Bass/Asx/Perc •ACA

ULRICH, Jürgen - *Spiel* (1974) (5') •Fl/Ob/Cl/Bsn/Sx/Hn/Tpt/Trb/Tuba •VDMK

VELLONES, Pierre - *Planisphère*, op. 23 (1930) •2 Sx: AT/Cl/2 Tpt/Trb/Bass (or Tuba)/Perc/Pno •JJ

WALTON, William - *Façade* (1922/26, 42) (34'30) •2 Narr/Fl+Picc/Cl/BsCl/Asx/Tpt/Vcl/Perc •OUP

WILDER, Alec - *Suite* •Bsx/Fl/Ob/Cl/2 Hn/Bsn/Bass/Drums

10 Musicians

BRANT, Henry - *Dialogue in the Jungle* (1964) (15') •Tenor Voice/Fl/Ob/Cl/Bsx/2 Tpt/Trb/Hn/Tuba •adr

BUMCKE, Gustav - *Präludium und Fuge*, op. 20 (1903) •Fl/Ob/EH/Sx/Cl/BsCl/2 Bsn/2 Hn

COE, Tony - *The Buds of Time* (1979) (20') •Cl+Sx/Cl+BsCl/2 Vln/Vla/Vcl/BsTrb/Pno/Bass/Perc •adr

COLE, Hugo - *Serenade...* (1965) (15') •2 Fl/Ob/2 Cl/Asx/2 Bsn/2 Hn

COSTEN, Roel van - *Prisma* (1984) (8') •Vla/Fl/Cl/Asx/BsCl/Trb/Vcl/Bass/Perc/Pno •Don

CUNNINGHAM, Michael - *Linear Ceremony* •2 Fl/2 Ob/2 Cl/Sx/Hn/2 Bsn •SeMC

Spring Sonnet •Fl/2 Cl/BsCl/2 Sx/3 Hn/Bass •SeMC

DEPELSENAIRE, Jean-Marie - *Dixtour* (1971) •2 Fl/2 Tpt/2 Sx/4 Cl •adr

GOODMAN, Alfred - *3 Gesänge für Gresang* •Soprano Voice/Fl/Ob/Asx/Cl/Vla/Vcl/Prepared Pno/Guit/Perc •adr

GOTTSCHALK, Arthur - *Cycloid* •Cl/Asx/Hn/Tpt/Harp/Vibr/2 Vln/Vla/Vcl •SeMC

GRAHN, Ulf - *Soundscape II* (1974) (7') •Fl/Cl/EH/Asx/2 Trb/2 Vln/Vcl/Bass •SMIC

HARTLEY, Walter - *Double Concerto* (1969) (7'30) •Asx/Tuba/Wind Octet (Fl/Ob/Cl/Bsn/Hn/2 Tpt/Trb) •PhiCo

HEIDEN, Bernhard - *Sonatina* •Fl/Cl/Tsx/Hn/Trb/Harp/Vibr/Pno/Bass/Perc •MJQ

HOVHANESS, Alan - *Is This Survival?*, op. 59 (1949) •4 Cl/Asx/4 Tpt/Perc

JOHNSON, J. J. - *Turnpike* (5') •Fl/Cl/3 Sx: ATB/Trb/Harp (or Guit)/Pno/Bass/Perc •MJQ

LACHARTE, Nicole - *La Geste inachevée* (1980) •Fl/Cl/Sx/Tpt/Trb/Pno/Perc/Vln/Vla/Vcl

LAZARUS, Daniel - *4 Mélodies* •Contralto Voice/Fl/Cl/Asx/Bsn/2 Vln/Vla/Vcl/Bass

LINDBERG, Nils - *Progression* (1985) (28') •Fl/Ob/Cl/Hn/Bsn/2 Sx: SA/Pno/Bass/Drums •SMIC

LUTYENS, Elisabeth - *Akapotik Rose*, op. 64 (1966) (18') •Soprano Voice/Picc/Fl/Cl/Bsn/Cl+Tsx/Vln/Vla/Vcl/Pno

MIMET, Anne-Marie - *Fanfare et divertissement* •Fl/Ob/Cl/Bsn/3 Sx: SAT/Tpt/Trb/Tuba

NILSSON, Bo - *Zeitpunkte* (1960) (5') •Fl/Alto Fl/Ob/EH/Cl/BsCl/2 Sx: AT/Bsn/CBsn

POOLE, Geoffrey - *Son of Paolo* (1971) •Fl/Picc/Cl/BsCl/Tsx/2 Vln/2 Vcl/Prepared Pno •BMIC

SCHAFFER, Boguslaw - *Permutations n° 27* (1956) •Fl/Ob/Cl/Sx/
Tpt/Trb/Vla/Perc/Harp/Pno •A&S
SCHULLER, Gunther - *12 by 11* (8'30) •Fl/Cl/Tsx/Hn/Trb/Vibr/Pno/
Harp/Bass/Perc •MJQ
SMITH, William - *Elegy for Eric* •Fl/2 Sx: AB/Cl/Tpt/Trb/Vibr/Vln/
Bass/Perc •MJQ
SPINO, P. - *Prelude of Woodwinds* •2 Fl/Ob (ad lib.)/3 Cl/BsCl/Bsn
(ad lib.)/4 Sx: AATB •StMU
TREMBLAY, George - *Epithalamium* (1962) •Fl/Ob/Cl/Sx/Bsn/Hn/
Tpt/Trb/Tuba/Perc •CFE
WILDER, Alec - *She'll Be Seven in May* •Fl/Ob/Asx/2 Cl/BsCl/Bsn/
Bass/Drums/Pno

11 Musicians

ANDRIESSEN, Jurriaan - *Hommage à Milhaud* (1945) (8') •Fl/Ob/
Cl/Bsn/Hn/Tpt/Trb/Asx/Vln/Vla/Vcl •Don
COLE, Bruce - *Pantomimes* (25') •Soprano Voice/Fl/Cl/BsCl/Ssx/
Perc/Pno/Guit/Vln/Vla/Vcl •B&H
HAZZARD, Peter - *Massage* •3 Voices (SAB)/3 Perc/Fl/Cl/Hn/Sx/
Trb •SeMC
KEULEN, Geert van - *Onkruid* (1981) (5') •Ob/Cl/2 Sx: AT/Bsn/Hn/
Tpt/Trb/Vln/Vla/Pno •Don
MESTRAL, Patrice - *Alliages* (1969) •Tpt Solo/Fl/Cl/Asx/2 Trb/2
Perc/Pno/Org/Bass
MONDELLO, Nuncio - *Suite* (1956) •Asx/2 Fl/Ob/Cl/Bsn/2 Hn/Tpt/
Trb/Perc •adr
SCHILLING, Otto-Erich - *Überall ist Wunderland* •Voice/Fl/Cl/Sx/
Tpt/2 Vln/Bass/Perc/Accordion/Pno •SeMC
SPINO, P. - *Prelude of Woodwinds* •2 Fl/Ob (ad lib.)/3 Cl/BsCl/Bsn
(ad lib.)/4 Sx: AATB •StMU

12 Musicians

BERIO, Luciano - *Novissimum Testamentum* (1991) •4 Sx: SATB/4
Voice/4 Cl
CECCONI, Monique - *Hommage à...* •Ob/Cl/Asx/Bsn/4 Vln/2 Vla/2
Vcl •Phi
CURTIS-SMITH, Curtis - *Sundry Dances* (1981) •Fl/Ob/Cl/3 Sx:
SAB/Bsn/CBsn/Tpt/Trb/Tuba/Bass •adr
HASQUENOPH, Pierre - *Inventions* •2 Vln/Vla/Vcl/Bass/Fl/Ob/Cl/
Asx/Bsn/Hn/Tpt •Heu
HOVHANESS, Alan - *After Water* •3 Cl/3 Tpt/3 Asx/Perc/Harp/Pno
•ACA
JAEGGI, Oswald - *Dum Clamarem* (1961) •Ob/EH/Cl/3 Sx/3 Tpt/3
Trb
LEWIS, Arthur - *Pieces of Eight* •Fl/2 Ob/3 Cl/Bsn/2 Tsx/Hn/Baritone
Hn/Perc •CAP
MASINI, Fabio - *"Nuvole e colori forti"* (1992) (18') •Fl/1 Sx: S+A/
BsCl/Fl/Ob/Cl/Bsn/2 Vln/Vla/Vcl/Harp
REA, John - *Treppenmusik* (1982) •4 Sx: SATB/4 Cl/Vln/Vla/Vcl/
Bass •CMC
RECK, David - *Number 1 for 12 Performers* (15') •Fl/Cl/Tsx/Hn/Guit/
Vibr/Pno/Bass/Perc •MJQ
ROBBINS, David - *Improvisation* •Fl/2 Cl/Tsx/Bsn/Tpt/Trb/Vln/Vla/
Vcl/Bass/Perc
SPINO, P. - *Prelude of Woodwinds* •2 Fl/Ob (ad lib.)/3 Cl/BsCl/Bsn
(ad lib.)/4 Sx: AATB •StMU
TOEPLITZ, Kasper - *Johnny Panic...* (25') •1 Sx: T+CBs/Mezzo
Soprano Voice/2 Fl/2 Cl/Hn/2 Vln/2 Vla/
Perc/Tape

13 Musicians

BENHAMOU, Maurice - *Musique pour 13 instruments* •Fl/2 Cl/
Harmonica/Sx/2 Vln/3 Guit/Pno 6 hands (à 6
mains)

EICHMANN, Dietrich - *George...* (1984) (35') •3 Fl/Cl/2 Sx: AT/2
Tpt/Trb/2 Perc/Pno/Bs Guit •adr
FINNISSY, Michael - *Babylon* (1971) (19') •Mezzo Soprano Voice/
Ob/Cl/Asx/Bsn/Guit/Harp/Pno/2 Perc/2 Vcl/
Bass •Uni
First sign a sharp white mons (1974-67) (45') •2 Fl/2 Cl/Asx/CBsn/
Hn/Accordion/Guit/Vln/2 Vcl/Pno •BMIC
HESPOS, Hans - *Keime und male* (9') •Picc/Fl/2 Cl/Asx/Hn/Guit/Vln/
Vla/Bass/3 Perc •JJ
HUREL, Philippe - *"Pour l'image"* •Fl/Ob/Cl/Asx/Hn/Tpt/Trb/Perc/
2 Vln/Vla/Vcl/Bass
MERKU, Pavle - *Tiare* •Baritone Voice/Sx/11 wind instruments •Piz
SEKON, Joseph - *Lemon Ice* (1972) •Fl/Ob/Cl/2 Sx: ST/Bsn/Tpt/Trb/
2 Perc/Vln/Vcl/Pno •adr
SPINO, P. - *Statement...* •Hn Solo/2 Fl/Ob/3 Cl/BsCl/Bsn/4 Sx:
AATB •StMu
WENDEL, Eugen - *Saphonospir* (15') •Asx/Fl/Cl/Ob/Tpt/Trb/2 Vln/
Vla/Vcl/Bass/2 Perc •adr

14 Musicians

HARBISON, John - *Confinement* (1965) (15'15) •Fl/Ob/EH/Cl/BsCl/
Asx/Tpt/Trb/Vln/Vla/Vcl/Bass/Pno/Perc
MIEREANU, Costin - *Clair de biche* (1986) (11') •Fl/Picc/Cl/1 Sx:
Sno+S+T/Brass Quintet/5 Perc •Sal
ROSSÉ, François - *Paléochrome* (1988) (22') •Vla principal/2 Fl/Cl/
BsCl/1 Sx: S+T/EH/Bsn/Hn/4 Perc/Bass •adr

15 Musicians

LUTYENS, Elisabeth - *Islands*, op. 80 (1971) •2 Narr: ST/Picc/Fl/Cl/
BsCl/Tsx/Hn/Pno/Celesta/Vln/Vla/Vcl/2
Perc
TEMPLE & SHAW - *Vanity Fair Suite* •Fl/Ob/4 Cl/BsCl/Asx/2 Vln/
Vla/Vcl/Bass/Perc/Pno •Mills

oOo

ANSIND, Caroline - *Het water...* (1986) (14'30) •Ob/Cl/2 Sx: AB/2
Trb/Perc/Pno/Choir •Don
BELLEMARE, Gilles - *La chasse-galerie* (1981) •Narr/Choir/2 Fl/2
Recorder/2 Cl/2 Tpt/1 Sx
Cailliet, Lucien - *Canzonetta* (TSCHAIKOVSKY) •Asx/Cl Choir •LCP/
South
CAVANA, Bernard - *Mariage* (1984) •1 Sx: Sno+S+T+Bs+CBs/Cl/
Pno/Singers
DAKIN, Charles - *Syra* (1979) (8'30) •2 Cl/2 Tsx/2 Tpt/2 Trb/4 Vla/
4 Vcl/2 Bass
DHAINE, Jean-Louis - *Fantaisies...* •4 Fl/4 Cl/4 Sx: AATT/2 Tpt/2
Trb
KONAGAYA, Sôichi - *Masquerade* •Cl Choir/4 Sx: SATB
LERSTAD, Terje - *Concerto No. 2*, op. 171 (1984) (20') •Asx/Cl
Choir •NMI
PEPIN, Clermont - *Pièces de circonstance* (1967) •Childrens chorus/
Fl/Ob/3 Cl/2 Sx/2 Hn •CMC
TELFER, Nancy - *The Golden Cage* (1979) •Mixed Choir/Fl/Cl/Sx/
3 Perc/Pno
VILLA-LOBOS, Heitor - *Nonetto*, op. 181 (1923) (18') •Fl/Ob/Cl/1
Sx: A+B/Bsn/Perc/Celesta/Harp/Pno/Mixed
Chorus •ME

Saxophone and Bass Clarinet

2 Musicians

BARKER, Warren - *CCI* •BsCl/Bsx •WWS
EYSER, Eberhard - *Watermusic...* (1979-84) •1 Sx: A+T/Cl+BsCl/
Tape •STIM

HYLA, Lee - *We Speak Etruscan* (8'30) •BsCl/Bsx •adr
MASSIAS, Gérard - *Dialogues* (1956) (6') •Asx/BsCl or 2 Sx •Bil
SEFFER, Yochk'o - *Techouba...* •Tsx Solo/1 to 8 BsCl
TESEI, Tonino - *Controcontrasti* (1993) •SnoSx/BsCl •INM

3 Musicians

ALBRIGHT, William - *Pit Band* (1993) •Asx/BsCl/Pno •INM
BÖRJESSON, Lars-Ove - *Interparolo III*, op. 45 (1986) •Asx/BsCl/
    Org •SMIC
CELERIANU, Michel - *Ouverture trio* •Sx/BsCl/Perc
FISCHER-MÜNSTER, Gerhard - *Fossilien* (1981) (9') •BsCl/Ssx/
    Perc •VDMK
MENCHERINI, Fernando - *Caravan trio* (1989) •SnoSx/BsCl/Pno
SCHWANTNER, Joseph - *Entropy* (1968) •Ssx/BsCl/Vcl •DP/ACA
SEFFER, Yochk'o - *Techouba...* •Tsx Solo/1 to 8 BsCl
SOTELO, Mauricio - *Nel suono indicible* (1989) •1 Sx: A+T/
    BsCl+CBsCl/Vcl/Live electronics •adr

4 Musicians

BANK, Jacques - *Finale* (1984) (30') •Baritone Voice/Asx/BsCl/Perc
    •Don
BOOGARD, Bernard van den - *Syntetisch Gedicht* (1971) (20')
    •Mezzo Soprano Voice/Asx/BsCl/Pno •Don
CALLHOFF, Herbert - *Facetten* (1986) •Asx/BsCl/Cl/Perc •adr
CASKEN, John - *Music for a Tawny-Gold Day* (1975-76) (10') •Asx/
    BsCl/Vla/Pno •Sch
CHARBONNIER, Janine - *Exercice* (4') •2Sx: SA/BsCl/Bsn •EFM
Corelli, Arcangelo - *Gigue* (HARRIS) •2 Cl/Asx/Bsn (or BsCl) •CF
Cui, César - *Orientale* (HARRIS) •2 Cl/Asx/Bsn (or BsCl) •CF
Denza, Luigi - Funiculi-Funicula (HARRIS) •2 Cl/Asx/Bsn (or BsCl)
    •CF
Dewit, A. - *Pieces* (HARRIS) •2 Cl/Asx/Bsn (or BsCl) •CF
DUBOIS, Pierre-Max - *Dessins animés* (1978) (16') •2 Sx: SA/Cl/
    BsCl •FroMu
EYSER, Eberhard - *Edictus to the...* (1985) •Fl/Ssx/Cl/BsCl •STIM
Glazounov, Alexander - *In modo religioso* (BETTONEY) •2 Cl/Asx/Bsn
    (or BsCl) •CF
GLOBOKAR, Vinko - *Plan* (1965) Tsx/BsCl/Cnt/Tbn •Pet
GREEN, Stuart - *Pipedreams* (1978) (7') •Fl/Asx/Ob/BsCl
HAMBURG, Jeff - *Elegie* (1985-86) (9') •Fl/BsCl/Bsx/Perc •Don
Handel, Georg-Friedrich - *Pieces* (STANG) •2 Cl/Asx/Bsn (or BsCl)
    •CF
HARRIS, Floyd - *Pieces* •2 Cl/Asx/Bsn (or BsCl) •CF
HOLZMANN, Rodolfo - *Suite* (1933) •Asx/BsCl/Tpt/Pno
LAMBRECHT, Homer - *Metaphrases* (1973) •1 Sx: S+A/Cl/BsCl/
    Bass
Macbeth, Allan - *Intermezzo* (HARRIS) •2 Cl/Asx/Bsn (or BsCl) •CF
MAGANINI, Quinto - *Rêverie* (HARRIS) •Fl or Cl/Ob or Cl/Asx/Bsn
    or BsCl •CF
Massenet, Jules - *Last Slumber...* (HARRIS) •2 Cl/Asx/Bsn (or BsCl)
    •CF
MERCURE, Pierre - *Tetrachromie* (1963) •Cl/Asx/BsCl/Perc/Tape
    •CMC
Meyerbeer, Giacomo - *Coronation March* (HARRIS) •2 Cl/Asx/Bsn (or
    BsCl) •CF
Molloy, James - *Kerry Dance* (HARRIS) •2 Cl/Asx/Bsn (or BsCl) •CF
Mozart, Wolfgang - *Pieces* (STEPHENS, TOLL) •2 Cl/Asx/Bsn (or BsCl)
    •CF
Pleyel, Ignace - *Andante aus rondo*, op. 48/1 •2 Cl/Asx/Bsn (or BsCl)
    •CF
ROLIN, Etienne - *Vocalise II* (1989) •Ssx/Pno/BsCl/Fl •adr
RUBBERT, Rainer - *Obstacle* (1992) (14') •Tsx/BsCl/Vln/Pno •adr
SEFFER, Yochk'o - *Techouba...* •Tsx Solo/1 to 8 BsCl
Silcher, Friedrich - *Loreley Paraphrase* (HARRIS) •2 Cl/Asx/Bsn (or
    BsCl) •CF

Stamitz, Anton - *Andante* (KESNAR) •2 Cl/Asx/Bsn (or BsCl) •CF
STROUD, Richard - *Capriccio* •Fl/Ob/Asx/BsCl •SeMC
Thome, François - *Pizzicato* (HARRIS) •2 Cl/Asx/Bsn (or BsCl) •CF
Verdi, Giuseppe - *Quartet* •2 Cl/Asx/Bsn (or BsCl) •CF
Walckiers, E. - *Rondo* (HARRIS) •2 Cl/Asx/Bsn (or BsCl) •CF
Weigl, Karl - *Sir Voire* (HARRIS) •2 Cl/Asx/Bsn (or BsCl) •CF

5 Musicians

ADAM, Adolphe - *Quintette* (185x) •3 Cl (Eb, Bb, Bs)/2 Sx
CHARRON, Damien - *Extraits du corps* (1985) •Mezzo Soprano
    Voice/Tsx/BsCl/Bass/Perc
ISTVAN, Miloslav - *Concertino...* (1982) (13') •Ob/Cl+Asx/BsCl/
    Perc/Pno
MEULEMANS, Arthur - *Rapsodie* (1961) •3 Cl/BsCl/Asx •CBDM
SEFFER, Yochk'o - *Techouba...* •Tsx Solo/1 to 8 BsCl
TREMBLAY, George - *Piece* •Fl/Ob/Cl/Tsx/BsCl

6 Musicians

BACHOREK, Milan - *Inspirace* (1983) (12') •Ob/Asx/Cl+BsCl/Perc/
    Pno/Electr. Guit •CHF
BAINBRIDGE, Simon - *People of the dawn* (1975) •Soprano Voice/
    Cl/Ssx/BsCl/Perc/Pno •UMPL
BENNETT, Richard Rodney - *Comedia I* (1972) •Fl/Asx/BsCl/Tpt/
    Vcl/Perc •Uni
BUMCKE, Gustav - *Sextet*, op. 19 (1903) •Cl/EH/Wald Horn/BsCl/
    Sx/Bsn •Diem
    Sextuor, op. 20 en Lab •2 Sx: AA/EH/Hn/BsCl/Bsn •VAB
HEDSTROM, Ase - *Close by* (1980) •Fl/Cl/BsCl/Ssx/Vln/Vcl •NMI
HURÉ, Jean - *2me Sextuor* •Tpt/2 Bugle/Cl/BsCl/Sx
SEFFER, Yochk'o - *Techouba...* •Tsx Solo/1 to 8 BsCl

7 Musicians

BERNARD, Jacques - *L'Opéra de l'espace* (1970) •Narr/Ob/Cl/BsCl/
    1 Sx: S+A+B/Bsn/Perc •adr
CANTON, Edgardo - *Phares et balises* •Fl/Ob/Sx/BsCl/Hn/Tpt/Trb
CERHA, Friedrich - *Fantasies nach Cardw's Herbst 60* •Cl/BsCl/Tsx/
    Vln/Vla/Vcl/Pno •EMod
HARVEY, Paul - *Concertino* (1973) (15') •Ssx/Orch or Cl Choir (3 Bb/
    Alto/Bs/CBs) or Pno •Mau
JEVERUD, Johan - *Chimaira* (1984) •BsCl/Tsx/Trb/3 Vcl/Pno •SMIC
NILSSON, Bo - *Zeiten im Umlauf*, op. 14 (1957) (3') •Fl/Ob/EH/Cl/
    BsCl/Tsx/Bsn •Uni
NORDENSTEN, Frank - *Sample and hold* (1978) (14') •Fl+Picc/
    Cl+BsCl/1 Sx: S+T/Vln+Vla/Vcl/Pno/Perc
PINOS-SIMANDL, Aloïs - *Euforie* (1983) (10') •Ob (or Fl)/Asx/Cl/
    BsCl/Pno/Perc/Bass •CHF
POOLE, Geoffrey - *Polter zeits* (1975) •Vla/2 Cl/BsCl/2 Sx: AB/
    Prepared Pno •BMIC
SEFFER, Yochk'o - *Techouba...* •Tsx Solo/1 to 8 BsCl
SKOUEN, Synne - *Hva sa Schopenhauer...* (1978) (8') •Narr/Fl/
    Cl+BsCl/Sx/Vln/Vcl/Perc •NMI
STRINDBERG, Henrik - *Coming* (1982) (6') •2 Sx: SA/BsCl/Tpt/
    Trb/2 Perc •SMIC

8 Musicians

BÖRJESSON, Lars - *Divertimento*, op. 38 (1983) •Asx/BsCl/Bsn/
    Guit/Harp/Marimba/Vln/Vcl •STIM
DEL PRINCIPE, Joseph - *Lyric Pieces for Octet* •Fl/Ob/Sx+Cl/BsCl/
    Tpt/Hn/Trb/Tuba •SeMC
EYSER, Eberhard - *3 Paraphrases* (1979) (8') 3 Sx: ATB/3 Cl/BsCl/
    CBsCl •EMa
    Petite suite [Liten suite für 8 blasure] (1978) (10') •3 Sx: SAB/2
        Cl/Basset Horn/BsCl/CBsCl •STIM
    Symphonie Orientale (1978) (18') •3 Sx: SAT/3 Cl/BsCl/CBsCl
        •EMa

NILSSON, Bo - *Frequenzen* (1957) •Fl/Picc/Ob/EH/Cl/BsCl/Tsx/
Bsn •Uni
PERSSON, Bob - *Om sommaren sköna II* (1965) •Fl/BsCl/Trb/2 Perc/
Vibr/Vcl/Jazz Sx/Tape
RABE, Folke - *Pajazzo* (1964) •Tpt/Asx/Pno/2 BsCl/3 Perc •STIM
SEFFER, Yochk'o - *Dépression* (1985) •Tsx improvised/4 Sx: SATB/
BsCl/Bass/Perc
Techouba... •Tsx Solo/1 to 8 BsCl
SPAHLINGER, Mathias - *Aussageverweigerung-Gegendarstellung*
•Cl/Bsx/Bass/Pno/BsCl/Tsx/Vcl/Pno •Peer

9 Musicians

ALLGEN, Claude - *Adagio och Fuga* (25') •Fl/Ob/EH/Cl/BsCl/2 Sx:
AB/Bsn/Hn •STIM
BORTOLOTTI, Mauro - *Studio per E.E. Cummings n° 2* (1964) •Vla/
Vcl/Bass/Ob/Cl/BsCl/Sx/Hn/Perc •adr
CERHA, Friedrich - *Exercices for Nine, No. 1* •BsCl/Bsx/Bsn/Tpt/
Trb/Tuba/Vcl/Bass/Harp •Uni
COLE, Helen - *Serenade* •Fl/Ob/2 Cl/BsCl/Hn/Asx/2 Bsn
CUSTER, Arthur - *Cycle for Nine Instruments* •Asx/BsCl/Tpt/Hn/
Vln/Vla/Vcl/Bass/Perc •JM
GRAINGER, Ella - *To Echo* (1945) •Soprano Voice/Picc/Fl/Cl+Asx/
Tsx/Vla/BsCl/Bass/Marimba •GS
GRANDERT, Johnny - *86 T* •Fl/EH/BsCl/Bsx/CBsn/2 Tpt/Perc/Pno
•STIM
NONO, Luigi - *Polifonica, Monodia, Ritmica* (1951) (10') •Fl/Cl/
BsCl/Asx/Hn/4 Perc •AVV
OOSTERVELD, Ernst - *Omaga* (1981/82) (19') •BsCl Solo/8 instru-
ments including [dont] 1 Asx •Don
RENOSTO, Paolo - *Dissolution* •Vla/Vcl/Bass/Ob/Cl/BsCl/Sx/Hn/
Perc
SAGVIK, Stellan - *Det Förlorade steget, op. 64* (1976) (20') •Fl/
Cl+BsCl/Asx/Cnt/Trb/Vln/Vla/Vcl/Perc
•SMIC
SCELSI, Jacinto - *Kya* (1959) (11') •Cl (or Ssx)/EH/Hn/BsCl/Tpt/
Trb/Vla/Vcl/Bass •Sal
SEFFER, Yochk'o - *Techouba...* •Tsx Solo/1 to 8 BsCl
TARENSKEEN, Boudewijn - *Nonet* (1982) (13') •Asx/Hn/BsCl/
Accordion/Banjo/Harp/Vla/Vcl/Bass •Don
WALTON, William - *Façade* (1922/26, 42) (34'30) •2 Narr/Fl+Picc/
Cl/BsCl/Asx/Tpt/Vcl/Perc •OUP

10 Musicians

BUMCKE, Gustav - *Präludium und Fuge, op. 20* (1903) •Fl/Ob/EH/
Sx/Cl/BsCl/2 Bsn/2 Hn
COE, Tony - *The Buds of Time* (1979) (20') •Cl+Sx/Cl+BsCl/2 Vln/
Vla/Vcl/BsTrb/Pno/Bass/Perc •adr
COSTEN, Roel van - *Prisma* (1984) (8') •Vla/Fl/Cl/Asx/BsCl/Trb/
Vcl/Bass/Perc/Pno •Don
CUNNINGHAM, Michael - *Spring Sonnet* •Fl/2 Cl/BsCl/2 Sx/3 Hn/
Bass •SeMC
KOX, Hans - *Concertino* (1982) •Asx/Picc/2 Fl/BsCl/2 Hn/2 Tpt/Trb
•Don
NILSSON, Bo - *Zeitpunkte* (1960) (5') •Fl/Alto Fl/Ob/EH/Cl/BsCl/2
Sx: AT/Bsn/CBsn
POOLE, Geoffrey - *Son of Paolo* (1971) •Fl/Picc/Cl/BsCl/Tsx/2 Vln/
2 Vcl/Prepared Pno •BMIC
SCHWERTSIK, Kurt - *Salotto romano, op. 5* (1961) •BsCl/Bsx/Bsn/
Hn/Trb/Tuba/Perc/Bass/Vcl/Guit •EMod
SPINO, P. - *Prelude of Woodwinds* •2 Fl/Ob (ad lib.)/3 Cl/BsCl/Bsn
(ad lib.)/4 Sx: AATB •StMU
WILDER, Alec - *She'll Be Seven in May* •Fl/Ob/Asx/2 Cl/BsCl/Bsn/
Bass/Drums/Pno

11 Musicians

COLE, Bruce - *Pantomimes* (25') •Soprano Voice/Fl/Cl/BsCl/Ssx/
Perc/Pno/Guit/Vln/Vla/Vcl •B&H
PABLO, Luis de - *Polar, op. 12* (1963) •Vln/Ssx/BsCl/Xylophone/
Trb/6 Perc •Tono/SeMC
SPINO, P. - *Prelude of Woodwinds* •2 Fl/Ob (ad lib.)/3 Cl/BsCl/Bsn
(ad lib.)/4 Sx: AATB •StMU

12 Musicians

MASINI, Fabio - *"Nuvole e colori forti"* (1992) (18') •Fl/1 Sx: S+A/
BsCl/Fl/Ob/Cl/Bsn/2 Vln/Vla/Vcl/Harp
SPINO, P. - *Prelude of Woodwinds* •2 Fl/Ob (ad lib.)/3 Cl/BsCl/Bsn
(ad lib.)/4 Sx: AATB •StMU

13 Musicians

SPINO, P. - *Statement...* •Hn Solo/2 Fl/Ob/3 Cl/BsCl/Bsn/4 Sx:
AATB •StMu

14 Musicians

HARBISON, John - *Confinement* (1965) (15'15) •Fl/Ob/EH/Cl/BsCl/
Asx/Tpt/Trb/Vln/Vla/Vcl/Bass/Pno/Perc
ROSSÉ, François - *Paléochrome* (1988) (22') •Vla principal/2 Fl/Cl/
BsCl/1 Sx: S+T/EH/Bsn/Hn/4 Perc/Bass •adr

15 Musicians

LUTYENS, Elisabeth - *Islands, op. 80* (1971) •2 Narr: ST/Picc/Fl/Cl/
BsCl/Tsx/Hn/Pno/Celesta/Vln/Vla/Vcl/2
Perc
TEMPLE & SHAW - *Vanity Fair Suite* •Fl/Ob/4 Cl/BsCl/Asx/2 Vln/
Vla/Vcl/Bass/Perc/Pno •Mills

oOo

KONAGAYA, Sôichi - *Masquerade* •Cl Choir/4 Sx: SATB
LERSTAD, Terje - *Concerto No. 2, op. 171* (1984) (20') •Asx/Cl
Choir •NMI

Saxophone and Bassoon

2 Musicians

BOURLAND, Roger - *Double Concerto* (1983) •Ssx/Bsn/Str/Harp
•ECS
LASTRA, Erich Eder de - *Divertissement* (1974) •Asx/Bsn •adr
MYERS, Robert - *Three Inventions* (1971) (5') •Asx/Bsn •SeMC
SMITH, Stuart - *One for J. C.* (6') •Asx/Bsn •SeMC
SULZER, Baldwin - *Suite* (1974) •Asx/Bsn
WOODBURN, James - *Piece in Three Sections* (1976) •Asx/Bsn •adr

3 Musicians

ALCALAY, Luna - *Trio* (1964) •Asx/CBsn/Bass
AMRAM, David Werner - *Trio* (1965) •Tsx/Hn/Bsn •Pet
Beethoven, Ludwig van - *Excepts from Rondo* •Cl/Asx/Bsn •CF
BLACHER, Boris - *Jazz-Koloraturen, op. 1* (1929) •Soprano Voice/
Asx/Bsn •B&B
BOUVARD, Jean - *4 Fabliaux* •Ob/Asx/Bsn •adr
CUNNINGHAM, Michael - *Serenade, op. 13a* (1961) (7') •Cl/Asx/
Bsn •SeMC
EISENMANN, Will - *Divertimento* (1954) •2 Sx: SA/Bsn •Uni
EYSER, Eberhard - *Salinas nocturnas* (1979) (11') •Ssx/Cl/Vcl (or
Bsn) •STIM
FRACKENPOHL, Arthur - *Trio* •Ssx/Hn/Bsn •DP
HOLEWA, Hans - *Lamenti* (1976) (5') •Asx/Bsn/Hn •STIM
Kibbe - *Divertimento* •Ob/EH (or Asx)/Bsn •Sha
KOUTZEN, Boris - *Music trio* (1940) •Asx/Bsn/Vcl
MYERS, Robert - *Trio* (1965) (8') •Asx/Bsn/Vcl •Art

POLIN, Claire - *A Klockwork Diurnal* (1977) •Asx/Bsn/Hn •DP
ROESGEN-CHAMPION, Marguerite - *Concert n° 1; Concert n° 2* (1945) •Asx/Bsn/Harps •FDP
SCHULZE, Werner - *2 Duos* (12') •Fl/Asx/Bsn •CA
 Transplantazioni •Fl/Asx/Bsn •CA
SIBBING, Robert - *Moments* (1974) •Sx/Bsn/Tuba (or Bass) •Eto
VAUGHAN WILLIAMS, Ralph - *Household Music* (1940-41) •Diverse combinations •B&H
ZINN, Michael - *Suspensions* (1973) •Asx/Bsn/Vibr •SeMC

4 Musicians

Also see Reed Quartet (Voir aussi quatuor d'anches), page 367.

ATOR, James Donald - *Woodwind Quartet* (1969) (11') •Fl/Cl/Sx/Bsn •SeMC
Bagley - *Thistledown* (HARRIS) •2 Cl/Asx/Bsn •CF
BARBAUD, Pierre - *Arthémise...* (6'30) •Cl/Bsn/2 Sx •EFM
BENTZON, Jörgen - *Raconto n° 1*, op. 25 (1935) (13') •Fl/Asx/Bsn/Bass •SOBM/BMCo
BROWN, Newel - *Figments* •Sx/Tpt/Bsn/Vcl •SeMC
CHARBONNIER, Janine - *Exercice* (4') •2Sx: SA/BsCl/Bsn •EFM
Corelli, Arcangelo - *Gigue* (HARRIS) •2 Cl/Asx/Bsn (or BsCl) •CF
Cui, César - *Orientale* (HARRIS) •2 Cl/Asx/Bsn (or BsCl) •CF
Denza, Luigi - *Funiculi-Funicula* (HARRIS) •2 Cl/Asx/Bsn (or BsCl) •CF
Dewit, A. - *Pieces* (HARRIS) •2 Cl/Asx/Bsn (or BsCl) •CF
Di Lasso, O. - *Matona...* (CHEYETTE) •2 Cl/Asx/Bsn (or Bsx) •Ken
ENGELMANN, Hans - *Permutagioni* •Fl/Ob/Sx/Bsn •A&S
GERSCHEFSKI, Edwin - *America*, op. 44, nos. 6 & 13 (1962) •Fl/Cl/Asx/Bsn •CFE
Glazounov, Alexander - *In modo religioso* (BETTONEY) •2 Cl/Asx/Bsn (or BsCl) •CF
GRANT, Jerome - *Classical Woodwind Quartet* (1966) (20') •Asx/Cl/Fl/Bsn •adr
HALETZKI, P. - *Father and Son* (1938) •Picc/Asx/Bsn/Pno •Sch
Handel, Georg-Friedrich - *Pieces* (STANG) •2 Cl/Asx/Bsn (or BsCl) •CF
HARRIS, Floyd - *Pieces* •2 Cl/Asx/Bsn (or BsCl) •CF
HARTLEY, Walter - *Quartet 1993* (1993) (8'15) •Asx/Ob/Hn/Bsn •DP
Haydn, Franz Joseph - *Adagio* (GEIGER) •Fl/Ob/Asx/Bsn •CF
Macbeth, Allan - *Intermezzo* (HARRIS) •2 Cl/Asx/Bsn (or BsCl) •CF
MAEGAARD, Jan - *Musica riservata II* (1976) •Ob/Cl/Sx/Bsn
MAGANINI, Quinto - *Rêverie* (HARRIS) •Fl or Cl/Ob or Cl/Asx/Bsn or BsCl •CF
Massenet, Jules - *Last Slumber...* (HARRIS) •2 Cl/Asx/Bsn (or BsCl) •CF
MASSET-LECOQ, Roselyne - *3 Pièces* (1977) •Cl/Asx/Hn/Bsn
Meyerbeer, Giacomo - *Coronation March* (HARRIS) •2 Cl/Asx/Bsn (or BsCl) •CF
Molloy, James - *Kerry Dance* (HARRIS) •2 Cl/Asx/Bsn (or BsCl) •CF
MORRISSON, Julia - *The Memorare* •Asx/Bsn/Harp/Alto Voice •CFE
Mozart, Wolfgang - *Pieces* (STEPHENS, TOLL) •2 Cl/Asx/Bsn (or BsCl) •CF
MYERS, Robert - *Quartet* (1966) •Fl/Asx/Bsn/Vcl •SeMC/AMu
Pleyel, Ignace - *Andante aus rondo*, op. 48/1 •2 Cl/Asx/Bsn (or BsCl) •CF
Rossini, Giacchino - *Quartet No. 2* (GEE) •Fl/Cl/Sx/Bsn •DP
Silcher, Friedrich - *Loreley Paraphrase* (HARRIS) •2 Cl/Asx/Bsn (or BsCl) •CF
Stamitz, Anton - *Andante* (KESNAR) •2 Cl/Asx/Bsn (or BsCl) •CF
STRAESSER, Joep - *Intersections V* (1977) (12') •Ob/Cl/Asx/Bsn •Don

Tenaglia, Antonio - *Aria* (CHEYETTE) •2 Cl/Asx/Bsn (or Bsx) •Ga
Thome, François - *Pizzicato* (HARRIS) •2 Cl/Asx/Bsn (or BsCl) •CF
Verdi, Giuseppe - *Quartet* •2 Cl/Asx/Bsn (or BsCl) •CF
Walckiers, E. - *Rondo* (HARRIS) •2 Cl/Asx/Bsn (or BsCl) •CF
Weigl, Karl - *Sir Voire* (HARRIS) •2 Cl/Asx/Bsn (or BsCl) •CF
WILSON, Donald - *Tetragon* (1990) •Fl/Asx/Cl/Bsn
ZLATIC, Slmavko - *Balum* (1936) •Ob/EH/Asx/Bsn •UKH

5 Musicians

ASCOUGH, R. - *Quintet* •Ssx/Fl/Ob/Cl/Bsn
BARGSTEM, Joey - *Quintet for Winds* •Ob/Cl/Asx/Trb/Bsn •DP
BROTONS, Soler - *Quinteto* (1978) •Fl/Ob/Asx/Hn/Bsn •EMEC
BUEL, Charles - *37 Dream Flowers* (1971-72) (9') •Asx/Bsn/Pno/Electr. Pno/Perc •adr
BUMCKE, Gustav - *Quintet*, op. 23b •Cl/EH/Wald Horn/Bsn/Bsx
CARPENTER, Gary - *Dances for Mutilated Toys* (1970) (15') •Fl/Ob/Cl/Asx/Bsn •BMIC
CONTI, Francis - *Quintet* (1972) •Fl/Picc/1 Sx: A+S/Cl/Bsn •adr
CUNNINGHAM, Michael - *Miro Gallery* •Fl/Ob/Cl/Asx/Bsn •SeMC
DEFOSSEZ, René - *Mélopée et Danse* •Asx/Pno or Fl/Ob/Cl/Asx/Bsn •An
FREE, John - *A Wind of Changes* (1990) •Cl/Bsn/Sx/Perc/Pno •CMC
GASTINEL, Gérard - *Quintette* (1977) •Ssx/Ob/Cl/Hn/Bsn
GHEZZO, Dinu - *Sound shapes* •Fl/Ob/Cl/Sx/Bsn •SeMC
HESPOS, Hans - *En-kin das fern-nahe* (1970) (5'30) •Ssx/Cl/Bsn/Bass/Perc •EMod
HOLZMANN, Rodolfo - *Divertimento* (1936) •Fl/Cl/Sx/Hn/Bsn
Joplin, Scott - *The Entertainer* (AXWORTHY) •2 Sx: ST/Hn/Bsn/Perc •DP
KAINZ, Walter - *Bläser Quintet*, op. 12 (1935) •Fl/Cl/Asx/Hn/Bsn •adr
KUNZ, Ernst - *25 pezzi per varie...* (1963) •Vcl/3 Sx/Bsn
LAUBA, Christian - *Ravel's raga* (1993) (15') •Vln/Cl/Asx/Bsn/Pno •adr
Laube, P. - *Alsacian Dance* •Fl/Ob/Asx/Bsn (or Hn)/Pno •CF
LAUBER, Anne - *5 Eléments* (1972) (6'15) •Fl/Ssx/Vln/Bsn/Tuba •CMC
LOEFFLER, Charles-Martin - *Ballade carnavalesque* (1904) •Fl/Ob/Asx/Bsn/Pno •South
MALHERBE, Claudy - *Non-sun* (1984-85) (10') •Picc/Tsx/Ob/Cl/Bsn
McKAY George - *American Street Scenes* (1935) •Cl/Tpt/Asx/Bsn/Pno or 4 Sx/Pno •CAP
NILSSON, Anders - *Cadenze* (1992) •Fl/Ob/Cl/Bsn/Sx
OLIVER, John - *Métalmorphose* (1983) •Ob/Cl/Bsn/Sx/Tpt •CMC
READE, Paul - *Quintet* (1976) •Fl/Ob/Asx/Hn/Bsn •adr
SODERO, Cesare - *Pieces* (1933) •Fl/Ob/Cl/Tsx/Bsn •AMPC
SPRONGL, Norbert - *Quintet*, op. 124 (1958) •Ob/Asx/Tpt/Hn/Bsn •adr
VOGEL, Wladimir - *La Ticinella...* (1941) •Fl/Ob/Cl/Asx/Bsn •SZ
WOLFE, George - *Persian Dance* (1982) •Asx/Picc/Bsn/Xylophone/Exotic Perc
YOUNG, Lynden de - *Chamber Music* (1972) •Asx/Bsn/Ob/Pno/Vibr •SeMC

6 Musicians

Also see Wind Sextet (Voir aussi sextuor à vent), page 368.

AMELLER, André - *Azuleros de Valencia* (1965) (13') •Fl/Ob/Cl/Asx/Hn/Bsn
BUMCKE, Gustav - *Sextet*, op. 19 (1903) •Cl/EH/Wald Horn/BsCl/Sx/Bsn •Diem
 Sextuor, op. 20 en Lab •2 Sx: AA/EH/Hn/BsCl/Bsn •VAB
CORY, Eleanor - *Waking* (1974) •Tsx/Bsn/Vln/Vcl/Bass/Perc

DINESCU-LUCACI, Violeta - *"Auf der Suche nach Mozart"* (1983) (19') •Fl/Sx/Bsn/Hn/Vln/Pno+Celesta •adr

FERRO, Pictro - *Amphitrion divertimento* •2 Fl/2 Sx/CBsn/Perc •Ric

GERSCHEFSKI, Edwin - *America*, op. 44, no. 14a •Fl/Cl/Asx/Tpt/Bsn/Pno •CFE

GOTKOVSKY, Ida - *Poème lyrique* (1987) •2 Voices: SB/Pno/Fl (or Vln)/Asx (or Vla)/Bsn (or Vcl)

GOTSKOSIK, Oleg - *Svit...* (1986) •Ob/Asx/Bsn/2 Vln/Pno •SMIC

LUNDEN, Lennart - *Quadrille*; *Queen Christina's Song* •2 Fl/2 Cl/Sx/Bsn •Che

LUROT, Jacques - *Sextuor* •Ob/Cl/Asx/Bsn/2 Voices: SA

MIEREANU, Costin - *Miroir liquide* (1986) (11') •1 Sx: Sno+S+A+T/Bsn/Perc/Harp/Pno/Bass •Sal

SCELSI, Jacinto - *Yamaon* (1954-58) (10') •Bass Voice/2 Sx: AB/CBsn/Bass/Perc •Sal

TAGGART, Mark - *Concerto for Chamber Ensemble* (1983) (20') •Cl/Asx/Bsn/Tpt/Bass/Pno

7 Musicians

ARGERSINGER, Charles - *Drastic Measures* •Fl/Ob/Cl/Asx/Bsn/Hn/Perc

BERNARD, Jacques - *L'Opéra de l'espace* (1970) •Narr/Ob/Cl/BsCl/1 Sx: S+A+B/Bsn/Perc •adr

BROWN, Anthony - *Soundscape 1* •Asx/Bsn/Tpt/Vln/Voice/Pno/Perc/Tape •SeMC

DANCEANU, Liviu - *Quasi concerto* (1983) (15') •1 Sx: S+T/Bsn/Trb/Vcl/Bass/Pno/Perc

KARKOFF, Maurice - *Djurens Karneval* (1974) (15') •Fl/Picc/2 Cl/Tsx/Bsn/Perc •STIM

KOECHLIN, Charles - *Septuor*, op. 165 (1937) (11'30) •Fl/Ob/EH/Cl/Asx/Hn/Bsn •Oil

LONGY, George - *Rhapsodie - Lento* (1904) •Harp/Bass/2 Cl/Bsn/Asx/Timp •South

MASON, Lucas - *A Quilt of Love* (1971) •Soprano Voice/Asx/Fl/Vln/Bsn/Trb/Vcl •adr

NILSSON, Bo - *Zeiten im Umlauf*, op. 14 (1957) (3') •Fl/Ob/EH/Cl/BsCl/Tsx/Bsn •Uni

RADULESCU, Horatiu - *X* (1984-85) •Sx/Cl/2 Bsn/2 Bass/Perc

SOMERS, Harry - *Limericks* (1979) •Voice/Fl/Cl/Sx/Bsn/Tpt/Euphonium •CMC

VILLA-LOBOS, Heitor - *Chôros n° 3 - Pica-Pào*, op. 189 (1925) (6') •Cl/Asx/Bsn/3 Hn/Trb •ME

WILLIS, Richard - *Irregular Resolutions* •Fl/Ob/Cl/Asx/Bsn/Hn/Perc •adr

8 Musicians

BÖRJESSON, Lars - *Divertimento*, op. 38 (1983) •Asx/BsCl/Bsn/Guit/Harp/Marimba/Vln/Vcl •STIM

BUMCKE, Gustav - *Suite G Dur*, op. 24 •Tenor Voice/Fl/Ob/Cl/Bsn/Hn/Bsx/Harp •VAB

FERRAND-TEULET, Denise - *Octuor* (1975) •4 Sx: SATB/3 Cl/Bsn

FRANCO, Clare - *Four Winds...* •Asx/Harp/Vibr/Fl/Ob/Cl/Hn/Bsn

GARCIN, Gérard - *Encore plus tard* (1984) (12') •1 Sx: Sno+A+Bs/Fl/Cl/Bsn/Vla/Vcl/Bass/Perc/Tape •Sal

GUY, Georges - *Concerto en forme de jazz* •Asx Solo/Pno Solo/Fl/Ob/Cl/Hn/Bsn/Bass

HESPOS, Hans - *Druckspuren - geschattet* (1970) (7'30) •Fl/Eb Cl/Asx/Bsn/2 Tpt/Trb/Bass •EMod

KORTE, Karl - *Matrix* (1968) (16') •Fl/Ob/Cl/Asx/Hn/Bsn/Pno/Perc •GSch

LAKE, Larry - *Filar il tuono* (1989) •Cl/3 Sx: ATB/Bsn/Tpt/Trb/Marimba •CMC

LANTIER, Pierre - *Fugue jazz* (1944) (3') •2 Cl/2 Sx: AT/Bsn/Tpt/Trb/Perc

LAURETTE, Marc - *Kaleïdoscope* •Cl/Bsn/2 Sx: SB/Hn/Vla/Bass/Vibr

MARIETAN, Pierre - *13 en concert* (1983) (15') •1 Sx: Sno+S+B/Cl/Bsn/Trb/Vcl/2 Bass/Pno

MONNET, Marc - *L'exercice de la bataille* (1991) (45') •2 Vln/2 Bsn/2 MIDI Sx/MIDI Guit/MIDI Pno

NILSSON, Bo - *Frequenzen* (1957) •Fl/Picc/Ob/EH/Cl/BsCl/Tsx/Bsn •Uni

RADULESCU, Horatiu - *Sky* (1984-85) •Sx/Cl/Fl/2 Bsn/2 Bass/Perc

RIEDEL, Georg - *Reflexioner* (1974) (8') •Woodwind Quintet/Jazz group (Cl+Asx/Pno/Bass) •SMIC

SAGVIK, Stellan - *Guenilles des jongleurs*, op. 74 (1977) (7'30) •Fl/Ob/3 Cl/Asx/Bsn/Cnt •STIM

VILLA-LOBOS, Heitor - *Chôros n° 7* (1924) (10') •Fl/Ob/Cl/Asx/Bsn/Vln/Vcl/Tam-tam •ME

9 Musicians

ALLGEN, Claude - *Adagio och Fuga* (25') •Fl/Ob/EH/Cl/BsCl/2 Sx: AB/Bsn/Hn •STIM

BUMCKE, Gustav - *"Der Spaziergang"*, op. 22 •Fl/Ob/EH/Cl/Bsn/Hn/BsTrb/Bsx/Harp

CAPLET, André - *Impressions d'Automne* (1905) (3') •Asx/Ob/2 Cl/Bsn/Harp/Org/2 Vcl

Légende (1903) (13') •Asx/Ob/Cl/Bsn/2 Vln/Vla/Vcl/Bass •Fuz

CERHA, Friedrich - *Exercices for Nine, No. 1* •BsCl/Bsx/Bsn/Tpt/Trb/Tuba/Vcl/Bass/Harp •Uni

COLE, Helen - *Serenade* •Fl/Ob/2 Cl/BsCl/Hn/Asx/2 Bsn

COX, Rona - *Two Expressions* (1968) •Fl/Ob/Cl/2 Sx: SB/Hn/Bsn/Bass/Perc •adr

DIEMENTE, Edward - *For Lady Day* •Fl/Ob/Cl/Tpt/Trb/Vln/Vla/Sx/Bsn/Tape •SeMC

GRANDERT, Johnny - *86 T* •Fl/EH/BsCl/Bsx/CBsn/2 Tpt/Perc/Pno •STIM

HAHN, Reynaldo - *Divertissement...* (1933) (25') •2 Vln/Vla/Vcl/Bass/Asx/Bsn/Timp/Perc •Sal

IVES, Charles - *Over the Pavements*, op. 20 (1906-13) •Picc/Cl/Bsx (or Bsn)/Tpt/3 Trb/Perc/Pno •PIC

LEGRAND, Michel - *Porcelaine de Sax* (1958) (3') •6 Sx: SnoSATBBs (or Eb Cl/Cl/3 Sx: ATB/Bsn) Trb/Bass/Perc •Mills

LEWIS, John Aaron - *The Queen's Fancy* (4') •Fl/Cl/Tsx/Bsn/Hn/Trb/Harp/Bass/Perc •MJQ

NATANSON, Tadeus - *3 Pictures for 7 Instruments* (1960) •Ob/Cl/Asx/Trb/Vcl/Tpt/Bsn/Pno/Perc •AMP

SILVERMAN, Faye - *Shadings* (1978) •Vln/Vla/Bass/Fl/Ob/Asx/Bsn/Hn/Tuba

ULRICH, Jürgen - *Spiel* (1974) (5') •Fl/Ob/Cl/Bsn/Sx/Hn/Tpt/Trb/Tuba •VDMK

WILDER, Alec - *Suite* •Bsx/Fl/Ob/Cl/2 Hn/Bsn/Bass/Drums

10 Musicians

BUMCKE, Gustav - *Präludium und Fuge*, op. 20 (1903) •Fl/Ob/EH/Sx/Cl/BsCl/2 Bsn/2 Hn

COLE, Hugo - *Serenade...* (1965) (15') •2 Fl/Ob/2 Cl/Asx/2 Bsn/2 Hn

CUNNINGHAM, Michael - *Linear Ceremony* •2 Fl/2 Ob/2 Cl/Sx/Hn/2 Bsn •SeMC

FORTNER, Jack - *S pr ING sur des poèmes de E. E. Cummings* (1966) (11') •Mezzo Soprano Voice/Fl/Asx/Bsn/Vla/Vcl/Bass/Vibr/Harp/Pno •JJ

HARTLEY, Walter - *Double Concerto* (1969) (7'30) •Asx/Tuba/Wind Octet (Fl/Ob/Cl/Bsn/Hn/2 Tpt/Trb) •PhiCo

LAZARUS, Daniel - *4 Mélodies* •Contralto Voice/Fl/Cl/Asx/Bsn/2 Vln/Vla/Vcl/Bass

LINDBERG, Nils - *Progression* (1985) (28') •Fl/Ob/Cl/Hn/Bsn/2 Sx:
SA/Pno/Bass/Drums •SMIC
LUTYENS, Elisabeth - *Akapotik Rose*, op. 64 (1966) (18') •Soprano
Voice/Picc/Fl/Cl/Bsn/Cl+Tsx/Vln/Vla/Vcl/
Pno
MASON, Benedict - *Coulour and information* (1993) •Fl/Ob/Sx/Bsn/
Hn/Tpt/Trb/Tuba/Perc/Electr. Bass
MIMET, Anne-Marie - *Fanfare et divertissement* •Fl/Ob/Cl/Bsn/3 Sx:
SAT/Tpt/Trb/Tuba
NILSSON, Bo - *Zeitpunkte* (1960) (5') •Fl/Alto Fl/Ob/EH/Cl/BsCl/2
Sx: AT/Bsn/CBsn
PAUMGARTNER, Bernhard - *Divertimento* •Picc/EH/Asx/Bsn/Hn/
Tpt/Pno/Vla/Vcl/Perc •Uni
SCHWERTSIK, Kurt - *Salotto romano*, op. 5 (1961) •BsCl/Bsx/Bsn/
Hn/Trb/Tuba/Perc/Bass/Vcl/Guit •EMod
TREMBLAY, George - *Epithalamium* (1962) •Fl/Ob/Cl/Sx/Bsn/Hn/
Tpt/Trb/Tuba/Perc •CFE
WILDER, Alec - *She'll Be Seven in May* •Fl/Ob/Asx/2 Cl/BsCl/Bsn/
Bass/Drums/Pno

11 Musicians

ANDRIESSEN, Jurriaan - *Hommage à Milhaud* (1945) (8') •Fl/Ob/
Cl/Bsn/Hn/Tpt/Trb/Asx/Vln/Vla/Vcl •Don
KEULEN, Geert van - *Onkruid* (1981) (5') •Ob/Cl/2 Sx: AT/Bsn/Hn/
Tpt/Trb/Vln/Vla/Pno •Don
MONDELLO, Nuncio - *Suite* (1956) •Asx/2 Fl/Ob/Cl/Bsn/2 Hn/Tpt/
Trb/Perc •adr
SPINO, P. - *Prelude of Woodwinds* •2 Fl/Ob (ad lib.)/3 Cl/BsCl/Bsn
(ad lib.)/4 Sx: AATB •StMU

12 Musicians

CECCONI, Monique - *Hommage à...* •Ob/Cl/Asx/Bsn/4 Vln/2 Vla/2
Vcl •Phi
CURTIS-SMITH, Curtis - *Sundry Dances* (1981) •Fl/Ob/Cl/3 Sx:
SAB/Bsn/CBsn/Tpt/Trb/Tuba/Bass •adr
DUREY, Louis - *Feu la mère de Madame*, op. 49 (1945) (5') •Fl/Ob/
Asx/Bsn/Tpt/Tuba/Perc/2 Vln/Vla/Vcl/Bass
•BRF
HASQUENOPH, Pierre - *Inventions* •2 Vln/Vla/Vcl/Bass/Fl/Ob/Cl/
Asx/Bsn/Hn/Tpt •Heu
LEWIS, Arthur - *Pieces of Eight* •Fl/2 Ob/3 Cl/Bsn/2 Tsx/Hn/Baritone
Hn/Perc •CAP
MASINI, Fabio - *"Nuvole e colori forti"* (1992) (18') •Fl/1 Sx: S+A/
BsCl/Fl/Ob/Cl/Bsn/2 Vln/Vla/Vcl/Harp
ROBBINS, David - *Improvisation* •Fl/2 Cl/Tsx/Bsn/Tpt/Trb/Vln/Vla/
Vcl/Bass/Perc
SPINO, P. - *Prelude of Woodwinds* •2 Fl/Ob (ad lib.)/3 Cl/BsCl/Bsn
(ad lib.)/4 Sx: AATB •StMU

13 Musicians

FINNISSY, Michael - *Babylon* (1971) (19') •Mezzo Soprano Voice/
Ob/Cl/Asx/Bsn/Guit/Harp/Pno/2 Perc/2 Vcl/
Bass •Uni
First sign a sharp white mons (1974-67) (45') •2 Fl/2 Cl/Asx/CBsn/
Hn/Accordion/Guit/Vln/2 Vcl/Pno •BMIC
MERKU, Pavle - *Tiare* •Baritone Voice/Sx/11 wind instruments •Piz
SEKON, Joseph - *Lemon Ice* (1972) •Fl/Ob/Cl/2 Sx: ST/Bsn/Tpt/Trb/
2 Perc/Vln/Vcl/Pno •adr
SPINO, P. - *Statement...* •Hn Solo/2 Fl/Ob/3 Cl/BsCl/Bsn/4 Sx:
AATB •StMu

14 Musicians

GRAINGER, Percy - *The Duke of Marlborough* (1905-39-49) •4 Tpt/
4 Hn (or 2 Sx: AT/2 Bsn)/3 Trb/Tuba/Bass/
Cymb. •Sch

ROSSÉ, François - *Paléochrome* (1988) (22') •Vla principal/2 Fl/Cl/
BsCl/1 Sx: S+T/EH/Bsn/Hn/4 Perc/Bass •adr

oOo

GRAINGER, Percy - *Stalt Vesselil* (1951) •Voice/Bsn/Sx/Str •GSch
VILLA-LOBOS, Heitor - *Nonetto*, op. 181 (1923) (18') •Fl/Ob/Cl/1
Sx: A+B/Bsn/Perc/Celesta/Harp/Pno/Mixed
Chorus •ME

Reed Quartet (Quatuor d'anches)

Oboe, Clarinet, Alto Saxophone, and Bassoon
(Hautbois, Clarinette, Saxophone Alto, et Basson).

ABBOTT, Alain - *Saxophonie* (1974) (8'45) •Bil
ARMA, Paul - *Transparences*
AURIOL Hubert d' - *Quatuor d'anches* •Bil
Bach, J. S. - *Pieces* (A. DOMIZI)
BAGOT, Maurice - *Transmutation* (1974)
BAGUERRE, Francis - *Et la source...* (1980)
Bartok, Béla - *Suite* (L. LIVI)
BAUMGARTNER, Jean-Paul - *Cycle IV* (1981) (15')
BERNARD, Jacques - *Dialogues d'anches* (1969) (13') •EFM
BERTAINA, Pier Michele - *5 Pezzi...* (1988)
BOUVARD, Jean - *Choral varié* •adr
3 Pièces brèves (1972) •adr
Suite montagnarde •adr
CALMEL, Roger - *Cantate "Liberté"* •Ob/Cl/Asx/Bsn/Chorus/Solo-
ists
Incantations thibétaines (1974) •adr
Messe du pays d'Oc •Ob/Cl/Asx/Bsn/Chorus/Soloists •adr
Quatuor d'anches •adr
7 Séquences (12'15) •4 Sx: SATB or Ob/Cl/Asx/Bsn •EFM
CARLES, Marc - *Fragmentaires* (1971) (12') •adr
CECCONI, Monique - *Silences* (1971) (10') •EFM/Bil
CHAGNON, Roland - *Image pour un enfant* (1974)
CHINI, André - *3 Cris pour 4* (1974) (7') •STIM
COCO, Remigio - *Rag-time* (1987)
Debussy, Claude - *Pieces* (TESEI)
DEPELSENAIRE, Jean-Marie - *Les métamorphoses d'Arlequin* •adr
DESLOGES, Jacques - *Prélude et danse* (1983) •4 Sx: SATB or Ob/
Cl/Asx/Bsn (or Vcl or Trb) •Arp
DUBOIS, Pierre-Max - *Les trois mousquetaires* (1966) (10') •Led
EYCHENNE, Marc - *Nuances et rythmes* (1968) (10') •adr
FALK, Julien - *Quatuor d'anches* •adr
FRACKENPOHL, Arthur - *Quartet* (1969) (12') •RPS/DP
GILLET, Bruno - *Hornpipes*
GOLDMANN, Marcel - *Hével II* (1970) (10') •EFM
Granados, Enrique - *Intermezzo des Goyescas* (LACOUR)
HARTLEY, Walter - *Quartet for Reeds* (1977) (9'30) •DP
HEKSTER, Walter - *Setting V* (1985) (8') •Ob+EH/Cl+BsCl/Asx/Bsn
•Don
HERBERG, Perig - *Pevar benveg*
HERSANT, Philippe - *Extraits* •adr
Joplin, Scott - *The Easy Winners* (DOMIZI)
JUELICH, Raimund - *In-formation* (1981) (12')
KEISER, Henk - *V.S.O.P.* (1984) (14') •Don
KOUZAN, Marien - *Nyaya*
LANTOINE, Louis - *Quatuor d'anches* •Ob+EH/Cl+BsCl/1 Sx: A+S/
Bsn •adr
LAUBA, Christian - *Douar* (1991) (16'30) •adr
LEJET, Edith - *Quatre petits poèmes chinois* (12') •Ob/Cl/Asx/Bsn/
Soprano Voice •adr
LEMELAND, Aubert - *Nocturne*, op. 10 (1970) (9'40) •EFM
LENOT, Jacques - *Pièce* •Ob/Cl/Asx/Bsn/Soprano Voice •adr

LERSY, Roger - *Pérégrination* (1969) (8') •adr
LOLINI, Ruggero - *Stanze d'Ambra* (1984)
LOUVIER, Alain - *5 Portraits et une image* (1973) •Led
MAEGAARD, Jan - *Musica riservata II* (1976)
Mancini, Henry - *The Pink Panther* (DOMIZI)
MARKOVITCH, Ivan - *Aulodisation* (1990)
MASSIAS, Gérard - *Variations* (1955) (11') •Bil
MATSUSHITA, Isao - *Ashi no sho II* (1981)
MEIER, Daniel - *Kuklos* (12') •EFM
MERANGER, Paul - *1er Quatuor d'anches* (1977)
NIHASHI, Jun-ichi - *Banka* (1981-86) •Led
PONJEE, Ted - *Quatuor d'anches* (1979) (9') •Don
PRIN, Yves - *Quatuor d'anches*
QUERAT, Marcel - *Quatuor d'anches* •adr
RIBAS, Rosa - *Quatuor de viento* (1981) (10') •adr
ROGER, Denise - *3 Mouvements* (11') •EFM
ROSSÉ, François - *Anchée* (1987) •Ob/Cl/1 Sx: S+A+B/Bsn •adr
SAGVIK, Stellan - *Roughs from the...*, op. 85 (1978) (7') •STIM
SALVATORE, Daniele - *Dal libro rosso del Signor Bagging* (1987)
SAMONOV - *Suite*
SCHOSER, Brian - *Traces*
SCIORTINO, Patrice - *Flammes* (1969) •Ob+EH/Cl+Basset Horn/1 Sx: A+B/Bsn+CBsn •adr
    Rapsodique
SEMLER-COLLERY, Jules - *Quatuor d'anches* (1964) (9')
STRAESSER, Joep - *Intersections V* (1977) (12') •Don
    Intersections V-1 (1974-79) (11'30) •4 Sx: SATB or Ob/Cl/Asx/Bsn •Don
Stravinsky, Igor - *Suite No. 1* (TESEI)
Tcherepnine, Alexandre - *Sonatine sportive* (E. YADZINSKI) •Led
TESEI, Tonino - *5 Piccoli pezzi* (1984) (7')
TOURNIER, Franz-André - *Quatuor d'anches* (1964) (14') •RR
TREBINSKY, Arkadi - *Deux mouvements* •adr
WALTER, D. - *Deux Silhouettes* (1975)
WEBER, Alain - *Epitames* (1974)
    Epodes (1974) •EFM
WIERNIK, Adam - *Feelings* (1981) (11') •STIM
ZOURABICHVILI, Nicolas - *Winterleid* (1984) (18')

Wind Sextet (Sextuor à vent)

Flute, Oboe, Clarinet, Alto Saxophone unless indicated otherwise, Horn, and Bassoon (Flute, Hautbois, Clarinette, Saxophone Alto sauf indication contraire, Cor, et Basson).

AMELLER, André - *Suite d'après Rameau* (1960) (9') •ET
    Azuleros de Valencia (1965) (13')
ANDERSON, Tommy Joe - *Nemesis*, op. 19 (1975) •Ssx •DP
ANGELINI, Louis - *Sextet*
BASSET, Leslie - *Wind Music* •THP
BAUZIN, Pierre-Philippe - *5 Mouvements...*, op. 19 (1960) (12') •adr
BEALL, John - *Shaker Tunes* (1992)
BECKLER, Stanworth - *Mixtures* •SeMC
BULL, Edward Hagerup - *Sextuor*, op. 31 (1965) (11') •NMI
CHILDS, Barney - *Four Pieces...* (1977) •1 Sx: S+A •WWS
    Interbalances V •CFE
CLERISSE, Robert - *Le P'tit Prince a dit...* •4 Sx: SATB or Fl/Ob/Cl/Asx/Hn/Bsn •adr
    Polka valaisanne •adr
DUBOIS, Pierre-Max - *Sinfonia da camera* (1964) (10') •Led
EYCHENNE, Marc - *Sextuor* (1964) (12'15) •Fuz
GRABNER, Hermann - *Sextet*, op. 33 •Tsx •K&S
HAGSTRÖM, Nils - *Suono per fiati* (1979) (11') •Fl+Picc/Ob+EH/Asx/Cl/Hn/Bsn

HARTLEY, Walter - *Chamber Music* (1960) (8'30) •Wi&Jo
HEDWALL, Lennart - *Une petite musique...* (1984) (21') •Fl+Picc/Ob+EH/Cl+BsCl/Asx/Hn/Bsn •SMIC
HEIDEN, Bernhard - *Intrada* (1970) (10') •South
HESPOS, Hans - *Profile* (1972) (11') •Ssx •EMod
HOBBS - *Sextet* •Tsx •DP
KABELAC, Miloslav - *Dechovy Sextet*, op. 8 (1940) (17') •CHF/JMD/SHF
KAVANAUGH, Patrick - *Hommage to C. S. Lewis* (1978)
KLEIN, Lothar - *Vaudeville* (1979) (12') •Ssx •CMC
KULESHA, Gary - *Concertante music* (1980) •CMC
LEVEL, Pierre-Yves - *Cheminements* •Lem
LIESENFELD, Paul - *Sérénade* (1965) (4') •adr
MARKOVITCH, Ivan - *Petite marche* (1963) (4')
    Variations (1964) (8')
MILHAUD, Darius - *Scaramouche* (STEWART) •Sal
ÖHLUND, Ulf - *Three Pieces...* (12') •Tons/SMIC
Rameau, Jean-Philippe - *Ordre pour les festes...* (LONDEIX)
RIEDEL, Georg - *Reflexioner* (1974) (8') •Woodwind Quintet/Jazz group (Cl+Asx/Pno/Bass) •SMIC
Rimsky-Korsakov, Nicolas - *Danse des bouffons* (LONDEIX)
    Snégourotchka - Chanson de Lel (LONDEIX)
SCHÖNBERG, Stig - *Sostetto per fiati*, op. 85 (1979-80) (14') •1 Sx: S+A •STIM
Schubert, Franz - *Schubertiade* (LONDEIX)
SNYDER, Randall - *Almagest* •DP
STEIN, Leon - *Sextet* (1958) (18') •CFE/CP
TOMASI, Henri - *Printemps* (1963) (10') •Led
WALKER, James J. - *Chamber Concerto*

Saxophone and Horn

2 Musicians

DUTKIEWICZ, Andrzzei - *Capriccio* (1984) (9') •Asx/Hn
SIBBING, Robert - *Pastiche* •Sx/Hn •Pres

3 Musicians

AMRAM, David Werner - *Trio* (1965) •Tsx/Hn/Bsn •Pet
BEUGNIOT, Jean-Pierre - *Anamorphose* (1976) (11') •Ob/Hn/Bsx •adr
COPLEY, Evan - *Trio* (1981) •Asx/Hn/Pno
FRACKENPOHL, Arthur - *Trio* •Ssx/Hn/Bsn •DP
HOLEWA, Hans - *Lamenti* (1976) (5') •Asx/Bsn/Hn •STIM
LEMELAND, Aubert - *Trio*, op. 98 (1979) (8') •Cl/Ssx/Hn •adr
POLIN, Claire - *A Klockwork Diurnal* (1977) •Asx/Bsn/Hn •DP
RADDATZ, Otto - *Pieces* (1982) •2 Hn/Asx •adr

4 Musicians

DADELSEN, Hans-Christian von - *Cries of Butterflies* (1979) (16') •Asx/Hn/Vla/Synth •Kodasi
HARTLEY, Walter - *Quartet 1993* (1993) (8'15) •Asx/Ob/Hn/Bsn •DP
MASSET-LECOQ, Roselyne - *3 Pièces* (1977) •Cl/Asx/Hn/Bsn
THOMAS, Ronald - *Occasion* •Fl/Ssx/Cl/Hn

5 Musicians

ARCURI, Serge - *Prologue* (1985) •Fl/Ssx/Cl/Hn/Perc/Tape •CMC
BROTONS, Soler - *Quinteto* (1978) •Fl/Ob/Asx/Hn/Bsn •EMEC
CHANDLER, Erwin - *Concert Music* •Asx/Ob/2 Hn/Pno
FONTAINE, Louis-Noël - *Musique* (1978) (8') •Cl/2 Hn/2 Sx: AB •Capri
Frescobaldi, Girolamo - *Gagliarda* (ARON) •4 Sx: ATTB/Hn •GSch
GASTINEL, Gérard - *Quintette* (1977) •Ssx/Ob/Cl/Hn/Bsn
HOLZMANN, Rodolfo - *Divertimento* (1936) •Fl/Cl/Sx/Hn/Bsn

JONES, Robert - *Divertimento* •Fl/Ob/Cl/Asx/Hn •WWS

Joplin, Scott - *The Entertainer* (Axworthy) •2 Sx: ST/Hn/Bsn/Perc •DP

KAINZ, Walter - *Bläser Quintet*, op. 12 (1935) •Fl/Cl/Asx/Hn/Bsn •adr

Laube, P. - *Alsacian Dance* •Fl/Ob/Asx/Bsn (or Hn)/Pno •CF

MULDOWNEY, Dominic - *Love Music for Bathsheba...* (1974) (20') •Fl/Ob/Cl/Asx/Hn (or Trb) •Nov

NIELSON, Lewis - *Dialectical Fantasy* (1981) •Fl/Ob/Cl/Tsx/Hn •ACA

OLBRISCH, Franz-Martin - *Quintett* (1989) •Ob+EH/2 Sx: AT/Hn/Perc •adr

READE, Paul - *Quintet* (1976) •Fl/Ob/Asx/Hn/Bsn •adr

SPRONGL, Norbert - *Quintet*, op. 124 (1958) •Ob/Asx/Tpt/Hn/Bsn •adr

TARLOW, Karen - *Music...* (1973) (12') •Fl/Ob/Cl/Asx/Hn •SeMC

YOUNG, Charles Rochester - *October in the Rain* (1989) (5') •MIDI Wind Controller/Hn/Pno/Synth/Perc •adr

6 Musicians

Also see Wind Sextet (Voir aussi sextuor à vent), page 368.

AMELLER, André - *Azuleros de Valencia* (1965) (13') •Fl/Ob/Cl/Asx/Hn/Bsn

BUMCKE, Gustav - *Sextuor*, op. 20 en La*b* •2 Sx: AA/EH/Hn/BsCl/Bsn •VAB

BRANDON, Seymour - *Chaconne and Variations* •Ob/Asx/2 Hn/Trb/Pno •MaPu

CARLOSEMA, Bernard - *Radiance* (1988) (5'30) •Fl/Asx/Hn/Tpt/Trb/Tuba •Fuz

DINESCU-LUCACI, Violeta - *"Auf der Suche nach Mozart"* (1983) (19') •Fl/Sx/Bsn/Hn/Vln/Pno+Celesta •adr

GOEHR, Alexander - *Shadowplay*, op. 30 (1976) (20') •Actor+Tenor Voice/Narr+Fl/Asx/Hn/Vcl/Pno •Sch

HARTLEY, Walter - *Concertino da Camera* (1994) •Ssx/2 Tpt/Hn/Trb/Tuba •adr

KARLINS, M. William - *Cantena II* (1982) (10') •Ssx/Brass Quintet •ACA

LESSER, Jeffrey - *Last Saxophone on Earth* (1979) •Asx/Brass Quintet

ORREGO SALAS, Juan - *Concerto da camera* (1987) •Asx/Brass Quintet

PELUSI, Mario - *Concert Piece* (1978) (12'30) •Bsx/Brass Quartet/Perc

ROKEACH, Martin - *Tango* •Ob/Cl/Asx/Hn/Trb/Vcl •DP

SIMS, Ezra - *Sextet* (1981) (22') •Cl/Asx/Hn/Vln/Vla/Vcl •ACA

TULL, Fisher - *Concertino da camera* •Asx/Brass Quintet •South

7 Musicians

ARGERSINGER, Charles - *Drastic Measures* •Fl/Ob/Cl/Asx/Bsn/Hn/Perc

BJORKLUND, Terje - *Herbarium* (1982) •Fl/Ssx/Vln/Hn/Bass/Pno/Perc •NMI

CANTON, Edgardo - *Phares et balises* •Fl/Ob/Sx/BsCl/Hn/Tpt/Trb

EYCHENNE, Marc - *Petite suite* •Ob/Ssx/5 Hn •adr

FINNISSY, Michael - *Evening* (1974) •Asx/Hn/Tpt/Perc/Harp/Vcl/Bass

HEYN, Volker - *Sandwich Gare de l'Est* (1986) (12'30) •1 Sx: Sno+CBs/2 Hn/2 Tpt/2 Trb •Br&Ha

KLEIN, Jonathan - *Hear O Israel* •Soprano Voice/Alto Voice/Sx/Hn/Pno/Perc/Bass •SeMC

KOECHLIN, Charles - *Septuor*, op. 165 (1937) (11'30) •Fl/Ob/EH/Cl/Asx/Hn/Bsn •Oil

LAYZER, Arthur - *Inner and Outer Forms* •2 Sx/3 Brass/2 Perc

MAJOS, Giulio di - *Passacaglia* •Fl/Asx/Hn/Guit/Vibr/Pno/Bass •Sch

MUSSEAU, Michel - *Les paupières rebelles* (1993) (40') •Fl/Cl/Ssx/Hn/Tpt/Trb/Tuba •Ed. Visage

SPROGIS, Eric - *Comme une légère inexactitude* (1992) •Asx/Hn/Tpt/Trb/Tuba/2 Perc

STEARNS, Peter - *Septet* (1959) •Cl/Tsx/Hn/Vln/Vla/Vcl/Bass •Pio/ACA

VILLA-LOBOS, Heitor - *Chôros n° 3 - Pica-Pào*, op. 189 (1925) (6') •Cl/Asx/Bsn/3 Hn/Trb •ME

WILLIS, Richard - *Irregular Resolutions* •Fl/Ob/Cl/Asx/Bsn/Hn/Perc •adr

8 Musicians

BUMCKE, Gustav - *Suite G Dur*, op. 24 •Tenor Voice/Fl/Ob/Cl/Bsn/Hn/Bsx/Harp •VAB

CHAGRIN, Francis - *Sarabande* (1951) (6') •Ob/Hn/Vln/Asx/Str Quartet •ALC

DEL PRINCIPE, Joseph - *Lyric Pieces for Octet* •Fl/Ob/Sx+Cl/BsCl/Tpt/Hn/Trb/Tuba •SeMC

FRANCO, Clare - *Four Winds...* •Asx/Harp/Vibr/Fl/Ob/Cl/Hn/Bsn

GHEZZO, Dinu - *Pontica II* •Fl/Sx/2 Tpt/2 Hn/Pno/Narr •SeMC

GUY, Georges - *Concerto en forme de jazz* •Asx Solo/Pno Solo/Fl/Ob/Cl/Hn/Bsn/Bass

HARTLEY, Walter - *Double Quartet* (1994) (7'30) •4 Sx: SATB/Hn/Tpt/Trb/Tuba •adr

KORTE, Karl - *Matrix* (1968) (16') •Fl/Ob/Cl/Asx/Hn/Bsn/Pno/Perc •GSch

LAURETTE, Marc - *Kaleïdoscope* •Cl/Bsn/2 Sx: SB/Hn/Vla/Bass/Vibr

RIEDEL, Georg - *Reflexioner* (1974) (8') •Woodwind Quintet/Jazz group (Cl+Asx/Pno/Bass) •SMIC

SAGVIK, Stellan - *Suite circuler*, op. 86 (1978) (10') •Picc/Asx/Tpt/Hn/2 Trb/Perc/Bass •STIM

SUTER, Robert - *Estampida* •Fl/Cl/Tsx/Hn/Tpt/Trb/Bass/Perc •EMod

TANENNBAUM, Elias - *Consort* •Fl/Hn/Asx/Electr. Guit/Vcl/Bass/Vibr/Jazz drums •ACA

TISNÉ, Antoine - *Dolmen* (1976) (30') •Fl/Cl/Asx/Hn/Tpt/Trb/Tuba/Pno •adr

TOMASSON, Haukur - *Octette* (1987) •Fl/Cl/Asx/Hn/Vla/Vcl/Pno/Perc (Vibr+Gong) •IMIC

9 Musicians

ALBRIGHT, William - *Introduction...* (14') •Pno/Fl/Cl/Asx/Hn/Tpt/Trb/Tuba/Perc •Pet

ALLGEN, Claude - *Adagio och Fuga* (25') •Fl/Ob/EH/Cl/BsCl/2 Sx: AB/Bsn/Hn •STIM

BORTOLOTTI, Mauro - *Studio per E.E. Cummings n° 2* (1964) •Vla/Vcl/Bass/Ob/Cl/BsCl/Sx/Hn/Perc •adr

BUMCKE, Gustav - *"Der Spaziergang"*, op. 22 •Fl/Ob/EH/Cl/Bsn/Hn/BsTrb/Bsx/Harp

COLE, Helen - *Serenade* •Fl/Ob/2 Cl/BsCl/Hn/Asx/2 Bsn

COX, Rona - *Two Expressions* (1968) •Fl/Ob/Cl/2 Sx: SB/Hn/Bsn/Bass/Perc •adr

CUSTER, Arthur - *Cycle for Nine Instruments* •Asx/BsCl/Tpt/Hn/Vln/Vla/Vcl/Bass/Perc •JM

DOMAZLICKY, Frantisek - *Suite danza*, op. 52 (17') •4 Sx/Hn/2 Tpt/Trb/Tuba

HARVEY, Paul - *Pieces for Nine* (1979) (5') •4 Sx: SATB/2 Tpt/Hn/Trb/Tuba •adr

HOFFER, Bernard - *Preludes and Fugues* (1977) (25') •4 Sx: SATB/Brass Quintet •Shir

LEWIS, John Aaron - *The Queen's Fancy* (4') •Fl/Cl/Tsx/Bsn/Hn/Trb/Harp/Bass/Perc •MJQ

McFARLAND, Gary - *Night Float* (4'30) •3 Sx: ATB/Tpt/Hn/Guit/
Pno/Bass/Drums •MJQ

NONO, Luigi - *Polifonica, Monodia, Ritmica* (1951) (10') •Fl/Cl/
BsCl/Asx/Hn/4 Perc •AVV

RENOSTO, Paolo - *Dissolution* •Vla/Vcl/Bass/Ob/Cl/BsCl/Sx/Hn/
Perc

SCELSI, Jacinto - *Kya* (1959) (11') •Cl (or Ssx)/EH/Hn/BsCl/Tpt/
Trb/Vla/Vcl/Bass •Sal

SILVERMAN, Faye - *Shadings* (1978) •Vln/Vla/Bass/Fl/Ob/Asx/
Bsn/Hn/Tuba

SÖDERLIND, Ragnar - *Eg hev funne...* (1982) (9'); *Legg ikkje ditt...*
(1983) •Soprano Voice/Fl+Picc/Ssx/Hn/Vln/
Vla/Bass/Pno/Perc •NMI

TARENSKEEN, Boudewijn - *Nonet* (1982) (13') •Asx/Hn/BsCl/
Accordion/Banjo/Harp/Vla/Vcl/Bass •Don

ULRICH, Jürgen - *Spiel* (1974) (5') •Fl/Ob/Cl/Bsn/Sx/Hn/Tpt/Trb/
Tuba •VDMK

WILDER, Alec - *Suite* •Bsx/Fl/Ob/Cl/2 Hn/Bsn/Bass/Drums

10 Musicians

ANDRIESSEN, Louis - *On Jimmy Yancey* (1973) (10') •Fl/2 Sx: AT/
Hn/Tpt/3 Trb/Bass/Pno •Don

BRANT, Henry - *Dialogue in the Jungle* (1964) (15') •Tenor Voice/
Fl/Ob/Cl/Bsx/2 Tpt/Trb/Hn/Tuba •adr

BUMCKE, Gustav - *Präludium und Fuge*, op. 20 (1903) •Fl/Ob/EH/
Sx/Cl/BsCl/2 Bsn/2 Hn

COLE, Hugo - *Serenade...* (1965) (15') •2 Fl/Ob/2 Cl/Asx/2 Bsn/2 Hn

COPPOOLSE, David - *Canto XVII* (1984) (12') •Asx/2 Hn/2 Trb/Vln/
Vla/Vcl/Bass/Pno •Don

CUNNINGHAM, Michael - *Linear Ceremony* •2 Fl/2 Ob/2 Cl/Sx/Hn/
2 Bsn •SeMC

Spring Sonnet •Fl/2 Cl/BsCl/2 Sx/3 Hn/Bass •SeMC

GOTTSCHALK, Arthur - *Cycloid* •Cl/Asx/Hn/Tpt/Harp/Vibr/2 Vln/
Vla/Vcl •SeMC

GRANDIS, Renato de - *Scotter Sud-est* •Vln/Vla/Vcl/Bass/Sx/Hn/
Tpt/Trb/Pno/Perc •SeMC

HARTLEY, Walter - *Double Concerto* (1969) (7'30) •Asx/Tuba/
Wind Octet (Fl/Ob/Cl/Bsn/Hn/2 Tpt/Trb)
•PhiCo

HEIDEN, Bernhard - *Sonatina* •Fl/Cl/Tsx/Hn/Trb/Harp/Vibr/Pno/
Bass/Perc •MJQ

HORWOOD, Michael - *Facets* (1974) (20') •Narr/Sx/Tpt/Hn/Trb/
Pno/Accordion/Electr. Bass/2 Electr. Guit
•CMC

KOPP, Frederick - *Terror Suite* •Brass/Sx/Timp/3 Perc •SeMC

KOX, Hans - *Concertino* (1982) •Asx/Picc/2 Fl/BsCl/2 Hn/2 Tpt/Trb
•Don

LINDBERG, Nils - *Progression* (1985) (28') •Fl/Ob/Cl/Hn/Bsn/2 Sx:
SA/Pno/Bass/Drums •SMIC

MASON, Benedict - *Coulour and information* (1993) •Fl/Ob/Asx/Bsn/
Hn/Tpt/Trb/Tuba/Perc/Electr. Bass

PAUMGARTNER, Bernhard - *Divertimento* •Picc/EH/Asx/Bsn/Hn/
Tpt/Pno/Vla/Vcl/Perc •Uni

SCELSI, Jacinto - *I Presagi* (1958) (9'30) •2 Hn/2 Tpt/Sx/2 Trb/2
Tuba/Perc •Sal

SCHULLER, Gunther - *12 by 11* (8'30) •Fl/Cl/Tsx/Hn/Trb/Vibr/Pno/
Harp/Bass/Perc •MJQ

SCHWERTSIK, Kurt - *Salotto romano*, op. 5 (1961) •BsCl/Bsx/Bsn/
Hn/Trb/Tuba/Perc/Bass/Vcl/Guit •EMod

TREMBLAY, George - *Epithalamium* (1962) •Fl/Ob/Cl/Sx/Bsn/Hn/
Tpt/Trb/Tuba/Perc •CFE

VRIES, Klaas de - *Moeilijkheden* (1977) (15') •Fl/2 Sx: AT/Hn/2 Tpt/
3 Trb/Pno •Don

11 Musicians

ANDRIESSEN, Jurriaan - *Hommage à Milhaud* (1945) (8') •Fl/Ob/
Cl/Bsn/Hn/Tpt/Trb/Asx/Vln/Vla/Vcl •Don

BOIS, Rob du - *Springtime* (1978) •Picc/3 Sx/Hn/2 Tpt/2 Trb/Tuba/
Pno •Don

BORSTLAP, Dick - *Fanfare II* (1975) (6'); *Over de verandering...*
(1974) (5') •Fl/Picc/2 Sx: AT/Hn/Tpt/2 Trb/
BsTrb/Pno/Bass •Don

Vrijheidslied (1978) (2') •Picc/3 Sx: SAT/Hn/2 Tpt/2 Trb/Tuba/
Pno •Don

HAZZARD, Peter - *Massage* •3 Voices (SAB)/3 Perc/Fl/Cl/Hn/Sx/
Trb •SeMC

KEULEN, Geert van - *Onkruid* (1981) (5') •Ob/Cl/2 Sx: AT/Bsn/Hn/
Tpt/Trb/Vln/Vla/Pno •Don

MENGELBERG, Misha - *Dressoir* (1977) (10') •Fl/3 Sx: S+A A T/
2 Tpt/Hn/2 Trb/Tuba/Pno •Don

MONDELLO, Nuncio - *Suite* (1956) •Asx/2 Fl/Ob/Cl/Bsn/2 Hn/Tpt/
Trb/Perc •adr

TARENSKEEN, Boudewijn - *Marchtelt suite* (1978) (30') •4 Sx:
AATT/Hn/2 Tpt/3 Trb/Bass •Don

ZONN, Paul Martin - *Voyage of Columbus* (1974) (13') •Tpt Solo/Fl/
Ob/Ssx/Hrn/Trb/2 Perc/Pno/Vln/Bass •ACA

12 Musicians

BENNETT, Richard Rodney - *A Jazz Calender* (1963-64) (31') •Fl/
3 Sx: ATB/2 Tpt/Hn/Trb/Tuba/Pno/2 Perc
•Uni

HASQUENOPH, Pierre - *Inventions* •2 Vln/Vla/Vcl/Bass/Fl/Ob/Cl/
Asx/Bsn/Hn/Tpt •Heu

LEWIS, Arthur - *Pieces of Eight* •Fl/2 Ob/3 Cl/Bsn/2 Tsx/Hn/Baritone
Hn/Perc •CAP

MEIJERING, Chiel - *Het ontblote feit* (1988-90) (8'30) •2 Fl/3 Sx:
ATB/ Hn/Tpt/Trb/Perc/Pno/Electr. Guit
•Don

RECK, David - *Number 1 for 12 Performers* (15') •Fl/Cl/Tsx/Hn/Guit/
Vibr/Pno/Bass/Perc •MJQ

TOEPLITZ, Kasper - *Johnny Panic...* (25') •1 Sx: T+CBs/Mezzo
Soprano Voice/2 Fl/2 Cl/Hn/2 Vln/2 Vla/
Perc/Tape

13 Musicians

FINNISSY, Michael - *First sign a sharp white mons* (1974-67) (45')
•2 Fl/2 Cl/Asx/CBsn/Hn/Accordion/Guit/
Vln/2 Vcl/Pno •BMIC

HESPOS, Hans - *Keime und male* (9') •Picc/Fl/2 Cl/Asx/Hn/Guit/Vln/
Vla/Bass/3 Perc •JJ

HUREL, Philippe - *"Pour l'image"* •Fl/Ob/Cl/Asx/Hn/Tpt/Trb/Perc/
2 Vln/Vla/Vcl/Bass

MERKU, Pavle - *Tiare* •Baritone Voice/Sx/11 wind instruments •Piz

MEULEN, Henk van der - *De profondis I* (1986) (15') •Fl/3 Sx: S+T
A A/Hn/3 Tpt/2 Trb/BsTrb/Bass/Pno •Don

SPINO, P. - *Statement...* •Hn Solo/2 Fl/Ob/3 Cl/BsCl/Bsn/4 Sx:
AATB •StMu

14 Musicians

JENNI, Donald - *Allegro...* •4 Hn/4 Tpt/3 Trb/Tuba/2 Bsx •Pio

MIEREANU, Costin - *Clair de biche* (1986) (11') •Fl/Picc/Cl/1 Sx:
Sno+S+T/Brass Quintet/5 Perc •Sal

ROSSÉ, François - *Paléochrome* (1988) (22') •Vla principal/2 Fl/Cl/
BsCl/1 Sx: S+T/EH/Bsn/Hn/4 Perc/Bass •adr

15 Musicians

LUTYENS, Elisabeth - *Islands*, op. 80 (1971) •2 Narr: ST/Picc/Fl/Cl/
BsCl/Tsx/Hn/Pno/Celesta/Vln/Vla/Vcl/2
Perc

oOo

BASSET, Leslie - *Designs in Brass* •2 Sx: BB/4 Hn/4 Tpt/3 Trb/Tuba/
Timp/Perc •Pio
KREMENLIEV, Boris - *Tune* •Asx/Hn/Str •adr
PEPIN, Clermont - *Pièces de circonstance* (1967) •Childrens chorus/
Fl/Ob/3 Cl/2 Sx/2 Hn •CMC

Saxophone and Trumpet

2 Musicians

DAKIN, Charles - *Kinnari* (1982) (5'35) •Ssx/Tpt
DEASON, David - *Double-take* (1979) (4'45) •Asx/Tpt •Pres
DELAMARRE, Pierre - *Inéquation* (1981) (2') •Asx/Tpt •adr
EICHMANN, Dietrich - *3 Dialoge* (1984-85) •Tpt/Tsx •adr
McBRIDE, David - *Inner Voices* •Asx/Tpt
ROTH, Wolfgang - *Drei Dialoge* (1993) •Asx/Tpt •INM
WALKER, Gregory - *Sonatine* (1981) •Asx/Tpt

3 Musicians

Beethoven, Ludwig van - *Menuet* (TRINKAUS) •Sx/Tpt (or Trb)/Pno
•CF
Bellini, Vincenzo - *Hear me Norma* (LEWIS) •Asx/Tpt (or Trb)/Pno
•CF
COENEN, Paul - *Trio* (22'30) •Asx/Tpt/BsTrb •Asto
DAKIN, Charles - *Leda and the Swan* (1977) (7') •Ssx/Tpt/Trb •DP
DEPELSENAIRE, Jean-Marie - *Trio surprise* (1975) (4') •Cl/Asx/
Tpt •Phi/Com
De Ville, Paul - *The Swiss Boy* •Ssx/Tpt/Pno •CF
DIEMENTE, Edward - *Trio* (1969) •Asx/Tpt/Perc •SeMC
DUPRÉ, René - *Trio en canon* •Cl/Asx/Tpt •adr
Elgar, Edward - *Love's Greeting* (TRINKAUS) •Sx/Tpt(or Trb)/Pno •CF
FICHER, Jacobo - *Sonatina*, op. 21 (1932) (8') •Asx/Tpt/Pno •NMSC
FIEVET, Paul - *Fantoche* (1962) •Tpt/Bugle/Asx or Asx/Pno •Com
GERBER, René - *Concertino* (1937) •Sx/Tpt/Pno
HEKSTER, Walter - *Windsong II* (1970) (8') •Fl/Asx/Tpt •Don
JONGHE, Marcel de - *Trio* (1980) •Asx/Tpt/Trb
Lemare, Edwin - *Andantino* (TRINKAUS) •Sx/Tpt (or Trb)/Pno •CF
PEPPING, Ernst - *Suite* (1925-26) •Tpt/Asx/Trb •Sch
PERRIN, Marcel - *Complainte - Trio* (1951) (3'15) •2 Sx: SA/Tpt
•Com
SEYRIG, François - *Concert en trio* •Asx/Tpt/Org
SMITH, Clay - *De die in diem* •1 Sx: A or T/Tpt (or Trb)/Pno •CF
STEINKE, Greg - *Tricinium* (1972) (8') •Asx/Tpt/Pno •SeMC
TRUAX, Bert - *Romance and Burlesque* (1985) (15') •Ssx/Tpt/Pno
VAUGHAN WILLIAMS, Ralph - *Household Music* (1940-41) •Di-
verse combinations •B&H
WASHBURN, Gary - *Solitudes...* (1974) •1 Sx: S+A/Tpt/Pno •SeMC
WILSON, G. - *Theater Trio* •Asx/Tpt/Pno

4 Musicians

BARBAUD, Pierre - *Pièces brèves...* (10') •Sx/Tpt/Trb/Tuba •EFM
BOOREN, Jo van den - *2 Pièces caractéristiques*, op. 84 (1992) (9')
•Sx/Tpt/Trb/Perc •Don
BROWN, Newel - *Figments* •Sx/Tpt/Bsn/Vcl •SeMC
CHAGRIN, Francis - *2 Studies...* (1959) •Tpt/Sx/Bass/Drums •BMIC
CHARBONNIER, Janine - *Prélude, Canon et Choral* (5') •Asx/Tpt/
Trb/Tuba •EFM
DELANNOY, Marcel - *Rapsodie* (1934) •Asx/Tpt/Vcl/Pno •Heu
Diaz, F. - *Meu Bem* •Sx/Tpt/Trb/Perc •PMP
DI PASQUALE, James - *Quartet* (1964) (10') •Tsx/Tpt/Vla/Vcl •adr
EITHLER, Estaban - *Quartet* (1945) •Picc/Fl/Tpt/Sx
ELLIS, Donald - *Improvisational Suite* •Tpt/Asx/Bass/Perc •MJQ
GLOBOKAR, Vinko - *Plan* (1965) Tsx/BsCl/Cnt/Tbn •Pet

GROSSE, Erwin - *Konzerte* •Tpt/Vln/Asx/Bass •adr
GUIMAUD, Olivier - *Sérénade...* (16'15) •Tpt/Sx/Vcl/Perc •adr
HOLZMANN, Rodolfo - *Suite* (1933) •Asx/BsCl/Tpt/Pno
IVES, Charles - *Tun Street* (1921) •Fl/Tpt/Bsx/Pno
KLEBE, Giselher - *Gratullations - tango*, op. 40a •Asx/Tpt/Pno/Perc
•B&B
LERSTAD, Terje - *Quartet*, op. 110 •Ssx/2 Tpt/Fluegelhorn •NMI
LOCKWOOD, Harry - *Lyric Piece* •Asx/Tpt/Vla/Tuba
MARTIN, Vernon - *Contingencies* (1969) •Asx/Tpt/Trb/Perc/Tape
•CAP
MICHEL-FREDERIC, Félix - *Micro-climat* (1981) •2 Sx: AB/Tpt/
Trb
PARTCH, Harry - *Ulysses at the Edge...* (1955) •Vln/Tsx/Tpt/Perc
PAYNE, Frank - *Quartet* •Asx/Tpt/Vla/Trb •SeMC
PLENEY, Bernard - *Toccata* •2 Sx: AB/Tpt/Trb/
SCHULTE, Peter - *Samba...* (1983) (5-10') •Asx/Tpt/Perc/Pno •adr
SJÖHOLM, Staffan - *Sommarlov...* (12') •Tpt/3 Sx/Tape •STIM
SMITH, William O. - *Schizophenic Scherzo* (1947) •Cl/Tpt/Asx/Trb
STEARNS, Peter - *Chamber Set II* •Asx/Vln/Tpt/Bass •ACA
WELLS, Thomas - *Comedia* (1978) •Fl/Sx/Tpt/Vcl
WOLPE, Stefan - *Quartet No. 1* (1950) •Tpt/Tsx/Perc/Pno •Gi&Ma/
MM

5 Musicians

AMBROSINI, Claudio - *Trobar clar* (1982) •Fl/Ob/Cl/Tpt/1 Sx: S+A
AYSCUE, Brian - *Permutations I* (1972) (6'30) •Fl/Ob/Cl/Tpt/Tsx
•adr
BRNCIC, Isaza - *Quodlibet I* (1966) •Sx/Vla/Tpt/Electr. Guit/Electr.
Org or 2 Asx/Vla/Vibr
BROWN, Newel Kay - *Pastorale and Dance* •Fl/Cl/Asx/Tpt/Trb
•SeMC
DHAINE, Jean-Louis - *4me Concertino* •2 Tpt/2 Sx: AT/Trb
DUBOIS, Pierre-Max - *Sonatine* (1974) (7') •Fl/Cl/Asx/Tpt/Trb •adr
DÜNKI, Jean-Jacques - *Lutezia, 1842* (1978) •Ssx/Tpt/Vcl/Pno/Perc
DUPRÉ, René - *Ballade chromatique* •4 Sx: AAAA/Tpt •adr
Canon perpétuel •4 Sx: AAAA/4 Tpt •adr
Intermède •3 Sx: ATB/Tpt/Trb •adr
FLOTHUIS, Marius - *Kleine Suite* (1952) •Ob/Cl/Ssx/Tpt/Pno •Don
GOODWIN, Gordon - *Levittation* •Sx/Tpt/Pno/Bass/Perc •adr
HAERL, Dan - *Quintet* •Fl/Asx/Tpt/Trb/Bass •adr
HAUTA-AHO, Teppo - *For Charles M.* (1980) (15') •Tpt/Asx/Trb/
Bass/Perc •FMIC
HOLZMANN, Rodolfo - *Suite a tres temas* •Asx/Tpt/Cl/Pno/Bongos
HOPKINS, Bill - *Sensation* (1965) •Voice/Tsx/Tpt/Harp/Vla
IRINO, Yoshiro - *Quintette* (1958) •Cl/Asx/Tpt/Vcl/Pno •OE
KUCHARZYK, Henry - *One for the Underdog* (1981) •Tpt/Sx/Pno/
Bass/Perc •CMC
LABURDA, Jiric - *Dixie...* (1990) (14') •Cl/Asx/Tpt/Trb/Pno •Com
LATHROP, Gayle - *Pieces 4-5* •Asx/Tpt/Vcl/Bass/Perc •CAP
MACERO, Teo - *Canzona No. 1* •4 Sx: AATB/Tpt or 2 Vln/Asx/Vcl/
Tpt •Pres
McKAY George - *American Street Scenes* (1935) •Cl/Tpt/Asx/Bsn/
Pno or 4 Sx/Pno •CAP
MILLS, Charles - *Paul Bunyan Jump* (1964) •Asx/Pno/Tpt/Bass/Perc
•ACA
OLIVER, John - *Métalmorphose* (1983) •Ob/Cl/Bsn/Sx/Tpt •CMC
REVUELTAS, Silvestre - *First Little Serious Piece* (2'45) •Picc/Ob/
Cl/Tpt/Bsx •MM/PIC/Peer
Second Little Serious Piece (1'15) •Picc/Ob/Cl/Tpt/Bsx •PIC/Peer
ROBERT, Lucie - *Géométrie* (1986) (12') •2 Sx: AB/Tpt/Trb/Perc
•adr
SCHIFRIN, Lalo - *Jazz Faust* (1963) (20') •Asx/Tpt/Pno/Bass/Perc
•MJQ
SCHREIBER, Frederic C. - *Concerto Grosso* (1955) •2 Coloratura
Soprano Voices/Asx/Tpt/Pno

SHEPPARD, James - *Bitter Ice* •Tpt/Sx/Pno/Bass/Perc •SeMC
SPRONGL, Norbert - *Quintet*, op. 124 (1958) •Ob/Asx/Tpt/Hn/Bsn •adr

6 Musicians

AKKERMANN, Michel - *"To be redreamed in colors pale but intense"* (1991) (10') •4 Sx: SATB/Tpt/Pno
ANDERSON, Thomas J. - *Variations on a Theme by M.B. Tolson* (1969) •Ssx/Tpt/Trb/Vln/Vcl/Pno
BARCE, Ramon - *Obertura fonética* (1968) (8'50) •Fl/Ob/Cl/Asx/Tpt/Trb •EMEC
BENNETT, Richard Rodney - *Comedia I* (1972) •Fl/Asx/BsCl/Tpt/Vcl/Perc •Uni
BERLIOZ, Hector - *Chant sacré* (1843/44) •2 Tpt/Bugle/2 Cl/Bsx
CARLOSEMA, Bernard - *Radiance* (1988) (5'30) •Fl/Asx/Hn/Tpt/Trb/Tuba •Fuz
CASANOVA, André - *Duo Canzoni* (1973) (10'30) •Asx/Cl/Tpt/Perc/Small Org/Electr. Bass Guit •adr
EICHMANN, Dietrich - *Damnation du Pouls* (1991) (19') •Tpt/Pno/4 Sx: SATB •adr
ERB, Donald - *Hexagon* (1962) (6') •Fl/Asx/Tpt/Trb/Vcl/Pno •CMC
GERSCHEFSKI, Edwin - *America*, op. 44, no. 14a •Fl/Cl/Asx/Tpt/Bsn/Pno •CFE
GOJKOVIC, Dusan - *Swinging macedonia* (1966) (35') •Tpt/2 Sx: AT/Pno/Bass/Perc •adr
GUINJOAN, Juan - *Musique intuitive - Diari* (1969) •Cl/Tsx/Tpt/Vln/Vcl/Pno
GÜRSCH, Günther - *Madison...* (1963) (3') •3 Sx/Tpt/Trb/Perc •adr
HARTLEY, Walter - *Concertino da Camera* (1994) •Ssx/2 Tpt/Hn/Trb/Tuba •adr
HELLAN, Arne - *Sextet* (1981) •Tpt/2 Sx/2 Guit/Perc •NMI
HODEIR, André - *Cadenze* (4') •Bsx/Tpt/Trb/Pno/Bass/Perc •MJQ
Osymetrios (3') •Tpt/Tsx/Trb/Pno/Bass/Drums •MJQ
Trope à St-Trop •Tpt/Tsx/Trb/Pno/Bass/Drums •MJQ
HOLMBERG, Peter - *Musica alta e bassa* (1979) (12') •Fl/Tpt/Bsx/Tuba/Vln/Vcl •STIM
HURÉ, Jean - *2me Sextuor* •Tpt/2 Bugle/Cl/BsCl/Sx
KÖPER, Heinz-Karl - *Musik...* •Fl/Cl/Asx/Tpt/Trb/Bass •EMBA
LEWIS, John A. - *Pieces* •Tsx/Tpt/Trb/Pno/Bass/Perc •MJQ
MILHAUD, Darius - *Caramel mou*, op. 68 (1921) (5') •Bb Sx (or Voice)/Cl/Tpt/Trb/Pno/Perc •ME
ORREGO SALAS, Juan - *Concerto da camera* (1987) •Asx/Brass Quintet
PELUSI, Mario - *Concert Piece* (1978) (12'30) •Bsx/Brass Quartet/Perc
SEIBER, Màtyàs - *Two Jazzolettes* (1929-33) •2 Sx/Tpt/Trb/Pno/Perc •WH
TAGGART, Mark - *Concerto for Chamber Ensemble* (1983) (20') •Cl/Asx/Bsn/Tpt/Bass/Pno
TULL, Fisher - *Concertino da camera* •Asx/Brass Quintet •South

7 Musicians

BENNETT, Richard Rodney - *Soliloquy* (1966) (14') •Voice/1 Sx: A+T/Tpt/Tuba/Pno/Bass/Perc •Uni
BROWN, Anthony - *Soundscape 1* •Asx/Bsn/Tpt/Vln/Voice/Pno/Perc/Tape •SeMC
CANTON, Edgardo - *Phares et balises* •Fl/Ob/Sx/BsCl/Hn/Tpt/Trb
CRAS, Jean - *Demain* (1929) •Asx/Tpt/Trb/Perc/Vln/Vcl/Bass •Sen
DHAINE, Jean-Louis - *3 Chants lyriques* •3 Voice/2 Tpt/Asx/Pno
DONATONI, Franco - *Hot* (1989) (14') •1 Sx: T+Sno/Cl+Eb Cl/Tpt/Trb/Perc/Bass/Pno •Ric
ESCAICH, Thierry - *Antiennes oubliées* (1994) •Vln/Fl/Asx/Tpt/Trb/Vcl/Vibr •Bil
FINNISSY, Michael - *Evening* (1974) •Asx/Hn/Tpt/Perc/Harp/Vcl/Bass

HARTWELL, Hugh - *Soul Piece* (1967) •2 Sx: AT/Tpt/2 Pno/Bass/Perc •CMC
HESPOS, Hans - *Passagen* (1969) (9') •Cl/Asx/Tpt/Trb/Vla/Bass/Perc •EMod
HEYN, Volker - *Sandwich Gare de l'Est* (1986) (12'30) •1 Sx: Sno+CBs/2 Hn/2 Tpt/2 Trb •Br&Ha
JENNEFELT, Thomas - *Stones* (1981) •Ob/Cl/Asx/Tpt/Guit/2 Perc
KOBLENZ, Babette - *Grey Fire* (1981) •Cl/2 Sx: AT/Tpt/Electr. Bass/Electr. Pno/Perc •adr
MACERO, Teo - *Structure no. 4* •3 Sx: ATB/Tpt/Trb/Tuba/Perc •ACA
MUSSEAU, Michel - *Les paupières rebelles* (1993) (40') •Fl/Cl/Ssx/Hn/Tpt/Trb/Tuba •Ed. Visage
SOMERS, Harry - *Limericks* (1979) •Voice/Fl/Cl/Sx/Bsn/Tpt/Euphonium •CMC
SPROGIS, Eric - *Comme une légère inexactitude* (1992) •Asx/Hn/Tpt/Trb/Tuba/2 Perc
STRINDBERG, Henrik - *Coming* (1982) (6') •2 Sx: SA/BsCl/Tpt/Trb/2 Perc •SMIC
Kommandez (1982-84) (6') •3 Sx: SAB/Tpt/Trb/2 Perc •SMIC/WIM
TAUTENAHN, Günther - *Septet* •Cl/Tpt/Tsx/Guit/Vcl/Pno/Perc •SeMC
WILLIAMSON, Malcolm - *Merry Wives of Windsor* (1964) •Fl+Picc/Cl/Tsx/Tpt/Perc/Bass/Pno •JW
WOLF, Hans - *Tip Kick - Swing Fox* (1964) (3') •4 Sx/Tpt/Trb/Perc •Moz

8 Musicians

ARMSTRONG, David - *The Protest* (1960) (9'30) •Cl/Trb/2 Asx/Tpt/Perc/Pno/Bass •BMIC
BABBITT, Milton - *All Set* (1957) •2 Sx: AT/Tpt/Trb/Vibr/Bass/Perc/Pno •adr
BARCE, Ramon - *Concierto de Lizara V* (1977) (10'45) •Cl/Tsx/Tpt/Trb/Harp/Pno/Vln/Vcl
BARK, Jan - *Ost-funk* (1964) (10') •Tpt/Asx/3 Perc/Pno/2 Bass •SMIC
BLATNY, Pavel - *D-E-F-G-A-H-C* •Fl/3 Sx: ATB/Pno/Bass/Tpt/Trb •CMIC
BULOW, Harry - *Crystal Cove* •Tpt/3 Sx: AAT/Pno/Bass/Guit/Drums •adr
DEL PRINCIPE, Joseph - *Lyric Pieces for Octet* •Fl/Ob/Sx+Cl/BsCl/Tpt/Hn/Trb/Tuba •SeMC
DEPELSENAIRE, Jean-Marie - *Octuor moderne* (1978) •2 Tpt/2 Asx/4 Perc •Chou
DUHAMEL, Antoine - *Le Transibérien* (1983) •Asx/Tpt/Pno/Perc/Harmonica/3 Armenian Instruments
DUPRÉ, René - *Canon chromatique...* •4 Sx: SATB/2 Tpt/2 Trb •adr
FABERMAN, Harold - *For Erik and Nick* (1964) •Tenor Voice/Asx/Vcl/Bass/Tpt/Trb/Vibr/Perc
GHEZZO, Dinu - *Pontica II* •Fl/Sx/2 Tpt/2 Hn/Pno/Narr •SeMC
HARTLEY, Walter - *Double Quartet* (1994) (7'30) •4 Sx: SATB/Hn/Tpt/Trb/Tuba •adr
HEKSTER, Walter - *Of mere being* (1982) (12') •Asx/Fl/Ob/Cl/2 Tpt/Perc/Electr. Guit •Don
HESPOS, Hans - *Druckspuren - geschattet* (1970) (7'30) •Fl/Eb Cl/Asx/Bsn/2 Tpt/Trb/Bass •EMod
HODEIR, André - *Ambiguité II* (8'); *Bicinium* (3') •3 Sx: ATB/2 Tpt/Trb/Bass/Perc •MJQ
KETTING, Otto - *Musik zu einen Tonfilm* (1982) (15') •2 Sx/Tpt/Trb/Perc/Pno/2 Vln •Don
LAKE, Larry - *Filar il tuono* (1989) •Cl/3 Sx: ATB/Bsn/Tpt/Trb/Marimba •CMC
LANTIER, Pierre - *Fugue jazz* (1944) (3') •2 Cl/2 Sx: AT/Bsn/Tpt/Trb/Perc

LASNE, George - *Ballade française* (1971) •Fl/Ob/2 Cl/Asx/2 Tpt/
Trb

NILSSON, Ivo - *Agnosi* (1988) (9') •Ob/Asx/Tpt/Harp/2 Vln/Vla/Vcl
•STIM

RABE, Folke - *Pajazzo* (1964) •Tpt/Asx/Pno/2 BsCl/3 Perc •STIM

SAGVIK, Stellan - *Guenilles des jongleurs*, op. 74 (1977) (7'30) •Fl/
Ob/3 Cl/Asx/Bsn/Cnt •STIM

   Suite circuler, op. 86 (1978) (10') •Picc/Asx/Tpt/Hn/2 Trb/Perc/
Bass •STIM

SUTER, Robert - *Estampida* •Fl/Cl/Tsx/Hn/Tpt/Trb/Bass/Perc •EMod

TISNÉ, Antoine - *Dolmen* (1976) (30') •Fl/Cl/Asx/Hn/Tpt/Trb/Tuba/
Pno •adr

9 Musicians

ALBRIGHT, William - *Introduction...* (14') •Pno/Fl/Cl/Asx/Hn/Tpt/
Trb/Tuba/Perc •Pet

ANDRIESSEN, Louis - *De Volharping* (1972) (23') •3 Sx/3 Tpt/3 Trb
•Don

CERHA, Friedrich - *Exercices for Nine, No. 1* •BsCl/Bsx/Bsn/Tpt/
Trb/Tuba/Vcl/Bass/Harp •Uni

CLARK, Thomas - *Dreamscape* •Fl/Ob/Cl/Sx/Tpt/Trb/Pno/Perc/
Bass •SeMC

CUSTER, Arthur - *Cycle for Nine Instruments* •Asx/BsCl/Tpt/Hn/
Vln/Vla/Vcl/Bass/Perc •JM

DIEMENTE, Edward - *For Lady Day* •Fl/Ob/Cl/Tpt/Trb/Vln/Vla/Sx/
Bsn/Tape •SeMC

DOMAZLICKY, Frantisek - *Suite danza*, op. 52 (17') •4 Sx/Hn/2 Tpt/
Trb/Tuba

FICHER, Jacobo - *Los invitados*, op. 26 •Fl/Cl/2 Sx: AT/2 Tpt/Tuba/
Pno/Perc

GRANDERT, Johnny - *86 T* •Fl/EH/BsCl/Bsx/CBsn/2 Tpt/Perc/Pno
•STIM

HARVEY, Paul - *Pieces for Nine* (1979) (5') •4 Sx: SATB/2 Tpt/Hn/
Trb/Tuba •adr

HODEIR, André - *Pieces* •3 Sx: ATB/2 Tpt/Trb/Vibr/Bass/Perc
•MJQ

HOFFER, Bernard - *Preludes and Fugues* (1977) (25') •4 Sx: SATB/
Brass Quintet •Shir

IVES, Charles - *Over the Pavements*, op. 20 (1906-13) •Picc/Cl/Bsx
(or Bsn)/Tpt/3 Trb/Perc/Pno •PIC

JELINEK, Hanns - *Blue Sketches*, op. 25 (1956) •Fl/Cl/2 Sx: AB/Tpt/
Trb/Vibr/Bass/Perc •EMod

LEWIS, John Aaron - *Little David's Fugue* (5'30) •Fl/Cl/3 Sx÷ATB/
Trb or Tpt/Harp or Pno/Bass/Perc •MJQ

MANOURY, Philippe - *Etude automatique 1* •Fl/Tpt/Sx/Tuba/Harp/
Vln/Vla/Vcl/Bass

MARCO, Tomàs - *Anna Blume* (1967) •2 Narr/Fl/Ob/Cl/Sx/Tpt/2
Perc

McFARLAND, Gary - *Night Float* (4'30) •3 Sx: ATB/Tpt/Hn/Guit/
Pno/Bass/Drums •MJQ

MELLNÄS, Arne - *Drones* (1967) (8') •Fl/Cl/3 Sx: ATB/Tpt/Perc/
Vcl/Bass •STIM

NATANSON, Tadeus - *3 Pictures for 7 Instruments* (1960) •Ob/Cl/
Asx/Trb/Vcl/Tpt/Bsn/Pno/Perc •AMP

SAGVIK, Stellan - *Det Förlorade steget*, op. 64 (1976) (20') •Fl/
Cl+BsCl/Asx/Cnt/Trb/Vln/Vla/Vcl/Perc
•SMIC

SCELSI, Jacinto - *Kya* (1959) (11') •Cl (or Ssx)/EH/Hn/BsCl/Tpt/
Trb/Vla/Vcl/Bass •Sal

ULRICH, Jürgen - *Spiel* (1974) (5') •Fl/Ob/Cl/Bsn/Sx/Hn/Tpt/Trb/
Tuba •VDMK

VELLONES, Pierre - *Planisphère*, op. 23 (1930) •2 Sx: AT/Cl/2 Tpt/
Trb/Bass (or Tuba)/Perc/Pno •JJ

   Prélude et fables de Florian, op. 28 (1930) •Tenor Voice/3 Sx:
SAB/2 Tpt/Trb/Tuba/Banjo •Dur

WALTON, William - *Façade* (1922/26, 42) (34'30) •2 Narr/Fl+Picc/
Cl/BsCl/Asx/Tpt/Vcl/Perc •OUP

YOSHIBA, Susumu - *Erka* •Fl/Ob/Sx/Tpt/Trb/Perc/Vcl/Guit/Pno

10 Musicians

ANDRIESSEN, Louis - *On Jimmy Yancey* (1973) (10') •Fl/2 Sx: AT/
Hn/Tpt/3 Trb/Bass/Pno •Don

BANKS, Donald - *Equation 1* (1964) (7') •Tpt/Asx/Pno/Harp/Guit/
Perc/2 Vln/Vla/Vcl •BMIC

BENNETT, Richard Rodney - *Jazz Pastorale* (1969) (25') •Voice/1
Sx: A+T/Bsx/2 Tpt/Trb/Tuba/Pno/Bass/Perc
•Uni

BRANT, Henry - *Dialogue in the Jungle* (1964) (15') •Tenor Voice/
Fl/Ob/Cl/Bsx/2 Tpt/Trb/Hn/Tuba •adr

DEPELSENAIRE, Jean-Marie - *Dixtour* (1971) •2 Fl/2 Tpt/2 Sx/4 Cl
•adr

GOTTSCHALK, Arthur - *Cycloid* •Cl/Asx/Hn/Tpt/Harp/Vibr/2 Vln/
Vla/Vcl •SeMC

GRANDIS, Renato de - *Scotter Sud-est* •Vln/Vla/Vcl/Bass/Sx/Hn/
Tpt/Trb/Pno/Perc •SeMC

HARTLEY, Walter - *Double Concerto* (1969) (7'30) •Asx/Tuba/
Wind Octet (Fl/Ob/Cl/Bsn/Hn/2 Tpt/Trb)
•PhiCo

HODEIR, André - *Jazz cantata* (10') •Soprano Voice/3 Sx: ATB/2
Tpt/Trb/Vibr/Bass/Perc •MJQ

HORWOOD, Michael - *Facets* (1974) (20') •Narr/Sx/Tpt/Hn/Trb/
Pno/Accordion/Electr. Bass/2 Electr. Guit
•CMC

HOVHANESS, Alan - *Is This Survival?*, op. 59 (1949) •4 Cl/Asx/4
Tpt/Perc

KOX, Hans - *Concertino* (1982) •Asx/Picc/2 Fl/BsCl/2 Hn/2 Tpt/Trb
•Don

LACHARTE, Nicole - *La Geste inachevée* (1980) •Fl/Cl/Sx/Tpt/Trb/
Pno/Perc/Vln/Vla/Vcl

Lecuona, Ernesto - *Andalucia* •2 Tpt/Trb/3Sx: AAT/2 Vln/Vcl/Bass

MASON, Benedict - *Coulour and information* (1993) •Fl/Ob/Sx/Bsn/
Hn/Tpt/Trb/Tuba/Perc/Electr. Bass

MIMET, Anne-Marie - *Fanfare et divertissement* •Fl/Ob/Cl/Bsn/3 Sx:
SAT/Tpt/Trb/Tuba

PAUMGARTNER, Bernhard - *Divertimento* •Picc/EH/Asx/Bsn/Hn/
Tpt/Pno/Vla/Vcl/Perc •Uni

SCELSI, Jacinto - *I Presagi* (1958) (9'30) •2 Hn/2 Tpt/Sx/2 Trb/2
Tuba/Perc •Sal

SCHAFFER, Boguslaw - *Permutations n° 27* (1956) •Fl/Ob/Cl/Sx/
Tpt/Trb/Vla/Perc/Harp/Pno •A&S

SMITH, Linda - *Periphery* (1979) •Fl/Sx/Tpt/Marimba/Vibr/Chimes/
Pno/Vln/Vcl/Bass •CMC

SMITH, William - *Elegy for Eric* •Fl/2 Sx: AB/Cl/Tpt/Trb/Vibr/Vln/
Bass/Perc •MJQ

TREMBLAY, George - *Epithalamium* (1962) •Fl/Ob/Cl/Sx/Bsn/Hn/
Tpt/Trb/Tuba/Perc •CFE

VRIES, Klaas de - *Moeilijkheden* (1977) (15') •Fl/2 Sx: AT/Hn/2 Tpt/
3 Trb/Pno •Don

WROCHEM, Klaus - *Oratorium meum plus praeperturi* •3 Voices/2
Vln/Vla/Vcl/Asx/Tpt/Perc •CAP

11 Musicians

ANDRIESSEN, Jurriaan - *Hommage à Milhaud* (1945) (8') •Fl/Ob/
Cl/Bsn/Hn/Tpt/Trb/Asx/Vln/Vla/Vcl •Don

BOIS, Rob du - *Springtime* (1978) •Picc/3 Sx/Hn/2 Tpt/2 Trb/Tuba/
Pno •Don

BORSTLAP, Dick - *Fanfare II* (1975) (6'); *Over de verandering...*
(1974) (5') •Fl/Picc/2 Sx: AT/Hn/Tpt/2 Trb/
BsTrb/Pno/Bass •Don

Vrijheidslied (1978) (2') •Picc/3 Sx: SAT/Hn/2 Tpt/2 Trb/Tuba/
Pno •Don
DIEMENTE, Edward - *3-31 '70* •Voice/Tpt/Trb/Sx/Guit/Bass/5 Perc
•SeMC
HESPOS, Hans - *Break* •Ob/3 Tpt/2 Sx: TB/Vcl/Bass/Trb/Pno/Perc
•EMod
KEULEN, Geert van - *Onkruid* (1981) (5') •Ob/Cl/2 Sx: AT/Bsn/Hn/
Tpt/Trb/Vln/Vla/Pno •Don
MENGELBERG, Misha - *Dressoir* (1977) (10') •Fl/3 Sx: S+A A T/
2 Tpt/Hn/2 Trb/Tuba/Pno •Don
MESTRAL, Patrice - *Alliages* (1969) •Tpt Solo/Fl/Cl/Asx/2 Trb/2
Perc/Pno/Org/Bass
MONDELLO, Nuncio - *Suite* (1956) •Asx/2 Fl/Ob/Cl/Bsn/2 Hn/Tpt/
Trb/Perc •adr
SCHILLING, Otto-Erich - *Überall ist Wunderland* •Voice/Fl/Cl/Sx/
Tpt/2 Vln/Bass/Perc/Accordion/Pno •SeMC
TARENSKEEN, Boudewijn - *Marchtelt suite* (1978) (30') •4 Sx:
AATT/Hn/2 Tpt/3 Trb/Bass •Don
ZONN, Paul Martin - *Voyage of Columbus* (1974) (13') •Tpt Solo/Fl/
Ob/Ssx/Hrn/Trb/2 Perc/Pno/Vln/Bass •ACA

12 Musicians

BENNETT, Richard Rodney - *A Jazz Calender* (1963-64) (31') •Fl/
3 Sx: ATB/2 Tpt/Hn/Trb/Tuba/Pno/2 Perc
•Uni
CURTIS-SMITH, Curtis - *Sundry Dances* (1981) •Fl/Ob/Cl/3 Sx:
SAB/Bsn/CBsn/Tpt/Trb/Tuba/Bass •adr
DUREY, Louis - *Feu la mère de Madame*, op. 49 (1945) (5') •Fl/Ob/
Asx/Bsn/Tpt/Tuba/Perc/2 Vln/Vla/Vcl/Bass
•BRF
HASQUENOPH, Pierre - *Inventions* •2 Vln/Vla/Vcl/Bass/Fl/Ob/Cl/
Asx/Bsn/Hn/Tpt •Heu
HOVHANESS, Alan - *After Water* •3 Cl/3 Tpt/3 Asx/Perc/Harp/Pno
•ACA
JAEGGI, Oswald - *Dum Clamarem* (1961) •Ob/EH/Cl/3 Sx/3 Tpt/3
Trb
LINKOLA, Jukka - *Alta* (1983) (8') •Vocal group: SATBs/2 Sx: AT/
Tpt/Trb/Pno/Bass/Drums/Perc •FMIC
MEIJERING, Chiel - *Het ontblote feit* (1988-90) (8'30) •2 Fl/3 Sx:
ATB/2 Hn/Tpt/Trb/Perc/Pno/Electr. Guit
•Don
ROBBINS, David - *Improvisation* •Fl/2 Cl/Tsx/Bsn/Tpt/Trb/Vln/Vla/
Vcl/Bass/Perc

13 Musicians

BOZZA, Eugène - *Ouverture pour une cérémonie* •3 Tpt/4 Sx/3 Trb/
BsTrb/Tuba/Perc •Led
DELANNOY, Marcel - *Le Marchand de notes* •3 Vln/Bass/4 Sx/2 Tpt/
Trb/Perc/Pno
EICHMANN, Dietrich - *George...* (1984) (35') •3 Fl/Cl/2 Sx: AT/2
Tpt/Trb/2 Perc/Pno/Bs Guit •adr
HUREL, Philippe - *"Pour l'image"* •Fl/Ob/Cl/Asx/Hn/Tpt/Trb/Perc/
2 Vln/Vla/Vcl/Bass
MERKU, Pavle - *Tiare* •Baritone Voice/Sx/11 wind instruments •Piz
MEULEN, Henk van der - *De profondis I* (1986) (15') •Fl/3 Sx: S+T
A A/Hn/3 Tpt/2 Trb/BsTrb/Bass/Pno •Don
SEKON, Joseph - *Lemon Ice* (1972) •Fl/Ob/Cl/2 Sx: ST/Bsn/Tpt/Trb/
2 Perc/Vln/Vcl/Pno •adr
WENDEL, Eugen - *Saphonospir* (15') •Asx/Fl/Cl/Ob/Tpt/Trb/2 Vln/
Vla/Vcl/Bass/2 Perc •adr

14 Musicians

GRAINGER, Percy - *The Duke of Marlborough* (1905-39-49) •4 Tpt/
4 Hn (or 2 Sx: AT/2 Bsn)/3 Trb/Tuba/Bass/
Cymb. •Sch

HARBISON, John - *Confinement* (1965) (15'15) •Fl/Ob/EH/Cl/BsCl/
Asx/Tpt/Trb/Vln/Vla/Vcl/Bass/Pno/Perc
HARVEY, Jonathan - *The Valley of Aosta* (1985) (13'30) •Fl/Ob/Ssx/
Tpt/2 Yamaha DX7 Synth/2 Harp/Pno/2 Vln/
Vla/Vcl/Perc •FM
JENNI, Donald - *Allegro...* •4 Hn/4 Tpt/3 Trb/Tuba/2 Bsx •Pio
MIEREANU, Costin - *Clair de biche* (1986) (11') •Fl/Picc/Cl/1 Sx:
Sno+S+T/Brass Quintet/5 Perc •Sal

oOo

BASSET, Leslie - *Designs in Brass* •2 Sx: BB/4 Hn/4 Tpt/3 Trb/Tuba/
Timp/Perc •Pio
BELLEMARE, Gilles - *La chasse-galerie* (1981) •Narr/Choir/2 Fl/2
Recorder/2 Cl/2 Tpt/1 Sx
DAKIN, Charles - *Syra* (1979) (8'30) •2 Cl/2 Tsx/2 Tpt/2 Trb/4 Vla/
4 Vcl/2 Bass
DHAINE, Jean-Louis - *Fantaisies...* •4 Fl/4 Cl/4 Sx: AATT/2 Tpt/2
Trb

Saxophone and Trombone

2 Musicians

MESSINA-ROSARYO, Antonio - *Dialogo* (5') •Sx/BsTrb •Asto
NILSSON, Ivo - *Passad* (1988) •Ssx/Trb •STIM
To no (1991) •Asx/Trb •SvM
PERNAIACHI, Gianfranco - *Realgar 1 & 2* (1984 & 1990) (8' + 5')
•Trb and/or Tsx/Electr. •EDP
SCHLAISH, Kennet - *9'65* •SMIC
TAYLOR, Clifford - *Duo* (1964) (3'30) •Asx/Trb •ACA

3 Musicians

AMY, Gilbert - *Trio* (1993) •Vln/Sx/Trb
Beethoven, Ludwig van - *Menuet* (TRINKAUS) •Sx/Tpt (or Trb)/Pno
•CF
Bellini, Vincenzo - *Hear me Norma* (LEWIS) •Asx/Tpt (or Trb)/Pno
•CF
COENEN, Paul - *Trio* (22'30) •Asx/Tpt/BsTrb •Asto
DAKIN, Charles - *Leda and the Swan* (1977) (7') •Ssx/Tpt/Trb •DP
Elgar, Edward - *Love's Greeting* (TRINKAUS) •Sx/Tpt (or Trb)/Pno •CF
EVERETT, Thomas - *Three Comments* (1970) (4-10') •Tsx/Bass/
BsTrb •SeMC
GOLDSTEIN, Malcolm - *Ludlow Blues* (1963) (12') •Asx/Fl/Trb/
Tape •adr
JONGHE, Marcel de - *Trio* (1980) •Asx/Tpt/Trb
LA ROSA, Michael - *Coming in Glory* (1974) •Asx/Trb/Vibr •SeMC
Lemare, Edwin - *Andantino* (TRINKAUS) •Sx/Tpt (or Trb)/Pno •CF
Mozart, Wolfgang - *Trio* •2 Sx: ST/Bass (or Trb) •Mil
MYERS, Robert - *Contrast* (1970) (7') •Tsx/Pno/Trb •Art
PEPPING, Ernst - *Suite* (1925-26) •Tpt/Asx/Trb •Sch
REDOLFI, Michel - *Swinging on a vine* (1974) •Trb/Sx/Synth
SCHUST, Alfred - *Trio* (1984) •Fl/Asx/Trb •adr
SMITH, Clay - *De die in diem* •1 Sx: A or T/Tpt (or Trb)/Pno •CF
VAUGHAN WILLIAMS, Ralph - *Household Music* (1940-41) •Di-
verse combinations •B&H
YATES, Ronald - *Triune* (1971) •Asx/Vla/BsTrb •adr

4 Musicians

ALBERT, Thomas - *Sound Frames* (1968) (6') •Asx/Ob/Trb/Vibr
•MP
ALSINA - *Rendez-vous* •Cl/Asx/Trb/Perc •Led
BARBAUD, Pierre - *Pièces brèves...* (10') •Sx/Tpt/Trb/Tuba •EFM
BOOREN, Jo van den - *2 Pièces caractéristiques*, op. 84 (1992) (9')
•Sx/Tpt/Trb/Perc •Don

CHARBONNIER, Janine - *Prélude, Canon et Choral* (5') •Asx/Tpt/Trb/Tuba •EFM

DESLOGES, Jacques - *Prélude et danse* (1983) •4 Sx: SATB or Ob/Cl/Asx/Bsn (or Vcl or Trb) •Arp

Diaz, F. - *Meu Bem* •Sx/Tpt/Trb/Perc •PMP

DIEMENTE, Edward - *Quartet in Memory Fl. O'Connor* (1967) •Asx/Trb/Bass/Perc •SeMC

EMMER, Huib - *Koud zoud* (1984) (5') •Ob/Asx/Trb/Bass •Don

GERMETEN, Gunnar - *Applaus* (1985) •Cl/Sx/Trb/Accordion

GLOBOKAR, Vinko - *Plan* (1965) Tsx/BsCl/Cnt/Tbn •Pet

HODEIR, André - *Paradoxe I* •Tsx/Trb/Bass/Perc •MJQ

LAUTH, Wolfgang - *Concertino* (1958) (14') •Tsx/Trb/Fl/Perc •adr

MARTIN, Vernon - *Contingencies* (1969) •Asx/Tpt/Trb/Perc/Tape •CAP

MICHEL-FREDERIC, Félix - *Micro-climat* (1981) •2 Sx: AB/Tpt/Trb

MUCI, Italo - *Quartetto* (1981) •Cl/Tsx/Trb/Bass

OLOFSSON, Kent - *The voice of one who calls...* (1991-92) •Fl/Asx/Trb/Synth •Tons

PAYNE, Frank - *Quartet* •Asx/Tpt/Vla/Trb •SeMC

PLENEY, Bernard - *Toccata* •2 Sx: AB/Tpt/Trb/

RADULESCU, Horatiu - *Sensual sky* (1985) •Asx/Trb/Vcl/Bass/Tape

SMITH, William O. - *Schizophenic Scherzo* (1947) •Cl/Tpt/Asx/Trb

5 Musicians

BARGSTEM, Joey - *Quintet for Winds* •Ob/Cl/Asx/Trb/Bsn •DP

BROWN, Newel Kay - *Pastorale and Dance* •Fl/Cl/Asx/Tpt/Trb •SeMC

DHAINE, Jean-Louis - *4me Concertino* •2 Tpt/2 Sx: AT/Trb

DUBOIS, Pierre-Max - *Sonatine* (1974) (7') •Fl/Cl/Asx/Tpt/Trb •adr

DUPRÉ, René - *Intermède* •3 Sx: ATB/Tpt/Trb •adr

FLODI, John - *Signals*, op. 22 (1968-69) (5'30) •2 Sx: ST/Trb/Perc/Pno •adr

HAERL, Dan - *Quintet* •Fl/Asx/Tpt/Trb/Bass •adr

HARTLEY, Walter - *Suite for 5 Winds* (1951) (7') •Fl/Ob/Cl/Asx/Trb •Wi&Jo

HAUTA-AHO, Teppo - *For Charles M.* (1980) (15') •Tpt/Asx/Trb/Bass/Perc •FMIC

KRIEGER, Edino - *Melopéia* (1949) •Soprano Voice/Ob/Tsx/Trb/Vla

LABURDA, Jiric - *Dixie Quintetto* (1990) (14') •Cl/Asx/Tpt/Trb/Pno •Com

LAVENDA, Richard - *The Weary Man Whispers* (1985) •Tenor Voice/Asx/Trb/Perc/Pno •Eto

MARIN, Amadeo - *Quintet* •Fl/Ob/Tsx/Vcl/Trb

MULDOWNEY, Dominic - *Love Music for Bathsheba...* (1974) (20') •Fl/Ob/Cl/Asx/Hn (or Trb) •Nov

OLBRISCH, Franz-Martin - *"Im Anfänglichen...* (1989) (90') •Vln/Fl/Trb/Sx/Perc/Electronics

ROBERT, Lucie - *Géométrie* (1986) (12') •2 Sx: AB/Tpt/Trb/Perc •adr

TALLET, Marc - *Estagari* (12') •Fl/Asx/Trb/Vla/Guit

6 Musicians

ANDERSON, Thomas J. - *Variations on a Theme by M.B. Tolson* (1969) •Ssx/Tpt/Trb/Vln/Vcl/Pno

BARCE, Ramon - *Obertura fonética* (1968) (8'50) •Fl/Ob/Cl/Asx/Tpt/Trb •EMEC

BERG, Paul - *To Teach His Own* (1984) (12') •Fl/Ob/Tsx/Trb/Vln/Vcl/Tape •Don

BRANDON, Seymour - *Chaconne and Variations* •Ob/Asx/2 Hn/Trb/Pno •MaPu

CARLOSEMA, Bernard - *Radiance* (1988) (5'30) •Fl/Asx/Hn/Tpt/Trb/Tuba •Fuz

COURTIOUX, Jean - *Manu reva* (1983) •2 Sx: TB/Flugelhorn/Trb/Bass/Drums •DP

ERB, Donald - *Hexagon* (1962) (6') •Fl/Asx/Tpt/Trb/Vcl/Pno •CMC

GEHLHAARD, Rolf - *Hélix* (1967) •Soprano Voice/Sx/Trb/Bass/Pno/Perc •FM

GRANDIS, Renato de - *Canti...* •Vln/Vcl/Tsx/Vibr/Trb/Perc •SeMC

GÜRSCH, Günther - *Madison...* (1963) (3') •3 Sx/Tpt/Trb/Perc •adr

HARTLEY, Walter - *Concertino da Camera* (1994) •Ssx/2 Tpt/Hn/Trb/Tuba •adr

HERMANSSON, Christer - *Aggjakten* (1979) •Narr/Tsx/Trb/Guit/Bass/Perc •STIM

HODEIR, André - *Cadenze* (4') •Bsx/Tpt/Trb/Pno/Bass/Perc •MJQ
Oblique (3'30) •2 Sx: AT/Trb/Pno/Bass/Perc •MJQ
Osymetrios (3') •Tpt/Tsx/Trb/Pno/Bass/Drums •MJQ
Trope à St-Trop •Tpt/Tsx/Trb/Pno/Bass/Drums •MJQ

KARLINS, M. William - *Cantena II* (1982) (10') •Ssx/Brass Quintet •ACA

KÖPER, Heinz-Karl - *Musik...* •Fl/Cl/Asx/Tpt/Trb/Bass •EMBA

LESSER, Jeffrey - *Last Saxophone on Earth* (1979) •Asx/Brass Quintet

LEWIS, John A. - *Pieces* •Tsx/Tpt/Trb/Pno/Bass/Perc •MJQ

MELLNÄS, Arne - *Per caso* (1963) (5'30) •Asx/Trb/Vln/Bass/2 Perc •SeMC

MICHAEL, Frank - *Kmk* •Fl/Ssx/Trb/Vln/Vla/Vcl •adr

MILHAUD, Darius - *Caramel mou*, op. 68 (1921) (5') •Bb Sx (or Voice)/Cl/Tpt/Trb/Pno/Perc •ME

NILSSON, Ivo - *Per-cept* (1989-91) •Fl/Ob+EH/1 Sx: S+A/Trb/Pno/Vln+Vla •SMIC

ORREGO SALAS, Juan - *Concerto da camera* (1987) •Asx/Brass Quintet

PELUSI, Mario - *Concert Piece* (1978) (12'30) •Bsx/Brass Quartet/Perc

ROKEACH, Martin - *Tango* •Ob/Cl/Asx/Hn/Trb/Vcl •DP

SCHUBACK, Peter - *A Priori* (1983) (45') •Sx/Trb/Perc/Vlc/Pno/Harps •Tons/SMIC

SEIBER, Màtyàs - *Two Jazzolettes* (1929-33) •2 Sx/Tpt/Trb/Pno/Perc •WH

TULL, Fisher - *Concertino da camera* •Asx/Brass Quintet •South

7 Musicians

ADDERLEY, Mark - *The Worm and the Toothache* (1986) •Asx/Tsx/Vln/Fl/Trb/Pno/Perc •NMI

CANTON, Edgardo - *Phares et balises* •Fl/Ob/Sx/BsCl/Hn/Tpt/Trb

CRAS, Jean - *Demain* (1929) •Asx/Tpt/Trb/Perc/Vln/Vcl/Bass •Sen

DANCEANU, Liviu - *Quasi concerto* (1983) (15') •1 Sx: S+T/Bsn/Trb/Vcl/Bass/Pno/Perc

DONATONI, Franco - *Hot* (1989) (14') •1 Sx: T+Sno/Cl+Eb Cl/Tpt/Trb/Perc/Bass/Pno •Ric

ESCAICH, Thierry - *Antiennes oubliées* (1994) •Vln/Fl/Asx/Tpt/Trb/Vcl/Vibr •Bil

HERMANSSON, Christer - *Rumba* (1979) •Narr/2 Sx: ST/Trb/Guit/Pno/Bass •STIM

HESPOS, Hans - *Passagen* (1969) (9') •Cl/Asx/Tpt/Trb/Vla/Bass/Perc •EMod

HEYN, Volker - *Sandwich Gare de l'Est* (1986) (12'30) •1 Sx: Sno+CBs/2 Hn/2 Tpt/2 Trb •Br&Ha

JEVERUD, Johan - *Chimaira* (1984) •BsCl/Tsx/Trb/3 Vcl/Pno •SMIC

LARSSON, Häkan - *Farleder - 4 pieces* (1993) •Fl/Tsx/Trb/Electr. Guit/Electr. Bass/Pno/Perc •SvM

LAYZER, Arthur - *Inner and Outer Forms* •2 Sx/3 Brass/2 Perc

LUDWIG, J. - *Stenogramme* •Fl/Tsx/Trb/Bass/Vibr/Harps/Perc •EMod

MACERO, Teo - *Structure no. 4* •3 Sx: ATB/Tpt/Trb/Tuba/Perc •ACA

MASON, Lucas - *A Quilt of Love* (1971) •Soprano Voice/Asx/Fl/Vln/Bsn/Trb/Vcl •adr

MUSSEAU, Michel - *Les paupières rebelles* (1993) (40') •Fl/Cl/Ssx/
Hn/Tpt/Trb/Tuba •Ed. Visage

NEMESCU, Octavian - *Septuor* (1983) •Fl/Cl/Trb/Tsx/Pno/Bass/
Perc

SCHWERTSIK, Kurt - *Liebesträume*, op. 7 (1963) •Asx/Trb/Pno/
Vibr/Marimba/Harmonium/Bass •EMod

SPROGIS, Eric - *Comme une légère inexactitude* (1992) •Asx/Hn/
Tpt/Trb/Tuba/2 Perc

STEVEN, Donald - *On the down side* (1982) •2 Sx: AB/Trb/2 Perc/
Pno/Electr. Bass •CMC

STOUT, Alan - *Four Antiphonies* •Fl/Trb/Asx/Org/Vln/Vla/Perc
•CFE

STRINDBERG, Henrik - *Coming* (1982) (6') •2 Sx: SA/BsCl/Tpt/
Trb/2 Perc •SMIC

    Kommandez (1982-84) (6') •3 Sx: SAB/Tpt/Trb/2 Perc •SMIC/
WIM

VILLA-LOBOS, Heitor - *Chôros n° 3 - Pica-Pào*, op. 189 (1925) (6')
•Cl/Asx/Bsn/3 Hn/Trb •ME

WOLF, Hans - *Lady Style* (1972) (3') •2 Asx/4 Trb/Perc •Moz

    Tip Kick - Swing Fox (1964) (3') •4 Sx/Tpt/Trb/Perc •Moz

8 Musicians

ARMSTRONG, David - *The Protest* (1960) (9'30) •Cl/Trb/2 Asx/Tpt/
Perc/Pno/Bass •BMIC

BABBITT, Milton - *All Set* (1957) •2 Sx: AT/Tpt/Trb/Vibr/Bass/Perc/
Pno •adr

BARCE, Ramon - *Concierto de Lizara V* (1977) (10'45) •Cl/Tsx/Tpt/
Trb/Harp/Pno/Vln/Vcl

BLATNY, Pavel - *D-E-F-G-A-H-C* •Fl/3 Sx: ATB/Pno/Bass/Tpt/Trb
•CMIC

CARL, Gene - *Gray Matter* (1983) (23') •2 Sx: AA/2 Pno/2 Bass Guit/
2 Trb •Don

DEL PRINCIPE, Joseph - *Lyric Pieces for Octet* •Fl/Ob/Sx+Cl/BsCl/
Tpt/Hn/Trb/Tuba •SeMC

DUPRÉ, René - *Canon chromatique...* •4 Sx: SATB/2 Tpt/2 Trb •adr

ERNRYD, Bengt - *Rödingsjön II* (1967) •Fl+Picc/Trb/Tsx+Perc/
Bsx+Perc/Vcl/Bass/2 Perc •SMIC

FABERMAN, Harold - *For Erik and Nick* (1964) •Tenor Voice/Asx/
Vcl/Bass/Tpt/Trb/Vibr/Perc

HARTLEY, Walter - *Double Quartet* (1994) (7'30) •4 Sx: SATB/Hn/
Tpt/Trb/Tuba •adr

HESPOS, Hans - *Druckspuren - geschattet* (1970) (7'30) •Fl/Eb Cl/
Asx/Bsn/2 Tpt/Trb/Bass •EMod

HODEIR, André - *Ambiguité II* (8'); *Bicinium* (3') •3 Sx: ATB/2 Tpt/
Trb/Bass/Perc •MJQ

KETTING, Otto - *Musik zu einen Tonfilm* (1982) (15') •2 Sx/Tpt/Trb/
Perc/Pno/2 Vln •Don

LAKE, Larry - *Filar il tuono* (1989) •Cl/3 Sx: ATB/Bsn/Tpt/Trb/
Marimba •CMC

LANTIER, Pierre - *Fugue jazz* (1944) (3') •2 Cl/2 Sx: AT/Bsn/Tpt/
Trb/Perc

LASNE, George - *Ballade française* (1971) •Fl/Ob/2 Cl/Asx/2 Tpt/
Trb

MARIETAN, Pierre - *13 en concert* (1983) (15') •1 Sx: Sno+S+B/Cl/
Bsn/Trb/Vcl/2 Bass/Pno

PERSSON, Bob - *Om sommaren sköna II* (1965) •Fl/BsCl/Trb/2 Perc/
Vibr/Vcl/Jazz Sx/Tape

PINOS-SIMANDL, Aloïs - *Geneze* (1970) (8') •Vln/Asx/Vcl/Trb/
Perc/Harp/Harps/Ionika •CHF

SAGVIK, Stellan - *Suite circuler*, op. 86 (1978) (10') •Picc/Asx/Tpt/
Hn/2 Trb/Perc/Bass •STIM

SUTER, Robert - *Estampida* •Fl/Cl/Tsx/Hn/Tpt/Trb/Bass/Perc •EMod

TISNÉ, Antoine - *Dolmen* (1976) (30') •Fl/Cl/Asx/Hn/Tpt/Trb/Tuba/
Pno •adr

9 Musicians

ALBRIGHT, William - *Introduction...* (14') •Pno/Fl/Cl/Asx/Hn/Tpt/
Trb/Tuba/Perc •Pet

ANDRIESSEN, Louis - *De Volharping* (1972) (23') •3 Sx/3 Tpt/3 Trb
•Don

BUMCKE, Gustav - *"Der Spaziergang"*, op. 22 •Fl/Ob/EH/Cl/Bsn/
Hn/BsTrb/Bsx/Harp

CERHA, Friedrich - *Exercices for Nine, No. 1* •BsCl/Bsx/Bsn/Tpt/
Trb/Tuba/Vcl/Bass/Harp •Uni

CLARK, Thomas - *Dreamscape* •Fl/Ob/Cl/Sx/Tpt/Trb/Pno/Perc/
Bass •SeMC

DIEMENTE, Edward - *For Lady Day* •Fl/Ob/Cl/Tpt/Trb/Vln/Vla/Sx/
Bsn/Tape •SeMC

DOMAZLICKY, Frantisek - *Suite danza*, op. 52 (17') •4 Sx/Hn/2 Tpt/
Trb/Tuba

HARVEY, Paul - *Pieces for Nine* (1979) (5') •4 Sx: SATB/2 Tpt/Hn/
Trb/Tuba •adr

HODEIR, André - *Pieces* •3 Sx: ATB/2 Tpt/Trb/Vibr/Bass/Perc
•MJQ

HOFFER, Bernard - *Preludes and Fugues* (1977) (25') •4 Sx: SATB/
Brass Quintet •Shir

IVES, Charles - *Over the Pavements*, op. 20 (1906-13) •Picc/Cl/Bsx
(or Bsn)/Tpt/3 Trb/Perc/Pno •PIC

JELINEK, Hanns - *Blue Sketches*, op. 25 (1956) •Fl/Cl/2 Sx: AB/Tpt/
Trb/Vibr/Bass/Perc •EMod

LEGRAND, Michel - *Porcelaine de Sax* (1958) (3') •6 Sx: SnoSATBBs
(or Eb Cl/Cl/3 Sx: ATB/Bsn) Trb/Bass/Perc
•Mills

LEWIS, John Aaron - *Little David's Fugue* (5'30) •Fl/Cl/3 Sx: ATB/
Trb or Tpt/Harp or Pno/Bass/Perc •MJQ

    The Queen's Fancy (4') •Fl/Cl/Tsx/Bsn/Hn/Trb/Harp/Bass/Perc
•MJQ

    Sun Dance (4') •Fl/Cl/3 Sx: ATB/Trb/Harp or Guit/Bass/Perc
•MJQ

NATANSON, Tadeus - *3 Pictures for 7 Instruments* (1960) •Ob/Cl/
Asx/Trb/Vcl/Tpt/Bsn/Pno/Perc •AMP

SAGVIK, Stellan - *Det Förlorade steget*, op. 64 (1976) (20') •Fl/
Cl+BsCl/Asx/Cnt/Trb/Vln/Vla/Vcl/Perc
•SMIC

SCELSI, Jacinto - *Kya* (1959) (11') •Cl (or Ssx)/EH/Hn/BsCl/Tpt/
Trb/Vla/Vcl/Bass •Sal

SVOBODA, Tomàs - *Seven Short Dances* •Fl/2 Cl/Asx/Trb/Vln/Bass/
Pno/Perc

ULRICH, Jürgen - *Spiel* (1974) (5') •Fl/Ob/Cl/Bsn/Sx/Hn/Tpt/Trb/
Tuba •VDMK

VELLONES, Pierre - *Planisphère*, op. 23 (1930) •2 Sx: AT/Cl/2 Tpt/
Trb/Bass (or Tuba)/Perc/Pno •JJ

    Prélude et fables de Florian, op. 28 (1930) •Tenor Voice/3 Sx:
SAB/2 Tpt/Trb/Tuba/Banjo •Dur

YOSHIBA, Susumu - *Erka* •Fl/Ob/Sx/Tpt/Trb/Perc/Vcl/Guit/Pno

10 Musicians

ANDRIESSEN, Louis - *On Jimmy Yancey* (1973) (10') •Fl/2 Sx: AT/
Hn/Tpt/3 Trb/Bass/Pno •Don

BENNETT, Richard Rodney - *Jazz Pastorale* (1969) (25') •Voice/1
Sx: A+T/Bsx/2 Tpt/Trb/Tuba/Pno/Bass/Perc
•Uni

BRANT, Henry - *Dialogue in the Jungle* (1964) (15') •Tenor Voice/
Fl/Ob/Cl/Bsx/2 Tpt/Trb/Hn/Tuba •adr

CHIARPARIN, Antonio - *Omaggio à Zoltan Kodaly* •2 Fl/6 Sx:
AAATTB/Bugle (Flicorno)/BsTrb •Piz

COE, Tony - *The Buds of Time* (1979) (20') •Cl/Sx/Cl+BsCl/2 Vln/
Vla/Vcl/BsTrb/Pno/Bass/Perc •adr

COPPOOLSE, David - *Canto XVII* (1984) (12') •Asx/2 Hn/2 Trb/Vln/
Vla/Vcl/Bass/Pno •Don

COSTEN, Roel van - *Prisma* (1984) (8') •Vla/Fl/Cl/Asx/BsCl/Trb/
Vcl/Bass/Perc/Pno •Don

GRAHN, Ulf - *Soundscape II* (1974) (7') •Fl/Cl/EH/Asx/2 Trb/2 Vln/
Vcl/Bass •SMIC

GRANDIS, Renato de - *Scotter Sud-est* •Vln/Vla/Vcl/Bass/Sx/Hn/
Tpt/Trb/Pno/Perc •SeMC

HARTLEY, Walter - *Double Concerto* (1969) (7'30) •Asx/Tuba/
Wind Octet (Fl/Ob/Cl/Bsn/Hn/2 Tpt/Trb)
•PhiCo

HEIDEN, Bernhard - *Sonatina* •Fl/Cl/Tsx/Hn/Trb/Harp/Vibr/Pno/
Bass/Perc •MJQ

HODEIR, André - *Jazz cantata* (10') •Soprano Voice/3 Sx: ATB/2
Tpt/Trb/Vibr/Bass/Perc •MJQ

HORWOOD, Michael - *Facets* (1974) (20') •Narr/Sx/Tpt/Hn/Trb/
Pno/Accordion/Electr. Bass/2 Electr. Guit
•CMC

JOHNSON, J. J. - *Turnpike* (5') •Fl/Cl/3 Sx: ATB/Trb/Harp (or Guit)/
Pno/Bass/Perc •MJQ

KOPP, Frederick - *Terror Suite* •Brass/Sx/Timp/3 Perc •SeMC

KOX, Hans - *Concertino* (1982) •Asx/Picc/2 Fl/BsCl/2 Hn/2 Tpt/Trb
•Don

LACHARTE, Nicole - *La Geste inachevée* (1980) •Fl/Cl/Sx/Tpt/Trb/
Pno/Perc/Vln/Vla/Vcl

Lecuona, Ernesto - *Andalucia* •2 Tpt/Trb/3 Sx: AAT/2 Vln/Vcl/Bass

MASON, Benedict - *Coulour and information* (1993) •Fl/Ob/Sx/Bsn/
Hn/Tpt/Trb/Tuba/Perc/Electr. Bass

MIMET, Anne-Marie - *Fanfare et divertissement* •Fl/Ob/Cl/Bsn/3 Sx:
SAT/Tpt/Trb/Tuba

SCELSI, Jacinto - *I Presagi* (1958) (9'30) •2 Hn/2 Tpt/Sx/2 Trb/2
Tuba/Perc •Sal

SCHAFFER, Boguslaw - *Permutations n° 27* (1956) •Fl/Ob/Cl/Sx/
Tpt/Trb/Vla/Perc/Harp/Pno •A&S

SCHULLER, Gunther - *12 by 11* (8'30) •Fl/Cl/Tsx/Hn/Trb/Vibr/Pno/
Harp/Bass/Perc •MJQ

SCHWERTSIK, Kurt - *Salotto romano*, op. 5 (1961) •BsCl/Bsx/Bsn/
Hn/Trb/Tuba/Perc/Bass/Vcl/Guit •EMod

SMITH, William - *Elegy for Eric* •Fl/2 Sx: AB/Cl/Tpt/Trb/Vibr/Vln/
Bass/Perc •MJQ

TREMBLAY, George - *Epithalamium* (1962) •Fl/Ob/Cl/Sx/Bsn/Hn/
Tpt/Trb/Tuba/Perc •CFE

VRIES, Klaas de - *Moeilijkheden* (1977) (15') •Fl/2 Sx: AT/Hn/2 Tpt/
3 Trb/Pno •Don

11 Musicians

ANDRIESSEN, Jurriaan - *Hommage à Milhaud* (1945) (8') •Fl/Ob/
Cl/Bsn/Hn/Tpt/Trb/Asx/Vln/Vla/Vcl •Don

BOIS, Rob du - *Springtime* (1978) •Picc/3 Sx/Hn/2 Tpt/2 Trb/Tuba/
Pno •Don

BORSTLAP, Dick - *Fanfare II* (1975) (6'); *Over de verandering...*
(1974) (5') •Fl/Picc/2 Sx: AT/Hn/Tpt/2 Trb/
BsTrb/Pno/Bass •Don

Vrijheidslied (1978) (2') •Picc/3 Sx: SAT/Hn/2 Tpt/2 Trb/Tuba/
Pno •Don

DIEMENTE, Edward - *3-31 '70* •Voice/Tpt/Trb/Sx/Guit/Bass/5 Perc
•SeMC

HAZZARD, Peter - *Massage* •3 Voices (SAB)/3 Perc/Fl/Cl/Hn/Sx/
1 rb •SeMC

HESPOS, Hans - *Break* •Ob/3 Tpt/2 Sx: TB/Vcl/Bass/Trb/Pno/Perc
•EMod

KEULEN, Geert van - *Onkruid* (1981) (5') •Ob/Cl/2 Sx: AT/Bsn/Hn/
Tpt/Trb/Vln/Vla/Pno •Don

MENGELBERG, Misha - *Dressoir* (1977) (10') •Fl/3 Sx: S+A A T/
2 Tpt/Hn/2 Trb/Tuba/Pno •Don

MESTRAL, Patrice - *Alliages* (1969) •Tpt Solo/Fl/Cl/Asx/2 Trb/2
Perc/Pno/Org/Bass

MONDELLO, Nuncio - *Suite* (1956) •Asx/2 Fl/Ob/Cl/Bsn/2 Hn/Tpt/
Trb/Perc •adr

PABLO, Luis de - *Polar*, op. 12 (1963) •Vln/Ssx/BsCl/Xylophone/
Trb/6 Perc •Tono/SeMC

TARENSKEEN, Boudewijn - *Marchtelt suite* (1978) (30') •4 Sx:
AATT/Hn/2 Tpt/3 Trb/Bass •Don

ZONN, Paul Martin - *Voyage of Columbus* (1974) (13') •Tpt Solo/Fl/
Ob/Ssx/Hrn/Trb/2 Perc/Pno/Vln/Bass •ACA

12 Musicians

BENNETT, Richard Rodney - *A Jazz Calender* (1963-64) (31') •Fl/
3 Sx: ATB/2 Tpt/Hn/Trb/Tuba/Pno/2 Perc
•Uni

CURTIS-SMITH, Curtis - *Sundry Dances* (1981) •Fl/Ob/Cl/3 Sx:
SAB/Bsn/CBsn/Tpt/Trb/Tuba/Bass •adr

JAEGGI, Oswald - *Dum Clamarem* (1961) •Ob/EH/Cl/3 Sx/3 Tpt/3
Trb

LINKOLA, Jukka - *Alta* (1983) (8') •Vocal group: SATBs/2 Sx: AT/
Tpt/Trb/Pno/Bass/Drums/Perc •FMIC

MEIJERING, Chiel - *Het ontblote feit* (1988-90) (8'30) •2 Fl/3 Sx:
ATB/2 Hn/Tpt/Trb/Perc/Pno/Electr. Guit
•Don

ROBBINS, David - *Improvisation* •Fl/2 Cl/Tsx/Bsn/Tpt/Trb/Vln/Vla/
Vcl/Bass/Perc

13 Musicians

BOZZA, Eugène - *Ouverture pour une cérémonie* •3 Tpt/4 Sx/3 Trb/
BsTrb/Tuba/Perc •Led

DELANNOY, Marcel - *Le Marchand de notes* •3 Vln/Bass/4 Sx/2 Tpt/
Trb/Perc/Pno

EICHMANN, Dietrich - *George...* (1984) (35') •3 Fl/Cl/2 Sx: AT/
Tpt/Trb/2 Perc/Pno/Bs Guit •adr

HUREL, Philippe - *"Pour l'image"* •Fl/Ob/Cl/Asx/Hn/Tpt/Trb/Perc/
2 Vln/Vla/Vcl/Bass

MERKU, Pavle - *Tiare* •Baritone Voice/Sx/11 wind instruments •Piz

MEULEN, Henk van der - *De profondis I* (1986) (15') •Fl/3 Sx: S+T
A A/Hn/3 Tpt/2 Trb/BsTrb/Bass/Pno •Don

SEKON, Joseph - *Lemon Ice* (1972) •Fl/Ob/Cl/2 Sx: ST/Bsn/Tpt/Trb/
2 Perc/Vln/Vcl/Pno •adr

WENDEL, Eugen - *Saphonospir* (15') •Asx/Fl/Cl/Ob/Tpt/Trb/2 Vln/
Vla/Vcl/Bass/2 Perc •adr

14 Musicians

GRAINGER, Percy - *The Duke of Marlborough* (1905-39-49) •4 Tpt/
4 Hn (or 2 Sx: AT/2 Bsn)/3 Trb/Tuba/Bass/
Cymb. •Sch

HARBISON, John - *Confinement* (1965) (15'15) •Fl/Ob/EH/Cl/BsCl/
Asx/Tpt/Trb/Vln/Vla/Vcl/Bass/Pno/Perc

JENNI, Donald - *Allegro...* •4 Hn/4 Tpt/3 Trb/Tuba/2 Bsx •Pio

MIEREANU, Costin - *Clair de biche* (1986) (11') •Fl/Picc/Cl/1 Sx:
Sno+S+T/Brass Quintet/5 Perc •Sal

oOo

ANSIND, Caroline - *Het water...* (1986) (14'30) •Ob/Cl/2 Sx: AB/2
Trb/Perc/Pno/Choir •Don

BASSET, Leslie - *Designs in Brass* •2 Sx: BB/4 Hn/4 Tpt/3 Trb/Tuba/
Timp/Perc •Pio

DAKIN, Charles - *Syra* (1979) (8'30) •2 Cl/2 Tsx/2 Tpt/2 Trb/4 Vla/
4 Vcl/2 Bass

DHAINE, Jean-Louis - *Fantaisies...* •4 Fl/4 Cl/4 Sx: AATT/2 Tpt/2
Trb

Saxophone and Tuba

2 Musicians

ATOR, James - *Duo* (1981) •Asx/Tuba •DP
GARCIA, Manuel - *Concert Duet* •Asx/Tuba •DP
HAUBENSTOCK-RAMATI, Roman - *Versione 9* (1981) •Sx/Tuba •Uni
HEUSSENSTAMM, George - *Dialogue*, op. 77 (1984) (13') •Asx/Tuba •DP
SMITH, Howie - *Schizerzo* (1983) •Sx/Tuba •Oa
VAN BEURDEN, Bernard - *Überwindung des toten Punktes* (1993) •1 Sx: S+A+T/Tuba •INM

3 Musicians

BIGOT, Eugène - *Carillon et Bourdon* •Tsx/Tuba/Pno
DEASON, David - *Sonata* (1980) •Asx/Tuba/Pno •DP
KARLINS, M. William - *Saxtuper* (1989) (9') •1 Sx: A+S/Tuba/Perc •ACA
SIBBING, Robert - *Moments* (1974) •Sx/Bsn/Tuba (or Bass) •Eto
YATES, Ronald - *Triune* (1971) •Asx/Vla/BsTrb •adr

4 Musicians

BARBAUD, Pierre - *Pièces brèves...* (10') •Sx/Tpt/Trb/Tuba •EFM
CHARBONNIER, Janine - *Prélude, Canon et Choral* (5') •Asx/Tpt/Trb/Tuba •EFM
Kahal & Raskin - *If I Give Up The Saxophone* (WOLFE) •Voice/Ssx/Pno/Tuba (optional) •Ron
KASPAR, Edward - *Quartet* (1972) •2 Sx: AT/Vibr/Tuba •adr
KRÖLL, Georg - *Quartett* (1993) •Bsx/Vcl/Tuba/Pno
LOCKWOOD, Harry - *Lyric Piece* •Asx/Tpt/Vla/Tuba
Schmidt, Joseph - *Finale* (BRINK) •2 Cl/Tsx/Tuba or 4 Sx: SATB •Mol

5 Musicians

LAUBER, Anne - *5 Eléments* (1972) (6'15) •Fl/Ssx/Vln/Bsn/Tuba •CMC

6 Musicians

BOUDREAU, Walter - *Variations* (1975) •Ssx/Asx+Fl/Tsx+Picc/Tuba/Pno+Celesta/Guit •CMC
CARLOSEMA, Bernard - *Radiance* (1988) (5'30) •Fl/Asx/Hn/Tpt/Trb/Tuba •Fuz
HARTLEY, Walter - *Concertino da Camera* (1994) •Ssx/2 Tpt/Hn/Trb/Tuba •adr
HOLMBERG, Peter - *Musica alta e bassa* (1979) (12') •Fl/Tpt/Bsx/Tuba/Vln/Vcl •STIM
KARLINS, M. William - *Cantena II* (1982) (10') •Ssx/Brass Quintet •ACA
LESSER, Jeffrey - *Last Saxophone on Earth* (1979) •Asx/Brass Quintet
OLIVEIRA, Willy Corrêa de - *Sugestoes* (1971) •Ob/Asx/Bandoneon/Tuba/Bass/Perc
ORREGO SALAS, Juan - *Concerto da camera* (1987) •Asx/Brass Quintet
PELUSI, Mario - *Concert Piece* (1978) (12'30) •Bsx/Brass Quartet/Perc
TULL, Fisher - *Concertino da camera* •Asx/Brass Quintet •South

7 Musicians

BENNETT, Richard Rodney - *Soliloquy* (1966) (14') •Voice/1 Sx: A+T/Tpt/Tuba/Pno/Bass/Perc •Uni
MACERO, Teo - *Structure no. 4* •3 Sx: ATB/Tpt/Trb/Tuba/Perc •ACA
MUSSEAU, Michel - *Les paupières rebelles* (1993) (40') •Fl/Cl/Ssx/Hn/Tpt/Trb/Tuba •Ed. Visage

SOTELO, Mauricio - *IX +... - de substantiis separatis* (1990) •Cl/Sx/Tuba/Vln/Vcl/Bass/Pno/Schtagzeng with live electronics •adr
SPROGIS, Eric - *Comme une légère inexactitude* (1992) •Asx/Hn/Tpt/Trb/Tuba/2 Perc

8 Musicians

DEL PRINCIPE, Joseph - *Lyric Pieces for Octet* •Fl/Ob/Sx+Cl/BsCl/Tpt/Hn/Trb/Tuba •SeMC
HARTLEY, Walter - *Double Quartet* (1994) (7'30) •4 Sx: SATB/Hn/Tpt/Trb/Tuba •adr
TISNÉ, Antoine - *Dolmen* (1976) (30') •Fl/Cl/Asx/Hn/Tpt/Trb/Tuba/Pno •adr

9 Musicians

ALBRIGHT, William - *Introduction...* (14') •Pno/Fl/Cl/Asx/Hn/Tpt/Trb/Tuba/Perc •Pet
CERHA, Friedrich - *Exercices for Nine, No. 1* •BsCl/Bsx/Bsn/Tpt/Trb/Tuba/Vcl/Bass/Harp •Uni
DOMAZLICKY, Frantisek - *Suite danza*, op. 52 (17') •4 Sx/Hn/2 Tpt/Trb/Tuba
FICHER, Jacobo - *Los invitados*, op. 26 •Fl/Cl/2 Sx: AT/2 Tpt/Tuba/Pno/Perc
HARVEY, Paul - *Pieces for Nine* (1979) (5') •4 Sx: SATB/2 Tpt/Hn/Trb/Tuba •adr
HOFFER, Bernard - *Preludes and Fugues* (1977) (25') •4 Sx: SATB/Brass Quintet •Shir
MANOURY, Philippe - *Etude automatique* 1 •Fl/Tpt/Sx/Tuba/Harp/Vln/Vla/Vcl/Bass
SILVERMAN, Faye - *Shadings* (1978) •Vln/Vla/Bass/Fl/Ob/Asx/Bsn/Hn/Tuba
ULRICH, Jürgen - *Spiel* (1974) (5') •Fl/Ob/Cl/Bsn/Sx/Hn/Tpt/Trb/Tuba •VDMK
VELLONES, Pierre - *Planisphère*, op. 23 (1930) •2 Sx: AT/Cl/2 Tpt/Trb/Bass (or Tuba)/Perc/Pno •JJ
 Prélude et fables de Florian, op. 28 (1930) •Tenor Voice/3 Sx: SAB/2 Tpt/Trb/Tuba/Banjo •Dur

10 Musicians

BENNETT, Richard Rodney - *Jazz Pastorale* (1969) (25') •Voice/1 Sx: A+T/Bsx/2 Tpt/Trb/Tuba/Pno/Bass/Perc •Uni
BRANT, Henry - *Dialogue in the Jungle* (1964) (15') •Tenor Voice/Fl/Ob/Cl/Bsx/2 Tpt/Trb/Hn/Tuba •adr
HARTLEY, Walter - *Double Concerto* (1969) (7'30) •Asx/Tuba/Wind Octet (Fl/Ob/Cl/Bsn/Hn/2 Tpt/Trb) •PhiCo
KOPP, Frederick - *Terror Suite* •Brass/Sx/Timp/3 Perc •SeMC
MASON, Benedict - *Coulour and information* (1993) •Fl/Ob/Sx/Bsn/Hn/Tpt/Trb/Tuba/Perc/Electr. Bass
MIMET, Anne-Marie - *Fanfare et divertissement* •Fl/Ob/Cl/Bsn/3 Sx: SAT/Tpt/Trb/Tuba
SCELSI, Jacinto - *I Presagi* (1958) (9'30) •2 Hn/2 Tpt/Sx/2 Trb/2 Tuba/Perc •Sal
SCHWERTSIK, Kurt - *Salotto romano*, op. 5 (1961) •BsCl/Bsx/Bsn/Hn/Trb/Tuba/Perc/Bass/Vcl/Guit •EMod
TREMBLAY, George - *Epithalamium* (1962) •Fl/Ob/Cl/Sx/Bsn/Hn/Tpt/Trb/Tuba/Perc •CFE

11 Musicians

BOIS, Rob du - *Springtime* (1978) •Picc/3 Sx/Hn/2 Tpt/2 Trb/Tuba/Pno •Don
BORSTLAP, Dick - *Vrijheidslied* (1978) (2') •Picc/3 Sx: SAT/Hn/2 Tpt/2 Trb/Tuba/Pno •Don

MENGELBERG, Misha - *Dressoir* (1977) (10') •Fl/3 Sx: S+A A T/
2 Tpt/Hn/2 Trb/Tuba/Pno •Don

12 Musicians

BENNETT, Richard Rodney - *A Jazz Calender* (1963-64) (31') •Fl/
3 Sx: ATB/2 Tpt/Hn/Trb/Tuba/Pno/2 Perc
•Uni
CURTIS-SMITH, Curtis - *Sundry Dances* (1981) •Fl/Ob/Cl/3 Sx:
SAB/Bsn/CBsn/Tpt/Trb/Tuba/Bass •adr
DUREY, Louis - *Feu la mère de Madame*, op. 49 (1945) (5') •Fl/Ob/
Asx/Bsn/Tpt/Tuba/Perc/2 Vln/Vla/Vcl/Bass
•BRF

13 Musicians

BOZZA, Eugène - *Ouverture pour une cérémonie* •3 Tpt/4 Sx/3 Trb/
BsTrb/Tuba/Perc •Led
MEULEN, Henk van der - *De profondis I* (1986) (15') •Fl/3 Sx: S+T
A A/Hn/3 Tpt/2 Trb/BsTrb/Bass/Pno •Don

14 Musicians

GRAINGER, Percy - *The Duke of Marlborough* (1905-39-49) •4 Tpt/
4 Hn (or 2 Sx: AT/2 Bsn)/3 Trb/Tuba/Bass/
Cymb. •Sch
JENNI, Donald - *Allegro...* •4 Hn/4 Tpt/3 Trb/Tuba/2 Bsx •Pio
MIEREANU, Costin - *Clair de biche* (1986) (11') •Fl/Picc/Cl/1 Sx:
Sno+S+T/Brass Quintet/5 Perc •Sal

oOo

BASSET, Leslie - *Designs in Brass* •2 Sx: BB/4 Hn/4 Tpt/3 Trb/Tuba/
Timp/Perc •Pio

Saxophone and Violin

2 Musicians

BRUCE, Neely - *Analogues* (1993) •Sx/Vln
BUSCH, Adolph - *Suite* (1926) •Asx/Vln •AmV
DUBOIS, Pierre-Max - *Feu de paille* (1986) (8') •Asx/Vln •Bil
EICHLER, Matthew - *Beach Dance* (1982) •Asx/Vln
KLAMMER, David - *Erwartingen oder...* (1993) •Vln/Sx •INM
MEIJERING, Chiel - *Niet doorslikken* (1985) (5') •Bsx/Vln •Don
    The Ugly Howling Monkey (1978) (7') •Bsx/Vln •Don
WREDE, Bert - *Miniature* (1993) •Asx/Vln •INM

3 Musicians

AMY, Gilbert - *Trio* (1993) •Vln/Sx/Trb
BRANT, Henry - *Nomads* (1974) •3 Soloists (Vln/Perc/Sx)/Brass
    Orch •adr
BOIS, Rob du - *Summer Music* (1967) (7'15) •Asx/Vln/Vcl •Don
BORCK, Edmund - *Introduktion und Capriccio*, op. 11 (1934) •Asx/
    Vln/Pno •IMD
BURSA, Lech - *Suite*, op. 3 (1928) •Vln/Sx/Pno
CARNES, Michael - *Before We Were...* •Asx/Vln/Pno •DP
EYCHENNE, Marc - *Cantilène et danse* (1961) (13') •Asx/Vln/Pno
    •Bil
FERRAND-TEULET, Denise - *Trio* •Asx/Vln/Pno
HARTLEY, Walter - *Dance Suite* (1985) (6'30) •Asx/Vln/Pno •Eth
JACOBS, Ivan - *Trio* •Soprano Voice (or Ssx)/Vln/Pno
KORBAR, Leopold - *Valse triste per trio* (1978) (5') •Vln (or Fl or Ob
    or Cl or Ssx)/Vcl (or Bsn or Tsx)/Pno •CHF
MACY, Charleton - *Connections* (1986) •Asx/Vln/Pno
MAXFIELD, Richard - *Perateia* •Asx/Vln/Pno/Tape
MAYUZUMI, Toshiro - *Metamusic* (1961) •Asx/Vln/Pno •Pet
MORITZ, Edvard - *Trio Sonata* (1963) •Asx/Vln/Pno
PRICE, Deon - *Augury* (1980) •Asx/Vln/Pno •CCP
ROTERS, Ernst - *Trio*, op. 26b (1926) •Asx/Vln/Vcl •Sim
RUSSELL, Armand - *Transfluent Forms* (1980) •Vln/Asx/Pno
SHAFFER, Sherwood - *Charades* •Vln/Tsx/Pno •adr
SHERMAN, Robert - *Trio Sonata* (1963) •Asx/Vln/Pno
STEIN, Leon - *Trio Concertante* (1961) (16') •Asx/Cl (or Vln)/Pno
    •CFE/ACA
TUROK, Paul - *Improvisation* (1988) (15'30) •Vln/Asx/Pno •SeMC
VAUGHAN WILLIAMS, Ralph - *Household Music* (1940-41) •Di-
    verse combinations •B&H
VEHAR, Persis - *A Day Off* •Asx/Vln/Pno
WEINHORST, Richard - *Trio Sonata* (1963) •Asx/Vln/Pno •ACF
WOODBURY, Arthur - *Remembrances* (1968) (16'30) •Asx/Vln/
    Vibr •CPE
WORLEY, John - *Trio* (1983) •Vln/Sx/Pno

4 Musicians

ADDERLEY, Mark - *Waver* (1986) •Fl/Cl/Tsx/Vln •NMI
ALBERTH, Rudolf - *Divertimento* (1941) •Asx/Str Trio •adr
BOEUF, Georges - *Em Misma...* (1971) (10') •Vln/Fl/Cl/Asx •adr
BOUVARD, Jean - *3 Images* •Fl/Vln/Asx/Pno •Bil
BRIZZI, Aldo - *D'après une esquisse* (1987) (8') •1 Sx: A+S/Vln/Cl/
    Pno
CALMEL, Roger - *Les Caractères* (15') •Vln/Asx/Vcl/Pno •adr
CONSTANT, Franz - *Rythme et Expression*, op. 49 (1972) (13') •Vln/
    Asx/Pno/Perc •CBDM
DAVID, Karl - *Quartets* (1934) (1946) •Vln/Asx/Vcl/Pno
DEFOSSEZ, René - *Suite "Souvenirs"* •Vln/Asx/Pno/Perc
DEPELSENAIRRE, J-M. - *Les approches de l'invisible* (1973) (4')
    •Vln/Asx/Pno/Perc •adr
DIJK, Jan van - *Concertino* •Vln/Fl/Cl/Asx •Don
DUBOIS, Pierre-Max - *Suite* •Vln/Asx/Pno/Perc •Mau
EKSTRÖM, Lars - *Vargtimen* (1990) •Cl/Asx/Vln/Pno •STIM

FRIED, Alexej - *Tympanon* (1982) (21') •Vln/SopranoVoice/Sx/Pno
GLASER, Werner Wolf - *Kvartett* (1950) •Asx/Vln/Vla/Vcl •STIM
    Linda - *Quartett* (1970-85) (17') •Bsx/Vln/Vla/Vcl •STIM
    Little Quartet (1970) •Asx/Vln/Vcl/Pno •STIM
GROSSE, Erwin - *Konzerte* •Tpt/Vln/Asx/Bass •adr
HEUSSENSTAMM, George - *Four Miniatures*, op. 57 (1975) (9')
    •Tsx/Fl/Ob/Vln •DP
KARLINS, M. William - *Variations* (1962-63) Ssx/Vln/Vla/Vcl
    •SeMC
KROL, Bernhard - *Suite* •Vln/Asx/Vcl/Pno •adr
LINDEMAN, Peter - *Gloxinta* •Vln/Cl/Tsx/Pno
MARCUSSEN, Kjell - *Quartet* (1983) •Ob (or Ssx)/Vln/Vcl/Pno
    •NMI
MEIJERING, Chiel - *I Hate Mozart* (1979) (4') •Fl/Asx/Harp/Vln
    •Don
MENGOLD, Paul - *Quartette* •Vln/Asx/Vcl/Pno
MOESCHINGER, Albert - *Images*, op. 85 (1958) (18') •Fl/Vln/Asx/
    Vcl •Bil
NOON, David - *Hymn Variations*, op. 108 (1991) (7') •Ssx/Vln/Vcl/
    Pno •TTF
OLBRISCH, Franz-Martin - *Trios* (1984) (21') •Vln/Cl/Tsx/Pno •adr
OLSON, Roger - *Cobwebs* (1983) •Narr/Guit/Asx/Vln
PARTCH, Harry - *Ulysses at the Edge...* (1955) •Vln/Tsx/Tpt/Perc
PRICE, Deon - *Allegro barbaro* (1980) •Vln/Ssx/Vla/Vcl
RICHMOND, Thomas - *Two Movements* (1964) •Vln/Vla/Asx/Vcl
RUBBERT, Rainer - *Obstacle* (1992) (14') •Tsx/BsCl/Vln/Pno •adr
SEVRETTE, Danielle - *L'Innomé* •Vln/Vcl/Asx/Org •adr
SLONIMSKY, Sergei - *Suite exotique* •2 Vln/Tsx Solo/Electr. Bass
STEARNS, Peter - *Chamber Set II* •Asx/Vln/Tpt/Bass •ACA
STEINBERG, Ben - *Suite Sephardi* (1979) •Ssx/Vln/Vla/Vcl •CMC
SUTHERLAND, Margaret - *Quartet* (1965) •Asx/Vln/Vla/Vcl
WEBERN, Anton - *Quartet*, op. 22 (1930) (8') •Vln/Cl/Tsx/Pno •Uni
WINKLER, Gerhard - *Aussenhäute* (1989) •Cl/Vln/Bsx/Vcl •adr
ZONN, Paul Martin - *Midnight Secrets* (1992) (20') •Ssx/Vln/Vla/Vcl
    •ACA

5 Musicians

Also see Saxophone and String Quartet (Voir aussi
quatuor à cordes), page 394.

D'ANGELO, Nicholas - *The Seventh Star of Paracelsus* (1968) (16')
    •Fl/Vln/Asx/Vcl/Pno •adr
DONDEYNE, Désiré - *Voyages imaginaires* (1989) (12') •Asx/Pno or
    Asx/2 Vln/Harp/Vcl •Com
DURBIN, Jean - *1ère suite de Alain Fournier* •Pno/Org/Vln/Vla/Sx
HRISANIDE, Alexandru - *M. P. 5* (1967) •Tsx+Cl/Vln/Vla/Vcl/Pno
    •IMD
JAEGER, Robert - *Quintet* (1969) •Asx/Vln/Vla/Vcl/Harp •adr
    Three Pieces (1967) (6'30) •Asx/Vln/Vla/Vcl/Harp (or Pno) •adr
KONOE, Hidétaké - *Quintet* (1968) •Sx/Vln/Vla/Vcl/Bass
    Sonata caprice (1970) •Asx/Vln/Vla/Vcl/Bass
LAUBA, Christian - *Ravel's raga* (1993) (15') •Vln/Cl/Asx/Bsn/Pno
    •adr
LAUBER, Anne - *5 Eléments* (1972) (6'15) •Fl/Ssx/Vln/Bsn/Tuba
    •CMC
LINDROTH, Scott - *Two Pieces* •Asx/Vln/Vla/Vcl/Pno •DP
MACCHI, Egisto - *Schemi* (1960) •2 Vln/2 Pno/Asx
MACERO, Teo - *Canzona No. 1* •2 Vln/Asx/Vcl/Tpt •Pres
MATSUDAIRA, Roh - *Quintette* (1968) •Asx/Vln/Vla/Vcl/Bass
OLBRISCH, Franz-Martin - *"Im Anfänglichen...* (1989) (90') •Vln/
    Fl/Trb/Sx/Perc/Electronics
PARISI, Stephen - *Quintet* (1988) •Vln/4 Sx: SATB
SCHAFFER, Boguslaw - *Proietto simultaneo* (1983) (12') •Soprano
    Voice/Vln/Pno/Ob/Sx/Tape
VOSK, Jay - *Le Nid* •Ssx/Vibr/Guit/Vln/Bass •SeMC

6 Musicians

ABECASSIS, Eryck - *Dans 3 nuits* (1984) •Asx/Fl/Cl/Vln/Vcl/Pno

ANDERSON, Thomas J. - *Variations on a Theme by M.B. Tolson* (1969) •Ssx/Tpt/Trb/Vln/Vcl/Pno

BERG, Paul - *To Teach His Own* (1984) (12') •Fl/Ob/Tsx/Trb/Vln/Vcl/Tape •Don

BOSSE, Denis - *...d'un léger souffle cosmique* (1987) (10') •1 Sx Solo: B+A+S/2 Vln/Vla/Vcl/Bass

CORY, Eleanor - *Waking* (1974) •Tsx/Bsn/Vln/Vcl/Bass/Perc

DAMICO, John - *Avilion* •Asx/2 Vln/Vla/Vcl/Bass •DP

DeBLASIO, Chris - *Prelude and Fugue* (1991) (9') •Ssx/Str Quintet •TTF

DESPORTES, Yvonne - *La maison abandonnée* (1961) (20') •Vln/Vla/Vcl/Asx/Perc/Pno •adr

DINESCU-LUCACI, Violeta - *"Auf der Suche nach Mozart"* (1983) (19') •Fl/Sx/Bsn/Hn/Vln/Pno+Celesta •adr

EYSER, Eberhard - *Livre des jeux...* (1959-86) (23'30) •Asx/Harp/Pno/Vibr/Guit/Vln •EMa

FUSTÉ-LAMBEZAT, Arnaud - *Catalogue d'étoiles* (1983) •Asx/Fl/Cl/Vln/Vcl/Pno •adr

GARCIN, Gérard - *SA* (1986) •Asx/Fl/Cl/Vln/Vcl/Pno

GAUTHIER, Brigitte - *Like the Sweet Blonde* (1983) •Fl/Asx/Cl/Vln/Vcl/Pno

GOTKOVSKY, Ida - *Poème lyrique* (1987) •2 Voices: SB/Pno/Fl (or Vln)/Asx (or Vla)/Bsn (or Vcl)

GOTSKOSIK, Oleg - *Svit...* (1986) •Ob/Asx/Bsn/2 Vln/Pno •SMIC

GRANDIS, Renato de - *Canti...* •Vln/Vcl/Tsx/Vibr/Trb/Perc •SeMC

GUINJOAN, Juan - *Musique intuitive - Diari* (1969) •Cl/Tsx/Tpt/Vln/Vcl/Pno

GULLIN, Peter - *Tre suma julsagor* (1988) •Bsx/2 Vln/Vla/Vcl/Bass

HEDSTROM, Ase - *Close by* (1980) •Fl/Cl/BsCl/Ssx/Vln/Vcl •NMI

HOLMBERG, Peter - *Musica alta e bassa* (1979) (12') •Fl/Tpt/Bsx/Tuba/Vln/Vcl •STIM

HUMBERT-CLAUDE, Eric - *Eux* (1983) •Asx/Fl/Cl/Vln/Vcl/Pno

LANZA, Alcides - *Modulos III* (1983) •Guit/Tsx/Vln/Vcl/Perc/Pno/Tape •CMC

MAXFIELD, Richard - *Domenon* (1961) •Fl/Sx/Pno/Vibr/Vln/Bass/Tape

McPEEK, Ben - *Trillium* (1979) •Ssx/Fl/Cl/Vln/Vcl/Pno

MELLNÄS, Arne - *Per caso* (1963) (5'30) •Asx/Trb/Vln/Bass/2 Perc •SeMC

MICHAEL, Frank - *Kmk* •Fl/Ssx/Trb/Vln/Vla/Vcl •adr

NILSSON, Ivo - *Per-cept* (1989-91) •Fl/Ob+EH/1 Sx: S+A/Trb/Pno/Vln+Vla •SMIC

RAYNAL, Gilles - *Ombilic* (1983) •Fl/Cl/Asx/Vln/Vcl/Pno

ROLIN, Etienne - *Tressage-Concerto* (1983-84) (10') •Ssx/Fl/Cl/Pno/Vln/Vcl •Lem

SCHWEYER, Bruno - *Konzerstück* (1983) •Tsx/Fl/Cl/Vln/Vcl/Pno

SIMS, Ezra - *Sextet* (1981) (22') •Cl/Asx/Hn/Vln/Vla/Vcl •ACA

SURIANU, Horia - *Esquisse pour un clair obscur* (1986) (11') •Ssx/Fl/Cl/Vln/Vcl/Pno •Sal

TOSI, Daniel - *Multiphony III* (1986) (6'30) •Fl/Cl/Asx/Pno/Vln/Vcl

7 Musicians

ADDERLEY, Mark - *The Worm and the Toothache* (1986) •Asx/Tsx/Vln/Fl/Trb/Pno/Perc •NMI

ALLGEN, Claude - *Praeludium och Carmen Perlotense* •Vln/Vla/Vcl/Asx/Pno/Harps/Org •STIM

BJORKLUND, Terje - *Herbarium* (1982) •Fl/Ssx/Vln/Hn/Bass/Pno/Perc •NMI

BOSSEUR, Jean-Yves - *43 Miniatures* (1992) •Vln/Cl/2 Sx: AB/Harp/Pno/Perc

BROTT, Alexander - *7 for seven* (1954) (14'30) •Narr/Cl/Asx/Vln/Vla/Vcl/Pno •CMC

BROWN, Anthony - *Soundscape 1* •Asx/Bsn/Tpt/Vln/Voice/Pno/Perc/Tape •SeMC

CERHA, Friedrich - *Fantasies nach Cardw's Herbst 60* •Cl/BsCl/Tsx/Vln/Vla/Vcl/Pno •EMod

COWELL, Henry - *Chrysanthemus* (1937) •Soprano Voice/2 Sx/2 Vln/Vla/Vcl

ESCAICH, Thierry - *Antiennes oubliées* (1994) •Vln/Fl/Asx/Tpt/Trb/Vcl/Vibr •Bil

CRAS, Jean - *Demain* (1929) •Asx/Tpt/Trb/Perc/Vln/Vcl/Bass •Sen

GRÄSBECK, Mannfred - *Rapsodia...* •2 Vln/Vla/Vcl/Sx/Pno/Perc

MASON, Lucas - *A Quilt of Love* (1971) •Soprano Voice/Asx/Fl/Vln/Bsn/Trb/Vcl •adr

MIEREANU, Costin - *Polymorphies 5 X 7 B* (1969-70) (9-10') •Fl+Picc/Cl+Tsx/Pno/Vln/Vla/Vcl/Bass •Sal

Milhaud, Darius - *La Création du monde* (LONDEIX) •2 Vln/Asx/Vcl/Bass/Perc/Pno •ME

NORDENSTEN, Frank - *Sample and hold* (1978) (14') •Fl+Picc/Cl+BsCl/1 Sx: S+T/Vln+Vla/Vcl/Pno/Perc

SAGVIK, Stellan - *Pastoral*, op. 65 (1976) (4') •Asx/2 Vln/2 Vla/2 Vcl •STIM

SKOUEN, Synne - *Hva sa Schopenhauer...* (1978) (8') •Narr/Fl/Cl+BsCl/Sx/Vln/Vcl/Perc •NMI

SOTELO, Mauricio - *Quando il cielo...* (1989) (18') •Asx/Perc/Pno/Vln/Vla/Vcl/Bass •ECA

IX +... - de substantiis separatis (1990) •Cl/Sx/Tuba/Vln/Vcl/Bass/Pno/Schtagzeng with live electronics •adr

STEARNS, Peter - *Septet* (1959) •Cl/Tsx/Hn/Vln/Vla/Vcl/Bass •Pio/ACA

STOUT, Alan - *Four Antiphonies* •Fl/Trb/Asx/Org/Vln/Vla/Perc •CFE

VOUILLEMIN, Sylvain - *Divertimento...* (1983) (8'30) •Ssx/2 Vln/Vla/Vcl/Bass/Perc or Ssx/Pno •Led

WENTING, Victor - *Raderwek...* (1973) (30') •4 wind or string instruments/Sx/Vln/Pno/Radio electronic

8 Musicians

BARCE, Ramon - *Concierto de Lizara V* (1977) (10'45) •Cl/Tsx/Tpt/Trb/Harp/Pno/Vln/Vcl

BIRTWISTLE, Harrison - *Medusa* (1969/70/78) •Fl/Cl/Ssx/Pno/Perc/Vln/Vla/Vcl/Tape

BÖRJESSON, Lars - *Divertimento*, op. 38 (1983) •Asx/BsCl/Bsn/Guit/Harp/Marimba/Vln/Vcl •STIM

CHAGRIN, Francis - *Sarabande* (1951) (6') •Ob/Hn/Vln/Asx/Str Quartet •ALC

FRANCESCONI, Luca - *Piccola trama* (1989) (14') •1 Sx: S+A/Fl/Cl/Guit/Perc/Vln/Vla/Vcl •Ric

KETTING, Otto - *Musik zu einen Tonfilm* (1982) (15') •2 Sx/Tpt/Trb/Perc/Pno/2 Vln •Don

MANDANICI, Marcella - *Extraits I* (1989) •Tsx/Fl/Cl/Pno/Perc/Vln/Vla/Vcl •adr

MAYUZUMI, Toshiro - *Sphenogramme* (1951) •Contralto Voice/Fl/Asx/Marimba/Vln/Vcl/Pno 4 hands [à 4 mains]

MICHEL, Paul - *Ultramorphoses* (1965) (12-15') •Fl/Cl/Asx/Perc/Pno/Vln/Vla/Vcl •CBDM

MONNET, Marc - *L'exercice de la bataille* (1991) (45') •2 Vln/2 Bsn/2 MIDI Sx/MIDI Guit/MIDI Pno

NICKLAUS, Wolfgang - *Die Antwort* (1986) (7'30) •Cl/Asx/2 Perc/Pno/Vln/Vcl/Bass •adr

NILSSON, Ivo - *Agnosi* (1988) (9') •Ob/Asx/Tpt/Harp/2 Vln/Vla/Vcl •STIM

PINOS-SIMANDL, Aloïs - *Geneze* (1970) (8') •Vln/Asx/Vcl/Trb/Perc/Harp/Harps/Ionika •CHF

SOTELO, Mauricio - *IX +...* (1990) •Cl/Sx/Tuba/Vln/Vcl/Bass/Pno/ Schtagzeng with live electronics •adr

VILLA-LOBOS, Heitor - *Chôros n° 7* (1924) (10') •Fl/Ob/Cl/Asx/ Bsn/Vln/Vcl/Tam-tam •ME

WOOLLETT, Henri - *Octuor n° 1* (1911) •Ob/Cl/Asx/2 Vln/Vla/Vcl/ Bass •South

9 Musicians

CAPLET, André - *Légende* (1903) (13') •Asx/Ob/Cl/Bsn/2 Vln/Vla/ Vcl/Bass •Fuz

CUSTER, Arthur - *Cycle for Nine Instruments* •Asx/BsCl/Tpt/Hn/ Vln/Vla/Vcl/Bass/Perc •JM

DANKWORTH, John - *Fairoak Fusion* (1979) (45') •4 Sx: SATB/ Vln/Jazz Quartet

DIEMENTE, Edward - *For Lady Day* •Fl/Ob/Cl/Tpt/Trb/Vln/Vla/Sx/ Bsn/Tape •SeMC

GUALDA JIMENEZ, Antonio - *Noneto Zarco* (1988) (16') •Vln/Vcl/ Cl/2 Sx: SA/Vibr/Marimba/Guit/Pno

HAHN, Reynaldo - *Divertissement...* (1933) (25') •2 Vln/Vla/Vcl/ Bass/Asx/Bsn/Timp/Perc •Sal

MANOURY, Philippe - *Etude automatique* 1 •Fl/Tpt/Sx/Tuba/Harp/ Vln/Vla/Vcl/Bass

MULDOWNEY, Dominic - *An Heavyweight Dirge* (1971) (25') •Voice/Fl/Asx/Perc/Pno/2 Vln/Vla/Vcl •Nov

RYTTERKVIST, Hans - *Lied ohne Worte* (1968) •3 Vln/Vla/2 Vcl/ Harps/Pno/Bsx •SMIC

SAGVIK, Stellan - *Det Förlorade steget*, op. 64 (1976) (20') •Fl/ Cl+BsCl/Asx/Cnt/Trb/Vln/Vla/Vcl/Perc •SMIC

SCHULLER, Gunther - *Abstraction* (1959) (5') •Asx/Guit/Perc/2 Vln/Vla/Vcl/2 Bass •MJQ

SCHWANTNER, Joseph - *Diaphona intervallum* (1966) (12') •Asx/ Pno/Fl/2 Vln/Vla/2 Vcl/Bass •ACA

SILVERMAN, Faye - *Shadings* (1978) •Vln/Vla/Bass/Fl/Ob/Asx/ Bsn/Hn/Tuba

SÖDERLIND, Ragnar - *Eg hev funne...* (1982) (9'); *Legg ikkje ditt...* (1983) •Soprano Voice/Fl+Picc/Ssx/Hn/Vln/ Vla/Bass/Pno/Perc •NMI

SVOBODA, Tomàs - *Seven Short Dances* •Fl/2 Cl/Asx/Trb/Vln/Bass/ Pno/Perc

TANENBAUM, Elias - *Trios I, II, III* •Fl/Ob/Cl/Vln/Vla/Vcl/Bass/ Asx/Perc •ACA

10 Musicians

BANKS, Donald - *Equation 1* (1964) (7') •Tpt/Asx/Pno/Harp/Guit/ Perc/2 Vln/Vla/Vcl •BMIC

COE, Tony - *The Buds of Time* (1979) (20') •Cl+Sx/Cl+BsCl/2 Vln/ Vla/Vcl/BsTrb/Pno/Bass/Perc •adr

COPPOOLSE, David - *Canto XVII* (1984) (12') •Asx/2 Hn/2 Trb/Vln/ Vla/Vcl/Bass/Pno •Don

GOTTSCHALK, Arthur - *Cycloid* •Cl/Asx/Hn/Tpt/Harp/Vibr/2 Vln/ Vla/Vcl •SeMC

GOUGEON, Denis - *Heureux qui comme...* (1987) •Soprano Voice/ Picc/EH/Bsx/2 Vln/Vla/Vcl/Bass/Perc •CMC

GRAHN, Ulf - *Soundscape II* (1974) (7') •Fl/Cl/EH/Asx/2 Trb/2 Vln/ Vcl/Bass •SMIC

GRANDIS, Renato de - *Scotter Sud-est* •Vln/Vla/Vcl/Bass/Sx/Hn/ Tpt/Trb/Pno/Perc •SeMC

LACHARTE, Nicole - *La Geste inachevée* (1980) •Fl/Cl/Sx/Tpt/Trb/ Pno/Perc/Vln/Vla/Vcl

LAZARUS, Daniel - *4 Mélodies* •Contralto Voice/Fl/Cl/Asx/Bsn/2 Vln/Vla/Vcl/Bass

Lecuona, Ernesto - *Andalucia* •2 Tpt/Trb/3Sx: AAT/2 Vln/Vcl/Bass

LEWIS, John Aaron - *The Milanese Story* •Fl/Tsx/Guit/Pno/Bass/2 Vln/Vla/Vcl/Perc •MJQ

LUTYENS, Elisabeth - *Akapotik Rose*, op. 64 (1966) (18') •Soprano Voice/Picc/Fl/Cl/Bsn/Cl+Tsx/Vln/Vla/Vcl/ Pno

MAROS, Miklos - *Coalottino* (1969) (5') •Bsx/Electr. instrum./2 Pno/ Harps/2 Vln/Vla/2 Vcl •STIM

POOLE, Geoffrey - *Son of Paolo* (1971) •Fl/Picc/Cl/BsCl/Tsx/2 Vln/ 2 Vcl/Prepared Pno •BMIC

SMITH, Linda - *Periphery* (1979) •Fl/Sx/Tpt/Marimba/Vibr/Chimes/ Pno/Vln/Vcl/Bass •CMC

SMITH, William - *Elegy for Eric* •Fl/2 Sx: AB/Cl/Tpt/Trb/Vibr/Vln/ Bass/Perc •MJQ

WROCHEM, Klaus - *Oratorium meum plus praeperturi* •3 Voices/2 Vln/Vla/Vcl/Asx/Tpt/Perc •CAP

11 Musicians

ANDRIESSEN, Jurriaan - *Hommage à Milhaud* (1945) (8') •Fl/Ob/ Cl/Bsn/Hn/Tpt/Trb/Asx/Vln/Vla/Vcl •Don

COLE, Bruce - *Pantomimes* (25') •Soprano Voice/Fl/Cl/BsCl/Ssx/ Perc/Pno/Guit/Vln/Vla/Vcl •B&H

KEULEN, Geert van - *Onkruid* (1981) (5') •Ob/Cl/2 Sx: AT/Bsn/Hn/ Tpt/Trb/Vln/Vla/Pno •Don

PABLO, Luis de - *Polar*, op. 12 (1963) •Vln/Ssx/BsCl/Xylophone/ Trb/6 Perc •Tono/SeMC

SCHILLING, Otto-Erich - *Überall ist Wunderland* •Voice/Fl/Cl/Sx/ Tpt/2 Vln/Bass/Perc/Accordion/Pno •SeMC

TRIMBLE, Lester - *Panels I* (1973) (6') •Picc/Bsx/Vln/Vla/Vcl/Bass/ 2 Perc/Electr. Guit/Electr. Org/Electr. Harp •Pet

ZONN, Paul Martin - *Voyage of Columbus* (1974) (13') •Tpt Solo/Fl/ Ob/Ssx/Hrn/Trb/2 Perc/Pno/Vln/Bass •ACA

12 Musicians

CECCONI, Monique - *Hommage à...* •Ob/Cl/Asx/Bsn/4 Vln/2 Vla/2 Vcl •Phi

DUREY, Louis - *Feu la mère de Madame*, op. 49 (1945) (5') •Fl/Ob/ Asx/Bsn/Tpt/Tuba/Perc/2 Vln/Vla/Vcl/Bass •BRF

HASQUENOPH, Pierre - *Inventions* •2 Vln/Vla/Vcl/Bass/Fl/Ob/Cl/ Asx/Bsn/Hn/Tpt •Heu

MASINI, Fabio - *"Nuvole e colori forti"* (1992) (18') •Fl/1 Sx: S+A/ BsCl/Fl/Ob/Cl/Bsn/2 Vln/Vla/Vcl/Harp

REA, John - *Treppenmusik* (1982) •4 Sx: SATB/4 Cl/Vln/Vla/Vcl/ Bass •CMC

ROBBINS, David - *Improvisation* •Fl/2 Cl/Tsx/Bsn/Tpt/Trb/Vln/Vla/ Vcl/Bass/Perc

TOEPLITZ, Kasper - *Johnny Panic...* (25') •1 Sx: T+CBs/Mezzo Soprano Voice/2 Fl/2 Cl/Hn/2 Vln/2 Vla/ Perc/Tape

13 Musicians

BENHAMOU, Maurice - *Musique pour 13 instruments* •Fl/2 Cl/ Harmonica/Sx/2 Vln/3 Guit/Pno 6 hands (à 6 mains)

DELANNOY, Marcel - *Le Marchand de notes* •3 Vln/Bass/4 Sx/2 Tpt/ Trb/Perc/Pno

FINNISSY, Michael - *First sign a sharp white mons* (1974-67) (45') •2 Fl/2 Cl/Asx/CBsn/Hn/Accordion/Guit/ Vln/2 Vcl/Pno •BMIC

HESPOS, Hans - *Conga* (1979) (15'30) •Tsx/5 Congas/2 Vln/2 Vla/ 2 Vcl/Bass •Hes

Keime und male (9') •Picc/Fl/2 Cl/Asx/Hn/Guit/Vln/Vla/Bass/3 Perc •JJ

HUREL, Philippe - *"Pour l'image"* •Fl/Ob/Cl/Asx/Hn/Tpt/Trb/Perc/
2 Vln/Vla/Vcl/Bass
SEKON, Joseph - *Lemon Ice* (1972) •Fl/Ob/Cl/2 Sx: ST/Bsn/Tpt/Trb/
2 Perc/Vln/Vcl/Pno •adr
WENDEL, Eugen - *Saphonospir* (15') •Asx/Fl/Cl/Ob/Tpt/Trb/2 Vln/
Vla/Vcl/Bass/2 Perc •adr

14 Musicians

HARBISON, John - *Confinement* (1965) (15'15) •Fl/Ob/EH/Cl/BsCl/
Asx/Tpt/Trb/Vln/Vla/Vcl/Bass/Pno/Perc
HARVEY, Jonathan - *The Valley of Aosta* (1985) (13'30) •Fl/Ob/Ssx/
Tpt/2 Yamaha DX7 Synth/2 Harp/Pno/2 Vln/
Vla/Vcl/Perc •FM
RUBBERT, Rainer - *Kammerkonzert* (1990) •4 Sx: SATB/4 Vln/2
Vla/2 Vcl/Bass/Pno •adr

15 Musicians

LUTYENS, Elisabeth - *Islands*, op. 80 (1971) •2 Narr: ST/Picc/Fl/Cl/
BsCl/Tsx/Hn/Pno/Celesta/Vln/Vla/Vcl/2
Perc
TEMPLE & SHAW - *Vanity Fair Suite* •Fl/Ob/4 Cl/BsCl/Asx/2 Vln/
Vla/Vcl/Bass/Perc/Pno •Mills

Saxophone and Viola

2 Musicians

DADELSEN, Hans von - *Kra / Dark* (1993) •Asx/Vla •INM
FREUDENTHAL, Otto - *Duo* (1978) •Ssx/Vla •SMIC
FRIEDRICH, Burkhard - *Liezwicht* (1993) •Tsx/Vla •B&N
FRISK, Henrik - *Variations in three parts* (1993) •Ssx/Vla •INM
LIEBMAN, David - *Untitled Duet* (1993) •Ssx/Vla •INM
SHIGERU, Kan-no - *Keycoy* (1993) •Tsx/Vla •INM
SMITH, Howie - *Life on Earth...* •Sx/Amplified Vla/Electronics •Oa

3 Musicians

AGNESENS, Udo - *Suite populaire* (1986) •Asx/Vla/Vcl •adr
BANASIK, Christian - *Begegbubg* •Asx/Vla/Perc
BOURLAND, Roger - *Three Dark Paintings* •Ssx/Vla/Vcl •ECS
BURGERS, Simon - *Trio* (1983) (10') •Asx/Vla/Pno •Don
DUPIN, Paul - *Chant* (1910) •Asx/Harps/Vla/Chorus
HARTLEY, Walter - *Lyric Suite* (1993) (8'15) •Tsx/Vla/Pno •adr
HINDEMITH, Paul - *Trio*, op. 47 (1928) •Tsx (or Heckelphone)/Vla/
Pno •ME/Sch
HOWARD, Robert - *Trilogue* •Asx/Vla/Harp •Art
JUGUET, Henri-Pierre - *Trio suite* (1986) •Ssx/Vla/Pno
LEMELAND, Aubert - *Mouvement concertant n° 3* (7'30) •Asx/Vla/
Vcl •Bil
LOEFFLER, Charles Martin - *The Lone Prairée* (c. 1930) (4') •Vla
d'amore (or Vla)/Tsx/Pno •TTF
RÜDINGER, Gottfried - *Divertimento*, op. 75 •Vla (or Cl)/Tsx/Pno
•BAUS
SAMAMA, Leo - *Trio marchese*, op. 24 (1984) (15') •Asx/Vla/Pno
•Don
VISSER, Peter - *Orient express* (1982) (12') •Sx+Cl/Vla/Pno •Don
YATES, Ronald - *Triune* (1971) •Asx/Vla/BsTrb •adr

4 Musicians

ALBERTH, Rudolf - *Divertimento* (1941) •Asx/Str Trio •adr
BARRIERE, Françoise - *A propos...* (1979) •Asx/Perc/Vla/Vcl/Tape
BOIS, Rob du - *Stuleken* (1960) •Fl/Tsx/Vla/Perc •Don
BOURLAND, Roger - *Stone Quartet* •Ssx/Vla/Vcl/Pno •ECS
BRNCIC, Isaza - *Quodlibet I* (1966) •Sx/Vla/Tpt/Electr. Guit/Electr.
Org or 2 Asx/Vla/Vibr

CASKEN, John - *Music for a Tawny-Gold Day* (1975-76) (10') •Asx/
BsCl/Vla/Pno •Sch
DADELSEN, Hans-Christian von - *Cries of Butterflies* (1979) (16')
•Asx/Hn/Vla/Synth •Kodasi
DI PASQUALE, James - *Quartet* (1964) (10') •Tsx/Tpt/Vla/Vcl •adr
FUSTÉ-LAMBEZAT, Michel - *Polyphonies* (1975) (15') •Cl/Asx/
Vla/Vcl •SeMC
GERBER, René - *Concertino* (1944) •Sx/Vla/Vcl/Pno
GLASER, Werner Wolf - *Kvartett* (1950) •Asx/Vln/Vla/Vcl •STIM
Linda - *Quartett* (1970-85) (17') •Bsx/Vln/Vla/Vcl •STIM
KARKOFF, Maurice - *Drömmeri/Poem*, op. 165 (1988) (17') •Cl/Vla/
Asx/Pno •STIM
KARLINS, M. William - *Variations* (1962-63) Ssx/Vln/Vla/Vcl
•SeMC
LEMELAND, Aubert - *Figures...*, op. 79 (10') •Asx/Vla/Vibr/Guit
•adr
LOCKWOOD, Harry - *Lyric Piece* •Asx/Tpt/Vla/Tuba
PAYNE, Frank - *Quartet* •Asx/Tpt/Vla/Trb •SeMC
PRICE, Deon - *Allegro barbaro* (1980) •Vln/Ssx/Vla/Vcl
RICHMOND, Thomas - *Two Movements* (1964) •Vln/Vla/Asx/Vcl
ROSENBLOOM, David - *Pocket Pieces* (1977) •Fl/Asx/Vla/Perc
•SeMC
SCIORTINO, Patrice - *Moulin du temps* •Vibr/Guit/Vla/Asx •adr
STEINBERG, Ben - *Suite Sephardi* (1979) •Ssx/Vln/Vla/Vcl •CMC
SUTHERLAND, Margaret - *Quartet* (1965) •Asx/Vln/Vla/Vcl
THEOBALD, James - *Plane 5* •Asx/Vla/Pno/Perc •SeMC
THILMAN, J. - *Das kleine Requiem*, op. 27 (1969) •EH/Asx/Vla/Pno
•Bar
ZONN, Paul Martin - *Midnight Secrets* (1992) (20') •Ssx/Vln/Vla/Vcl
•ACA

5 Musicians

Also see Saxophone and String Quartet (Voir aussi
quatuor à cordes), page 394.

ANDERSON, Thomas - *Re-creation* (1978) •Asx/Vla/Vcl/Pno/Tamtam
BENHAMOU, Maurice - *Mouvement* (1979) •Fl/Sx/Vla/Vcl/Perc/
Tape
BRNCIC, Isaza - *Quodlibet I* (1966) •Sx/Vla/Tpt/Electr. Guit/Electr.
Org or 2 Asx/Vla/Vibr
DURBIN, Jean - *1ère suite de Alain Fournier* •Pno/Org/Vln/Vla/Sx
HALL, Neville - *For a Single Point* (1990) (11') •Cl/Tsx/Pno/Vla/Vcl
•adr
HESPOS, Hans - *Einander* (1966) (12-13') •Fl/Cl/Guit/Tsx/Vla
•EMod
HOPKINS, Bill - *Sensation* (1965) •Voice/Tsx/Tpt/Harp/Vla
HRISANIDE, Alexandru - *M. P. 5* (1967) •Tsx+Cl/Vln/Vla/Vcl/Pno
•IMD
JAEGER, Robert - *Quintet* (1969) •Asx/Vln/Vla/Vcl/Harp •adr
Three Pieces (1967) (6'30) •Asx/Vln/Vla/Vcl/Harp (or Pno) •adr
KONOE, Hidétaké - *Quintet* (1968) •Sx/Vln/Vla/Vcl/Bass
Sonata caprice (1970) •Asx/Vln/Vla/Vcl/Bass
KRIEGER, Edino - *Melopéia* (1949) •Soprano Voice/Ob/Tsx/Trb/
Vla
KUNZ, Ernst - *Nachtkonzert* •3 Sx/Vla/Guit
LINDROTH, Scott - *Two Pieces* •Asx/Vln/Vla/Vcl/Pno •DP
MATSUDAIRA, Roh - *Quintette* (1968) •Asx/Vln/Vla/Vcl/Bass
MOORTEL, Arie van de - *Nocturne*, op. 18 (1956) •Cl/Asx/Vla/Vcl/
Pno •Mau
OSTERC, Slavko - *Ave Maria* (1930) •Soprano Voice/Vla/Ob/Cl/Sx
TALLET, Marc - *Estagari* (12') •Fl/Asx/Trb/Vla/Guit

6 Musicians

ASHEIM, Nils Henrik - *Midt iblant os...* (1978) •Fl/Asx/Vla/Vcl/
Bass/Perc •NMI

BOSSE, Denis - *...d'un léger souffle cosmique* (1987) (10') •1 Sx
Solo: B+A+S/2 Vln/Vla/Vcl/Bass
DAMICO, John - *Avilion* •Asx/2 Vln/Vla/Vcl/Bass •DP
DeBLASIO, Chris - *Prelude and Fugue* (1991) (9') •Ssx/Str Quintet
•TTF
DESPORTES, Yvonne - *La maison abandonnée* (1961) (20') •Vln/
Vla/Vcl/Asx/Perc/Pno •adr
GULLIN, Peter - *Tre suma julsagor* (1988) •Bsx/2 Vln/Vla/Vcl/Bass
HAMBRAEUS, Bengt - *Kammarmusik for 6*, op. 28 (1950) (8') •Fl/
Ob/Cl/Asx/Vla/Harp •STIM/Ehr
MICHAEL, Frank - *Kmk* •Fl/Ssx/Trb/Vln/Vla/Vcl •adr
NILSSON, Ivo - *Per-cept* (1989-91) •Fl/Ob+EH/1 Sx: S+A/Trb/Pno/
Vln+Vla •SMIC
SIMS, Ezra - *Sextet* (1981) (22') •Cl/Asx/Hn/Vln/Vla/Vcl •ACA

7 Musicians

ALLGEN, Claude - *Praeludium och Carmen Perlotense* •Vln/Vla/
Vcl/Asx/Pno/Harps/Org •STIM
BROTT, Alexander - *7 for seven* (1954) (14'30) •Narr/Cl/Asx/Vln/
Vla/Vcl/Pno •CMC
CERHA, Friedrich - *Fantasies nach Cardw's Herbst 60* •Cl/BsCl/Tsx/
Vln/Vla/Vcl/Pno •EMod
COWELL, Henry - *Chrysanthemus* (1937) •Soprano Voice/2 Sx/2
Vln/Vla/Vcl
GRÄSBECK, Mannfred - *Rapsodia...* •2 Vln/Vla/Vcl/Sx/Pno/Perc
HESPOS, Hans - *Passagen* (1969) (9') •Cl/Asx/Tpt/Trb/Vla/Bass/
Perc •EMod
HILLBORG, Anders - *Variations* (1991) •Soprano Voice/Mezzo
Soprano Voice/Fl/Sx/Perc/Vla/Bass •SMIC
MIEREANU, Costin - *Polymorphies 5 X 7 B* (1969-70) (9-10')
•Fl+Picc/Cl+Tsx/Pno/Vln/Vla/Vcl/Bass •Sal
NORDENSTEN, Frank - *Sample and hold* (1978) (14') •Fl+Picc/
Cl+BsCl/1 Sx: S+T/Vln+Vla/Vcl/Pno/Perc
POOLE, Geoffrey - *Polter zeits* (1975) •Vla/2 Cl/BsCl/2 Sx: AB/
Prepared Pno •BMIC
ROLIN, Etienne - *Quètes ancestrales* (1989) (14') •Tsx/Vla/2 Vcl/
Bass/Harp/Marimba •Fuz
SAGVIK, Stellan - *Pastoral*, op. 65 (1976) (4') •Asx/2 Vln/2 Vla/2
Vcl •STIM
SOTELO, Mauricio - *Quando il cielo...* (1989) (18') •Asx/Perc/Pno/
Vln/Vla/Vcl/Bass •ECA
STEARNS, Peter - *Septet* (1959) •Cl/Tsx/Hn/Vln/Vla/Vcl/Bass •Pio/
ACA
STOUT, Alan - *Four Antiphonies* •Fl/Trb/Asx/Org/Vln/Vla/Perc
•CFE
VOUILLEMIN, Sylvain - *Divertimento...* (1983) (8'30) •Ssx/2 Vln/
Vla/Vcl/Bass/Perc or Ssx/Pno •Led

8 Musicians

BERG, Olav - *Fragments* (1977) (8') •Fl/Cl/Asx/Vla/Vcl/Pno/2 Perc
•NMJ
BIRTWISTLE, Harrison - *Medusa* (1969/70/78) •Fl/Cl/Ssx/Pno/
Perc/Vln/Vla/Vcl/Tape
CHAGRIN, Francis - *Sarabande* (1951) (6') •Ob/Hn/Vln/Asx/Str
Quartet •ALC
FRANCESCONI, Luca - *Piccola trama* (1989) (14') •1 Sx: S+A/Fl/
Cl/Guit/Perc/Vln/Vla/Vcl •Ric
GARCIN, Gérard - *Encore plus tard* (1984) (12') •1 Sx: Sno+A+Bs/
Fl/Cl/Bsn/Vla/Vcl/Bass/Perc/Tape •Sal
HACHIMURA, Yoshiro - *Concerto per 8 soli* •Fl/Cl/Sx/Vibr/Vcl/
Vla/2 Perc •OE
LAURETTE, Marc - *Kaleïdoscope* •Cl/Bsn/2 Sx: SB/Hn/Vla/Bass/
Vibr
MANDANICI, Marcella - *Extraits I* (1989) •Tsx/Fl/Cl/Pno/Perc/Vln/
Vla/Vcl •adr

MICHEL, Paul - *Ultramorphoses* (1965) (12-15') •Fl/Cl/Asx/Perc/
Pno/Vln/Vla/Vcl •CBDM
NILSSON, Ivo - *Agnosi* (1988) (9') •Ob/Asx/Tpt/Harp/2 Vln/Vla/Vcl
•STIM
TOMASSON, Haukur - *Octette* (1987) •Fl/Cl/Asx/Hn/Vla/Vcl/Pno/
Perc (Vibr+Gong) •IMIC
WOOLLETT, Henri - *Octuor n° 1* (1911) •Ob/Cl/Asx/2 Vln/Vla/Vcl/
Bass •South

9 Musicians

BORTOLOTTI, Mauro - *Studio per E.E. Cummings n° 2* (1964) •Vla/
Vcl/Bass/Ob/Cl/BsCl/Sx/Hn/Perc •adr
CAPLET, André - *Légende* (1903) (13') •Asx/Ob/Cl/Bsn/2 Vln/Vla/
Vcl/Bass •Fuz
CUSTER, Arthur - *Cycle for Nine Instruments* •Asx/BsCl/Tpt/Hn/
Vln/Vla/Vcl/Bass/Perc •JM
DIEMENTE, Edward - *For Lady Day* •Fl/Ob/Cl/Tpt/Trb/Vln/Vla/Sx/
Bsn/Tape •SeMC
GRAINGER, Ella - *To Echo* (1945) •Soprano Voice/Picc/Fl/Cl+Asx/
Tsx/Vla/BsCl/Bass/Marimba •GS
HAHN, Reynaldo - *Divertissement...* (1933) (25') •2 Vln/Vla/Vcl/
Bass/Asx/Bsn/Timp/Perc •Sal
MANOURY, Philippe - *Etude automatique* 1 •Fl/Tpt/Sx/Tuba/Harp/
Vln/Vla/Vcl/Bass
MULDOWNEY, Dominic - *An Heavyweight Dirge* (1971) (25')
•Voice/Fl/Asx/Perc/Pno/2 Vln/Vla/Vcl •Nov
RENOSTO, Paolo - *Dissolution* •Vla/Vcl/Bass/Ob/Cl/BsCl/Sx/Hn/
Perc
RYTTERKVIST, Hans - *Lied ohne Worte* (1968) •3 Vln/Vla/2 Vcl/
Harps/Pno/Bsx •SMIC
SAGVIK, Stellan - *Det Förlorade steget*, op. 64 (1976) (20') •Fl/
Cl+BsCl/Asx/Cnt/Trb/Vln/Vla/Vcl/Perc
•SMIC
SCELSI, Jacinto - *Kya* (1959) (11') •Cl (or Ssx)/EH/Hn/BsCl/Tpt/
Trb/Vla/Vcl/Bass •Sal
SCHULLER, Gunther - *Abstraction* (1959) (5') •Asx/Guit/Perc/2
Vln/Vla/Vcl/2 Bass •MJQ
SCHWANTNER, Joseph - *Diaphona intervallum* (1966) (12') •Asx/
Pno/Fl/2 Vln/Vla/2 Vcl/Bass •ACA
SILVERMAN, Faye - *Shadings* (1978) •Vln/Vla/Bass/Fl/Ob/Asx/
Bsn/Hn/Tuba
SÖDERLIND, Ragnar - *Eg hev funne...* (1982) (9'); *Legg ikkje ditt...*
(1983) •Soprano Voice/Fl+Picc/Ssx/Hn/Vln/
Vla/Bass/Pno/Perc •NMI
TANENBAUM, Elias - *Trios I, II, III* •Fl/Ob/Cl/Vln/Vla/Vcl/Bass/
Asx/Perc •ACA
TARENSKEEN, Boudewijn - *Nonet* (1982) (13') •Asx/Hn/BsCl/
Accordion/Banjo/Harp/Vla/Vcl/Bass •Don

10 Musicians

BANKS, Donald - *Equation 1* (1964) (7') •Tpt/Asx/Pno/Harp/Guit/
Perc/2 Vln/Vla/Vcl •BMIC
COE, Tony - *The Buds of Time* (1979) (20') •Cl+Sx/Cl+BsCl/2 Vln/
Vla/Vcl/BsTrb/Pno/Bass/Perc •adr
COPPOOLSE, David - *Canto XVII* (1984) (12') •Asx/2 Hn/2 Trb/Vln/
Vla/Vcl/Bass/Pno •Don
COSTEN, Roel van - *Prisma* (1984) (8') •Vla/Fl/Cl/Asx/BsCl/Trb/
Vcl/Bass/Perc/Pno •Don
FORTNER, Jack - *S pr ING sur des poèmes de E. E. Cummings* (1966)
(11') •Mezzo Soprano Voice/Fl/Asx/Bsn/
Vla/Vcl/Bass/Vibr/Harp/Pno •JJ
GOODMAN, Alfred - *3 Gesänge für Gresang* •Soprano Voice/Fl/Ob/
Asx/Cl/Vla/Vcl/Prepared Pno/Guit/Perc •adr
GOTTSCHALK, Arthur - *Cycloid* •Cl/Asx/Hn/Tpt/Harp/Vibr/2 Vln/
Vla/Vcl •SeMC

GOUGEON, Denis - *Heureux qui comme...* (1987) •Soprano Voice/
    Picc/EH/Bsx/2 Vln/Vla/Vcl/Bass/Perc
    •CMC

GRANDIS, Renato de - *Scotter Sud-est* •Vln/Vla/Vcl/Bass/Sx/Hn/
    Tpt/Trb/Pno/Perc •SeMC

LACHARTE, Nicole - *La Geste inachevée* (1980) •Fl/Cl/Sx/Tpt/Trb/
    Pno/Perc/Vln/Vla/Vcl

LAZARUS, Daniel - *4 Mélodies* •Contralto Voice/Fl/Cl/Asx/Bsn/2
    Vln/Vla/Vcl/Bass

LEWIS, John Aaron - *The Milanese Story* •Fl/Tsx/Guit/Pno/Bass/2
    Vln/Vla/Vcl/Perc •MJQ

LUTYENS, Elisabeth - *Akapotik Rose*, op. 64 (1966) (18') •Soprano
    Voice/Picc/Fl/Cl/Bsn/Cl+Tsx/Vln/Vla/Vcl/
    Pno

MAROS, Miklos - *Coalottino* (1969) (5') •Bsx/Electr. instrum./2 Pno/
    Harps/2 Vln/Vla/2 Vcl •STIM

PAUMGARTNER, Bernhard - *Divertimento* •Picc/EH/Asx/Bsn/Hn/
    Tpt/Pno/Vla/Vcl/Perc •Uni

SCHAFFER, Boguslaw - *Permutations n° 27* (1956) •Fl/Ob/Cl/Sx/
    Tpt/Trb/Vla/Perc/Harp/Pno •A&S

WROCHEM, Klaus - *Oratorium meum plus praeperturi* •3 Voices/2
    Vln/Vla/Vcl/Asx/Tpt/Perc •CAP

11 Musicians

ANDRIESSEN, Jurriaan - *Hommage à Milhaud* (1945) (8') •Fl/Ob/
    Cl/Bsn/Hn/Tpt/Trb/Asx/Vln/Vla/Vcl •Don

COLE, Bruce - *Pantomimes* (25') •Soprano Voice/Fl/Cl/BsCl/Ssx/
    Perc/Pno/Guit/Vln/Vla/Vcl •B&H

KEULEN, Geert van - *Onkruid* (1981) (5') •Ob/Cl/2 Sx: AT/Bsn/Hn/
    Tpt/Trb/Vln/Vla/Pno •Don

TRIMBLE, Lester - *Panels I* (1973) (6') •Picc/Bsx/Vln/Vla/Vcl/Bass/
    2 Perc/Electr. Guit/Electr. Org/Electr. Harp
    •Pet

12 Musicians

CECCONI, Monique - *Hommage à...* •Ob/Cl/Asx/Bsn/4 Vln/2 Vla/2
    Vcl •Phi

DUREY, Louis - *Feu la mère de Madame*, op. 49 (1945) (5') •Fl/Ob/
    Asx/Bsn/Tpt/Tuba/Perc/2 Vln/Vla/Vcl/Bass
    •BRF

HASQUENOPH, Pierre - *Inventions* •2 Vln/Vla/Vcl/Bass/Fl/Ob/Cl/
    Asx/Bsn/Hn/Tpt •Heu

MASINI, Fabio - *"Nuvole e colori forti"* (1992) (18') •Fl/1 Sx: S+A/
    BsCl/Fl/Ob/Cl/Bsn/2 Vln/Vla/Vcl/Harp

REA, John - *Treppenmusik* (1982) •4 Sx: SATB/4 Cl/Vln/Vla/Vcl/
    Bass •CMC

ROBBINS, David - *Improvisation* •Fl/2 Cl/Tsx/Bsn/Tpt/Trb/Vln/Vla/
    Vcl/Bass/Perc

TOEPLITZ, Kasper - *Johnny Panic...* (25') •1 Sx: T+CBs/Mezzo
    Soprano Voice/2 Fl/2 Cl/Hn/2 Vln/2 Vla/
    Perc/Tape

13 Musicians

HESPOS, Hans - *Conga* (1979) (15'30) •Tsx/5 Congas/2 Vln/2 Vla/
    2 Vcl/Bass •Hes

   Keime und male (9') •Picc/Fl/2 Cl/Asx/Hn/Guit/Vln/Vla/Bass/3
    Perc •JJ

HUREL, Philippe - *"Pour l'image"* •Fl/Ob/Cl/Asx/Hn/Tpt/Trb/Perc/
    2 Vln/Vla/Vcl/Bass

WENDEL, Eugen - *Saphonospir* (15') •Asx/Fl/Cl/Ob/Tpt/Trb/2 Vln/
    Vla/Vcl/Bass/2 Perc •adr

14 Musicians

HARBISON, John - *Confinement* (1965) (15'15) •Fl/Ob/EH/Cl/BsCl/
    Asx/Tpt/Trb/Vln/Vla/Vcl/Bass/Pno/Perc

HARVEY, Jonathan - *The Valley of Aosta* (1985) (13'30) •Fl/Ob/Ssx/
    Tpt/2 Yamaha DX7 Synth/2 Harp/Pno/2 Vln/
    Vla/Vcl/Perc •FM

ROSSÉ, François - *Paléochrome* (1988) (22') •Vla principal/2 Fl/Cl/
    BsCl/1 Sx: S+T/EH/Bsn/Hn/4 Perc/Bass •adr

RUBBERT, Rainer - *Kammerkonzert* (1990) •4 Sx: SATB/4 Vln/2
    Vla/2 Vcl/Bass/Pno •adr

15 Musicians

LUTYENS, Elisabeth - *Islands*, op. 80 (1971) •2 Narr: ST/Picc/Fl/Cl/
    BsCl/Tsx/Hn/Pno/Celesta/Vln/Vla/Vcl/2
    Perc

TEMPLE & SHAW - *Vanity Fair Suite* •Fl/Ob/4 Cl/BsCl/Asx/2 Vln/
    Vla/Vcl/Bass/Perc/Pno •Mills

oOo

DAKIN, Charles - *Syra* (1979) (8'30) •2 Cl/2 Tsx/2 Tpt/2 Trb/4 Vla/
    4 Vcl/2 Bass

DUPIN, Paul - *Chant* (1910) •Asx/Harps/Vla/Chorus

Saxophone and Cello

2 Musicians

AGNESENS, Udo - *Petite sonate* (1986) •Asx/Vcl •adr
BERNAUD, Alain - *Sonate en Duo* •Ssx/Vcl •adr
BRAXTON, Anthony - *RKM* •Ssx/Vcl
CHATILLON, Jean - *Suite renaissance* (1966) •Asx/Vcl •Reb
DAKIN, Charles - *Ragamala* (1980) (2'30) •Ssx/Vcl
GLASER, Werner Wolf - *Duo* (1981) (9') •Asx/Vcl •STIM
GOODMAN, Alfred - *We Two* •1 Sx: S+T/Vcl
HEKSTER, Walter - Monologues et conversation (1970-78) (4')
    •Asx/Vcl •Don
KANZLEITER, Dieter - *Les mouvements...* (1993) •Asx/Vcl •INM
KASEMETS, Udo - *Cascando-Poem* (1965) •Asx/Vcl
KOPROWSKI, Peter - *Vigoresque* (1967) (8') •Asx/Vcl •MPC/CMC
LERSY, Roger - *3 Esquisses en deux...* (1971) (7'30) •Asx/Vcl •adr
LUNDE, Lawson - *Pieces* •adr
MacLEAN, John T. - *Duo* (1982/92) •Tsx/Vcl
MOODY, Ivan - *Evocaczon de Silves* (1993) •Asx/Vcl •INM
RAPHAEL, Günter - *Divertimento*, op. 74 (1952) (13'30) •Asx/Vcl
    •Br&Ha
ROGER, Denise - *Duo* •Asx/Vcl •adr
ROLIN, Etienne - *Dialogue* (1985-86) •Asx/Vcl •Sal
ROSSÉ, François - *3L19L501X* (1993) (11') •Bsx/Vcl •B&N
SALM, Andreas - *Mah Jonhg* (1993) •Asx/Vcl •INM
SAVOURET, Alain - *Phil cello Joe Sax chez les...* •Asx/Vcl/Tape
SCHLUMPF, Martin - *Onyx* (1983) •Asx/Vcl •Hug
SHCHETINSKY, Alexander - *Crosswise* (1993) •Asx/Vcl •INM
STALLAERT, Alphonse - *Bestiaire* (1966) (14') •Asx/Vcl •Bil
VALK, Adriaan - *Dialogue* (1980) •Asx/Vcl •BVP
VITAKIS, Manolis - *Stück* (1992) •Asx/Vcl •INM
WISZNIEWSKI, Zbigniew - *Bicinium* (1993) •Asx/Vcl •INM
   Duo (1983) (14') •Asx/Vcl

3 Musicians

AGNESENS, Udo - *Suite populaire* (1986) •Asx/Vla/Vcl •adr
APIVOR, Denis - *Trio* (1981) •Ssx/Vcl/Pno
ARNOLD, Hubert - *Piano Trio* (1992) •Ssx+EH/Vcl/Pno
BOIS, Rob du - *Summer Music* (1967) (7'15) •Asx/Vln/Vcl •Don
BOIZARD, Gilles - *Concert* (1981) (14') •Asx/Vcl/Harp
BONNARD, Alain - *Pieces* •Ob/Sx/Vcl •Chou/adr
BOURLAND, Roger - *Three Dark Paintings* •Ssx/Vla/Vcl •ECS
BUSSEUIL, Patrick - *Trio - Inertie* (1981) •Ob/Asx/Vcl

CHAN, Francis - *Wild nights wild nights* (1978) •Soprano Voice/Sx/Vcl •CMC

CHARPILLE, Jean-Louis - *Jardins provisoires* (1991) •Bsx/Vcl/Perc

DAKIN, Charles - *Epona* (1981) (11') •Ssx/Vcl/Pno •DP

DUBOIS, Pierre-Max - *Trio* •Ob/Asx/Vcl •adr

EYSER, Eberhard - *Salinas nocturnas* (1979) (11') •Ssx/Cl/Vcl (or Bsn) •STIM

GASTINEL, Gérard - *8 Pièces en trio* (1981) (8') •Asx/Ob/Vcl

GINER, Bruno - *Con brio* (1991) (13-17') •Vcl/Bsx/Perc/Tape

GLASER, Werner Wolf - *Trio* (1981) (14') •Ob/Asx/Vcl •STIM

HARBISON, John - *Bermuda Triangle* (1970) •Vcl/Tsx/Electr. Org

JOLAS, Betsy - *Plupart du temps II* (1989) (10') •Tenor Voice/Tsx/Vcl •Led

JOLLET, Jean-Clément - *Amuse-gueules* (1988) (10'30) •Ob/Asx/Vcl •Bil

KORBAR, Leopold - *Valse triste per trio* (1978) (5') •Vln (or Fl or Ob or Cl or Ssx)/Vcl (or Bsn or Tsx)/Pno •CHF

KOUTZEN, Boris - *Music trio* (1940) •Asx/Vcl/Bsn •Bro/AMP

LAUBA, Christian - *Variation-Couleurs* (1986) •Ssx/Vcl (or Bass)/Perc •adr

LEMAIRE, Félix - *Trio*, op. 106 (1982) •Ob/Sx/Vcl •adr

LEMELAND, Aubert - *Mouvement concertant n° 3* (7'30) •Asx/Vla/Vcl •Bil

LEROUX, Philippe - *Phonice douce* (1991) •Ob/Asx/Vcl •Bil

MIGNION, René - *Pieces* •Ob/Asx/Vcl

MINAMIKAWA, Mio - *Ondulation* (1981) •Ob/Asx/Vcl •adr

MORRISSON, Julia - *Psalm 122* •Baritone Voice/Asx/Vcl •CFE

MYERS, Robert - *Trio* (1965) (8') •Asx/Bsn/Vcl •Art

NATANSON, Tadeus - *Trio* (1977) (11'30) •Asx/2 Vcl •AAW

PAVLENKO, Serguei - *Dedication* (1989) (17') •Ob/Asx/Vcl

ROBERT, Lucie - *Supplications* (1981) (10') •Ob/Asx/Vcl •DP

ROLIN, Etienne - *Jeu de trèfle* (1981) (11') •Ob/Sx/Vcl •adr
  Toile en trois couleurs (1976) (8') •Asx/Vcl/Pno •adr

ROTERS, Ernst - *Trio*, op. 26b (1926) •Vln/Asx/Vcl •Sim

RUBBERT, Rainer - *Trio "...le fou"* (1979-88) (11') •Ob/Asx/Vcl •adr

RUDAJEV, Alexandre - *5 Episodes* (1989) •Ob/Asx/Vcl •adr

SCHWANTNER, Joseph - *Entropy* (1968) •Ssx/BsCl/Vcl •DP/ACA

SMIRNOV, Dimitry - *Sérénade - trio* (1981) •Ob/Sx/Vcl •ECS

SOTELO, Mauricio - *Nel suono...* (1989) •1 Sx: A+T/BsCl+CBsCl/Vcl/Live electronics •adr

STRADOMSKI, Rafal - *Trio* (1989) (9') •Ob (or Ssx)/Asx/Vcl

VAUGHAN WILLIAMS, Ralph - *Household Music* (1940-41) •Diverse combinations •B&H

WEBER, Alain - *Assonances* (1980) •Asx/Ob/Vcl

WESTRUP, Jack - *Divertimento* (1948) •Tsx/Vcl/Pno •Ga

4 Musicians

ALBERTH, Rudolf - *Divertimento* (1941) •Asx/Str Trio •adr

ALEXANDER, Joseph - *Masks and Mirrors* (1986) •Ssx/Vcl/Perc/Pno

ATOR, James - *Haikansona* (1974) (10') •Mezzo Soprano Voice/Ob/Asx/Vcl •SeMC

BARRIERE, Françoise - *A propos...* (1979) •Asx/Perc/Vla/Vcl/Tape

BAUCKHOLT, Carola - *Schraubdichtung* (12') •CBsSx/Vcl/Perc/Voice

BEAL, Jeff - *Circular Logic* (1986) (10') •Asx/Soprano Voice/Vcl/Pno •PMCP

BLOOM, Shirley - *Suryanamaskar* (1971) (10') •Asx/Vcl/Chanter/Dancer •DP

BLYTON, Carey - *Market* (1964) (30') •Ob/Asx/Harp/Vcl •adr

BOURDIN, François - *Choral en canon* •Ob/Asx (or Tsx)/Vcl/Bass

BOURLAND, Roger - *Stone Quartet* •Ssx/Vla/Vcl/Pno •ECS

BROWN, Newel - *Figments* •Sx/Tpt/Bsn/Vcl •SeMC

CALMEL, Roger - *Les Caractères* (15') •Vln/Asx/Vcl/Pno •adr

CONYNGHAM, Barry - *Mirror Images* (1975) •4 Actors/Asx/Vcl/Bass/Perc •Uni

DAVID, Karl - *Quartets* (1934) (1946) •Vln/Asx/Vcl/Pno

DELANNOY, Marcel - *Rapsodie* (1934) •Asx/Tpt/Vcl/Pno •Heu

DESLOGES, Jacques - *Prélude et danse* (1983) •4 Sx: SATB or Ob/Cl/Asx/Bsn (or Vcl or Trb) •Arp

DI PASQUALE, James - *Quartet* (1964) (10') •Tsx/Tpt/Vla/Vcl •adr

FUSTÉ-LAMBEZAT, Michel - *Polyphonies* (1975) (15') •Cl/Asx/Vla/Vcl •SeMC

GERBER, René - *Concertino* (1944) •Sx/Vla/Vcl/Pno

GLASER, Werner Wolf - *Kvartett* (1950) •Asx/Vln/Vla/Vcl •STIM
  Linda - *Quartett* (1970-85) (17') •Bsx/Vln/Vla/Vcl •STIM
  Little Quartet (1970) •Asx/Vln/Vcl/Pno •STIM
  5 Strukturer •Soprano Voice/Fl/Sx/Vcl •STIM

GUIMAUD, Olivier - *Sérénade alla Lupesca* (16'15) •Tpt/Sx/Vcl/Perc •adr

HEYN, Volker - *Blues two* (1983) •Voice/Vcl/Sx/Perc •Br&Ha

KARLINS, M. William - *Variations* (1962-63) Ssx/Vln/Vla/Vcl •SeMC

KRIVITSKI, D. - *December Song* (1976) •Baritone Voice/Ssx/Vcl/Pno

KROL, Bernhard - *Suite* •Vln/Asx/Vcl/Pno

KRÖLL, Georg - *Quartett* (1993) •Bsx/Vcl/Tuba/Pno

LERSY, Roger - *Vitraux* (1972) (35') •Cl/Asx/Vcl/Perc •adr

MARCUSSEN, Kjell - *Quartet* (1983) •Ob (or Ssx)/Vln/Vcl/Pno •NMI

MENGOLD, Paul - *Quartette* •Vln/Asx/Vcl/Pno

MIEREANU, Costin - *Jardins retrouvés* (1985) (20') •Electr. Ssx/Vcl/Perc/Harp/Tape •Sal

MOESCHINGER, Albert - *Images*, op. 85 (1958) (18') •Fl/Vln/Asx/Vcl •Bil

MORRISSON, Julia - *Psalm 130* •2 Voices: AB/Asx/Vcl •CFE

MYERS, Robert - *Quartet* (1966) •Fl/Asx/Bsn/Vcl •SeMC/AMu

NOON, David - *Hymn Variations*, op. 108 (1991) (7') •Ssx/Vln/Vcl/Pno •TTF

PRICE, Deon - *Allegro barbaro* (1980) •Vln/Ssx/Vla/Vcl

RADULESCU, Horatiu - *Sensual sky* (1985) •Asx/Trb/Vcl/Bass/Tape

RICHMOND, Thomas - *Two Movements* (1964) •Vln/Vla/Asx/Vcl

SEVRETTE, Danielle - *L'Innomé* •Vln/Vcl/Asx/Org •adr

STEINBERG, Ben - *Suite Sephardi* (1979) •Ssx/Vln/Vla/Vcl •CMC

SUTHERLAND, Margaret - *Quartet* (1965) •Asx/Vln/Vla/Vcl

TAGGART, Mark - *Death* (1978) (19') •Mezzo Voice/Sx/Vcl/Pno •adr

WELLS, Thomas - *Comedia* (1978) •Sx/Fl/Tpt/Vcl

WILSON, Dana - *Sati* (1982) •Asx/Vcl/2 Perc •DP

WINKLER, Gerhard - *Aussenhäute* (1989) •Cl/Vln/Bsx/Vcl •adr

YAMANOUCHI, Tadashi - *Epistoraphe* (1968) •Asx/Marimba/Vibr/Vcl

ZONN, Paul Martin - *Midnight Secrets* (1992) (20') •Ssx/Vln/Vla/Vcl •ACA

5 Musicians

Also see Saxophone and String Quartet (Voir aussi quatuor à cordes), page 394.

ANDERSON, Thomas - *Re-creation* (1978) •Asx/Vla/Vcl/Pno/Tamtam

ATOR, James - *Life Cycle* (1973) (18') •Mezzo Soprano Voice/Asx/Ob/Perc/Vcl •SeMC

BENHAMOU, Maurice - *Mouvement* (1979) •Fl/Sx/Vla/Vcl/Perc/Tape

BUCZKOWNA, Anna - *Hipostaza* (1984/85) (15') •1 Sx: S+A+T/Fl/Vcl/Vibr/Soprano Voice

D'ANGELO, Nicholas - *The Seventh Star of Paracelsus* (1968) (16') •Fl/Vln/Asx/Vcl/Pno •adr

DONDEYNE, Désiré - *Voyages imaginaires* (1989) (12') •Asx/Pno or Asx/2 Vln/Harp/Vcl •Com

DÜNKI, Jean-Jacques - *Lutezia, 1842* (1978) •Ssx/Tpt/Vcl/Pno/Perc

FONTAINE, Louis-Noël - *Mauresque* (1992) (8') •Fl/Ssx/Cl/Vcl/Perc •Capri

HALL, Neville - *For a Single Point* (1990) (11') •Cl/Tsx/Pno/Vla/Vcl •adr

HEKSTER, Walter - *A song of peace* •Voice/Cl/Asx/Vcl/Perc •Don

HESPOS, Hans-Joachim - *Frottages* •Asx/Vcl/Harp/Mandolin/Perc •EMod

HRISANIDE, Alexandru - *M. P. 5* (1967) •Tsx+Cl/Vln/Vla/Vcl/Pno •IMD

IRINO, Yoshiro - *Quintette* (1958) •Cl/Asx/Tpt/Vcl/Pno •OE

JAEGER, Robert - *Quintet* (1969) •Asx/Vln/Vla/Vcl/Harp •adr
 Three Pieces (1967) (6'30) •Asx/Vln/Vla/Vcl/Harp (or Pno) •adr

JANSEN, Guus - *Juist daarom* (1981) (7') •Ob/Cl/Ssx/Vcl/Pno •Don

KONOE, Hidétaké - *Quintet* (1968) •Sx/Vln/Vla/Vcl/Bass
 Sonata caprice (1970) •Asx/Vln/Vla/Vcl/Bass

KUNZ, Ernst - *25 pezzi per varie...* (1963) •Vcl/3 Sx/Bsn

LATHROP, Gayle - *Pieces 4-5* •Asx/Tpt/Vcl/Bass/Perc •CAP

LINDROTH, Scott - *Two Pieces* •Asx/Vln/Vla/Vcl/Pno •DP

MACERO, Teo - *Canzona No. 1* •2 Vln/Asx/Vcl/Tpt •Pres

MARIN, Amadeo - *Quintet* •Fl/Ob/Tsx/Vcl/Trb

MATSUDAIRA, Roh - *Quintette* (1968) •Asx/Vln/Vla/Vcl/Bass

MOORTEL, Arie van de - *Nocturne*, op. 18 (1956) •Cl/Asx/Vla/Vcl/Pno •Mau

NICKLAUS, Wolfgang - *Der Priwall* (1984) (9') •Voice/Asx/Perc/Cl/Vcl •adr

NIKIPROWETZKY, Tolia - *Auto-stop* •Soprano Voice/Tenor Voice/Perc/Vcl/1 Sx: A+S •adr

POMORIN, Sibylle - *Zwei Lieder nach Anne Waldman* (1989) (19') •Voice/Asx/Perc/Vcl/Bass •adr

ROSENBLOOM, David - *The thud, thud, thud...* (1966) •Sx/Electric Vcl/Pno/Celesta/Perc/Tape/Lights •SeMC

RUBBERT, Rainer - *Vocalise* (1992) •Asx/Fl/Vcl/Perc/Pno •adr

WOOLLETT, Henri - *Danses païennes* (19xx) •2 Fl/Asx/Vcl/Harp

WYMAN, Laurence - *Deltangi* (1964) •Asx/4 Vcl •adr

6 Musicians

ABECASSIS, Eryck - *Dans 3 nuits* (1984) •Asx/Fl/Cl/Vln/Vcl/Pno

ANDERSON, Thomas J. - *Variations on a Theme by M.B. Tolson* (1969) •Ssx/Tpt/Trb/Vln/Vcl/Pno

ASHEIM, Nils Henrik - *Midt iblant os...* (1978) •Fl/Asx/Vla/Vcl/Bass/Perc •NMI

BENNETT, Richard Rodney - *Comedia I* (1972) •Fl/Asx/BsCl/Tpt/Vcl/Perc •Uni

BERG, Paul - *To Teach His Own* (1984) (12') •Fl/Ob/Tsx/Trb/Vln/Vcl/Tape •Don

BERGEIJK, Gilius van - *Life of Rosa Luxembourg* •Pno/Vcl/4 Instr./Tape

BOSSE, Denis - *...d'un léger souffle cosmique* (1987) (10') •1 Sx Solo: B+A+S/2 Vln/Vla/Vcl/Bass

CORY, Eleanor - *Waking* (1974) •Tsx/Bsn/Vln/Vcl/Bass/Perc

DAMICO, John - *Avilion* •Asx/2 Vln/Vla/Vcl/Bass •DP

DeBLASIO, Chris - *Prelude and Fugue* (1991) (9') •Ssx/Str Quintet •TTF

DE MARS, James - *Desert Songs* (1983) •Soprano Voice/Asx/Vcl/2 Perc/Pno •adr
 Premonitions... (16'30) •Native American Fl/African Perc/Asx/Vcl/Pno/Perc •adr

DESPORTES, Yvonne - *La maison abandonnée* (1961) (20') •Vln/Vla/Vcl/Asx/Perc/Pno •adr

ERB, Donald - *Hexagon* (1962) (6') •Fl/Asx/Tpt/Trb/Vcl/Pno •CMC

FUSTÉ-LAMBEZAT, Arnaud - *Catalogue d'étoiles* (1983) •Asx/Fl/Cl/Vln/Vcl/Pno •adr

GARCIN, Gérard - *SA* (1986) •Asx/Fl/Cl/Vln/Vcl/Pno

GAUTHIER, Brigitte - *Like the Sweet Blonde* (1983) •Fl/Asx/Cl/Vln/Vcl/Pno

GOEHR, Alexander - *Shadowplay*, op. 30 (1976) (20') •Actor+Tenor Voice/Narr+Fl/Asx/Hn/Vcl/Pno •Sch

GOTKOVSKY, Ida - *Poème lyrique* (1987) •2 Voices: SB/Pno/Fl (or Vln)/Asx (or Vla)/Bsn (or Vcl)

GRANDIS, Renato de - *Canti...* •Vln/Vcl/Tsx/Vibr/Trb/Perc •SeMC

GUINJOAN, Juan - *Musique intuitive - Diari* (1969) •Cl/Tsx/Tpt/Vln/Vcl/Pno

GULLIN, Peter - *Tre suma julsagor* (1988) •Bsx/2 Vln/Vla/Vcl/Bass

HEDSTROM, Ase - *Close by* (1980) •Fl/Cl/BsCl/Ssx/Vln/Vcl •NMI

HOLMBERG, Peter - *Musica alta e bassa* (1979) (12') •Fl/Tpt/Bsx/Tuba/Vln/Vcl •STIM

HUMBERT-CLAUDE, Eric - *Eux* (1983) •Asx/Fl/Cl/Vln/Vcl/Pno

KUPFERMAN, Meyer - *Jazz Cello Concerto* (1962) (25') •Vcl/3 Sx/Bass/Perc •GMP

LANZA, Alcides - *Modulos III* (1983) •Guit/Tsx/Vln/Vcl/Perc/Pno/Tape •CMC

LE SIEGE, Annette - *Ordinary Things* •Voice/Fl/Sx/Vibr/Vcl/Pno •SeMC

McPEEK, Ben - *Trillium* (1979) •Ssx/Fl/Cl/Vln/Vcl/Pno

MICHAEL, Frank - *Kmk* •Fl/Ssx/Trb/Vln/Vla/Vcl •adr

POMORIN, Sibylle - *Rabengold - Goldraben* (1989) (80') •2 Sx: AT/Perc/Pno/Org/Vcl •adr

RAYNAL, Gilles - *Ombilic* (1983) •Fl/Cl/Asx/Vln/Vcl/Pno

ROKEACH, Martin - *Tango* •Ob/Cl/Asx/Hn/Trb/Vcl •DP

ROLIN, Etienne - *Tressage-Concerto* (1983-84) (10') •Ssx/Fl/Cl/Pno/Vln/Vcl •Lem

RUDAJEV, Alexandre - *Variations et Thème* (1991) (10') •Asx/5 Vcl •adr

SCHUBACK, Peter - *A Priori* (1983) (45') •Sx/Trb/Perc/Vlc/Pno/Harps •Tons/SMIC

SCHWEYER, Bruno - *Konzerstück* (1983) •Tsx/Fl/Cl/Vln/Vcl/Pno

SIMS, Ezra - *Sextet* (1981) (22') •Cl/Asx/Hn/Vln/Vla/Vcl •ACA

SURIANU, Horia - *Esquisse pour un clair obscur* (1986) (11') •Ssx/Fl/Cl/Vln/Vcl/Pno •Sal

TOSI, Daniel - *Multiphony III* (1986) (6'30) •Fl/Cl/Asx/Pno/Vln/Vcl

7 Musicians

ALLGEN, Claude - *Praeludium och Carmen Perlotense* •Vln/Vla/Vcl/Asx/Pno/Harps/Org •STIM

BROTT, Alexander - *7 for seven* (1954) (14'30) •Narr/Cl/Asx/Vln/Vla/Vcl/Pno •CMC

CERHA, Friedrich - *Fantasies nach Cardw's Herbst 60* •Cl/BsCl/Tsx/Vln/Vla/Vcl/Pno •EMod

COWELL, Henry - *Chrysanthemus* (1937) •Soprano Voice/2 Sx/2 Vln/Vla/Vcl

CRAS, Jean - *Demain* (1929) •Asx/Tpt/Trb/Perc/Vln/Vcl/Bass •Sen

DANCEANU, Liviu - *Quasi concerto* (1983) (15') •1 Sx: S+T/Bsn/Trb/Vcl/Bass/Pno/Perc

ESCAICH, Thierry - *Antiennes oubliées* (1994) •Vln/Fl/Asx/Tpt/Trb/Vcl/Vibr •Bil

FINNISSY, Michael - *Evening* (1974) •Asx/Hn/Tpt/Perc/Harp/Vcl/Bass

GRÄSBECK, Mannfred - *Rapsodia...* •2 Vln/Vla/Vcl/Sx/Pno/Perc

JEVERUD, Johan - *Chimaira* (1984) •BsCl/Tsx/Trb/3 Vcl/Pno •SMIC

MASON, Lucas - *A Quilt of Love* (1971) •Soprano Voice/Asx/Fl/Vln/Bsn/Trb/Vcl •adr

MIEREANU, Costin - *Polymorphies 5 X 7 B* (1969-70) (9-10') •Fl+Picc/Cl+Tsx/Pno/Vln/Vla/Vcl/Bass •Sal

MILHAUD, Darius - *La Création du monde* (LONDEIX) •2 Vln/Asx/Vcl/Bass/Perc/Pno •ME

NORDENSTEN, Frank - *Sample and hold* (1978) (14') •Fl+Picc/Cl+BsCl/1 Sx: S+T/Vln+Vla/Vcl/Pno/Perc

ROLIN, Etienne - *Quètes ancestrales* (1989) (14') •Tsx/Vla/2 Vcl/ Bass/Harp/Marimba •Fuz

SAGVIK, Stellan - *Pastoral*, op. 65 (1976) (4') •Asx/2 Vln/2 Vla/2 Vcl •STIM

SKOUEN, Synne - *Hva sa Schopenhauer...* (1978) (8') •Narr/Fl/ Cl+BsCl/Sx/Vln/Vcl/Perc •NMI

SOTELO, Mauricio - *Quando il cielo...* (1989) (18') •Asx/Perc/Pno/ Vln/Vla/Vcl/Bass •ECA

  IX +... - de substantiis separatis (1990) •Cl/Sx/Tuba/Vln/Vcl/ Bass/Pno/Schtagzeng with live electronics •adr

STEARNS, Peter - *Septet* (1959) •Cl/Tsx/Hn/Vln/Vla/Vcl/Bass •Pio/ ACA

TAUTENAHN, Günther - *Septet* •Cl/Tpt/Tsx/Guit/Vcl/Pno/Perc •SeMC

VOUILLEMIN, Sylvain - *Divertimento...* (1983) (8'30) •Ssx/2 Vln/ Vla/Vcl/Bass/Perc or Ssx/Pno •Led

8 Musicians

BARCE, Ramon - *Concierto de Lizara V* (1977) (10'45) •Cl/Tsx/Tpt/ Trb/Harp/Pno/Vln/Vcl

BERG, Olav - *Fragments* (1977) (8') •Fl/Cl/Asx/Vla/Vcl/Pno/2 Perc •NMJ

BIRTWISTLE, Harrison - *Medusa* (1969/70/78) •Fl/Cl/Ssx/Pno/ Perc/Vln/Vla/Vcl/Tape

BÖRJESSON, Lars - *Divertimento*, op. 38 (1983) •Asx/BsCl/Bsn/ Guit/Harp/Marimba/Vln/Vcl •STIM

BREGENT, Michel - *Melorytharmundi* (1984) •Fl/Cl/Sx/2 Perc/Pno/ Vcl/Guit •CMC

CHAGRIN, Francis - *Sarabande* (1951) (6') •Ob/Hn/Vln/Asx/Str Quartet •ALC

ERNRYD, Bengt - *Rödingsjön II* (1967) •Fl+Picc/Trb/Tsx+Perc/ Bsx+Perc/Vcl/Bass/2 Perc •SMIC

FABERMAN, Harold - *For Erik and Nick* (1964) •Tenor Voice/Asx/ Vcl/Bass/Tpt/Trb/Vibr/Perc

FONTYN, Jacqueline - *Cheminement* (1986) (15') •Soprano Voice/ Fl/Cl/Hn (or Asx)/Vcl/Bass/Perc/Pno

FRANCESCONI, Luca - *Piccola trama* (1989) (14') •1 Sx: S+A/Fl/ Cl/Guit/Perc/Vln/Vla/Vcl •Ric

GARCIN, Gérard - *Encore plus tard* (1984) (12') •1 Sx: Sno+A+Bs/ Fl/Cl/Bsn/Vla/Vcl/Bass/Perc/Tape •Sal

HACHIMURA, Yoshiro - *Concerto per 8 soli* •Fl/Cl/Sx/Vibr/Vcl/ Vla/2 Perc •OE

HARBISON, John - *The Flower-fed Buffaloes* (1976) •Voice/Cl/Tsx/ Fl/Vcl/Bass/Pno/Perc

MANDANICI, Marcella - *Extraits I* (1989) •Tsx/Fl/Cl/Pno/Perc/Vln/ Vla/Vcl •adr

MARIETAN, Pierre - *13 en concert* (1983) (15') •1 Sx: Sno+S+B/Cl/ Bsn/Trb/Vcl/2 Bass/Pno

MAYUZUMI, Toshiro - *Sphenogramme* (1951) •Contralto Voice/Fl/ Asx/Marimba/Vln/Vcl/Pno 4 hands [à 4 mains]

MICHEL, Paul - *Ultramorphoses* (1965) (12-15') •Fl/Cl/Asx/Perc/ Pno/Vln/Vla/Vcl •CBDM

NICKLAUS, Wolfgang - *Die Antwort* (1986) (7'30) •Cl/Asx/2 Perc/ Pno/Vln/Vcl/Bass •adr

NILSSON, Ivo - *Agnosi* (1988) (9') •Ob/Asx/Tpt/Harp/2 Vln/Vla/Vcl •STIM

PERSSON, Bob - *Om sommaren sköna II* (1965) •Fl/BsCl/Trb/2 Perc/ Vibr/Vcl/Jazz Sx/Tape

PINOS-SIMANDL, Aloïs - *Geneze* (1970) (8') •Vln/Asx/Vcl/Trb/ Perc/Harp/Harps/Ionika •CHF

SOTELO, Mauricio - *IX +...* (1990) •Cl/Sx/Tuba/Vln/Vcl/Bass/Pno/ Schtagzeng with live electronics •adr

SPAHLINGER, Mathias - *Aussageverweigerung-Gegendarstellung* •Cl/Bsx/Bass/Pno/BsCl/Tsx/Vcl/Pno •Peer

TANENNBAUM, Elias - *Consort* •Fl/Hn/Asx/Electr. Guit/Vcl/Bass/ Vibr/Jazz drums •ACA

TOMASSON, Haukur - *Octette* (1987) •Fl/Cl/Asx/Hn/Vla/Vcl/Pno/ Perc (Vibr+Gong) •IMIC

VILLA-LOBOS, Heitor - *Chôros n° 7* (1924) (10') •Fl/Ob/Cl/Asx/ Bsn/Vln/Vcl/Tam-tam •ME

WOOLLETT, Henri - *Octuor n° 1* (1911) •Ob/Cl/Asx/2 Vln/Vla/Vcl/ Bass •South

9 Musicians

BORTOLOTTI, Mauro - *Studio per E.E. Cummings n° 2* (1964) •Vla/ Vcl/Bass/Ob/Cl/BsCl/Sx/Hn/Perc •adr

CAPLET, André - *Impressions d'Automne* (1905) (3') •Asx/Ob/2 Cl/ Bsn/Harp/Org/2 Vcl

  Légende (1903) (13') •Asx/Ob/Cl/Bsn/2 Vln/Vla/Vcl/Bass •Fuz

CERHA, Friedrich - *Exercices for Nine, No. 1* •BsCl/Bsx/Bsn/Tpt/ Trb/Tuba/Vcl/Bass/Harp •Uni

CUSTER, Arthur - *Cycle for Nine Instruments* •Asx/BsCl/Tpt/Hn/ Vln/Vla/Vcl/Bass/Perc •JM

DAVIDSON, Tina - *Berceuse* (1991) •Asx/8 Vcl

GUALDA JIMENEZ, Antonio - *Noneto Zarco* (1988) (16') •Vln/Vcl/ Cl/2 Sx: SA/Vibr/Marimba/Guit/Pno

HAHN, Reynaldo - *Divertissement...* (1933) (25') •2 Vln/Vla/Vcl/ Bass/Asx/Bsn/Timp/Perc •Sal

MANOURY, Philippe - *Etude automatique* 1 •Fl/Tpt/Sx/Tuba/Harp/ Vln/Vla/Vcl/Bass

MELLNÄS, Arne - *Drones* (1967) (8') •Fl/Cl/3 Sx: ATB/Tpt/Perc/ Vcl/Bass •STIM

MULDOWNEY, Dominic - *An Heavyweight Dirge* (1971) (25') •Voice/Fl/Asx/Perc/Pno/2 Vln/Vla/Vcl •Nov

NATANSON, Tadeus - *3 Pictures for 7 Instruments* (1960) •Ob/Cl/ Asx/Trb/Vcl/Tpt/Bsn/Pno/Perc •AMP

RACOT, Gilles - *Jubilad'a* (1985) (23'30) •1 Sx: Bs+Sno/Vcl/Fl/6 Voices

RENOSTO, Paolo - *Dissolution* •Vla/Vcl/Bass/Ob/Cl/BsCl/Sx/Hn/ Perc

RYTTERKVIST, Hans - *Lied ohne Worte* (1968) •3 Vln/Vla/2 Vcl/ Harps/Pno/Bsx •SMIC

SAGVIK, Stellan - *Det Förlorade steget*, op. 64 (1976) (20') •Fl/ Cl+BsCl/Asx/Cnt/Trb/Vln/Vla/Vcl/Perc •SMIC

SCELSI, Jacinto - *Kya* (1959) (11') •Cl (or Ssx)/EH/Hn/BsCl/Tpt/ Trb/Vla/Vcl/Bass •Sal

SCHULLER, Gunther - *Abstraction* (1959) (5') •Asx/Guit/Perc/2 Vln/Vla/Vcl/2 Bass •MJQ

SCHWANTNER, Joseph - *Diaphona intervallum* (1966) (12') •Asx/ Pno/Fl/2 Vln/Vla/2 Vcl/Bass •ACA

TANENBAUM, Elias - *Trios I, II, III* •Fl/Ob/Cl/Vln/Vla/Vcl/Bass/ Asx/Perc •ACA

TARENSKEEN, Boudewijn - *Nonet* (1982) (13') •Asx/Hn/BsCl/ Accordion/Banjo/Harp/Vla/Vcl/Bass •Don

WALTON, William - *Façade* (1922/26, 42) (34'30) •2 Narr/Fl+Picc/ Cl/BsCl/Asx/Tpt/Vcl/Perc •OUP

YOSHIBA, Susumu - *Erka* •Fl/Ob/Sx/Tpt/Trb/Perc/Vcl/Guit/Pno

10 Musicians

BANKS, Donald - *Equation 1* (1964) (7') •Tpt/Asx/Pno/Harp/Guit/ Perc/2 Vln/Vla/Vcl •BMIC

COE, Tony - *The Buds of Time* (1979) (20') •Cl+Sx/Cl+BsCl/2 Vln/ Vla/Vcl/BsTrb/Pno/Bass/Perc •adr

COPPOOLSE, David - *Canto XVII* (1984) (12') •Asx/2 Hn/2 Trb/Vln/ Vla/Vcl/Bass/Pno •Don

COSTEN, Roel van - *Prisma* (1984) (8') •Vla/Fl/Cl/Asx/BsCl/Trb/
Vcl/Bass/Perc/Pno •Don

FORTNER, Jack - *S pr ING sur des poèmes de E. E. Cummings* (1966)
(11') •Mezzo Soprano Voice/Fl/Asx/Bsn/
Vla/Vcl/Bass/Vibr/Harp/Pno •JJ

GOODMAN, Alfred - *3 Gesänge für Gresang* •Soprano Voice/Fl/Ob/
Asx/Cl/Vla/Vcl/Prepared Pno/Guit/Perc •adr

GOTTSCHALK, Arthur - *Cycloid* •Cl/Asx/Hn/Tpt/Harp/Vibr/2 Vln/
Vla/Vcl •SeMC

GOUGEON, Denis - *Heureux qui comme...* (1987) •Soprano Voice/
Picc/EH/Bsx/2 Vln/Vla/Vcl/Bass/Perc
•CMC

GRAHN, Ulf - *Soundscape II* (1974) (7') •Fl/Cl/EH/Asx/2 Trb/2 Vln/
Vcl/Bass •SMIC

GRANDIS, Renato de - *Scotter Sud-est* •Vln/Vla/Vcl/Bass/Sx/Hn/
Tpt/Trb/Pno/Perc •SeMC

LACHARTE, Nicole - *La Geste inachevée* (1980) •Fl/Cl/Sx/Tpt/Trb/
Pno/Perc/Vln/Vla/Vcl

LAZARUS, Daniel - *4 Mélodies* •Contralto Voice/Fl/Cl/Asx/Bsn/2
Vln/Vla/Vcl/Bass

Lecuona, Ernesto - *Andalucia* •2 Tpt/Trb/3Sx: AAT/2 Vln/Vcl/Bass

LEWIS, John Aaron - *The Milanese Story* •Fl/Tsx/Guit/Pno/Bass/2
Vln/Vla/Vcl/Perc •MJQ

LUTYENS, Elisabeth - *Akapotik Rose*, op. 64 (1966) (18') •Soprano
Voice/Picc/Fl/Cl/Bsn/Cl+Tsx/Vln/Vla/Vcl/
Pno

MAROS, Miklos - *Coalottino* (1969) (5') •Bsx/Electr. instrum./2 Pno/
Harps/2 Vln/Vla/2 Vcl •STIM

PAUMGARTNER, Bernhard - *Divertimento* •Picc/EH/Asx/Bsn/Hn/
Tpt/Pno/Vla/Vcl/Perc •Uni

POOLE, Geoffrey - *Son of Paolo* (1971) •Fl/Picc/Cl/BsCl/Tsx/2 Vln/
2 Vcl/Prepared Pno •BMIC

SCHWERTSIK, Kurt - *Salotto romano*, op. 5 (1961) •BsCl/Bsx/Bsn/
Hn/Trb/Tuba/Perc/Bass/Vcl/Guit •EMod

SMITH, Linda - *Periphery* (1979) •Fl/Sx/Tpt/Marimba/Vibr/Chimes/
Pno/Vln/Vcl/Bass •CMC

WROCHEM, Klaus - *Oratorium meum plus praeperturi* •3 Voices/2
Vln/Vla/Vcl/Asx/Tpt/Perc •CAP

11 Musicians

ANDRIESSEN, Jurriaan - *Hommage à Milhaud* (1945) (8') •Fl/Ob/
Cl/Bsn/Hn/Tpt/Trb/Asx/Vln/Vla/Vcl •Don

COLE, Bruce - *Pantomimes* (25') •Soprano Voice/Fl/Cl/BsCl/Ssx/
Perc/Pno/Guit/Vln/Vla/Vcl •B&H

HALL, Helene - *Pieces* •5 Soprano Voices/3 Sx: SAB/Vcl/2 Perc
•CMC

HESPOS, Hans - *Break* •Ob/3 Tpt/2 Sx: TB/Vcl/Bass/Trb/Pno/Perc
•EMod

TRIMBLE, Lester - *Panels I* (1973) (6') •Picc/Bsx/Vln/Vla/Vcl/Bass/
2 Perc/Electr. Guit/Electr. Org/Electr. Harp
•Pet

12 Musicians

CECCONI, Monique - *Hommage à...* •Ob/Cl/Asx/Bsn/4 Vln/2 Vla/2
Vcl •Phi

DUREY, Louis - *Feu la mère de Madame*, op. 49 (1945) (5') •Fl/Ob/
Asx/Bsn/Tpt/Tuba/Perc/2 Vln/Vla/Vcl/Bass
•BRF

HASQUENOPH, Pierre - *Inventions* •2 Vln/Vla/Vcl/Bass/Fl/Ob/Cl/
Asx/Bsn/Hn/Tpt •Heu

MASINI, Fabio - *"Nuvole e colori forti"* (1992) (18') •Fl/1 Sx: S+A/
BsCl/Fl/Ob/Cl/Bsn/2 Vln/Vla/Vcl/Harp

REA, John - *Treppenmusik* (1982) •4 Sx: SATB/4 Cl/Vln/Vla/Vcl/
Bass •CMC

ROBBINS, David - *Improvisation* •Fl/2 Cl/Tsx/Bsn/Tpt/Trb/Vln/Vla/
Vcl/Bass/Perc

13 Musicians

FINNISSY, Michael - *Babylon* (1971) (19') •Mezzo Soprano Voice/
Ob/Cl/Asx/Bsn/Guit/Harp/Pno/2 Perc/2 Vcl/
Bass •Uni

First sign a sharp white mons (1974-67) (45') •2 Fl/2 Cl/Asx/CBsn/
Hn/Accordion/Guit/Vln/2 Vcl/Pno •BMIC

HESPOS, Hans - *Conga* (1979) (15'30) •Tsx/5 Congas/2 Vln/2 Vla/
2 Vcl/Bass •Hes

HUREL, Philippe - *"Pour l'image"* •Fl/Ob/Cl/Asx/Hn/Tpt/Trb/Perc/
2 Vln/Vla/Vcl/Bass

SEKON, Joseph - *Lemon Ice* (1972) •Fl/Ob/Cl/2 Sx: ST/Bsn/Tpt/Trb/
2 Perc/Vln/Vcl/Pno •adr

WENDEL, Eugen - *Saphonospir* (15') •Asx/Fl/Cl/Ob/Tpt/Trb/2 Vln/
Vla/Vcl/Bass/2 Perc •adr

14 Musicians

HARBISON, John - *Confinement* (1965) (15'15) •Fl/Ob/EH/Cl/BsCl/
Asx/Tpt/Trb/Vln/Vla/Vcl/Bass/Pno/Perc

HARVEY, Jonathan - *The Valley of Aosta* (1985) (13'30) •Fl/Ob/Ssx/
Tpt/2 Yamaha DX7 Synth/2 Harp/Pno/2 Vln/
Vla/Vcl/Perc •FM

RUBBERT, Rainer - *Kammerkonzert* (1990) •4 Sx: SATB/4 Vln/2
Vla/2 Vcl/Bass/Pno •adr

15 Musicians

LUTYENS, Elisabeth - *Islands*, op. 80 (1971) •2 Narr: ST/Picc/Fl/Cl/
BsCl/Tsx/Hn/Pno/Celesta/Vln/Vla/Vcl/2
Perc

TEMPLE & SHAW - *Vanity Fair Suite* •Fl/Ob/4 Cl/BsCl/Asx/2 Vln/
Vla/Vcl/Bass/Perc/Pno •Mills

oOo

DAKIN, Charles - *Syra* (1979) (8'30) •2 Cl/2 Tsx/2 Tpt/2 Trb/4 Vla/
4 Vcl/2 Bass

MORRISSON, Julia - *De profundis* •Asx/Vcl/Voices •CFE

WALLACH, Joelle - *Sweet Briar Elegies* •Ssx/Vcl Ensemble

Saxophone and Bass

2 Musicians

BEUGER, Antoine - *Things taking place* (1993) •Bsx/Bass •INM

ESSLINGER, Paul - *Yak* (1993) •1 Sx: A+S/Bass •INM

FUCHS, Christina - *Suite I* (1993) •Ssx/Bass •INM

GIORGIO, Babbini - *Suite Medioevale* •Sx/Bass

HAUBRUCK, Joachim - *5 Touken* (1993) •Ssx/Electr. Bass •INM

LEANDRE, Joëlle - *Duo n° 1* (6') •Asx/Bass

LEGUAY, Jean-Pierre - *Scabbs* (1984) •Asx/Bass (or Bsx) •Lem

MACCHIA, Salvatore - Duo •Asx/Bass

MILLS, Charles - *Music; Music for Recorder* •Sx/Bass •Pio/CFE/
ACA

PETROJ, Lionel - *11 Actes* (20') •Sx/Bass

REA, Melvin - *Goodbye Mr. Penguin* (1993) •Asx/Bass •INM

SMITH, Howie - *Indian Orange* •Tsx/Bass

UCHIMOTO, Yoshio - *Afro-blue* (1993) •1 Sx: S+T/Bass •INM

VALENTI, William - *Duo* •Asx/Bass

WARZECHA, Piotr - *Dialoghi* (1993) •Bsx/Bass •INM

3 Musicians

ALCALAY, Luna - *Trio* (1964) •Asx/CBsn/Bass

BARKIN, Elaine - *Media Speak* (1981) •Fl/Asx/Bass/Tape

BLUMENTHALER, Volker - *Elégie* (1981) •Tsx/Bass/Vibr •B&B

EITHLER, Estaban - *Trio* (1944) •Fl/Asx/Bass •BBC

EVERETT, Thomas - *Three Comments* (1970) (4-10') •Tsx/Bass/
BsTrb •SeMC
GARCIN, Gérard - *Le retour d'Uswann* (1987) •Sx+BsCl/Perc/Bass
GONZALES, Jean-François - *Page d'album* •Sx/Harp/Bass
GRUBER, Heinz - *Concerto No. 2* (1961) •Tsx/Bass/Perc •B&H
HOFFMAN, Allan - *6 Versions* •Asx/Bass/Vibr
JOHNSON, Roger - *Fantasy* •Asx/Perc/Bass •DP
KILAR, Wojciech - *1 Dla 3* (1963) •Asx/Vibr/Bass
KUNZ, Ernst - *25 pezzi per varie...* (1962) •Asx/Bass/Perc
LAUBA, Christian - *Variation-Couleurs* (1986) •Ssx/Vcl (or Bass)/
Perc •adr
LEUCHTER, Heibert - *Diamonds in the water* (1981) (5'30) •Asx/Bs
Guit/Perc •adr
MITREA-CELARIANU, Mihai - *Ouverture* •Asx/Bass/Perc •Sal
MORRISSON, Julia - *Julia Street* (1969) (12') •Asx/Pno/Bass •CFE
October Music (1969) (5') •Asx/Pno/Bass •CFE
Subjective Objective (1970) (6') •Tsx/Bass/Electr. Guit •CFE
Mozart, Wolfgang - *Trio* •2 Sx: ST/Bass (or Trb) •Mil
SCHWARTZ, Francis - *Daiamoni* (5') •Asx/Fl/Bass
SIBBING, Robert - *Moments* (1974) •Sx/Bsn/Tuba (or Bass) •Eto
STEINKE, Günter - *Nachklang* (10') •Bsx/Perc/Bass
YAMANOUCHI, Tadashi - *Correlation* (1979) •Marimba/Asx/Bass

4 Musicians

Bach, J. S. - *Quartet*, op. 17, no. 6 (CUNNINGHAM) •SATB or SAT/Bass
•Eto
BENTZON, Jørgen - *Raconto n° 1*, op. 25 (1935) (13') •Fl/Asx/Bsn/
Bass •SOBM/BMCo
BOURDIN, François - *Choral en canon* •Ob/Asx (or Tsx)/Vcl/Bass
CAMPBELL, John - *Voices of America* (1984) •Voice/Ssx/Vibr/Bass
•adr
CHAGRIN, Francis - *2 Studies for Jazz Quartet* (1959) •Tpt/Sx/Bass/
Drums •BMIC
CHEN, Qijang - *Feu d'ombres* (1991) •Ssx/Instr. Ensemble/Harp/
Bass/Perc •Bil
CONYNGHAM, Barry - *Mirror Images* (1975) •4 Actors/Asx/Vcl/
Bass/Perc •Uni
DIEMENTE, Edward - *Quartet in Memory Fl. O'Connor* (1967)
•Asx/Trb/Bass/Perc •SeMC
ELLIS, Donald - *Improvisational Suite* •Tpt/Asx/Bass/Perc •MJQ
EMMER, Huib - *Koud zoud* (1984) (5') •Ob/Asx/Trb/Bass •Don
ERB, Donald - *Quartet* (1962) (7') •Fl/Ob/Asx/Bass •CMC
FIORENZA, Eduard - *Soundscape Suite...* •Tsx/Pno/Bass/Perc •DP
GASLINI, Giorgio - *Magnificat* (1963) (4') •Soprano Voice/Asx/Pno/
Bass •Uni
GODAR, Vladimir - *2 Frammenti* (1977) •Narr/Sx/Bass/Pno
GOODMAN, Alfred - *Suite* (1990) (13') •2 Sx: SA/Harp/Bass •adr
GOTTSCHALK, Arthur - *The Sessions* •Fl/Asx/Vibr/Bass •SeMC
GROSSE, Erwin - *Konzerte* •Tpt/Vln/Asx/Bass •adr
HODEIR, André - *Paradoxe I* •Tsx/Trb/Bass/Perc •MJQ
KARLINS, M. William - *Reflux* (1970) •Amplified Bass/3 Sx •adr
KUPFERMAN, Meyer - *Jazz Infinities Three* (1961) (90') •Asx/Pno/
Bass/Perc •GMP
LAMBRECHT, Homer - *Metaphrases* (1973) •1 Sx: S+A/Cl/BsCl/
Bass
LAUBA, Christian - *Atlas* (1984) (20') •1 Sx: A+B/Pno/Perc/Bass
•adr
LERSY, Roger - *Kandinsky* (1973) •Asx/Bass/Perc/Pno •adr
MACHOVER, Tod - *Valise's Song* (1989) (5') •1 Sx: S+T/Electr.
Guit/Perc/Electr. Bass/Computer tape •adr
MIGOT, Georges - *2 Stèles de Victor Segalen* (1925) (15') •Voice (or
Asx)/Celesta/Bass/Perc •Led
MUCI, Italo - *Quartetto* (1981) •Cl/Tsx/Trb/Bass
MANSHIP, Munch - *Four Songs* •Bb or Eb Sx/Pno/Bass/Drums •PBP
RADULESCU, Horatiu - *Sensual sky* (1985) •Asx/Trb/Vcl/Bass/Tape

SHOUT, Vladislav - *Metamorphosis* (1979) •Asx/Bass/Harp/Perc
•ECS
SLEZAK, Milan - *3 Pisnê pro nizsi a Vyssi* •Pno/Cymbals/Sx/Bass
SLONIMSKY, Sergei - *Suite exotique* •2 Vln/Tsx Solo/Electr. Bass
STEARNS, Peter - *Chamber Set II* •Asx/Vln/Tpt/Bass •ACA

5 Musicians

CAMPANA, José-Luis - *Insight* (1987) (18') •Fl/Voice/Sx/Bass/
Perc/Tape/Video •Bil
CELERIANU, Michel - *Janvier* (1983) •Ssx/Fl/2 Bass/Perc •Sal
CHARRON, Damien - *Extraits du corps* (1985) •Mezzo Soprano
Voice/Tsx/BsCl/Bass/Perc
CONYNGHAM, Barry - *Jazz Ballet* (1964) •Fl/Asx/Bass/Perc/Pno
•Uni
FERRITO - *Concertino* •Asx/Ob/2 Perc/Bass •DP
FLETA POLO, Francisco - *Divertimento 26* (1985) •Sx/Cl/Accor-
dion/Bass/Timp
GARCIN, Gérard - *Méditations* (1971) •2 Sx/Pno/Bass/Perc
GOODWIN, Gordon - *Levittation* •Sx/Tpt/Pno/Bass/Perc •adr
GREENE - *From Out of Bartok* •Asx/2 Bass/Perc/Pno
GULLIN, Peter - *Adventures* •2 Sx: AT/Pno/Bass/Perc •SMIC/WIM
HAERL, Dan - *Quintet* •Fl/Asx/Tpt/Trb/Bass •adr
HAUTA-AHO, Teppo - *For Charles M.* (1980) (15') •Tpt/Asx/Trb/
Bass/Perc •FMIC
HESPOS, Hans - *En-kin das fern-nahe* (1970) (5'30) •Ssx/Cl/Bsn/
Bass/Perc •EMod
HODKINSON, Sidney - *Interplay* (1966) (12'30) •Fl+Picc/Cl/Asx/
Perc/Bass •CMC
KONOE, Hidétaké - *Quintet* (1968) •Sx/Vln/Vla/Vcl/Bass
Sonata caprice (1970) •Asx/Vln/Vla/Vcl/Bass
KUCHARZYK, Henry - *One for the Underdog* (1981) •Tpt/Sx/Pno/
Bass/Perc •CMC
LATHROP, Gayle - *Pieces 4-5* •Asx/Tpt/Vcl/Bass/Perc •CAP
LONARDONI, Markus - *Modal interchange* (1987) (6') •Sx/Perc/
Pno/Guit/Bass
MABRY, Drake - *9.10.89* •Ssx/Electr. Guit/Bass Guit/Synth/Perc
MACERO, Teo - *Exploration* •Asx/Cl/Bass/Perc/Accordion
MATSUDAIRA, Roh - *Quintette* (1968) •Asx/Vln/Vla/Vcl/Bass
MIEREANU, Costin - *Ricochets* (1989) •1 Sx: Sno+S+A+T+B/
Electr. Guit/Bass Guit/Synth/Perc/Régie
électr. •Sal
MILLS, Charles - *Paul Bunyan Jump* (1964) •Asx/Pno/Tpt/Bass/Perc
•ACA
POMORIN, Sibylle - *Zwei Lieder nach Anne Waldman* (1989) (19')
•Voice/Asx/Perc/Vcl/Bass •adr
RACKLEY-SMITH, Lawrence - *Kay-Vee-Si-Si* •2 Sx: AT/Pno/Bass/
Perc/Tape
RECK, David - *Blues and Screamer* (1965-66) •Fl+Picc/Harmonica/
Asx/Bass/Perc •CPE
SCHIFRIN, Lalo - *Jazz Faust* (1963) (20') •Asx/Tpt/Pno/Bass/Perc
•MJQ
Mount Olive (3') •Asx/Guit/Pno/Bass/Perc •MJQ
SHEPHERD, Stu - *Birthday Music III* (1986) •1 Sx: A+T/Guit/Synth/
Bass/Perc •CMC
SHEPPARD, James - *Bitter Ice* •Tpt/Sx/Pno/Bass/Perc •SeMC
STEELE, Jan - *Temporary farewell* (1971) (5') •1 Sx: S+A/Electr.
Guit/Pno/Bass/Perc
Sternberg - *Variations on German Folk Songs* •Sx/Bass/Guit/Pno/
Perc •DV
SYMONDS, Norman - *Sylvia* (1974) •Narr/Tsx/Fl/Pno/Bass •CMC
TSOUPAKI, Calliope - *Kentavros* (1991) (17') •3 Sx/Pno/Bass •Don
VOSK, Jay - *Le Nid* •Ssx/Vibr/Guit/Vln/Bass •SeMC
WATANABE, Hiroshi - *Q-I-love* •4 Sx: AATB/Bass

6 Musicians

ASHEIM, Nils Henrik - *Midt iblant os...* (1978) •Fl/Asx/Vla/Vcl/
Bass/Perc •NMI

BOSSE, Denis - *...d'un léger souffle cosmique* (1987) (10') •1 Sx
Solo: B+A+S/2 Vln/Vla/Vcl/Bass

CASANOVA, André - *Duo Canzoni* (1973) (10'30) •Asx/Cl/Tpt/
Perc/Small Org/Electr. Bass Guit •adr

CHINI, André - *Pieces* (1992) •Fl/Sx/2 Perc/Pno/Bass

CORY, Eleanor - *Waking* (1974) •Tsx/Bsn/Vln/Vcl/Bass/Perc

COURTIOUX, Jean - *Manu reva* (1983) •2 Sx: TB/Flugelhorn/Trb/
Bass/Drums •DP

DAMICO, John - *Avilion* •Asx/2 Vln/Vla/Vcl/Bass •DP

DeBLASIO, Chris - *Prelude and Fugue* (1991) (9') •Ssx/Str Quintet
•TTF

DORNBY, Finn - *Musickus dornby* •2 Sx: AB/Org/Electr. Guit/Electr.
Bs Guit/Perc

EISMA, Will - *Affairs no. 1* •Fl/Asx/Vibr/Pno/Bass/Perc •Don

ERIKSON, Ake - *The rest is silence* (1971/73) •Fl/Asx/Cl/Pno/Bass/
Perc •SMIC

FUKUDA, Wakako - *Divertissement* •4 Sx/Bass/Perc

GEHLHAARD, Rolf - *Hélix* (1967) •Soprano Voice/Sx/Trb/Bass/
Pno/Perc •FM

GOJKOVIC, Dusan - *Swinging macedonia* (1966) (35') •Tpt/2 Sx:
AT/Pno/Bass/Perc •adr

GOODWIN, Gordon - *Heterophonie Conuberations* •5 Sx: SATTB/
Electr. Bass •adr

GULLIN, Peter - *Tre suma julsagor* (1988) •Bsx/2 Vln/Vla/Vcl/Bass

HAAS, Konrad - *Steinwolke* (1983) (45') •Voice/Sx/Perc/Pno/Guit/
Bass •Holz

HERMANSSON, Christer - *Aggjakten* (1979) •Narr/Tsx/Trb/Guit/
Bass/Perc •STIM

HODEIR, André - *Cadenze* (4') •Bsx/Tpt/Trb/Pno/Bass/Perc •MJQ
Oblique (3'30) •2 Sx: AT/Trb/Pno/Bass/Perc •MJQ
Osymetrios (3') •Tpt/Tsx/Trb/Pno/Bass/Drums •MJQ
Trope à St-Trop •Tpt/Tsx/Trb/Pno/Bass/Drums •MJQ

KÖPER, Heinz-Karl - *Musik...* •Fl/Cl/Asx/Tpt/Trb/Bass •EMBA

KUPFERMAN, Meyer - *Jazz Cello Concerto* (1962) (25') •Vcl/3 Sx/
Bass/Perc •GMP

LEWIS, John A. - *Pieces* •Tsx/Tpt/Trb/Pno/Bass/Perc •MJQ

MAXFIELD, Richard - *Domenon* (1961) •Fl/Sx/Pno/Vibr/Vln/Bass/
Tape

MELLNÄS, Arne - *Per caso* (1963) (5'30) •Asx/Trb/Vln/Bass/2 Perc
•SeMC

MIEREANU, Costin - *Miroir liquide* (1986) (11') •1 Sx: Sno+S+A+T/
Bsn/Perc/Harp/Pno/Bass •Sal

ÖHLUND, Ulf - *Simplicity musik* (1983) (10') •4 Perc/Ssx/Bass
•STIM

OLIVEIRA, Willy Corrêa de - *Sugestoes* (1971) •Ob/Asx/Bandoneon/
Tuba/Bass/Perc

PAICH, Marty - *Toccata in F* •4 Sx: SATB/Bass/Perc •Eto

Rodgers - *Dancing on the Ceiling* •4 Sx: SATB/Bass/Drums •DP

RODRIGUEZ-PICO, Jesùs - *Sextet* (1992) •Fl/2 Cl/2 Sx: AT/Bass

SCELSI, Jacinto - *Yamaon* (1954-58) (10') •Bass Voice/2 Sx: AB/
CBsn/Bass/Perc •Sal

TAGGART, Mark - *Concerto for Chamber Ensemble* (1983) (20')
•Cl/Asx/Bsn/Tpt/Bass/Pno

7 Musicians

BENNETT, Richard Rodney - *Soliloquy* (1966) (14') •Voice/1 Sx:
A+T/Tpt/Tuba/Pno/Bass/Perc •Uni

BJORKLUND, Terje - *Herbarium* (1982) •Fl/Ssx/Vln/Hn/Bass/Pno/
Perc •NMI

BYTZEK, Peter - *Gefühle auf dem Eis* (1985) (3'45) •2 Voice/Guit/
Pno/Sx/Perc/Bass •adr

CRAS, Jean - *Demain* (1929) •Asx/Tpt/Trb/Perc/Vln/Vcl/Bass •Sen

DANCEANU, Liviu - *Quasi concerto* (1983) (15') •1 Sx: S+T/Bsn/
Trb/Vcl/Bass/Pno/Perc

DONATONI, Franco - *Hot* (1989) (14') •1 Sx: T+Sno/Cl+Eb Cl/Tpt/
Trb/Perc/Bass/Pno •Ric

ESCOT, Pozzi - *Visione* (1964-87) •Fl/Asx/Vibr/Soprano Voice/
Bass/Perc/Narr

FINNISSY, Michael - *Evening* (1974) •Asx/Hn/Tpt/Perc/Harp/Vcl/
Bass

GIUFFRE, James - *Fine* •Tsx/Guit/Vibr/Pno/2 Bass/Perc •MJQ

HAAS, Konrad - *Pieces* •Voice/Fl/Sx/Pno/Perc/Guit/Bass •Holz

HARTWELL, Hugh - *Soul Piece* (1967) •2 Sx: AT/Tpt/2 Pno/Bass/
Perc •CMC

HERMANSSON, Christer - *Rumba* (1979) •Narr/2 Sx: ST/Trb/Guit/
Pno/Bass •STIM

HESPOS, Hans - *Passagen* (1969) (9') •Cl/Asx/Tpt/Trb/Vla/Bass/
Perc •EMod

HILLBORG, Anders - *Variations* (1991) •Soprano Voice/Mezzo
Soprano Voice/Fl/Sx/Perc/Vla/Bass •SMIC

HODKINSON, Sidney - *Funks* (1969) (5') •4 Sx: AATB/Guit/Bass/
Perc •adr

KLEIN, Jonathan - *Hear O Israel* •Soprano Voice/Alto Voice/Sx/Hn/
Pno/Perc/Bass •SeMC

KOBLENZ, Babette - *Grey Fire* (1981) •Cl/2 Sx: AT/Tpt/Electr. Bass/
Electr. Pno/Perc •adr

LARSSON, Häkan - *Farleder - 4 pieces* (1993) •Fl/Tsx/Trb/Electr.
Guit/Electr. Bass/Pno/Perc •SvM

LONGY, George - *Rhapsodie - Lento* (1904) •Harp/Bass/2 Cl/Bsn/
Asx/Timp •South

LUDWIG, J. - *Stenogramme* •Fl/Tsx/Trb/Bass/Vibr/Harps/Perc •EMod

MAJOS, Giulio di - *Passacaglia* •Fl/Asx/Hn/Guit/Vibr/Pno/Bass
•Sch

MIEREANU, Costin - *Polymorphies 5 X 7 B* (1969-70) (9-10')
•Fl+Picc/Cl+Tsx/Pno/Vln/Vla/Vcl/Bass •Sal

MILHAUD, Darius - *La Création du monde* (LONDEIX) •2 Vln/Asx/
Vcl/Bass/Perc/Pno •ME

NEMESCU, Octavian - *Septuor* (1983) •Fl/Cl/Trb/Tsx/Pno/Bass/
Perc

PINOS-SIMANDL, Aloïs - *Euforie* (1983) (10') •Ob (or Fl)/Asx/Cl/
BsCl/Pno/Perc/Bass •CHF

RADULESCU, Horatiu - *X* (1984-85) •Sx/Cl/2 Bsn/2 Bass/Perc

ROLIN, Etienne - *Quètes ancestrales* (1989) (14') •Tsx/Vla/2 Vcl/
Bass/Harp/Marimba •Fuz

ROSSÉ, François - *OEM* (1988) (21') •Soprano Voice/1 Sx: S+Bs/
EH/Accordion/Bass/Jazz Guit/Pno/Disposi-
tif électro-acoust. •adr

SCHWERTSIK, Kurt - *Liebesträume, op. 7* (1963) •Asx/Trb/Pno/
Vibr/Marimba/Harmonium/Bass •EMod

SOLAL, Martial - *Triptyque* (1989) (55') •4Sx: SATB/Pno/Bass/Perc

SOTELO, Mauricio - *Quando il cielo...* (1989) (18') •Asx/Perc/Pno/
Vln/Vla/Vcl/Bass •ECA

IX +... - de substantiis separatis (1990) •Cl/Sx/Tuba/Vln/Vcl/
Bass/Pno/Schtagzeng with live electronics
•adr

STEARNS, Peter - *Septet* (1959) •Cl/Tsx/Hn/Vln/Vla/Vcl/Bass •Pio/
ACA

STEVEN, Donald - *On the down side* (1982) •2 Sx: AB/Trb/2 Perc/
Pno/Electr. Bass •CMC

VOUILLEMIN, Sylvain - *Divertimento...* (1983) (8'30) •Ssx/2 Vln/
Vla/Vcl/Bass/Perc or Ssx/Pno •Led

WILLIAMSON, Malcolm - *Merry Wives of Windsor* (1964) •Fl+Picc/
Cl/Tsx/Tpt/Perc/Bass/Pno •JW

8 Musicians

ARMSTRONG, David - *The Protest* (1960) (9'30) •Cl/Trb/2 Asx/Tpt/ Perc/Pno/Bass •BMIC

AYOUB, Nick - *Saxtet* •6 Sx: SAATTB/Bass/Drums •DP

BABBITT, Milton - *All Set* (1957) •2 Sx: AT/Tpt/Trb/Vibr/Bass/Perc/ Pno •adr

BARK, Jan - *Ost-funk* (1964) (10') •Tpt/Asx/3 Perc/Pno/2 Bass •SMIC

BLATNY, Pavel - *D-E-F-G-A-H-C* •Fl/3 Sx: ATB/Pno/Bass/Tpt/Trb •CMIC

BULOW, Harry - *Crystal Cove* •Tpt/3 Sx: AAT/Pno/Bass/Guit/ Drums •adr

CARL, Gene - *Gray Matter* (1983) (23') •2 Sx: AA/2 Pno/2 Bass Guit/ 2 Trb •Don

DELAMARRE, Pierre - *La 8* (1981) (3') •Fl/Ob/Cl/Asx/Pno 4 hands [à 4 mains]/Bass/Perc •adr

ERNRYD, Bengt - *Rödingsjön II* (1967) •Fl+Picc/Trb/Tsx+Perc/ Bsx+Perc/Vcl/Bass/2 Perc •SMIC

FABERMAN, Harold - *For Erik and Nick* (1964) •Tenor Voice/Asx/ Vcl/Bass/Tpt/Trb/Vibr/Perc

FONTYN, Jacqueline - *Cheminement* (1986) (15') •Soprano Voice/ Fl/Cl/Hn (or Asx)/Vcl/Bass/Perc/Pno

GARCIN, Gérard - *Encore plus tard* (1984) (12') •1 Sx: Sno+A+Bs/ Fl/Cl/Bsn/Vla/Vcl/Bass/Perc/Tape •Sal

GUY, Georges - *Concerto en forme de jazz* •Asx Solo/Pno Solo/Fl/Ob/ Cl/Hn/Bsn/Bass

HARBISON, John - *The Flower-fed Buffaloes* (1976) •Voice/Cl/Tsx/ Fl/Vcl/Bass/Pno/Perc

HESPOS, Hans - *Druckspuren - geschattet* (1970) (7'30) •Fl/Eb Cl/ Asx/Bsn/2 Tpt/Trb/Bass •EMod

HODEIR, André - *Ambiguité II* (8'); *Bicinium* (3') •3 Sx: ATB/2 Tpt/ Trb/Bass/Perc •MJQ

HOUNSELL - *Showcase for Saxes* •5 Sx/Pno/Bass/Perc •TMPI

LAURETTE, Marc - *Kaleïdoscope* •Cl/Bsn/2 Sx: SB/Hn/Vla/Bass/ Vibr

MARIETAN, Pierre - *13 en concert* (1983) (15') •1 Sx: Sno+S+B/Cl/ Bsn/Trb/Vcl/2 Bass/Pno

NAULAIS, Jérôme - *Mise à sax* •5 Sx: SATTB/Pno/Bass/Drums •Arp

NICKLAUS, Wolfgang - *Die Antwort* (1986) (7'30) •Cl/Asx/2 Perc/ Pno/Vln/Vcl/Bass •adr

RADULESCU, Horatiu - *Sky* (1984-85) •Sx/Cl/Fl/2 Bsn/2 Bass/Perc

RIEDEL, Georg - *Reflexioner* (1974) (8') •Woodwind Quintet/Jazz group (Cl+Asx/Pno/Bass) •SMIC

SAGVIK, Stellan - *Suite circuler*, op. 86 (1978) (10') •Picc/Asx/Tpt/ Hn/2 Trb/Perc/Bass •STIM

SCOTT, Andy - *Pieces* •5 Sx: AATTB or SATTB/Pno/Bass/Drums •PBP

SEFFER, Yochk'o - *Alpha-gamma* (1990) •Tsx improvised/5 Sx:SnoSATB/Bass/Perc

Dépression (1985) •Tsx improvised/4 Sx: SATB/BsCl/Bass/Perc

SOTELO, Mauricio - *IX +...* (1990) •Cl/Sx/Tuba/Vln/Vcl/Bass/Pno/ Schtagzeng with live electronics •adr

SPAHLINGER, Mathias - *Aussageverweigerung-Gegendarstellung* •Cl/Bsx/Bass/Pno/BsCl/Tsx/Vcl/Pno •Peer

SUTER, Robert - *Estampida* •Fl/Cl/Tsx/Hn/Tpt/Trb/Bass/Perc •EMod

TANENNBAUM, Elias - *Consort* •Fl/Hn/Asx/Electr. Guit/Vcl/Bass/ Vibr/Jazz drums •ACA

VELLONES, Pierre - *A Cadix*, op. 102 (1938) (4') •3 Sx/2 Ondes Martenot/Bass/Harp/Perc

Cinq poèmes de Mallarmé, op. 24 (1929) (28') •High Voice/4 Harp/ 2 Sx: AT/Bass •Lem

WOOLLETT, Henri - *Octuor n° 1* (1911) •Ob/Cl/Asx/2 Vln/Vla/Vcl/ Bass •South

9 Musicians

BORTOLOTTI, Mauro - *Studio per E.E. Cummings n° 2* (1964) •Vla/ Vcl/Bass/Ob/Cl/BsCl/Sx/Hn/Perc •adr

CAPLET, André - *Légende* (1903) (13') •Asx/Ob/Cl/Bsn/2 Vln/Vla/ Vcl/Bass •Fuz

CERHA, Friedrich - *Exercices for Nine, No. 1* •BsCl/Bsx/Bsn/Tpt/ Trb/Tuba/Vcl/Bass/Harp •Uni

CLARK, Thomas - *Dreamscape* •Fl/Ob/Cl/Sx/Tpt/Trb/Pno/Perc/ Bass •SeMC

COX, Rona - *Two Expressions* (1968) •Fl/Ob/Cl/2 Sx: SB/Hn/Bsn/ Bass/Perc •adr

CUSTER, Arthur - *Cycle for Nine Instruments* •Asx/BsCl/Tpt/Hn/ Vln/Vla/Vcl/Bass/Perc •JM

DANKWORTH, John - *Fairoak Fusion* (1979) (45') •4 Sx: SATB/ Vln/Jazz Quartet

GRAINGER, Ella - *To Echo* (1945) •Soprano Voice/Picc/Fl/Cl+Asx/ Tsx/Vla/BsCl/Bass/Marimba •GS

HAHN, Reynaldo - *Divertissement...* (1933) (25') •2 Vln/Vla/Vcl/ Bass/Asx/Bsn/Timp/Perc •Sal

HODEIR, André - *Pieces* •3 Sx: ATB/2 Tpt/Trb/Vibr/Bass/Perc •MJQ

JELINEK, Hanns - *Blue Sketches*, op. 25 (1956) •Fl/Cl/2 Sx: AB/Tpt/ Trb/Vibr/Bass/Perc •EMod

LEGRAND, Michel - *Porcelaine de Sax* (1958) (3') •6 Sx: SnoSATBBs (or Eb Cl/Cl/3 Sx: ATB/Bsn) Trb/Bass/Perc •Mills

LEWIS, John Aaron - *Little David's Fugue* (5'30) •Fl/Cl/3 Sx: ATB/ Trb or Tpt/Harp or Pno/Bass/Perc •MJQ

The Queen's Fancy (4') •Fl/Cl/Tsx/Bsn/Hn/Trb/Harp/Bass/Perc •MJQ

Sun Dance (4') •Fl/Cl/3 Sx: ATB/Trb/Harp or Guit/Bass/Perc •MJQ

MANOURY, Philippe - *Etude automatique 1* •Fl/Tpt/Sx/Tuba/Harp/ Vln/Vla/Vcl/Bass

McFARLAND, Gary - *Night Float* (4'30) •3 Sx: ATB/Tpt/Hn/Guit/ Pno/Bass/Drums •MJQ

MELLNÄS, Arne - *Drones* (1967) (8') •Fl/Cl/3 Sx: ATB/Tpt/Perc/ Vcl/Bass •STIM

RENOSTO, Paolo - *Dissolution* •Vla/Vcl/Bass/Ob/Cl/BsCl/Sx/Hn/ Perc

SCELSI, Jacinto - *Kya* (1959) (11') •Cl (or Ssx)/EH/Hn/BsCl/Tpt/ Trb/Vla/Vcl/Bass •Sal

SCHULLER, Gunther - *Abstraction* (1959) (5') •Asx/Guit/Perc/2 Vln/Vla/Vcl/2 Bass •MJQ

SCHWANTNER, Joseph - *Diaphona intervallum* (1966) (12') •Asx/ Pno/Fl/2 Vln/Vla/2 Vcl/Bass •ACA

SILVERMAN, Faye - *Shadings* (1978) •Vln/Vla/Bass/Fl/Ob/Asx/ Bsn/Hn/Tuba

SÖDERLIND, Ragnar - *Eg hev funne...* (1982) (9'); *Legg ikkje ditt...* (1983) •Soprano Voice/Fl+Picc/Ssx/Hn/Vln/ Vla/Bass/Pno/Perc •NMI

SVOBODA, Tomàs - *Seven Short Dances* •Fl/2 Cl/Asx/Trb/Vln/Bass/ Pno/Perc

TANENBAUM, Elias - *Trios I, II, III* •Fl/Ob/Cl/Vln/Vla/Vcl/Bass/ Asx/Perc •ACA

TARENSKEEN, Boudewijn - *Nonet* (1982) (13') •Asx/Hn/BsCl/ Accordion/Banjo/Harp/Vla/Vcl/Bass •Don

VELLONES, Pierre - *Planisphère*, op. 23 (1930) •2 Sx: AT/Cl/2 Tpt/ Trb/Bass (or Tuba)/Perc/Pno •JJ

WILDER, Alec - *Suite* •Bsx/Fl/Ob/Cl/2 Hn/Bsn/Bass/Drums

10 Musicians

ANDRIESSEN, Louis - *On Jimmy Yancey* (1973) (10') •Fl/2 Sx: AT/ Hn/Tpt/3 Trb/Bass/Pno •Don

BENNETT, Richard Rodney - *Jazz Pastorale* (1969) (25') •Voice/1
Sx: A+T/Bsx/2 Tpt/Trb/Tuba/Pno/Bass/Perc
•Uni

COE, Tony - *The Buds of Time* (1979) (20') •Cl+Sx/Cl+BsCl/2 Vln/
Vla/Vcl/BsTrb/Pno/Bass/Perc •adr

COPPOOLSE, David - *Canto XVII* (1984) (12') •Asx/2 Hn/2 Trb/Vln/
Vla/Vcl/Bass/Pno •Don

COSTEN, Roel van - *Prisma* (1984) (8') •Vla/Fl/Cl/Asx/BsCl/Trb/
Vcl/Bass/Perc/Pno •Don

CUNNINGHAM, Michael - *Spring Sonnet* •Fl/2 Cl/BsCl/2 Sx/3 Hn/
Bass •SeMC

FORTNER, Jack - *S pr ING sur des poèmes de E. E. Cummings* (1966)
(11') •Mezzo Soprano Voice/Fl/Asx/Bsn/
Vla/Vcl/Bass/Vibr/Harp/Pno •JJ

GOUGEON, Denis - *Heureux qui comme...* (1987) •Soprano Voice/
Picc/EH/Bsx/2 Vln/Vla/Vcl/Bass/Perc
•CMC

GRAHN, Ulf - *Soundscape II* (1974) (7') •Fl/Cl/EH/Asx/2 Trb/2 Vln/
Vcl/Bass •SMIC

GRANDIS, Renato de - *Scotter Sud-est* •Vln/Vla/Vcl/Bass/Sx/Hn/
Tpt/Trb/Pno/Perc •SeMC

HEIDEN, Bernhard - *Sonatina* •Fl/Cl/Tsx/Hn/Trb/Harp/Vibr/Pno/
Bass/Perc •MJQ

HODEIR, André - *Jazz cantata* (10') •Soprano Voice/3 Sx: ATB/2
Tpt/Trb/Vibr/Bass/Perc •MJQ

HORWOOD, Michael - *Facets* (1974) (20') •Narr/Sx/Tpt/Hn/Trb/
Pno/Accordion/Electr. Bass/2 Electr. Guit
•CMC

JOHNSON, J. J. - *Turnpike* (5') •Fl/Cl/3 Sx: ATB/Trb/Harp (or Guit)/
Pno/Bass/Perc •MJQ

LAZARUS, Daniel - *4 Mélodies* •Contralto Voice/Fl/Cl/Asx/Bsn/2
Vln/Vla/Vcl/Bass

Lecuona, Ernesto - *Andalucia* •2 Tpt/Trb/3Sx: AAT/2 Vln/Vcl/Bass

LEWIS, John Aaron - *The Milanese Story* •Fl/Tsx/Guit/Pno/Bass/2
Vln/Vla/Vcl/Perc •MJQ

LINDBERG, Nils - *Progression* (1985) (28') •Fl/Ob/Cl/Hn/Bsn/2 Sx:
SA/Pno/Bass/Drums •SMIC

MASON, Benedict - *Coulour and information* (1993) •Fl/Ob/Sx/Bsn/
Hn/Tpt/Trb/Tuba/Perc/Electr. Bass

SCHULLER, Gunther - *12 by 11* (8'30) •Fl/Cl/Tsx/Hn/Trb/Vibr/Pno/
Harp/Bass/Perc •MJQ

SCHWERTSIK, Kurt - *Salotto romano*, op. 5 (1961) •BsCl/Bsx/Bsn/
Hn/Trb/Tuba/Perc/Bass/Vcl/Guit •EMod

SMITH, Linda - *Periphery* (1979) •Fl/Sx/Tpt/Marimba/Vibr/Chimes/
Pno/Vln/Vcl/Bass •CMC

SMITH, William - *Elegy for Eric* •Fl/2 Sx: AB/Cl/Tpt/Trb/Vibr/Vln/
Bass/Perc •MJQ

VELLONES, Pierre - *Deux Pièces...*, op. 67 (1935) (6'30) •2 Fl/4 Sx/
Pno/Bass/Perc/Ondes Martenot •Sal

WILDER, Alec - *She'll Be Seven in May* •Fl/Ob/Asx/2 Cl/BsCl/Bsn/
Bass/Drums/Pno

11 Musicians

BORSTLAP, Dick - *Fanfare II* (1975) (6'); *Over de verandering...*
(1974) (5') •Fl/Picc/2 Sx: AT/Hn/Tpt/2 Trb/
BsTrb/Pno/Bass •Don

DIEMENTE, Edward - *3-31 '70* •Voice/Tpt/Trb/Sx/Guit/Bass/5 Perc
•SeMC

HESPOS, Hans - *Break* •Ob/3 Tpt/2 Sx: TB/Vcl/Bass/Trb/Pno/Perc
•EMod

MARTIRANO, Salvatore - *Underworld* (1959) •4 Actors/Tsx/4 Perc/
2 Bass/2 Track tape

MESTRAL, Patrice - *Alliages* (1969) •Tpt Solo/Fl/Cl/Asx/2 Trb/2
Perc/Pno/Org/Bass

PÜTZ, Eduard - *Kon-Takte* •Vocal Quartet (SATB)/Fl/Sx/Vibr/Guit/
Perc/Pno/Bass •SeMC

SCHILLING, Otto-Erich - *Überall ist Wunderland* •Voice/Fl/Cl/Sx/
Tpt/2 Vln/Bass/Perc/Accordion/Pno •SeMC

TARENSKEEN, Boudewijn - *Marchtelt suite* (1978) (30') •4 Sx:
AATT/Hn/2 Tpt/3 Trb/Bass •Don

TRIMBLE, Lester - *Panels I* (1973) (6') •Picc/Bsx/Vln/Vla/Vcl/Bass/
2 Perc/Electr. Guit/Electr. Org/Electr. Harp
•Pet

ZONN, Paul Martin - *Voyage of Columbus* (1974) (13') •Tpt Solo/Fl/
Ob/Ssx/Hrn/Trb/2 Perc/Pno/Vln/Bass •ACA

12 Musicians

CURTIS-SMITH, Curtis - *Sundry Dances* (1981) •Fl/Ob/Cl/3 Sx:
SAB/Bsn/CBsn/Tpt/Trb/Tuba/Bass •adr

DUREY, Louis - *Feu la mère de Madame*, op. 49 (1945) (5') •Fl/Ob/
Asx/Bsn/Tpt/Tuba/Perc/2 Vln/Vla/Vcl/Bass
•BRF

HASQUENOPH, Pierre - *Inventions* •2 Vln/Vla/Vcl/Bass/Fl/Ob/Cl/
Asx/Bsn/Hn/Tpt •Heu

LINKOLA, Jukka - *Alta* (1983) (8') •Vocal group: SATBs/2 Sx: AT/
Tpt/Trb/Pno/Bass/Drums/Perc •FMIC

REA, John - *Treppenmusik* (1982) •4 Sx: SATB/4 Cl/Vln/Vla/Vcl/
Bass •CMC

RECK, David - *Number 1 for 12 Performers* (15') •Fl/Cl/Tsx/Hn/Guit/
Vibr/Pno/Bass/Perc •MJQ

ROBBINS, David - *Improvisation* •Fl/2 Cl/Tsx/Bsn/Tpt/Trb/Vln/Vla/
Vcl/Bass/Perc

TORSTENSSON, Klas - *Spâra* (1984) (13') •3 Sx/3 Bs Guit/2 Electr.
Pno/4 Perc •Don

13 Musicians

DELANNOY, Marcel - *Le Marchand de notes* •3 Vln/Bass/4 Sx/2 Tpt/
Trb/Perc/Pno

EICHMANN, Dietrich - *George...* (1984) (35') •3 Fl/Cl/2 Sx: AT/2
Tpt/Trb/2 Perc/Pno/Bs Guit •adr

FINNISSY, Michael - *Babylon* (1971) (19') •Mezzo Soprano Voice/
Ob/Cl/Asx/Bsn/Guit/Harp/Pno/2 Perc/2 Vcl/
Bass •Uni

HESPOS, Hans - *Conga* (1979) (15'30) •Tsx/5 Congas/2 Vln/2 Vla/
2 Vcl/Bass •Hes

Keime und male (9') •Picc/Fl/2 Cl/Asx/Hn/Guit/Vln/Vla/Bass/3
Perc •JJ

HUREL, Philippe - *"Pour l'image"* •Fl/Ob/Cl/Asx/Hn/Tpt/Trb/Perc/
2 Vln/Vla/Vcl/Bass

MEULEN, Henk van der - *De profondis I* (1986) (15') •Fl/3 Sx: S+T
A A/Hn/3 Tpt/2 Trb/BsTrb/Bass/Pno •Don

WENDEL, Eugen - *Saphonospir* (15') •Asx/Fl/Cl/Ob/Tpt/Trb/2 Vln/
Vla/Vcl/Bass/2 Perc •adr

14 Musicians

GRAINGER, Percy - *The Duke of Marlborough* (1905-39-49) •4 Tpt/
4 Hn (or 2 Sx: AT/2 Bsn)/3 Trb/Tuba/Bass/
Cymb. •Sch

HARBISON, John - *Confinement* (1965) (15'15) •Fl/Ob/EH/Cl/BsCl/
Asx/Tpt/Trb/Vln/Vla/Vcl/Bass/Pno/Perc

ROSSÉ, François - *Paléochrome* (1988) (22') •Vla principal/2 Fl/Cl/
BsCl/1 Sx: S+T/EH/Bsn/Hn/4 Perc/Bass •adr

RUBBERT, Rainer - *Kammerkonzert* (1990) •4 Sx: SATB/4 Vln/2
Vla/2 Vcl/Bass/Pno •adr

15 Musicians

TEMPLE & SHAW - *Vanity Fair Suite* •Fl/Ob/4 Cl/BsCl/Asx/2 Vln/
Vla/Vcl/Bass/Perc/Pno •Mills

oOo

ALLA, Thierry - *La terre et la Comète* (1991) •Fl/Cl/Asx/Pno/Bass/ Synth/Perc/Tape/Children's Choir •adr

BANK, Jacques - *Requiem voor een Levende* (1985) (50') •Récit. Choeur/4 Sx/9 Accordion/3 Bass/3 Perc •Don

DAKIN, Charles - *Syra* (1979) (8'30) •2 Cl/2 Tsx/2 Tpt/2 Trb/4 Vla/ 4 Vcl/2 Bass

FISCHER, Eric - *Spleen...* (1984) •Jazz Group including [dont] 4 Sx: SATB/Electr. Bass/Perc •adr

LUEDEKE, Raymond - *"Of him I love day and night"* & *"A noiseless, patient spider"* •Chorus (SATB)/4 Sx: SATB/Bass/2 Perc

Saxophone and String Quartet

Alto saxophone unless otherwise indicated (Saxo-phone-alto, sauf indication contraire).

BENSON, Warren - *The Dream Net* (1972) •Bel
   Quintette •Ssx •adr

BOTTJE, Will Gay - *Concertino* (1958) (13') •Pio

BOURLAND, Roger - *Quintet* (1985) (15') •Ssx •ECS

BOUVARD, Jean - *Petit concerto* (1984) •Mar

BUSCH, Adolph - *Quintett*, op. 24 (1927-28) •HD/Tong
   Quintette Es-Dur, op.34 (1925) (20'15) •PJT

CANGINI, Giuseppe - *Spiandoti e ciecamente...!!* (1992)

CHAGRIN, Francis - *4 Lyric Interludes* (1963) (5') •Any solo instrument •Nov

CHERNEY, Brian - *Quintet* (1962) (20') •CMC

COWELL, Henry - *Chrysanthemus* (1937) •Soprano Voice/2 Sx

COWLES, Colin - *Concertante* (1973) •4 Sx: SATB •adr
   Sarabande, Ben ritmico... (1975) (8') •1 Sx: S+A+T+B • adr

DEAK, Csaba - *Quintet* (1989) (15') •SUE

DEGASTYNE, Serge - *Suite rhétaise*, op. 26 (1961) •FP/SMC

FRIED, Alexej - *Guernica* (1978) (15') •Ssx •CHF

GROSS, Eric - *Quintet*, op. 102 (1977) •Lee

HARRIS, Arthur - *Quintette*

HARTLEY, Walter - *Rhapsody* (1979) (6'15) •Tsx/Str Quartet or Str Orch •DP

HAUBIEL, Charles - *Suite Concertante* (1975) (22') •TCP

HILDEMANN, Wolfgang - *Farben und Klänge* (1982) •adr

KARLINS, M. William - *Music* (1969) (13') •Tsx •South
   Quintet (1973-74) (15') •SeMC

KIANOVSKY, Raphael - *Quintet* (1972)

KIRSCHENMANN, Mark - *Paradigm Shift* (1993) •Ssx •INM

LEMELAND, Aubert - *Quintette*, op. 37 (1978) (15'30) •adr

MASLANKA, David - *Heaven to clear when day did close* •Tsx

MORITZ, Edvard - *Quintette*, op. 99 (1940) •South

MÜLLER, Gottfried - *Fantasie* •adr

NAKAMURA, Koya - *Hida* (1980)

NUIX, Jep - *Pièce* (1992) (10')

PATCH, Marc - *Magic spell* (1992) •1 Sx: A+S

PÜTZ, Eduard - *Blues* •adr
   Cries in the dark (1993) •Tong

RAHN, John - *Games* (1969) (8') •adr

ROBERT, Lucie - *Quintette* (1960) (19') •Bil

ROSEN, Robert - *Three Miniatures* •2 Sx: SA •CMC

SAGVIK, Stellan - *Lamento, marsch & scherzo*, op. 115 (1982) (11'30) •Ssx •STIM

SAHL, Michael - *Storms* (1985) •4 Sx: SATB

SAPIEYEVSKI, Jerzy - *Air* (1974) (10')

SMITH, Howie - *Passages* (1981) •Oa

SNYDER, Randall - *Quintet* (1972) •DP

STALLAERT, Alphonse - *Quintette* (1960) (19') •Bil

STEIN, Leon - *Quintet* (1956) (25') •CFE/CP

TREBINSKY, Arkadi - *Double quatuor* (1977) •4 Sx: SATB •adr

VAN VACTOR, David - *Andante and Allegro* (1972)

VIGELAND, Nils - *Classical music* (1986) •4 Sx: SATB

Saxophone and Percussion

2 Musicians

AATZ, Michel - *Engrenages* (6') •Sx/Mallet Perc [Claviers]

AKI, Touru - *Réla* •Ssx/Perc

ALKEMA, Henk - *Just music* (1986) (12') •Sx/Marimba •Don

AMEELE - *Sound poem* •Sx/Perc

AMON, Klemens - *Sax with Mr. X* (1993) •Asx/Perc •INM

ARMA, Paul - *Résonnance* (1973) (16') •Ssx/Perc •DP

ATOR, James Donald - *Enuffispluntee* (1972) (9') •Asx/Perc •SeMC

AUSTIN, John - *Farewell Music...* (1985) •Asx/Perc •DP

    In Memoriam (1979) •Asx/Timp

BABCOCK, David - *Fenêtres prismatiques*, op. 8 (1982) •Sx+BsCl/Marimba+Vibr

BARDEZ, Jean-Michel - *Saxyphrage* (1984) (1'45) •Asx/Xylophone

BARGIELSKI, Zbigniew - *Ikar* (1981) •Sx+BsCl/Marimba+Vibr

BAXTER, L. - *Nocturne* (5'30) •Sx/Vibr

BERGMAN, Erik - *Solfatara*, op. 81 (1977) (15') •Asx/Perc •Pa/FMIC

BERNARD, Jacques - *Climats* (1975) •Asx/Perc •adr

BESTOR, Charles - *Suite* (1982) •Asx/Perc •DP

BLEUSE, Marc - *Proper* (1980) •Asx/Perc

BLOCH, Augustin - *A Due* (1984) (7'30) •Asx/BsCl/Vibr/Marimba •PNS

BLUMENTHALER, Volker - *Tez Thelon...* (1993) •Asx/Vibr •INM

BORSODY, Làszlo - *Duo* (1983) •Asx/Vibr

BRIGGS, Thomas - *Festival* •Ssx/Marimba •DP

    Montage •Asx/Vibr •DP

BRIZZI, Aldo - *Mi ha sefer* (12') •Sx/Perc •Sal

CADEE, J. L. - *Suite* (1986) (6'30) •Ssx/Perc •SL

CAMPANA, José Luis - *Du sonore* (1986) (7') •Asx/Perc •Lem

CARLOSEMA, Bernard - *Zeugma* (1986) (3'10) •Asx (or Tsx)/Perc •Fuz

CASTEREDE, Jacques - *Libre parcours* (1984) •Sx/Perc •Led

CHATMAN, Stephen - *O lo velo!* (1973) (9') •Asx/Perc •Eto

    Quiet Exchange (1976) •Asx/Cymbals •DP

CIBULKA, Franz - *Garuda...* (1991) (6') •Asx/Org+Marimba

COLARDO, Giuseppe - *Divertimento* (1983) •Sx+Cl/Marimba+Vibr

CONSTANTINIDES, Dinos - *Legend* (1988) (11') •Asx/Perc

Corea, Chick - *Crystal Silence* •Asx/Perc

CORNU, Françoise - *Sentiers* (1988) (2'15) •Asx/Perc •Lem

COYNER, Lou - *Music-Piva* •Asx/Perc/Tape

CULBERTSON, D. C. - *Dream Music I* (1979) •Sx/Vibr

DEPELSENAIRE, Jean-Marie - *Petit rituel occidental* (1974) (2'30) •Asx/Perc

    Vers la lumière (1979) (5') •1 Sx: S+A+T+B/Perc

DESPORTES, Yvonne - *Per sa pia* (1978) •Sx/Perc •adr

    Un choix difficile (17') •Asx/Marimba+Vibr •DP

DIEDERICHS, Yann - *Pentes* (1985/88) (12'30) •Ssx/Perc

    SPC 834 (1984) (5') •Bsx/Perc

DOBROWOLSKI, Andrzej - *Passacaglia* (1988) (16') •Tsx/Perc

DUBOIS, Pierre-Max - *Circus parade* (1965) (15') •Asx/Perc •Led

ELLIS, Merrill - *Dream Fantasy* (1974) •Asx+Cl/Prepared Tape/Perc/Visuals •CF

ELOY, Christian - *Deux Pièces* •Asx/Perc •Lem

ENGEBRETSON, Mark - *For Anders* (1991) (9') •Asx/Perc •adr

ENGELMANN, Hans - *Interlineas*, op. 50b (1985) (16') •Sx/Perc •Br&Ha

EYSER, Eberhard - *Aubade* (1981) (4'30) •Asx/Vibr •STIM

    Dosonat (1986) •Tsx/Marimba •EMa

    Nocturne (1981) (6') •Asx/Vibr •STIM

    Notados (1993) •Tsx/Marimba •INM

FAITH, Walter - *Phantasies* (1966) •Asx/Perc

FEILER, Dror - *Too much too soon* •Asx/Perc/Tape •Tons

FLORIAN - *Pacific Poem...* (1983) •1 Sx: S+B/Perc/Tape

FONTAINE, Louis-Noël - *Folia* (1992) (12') •Asx/Perc •Capri

FONTYN, Jacqueline - *Controverse* (1983) (7') •Tsx/Perc •B&B

FORD, Andrew - *Boatsong* (1982) •Sx+BsCl/Marimba •Don

FORENBACH, Jean-Claude - *Week Chronicle* •Asx/Perc

FOURNIER, Marie-Hélène - *Deux Pièces...* (1987) •Asx/Perc •Lem

    Hippogriffe IV (1991) (11') •Sx/Perc/Tape

FRAZEUR, Theodore - *Frieze* (1972) •Tsx/Perc •adr

FREUDENTHAL, Otto - *Intermezzo & Scherzoso* (1992) •Asx/Perc •SMIC

FRID, Geza - *Vice versa*, op. 96 (1982) •Sx/Marimba •Don

GARCIA, Manuel - *Crucibus* (1984) •Asx/Perc

GARIN, Didier-Marc - *Aï fec* (1985) •1 Sx: Sno+S+B+Bs/Perc/Tape

GENZMER, Harald - *Konzertantes Duo* •Asx/Perc •R&E

GIEFER, Willy - *Saxopercumovi* (1993) •1 Sx: S+A+T/Perc •INM

GRAEF, Friedemann - *Duos* •Asx/Perc •adr

    Sonata urbanisata (1993) •1 Sx: T+S/Perc •INM

GRAINGER, Christian - *Introduction and Allegro* •Asx/Marimba

GRIFFITHS, James - *Dialogue on a Tone Row* (1969) (4') •Asx/Perc

GYSELYNCK, Jean - *Sorrow* •Asx/Vibr

HAASE, Milos - *Echoes* (1982) •Sx/Vibr

HALL, Neville - *For Two* (1990) •Tsx/Perc •adr

HARTLEY, Walter - *Cantelina* (1984) (2'40) •Asx/Marimba •Eth

HARTZELL, Eugene - *Monologue V* (1965) •1 Sx: A or T/Perc •AMP/VD

    Variants (1965) (7') •1 Sx: A or T/Perc •ECA

HARTZELL, L. - *Jefferson Variations* •Sx/Perc

HEINIO, Mikko - *"...in spe" - Diaphony* (1984) (8'30) •Asx/Marimba+Vibr •JO/FMIC

HEKSTER, Walter - *Setting VII* (1985) (9') •Bsx/Perc •Don

HELLER, Richard - *Dialog* •BsCl+Asx/Vibr+Marimba •adr

HELSIP, G. - *West 10th* •Sx/Perc

HEUSSENSTAM, George - *Duo*, op. 71 (1981) (11') •Asx/Perc •DP

    Duo, op. 89 (1988) •Sx/Perc •DP

    Playphony, op. 56 (1975) (12') •Asx/Perc •DP

HOLE, Rob - *Toby and Pooh Bear* (1993) •Tsx/Perc •INM

HORWOOD, Michael - *Microduet No. 6* (1978) (2'30) •Sx/Perc •CMC

HWANG, Serra - *Duet* (1989) (12') •Asx/Marimba •adr

IRIK, Mike - *Interaction III* (1983) •Sx+Cl/Marimba+Vibr

ISRAEL, Hovav - *No name for it...* (1985) •Asx/Perc •adr

JESTL, Bernhard - *Isaak* (1993) •1 Sx: S+A/Perc •INM

JU, Yong-Su - *Winterliche Impressionen* (1993) •Ssx/Vibr •INM

JUELICH, Raimund - *Amok* (1993) •Sx/Perc •INM

KALAF, Jerry - *3 Movements* (1979) •Asx/Perc

KANEKO, S. - *Damnoen sakuak floating market* (14') •Sx/Perc

KARKOFF, Ingvar - *2 Danses exotiques* (1990) •Asx/Perc •STIM

KARLINS, M. William - *Fantasia* (1978-79) (9'30) •Tsx/Perc •ACA/NP

KASPAR, Edward - *Abyss* (1971) (5') •Asx/Vibr •adr

KESSNER, Daniel - *Arabesque* (1983) •Sx/Vibr

KIRCK, George - *Song to Wind* (1971) (10') •Asx/Perc/Tape •adr

KNAKKERGARD, Martin - *Monrovida discount replacement* (1989) (15') •Tsx/Marimba

KOSUT, Michal - *Honeymoon* (1981) •Sx/Marimba+Vibr

KOVARIK, Jàn - *if (her Word = "Ay me!")* (1993) •Asx/Perc •INM

KRAFT, Leo - *Encounters IX* (1982) •Asx/Perc

KUPFERMAN, Meyer - *Sound Phantoms No. 7* (1980) •Ssx/Perc

LACERDA, Osvaldo - *Variacoes sobre...* (1979) •Sx/Marimba

LACOUR, Guy - *Divertissement* (1968) (13') •Asx/1 or 6 Perc •Bil

LAMB, John - *Three Antique Dances* (1961) •Asx/Perc

LARSSON, M. - *Whirls in crouching positions* (1990) •Sx/Marimba

LAUBA, Christian - *Dream in the bar* (1992) (14'30) •Bsx/Perc •Bil

    Parcours (1986) (2'30) •Asx/Perc •Bil

LEE, Chol-Woo - *Meditation II* (1993) •Tsx/Perc •INM

LEE, Thomas Oboe - *The MacGuffin* (10') •1 Sx: S+A/Perc •adr
LEJET, Edith - *Jade* (1981) (3'30) •Asx/Perc •Sal
LEMAY, Robert - *Les yeux de la...* (1987) (16') •Asx/Perc •CMC
LEMELAND, Aubert - *Walkings*, op. 105 (8'30) •Ssx/Vibr •Bil
LEWIS, J. - *Tampanera* (1976) •Sx/Perc
LOMBARDO, Robert - *Cantabile* (1980) •Asx/Vibr •adr
LUKAS, Zdenek - *2 + 2* (1982) (14') •Sx+BsCl/Marimba+Vibr
MARBE, Myriam - *Überzeitliches God* (1993) •Soprano Voice+Perc/
Ssx
MARIOTTI, Christian - *Resurgence* (1991) •Ssx/Vibr
MARTHINSEN, Niels - *Burst* (1990) •Asx/Perc
MATSUO, M. - *Phono* •Sx/Perc
MEIJERING, Chiel - *Frequente...* (1985) (9') •Sx/Marimba •Don
METRAL, Pierre - *Sonatine No. 2* (1976) •Asx/Perc •SeMC
MEUNIER, R. - *Metamorphosis* (1982) •Sx/Perc
MICHEL, Paul - *Masscom* (1983) •Sx/Vibr •adr
MIEREANU, Costin - *Boléro des Balkans* (1984) (13') •1 Sx:
CBs+Bs+T+S+Sno/Perc/Tape •Sal
Distance zero (1987) (10') •Cl+Asx/Perc •Sal
MILOVIC, Janko - *Metallochronie* (1980) •Asx/Perc
MORYL, Richard - *Sunday Morning* (1971) (12') •Asx/Perc/Tape
•CFE/ACA
MÖSS, Piotr - *Avant le départ* (1982) (10') •Ssx/Perc •Bil
MYERS, Robert - *Fantasy Duos* (1968) •Asx/Perc •Art
NAKAMURA, Hitoshi - *Gradation* (1993) •Tsx/Perc •INM
NAKAZAWA, Michiko - *Amber* •Asx/Marimba
NICHIFOR, Serban - *Chimaera* (1993) (18') •Asx/Vibr •INM
NICOLAU, Dimitri - *Strassemusik n° 8* (1989) •1 Sx: A+T+S/Perc
NIEDER, Fabio - *Lega* (1983) •Sx/Marimba
NIELSON, Lewis - *Ain't Misbehavin'* (1980) (9') •Ssx/Perc •ACA
NILOVIC, J. - *Métallochromie* (1986) (6'40) •Asx/Perc •SL
NOMURA, Mikiko - *In the rain* (1993) •Tsx/Marimba
NORGÂRD, Per - *Protens* (1983) •Sx/Perc
OCKENFELS, Helmut - *Opusculum* (1980) •Tsx/Perc
OLAH, Tiberiu - *Concerto notturno* (1983) •Sx+BsCl/Marimba+Vibr
PALMER, Glenn - *1990 Ballroom Blitz* (1990) (10') •Asx/Perc •Ron
PARKS, Ron - *Increments* (1993) •Asx/Perc/Tape
PENHERSKI, Zbigniew - *Jeux parties* (1984) (11') •Asx/Perc •CPM
PERRIER, Alain - *Otinavari* •Asx/Perc
PERRON, Alain - *Cycle 1* (1992) (8') •1 Sx: S+A+T+B/Perc
PETIT, Jean-Louis - *Treize Passages* (1985) •Asx/Vibr+Marimba
PONJEE, Ted - *Autumn themes II* (1986-91) (7') •Asx/Marimba •Don
PRESCOTT, John - *Transmigrations* •Sx/Marimba
PRIESNER, Vroni - *Conversation* (1974) (6') •Bsx/Perc
QUATE, Amy - *Ace of Swords* (1992) •Sx/Perc
QUEYROUX, Yves - *Sonate* •Ssx/Perc
QUINT, Johannes - *Mögliche Welten* (1993) •1 Sx: S+B/Perc •INM
RADOVANOVIC, Vladan - *Duet* (1983) •Sx+Cl/Marimba+Vibr
RAN, Shulamit - *Encounter* (1979) •Asx/Perc
REASER, Ronald - *Liberare sonare* (1978) (20') •Asx/Perc •WWS
REINER, Thomas - *Moth and Spider* (1988) (21') •Sx/Perc •AuMC
Movements in Time (1993) •Asx/Perc •INM/adr
REYNOLDS, Verne - *Five Duos* (1981) •Asx/Perc
RILEY, Terry - *Persian Surgery Dervishes* (1971) •Sx/Perc/Tape
ROLIN, Etienne - *Tourbillons* (1981) (8') •1 Sx: S+A+T+B/Perc •adr
ROSEN, Alex - *Tensoren* (1993) •1 Sx: S+B/Perc •INM
ROSSÉ, François - *Etki en Droutzy* (1986) (12') •1 Sx: S+Bs/Perc •adr
ROWLAND, David - *Projections I* (1987) (13') •Sx/Perc •Don
RÜGER, Tobias - *Festgesang* (1993) •Tsx/Marimba •INM
RUGGERI, Gianluca - *Esercizio...* (1990) (13') •Ssx/Perc/Tape •adr
RUZDJAK, Marko - *Passamezzo* (1986) •Asx/Tam-tam •DSH/HG
SAGVIK, Stellan - *Nocturne*, op. 117d (1983) (6') •Ssx or Asx/Vibr
•STIM
SCHLIEPHACKE, Jan Jakob - *Zwang* (1993) •Asx/Perc •INM

SCHMIDT-HAMBROCK, Jochen - *How could it happen* (1983) (7')
•Sx/Perc •adr
SCHMIDT-MECHAU, Friedman - *Differenz und begegnung* (1993)
•Tsx/Perc •INM
SCHWARZ Gunter - *Nr. 37* (1993) •Sx/Gong •INM
SCIORTINO, Patrice - *Falw* (1984) (7') •Bsx (or Asx or Tsx)/1 Perc
(Cymbal/Temple blocks/Toms) •Led
SEGERSTAM, Leif - *Episode n° 7* (1979) (10') •Asx/Perc •FMIC
SLETTHOLM, Yngve - *Introduction og toccata* (1981) (14') •Asx/
Perc •NMI
STEELE, Jan - *Aesir* (1963) (10') •Asx/Perc
STINE, R. - *Duo* (1983) (6'30) •Asx/Perc
STOUT, Gordon - *Duo Dance-Song* (1991) •Ssx/Marimba
STRAESSER, Joep - *Points of contact II* (1988) (11') •Sx/Perc •Don
STROE, Aurel - *Sonate* (17') •Sx/Perc
SZEKELY, Endre - *He Bem-Music* (1982) •Sx+Cl/Marimba+Vibr
TADA, Eiichi - *Tonality* (1993) •Asx/Perc •INM
TAJINO, Masato - *Collage mode key* (8') •Asx/Perc
TAMBA, Akira - *Elemental II* (1978) •Sx/Perc
THEBERGE, Paul - *A Void...* (1983) (16'15) •Asx/Pno or Sx/Perc
THEOBALD, James - *Lewis Carrolls* (1983) •Sx+BsCl/Marimba+Vibr
TISNÉ, Antoine - *Point fixe* (1982) •BsCl+Asx/Perc à claviers •adr
TORREBRUNO, Leonida - *Scemiary* •Asx/Perc
TOWNER, Ralph - *Icarus* •Asx/Vibr
TULL, Fisher - *Colloquy* (1982) •Asx/Perc
UDOW, Michael - *Sandsteps I* (1989) (15') •Asx/Marimba •adr
VALK, Adriaan - *Circles - Impressions* (1979) •Asx/Perc •BVP
VASSILIADIS, Anastassios - *Kyklorythmia II* (1993) •Asx/Marimba
•INM
VERHAEGEN, Mark - *Etchings* (1982) •Sx+Cl/Marimba+Vibr
VERHIEL, Ton - *Kinderstücke* (1989) •Asx/Vibr
VIERU, Anatol - *Diathlon* (20) •Sx/Perc
Double duos (1983) •Sx+Cl/Marimba+Vibr
WEISS, Ferdinand - *Méditation et danse* (1982) •Sx/Vibr
WENDEL, Eugene - *Diason* (15') •Asx/Perc •adr
WERNER, S. E. - *Lettres de voyage* (1987) (17') •Sx/Vibr
WHITICKER, Michael - *Redror* (1989) •Asx/Perc
WILLIS, Richard - *Colloquy III* (1982) •Asx/Perc •adr
WISZNIEWSKI, Zbigniew - *Duo* (1982) (12') •Asx/Marimba
WRIGHT, Rayburn - *Verberations* •Ssx/Perc
YOUNG, Charles Rochester - *Excursions* (1989) (6') •Asx/Marimba
•adr
YUYAMA, Akira - *Divertimento* (1968) (9') •Asx/Marimba •JCC/
B&B
ZAKREVSKY, Vadim - *Softmusic* (1992) •Asx/Vibr •INM

3 Musicians

ARTIOMOV, Vyatcheslav - *Caprice...* (18-20') •2 Sx: SB/Perc •ECS
BANASIK, Christian - *Begegbubg* •Asx/Vla/Perc
BASSKIN, Ali - *Abushina* (1983) (15') •Asx/2 Perc •adr
BAUCHWITZ, Peter - *You came into my life* (1986) (3'40) •Voice/Sx/
Perc •adr
BENSON, Warren - *Invocation and Dance* (1960) (5') •2 Sx: SA/Perc
•MCA
BIELER, Helmut - *Reprisen* (1982) (12') •Asx/Perc/Pno •adr
BLOMENKAMP, Thomas - *Background Music* (12') •2 Sx: AT/Perc
•Asto
Vier Stücke (13'30) •Asx/Marimba/Tam-tam •Asto
BLUMENTHALER, Volker - *Elégie* (1981) •Tsx/Bass/Vibr •B&B
BORROFF, Edith - *Trio* (1982) •Tsx/Pno/Perc
BRAXTON, Anthony - *G 10 4 ZI; S-37 C-67B* •2 Sx: ABs/Perc
BROWN, Newel - *Four Meditations* (1982) •Voice/Asx/Perc •DP
BUBALO, Rudolph - *Organic Concretion* •Asx/Org/Perc/Tape
CABUS, Peter - *Rapsodie* (1974) 1 Sx: A+T/Pno/Perc
CELERIANU, Michel - *Ouverture trio* •Sx/BsCl/Perc

CHARPILLE, Jean-Louis - *Jardins provisoires* (1991) •Bsx/Vcl/Perc
CLARK, Keith - *Different Callings* (1977) •Asx/Pno/Perc
COCCO, Enrico - *Il Sogno di Chuang Tzu* (1989/91) (40') •Dancer/ Perc/1 Sx: S+A+T+B/Electronics •adr
DETTLEFSEN, H. C. - *Mirage* (1982) (13') •Asx/Pno/Perc •Don
DIEMENTE, Edward - *Trio* (1969) •Asx/Tpt/Perc •SeMC
DUBOIS, Pierre-Max - *Danses provençales* •2 Sx: AA/Perc •adr
EK, Hans - *And down goes the bandit* (1989) •Asx/2 Perc. •SvM
ELLO, William - *The Eyes of the Dragon* (1977) •Asx/Perc/Pno
ENGELMANN, Hans - *Incanto*, op. 19 (1959) •Soprano Voice/Asx/ Perc •A&S
    Inter-lineas, op. 50b (1985) •Cl/Sx/Perc •Br&Ha
FAULCONER, Bruce - *Music* (1972) •Tsx/2 Perc •DP
FINGER, Peter - *Neue Wege* (1983) (11') •Guit/Ssx/Perc •adr
FISCHER, Eric - *Blues* (1980) •Ssx/Vibr/Org •adr
FISCHER-MÜNSTER, Gerhard - *Fossilien* (1981) (9') •BsCl/Ssx/ Perc •VDMK
FLADT, Hartmut - *Im Fabelreich* (1982) •Voice/Sx/Perc •adr
FRANCIS, Mark - *Divertimento* •Cl/Asx/Perc
FURRER-MÜNCH, Franz - *Momenti...* (1989) •Tsx/Harps/Perc •adr
GARCIN, Gérard - *Le retour d'Uswann* (1987) •Sx+BsCl/Perc/Bass
GEELEN, Mathieu - *Invention* (1983) (6') •Asx/Electr. Org/Perc •Don
GEUSEN, F. - *Saxo trio* •1 Sx: A+T/Pno/Perc
GINER, Bruno - *Con brio* (1991) (13-17') •Vcl/Bsx/Perc/Tape
GLASER, Werner Wolf - *Triade* (1992) •Fl/Marimba/Bsx
GRUBER, Heinz - *Concerto No. 2* (1961) •Tsx/Bass/Perc •B&H
GYSELYNCK, Jean - *Adagio et Allegro* •Asx/Perc/Pno
HANNAY, Roger - *Cabaret Voltaire* •Female Voice/Ssx/Perc •SeMC
HOFFMAN, Allan - *6 Versions* •Asx/Bass/Vibr
HOLSTEIN, Jean-Paul - *Suite en bleu* (1991) •Asx/Pno/Perc/Ondes martenot (ad lib.) •Bil
HUTCHESON, Jere - *Interplay* •Asx/Marimba/Vibr •DP
ICHIYANAGI, Toshi - *Trichotomy* (1978) •Asx/Pno/Perc
JAHR, New - *Scherzo* (1979) •2 Sx: SB/Perc
JEVERUD, Johan - *2 Pieces...* (1992) •Fl/Asx/Perc •SMIC
JOHNSON, Roger - *Fantasy* •Asx/Perc/Bass •DP
KARLINS, M. William - *Saxtuper* (1989) (9') •1 Sx: A+S/Tuba/Perc •ACA
KELKEL, Manfred - *Lanterna magica* •Asx/Perc/Pno
KILAR, Wojciech - *1 Dla 3* (1963) •Asx/Vibr/Bass
KUNZ, Ernst - *25 pezzi per varie...* (1962) •Asx/Bass/Perc
LA ROSA, Michael - *Coming in Glory* (1974) •Asx/Trb/Vibr •SeMC
LAUBA, Christian - *Passage* •2 Sx/Perc •adr
    Variation-Couleurs (1986) •Ssx/Vcl (or Bass)/Perc •adr
LEMAY, Robert - *Tryptique écarlate* (1991) (18') •1 Sx: S+T+B/ Harp/Perc •adr
LEUCHTER, Heibert - *Diamonds in the water* (1981) (5'30) •Asx/Bs Guit/Perc •adr
LIMA, Candido - *Cantica II* (1987) •Cl/Sx/Perc
LINKE, Norbert - *Matinée de jazz* (12') •Asx/Pno/Perc •adr
LUKAS, Zdenek - *Racontino* (1980) (10') •Bsx or Tsx/2 Perc •CHF
MARCOUX, Isabelle - *Ofaeruffoss* (1992) (12') •Ssx/Harp or Pno or 2 Vibr •adr
MAXWELL - *Acousma IV* •Tsx/Perc/Pno •DP
MAZUREK, Micezyslaw - *Ewokacje* (1986) (8') •Asx/Vibr/Perc
MENSING, Eberhard - *Tennis ist toll* (1978) (44') •Cl/Sx/Perc •adr
MEULEN, Henk van der - *Desert journey* (1982) (15') •2 Sx: AT/Perc •Don
MICHAEL, Edward - *Nocturne* •Asx/Pno/Perc
MITREA-CELARIANU, Mihai - *Ouverture* •Asx/Bass/Perc •Sal
MIYAZAWA, Kazuto - *Paragraphen* (1988) •Asx/Vibr/Harp or Asx/ Pno
MOORE, David - *"Le Rêve"...* •Asx/2 Perc •WWS
NEWHOUSE, Dana - *Sonata Sentimentale* (1979) •Asx/Pno/Perc

NODA, Ryo - *Guernica...*, op. 4 •Asx/Perc/Speaking Voice
PAVLENKO, Serguei - *Intermezzo* (1985) (12') •Asx/Harp/Perc
POLK, Marlyce - *Chromasia* •Asx/2 Perc •SeMC
RUELLE, Fernand - *Le Gille* (1976) •Asx+Perc/Tsx+Perc/Pno •adr
SCELSI, Jacinto - *Canti del Capricorno* •Soprano Voice/Perc/Sx
SCHMIDT, William - *Jazz Suite* •2 Tsx/Perc •WIM
SCHMIDT-HAMBROCK, Jochen - *Ozie* (1982) (10') •Sx/Guit/Perc •adr
SCHULTE, Peter - *Du* (1983) (10') •Asx/Pno/Perc •adr
SCOTT, Richard - *En kloyennes...* (1984) •Asx/Org/Perc •STIM
SHAFFER, Sherwood - *Vision...* (1971) (15') •Actress+Dancer/Asx/ Tape (or 3 Asx)/Perc •DP/adr
SMITH, Stuart - *A Fine Old Tradition* (6-7') •Asx/Pno/Perc •MP
STEINKE, Günter - *Nachklang* (10') •Bsx/Perc/Bass
STRAESSER, Joep - *Grand Trio* (1984) (18') •Asx/Harp/Perc •Don
SZEREMETA, Ryszard - *Trickstar* (1989) (12') •Sx/Synth/Perc
TAGGART, Mark - *Red and White* (1978) (10') •Tenor Voice/Sx/Vibr •adr
THOMSON, B. - *Temple Song* •Sx/Perc/Pno
TON-THAT, Tiêt - *Moments rituels* (1991) •Tsx/Marimba/Synth
TOSI, Daniel - *Multitude III* (1984) (20') •Fl/Asx/Vibr
VEERHOFF, Carlos - *Moments musicaux*, op. 50 •Asx/Accordion/ Perc
VOIRPY, Alain - *Offrandes* (1982) •Ssx/Perc/Pno •Lem
VOSK, Jay - *Chimera* (1983) •2 Sx: AT/Marimba •DP
VUATAZ, Roger - *Destin...*, op. 91 (1954) (23') •Asx/Harp/Perc
WALLIN, Peter - *Scäövu po màrrànànn...* (1989) •Asx/2 Perc •SMIC
WILEY, Frank - *Ritual Music* •Cl/Asx/Perc
WOLF, Hans - *Honey Polka* (1971) (3') •Asx/Accordion/Perc •Figurata
WOLFE, George - *Randomization No. 1* (1982) •Ssx/Marimba/Perc
WOODBURY, Arthur - *Remembrances* (1968) (16'30) •Asx/Vln/ Vibr •CPE
YAMANOUCHI, Tadashi - *Correlation* (1979) •Marimba/Asx/Bass
ZINN, Michael - *Suspensions* (1973) •Asx/Bsn/Vibr •SeMC

4 Musicians

ABSIL, Jean - *Phantasmes*, op. 22 & 72 (1936-50) (12') •Contralt. Voice/Asx/Pno/Perc •CBDM
AHO, Kalevi - *Quartet* (1982) (22') •Fl/Asx/Guit/Perc •FMIC
ALBERT, Thomas - *Sound Frames* (1968) (6') •Asx/Ob/Trb/Vibr •MP
ALEXANDER, Joseph - *Masks and Mirrors* (1986) •Ssx/Vcl/Perc/ Pno
ALSINA - *Rendez-vous* •Cl/Asx/Trb/Perc •Led
ANDRIESSEN, Louis - *Song lines* (1989) •3 Sx: TTB or 6 Sx: TTTTBB/Perc •JG
BANK, Jacques - *Finale* (1984) (30') •Baritone Voice/Asx/BsCl/Perc •Don
BARRIERE, Françoise - *A propos...* (1979) •Asx/Perc/Vla/Vcl/Tape
BAUCKHOLT, Carola - *Schraubdichtung* (12') •CBsSx/Vcl/Perc/ Voice
BERGMAN, Erik - *Mipejupa*, op. 96 (1981) (17') •Fl/Asx/Guit/Perc •FMIC
BERNAOLA, Carmelo - *Superficie n° 3* (1963) •Asx/Picc/Xylo-phone/Bongos •Alp
BOIS, Rob du - *Stuleken* (1960) •Fl/Tsx/Vla/Perc •Don
BOOREN, Jo van den - *2 Pièces caractéristiques*, op. 84 (1992) (9') •Sx/Tpt/Trb/Perc •Don
BRNCIC, Isaza - *Quodlibet I* (1966) •Sx/Vla/Tpt/Electr. Guit/Electr Org or 2 Asx/Vla/Vibr
CALLHOFF, Herbert - *Facetten* (1986) •Asx/BsCl/Cl/Perc •adr
CAMPBELL, John - *Voices of America* (1984) •Voice/Ssx/Vibr/Bass •adr
CAPDEVIELLE, Pierre - *Danse des 7...* (1956) (4') •Asx/3 Timp •Bil
CHAGRIN, Francis - *2 Studies...* (1959) •Tpt/Sx/Bass/Drums •BMIC

CHEN, Qijang - *Feu d'ombres* (1991) •Ssx/Instr. Ensemble/Harp/ Bass/Perc •Bil

CONSTANT, Franz - *Rythme et Expression*, op. 49 (1972) (13') •Vln/ Asx/Pno/Perc •CBDM

CONYNGHAM, Barry - *Mirror Images* (1975) •4 Actors/Asx/Vcl/ Bass/Perc •Uni

DEFOSSEZ, René - *Suite "Souvenirs"* •Vln/Asx/Pno/Perc

DELAGE, Jean-Louis - *Illusions, Rêves et Caprices* (1990) (12') •Asx/Pno/Synth/Perc or Asx/Pno •Bil

DEPELSENAIRRE, J-M. - *Les approches de l'invisible* (1973) (4') •Vln/Asx/Pno/Perc •adr

Diaz, F. - *Meu Bem* •Sx/Tpt/Trb/Perc •PMP

DIEMENTE, Edward - *Quartet in Memory Fl. O'Connor* (1967) •Asx/Trb/Bass/Perc •SeMC

DUBOIS, Pierre-Max - *Suite* •Vln/Asx/Pno/Perc •Mau

ELLIS, Donald - *Improvisational Suite* •Tpt/Asx/Bass/Perc •MJQ

FIORENZA, Eduard - *Soundscape Suite...* •Tsx/Pno/Bass/Perc •DP

FLADT, Hartmut - *Die Abnehmer* (1980) •2 Voice/Sx/Perc •adr

FOX, Frederick - *Shaking the Pumpkin* (1987) •Asx/Pno/2 Perc

FUENTES, Tristan - *Auerbachs Keller* •Ssx/Pno/Vibr/Marimba •HMC
Gretchen •Cl+Sx/Synth/Vibr+Sgl-lead/Marimba+Steel Drum
Pan Am •BsCl+Ssx/Synth/Vibr+Steel Drum/Marimba+Accordion/ Tape •HMC
Quartet •BsCl+Asx/Synth/Vibr+Tabla/Marimba+Drums
Risas de los Incas •BsCl+Ssx/Pno/Vibr/Marimba+Bass Drum •HMC

GARIN, Didier-Marc - *Da caccia IV* (1992) •Fl/2 Sx: AT/Perc

GOTTSCHALK, Arthur - *The Sessions* •Fl/Asx/Vibr/Bass •SeMC

GUICHARD, Christophe - *Glu et gli* (1991) (10') •Soprano Voice/ Baritone Voice/Bsx/Perc

GUIMAUD, Olivier - *Sérénade...* (16'15) •Tpt/Sx/Vcl/Perc •adr

HAMBURG, Jeff - *Elegie* (1985-86) (9') •Fl/BsCl/Bsx/Perc •Don

HÄMEENIEMI, Aero - *Chamber Music Book* (1980) •Fl/Guit/Asx/ Perc •FMIC

HARVEY, Paul - *Common Market Suite* •2 Sx: AT/Perc/Pno •Mau

HAVEL, Christophe - *AER (la danse)* (1994) (10') •Picc/SnoSx/ Celesta/Perc •adr
RamDam (1992) (15') •Fl/1 Sx: S+B/Perc/Pno/Transformation électroacoustique •adr

HEWITT, Harry - *34 Preludes*, op. 439 (1972) (90') •Pno/Guit/Perc/ Sx •DP

HEYN, Volker - *Blues two* (1983) •Voice/Vcl/Sx/Perc •Br&Ha

HODEIR, André - *Paradoxe I* •Tsx/Trb/Bass/Perc •MJQ

HOLSTEIN, Jean-Paul - *Suite en bleu* (1991) •Asx/Pno/Perc/Ondes martenot (ad lib.) •Bil

HOVHANESS, Alan - *The Flowering Peach*, op. 125 (1954) (21') •Asx+Cl/Vibr/Perc/Harp or Pno •AMP

ILLASOVAY, Elsor von - *2 Songs* •Soprano Voice/Asx/Vibr/Perc •IMD

KAIPAINEN, Jouni - *Far from home*, op. 17 (1981) (10') •Fl/Asx/ Guit/Perc •WH

KARPMAN, Laura - *Matisse and Jazz* (1987) (18') •Voice/1 Sx: S+A/ Perc/Pno •Eto

KASPAR, Edward - *Quartet* (1972) •2 Sx: AT/Vibr/Tuba •adr

KLEBE, Giselher - *Gratullations - tango*, op. 40a •Asx/Tpt/Pno/Perc •B&B

KÖHLER, Wolfgang - *Morgen hol'ich mir die Rosen* (1986) (3'30) •Voice/Sx/Perc/Synth •adr

KUBINSKY, Richard - *Invention* •2 Sx: AT/Pno/Vibr •NYPL

KUPFERMAN, Meyer - *Jazz Infinities Three* (1961) (90') •Asx/Pno/ Bass/Perc •GMP

KURTZ, Arthur - *Isaiah VI*, op. 31 (1971) (7'30) •Narr/Asx/Pno/Perc •adr

LANCEN, Serge - *Petit concert* (1984) •3 voice: instrumentation variable/Perc •Mol

LAUBA, Christian - *Atlas* (1984) (20') •1 Sx: A+B/Pno/Perc/Bass •adr
Autographie (1985) •Asx/Perc/Electr. Pno/Synth/Tape •adr

LAUTH, Wolfgang - *Concertino* (1958) (14') •Tsx/Trb/Fl/Perc •adr

LEDUC, Jacques - *Sortilèges africains* (1967) (10') •4 Sx: SATB or Voice/Sx/Pno/Perc

LEMELAND, Aubert - *Figures...*, op. 79 (10') •Asx/Vla/Vibr/Guit •adr

LERSY, Roger - *Kandinsky* (1973) •Asx/Bass/Perc/Pno •adr
Vitraux (1972) (35') •Cl/Asx/Vcl/Perc •adr

LINDBERG, Magnus - *Linea d'ombra* (1981) (15') •Fl/Asx/Guit/ Perc •WH/FMIC

MACHOVER, Tod - *Valise's Song* (1989) (5') •1 Sx: S+T/Electr. Guit/Perc/Electr. Bass/Tape •Ric/adr

MAROS, Miklos - *Clusters...* (1981) •Fl/Ssx/Guit/Perc •SMIC

MARRA, James - *To Suffer...* (1978) (11') •Tsx/Pno/2 Perc •DP

MARTIN, Vernon - *Contingencies* (1969) •Asx/Tpt/Trb/Perc/Tape •CAP

MEIJERING, Chiel - *Schudden voor gebruik* (1985) (8') •Asx/Perc/ Pno/Harp •Don

MERCURE, Pierre - *Tetrachromie* (1963) •Cl/Asx/BsCl/Perc/Tape •CMC

MERILÄINEN, Usko - *Simultanus for four* (1979) (16') •Fl/Asx/ Guit/Perc •Pan/FMIC

MIEREANU, Costin - *Jardins retrouvés* (1985) (20') •Electr. Ssx/ Vcl/Perc/Harp/Tape •Sal

MIGOT, Georges - *2 Stèles de Victor Segalen* (1925) (15') •Voice (or Asx)/Celesta/Bass/Perc •Led

MANSHIP, Munch - *Four Songs* •Bb or Eb Sx/Pno/Bass/Drums •PBP

PARTCH, Harry - *Ulysses at the Edge...* (1955) •Vln/Tsx/Tpt/Perc

PERRUCCI, Mario - *Piccola serenata* (1970) •2 Tsx/Timp/Pno

ROSENBLOOM, David - *Pocket Pieces* (1977) •Fl/Asx/Vla/Perc •SeMC

SCHMIDT-HAMBROCK, Jochen - *ARD - Sportschau* (1984) (10') •Guit/Asx/Perc/Synth •adr

SCHULTE, Peter - *Samba...* (1983) (5-10') •Asx/Tpt/Perc/Pno •adr

SCIORTINO, Patrice - *Moulin du temps* •Vibr/Guit/Vla/Asx •adr

SCOTT, Ronnie - *Dark Flowers* (1988) (13') •Fl/Asx/Guit/Perc

SHOUT, Vladislav - *Metamorphosis* (1979) •Asx/Bass/Harp/Perc •ECS

SLEZAK, Milan - *3 Pisně pro nizsi a Vyssi* •Pno/Cymbals/Sx/Bass

STOKES, Eric - *Susquehanna* (1985) (16') •2 Perc/Cl+Sx/Pno •HMC

SUDLOW, Paul - *Pieces* (1978) (5-6') •Asx/Pno (4 hands)/Perc ad lib. •adr

THEOBALD, James - *Plane 5* •Asx/Vla/Pno/Perc •SeMC

WARING, Kate - *Psalmance* (1978) (5') •Fl/Ssx/Guit/Perc

WASHBURN, Gary - *Quintet I* (1960) (6'); *Quintet II* •2 Bsx/2 Perc/ Tape •SeMC

WILSON, Dana - *Sati* (1982) •Asx/Vcl/2 Perc •DP

WOLPE, Stefan - *Quartet No. 1* (1950) •Tpt/Tsx/Perc/Pno •Gi&Ma/ MM

YAMANOUCHI, Tadashi - *Epistoraphe* (1968) •Asx/Marimba/Vibr/ Vcl

5 Musicians

ALLA, Thierry - *Aérienne* (1994) (8') •Fl/2 Sx/Pno/Perc/dispositif électroacoustique

ANDERSON, Thomas - *Re-creation* (1978) •Asx/Vla/Vcl/Pno/Tamtam

ARCURI, Serge - *Prologue* (1985) •Fl/Ssx/Cl/Hn/Perc/Tape •CMC

ASHEIM, Nils - *Kvad* (1975) (10') •4 Sx: SATB/Perc •NMI/DP

ATOR, James - *Life Cycle* (1973) (18') •Mezzo Soprano Voice/Asx/ Ob/Perc/Vcl •SeMC

BEAVERS, Kevin - *Shadowplays* (1994) •Sx/Pno/3 Perc

BENHAMOU, Maurice - *Mouvement* (1979) •Fl/Sx/Vla/Vcl/Perc/ Tape

BUCZKOWNA, Anna - *Hipostaza* (1984/85) (15') •1 Sx: S+A+T/Fl/
Vcl/Vibr/Soprano Voice

BUEL, Charles - *Chimera, Avatars and Beyond* (1972) (15-20') •Fl/
Ob/2 Sx: AT/Perc •adr
37 Dream Flowers (1971-72) (9') •Asx/Bsn/Pno/Electr. Pno/Perc
•adr

CAMPANA, José-Luis - *Insight* (1987) (18') •Fl/Voice/Sx/Bass/
Perc/Tape/Video •Bil

CELERIANU, Michel - *Janvier* (1983) •Ssx/Fl/2 Bass/Perc •Sal

CHARRON, Damien - *Extraits du corps* (1985) •Mezzo Soprano
Voice/Tsx/BsCl/Bass/Perc

CONYNGHAM, Barry - *Jazz Ballet* (1964) •Fl/Asx/Bass/Perc/Pno
•Uni

CRUMB, George - *Quest* (25') •Guit/1 Sx: S+A+T+Harmonica/2
Perc/Harp •BR

DAETVYLER, Jean - *Concerto* (1980) •4 Sx: SATB/Perc

DEDRICK, Rusty - *Saxafari* •4 Sx: SATB/Optional Perc •Ken

DESPORTES, Yvonne - *Sonate pour un baptême* (1959) (18') •Fl/
Asx/Soprano Voice (or EH)/Perc/Pno •Bil

DÜNKI, Jean-Jacques - *Lutezia, 1842* (1978) •Ssx/Tpt/Vcl/Pno/Perc

FEILER, Dror - *Om* (1985) •Ssx/Electr. Guit/3 Perc •Tons/SMIC
Schlafbeand (1985) •Ssx/Electr. Guit/3 Perc •Tons/SMIC
Tändstickorna... (1979-80) •Ssx/2 Electr. Guit/2 Perc •SMIC
Yad (1984) •2 Ssx/Electr. Guit/2Perc •Tons/SMIC

FERRITO - *Concertino* •Asx/Ob/2 Perc/Bass •DP

FISCHER, Eric - *Visions du Christ* •4 Sx: SATB/Mallet Perc [Perc à
clavier] •adr

FISHER, Alfred - *5 Time Prisme* •3 Sx: STBs/Vibr/Pno •SeMC

FLETA POLO, Francisco - *Divertimento 26* (1985) •Sx/Cl/Accor-
dion/Bass/Timp

FLODI, John - *Signals*, op. 22 (1968-69) (5'30) •2 Sx: ST/Trb/Perc/
Pno •adr

FONTAINE, Louis-Noël - *Mauresque* (1992) (8') •Fl/Ssx/Cl/Vcl/
Perc •Capri

FOURNIER, Marie Hélène - *Supplément nécessaire* (1990) (50') •2
Perc/Bsx/Harp/Soprano Voice

FREE, John - *A Wind of Changes* (1990) •Cl/Bsn/Sx/Perc/Pno •CMC

GARCIN, Gérard - *Méditations* (1971) •2 Sx/Pno/Bass/Perc

GAY, Harry - *Quartet with Percussion* (1972) (8') •4 Sx: SATB/Perc
•Eri

GOODWIN, Gordon - *Levittation* •Sx/Tpt/Pno/Bass/Perc •adr

GREENE - *From Out of Bartok* •Asx/2 Bass/Perc/Pno

GUILLONNEAU, Christian - *Eolithes* (1988) (7') •4 Sx: AAAA/
Perc/Tape

GULLIN, Peter - *Adventures* •2 Sx: AT/Pno/Bass/Perc •SMIC/WIM

HARRIS, Roger - *Caliban in Apartment 112* •Tenor Voice/Asx/Pno/
2 Perc •SeMC

HAUTA-AHO, Teppo - *For Charles M.* (1980) (15') •Tpt/Asx/Trb/
Bass/Perc •FMIC

HEIDEN, Bernhard - *Four Movements* (1976) •4 Sx: SATB/Timp
•Eto

HEININEN, Paavo - *Quintetto*, op. 7 (1961) (18') •Fl/Sx/Pno/Vibr/
Perc •Tie/FMIC

HEKSTER, Walter - *A song of peace* •Voice/Cl/Asx/Vcl/Perc •Don

HESPOS, Hans - *En-Kin...* (1970) (5'30) Ssx/Cl/Bsn/Bass/Perc
•EMod
Frottages •Asx/Vcl/Harp/Mandolin/Perc •EMod

HISCOTT, James - *Variations on O. Cèlestin's...* (1978) (9') •Fl/Cl/
Sx/Perc/Pno •CMC

HODKINSON, Sidney - *Interplay* (1966) (12'30) •Fl+Picc/Cl/Asx/
Perc/Bass •CMC

HOLZMANN, Rodolfo - *Suite a tres temas* •Asx/Tpt/Cl/Pno/Bongos

HOVHANESS, Alan - *The World Beneath the Sea*, op. 133/1 (1953)
•Asx/Harp/Vibr/Timp/Gong

ISTVAN, Miloslav - *Concertino...* (1982) (13') •Ob/Cl+Asx/BsCl/
Perc/Pno

Joplin, Scott - *The Entertainer* (Axworthy) •2 Sx: ST/Hn/Bsn/Perc
•DP

KORTE, Karl - *Symmetrics* (1973) •Asx/4 Perc •SeMC

KUCHARZYK, Henry - *One for the Underdog* (1981) •Tpt/Sx/Pno/
Bass/Perc •CMC

LATHROP, Gayle - *Pieces 4-5* •Asx/Tpt/Vcl/Bass/Perc •CAP

LAUBA, Christian - *Rif* (1991) (14') •Fl/2 Sx: SA/Pno/Perc •Fuz

LAUZURICA, Antonio - *El movimento...* (1991) •4 Sx: SATB/Perc

LAVAL, Philippe - *1,0544876* (1992) •Soprano Voice/2 Sx: AT/Guit/
Vibr

LAVENDA, Richard - *The Weary Man Whispers* (1985) •Tenor
Voice/Asx/Trb/Perc/Pno •Eto

LILJEHOLM, Thomas - *Turnings* (1989) (11') •Asx/4 Perc •SMIC

LONARDONI, Markus - *Modal interchange* (1987) (6') •Sx/Perc/
Pno/Guit/Bass

MABRY, Drake - *9.10.89* •Ssx/Electr. Guit/Bass Guit/Synth/Perc

MACERO, Teo - *Exploration* •Asx/Cl/Bass/Perc/Accordion

MANZO, Silvio - *2 Tempi* •4 Sx: SATB/Timp ad lib. •Pet

MEIJERING, Chiel - *Meine Lippen die...* (1984) (10') •Fl/Ob/Asx/
Pno/Perc •Don

MEULEN, Henk van der - *Quintet* (1981/84) (48') •2 Sx: SA/3 Perc
•Don

MIEREANU, Costin - *Ricochets* (1989) •1 Sx: Sno+S+A+T+B/
Electr. Guit/Bass Guit/Synth/Perc/Régie
électr. •Sal

MILLS, Charles - *Paul Bunyan Jump* (1964) •Asx/Pno/Tpt/Bass/Perc
•ACA

NICKLAUS, Wolfgang - *Der Priwall* (1984) (9') •Voice/Asx/Perc/
Cl/Vcl •adr

NIKIPROWETZKY, Tolia - *Auto-stop* •Soprano Voice/Tenor Voice/
Perc/Vcl/1 Sx: A+S •adr

OLBRISCH, Franz-Martin - *"Im Anfänglichen...* (1989) (90') •Vln/
Fl/Trb/Sx/Perc/Electronics
Quintett (1989) •Ob+EH/2 Sx: AT/Hn/Perc •adr

OSTENDORF, Jens-Peter - *Johnny reitet westwärts* •Cl/2 Sx: AT/
Perc/Prepared Pno •Sik

PILON, Daniel - *Oleum perdidisti* (1987-88) (21') •4 Sx: SATB/Perc
•adr

POMORIN, Sibylle - *Zwei Lieder nach Anne Waldman* (1989) (19')
•Voice/Asx/Perc/Vcl/Bass •adr

RACKLEY-SMITH, Lawrence - *Kay-Vee-Si-Si* •2 Sx: AT/Pno/Bass/
Perc/Tape

REA, John - *Fantasies...* (1969) •4 Sx: SATB/Perc ad lib. •CMC

REBEL, Meeuwis - *Sextet à 5* (1984) (15') •4 Sx: SATB/Perc •Don

RECK, David - *Blues and Screamer* (1965-66) •Fl+Picc/Harmonica/
Asx/Bass/Perc •CPE

RISSET, Jean-Claude - *Glissements* (10'10) •3 melody instruments of
choice [instruments monodiques au choix]/
Perc/Pno/Tape

ROBERT, Lucie - *Géométrie* (1986) (12') •2 Sx: AB/Tpt/Trb/Perc
•adr

ROSENBLOOM, David - *The thud, thud, thud...* (1966) •Sx/Electric
Vcl/Pno/Celesta/Perc/Tape/Lights •SeMC

RUBBERT, Rainer - *Vocalise* (1992) •Asx/Fl/Vcl/Perc/Pno •adr

SAUCEDO, Victor - *Four Bagatelles* •2 Sx: AT/2 Pno/Perc •adr

SCHIFRIN, Lalo - *Jazz Faust* (1963) (20') •Asx/Tpt/Pno/Bass/Perc
•MJQ
Mount Olive (3') •Asx/Guit/Pno/Bass/Perc •MJQ

SCHUDEL, Thomas - *Pentagram* (1987) (14') •4 Sx:SATB/Perc
•DP/CMC

SEFFER, Yochk'o - *Galère assymétrique* (7'30) •4 Sx: SATB/Perc

SHEPHERD, Stu - *Birthday Music III* (1986) •1 Sx: A+T/Guit/Synth/
Bass/Perc •CMC

SHEPPARD, James - *Bitter Ice* •Tpt/Sx/Pno/Bass/Perc •SeMC

SORG, Margarete - *Cantica Catulliana* (1986) (11') •Soprano Voice/ Baritone Voice/Tsx/Pno+Harps/Perc •adr

STEELE, Jan - *Temporary farewell* (1971) (5') •1 Sx: S+A/Electr. Guit/Pno/Bass/Perc

Sternberg - *Variations on German Folk Songs* •Sx/Bass/Guit/Pno/ Perc •DV

TOSI, Daniel - *Multitude II* (1984-85) •1 Sx: S+A+T/Fl/Vibr/Tape/2 Perc - 3 soloists

VOSK, Jay - *Le Nid* •Ssx/Vibr/Guit/Vln/Bass •SeMC

WARE, Peter - *Libera me domine* (1981) •2 Sx/3 Perc •CMC

WEDDINGTON, Maurice - *Fire in the Lake*, op. 43 (1978) •4 Sx: SATB/Perc

WERDER, Felix - *Komposition* (1987) (10') •4 Sx/Perc •adr

WINZENBURGER, Walter - *Quartet* •4 Sx: AATB/Perc •adr

WOLFE, George - *Persian Dance* (1982) •Asx/Picc/Bsn/Xylophone/ Exotic Perc

YOUNG, Charles Rochester - *October in the Rain* (1989) (5') •MIDI Wind Controller/Hn/Pno/Synth/Perc •adr

YOUNG, Lynden de - *Chamber Music* (1972) •Asx/Bsn/Ob/Pno/Vibr •SeMC

6 Musicians

ASHEIM, Nils Henrik - *Midt iblant os...* (1978) •Fl/Asx/Vla/Vcl/ Bass/Perc •NMI

BACHOREK, Milan - *Inspirace* (1983) (12') •Ob/Asx/Cl+BsCl/Perc/ Pno/Electr. Guit •CHF

BAINBRIDGE, Simon - *People of the dawn* (1975) •Soprano Voice/ Cl/Ssx/BsCl/Perc/Pno •UMPL

BENNETT, Richard Rodney - *Comedia I* (1972) •Fl/Asx/BsCl/Tpt/ Vcl/Perc •Uni

CASANOVA, André - *Duo Canzoni* (1973) (10'30) •Asx/Cl/Tpt/ Perc/Small Org/Electr. Bass Guit •adr

CHINI, André - *Pieces* (1992) •Fl/Sx/2 Perc/Pno/Bass

CORY, Eleanor - *Waking* (1974) •Tsx/Bsn/Vln/Vcl/Bass/Perc

COURTIOUX, Jean - *Manu reva* (1983) •2 Sx: TB/Fluegelhorn/Trb/ Bass/Drums •DP

DE MARS, James - *Desert Songs* (1983) •Soprano Voice/Asx/Vcl/2 Perc/Pno •adr

Premonitions... (16'30) •Native American Fl/African Perc/Asx/ Vcl/Pno/Perc •adr

DESPORTES, Yvonne - *La maison abandonnée* (1961) (20') •Vln/ Vla/Vcl/Asx/Perc/Pno •adr

DORNBY, Finn - *Musickus dornby* •2 Sx: AB/Org/Electr. Guit/Electr. Bs Guit/Perc

EISMA, Will - *Affairs no. 1* •Fl/Asx/Vibr/Pno/Bass/Perc •Don

ELIASSON, Anders - *The Green Rose* (1976) (11'15) •Soprano Voice/4 Sx: SATB/Perc •STIM

ERIKSON, Ake - *The rest is silence* (1971/73) •Fl/Asx/Cl/Pno/Bass/ Perc •SMIC

EYSER, Eberhard - *Livre des jeux...* (1959-86) (23'30) •Asx/Harp/ Pno/Vibr/Guit/Vln •EMa

FEILER, Dror - *Hive* (1985) •2 Ssx/2 Electr. Guit/2 Perc. •Tons/ SMIC

FERRO, Pietro - *Amphitrion divertimento* •2 Fl/2 Sx/CBsn/Perc •Ric

FUKUDA, Wakako - *Divertissement* •4 Sx/Bass/Perc

GEHLHAARD, Rolf - *Hélix* (1967) •Soprano Voice/Sx/Trb/Bass/ Pno/Perc •FM

GLASER, Werner Wolf - *Tale* (1977) (12') •Bsx/5 Perc •STIM

GOJKOVIC, Dusan - *Swinging macedonia* (1966) (35') •Tpt/2 Sx: AT/Pno/Bass/Perc •adr

GRANDIS, Renato de - *Canti...* •Vln/Vcl/Tsx/Vibr/Trb/Perc •SeMC

GÜRSCH, Günther - *Madison...* (1963) (3') •3 Sx/Tpt/Trb/Perc •adr

HAAS, Konrad - *Steinwolke* (1983) (45') •Voice/Sx/Perc/Pno/Guit/ Bass •Holz

HELLAN, Arne - *Sextet* (1981) •Tpt/2 Sx/2 Guit/Perc •NMI

HERMANSSON, Christer - *Aggjakten* (1979) •Narr/Tsx/Trb/Guit/ Bass/Perc •STIM

HISCOTT, James - *Ballad No. 1* (1978) (14') •Fl/Cl/Sx/Perc/Accor- dion/Pno •CMC

HODEIR, André - *Cadenze* (4') •Bsx/Tpt/Trb/Pno/Bass/Perc •MJQ

Oblique (3'30) •2 Sx: AT/Trb/Pno/Bass/Perc •MJQ

Osymetrios (3') •Tpt/Tsx/Trb/Pno/Bass/Drums •MJQ

Trope à St-Trop •Tpt/Tsx/Trb/Pno/Bass/Drums •MJQ

HORWOOD, Michael - *Interphases* (1975) (13') •Fl/Sx/Accordion (or Org)/Pno/2 Perc •CMC

KARKOFF, Ingvar - *Konsert* (1988) (17') •Asx/5 Perc •SUE

KUPFERMAN, Meyer - *Jazz Cello Concerto* (1962) (25') •Vcl/3 Sx/ Bass/Perc •GMP

LANZA, Alcides - *Interferences III* (1983-84) •Fl/Cl/Sx/Guit/Pno/ Perc •ShP

Modulos III (1983) •Guit/Tsx/Vln/Vcl/Perc/Pno/Tape •CMC

LE SIEGE, Annette - *Ordinary Things* •Voice/Fl/Sx/Vibr/Vcl/Pno •SeMC

LEWIS, John A. - *Pieces* •Tsx/Tpt/Trb/Pno/Bass/Perc •MJQ

MALLIE, Loïc - *Sextuor* (1989) •Fl/Cl/Asx/Pno/Guit/Perc

MAXFIELD, Richard - *Domenon* (1961) •Fl/Sx/Pno/Vibr/Vln/Bass/ Tape

MELLNÄS, Arne - *Per caso* (1963) (5'30) •Asx/Trb/Vln/Bass/2 Perc •SeMC

MIEREANU, Costin - *Miroir liquide* (1986) (11') •1 Sx: Sno+S+A+T/ Bsn/Perc/Harp/Pno/Bass •Sal

MILHAUD, Darius - *Caramel mou*, op. 68 (1921) (5') •Bb Sx (or Voice)/Cl/Tpt/Trb/Pno/Perc •ME

ÖHLUND, Ulf - *Simplicity musik* (1983) (10') •4 Perc/Ssx/Bass •STIM

OLIVEIRA, Willy C. de - *Sugestoes* (1971) •Ob/Asx/Bandoneon/ Tuba/Bass/Perc

PAICH, Marty - *Toccata in F* •4 Sx: SATB/Bass/Perc •Eto

PELUSI, Mario - *Concert Piece* (1978) (12'30) •Bsx/Brass Quartet/ Perc

PENTLAND, Barbara - *Variable Winds* (1979) (5') •Fl (or Ob)/Asx/ 3 Tom-toms/Bongos •CMC

POMORIN, Sibylle - *Rabengold - Goldraben* (1989) (80') •2 Sx: AT/ Perc/Pno/Org/Vcl •adr

Rodgers - *Dancing on the Ceiling* •4 Sx: SATB/Bass/Drums •DP

SCELSI, Jacinto - *Yamaon* (1954-58) (10') •Bass Voice/2 Sx: AB/ CBsn/Bass/Perc •Sal

SCHUBACK, Peter - *A Priori* (1983) (45') •Sx/Trb/Perc/Vlc/Pno/ Harps •Tons/SMIC

SECO, Manuel - *Concierto...* (1988) (12') •4 Sx: SATB/Pno/Perc

SEIBER, Màtyàs - *Two Jazzolettes* (1929-33) •2 Sx/Tpt/Trb/Pno/Perc •WH

SOLAL, Martial - *Ballade* (1987) (5') •5 Sx: SAATB/Perc ad lib. •Mar

STOUT, Alan - *Toccata* (1965) (10') •Asx/5 Perc •ACA

7 Musicians

ADDERLEY, Mark - *The Worm and the Toothache* (1986) •Asx/Tsx/ Vln/Fl/Trb/Pno/Perc •NMI

ALLA, Thierry - *Météore* (1986) •6 Sx: SAATBBs/Perc •adr

ANDRIESSEN, Louis - *Song lines* (1989) •3 Sx: TTB or 6 Sx: TTTTBB/Perc •JG

ARGERSINGER, Charles - *Drastic Measures* •Fl/Ob/Cl/Asx/Bsn/ Hn/Perc

ARTIOMOV, Vyacheslav - *Little Concerto* •Ssx/6 Perc

BENNETT, Richard Rodney - *Soliloquy* (1966) (14') •Voice/1 Sx: A+T/Tpt/Tuba/Pno/Bass/Perc •Uni

BERGHMANS, José - *Telle qu'en...* (1977) •Tsx/Pno/5 Perc •Chou

BERNARD, Jacques - *L'Opéra de l'espace* (1970) •Narr/Ob/Cl/BsCl/ 1 Sx: S+A+B/Bsn/Perc •adr

BJORKLUND, Terje - *Herbarium* (1982) •Fl/Ssx/Vln/Hn/Bass/Pno/ Perc •NMI

BOSSEUR, Jean-Yves - *43 Miniatures* (1992) •Vln/Cl/2 Sx: AB/ Harp/Pno/Perc

BROWN, Anthony - *Soundscape 1* •Asx/Bsn/Tpt/Vln/Voice/Pno/ Perc/Tape •SeMC

Byrd, William - *Fantasie* (AXWORTHY) •6 Sx: SSAATB/Optional Perc

BYTZEK, Peter - *Gefühle auf dem Eis* (1985) (3'45) •2 Voice/Guit/ Pno/Sx/Perc/Bass •adr

CRAS, Jean - *Demain* (1929) •Asx/Tpt/Trb/Perc/Vln/Vcl/Bass •Sen

DANCEANU, Liviu - *Quasi concerto* (1983) (15') •1 Sx: S+T/Bsn/ Trb/Vcl/Bass/Pno/Perc

DENISOV, Edison - *Concerto piccolo* (1977) (22') •1 Sx: S+A+T+B/ 6 Perc •Led

DONATONI, Franco - *Hot* (1989) (14') •1 Sx: T+Sno/Cl+Eb Cl/Tpt/ Trb/Perc/Bass/Pno •Ric

ESCAICH, Thierry - *Antiennes oubliées* (1994) •Vln/Fl/Asx/Tpt/Trb/ Vcl/Vibr •Bil

ESCOT, Pozzi - *Visione* (1964-87) •Fl/Asx/Vibr/Soprano Voice/ Bass/Perc/Narr

FINNISSY, Michael - *Evening* (1974) •Asx/Hn/Tpt/Perc/Harp/Vcl/ Bass

GRÄSBECK, Mannfred - *Rapsodia...* •2 Vln/Vla/Vcl/Sx/Pno/Perc

GIUFFRE, James - *Fine* •Tsx/Guit/Vibr/Pno/2 Bass/Perc •MJQ

HAAS, Konrad - *Pieces* •Voice/Fl/Sx/Pno/Perc/Guit/Bass •Holz

HARTWELL, Hugh - *Soul Piece* (1967) •2 Sx: AT/Tpt/2 Pno/Bass/ Perc •CMC

HAYAKAWA, Masaaki - *Four Little Poems* (1979) (9'30) •4 Sx: SATB/Soprano Voice/Harp/Perc •SFC

HESPOS, Hans - *Passagen* (1969) (9') •Cl/Asx/Tpt/Trb/Vla/Bass/ Perc •EMod

HILLBORG, Anders - *Variations* (1991) •Soprano Voice/Mezzo Soprano Voice/Fl/Sx/Perc/Vla/Bass •SMIC

HODKINSON, Sidney - *Funks* (1969) (5') •4 Sx: AATB/Guit/Bass/ Perc •adr

ISHIHARA, Taduoki - *Successions* (1980) •Asx/6 Perc

JANSSEN, Werner - *Obsequies of a Saxophone* (1929) •6 Wind Instruments/Snare Drum

JENNEFELT, Thomas - *Stones* (1981) •Ob/Cl/Asx/Tpt/Guit/2 Perc

KARKOFF, Maurice - *Djurens Karneval* (1974) (15') •Fl/Picc/2 Cl/ Tsx/Bsn/Perc •STIM

KLEIN, Jonathan - *Hear O Israel* •Soprano Voice/Alto Voice/Sx/Hn/ Pno/Perc/Bass •SeMC

KOBLENZ, Babette - *Grey Fire* (1981) •Cl/2 Sx: AT/Tpt/Electr. Bass/ Electr. Pno/Perc •adr

LACOUR, Guy - *Divertissement* (1968) (13') •Asx/1 or 6 Perc •Bil

LARSSON, Häkan - *Farleder - 4 pieces* (1993) •Fl/Tsx/Trb/Electr. Guit/Electr. Bass/Pno/Perc •SvM

LAYZER, Arthur - *Inner and Outer Forms* •2 Sx/3 Brass/2 Perc

LONGY, George - *Rhapsodie - Lento* (1904) •Harp/Bass/2 Cl/Bsn/ Asx/Timp •South

LUDWIG, J. - *Stenogramme* •Fl/Tsx/Trb/Bass/Vibr/Harps/Perc •EMod

MACERO, Teo - *Structure no. 4* •3 Sx: ATB/Tpt/Trb/Tuba/Perc •ACA

MAJOS, Giulio di - *Passacaglia* •Fl/Asx/Hn/Guit/Vibr/Pno/Bass •Sch

MARCO, Tomàs - *Jabberwochy* (1967) •Voice/Tsx/Pno/4 Perc/Tape

Milhaud, Darius - *La Création du monde* (LONDEIX) •2 Vln/Asx/Vcl/ Bass/Perc/Pno •ME

NEMESCU, Octavian - *Septuor* (1983) •Fl/Cl/Trb/Tsx/Pno/Bass/ Perc

NORDENSTEN, Frank - *Sample and hold* (1978) (14') •Fl+Picc/ Cl+BsCl/1 Sx: S+T/Vln+Vla/Vcl/Pno/Perc

PINOS-SIMANDL, Aloïs - *Euforie* (1983) (10') •Ob (or Fl)/Asx/Cl/ BsCl/Pno/Perc/Bass •CHF

RADULESCU, Horatiu - *X* (1984-85) •Sx/Cl/2 Bsn/2 Bass/Perc

ROLIN, Etienne - *Quètes ancestrales* (1989) (14') •Tsx/Vla/2 Vcl/ Bass/Harp/Marimba •Fuz

SAGVIK, Stellan - *Sma gyckelvisor...*, op. 112 (1981) (8') •Fl/2 Cl/ Asx/Mandolin/2 Perc •STIM

SCHWERTSIK, Kurt - *Liebesträume*, op. 7 (1963) •Asx/Trb/Pno/ Vibr/Marimba/Harmonium/Bass •EMod

SEFFER, Yochk'o - *Dromüs* (1991) •Pno/Cl/Perc/4 Sx: SATBs *Torma* (7'30) •6 Sx: SnoSATBCBs/Perc

SKOUEN, Synne - *Hva sa Schopenhauer...* (1978) (8') •Narr/Fl/ Cl+BsCl/Sx/Vln/Vcl/Perc •NMI

SOLAL, Martial - *Triptyque* (1989) (55') •4Sx: SATB/Pno/Bass/Perc

SOTELO, Mauricio - *Quando il cielo...* (1989) (18') •Asx/Perc/Pno/ Vln/Vla/Vcl/Bass •ECA

SPROGIS, Eric - *Comme une légère inexactitude* (1992) •Asx/Hn/ Tpt/Trb/Tuba/2 Perc

STEVEN, Donald - *On the down side* (1982) •2 Sx: AB/Trb/2 Perc/ Pno/Electr. Bass •CMC

STOCKHAUSEN, Karlheinz - *Linker Augentanz* (1983) •6 Sx: SSAA T+B Bs/1 Perc •Stv

STOUT, Alan - *Four Antiphonies* •Fl/Trb/Asx/Org/Vln/Vla/Perc •CFE

STRINDBERG, Henrik - *Coming* (1982) (6') •2 Sx: SA/BsCl/Tpt/ Trb/2 Perc •SMIC
Kommandez (1982-84) (6') •3 Sx: SAB/Tpt/Trb/2 Perc •SMIC/ WIM

TAUTENAHN, Günther - *Septet* •Cl/Tpt/Tsx/Guit/Vcl/Pno/Perc •SeMC

TERRY, Peter - *Windows Looking...* •4 Sx: SATB/Pno/2 Perc •DP

VOUILLEMIN, Sylvain - *Divertimento...* (1983) (8'30) •Ssx/2 Vln/ Vla/Vcl/Bass/Perc or Ssx/Pno •Led

WILLIAMSON, Malcolm - *Merry Wives of Windsor* (1964) •Fl+Picc/ Cl/Tsx/Tpt/Perc/Bass/Pno •JW

WILLIS, Richard - *Irregular Resolutions* •Fl/Ob/Cl/Asx/Bsn/Hn/ Perc •adr

WOLF, Hans - *Lady Style* (1972) (3') •2 Asx/4 Trb/Perc •Moz
Tip Kick - Swing Fox (1964) (3') •4 Sx/Tpt/Trb/Perc •Moz

8 Musicians

ARMSTRONG, David - *The Protest* (1960) (9'30) •Cl/Trb/2 Asx/Tpt/ Perc/Pno/Bass •BMIC

AYOUB, Nick - *Saxtet* •6 Sx: SAATTB/Bass/Drums •DP

BABBITT, Milton - *All Set* (1957) •2 Sx: AT/Tpt/Trb/Vibr/Bass/Perc/ Pno •adr

BARK, Jan - *Ost-funk* (1964) (10') •Tpt/Asx/3 Perc/Pno/2 Bass •SMIC

BERG, Olav - *Fragments* (1977) (8') •Fl/Cl/Asx/Vla/Vcl/Pno/2 Perc •NMJ

BIRTWISTLE, Harrison - *Medusa* (1969/70/78) •Fl/Cl/Ssx/Pno/ Perc/Vln/Vla/Vcl/Tape

BÖRJESSON, Lars - *Divertimento*, op. 38 (1983) •Asx/BsCl/Bsn/ Guit/Harp/Marimba/Vln/Vcl •STIM

BREGENT, Michel - *Melorytharmundi* (1984) •Fl/Cl/Sx/2 Perc/Pno/ Vcl/Guit •CMC

BULOW, Harry - *Crystal Cove* •Tpt/3 Sx: AAT/Pno/Bass/Guit/ Drums •adr

CHATMAN, Stephen - *Outer Voices* (1978) •Fl/Cl/Asx/2 Perc/ Celesta/Guit/Harp/Tape •CMC

DECOUST, Michel - *Ombres portées* (1986) (9') •2 Ob/Cl/2 Asx/ Harp/Pno/Perc •Sal

DELAMARRE, Pierre - *La 8* (1981) (3') •Fl/Ob/Cl/Asx/Pno 4 hands [à 4 mains]/Bass/Perc •adr

DEPELSENAIRE, Jean-Marie - *Octuor moderne* (1978) •2 Tpt/2 Asx/4 Perc •Chou

DESCARPENTRIES, Hugues - *ô* (1993) (3'30) •Voice/5 Sx: SATBBs/ Pno/Perc

DUHAMEL, Antoine - *Le Transibérien* (1983) •Asx/Tpt/Pno/Perc/ Harmonica/3 Armenian Instruments

EMMER, Huib - *Camera eye* (1978-79) (15') •2 Sx/2 Guit/2 Pno/2 Perc •Don

ERNRYD, Bengt - *Rödingsjön II* (1967) •Fl+Picc/Trb/Tsx+Perc/ Bsx+Perc/Vcl/Bass/2 Perc •SMIC

FABERMAN, Harold - *For Erik and Nick* (1964) •Tenor Voice/Asx/ Vcl/Bass/Tpt/Trb/Vibr/Perc

FONTYN, Jacqueline - *Cheminement* (1986) (15') •Soprano Voice/ Fl/Cl/Hn (or Asx)/Vcl/Bass/Perc/Pno

FRANCESCONI, Luca - *Piccola trama* (1989) (14') •1 Sx: S+A/Fl/ Cl/Guit/Perc/Vln/Vla/Vcl •Ric

FRANCO, Clare - *Four Winds...* •Asx/Harp/Vibr/Fl/Ob/Cl/Hn/Bsn

GARCIN, Gérard - *Encore plus tard* (1984) (12') •1 Sx: Sno+A+Bs/ Fl/Cl/Bsn/Vla/Vcl/Bass/Perc/Tape •Sal

GUY, Georges - *Concerto en forme de jazz* •Asx Solo/Pno Solo/Fl/Ob/ Cl/Hn/Bsn/Bass

HACHIMURA, Yoshiro - *Concerto per 8 soli* •Fl/Cl/Sx/Vibr/Vcl/ Vla/2 Perc •OE

HARBISON, John - *The Flower-fed Buffaloes* (1976) •Voice/Cl/Tsx/ Fl/Vcl/Bass/Pno/Perc

HEKSTER, Walter - *Of mere being* (1982) (12') •Asx/Fl/Ob/Cl/2 Tpt/ Perc/Electr. Guit •Don

HODEIR, André - *Ambiguité II* (8'); *Bicinium* (3') •3 Sx: ATB/2 Tpt/ Trb/Bass/Perc •MJQ

HOUNSELL - *Showcase for Saxes* •5 Sx/Pno/Bass/Perc •TMPI

KETTING, Otto - *Musik zu einen Tonfilm* (1982) (15') •2 Sx/Tpt/Trb/ Perc/Pno/2 Vln •Don

KORTE, Karl - *Matrix* (1968) (16') •Fl/Ob/Cl/Asx/Hn/Bsn/Pno/Perc •GSch

LAKE, Larry - *Filar il tuono* (1989) •Cl/3 Sx: ATB/Bsn/Tpt/Trb/ Marimba •CMC

LANTIER, Pierre - *Fugue jazz* (1944) (3') •2 Cl/2 Sx: AT/Bsn/Tpt/ Trb/Perc

LAURETTE, Marc - *Kaleïdoscope* •Cl/Bsn/2 Sx: SB/Hn/Vla/Bass/ Vibr

MANDANICI, Marcella - *Extraits I* (1989) •Tsx/Fl/Cl/Pno/Perc/Vln/ Vla/Vcl •adr

MAYUZUMI, Toshiro - *Sphenogramme* (1951) •Contralto Voice/Fl/ Asx/Marimba/Vln/Vcl/Pno 4 hands [à 4 mains]

MICHEL, Paul - *Ultramorphoses* (1965) (12-15') •Fl/Cl/Asx/Perc/ Pno/Vln/Vla/Vcl •CBDM

NAULAIS, Jérôme - *Mise à sax* •5 Sx: SATTB/Pno/Bass/Drums •Arp

NICKLAUS, Wolfgang - *Die Antwort* (1986) (7'30) •Cl/Asx/2 Perc/ Pno/Vln/Vcl/Bass •adr

NIHASHI, Jun-ichi - *Pratinade* •Sx/6 Perc/Tablas

PERSSON, Bob - *Om sommaren sköna II* (1965) •Fl/BsCl/Trb/2 Perc/ Vibr/Vcl/Jazz Sx/Tape

PINOS-SIMANDL, Aloïs - *Geneze* (1970) (8') •Vln/Asx/Vcl/Trb/ Perc/Harp/Harps/Ionika •CHF

RABE, Folke - *Pajazzo* (1964) •Tpt/Asx/Pno/2 BsCl/3 Perc •STIM

RADULESCU, Horatiu - *Sky* (1984-85) •Sx/Cl/Fl/2 Bsn/2 Bass/Perc

SAGVIK, Stellan - *Suite circuler*, op. 86 (1978) (10') •Picc/Asx/Tpt/ Hn/2 Trb/Perc/Bass •STIM

SCOTT, Andy - *Pieces* •5 Sx: AATTB or SATTB/Pno/Bass/Drums •PBP

SEFFER, Yochk'o - *Alpha-gamma* (1990) •Tsx improvised/5 Sx:SnoSATB/Bass/Perc

Dépression (1985) •Tsx improvised/4 Sx: SATB/BsCl/Bass/Perc

SUTER, Robert - *Estampida* •Fl/Cl/Tsx/Hn/Tpt/Trb/Bass/Perc •EMod

TANENNBAUM, Elias - *Consort* •Fl/Hn/Asx/Electr. Guit/Vcl/Bass/ Vibr/Jazz drums •ACA

TOMASSON, Haukur - *Octette* (1987) •Fl/Cl/Asx/Hn/Vla/Vcl/Pno/ Perc (Vibr+Gong) •IMIC

VELLONES, Pierre - *A Cadix*, op. 102 (1938) (4') •3 Sx/2 Ondes Martenot/Bass/Harp/Perc

VILLA-LOBOS, Heitor - *Chôros n° 7* (1924) (10') •Fl/Ob/Cl/Asx/ Bsn/Vln/Vcl/Tam-tam •ME

9 Musicians

ALBRIGHT, William - *Introduction...* (14') •Pno/Fl/Cl/Asx/Hn/Tpt/ Trb/Tuba/Perc •Pet

BORTOLOTTI, Mauro - *Studio per E.E. Cummings n° 2* (1964) •Vla/ Vcl/Bass/Ob/Cl/BsCl/Sx/Hn/Perc •adr

CLARK, Thomas - *Dreamscape* •Fl/Ob/Cl/Sx/Tpt/Trb/Pno/Perc/ Bass •SeMC

COX, Rona - *Two Expressions* (1968) •Fl/Ob/Cl/2 Sx: SB/Hn/Bsn/ Bass/Perc •adr

CUSTER, Arthur - *Cycle for Nine Instruments* •Asx/BsCl/Tpt/Hn/ Vln/Vla/Vcl/Bass/Perc •JM

DANKWORTH, John - *Fairoak Fusion* (1979) (45') •4 Sx: SATB/ Vln/Jazz Quartet

FICHER, Jacobo - *Los invitados*, op. 26 •Fl/Cl/2 Sx: AT/2 Tpt/Tuba/ Pno/Perc

FISCHER, Eric - *Tango* (1982) •2 Cl/4 Sx: SATB/Mallet Perc [Perc à clavier]/Synth/Pno •adr

GRAINGER, Ella - *To Echo* (1945) •Soprano Voice/Picc/Fl/Cl+Asx/ Tsx/Vla/BsCl/Bass/Marimba •GS

GRANDERT, Johnny - *86 T* •Fl/EH/BsCl/Bsx/CBsn/2 Tpt/Perc/Pno •STIM

GUALDA JIMENEZ, Antonio - *Noneto Zarco* (1988) (16') •Vln/Vcl/ Cl/2 Sx: SA/Vibr/Marimba/Guit/Pno

HAHN, Reynaldo - *Divertissement...* (1933) (25') •2 Vln/Vla/Vcl/ Bass/Asx/Bsn/Timp/Perc •Sal

HODEIR, André - *Pieces* •3 Sx: ATB/2 Tpt/Trb/Vibr/Bass/Perc •MJQ

IVES, Charles - *Over the Pavements*, op. 20 (1906-13) •Picc/Cl/Bsx (or Bsn)/Tpt/3 Trb/Perc/Pno •PIC

JELINEK, Hanns - *Blue Sketches*, op. 25 (1956) •Fl/Cl/2 Sx: AB/Tpt/ Trb/Vibr/Bass/Perc •EMod

LEGRAND, Michel - *Porcelaine de Sax* (1958) (3') •6 Sx: SnoSATBBs (or Eb Cl/Cl/3 Sx: ATB/Bsn) Trb/Bass/Perc •Mills

LEWIS, John Aaron - *Little David's Fugue* (5'30) •Fl/Cl/3 Sx: ATB/ Trb or Tpt/Harp or Pno/Bass/Perc •MJQ

The Queen's Fancy (4') •Fl/Cl/Tsx/Bsn/Hn/Trb/Harp/Bass/Perc •MJQ

Sun Dance (4') •Fl/Cl/3 Sx: ATB/Trb/Harp or Guit/Bass/Perc •MJQ

MARCO, Tomàs - *Anna Blume* (1967) •2 Narr/Fl/Ob/Cl/Sx/Tpt/2 Perc

McFARLAND, Gary - *Night Float* (4'30) •3 Sx: ATB/Tpt/Hn/Guit/ Pno/Bass/Drums •MJQ

MELLNÄS, Arne - *Drones* (1967) (8') •Fl/Cl/3 Sx: ATB/Tpt/Perc/ Vcl/Bass •STIM

MULDOWNEY, Dominic - *An Heavyweight Dirge* (1971) (25') •Voice/Fl/Asx/Perc/Pno/2 Vln/Vla/Vcl •Nov

NATANSON, Tadeus - *3 Pictures for 7 Instruments* (1960) •Ob/Cl/ Asx/Trb/Vcl/Tpt/Bsn/Pno/Perc •AMP

NONO, Luigi - *Polifonica, Monodia, Ritmica* (1951) (10') •Fl/Cl/ BsCl/Asx/Hn/4 Perc •AVV

ODSTRCIL, Karl - *Transit* •8 Sx/Perc

RENOSTO, Paolo - *Dissolution* •Vla/Vcl/Bass/Ob/Cl/BsCl/Sx/Hn/ Perc

SAGVIK, Stellan - *Det Förlorade steget*, op. 64 (1976) (20') •Fl/
Cl+BsCl/Asx/Cnt/Trb/Vln/Vla/Vcl/Perc
•SMIC

SCHULLER, Gunther - *Abstraction* (1959) (5') •Asx/Guit/Perc/2
Vln/Vla/Vcl/2 Bass •MJQ

SÖDERLIND, Ragnar - *Eg hev funne...* (1982) (9'); *Legg ikkje ditt...*
(1983) •Soprano Voice/Fl+Picc/Ssx/Hn/Vln/
Vla/Bass/Pno/Perc •NMI

SVOBODA, Tomàs - *Seven Short Dances* •Fl/2 Cl/Asx/Trb/Vln/Bass/
Pno/Perc

TANENBAUM, Elias - *Trios I, II, III* •Fl/Ob/Cl/Vln/Vla/Vcl/Bass/
Asx/Perc •ACA

VELLONES, Pierre - *Planisphère*, op. 23 (1930) •2 Sx: AT/Cl/2 Tpt/
Trb/Bass (or Tuba)/Perc/Pno •JJ

WALTON, William - *Façade* (1922/26, 42) (34'30) •2 Narr/Fl+Picc/
Cl/BsCl/Asx/Tpt/Vcl/Perc •OUP

WILDER, Alec - *Suite* •Bsx/Fl/Ob/Cl/2 Hn/Bsn/Bass/Drums

YOSHIBA, Susumu - *Erka* •Fl/Ob/Sx/Tpt/Trb/Perc/Vcl/Guit/Pno

10 Musicians

BANKS, Donald - *Equation 1* (1964) (7') •Tpt/Asx/Pno/Harp/Guit/
Perc/2 Vln/Vla/Vcl •BMIC

BENNETT, Richard Rodney - *Jazz Pastorale* (1969) (25') •Voice/1
Sx: A+T/Bsx/2 Tpt/Trb/Tuba/Pno/Bass/Perc
•Uni

COE, Tony - *The Buds of Time* (1979) (20') •Cl+Sx/Cl+BsCl/2 Vln/
Vla/Vcl/BsTrb/Pno/Bass/Perc •adr

COSTEN, Roel van - *Prisma* (1984) (8') •Vla/Fl/Cl/Asx/BsCl/Trb/
Vcl/Bass/Perc/Pno •Don

FORTNER, Jack - *S pr ING sur des poèmes de E. E. Cummings* (1966)
(11') •Mezzo Soprano Voice/Fl/Asx/Bsn/
Vla/Vcl/Bass/Vibr/Harp/Pno •JJ

GOODMAN, Alfred - *3 Gesänge für Gresang* •Soprano Voice/Fl/Ob/
Asx/Cl/Vla/Vcl/Prepared Pno/Guit/Perc •adr

GOTTSCHALK, Arthur - *Cycloid* •Cl/Asx/Hn/Tpt/Harp/Vibr/2 Vln/
Vla/Vcl •SeMC

GOUGEON, Denis - *Heureux qui comme...* (1987) •Soprano Voice/
Picc/EH/Bsx/2 Vln/Vla/Vcl/Bass/Perc
•CMC

GRANDIS, Renato de - *Scotter Sud-est* •Vln/Vla/Vcl/Bass/Sx/Hn/
Tpt/Trb/Pno/Perc •SeMC

HEIDEN, Bernhard - *Sonatina* •Fl/Cl/Tsx/Hn/Trb/Harp/Vibr/Pno/
Bass/Perc •MJQ

HODEIR, André - *Jazz cantata* (10') •Soprano Voice/3 Sx: ATB/2
Tpt/Trb/Vibr/Bass/Perc •MJQ

HOVHANESS, Alan - *Is This Survival?*, op. 59 (1949) •4 Cl/Asx/4
Tpt/Perc

JOHNSON, J. J. - *Turnpike* (5') •Fl/Cl/3 Sx: ATB/Trb/Harp (or Guit)/
Pno/Bass/Perc •MJQ

KOPP, Frederick - *Terror Suite* •Brass/Sx/Timp/3 Perc •SeMC

LACHARTE, Nicole - *La Geste inachevée* (1980) •Fl/Cl/Sx/Tpt/Trb/
Pno/Perc/Vln/Vla/Vcl

LEWIS, John Aaron - *The Milanese Story* •Fl/Tsx/Guit/Pno/Bass/2
Vln/Vla/Vcl/Perc •MJQ

LINDBERG, Nils - *Progression* (1985) (28') •Fl/Ob/Cl/Hn/Bsn/2 Sx:
SA/Pno/Bass/Drums •SMIC

MASON, Benedict - *Coulour and information* (1993) •Fl/Ob/Sx/Bsn/
Hn/Tpt/Trb/Tuba/Perc/Electr. Bass

NILSSON, Anders - *Krasch!* (1993) •4 Sx: SATB/6 Perc/Tape •SMIC

PAUMGARTNER, Bernhard - *Divertimento* •Picc/EH/Asx/Bsn/Hn/
Tpt/Pno/Vla/Vcl/Perc •Uni

SCELSI, Jacinto - *I Presagi* (1958) (9'30) •2 Hn/2 Tpt/Sx/2 Trb/2
Tuba/Perc •Sal

SCHAFFER, Boguslaw - *Permutations n° 27* (1956) •Fl/Ob/Cl/Sx/
Tpt/Trb/Vla/Perc/Harp/Pno •A&S

SCHULLER, Gunther - *12 by 11* (8'30) •Fl/Cl/Tsx/Hn/Trb/Vibr/Pno/
Harp/Bass/Perc •MJQ

SCHWERTSIK, Kurt - *Salotto romano*, op. 5 (1961) •BsCl/Bsx/Bsn/
Hn/Trb/Tuba/Perc/Bass/Vcl/Guit •EMod

SMITH, Linda - *Periphery* (1979) •Fl/Sx/Tpt/Marimba/Vibr/Chimes/
Pno/Vln/Vcl/Bass •CMC

SMITH, William - *Elegy for Eric* •Fl/2 Sx: AB/Cl/Tpt/Trb/Vibr/Vln/
Bass/Perc •MJQ

TREMBLAY, George - *Epithalamium* (1962) •Fl/Ob/Cl/Sx/Bsn/Hn/
Tpt/Trb/Tuba/Perc •CFE

VELLONES, Pierre - *Deux Pièces...*, op. 67 (1935) (6'30) •2 Fl/4 Sx/
Pno/Bass/Perc/Ondes Martenot •Sal

WILDER, Alec - *She'll Be Seven in May* •Fl/Ob/Asx/2 Cl/BsCl/Bsn/
Bass/Drums/Pno

WROCHEM, Klaus - *Oratorium meum plus praeperturi* •3 Voices/2
Vln/Vla/Vcl/Asx/Tpt/Perc •CAP

11 Musicians

COLE, Bruce - *Pantomimes* (25') •Soprano Voice/Fl/Cl/BsCl/Ssx/
Perc/Pno/Guit/Vln/Vla/Vcl •B&H

DIEMENTE, Edward - *3-31 '70* •Voice/Tpt/Trb/Sx/Guit/Bass/5 Perc
•SeMC

HALL, Helene - *Pieces* •5 Soprano Voices/3 Sx: SAB/Vcl/2 Perc
•CMC

HAZZARD, Peter - *Massage* •3 Voices (SAB)/3 Perc/Fl/Cl/Hn/Sx/
Trb •SeMC

HESPOS, Hans - *Break* •Ob/3 Tpt/2 Sx: TB/Vcl/Bass/Trb/Pno/Perc
•EMod

MARTIRANO, Salvatore - *Underworld* (1959) •4 Actors/Tsx/4 Perc/
2 Bass/2 Track tape

MESTRAL, Patrice - *Alliages* (1969) •Tpt Solo/Fl/Cl/Asx/2 Trb/2
Perc/Pno/Org/Bass

MONDELLO, Nuncio - *Suite* (1956) •Asx/2 Fl/Ob/Cl/Bsn/2 Hn/Tpt/
Trb/Perc •adr

PABLO, Luis de - *Polar*, op. 12 (1963) •Vln/Ssx/BsCl/Xylophone/
Trb/6 Perc •Tono/SeMC

PÜTZ, Eduard - *Kon-Takte* •Vocal Quartet (SATB)/Fl/Sx/Vibr/Guit/
Perc/Pno/Bass •SeMC

SCHILLING, Otto-Erich - *Überall ist Wunderland* •Voice/Fl/Cl/Sx/
Tpt/2 Vln/Bass/Perc/Accordion/Pno •SeMC

TRIMBLE, Lester - *Panels I* (1973) (6') •Picc/Bsx/Vln/Vla/Vcl/Bass/
2 Perc/Electr. Guit/Electr. Org/Electr. Harp
•Pet

ZONN, Paul Martin - *Voyage of Columbus* (1974) (13') •Tpt Solo/Fl/
Ob/Ssx/Hrn/Trb/2 Perc/Pno/Vln/Bass •ACA

12 Musicians

BENNETT, Richard Rodney - *A Jazz Calender* (1963-64) (31') •Fl/
3 Sx: ATB/2 Tpt/Hn/Trb/Tuba/Pno/2 Perc
•Uni

DUREY, Louis - *Feu la mère de Madame*, op. 49 (1945) (5') •Fl/Ob/
Asx/Bsn/Tpt/Tuba/Perc/2 Vln/Vla/Vcl/Bass
•BRF

HOVHANESS, Alan - *After Water* •3 Cl/3 Tpt/3 Asx/Perc/Harp/Pno
•ACA

LEWIS, Arthur - *Pieces of Eight* •Fl/2 Ob/3 Cl/Bsn/2 Tsx/Hn/Baritone
Hn/Perc •CAP

LINKOLA, Jukka - *Alta* (1983) (8') •Vocal group: SATBs/2 Sx: AT/
Tpt/Trb/Pno/Bass/Drums/Perc •FMIC

MEIJERING, Chiel - *Het ontblote feit* (1988-90) (8'30) •2 Fl/3 Sx:
ATB/2 Hn/Tpt/Trb/Perc/Pno/Electr. Guit
•Don

PAPE, Gérard - *Pour un tombeau d'Anatole* (1985) •Soprano Voice/
Perc/Sx Orch: SSAAATTTBBs

RECK, David - *Number 1 for 12 Performers* (15') •Fl/Cl/Tsx/Hn/Guit/
        Vibr/Pno/Bass/Perc •MJQ
ROBBINS, David - *Improvisation* •Fl/2 Cl/Tsx/Bsn/Tpt/Trb/Vln/Vla/
        Vcl/Bass/Perc
TOEPLITZ, Kasper - *Johnny Panic...* (25') •1 Sx: T+CBs/Mezzo
        Soprano Voice/2 Fl/2 Cl/Hn/2 Vln/2 Vla/
        Perc/Tape
TORSTENSSON, Klas - *Spâra* (1984) (13') •3 Sx/3 Bs Guit/2 Electr.
        Pno/4 Perc •Don

13 Musicians

BOZZA, Eugène - *Ouverture pour une cérémonie* •3 Tpt/4 Sx/3 Trb/
        BsTrb/Tuba/Perc •Led
DELANNOY, Marcel - *Le Marchand de notes* •3 Vln/Bass/4 Sx/2 Tpt/
        Trb/Perc/Pno
EICHMANN, Dietrich - *George...* (1984) (35') •3 Fl/Cl/2 Sx: AT/2
        Tpt/Trb/2 Perc/Pno/Bs Guit •adr
FINNISSY, Michael - *Babylon* (1971) (19') •Mezzo Soprano Voice/
        Ob/Cl/Asx/Bsn/Guit/Harp/Pno/2 Perc/2 Vcl/
        Bass •Uni
GRAEF, Friedemann - *Kammersinfonie* (1992) (20') 3 Voices/Str
        Quartet/4 Sx: SATB/2 Perc
HESPOS, Hans - *Conga* (1979) (15'30) •Tsx/5 Congas/2 Vln/2 Vla/
        2 Vcl/Bass •Hes
    Keime und male (9') •Picc/Fl/2 Cl/Asx/Hn/Guit/Vln/Vla/Bass/3
        Perc •JJ
HUREL, Philippe - *"Pour l'image"* •Fl/Ob/Cl/Asx/Hn/Tpt/Trb/Perc/
        2 Vln/Vla/Vcl/Bass
LEMAY, Robert - *Vagues vertiges* (1989) (21') •12 Sx:
        SnoSSAAATTTBBBs/1 Perc •adr
McKINLEY, Thomas - *Emsdettener Totentanz* •3 Voices/Str Quartet/
        4 Sx: SATB/2 Perc
SAMAMA, Leo - *Soit que l'abîme*, op. 19 (1983) (20') •5 Sx: SAATB/
        8 Perc •Don
SEKON, Joseph - *Lemon Ice* (1972) •Fl/Ob/Cl/2 Sx: ST/Bsn/Tpt/Trb/
        2 Perc/Vln/Vcl/Pno •adr
WENDEL, Eugen - *Saphonospir* (15') •Asx/Fl/Cl/Ob/Tpt/Trb/2 Vln/
        Vla/Vcl/Bass/2 Perc •adr

14 Musicians

GRAINGER, Percy - *The Duke of Marlborough* (1905-39-49) •4 Tpt/
        4 Hn (or 2 Sx: AT/2 Bsn)/3 Trb/Tuba/Bass/
        Cymb. •Sch
HARBISON, John - *Confinement* (1965) (15'15) •Fl/Ob/EH/Cl/BsCl/
        Asx/Tpt/Trb/Vln/Vla/Vcl/Bass/Pno/Perc
HARVEY, Jonathan - *The Valley of Aosta* (1985) (13'30) •Fl/Ob/Ssx/
        Tpt/2 Yamaha DX7 Synth/2 Harp/Pno/2 Vln/
        Vla/Vcl/Perc •FM
HAVEL, Christophe - *Amers I* (1992) (12') •12 Sx: SnoSSAAATTT
        BBBs/2 Perc •adr
MIEREANU, Costin - *Clair de biche* (1986) (11') •Fl/Picc/Cl/1 Sx:
        Sno+S+T/Brass Quintet/5 Perc •Sal
MINAMIKAWA, Mio - *Métaplasm* (1982) •12 Sx: SnoSSAAATTT
        BBBs/2 Perc •adr
NICOLAU, Dimitri - *Concerto...*, op. 77 (1988) •Pno/12 Sx:
        SnoSSAAATTTBBBs/Perc •adr
    Quarta sinfonia, op. 70 (1987) (10') •Sx Orch:
        SnoSSAAATTTBBBs/Soprano Voice/Perc
ROSSÉ, François - *Paléochrome* (1988) (22') •Vla principal/2 Fl/Cl/
        BsCl/1 Sx: S+T/EH/Bsn/Hn/4 Perc/Bass •adr
UDOW, Michael - *Understanding* (1969) (15') •6 Unspecified instru-
        ments/8 Perc/Tape •MP

15 Musicians

LAMB, John David - *Cenotaph* (1987) (30') •13 Sx: SSSAAAATTT
        BBBs/2 Perc
LUTYENS, Elisabeth - *Islands*, op. 80 (1971) •2 Narr: ST/Picc/Fl/Cl/
        BsCl/Tsx/Hn/Pno/Celesta/Vln/Vla/Vcl/2
        Perc
TEMPLE & SHAW - *Vanity Fair Suite* •Fl/Ob/4 Cl/BsCl/Asx/2 Vln/
        Vla/Vcl/Bass/Perc/Pno •Mills

16 Musicians

BASSET, Leslie - *Designs in Brass* •2 Sx: BB/4 Hn/4 Tpt/3 Trb/Tuba/
        Timp/Perc •Pio
GROUVEL, Pierre - *Volcan* (1993) (16'15) •Sx Solo: A+T+B/12 Sx:
        SnoSSAAATTTBBBs/3 Perc

oOo

ALLA, Thierry - *La terre et la Comète* (1991) •Fl/Cl/Asx/Pno/Bass/
        Synth/Perc/Tape/Children's Choir •adr
ANSIND, Caroline - *Het water...* (1986) (14'30) •Ob/Cl/2 Sx: AB/2
        Trb/Perc/Pno/Choir •Don
BANK, Jacques - *Requiem voor een Levende* (1985) (50') •Récit.
        Choeur/4 Sx/9 Accordion/3 Bass/3 Perc •Don
FISCHER, Eric - *Spleen...* (1984) •Jazz Group including [dont] 4 Sx:
        SATB/Electr. Bass/Perc •adr
HEUSSENSTAMM, George - *Periphony No. 3*, op. 70 (1980) (18')
        •16 Sx: 4 x SATB/4 Perc •DP
HOFFER, Bernard - *The River* (1984) (30') •4 Sx: SATB/Large Perc
        Ensemble •Shir
KOPP, Frederick - *Terror Suite* •Brass/Sx/Timpani/3 Perc •SeMC
LUEDEKE, Raymond - *"Of him I love day and night"* & *"A noiseless,
        patient spider"* •Chorus (SATB)/4 Sx:
        SATB/Bass/2 Perc
MELLÉ, Patrick - *Seriotis*, op. 4 (1985) (10') •2 Sx: TB/Men's chorus
        [Choeur d'hommes]/Soprano Voice Solo/
        Perc/Pno/Synth/Tape
PARKER, Phillip - *Sketches* (1990) •Asx/Perc Ensemble
RILEY, Terry - *A Rainbow in Curved Air* (1970) •Partly improvised
        Sx/Keyboards/Perc/Tapes
TELFER, Nancy - *The Golden Cage* (1979) •Mixed Choir/Fl/Cl/Sx/
        3 Perc/Pno
VELLONES, Pierre - *Fête fantastique*, op. 83 (1937) (18') •2 Sx: AT/
        3 Ondes Martenot/Pno/Fl/2 Cl/Bsn/3 Tpt/2
        Trb/Tuba/2 Bass/Perc/Exotic Perc
VILLA-LOBOS, Heitor - *Nonetto*, op. 181 (1923) (18') •Fl/Ob/Cl/1
        Sx: A+B/Bsn/Perc/Celesta/Harp/Pno/Mixed
        Chorus •ME
WEISS, Adolph - *Tone Poem* •2 Sx/Brass/Perc •ACA

Saxophone and Accordion

2 Musicians

DESPORTES, Yvonne - *L'Homme des cavernes* (6') •Tsx/Accordion
        or Pno •DP
DHAINE, Jean-Louis - *Cantabile* •Asx/Accordion (or Pno)
FIALA, George - *Sonata...* (1971) (14'30) •Ssx/Accordion •CMC
HISCOTT, James - *Mac Crimmon Will Never Return* (1977) (4'30)
        •Asx/Accordion •CMC
LEUCHTER, Heibert - *Contemplativo* (1993) •1 Sx: A+B/Accordion
        •INM
MOTZ, Wolfgang - *Goranî-gazîn* (1993) •Asx/Accordion •INM

3 Musicians

MOLAND, Eirik - *Trio* (1982) •Fl/Asx/Accordion •NMI

VEERHOFF, Carlos - *Moments musicaux*, op. 50 •Asx/Accordion/
Perc

WOLF, Hans - *Honey Polka* (1971) (3') •Asx/Accordion/Perc •Figurata

4 Musicians

FUENTES, Tristan - *Pan Am* •BsCl+Ssx/Synth/Vibr+Steel Drum/
Marimba+Accordion/Tape •HMC

GERMETEN, Gunnar - *Applaus* (1985) •Cl/Sx/Trb/Accordion

5 Musicians

FLETA POLO, Francisco - *Divertimento 26* (1985) •Sx/Cl/Accordion/Bass/Timp

MACERO, Teo - *Exploration* •Asx/Cl/Bass/Perc/Accordion

6 Musicians

HISCOTT, James - *Ballad No. 1* (1978) (14') •Fl/Cl/Sx/Perc/Accordion/Pno •CMC

HORWOOD, Michael - *Interphases* (1975) (13') •Fl/Sx/Accordion
(or Org)/Pno/2 Perc •CMC

7 Musicians

ROSSÉ, François - *OEM* (1988) (21') •Soprano Voice/1 Sx: S+Bs/
EH/Accordion/Bass/Jazz Guit/Pno/Dispositif électro-acoust. •adr

9 Musicians

TARENSKEEN, Boudewijn - *Nonet* (1982) (13') •Asx/Hn/BsCl/
Accordion/Banjo/Harp/Vla/Vcl/Bass •Don

10 Musicians

HORWOOD, Michael - *Facets* (1974) (20') •Narr/Sx/Tpt/Hn/Trb/
Pno/Accordion/Electr. Bass/2 Electr. Guit
•CMC

11 Musicians

SCHILLING, Otto-Erich - *Überall ist Wunderland* •Voice/Fl/Cl/Sx/
Tpt/2 Vln/Bass/Perc/Accordion/Pno •SeMC

13 Musicians

FINNISSY, Michael - *First sign a sharp white mons* (1974-67) (45')
•2 Fl/2 Cl/Asx/CBsn/Hn/Accordion/Guit/
Vln/2 Vcl/Pno •BMIC

oOo

BANK, Jacques - *Requiem...* (1985) (50') •Récit. Choeur/4 Sx/9
Accordion/3 Bass/3 Perc •Don

QUELLE, Ernst-August - *"Kommissar Maigret-valse"* (1964) (2'30)
•Accordion/Sx/Perc/Str Orch •adr

Saxophone and Celesta

2 Musicians

GOLDSTAUB, Paul - *Graphic IV* (1973) •Asx/Celesta or Pno •DP
Sonata (1972) (8'30) •Asx/Pno or Celesta •adr

3 Musicians

MORRISSON, Julia - *John I, 19-23* •Alto Voice/Asx/Celesta •CFE

VELLONES, Pierre - *Rapsodie*, op. 92 (1937) (4'30) •Asx/Harp/
Celesta or Asx/Pno •Lem

4 Musicians

HAVEL, Christophe - *AER (la danse)* (1994) (10') •Picc/SnoSx/
Celesta/Perc •adr

MIGOT, Georges - *2 Stèles de Victor Segalen* (1925) (15') •Voice (or
Asx)/Celesta/Bass/Perc •Led

VILLA-LOBOS, Heitor - *Quatuor*, op. 168 (1921) (20') •Fl/Asx/
Celesta/Harp •ME

5 Musicians

ROSENBLOOM, David - *The thud, thud, thud...* (1966) •Sx/Electric
Vcl/Pno/Celesta/Perc/Tape/Lights •SeMC

6 Musicians

BOUDREAU, Walter - *Variations* (1975) •Ssx/Asx+Fl/Tsx+Picc/
Tuba/Pno+Celesta/Guit •CMC

DINESCU-LUCACI, Violeta - *"Auf der Suche nach Mozart"* (1983)
(19') •Fl/Sx/Bsn/Hn/Vln/Pno+Celesta •adr

VILLA-LOBOS, Heitor - *Sexteto mistico*, op. 123 (1917) (9') •Fl/Ob/
Asx/Guit/Celesta/Harp •ME

8 Musicians

CHATMAN, Stephen - *Outer Voices* (1978) •Fl/Cl/Asx/2 Perc/
Celesta/Guit/Harp/Tape •CMC

15 Musicians

LUTYENS, Elisabeth - *Islands*, op. 80 (1971) •2 Narr: ST/Picc/Fl/Cl/
BsCl/Tsx/Hn/Pno/Celesta/Vln/Vla/Vcl/2
Perc

oOo

VILLA-LOBOS, Heitor - *Nonetto*, op. 181 (1923) (18') •Fl/Ob/Cl/1
Sx: A+B/Bsn/Perc/Celesta/Harp/Pno/Mixed
Chorus •ME

Saxophone and Harpsichord (Clavecin)

2 Musicians

CHATMAN, Stephen - *Whisper Rachel* (1976) (8') •Asx/Harps •DP

FURRER-MÜNCH, Franz - *Aufgebrochene Momente* (1991) •Tsx/
Harps •adr

GOODMAN, Alfred - *Universum* (1993) •Asx/Harps •INM

GROSSE-SCHWARE, Hermann - *Fantasiestück* •Asx/Harps •PJT

RESCHTNEFKI, Markus - *Psychosomatik* (1993) •Ssx/Harps •INM

3 Musicians

FURRER-MÜNCH, Franz - *Momenti...* (1989) •Tsx/Harps/Perc •adr

ROESGEN-CHAMPION, Marguerite - *Concert n° 1; Concert n° 2*
(1945) •Asx/Bsn/Harps •FDP

5 Musicians

SORG, Margarete - *Cantica Catulliana* (1986) (11') •Soprano Voice/
Baritone Voice/Tsx/Pno+Harps/Perc •adr

6 Musicians

SCHUBACK, Peter - *A Priori* (1983) (45') •Sx/Trb/Perc/Vlc/Pno/
Harps •Tons/SMIC

7 Musicians

ALLGEN, Claude - *Praeludium och Carmen Perlotense* •Vln/Vla/
Vcl/Asx/Pno/Harps/Org •STIM

LUDWIG, J. - *Stenogramme* •Fl/Tsx/Trb/Bass/Vibr/Harps/Perc •EMod

8 Musicians

PINOS-SIMANDL, Aloïs - *Geneze* (1970) (8') •Vln/Asx/Vcl/Trb/
Perc/Harp/Harps/Ionika •CHF

9 Musicians

RYTTERKVIST, Hans - *Lied ohne Worte* (1968) •3 Vln/Vla/2 Vcl/
Harps/Pno/Bsx •SMIC

10 Musicians

MAROS, Miklos - *Coalottino* (1969) (5') •Bsx/Electr. instrum./2 Pno/ Harps/2 Vln/Vla/2 Vcl •STIM

oOo

DUPIN, Paul - *Chant* (1910) •Asx/Harps/Vla/Chorus

Saxophone and Organ or Harmonium

2 Musicians

ALBERTH, Rudolf - *Piece* •Asx/Org

Albinoni, Tomaso - *Adagio* (GIAZOTTO-LONDEIX) •Asx/Org •Lem

ANDRES, Edouard - *Méditation* (5') •Asx/Org

ARNOLD, André - *Thème varié* (1979) •Asx/Org

Aubigny, L. d' - *Prière* (1890) •Ob or Asx/Pno or Org

Bach, J. S. - *Pieces* (GEE) •Asx/Pno or Org •Ken/Lud

BACKE, Ruth - *Fantasia...* (1982) •Asx/Org

BEUGNIOT, Jean-Pierre - *Omenage* (5'30) •Ssx/Org •adr

BIELER, Helmet - *Fantasia* (1987) (12') •Asx/Org •adr

BOUVARD, Jean - *Andantino* (1976) •Asx/Org •adr

  3 Paraphrases •Asx/Org •adr

  3 Pièces rustiques (1971) (6') •Asx/Org •adr

BROWN, Rayner - *Sonata* (1981) •Asx/Org •WIM

  Sonata (1987) •Ssx/Org

Brunard, Gaston - *Offertoire* •1 Sx: A or T/Org or Pno •Mil

BUOT, Victor - *Morceau d'élévation* (1880) •Asx/Org or Pno or Harmonie •ES

BUWEN, Dieter - *Die Sephiroth* (1991) (18') •Asx/Org •adr

CIBULKA, Franz - *Garuda, Phantasia...* •Asx/Org+Marimba

COLIN, Jean-Marie - *Médecines douces* (1984) •Sx/Org

CRESTON, Paul - *Rapsodie*, op. 108 (1976) (10') •Asx/Org •Sha

DeBLASIO, Chris - *Music...* (1990) (8') •Ssx/Org •TTF

DESPORTES, Yvonne - *Souvenir...* (20'15) •Ssx/Org •DP

DHAINE, Jean-Louis - *Grave* (3') •Bb Sx/Org or Pno

  3 Hymnes (14') •Asx/Org

DJORDJEVIC, Aleksandra - *Menace...* (1993) •Asx/Org •INM

DOYEN, Henri - *Canzona* •Asx/Org •adr

EBEN, Pets - *Dré Invokace* •Ssx (or Tsx)/Org

ESCUDIER, H. - *6 Andantes...* (1875) •Asx/Org or Pno •Mar

  Le chant des vaux, op. 48 (1878) •Asx/Org or Pno •Cos/Bil

FANTONI, Corrado - *4 Della vergino* (1993) (13'45) •Bsx/Org

FISCHER, Eric - *Prière* (1979) •Ssx/Org

  Prière au Christ (1980) •Asx/Org •adr

FORSSELL, Jonas - *Epitaphinum* (1978) •Asx/Org •STIM

FRIIS, Flemming - *Angelus* (1988) (6') •Asx/Org

GENZMER, Harald - *Konzertantes duo* •Bsx/Org •R&E

GINGRAS, Guy - *Choral et variations* (1984) •Asx/Org •Med

GOODE, Jack C. - *Dance of Joy* •Sx/Org

GRAEF, Friedemann - *Canzona...* (1990) (6') •Ssx/Org •R&E

  Nocturne (1988) (11'30) •Bsx/Org •B&B

HAIDMAYER, Karl - *Pieces* •Asx/Org

HAÏK-VANTOURA, Suzanne - *Adagio* (1962) (4'30) •Asx/Org •Bil

HARTL, Henrich - *Meditation*, op. 42 (1989) •Bsx/Org

HARTLEY, Walter - *Seven "Sacred Harp" Songs* (1992) •Asx/ Keyboard •EK

HEILMANN, Harald - *Pastorale* (1991) (5') •Asx/Org •Tong

  Sonata breve (1982) (7') •Asx/Org •Tong

HILDEMANN, Wolfgang - *Partita coloratura* (1978) •Asx/Org or Harp or Pno •Mau

HIRANUMA, Yuri - *Tiki Tiki-Ta* •Asx/Electr. Org

HOAG, Charles - *An Elegy in Troubled...* (1972) (4') •Asx/Org •adr

KARLINS, M. William - *Impromptu* (12') •Asx/Org or Electr. Pno or Pno •ACA

KOPKA, Ulrico - *Sonata da chiesa* (12'30) •Tsx/Org •Asto

KORN, Peter - *Ruft uns die Stimme*, op. 81 •Tsx (or Ssx)/Org •adr

KROL, Bernhard - *Antifona*, op. 53a (7') •Asx/Org •B&B

  Elegia passionata, op. 69a (1979) (9') •Asx/Org •B&B

  Litania pastorale, op. 62 •Ssx/Org •B&B

LAMPROYE, André - *Messe de St Hadelin* (1988) (16') •Ssx/Org

LASNE, George - *2 Esquisses...* (1946) •Asx (or Ssx)/Org or Pno

LAUBA, Christian - *Dies Irae* (1990) (12'30) •Ssx/Org or Orch •adr

  Pulsar (1985-90) (8') •Ssx/Org •adr

LECLERC, Michel - *Variations sur Harbouya* •Ssx/Org

LEHMANN, Markus - *Elegie* (1989) (8') •Asx/Org •Asto

LIMBERG, Hans Martin - *Pieces* (1990) •Tsx/Org •Eres

LIONCOURT, Guy de - *3 mélodies...*, op. 60 (1923) •Asx/Org •SAE

Londeix, Jean-Marie - *Eclesia II* •1 Sx: A or S/Org or Pno •Fuz

LOWRY, Richard - *Pièce* (1982) •Asx/Org

LUTTMANN, Reinhard - *Méditation II* (1972-77) •Asx/Org •Led

LUYO, C. - *Geometriche etudie* (1981) •Asx/Org

MARGONI, Alain - *In memoriam* (1982) •Asx/Org •Bil

MARI, Pierrette - *Paysage nocturne* (1961) (4') •Asx/Org •adr

MARTIN, Victor - *Orbitales III* (1982) (8') •Asx/Org

MATOT, Pierre - *Spleen* •Asx/Org

MEYER, Lucien - *Assomption...* •Asx/Org or Pno •ES

Mozart, Wolfgang - *Ceremonial Adagio* (GEE) •Asx/Pno or Org •adr

PERRIN, Marcel - *Esquisse* (1983) (2'45) •Asx/Pno or Org •DP

  Nocturne (1945) (7'30) •Asx/Orch or Org or Pno •GD

  Prière •Asx/Org •DP

PILLEVESTRE - *2me Offertoire* (1890) •Bb Sx or Eb Sx/Pno or Org

PRESSL, Herman - *N.N. 4/1* (1991) (4'30) •Asx/Org •INM

QUATE, Amy - *Light of Sothis* (1982) (11') •Asx/Org or Pno •Led

Rivier, Jean - *Aria* (5') (LONDEIX) •1 Sx: S or A/Org •ET

ROLIN, Etienne - *Sous les cieux* (1993) (7') •Ssx/Org •adr

SAGVIK, Stellan - *Tre Ballader*, op. 112 (1983) (12') •Asx/Org or Guit •STIM

SALBERT, Dieter - *3 Elegien* (1989) (8') •1Sx: S+T+B/Org •adr

SARS, Gerard - *Music* (1992) •Asx/Org

SAUGUET, Henri - *Oraisons* (1976) (11') •1 Sx: S+A+T+B/Org •Bil

SCHILLING, Hans - *Dialogue* (1983) •Asx/Org

  4 Dialogue (1976) (8') •Sx/Org •adr

  Intonation und Partita... (1982) (12') •Asx/Org •B&B

  Passions - Partita (1992) (10') •Asx/Org •adr

SCHMIDT, William - *Variegations* (1973) (10') •Asx/Org •adr

SENGSTSCHMID, Johann - *Meditation* (1991) (4'30) •Asx/Org

SMITH, Stuart - *One for Two* (6') •Asx/Org •SeMC

STEVENS, C. - *Mourning his brother* •Asx/Org

STOCKMEIER, Wolfgang - *Sonate* (1981) (6') •Asx/Org •PJT

STOUT, Alan - *Suite* (1972) (6'45) •Asx/Org •adr

TERRENI, Ottavio - *Xeres* (1981) •Asx/Org

TOURNIER, Franz-André - *Prophéties* (1982) (10') •Asx/Org •adr

VERHEIL, Ton - *Meditation* (1984) (3'50) •Asx/Org •Eres

  Partita breve (1990) (7'15) •Asx/Org •*Eres*

  Suite (1982) •Ssx/Pno or Org

VOIRPY, Alain - *Méditation sur un...* (1982) (4'30) •Asx/Org •Lem

WALLNER, Alarich - *Fünf Ludi* (1991) (18') •Asx/Org

  Konzert •1 Sx: A+B/Org

WARING, Kate - *Plainte* (1985) (4') •Ssx or Asx/Pno or Org

Woodcock, Robert - *Concerto No. 2* (V. WÜRTH) •1 Sx: S or A/Pno or Org •VW

ZEBINGER, Franz - *Pieces* •Asx/Org •INM

3 Musicians

BÖRJESSON, Lars-Ove - *Interparolo III*, op. 45 (1986) •Asx/BsCl/ Org •SMIC

BUBALO, Rudolph - *Organic Concretion* •Asx/Org/Perc/Tape

CARAVAN, Ronald - *Love* (1973) (4') •2 Sx: AT/Org •adr

FISCHER, Eric - *Blues* (1980) •Ssx/Vibr/Org •adr

GEELEN, Mathieu - *Invention* (1983) (6') •Asx/Electr. Org/Perc
•Don
HARBISON, John - *Bermuda Triangle* (1970) •Vcl/Tsx/Electr. Org
MARCHAL, Dominique - *Bonus est dominus* (1980) (5') •Soprano
Voice/Asx/Org •adr
MARGONI, Alain - *Triple fugue* (1981) •2 Sx: AB/Org
MOORE, David - *Sicut cervus* •2 Sx: AT/Org •WWS
SCOTT, Richard - *En kloyennes...* (1984) •Asx/Org/Perc •STIM
SEYRIG, François - *Concert en trio* •Asx/Tpt/Org

4 Musicians

SEVRETTE, Danielle - *L'Innomé* •Vln/Vcl/Asx/Org •adr

5 Musicians

ALBRIGHT, William - *From Dawn to Dusk in the Valley of Fire*
(1989) (6'30) •4 Sx: SATB/Org •Hen/Pet
Bach, J. S. - *Koraalbewerking* •4 Sx: SATB/Org •Lis
BIRKNER, Rudolf - *Pastorale und Fughetta* (1992) •4 Sx: SATB/Org
BRNCIC, Isaza - *Quodlibet I* (1966) •Sx/Vla/Tpt/Electr. Guit/Electr.
Org or 2 Asx/Vla/Vibr
DURBIN, Jean - *1ère suite de Alain Fournier* •Pno/Org/Vln/Vla/Sx
HAIDMAYER, Karl - *Popludium III* (1991) (11') •4 Sx: SATB/Org
HARTLEY, Walter - *Pieces* •4 Sx: SATB/Org •Eth
MABIT, Alain - *Fragment pour un...* (1992) •4 Sx: SATB/Org
PRESSL, Herman - *Sprang N.N. 6* (1992) •4 Sx: SATB/Org
WALLNER, Alarich - *Siciliana* (1992) •4 Sx: SATB/Org

6 Musicians

CASANOVA, André - *Duo Canzoni* (1973) (10'30) •Asx/Cl/Tpt/
Perc/Small Org/Electr. Bass Guit •adr
DORNBY, Finn - *Musickus dornby* •2 Sx: AB/Org/Electr. Guit/Electr.
Bs Guit/Perc
HORWOOD, Michael - *Interphases* (1975) (13') •Fl/Sx/Accordion
(or Org)/Pno/2 Perc •CMC
POMORIN, Sibylle - *Rabengold - Goldraben* (1989) (80') •2 Sx: AT/
Perc/Pno/Org/Vcl •adr
WELSH, Wilmer - *Mosaic Portraits II...* •4 Sx/Org/Narr

7 Musicians

ALLGEN, Claude - *Praeludium och Carmen Perlotense* •Vln/Vla/
Vcl/Asx/Pno/Harps/Org •STIM
SCHWERTSIK, Kurt - *Liebesträume*, op. 7 (1963) •Asx/Trb/Pno/
Vibr/Marimba/Harmonium/Bass •EMod
STOUT, Alan - *Four Antiphonies* •Fl/Trb/Asx/Org/Vln/Vla/Perc
•CFE

9 Musicians

CAPLET, André - *Impressions d'Automne* (1905) (3') •Asx/Ob/2 Cl/
Bsn/Harp/Org/2 Vcl

11 Musicians

MESTRAL, Patrice - *Alliages* (1969) •Tpt Solo/Fl/Cl/Asx/2 Trb/2
Perc/Pno/Org/Bass
TRIMBLE, Lester - *Panels I* (1973) (6') •Picc/Bsx/Vln/Vla/Vcl/Bass/
2 Perc/Electr. Guit/Electr. Org/Electr. Harp
•Pet

oOo

HILDEMANN, Wolfgang - Psalmodia III •Asx/Org/Chorus •MV

Saxophone and Harp

2 Musicians

ABSIL, Jean - *Sicilienne* (1950) (9') •1 Sx: A or T/Orch or Harp or Pno
•An/Ger

ALIPRANDI, Paul - *Paysages* •Asx/Harp •Chap
BACULEWSKI, Krzysztof - *Partita* (1980) (12'-15') •Asx/Harp or
Prepared Pno •CPWN
BROGUE, Roslyn - *Equipoise* (1971) (10') •Asx/Harp
BUMCKE, Gustav - *Notturno*, op. 45 •Asx/Harp •R&E
Scherzo, op. 67 (1937/38) •Asx Solo/Pno or Harp or Orch or Wind
Ensemble
COWLES, Colin - *Recitative and Air* (3') •Ssx/Harp •adr
DENIZOT, Anne-Marie - *Trois petits sons et puis s'en vont* (1993) •1
Sx: S+A/Harp or Pno •INM
DESPORTES, Yvonne - *Le Noir...* (5'30) •Tsx/Harp or Pno •DP
Une fleur sur l'étang (1977) (12') •Asx/Harp •Dom
DI BETTA, Philippe - *Fissures* (1991) (3') •BsSx/Harp •adr
EYSER, Eberhard - *Liebeslied im Regen* (1993) •Ssx/Harp •INM
Petit caprice & Cavatina (1977-79) (9') •Asx/Harp or Pno •EMa
FONTYN, Jacqueline - *Fougères* (1981) (5') •1 Sx: S+A/Pno or Harp
•Sal
GOODMAN, Alfred - *Duo* (1968) (11'30) •Asx/Harp •adr
GOTKOVSKY, Ida - *Eolienne* (1979) (15') •Asx/Harp •Bil
HILDEMANN, Wolfgang - *Partita coloratura* (1978) •Asx/Org or
Harp or Pno •Mau
Joplin, Scott - *Maple Leaf Rag* (AXWORTHY) •1 Sx: S or A or T/Harp
(or Pno) •DP/TVA
KAGEL, Mauricio - *2 Akte* - Grand duo (1988-89) •Asx/Harp •Pet
KENNELL, Richard - *Lamentations* •Sx/Harp
KRICKEBERG, Dieter - *Zummara* (1987-88) (8') •Tsx/Harp
LUC, Francis - *Eliantheme* (8') •Asx/Harp/Tape
MAGANINI, Quinto - *La romanesca* •Tsx/Guit or Harp •Mus
MARCOUX, Isabelle - *Ofaeruffoss* (1992) (12') •Ssx/Harp •adr
McCLINTOCK, Robert - *Pieces* •Asx/Harp •adr
MICHEL, Paul - *Mouvement intérieur* (1977) •Asx/Harp •adr
MIMET, Anne-Marie - *Pieces* •Asx/Harp or Pno •Bil
MÖSS, Piotr - *4 Poèsies* (1983) (23'30) •Asx/Harp
RABINSKI, Jacek - *Rosa dei venti* (1993) •Asx/Harp •INM
ROSSÉ, François - *Séaodie III* (1985) (3') •Asx/Harp •Bil
Schware - *Fantasiestück* •Asx/Harp •WWS
SPROGIS, Eric - *Comme un drame dérisoire* (1992) •Asx/Harp
STAMPFLI, Edward - *5 Nocturnes* (1983) (11') •Asx/Harp
TALLET, Marc - *Chrysalides* (1984) (7') •Asx/Harp
TAUTENHAHN, Günther - *Elegy* (1969) (2'30) •Tsx/Harp •SeMC

3 Musicians

BARON, Maurice - *Elegy* •Fl/Asx/Harp or Pno •MBCo
BOIZARD, Gilles - *Concert* (1981) (14') •Asx/Vcl/Harp
BON, André - *Fragments* (1984) (25') •Tsx/2 Harp/Processeur de son
numérique
DEPELSENAIRE, Jean-Marie - *Mosaïque* (1979) (2'30) •Fl/1 Sx:
A+T+B/Harp •adr
DUBOIS, Pierre-Max - *Trio* •Fl/Tsx/Harp •adr
DUPIN, Paul - *Chant* (1910) •Asx/Harps/Vla/Chorus
GONZALES, Jean-François - *Page d'album* •Sx/Harp/Bass
GOODMAN, Alfred - *3 Chants* •Voice/Sx/Harp or Pno •adr
HAVEL, Christophe - *L'canton'ier* (1990) •Soprano Voice/Ssx/Harp
•adr
HOWARD, Robert - *Trilogue* •Asx/Vla/Harp •Art
LEMAY, Robert - *Tryptique écarlate* (1991) (18') •1 Sx: S+T+B/
Harp/Perc •adr
MIYAZAWA, Kazuto - *Paragraphen* (1988) •Asx/Vibr/Harp or Asx/
Pno
PAVLENKO, Serguei - *Intermezzo* (1985) (12') •Asx/Harp/Perc
SAUGUET, Henri - *Concert...* (1979) (12') •Fl/Asx/Harp •Fuz
STRAESSER, Joep - *Grand Trio* (1984) (18') •Asx/Harp/Perc •Don
TAUTENHAN, Günther - *Trio Sonata* •Asx/Harp/Pno •SeMC
VELLONES, Pierre - *Rapsodie*, op. 92 (1937) (4'30) •Asx/Harp/
Celesta or Asx/Pno •Lem

VUATAZ, Roger - *Destin...*, op. 91 (1954) (23') •Asx/Harp/Perc

4 Musicians

BLYTON, Carey - *Market* (1964) (30') •Ob/Asx/Harp/Vcl •adr
COWLES, Colin - *Suite* (1978) (20') •4 Sx: SATB/Harp or Pno •adr
GOODMAN, Alfred - *Suite* (1990) (13') •2 Sx: SA/Harp/Bass •adr
HOVHANESS, Alan - *The Flowering Peach*, op. 125 (1954) (21')
    •Asx+Cl/Vibr/Perc/Harp or Pno •AMP
MEIJERING, Chiel - *I Hate Mozart* (1979) (4') •Fl/Asx/Harp/Vln
    •Don
    Schudden voor gebruik (1985) (8') •Asx/Perc/Pno/Harp •Don
MIEREANU, Costin - *Jardins retrouvés* (1985) (20') •Electr. Ssx/
    Vcl/Perc/Harp/Tape •Sal
MORRISSON, Julia - *The Memorare* •Asx/Bsn/Harp/Alto Voice
    •CFE
PROVOST, Serge - *Tétractys* •Fl/Asx/Pno/Harp
SHOUT, Vladislav - *Metamorphosis* (1979) •Asx/Bass/Harp/Perc
    •ECS
VILLA-LOBOS, Heitor - *Quatuor*, op. 168 (1921) (20') •Fl/Asx/
    Celesta/Harp •ME
WALKER, Robin - *HB TO HB* (11') •3 Sx/Harp

5 Musicians

ARMA, Paul - *Musique* (1980) (13') •4 Sx: SATB/Harp
BIRTWISTLE, Harrison - *Dinah & Nick's Love Song* (1972) (5') •3
    Sx: SSS/EH/Harp •Uni
CRUMB, George - *Quest* (25') •Guit/1 Sx: S+A+T/Harmonica/2
    Perc/Harp •BR
DONDEYNE, Désiré - *Voyages imaginaires* (1989) (12') •Asx/Pno or
    Asx/2 Vln/Harp/Vcl •Com
FOURNIER, Marie Hélène - *Supplément nécessaire* (1990) (50') •2
    Perc/Bsx/Harp/Soprano Voice
HESPOS, Hans-Joachim - *Frottages* •Asx/Vcl/Harp/Mandolin/Perc
    •EMod
HOPKINS, Bill - *Sensation* (1965) •Voice/Tsx/Tpt/Harp/Vla
HOVHANESS, Alan - *The World Beneath the Sea*, op. 133/1 (1953)
    •Asx/Harp/Vibr/Timp/Gong
JAEGER, Robert - *Quintet* (1969) •Asx/Vln/Vla/Vcl/Harp •adr
    Three Pieces (1967) (6'30) •Asx/Vln/Vla/Vcl/Harp or Pno •adr
WOOLLETT, Henri - *Danses païennes* (19xx) •2 Fl/Asx/Vcl/Harp

6 Musicians

EYSER, Eberhard - *Livre des jeux...* (1959-86) (23'30) •Asx/Harp/
    Pno/Vibr/Guit/Vln •EMa
HAMBRAEUS, Bengt - *Kammarmusik for 6*, op. 28 (1950) (8') •Fl/
    Ob/Cl/Asx/Vla/Harp •STIM/Ehr
MIEREANU, Costin - *Miroir liquide* (1986) (11') •1 Sx: Sno+S+A+T/
    Bsn/Perc/Harp/Pno/Bass •Sal
VILLA-LOBOS, Heitor - *Sexteto mistico*, op. 123 (1917) (9') •Fl/Ob/
    Asx/Guit/Celesta/Harp •ME

7 Musicians

BOSSEUR, Jean-Yves - *43 Miniatures* (1992) •Vln/Cl/2 Sx: AB/
    Harp/Pno/Perc
FINNISSY, Michael - *Evening* (1974) •Asx/Hn/Tpt/Perc/Harp/Vcl/
    Bass
HAYAKAWA, Masaaki - *Four Little Poems* (1979) (9'30) •4 Sx:
    SATB/Soprano Voice/Harp/Perc •SFC
LONGY, George - *Rhapsodie - Lento* (1904) •Harp/Bass/2 Cl/Bsn/
    Asx/Timp •South
ROLIN, Etienne - *Quètes ancestrales* (1989) (14') •Tsx/Vla/2 Vcl/
    Bass/Harp/Marimba •Fuz

8 Musicians

BARCE, Ramon - *Concierto de Lizara V* (1977) (10'45) •Cl/Tsx/Tpt/
    Trb/Harp/Pno/Vln/Vcl
BÖRJESSON, Lars - *Divertimento*, op. 38 (1983) •Asx/BsCl/Bsn/
    Guit/Harp/Marimba/Vln/Vcl •STIM
BUMCKE, Gustav - *Suite G Dur*, op. 24 •Tenor Voice/Fl/Ob/Cl/Bsn/
    Hn/Bsx/Harp •VAB
CHATMAN, Stephen - *Outer Voices* (1978) •Fl/Cl/Asx/2 Perc/
    Celesta/Guit/Harp/Tape •CMC
DECOUST, Michel - *Ombres portées* (1986) (9') •2 Ob/Cl/2 Asx/
    Harp/Pno/Perc •Sal
FRANCO, Clare - *Four Winds...* •Asx/Harp/Vibr/Fl/Ob/Cl/Hn/Bsn
NILSSON, Ivo - *Agnosi* (1988) (9') •Ob/Asx/Tpt/Harp/2 Vln/Vla/Vcl
    •STIM
PINOS-SIMANDL, Aloïs - *Geneze* (1970) (8') •Vln/Asx/Vcl/Trb/
    Perc/Harp/Harps/Ionika •CHF
VELLONES, Pierre - *A Cadix*, op. 102 (1938) (4') •3 Sx/2 Ondes
    Martenot/Bass/Harp/Perc
    Cinq poèmes de Mallarmé, op. 24 (1929) (28') •High Voice/4 Harp/
    2 Sx: AT/Bass •Lem

9 Musicians

BUMCKE, Gustav - *"Der Spaziergang"* •Fl/Ob/EH/Cl/Bsn/Hn/
    BsTrb/Bsx/Harp
CAPLET, André - *Impressions d'Automne* (1905) (3') •Asx/Ob/2 Cl/
    Bsn/Harp/Org/2 Vcl
CERHA, Friedrich - *Exercices for Nine, No. 1* •BsCl/Bsx/Bsn/Tpt/
    Trb/Tuba/Vcl/Bass/Harp •Uni
LEWIS, John Aaron - *Little David's Fugue* (5'30) •Fl/Cl/3 Sx: ATB/
    Trb or Tpt/Harp or Pno/Bass/Perc •MJQ
    The Queen's Fancy (4') •Fl/Cl/Tsx/Bsn/Hn/Trb/Harp/Bass/Perc
    •MJQ
    Sun Dance (4') •Fl/Cl/3 Sx: ATB/Trb/Harp or Guit/Bass/Perc
    •MJQ
MANOURY, Philippe - *Etude automatique* 1 •Fl/Tpt/Sx/Tuba/Harp/
    Vln/Vla/Vcl/Bass
MIEREANU, Costin - *Kammer-koncert n° 1* (1984-85) (16') •1 Sx:
    Sno+A+T+Bs/Orch (1010/000/1001/Guit/
    Mandolin/Harp/Perc •Sal
TARENSKEEN, Boudewijn - *Nonet* (1982) (13') •Asx/Hn/BsCl/
    Accordion/Banjo/Harp/Vla/Vcl/Bass •Don

10 Musicians

BANKS, Donald - *Equation 1* (1964) (7') •Tpt/Asx/Pno/Harp/Guit/
    Perc/2 Vln/Vla/Vcl •BMIC
FORTNER, Jack - *S pr ING sur des poèmes de E. E. Cummings* (1966)
    (11') •Mezzo Soprano Voice/Fl/Asx/Bsn/
    Vla/Vcl/Bass/Vibr/Harp/Pno •JJ
GOTTSCHALK, Arthur - *Cycloid* •Cl/Asx/Hn/Tpt/Harp/Vibr/2 Vln/
    Vla/Vcl •SeMC
HEIDEN, Bernhard - *Sonatina* •Fl/Cl/Tsx/Hn/Trb/Harp/Vibr/Pno/
    Bass/Perc •MJQ
JOHNSON, J. J. - *Turnpike* (5') •Fl/Cl/3 Sx: ATB/Trb/Harp (or Guit)/
    Pno/Bass/Perc •MJQ
SCHAFFER, Boguslaw - *Permutations n° 27* (1956) •Fl/Ob/Cl/Sx/
    Tpt/Trb/Vla/Perc/Harp/Pno •A&S
SCHULLER, Gunther - *12 by 11* (8'30) •Fl/Cl/Tsx/Hn/Trb/Vibr/Pno/
    Harp/Bass/Perc •MJQ

11 Musicians

TRIMBLE, Lester - *Panels I* (1973) (6') •Picc/Bsx/Vln/Vla/Vcl/Bass/
    2 Perc/Electr. Guit/Electr. Org/Electr. Harp
    •Pet

12 Musicians

HOVHANESS, Alan - *After Water* •3 Cl/3 Tpt/3 Asx/Perc/Harp/Pno •ACA

MASINI, Fabio - *"Nuvole e colori forti"* (1992) (18') •Fl/1 Sx: S+A/ BsCl/Fl/Ob/Cl/Bsn/2 Vln/Vla/Vcl/Harp

13 Musicians

FINNISSY, Michael - *Babylon* (1971) (19') •Mezzo Soprano Voice/ Ob/Cl/Asx/Bsn/Guit/Harp/Pno/2 Perc/2 Vcl/ Bass •Uni

14 Musicians

HARVEY, Jonathan - *The Valley of Aosta* (1985) (13'30) •Fl/Ob/Ssx/ Tpt/2 Yamaha DX7 Synth/2 Harp/Pno/2 Vln/ Vla/Vcl/Perc •FM

oOo

VILLA-LOBOS, Heitor - *Nonetto*, op. 181 (1923) (18') •Fl/Ob/Cl/1 Sx: A+B/Bsn/Perc/Celesta/Harp/Pno/Mixed Chorus •ME

Saxophone and Guitar or Mandolin

2 Musicians

ANEST, Alex - *Last* (1993) •Ssx/Guit •INM

BAUER, Robert - *Three Pieces* (1975) (9') •Ssx/Guit •CMC

BOND, Victoria - *Scat* (1985) •Sx/Pno or Guit •SeMC

DESPORTES, Yvonne - *L'Horloge...* (1984) (8') •Asx/Guit •Bil

FEILER, Dror - *Slichot* (1986) (4') •Sx/Guit •SMIC

HOVHANESS, Alan - *Suite*, op. 291 (1976) (7') •Asx/Guit •adr

KECHLEY, David - *In the Dragon's Garden* (1992) (15'55) •Asx/ Guit •PV

KHALADJI, Iwan - *Solstice* (1986) •Asx/Guit

MAGANINI, Quinto - *La romanesca* •Tsx/Guit or Harp •Mus

MASON, Lucas - *Romance* (1978) •Asx/Guit •DP

NOON, David - *Partita*, op. 103b (1989) (8') •Ssx/Guit •TTF

NOSSE, Carl - *Sonnet* (1978) •Asx/Guit •DP

PADWA, Vladimir - *Concertino* •Asx/Guit •adr

PRICE, Deon - *Mesurée* (1979) •Ssx/Guit •DP

SAGVIK, Stellan - *Tre Ballader*, op. 112 (1983) (12') •Asx/Org or Guit •STIM

SCHNEIDER, Stephan - *Tripes de roche* (1993) •Asx/Electr. Guit •INM

STAUDE, Christoph - *Memoire* (1985) •Asx/Guit •adr

VERHIEL, Ton - *Brie bagatellen* (1990) (1'40) •Asx/Guit

3 Folkdances (1989) •Asx/Guit

Introduktie en scherzo (1990) (2'30) •Asx/Guit

WALTER, Wolfgang - *La cité...* (1993) •1 Sx: A+T+B/Guit •INM

ZELLER, Fredrik - *Geteiltes Lied...* (1992) •Bsx/Electr. Guit

3 Musicians

ELOY, Christian - *Archipel* (1990) •Fl/Asx/Guit •adr

FINGER, Peter - *Neue Wege* (1983) (11') •Guit/Ssx/Perc •adr

FRID, Geza - *3 Poemes* (1976) •Narr/Asx/Guit •Don

LENNERS, Claude - *Frammenti fugativi* (1987) •Ssx/2 Guit •adr

MORRISSON, Julia - *Subjective Objective* (1970) (6') •Tsx/Bass/ Electr. Guit •CFE

SCHMIDT-HAMBROCK, Jochen - *Ozte* (1982) (10') •Sx/Guit/Perc •adr

4 Musicians

AHO, Kalevi - *Quartet* (1982) (22') •Fl/Asx/Guit/Perc •FMIC

ANDERSON, Beth - *Hallophone* (1973) •Dancer/Voice/Sx/Guit/ Tape

BERGMAN, Erik - *Mipejupa*, op. 96 (1981) (17') •Fl/Asx/Guit/Perc •FMIC

HÄMEENIEMI, Aero - *Chamber Music Book* (1980) •Fl/Guit/Asx/ Perc •FMIC

HEWITT, Harry - *34 Preludes*, op. 439 (1972) (90') •Pno/Guit/Perc/ Sx •DP

KAIPAINEN, Jouni - *Far from home*, op. 17 (1981) (10') •Fl/Asx/ Guit/Perc •WH

KOTONSKI, Wladzimierz - *Pieces* (1962) •Electr. Guit/2 Sx: AT/Cl •B&H/PWM

LAUBA, Christian - *Atlantis* (1990) (14') •Fl (+Tam)/Tsx/2 Guit •adr

LEMELAND, Aubert - *Figures...*, op. 79 (10') •Asx/Vla/Vibr/Guit •adr

LINDBERG, Magnus - *Linea d'ombra* (1981) (15') •Fl/Asx/Guit/ Perc •WH/FMIC

MACHOVER, Tod - *Valise's Song* (1989) (5') •1 Sx: S+T/Electr. Guit/Perc/Electr. Bass/Computer tape •adr

MAROS, Miklos - *Clusters...* (1981) •Fl/Ssx/Guit/Perc •SMIC

MERILÄINEN, Usko - *Simultanus for four* (1979) (16') •Fl/Asx/ Guit/Perc •Pan/FMIC

OLSON, Roger - *Cobwebs* (1983) •Narr/Guit/Asx/Vln

SCHMIDT-HAMBROCK, Jochen - *ARD - Sportschau* (1984) (10') •Guit/Asx/Perc/Synth •adr

SCIORTINO, Patrice - *Moulin du temps* •Vibr/Guit/Vla/Asx •adr

SCOTT, Ronnie - *Dark Flowers* (1988) (13') •Fl/Asx/Guit/Perc

WARING, Kate - *Psalmance* (1978) (5') •Fl/Ssx/Guit/Perc

5 Musicians

BRNCIC, Isaza - *Quodlibet I* (1966) •Sx/Vla/Tpt/Electr. Guit/Electr. Org or 2 Asx/Vla/Vibr

CRUMB, George - *Quest* (25') •Guit/1 Sx: S+A+T+Harmonica/2 Perc/Harp •BR

FEILER, Dror - *Om* (1985) •Ssx/Electr. Guit/3 Perc •Tons/SMIC

Schlafbeand (1985) •Ssx/Electr. Guit/3 Perc •Tons/SMIC

Tändstickorna... (1979-80) •Ssx/2 Electr. Guit/2 Perc •SMIC

Yad (1984) •2 Ssx/Electr. Guit/2Perc •Tons/SMIC

HESPOS, Hans - *Einander* (1966) (12-13') •Fl/Cl/Guit/Tsx/Vla •EMod

Frottages •Asx/Vcl/Harp/Mandolin/Perc •EMod

KÖHLER, Wolfgang - *Schwerenöters Liä-song* (1986) (2'50) •Cl/Sx/ Electr Guit/Guit/Synth •adr

KUNZ, Ernst - *Nachtkonzert* •3 Sx/Vla/Guit

LAVAL, Philippe - *1,0544876* (1992) •Soprano Voice/2 Sx: AT/Guit/ Vibr

LONARDONI, Markus - *Modal interchange* (1987) (6') •Sx/Perc/ Pno/Guit/Bass

MABRY, Drake - *9.10.89* •Ssx/Electr. Guit/Bass Guit/Synth/Perc

MIEREANU, Costin - *Ricochets* (1989) •1 Sx: Sno+S+A+T+B/ Electr. Guit/Bass Guit/Synth/Perc/Régie électr. •Sal

SCHIFRIN, Lalo - *Mount Olive* (3') •Asx/Guit/Pno/Bass/Perc •MJQ

SHEPHERD, Stu - *Birthday Music III* (1986) •1 Sx: A+T/Guit/Synth/ Bass/Perc •CMC

STEELE, Jan - *Temporary farewell* (1971) (5') •1 Sx: S+A/Electr. Guit/Pno/Bass/Perc

Sternberg - *Variations on German Folk Songs* •Sx/Bass/Guit/Pno/ Perc •DV

TALLET, Marc - *Estagari* (12') •Fl/Asx/Trb/Vla/Guit

VOSK, Jay - *Le Nid* •Ssx/Vibr/Guit/Vln/Bass •SeMC

6 Musicians

BACHOREK, Milan - *Inspirace* (1983) (12') •Ob/Asx/Cl+BsCl/Perc/ Pno/Electr. Guit •CHF

BOUDREAU, Walter - *Variations* (1975) •Ssx/Asx+Fl/Tsx+Picc/ Tuba/Pno+Celesta/Guit •CMC

DORNBY, Finn - *Musickus dornby* •2 Sx: AB/Org/Electr. Guit/Electr. Bs Guit/Perc

EYSER, Eberhard - *Livre des jeux...* (1959-86) (23'30) •Asx/Harp/Pno/Vibr/Guit/Vln •EMa

FEILER, Dror - *Hive* (1985) •2 Ssx/2 Electr. Guit/2 Perc. •Tons/SMIC

HELLAN, Arne - *Sextet* (1981) •Tpt/2 Sx/2 Guit/Perc •NMI

HERMANSSON, Christer - *Aggjakten* (1979) •Narr/Tsx/Trb/Guit/Bass/Perc •STIM

LANZA, Alcides - *Interferences III* (1983-84) •Fl/Cl/Sx/Guit/Pno/Perc •ShP

Modulos III (1983) •Guit/Tsx/Vln/Vcl/Perc/Pno/Tape •CMC

MALLIE, Loïc - *Sextuor* (1989) •Fl/Cl/Asx/Pno/Guit/Perc

STEVENS, James - *Girl in scena* (1973) •Voice/Sx+Cl/Asx+Cl/Tsx+BsCl+Fl/Electr. Guit/Pno •BMIC

VILLA-LOBOS, Heitor - *Sexteto mistico*, op. 123 (1917) (9') •Fl/Ob/Asx/Guit/Celesta/Harp •ME

7 Musicians

BYTZEK, Peter - *Gefühle auf dem Eis* (1985) (3'45) •2 Voice/Guit/Pno/Sx/Perc/Bass •adr

GIUFFRE, James - *Fine* •Tsx/Guit/Vibr/Pno/2 Bass/Perc •MJQ

HAAS, Konrad - *Pieces* •Voice/Fl/Sx/Pno/Perc/Guit/Bass •Holz

HERMANSSON, Christer - *Rumba* (1979) •Narr/2 Sx: ST/Trb/Guit/Pno/Bass •STIM

HODKINSON, Sidney - *Funks* (1969) (5') •4 Sx: AATB/Guit/Bass/Perc •adr

JENNEFELT, Thomas - *Stones* (1981) •Ob/Cl/Asx/Tpt/Guit/2 Perc

LARSSON, Häkan - *Farleder - 4 pieces* (1993) •Fl/Tsx/Trb/Electr. Guit/Electr. Bass/Pno/Perc •SvM

MAJOS, Giulio di - *Passacaglia* •Fl/Asx/Hn/Guit/Vibr/Pno/Bass •Sch

ROSSÉ, François - *OEM* (1988) (21') •Soprano Voice/1 Sx: S+Bs/EH/Accordion/Bass/Jazz Guit/Pno/Dispositif électro-acoust. •adr

SAGVIK, Stellan - *Sma gyckelvisor...*, op. 112 (1981) (8') •Fl/2 Cl/Asx/Mandolin/2 Perc •STIM

TAUTENAHN, Günther - *Septet* •Cl/Tpt/Tsx/Guit/Vcl/Pno/Perc •SeMC

8 Musicians

BÖRJESSON, Lars - *Divertimento*, op. 38 (1983) •Asx/BsCl/Bsn/Guit/Harp/Marimba/Vln/Vcl •STIM

BREGENT, Michel - *Melorytharmundi* (1984) •Fl/Cl/Sx/2 Perc/Pno/Vcl/Guit •CMC

BULOW, Harry - *Crystal Cove* •Tpt/3 Sx: AAT/Pno/Bass/Guit/Drums •adr

CHATMAN, Stephen - *Outer Voices* (1978) •Fl/Cl/Asx/2 Perc/Celesta/Guit/Harp/Tape •CMC

EMMER, Huib - *Camera eye* (1978-79) (15') •2 Sx/2 Guit/2 Pno/2 Perc •Don

FRANCESCONI, Luca - *Piccola trama* (1989) (14') •1 Sx: S+A/Fl/Cl/Guit/Perc/Vln/Vla/Vcl •Ric

HEKSTER, Walter - *Of mere being* (1982) (12') •Asx/Fl/Ob/Cl/2 Tpt/Perc/Electr. Guit •Don

MONNET, Marc - *L'exercice de la bataille* (1991) (45') •2 Vln/2 Bsn/2 MIDI Sx/MIDI Guit/MIDI Pno

NICULESCU, Stefan - *Octoplum* (1985) (10') •1 Sx: S+A/Ensemble (1010/000/00101/Guit/Mandolin/Perc)

TANENNBAUM, Elias - *Consort* •Fl/Hn/Asx/Electr. Guit/Vcl/Bass/Vibr/Jazz drums •ACA

9 Musicians

GUALDA JIMENEZ, Antonio - *Noneto Zarco* (1988) (16') •Vln/Vcl/Cl/2 Sx: SA/Vibr/Marimba/Guit/Pno

LEWIS, John Aaron - *Sun Dance* (4') •Fl/Cl/3 Sx: ATB/Trb/Harp or Guit/Bass/Perc •MJQ

McFARLAND, Gary - *Night Float* (4'30) •3 Sx: ATB/Tpt/Hn/Guit/Pno/Bass/Drums •MJQ

SCHULLER, Gunther - *Abstraction* (1959) (5') •Asx/Guit/Perc/2 Vln/Vla/Vcl/2 Bass •MJQ

YOSHIBA, Susumu - *Erka* •Fl/Ob/Sx/Tpt/Trb/Perc/Vcl/Guit/Pno

10 Musicians

BANKS, Donald - *Equation 1* (1964) (7') •Tpt/Asx/Pno/Harp/Guit/Perc/2 Vln/Vla/Vcl •BMIC

GOODMAN, Alfred - *3 Gesänge für Gresang* •Soprano Voice/Fl/Ob/Asx/Cl/Vla/Vcl/Prepared Pno/Guit/Perc •adr

HORWOOD, Michael - *Facets* (1974) (20') •Narr/Sx/Tpt/Hn/Trb/Pno/Accordion/Electr. Bass/2 Electr. Guit •CMC

JOHNSON, J. J. - *Turnpike* (5') •Fl/Cl/3 Sx: ATB/Trb/Harp (or Guit)/Pno/Bass/Perc •MJQ

LEWIS, John Aaron - *The Milanese Story* •Fl/Tsx/Guit/Pno/Bass/2 Vln/Vla/Vcl/Perc •MJQ

SCHWERTSIK, Kurt - *Salotto romano*, op. 5 (1961) •BsCl/Bsx/Bsn/Hn/Trb/Tuba/Perc/Bass/Vcl/Guit •EMod

11 Musicians

COLE, Bruce - *Pantomimes* (25') •Soprano Voice/Fl/Cl/BsCl/Ssx/Perc/Pno/Guit/Vln/Vla/Vcl •B&H

DIEMENTE, Edward - *3-31 '70* •Voice/Tpt/Trb/Sx/Guit/Bass/5 Perc •SeMC

PÜTZ, Eduard - *Kon-Takte* •Vocal Quartet (SATB)/Fl/Sx/Vibr/Guit/Perc/Pno/Bass •SeMC

TRIMBLE, Lester - *Panels I* (1973) (6') •Picc/Bsx/Vln/Vla/Vcl/Bass/2 Perc/Electr. Guit/Electr. Org/Electr. Harp •Pet

12 Musicians

MEIJERING, Chiel - *Het ontblote feit* (1988-90) (8'30) •2 Fl/3 Sx: ATB/2 Hn/Tpt/Trb/Perc/Pno/Electr. Guit •Don

RECK, David - *Number 1 for 12 Performers* (15') •Fl/Cl/Tsx/Hn/Guit/Vibr/Pno/Bass/Perc •MJQ

13 Musicians

BENHAMOU, Maurice - *Musique pour 13 instruments* •Fl/2 Cl/Harmonica/Sx/2 Vln/3 Guit/Pno 6 hands (à 6 mains)

FINNISSY, Michael - *Babylon* (1971) (19') •Mezzo Soprano Voice/Ob/Cl/Asx/Bsn/Guit/Harp/Pno/2 Perc/2 Vcl/Bass •Uni

First sign a sharp white mons (1974-67) (45') •2 Fl/2 Cl/Asx/CBsn/Hn/Accordion/Guit/Vln/2 Vcl/Pno •BMIC

HESPOS, Hans - *Keime und male* (9') •Picc/Fl/2 Cl/Asx/Hn/Guit/Vln/Vla/Bass/3 Perc •JJ

oOo

CUNNINGHAM, Michael - *Pieces* •5 Sx/4 Tpt/4 Trb/Guit/Pno/Bass/Drum •SeMC

Saxophone and Harmonica

5 Musicians

CRUMB, George - *Quest* (25') •Guit/1 Sx: S+A+T+Harmonica/2 Perc/Harp •BR

RECK, David - *Blues and Screamer* (1965-66) •Fl+Picc/Harmonica/Asx/Bass/Perc •CPE

8 Musicians

DUHAMEL, Antoine - *Le Transibérien* (1983) •Asx/Tpt/Pno/Perc/
Harmonica/3 Armenian Instruments

13 Musicians

BENHAMOU, Maurice - *Musique pour 13 instruments* •Fl/2 Cl/
Harmonica/Sx/2 Vln/3 Guit/Pno 6 hands (à 6
mains)

Saxophone and Synthesizer

2 Musicians

BERTOCCHI, Serge - *Axolotl* (1987) (4') •Ssx/Synth
CHEVALIER, Christina - *Iris* •Ssx/Synth
COCCO, Enrico - *Actings* (1990) (10') •1 Sx: A+B/Electronics •adr
DUFOUR, Denis - *Cueillir à l'arbre...* (1978) (8') •Asx/Synth
GALANTE, Steven - *Shu Gath Manna* (1987) (12') •Asx/Yamaha
DX7 Synth •adr
GELLER, Gabriel - *Osculum infame* (1993) •Ssx/Pno+Synth •INM
GINER, Bruno - *Entrechocs I* (1985) (14') •1 sx: Sno+S+B/Tape/
Synth
HAIDMAYER, Karl - *Romanze* (1989) •Asx/Synth
LENFANT, Patrick - *Sequencadenza IV* (1986) •Sx/Synth
MANSHIP, Munch - *Dance Suite No. 3* •MIDI Wind Controller/Synth
•PBP
NITTMAR, Zbigniew - *Piton* (1993) •Ssx/Synth •INM
SZEREMETA, Ryszard - *Agent Orange* (1987) (13') •Sx/Synth
TOENSING, Richard - *Concerto* (1990) •Asx/Synth •CF
TOSI, Daniel - *Surimpressions II...* (1982) (15') •1 Sx: A+T+B+S/
Synth/Tape •Sal

3 Musicians

COCCO, Enrico - *Il Sogno di Chuang Tzu* (1989/91) (40') •Dancer/
Perc/1 Sx: S+A+T+B/Electronics •adr
COLIN, Jean-Marie - *SaXaf* (1991) •1 Sx: S+T/African Instruments/
Tape or Synth
REDOLFI, Michel - *Swinging on a vine* (1974) •Trb/Sx/Synth
SZEREMETA, Ryszard - *Trickstar* (1989) (12') •Sx/Synth/Perc
TON-THAT, Tiêt - *Moments rituels* (1991) •Tsx/Marimba/Synth

4 Musicians

DADELSEN, Hans-Christian von - *Cries of Butterflies* (1979) (16')
•Asx/Hn/Vla/Synth •Kodasi
DELAGE, Jean-Louis - *Illusions, Rêves et Caprices* (1990) (12')
•Asx/Pno/Synth/Perc or Asx/Pno •Bil
FUENTES, Tristan - *Gretchen* •Cl+Sx/Synth/Vibr+Sgl-lead/
Marimba+Steel Drum
Pan Am •BsCl/Ssx/Synth/Vibr+Steel Drum/Marimba+Accordion/
Tape •HMC
Quartet •BsCl+Asx/Synth/Vibr+Tabla/Marimba+Drums
HOLSTEIN, Jean-Paul - *Suite en bleu* (1991) •Asx/Pno/Perc/Ondes
martenot (ad lib.) •Bil
KÖHLER, Wolfgang - *Morgen hol'ich mir die Rosen* (1986) (3'30)
•Voice/Sx/Perc/Synth •adr
LAUBA, Christian - *Autographie* (1985) •Asx/Perc/Electr. Pno/
Synth/Tape •adr
OLOFSSON, Kent - *The voice of one who calls...* (1991-92) •Fl/Asx/
Trb/Synth •Tons
ROSSÉ, François - *Level 01-84* (1984) •Fl-à-bec/Fl/Asx/1 or 2 Synth/
Chambre d'écho & reverb. •adr
SCHMIDT-HAMBROCK, Jochen - *ARD - Sportschau* (1984) (10')
•Guit/Asx/Perc/Synth •adr

5 Musicians

KÖHLER, Wolfgang - *Schwerenöters Liä-song* (1986) (2'50) •Cl/Sx/
Electr Guit/Guit/Synth •adr
MABRY, Drake - *9.10.89* •Ssx/Electr. Guit/Bass Guit/Synth/Perc
MORTHENSON, Jan W. - *Scena* (1990) (17') •4 Sx: SATB/Synth
ROSSÉ, François - *Level 01-84* (1984) •Fl-à-bec/Fl/Asx/1 or 2 Synth/
Chambre d'écho & reverb. •adr
SHEPHERD, Stu - *Birthday Music III* (1986) •1 Sx: A+T/Guit/Synth/
Bass/Perc •CMC
YOUNG, Charles Rochester - *October in the Rain* (1989) (5') •MIDI
Wind Controller/Hn/Pno/Synth/Perc •adr

6 Musicians

MIEREANU, Costin - *Ricochets* (1989) •1 Sx: Sno+S+A+T+B/
Electr. Guit/Bass Guit/Synth/Perc/Régie
électr. •Sal

7 Musicians

ALLA, Thierry - *La terre et la Comète* (1991) •Fl/Cl/Asx/Pno/Bass/
Synth/Perc/Tape/Children's Choir •adr

8 Musicians

STOCKHAUSEN, Karlheinz - *Linker Augentanz* (1990) •7 to 12 Sx:
SS(S)AA(A)T(TT)B(B)Bs/1 Synth ad lib.
•Stv

9 Musicians

FISCHER, Eric - *Tango* (1982) •2 Cl/4 Sx: SATB/Mallet Perc [Perc
à clavier]/Synth/Pno •adr
STOCKHAUSEN, Karlheinz - *Linker Augentanz* (1990) •7 to 12 Sx:
SS(S)AA(A)T(TT)B(B)Bs/1 Synth ad lib.
•Stv

10 Musicians

STOCKHAUSEN, Karlheinz - *Linker Augentanz* (1990) •7 to 12 Sx:
SS(S)AA(A)T(TT)B(B)Bs/1 Synth ad lib.
•Stv

11 Musicians

STOCKHAUSEN, Karlheinz - *Linker Augentanz* (1990) •7 to 12 Sx:
SS(S)AA(A)T(TT)B(B)Bs/1 Synth ad lib.
•Stv

12 Musicians

ROY, Myke - *Ne pas plier, brocher...* (1987) •4 Sx/8 Synth •CMC
STOCKHAUSEN, Karlheinz - *Linker Augentanz* (1990) •7 to 12 Sx:
SS(S)AA(A)T(TT)B(B)Bs/1 Synth ad lib.
•Stv

13 Musicians

STOCKHAUSEN, Karlheinz - *Linker Augentanz* (1990) •7 to 12 Sx:
SS(S)AA(A)T(TT)B(B)Bs/1 Synth ad lib.
•Stv

14 Musicians

HARVEY, Jonathan - *The Valley of Aosta* (1985) (13'30) •Fl/Ob/Ssx/
Tpt/2 Yamaha DX7 Synth/2 Harp/Pno/2 Vln/
Vla/Vcl/Perc •FM

oOo

MELLÉ, Patrick - *Seriotis*, op. 4 (1985) (10') •2 Sx: TB/Men's chorus
[Choeur d'hommes]/Soprano Voice Solo/
Perc/Pno/Synth/Tape

Saxophone and Voice

2 Musicians

BASEVI, Andrea - *6 Brecht-lieder* (1993) •Voice/1 Sx: S+T •INM

BAUER, Robert - *Serenata Nerak* (1972) (5') •Mezzo Soprano Voice/Ssx •CMC

DEDIU, Dan - *Parerga agonica* (1993) •Mezzo Soprano Voice/1 Sx: S+A+B •INM

DEMERSSEMAN, Jules - *Ave Maria* (1865) •Voice/Asx

DINESCU-LUCACI, Violeta - *Mondnacht* (12') •Mezzo Soprano Voice/Sx •adr

HILLE, Wolfgang - *Es wäre besser...* (1993) •Sx/Voice •INM

HOUBEN, Guido - *Sax mit Worten* (1993) •Baritone Voice/Tsx •INM

KARPMAN, Laura - *Song Pictures* (1989) (8') •2 performers: Yamaha WX7 MIDI wind controller/Yamaha TX81Z tone generator/Sequencer/Soprano Voice •MMB

KAUFMANN, Waldemar - *Sein Weg* (1993) •Bsx/Voice •INM

KLOIBER, Anton - *Bekenntnisse eines Liebenden* (1993) •Soprano Voice/Bsx •INM

KOPELENT, Marek - *Snehah* (1967) •Soprano Voice/Asx/Tape

LOPEZ, Tom - *"In what far part...* (1994) •Soprano Voice/Asx

MARBE, Myriam - *Hell, Klar...* (10') •Mezzo Soprano Voice/Sx
   Überrzeitliches God (1993) •Soprano Voice+Perc/Ssx

MARSH, Roger - *Chamber Music* (1981) •Soprano Voice/Asx

MARTINEAU, Christine - *Soprani-une-ni-deux* (1989) •Voice/Sx/Tape

MELLÉ, Patrick - *Verbiages...* (1992) (13') •Soprano Voice/Bsx/Transf. en direct/Tape

MORRISSON, Julia - *Psalm 131* •Baritone Voice/Asx •CFE

NISHIKAZE, Makiko - *Liebeslied* (1993) •Soprano Voice/Ssx •INM

ROSEN, Jerome - *Serenade* (1964) (8') •Soprano Voice/Asx •ACA

ROSSÉ, François - *Atemkreis* (1990) (8') •Soprano Voice/Bsx •adr

STELZENBACH, Susanne - *Imagination* (1993) •Soprano Voice/Tsx

STROE, Aurel - *Quatre chansons* (10') •Soprano Voice/Asx

TAGGART, Mark - *Welcome Traveler* (1985) •Soprano Voice/Tsx •adr

TIPTON, Clyde - *Three Whitman Songs on Death* •Bass Voice/Tsx

TYSSENS, Albert - *3 Excerpts from 'Phantasmes'* (1983) •Asx/Voice/Tape •adr

VIERU, Anatol - *Siehe du bist...* (8') •Mezzo Soprano Voice/Asx

ZIMMERMANN, Keith - *The Paradoxes of Love* (1987) (7') •Soprano Voice/Ssx •adr

3 Musicians

BAUCHWITZ, Peter - *You came into my life* (1986) (3'40) •Voice/Sx/Perc •adr

BLACHER, Boris - *Jazz-Koloraturen*, op. 1 (1929) •Soprano Voice/Asx/Bsn •B&B

BLOOM, Shirley - *Suryanamaskar* (1971) (10') •Asx/Vcl/Chanter/Dancer •DP

BROWN, Newel - *Four Meditations* (1982) •Voice/Asx/Perc •DP

BUMCKE, Gustav - *Liedbearbeitung*, op. 64 (1937) •Voice/Sx/Pno
   3 Lieder..., op. 63 •Low Voice/Asx/Pno

BURRITT, Lloyd - *Crystal Earth* (1990) •Soprano Voice/1 Sx: S+A/Pno •CMC

CAVANA, Bernard - *Sax déminé* •2 Soprano Voices/1 Sx: Sno+S+T+Bs/Echo Chamber

CHALFONTE, Richard - *Sorrows of Werther* (1961) •Asx/Pno/Soprano Voice •adr

CHAN, Francis - *Wild nights...* (1978) •Soprano Voice/Sx/Vcl •CMC

DERR, Ellwood - *I Never Saw Another Butterfly*, op. 11 (1966) •Soprano Voice/Asx/Pno •UMM/DP

DESPORTES, Yvonne - *Discordances* •2 Voices/1 Sx: S+A+B •EFM/Bil

EHRLICH, Abel - *The Answer* (1970) •Tenor Voice/Fl/Sx

ENGELMANN, Hans - *Incanto*, op. 19 (1959) •Soprano Voice/Asx/Perc •A&S

EYSER, Eberhard - *The Seasons* (1988) (8') •Voice/2 Sx •EMa

FLADT, Hartmut - *Im Fabelreich* (1982) •Voice/Sx/Perc •adr

FLOTHUIS, Marius - *Negro Lament* (1953) •Contralto Voice/Asx/Pno •Don

GLINKOWSKI, Aleksander - *Capriccio* •Contralto Voice/Bsx/Pno •adr

GOODMAN, Alfred - *3 Chants* •Voice/Sx/Harp or Pno •adr

GREIF, Olivier - *Bomber auf Engelland* •Soprano Voice/Asx/Pno

HANNAY, Roger - *Cabaret Voltaire* •Female Voice/Ssx/Perc •SeMC

HAVEL, Christophe - *L'canton'ier* (1990) •Soprano Voice/Ssx/Harp •adr

HEWITT, Harry - *I Want My Karma* (1971) (8') •Sx/Actress+Singer/Dancer •DP

HOIBY, Lee - *Three Monologues* (15') •Soprano Voice/Asx/Pno •AMP

JACOBI, Wolfgang - *Cantata* •Soprano Voice/Asx/Pno
   Pastorale (1936) •Soprano Voice/Asx/Pno

JOLAS, Betsy - *Plupart du temps II* (1989) (10') •Tenor Voice/Tsx/Vcl •Led

Kahal & Raskin - *If I Give Up The Saxophone* (WOLFE) •Voice/Ssx/Pno/Tuba (optional) •Ron

MARCHAL, Dominique - *Bonus est dominus* (1980) (5') •Soprano Voice/Asx/Org •adr

MEFANO, Paul - *Scintillante, Mémoire...* (1993) •Bass Voice/2 Sx

MORRISSON, Julia - *John I, 19-23* •Alto Voice/Asx/Celesta •CFE
   Long John Brown and Little Mary Bell •Asx/Pno/Bass Voice •CFE
   Psalm 122 •Baritone Voice/Asx/Vcl •CFE

MYERS, Theldon - *Vocalise* (1986) (6'30) •Soprano Voice/Asx/Pno •DP

NIN, Joaquin - *Le Chant du veilleur* (1933) (4') •Mezzo Soprano Voice/Asx (or Vln)/Pno •ME

NODA, Ryo - *Guernica...*, op. 4 •Asx/Perc/Speaking Voice

OLSEN, Rovsing - *Aria*, op. 76 (1976) •Mezzo Soprano Voice/Asx/Pno

PANDELÉ, Thierry - *Le Fils apprête, à la mort, son chant* (1993) (10') •Soprano Voice/Fl/Sx

READE, Paul - *Bienvenue prelude* (1978) (2'35); *Cartoons* (1980) (3') •Mezzo Soprano Voice/Asx/Pno •adr

Rimsky-Korsakov, Nicolas - *Aimant la rose et le rossignol* (VIARD) •Mezzo Soprano Voice/Asx/Pno

RUEGER, Christoph - *Chansonabend Erich Mühsam* (1975) (2 Std.) •Voice/Sx/Pno •adr

SCELSI, Jacinto - *Canti del Capricorno* •Soprano Voice/Perc/Sx

SNOKE, Craig - *Within a Dream* (1990/93) •Soprano Voice/Sx/Pno

TAGGART, Mark - *Red and White* (1978) (10') •Tenor Voice/Sx/Vibr •adr

TAYLOR, Clifford - *Quattro Liriche* (1970) (13') •Medium Voice/Asx/Pno •ACA

VALK, Adriaan - *4 Miniatures* (1988) •Cl/Asx/Voice ad lib. •TM

VOGEL, Roger - *One Flesh* (1988) •Ssx/Bass Voice/Pno •adr

4 Musicians

ABSIL, Jean - *Phantasmes*, op. 22 & 72 (1936-50) (12') •Contralt. Voice/Asx/Pno/Perc •CBDM

ANDERSON, Beth - *Hallophone* (1973) •Dancer/Voice/Sx/Guit/Tape

ATOR, James - *Haikansona* (1974) (10') •Mezzo Soprano Voice/Ob/Asx/Vcl •SeMC

BANK, Jacques - *Finale* (1984) (30') •Baritone Voice/Asx/BsCl/Perc •Don

BAUCKHOLT, Carola - *Schraubdichtung* (12') •CBsSx/Vcl/Perc/ Voice

BEAL, Jeff - *Circular Logic* (1986) (10') •Asx/Soprano Voice/Vcl/ Pno •PMCP

BOOGARD, Bernard van den - *Syntetisch Gedicht* (1971) (20') •Mezzo Soprano Voice/Asx/BsCl/Pno •Don

BROWN, Newel - *Déjeuner sur l'herbe* (14') •Mezzo Voice/Fl/Sx/ Pno •SeMC

BUMCKE, Gustav - *4 Volksliedbearbeitungen*, op. 59 •Soprano Voice/Tenor Voice/Sx/Pno

CAMPBELL, John - *Voices of America* (1984) •Voice/Ssx/Vibr/Bass •adr

COLIN, Jean-Marie - *L'homme cage* (1976) •Soprano Voice/2 Cl/Sx

EYSER, Eberhard - *Canciones Nuevas* (1988) (10') •Mezzo Soprano Voice/4 Sx: SATB •EMa

FLADT, Hartmut - *Die Abnehmer* (1980) •2 Voice/Sx/Perc •adr

FRIED, Alexej - *Tympanon* (1982) (21') •Vln/Soprano Voice/Sx/Pno

GASLINI, Giorgio - *Magnificat* (1963) (4') •Soprano Voice/Asx/Pno/ Bass •Uni

GLASER, Werner Wolf - *5 Strukturer* •Soprano Voice/Fl/Sx/Vcl •STIM

GUACCERO, Domenico - *Quartetto* •Tsx/Cl/2 Voices: ST •DP

GUICHARD, Christophe - *Glu et gli* (1991) (10') •Soprano Voice/ Baritone Voice/Bsx/Perc

HEYN, Volker - *Blues two* (1983) •Voice/Vcl/Sx/Perc •Br&Ha

ILLASOVAY, Elsor von - *2 Songs* •Soprano Voice/Asx/Vibr/Perc •IMD

Kahal & Raskin - *If I Give Up The Saxophone* (WOLFE) •Voice/Ssx/ Pno/Tuba (optional) •Ron

KARPMAN, Laura - *Matisse and Jazz* (1987) (18') •Voice/1 Sx: S+A/ Perc/Pno •Eto

KÖHLER, Wolfgang - *Morgen hol'ich mir die Rosen* (1986) (3'30) •Voice/Sx/Perc/Synth •adr

KRIVITSKI, D. - *December Song* (1976) •Baritone Voice/Ssx/Vcl/ Pno

LEDUC, Jacques - *Sortilèges africains* (1967) (10') •4 Sx: SATB or Voice/Sx/Pno/Perc

MASON, Lucas - *Lay-Alla-Allah* (1972) •Soprano Voice/Asx/Fl/Pno •adr

MORRISSON, Julia - *The Memorare* •Asx/Bsn/Harp/Alto Voice •CFE

Psalm 130 •2 Voices: AB/Asx/Vcl •CFE

ROSSÉ, François - *...ces berges voyantes* (1988) (12') •2 Voice: AB/ 1 Sx: A+B/Prepared Pno/Tape •adr

TAGGART, Mark - *Death* (1978) (19') •Mezzo Voice/Sx/Vcl/Pno •adr

TAILLEFERRE, Germaine - *Fox* •2 Baritone Voices/2 Sx: SA •EFM

5 Musicians

ATOR, James - *Life Cycle* (1973) (18') •Mezzo Soprano Voice/Asx/ Ob/Perc/Vcl •SeMC

BUCZKOWNA, Anna - *Hipostaza* (1984/85) (15') •1 Sx: S+A+T/Fl/ Vcl/Vibr/Soprano Voice

CAMPANA, José-Luis - *Insight* (1987) (18') •Fl/Voice/Sx/Bass/ Perc/Tape/Video •Bil

CAVANA, Bernard - *Mariage* (1984) •1 Sx: Sno+S+T+Bs+CBs/Cl/ Pno/Singers

CHARRON, Damien - *Extraits du corps* (1985) •Mezzo Soprano Voice/Tsx/BsCl/Bass/Perc

CONDÉ, Gérard - *Invocations* (1983) (12'30) •Baritone Voice/4 Sx: SATB •Sal

DESPORTES, Yvonne - *Sonate pour un baptême* (1959) (18') •Fl/ Asx/Soprano Voice (or EH)/Perc/Pno •Bil

EYSER, Eberhard - *Canciones Nuevas* (1988) (10') •Mezzo Soprano Voice/4 Sx: SATB •EMa

FIRSOVA, Elena - *La Nuit* (1978) •Soprano Voice/4 Sx: SATB

FOURNIER, Marie Hélène - *Supplément nécessaire* (1990) (50') •2 Perc/Bsx/Harp/Soprano Voice

GAMSTORP, Göran - *Barnet i skogen...* (1987) (9'30) •Mezzo Soprano Voice/4 Sx: SATB •SMIC

HAMPTON, Calvin - *Labyrinth* (1986) (6') •Soprano Voice/4 Sx: SATB •NYSQ

HARRIS, Roger - *Caliban in Apartment 112* •Tenor Voice/Asx/Pno/ 2 Perc •SeMC

HEKSTER, Walter - *A song of peace* •Voice/Cl/Asx/Vcl/Perc •Don

HOPKINS, Bill - *Sensation* (1965) •Voice/Tsx/Tpt/Harp/Vla

KRIEGER, Edino - *Melopéia* (1949) •Soprano Voice/Ob/Tsx/Trb/ Vla

LAVAL, Philippe - *1,0544876* (1992) •Soprano Voice/2 Sx: AT/Guit/ Vibr

LAVENDA, Richard - *The Weary Man Whispers* (1985) •Tenor Voice/Asx/Trb/Perc/Pno •Eto

LEJET, Edith - *Quatre petits poèmes chinois* (12') •Soprano Voice/ Ob/Cl/Asx/Bsn •adr

LENOT, Jacques - *Pièce* •Soprano Voice/Asx/Ob/Cl/Bsn •adr

NICKLAUS, Wolfgang - *Der Priwall* (1984) (9') •Voice/Asx/Perc/ Cl/Vcl •adr

NIKIPROWETZKY, Tolia - *Auto-stop* •Soprano Voice/Tenor Voice/ Perc/Vcl/1 Sx: A+S •adr

OSTERC, Slavko - *Ave Maria* (1930) •Soprano Voice/Vla/Ob/Cl/Sx

POMORIN, Sibylle - *Zwei Lieder nach Anne Waldman* (1989) (19') •Voice/Asx/Perc/Vcl/Bass •adr

SCHAFFER, Boguslaw - *Proietto simultaneo* (1983) (12') •Soprano Voice/Vln/Pno/Ob/Sx/Tape

Schoenberg, Arnold - *Von heute auf Morgen*, op. 32 (PENNETIER) •2 Voices/Cl/Asx/Pno

SCHREIBER, Frederic C. - *Concerto Grosso* (1955) •2 Coloratura Soprano Voices/Asx/Tpt/Pno

SORG, Margarete - *Cantica Catulliana* (1986) (11') •Soprano Voice/ Baritone Voice/Tsx/Pno+Harps/Perc •adr

6 Musicians

BACULIS, Alphonse - *Three Folk Songs* •Soprano Voice/5 Sx: SAATB

BAINBRIDGE, Simon - *People of the dawn* (1975) •Soprano Voice/ Cl/Ssx/BsCl/Perc/Pno •UMPL

BUMCKE, Gustav - *2 Volksliedbearbeitungen...*, op. 58 •Tenor Voice/Baritone Voice/4 Sx

DE MARS, James - *Desert Songs* (1983) •Soprano Voice/Asx/Vcl/2 Perc/Pno •adr

ELIASSON, Anders - *The Green Rose* (1976) (11'15) •Soprano Voice/4 Sx: SATB/Perc •STIM

GASTINEL, Gérard - *5 Poèmes...* (1974) •Mezzo Soprano Voice/4 Sx: SATB/Pno •Chou

GEHLHAARD, Rolf - *Hélix* (1967) •Soprano Voice/Sx/Trb/Bass/ Pno/Perc •FM

GOEHR, Alexander - *Shadowplay*, op. 30 (1976) (20') •Actor+Tenor Voice/Narr+Fl/Asx/Hn/Vcl/Pno •Sch

GOTKOVSKY, Ida - *Poème lyrique* (1987) •2 Voices: SB/Pno/Fl (or Vln)/Asx (or Vla)/Bsn (or Vcl)

HAAS, Konrad - *Steinwolke* (1983) (45') •Voice/Sx/Perc/Pno/Guit/ Bass •Holz

Ingalls, Jeremiah - *Northfield* (1800) (HARTLEY) •1 Voice/5 Sx: BsBsBsBsBs

LE SIEGE, Annette - *Ordinary Things* •Voice/Fl/Sx/Vibr/Vcl/Pno •SeMC

LUROT, Jacques - *Sextuor* •Ob/Cl/Asx/Bsn/2 Voices: SA

OSTENDORF, Jens-Peter - *Minnelieder* (1987) •Soprano Voice/ Tenor Voice/4 Sx: SATB •Sik

SCELSI, Jacinto - *Yamaon* (1954-58) (10') •Bass Voice/2 Sx: AB/
    CBsn/Bass/Perc •Sal
STEVENS, James - *Girl in scena* (1973) •Voice/Sx+Cl/Asx+Cl/
    Tsx+BsCl+Fl/Electr. Guit/Pno •BMIC
Walker, Billy - *Hallelujah* (1835) •1 Voice/5 Sx: BsBsBsBsBs •adr

7 Musicians

BENNETT, Richard Rodney - *Soliloquy* (1966) (14') •Voice/1 Sx:
    A+T/Tpt/Tuba/Pno/Bass/Perc •Uni
BROWN, Anthony - *Soundscapes 1* •Asx/Bsn/Tpt/Vln/Voice/Pno/
    Perc/Tape •SeMC
BYTZEK, Peter - *Gefühle auf dem Eis* (1985) (3'45) •2 Voice/Guit/
    Pno/Sx/Perc/Bass •adr
COWELL, Henry - *Chrysanthemus* (1937) •Soprano Voice/2 Sx/2
    Vln/Vla/Vcl
DHAINE, Jean-Louis - *3 Chants lyriques* •3 Voice/2 Tpt/Asx/Pno
ESCOT, Pozzi - *Visione* (1964-87) •Fl/Asx/Vibr/Soprano Voice/
    Bass/Perc/Narr
HAAS, Konrad - *Pieces* •Holz
HAYAKAWA, Masaaki - *Four Little Poems* (1979) (9'30) •4 Sx:
    SATB/Soprano Voice/Harp/Perc •SFC
HILLBORG, Anders - *Variations* (1991) •Soprano Voice/Mezzo
    Soprano Voice/Fl/Sx/Perc/Vla/Bass •SMIC
KLEIN, Jonathan - *Hear O Israel* •Soprano Voice/Alto Voice/Sx/Hn/
    Pno/Perc/Bass •SeMC
MARCO, Tomàs - *Jabberwochy* (1967) •Voice/Tsx/Pno/4 Perc/Tape
MASON, Lucas - *A Quilt of Love* (1971) •Soprano Voice/Asx/Fl/Vln/
    Bsn/Trb/Vcl •adr
ROSSÉ, François - *OEM* (1988) (21') •Soprano Voice/1 Sx: S+Bs/
    EH/Accordion/Bass/Jazz Guit/Pno/Disposi-
    tif électro-acoust. •adr
SOMERS, Harry - *Limericks* (1979) •Voice/Fl/Cl/Sx/Bsn/Tpt/Eupho-
    nium •CMC

8 Musicians

BUMCKE, Gustav - *Suite G Dur*, op. 24 •Tenor Voice/Fl/Ob/Cl/Bsn/
    Hn/Bsx/Harp •VAB
DESCARPENTRIES, Hugues - *ô* (1993) (3'30) •Voice/5 Sx: SATBBs/
    Pno/Perc
FABERMAN, Harold - *For Erik and Nick* (1964) •Tenor Voice/Asx/
    Vcl/Bass/Tpt/Trb/Vibr/Perc
FONTYN, Jacqueline - *Cheminement* (1986) (15') •Soprano Voice/
    Fl/Cl/Hn (or Asx)/Vcl/Bass/Perc/Pno
FRANCAIX, Jean - *Paris à nous deux* (1954) (30') •4 Voices/4 Sx:
    SATB •ET
HARBISON, John - *The Flower-fed Buffaloes* (1976) •Voice/Cl/Tsx/
    Fl/Vcl/Bass/Pno/Perc
MAYUZUMI, Toshiro - *Sphenogramme* (1951) •Contralto Voice/Fl/
    Asx/Marimba/Vln/Vcl/Pno 4 hands [à 4
    mains]
VELLONES, Pierre - *Cinq poèmes de Mallarmé*, op. 24 (1929) (28')
    •High Voice/4 Harp/2 Sx: AT/Bass •Lem
VOGEL, Wladimir - *Wagadu's Untergang durch die Eitelkeit* (1930)
    •Soli Voices: SAB/5 Sx: SAATB/Singing
    Chorus/Speaking Chorus •adr

9 Musicians

BERIO, Luciano - *Prière* (1970) (15') •Voice/Instruments •Uni
GRAINGER, Ella - *To Echo* (1945) •Soprano Voice/Picc/Fl/Cl+Asx/
    Tsx/Vla/BsCl/Bass/Marimba •GS
MULDOWNEY, Dominic - *An Heavyweight Dirge* (1971) (25')
    •Voice/Fl/Asx/Perc/Pno/2 Vln/Vla/Vcl •Nov
RACOT, Gilles - *Jubilad'a* (1985) (23'30) •1 Sx: Bs+Sno/Vcl/Fl/6
    Voices

SÖDERLIND, Ragnar - *Eg hev funne...* (1982) (9'); *Legg ikkje ditt...*
    (1983) •Soprano Voice/Fl+Picc/Ssx/Hn/Vln/
    Vla/Bass/Pno/Perc •NMI
STROE, Aurel - *Orestia III* (60') •1 Sx: Sno+S+A+CBs/8 Voices
VELLONES, Pierre - *Prélude et fables...*, op. 28 (1930) •Tenor Voice/
    3 Sx: SAB/2 Tpt/Trb/Tuba/Banjo •Dur

10 Musicians

BENNETT, Richard Rodney - *Jazz Pastorale* (1969) (25') •Voice/1
    Sx: A+T/Bsx/2 Tpt/Trb/Tuba/Pno/Bass/Perc
    •Uni
BRANT, Henry - *Dialogue in the Jungle* (1964) (15') •Tenor Voice/
    Fl/Ob/Cl/Bsx/2 Tpt/Trb/Hn/Tuba •adr
FORTNER, Jack - *S pr ING sur des poèmes de E. E. Cummings* (1966)
    (11') •Mezzo Soprano Voice/Fl/Asx/Bsn/
    Vla/Vcl/Bass/Vibr/Harp/Pno •JJ
GOODMAN, Alfred - *3 Gesänge für Gresang* •Soprano Voice/Fl/Ob/
    Asx/Cl/Vla/Vcl/Prepared Pno/Guit/Perc •adr
GOUGEON, Denis - *Heureux qui comme...* (1987) •Soprano Voice/
    Picc/EH/Bsx/2 Vln/Vla/Vcl/Bass/Perc
    •CMC
HODEIR, André - *Jazz cantata* (10') •Soprano Voice/3 Sx: ATB/2
    Tpt/Trb/Vibr/Bass/Perc •MJQ
LAZARUS, Daniel - *4 Mélodies* •Contralto Voice/Fl/Cl/Asx/Bsn/2
    Vln/Vla/Vcl/Bass
LUTYENS, Elisabeth - *Akapotik Rose*, op. 64 (1966) (18') •Soprano
    Voice/Picc/Fl/Cl/Bsn/Cl+Tsx/Vln/Vla/Vcl/
    Pno
WROCHEM, Klaus - *Oratorium meum plus praeperturi* •3 Voices/2
    Vln/Vla/Vcl/Asx/Tpt/Perc •CAP

11 Musicians

COLE, Bruce - *Pantomimes* (25') •Soprano Voice/Fl/Cl/BsCl/Ssx/
    Perc/Pno/Guit/Vln/Vla/Vcl •B&H
DIEMENTE, Edward - *3-31 '70* •Voice/Tpt/Trb/Sx/Guit/Bass/5 Perc
    •SeMC
HALL, Helene - *Pieces* •5 Soprano Voices/3 Sx: SAB/Vcl/2 Perc
    •CMC
HAZZARD, Peter - *Massage* •3 Voices (SAB)/3 Perc/Fl/Cl/Hn/Sx/
    Trb •SeMC
PÜTZ, Eduard - *Kon-Takte* •Vocal Quartet (SATB)/Fl/Sx/Vibr/Guit/
    Perc/Pno/Bass •SeMC
SCHILLING, Otto-Erich - *Überall ist Wunderland* •Voice/Fl/Cl/Sx/
    Tpt/2 Vln/Bass/Perc/Accordion/Pno •SeMC

12 Musicians

BERIO, Luciano - *Novissimum Testamentum* (1991) •4 Sx: SATB/4
    Voice/4 Cl
PAPE, Gérard - *Pour un tombeau d'Anatole* (1985) •Soprano Voice/
    Perc/Sx Orch: SSAAATTTBBs
TOEPLITZ, Kasper - *Johnny Panic...* (25') •1 Sx: T+CBs/Mezzo
    Soprano Voice/2 Fl/2 Cl/Hn/2 Vln/2 Vla/
    Perc/Tape

13 Musicians

FINNISSY, Michael - *Babylon* (1971) (19') •Mezzo Soprano Voice/
    Ob/Cl/Asx/Bsn/Guit/Harp/Pno/2 Perc/2 Vcl/
    Bass •Uni
GRAEF, Friedemann - *Kammersinfonie* (1992) (20') 3 Voices/Str
    Quartet/4 Sx: SATB/2 Perc
McKINLEY, Thomas - *Emsdettener Totentanz* •3 Voices/Str Quartet/
    4 Sx: SATB/2 Perc
MERKU, Pavle - *Tiare* •Baritone Voice/Sx/11 wind instruments •Piz

14 Musicians

NICOLAU, Dimitri - *Quarta sinfonia*, op. 70 (1987) (10') •Sx Orch: SnoSSAAATTTBBBs/Soprano Voice/Perc

15 Musicians

MOSER, Roland - *Wortabend* (1979) (21'30) •2 Voices/13 instruments including 1 Asx

oOo

ALLA, Thierry - *La Terre et la Comète* (1991) •Children's Choir (Choeur d'enfants)/Fl/Cl/Asx/Pno/Bass/ Synth/Perc/Tape •adr

ANSIND, Caroline - *Het water...* (1986) (14'30) Choir/Ob/Cl/2 Sx: AB/2 Trb/Perc/Pno •Don

BANK, Jacques - *Requiem...* (1985) (50') •Récit. Choeur/4 Sx/9 Accordion/3 Bass/3 Perc •Don

BELLEMARE, Gilles - *La chasse-galerie* (1981) •Narr/Choir/2 Fl/2 Recorder/2 Cl/2 Tpt/Sx

BEURLE, Jürgen - *Variable Realisationen* (1967) •Voice/Chamber Ensemble/Chamber Choir •EMod

BLYTON, Carey - *Rainbow Snake - Cantata* (1974) •Voices/4 Sx: SATB •BBC

BRANT, Henry - *Barricades* (1961) •Tenor Voice/Ob/Ssx/Cl/Bsn/ Trb/Pno/Xylophone/Str •adr

Millennium •Soprano Voice/10 Tpt/10 Trb/8 Hn/2 Tuba/6 Sx/5 Perc •MCA

BRAXTON, Anthony - *W12-B46* •Voice/Reeds/BsTrb/Perc

CALMEL, Roger - *Cantate "Liberté"* •Ob/Cl/Asx/Bsn/Chorus/Soloists •adr

Messe du Pays d'Oc •Ob/Cl/Asx/Bsn/Chorus/Soloists •adr

CAVANA, Bernard - *Mariage* (1984) •1 Sx: Sno+S+T+Bs+CBs/Cl/ Pno/Singers

CELERIANU, Michel - *Aus* (1985) •1 Sx: S+Bs/Ensemble/Choir

DUPIN, Paul - *Chant* (1910) •Asx/Harps/Vla/Chorus

GRAEF, Friedemann - *Lieder...* (1989) (18') •Chorus/4 Sx: SATB •adr

GRAINGER, Percy - *Stalt Vesselil* (1951) •Voice/Bsn/Sx/Str •GSch

HAUBIEL, Charles - *Jungle Tale* •Asx/Pno/Male Choir (TTBB) •SeMC

HAZON, Roberto - *Cantata spirituale* (1955) •Contralto Voice/4 Sx/ Org/Str

HILDEMANN, Wolfgang - *Psalmodia III* (1973) •Asx/Org/Chorus •MV

KUERGEL, Hannes - *Konzert* •Asx/Winds/Male Choir

LETASSEY, Laurent - *Sempre tutti* (1991) (17') •Asx Ensemble/8 Voices •Bil

LUEDEKE, Raymond - *"Of him I love day and night"* & *"A noiseless, patient spider"* •Chorus (SATB)/4 Sx: SATB/Bass/2 Perc

MAIS, Chester - *Poem* (1974) •Asx/Chorus •adr

MARCHAL, Dominique - *Jesus dulcis memoriam* •Soprano Voice/ Asx/Choir/Str •adr

MELLÉ, Patrick - *Seriotis*, op. 4 (1985) (10') •2 Sx: TB/Men's chorus [Choeur d'hommes]/Soprano Voice Solo/ Perc/Pno/Synth/Tape

MILHAUD, Darius - *Etude poétique*, op. 333 (1954) •2 Sx/Voice/ Orch/Tape

MORRISSON, Julia - *De profundis* •Asx/Vcl/Voices •CFE

Psalm 29 •Fl/Tsx/Voices •CFE

NILSSON, Bo - *La Bran - Anagramme sur Ilmar Laaban* (1963-76) (16') •Sx Solo: S+A/Chorus/Orch/Tape/ Electr. •STIM

Szene IV (1975) •Jazz Sx/Chorus

PELLMAN, Samuel - *Horizon* (1978) •Ssx/Wind Ensemble/Mixed Chorus/Narr

PEPIN, Clermont - *Pièces de circonstance* (1967) •Childrens chorus/ Fl/Ob/3 Cl/2 Sx/2 Hn •CMC

POLIN, Claire - *Infinito - a requiem* (1972) (23') •Soprano Voice/Asx/ Narr/Mixed chorus •SeMC

Prevost, André - *'Il fait nuit lente'* (LONDEIX) (16') •Chorus/10 Sx: SnoSSAATTBBBs

RAYNAL, Gilles - *L'ordre et la lumière* (6') •4 Sx: SATB/Choeur

REBOTIER, J. - *Le Bestiaire marin* •Children's Choir/4 Fl/4 Sx: SATB •Dur

SMITH, Stuart - *A Pool of...* (1973) •Asx/Chorus •adr

STROE, Aurel - *Orestia III* (60') •Voices (T/M-S/H-C)/Mixed choir of 6 voices/1 Sx: Sno+A+B+CBs

TELFER, Nancy - *The Golden Cage* (1979) •Mixed Choir/Fl/Cl/Sx/ 3 Perc/Pno

VILLA-LOBOS, Heitor - *Nonetto*, op. 181 (1923) (18') •Fl/Ob/Cl/1 Sx: A+B/Bsn/Perc/Celesta/Harp/Pno/Mixed Chorus •ME

VOGEL, Wladimir - *Wagadu's Untergang durch die Eitelkeit* (1930) •Soli Voices/Singing Chorus/Speaking Chorus/5 Sx: SAATB •adr

Saxophone and Narrator

2 Musicians

GAY, Harry Wilbur - *Ishtar* (1971) (12') •Sx/Tape/Narr •Eri

GOLDBERG, William - *Pelagos* (1971) •Asx/Tape/Narr •adr

HEILNER, Irwin - *Pieces* •Sx/Narr

HOFFMAN, Allan - *Duo* •Sx/Narr •DP

OSTRANDER, Linda - *Tarot* •Asx/Narr+Dancer/Tape •DP

SMITH, Stuart - *Hey, Did You Hear the One About...* •Sx/Narr •adr

STOCKHAUSEN, Karlheinz - *Aus den 7 Tagen n° 26* (1968) (60') •Narr/1 Instrument (Improvised) •Uni

3 Musicians

DUKE, Lewis Byron - *Eingang* (1969/71) •2 Sx: AB/Narr •BPb

FRID, Geza - *3 Poemes* (1976) •Narr/Asx/Guit •Don

NODA, Ryo - *Guernica - Hommage à Picasso*, op. 4 (1973) •Asx/ Perc/Speaking Voice

4 Musicians

GODAR, Vladimir - *2 Frammenti* (1977) •Narr/Sx/Bass/Pno

KURTZ, Arthur - *Isaiah VI*, op. 31 (1971) (7'30) •Narr/Asx/Pno/Perc •adr

MUCZYNSKI, Robert - *Fuzzette...* (1962) (12') •Narr/Fl/Asx/Pno

OLSON, Roger - *Cobwebs* (1983) •Narr/Guit/Asx/Vln

WILMAUT, Jean-Marie - *La complainte...* •Narr/Ob/Cl/Asx

5 Musicians

HARVEY, Paul - *The Tale of Billy Goats and the Troll* (1973) (15') •4 Sx: SATB/Narr •adr

SYMONDS, Norman - *Sylvia* (1974) •Narr/Tsx/Fl/Pno/Bass •CMC

6 Musicians

GOEHR, Alexander - *Shadowplay*, op. 30 (1976) (20') •Actor+Tenor Voice/Narr+Fl/Asx/Hn/Vcl/Pno •Sch

HERMANSSON, Christer - *Aggjakten* (1979) •Narr/Tsx/Trb/Guit/ Bass/Perc •STIM

WELSH, Wilmer - *Mosaic Portraits II...* •4 Sx/Org/Narr

7 Musicians

BERNARD, Jacques - *L'Opéra de l'espace* (1970) •Narr/Ob/Cl/BsCl/ 1 Sx: S+A+B/Bsn/Perc •adr

BROTT, Alexander - *7 for seven* (1954) (14'30) •Narr/Cl/Asx/Vln/ Vla/Vcl/Pno •CMC

ESCOT, Pozzi - *Visione* (1964-87) •Fl/Asx/Vibr/Soprano Voice/Bass/Perc/Narr

HERMANSSON, Christer - *Rumba* (1979) •Narr/2 Sx: ST/Trb/Guit/Pno/Bass •STIM

8 Musicians

GHEZZO, Dinu - *Pontica II* •Fl/Sx/2 Tpt/2 Hn/Pno/Narr •SeMC

ORTEGA, Sergio - *Récit d'un naufragé* (1990) (15') •7 Sx: SnoSATBBsCBs/Narr

9 Musicians

MARCO, Tomàs - *Anna Blume* (1967) •2 Narr/Fl/Ob/Cl/Sx/Tpt/2 Perc

WALTON, William - *Façade* (1922/26, 42) (34'30) •2 Narr/Fl+Picc/Cl/BsCl/Asx/Tpt/Vcl/Perc •OUP

10 Musicians

HORWOOD, Michael - *Facets* (1974) (20') •Narr/Sx/Tpt/Hn/Trb/Pno/Accordion/Electr. Bass/2 Electr. Guit •CMC

15 Musicians

LUTYENS, Elisabeth - *Islands*, op. 80 (1971) •2 Narr: ST/Picc/Fl/Cl/BsCl/Tsx/Hn/Pno/Celesta/Vln/Vla/Vcl/2 Perc

oOo

BELLEMARE, Gilles - *La chasse-galerie* (1981) •Narr/Choir/2 Fl/2 Recorder/2 Cl/2 Tpt/Sx

COWLES, Colin - *From the King's Chamber* •Tsx/Narr/Chamber Orch •adr

PELLMAN, Samuel - *Horizon* (1978) •Ssx/Wind Ensemble/Mixed Chorus/Narr

POLIN, Claire - *Infinito - a requiem* (1972) (23') •Soprano Voice/Asx/Narr/Mixed chorus •SeMC

POPP, André - *Pieces* •Narr/4 Sx: SATB/Orch

SHAFFER, Sherwood - *Stargaze* •Narr/Tsx/Orch •adr

VALEK, Jiri - *Symphony III* (1963) (28') •2 Sx: ST/Narr/Orch •CHF

Saxophone and Tape or Electronics
(Bande magnetique ou appareillage electronique)

1 Musician

ABLINGER, Peter - *7 X 7* (1993) •Ssx/Tape •INM

ALLIK, Kristi - *Integra* (1986) •Ssx (or Asx)/Tape •CMC

ANGULO, Manuel - *Bucolica* (1985) (13') •Ssx/Tape

ARMA, Paul - *2 Convergences* (1976) (7'30) •Asx/Tape (African instruments)

AUBART, Michael - *Duo* (1982) •Asx/Tape

AUSTIN, Larry - *J.B. Larry Plus* •Improvisational Sx/Tape •DP

BABBITT, Milton - *Images* (1979) (10'30) •1 Sx: Sno+S+A/Synth Tape •adr

BARROSO, Sergio - *Yantra IX* (1979) •Sx/Tape

BATTISTA, Tonino - *Narcisso* (1989/91) •1 Sx: S+B/Live Electron.

BEERMAN, Burton - *Concerto I* (1980) •Asx/Tape

BELLINI, Luciano - *Phos* (1991) •Asx/Tape •adr

BENNETT, Wilhelmine - *Five Quick Visions...* (1971) (25') •Sx/Actress/Tape

BERENGUER, José-Manuel - *Fuego* (1989) (8') •BsSx/Tape

BEVELANDER, Brian - *Synthecisms* (1988) •1 Sx: S+A/Tape

BIANCHINI, Laura - *NO.DI - Note differenze* (1987/88) (10') •1 Sx (S+A+T)/Computer "Fly" •adr

BLANCO, Juan - *Bucolica* •Ssx/Tape

BOEUF, Georges - *Phrases* (1975) (15') •Ssx/Tape •adr

BORENSTEIN, Daniel - *M-Tango* (1982) (6') •1 Instrument/Electronics •Sal

BRABANT, Eric - *Saxodrome* (1982) (22') 1 Sx: Sno+S+A+T+B/Tape

BRINDUS, Nicolae - *Kitsh II-N* (20') •1 Sx: Sno+S+A+T+B/Tape

BRNCIC, Isaza Gabriel - *Kientzy - Concert* (1989) (12') •Tsx/Tape

BROSH, Thomas - *Aeolian Suite* (1985) •Tsx/Tape

BROWN, Anthony - *Beyond Oblivion* •Asx/Chamber Orch or Tape •SeMC

Interpolations •Asx/Film/Lights •SeMC

Soundscapes 3 •Ssx/Tape •SeMC

BUBALO, Rudolph - *Electrum* (1977) (5'45) •Asx/Tape

CAVANA, Bernard - *Goutte d'or blues* (1985) (7') •1 Sx: Sno+S/Tape or 12 Sx •Sal

La Villette (1984-85) •1 Sx: S+T+CBs/Tape

CECCARELLI, Luigi - *Neuromante* (1993) •Asx/Tape •INM

CIBULKA, Franz - *Solo* (1982); *Studie...* (1982) •Asx/Tape

CLAYTON, Laura - *Simichai-ya* (1976) •Asx/Tape

COLIN, Jean-Marie - *Saxanzesse* (1990) (10') •Bsx/Tape

CONRAD, Tony - *3 Loops for Performers and Tape* •Performer/Tape

CORNER, Philip - *Composition...* •Sx/Tape

CRUZ, Zulema de la - *Chio* (1989) •BsSx/Tape

DAVIES, Terry - *Whale* (1990) •Sx+WX7 MIDI Wind Controller/Tape

DECOUST, Michel - *Olos* (1983-84) (11') •Tsx/Dispositif électro-acoust. •Sal

DELACRUZ, Zulema - *Chio* (1989) (7'30) •1 Sx: S+A+B/Tape

DEL CERRO, Emiliano - *Quejumbroso metal* (1992) (8') •Asx/Tape

DE MARS, James - *Seven Healing Songs...* (1982) (9'20) •Asx/Tape •adr

DESJARDINS, Luc - *Autodafé* •Ssx/Tape

DIEDERICHS, Yann - *Pieces* •Sx/Dispositif électro-acoust.

DIEMENTE, Edward - *Dimensions II*; *Dimensions III* (1971) •SeMC

DOLDEN, Paul - *Revenge of repressed...* (1993) •Ssx/Tape •INM

D'OMBRAIN, Geoffrey - *Continuo* (1982) •Asx/Tape

Introspections (1975) •Asx/Tape

DROZIN, Garth - *Parabolics* (1981) •Ssx/Tape •ACA

DUBEDOUT, Bertrand - *Cycles de transparence* (1984-85) (8') •Asx/Tape

DUCKWORTH, William - *Midnight Blue* (1976) (4'30) •Asx/Tape •adr

DYFFORT, Jens-Uwe - *Bewegtes Stück* (1993) •Asx/Tape •INM

EHLE, Robert - *Hypothetical Orbits* •Asx/Tape •DP

EICHLER, Matthew - *"(Colloquy) (Charter) 1980"* •Asx/Tape

ELOY, Christian - *Moai* (1986) (5') •Asx/Electronics

EVANS, Stanford - *Chor* •Sx/Tape •adr

EVERTT, Steven - *Interactive Electronics* •Asx+MIDI Wind Controller+Narr/Computer

FEILER, Dror - *Antafada* (1988) •Asx/Electronics •Tons

Gavona (1984) •Ssx/Tape •STIM

The Heart (1991) •Sx/Tape •Tons

Sendero Luminoso II (1991) •Sx/Live Electronics/Tape •Ton

FONGAARD, Bjorn - *Sonata*, op. 95 (1971) (8') •Asx/Tape •HL/Pet

FOURNIER, Marie-Hélène - *Aliènage* (1987) (20') •Ad lib./Tape

Hippogriffe III (1988) (11') •1 Sx comédien: S+B/Tape

Les muses inconnues •1 Sx: A+S+T/Tape

FRANCESCHINI, Romulus - *Celebrations* •Sx/Tape

GABURO, Kenneth - *The Flight of Sparrow* •Asx/Tape

GAGNEUX, Renaud - *Babel* (1978) (7') •1 Sx: A+S/Dispositif électro-acoustique simple

Première •Asx/Tape

GARCIN, Gérard - *Après...* (1981) (14') •Asx/Tape •Sal

Elle arriva... (1981) •Bsx/Tape •Sal

Enfin... (1981) (13') •Sno Sx/Tape •Sal
6me musique... (1984) (6') •1 to 7 Asx/Tape •Sal
GIARO, Paolo - *Su in aire* (1992) •Asx/Live electronics
GIULIANO, Giuseppe - *Tempi della mente* (1986) (11') •1 Sx: Sno+S/Tape
GLEMINOV, Michail - *Coyote* (1993) •Bsx/Tape •INM
GOLDBERG, Theo - *Anti thesis* (1974) •Asx/Pno or Tape
GRANT, Jerome - *Duo I* •Eb Sx or Bb Sx/Tape •DP
GRANT, Parks - *Varied Obstinacy*, op. 61 (1972) (3'30) •Asx/Tape •ACA
GRATZER, Carlo - *Failles flourescentes* (1990) (16') •Asx/Tape
GREENWOOD, Allan - *Junctions* (1992) (8') •Sx/Yamaha WX7 MIDI Wind Controller/Tape
GREUSSAY, Patrick - *L'Itinéraire* •Sx/Tape
GUACCERO, Domenico - *Luz* (1973) (7-10') •1 Low Instrument/Tape •CRM
GUTWEIN, Daniel - *Reliquary for Rahshaan* •Tsx/Tape •DP
HANLON, Kevin - *Variations...* •Asx/Tape Delay
HARRISON, Jonty - *EQ* (1980) (13'30) •Ssx/Tape
HAVEL, Christophe - *S* (1993) •Tsx/Computer •INM
Xaps (1991) •Ssx/Transformation électroacoustique •adr
HEILNER, Irwin - *The Ghost of Amsterdam* •Sx/Tape
HEUSSENSTAMM, George - *Saxoclone*, op. 42 (1971) (11') •1 Sx: A+T/Tape •SeMC
HEUTBERG, Cortland - *Improvisation...* •Any instrument/Tape
HEWITT, Harry - *Adornments* (1971) (20') •Sx/Tape •DP
Saxercises, op. 438, no. 5 (1971) (60') •Sx/Tape •DP
Venus in Transit (1971) (15') •Sx/Tape •DP
HORVIT, Michael - *Antiphon* (1971) •Asx/Tape •DP
INGHAM, Richard - *Still Life* (1992) (7') •Sx+Yamaha WX7 MIDI Wind Controller/Tape
IOACHIMESCU, Calin - *Musique spectrale* •1 Sx: S+Bs/Tape
JUSTEL, Elsa - *Sikxo* (1989) (11') •Bsx/Tape •INM
KAGEL, Mauricio - *Atem* (1970) (25') •1 Wind instrument/Tape •Uni
KARPEN, Richard - *Saxonomy* •1 Sx: A+T+B/Tape
KAVANAUGH, Patrick - *Quintus rotus* (1980) •Asx/Tape
KEANE, David - *Saxophonies* (1987/90) (13') •Ssx/Computer •CMC
KERGOMARD, Henri - *Anem* (1989) (8') •Ssx/Tape
KLEIN, Georg - *Nuit...* (1993) •1 Sx: S+T/Live electronics •INM
KOCH, Frederick - *Three Dance Episodes* (1971) •Asx/Tape •SeMC
KORTE, Karl - *Dialogue* (1969) (19') •Asx/Tape •Ga/DP
Study •Asx/Tape •SeMC
KORTH, Thomas - *Disparities II* (1974) •Asx/Tape •adr
KUNDRATS, Vilnis - *Emotions...* (1993) •Sx/Electronics •INM
KURTAG, György - *Interrogation* (1983) (11'30) •1 Sx: T+Bs+CBs/Tape •Sal
LASAGNA, Marco - *"Il nastro delle tredici lune"* •Asx/Tape
LE FASSE, Roger - *Le Biniou et le labo* •Sx/Tape
LEVINAS, Michael - *Les rires du Gilles* (1981) (7') •Ssx/Tape •Sal
LONG, Duncan - *Future past perfect* (1971) (8'30) •Sx/Tape •adr
Weep dark flame (1976) •Asx/Tape •adr
LOPEZ-LOPEZ, José-Manuel - *Con Cadencia...* (1989) (9') •Bsx/Tape
LUC, Francis - *Concerto* (1981) (15') •1 Sx: Sno+A+T+B/Tape
LUKASIK, Joseph - *Concertino* (1992) (16') •Asx/Computer
LUQUE, Francisco - *Saxofonia* (1989) (7') •1 Sx: Sno+B/Tape
LUSTGARTEN, Dan - *Parole de Dieu* (1982) (25') •Sx/Dispositif électron.
LUTZ-RIJEKA, Wilhelm - *Psy* (1993) •Tsx/Computer •INM
MACHE, François-Bernard - *Aulodie* (1983) (11') •Ssx/Tape •Dur
MAIGUASCHCA, Mesias - *Lindgrend* (1985) (13') •Bsx/Tape
MARIASY, David - *Private Eye* (1982) •Ssx/Tape
MARIETAN, Pierre - *Concert III* (1989) (7') •1 Sx: Sno+S/Magnétoph. multipistes
Duo (1985) •1 Sx: Sno+A+T+B+Bs+CBs/Tape

MARKOVITCH, Ivan - *Appels* (1985) (15') •1 player: Sx+Chanteur [Singer]/Tape
MAXFIELD, Richard - *Wind* •Sx/Tape
McGUIRE, Edward - *Music...* (1976) (8') •1 to 4 Sx (SATB)/Tape •SMPL
McLEAN, Barton - *Dimensions III/IV* (1979) •Asx/Tape
McTEE, Cindy - *Etudes* (1992) •Asx/Tape
MELBY, John - *Rhapsody* (1987) •Asx/Tape
MELILLO, Peter - *Diane Piece* •Ssx/Tape
MESSIERI, Massimiliano - *Espressione I* (1993) •Asx/Live Tape •INM
MIEREANU, Costin - *Do-Mi-Si-La-Do-Ré* (1980-81) (16'30) •1 player: Cl+BsCl+Sx/Tape or 5 Sx: SATBBs/Tape •Sal
Variants - Invariants (1982) (14') •Asx or Ssx/Echo Chamber •Sal
MILICEVIC, Mladen - *Solo* (1986) (8') •Ssx/Tape
MOBBERLEY, James - *Spontaneous Combustion* •1 Sx:S+A/Tape
MOLINO, Andréa - *Unité K* (7') •1 Sx: S+B/Tape
MOLTENI, Marco - *Saturna pyri* (1986) (6') •1 Sx: A+Bs/Tape
MORRIL, Dexter - *Getz Variations* (1984) (22') •Tsx/Tape •CVMP
Six Studies and an Improvisation •Tsx/Tape
MORYL, Richard - *Chamber II* (1972) (11') •Asx/Tape •ACA
MOSS, Lawrence - *Evocation and Song* (1972) (9'45) •Ron
Saxpressivo (1992) (8'10) •Asx/Tape •Ron
MOYLAN, William - *Suite...* (1979) (13') •1 Sx: B or A/Tape •SeMC/DP
NEMESCU, Octavian - *Metabyzantiniricon* (1983-84) (19') •Asx/Tape
NIELSON, Lewis - *Fantaisies* (1983) (17'30) •Ssx/Tape •ACA
NUNEZ, Adolfo - *Cambio de saxo* (1989) (6') •1 Sx: B+S/Tape
OLAH, Tiberiu - *Rimes* (1985) (8') •1 Sx: Sno+A/Matériel électr.
OTT, Joseph - *Quartet* (1972) (9') •Asx Solo/Tape Recorder •DP
PARSCH, Arnost - *Kure krakore* (1970) •Asx/Tape •DP
PATACHICH, Ivan - *Modsaxyn* (1989) (9') •Tsx/Tape
Patience (9') •Asx/Tape
PAYNE, Frank - *Sax Prepared Tape* •Asx/Tape •NTS
PECK, Russell - *Time Being* •Sx/Tape
PELLMAN, Samuel - *Pentacle* (1976) •Asx/Tape •DP
PENNYCOOK, Bruce - *3 Pièces* (1982) (10') •1 Sx: S+A/Tape •CMC
PEREZ-MASEDA, Eduardo - *My echo, my shadow* (1989) (10') •1 Sx: S+B/Tape
PERNAIACHI, Gianfranco - *Realgar 1 & 2* (1984 & 1990) (8' + 5') •Trb and/or Tsx/Electr. •EDP
POLONIO, Eduardo - *Errance* (1989) (8') •Bsx/Tape
RABINOWITZ, Robert - *Echoes for Forever* (1983) •Asx/Tape
RACOT, Gilles - *Ité* •Tsx/Tape
RADULESCU, Horatiu - *Astray* (1984-85) (23') •1 Sx: Sno+S+A+T+B+Bs/matériel électron. (or Prepared Pno)
Capricorn's... (1974-83) (22') •Asx/matériel électron.
REICH, Steve - *Reed Phase* (1967) •Any reed instrument/Tape
RILEY, Terry - *Peppy Naggod's Phantom Band* (1970) •Asx/Tape
RISSET, Jean-Claude - *Saxatile* •Ssx/2 Tapes •Sal
Voilements (1987) (14') •Tsx/Tape •Sal
ROLIN, Etienne - *Ost Schatten* (1993) (10') •Ssx/Tape •adr
ROQUIN, Louis - *Machination VIII* (1983) •1 Sx: S+A+T+B+Bs/Tape
Soli... (1984-85) (10') •1 Sx: S+A+T+CBs/Tape
ROSS, Walter - *Toward the Empyreans* •Sx/Tape •DP
ROSSÉ, François - *Epiphanies* (1990) (10') •1 Sx: S+B+Bs/Dispositif électro-acoust. •adr
Ost Atem (1992) (8') •Bsx/Tape •adr
Udel 05.89 (1989) (12') •SnoSx or Ssx/Tape •adr
RUEDA, Enrique - *La Otra zona* (1992) •Sx/Tape

RUGGIERO, Charles - *Interplay* •Ssx/Pno or Yamaha WX7 MIDI Wind Controller/Tape

RUIZ, Pierre - *Another Lifetime* (1972) •Asx/Tape •DP

RUZICKA, Rudolf - *Tibia 1* (1984) (11') •Ssx/Dispositif électro-acoustique

RYDBERG, Bo - *Illuminated bodies* (1985) (15') •1 Sx: T+S/Tape •SMIC

SAUCEDO, Victor - *Philolicia Comica* (1971) (10') •Ssx/Tape •adr

SCHAAD, Roar - *Study* (1972) (8'30) •Asx/Tape •DP
  20:50 (1971) (20'50) •Sx/Tape •DP

SCHALLOCK, Ralf - *So ach... chaos* (1993) •Tsx/Tape •INM

SCHWARTZ, Francis - *Sex-Six-Sax* (1990) (5') •Asx/Dispositif électro-acoustique

SERMILÄ, Jarno - *Contemplation II* (1978) (11') •Asx/Tape •FMIC

SHINOHARA, Makoto - *Situations* (1993) •Asx/Electronics •INM

SMITH, Howie - *Metaforest* (1978) •Sx/Electronics/Tape •Oa

SOUFFRIAU, Arsène - *Structures*, op. 223 (1971) •Asx/Tape •adr

STEDRON, Milos - *Jazz pieces* •Sx/Tape

STEINBERG, Paul - *Troika* (1983) •Asx/Tape •DP

STOKES, Eric - *Eldey Island...* (1971) (8') •MP
  Tag (1982) (5'35) •Asx/Tape •HMC

STROE, Aurel - *La cité ouverte* (1983) (9'30) •1 Sx: Sno+S+B/Tape

SUBOTNICK, Morton - *In Two Worlds* - Concerto (1988) (25') •Asx/Computer/Orch or Yamaha WX7 MIDI Wind Controller/Computer or Asx/Computer •EAM

SURIANU, Horia - *Vagues...* (1984) (11') •Asx/Tape or 6 Sx •Sal

SYVERUD, Stephen - *Pieces* •Asx/Tape

SZEREMETA, Ryszard - *Amphora Snake Dance* (1984) •Tsx/Tape

TALLET, Marc - *Mnémosyne et l'oubli* (1982) (6'30) •Asx/Chambre d'echo •Sal

TENNEY, James - *Saxony* (1978) •Sx/Tape •CMC

TERRY, Peter - *Spider Kiss* (1984) •Asx/Tape •adr

TERUGGI, Daniel - *Xatys* (1988) (18'30) •1 Sx: Bs+T+S/Dispositif électronique

TOKUNAGA, Hidenori - *Eidos* •1 Sx: S+A+T+B/Tape •adr

TORRE, Salvador - *Bira* (1987) (15') •Asx/Tape

TRAVERSA, Martino - *Fragment* (1992) •Ssx/Live electronics

TUREK, Ralph - *Pieces* •Asx/Tape

UNGVARY, Tamas - *Pignon, Paul Olarra* (1983) (10') •Ssx/Live computer •SMIC

USSACHEVSKY, Vladimir - *Mimicry* (1982) •Asx/Tape

VAGGIONE, Oracio - *Thema* (1985) (10') •BsSx/Dispositif électroacoust. •Sal

VANDENBOGAERDE, Fernand - *Tezcatlipoca II* (1986) •Sx/Tape •Mor

VAN TUONG, Nguyen - *Synthese* (1975) •Asx/Tape

VILLA-ROJO, Jésus - *Lamento* (1989) (8'15) •Tsx/Tape

WEIDENAAR, Reynold - *The Stillness* (1985) (12'45) •Asx/Tape/Color video •adr

WELLS, Thomas - *Nocturne* (1985) •Sx/Computer generated sound

WESLEY-SMITH, Martin - *Doublets II* (1974) (8') •Asx/Tape
  For Alto Saxophone and Tape (1988) •Asx/Tape

WIER, Albert - *Pièces* •Asx/Tape •HaBr/AC

WILLIAMS, Jay - *Looking at Number* •Sx/Tape

WONG, Vincent - *Music* (1983-84) •Asx/Tape

WYATT, Scott - *Counterpoints* (1992) •Ssx/Tape •adr
  Vignettes (1989) •MIDI Wind Controller/Tape •adr

XANTHOUDAKIS, Charis - *Les visages...* (1989) (8') •CBsSx/Tape

YERGEAU, Liette - *Dans les spirales du silence* (1992) •Ssx/Tape

ZOURABICHVILI, Nicolas - *Pointillés* (1974) •Asx/Tape •adr

2 Musicians

BURRITT, Lloyd - *The Electric Chair* (1971) (5') •Asx/Actress/Tape •Ken

CARLOSEMA, Bernard - *Vésanie II* (1985) (5') •Asx/Pno/Tape

COHEN, Veronika - *I Remember* •Sx/Dancer/Tape

COLIN, Jean-Marie - *SaXaf* (1991) •1 Sx: S+T/African Instruments/Tape or Synth

COYNER, Lou - *Music-Piva* •Asx/Perc/Tape

COX, Rona - *A Saxophone* (1968) (6') •2 Sx: AT/Tape

DIEMENTE, Edward - *Diary Part II* (1972) •2 Asx/Tape •DP
  Dimensions II •Any 1 to 6 Instruments/Tape •SeMC

ELLIS, Merrill - *Dream...* (1974) •Asx+Cl/Tape/Perc/Visuals •CF

ERB, Donald - *I "Mixed-Media": Fission* (1968) (13') •Ssx/Pno/Tape •adr

EVANS, Stanford - *Each Tolling Sun* (1972) (17') •Sx/Tape/Actress •adr

EYSER, Eberhard - *Watermusic - Submarine* (1979-84) •1 Sx: A+T/Cl+BsCl/Tape •STIM

FEILER, Dror - *Too much too soon* •Asx/Perc/Tape •Tons

FLORIAN - *Pacific Poem...* (1983) •1 Sx: S+B/Perc/Tape

FOURNIER, Marie-Hélène - *Hippogriffe IV* (1991) (11') •Sx/Perc/Tape

FREUND, Donald - *Killing Time* (1980) •Amplified Asx/Amplified Pno/Tape •adr

GARCIN, Gérard - *6me Musique...* (1984) (6') •1 to 7 Asx/Tape •Sal

GARIN, Didier-Marc - *Aï fec* (1985) •1 Sx: Sno+S+B+Bs/Perc/Tape

GAY, Harry Wilbur - *Ishtar* (1971) (12') •Sx/Tape/Narr •Eri

GINER, Bruno - *Entrechocs I* (1985) (14') •1 sx: Sno+S+B/Tape/Synth

GOLDBERG, William - *Pelagos* (1971) •Asx/Tape/Narr •adr

HENRY, Otto - *New Adventures* (1982) •Ob/Asx/Tape •RKM

IWAMOTO, Wataru - *Image* (1990) •2 Sx: AA/Tape

JOY, Jérôme - *Départ errance retour* (1992) (13') •Fl/Asx/Transf. du son en direct/Tape

KEIG, Betty - *After the Circus* (1972) (10') •Sx/Tape/Pno •adr

KIRCK, George - *Song to Wind* (1971) (10') •Asx/Perc/Tape •adr

KOMOROUS, Rudolf - *Dingy yellow* (1972) •Ssx/Pno/Tape •CMC

KOPELENT, Marek - *Snehah* (1967) •Soprano Voice/Asx/Tape

KOSUGI, Takehisa - *Mano-dharma with Takeda III* •Asx/Cl/Tape

LUC, Francis - *Eliantheme* (8') •Asx/Harp/Tape

MALONEY, Michael - *Music* (1982) •Fl/Asx/Tape

MARIETAN, Pierre - *La Rose des vents* (1982-83) (16') •Sx/Lyricon/Tape or 7 Sx: SnoSATBBsCBs/Tape

MARTINEAU, Christine - *Soprani-une-ni-deux* (1989) •Voice/Sx/Tape

McCARTHY, Daniel - *Sonata* •1 Sx: S+A/Pno/Tape •adr

McGUIRE, Edward - *Music...* (1976) (8') •1 to 4 Sx (SATB)/Tape •SMPL

MELLÉ, Patrick - *Verbiages...* (1992) (13') •Soprano Voice/Bsx/Transf. en direct/Tape

MIEREANU, Costin - *Boléro des Balkans* (1984) (13') •1 Sx: CBs+Bs+T+S+Sno/Perc/Tape •Sal

MORYL, Richard - *Sunday Morning* (1971) (12') •Asx/Perc/Tape •CFE/ACA

OSTRANDER, Linda - *Tarot* •Asx/Narr+Dancer/Tape •DP

PARKS, Ron - *Increments* (1993) •Asx/Perc/Tape

PERNAIACHI, Gianfranco - *Realgar 1 & 2* (1984 & 1990) (8' + 5') •Trb and/or Tsx/Electr. •EDP

POLIN, Claire - *Aderyn pur* (1972) (14') •Fl/Asx/Optional Tape •SeMC

RACOT, Gilles - *Exultitudes* (1985) (20') •2 Sx/live electronics

RILEY, Terry - *Persian Surgery Dervishes* (1971) •Sx/Perc/Tape

ROLIN, Etienne - *Caccia* (1991) (11') •2 Sx: AT/Echantilloneur [sampler] •adr

RUGGERI, Gianluca - *Esercizio...* (1990) (13') •Ssx/Perc/Tape •adr

SAVOURET, Alain - *Phil cello Joe Sax chez les...* •Asx/Vcl/Tape

SCOTT, Cleve - *Rimes, rilles, rings* (1988) •Asx/Pno/Tape

SMITH, Howie - *Life on Earth...* •Sx/Amplified Vla/Electronics •Oa

TOSI, Daniel - *Surimpressions II...* (1982) (15') •1 Sx: A+T+B+S/ Synth/Tape •Sal

TYSSENS, Albert - *3 Excerpts...* (1983) •Asx/Voice/Tape •adr

3 Musicians

BARKIN, Elaine - *Media Speak* (1981) •Fl/Asx/Bass/Tape

BON, André - *Fragments* (1984) (25') •Tsx/2 Harp/Processeur de son numérique

BUBALO, Rudolph - *Organic Concretion* •Asx/Org/Perc/Tape

CAVANA, Bernard - *Sax déminé* •2 Soprano Voices/1 Sx: Sno+S+T+Bs/Echo Chamber

CHANCE, Nancy - *Bathseba's Song* (1972) (7') •Asx/Tape/Speaker/ Dancer •SeMC

COCCO, Enrico - *Il Sogno di Chuang Tzu* (1989/91) (40') •Dancer/ Perc/1 Sx: S+A+T+B/Electronics •adr

DIEMENTE, Edward - *Dimensions II* •Any 1 to 6 instruments/Tape •SeMC

GARCIN, Gérard - *6me Musique...* (1984) (6') •1 to 7 Asx/Tape •Sal

GINER, Bruno - *Con brio* (1991) (13-17') •Vcl/Bsx/Perc/Tape

GOLDSTEIN, Malcolm - *Ludlow Blues* (1963) (12') •Asx/Fl/Trb/ Tape •adr

MAXFIELD, Richard - *Perateia* •Asx/Vln/Pno/Tape

McGUIRE, Edward - *Music...* (1976) (8') •1 to 4 Sx (SATB)/Tape •SMPL

MIEREANU, Costin - *Tercafeira* (1984-85) (16') •3 Sx Players: Sno+S+A, S+A+T, S+A+T+B/Tape •Sal

SHAFFER, Sherwood - *Vision...* (1971) (15') •Actress+Dancer/Asx/ Tape (or 3 Asx)/Perc •DP/adr

SOTELO, Mauricio - *Nel suono...* (1989) •1 Sx: A+T/BsCl+CBsCl/ Vcl/Live electronics •adr

4 Musicians

ABBOTT, Alain - *Le Tombeau de Bach* (1984) •4 Sx: SATB/Tape

ANDERSON, Beth - *Hallophone* (1973) •Dancer/Voice/Sx/Guit/ Tape

BARRIERE, Françoise - *A Propos...* (1979) •Asx/Perc/Vla/Vcl/Tape

BEGLARIAN, Eve - *Fresh Air* •4 Sx: SATB/Tape •NP

BIANCHINI, Laura - *Tra le voci* (1990) (15') •4 Sx: SATB/Tape •adr

BOESWILLWALD, Pierre - *La vie des Saints...* (1989) (45') •2 Sx: AT/Cl/Tape/Comédienne

BOTTJE, Will Gay - *Modalities* •4 Sx: AATB/Tape •AMA

BREGENT, Michel-Georges - *Mitzvot...* (1982) •SATB/Tape

BROWN, Anthony - *Quartet No. 2* •4 Sx: SATB/Tape •SeMC

DASKE, Martin - *Sisaxason* (1991) (13') •4 Sx: SATB/Tape

DIEMENTE, Edward - *Dimensions II* •Any 1 to 6 instruments/Tape •SeMC

FUENTES, Tristan - *Pan Am* •BsCl/Ssx/Synth/Vibr+Steel Drum/ Marimba+Accordion/Tape •HMC

GARCIN, Gérard - *Après, bien après, enfin...* (1981) •4 Reeds (SATB or other combinations)/Tape •Sal

6me Musique... (1984) (6') •1 to 7 Asx/Tape •Sal

HAJDU, Georg - *Die Stimmen...* (1990) (12') •4 Sx/Tape •Peer

HARRIS, Roger - *Sopwith Hemke* (1972) •4 Sx: SSSS/Tape •Bou

HAVEL, Christophe - *RamDam* (1992) (15') •Fl/1 Sx: S+B/Perc/Pno/ Transformation électroacoustique •adr

LAUBA, Christian - *Autographie* (1985) •Asx/Perc/Electr. Pno/ Synth/Tape •adr

MACHOVER, Tod - *Valise's Song* (1989) (5') •1 Sx: S+T/Electr. Guit/Perc/Electr. Bass/Computer tape •adr

MADDOCKS, David - *Octet...* (1977) •4 Sx: SATB/Tape (SnoATBs)

MARTIN, Vernon - *Contingencies* (1969) •Asx/Tpt/Trb/Perc/Tape •CAP

McGUIRE, Edward - *Music...* (1976) (8') •1 to 4 Sx (SATB)/Tape •SMPL

MERCURE, Pierre - *Tetrachromie* (1963) •Cl/Asx/BsCl/Perc/Tape •CMC

MIEREANU, Costin - *Jardins retrouvés* (1985) (20') •Electr. Ssx/ Vcl/Perc/Harp/Tape •Sal

NYKOPP, Lauri - *New music...* (14-40') •4 Sx/Tape •FMIC

PARENT, Nil - *Inter-modul-action* (1973) (26') •4 Sx: SATB/Electr. equipment

RADULESCU, Horatiu - *Sensual sky* (1985) •Asx/Trb/Vcl/Bass/Tape

ROLIN, Etienne - *Sax over seas* (1992) (20') •SATB/Tape •adr

ROSSÉ, François - *...ces berges voyantes* (1988) (12') •2 Voice: AB/ 1 Sx: A+B/Prepared Pno/Tape •adr

Level 01-84 (1984) •Fl-à-bec/Fl/Asx/1 or 2 Synth/Chambre d'écho & reverb. •adr

RYDBERG, Bo - *Link/Sequence* (1990) •4 Sx: SATB/Computer/Live electronics •Tons

SBACCO, Franco - *Equinst* (1990) (13') •4 Sx: SATB/Electron. •adr

SJÖHOLM, Staffan - *Sommarlov...* (12') •Tpt/3 Sx/Tape •STIM

THIBAULT, Alain - *E.L.V.I.S.* (1984) •4 Sx: SATB/Tape

WASHBURN, Gary - *Quintet I* (1960) (6'); *Quintet II* •2 Bsx/2 Perc/ Tape •SeMC

5 Musicians

ALLA, Thierry - *Aérienne* (1994) (8') •Fl/2 Sx/Pno/Perc/dispositif électroacoustique

ARCURI, Serge - *Prologue* (1985) •Fl/Ssx/Cl/Hn/Perc/Tape •CMC

BENHAMOU, Maurice - *Mouvement* (1979) •Fl/Sx/Vla/Vcl/Perc/ Tape

CAMPANA, José-Luis - *Insight* (1987) (18') •Fl/Voice/Sx/Bass/ Perc/Tape/Video •Bil

DIEMENTE, Edward - *Dimensions II* •Any 1 to 6 instruments/Tape •SeMC

GARCIN, Gérard - *6me Musique...* (1984) (6') •1 to 7 Asx/Tape •Sal

GUILLONNEAU, Christian - *Eolithes* (1988) (7') •4 Sx: AAAA/ Perc/Tape

MIEREANU, Costin - *Do-Mi-Si-La-Do-Ré* (1980-81) (16'30) •1 player: Cl+BsCl+Sx/Tape or 5 Sx: SATBBs/ Tape •Sal

Ricochets (1989) •1 Sx: Sno+S+A+T+B/Electr. Guit/Bass Guit/ Synth/Perc/Régie électr. •Sal

OLBRISCH, Franz-Martin - *"Im Anfänglichen...* (1989) (90') •Vln/ Fl/Trb/Sx/Perc/Electronics

RACKLEY-SMITH, Lawrence - *Kay-Vee-Si-Si* •2 Sx: AT/Pno/Bass/ Perc/Tape

ROSENBLOOM, David - *The thud, thud, thud...* (1966) •Sx/Electric Vcl/Pno/Celesta/Perc/Tape/Lights •SeMC

ROSSÉ, François - *Level 01-84* (1984) •Fl-à-bec/Fl/Asx/1 or 2 Synth/ Chambre d'écho & reverb. •adr

RYDBERG, Bo - *Link/Sequence* (1990) •4 Sx: SATB/Computer/Live electronics •Tons

SCHAFFER, Boguslaw - *Proietto simultaneo* (1983) (12') •Soprano Voice/Vln/Pno/Ob/Sx/Tape

6 Musicians

BERG, Paul - *To Teach His Own* (1984) (12') •Fl/Ob/Tsx/Trb/Vln/ Vcl/Tape •Don

BERGEIJK, Gilius van - *Life of Rosa...* •Pno/Vcl/4 Instr./Tape

DIEMENTE, Edward - *Dimensions II* •Any 1 to 6 instruments/Tape •SeMC

GARCIN, Gérard - *6me Musique...* (1984) (6') •1 to 7 Asx/Tape •Sal

LANZA, Alcides - *Modulos III* (1983) •Guit/Tsx/Vln/Vcl/Perc/Pno/ Tape •CMC

MAXFIELD, Richard - *Domenon* (1961) •Fl/Sx/Pno/Vibr/Vln/Bass/ Tape

RISSET, Jean-Claude - *Glissements* (10'10) •3 melody instruments of choice [instruments monodiques au choix]/Perc/Pno/Tape

7 Musicians

BROWN, Anthony - *Soundscape 1* •Asx/Bsn/Tpt/Vln/Voice/Pno/Perc/Tape •SeMC

MARCO, Tomàs - *Jabberwochy* (1967) •Voice/Tsx/Pno/4 Perc/Tape

MARIETAN, Pierre - *La Rose des vents* (1982-83) (16') •Sx/Lyricon/Tape or 7 Sx: SnoSATBBsCBs/Tape

ROSSÉ, François - *OEM* (1988) (21') •Soprano Voice/1 Sx: S+Bs/EH/Accordion/Bass/Jazz Guit/Pno/Dispositif électro-acoust. •adr

SOTELO, Mauricio - *IX +... de substantiis separatis* (1990) •Cl/Sx/Tuba/Vln/Vcl/Bass/Pno/Schtagzeng with live electronics •adr

VANDENBOGAERDE, Fernand - *Tezcatlipoca I* (1986) •7 Sx: SnoSATBBsCBs/Tape •Mor

WENTING, Victor - *Raderwek...* (1973) (30') •4 wind or string instruments/Sx/Vln/Pno/Radio electronic

8 Musicians

BIRTWISTLE, Harrison - *Medusa* (1969/70/78) •Fl/Cl/Ssx/Pno/Perc/Vln/Vla/Vcl/Tape

CHATMAN, Stephen - *Outer Voices* (1978) •Fl/Cl/Asx/2 Perc/Celesta/Guit/Harp/Tape •CMC

GARCIN, Gérard - *Encore plus tard* (1984) (12') •1 Sx: Sno+A+Bs/Fl/Cl/Bsn/Vla/Vcl/Bass/Perc/Tape •Sal

PERSSON, Bob - *Om sommaren sköna II* (1965) •Fl/BsCl/Trb/2 Perc/Vibr/Vcl/Jazz Sx/Tape

9 Musicians

DIEMENTE, Edward - *For Lady Day* •Fl/Ob/Cl/Tpt/Trb/Vln/Vla/Sx/Bsn/Tape •SeMC

10 Musicians

NILSSON, Anders - *Krasch!* (1993) •4 Sx: SATB/6 Perc/Tape •SMIC

11 Musicians

MARTIRANO, Salvatore - *Underworld* (1959) •4 Actors/Tsx/4 Perc/2 Bass/2 Track tape

12 Musicians

MALEC, Ivo - *Lumina* (1968-89) •12 Sx: SnoSSAAATTTBBBs/Tape •Sal

ROLIN, Etienne - *Machine à sons* (1990) (12') •12 Sx (solo bass)/Tape •adr

TOEPLITZ, Kasper - *Johnny Panic...* (25') •1 Sx: T+CBs/Mezzo Soprano Voice/2 Fl/2 Cl/Hn/2 Vln/2 Vla/Perc/Tape

14 Musicians

UDOW, Michael - *Understanding* (1969) (15') •6 Unspecified instruments/8 Perc/Tape •MP

oOo

ALLA, Thierry - *La terre et la Comète* (1991) •Fl/Cl/Asx/Pno/Bass/Synth/Perc/Tape/Children's Choir •adr

FOURNIER, Marie-Hélène - *Cinq Muses* (1990) (20') •Saxophones/Tape

KAGEL, Mauricio - *Musik aus diaphonie* (1962-64) (12' minimum) •6-10 Instrumentalists or singers/diapositives •Uni

KASEMETS, Udo - *Cumulus* (1964) •Any solo ensemble/2 Tape Recorders

KNAIFEL, Alexandre Aronovitch - *Agnus Dei* (1985) (120-150') •Sx/Orch/Perc/Tape

MELLÉ, Patrick - *Seriotis*, op. 4 (1985) (10') •2 Sx: TB/Men's chorus [Choeur d'hommes]/Soprano Voice Solo/Perc/Pno/Synth/Tape

MILHAUD, Darius - *Etude poètique*, op. 333 (1954) •2 Sx/Voice/Orch/Tape

NILSSON, Bo - *La Bran - Anagramme sur Ilmar Laaban* (1963-76) (16') •Sx Solo: S+A/Chorus/Orch/Perc/Pno/Tape/Electr.) •STIM

RILEY, Terry - *A Rainbow in Curved Air* (1970) •Partly improvised Sx/Keyboards/Perc/Tapes

SCELSI, Jacinto - *Pranam 1* •Asx/Orch/Tape

TERRY, Peter - *Into Light...* (1986) •Ssx/Chamber Orch/Tape •adr

TOSI, Daniel - *Multitude II* (1984-85) •1 Sx: S+A+T/Fl/Vibr/Tape/2 Perc - 3 soloists

Music for MIDI Wind Controller

1 Musician

APFELSTADT, Marc - *Industrial.Orient.90* (1990) •Yamaha WX7 MIDI Wind Controller •adr

BALL, Leonard V. - *and they spoke of things transfigured...* (10') •Yamaha WX11 MIDI Wind Controller and Korg Wavestation Synth •adr

BAUR, John - *Colors–O'Keefe* •MIDI Wind Controller/MIDI Sequencer

BEERMAN, Burton - *Fragments* (1988) •MIDI Wind Controller/Yamaha TX81Z Synth/Digital Delay •ACA

DAVIES, Terry - *Whale* (1990) •Sx+Yamaha WX7 MIDI Wind Controller/Tape

DURANT, Douglas - *Skelter Memory* (1994) •MIDI Wind Controller Solo •adr

EVERTT, Steven - *Interactive Electronics* •Asx+MIDI Wind Controller+Narr/Computer

FISH, Greg - *The Hammer and the Arrow* (1990) •adr

FREUND, Donald - *Not Gentle* •MIDI Wind Controller/Computer

GREENWOOD, Allan - *Junctions* (1992) (8') •Sx/Yamaha WX7 MIDI Wind Controller/Tape

HERTZOG, Christian - *Angry Candy* (1989) (7') •adr

INGHAM, Richard - *Still Life* (1992) (7') •Yamaha WX7 MIDI Wind Controller/Tape

MAHIN, Bruce - *Synapse* •MIDI Wind Controller/Computer

MOYLAN, William - *Two Suspended Images* (1990) (8') •Ron

RUGGIERO, Charles - *Interplay* •Ssx/Pno or Yamaha WX7 MIDI Wind Controller/Tape

SUBOTNICK, Morton - *In Two Worlds* - Concerto (1988) (25') •Asx/Computer/Orch or Yamaha WX7 MIDI Wind Controller/Computer or Asx/Computer •EAM

TRYTHALL, Gil - *Rima's Song* (1994) •MIDI Wind Controller/Computer

WYATT, Scott - *Vignettes* (1989) •MIDI Wind Controller/Tape •adr

2 Musicians

APFELSTADT, Marc - *Duo* (1990) •2 MIDI Wind Controllers •adr

Bizet, Georges - *Suite from Carmen* (RONKIN) •MIDI Wind Controller/Pno •adr

KARPMAN, Laura - *Song Pictures* (1989) (8') • Yamaha WX7 MIDI Wind Controller/Soprano Voice •MMB

Lennon, John & Paul McCartney - *Yesterday* (RONKIN) •MIDI Wind Controller/Pno •adr

MANSHIP, Munch - *Dance Suite No. 3* •MIDI Wind Controller/Synth •PBP

MOYLAN, William - *Future Echoes from the Ancient Voices of Turtle Island* (1992) (14') •MIDI Wind Controller/ Pno •Ron

RONKIN, Bruce - *Transient States* (1993) (10'30) •MIDI Wind Controller/Pno •adr

5 Musicians

YOUNG, Charles Rochester - *October in the Rain* (1989) (5') •MIDI Wind Controller/Hn/Pno/Synth/Perc •adr

8 Musicians

MONNET, Marc - *L'exercice de la Bataille* (1991) (45') •2 Vln/2 Bsn/ 2 MIDI Sx/MIDI Guit/MIDI Pno

oOo

SANDROFF, Howard - *Concerto* (1988) (to F. Hemke) •Yamaha WX7 MIDI Wind Controller+Sx/Str Orch •adr

Unspecified Instrumentation
(Instruments non déterminés)

1 Musician

BORENSTEIN, Daniel - *M-Tango* (1982) (6') •1 Instrument/Electronics •Sal

CAGE, John - *4'33"* (1952); *4'33" (no. 2)* (1962)
Theatre Piece (1960) •1 to 8 Performers •Pet

CHADABE, Joel - *Sean* •Any instrument, any number

DIEMENTE, Edward - *Dimensions II* •Any 1 to 6 Instruments/Tape •SeMC

HAMMAN, Michael - *Variant Forms-Derivatives I* (1985)

KASEMETS, Udo - *Cumulus* (1964) •Any solo ensemble/2 Tape recorders
Timepiece (1964) •BMI
Trigon (1963) •1, 3, or 9 Performers •BMI

MORAN, Robert - *L'après-midi de Dracoula* (1966) •SS

REICH, Steve - *Reed Phase* (1967) •Any reed instrument/Tape or 3 reeds

SCELSI, Jacinto - *Ixor* (1956) (4') •Sal
Maknongan (1976) (4') •Low instrument [instrument grave] •Sal

SCHAFFER, Boguslaw - *Confrontations n° 148* (1972) •Any solo instrument/Orch •AMP

SIMONS, Netty - *Buckeye...* (1971) •1 to any number of players •Pres
Silver Thaw (1969) (8') •1 to 8 players •Pres

STOCKHAUSEN, Karlheinz - *Solo n° 19* (1965-66) (6-10') •Uni
Spiral n° 27 (1969) (15') •1 Soloist/1 Recepteur à O. C.) •Uni
Tierkreiss (1977) (11') •1 Solo instr./Pno ad lib. •Uni

WILLIAMS, Joan - *Etude from Moscow Idaho* •ACA

WOLFF, Christian - *For 1, 2 or 3 People* (1964) •Pet

2 Musicians

CAGE, John - *Sonata for 2 Voices* (1933) •2 or more instruments •Pet
Theatre Piece (1960) •1 to 8 Performers •Pet

CARDEW, Cornelius - *Solo with Accompaniment* (1964) (10') •Uni

CHAGRIN, Francis - *4 Lyric Interludes* (1963) (5') •Any solo instrument/Str Quartet or Pno •Nov

DE JONG, Conrad - *Fun and Games* (1967/70) •Any instrument/Pno •MP

DIEMENTE, Edward - *Dimensions II* •Any 1 to 6 Instruments/Tape •SeMC

HAUBENSTOCK-RAMATI, Roman - *Multiple IV* (1969) (10')
Multiple V (1969) (10') •Uni

HELLERMAN, William - *Circle Music II* •Any 2 or more instruments •ACA
Round and About •Any 2 or more instruments •ACA

HOFFMANN, Robin - *Inquisition I* (1993) •Asx/1 Performer obbligato •INM

KURTZ, Arthur - *Duets*, op. 6 •adr

MADERNA, Bruno - *Dialodia* (1972) (2'15) •Ric

NELHYBEL, Vaclav - *Four Duos* •Heu

SCARMOLIN, Louis - *Duet Time* •2 Woodwind instruments •Lud

SIMONS, Netty - *Design Group No. 2* (1968) (8-10') •Pres
Silver Thaw (1969) (8') •1 to 8 players •Pres

STAHMER, Klaus - *Rhapsodia piccola* (1976) (8') •Melodic instrument/Pno •Hei

STOCKHAUSEN, Karlheinz - *Aus den 7 Tagen n° 26* (1968) (60') •Narr/1 Instrument •Uni
Pole (1969-70) •Uni
Tierkreiss (1977) (11') •1 Solo instr./Pno ad lib. •Uni

STOKER, Richard - *Little Suite* (1966) •2 or more equal instruments •Hin

WOLFF, Christian - *For 1, 2 or 3 People* (1964) •Pet
Pairs (1968) •Pet

3 Musicians

BARREL, Bernard - *A Shottisham Suite*, op. 23 (1960) (4')
A Suffolk Suite, op. 24 (1960) (4')

BEEKUM, Jan van - *Fair Play* (1984) •Mol

BERGER, Jean - *Divertimento* •Bou

BLANK, Allan - *Music for 3 Players* •ACA

CAGE, John - *Solo with Obbligato...* (1933) •3 or more instruments •Pet
Theatre Piece (1960) •1 to 8 Performers •Pet

CASKEN, John - *Visu for Three* (1974) •BMIC

CHILDS, Barney - *Operation Flappy...* •3 or more instruments •ACA

COWELL, Henry - *Hymn and Fuguing Tune No. 4* (1945) •ACA

DIEMENTE, Edward - *Dimensions I* •SeMC
Dimensions II •Any 1 to 6 Instruments/Tape •SeMC

EYSER, Eberhard - *Tremelin* (1974) (3'30) •STIM

GLOBOKAR, Vinko - *Vostellung* (1976) •1 Soloist/2 Instruments •Pet

HARRIS, Roger - *4 Pieces for 3* •Bou

HEUSSENSTAMM, George - *Canonograph 1* •Any 3 Winds: Fl/Ob/Cl/Sx/Bsn •SeMC

Honegger, Arthur - *Petite suite n° 1* (1934) (2'30) •2 instruments/Pno •CDM

KAGEL, Mauricio - *Acustica III* (1968-70) (25') •2-5 Woodwind instruments/Perc •Uni

KARLINS, M. William - *Graphic Mobile* (1970) •Any 3 or more instruments •MP

KASEMETS, Udo - *Trigon* (1963) •1, 3, or 9 Performers •BMI

LANCEN, Serge - *Pieces* •Mol

NILSSON, Bo - *20 Gruppen* (1958) •3 or more instruments

PHIFER, Larry - *Construction II* •3, 6 instruments

REICH, Steve - *Reed Phase* (1967) •Any reed instrument/Tape or 3 reeds

SCHOLLUM, Robert - *Veränderungen*, op. 81a •2 Melodic instruments/Perc •Dob

SIMONS, Netty - *Silver Thaw* (1969) (8') •1 to 8 players •Pres

STOCKHAUSEN, Karlheinz - *Expo* (1969-70) •Uni

SYDEMAN, William - *Trio* •3 Treble instruments •SeMC

WOLFF, Christian - *For 1, 2 or 3 People* (1964) •Pet
In Between Pieces (1963) •Pet

4 Musicians

APERGHIS, G. - *Signaux* (1978) •Quatuor d'instruments de même timbre et tessiture •Sal

BUDD, Harold - *Black Flowers* (1968)

CAGE, John - *Theatre Piece* (1960) •1 to 8 Performers •Pet

DIEMENTE, Edward - *Dimensions II* •Any 1 to 6 Instruments/Tape •SeMC

DUCKWORTH, William - *Pitch City* •Any 4 instruments •MP

FOSS, Lukas - *Map* •CF

HELLERMAN, William - *Circle Music I* •ACA

KAGEL, Mauricio - *Acustica III* (1968-70) (25') •2-5 Woodwind instruments/Perc •Uni

LANCEN, Serge - *Quatre par quatre* (1990) •Mar

MILLER, Edward - *Quartet Variations*

SIMONS, Netty - *Silver Thaw* (1969) (8') •1 to 8 players •Pres

STRANG, Gerald - *Variations* •ACA

WOLFF, Christian - *Pairs* (1968) •Pet

5 Musicians

CAGE, John - *Theatre Piece* (1960) •1 to 8 Performers •Pet

CHAGRIN, Francis - *4 Lyric Interludes* (1963) (5') •Any solo instrument/Str Quartet or Pno •Nov

DIEMENTE, Edward - *Dimensions II* •Any 1 to 6 Instruments/Tape •SeMC

GERSCHEFSKI, Edwin - *America*, op. 44, nos. 8 & 9 •Ensemble of
4 Winds/Pno
KAGEL, Mauricio - *Acustica III* (1968-70) (25') •2-5 Woodwind
instruments/Perc •Uni
MANNEKE, Danièl - *Vice versa* (1979) (14') •Don
RISSET, Jean-Claude - *Glissements* (10'10) •3 melody instruments of
choice [instruments monodiques au choix]/
Perc/Pno/Tape
SIMONS, Netty - *Silver Thaw* (1969) (8') •1 to 8 players •Pres
WOLFF, Christian - *For 5 or 10 People* (1962) •Pet

6 Musicians

BERGEIJK, Gilius van - *Life of Rosa Luxembourg* •Pno/Vcl/4 Instr./
Tape
CAGE, John - *Theatre Piece* (1960) •1 to 8 Performers •Pet
DIEMENTE, Edward - *Dimensions II* •Any 1 to 6 Instruments/Tape
•SeMC
FOSS, Lukas - *Music for 6* •CF
HELLERMAN, William - *Circle Music III* •ACA
KAGEL, Mauricio - *Acustica III* (1968-70) (25') •2-5 Woodwind
instruments/Perc •Uni
Musik aus diaphonie (1962-64) (12' minimum) •6-10 Instrumen-
talists or singers/diapositives •Uni
MEIJERING, Chiel - *Tripppette trippetic* (1976) (15') •Don
OAKES, Rodney - *Six By Six* •CAP
PHIFER, Larry - *Construction II* •3, 6 instruments
SIMONS, Netty - *Silver Thaw* (1969) (8') •1 to 8 players •Pres
WOLFF, Christian - *Pairs* (1968) •Pet

7 Musicians

CAGE, John - *Theatre Piece* (1960) •1 to 8 Performers •Pet
HAUBENSTOCK-RAMATI, Roman - *Multiple II* (1969) (12') •Uni
Multiple III (1969) (10') •Uni
JANSSEN, Werner - *Obsequies of a Saxophone* (1929) •6 Wind
Instruments/Snare Drum
KAGEL, Mauricio - *Musik aus diaphonie* (1962-64) (12' minimum)
•6-10 Instrumentalists or singers/diapositives
•Uni
MAREZ OYENS-WANSINK, Tera de - *Mahpoochah...* (1978) (8')
•7 or more instruments •Don
SIMONS, Netty - *Silver Thaw* (1969) (8') •1 to 8 players •Pres
WENTING, Victor - *Raderwek...* (1973) (30') •4 wind or string
instruments/Sx/Vln/Pno/Radio electronic
WOLFF, Christian - *Septet* (1964) •Pet

8 Musicians

CAGE, John - *Theatre Piece* (1960) •1 to 8 Performers •Pet
KAGEL, Mauricio - *Musik aus diaphonie* (1962-64) (12' minimum)
•6-10 Instrumentalists or singers/diapositives
•Uni
SIMONS, Netty - *Silver Thaw* (1969) (8') •1 to 8 players •Pres
WOLFF, Christian - *Pairs* (1968) •Pet

9 Musicians

KAGEL, Mauricio - *Musik aus diaphonie* (1962-64) (12' minimum)
•6-10 Instrumentalists or singers/diapositives
•Uni
KASEMETS, Udo - *Trigon* (1963) •1, 3, or 9 Performers •BMI
DROGOZ - *Triptyque pour 3 fois 3 instruments* •Led

10 Musicians

KAGEL, Mauricio - *Musik aus diaphonie* (1962-64) (12' minimum)
•6-10 Instrumentalists or singers/diapositives
•Uni
WOLFF, Christian - *For 5 or 10 People* (1962) •Pet

12 Musicians

ROGERS, Lloyd - *Alma redemptoris mater*

14 Musicians

UDOW, Michael - *Understanding* (1969) (15') •6 Unspecified instru-
ments/8 Perc/Tape •MP

oOo

BUDD, Alain - *Intermission Piece* (1968); *September Music* (1967);
•Any number of players
CAGE, John - *Solo with Obbligato...* (1933) •3 or more instruments
•Pet
Sonata for 2 Voices (1933) •2 or more instruments •Pet
Variations I and II (1958) (1961) •Any number of players •Pet
Variations III; Variations IV (1963) •Any number of players
CARDEW, Cornelius - *Autumn '60* (1960) (10') •Any ensemble •Uni
Material (1960) (10') •Any ensemble •Uni
CHADABE, Joel - *Sean* •Any instrument, any number
CHILDS, Barney - *Operation Flappy...* •3 or more instruments •ACA
COPE, David - *Towers* (1968) •Unspecified Ensemble •MP
DI BETTA, Philippe - *Tempête de souffleurs* (1993) •Ensemble ad lib
of wind instruments •adr
FERRARI, Luc - *Tautologos III* (1969) •Choice and number of various
instruments
HELLERMAN, William - *Circle Music II* •Any 2 or more instruments
•ACA
Round and About •Any 2 or more instruments •ACA
KARLINS, M. William - *Graphic Mobile* (1970) •Any 3 or more
instruments •MP
KUPKOVIC, Ladislav - *Interpretation einer Kritik* (15') •Any instru-
ments •Uni
Weniger und Mehr (15') •Any 6 groups of instruments •Uni
MAREZ OYENS-WANSINK, Tera de - *Mahpoochah...* (1978) (8')
•7 or more instruments •Don
MORAN, Robert - *Elegant Journey...* (1965) •SS
Interiors (1964) •Pet
NILSSON, Bo - *20 Gruppen* (1958) •3 or more instruments
OAKES, Rodney - *Introspectum in Six Refractions* •Any number of
musicians, audience and conductor •CAP
ROLIN, Etienne - *Wind flight* (1986) •Free instrumentation including
1 Asx minimum •Lem
RZEWSKI, Frederick - *Les moutons de Panurge* (1969) •Soloist/Perc/
Any ensemble
SCHAFFER, Boguslaw - *Collage...* •8 Jazz players/Orch •AMP
Confrontations n° 148 (1972) •Any solo instrument/Orch
SIMONS, Netty - *Buckeye has Wings* (1971) •1 to any number of
players •Pres
STOKER, Richard - *Little Suite* (1966) •2 or more equal instruments
•Hin
SYMONDS, Norman - *The Nameless Hour* •Jazz Soloist/Orch •CMC
WOLFF, Christian - *Tilbury 2 and 3* (1969) •Pet

Double Concertos

Orchestra unless otherwise indicated (Orchestre, sauf
indication contraire).

ATWOOD, Charles - *Alienated Thing* (1989) •Asx/Electr.Vln •CMA
BECKER, Günter - *Correspondances* (1966/68) (triple concerto) •Eb
Cl/BsCl/Asx/Chamber Orch •HG/IMD
BEERS, Jacobus - *Concerto* •Voice/Asx
BENTZON, Niels Viggo - *Climatic Changes*, op. 474 (1985) (20')
•Bsx/Pno •Hire/Sal
BLATNY, Pavel - *Pour Ellis* (1966) •Tpt/Ssx/Jazz Orch •IMD
BOURLAND, Roger - *Double Concerto* (1983) (11') •Ssx/Bsn •ECS

BRANDON, Seymour - *Bachburg Concerto No. 2* (1978) •Asx/Pno
BRANT, Henry - *Nomads* (1974) (triple concerto) •Vln/Perc/Sx/Brass Orch •adr
BREVER, Karl - *Atonalyse II* (1957) •5 Soloists: Tpt/Cl/Vln/Vla/Sx/ Str Orch •Led
CHATTAWAY, Jay - *Double Star* (1985) •2 Sx: AT/Band
CHEVREUILLE, Raymond - *Double Concerto*, op. 34 (1946) (21') •Pno/Asx •CBDM
COHN, Arthur - *Variations* (1945) •Cl/Asx/Str Orch •EV
COWLES, Colin - *From the King's Chamber* •Tsx/Narr/Chamber Orch •adr
DELDEN, Lex van - *Concerto*, op. 91 (1967) •2 Sx: SS •Don
DEPELSENAIRE, Jean-Marie - *Concertino* (1969) (9') •Ob/Asx •Chou
   Concertino (1972) (9') (triple concerto) •3 Sx: AAA •ET
   Dialogue (1966) (6'30) •Tpt/Asx •ET
DRESSEL, Erwin - *Concerto* (1965) •2 Sx: SA
EBERT, Hans - *Concerto* •2 Sx
EISENMANN, Will - *Konzert* (1962) (12') •2 Sx: SA
FAITH, Walter - *Divertimento* (1951) (triple concerto) •Asx/Pno/Tpt •adr
FLOTHUIS, Marius - *Sinfonietta concertante*, op. 55 (1954-55) (15') •Cl/Asx •Don
FREEDMAN, Harry - *Scenario* (1970) •Asx/Electr. Bs Guit •CMC
GIRARDIN, Jean-Paul - *L'Insolitude* (1983) •Asx/Vibr/Str orch
GÖRNER, Hans Georg - *Concertino*, op. 31 (1957) •2 Sx: AT •Hof
GREEN, John - *Mine Eyes Have Seen* (1978) (37') (triple concerto) •Tsx/Tpt+Flugelhorn/Electr. Guit •B&H
GULDA, Friedrich - *Music...* (triple concerto) •Trb/Bugle/Sx
GUY, Georges - *Concerto en forme de jazz* •Asx/Pno
HARTLEY, Walter - *Double Concerto* (1969) (7'30) •Asx/Tuba/ Wind Octet •PhiCo
HESPOS, Hans-Joachim - *Ka* (1972) (8'30) •Bsx/Bass •EMod
HOFFMAN, Norbert - *Suite concertante* (1980) •2 Sx: AA/Band
HOFMANN, Thomas - *Konzertantes* (1988) (20') •Pno/Asx/Str Orch
HOLLOWAY, Robin - *Double Concerto* (1987) •Cl/Asx
HOLVICH, Karl - *Sarabande* •2 Sx/Band
Honegger, Arthur - *Concerto da camera* (1948) (12'30) (LONDEIX) •Fl (or Ssx)/Asx (or EH)/Str Orch •Sal
ISRAEL, Brian - *Double Concerto* (1984) •2 Sx: Sno Bs/Band
KAZANDJIEV, Vasil - *Double concerto* (1962) •Asx/Pno
KREMENLIEV, Boris - *Tune* •Asx/Hn/Str •adr
KRUSE, Bjorne - *Metal* (1984) (10') •Voice/Tsx •NMI
LATHAM, William - *Concerto Grosso* (1960) (18') •2 Sx: SA/Orch or Band
LEGLEY, Victor - *Concerto grosso* (1976) •Vln/Asx/Chamber Orch •Bil/Mau
LEVITIN, Jurij - *Concerto* (1951) •Asx/Tpt/Orch de variété
LUTYENS, Elisabeth - *Chamber Concerto*, op. 8/2 (1940-41) (triple concerto) •Cl/Tsx/Pno/Str •Che
MARCHAL, Dominique - *Jesus dulcis memoriam* •Soprano Voice/ Asx/Choir/Str •adr
MARINUZZI, Gino - *Concertino* (1936) (triple concerto) •Pno/Ob/ Sx/Str Orch
MIEREANU, Costin - Doppelkammerkonzert (1985) (17') •1 Sx: Sno+A+T+Bs/Perc •Sal
NATANSON, Tadeus - *Kincert Podwojny* (1959) •2 Sx: AT •AAW/ AMP
NIEHAUS, Manfred - *Concertino* (1981) (18') •2 Sx: SS •adr
OLIVE, Vivienne - *Music* (1981) •2 Sx: AA •DP
OWEN, Jerry - *Diversion* (1982) •2 Sx: AT/Band •DP
PERDER, Kjell - *Flexica* (1985) (12') •5 Soloists: Fl-à-bec/Soprano Voice/Guit/Vcl/Sx/Orch (variable instrumentation)

QUELLE, Ernst-August - *"Kommissar Maigret-valse"* (1964) (2'30) •Accordion/Sx/Str Orch/Perc •adr
RIVIER, Jean - *Concerto* (1955) (17'30) •Asx/Tpt •Bil
   Concerto (DECOUAIS) •Asx/Tpt/Band •Bil
ROBERT, Lucie - *Double Concerto* (1968) (28') •Asx/Pno •Bil
ROCCISANO, Joe - *Contrasts* (1984) •2 Sx: AT/Band or Pno
ROLIN, Etienne - *Maschera* (1980) (17') •1 Sx: S+A+B/Pno/Chamber Orch •adr
   Rideau de feu (1993) (18') 2 Sx: ST •adr
ROSSÉ, François - *Vestiges...* (1993) •Vln/Pno/BsCl/Fl/Fl-à-bec/Sx •adr
RUSHANT, Ian - *This Side Up* (1986) (15') •2 Sx: SA/Chamber ensemble
SIVERTSEN, Kenneth - *Largo...* (1981) •Tsx/Pno/Str •NMI
SMIT, Sytze - *Double concerto* •Vln/Asx •Don
SOTELO, Mauricio - *Due voci* (1990) •Tsx/BsCl+CBsCl •Uni
SPRATLAN, Lewis - *Penelope's Knees* (1985) (23') •Asx/Bass/ Chamber Orch •MMI
STÄBLER, Gerhard - *Traum...* (1992) •Ssx/Vcl/Pno/Ensemble •Ric
SUTER, Robert - *Conversazioni concertanti* (1978) (18'15) •Asx/ Vibr/Str Orch
THOMPSON, Terence - *Comedy Flick* (1977) •2 Sx: AA
VALEK, Jiri - *Symphony III* (1963) (28') •2 Sx: ST/Narr/Orch •CHF
ZLATO, Pibernick - *Koncertantna* •Fl/Sx/Harp/Str •YUC

Music Publishers - Éditeurs de musique

AA   Albert Andraud: 1100 Broadway, San Antonio TX 78206, USA

AAR   Agencja Autorska Rocznica: Ul. Hipoteczna 2, 950 Warsawa, Poland

AAW   Agencja Autorska Warsawa: Warsawa, Poland

ABC   ABC Music Corp. =Bou

AC   Appleton & Co.: New York NY, USA

ACA   American Composers Alliance: 170 W. 74th Street, New York NY 10023, USA

ACE   American Composers Edition =ACA

ACF   American Composers Facsimile =ACA

ACS   Association des Compositeurs Suédois: Stockholm, Sweden

ADE   Arbeitsgemeinschaft der Eigenverleger

AdMu   Advance Music: Rottenburg, D-7407, Germany

adr   See Addresses of Unpublished Composers (Voir adresses de compositeurs inédits), page 432.

AE   Alpuerto Edit.: Canos del Peral 7-1-D, Madrid-2280 13, Spain

AEN   Autograph Edition New York: 11 West End Road, Totowa NJ 07512, USA

AI   Alpheus Music Corp.: 143 N. Cole Place, Hollywood CA 90029, USA

ALC   Alfred Lengnick & Co.: 14 Berners Street, London W1, England

Alf   Alfred Music Company: 16380 Roscoe Blvd., Suite 200, Van Nuys CA 91410, USA

Alp   Alpuerto =AE

AM   Accura Music: P. O. Box 4260, Athens OH 45701, USA

AMC   American Music Center; 2109 Broadway, Suite 15, New York NY, USA

AMCP   =AMP

AMI   Almitra Music Company, Inc.: P. O. Box 278, Delevan NY 14042, USA

AMP   Associated Music Publishers: 7777 West Bluemond Road, Milwaukee WI 53213, USA; 225 Park Avenue South, New York NY 10003, USA

Ams   Amsco Music Publishing: =MSC

AMu   Atlantic Music Corp.: Criterion Music Corp., 6124 Selma Avenue, Hollywood CA 90028, USA

AmV   Amadeus Verlag: Adliswil, Zurich, Switzerland; USA=FMD

An   Andel Uitgave: 26 Madseliefjeslaan, B-8400 Oostende, Belgium

And   =Mar

APA   Ardito Public.: Amsterdam, Netherlands

APC   Armstrong Publishing Company: Hansen House, 1804 West Avenue, Miami Beach FL 33139, USA

ApE   Apoll-Edition: Kleine Stadtgutgasse 10/4, A-1020 Wien, Austria

Ara   Arambol, Spain

Arp   IMD Diffusion Arpeges: 24, rue Etex, 75018 Paris, France

Art   Artisan Music Press: New York, USA

A&S   Ahn & Simrock: Berlin; Wiesbaden, Germany; France=Sal

Asto   Astoria Verlag: Berlin, Germany

Aug   Ediz. Musicale Augusta: Via Po 3, Torina, Italy

AuMC   Australian Music Center

AvMu   =WIM

AVV   Ars Viva Verlag: Mainz, Germany; USA=EAM

AZM   A. Z. Mathot: 11, rue Bergère, 75009 Paris, France

Band   Bandland Inc.: =CPP

Bar   C. L. Barnhouse Co.: 205 Cowan Avenue West, Box 680, Oskaloosa IA 52577, USA

BAUS   Bohm Anthon U Solm: Laggestrasse 26, 89 Augsburg 2, Germany

B&B   Bote & Bock KG: Hardenbergstrasse 9a, 1000 Berlin 12, Germany; USA=HLe

BBC   British Broadcasting Corp. Library: London, England

BC   BAJUS & Co.

BCM   British and Continental Music Agencies: 8 Horse & Dolphin Yard, London W1V 7LG, England

BD   Byron-Douglas Publ.: =CPP

Bel   Belwin: =CPP; M230 Purley Way, Croydon CR9 4QD, England

Belai   M. P. Belaieff: 26 Kronprinzallee, Bonn, Germany; USA=Pet

Ber   Edizioni Bèrben: Via Redipuglia 65, 60100 Ancona, Italy; USA=Pres

Bes   Besson & Co., Ltd.: England; USA=B&H

Bet   =CF

BFS   Blasmusikverlag Fritz Schultz: Am Märzengraben 6, D-78000 Frieburg Tiengen, Germany

B&H   Boosey & Hawkes: 52 Cooper Square, New York NY 10003, USA; 295 Regent Street London W1R-8JH, England; 7, rue Boutard, 92200 Neuilly, France; 279 Yorkland Blvd., Willowdale 425, Ontario, Canada

Bil   Billaudot: 14, rue de l'Echiquier, 75010 Paris; USA=Pres

Blen   Blenheim Press: 8 Storey's Gate, London SW1, England

BM   Belwin Mills: =CPP

BMCo   =MBCo

BMI   BMI Canada Ltd: Don Mills, 41 Vallybrook Drive, Ontario, Canada

BML   Berandol Music Ltd.: 11 St. Joseph Street, Toronto Ontario M4Y 1J8, Canada

BMP   Brightstar Music Publications =WIM

B&N   Bärenreiter & Neuwerk: Heinrich Schütz allee 35, 3500 Kassel Wilhemshöhe 1, Germany; USA=FMD

Boi   Boileau: Provenza 287, 08037 Barcelona, Spain

Bos   Boston Music Co.: P. O. Box 131, Airport Drive, Hopedale MA 11735, USA

Bosw   Bosworth: 45, rue de Ruysbroeck, Bruxelles, Belgium; 14-18 Heddon Street, Regent Street, London W1R-8DP, England; USA=Brodt Music Co.: P. O. Box 9345, Charlotte NC 28299, USA

Bou   Bourne Co.: 5 West 37th Street, New York NY 10018, USA

BP   Berklee Press Publ.: =HLe

BPb   Byron Publ.: P.O. Box 4193, Covina CA 91722, USA

BR   Bridge Records: Becky Starobim, JAF Box 1864, New York NY 10116, USA

Braun   Braun M. R.; France=Bil

BRF   Bibliothèque Radio France: 116 Blvd du Prés. Kennedy, 75016 Paris, France

Br&Ha   Breitkopf & Härtel: Karlstrasse 10, 701 Leipzig, Germany; 8 Horse & Dolphin Yard, London W1V 7LG, England; USA=FMD/Brou/HLe

Bri   Briegel, Inc.: 4 Summit Court, Flushing NY 11355, USA

Bro   Broadcast Music =AMP

Brou   Broude Brothers Ltd.: 141 White Oaks Road, Williamstown MA 01267, USA

Buff   Editions Buffet-Crampon: Paris, France

BVP   Broekmans & Van Poppel: Van Baererstraat 92-94, Amsterdam 7, Netherlands

CA	Contemp-Art: Linke Wienzeile 6/16, A-1060 Wien, Austria; =ApE		CP	Cor Publishing Co: 67 Bell Place, Massapequa NY 11758, USA
CANF	Centre d'Art National Français: BP 44, 31012 Toulouse, France		CPC	=Co
CAP	Composers Autograph Publ.: 1527-1/2 N. Vine Street, Hollywood CA 90028, USA		CPE	Composers Performer Editions: 330 University Avenue, Davis CA 95616, USA
Capri	Ordinateurs et Musique Capricorne: 5284 rue Jueles Fournier, Montreal-Nord H1G 2W7, Canada		CPM	Contemporary Polish Music: Warsaw, Poland
Car	Carisch: 399 Via general Fara, Milano, Italy; USA=B&H		CPP	CPP/Belwin Music: 15800 N.W. 48th Avenue, Miami FL 33014, USA
Carco	Carey & Co: 13-15 Mortimer Street, London W1, England		CPWM	Crakow Polskie Wydawnictwo Muzyczne, Poland; USA=HLe/EM

CA — Contemp-Art: Linke Wienzeile 6/16, A-1060 Wien, Austria; =ApE

CANF — Centre d'Art National Français: BP 44, 31012 Toulouse, France

CAP — Composers Autograph Publ.: 1527-1/2 N. Vine Street, Hollywood CA 90028, USA

Capri — Ordinateurs et Musique Capricorne: 5284 rue Jueles Fournier, Montreal-Nord H1G 2W7, Canada

Car — Carisch: 399 Via general Fara, Milano, Italy; USA=B&H

Carco — Carey & Co: 13-15 Mortimer Street, London W1, England

CasM — Cascade Music: 30 College Green, Bristol, England

CBDM — CeBeDeM: 75, rue d'Arlon, B-1040 Bruxelles, Belgium; USA=HE

CBet — Cundy-Bettoney Co.: =CF

CC — Charles Colin Music Publ.: 315 W. 53rd. Street, New York NY 10019, USA

CCP — Culver Crest Publ.: 10701 Ranch Road, Culver City CA 90230, USA

CDM — Chant du Monde: 32, rue Beaujon, 75008 Paris, France

Cen — Century Music Publ.: c/o Ashley Dealers Inc., 263 Veterans Blvd, Carlstadt NJ 07072, USA

CF — Carl Fischer: 62 Cooper Square, New York NY 10003, USA; England=OUP

CFE — Composers Facsimile Edition: =ACA

CFI — Charles Foley, Inc.: =CF/CPP

CG — Carl Gehrmans: Box 6005, 10231 Stockholm, Sweden; USA=B&H

CH — Carl Haslinger: Wien, Austria

Cha — Chabal: 10, Blvd. des Italiens, 75009 Paris, France

Cham — Champel: BP n° 2, Neuville sur Ain 01160 Pont d'Ain, France

Chap — Chappel & Co: 50 New Bond Street, London W1, England; USA=HLe; 4, rue d'Arsonval, 75008 Paris, France

Chart — Chart Music Publishing House: 506 S. Wabash Avenue, Chicago IL, USA; =Wab

Che — J&W Chester Music: 7-9 Eagle Court, London EC1M-5QD, England; France=B&H; USA=MSC

CHF — Cesky Hudebni Ford Arch: Pariska ul. 13, 11000 Praha 1, Czechoslovakia; USA=B&H

ChFo — =CFI

ChH — Charles Hansen: 1842 West Avenue, Miami Beach FL 33139, USA

Chou — Choudens & C°: 38, rue Jean Mermoz, 75008 Paris, France; USA & Canada=Pet

CI — Composer's Ink: 84 N. James Street, Hazleton PA 18201, USA

Cil — Cilvis: Côrgeca, 619 Bajos, Barcelona 08025, Spain

CM — J. Christopher Music Co.: =Pres

CMA — College of Musical Arts, Bowling Green State University, Bowling Green OH 43403, USA

CMC — Canadian Music Center: 1263 Bay Street, Toronto, Ontario M5R 2C1, Canada; 430 St. Pierre, Suite 300, Montreal, Quebec H2Y-2M5, Canada

CMIC — Czechoslovak Musik Info. Center: Besedni 3, Prague 1, Czechoslovakia

Co — Cole Publishing Co: 251 E. Grand Avenue, Chicago IL 60611, USA

ColM — =CoMu

Com — Marcel Combre: 24, Blvd Poissonnière, 75009 Paris, France; USA=Pres

Comp — ASCAP: 1 Lincoln Plaza, New York NY 10023, USA

CoMu — College Music: Via A. Billalducci 43, 47100 Forli, Italy

Cons — Consolidated Music Publishers: =MSC

Cos — COSTALLAT & Cie: France=Bil; USA=Pres

CP — Cor Publishing Co: 67 Bell Place, Massapequa NY 11758, USA

CPC — =Co

CPE — Composers Performer Editions: 330 University Avenue, Davis CA 95616, USA

CPM — Contemporary Polish Music: Warsaw, Poland

CPP — CPP/Belwin Music: 15800 N.W. 48th Avenue, Miami FL 33014, USA

CPWM — Crakow Polskie Wydawnictwo Muzyczne, Poland; USA=HLe/EM

CRA — Cranz: 30, rue St. Christophe, 1000 Bruxelles, Belgium; USA=Pres

Cres — Crescendo Music Sales Co.: =FEMA

CRM — Centro Riocerche Musicali: Via Lamarmora 18, 08185 Rome, Italy

CT — Cahiers du Tourdion: 111, Grand-Rue, 67000 Strasbourg, France

CVMP — Chenango Valley Music Press: Box 251, Hamilton NY 13346, USA

Cur — Curci Editions

Cz — Czech Music Fund: Parizska 3, 11000 Prague 1, Czechoslovakia; USA=B&H

DBM — Dedrick Brothers Music Co.: =Ken

Dec — Maurice Decruck

DG — David Gornston: =Ply

DMC — Derry Music Co.: 240 Stockton Street, San Francisco CA, USA; =CPP

Do — Doberman (CAPAC): CO 2021, St. Nicolas, P. Q. GOS 320, Canada; USA=B&H

Dob — Ludwig Doblinger Verlag: Dorotheergasse 10, Postfach 882, 1011 Wien, Austria; Wiesbaden, Germany; USA=FMD

Don — Donemus: Jacob Obrechtstraat 51, 1071 KJ Amsterdam, Netherlands; USA=Pres; Germany=Br&Ha; France=ET; British Commonwealth=Nov; Scandinavia=Reim

DP — Dorn Publications: P. O. Box 206, Medfield MA 02052, USA

DS — DeSantis: Via Cassia 13, 00191 Rome, Italy; USA=Pet

DSH — Drustvo Skladatelja Hrvatske: 9 Berislaviceva, Zagreb, Croatia

DSS — Trg. Franc. Revolucije: 6/1 YU, 6100 Ljubliana, Slovenia

Dur — Durand: 215, rue du Fg-St-Honoré, 75008 Paris. France; USA=Pres

Dus — Dusiorane Music: 72 Cambridge Road, Montclair NJ 07042, USA

DV — Deutscher Verlag: Postfach 147-701, Leipzig, Germany; USA=FMD

DWM — Detroit Wayne Music: 14201 Gratiot Avenue, Detroit MI 48205, USA

EAM — European American Music: 2480 Industrial Blvd., Paoli PA 19301, USA

EBMM — =EM

ECA — =ApE

ECANF — =CANF

ECP — Edition des Compositeurs Soviètiques

ECS — E. C. Schirmer: 138 Ipswich Street, Boston MA 02215, USA; France=Sal

EDF — Edi-Pan: Viale Mazzini 6, Rome 00195, Italy

EFM — Editions Françaises de Musique =Bil; USA=Pres

EG — Everett Gates: =GM

EH — Edition Helios: Mark Foster Music Co., 28 E. Springfield Avenue, Champaign IL 61820, USA

Ehr — Ehrlingforlagen: Linnegatan 9-11, Stockholm, Sweden

EK — Edwin Kalmus: P. O. Box 5011, Boca Raton FL 33433, USA

ELC — Edition La Comète

ELK — =HE

ElVo   Elkan-Vogel Co.: =Pres
EM   Edward B. Marks Music Company: 1619 Broadway, 11th Floor, New York NY 10019, USA; =HLe
EMa   Edition Margana: Karlbergsvägen 71B, S11335 Stockholm, Sweden
EMB   Edition Musicales Brogneaux: 73 Av. Paul Janson, Bruxelles, Belgium; USA=HE
EMBA   Edition Musicales Buenos-Aires: Buenos-Aires, Argentina
EMEC   Edition Musica Espanola Contemporane: 70 rue Alcala, 28009 Madrid; 45 rue Canada, Barcelona, Spain
EMF   Eriks Musikhandel & Forlag AB: Karlavagen 40, Stockholm, Sweden
EMod   Edition Modernes: Franz-Joseph Strasse 2, 8000 Munich, Germany
EMP   Encora Music Press: P. O. Box 6018, Ann Arbor MI 48108, USA
EMRF   Edition Musicale Radio-France: 116 Blvd. Kennedy, 75786 Paris Cedex 16, France
EMu   Edition Muzicala: Bucharest, Rumania
En   Enoch & Cie: 27 Blvd, des Italiens, 75009 Paris, France; USA=Pres/SMPC
Enc   Enchante Publications: Cary IL, USA
EP   Editions de Paris: 8, rue de la Renaissance, 75008 Paris, France
EPA   Editions du Palais des Académies: 1 rue Ducale, Bruxelles, Belgium
EPN   Editions Pro Nova: Munich, Germany
Eres   Eres Editions: D-2804 Lilienthal-Bremen, Germany
Eri   Erico Music Publications: Memphis TN, USA
ES   Evette & Schaeffer =Led; USA=AA
ET   Editions Musicales Transatlantiques: 151-153 av. Jean-Jaurès, 75019 Paris, France; USA=Pres; Germany=OJ; Italy=Car; England=UMu
Eth   Ethos Publications: P. O. Box 2043, Oswego NY 13126, USA
Eto   Etoile Music: =MMB
EV   Elkan-Vogel Company Inc.: =Pres; France=Dur
ExMu   Experimental Music: 208 Ladbroke Grove, London W10, England
FaM   Fana Music: P. O. Box 393, Amherst MA 01004, USA
FBC   Finnish Broadcasting Co.: Unionink 16, 00130 Heksinki 13, Finland
FC   Franco Colombo: 16 W. 61 Street, New York NY 10023, USA; USA=CPP; France=Sal
FDi   First Division Publishing Corp.: =CPP
FDP   A la Flûte de Pan: 49, rue de Rome, 75008 Paris, France
FEMA   FEMA Music Publications: Box 395, Naperville IL 60566, USA
FF   F. Friede CP: Berlin, Germany
FHV   =Hof
Fit   H. T. FitzSimons Co.: 615 N. Lasalle Street, Chicago IL 60610, USA; P. O. Box 210, Alexandria IN 46001, USA
Fle   Fleischer Collection: Philadelphia Public Library, Philadelphia PA, USA
FM   Faber Music Ltd.: 3 Queen Square, London WC1N-3AU, England; USA=HLe
FM   Filmkunst-Musikverlag: Bahnhofstrasse 28, D-8043 Unterföhring, Germany
FMH   Frederick Harris Music Co.: 529 Speers Road, Oakville, Ontario L6K 2G4, Canada; 340 Nagel Drive, Buffalo NY 14225, USA
FMIC   Finnish Music Information Centre: Runneberginkatu 15 A 1, SF 00100 Helsinki JO, Finland
FMD   Foreign Music Distributors: 13 Elkay Drive, Chester NY 10918, USA

FMH   Fillmore Music House =CF
FMP   =FEMA
FMT   Fonds Musical Tchèque: Staré Mesto, Parizska 13, Praha 1, Czechoslovakia; USA=B&H
FP   Ferol Publications: P. O. Box 6007, Alexandria VA 22306, USA
Fro   Frolisch: Ansbacherstrasse 52, 1000 Berlin W30, Germany
FroMu   Frost Music: P. B. 38, Redfstad - Oslo 5, Norway
FS   Foreningen Svenka
F&U   Finder & Urbanek: =HLe
Fuz   Jean-Marc Fuzeau: B. P. 6, 79440 Courlay, France
Ga   Galaxy Music Corp.: =ECS
Gach   G. Gacher: 69, rue du Fg St-Martin, 75010 Paris, France
Gaz   Gazebo Series: Musicians Publications, 1076 River Road, Trenton NJ 08628, USA
GB   Georg Bauer: D-7500, Karlsruhe 1, Germany; USA=Gaz
GD   Georges Delrieu: Palais Bellecour, 14 rue Trachel, 06000 Nice, France; USA=ECS
Ger   Gervan: =An
G&F   Gallet & Fils: 6 rue Vivienne, 75002 Paris, France
GHS   George H. Sanders: 408 2nd Avenue, New York NY, USA
Gi&Ma   McGinnis & Marx Music: 236 W. 26th Street, Suite 11S, New York NY 10001, USA
Gly   Glyphic Press: 665 Killarney Drive, Morgantown WV 26505, USA
GM   Gates Music Inc.: 1845 N. Clinton Avenue, Rochester NY 14580, USA
GMP   General Music Publishing Co.: =Bos
Gras   Editions Gras: 12 rue de la Chaussée d'Antin, 75009 Paris, France; USA=South
GrB   Gravis Bad Schwalbach, Germany
GSch   G. Schirmer: 225 Park Avenue South, New York NY 10003; =HLe
GW   George Wahr Publishing Co.: 304½ S. State Street, Ann Arbor MI 48108, USA
GZ   Guglielmo Zanibon: Piazza del Signori 24, 35100 Padore, Italy
HaBr   Harcourt Brace =MBCo
Hag   Hage, Germany
Hal   Wilhelm Halter Musikverlag: BP 21 06 62, D-76156 Karlsruhe, Germany
Ham   Hamelle & Cie: 24 Blvd. Mallesherbes, 75009 Paris, France; USA=Pres
HB   HB Publications: P. O. Box 393, Keene NH 03431, USA
HD   Heinz Dreschler: =KuD
HE   Henri Elkan Music: 7720 FDR Station, New York NY 10150, USA
Hei   Heinrichshofen Verlag: Wilhelmshaven, Germany; USA=Pet
Heil   Heilman Music: P. O. Box 1044, Fairmont WV 26544, USA
Hen   Henmar, Germany; USA=Pet
Henn   Henn: 4 rue de Hesse, Geneve, Switzerland
Her   Heritage Music Press: The Lorenz Corp., 501 E. Third Street, Dayton OH 45401, USA
Hes   Hespos, Germany
Heu   Heugel =Led; USA=Pres/RKM
HG   Hans Gerig: Köln, Germany; USA=HLe
Hilcol Hill Coleman: 66 W. 55th Street, New York NY, USA
Hin   Hinrichsen, England; USA=Pet
HL   Harold Lyche: Kongensgate 2, Oslo, Norway
HLe   Hal Leonard Publ. Corp.: 7777 West Bluemond Road, Milwaukee, WI 53213, USA
HM   Hebra Music: 30, rue St. Christophe, 1000 Bruxelles, Belgium
Hnr   Henkar

Hof	Hofmeister: Friedrich Hofmeister Verlag: Ubierrstrasse 20, 6238 Hofheim-am-Taunus, Germany; Seilergasse 12a, Postfach 130, 1015 Wien, Austria; USA=FMD;
HP	Halmiles Publications: 1458 Morris Avenue, New York NY, USA
HR	H. Riedel: Uhlanstrasse 38, Berlin W 15, Germany
HS	Henri Selmer Editions: =Selm
Hug	Hug & Co. Musikverlage: Flughofstrasse 61, CH-8152 Glattbrugg/Zürich, Switzerland; Limmatquai 28, 8022 Zürich, Switzerland; USA=Mag/South
HV	Hänsler Verlag: Neuhaussen, Stuttgart, Germany; P. O. Box 210, Alexandria IN 46001, USA; USA=TMPI
HZ	Heuwekemeijer en Zoon: Groest 112, 1211 EE Hilversum, Netherlands; USA=Pres
IAC	Inter Art Company Ltd.: 10-16 Rathbone Street, London W1P 2BJ, England; USA=CPP
IC	Ithaca College: Ithaca NY 14850, USA
IMC	International Music Company: =Bou
IMD	International Musikinstitut Darmstadt: Nieder-Ramstadter Strasse 190, 6100 Darmstadt, Germany; 24 rue Etex, 75018 Paris, France
IMIC	Island Music Information Center
INM	Institut Für Neue Musik: Hardenbergstrasse 9, 10623 Berlin, Germany
Int	Interlochen Press: Interlochen MI 49643, USA; =FEMA
Ir	Iritonus: Luxembourg
ISM	Israel Music Institute: P.O. Box 11253, Tel Aviv, Israel; USA=Pres; France=Heu; England=Che
IUP	Indiana University Press: 10th and Morton Streets, Bloomington IN 47405, USA
JB	Joseph Boonin: =HLe
JCC	Japan Composer Council
JCCC:	J. C. Christopher Co.: RFD No. 4 Hibarlow Road, Newtown CT 06470, USA; =Pres
JE	June Emerson: Ampleforth, North Yorkshire YO6 4HF, England; USA=Pres
JFC	Japan Federation of Composers: c/o Ohrinato Bldg. 14, Suga-Cho Shinsuku-ku, Tokyo, Japan
JG	Judy Green: Netherlands
JJ	Jean Jobert: 76 rue Quincampoix, 75003 Paris, France; USA=Pres
JL	Josette Lyon: 11bis rue Georges Saché, 75014 Paris, France
JM	Joshua Music: Hasting-on-Hudson NY 10706, USA
JO	Jasemusiikki Oy: Pl 136, SF 13101 Hämeenlinna, Finland
JP	Jenson Publications Inc.: =HLe
JR	JRPublishers: 4182 Ursa Course, Liverpool NY, USA
JS	Jack Spratt Music Publishers: 77 W. Broad Street, Stamford CT, USA; =Ply
JW	Josef Weinberger: 10 Rathbone Street, London W1, England; Oederweg 26, 6000 Frankfurt 1, Germany; USA=B&H
Ka	Kali Yuga Music: P. O. Box 305, Garden City NY, USA
Kal	Kalmus: 2/3 Fareham Street, London W1, England
KD	=Ken
Ken	Kendor Music: P. O. Box 278, Delevan NY 14042, USA
KF	Kufstein
KG	=CG
Kjos	Neil Kjos Music Co.: 4382 Jutland Drive, San Diego CA 92117, USA
Klen	Klenheim Press: Cockertons, Gt Bradley, Newmarket, Suffolk, England
KMP	Kiodo Music Publ.: Tokyo, Japan
Kli	Klimet: Wien, Austria; Leipzig, Germany
Kneu	Edition Kneusslin: Basel, Switzerland; USA=FMD
Kon	Kontrapunkt Edit.: Stotsalleen 16, DK-Klampenborg, Denmark
KP	Keith Prowse: 21 Danemark Street, London WC2 H8NE, England; USA=CF
K&S	Kistner und Siegel: USA=Concordia Publishing House, 3558 S. Jefferson Avenue, St. Louis MO 63118, USA
Ku	Edition Kunzelmann: Grüstrasse 28, Postfach 8134, Adliswil 2H, Switzerland; USA=FMD
KuD	Isa Küffner & Heinz Dreschler: Peter-Henlein Strasse 37, 8500 Nürnberg 70, Germany
LC	Leonard Carrol
LCM	Library of Czech Music: Charles University, Library of Music, Theater and Film Dept., Nám Krasnoarmejcu 2, 110 00 Praha, Czechoslovakia
LCP	Lucien Cailliet: =South
Leba	Lebanon: =SP
Lebl	Leblanc Publications Inc.: 7001 Leblanc Blvd., Kenosha WI 53141, USA; =South
Led	Alphonse Leduc: 175 rue St-Honoré, 75040 Paris Cedex 01, France; USA=RKM/Pres/MBCo
Lee	Leeds Music Corp.: =HLe/MCA
Lem	Henri Lemoine: 17, rue Pigalle, 75009 Paris; USA=Pres
LEP	Les Editions de Paris: =EP
LF	Lino Florenzo: Lille, France
Lis	Lispet: =TM
LK	Ludwig Krenn: Wien, Austria
LM	Lorimar Music: London, England; USA=Wab
LMe	Le Menestrel: Paris, France
LMP	Lang Music Publications: P.O. Box 11021, Indianapolis IN 46201, USA
Lud	Ludwig Music Publishing: 557-67 E. 140th. Street, Cleveland OH 44110, USA
LY	=HL
Ma	=MMB
Mag	Magnamusic Distributors: Route 41, Sharon CT 06069, USA
Map	Mappemonde: 17, Clos Noblet, 91200 Atis Mons, France
MaPu	Manuscript Publications: 3201 E. Greenlee Road No. 32, Tucson AZ 85716, USA
Mar	Editions Robert Martin: BP 502, 71009 Macon, France; USA=Pres
Marc	Marcato Music: P. O. Box 13462, Pittsburgh PA 15243, USA
Marg	Marguerita: 290 Av. Victor Hugo, 94120 Fontenay-sous-Bois, France
Mau	Maurer: 7 Av du Verseau, Bruxelles 15, Belgium; USA=MBCo
MB	Musica Budapest: Kultura P. O. B. 149, H-1389 Budapest 62, Hungary; France=VV; USA=Pres
MBCo	M. Baron Company: P. O. Box 149, Oyster Bay NY 11771, USA
MCA	MCA Music Publishing: 1755 Broadway, 8th Floor, New York NY 10019, USA; =HLe
McK	McKinley Publ.: 401 5th Avenue, New York NY 10016, USA
MDM	Martino-Dantalian Music: 11 Pembroke Street, Newton MA 02158, USA
ME	Max Eschig: 48, rue de Rome, 75008 Paris; USA=HLe/GSch
Med	Medem: 1, 259 Richelieu, Quebec G1R 1J7, Canada
MeM	Merion Music: =Pres
MeP	Mediterranean Press: 11204 Oakleaf Drive, Silver Spring MD 20901, USA
Merc	Mercury Music Corporation: =Pres
Meri	Meridian: 7 rue Lincoln, 75008 Paris, France
Met	Metropolis: Van Erbornstrasse 5, Anvers, Belgium; USA=HE
MF	Ed. des Maîtres Français

Mil	Millereau
Mills	Mills Music: =CPP
Min	Minea: Budapest, Hungary
Mis	=Led
MJ	Merle Johnston: 151 W. 46th Street, New York NY, USA
MJQ	MJQ Music: 881 10th Avenue, New York NY 10019, USA
ML	McLellan: 7 Rowanstree Road, Enfield, Middlesex, England
MM	=Gi&Ma
MMB	MMB Music Inc.: 10370 Page Industrial Blvd, St. Louis MO 63132, USA
MMC	Marks Music Corp.: =EM
MMI	Margun Music Inc.: 167 Dudley Road, Newton Centre MA 02159, USA; c/o Jerona Music Corp., P. O. Box 5010, S. Hackensack NJ 07606, USA
MMP	Medici Music Press: 100 W. 24th Street, Owensboro KY 42301, USA
MMS	Modern Music School: 2979 Woodhill Road, Cleveland OH 44104, USA
Mol	Molenaar: Postbus 19, 1520 AA Wormerveer, Netherlands; USA=HE; France=Mar
Mor	Mordant Editions
MP	Media Press: Champaign IL 61820, USA
MPC	Music Publishers Co.: 529 Speers Road, Oakville, Ontario L6K 2G4, Canada
MPHC	Music Publishers Holding Corp.: 488 Madison Avenue, New York NY, USA; =Wab
MR	Musikverlag Rubato: Meppen, Germany
MV	Mavlo Sanco: Via Parma 78, 39100 Bolzano, Italy
MSA	Musicinco S. A.: Akala 70, 28009 Madrid, Spain
MSC	Music Sales Corp.: 5 Bellvale Road, Chester NY 10918
Mt	Marbot Edit.: Hamburg 13, Germany
Mu	Muzyka: Moscow; St. Petersburg, Russia
Mun	Mundimusica: Espejo 4, 28013 Madrid, Spain
Mur	Muraille: Liege, Bruxelles, Belgium
Mus	Edition Musicus: P. O. Box 1341, Stamford CT 06904, USA
Musi	Editio Musica Budapest: Budapest, Hungary; USA=B&H/Pres
MusPr	Music Press =Pres
Mut	Mutual Music Society: 1270 6th Avenue, New York NY, USA
MV	Möseler Verlag: Wolfenbüttel, Germany
NA	NACWPI Library: 1201 16th Street NW, Washington DC 20036, USA
NASA	Allyn Reilly, Dir. of Scholarly Publ., School of Music, Ohio University, Athens OH 45701, USA
NGlani	Edition NGlani: P. O. Box 5684, Takoma Park MD 20913, USA
NK	North Komponistforening: Klingenbergsaten 5, Oslo 1, Norway
NM	Nicomede Music, USA
NMI	Norsk Musikinformatjon: Toftesgt. 69, N-0552 Oslo 5, Norway
NMO	Norsk Musikforlag: A/S Oslo, Norway; USA=MMB
NMSC	New Music Society of California: Box 2888, Los Angeles CA; 250 W. 57th Street, New York NY, USA
NoE	Noetzel Edit.: Wilhelmshaven, Germany
NoMu	Norruth Music: =MMB
Nor	Norcat Music Press: 7402 Wells Blvd., Hyattsville MD 20783, USA
Nov	Novello & Co.: Borough Green, Seven Oaks, Kent T15-8DT, England; USA=Pres; France=Sal
NP	Needham Publishing Co.: =DP
NSM	North Star Music: P. O. Box 317, Park Ridge IL 60068, USA

NTS	North Texas State: University of North Texas, Denton TX 76203, USA
NYPL	New York Public Library: 5th Avenue, New York NY 10019, USA
NYSQ	New York Saxophone Quartet: 320 W. 87th Street, New York NY 10024, USA
NWM	New Wind Music Co.: England; USA=B&H
Oa	Otama, USA
OE	Ongako-No-Toma-Sha: Kagurazaka 6-30, Shinjuku, Tokyo, Japan; USA=Pres
Oil	L'Oiseau Lyre: B. P. 515, MC-98015 Monaco Cedex; USA=Mag
OJ	Otto June: München, Germany
OKM	Okra Music: 177 E. 87th Street, New York NY 10028, USA; =SeMC
OM	Oscar Music: 20 rue Duperré, 75009 Paris, France
OMC	Omega Music Co.: 353 E. 52nd Street, New York NY 10022, USA
OMP	Olympia Music Publishing: 909 Dafney Drive, Lafayette LA 70503, USA
ONT	=OE
OP	Olivan Press: 49 Selvage Lane, London NW7, England
Or	Orpheus, Netherlands; USA=Ply
Ot	Opera tres: Plaza Isabel 11 n° 3, 28013 Madrid, Spain
OUP	Oxford University Press: 7-8 Hatherley Street, London SW1P-2QT, England; 36 Soho Square, London W1, England; 200 Madison Avenue, New York NY 10016, USA; 2001 Evans Road, Cary NC 27513
OWR	Otto Wrede Regina: Wiesbaden, Germany
PA	Pro-Art Publications: 143 W. Broadway, New York NY, USA; =CPP
Pag	=PEMD
Pan	Pan: Helsinki, Finland
PAS	Paul A. Schmitt Marie: 110 N. 5th Street, Minneapolis MN 55403, USA
PB	Paul Beuscher: 25-27 Blvd Beaumarchais, 75004 Paris, France
PBP	Peter Birkby Publishing: 40 Park Avenue, South Kirkby, Pontefract, West Yorkshire WF9-3PG, England
PC	=Cil
Peer	Peer Music Verlag: Muhlennkamp 43, D-2000 Hamburg, Germany; USA=SMPC
PEM	Piles Editorial de Musica: Archena 33, 46014 Valencia, Spain
PEMD	Pagani Edizioni Musicali e Discografiche: 20090 Cesano Boscone, Milano, Italy
Pet	C. F. Peters Corp.: 373 Park Avenue South, New York NY 10016, USA; Kennedy-Allee 101, 6000 Frankfurt-am-Main 70, Germany; France=Sch
PG	Percy Grainger: 7 Commwell Place, White Plains NY, USA
PGM	Ph. Grosch Musikverlag: 8000 Munich, Germany
Phi	Philippo: =Com; USA=Pres
PhiCo	Philharmusica Corpration: 250 W. 57 Street, Suites 1527-195, New York NY 10107, USA; Sec 822 Duo Sonatas, Monaco
PHIL	Philharmonia: Wien, Austria; USA=EAM
PIC	Peer International Corp.: =Pres/SMPC
Pied	Piedmont Music Co.: =HLe/EM
Pio	Pioneer Editions: =ACA
Piz	Pizzicato Editions: Via M. Ortigara 10, 33100 Udine, Italy
PJT	P. J. Tonger: Auf dem Brand 3, 5000 Köln Rodenkirch, Germany; USA=CPP
Ply	Plymouth Music Company: 170 N. E. 33rd Street, Fort Lauderdale FL 33334, USA

PM	Podium Music: 360 Port Washington Blvd., Port Washington NY 11050, USA
PMCP	Penfield Music Commissioning Project, Penfield High School, Penfield NY 14516, USA
PMP	Providence Music Press: P. O. Box 2362, East Side Station, Providence RI 02906, USA
PMu	Pembroke Music Inc.: =CF
PMV	Pro Musica Verlag: Karl-Liebkechstrasse 12, 701 Leipzig, Germany; USA=Brou
PN	Pierre Noel: =Bil; USA=MBCo
PNS	Pro Nova Sonoton: Schlesibingerstrasse 10, D-8000 München 80, Germany
Por	Porret =Mol
PP	Paul Price Publications: =Ply
Pres	Theodore Presser Company: Presser Place, Bryn Mawr PA 19010, USA
Pro	=PA
PT	Primo Tema: Strada del Palazzo 91, 65125 Pescara, Italy
Pub	Publ. Bonnart: P. O. Box 6135, Montreal 3, Quebec, Canada
PV	Pine Valley Press: 69 Lindley Terrace, Williamstown MA 01267, USA
PWM	Polskie Wydawnictwo Muzyczne: Senatorska 13, Warsawa, Poland; USA=HLe/Pres/CPP/EM
Ram	Ramsey/Roberton Publications, England; USA=Pres
RB	Richard Birnbach Musik : Dürerstrasse 28, 1000 Berlin 45, Germany
RE	Ries & Erler: Charlottenbrunner Strasse 42, 1000 Berlin 33, Germany; USA=Pet
Reb	Rebec Editions: CP 246 Ancienne-Lorette, Quebec, Canada
Rebo	Rebo Music Publications: P. O. Box 9481, Denver CO 80209, USA
Reed	Reedmate: P. O. Box 1512, Decatur IL 62525, USA
Reg	Regent: Paris, France; USA=HLe
Reim	Reimers A. B.: P. O. Box 150-30, 161-15 Bromma 15, Stockholm, Sweden; USA=Pres
Rem	Remick Music Corp.: =Wab
RG	Richard Gatenmaire: München, Germany
Ric	Ricordi & Co.: Milano, Italy; USA=B&H; France=Sal
RIM	Rhode Island Music, USA
RKM	Robert King Music Co: 28 Main Street, Bldg. 15, N. Easton MA 02356, USA
RM	Repertory Music: Hollywood CA, USA
RME	Real Musical Edit.: Carlos III n° 1, 28013 Madrid, Spain
RMP	Rochester Music Publishers: P. O. Box 887, Athens OH 45701, USA; 358 Aldrich Road, Fairport NY 14450, USA; =AM
Rob	Robbins Music Corp.: =CPP
RoMu	=Rob
Ron	Roncorp Inc.: P. O. Box 724, Cherry Hill NJ 08003, USA
Rot	Rotvöpchen: Berlin, Germany
RPS	Rochester Photo Service: Maidenlane, Sodus Pt. NY 14555, USA
RR	Rideau Rouge: 23 rue de Longchamp, 75116 Paris; USA=Pres
RS	Robert Sibbing: Rte 4, Macomb IL 61455, USA
RSC	R. Smith & Co: P. O. Box 210, Watford-Herts WDZ-4YG, England; USA=William Allen Music Inc., P. O. Box 790, Newington VA 22122, USA
RTB	Edit. Radio Télévision Belge: Bruxelles, Belgium
Ru	Ruggimenti: Milano, Italy
Rub	Rubank Inc.: 16215 N.W. 15th Av., Miami FL 33169, USA; =HLe
Run	Rundel Musikverlag: D-7955 Rot an der Rot, Germany
SAE	Société Anonyme d'Edit.: 7 rue Gambetta, 54000 Nancy, France
SAGEM	SAGEM: 7 rue Boutard, 92200 Neuilly, France
Sal	Editions Salabert: 22 rue Chauchat, 75009 Paris, France; USA=HLe/GSch
Sax	Chez Adolphe Sax, Paris, France
SB	Shapiro, Bernstein & Co.: 10 E. 53rd Street, New York NY 10022, USA; =Ply
SBC	Summy-Birchard: =Wab
Sbg	Schonenberger Editions
SBM	Skandanavisk & Borups Musik: Copenhagen, Denmark; USA=MBCo
SC	Sprague Coleman: New York; USA=Lee
Sch	Schott: 30 rue Saint Jean, Bruxelles, Belgium; 35 rue Jean Moulin, BP 85, 94300 Vincennes, France; 48 Great Marlborough Street, London W1, England; USA=EAM
Schu	=BFS
SCo	Sax et Cie: =CT
Scz	Scherzo: 20-22 rue Lovelingstr., B-2008 Anvers, Belgium; USA=HE
SEDIM	SEDIM: 151-153 Avenue Jean-Jaurès, 75019 Paris, France
Selm	Editions Henri Selmer: P. O. Box 310, 1119 N. Main Street, Elkhart IN 46514, USA; USA=MBCo
SeMC	Seesaw Music Corp.: 2067 Broadway, New York NY 10023, USA
Sen	Maurice Senart: 20 rue du Dragon, 75006 Paris, France
SF	Sam Fox Publishing Co. =Ply
Sha	Shawnee Press: Waring Drive, Delaware Water Gap PA 18327, USA
Shir	=GSch
SH&MC	Schmitt, Hall & McCreary Co.: 527 Park Avenue, Minneapolis MN 55415, USA; =CPP
ShP	Shelan Publications
Shu	Shuebuck Editions
Sib	=RS
Sik	Hans Sikorski Musikverlag: Johnsallee 23, Postfach 132001, 2000 Hamburg 13, Germany; USA=HLe/GSch
Sil	Silver Mace Publications, USA
Sim	Simrock: London, England; Werdestrasse 44, Postfach 2561, 2000 Hamburg 13, Germany; USA=Pres
SiMC	Sintafest Music Company: 8729 Contee Road #303, Laurel MD 20708, USA
SJ	Szerzoï Joguero: Hivatal, Budapest, Hungary
SK	Sevetskij Kompozitor: Moscow, Russia
SKJ	Savez Kompozitora Jugoslavise: Marsala Tita 14, 11000 Belgrad, Serbia; 17 W. 60th Street, New York NY 10023, USA
SL	Symphony Land: 74, Quai de Jemmapes, 75010 Paris, France
SM	Stanza Music: 11 Victor Road, Harrow, Middlesex, England; USA=Ken
SMC	Studio Music & Co.: 77 Dudden Hill Lane, London NW 10, England; USA=Gaz
SMIC	Swedish Music Information Center: Sandhamnsgatan 79, P. O. Box 27327, S-10254, Stockholm, Sweden
SMP	Staff Music Publishing: =Ply
SMPC	Southern Music Publishing Company: 810 Seventh Avenue, New York NY 10019, USA; =Pres; France=En
SMPL	Scotus Music Publ.: 28 Dalrymple Crescent, Edinburg EH9-2NX, Scotland
Smt	Smith Publications: 2617 Gwynndale Avenue, Baltimore MD 21207, USA
SN	Statni Nakladatelstvi: Kraashe Litteratury, Hundby a Umeni Prague, Czechoslovakia
SOBM	=SBM
SOC	Soviet Composers: Moscow, Russia
SOMI	School of Music, Indiana University, Bloomington IN 47405, USA

South	Southern Music Co.: P. O. Box 329, San Antonio TX 78292, USA	VB	Van Beethoven: 115 rue Raymond Rivel, 92400 Courbevoie, France
SP	Studio PR Inc.: 224 S. Lebanon, Lebanon IN 46052, USA; =CPP	VCD	Verseau Centre d'Art: Paris, France
		VD	Verlag Doblinger: =Dob
SPAM	Society for the Publication of American Music: P. O. Box 269, Wall Street Station, New York NY 10005; =Pres	VDMK	VDMK: Landsbergerstrasse 425, 8000 München, Germany
		Ver	Verhoeven Editions: 80 rue du Prétoire, Bruxelles 1070, Belgium
SPM	=JS		
SR	Sveriges Radios Musikbibliotek: Stockholm, Sweden	VF	Vogt & Fritz Musik Verlag: Germany
SRU	=Run	Vog	Voggenreiter
SS	Schott's Söhne: Weihergarten 1-9, Postfach 3640, 6500 Mainz 1, Germany; France=Sch; USA=EAM	Volk	Volkwein Bros: 117 Sandusky Street, Pittsburgh PA 15212, USA; =CPP
Ste	Sterling Music: Kansas, USA	VV	Van de Velde: BP 22, Fondettes, 37230 Luynes, France
STI	STIMS Info Central for Swedish Music: Sandhamnsgatan 79, P. O. Box 27327, S-10254, Stockholm, Sweden	VW	Volker Würth: Wönder Hauptstrasse 46, 8500 Nürnberg 20, Germany
STIM	=STI	Wa	Waterloo Music: Waterloo, Ontario, Canada
StMu	Standard Music Publishing Inc: P. O. Box 1043, Whitman Square, Turnersville NJ 08012, USA	Wab	Warner Brothers Publications: 265 Secaucus Road, Secaucus NJ 07096, USA; 810 Seventh Avenue, New York NY 10019, USA
StV	Stockhausen Verlag: 5073 Kurten, Germany		
SUE	Suecia: Sandhamnsgatan 79, P. O. Box 27327, S-10254, Stockholm, Sweden	WB	Ward-Brodt Music Co.: 2200 West Beltline Highway, Madison WI 53713, USA
SV	Sirius Verlag: Wiclefstrasse 67, 1 Berlin 21, Germany	WH	Wilhelm Hansen: 9-11 Gothersgade, 1123 Copenhagen, Denmark; Eschenheimer Landstrasse, Postfach 2684, 6 Frankfurt-am-Main 1, Germany; USA=MSC; England=Che
SvM	Svensk Musik: Sandhamnsgatan 79, P. O. Box 27327, S-10254, Stockholm, Sweden		
SZ	Suvini Zerboni: Via M. F. Quintiliano 40, 20138 Milano, Italy; USA=B&H; France=SAGEM	WHi	William Hill: 1125 South 5th Avenue, Arcadia CA 91006, USA
		Wie	Rudy Wiedoeft Publishing: =Rob
TCP	The Composer's Press: Opus Music, 1880 Holste Road, Northbrooke IL 60062, USA	Wi&Jo	Wingert-Jones Music: 2026 Broadway, P. O. Box 419878, Kansas City MO 64141, USA
Tech	Technisonor: =EFM/Bil	WIM	Western International Music: 3707 65th Avenue, Greeley CO 80634, USA
Tem	Templeton Publishing Co.: =Sha		
Ten	Tenuto Publications: =Pres	Wis	Wissenschaft: Sofia, Bulgaria
Tie	Musikin Tiedotuskeskus: Runeberginkatu 15 A 11, 00100 Helsinki, Finland	Wit	Witmark & Sons: =Wab
		WJ	Walter Jacob: 6425 Hollywood Blvd., Hollywood CA, USA
TM	Tierolff Muziekcentrale: Markt 90-92, Postbus 18, 4700 AA ROOSENDAAL, Netherlands; USA=HE	WM	Wimbledon Music: 1888 Century Park East, Century City CA 90067, USA
TMPI	Tempo Music Publications: 3773 W. 95th Street, Leawood KS 66206, USA	WMP	Windsor Music Press: 426 W. 55th. Street, New York NY, USA
Ton	Tonsaffare	WOC	Winds of Change: c/o Richard Addison, 68 Huntington Road, London NZ, England
Tong	=PJT		
Tono	Tonos Editions: Ahastrasse 7 U9, Darmstadt 6100, Germany; USA=SeMC	WR	Will Rositer: Chicago, USA
		WWS	Woodwind Service: P. O. Box 206, Medfield MA 02052, USA
TP	Tritone Press: =Pres		
Tro	Tropic: Pujades 13, 08018 Barcelona, Spain	Wu	=VW
TTF	To The Fore Publishers: 43 Van Buskirk Road, Teaneck NJ 07666, USA	Yb	Ybarra Music: P. O. Box 665, Lemon Grove CA 92045, USA
TVA	Thomas V. Axworthy: 9354 S. Pioneer Blvd., Santa Fe Springs CA 90670, USA	YUC	Yugoslav Union of Composers: =SKJ
		Zan	=GZ
Ty	Maison Tyssens: 30, rue des Clarisses, 4000 Liege, Belgium	Zim	Wilhelm Zimmerman: P. O. Box 940183, D-6000 Frankfurt, Germany; USA=EAM
UGDAL	Union Grand-Duc Adolph Luxembourg: Café de la Paix, Pl. d'Armes, Luxembourg		
UKH	Association des Compositeurs de Croatie	ZOM	Zen-On Music Co., Japan; USA=EAM/Mag
UME	Union Musicale Espanola: Carrera de San Jerimo, 26 y Arsenal, 28014 Madrid, Spain; USA=MSC	Zu	Editions August Zurfluh: 73 Blvd. Raspail, 75006 Paris, France
UMM	=UMP		
UMP	University Music Press: P. O. Box 1267, Ann Arbor MI 48106, USA		
UMPL	United Music Publishers Ltd: 1 Montague Russel Square, London WC1B-5BS, England; USA=Pres		
UMu	=UMPL		
Uni	Universal: Postfach 130, Karlsplatz 6, 1015 Wien, Austria; 2 Fareham Street, London W1, England; France=SAGEM/Dur/Heu; USA=EAM		
USC	University of Southern California: Los Angeles CA 90089, USA		
VAB	Verlag Anton Benjamin: =Pres		

For information contact:
Pour toutes informations:

Centre Européen de Saxophone
22, Quai Sainte-Croix
33800 Bordeaux, France
Fax: 56.92.22.30

Addresses of Unpublished Composers - Adresses de compositeurs inédits

AARON, Yvonne: 16, rue Alphonse de Neuville, 75017 Paris, France

ABLINGER, Peter: Koloniestrasse 40, 1000 Berlin 65, Germany

AGNESENS, Udo: Graegestrasse 33, 1000 Berlin 61, Germany

ALBERT, Karel: 41, rue Rotterdam, Antwerpen, Belgium

ALBERTH, Rudolph: Frauenchiemseestrasse 7, 8000 München 80, Germany

ALLA, Thierry: "Le Basque", 33141 Villegouge, France

ANDERSON, Garland: 44 NW 6th Street, Richmond IN 47374, USA

ANTONINI, Félix: 7, rue du Jardin des Plantes 69001 Lyon, France

APFELSTADT, Marc: 2119 Tarrywood Drive, Greensboro NC 27408, USA

APOTHELOZ, Jean: Association des Musiciens Suisses, Zurich, Alpenquai 38, Switzerland

APPARAILLY, Yves: Citon. 33370 Pompignac, France

ARNOLD, André: 60, rue d'Alsace, 78200 Mantes-la-Jolie, France

AUSTIN, Larry: Music Dept., University of California Davis, Davis CA 95616, USA

AYSCUE, Brian: 1217 Sylvan Drive, Haddon Heights NJ 08035, USA

BABBITT, Milton: Woolworth Centre, Princeton NJ 08540, USA

BALL, Leonard - School of Music, University of Georgia, Athens GA 30602, USA

BASSETT, Leslie: School of Music, University of Michigan, Ann Arbor MI 48109, USA

BAILLY, Jean-Guy: 14, rue Jules Verne, 69003 Lyon, France

BANTER, Harald: Wieselweg 10, 5000 Köln 91, Germany

BARAT, Jacques: 5, Allées Aubert, 91200 Athis Mons, France

BARONIJAN, Vartkes: Dorda Javosionica, 6 Beograd, Yugoslavia

BASSKIN, Ali: Rotwandstrasse 24, 8000 München 90, Germany

BAUCHWITZ, Peter: Iversheimerstrasse 27, 5353 Mechernich-Wachendorf, Germany

BAUZIN, Pierre-Philippe: 51, Allée des Micocouliers, Hameau de Puissanton 06220 Vallauris, France

BEALL, John: College of Creative Arts, West Virginia University, Morgantown WV 26506, USA

BECKRATH, Alfred: Werneckstrasse 51, 8 München 23 , Germany

BEINKE, Eckart: Krumme Strasse 29a, D26131 Oldenburg, Germany

BELLINI, Luciano: Via A. Faustina 14/a, 00153 Rome, Italy

BELLISARIO, Angelo: Via Ardigo 4/6, 22052 Monza, Italy

BENCRISCUTTO, Frank: School of Music, University of Minnesota, Minneapolis MN 55455, USA

BENEJAM, Luis: c/o Dr. John Stewart, College of Fine Arts, University of Montevallo, Montevallo AL 35115, USA

BENSON, Warren: Eastman School of Music, 26 Gibbs Street, Rochester NY 14604, USA

BERG, Gunnar: Linoved gl. skole, 8783 Hornsyld, Denmark

BERGERON, Thomas: Department of Music, Western Oregon State College, Monmouth OR 97361, USA

BERNARD, Jacques: 194, Av. du Gal Giraud, 94100 St-Maur des Fosses, France

BERNARD, Robert: 32, Blvd Wilson, 06000 Antibes, France

BERNAUD, Alain: 20, Av. du Bois, 92430 Marnes-la-Coquette, France

BEUGNIOT, J-Pierre: 11, rue d'Ourches, 78100 St-Germain-en-Laye, France

BEYER, Frank Michael: Söhtstrasse 6, 1000 Berlin 45, Germany

BIANCHINI, Laura: c/o C.R.M., via Lamarmora 18, Rome, Italy

BIELER, Helmut: Humboldt Strasse 10, D-8580 Bayreuth, Germany

BIENVENU, Lily: 11, rue Gît-le-Coeur, 75006 Paris, France

BINNEY, Oliver: P. O. Box 128, Jupiter, Kent BR8 8HH, England

BLYTON, Carey: Hawthornden, 55 Goldsel Road, Swanley, England

BOEUF, Georges: Allé Granados 'L'Estramadure' 13008 Marseille, France

BOISSELET, Paul: 12, rue Garnier, 92200 Neuilly/Seine, France

BOLIART, Xavier: Tallers, 32 2n,2a, 08001 Barcelona, Spain

BONGIORNO, Frank - Department of Creative Arts, Division of Music, University of North Carolina at Wilmington, Wilmington NC 28403, USA

BONNARD, Alain: 26, Cours Mongolfier, 42400 St-Chamond, France

BOONE, Ben: 704 Oakdale Drive, Statesville NC 28677, USA

BORCHARD, Adolphe: 48, rue G. Mandel, 75016 Paris, France

BORTOLOTTI, Mauro: via S. Gregorio VII 89, 00165 Rome, Italy

BOUCHARD, Marcel: 101, Fg. Taillebourg, 17400 St-Jean D'Angely, France

BOUTRY, Roger: 3, rue des Pâtures, 75016 Paris, France

BOUVARD, Jean: 74, rue Garibaldi, 69006 Lyon, France

BRANDOLICA, Ljubomir: Ivo Lola Riber br45 VII, Skopje, Yugoslavia

BRANDON, Seymour: P. O. Box 150A, R.D. No. 2, Wrightsville PA 17368, USA

BRANT, Henry: Department of Music, Bennington College, Bennington VT 05201, USA

BROEGE, Timothy: 612 Rankin Road, Brielle NJ 08730, USA

BUEL, Charles: 1831 Lexington Avenue, San Mateo CA 94402, USA

BUESS, Alex: Güterstrasse 281, 4000 Basel, Switzerland

BULL, Edvard Hagerup: Kringsjävn 6., 1342 Jar (Baerum), Norway

BULOW, Harry: P. O. Box 561604, Charlotte NC 28256, USA

BURNETTE, Sonny: Department of Music, Georgetown College, 400 East College Street, Georgetown KY 40324, USA

BUWEN, Dieter: Philip-kittler Strasse 9, 8500 Nürnberg, Germany

BYTZEK, Peter: Schillerstrasse 12, 1000 Berlin 45, Germany

CADEE, J-L.: Symphony Land, Immeuble Cezanne, 24, rue Utrillo, 93370 Montfermeil, France

CADWALLADER, Rex: 2607 23rd. Avenue No. 22, Greeley CO 80631, USA

CAILLET, Lucien: 8913 Sunset Blvd., Hollywood CA, USA

CALLHOFF, Herbert: Lotosweg 35, 5000 Köln 50, Germany

CALMEL, Roger: 317, rue Belleville, 75019 Paris, France

CAMPBELL, John: Schwalbacher Strasse 8, 1000 Berlin 41, Germany

CARAVAN, Ronald: 702 Highland Street, Fulton NY 13069, USA

CARLES, Marc: 33, rue André Cayron, 92600 Asnieres, France

CARPENTER, Kurt: 4029 Clarendon Road, Indianapolis IN 46208, USA

CASANOVA, André: 4 Rés. des Grands-Prés, 78430 Louveciennes, France

CECCARELLI, Luigi: Via Tevere 15, Rome, Italy

CERVELLO, Jordi: rue St-Magdalena Sofia n° 14 Atico, Barcelona, Spain

CEUGNART, Robert: 119, rue du Chemin Vert, 75011 Paris, France

CHALFONTE, Richard: 1308 Madison Avenue, Lakewood NJ 08701, USA

CLELLAND, Kenneth: 130 Old Stone House Road, Carlisle PA 17013, USA

CLERISSE, Robert: 50, rue de Lausanne, 1950 Sion, Switzerland

COCCO, Enrico: Via Sampieri di Bastelica 38, Rome, Italy

CODINA, M-A.: c/o Viladomat 63, pral 2°, Barcelona 15, Spain

COE, Tony: 22 Glenton Road, London SE1 3, England

COHEN, Paul: 43 Van Buskirk Road, Teaneck NJ 07666, USA

CONSTANT, Franz: Drève Vanderborght 1A, 1160 Bruxelles, Belgium

CONTI, Francis: Johnsburg Central School, N. Creek NY 12853, USA

COOLIDGE, Richard: P. O. Box 6220, SFA Station, Nacogdoches TX 75962, USA

COPE, David: 3705 Standhill Road, Cleveland OH 44122, USA

CORINA, John: 396 Hancock, Rte 3, Athens GA 30601, USA

COSTANTINI, Andreina: Via Bezzecca 5, 40139 Bologna, Italy

COUINEAU, Patrice: 12, rue de Versailles, 15000 Aurillac, France

COURROYER, Bernard: 8, rue Sylvain Denayer, 1070 Bruxelles, Belgium

COWLES, Colin: Barrack Hill Nether Winchendon, Aylesbury Burks HP18-0DU, England

COX, Rona: 1114A W. Hickory, Denton TX, USA

CRAWFORD, Jerry: Department of Music, Sam Houston State University, Huntsville TX 77341, USA

CUNCHE, Jean: 198, Quartier de l'Europe, 6070 Chatelineau, Belgium

CURTIS-SMITH, Curtis: School of Music, Western Michigan University, Kalamazoo MI 49008, USA

D'ANGELO, Nicholas: 283 Pulteney Street, Geneva NY 14456, USA

DELAMARRE, Pierre: 7, rue de Toutes-Aides, 44600 St Nazaire, France

DELGIUDICE, Michel: Chef de Musique 7° R. M., 9° C. R. T. Montfuron 13, Marseille 9°, France

DE MARS, James: School of Music, Arizona State University, Tempe AZ 85287, USA

DEMUTH, Norman: 4 Elfin Grove, Bognor-Regis, Sussex, England

DEPELSENAIRE, Jean-Marie: Le Parc, Les Pinsons, 59600 Maubeuge, France

DERR, Ellwood: School of Music, University of Michigan, Ann Arbor MI 48109, USA

DESCHAMPS, Jean-Henri: 3, rue Coysevox, 75018 Paris, France

DESPORTES, Yvonne: 16, Av. du Gal-Leclerc, 75014 Paris, France

DEVEVEY, Pierre: 10, Av. du Père-Lachaise, 75020 Paris, France

DI BETTA, Philippe: 5, rue Jean Preschey - 95150 Taverny, France

DIESSEL, Karl: 7, rue de la Trémouille, 75008 Paris, France

DINESCU, Violeta: c/o V. Knorr, Jahnstrasse 3, 6907 Nossbloch, Germany

DININNY, John: RD 3, Smithport PA 16749, USA

DI PASQUALE, James: 5120 Suffield Court, Skokie IL 60076, USA

DJEMIL, Anyss: Dir. du Conservatoire, 3 rue du Marl. Joffre, 63000 Clermont-Ferrand, France

DMITRIEV, Gueorgui Petrovitch: Nezdanovoy Street, Bldg. 8/10 KS2, Apt. No. 24, Moscow 103009, Russia

DOMAGALA, Jacek: Hasburger Strasse 8, 1000 Berlin 30, Germany

DONDEYNE, Désiré: 206, rue du Fg. St-Honoré, 75008 Paris, France

DORSSELAER, Willy: 2, rue de l'Est, 68000 Colmar, France

DOTT, Hans-Peter: Bergheimerstrasse 28, 6900 Heidelberg, Germany

DOYEN, Henri: Maître de Chapelle à la Cathédrale, 02200 Soissons, France

DROUET, Raymond: 49, rue Gambetta, 79200 Parthenay, France

DUBOIS, Pierre-Max: 10, rue des Erables, 78150 Rocquencourt, France

DUBUS, Georges: 88, rue Ch. Infroit, 94400 Vitry, France

DUCKWORTH, William: 907 Anderson Street, Wilson NC 27893, USA

DUPRE, René: Sous-chef de musique, 1er R. I. M., 57230 Bitche, France

DURAND, André: 28, rue de l'Abbé de l'Epée, 13000 Marseille, France

DURANT, Douglas: Department of Music, Northeastern University, Boston MA 02115, USA

EICHMANN, Dietrich: Stephanientrasse 84, 7500 Karlsruhe 1, Germany

EISENMANN, Will: Chalet Alpina, 6103 Schwarzenberg/LU, Switzerland

ELOY, Christian: Conservatoire de Bordeaux, 22 Quai Ste Croix, 33000 Bordeaux, France

EMMERECHTS, Raymond: 66, Av. de Clichy, 75017 Paris, France

ENGEBRETSON, Mark: Novaragasse 21/1/11, A-1020 Wien , Austria

ERB, Donald: 1681 Cumberland Road, Cleveland Heights OH 44118, USA

ESSL, Karlheinz: Radeckgasse 118, 1040 Wien, Austria

EVANS, Stanford: Music Department, University of California San Diego, La Jolla CA 92031, USA

EYCHENNE, Marc: 9, rue de La Croix, 27140 Gisors, France

FAITH, Walter: Fasolstrasse 1, 8 München 38, Germany

FALK, Julien: 8, rue Tourlaque, 75018 Paris, France

FIEBIG, Kurt: Görlitzer Strasse 30, 2000 Hamburg 70, Germany

FILIPOVITCH, Remy: Springberg 32, 4300 Essen-Kettwig, Germany

FINGER, Peter: Ostrass. 92, 4500 Osnabrück, Germany

FISCHER, Clare: 3832 Laurel Canyon Blvd., Studio City CA 91604, USA

FISCHER, Eric: 5, rue du Calvaire, 77400 Lagny/Marne, France

FISCHER-MÜNSTER, Gerhard: Auf den Zeilen 11, 6538 Münster-Sarmsheim, Germany

FISH, Greg: 15454 Chatsworth Street #28, Mission Hills CA 91345, USA

FLADT, Hartmut: Ihnestrasse 58, 1000 Berlin, Germany

FLETCHER, Grant: School of Music, Arizona State University, Tempe AZ 85287, USA

FLYNN, George: 33 Tower Place, Mount Vernon NY 10552, USA

FONTAINE, Louis-Noël: 10337 Larose, Montreal H2B 2Y9, Canada

FORTNER, Wolfgang: 115 Bergstrasse, Heidelberg, Germany

FRACKENPOHL, Arthur: Crane School of Music, SUNY, Potsdam, NY 13676, USA

FRANCHETTI, Arnold: Lyme CT, USA

FRAZEUR, Theodore: School of Music, State University College, Fredonia NY 14063, USA

FREUND, Donald: Music Department, Memphis State University, Memphis TN 38152, USA

FURRER-MÜNCH, Franz: Hohfurristrasse 4, 8172 Niederglatt, Switzerland

FUSTÉ-LAMBEZAT, Michel: Dir. CNR, 22 Quai Ste Croix, 33000 Bordeaux, France

GAGO, José: Po Maragall, 243-41 Barcelona, Spain

GALANTE, Steven: 8315 Kimball Avenue, Skokie IL 60076, USA

GALLAHER, Christopher: Department of Music, Morehead State University, Morehead KY 40351, USA

GEBHARDT, Rochus: Thymianweg 4, 8000 München 70, Germany

GEE, Harry: 419 S. 32nd Street, Terre Haute IN 47803, USA

GENEST, Pierre: 82, rue St. Thomas, Montmagny Québec, Canada

GHIDONI, Armando: Via Brennero 52, 38100 Tento, Italy

GILARDIN, Jean-Paul: 266, rue E. Poulet, 69400 Villefranche/Saône, France

GIRARD, Anthony: 85, rue Legendre, 75017 Paris, France

GISSELMAN, Philippe: 47, Av. G. Clémenceau, 95100 Argenteuil, France

GLINKOWSKI, Aleksander: Ul. Szeligiewcza 15/5, Katowice, Poland

GODEL, Didier: 25, Bd. des Promenades, CH 1227 Carouge, Switzerland

GOJKOVIC, Dusan: Regina Ullmannstrasse 42, 8000 München 81, Germany

GOLDBERG, William: 11 5th Avenue, Northport NY 11768, USA

GOLDSTAUB, Paul: 433 Elmwood Avenue, Maplewood NJ 07040, USA

GOLDSTEIN, Malcolm: Shefield VT, USA

GOODE, Jack: 2742 Helen Street, Glenview IL 60025, USA

GOODMAN, Alfred: Clemens Krauss Strasse 22, 8000 München 60, Germany

GOODWIN, Gordon: Department of Music, University of Texas, Austin TX 78712, USA

GRAEF, Friedemann: Neue Kantstrasse 20, 1000 Berlin 19, Germany

GRANT, Jerome: 4720 Radford, Hollywood CA 91607, USA

GROBA, Rogelio: rue Fernandez Latorre n° 20, La Coruna, Spain

GROSSE, Erwin: Vordersteig 7a, 7505 Ettlingen, Germany

GROSSI, Daniel: 3, clos Vericier, 91370 Verrieres-les-Buissons, France

GUIMAUD, Olivier: 6, Carré Gomand, 1328 Lasne, Belgium

GÜRSCH, Günther: Delbrückstrasse 43, 1000 Berlin 33, Germany

HAENSCH, Gerhard Delle: Feichthofstrasse 20, 8000 München, Germany

HAERL, Dan: Monterey Peninsula C. 980, Monterey CA 93940, USA

HAIK-VANTOURA, Suzanne: 9, rue d'Artois, 75008 Paris, France

HALL, Neville: P. O. Box 46-131, Herne Bay, Auckland, New Zealand

HARREX, Patrick: 100 Tynemouth Road, Mitcham Surrey CR4-2BP, England

HARRISON, Jonty: Music Department, University of Birmingham "Edgbaston", Birmingham, England

HARTLEY, Walter: 27 Lowell Place, Fredonia NY 14063-1215, USA

HARTMANN, Otto: Corso italia 25, 6911 Campione d'It, Switzerland

HARVEY, Paul: 36 Alton Gardens, Twickenham Middlesex TW2-7PD, England

HAVEL, Christophe: CNR. 23, Quai Ste Croix, 33800 Bordeaux, France

HECKMANN, Heinz: Bergstrasse 45, 5501 Butzweiler, Germany

HEINICK, David: Crane School of Music, SUNY, Potsdam NY 13676, USA

HELLER, Richard: Ausstellungsstrasse 21/20, 1020 Wien, Austria

HEMKE, Frederick: School of Music, Northwestern University, Evanston IL 60201, USA

HEMMER, René: 34, rue de la Forêt, Luxembourg, Luxembourg

HENRY, Otto: School of Music, East Carolina University, Greenville NC 27858, USA

HERSANT, Philippe: 134 Quai Blériot, 75016 Paris, France

HERTZOG, Christian: 9240 Regents Road, Apt. H, La Jolla CA 92037, USA

HEWITT, Harry: 345 S. 19th Street, Philadelphia PA 19103, USA

HILDEMANN, Wolfgang: Aachener Strasse 311, Monchengladbach 1, D-4045, Germany

HILMY, Steven: 530 N. Division No. 3, Ann Arbor MI 48104, USA

HINES, Malcolm: 364 Valleyview Avenue, London Ontario, Canada

HOAG, Charles: 836 W. 21st, Lawrence KS 66044, USA

HODKINSON, Sydney: Eastman School of Music, 26 Gibbs Street, Rochester NY 14604, USA

HOLLAND, Dulcie: 67 Kameruka Road, Northbridge, NSW 2063, Australia

HÖLSZKY, Adriana: Urbanstrasse 80 A, 7000 Stuttgart 1, Germany

HOVHANESS, Alan: c/o Gary Scudder, 3166 Garnet Lane, Fullerton CA 92631, USA

HUMMEL, Berthold: Anne-Frank-Strasse 5, 8700 Würzburg, Germany

HWANG, Serra Mijeun: School of Music, University of Michigan, Ann Arbor MI 48109, USA

HYLA, Lee: 43 Bond Street, New York NY 10012, USA

ISRAEL, Hovav: Box 7183, Jerusalem 91071, Israel

ITURRALDE, Pedro: Real Musical, Carlos III n° 1, Madrid, Spain

JAEGER, Robert: School of Music, State University College, Fredonia NY 14063, USA

JARNIAT, Raymond: 101a, Chemin des Choulans, 69 Lyon 5e, France

JAY, Charles: 3, rue des Desprez, 80000 Amiens, France

JEAN, André: 5, Romiingin Astridlaan, 82000 Brugge, Belgium

JEANNEAU, François: 21, route de Coulommier, La Houssaie-en-Brie -77160 Fontenay Tresigny, France

JENNY, Albert: Association des Compositeurs Suisses, 38 Alpenquai, Zurich, Switzerland

JENTZSCH, Wilfried: Benekestrasse 50, 8500 Nürnberg, Germany

JOHNER, Hans-Rudolf: Kloppenheimer Strasse 56, 6800 Mannheim 61, Germany

JOHNSON, Allen: 5501 Glen Cove Drive, Knoxville TN 37919, USA

JONES, Kenneth V.: Hickwells Chailey, NR Lewes, Sussex, England

JONES, Martin: 11 Llwyn-Grant Road, Penylan, Cardiff CF3-7ET (UK3), England

JUELICH, Raimund: Pastetr. 9-403, Ratingen, Germany

KACINSKAS, Jeronimas: 16 Thomas Pk. So., Boston MA 02127, USA

KAINZ, Walter: A 8561, Soding 122, Austria

KARLINS, M. William: 1809 Sunnyside Circle, Northbrook IL 60062, USA

KASPAR, Edward: 27 Walker Street, Falmouth MA, USA

KEIG, Betty: 8825 NW 4th Place, Gainesville FL 32601, USA

KERN, Matthias: Kreuzwippe 17 (Engelbostel), 3012 Langenhagen 4, Germany

KIRCHSTEIN, Harold Manfred: 1081 Lighthouse Avenue, Pacific Grove CA 93950, USA

KIRCK, George: c/o Reedmate, P. O. Box 1512, Decatur IL 62525, USA

KLIER, Gottfield: Hedwigstrasse 15, 1000 Berlin 45, Germany

KNIGHT, Morris: 24243 Petty Road, Muncie IN 47304, USA

KNORR, Ernst-Lothar von: Jahnstrasse 3, 6907 Nussloch-Heidelberg, Germany

KNOSP, Erwin: 18, rue de la Kurvau, Strasbourg, France

KOBAYASHI, Hidéo: Higashi Kanamachi 4.22.14, Katsushika-ku, Tokyo 125, Japan

KOBLENZ, Babette: Hans-Christ-van Nag-dalenstrasse 50, D-2000 Hamburg 13, Germany

KÖBNER, Andreas: Reutterstrasse 84a, 8000 München 21, Germany

KOERBLER, Milivoj: Joze Laurencica 16, Zagreb, Yugoslavia

KÖHLER, Wolfgang: Domeneckerstrasse 3, 7109 Roigheim, Germany

KOLDITZ, Hans: Langenbergring 53, 5503 Konz, Germany

KÖPER, Heinz: Schneekoppenweg 12, 3001 Isernhagen NB/Hannover, Germany

KORN, Peter Jona: 123 Rosemheimerstrasse, D-8000 München 80, Germany

KORTH, Thomas: 11418 Pitsea Drive, Beltsville MD, USA

KREMENLIEV, Boris: Department of Music, University of California, Los Angeles CA 90024, USA

KRIPS, Henry: c/o Australian Broadcasting Commission, Hindmarsh, Adelaide, Australia

KROL, Bernhard: Friedrichstrasse 54, 7302 Ostfildern-Kemnat, Germany

KRUMLOVSKY, Claus: 24, rue Ouradour, Luxembourg, Luxembourg

KULLMANN, Wilton: Wasserstrasse 8-10, 6550 Bad Kreunach, Germany

KURTZ, Arthur: 685 Oakwood Avenue, Webster Groves MO 63119, USA

KURZ, Karl-Wieland: Geiselsteinweg 22, 6000 Frankfürt 50, Germany

KYLE, Mattews: 108 East Kenilworth Drive, Greenville SC 29615, USA

LANERI, Roberto: Lungotevere delle Navi 22, 00196 Rome, Italy

LANTOINE, Louis: Prof. Conservatoire, rue Deprez, 8000 Amiens, France

LAROCQUE, Jacques: Univers. 3351 Bd. des Forges, Trois Rivieres, Canada

LASTRA, Erich: Lessingstrasse 9, 1-4020 Linz, Austria

LAUBA, Christian: 25, rue Armand Gayral, 33700 Merignac, France

LAUTH, Wolfgang: Eugen-Bolzstrasse 1, 6800 Mannheim, Germany

LEE, Thomas Oboe: 9 Remington #2, Cambridge MA 02138, USA

LEENEN, Ulrich Jakob: Alter Kirchweg 28, 4005 Meerbusch 1, Germany

LEHMANN, Markus: Urach Strasse 39, D-7800 Freiburg, Germany

LEJET, Edith: 11/13 rue Cino del Luca, 75017 Paris, France

LEMAIRE, Félix: 13, rue des Dames de Metz, 57000 Metz, France

LEMELAND, Aubert: 77, Av. de la République, 75011 Paris, France

LENNERS, Claude: 1, rue de la Forêt, 1534 Luxembourg, Luxembourg

LENOT, Jacques: 45, Blvd. Aristide Briand, 17200 Royan, France

LENTZ, Daniel: 67 La Vuelta Road, Santa Barbara CA 93108, USA

LEONARD, J. Michael - 11 Sunset Road, Wayland MA 01778, USA

LERSY, Roger: Rue de Launay 91, Forges les Bains, France

LEUCHTER, Heibert: Lousbergstrasse 36, 5100 Aachen, Germany

LIC, Leslaw: K. Zclechowskirgo 4.1.9., Krakow, Poland

LIESENFELD, Paul: 1, rue de la Gendarmerie, 71 Montceau-les-Mines, France

LINKE, Norbert: Torfstuela 23, D-2000 Hamburg 62, Germany

LIPTAK, David: Eastman School of Music, 26 Gibbs Street, Rochester NY 14604, USA

LIST, Andrew: 75 St. Rose, Boston MA 02130, USA

LLOYD, Cy: 184 Elmhurst Mansion, Edgeley Road, Clapham, London SW4, England

LOMBARDO, Robert: 1040 W. Wellington Street, Chicago IL 60657, USA

LONDEIX, Jean-Marie: 59, rue Mondenard, 33000 Bordeaux, France

LONDON, Edwin: 910 W. Hill Street, Champaign IL 61820, USA

LONG, Duncan: P. O. Box 212, Alden KS 67512, USA

LUBIN, Ernest: 336 Ft. Washington Avenue, New York NY, USA

LUNDE, Lawson: 341 Lance Drive, Des Plaines IL 60016, USA

LUYPAERTS, Guy: 16, rue P. Féval, 75018 Paris, France

MABRY, Drake: 41, rue des Appenins, 75017 Paris, France

MACHOVER, Tod: Becky Starobin, Bridge Records JAF Box 1864, New York NY 10116, USA

MAHDI, Salah: Conservatoire de Musique, 16 Av. Mahomed V, Tunis, Tunisia

MAIS, Chester: Department of Music, Daemen College, 4380 Main Street, Amherst NY 14226, USA

MANDANICI, Marcella: c/o Nuovi Spazi Sonori c.p.n. 196, 25100 Brescia, Italy

MARCHAL, Dominique: 2, rue Fodéré, 06300 Nice, France

MARCHAND, Jean-Christophe: St Gilles de Crétot, 76490 Caudeberc en Caux, France

MARCOUX, Isabelle: 204, de la Seigneurie, Aylmer, Quebec J9J 1R2, Canada

MARI, Pierrette: 14bis rue Pierre Niciole, 75005 Paris, France

MARTIN, Vernon: c/o ASCAP, 1 Lincoln Plaza, New York NY 10023, USA

MAROCCHINI, Enrico: Via Capo d'Africa 15, 00184 Rome, Italy

MARTINO, Donald: Dantalian Music, 11 Pembroke Street, Newton MA 02158, USA

MASON, Lucas: 234 W. 13th Street, New York NY 10011, USA

MATITIA, Jean: 25, rue Armand Gayral, 33700 Merignac, France

MATZKE, Rex - Department of Music, University of Missouri-St. Louis, 8001 Natural Bridge Rd., St. Louis MO 63121, USA

MAUK, Steven: School of Music, Ithaca College, Ithaca NY 14850, USA

McCARTHY, Daniel - Department of Music, Indiana State University, Terre Haute IN 47809, USA

McCARTY, Frank: 549 S. Braddock, Pittsburgh PA 15221, USA

McCLINTOCK, Robert: 3851B Fair Oaks Blvd., Sacramento CA 95825, USA

MEAD, Andrew: School of Music, University of Michigan, Ann Arbor MI 48109, USA

MENSING, Eberhard: Marzlinger Fussweg 4, 8050 Freising, Germany

MERSSON, Boris: Engimatt Strasse 22, CH-8002 Zurich, Switzerland

MEYER, Jean-Michel: 83, rue Jean Jaurès, 29200 Brest, France

MICHAEL, Frank: Flaunserstrasse 3A, 7801 Stegen-Eschbach, Germany

MICHEL, Paul: 30, rue du Zéphyr, 1200 Bruxelles, Belgium

MILLER, Dennis: Department of Music, Northeastern University, Boston MA 02115, USA

MINIKAWA, Mio: 7.28.15 Nakayamate Cicah-ku, 650 Kobe, Japan

MINTCHEV, Gueorgui: 34, rue Asparoukh, Sofia 1000, Bulgaria

MONDELLO, Nuncio: 325 W. 45 Street, New York NY 10036, USA

MONTALTO, Richard: 905 6th Avenue S. #10, Columbus MS 39701, USA

MOQUÉ, Xavier: Bloc C, Appart.47, 47 rue Th. de Bèze, 45000 Orleans, France

MUELLER, Florian: School of Music, University of Michigan, Ann Arbor MI 48109, USA

MUELLER, Frederick: 4900 Brittany Dr. South, Apt. 205, St. Petersburg FL 33715, USA

MÜLLER, Gottfried: Güntherstrasse 17, 8500 Nürnberg 40, Germany

MYERS, Robert: Lot 10, 2752 W. No., Union Midland MI, USA

MYERS, Theldon: 5 Omera Place, Hampton VA 23366, USA

NÄTHER, Giesbert: W-Külz Strasse 23/85, 1560 Potsdam, Germany

NEWTON, Rodney: 13 Chetwynd Avenue E., Barnet Herts EN4 8N6, England

NICKLAUS, Wolfgang: Lohbrüggerstrasse 21b, 2057 Reinbek, Germany

NICOLAU, Dimitri: Via di Grotta Pinta 14, 00186 Rome, Italy

NICOLAUS, Louis: 7, Villa Maris, 92 Colombes, France

NIEHAUS, Manfred: Herkenratherstrasse 1, 5060 Bergish, Gladbach 2, Germany

NIKIPROWETSKY, Tolia: 65, rue La Fontaine, 75016 Paris, France

NODA, Ryo: 1.16.23. Nishinaniwa-ho, Amagasaki, Japan

OCKENFELS, Helmut: Siegtalstrasse 14, 5202 Hennef 1, Germany

OLBRISCH, Franz-Martin: 40 Grossgörschentstrasse, 1 Berlin, Germany

PACALET, Jean: c/o Monique Thevenet, 22, rue Cartelet, 26000 Valence, France

PADWA, Vladimir: 736 Riverside Drive, New York NY 10031, USA

PANTON, David: 63, Fountain Road, Birmingham 17, England

PARRIS, Herman: 3600 Conshohocken Avenue, Philadelphia PA 19131, USA

PATTERSON, Paul: 2 Jadesa Ct., 43 Somerset Road, Barnet Herts, England

PAVLENKO, Serguei: Ul. Shablovka 30/12, KV4 Moscow 117419, Russia

PENBERTHY, James: c/o Australian Broadcasting Commission, Hindmarsh, Adelaide, Australia

PFENNINGER, Rik: Department of Music, Plymouth State College, Plymouth MA 03264, USA

PHAN, P. Q.: School of Music, University of Michigan, Ann Arbor MI 48109, USA

PIERSON, Thomas: 5909 Fenway Drive, Corpus Christi TX 78413, USA

PILON, Daniel: 2106 Apt. 43 rue Clarmont, Montreal H3Z-2P8, Canada

POLIET, Lucien: 40, rue des Cygnes, 1050 Bruxelles, Belgium

POMORIN, Sibylle: Arndtstrasse 18, 1000 Berlin 61, Germany

PRESSER, William: Box 158 S. Station, Hattiesburg MS 39401, USA

PRODIGO, Sergio: Conservatorio di Musica 'A. Casella', L'Aquila, Italy

PROHASKA, Miljenko: Bogovice va 1, Zagreb, Yugoslavia

PÜTZ, Eduard: Mozartstrasse 15, 5308 Rheinbach, Germany

QUELLE, Ernst-August: Urspringerstrasse 14, 8021 Strasslach, Germany

QUERAT, Marcel: 13-18, rue du Gal de Larminat, 94000 Creteil, France

RADDATZ, Otto: Breslauerstrasse 47, 7180 Crailsheim, Germany

RAHN, John: 218B Eisenhower Street, Princeton NJ 08540, USA

READE, Paul: 12 Clorane Gardens, London NW3, England

REINER, Thomas: Am Platzenberg 3, 6380 Bad Homburg, Germany

REX, Harley: Department of Music, Sam Houston State University, Huntsville TX 77341, USA

REYMOND, Roger: 33, rue René Leynaud, 69001 Lyon, France

RIBAS, Rosa: C/Calabria 137, Barcelona 15, Spain

RIEMER, Franz: Ringbahnstrasse 58, 1000 Berlin 42, Germany

ROBERT, Lucie: 9, rue Soyer, 92000 Neuilly/Seine, France

RODRIGUEZ, Robert: 531 Winchester Drive, Richardson TX 75080, USA

ROGER, Denise: 94, rue de Miromesnil, 75008 Paris, France

ROLIN, Etienne: 1 Blvd. Thiers, 16000 Angouleme, France

RONKIN, Bruce: Department of Music, Northeastern University, Boston MA 02115, USA

ROSSÉ, François: Rue Rolland, 33850 Leognan, France

RUBBERT, Rainer: Gneisenaustrasse 112, D-10961 Berlin, Germany

RUDAJEV, Alexandre: 1207 Druid Lane, Tampa FL 33629, USA

RUEGER, Christoph: Xantenerstrasse 20, 1000 Berlin 15, Germany

RUELLE, Fernand: 16, rue d'Epinlieu. Mons 7000, Belgium

RUGGERI, Gianluca: Monte Zeda, Rome, Italy

RUNSWICK, Daryl: 19 Bittacy Park Avenue, London NW7, England

SABINA, Leslie: Saint Bonaventure University, Saint Bonaventure NY 14778, USA

SADLER, Helmut: J-S. Bach Strasse 11, 6901 Mauer, Germany

SALBERT, Dieter: Reiherweg 3, 3174 Meine, Germany

SALLUSTIO, Eraclio: Via Martoglio 60, 00137 Rome, Italy

SAMORI, Aurelio: Via D. Luigi Sturzo 9, 48018 Faenza (Ra), Italy

SAMYN, Noël: 988 Av. Beraud, Val d'Or, Québec, Canada

SANDROFF, Howard: Department of Music, University of Chicago, 5845 S. Ellis Avenue, Chicago IL 60637, USA

SAUCEDO, Victor: 1866 Loyola Court, Chula Vista CA 92010, USA

SBACCO, Franco: Via Gregorio XIII n° 51, Rome, Italy

SCHAFFER, Boguslaw: 31-938 Krakow, Kolorowe 4, Poland

SCHILLING, Hans: Norijestrasse 1933, 85000 Nürnberg, Germany

SCHMADTKE, Harry: Züricherstrasse 50, 2800 Bremen, Germany

SCHMELZER, August: Freinsheimerstrasse 9, 6700 Ludwigshafen, Germany

SCHMIDT, William: 3707 65th Avenue, Greeley CO 80634, USA

SCHMIDT-HAMBROCK Jochen: Kaisersescherstrasse 6, 5000 Köln 41, Germany

SCHÖNBACH, Dieter: Königsallee 72, 4630 Bochum, Germany

SCHULTE, Peter: Feldstrasse 53, 5870 Hemer, Germany

SCHUST, Alfred: Kleineweg 7, 1000 Berlin 42, Germany

SCHWARTZ, Elliott: School of Music, Ohio State University, Columbus OH 43210, USA

SCIORTINO, Patrice: 49, rue Rouelle, 75015 Paris, France

SEKON, Joseph: Department of Music, Cabrillo College, Aptos CA 95003, USA

SEMLER-COLLERY, Armand: "Le Chalet" 30, La Levade, France

SEVRETTE, Danielle: 20, Av. Mozart, 75016 Paris, France

SHAFFER, Sherwood: North Carolina School of the Arts, School of Music, P. O. Box 12189, Winston-Salem NC 27117, USA

SHRUDE, Marilyn: College of Musical Arts, Bowling Green State University, Bowling Green OH 43403, USA

SIEBERT, Robert: 302 High Street H4, Fair Lawn NJ, USA

SIGEL, Allen: 40 Brookedge Drive, Williamsville NY 14221, USA

SIMIC, Vojislaw: Karsrska 13, Belgrade, Yugoslavia

SIMONS, Netty: 374 S. Mountain Road, New City NY 10956, USA

SIVIC, Pavel: Académie de Musique, Gosposka Ulisa 8, Ljubljana, Slovenia

SLEICHIM, Eric: c/o MOTUS VZW, Boerenstraat 60, B-1040 Bruxelles, Belgium

SMIRNOV, Dmitry: Y1 Poroba 7.6.5., Cmnphoby-A.H., 123479 Moscow, Russia

SMITH, Edwin: Department of Music, University of Wisconsin, Eau Claire WI 54702, USA

SMITH, Stuart: UMBC, 5401 Wilkens Avenue, Baltimore MD 21228, USA

SORG, Margarete: Rheinallee 12, 6500 Mainz, Germany

SOTELO, Mauricio: Westbahnstrasse 32/20, 1000 Wien, Austria

SOUFFRIAU, Arsène: 42, Drène du Caporal, 1180 Bruxelles, Belgium

SOULE, Edmund: School of Music, University of Oregon, Eugene OR 97403, USA

SPRONGL, Norbert: Pfarrgasse 8, 2340 Mödling, Austria

STAEHLIN, Pierre: 15, Av. des Tilleuls, 64200 Biarritz, France

STAHMER, Klaus Hinrich: Am Pfad 12b, 8706 Höchberg, Germany

STAUDE, Christoph: Auf dem Berg 4 - 6229 Wambach, Germany

STERN, Max: P. O. Box 10504, Jerusalem 91103, Israel

STOLTIE, James: Crane School of Music, SUNY, Potsdam NY 13676, USA

STÖRRLE, Heinz: Pössenbacher Strasse 15, 8000 München 71, Germany

STOUT, Alan: 2600 1/2 Central Street, Evanston IL 60201, USA

STRAWSER, Richard: Eastman School of Music, 26 Gibbs Street, Rochester NY 14604, USA

SUDLOW, Paul: 80 Southam Road, Radford Semele Royal Leamington Spa, Warwickshire, England

TAGGART, Mark Alan: 110 S. Handing Street, Greenville NC 27834, USA

TANNER, David: 2062 Baffin Avenue, Ottawa, Ontario, Canada

TARP, Svend: Prinsessestien 1 Kgs, Lyngby, Denmark

TERRY, Peter: Department of Music, California State University, Los Angeles CA 90032, USA

THEOFANIDIS, Chris: c/o Kenneth Radnofsky WWCPCF, P. O. Box 1016, East Arlington MA 02174, USA

THOMAS, Robert: 85 Peplin's Way, Kings Norton, Birmingham 30, England

TICHELI, Frank: 1505 Northbrook, Ann Arbor MI 48103, USA

TISNÉ, Antoine: 32, rue du Cotentin, 75015 Paris, France

TOKUNAGA, Hidenori: 240 Noma Hatanaka Itam-shi, Hyogo-Ken 664, Japan

TOMLINSON, Ernest: Lancaster Farm, Chipping Road, Longridge, Preston Lanes PR3-2NB, England

TOURNIER, Franz: CNR, 26 rue Hoche, 35000 Rennes, France

TREBINSKY, Arkadi: 10, rue des Bruyères, 92600 Asnieres, France

TROUILLARD, Raymond: 29, Grande rue, 77 Villevande, France

TYSSENS, Albert: 5, rue Louis de Brouckère, B-4300 Ans, Belgium

UDOW, Michael: School of Music, University of Michigan, Ann Arbor MI 48109, USA

ULBEN, Denize: Manhattan School of Music, 120 Claremont Avenue, New York NY 10027, USA

VALLIER, Jacques: 17, Av. Schaeffer, 95 Deuil, France

VAN MAELE, Gérard: 34, rue de la Libération, 68 Brunstatt, France

VENTAS, Adolfo: C/Padilla 290-2-2, 08025 Barcelona, Spain

VERDI, Ralph: Department of Music, St. Josephs College, Rensselaer IN 47978, USA

VICTORY, Gérard: 29 Lannswood Pk, Stillorgan Co, Dublin, Ireland

VINCENT-DEMOULIN, Jean: 13 Blvd. République, 71100 Chalon-a-Saône, France

VOGEL, Roger: University of Georgia, School of Music, Athens GA 30602, USA

VOGEL, Wladimir: Oetlisbergstrasse 7, 8053 Zurich, Switzerland

VOIRPY, Alain: 132, Blvd. de la Liberté, 59800 Lille, France

WALDEN, D.E.: 64 Langley Avenue, Toronto 6, Ontario, Canada

WALTER, Richard: 8 Redhill Court, Palace Road, London SW2, England

WARNER, Scott: 114 Longman Lane, Ann Arbor MI 48103, USA

WATERS, Renee Silas: P. O. Box 589, McCaysville GA 30555, USA

WEIDENAAR, Reynold: 5 Jones Street No. 4, New York NY 10014, USA

WENDEL, Eugen: Siebengebirgsring 46, 5204 Lohmar 21, Germany

WERDER, Felix: Im Dol 44 c/o Manasse, 1000 Berlin, Germany

WHEELER, Kenneth: 141 Wallwood Road, London E11, England

WIENER, Gaston: 109bis Av. Gal de Gaulle, 92000 Neuilly, France

WILLIS, Richard: 1010 Southwood, Waco TX 76710, USA

WINKLER, Gerhard: Bründlweg 3, 5020 Salzburg, Austria

WINZENBURGER, Walter: Conservatory of Music, Baldwin-Wallace College, Berea OH 44017, USA

WIRTH, Carl Anton: c/o William Trimble, 138 Kageman Avenue, Santa Cruz CA 95062-2213, USA

WISHART, Peter: Bridge House, Great Elm, Somerset, England

WOODBURN, James: 35 Argyll Street, Kettering, Northhamptonshire, England

WYATT, Scott: School of Music, University of Illinois, Urbana IL 61801, USA

WYMAN, Laurence: School of Music, State University College, Fredonia NY 14063, USA

YATES, Ronald: 5126B, Matorral Way, Santa Barbara CA, USA

YOSHIOKA, Emmett G.: 3364 Hardesty Street, Honolulu HI 96816, USA

YOUNG, Charles Rochester: Department of Music, University of Wisconsin, Stevens Point WI 54481, USA

ZAJDA, Edward: 3709 S. 60th Court, Cicero IL 60650, USA

ZANDER, Heinz Joachim: Bethesdastrasse 25a, 2000 Hamburg 26, Germany

ZEMP, Joseph: 3, rue du Foyer, 9000 Belfort, France

ZENDER, Hans: Heimhuderstrasse 13, 2000 Hamburg, Germany

ZIMMERMAN, Keith: 108 Fayette Court, Washington IL 61571-1129, USA

ZOURABICHVILI, Nicolas: 107, rue de By, 77810 Thomery, France

For information contact:
Pour toutes informations:

Centre Européen de Saxophone
22, Quai Sainte-Croix
33800 Bordeaux, France
Fax: 56.92.22.30

Bibliography

Arnold, D. *Dictionnaire encyclopédique de la musique*. Editions R. Laffont, 1988.

Encyclopédie de la Musique. Editions Garzanti, 1992.

Fousnaquer, Jacques-Emmanuel, Claude Glayman and Christian Leblé. *Musiciens de notre temps, depuis 1945*. Paris: Editions Plume, 1992.

Gee, Harry R. *Saxophone Soloists and their Music, 1844-1985—An Annotated Bibliography*. Bloomington, Indiana: Indiana University Press, 1986.

Griffiths, Paul. *Brève histoire de la musique moderne*. Paris: Editions Fayard, 1992.

Honegger, Marc. *Dictionnaire de la musique*." [Paris]: Bordas, 1970.

Komponisten der Gegenwart. Editions Cip, 1985.

Massin, Jean & Brigitte. *Histoire de la Musique occidentale*. Paris: Editions Fayard, 1985.

Meynaerts-Wathelet, E. *Les Musiciens wallons*. Editions J. Destrée, 1963.

The New Grove Dictionary of Music and Musicians, ed. Stanley Sadie. New York: Macmillan, 1980.

Roland-Manuel. *Histoire de la musique*. Paris: Editions La Pléiade Gallimard, 1986.

Rostand, Claude. *Dictionnaire de la musique contemporaine*. Paris: Editions Larousse, 1970.

Siron, Paul-Louis. *Aspects de la musique contemporaine: 1960-1981*. Lausanne: Editions de l'Aire, 1981.

Tranchefort, François-René. *Guide de la musique de chambre*. Paris: Editions Fayard, 1989.

_____. *Guide de la musique symphonique*. Paris: Editions Fayard, 1986.

Vannes, René. *Dictionnaire des musiciens*. Bruxelles, Maison Larcier, 1947.

Vignal, Marc. *Dictionnaire de la musique allemande et autrichienne*. Paris: Editions Larousse, 1988.

_____. *Dictionnaire de la musique française*. Paris: Editions Larousse, 1988.

_____. *Dictionnaire de la musique italienne*. Paris: Editions Larousse, 1988.

Weid, J-N. von der. *La Musique du XX° siècle*. Editions Hachette, 1992.